D0349657

PASSPORT
A NOVEL OF THE COLD WAR

PASSPORT
A NOVEL OF THE COLD WAR

By

BRUCE HERSCHENSOHN

new york
www.ibooks.net
DISTRIBUTED BY SIMON & SCHUSTER

An ibooks, inc. Book

Distributed by Simon & Schuster, Inc.
1230 Avenue of the Americas, New York, NY 10020

ibooks, inc.
24 West 25th Street
New York, NY 10010

The ibooks World Wide Web Site address is:
http://www.ibooks.net

ISBN: 0-7434-7984-X
First ibooks printing October 2003
10 9 8 7 6 5 4 3 2 1

Dedicated to those Americans who have lived the highest morality by risking their lives for the liberty of strangers.

My deepest thanks to Byron Preiss and his superb and supportive publishing staff.

During the final years of writing *Passport,* while I often put myself in self-imposed isolation, there were those who maintained their consistent understanding, encouragement, backing and friendship, all of which mean so much to me. I thank the late Jerry Dunphy, Jim Neuman, Larry Adamy, Jay and Dulce Hoffman, Leila Suerth, Michael Warder, John and Colleen Gizzi, Howard and Janet Klein, and John and Maureen Nunn.

And, of course, my angelic sister, Vi Logan, and the late titan of an artist and titan of a brother, Wes Herschensohn.

And my eternal appreciation and love to Janet Bresnahan.

CONTENTS

INTRODUCTION

The main character of this book is not a person. *Passport* is a biography of a giant that had an effect on practically every person who lived during the last four decades of the twentieth century: the foreign policy of the United States of America. This book follows that mammoth figure from 1960 through 1997 through the lives of twelve people whose passions and careers mandated travel throughout the world.

Those twelve people and many others are fictional but they are based on people I have known during those 37 years. Other than historical and public figures, this book does not use real names, and I also changed some further identification of non-public figures. At times I used composites of people. But they are not imaginary. We follow them through the presidential campaigns of Vice President Richard Nixon and Senator John F. Kennedy, the Cuban Missile Crisis, the 1967 Mideast War, the wars of Vietnam, Laos, and Cambodia, the impact of Watergate on foreign affairs, the Iran Hostage Crisis, the wars of Nicaragua and El Salvador, the debates over a Nuclear Freeze, the Iran-Contra connection, the Tiananmen Square Massacre, the dismemberment of the Soviet Union, the Persian Gulf War, and the handover of Hong Kong to the People's Republic of China.

All of this started in 1960 when I was given a contract from the International Communications Foundation to make a documentary film in India. Since India was on the opposite side of the globe from my home in Los Angeles, I was provided with an around-the-world airline ticket. The director of the foundation, Lawrence van Mourick, Jr., told me to take my time with stops going to and coming from India. He further advised that I should take notes of everything I witnessed in the countries I would visit because "these are historical times, and details are often forgotten unless they are recorded before memories fade." It was advice I accepted.

That's when I started my note-keeping of historical times, incidents, episodes, people, and places. I thought that when I returned home from the trip, the note-taking would be done and I would be free of the writing-down ritual. But as the years went on, some of the people I met on that trip became more and more involved in world events, the times became more and more historical and, therefore, my notes became more and more extensive. For years, I had absolutely no idea what I would do with the notes, if anything. I continued as habit rather than destination.

Because the foreign service is a very tight community, as is the world of politics, those who choose either as a career do not simply meet new people as the years go on, but they see the same people with great frequency, often in unexpected countries and involved in unexpected world events. Therefore, in time I knew exactly what I wanted to do with the continuing notes.

Passport was being written all by itself. The details of the cities of the world are accurate with precision for the times in which this book takes place. Some scenes, references, and conversations with historical and public figures are not word-for-word actualities. Moreover, often conversations and incidents are portrayed as being *between* public and fictional characters and in those cases, whenever known, the public figure's dialogue is adapted from those things said by the public figure to another and, at times, on other occasions. Much of the book is based on my own experiences or from knowing well those who took part in segments in which I was not present. Fictional segments were added to give continuity and cohesion to the structure of the total. It would not be accurate to say the book took 37 years to write, but it would be accurate to say it was written over a period of 37 years.

Above the turbulence of those historical times, it was the people who took precedence over headlines. They used their times as their palette, as all people do:

There was Adam Orr, a man who worked at Cape Canaveral but had other and more covert interests during the Cold War, particularly in South Vietnam.

There was Anne Whitney, a young woman who changed her outlook of men and women and romance, and changed her radical political beliefs in a metamorphosis that was total.

There was Cody Cooper who was dedicated to the candidacy of Senator John F. Kennedy, and realized his dream by becoming an appointee on President Kennedy's White House staff.

There was Ambassador Gerald Fairbanks and his wife, Mary, who knew well the world of diplomacy and was respected at U.S. embassies and consulates around the world.

There was Tso Wai-yee, a beautiful young Chinese woman in Hong Kong whose devotion to that British colony was greater than any personal love or affection.

There was the newlywed Ted Murphy, a syndicated writer of political columns. As television increasingly became the medium of nightly importance, he became a television newscaster and commentator, giving him the opportunity to express his views on the international scene to millions. His politics were contagious and became the views of his wife, Linda, who would have a prominent future independent of Ted.

There was Moose Dunston, who was contracted by the Department of Defense, and uniquely became an appointee of both President Johnson and President Nixon.

There was Mark Daschle, the bow-tied Public Affairs Officer who had climbed the ladder of the foreign service, but never became an ambassador, and eventually was forced to leave the foreign service.

There was Irene Goodpastor who had a talent for giving Washington parties with prominence being the criterion of her invitation list. As she grew older and the Washington scene changed, her memories exceeded her dreams and her life became dominated by a loss of her celebrity.

There was Jonas Valadovich, the young Air Force lieutenant who would make a career of military service, and face total frustration when he retired until he was rescued by President Reagan.

The major events of *Passport* take place during 37 years that changed the world. And that time span became a chain of strong links that extend well beyond the back cover of this book:

One of those links was the U.S. abandonment of the Shah of Iran that brought about the first Islamic Fundamentalist Revolutionary Government in 1979. That revolution spread to other governments with the expansion of terrorism as an integral part of that fundamentalism.

The habit of bringing totalitarian governments to diplomatic agreements throughout those 37 years revealed with consistency that successful negotiations were never worthy of celebrations. Instead, their signatures proved to be nothing more or less than a decoy for the coming victory of tyrannies.

There were few apologies from street demonstrators and media celebrities when their advocacies helped bring about the defeat of allies and the victory of conquerors who then built and filled concentration camps, committed genocide, and thanked the U.S. demonstrators and celebrities for helping them to achieve their win.

The United Nations organization was given unjustified prestige as its resolutions upheld the quests of the Soviet Union until it died, and then the U.N. granted the quests of remaining expansionist governments while condemning democracies.

The rejection of a ballistic missile defense system assumed there would not be missiles that could endanger the United States or its allies, and cutting the military budget with a "peace-dividend" assumed that serious dangers of conflict were done.

The decision to bring the troops home after the liberation of Kuwait without going on to Iraq left a dangling link of 1991 that would be clasped to the next century.

Under the disguise of encouraging human rights, many in free nations traded with the People's Republic of China in the hope of enriching themselves, but simultaneously guaranteeing a coming superpower status of that government.

If new generations grasp the victories, the defeats, the debates, the bureaucracy, the international organizations, the geopolitics, the people and the places of those years, those new generations will be better able to avoid proven errors before their own entry into world affairs.

One other note: While some world events were acclaimed and others despised, I loved living through those times. I can still remember the aroma of those years and places. But the aroma is becoming fainter, even in some of the more prominent cities. If nothing else, I'm glad that *Passport* is finished before the hunters come and revise the record of those years into something they weren't.

Bruce Herschensohn
May 2003

PROLOGUE
THE HANDOVER
1997

Although the last scriptures of the Bible had been written some two thousand years before the Regent Hotel was built in Hong Kong, there was a crowd there one night with revelers who had an unholy similarity to those who angered the prophets in books from Leviticus to Corinthians.

A Golden Dragon at another time for another event might well have been worthy of its presence, but on that night the display of a golden dragon by the hotel's base of Victoria Harbor was too much like the exhibition of the molten calf at the base of Mount Sinai.

There were hoards of people in both formal dress and costume in the Regent eating, drinking, laughing, and toasting the city's reunification with China. But most of those who lived in Hong Kong had risked their lives to escape from China or they were descended from those who did. Some at the Regent who were Hong Kong residents were celebrating along with the hotel's guests to disguise the inevitability of such a dreaded midnight that was only hours away. And some were celebrating out of fear not to celebrate. And some business people were celebrating in the hope that their new masters would, somehow, know of their toasts and they would be rewarded for their exhibition of pleasure. Most of the visitors who were there were celebrating because it was fun. Through the Regent's huge glass south edifice was the sight across the harbor of the most magnificent architectural collaboration between God and Man. God had created the waterway that separated the peninsula from the island in view of each other, and He had built the mountains on the island, topped by the Peak. Then, those who escaped from China used His work as a canvas for their dreams. They designed and constructed the buildings and the roads on the island and ignited the lights across their skyline's width that traveled from horizon to horizon and illuminated all the towering steel and glass heights that touched the clouds, some going through them.

Cities imitate each other, but those who constructed Hong Kong forgot or never knew what other cities looked like.

In Room 1614 of the Regent, Brigadier General Jonas Valadovich, United States Air Force, Retired, was sitting on one of the room's yellow chairs with his back to the window. He was staring at the wall while behind him was not only the magnificence of the harbor and the skyline, but the largest fireworks exhibition since the Chinese started using them for celebration. Most of the explosions shook the window and some of them even shook the room. It was as though General Valadovich couldn't hear them and for sure, from his chosen position, he couldn't see them. His weathered, tanned, and strong face showed little emotion. Beneath one explosion after another, he could hardly hear his own voice: "Clocks and calendars always win. Even if I could put on my old uniform and fight and claim victory over all the armies of the world, the timepieces of every fallen soldier would laugh. There is no weapon to kill them."

With some effort, General Valadovich raised himself, pushing his hands against the low wooden arms of the chair. Fully standing, he took a final look at the colors reflecting against the sepia wallpaper in front of him, changing into an animated palette of moving colors, and he turned from the wall to the window. It was beyond the promise of the wallpaper's reflections. It was difficult to believe it was real. There were explosions of reds and then greens and then yellows and then all of them together and there were falling spears of lights into the water.

He could hear cheering. He walked to the window's edge and looked straight down and he could see the tops of thousands and thousands of motionless umbrellas held by observers on the Promenade Harbor Walk. Those unseen figures beneath the umbrellas were doing the cheering.

And then General Valadovich grabbed the drawstring by the window and pulled it to close the curtains. Midnight would be invisible to him.

At 2:45 in the morning, General Valadovich walked the short distance to Room 1600, which was the headquarters of World News Network. With the handover of Hong Kong from Great Britain to China done, it was the prescribed time for his television interview.

"General Valadovich! Come right in!" He did, and as soon as he crossed the threshold, the young woman put a can of unrequested Diet Coke in his hand. "Have one!" She had on red slacks and a Tee-shirt with a picture of the Union Jack over one breast, and a picture of the flag of the People's Republic of China over the other breast, with "1997" written above them. The room was full of cables, slates, camera batteries, cups, Coke cans and open white boxes with pizza slices in them. "We were getting worried about you. I was just going to call your room. Wasn't it exciting? Did you see the Royal Yacht *Britannia* leave?"

"No. I missed it. I don't want any Coke, thank you." He handed it back to her.

"Coffee?"

"No. I'm okay."

"We have a room full of stuff. Did you see the *Britannia* leave?" she repeated. "Prince Charles sailed away with Governor Patten."

"I know. I missed it. I didn't want to see them sail away."

She wasn't listening to him. "Wasn't it exciting?"

"I don't know. I didn't see it."

"It was so exciting. Now, you just need to get into makeup right away and then we'll get you on the roof. It's still raining out there so it's sort of a mess, but we have a tarp so you won't get wet while you're on-camera."

"Is Mrs. Goodpastor here yet?"

"Oh, yes. She's in place outside. She's on a wheelchair you know."

"I know."

"Poor thing. How old is she?"

"She's up there. I think she's passed her ninetieth birthday."

"She has a young man who's taking care of her out there."

"That's Brian Nestande. I met him earlier today."

Whatever he had to say was unimportant. "You'll be interviewed by Laurie Lespada," she said with raised eyebrows, a smile, and a nod, as though the general was to be awed by such a presence. He nodded in pretense that he had heard of Laurie Lespada. He hadn't, although most of the world knew who she was. "Now," she added, "let's get to makeup. Would you like a Diet Coke?"

Was this woman listening to anything except her own voice?

The camera was capturing the image of Laurie Lespada with the brilliantly lit skyline of Hong Kong Island behind her from across the harbor. Rain was beating on the tarp above her, and while the camera didn't show the tarp, the microphone couldn't deafen the noise of the rain beating on it. Laurie Lespada looked at the camera with a wide smile. "Welcome back to World Network News and *Above the Fold*'s coverage of the Hong Kong handover! And where else could we be but Hong Kong on this historical night? WNN continues its coverage from the roof of the Regent Hotel. Sitting with me now on this rainy night are two distinguished Americans who have become very familiar to all of us through the years, and who should have some valuable insights into what's happening here in Hong Kong. Irene Goodpastor is here, founder of the Goodpastor Center in Washington." The director cut to Mrs. Goodpastor who had her eyes closed and her mouth open. He held on her until he realized she was not about to open her eyes or close her mouth, and he cut to the camera that was on General Valadovich as the anchorwoman promptly continued, "And we have with us retired Brigadier General Jonas Valadovich. General, let's start with you." Could she do otherwise? "What's your feeling about the handover? Optimistic? Pessimistic?"

"I'm saddened by it. How can we celebrate the reunification of Hong Kong people with China when it was the Hong Kong people who escaped so as to be disunited from the PRC?"

"The PRC—the People's Republic of China." She felt her responsibility to the audience to show how knowledgable she was. "The government there."

"Yes, ma'am." *Ma'am* for Laurie Lespada?

"But why should things change here in Hong Kong, General? The late Deng Xiaoping promised One Country, Two Systems. Doesn't that give you some assurance?"

"Tragically, the world is defining Hong Kong's system as capitalism, and that's the way Deng Xiaoping thought of the system here. But Hong Kong's system is liberty. Capitalism is no less or more than the economic dimension of liberty. It's part of liberty but not its roots." He knew television well enough to just keep talking about what he wanted to say or the anchor would turn to another subject. "And although you can't have liberty without capitalism, you can have capitalism without liberty. That's what Deng brought to his own people. It's true that China is turning more and more to capitalism, but without political as well as economic change, China is becoming more of a fascist state than a communist state."

Laurie Lespada dismissed that. "Jiang Zemin and Li Peng said that this night ends a century and one-half of China's shame and humiliation from the British Opium Wars. Isn't that true? Now the shame and humiliation is over."

"What they're really ashamed of is how well these Chinese people did without the government of the People's Republic. This is the pearl of Asia. The pearl is not Shanghai and not Guangzchou and not Beijing. That's the PRC's shame. And there's more reason for shame; shame for their support of Pol Pot's genocide in Cambodia. That happened in this generation, not 156 years ago during the Opium Wars by people who have long been dead. Why aren't they ashamed of what they did in 1978 to kids who were putting up posters on Democracy Wall? Why aren't they ashamed of their massacre in 1989 at Tiananmen Square? That was ordered by Deng Xiaoping and Li Peng. Li Peng is here tonight! He did tonight what you just did, ma'am. He talked about the shame of the Opium Wars and by saying that, he allowed himself to avoid the obvious. The British shamed his government all right—by the British letting Chinese people be free. And look what they built!"

Enough of that for Laurie Lespada. "Mrs. Goodpastor, tell us why you and the General and some of your other friends are here. We know about your Institute in Washington—the Goodpastor Center—but I understand you aren't here for the Center. There's a fascinating story behind this visit of yours, isn't there?"

Too bad, but Mrs. Goodpastor didn't answer. She wasn't rude, she simply didn't hear her. Her eyes were open now but she wasn't looking at anything special, certainly not at Laurie Lespada or at the camera. Her mouth was still wide open. The director knew enough now to cut back quickly to a two-shot of Laurie Lespada and General Valadovich.

General Valadovich put his hand on top of Irene Goodpastor's off-camera hand and she gave an off-camera start. Then, surprisingly, she started talking very clearly, although her thoughts were a little off subject. "Is General MacArthur dead yet?"

The director quickly cut back to her.

General Valadovich tightened his hand on hers. "Oh, yes. He's been gone for a long time," General Valadovich answered.

"Thank God!" It was a little difficult to figure out what she meant.

The director cut to a tight close-up of Laurie Lespada who performed her duties perfectly, as though Irene Goodpastor had said something of note. "Well," she said, "you never stop being controversial! Now, tell me, Mrs. Goodpastor or General Valadovich, either of you—tell me about that fascinating story behind this visit of yours."

General Valadovich nodded. The director cut back to the two-shot.

"Yes, ma'am, it is fascinating. Irene Goodpastor was visiting here in 1960. That's 37 years ago now. So were some others here then, including me. Most of us didn't know each other, but nine of us were invited to the American Consulate to listen to one of the Kennedy-Nixon debates on Voice of America. I forgot by now which debate of theirs it was, but we all sat around a conference table and listened to it with three people from the consulate. So there were twelve of us all together. Afterwards we had a discussion about what would happen here in Hong Kong in 1997. Somehow, and again, I don't remember exactly how it happened, but we pledged to come back here–to be together during the transition of Hong Kong from Britain to China."

"It was my idea!" Mrs. Goodpastor yelled out. There wasn't any warning so the camera wasn't on her, but she was heard.

"That's right," General Valadovich said. "Now, the ones that are still left–who are still alive–were reminded of the occasion continually by Mrs. Goodpastor, not that we needed a reminder. The living are here. Some of the kids of the originals are here, too."

"She didn't have the Goodpastor Center back in 1960, did she?"

"Oh, no. Not back then. I don't believe there were many real Think Tanks back then. Maybe just the Brookings Institution. Anyway, we all fell in love with Hong Kong. What American wouldn't? This city has come a long way since then and this night is a sad one. God made it rain."

"What did you do tonight during the handover, General?"

"Prayed."

"You're a very religious man, aren't you?"

He hesitated as though he didn't want to answer. Then he nodded.

"Were you in the service back then at that 1960 meeting, General?"

"Yes, ma'am. I was a lieutenant then."

"That was quite a prominent group here, wasn't it?"

"At the time, not really. Other than Mrs. Goodpastor, none of the others in the group were well known back then."

"Well, the years have changed all that! They practically all had brilliant futures, didn't they?"

"Yes. Two of them went on to be assistants to U.S. presidents; Moose Dunston, and he's here in Hong Kong tonight, he's a close friend, and Cody Cooper. His son is here."

"Cody Cooper was a presidential assistant? What president?"

"President Kennedy."

She lurched her head back in a start. "I didn't know that."

"You weren't born then, ma'am. Cody was quite a young fellow himself back at that meeting. He went on to go to the White House, then the State Department, then he left government to become the man that gained such great prominence."

"Congresswoman Murphy was with you too, wasn't she?"

"Yes, ma'am. She was here back in 1960 with her husband, Ted. They were on their honeymoon. He did very well on your medium, didn't he?"

"Absolutely! One of the best television journalists of all time!"

There was no reaction on General Valadovich's face. And he didn't say anything.

Laurie Lespada didn't like pauses, so she added, "Congresswoman Murphy is in town now to be with all of you?"

"She was over at the handover ceremony tonight as a guest. The government of the People's Republic of China invited her. She's a guest of Li Peng."

"Really? That's prestige!"

Again, General Valadovich ignored a remark of Laurie Lespada. "Did you ever hear of a man named Adam Orr? He was here then."

The camera cut back to a close-up of her. She was squinting and giving a slight shake of her head. "No. I don't think so." The camera zoomed back.

"He's become my mentor. Whatever I am, I learned from him. He became my teacher. Not just mine. He did the same for Moose Dunston."

"Go on, General. Who were the others, although I think I know who some of them were."

"You know who Anne Whitney is?"

"Oh, yes. She was the one in Iran during the hostage crisis–and then she–"

"Anne's here," he interrupted. "She's here. In those days she worked at the Consulate with a Chinese girl who, indeed, became very celebrated. Do you know who I'm talking about?"

"I certainly do, General. I'm afraid I forgot her name, some Chinese name–I just don't remember, but she was the one who was in Tiananmen Square, wasn't she?"

"Yes. Tso Wai-yee. Her daughter is here. She lives here. Back in 1960 her mother and Anne worked for our Public Affairs Officer at the Consulate, Mark Daschle. And back then, there was a visiting Ambassador and his wife at the Consulate too; the Fairbanks. He was never known among the general public but he was known among practically all the foreign service officers back then."

"And you all kept in contact with each other through the years?"

"Irene kept in contact with all of us but, for the most part, because of our careers–foreign service, military, television, some who became a part of one administration or another, our lives couldn't help but cross–in different places throughout the world."

Suddenly Mrs. Goodpastor yelled out, "How about Johnny Carson?" The camera zoomed back to include Mrs. Goodpastor in the shot.

"Ma'am?" General Valadovich asked Mrs. Goodpastor.

"Is he dead yet?" she yelled.

"No. No. He's alive. He's fine. He's retired but he's fine."

"That's good," Irene Goodpastor said with a sigh of relief. The Assistant Director gave Laurie Lespada a hand gesture of expanding his fingers on both hands, then closing them and expanding them four times, in a sign that she had forty seconds left.

Again Irene Goodpastor yelled out, this time looking off to the side to her off-screen escort. "Tell Sonny Bono the fireworks were beautiful!"

It was not exactly the way Laurie Lespada wanted the show to wind down. "General, Hong Kong was a great deal different back then, I'll bet." She was struggling to quickly get the show back on base. "I'll bet there were no skyscrapers here back then, were there?"

"No, ma'am. But not just that. Everything was a great deal different back then. Every city. Every life. It was another world."

"Better or worse? Can you tell me in fifteen seconds? We have to go to a break."

"No, I can't," General Valadovich smiled. "The different world took 37 years to get here. It would take less time to tell you those things that are the same. Time changes so much we used to know. And it will change again from what you know tonight. It has to be that way. We can only assume that's what God wants. So Hong Kong's face will change. And so will all of our faces change. Are my fifteen seconds up?"

She turned from him to the camera. "This is Laurie Lespada for *Above the Fold* at the Hong Kong handover for World Network News, on the roof of the Regent Hotel in Hong Kong. And now, on this exciting night, we can say it differently than we ever said it before—we're broadcasting from Hong Kong, a Special Administrative Region of the People's Republic of China."

PART ONE

THE 1960s

ONE
AT THE START
1960

In 1960 United States passports had a green and cloth-like cover. There were also a lesser amount of maroon passports that were called Official, issued to foreign service officers of most ranks, and there were a very small amount of black ones for top-ranking diplomats.

No matter their color, those passports had good reason to have a strong protective cover because they were held tightly by their owners; tighter than a person would hold on to a loose piece of gold.

Inside all of them was a message from Christian Herter stating that "I, the undersigned, Secretary of State of the United States of America, hereby request all whom it may concern to permit safely and freely to pass, and in case of need to give all lawful aid and protection to the above named citizen of the United States."

It was a prized message.

That was when flying overseas was an adventure, not a task. There were no security devices to walk through or long corridors to an airliner's gate, and passengers dressed up for flights, and they were seen off by families who stayed at the gate until the airliner became a speck in the sky, and the families waved. It was when in-flight certificates were given to each passenger as the International Date Line was crossed, and airlines had flight attendants who were called stewardesses, and they looked like Hollywood starlets because being gorgeous was a requirement for stewardesses. Of course it wasn't fair to those applicants who weren't gorgeous, but justice isn't everything.

And it was when Ho Chi Minh City was called Saigon, Vietnam was called South Vietnam and North Vietnam, Santo Domingo was called Ciudad Trujillo, Zaire was called the Belgian Congo, Burkina Faso was called Upper Volta, Myanmar was called Burma, Namibia was called SouthWest Africa, Zimbabwe was called Rhodesia, Tanzania was called Tanganyika and Zanzibar, Botswana was called Bechuanaland, Germany was called East Germany and West Germany, Volgograd was called Stalingrad, Saint Petersberg was called Leningrad, 15 countries were called the Soviet Union, Beijing was called Peking, Guangzhou was called Canton, and Hong Kong, Special Administrative Region of the People's Republic of China was called Hong Kong, British Crown Colony.

At home young people were called kids, African-Americans were called Negroes, joggers were called runners, zip codes were called zones, pot was called marijuana, gays were called homosexuals, ghettoes were called slums, JFK Airport was called Idlewild, malls were called shopping centers, condoms were called rubbers, wimps were called squares, venues were called sites, chairpersons were called chairmen, consumers were called buyers, mentally challenged were called cuckoo, mid-life crisis was called dirty old man, rain-forests were called jungles, user-friendly was called easy, second-hand smoke was called smoke, option was called choice, choice was called abortion, Native Americans were called Indians, sexual harassment was called flirting, the get-go was called the beginning, closure was called the end, hegemony was called expansionism, graffiti was called painted messages, cost-effective was called cheap, input was called access, homeless were called hobos, stereos were called hi-fi's, promiscuity was called making-out, macho was called virile, Attention Deficit Disorder was called not paying attention, Hippies and Yippees were called Beatniks, prioritize was called order of importance, role-model was called admirable, sexually transmitted infections were called V.D., undocumented workers were called illegal aliens, entrepreneurial was called business-savvy, the environment was called Mother Nature, and the moon was called far away.

By those measurements, it was a long time ago.

On Saturday, October 8, 1960, the twelve people who came together in Hong Kong were showing a mix of green, maroon, and black passports to the U.S. Marine Guard at the U.S. Consulate for entrance. It was not the October meeting of the twelve that brought any of them to Hong Kong; their presence in Hong Kong created the meeting.

The night before the gathering of the twelve, Ted and Linda Murphy were dancing at the Repulse Bay Hotel, Lieutenant Jonas Valadovich was at the border area of Hong Kong looking through field-glasses at Red China, Irene Goodpastor was gambling in Macau, Cody Cooper was window shopping for a camera on Queen's Road Central, Moose Dunston was in a Wanchai bar, Ambassador and Mrs. Fairbanks were eating on a sampan in Aberdeen Harbor, while Mark Daschle, Anne Whitney, and Tso Wai-yee were working late at the U.S. Consulate. Adam Orr had yet to arrive in Hong Kong. He was on a Pan American Airways Clipper flying through the night to Kai Tak, Hong Kong's airport.

Black.

Through the window of the airliner there was nothing to see, but he stared at the black with intensity, as though he would miss something if he looked away from that window to his left.

"Where are we?" he heard from the woman on the seat next to him but he paid no attention to the question until it was asked again. "Where are we?"

He turned away from the window but didn't look at her. He looked down and then straight ahead. "Lean over and look through the window and you'll see." He pushed the shade all the way up to the top so it would be easier for her, and she leaned toward him, almost standing up.

"I can't see anything. There's nothing to see. But we aren't over land so that makes sense. Wait. I think I see a light down there. No. No it isn't. It's a light up here. It's on our plane, on the wing I think."

"We're nowhere."

"Nowhere? How can we be nowhere? We have to be somewhere."

"We're nowhere. Enjoy it."

She didn't. Fate had given her an assignment of an aisle seat next to an unsociable man who was probably old enough to be her father, but not old enough to have lost his interest in women. His total disinterest in her was not a boost for the confidence she had enjoyed for so many years based, in large part, on her ability to use her feminine allure. She could have moved to another seat since almost half of them were empty but that would have been a surrender. After all, she had intentionally dressed in a new tailored black dress with white trim along with shoes and purse to match just in case she met some man on the plane that she would want to entice even further than her natural appeal. None of it was working.

Two more hours of the flight had passed and not one more word had been said between the two. They both had drinks. They both ate. They both smoked. They both read magazines. But not a word. She noticed he had piercing blue eyes when he looked at anything, but he wouldn't look at her. When the stewardess asked if he wanted a drink or asked what he wanted to eat, his answer was made with style. Everything he said was an absolute and final decision. Had he said "hello" there would have been no need to answer him because "hello" had already been decided, his mind was made up and that was all there was to it. If he smiled, which he did at times at something he read, the smile was done quickly and automatically and the smile disappeared in the same manner. That, too, was a decision, and when his face disengaged from the smile he might just as well have said, "That's completed. Now I will decide other things."

In a quick and daring phrase she did it: "Pardon me," she said, "but I'm taking a night course in psychology at UCLA and I want to ask you something."

"Yes?"

"This is a great question, this is really a great question: if you could do it, what day of your life would you re-live?"

Without any hesitation at all he answered, "Last December, there was a day last December."

"Oh?" She smiled. "And what happened then?"

"I was on an airplane and the person sitting next to me left me alone."

That insult would have been enough to set a roadblock for any normal person. But she liked to jump roadblocks and prided herself in her ability to leap them. She let one more hour pass before making another jump. "Are we still nowhere?" she asked him as her last attempt at nurturing some civility from him, choosing to talk on his terms, pretending she believed they were nowhere.

"You don't understand," he looked at her directly for the first time. Now she could see how penetrating his eyes could look into hers.

He wished she was ugly. It would be easier to continue his disinterest. She wasn't ugly.

"What is it I don't understand?" she asked in a tone that sounded like she was a helpless maiden tied to a bedpost, asking her captor what he wanted of her.

"We are nowhere but you're too used to the world to enjoy what we have here in the cabin."

"What do you mean?" At last she had broken his resistance to conversation. Or maybe it was simply time rather than her charm that had broken him.

"Flying over the sea at night is the nearest you can come to feeling what it was like before you were born, and after you die. Up here we are without time and place."

"I don't get it."

"I'll prove it to you. What time is it?"

She looked at her watch, she looked confused, she smiled, she looked back at him. "Well, what time is it where? I already re-set my watch to Hong Kong time. Do you mean the time there?"

"No. I mean here. What time is it here?"

"But I don't know where we are."

No, she wasn't ugly. "You don't know what time it is even though you looked at your watch and it's working properly. You see? Even if you know exactly where we are, you won't know what time it is here. This airliner is full of people with watches and the watches read different times for different places. Time and place become unknown up here. So while you're here, don't search for the world. There's plenty of that where you were and where you're going. It isn't here. On these plane rides I used to do what you're doing now. I used to think of times and places I had left and times and places that were ahead of me, but in doing that I so vastly underrated the current. Then I realized the adventure that's in the cabin. Now I plan for it. Enjoy the fact that in this constantly moving aircraft there is a unique existence. Now I make the trip as frequently as I can."

"To where? To Hong Kong?"

He nodded. "I buy a ticket that takes me from home through this wonderful interlude, and then back into time and place in Hong Kong. And then, when it's done, I go back through another interlude to return to the time and place of home." He seemed to know something that she didn't know.

"Which do you prefer?"

"Which what do I prefer?"

"The life you left, or Hong Kong?"

"The life I left because home is best. It's the people I love and the habits I've acquired in all these years; the duties, the patterns, the times, all the normality that I've chosen. But it's not everything of life. It's Life Number One. Hong Kong is my Life Number Two. Secretive. Terrible. Wonderful. It's my secret place in my secret times. Everyone should have a secret place in secret times. Everyone should find their own Life Number Two. Why be content with what you know by habit when life is so brief and so much can be lived that generally goes unknown?"

"Are you married?" That was bold.

"Of course not." He looked sharply at her.

"Why of course not?" She smiled.

"Because honesty is important. I would have to give up Life Number Two to be honest in Life Number One."

"That's admirable."

"Not admirable; just livable. And there's another reason."

"What?"

"I can't marry because I believe in romance, and marriage turns romanticists into bankers."

She was silent for a while. But only for a while. "Bankers?"

He didn't answer her.

She felt she was losing him again.

"You know," and he squinted at her as he gave a short nod, "when Sigmund Freud was on his deathbed he said, 'I still don't know what women want.' Well, I do."

She hadn't lost him. "Oh?"

"What they want is only one word."

"Money? Is that what you think?"

"No."

"All right. I'll bite–what's the one word?"

"More."

She thought about it for a while. "More of what?"

"More of anything. They want more of it."

There was a silence again. He turned his face away from her. She tried to catch the silence before his memory of what he said was lost. "Anything?"

He still didn't look at her. "Give them your time and they want more of your time. Stay with them until two in the morning and they want you to stay until four. Stay with them until four and they want you to stay with them until eight. Stay with them through the morning and they want you to stay into the afternoon. Give them a one carat diamond and they want a two carat diamond. Give them a Chevrolet and they want a Cadillac. Give them a house and they want a mansion. A man wants to make a woman happy. All men should know that it's futile."

"What do you want? Sex? Is that all?"

He looked directly in her eyes again. She was prepared for his anger, but didn't receive it. Instead he said, "I spent half my youth searching for someone who would sell me Spanish Fly. I still don't know if there is such a thing."

She laughed. "And you call yourself a romanticist?"

"I call myself a realist. Why can't women be content with sex? Give them lovemaking, and when it's done they say 'hold me.' and they want more physical affection. Don't they know that it's like demanding someone who just had his arm amputated to pick up a boulder? All I want then is a cigarette. They always want more."

"You are such a cynic!"

"It's not cynicism. It's that I understand the differences between men and women. It's why I never celebrate the wedding of a friend. Women want security, men want liberty, and that's the conflict that will never be resolved. They tease him out of liberty. They bait him. They drive him crazy until he gives it up. It's done in the most careful steps. A man wants sex, affection, and support from a woman. Women pretend that's all they want. But they want to be a partner, an adviser, a critic. I can hire people to fill those positions if I want them filled. I want to be free. I'm not even as free as I was before you started talking to me. I can't be immersed in my own thoughts as long as I have to answer you. Do you think I'd be talking to a man this much?"

She liked that. He had proven her femininity was still intact. "Are you telling me that I'm encroaching on your liberty by talking to you?"

"Yes," he answered.

"I'm destroying your adventure by asking questions?"

"Yes," he answered.

"Then I'll be quiet."

"Good."

She reached for her cigarettes from her purse and then hunted for matches. "Do you have a light?" she asked. She knew he did because he was using a lighter throughout the flight, never offering to light her cigarettes with it.

He took the lighter from his inside breast pocket, and this time lit her cigarette with it. "I knew you couldn't be quiet." But he said it with a smile. He cupped his hand around the lighter, and she cupped her hand around his. There wasn't that much of a breeze from the overhead air nozzle to call for all that but he did it and she did it.

"I like your lighter," she said. "That's that new kind without flints and wicks and things, isn't it?"

"Gas. It works on gas. It's butane."

"What is it called?"

"Wyatt."

"Wyatt?"

"Wyatt."

"I never heard of that company."

"It's not a company. It's made by Ronson. I named him Wyatt."

She laughed. And when she stopped, her whole face was smiling, not just her lips. "Why did you name it at all?"

"He deserved a name. I name most of my inanimate things."

"You do?"

"Of course. Don't you?"

"No. No I don't. I had a doll once that I named Lov-ee, but that was a long time ago."

"Not too long ago."

She smiled like a woman. No, like a girl. "Thank you. How old are you?"

"There is no age on an airplane."

"Aren't you going to ask me how old I am? Who I am? What I do? Don't you even want to know my name?"

"No. You don't have any of that up here."

"All right. I'm not going to argue with you. You don't bend."

He reached in his other breast pocket, and took out his green passport. "See this passport?" He held it in front of him, tilting it in her direction.

"Yes."

"He has a name. He's Lawrence Pell the Fifth."

"What do you mean?"

"That's his name. Larry." And he put the passport back in his breast pocket.

She laughed. "Is that your name too? Are you Lawrence Pell?"

"No!"

"Why the Fifth?"

"A direct relation to the First. It's my sixth passport. They were all Larry except for my second one who was Walter Johnson. That was a mistake I suppose. In retrospect I should have named him Lawrence Pell the Second but as soon as I saw him, as soon as he was issued, I said, 'Walter!' and he looked so glad. I suppose if I had it to do over again I would have named him Lawrence Pell the Second and he would have gotten used to it and then I would have named my next passport Larry the Third instead of the Second. The way I did it got everything out of sequence."

"Are you crazy?"

"Yes," he said. "Have you never known a crazy man?"

She smiled and slowly nodded. "I think they've all been crazy."

"Good."

"And now another crazy man. This time on an airplane," she said through a slight giggle.

"This isn't just any airplane. This is Jerry Untemeyer."

"The plane is Jerry Undemeyer?"

"No 'd'. Untemeyer. With a 't'."

"Your lighter has a name and the plane has a name but the passengers don't?"

"It makes more sense because in a generation's time this plane, unless it crashes or is renovated, will still be the same. But if you and I live, you won't be the same as you are now and I won't be the same as I am now and no city will be the same as it is now. Are you or me or Los Angeles or Hong Kong the same as we were in 1940? Will we be the same as we are now when the year is 1980? We aren't just people and places. We are mixed with the times. It's why gravestones tell the years of birth and death. Time is part of the person. But inanimate objects stay the same as long as they last without observance of time, and so they deserve a name that lasts longer than we do. Untemeyer."

"Maybe you have something." She meant it.

"I do have something. And inanimate objects don't quest to hurt people or destroy places. They serve them. They have no secret motives."

"Can you hurt someone on a plane?" By asking him that question she intentionally was showing a submissiveness to his thoughts. She not only knew what she was doing but she added something to it. She gave a look that only women can give–or at least some women can give. Her lower lip kept moving although she was saying nothing.

"No. There's no hurt on an airplane. There can't be."

Her femininity had overtaken the entire aura. She reeked of it, smelled of it, her eyes daring his. "Why can't there be hurt up here?"

"Because it's away from hurt. We're too high." And he moved his right hand from the arm of the seat between them and slowly raised his hand until it cupped her left cheek. She closed her eyes, but just briefly and then she opened them again. She left his hand there, and she left her cheek there. Almost a minute passed before she slowly leaned her face tighter onto his hand. And then one of her hands came over his hand and then his other hand moved and her other hand moved and everything was slow and fast and slow and fast and if there was time, minutes passed and hours passed, but there was no time. Then she was on his assigned seat while he was still on it. Was anyone watching? It was of no significance and neither of them even glanced to find out. They didn't stop until the passion was entirely spent, and the plane started descending and the announcement was made over the loudspeaker to "please put your seat in an upright position and buckle your seat belt," and "it is 10:22 P.M. in Hong Kong on October the 7th and it has been a pleasure for all of us on Pan American Airways to serve you."

"Don't hold me," she said. "I know you don't want to. Let's have a cigarette–real quick before the 'no smoking' signs come on." She settled back in her seat and straightened the mess that had been her dress.

He lit a cigarette for her and one for him and then he handed her the lighter. "Wyatt likes you. Take him."

"You're giving him to me?"

"He likes you. He thinks you're softer than me."

"You're giving me Wyatt?"

"Take good care of him. He's a fine fellow. Don't give him any unsolicited advice. That's the mistake most women make. And don't ask him to give you a light unless you've filled him with fluid."

"What do you mean by that?"

"Take good care of him."

"I will. Thank you. Thank you for Wyatt," and she carefully put Wyatt in her purse. "Will I see you again?" she asked.

"Never."

"Never ever?"

"Never ever."

"Why not?"

"Because we, as we know each other, will never exist again."

"And that's final?"

"Unless we meet on a plane going across the ocean again where time and space and names are gone again."

And then the plane landed at Kai Tak Airport and he was back to being his age of 51 years and she was back to being her age of 32 and he and she and all the other passengers were back in 1960, and they were all their 1960 ages and they all took a 1960 motor-driven cart to the terminal and they rushed to go through Hong Kong's 1960 Passport Control and they waited for their luggage and they took taxis to their 1960 destinations and they all knew what time it was and where they were.

The journey without time and space was done.

They both went their separate ways. He was back to being Adam Orr and he would keep his word to never contact the woman he met when he wasn't.

And now he was in his Life Number Two: Hong Kong.

TWO
THE MEETING
1960

Adam Orr was up early, standing next to the Kowloon Clock Tower, looking across the harbor with the morning light revealing dozens and dozens of junks sailing from east to west and west to east with their brown weathered canvas sails on black wooden hulls making proud statements of their presence, as peacocks would. Beyond the junks was the island with its colonial-style buildings at the water's edge set against tall and rolling mountains, and some of the buildings were on ill-paved roads and alleyways that were going diagonally up as steep as tilted ladders. In the morning streets old men were pulling black-wheeled, red rickshaws carrying human cargoes, the rickshaw-pullers running to bring those passengers to their destinations. There were even some passengers who sat on wheeless sedan chairs suspended between two runners. Sedan chairs had more comfortable seats than the rickshaws. Between Kowloon and the island were the Star Ferries passing each other in the harbor bringing passengers from Kowloon to Hong Kong Island, and bringing passengers from Hong Kong Island to Kowloon. The ferries, never bored by their seven minute voyages that had been going one way and then the other since 1870 were filled with people, one departure only minutes after another, each ship named after a star: *Twinkling Star* and *Morning Star* and *Evening Star* and *Meridian Star* and all kinds of stars.

To Adam Orr, the procedure in taking the Star Ferry was an ecstasy revisited. The comforting familiarity was magnified by the uniqueness of the procedure: to walk down the concrete walkway and wait by the gated barrier until a small man in a dark blue uniform with white stripes on his sailored lapels opened the gateway, and the large warning-light above it turned from red to green. To be one of the first by the gateway was a loneliness that lasted no more than seconds, as the lonely would be surrounded by waiting people, and then would be swallowed by the pouring passengers as they passed the open gateway and down the ramp to the gangplank and onto the *Star Ferry.*

Each of the first ones aboard were expected, by tradition, to reverse the back of whatever long bench on which the oncoming passenger would decide to sit, so as to make all those who will sit there, face the direction of destination. As soon as the passengers sat down and before the gate was closed, early morning men were already reading their *South China Morning Post* and *Hong Kong Standard* and dozens of newspapers in Chinese. And early morning women dressed in brightly colored cheongsams with high collars and slit skirts sat like proper and erotic goddesses. All of this while it was only the morning. My God, what would later hours be like, not even to dare think of the nights? Other cities would writhe in jealousy if they had only known what happened here off the South China Sea.

Adam Orr went through those comforting procedures known nowhere else on earth and then, in the continuation of the unmatched, a loud bell rang to warn anymore prospective passengers that soon the gateway would be closed and the dark red gangplank would be raised and they better run. Finally there was the awkward, rocking start of the forward motion with the accompanying noise of water lapping against the wooden hull of the *Star Ferry*. Then Hong Kong Island started to come closer, getting larger and larger and larger.

The only awkward out-of-context interruption of this magnificent short journey was a sign that read, "Do Not Spit. Beware of Pickpockets." The warning seemed to be effective. No one spit, and at least no one could be seen picking anyone's pocket.

The ride was all too quick. The small man in the deep-blue uniform put on his thick, dirty, worn gloves and heaved the ship's rope and there was a bump of the ship and its motors stopped, and there was the boat's uneven swaying as it started being pulled toward the Hong Kong Island side of the harbor. As the rope was being wrapped around the protruding cleat of iron on the dock, the passengers rose, rushing to stand in mass by the small man in the uniform who was waiting for the signal that the boat would stop hitting the side of the dock so he could free the gangplank barrier and lower it. When it was lowered, the crowd poured out like a torrent of freed water, heading up the walkway to a myriad of destinations, Adam Orr making the short walk up to 26 Garden Road.

"Good to see you. Good to see you," Mark Daschle greeted each visitor as they walked in the windowless Conference Room of the United States Consulate. He had been trained to always say "good to see you" rather than "good to meet you," in case he forgot that he had already met whomever he was greeting. "Have some coffee and pastries, just help yourself, and then sit down with your snacks anywhere you'd like. So good to see you."

With the exception of one couple who stood at the coffee and pastry table talking to each other, they did as they were told, seating themselves around the oval conference table in the middle of the room.

Mark Daschle walked to take his place standing at the head of the table, totally at ease in that role. With suit and blue bow-tie with white dots on it, and an engaging smile and kind eyes, there was no question that he was the host, and that he had considerable experience in taking charge of events like this on behalf of the United States government. His face looked like so many other men in their early forties who were coming into their way in the world and who acted appropriately for the positions they had reached. What made him obvious as a foreign service officer was that bow-tie. He straightened it, smoothed back his brown hair, fiddled with the flaps of his jacket pockets to make sure they weren't tucked in and said, "Good morning, ladies and gentlemen. On behalf of the Consul

General and all of us at the U.S. Consulate, we're so glad to have you here this bright Saturday morning. For those of you who don't know, I'm Mark Daschle, the Public Affairs Officer here.

"Why don't you come around the table, Mr. and Mrs. Murphy? There's plenty of room. Please sit down and be comfortable." Since he was in authority, the couple that was still standing went to the conference table and sat down. Mark Daschle nodded and sat down, himself. "I recognize that most of you don't know each other. I also recognize that most of you don't know why you were singled out, rather than others, to receive the invitation to come here this morning to hear the Presidential Candidates Debate as it happens, back in the United States. What we did was ask the State Department, the United States Information Agency, and the Department of Defense to each suggest a few important Americans they knew would be in Hong Kong this morning and would be especially interested in hearing this debate between Vice President Nixon and Senator Kennedy. You were the names they recommended to us—and we're delighted to have you here.

"As you know, this morning the second Presidential Debate will be held, this one in D.C., at 7:30 in the evening, their time. Curly here," and he nodded to a young Chinese man also in a suit but without a tie, "Curly Kwang has rigged up a couple speakers to our rather archaic short-wave radio that I think we purchased here during F.D.R.'s administration," and he smiled and looked around the table, "but it still works. These debates, you know, are quite historical. It will be seen live on television throughout much of the United States for those who have television sets, and we'll get kinescopes of it here in about a week. Both Vice President Nixon and Senator Kennedy have agreed to have four of them—four debates, and the first one, a week and a half ago, was in Chicago and was intended to deal exclusively with domestic affairs, although they did talk quite a bit about foreign relations. This one has no restriction, they're going to discuss anything that's asked of them, any subject, so I suspect there will be a lot more on foreign relations, and I know that everyone here is particularly interested in that. And it won't have the tight format of the first one. This time no opening or closing statements, just answering questions of the press. It's an hour again. Now, above all, we want you to feel comfortable here, so let's keep it informal."

That was a strange request since Mark Daschle didn't know how to be informal. He was the type whose first words weren't "Ma-ma" and "Dada" but "I trust you must be my parents. Good to see you. My name is Mark Daschle. Please sit down."

He continued. "By now I'm sure you've found that Hong Kong is a fascinating place. There's a stack of brochures on Hong Kong by the door if you want to take one. It has good information in it on this wonderful city. As a foreign service officer from Washington, I just hope that no one back in Washington remembers I'm stationed here or they may demand I come back home!" The guests knew they were supposed to laugh, so they did.

"Anyone can stay after the debate is over, if you want to, and we'll discuss the debate among ourselves here. We'll see what, if anything, the two candidates say that might directly affect Hong Kong.

"Now while we still have a few minutes before the debate starts and Curly is still plugging things in, why don't we go around the table and introduce ourselves? Just tell us your name and what brings you to Hong Kong on this beautiful October day.

"I'll start by introducing our J.O.T., our Junior Officer Trainee, Anne Whitney from Pennsylvania, who graduated with honors from Penn State last year and immediately went to work at the State Department and then the U.S.I.A. She was sent here just last month."

"Thank you," Anne Whitney said with pretended maturity. "As a J.O.T. I do a little of everything here. While I'm doing just about everything, I'm living in the Shamshuipo area where I'm the only American. It's above Boundary Street which is where Kowloon ends and the New Territories begin. I'm the only white woman there in the housing unit, yet I am very much at home. Most people are very poor here and there are a few rich, with no middle class. As I'm sure you know, this is a British Crown Colony, that's what 'B.C.C.' means that you see on everything. Colonialists and their friends are the rich." No one asked her for her appraisal on economics. With her remarks done, she put on a pair of glasses that seemed bigger than her face, and she put them on so quick and abruptly that it was as though she was adding a visual period at the end of her statement. Her short, cropped blond hair was also a statement, saying she was competitive and professional, not interested in turning the heads of men, although it would have been easy for her to do that if that's what she wanted.

The tall young man in blue uniform with a silver first lieutenant's bar on each shoulder, was next. That uniform looked as though it just came from the cleaners without one wrinkle, and he was its equal in orderliness all the way to the top of his butch-cut hair. His voice was surprising in that it was a good octave lower than would be expected. "I'm Lieutenant Jonas Valadovich, U.S. Air Force, sir," he said looking directly at Mark Daschle. "I'm here on Rest-and-Relaxation from duty in Japan where I serve with the Occupation Forces. I'm just going to be here in Hong Kong for four days." It was obvious that his rest and relaxation was not going to be bar-hoping or doing anything that would embarrass his uniform that he wore with immense pride.

If there had been a high-cost ticket required to attend this meeting, the sight of the one sitting next to the airman would have made any man surrender his entire wallet. She was a beautiful young Chinese woman dressed in a red silk cheong-sam, her long black hair flowed over the back of her cheong-sam's high collar and then continued on and on, down to somewhere below the field of vision of those sitting around the table. She was the only one drinking tea rather than coffee, which seemed right for her. It was all part of her Chinese femininity. "My name is Tso Wai-yee," and she told her name almost in a whisper but easily heard as no one would have dared to make a noise while she was talking. "My little sister and I escaped from Red China right after the Communist Revolution. I was only 12 years old at the time." That automatically made most of the men there move their hands below the table to start counting on their fingers to figure out she was 23 years old now. "We are so grateful to live in a place that is free, and I'm especially proud to work for the Consulate of the United States of America."

"Wai-yee is an expert of the history of Hong Kong," Mark Daschle explained. "She wrote the history section in our brochure that we've stacked by the door for you. She's a real historian. And, of course, she speaks perfect Cantonese, and she also speaks perfect Mandarin, as well as English. She's been a tremendous help to us here at the Consulate." Mark Daschle said all this as though he was justifying the fact that she had been hired when he knew everyone sitting around the table was suspicious that she was hired because it would have been impossible for any man to refuse her a job with those looks. Even the women around the table were fascinated by her.

Next to Tso Wai-yee was a young man chewing gum with his mouth open. "I'm Ted Murphy and this is my bride, Linda." He took a couple more chews of his gum, then used his tongue to set it in a temporary resting place inside his mouth, for later use. "We live in New York City and I write a syndicated political column for King Features called 'Murphy's Law' about world events and it's in 108 newspapers now. We're havin' a great time here. I'm not writin' on this trip. Linda and I are on our honeymoon." Ted Murphy didn't sound like the writer he was, nor did he look like a writer. He was small and tough looking and it was apparent that he was a man who probably knew New York's worst streets. He had a nose that God did not create in the form in which it was now shaped. At least one fist, and maybe more than one, had transformed it into something unique. Ted Murphy looked like he would relish another fight, but since he was on his honeymoon, he had his temper under control. "We're stayin' at the Hong Kong home of the editor of the *Far Eastern Economic Review*, Dick Wilson. From here we go to Bangkok and to Angkor Wat in Cambodia, and—around the world."

Linda Murphy smiled and, with a lilt in her voice, said no more than, "And I'm Linda Murphy. It still sounds so strange to say it!" She was a little overweight and was adding to that weight by eating the pastry in front of her with great enthusiasm, only stopping long enough to tell her new name.

Before the introductions went across the table, Anne Whitney impulsively leaned forward to catch Ted Murphy's eyes. "I love your columns, Mr. Murphy. I look forward to them. We think alike, and it's so good to finally meet you." Ted Murphy turned his face directly at Anne, leaving the back of his head all that his wife, Linda, could see of him. While she was blind to his face, he winked at Anne Whitney.

Mark Daschle heard and saw the exchange and was ready to explode, but he contained himself. Anne Whitney's dialogue was not in the best interest of the Consulate.

Across the table was a very tall, distinguished gray-mustached man. He stood up before introducing himself and other than the host, Mark Daschle, no one before him had stood up for an introduction. He wore a vest and had a pocket watch with its gold chain dangling from one pocket of his vest to the pocket on the other side of his vest. He cleared his throat and nodded at Mark Daschle, while he seemed to tilt forward as he stood with a marked bend in his back. "Thank you for inviting us, Mark," and then he turned from Mark Daschle and roamed his view around the table. Then he cleared his throat again. "I'm Gerald Fairbanks and this is Mary Fairbanks, and we are not on our honeymoon!" There was scattered, polite laughter. "We've been married now for 36 years. We come from Austin, Texas but I suppose we could say we now live in Washington, D.C.–that is, when we're home. We live in the area called Foggy Bottom, not far from the Potomac River–and I don't know how George Washington did it. I've tried throwing a dollar across it so many times I'm broke!" Again there was some polite laughter. "I have ten more years before retirement and then Mrs. Fairbanks and I will go back to Austin. As for now, I'm with the State Department on the Far East Desk and–"

"Gerry's being modest," Mark Daschle interrupted. "He's Ambassador Gerald Fairbanks. He's not just on the Far East Desk he's–"

Gerald Fairbanks interrupted the interruption. "I was an Ambassador for a mere three months. President Truman appointed me and I was barely confirmed when Ike came in and he wisely appointed someone else and I went back to the State Department. I'm a careerist who has the honor of being called Mr. Ambassador, but only by my close friends who remember that I was one!" He sat down.

Mark Daschle shook his head. "Gerry's a top-ranking foreign service officer. And however brief, he was a great Ambassador." He turned his eyes to Mrs. Fairbanks, and nodded.

"And I'm Mary Fairbanks. I'm just thrilled to be here in Hong Kong with Gerald. It's been a dream of mine to see it and I have not been disappointed. And, Mr. Daschle, it's wonderful to be able to hear the presidential debate while we're away from home, so I thank you." She was perfect. She was skilled in the world of the foreign service. Every word was said with care and precision, and entirely correct.

Mark Daschle smiled and nodded. "It's our pleasure to have both of you here with us. Gerry and Mary are old friends of mine. The Ambassador and I served together in Lagos. Adam, go ahead."

Adam said, "Adam Orr from Florida," and that was that. He looked around the table with a dagger-like stare at the entire group and he gave one nod, the nod indicating that it was all he had to say, there was nothing else anyone needed to know, and don't ask questions.

Next to Adam was a man who was so big he almost took the room of two. Moose Dunston wasn't fat, just big, and needed no weapon other than his appearance to make a possible assailant look for victims elsewhere. He had lit and re-lit his big black Dunhill sandblasted pipe and he re-lit it again just before he gave himself an introduction while staring at Tso Wai-yee, his recitation given entirely for her reaction. He didn't for a moment look around the table or at Mark Daschle. "My name is Moose Dunston. They've called me Moose ever since my high school football days," he said as though Tso Wai-yee was anxious to know why he was called Moose. "I served in the 40th Division in the Korean War. Then near the end of the war I went to the Department of Defense, and got an appointment from Ike—not personally but his administration as a non-military liaison with some of the folks setting up defenses in South Vietnam. I'm here at the Miramar Hotel for a few days en route to Saigon. Just a few days there I think, and then back home. I do a little writing myself. Not like Mr. Murphy. I write reports for the D.O.D." He breathed in a large draw from his pipe, but his pipe did not obey. With or without his pipe lit, he was successful at doing what he wanted most to do since Tso Wai-yee seemed impressed, and she smiled at him when he finished. He said everything he wanted her to know except his room number at the Miramar Hotel.

Now came the thin, almost scrawny young man of extreme and unorthodox interest in every one seated at the table as they gave their introductions. No matter what they said, no matter how mundane, his eyes would enlarge to the point that they were in peril of falling from their sockets, looking at them as if to say, "What do you mean? That can't be! That just can't be!" His disproportionate interest in whatever was said, made the more impressionable speakers feel important. "I'm Cody Cooper. I've been with the Kennedy Campaign for the past two months and before that, the University of Michigan where I finished Pre-Med. I was going to go to Medical School but when Senator Kennedy won the nomination for the Presidency, I changed directions. I was born and raised in Detroit and I'm here because this is a city of refugees that I had to see before Senator Kennedy gets in the White House. I've been to Europe and I want to have more qualifications to work for him. From here I'm going to Africa and then in December to Latin America." His problem was not a lack of overseas travel, his problem was that his voice was cracking as though he was still in adolescence. His face that looked like it had no reason to ever meet a razor, and his frail frame, didn't argue with the impression given by his voice. But there was a goodness in him that was apparent, and his attentiveness with an obvious quest to absorb everything he could learn, was noted with appreciation by others.

When it got to the last person at the table, a small gray-haired woman in her mid-fifties who looked older than that, and who everyone there recognized as the Washington socialite, Irene Goodpastor, the radio blared out throughout the room by way of Curly Kwang's magically rigged up machinery.

From the speakers, a voice loudly bounced off the walls saying, "Good evening. This is Frank McGee, NBC News in Washington. This is the second of programs unmatched in history..."

"Shhh!" Mark Daschle signaled. "We'll get back to introductions later.

This is it." Curly lowered the volume to a reasonable level, then diplomatically left the room.

It was foreign affairs right away. Paul Niven of CBS asked Vice President Nixon who he thought was responsible for the loss of Cuba to Castro, in view of a speech the night before by Senator Kennedy in which he said, "The administration must take responsibility for the loss of Cuba."

The vice president answered, "there isn't any question but that we will defend Guantanamo if it's attacked. There also isn't any question but that the free people of Cuba—the people who want to be free—are going to be supported and that they will attain their freedom. No, Cuba is not lost, and I don't think this kind of defeatist talk by Senator Kennedy helps the situation one bit."

Ted Murphy, the bent-nosed columnist for King Features Syndicate, was the only one in the room who was taking notes. "Why is that defeatist?" he asked no one in particular. "Kennedy wasn't being defeatist!"

"In the first place," Senator Kennedy responded, "I've never suggested that Cuba was lost except for the present. In my speech last night I indicated that Cuba one day again would be free."

"So is that supposed to be defeatist?" Ted Murphy looked around the table. "That's not defeatist."

"I hope some day it will rise," Senator Kennedy said, "but I don't think it will rise if we continue the same policies toward Cuba that we did in recent years, and in fact towards all of Latin America when we've ignored the needs of Latin America. We've beamed not a single Voice of America program in Spanish to all of Latin America in the last eight years, except for the three months of the Hungarian revolution."

Then there was the subject of the Eisenhower Administration's first reaction of denial that the U.S. plane shot down by the Soviet Union was a U-2 spy plane, and Soviet Chairman Nikita Khrushchev's subsequent refusal to attend the planned summit meeting.

Senator Kennedy said, "The U-2 flights were proper from the point of view of protecting our security, but they were not in accordance with international law."

"You bet they weren't," Anne Whitney, the young Junior Officer Trainee with big glasses, muttered.

"Shhh!" Mark Daschle looked over at her clenching his lips. Then he said, "No side remarks, Anne! No remarks from our staff."

Senator Kennedy continued, "My judgment is that we should follow the advice of Theodore Roosevelt to be strong, maintain a strong position; but also speak softly."

Anne excitedly hit the air with her fist. Then she looked down so as not to see Mark Daschle's reaction.

"I believe we should be stronger than we now are," Senator Kennedy said. "I believe we should have a stronger military force. I believe we should increase our strength all over the world."

"Et tu, Brute?" Ted Murphy asked sarcastically, looking up from his note-taking.

"But I don't confuse words with strength," the senator added, "and in my judgment if the summit was useful, if it would have brought us closer to peace, than rather than the lie that we told, which has been criticized by all responsible people afterwards, it would have been far better for us to follow the common diplomatic procedure of expressing regrets and then try to move on."

Anne Whitney nodded. Nods of the Consulate staff had not yet been forbidden. Then Ted Murphy nodded. No danger there, he was a guest. The Washington socialite, Mrs. Goodpastor, seeing the nods and noticing that Mark Daschle didn't say anything about the movements of their heads, joined in the nodding-brigade and she dared to say softly, "Kennedy is a brilliant young man."

Vice President Nixon responded, "Whenever we do anything that's wrong, we can express regrets. But when the president of the United States is doing something that's right, something that is for the purpose of defending the security of this country against surprise attack, he can never express regrets or apologize to anybody, including Mr. Khrushchev."

Adam Orr couldn't resist saying something balancing the previous remarks around the table. "Good for you! We owe Khrushchev nothing!"

Vice President Nixon added, "I don't intend to see to it that the United States is ever in a position where, while we're negotiating with the Soviet Union, that we discontinue our intelligence effort. And I don't intend ever to express regrets to Mr. Khrushchev or anybody else if I'm doing something that has the support of the congress and that is right for the purpose of protecting the security of the United States."

"Oh, please," Anne said.

"Anne!" Tso Wai-yee, her consulate co-worker, looked angrily at Anne.

Vice President Nixon continued since, fortunately, he could not hear Anne Whitney. "Senator Kennedy a moment ago referred to the fact that there was not an adequate Voice of America program for Latin America. I'd like to point out that in the last six years the Democratic Congresses, of which he'd been a member, have cut twenty million dollars off the Voice of America programs. They also have cut four billion dollars off of mutual security in these last six years. They also have cut two billion dollars off of defense. Now when they talk about our record here, it is well that they recognize that they have to stand up for their record as well. So let me summarize by saying this: I'm not satisfied with what we're doing in the Cold War because I believe we have to step up our activities and launch an offensive for the minds and hearts and souls of men. It must be economic; it must be technological; above all it must be ideological. But we've got to get help from the Congress in order to do this."

"You and Ike had eight years," Cody Cooper, the young campaigner for Senator Kennedy offered, looking around the table for approval. "If you couldn't do it in all that time, Dick Nixon, what makes you think you can do it now?"

"The administration needs the Congress to do it, Nixon said," Moose

Dunston, the man whose big frame took up the room of two, responded to Cody. "Aren't you listening?" Then Moose looked over at Tso Wai-yee to see if she was impressed with what he said to Cody. She gave a smile of endorsement.

Senator Kennedy took all this less emotionally than Cody Cooper. "Of course Mr. Nixon is wholly inaccurate when he says that the Congress has not provided more funds in fact than the president requested for national defense. In 1953 we tried to put an appropriation of five billion dollars for our defenses."

This time it was Ambassador Fairbanks who felt compelled to say something. "Five billion? What does he mean five billion? Our defense budget is close to 44 billion. I don't know what it was in '53, but it couldn't have been only five billion."

"No, Gerry," Mark Daschle answered. "He's talking about an additional appropriation, not the whole budget."

Ambassador Fairbanks nodded. "I see. I see. He didn't make that clear."

"I was responsible for the amendment with Senator Monroney in 1954 to strengthen our ground forces," Senator Kennedy continued. "The Congress of the United States appropriated six hundred and seventy-seven million dollars more than the President was willing to use, up till a week ago."

"See?" Mark said to Ambassador Fairbanks.

"I see, I see," and Ambassador Fairbanks cleared his throat.

"What are you guys talkin' about?" Ted Murphy asked.

"Wait–wait," Mark Daschle said. "Let's hear what the Senator is saying."

"The relative strength of the United States compared to that of the Soviet Union and the Chinese Communists together has deteriorated in the last eight years and we should know it, and the American people should be told the facts."

"They sure should," Moose Dunston said. "Kennedy's right there. Our strength is chicken feed compared to Moscow and Peking. It's a scandal."

Lieutenant Valadovich gave a very short nod, hesitant because he didn't want to offend either his current commander in chief or any prospective commander in chief, be it Vice President Nixon or Senator Kennedy.

Senator Kennedy added, "We ought to know now that Laos is moving from neutralism in the direction of the Communists."

"That's for sure," Moose Dunston added.

Near the end of the hour-long debate came the issue of where the two candidates would draw the line in the defense of Taiwan (which was generally referred to by the name given to it by the Portuguese: Formosa,) and its outlying territory, most particularly the islands of Quemoy and Matsu.

"I believe strongly in the defense of Formosa," Senator Kennedy said. "But these islands are a few miles, five or six miles off the coast of Red China within a general harbor area and more than a hundred miles from Formosa."

"So what?" Moose said. "Do we give them up?"

"I believe that we should defend Formosa," Senator Kennedy said. "We should come to its defense."

"Good!" Moose said.

"I would not suggest the withdrawal at the point of the Communist gun."

"But how about the islands?" Moose asked the radio. "How about Quemoy and Matsu?"

The senator appeared to answer him. "It is a decision finally that the Nationalists should make and I believe that we should consult with them and attempt to work out a plan by which the line is drawn at the island of Formosa."

"Did you get that, friend? That's where he wants to draw the line. That's danger." Moose leaned to Adam. "He doesn't want to draw it at Quemoy and Matsu. He's saying he wouldn't do anything if they take over Quemoy and Matsu. That's what he's saying."

"Hold it down a second," Mark Daschle said. "Let's listen."

"I believe we should meet our commitments to every country whose security we've guaranteed," the senator explained. "But I do not believe that that line in case of war should be drawn on those islands, but instead on the island of Formosa."

"Wow!" Moose said. "I hope Mao didn't hear him, or Khrushchev for that matter. They'll think we have a lightweight if he wins."

"I disagree with Senator Kennedy completely on this point," Vice President Nixon said. "These two islands are in the area of freedom. The Nationalists have these two islands. We should not force our Nationalist allies to get off of them and give them to the Communists. If we do that, we start a chain reaction; because the Communists aren't after Quemoy and Matsu, they're after Formosa. In my opinion this is the same kind of woolly thinking that led to disaster for America in Korea. I am against it. I would never tolerate it as president of the United States, and I will hope that Senator Kennedy will change his mind if he should be elected."

When the debate was over, Frank McGee thanked Vice President Nixon and Senator Kennedy for their appearances, and said, "We hope this series of radio and television programs will help you toward a fuller understanding of the issues facing our country today and that on election day, November Eighth, you will vote for the candidate of your choice." The audience in the U.S. Consulate's Conference Room in Hong Kong, applauded.

"They were both good," Mark Daschle summarized diplomatically. "Don't you agree?" he asked the table at large. "Adam?" He shouldn't have asked.

"Superb!" Adam said. His voice prompted absolute quiet from the others in the room. "Nixon was right. If Mao Tse-tung thinks of attacking those off-shore islands he should know we'll attack Peking. It's that simple. We, too, are on an island here. If they feel they can take Quemoy and Matsu, they'll take Taiwan—and Hong Kong. We wouldn't have to concern ourselves with any of this if General MacArthur did what he wanted to do and went all the way to China when we were fighting North Korea. We didn't finish the job, we left Kim Il Sung in power in North Korea, and we're going to pay a price for that."

Mark Daschle looked uncomfortable and he shifted in his chair. "What do you think, Mrs. Goodpastor?" He couldn't leave her out. "Oh, and listen, we never got to you when we introduced ourselves around the table—but there isn't anyone here, I'm sure, who doesn't know who you are and hasn't, at least, read about your marvelous parties. They've become Washington institutions, particularly your annual April Fools Day parties. We're delighted to have you, Mrs. Goodpastor, and I'd be anxious to hear what you have to say about the debate."

She smiled and scanned the people at the table. Mrs. Irene Goodpastor was the widow of Senator Harry Goodpastor who died fifteen years ago on the same day FDR. died. Since celebrities are not excluded from death (which many celebrities feel is an unfair equality with others) one of their worst fates is to die at a time when a larger celebrity dies, over-shadowing and minimizing the lesser celebrity's public tributes. By 1960 no one remembered if Senator Goodpastor was a particularly good or bad senator. What was known was that Mrs. Goodpastor was more prominent in Washington social circles than the senator ever was and, in Mrs. Goodpastor's circles, prominence was more important than legislation. There wasn't a person at the conference table in Hong Kong who didn't know that last July she had been at the new Los Angeles Memorial Sports Arena for the Democratic National Convention, leading a troop of young Stevenson supporters. Television cameras had focused on her as she patiently waited for Senator Eugene McCarthy to place Adlai Stevenson's name in nomination and then she screamed in delight, she whistled, and she gave an obscene gesture to a Symington man. He put his banner down and faded back into the crowd. It was obvious that he would sooner have received that gesture from Floyd Patterson than from Irene Goodpastor. When Adlai Stevenson lost the nomination, she didn't think she could ever support John Kennedy, but it didn't take long.

"Senator Kennedy was absolutely right. Keep in mind, sir," and Mrs. Goodpastor leaned over to look directly at Adam Orr, "that the Senator from Massachusetts is not soft on communism. He's not only willing but advocating that if Red China attacks Formosa we, indeed, would attack Red China. There is no dispute there between the senator and the vice president, but Senator Kennedy believes, as I do, that those small itty-bitty islands where hardly anyone lives and are closer to the mainland than to Formosa, should not send us to war—while he's president. And that's being responsible. As for MacArthur, I can't stand a man who makes a career out of dying. I wish he would hurry up and fade away as he keeps warning us he will."

There was some uncomfortable laughter and the only one who was laughing loudly was Anne Whitney. As a Consulate representative she shouldn't have laughed at that one. Mark Daschle gave her his cold stare. Cody Cooper, the young man with the big eyes looked at Mrs. Goodpastor as though he had just witnessed the building of the Eighth Wonder of the World.

"Well," Mark Daschle said with his usual brand of tact, "I think both candidates made valuable points on that issue and, of course, it's a significant question for Hong Kong. But, you know, I wish the candidates had been asked about what their policy would be if there was any incursion here from Red China. You know, you can see Red China from here. You can see its mountains from this Consulate. If you haven't been up to Lok Ma Chau at the border, you ought to go there to see how fragile, how volatile this place is."

"If we want peace in the world, and I assume we do," Ted Murphy, the syndicated columnist with the contorted nose said, "or at least I hope we do, then we should stop preparin' for war and stop talkin' about war all the time as though that's what destiny or some Supreme Being has ordered for us."

"Right on!" Anne Whitney yelled out without even glancing at Mark Daschle for his reaction to her statement.

"No civilized person wants war," Adam Orr said to Ted Murphy, "least of all our country, your country—the United States. But the way to prevent war is to make those who do want it, reject the thought, because of our potential. The greatest weapon in the world, bar none, bar none, is fear. If an enemy fears us, he'll be restrained. If he has no fear of us, he'll just go further and further."

Anne looked disgusted. Ted Murphy shook his head and said, "Do we have to have an enemy? How do you define an enemy? Someone who believes in things different than you do? God!"

Curly Kwang re-entered, pushing a cart carrying a coffee pot, a tea kettle, and some clean cups. He went from each guest to the next with his offer of either drink. That suspended the group discussion, splitting up the conversation into softer words between those sitting next to each other.

Moose Dunston put his pipe in the large government-issued brown glass ash tray on the conference table. "That was good stuff, friend," Moose Dunston said to Adam Orr. "You said it just right. Fear is the greatest weapon in the world."

Adam gave his steel gaze to Moose Dunston. "That's true for a nation—and true for a man."

Moose nodded. He extended his hand. "Dunston here." Adam Orr smiled and they shook hands. "You said you live in Florida?"

"I do," Adam answered.

"Where? What city?"

"Cocoa Beach."

"Good town. I've been there when ever I've been to the Cape—Cape Canaveral." Moose Dunston reamed a pipe-cleaner through the stem of his Dunhill.

"Cocoa Beach is a good place to watch people. People come and go there. And, my man, I've been watching you this morning."

"You have?"

"And you are in trouble deep."

Moose smiled. "Why do you say that?"

"Have you ever been to an Arab country?"

"No. Why?" He pulled out the browned pipe-cleaner from the stem of his pipe.

"The Arabs say that there are three things you can't hide: love, smoke, and a man riding on a camel. They're wrong. I've done all three and the old Arab proverb only got one right out of three, because there are ways to hide smoke, and there are ways to hide a man riding on a camel."

"What does that mean?"

"You're taken with that girl across the table," and he nodded toward Tso Wai-yee who was sipping her tea. "And that's all she is, you know. She's a girl."

"I just met her, just like you."

"But it's here. It's in the room. If I can feel what's going on between you, I'm sure that you can feel it–and that's too bad."

"Frankly, if you're right–I think it's pretty good."

"You'll catch her. You'll catch her. I can tell. And then like any other man who catches his woman, you'll spend your life as the master of trivia."

"I just met her. I'm not going to marry her! I just met her."

"Have you ever been to East Pakistan?"

"No. What's there? More camels?"

"You should see it. That's because marriage is just like East Pakistan. If you haven't been there you can't imagine it. If you have been there you can't believe it."

"Why these warnings? I can look at her, can't I?"

"Do me a favor, man."

"What?"

"When you decide to ask her to marry you, don't do it until 8:45 in the morning."

"Why?"

"Because you can think clearly then, unburdened by midnight and the tempting hours. If there was a law that men could only ask women to marry them at 8:45 in the morning there would hardly be any marriages. Men have their senses then."

Ambassador Fairbanks stood up and interrupted every one's private conversations. He cleared his throat twice and then said, "Mark, here we are in the most beautiful city in the world, sitting inside a room without windows, talking. Why don't we all go up to the Peak? The tram is just across the street and Mrs. Fairbanks and I will take care of an early lunch up there or a brunch or whatever you want to call it–for everyone here–and we can continue talking up there over a sandwich or whatever, but from Victoria Peak you can see all of Hong Kong. Will you join Mary and me up there?"

Mark Daschle looked around the table to get a sense of whether or not the guests wanted to go. Their faces didn't give an indication except for a quick nod by Mrs. Goodpastor, with her eyebrows raised.

"That's kind of you, Gerry," Mark Daschle said in his "I'm the Voice of the Consulate" style. "And I have to admit that sounds inviting, but I have a meeting with Consul General Holmes and John Murray of the British Information Services to discuss how we're going to release material on this debate but—please go ahead, whoever wants to go, and I'll join you up there around noon when our meeting's over—at least somewhere around noon if you'll still be up there."

"Are you going?" Moose Dunston asked Adam Orr, not that he cared, but he felt he had to ask him since he was sitting next to him, and that would make it less noticeable when he would ask Tso Wai-yee, across the table.

Adam Orr nodded. "Yes. I want to hear what old lady Goodpastor has to say."

Unfortunately old lady Goodpastor heard him. "This old lady, Mr. Orr, is younger than you. Wiser but younger."

Moose Dunston looked across the table at Tso Wai-yee, her face centered perfectly in its frame of long black hair. "Would you like to go?" as though he was asking her out on a date.

She smiled and nodded. "I'm going. I love the Peak."

That statement and nod meant everyone in the room who heard her or saw her nod would be walking across the street and going to the entrance to the tram that would take them to Victoria Peak. Neither Vice President Nixon nor Senator Kennedy could have had that unifying influence over such a diverse group, but she did. Her voter approval was a landslide.

THREE
ON VICTORIA PEAK
1960

The tram was not simply a way to get up to Victoria Peak, it was an incredible experience that put amusement park rides to shame. That funicular railway had run accident-free since 1888 on an endless looped-together wire rope. The tram would struggle to climb to each successive stop and halt in absolute suspended soundlessness at a seventy degree angle, and then successfully proceed up again. The eight minute ride was so steep that an illusion was created that the tram was pushing ahead on level ground while the colonial buildings of Hong Kong were tilting down, ready to fall.

When the top was reached by the green tram on that October 1960 day, the most magnificent panorama of any city in the world was in front of the riders. It was important to remember the date when the sight was seen because the view changed so frequently as one road replaced another road and one building replaced another building and reclaimed land was added where once there was sea.

"It's fantastic!" Mrs. Goodpastor said as they stood outside before going into the Peak's restaurant. She was taking pictures with a small black Leica.

"But do you see those squatter's huts on top of practically every building?" Anne Whitney pointed out. "People just stake out there. They live there. They don't have a cent. Now–look way back there all the way. Those mountains–that's China!" She said that with a sense of longing. With her boss still at the consulate she felt free to add, "Do you know how Great Britain got this place? They were selling opium in China and when they were caught at it and forced to stop, the Brits bombarded China, and forced China into giving them this place. That's how they got all this!" Having accomplished her personal mission, she went on to what she was expected to do. "Now, do you know exactly where you are? Everything this side of those distant mountains is what's called Hong Kong, but it's deceiving. See? Hong Kong is really three places all put together. We're on Hong Kong Island and right across the harbor–there–that's Kowloon and then beyond Boundary Street which you can see–there–that's where I live and that's what starts the New Territories, but all three; this island, and Kowloon, and the New Territories, were called Hong Kong by the Brits when they wangled that lease of the New Territories by gun-power. You get it?"

"Do you see now why I love it up here?" Tso Wai-yee asked Moose Dunston, who was having the time of his life jusy by standing next to her. All the others on the mountain were reduced into non-entities as he inhaled her perfume and stood close to her softness.

Ted Murphy, including his mashed nose, and Linda Murphy, including her hunger, hugged each other, as the view made their honeymoon into the kind of memory they had sought.

Ambassador Fairbanks was pointing out where the Governor's House was and where the Supreme Court was and where the Peninsula Hotel was and where the India Club was and where Kai Tak Airport was and he explained why Cheng Chau Island was called Dumbbell Island. "See its shape?" Mrs. Fairbanks had no interest in his pointed-finger tour. "It's like a dumbbell!"

Adam Orr turned to Jonas Valadovich and said, "Lieutenant, take a good look at it. Some day you, or maybe your son or grandson, may be fighting to keep it free."

"This would be worth fighting for, sir," Jonas Valadovich said.

Cody Cooper was nodding. "Kennedy has got to come here!"

"Why don't you just tell him about it?" Adam Orr said, pretending he thought that Senator Kennedy and Cody Cooper were buddies.

"I will. I will."

Adam nodded. "Good. Tell Harry Truman, too, when you see him. I'll take care of Ike and the Pope."

"Dear," Mrs. Fairbanks asked Anne Whitney, "what does Hong Kong translate to—in English?"

Anne Whitney was complimented that the question was addressed to her, and by no less than the wife of Ambassador Fairbanks. "It means 'Fragrant Harbor,' Mrs. Fairbanks. And Kowloon means 'Nine Dragons,' one for each of eight mountains in Kowloon, plus one for the Emperor who at the time was considered to be a dragon himself—don't ask me—and the New Territories are called the New Territories because that's what they were for the Brits when they got the lease from China. Get it? Do you know what I mean?"

"I see, I see," Mrs. Fairbanks answered.

"And there's Tiger Balm Gardens, dear," Ambassador Fairbanks said, pointing down to a small group of buildings and pagodas and spires. Somehow it bothered Mary Fairbanks when her own husband answered what he wasn't asked.

"Anne—come here," and Mrs. Fairbanks guided Anne a few feet away where they couldn't be overheard. "Dear, I sense a kind of friction between you and Mark—Mr. Daschle."

"There is. A lot of it. He's very bossy."

"You have to understand that Mark Daschle has had a very difficult time in the last number of years. He's a wonderful man, honey, and you have to understand him."

"What do you mean a difficult time—here? Not here!"

"Gerry served with him in Lagos, Nigeria. That's when Betty and Mark got divorced. Betty did what a lot of foreign service wives do—they get bored and a lot of them start drinking that tax-free liquor they get at the Embassy commissary. It's a very tough life for a foreign service wife. I'm glad it never happened to me but it could have. The Daschles never had any children so Betty was alone so much of the time. She hated Lagos. Mark was working all the time at the Embassy and there were parties and receptions and she had to be the hostess and–it just happened. They suddenly found they had nothing in common anymore. At the same time the foreign service hasn't been particularly kind to Mark. He's from the old school, just like Gerry. They believe they're overseas to represent the United States. A lot of the newer foreign service officers start representing the country to which they've been sent. So a lot of the foreign service looks down on Gerry–and Mark. He's had difficult times. Maybe he's bossy at times, Anne, but bear with him. He's a very good man. Be patient with him."

Anne shrugged. "Mrs. Fairbanks, he is impossible to work for."

"No he isn't. Remember–you're the Junior Officer Trainee. He is responsible for your conduct. Make him proud of you."

It wasn't long before Ted Murphy walked Linda-less to Anne Whitney. "Take off your glasses," he said to her. "It will be an advantage for both of us. You won't be able to see me as well, and I'll be able to see you better."

If any other man had said that, Anne would have pushed him off the mountain. For Ted, she smiled and took off her glasses.

Linda walked over to them and Ted hugged Linda and said, "Isn't this city somethin'?"

With that view, it wasn't going to be an early lunch for any of them. It turned into a morning walk with a separation of the guests until noon when they met again in the Peak's restaurant. Mark Daschle didn't get there for another hour, so they spent that hour having drinks. When Mark Daschle came in he declined a drink. "I'm still working. Let's have lunch."

There was lunch and for most of them, after-lunch drinks, and mid-afternoon drinks and before-dinner drinks. After all that, they felt as though they had known each other for years.

Anne Whitney was talking to whomever would listen to her. With that habit restored of taking off and putting on her big eyeglasses, she also had her share of drinking glasses going to and from her lips, and their contents were having an effect on her. While Cody Cooper was talking about Senator Kennedy's war-time experiences on PT-109, Anne interrupted him with something that had nothing to do with it. "Ike lied about the U-2." Maybe it was just the initials that made her think of the U-2 when he was talking about PT-109. "It was a spy plane and he lied. I think Kennedy was too gentle with Nixon when it got to the U-2. Imagine, Eisenhower telling the world that it was a weather research plane and it–and it 'wandered' into Soviet airspace. Please, oh, please. I knew what it was when I heard about it. Did anyone believe the explanation? What a terrible error! But that isn't what Francis Gary Powers says, is it? And he ought to know since he was the spy. The spy, period! If I was Khrushchev I would have canceled the Summit, too, unless Eisenhower apologized and said it would never happen again, and punished Powers. Those were the things Khrushchev wanted and he said he'd go to the

Summit if Eisenhower did those things. I would have said the same things if I was Khrushchev."

"I think you *are* Khrushchev," Adam Orr said.

"And another thing," Anne Whitney said as though everyone needed another thing. "Eisenhower waited too long before he got those nine Negro kids into Central High School in Little Rock and I'll never forgive him for waiting, and I don't know why Kennedy didn't bring that up."

Mrs. Goodpastor reluctantly and slowly nodded, and Mark Daschle, tired of being publicly angry at Anne, shifted the discussion back to one of non-partisanship. "They were both fine. They did a good job. My problem is with the questions. I suppose the press has to ask the questions on the minds of the people, but I wish they'd get ahead of the people. Maybe it's just my immersion in this place, but Hong Kong has a special importance in the future of the world. Remember, Great Britain has this island and Kowloon in perpetuity–forever–by virtue of two treaties with China. It is forever the property of Great Britain. But the New Territories are only held by a lease that was signed in 1898 for 99 years. Now, in the meantime, Mao Tse-tung doesn't recognize those two treaties of perpetuity–and even if he did, in 1997 China gets the New Territories back. The New Territories are ninety-two percent of what we call Hong Kong, and God knows, he may take Kowloon and this island, too, when the time comes in 1997. Can you imagine, in 37 years this place–this paradise–the whole thing could go to Red China. That eventuality is a giant weight on everyone living here." Then he took from his breast pocket a folded copy of a worn page from the *Hong Kong Standard*. "I've carried this with me since the end of April when this editorial was published. Listen:

"'We could allow 1997 to worry us into hysteria; we could let it convince us that it is futile to work and live, we could fold our hands now and wait for the takeover 37 years hence. But how would such a course of action help? If we tormented ourselves into worries of 1997, it would merely make us less capable of tackling the real problems of the day and more vulnerable to Red China's threats and demands. Being incapable of averting the inevitable, Hong Kong has no choice but to continue to live on the premise that in the changeableness of the situation on the mainland, a lot can happen in 37 years.'"

"Changeableness?" Adam Orr asked. "I never heard of that word. Mao Tse-tung is not going to change. He's said too many times that all Chinese territories will be back in the embrace of the Motherland. His words. Do you know what he means by all Chinese territories? He means not only Tibet that he's still massacring right at this minute, but he means Hong Kong and he means Macau and he means Formosa and God knows what else. For all we know he means Mongolia and the Pacific Ocean."

"Mao is a great revolutionary," Anne Whitney said after a quick gulp of her drink.

"No," Mark Daschle quickly interjected. "No, Anne, he's a tyrant and you better understand that." He was reminding her that she was a Junior Officer Trainee.

"Well, of course," said Ambassador Fairbanks, taking the role of mediator. "I think Miss Whitney means he succeeded in his revolution, not that it was a good revolution. I'm sure Miss Whitney meant only that, and he did succeed."

Anne was surprised and delighted that he came to her defense. Mary Fairbanks smiled at her. Anne smiled back, but didn't know how to be content with acceptance. She took another sip of whatever it was that was in front of her and said, "I'd rather quit the Consulate than take back what I said." She didn't know it but her experience at the Consulate was on the edge of being very brief, and not because she was going to quit.

"Anne," Mark Daschle said while he was breathing hard, "why do you suppose two-and-one-half-million Chinese have risked their lives to come south to Hong Kong and no one–not one has gone north to China?"

"I think they'll go back when the revolution is complete," she said in justification of her position.

"When will that be?" Adam Orr asked. "I can't wait. By 1997?"

Ted Murphy wiped his uniquely-shaped nose and offered, "Mao will be dead in 1997, deader than a doorknob. So I wouldn't worry about what he does in 1997."

"Doornail," Adam Orr corrected.

"Doorknob is fine," Mrs. Goodpastor said, nodding assuringly at Ted Murphy.

"The question is–who will come after him?" Mark Daschle asked.

"Liu Shao-chi," Ambassador Fairbanks said, "or Chou En-lai or Lin Piao,"

"They'll be dead by 1997, too," Mark Daschle said. "There'll be an entire new generation."

"What do you think, Tso?" Moose Dunston asked Tso Wai-yee.

She realized that he asked her only to have another contact with her. "Anyone who thinks Mao is great knows nothing. He killed thirty million Chinese by starvation and execution, and he's still killing more. He is a murderer. He killed my grandparents after torturing them in the worst ways." She shifted her look from Moose to Anne. "You, Anne, are fooled. You don't know anything about communism. You haven't lived under it. I have. Communism is a murderer. And it can murder Hong Kong, too, because Hong Kong can become fooled like you."

"I don't get it, Mr. Daschle," Mrs. Fairbanks said. "Why this hoop-la about 1997 when all Great Britain has to do is give back the New Territories then? They have those treaties to keep this island and Kowloon forever, you said. So why not learn to live without the New Territories in the remaining 37 years? Gerry and I have been up there and there's nothing there. Other than maybe where Anne lives, in Shoo-shoo-poop or whatever it is–"

"Shamshuipo," Anne corrected with a smile.

"Well, other than where you live I guess," Mrs. Fairbanks continued, miffed that Anne had not taken her advice in respecting Mark Daschle. "By and large, the New Territories look exactly the way we've always thought China looks, not like Hong Kong, not here. There's rice paddies up there and a smelly walled city where the people all look like cut-throats. There's hardly anything up there."

Mark Daschle nodded. "Well, maybe you're right. Maybe Hong Kong should learn to live without the New Territories while there's time. But don't forget what I told you, that Mao says all those treaties were forced on China and can't be recognized. 'Unequal Treaties' he calls them. What do you think? Let's take a little survey while we have some brain-power assembled here. What do you think is going to happen? We won't ask our own staff people here," he quickly added so as to avoid any comment from Anne Whitney who surely would celebrate the red flag over Government House, and 37 years would be much too long for her to wait for that event.

Moose Dunston led off. "My guess is there won't be a People's Republic of China in 37 years. Maybe I'm too much of an optimist but I think communism is going to die by its own weight. It will die in the Soviet Union and China and everywhere else. So this place will remain just the way we see it today—free, and with the New Territories as part of it—as a piece of the government of Nationalist China that will, by that time, be back on the mainland."

"There'll be a war," Mrs. Goodpastor warned. "Don't get me wrong, I think we'll win, but there'll be a terrible nuclear war many years before 1997 the way things are going, with the Soviets and Red China against us. Hong Kong won't even be an issue. It's too small."

Ted and Linda Murphy both started talking at the same time, and Linda stopped short to allow Ted to be heard. "I'm no prophet," Ted Murphy said, "but the way things are goin', if someone who wants to press the button, like if Nixon gets in the White House, what Mrs. Goodpastor said'll come true. There'll be a war. I don't think Kennedy's ideal. He wasn't my man and if I remember right, Mrs. Goodpastor was originally for Stevenson." She nodded at him. "But I'll take Kennedy to Nixon any day. I'll predict one thing. It's goin' to be a landslide for Kennedy this November because the American people are goin' to wake up to who wants war and who wants peace."

His bride, Linda Murphy, was nodding all the way through her husband's remarks. "Ted said it the way it is. It's the way I feel, too."

Mrs. Fairbanks said, "I don't know, but I think things will work out well for this place no matter who becomes President. There's a lot of time between now and 1997. I don't think the Cold War will ever become a Hot War because neither side will start it. We won't, and Khrushchev is smart enough to know what could happen to his own country if there was a nuclear war. When 1997 comes I think Hong Kong will remain the same as it is right now and the New Territories won't go to anybody except the people of Hong Kong. I don't know how, but that's what I think."

Lieutenant Valadovich shook his head. "All three. I think China will take all three. Not just the New Territories but they'll take Kowloon and Hong Kong Island, too. Strategically, there's no threat here to stop them.

I can't see them stopping themselves at the New Territories. They'll take all three."

Ambassador Fairbanks said, "I'll put in my vote for a sigh of relief heard 'round the world long before 1997, making the issue of Hong Kong into a non-issue!"

"You agree with me, Mr. Ambassador?" Moose Dunston asked, hoping Tso Wai-yee noticed that the ambassador seemed to echo Moose's analysis.

"Not exactly, Mr. Dunston. I do agree with you that communism will die, but not just by its own weight. It's my belief–in fact it's my quest–that in time, perhaps in this new decade, that a new international organization will be formed that will make the U.N. irrelevant, and that organization will end all totalitarian regimes."

"How?" Moose Dunston asked.

"And what's wrong with the U.N.?" Anne Whitney asked.

Ambassador Fairbanks turned quickly to Anne. "What's wrong, Miss Whitney, is that the U.N. is not an organization that gives a forum to the people of the world as it claims–but only to the governments of the world–most of them unelected and unrepresentative of the people they pretend to represent. Its Charter starts out with a bit of plagiarism from the United States Constitution. Instead of 'We the people of the United States,' it reads, 'We the peoples of the United Nations.' But the United Nations Organization has nothing to do with 'We the peoples.' To be accurate it should read, 'We the governments, whether or not we were chosen by the people of our nations.' Most of those governments got there by force of arms. Now, I'm not one of those who advocates that we get out of the U.N. and the U.N. out of the U.S. Horrors, no! I don't agree with those posters you see all over Mississippi and Alabama and Florida–and even in my home state of Texas. Instead, I believe there should be a new organization only open to democracies–countries who have free, fair, and frequent elections. To be in that organization would be such a medal of honor–such a piece of prestige–that it would make the U.N. unimportant–unless it wanted to adopt the criteria of the new organization."

Mark Daschle was staring at his friend. "This is an idea that Ambassador Fairbanks has been working on for a long time. He even proposed it to Dag Hammarskjold."

"And Hammarskjold liked it!" Mrs. Fairbanks added.

"Yes," Ambassador Fairbanks was shaking his head. "But nothing has happened with it. But let me get back to the point–"

"The only thing wrong with the U.N.," Anne Whitney said in a loud voice, "is that the wrong China is in the U.N. Mao's government should be in it, not Chiang Kai-shek's petty government on Formosa. We better come to accept that he's off the mainland and Mao isn't, and Mao deserves a seat at the U.N. That's all that's wrong with the U.N.!"

"Cut it!" said Mark Daschle, and he clenched his lips. He glowered at Anne who wouldn't look at him. Ambassador Fairbanks looked down at his drink, and he turned it on the table in a nervous gesture. Mark Daschle continued for him. "What Gerry means by all that, in relation to Hong Kong, is that Red China will be forced by a democratic world organization to tow the mark. He thinks, and I'm inclined to agree with him, that Red China, under threat of that organization, will turn to democracy. Great Britain will go home, and Hong Kong will either join a free China as a part of its democracy, or become an independent democracy of its own. Either way, it will be for Hong Kong's good—and the good of the world."

That explanation gave Ambassador Fairbanks the opportunity to collect himself. "Well, let's assume my idea for a world organization of democracies doesn't work—that it doesn't come to be. Then my bet is the Chinese will give Britain a new long-term lease of the whole place. In that way Red China will be rid of the perpetuity clauses for Hong Kong Island and Kowloon, but Great Britain will have what it wants for another 99 years or more. And, frankly, if that happens, before the new 99-year cycle ends in—what would it be—2096, Hong Kong will probably become an independent state. I don't doubt that could happen. An independent state of Hong Kong. That isn't the best scenario, but maybe it's the second-best, at least for Hong Kong."

"May I say something?" Anne asked.

Mark Daschle quickly answered. "No. Neither you nor Wai-yee. This isn't the Consulate's forum. Who hasn't talked? Adam?"

"Cooper's aching to talk," Adam said. "You go ahead, Cooper. You seem to have an inside track on Senator Kennedy's thinking."

"I don't have an inside track," Cody Cooper said, "but I thought Senator Kennedy was right about Quemoy and Matsu. They're not worth a war. But if it comes to Formosa we should defend it, just the way he said this morning. And I'm sure when it comes to Hong Kong he'll defend it, too. He won't let it go to China in 1997."

"Cooper," Adam Orr said, "it's my guess that even if Kennedy does win the election, he won't still be president in 1997. I admit I'm going out on a limb and he may be so good that the American people will demand the repeal of the 22nd Amendment and give him ten terms, but I wouldn't bet on it. So as for 1997, if the Communists are still in control by then—as the lieutenant suggested, they'll take all three entities—this island, Kowloon, and the New Territories. Mao and whomever follows him will continue to say those treaties of perpetuity are void. And again, as the Lieutenant suggested, this would be a tough place to defend militarily against what could come from that northern border."

Lieutenant Valadovich added, "They'd pour down here and take this place in ten minutes, sir. But that doesn't mean we couldn't stop them if we really want to stop them. Troops can be stopped, but only with power. You have to have both the military, and the will to use it."

"What do you mean?" Anne Whitney said as quick as she could before Mark Daschle could stop her. "The bomb? I suppose you think we ought to use the bomb?" She looked at Ambassador and Mrs. Fairbanks for approval of her disgust but they wisely weren't looking at her.

Adam Orr nodded in a move solely designed to cause Anne Whitney a quick ulcer. "I don't know about the lieutenant, but I'd blow Peking to smithereens! I can see the mushroom cloud now!"

Mark Daschle said. "It's getting late and I have piles of things at the Consulate that I should have taken care of this afternoon and I didn't. That's what I do on Saturdays–take care of all the papers I didn't get to during the week." He stood up. "But how could I resist this invitation and this conversation? So I thank you, Gerry and Mrs. Fairbanks, and I'm delighted that–"

"Let's come back here," Tso Wai-yee interrupted and she had never interrupted Mark Daschle before, so there was importance to what she was saying.

"Come back?" he asked.

"Yes–in 1997. All of us."

There was a long silence. Then some smiles and some nods.

"Why not?" Tso Wai-yee continued. "Let's do this again in 1997 and see who's right!"

"I'll be dead," Adam Orr said, "and so will Mrs. Goodpastor."

"I won't be dead!" Mrs. Goodpastor said.

"You'll be dead," he said as a remark of confirmation of her current age.

"Let's see how old we'll all be," Anne Whitney said who could easily afford to call for such a computation. "Add 37 years to your age. Wwww–I'm 22 now so I'll be 59."

It was irresistible. Everyone started adding 37 to their age. Only Mrs. Goodpastor found it necessary to figure it out by pen and paper, using a napkin and a ball-point pen. It was for sure she wasn't simply adding, but she was fiddling with figures.

"Mrs. Fairbanks and I will both be 89," Ambassador Fairbanks said with a smile. "We'll join you here in 1997. You can count on it."

"Linda will be 63 and I'll be 65," Ted Murphy said.

"I'll be 78," Mark Daschle said slowly, and he sat back down.

"I'll be around the same age as you," Mrs. Goodpastor said to Mark Daschle. "No, I'll actually be 80 by then."

"You'll have passed 90," Adam corrected.

"Mr. Orr!" she said.

He pointed to himself with his thumb. "I won't be too far behind you. I'll be 88."

Lieutenant Valadovich said, "I'll be 64."

Cody Cooper said, "Sixty-one for me. Kennedy will be 80."

Adam shook his head. "I'm glad you gave Senator Kennedy a place at this table."

Moose Dunston said, "I'll be 70. And Tso here, I think she'll be 40."

"No," she smiled. "That would make me 3 years old today. I'll be 60. I already know. I already figured it out before suggesting the idea," and she cocked her head, then giggled, and quickly put her hand in front of her mouth. Wonderful. God didn't kid around when he created her.

Mark Daschle smiled at all this. "It's a great idea! Wouldn't it be wonderful if the Agency lets me stay here until I'm 78? I'm all for it."

Adam didn't want to leave things as they were between Irene Goodpastor and him. His conscience was bothering him. "Mrs. Goodpastor?"

"Yes?"

"I'm sorry and I apologize. I respect you very much. I should have recognized that there was no way you could have known that I only insult the people I like. Believe it or not, my joking is a sign of affection. Besides—you have good ankles."

After Mrs. Goodpastor's initial shock wore off, she smiled. "Do you mean—for a woman of my age?"

Adam shook his head. "I mean good ankles for a woman of any age."

"Well, it's too bad I find you so physically unappealing," she lied.

Adam laughed. "Very good! Very good!"

Mark Daschle stood up again, but before he left, he looked slowly around the table. "I didn't know it would go this way between all of you. I suppose most of you know that the international community of Americans is very small, and that all of us are bound to intersect with each other long before 1997. Travelers like us are a part of a small world. Between Gerry and me—Ambassador Fairbanks and me—I think we know practically every FS-1, that's the top-ranking U.S. foreign service officers in the world. We always run into each other from place to place and time to time. So it will be unavoidable for those in this group to cross each other's lives. That's simply the way it is among those who stay in international life. I like the idea of being here together again in 1997, but take it from me, it won't be the next time for most of you.

"And something else that you should know," Mark Daschle added. "Now that you've been in Hong Kong, there will be a magnetism that will pull you back here when you're away from it. You won't be able to fight it. That magnetism is in you now, a part of you. It will answer only to coming back here. I pity anyone of our times who has never been to Hong Kong." There was absolute silence at the table for the first time since they gathered there.

Mrs. Goodpastor broke the spell. "Every one of you," Mrs. Goodpastor said, as though she was giving an order. "I'm going to pass around a piece of paper," and she reached for a green spiral pad from her purse, "and I want you to write your names and addresses and I promise you I will keep in contact with you— particularly when 1997 comes closer. I love the idea. Just write it out in your own handwriting. I suppose you know, it's been published so many times, that I collect signatures, so I'll frame this document—and I'll give you my address so you can tell me if you move."

"Then we meet again," Tso Wai-yee smiled. "Now, remember your prophecies of what will happen then."

"But we didn't hear yours," Moose Dunston said with more affection in his voice than warranted.

"Mr. Daschle said for me not to tell. I'm working for the Consulate. But Mr. Orr, I like the word you used in your prophecy."

"What word?" Adam asked.

"Smithereens!" she said. She gave a big closed-lips smile, then she put her hand up to cover her mouth and moved her head downward, lifting only her eyes to look up at Adam and then at Moose Dunston. Who on earth could be mad at her remark? No one, not with that smile, not with that face, not with that gesture of her hand, not with that head motion down and that look up, not with that red silk cheong-sam, not with the way she then removed her hand from in front of her lips and cocked her head in a tilt. For Moose Dunston, a couple nuclear mushroom clouds would be of no importance compared to the importance of Tso Wai-yee. Surely any man with a reasonable sense of values would see it that way.

The tram took them back to the streets of Hong Kong where they went their separate ways, but as Mark Daschle knew, their separation tonight would be temporary.

That night Mark Daschle went back to the Consulate to figure out what to do about Anne Whitney's policy insubordination.

Moose Dunston went to his room at the Miramar Hotel with his mind enveloped in thoughts of Tso Wai-yee who was in her apartment at a government resettlement building, combing her long, black hair.

Cody Cooper went to the Night Market to immerse himself in a foreign land and become integrated with the people.

Former Ambassador and Mrs. Fairbanks had a night-cap at the Consul General's house where they were staying, and along with Consul General Holmes and Mrs. Holmes, the four of them were composing a list of ideal foreign capitals in which the Fairbanks should try to be posted in the decade before the Ambassador's retirement from the foreign service.

Lieutenant Valadovich took a walk by the harbor, drafting a contingency proposal on the defense of Hong Kong that he would present when he got back to Tokyo.

Ted and Linda Murphy made love in the guest room of the home of Dick Wilson, the editor of the *Far Eastern Economic Review.*

Anne Whitney took a cab to Shamshuipo where she cursed Mark Daschle to the taxi driver who had no idea what she was talking about.

Irene Goodpastor went to a street-based fortune-teller to find out if she would be alive in 1997.

Adam Orr did none of those things.

FOUR
HAPPY LEE
1960

Whenever Adam entered his second life: the secret one, he could smell a distinct aroma. It had no scientific basis, but it was real.

After he left the crowd at the Peak and was done with the tram and walked the late-night streets toward his destination in the Wanchai district of Hong Kong, the smell was intense.

He passed by the bars and clubs and drunks of Wanchai, much too interested in where he was going and what he would be receiving to care about the promise that was hawked from the men yelling in front of the bars of "a night with beautiful women without minimum or cover charge." He passed the hawkers and went to the corner and a right and a quick left to a ramshackle apartment building. There were big chips of paint hanging from the front of the building and there was laundry hanging outside its scores of windows. The windows were covered with either canvas or newspaper and some were covered with nothing. Through the ones with nothing, bare bulbs were exhibiting rooms that would best be unoccupied by man or beast.

He walked up one wooden flight of stairs after another. Of course, there was no elevator, but even if there had been one he wouldn't have chanced taking it in that building. The walk was enveloping him in that Life Number Two-trance mixed with new odors from each floor as he passed them on his way up.

There was an old Chinese woman in a loose, buttoned, black jacket and black pants seated on the stairwell leading to the entrance of the fourth floor, slurping some noodles from a black pot. She looked up and some noodles dropped from her lips back to the pot, too late to recover the noodles either with her chop sticks or by sucking in.

"Good evening," Adam said, smiling and nodding in pure American style. Her reaction was a puzzled stare and she put her face closer to the bowl, almost in it, as though she wanted to be unseen.

On the sixth floor, he gave a knock on a heavily painted shiny green door and it was opened by a small Chinese man who had so many marks and wrinkles on his face that they obscured his eyes, nose, and mouth. When the Chinese man saw his visitor was caucasian he said, "Name? Name? Name?"

"Orr," Adam Orr answered.

"Spell. Spell. Spell."

"O-R-R. Adam Orr. What's your name?"

The small Chinese man gave a broad smile, devoid of most teeth. There were a few oddly shaped and deeply yellowed things that looked like maybe they were teeth. There was one on the top in the middle of his mouth, and there were two bottom ones, both on the right side and both with gold crowns, and obviously none of them served a chewing purpose since none of them would meet resistance when he closed his mouth. "Happy," he said. "My name, Happy Lee. Come in, come in, come in." He seemed to speak in threes, one for each tooth-like thing suspended from his gums.

Adam walked into the hovel that was filled with oil-stained cardboard cartons, two cushioned chairs, and one sofa, all ripped, and hundreds of Kleenex boxes against one wall. Happy Lee either sold them or was anticipating catching a terrible cold.

"Sit, sit, sit," Happy, Happy, Happy said to Adam. Adam sat. Now the smell of Adam's mission was becoming mixed with the smell of the room and the combination was almost beyond endurance.

"Smoke?" His host offered from a pack of Japanese cigarettes. "Mild Sevens?"

"No thanks. I just put one out."

His host put a cigarette in his mouth and used his top tooth to balance it against his lower lip, although his upper lip would have done the job just fine. He lit the cigarette with a wooden match, and it was Adam's cue to say the rehearsed words. "Why do the Chinese put cigarettes in the middle of their lips rather than at the side like Americans?"

His host laughed and said, "Yes, yes, yes, you are Adam Orr. Do you want tea?"

"No," Adam said, and then added, "Thank you." Tea wasn't part of the script, and he was glad it wasn't since he couldn't trust either Happy Lee's recipe or equipment in making anything to put in his mouth.

"You have come for the what?" Happy Lee asked with his smile exposing again the protrusions in his mouth.

"For the envelope."

"Which one?"

"Not the red one or the green one, but the brown one."

"Only the brown. Good."

Happy Lee was totally satisfied that his guest was Adam Orr and Adam Orr was satisfied he was with Happy Lee. Happy Lee went to one of the oil-stained cardboard boxes and pulled out a letter-sized envelope. "The envelope for Mr. Orr, just what you ask for."

"Thank you, Happy." Adam Orr stood up, putting the envelope in his inner jacket pocket next to his leather secretary. That was all there was to it at this place. Mission accomplished. In truth, the short meeting was already too long since he was becoming nauseated from the smell of the surroundings.

They shook hands. Happy Lee smiled and said, "Good luck, Mr. Orr." He then showed his guest to the door, they shook hands again, and Adam Orr walked down the stairwell with speed, almost tripping over the woman in black. "Good Evening," he said to her again. By the time she gave another mystified look and lost some more noodles from her mouth, he had already passed her.

Once outside, relieved to be in the air of Wanchai, it was only the aroma of his mission that filled him. As he turned the first corner, some man bumped into him. Adam Orr, who made a career of being composed, almost shouted in fear, and put his hand in his jacket to feel if the envelope was still there. It was. The man hadn't reached for it. He was just walking in the opposite direction too fast to stop in time to permit Adam to pass by without obstruction.

In the safe haven of his room at the Peninsula Hotel, he sat on the edge of his bed and took the documents from the envelope. The two pages told him what to do next, and how to get to where he had to go.

He read them and then read them again and again and again. Then he tore them length-wise into vertical strands. He went into the hotel room's bathroom and Adam put each strand, one by one, over the sink and to the flame of wooden matches. Rolling some sheets of toilet paper into a wad, he gathered the ashes from the bottom and sides of the sink, and then threw the wad into the toilet. In one flush the wad with their watered ashes were on their voyage to somewhere in the sewers of Hong Kong.

Back in the main room he sat again on the edge of the bed, this time going into a strange ritual that he had practiced every night for the past two months before leaving the United States. He said as if reciting a mantra, "The U.S. Capitol Building. The Robert Taft Carillon. The White House. The Washington Monument. The Jefferson Memorial. The Lincoln Memorial. Arlington Bridge. The Pentagon. The South Gate Motel. Mount Vernon." He pictured each one of them in his mind, in a ten-item tour of the Washington, D.C. area, geographically moving west and then southward. Then he itemized ten New York places in geographical order, then ten places in Paris, then ten places in London, until ten places in thirty cities were itemized from memory.

After all three hundred places were pictured in his mind, and said in order, he went through a list of 59 household objects.

With that ritual accomplished, his rehearsal for what was ahead was done. He was ready to go to sleep.

It was a good day and a better night.

FIVE
I LIKE IKE
1960

"Good morning, Anne." Mark Daschle stood up when Anne walked in. His office was outfitted with the standard government desk, the American flag, three bookcases, a small coffee table, two chairs and a couch. And there were the framed pictures on the wall of President Eisenhower and Vice President Nixon. But this office had more: there was the wonderful window through which could be seen the edge of the island and the harbor with its junks and ferries, and across the harbor to Kowloon's dock and clock tower.

"Hi, Mr. Daschle." She was wearing white slacks, knowing well that Mark Daschle didn't like the women at the Consulate to wear slacks but, after all, it was Sunday. Sunday's didn't change the wardrobe of Mark Daschle. He was, as always, in suit and bow-tie. Today, a red and white striped one. Anne shook her head. "God, you wear your bow-tie on Sundays?"

"Sit down, Anne." He walked from behind his desk to a chair at the coffee table opposite the couch where she sat with one leg casually under the other.

"Oh, oh!" she said. "Calling me in on a Sunday morning is a bad enough sign but you just said 'Anne' twice, and you're not going to sit back at your desk. That's the 'this is serious' government stance, isn't it?"

He nodded. "What you did yesterday was very serious."

"I think I might have had a little too much to drink up at The Peak. I shouldn't have, I know. And, don't worry, I won't drink like that again when I'm out on Consulate business."

"Good. But I hope that isn't all you have to say to me."

She thought for a while and couldn't understand what he meant. "It is. Why?"

"It wasn't only your drinking, Anne. You started talking before you were drinking. You started when we were in the conference room listening to the debate. You had no business saying what you did. I had no interest yesterday, and no interest today, in what you think of the President of the United States or his handling of the U-2 incident or Little Rock or anything else. And I don't care how impressed you may be with Mao Tse-tung."

"Then don't be interested." She untucked her leg to put both feet on the floor, almost sitting at attention. "I can't make you interested in my opinion, Mr. Daschle, but it's as good as yours or anyone else's. And I'll say it if I'm roaring drunk–which I won't be–or I'm stone-faced sober–and I will be."

"You have no idea why we're having this meeting, do you?"

"Because you don't like what I said. You're making that clear, Mr. Daschle. Well, I said those things because I believe them, and to be able to say what I believe means everything to me."

"Then you shouldn't be part of the foreign service."

"Does being part of the foreign service mean I give up my First Amendment right of freedom of speech?"

"Absolutely."

"What do you mean, 'absolutely'?"

"The foreign service is like the military in that we are not entitled to every right of the people. We have obligations the people don't have. We are paid by the people. I have the obligation to choose those people who can speak for the United States at this Consulate."

Anne nodded. "Okay, but there are a lot of taxpayers who don't like Eisenhower. And I don't doubt there are a lot of them who recognize that Mao Tse-tung is not the evil, evil man with fire coming out of his mouth that our government makes him out to be. Do you think everyone who represents the United States has to feel the same way you do? Or the President does? What happens to representing all the other people? Don't they pay taxes, too? Don't they get representation overseas? Isn't it supposed to be a government of the people, by the people and–and–." It was just what she didn't want. She simply couldn't remember it, and she knew it was the simplest thing to remember.

"For the people, I'll help you there."

"For the people. Isn't that what the Constitution says?"

"That's the Gettysburg Address."

Oh, no. Another mistake. "Well, I'm sorry," she said sarcastically. "The Gettysburg Address then. Lincoln then. But isn't that the way our system works? Of the people, by the people, and for the people?" She took the opportunity to say it right.

"Yes. The people back home elect a president, and he has a professional career service at his disposal to carry out policy directives as he sees fit. That's where we come in. You work for me, I work for Consul General Holmes, Consul General Holmes works for Secretary of State Herter, Secretary of State Herter works for President Eisenhower, and the president is elected by the people. You don't work directly for the people. Do you understand that?"

"I can still represent some of the people."

"Anne, who won the last presidential election, you or President Eisenhower?"

"I know who won the election."

"If you can do the job better, you ought to run for the office."

"I'm not 35 years old yet."

"Until you qualify, and until you become elected by the people, knock it off, Anne. I'm giving you a warning. Your last one. And I don't like you publicly complimenting Ted Murphy's column like you did yesterday. Every one of his columns attacks the president and his policies. You don't do that publicly while you work for the Consulate. Not any more." The phone rang. "Wait a minute. Wait." Mark walked to his desk and picked up the phone's receiver. "This is Mark Daschle," he said. "Yes....Good morning, Moose....Oh no, I can't do that.... No.... The only thing you can do is call the Marine Guard here and ask him to phone her and he can ask her to phone you. That's the only way we can do it...I can't switch you over, it's Sunday, the system doesn't work on Sunday. So hang up and then call us again at 38026.... Add a 5 at the start of it if you're calling from Kowloon.... She spells it T-S-O. Then W-A-I-dash-Y-E-E.... Don't worry about it. He knows her. Moose, I have a meeting going on right now so.... Okay, good.... Yes.... Good luck." He hung up, shook his head and went back to the chair opposite Anne. "My job is a little of everything. What am I supposed to be, a match-maker? A representative of Cupid? Now, go ahead. Where were we?"

"That guy has the hots for Wai-yee, doesn't he?"

"Let's get back to where we were. This is your last warning."

"Mr. Daschle, I represent the United State very well." During the time he was on the phone, she felt a resurgence of audacity. "While you live half way up the Peak with all the Brits, and the Consul General lives even higher up the Peak going to the Royal Jockey Club or whatever it is, do you know where I'm living? I live in Shamshuipo with the people. The Chinese. And I'm studying Cantonese. I'm an American who loves the people here. That's why I'm glad I live in Shamshuipo and not in some western style villa."

"You advertise where you live so often, Anne, that it defeats your purpose. And, frankly, I wish you didn't live there."

"Why shouldn't I?"

"Because–and correct me if I'm wrong–because you probably say to those people who live there just what you said at the Peak yesterday."

"That's right. And they love me for it. I'm an American and I want them to love Americans, so I'm serving America."

"No. You want them to love you, not the United States. You're so inexperienced you think they care about you. I don't give one hoot if Hong Kong loves or hates Anne Whitney–or Mark Daschle. I want them to understand and respect U.S. policy. Do you get it?"

She looked around the office. She didn't want to look in his eyes.

"And I'll tell you what you did that was more destructive than anything else you did yesterday."

"Oh, tell me," she said with her sarcastic tone. "What was the most destructive thing I did all day? Tell me."

"To Ambassador Fairbanks."

"To Ambassador Fairbanks? I like him!"

"You hurt him. He was telling his idea that he's worked on since 1945. He was so pleased to have a distinguished, unexpected audience to present his idea for a different world organization, and you slashed it–just slashed it. Didn't you notice? He became flustered. He stopped talking about it. That was a terrible thing to do to him. What do you know?"

That got to her. She bit her lower lip, then shrugged. "I didn't mean to do that. I–I didn't think, then. He's a nice man."

"Anne, you simply don't know enough to offer your views to people–your views about things you don't know."

"So?" She recovered her grit.

"So I'm going to have to send you back to Washington, Anne." He surprised himself with that statement. It just seemed to come out by itself.

She pulled her head back with a start. "You're firing me?"

"I don't have the authority to do that. I only have the authority to get you out of here and to send you back home, and I'll let others decide whether or not you have a future with the foreign service. I don't think you do, and my report isn't going to be anything less than totally honest. I'm not here to protect your job."

There was a long silence. "Okay. Okay. Honesty–that's a new one. They'll hate America in Shamshuipo when they find out why I have to leave. Do you want me to make up a reason why I'm leaving? Is it my job to lie? If the president of the United States can lie, I suppose that's what's expected of me."

"And that's why you're going, Anne. You still don't get it."

"I thought you said you were giving me a warning, not–not–"

"You made me change my mind. I can't have this here. I want you out of here as quickly as you can get out. We don't need a beatnik here. What kind of passport do you have?"

"What do you mean?"

"Just what I asked."

"Well, I don't have a black one like you. They didn't give me a Diplomatic Passport. I don't rank."

"You on an Official one?"

"Yes."

"I have every instinct, every–" and he couldn't think of another word "–instinct to cancel it on you, and give you a tourist one for your trip home, but I won't. Don't misuse it, Anne. I'm warning you that as long as you hold an Official Passport, you represent our country."

"I can't believe this is happening!"

"You made it happen."

"By when do I have to leave Hong Kong?"

"I'll tell the Agency that you'll be back to report to them–" and he tried to arrive at an appropriate date to tell her, "on November the 1st. You can leave here when ever you want between now and then."

"You're a very mean man and–you're acting so–so–bossy."

Mark Daschle shook his head. "My responsibility is to help the United States and nothing is going to interfere with that assignment–not Mao Tse-tung, not Chou En-Lai, and for sure, not Anne Whitney who, unlike Mao and Chou, even gets paid by the people of the United States. Do you understand?"

"You said that a million times."

"I'm cabling the Agency today that you're coming home, and that you'll be at the Agency at 9:00 A.M. on November the 1st, if it isn't a Saturday or Sunday, I don't even know, I didn't know I was going to do this." He got up and walked behind his desk and flipped the pages of his desk calendar. "It's a Tuesday—that you'll be reporting in on Tuesday, November the 1st."

"Mr. Daschle, this can mean my career."

He nodded. "You bet it can. You don't have the maturity to be a foreign service officer. And I'm putting that in my report. Sorry. Now go say good-bye to all your friends in Shamshuipo." He remained standing behind his desk.

"You are so—I'm going to—You are so—"

"I'm so what, Anne?"

And then she did what she didn't want to do. She started crying.

"I'm sorry, Anne." He meant it. He despised it when a woman cried and he generally weakened when it happened.

She put her fingers under her glasses to wipe away the tears. "It's you who has the power. I don't have any." She should have been quiet. Her remark made him regard her tears with less interest.

"I'll get your travel orders. You'll have them tomorrow morning. No. Tuesday. Tomorrow's a holiday, Double Ten. On Tuesday morning you arrange your route with Mrs. Tien in the Travel Office." Then his voice got softer. "There's a lot of good in you, Anne. This isn't fun for me."

"No. I'm sure you're very sad," she said with that too-familiar caustic inflection.

"I don't want to argue with you anymore, Anne. That's enough. You take care of what you have to do and I'll take care of what I have to do."

She stood up, gave another quick wipe under her glasses, turned to the door, and said, "Good-bye, Mr. Daschle. Nice knowing you."

Anne Whitney went to her office at the Consulate and cried.

After the crying was done, she started writing an itinerary for her departure back to Washington. She wrote down New Delhi, then Karachi, then Munich, then Paris, then London, and then D.C. She wanted to make the best of leaving Hong Kong, but it was a route she had planned on putting on a travel order two years from now, not two days from now.

The tears started again.

Then it hit her.

She wiped her most recent tear, picked up the phone's receiver and asked the Marine Guard to connect her to the residence of Dick Wilson, the editor of *The Far Eastern Economic Review.* Within a minute the connection was complete. Some woman, maybe it was a servant, answered the phone. Anne asked if she could talk to Ted Murphy. Another minute passed and another woman got on the line. "This is Linda Murphy."

"Mrs. Murphy, this is Anne Whitney at the U.S. Consulate. It was so good to be with you and your husband yesterday. Is your husband right there?"

"Oh, how nice to hear from you. We enjoyed yesterday so much. He's here, but he's in the shower. Can I take a message for him or have him call you?"

"Mrs. Murphy, please tell him I have a story for him, a real story for his column and I want to meet with him because I can't tell him over the phone."

"Really?"

"Oh, yes."

"We're going to Tiger Balm Gardens today. Do you want to meet us there?"

"You tell me at what time and I'll be there."

"Let me talk to Ted."

They sat outside at Tiger Balm Gardens, sipping the thickest coffee in Hong Kong in the smallest cups in Asia under the most outrageous Buddha in the world. It was the only one with a huge smile and raised eyebrows and a multi-colored cape, set near a seven tiered white pagoda that was plopped right in the middle of smaller pagodas and hundreds of smaller statues of Buddha and tigers and Tamarix's and one spire after another, all of those things seeming to be as unpatterned and as disordered as the thought process of Anne Whitney.

"You don't have a story, Anne," Ted Murphy said. "There's nothin' there. You're a Junior Officer Trainee. He's your boss. He doesn't like what you're doin'. He's tellin' you to go home. So what? There's no story there."

"He even insulted you. He said he didn't like me complimenting your columns–when I was at the table."

Ted laughed. "Well then, they're havin' an impact!" He wanted to dismiss the remark because he remembered he winked at her when she complimented him, and he flirted with her on the Peak, and in her current state she might be liable to mention those things in front of Linda.

"But isn't this unconstitutional or something? It's against my First Amendment rights."

Ted laughed again. He felt secure again. She wouldn't spill the beans. Linda jumped in. "Well, wait a minute, Ted. I see what she means. And it isn't funny."

"Honey, please. Annie, listen. I love your spunk and I'm on your side, but he likes Ike. What do you think he's goin' to do? Tell you to say anything you want here? He's a bureaucratic bozo. So you got to take the medicine from the clown. If you don't, then you got to get out of the bureaucracy. It's the system. You're just unlucky, that's all. Most of the new foreign service officers feel like you do but you hit an Ike-lover. He's in his forties so two bits he fought in Europe and Ike was his God or somethin'."

Linda shook her head at her husband. "Well, it's awful."

"I know it's awful, honey," Ted said. "I know. It's terrible. But it isn't a story. Look, Anne. It happens every day in every business. You've been told by your boss to T.O. 'Take off, lady,' he's sayin'. So you go to

Washington, Annie. And if you run into anything there that's a story, you call me, will you? This isn't it."

"My friends at the housing building I live in, in Shamshuipo, aren't going to accept this easily. It's going to be very sad. I don't know how to tell them."

"Tell them you're takin' off," Ted advised.

"Oh, Ted," Linda said. "This is very painful for her. And it would be for you, too. You remember how you felt when you had to leave *The New York Post*. And it's worse for her because she has to leave the city and the neighbors who she loves and they love her. I know it will be hard and terribly sad to tell them. Anne, you have to understand that Ted's just being–Ted."

"Do you want to be there when I tell my friends in Shamshuipo?" Anne dared to ask as she looked back and forth between them with what she should have known was an invitation that would not be accepted. She was treating it as though it was a prized opportunity for them to witness a tragic event in the history of Hong Kong.

"No, Annie," Ted said, "this is somethin' I think you better handle alone. It's best that way." He looked quickly at Linda and when he was certain she was looking away and not at him, he gave a quick wink to Anne.

Anne thought she had drained herself of every tear, but there had been a quick replenishment from some unknown storage area. The new supply was eager to prove itself that night in the bed of her rented room. She cried not only because she was ordered out of Hong Kong, and not only because Ted Murphy wasn't interested in doing anything about her crisis except to wink at her, but because of the reaction of her friends living in the housing unit of Shamshuipo. Although they said they were sorry that she would have to move back to the United States, their eyes flashed when she spoke about leaving some of her possessions behind. They showed more interest in the possibility of inheriting her couch and chairs and particularly her Persian Rug than about the ordered departure of their American neighbor.

She lay in bed looking at the ceiling through the haze of what surely had to be the last of her tears unless her entire body was filled with them, pushing to exit through her eyes.

What Mark Daschle hadn't taught her, Shamshuipo did.

SIX
DOUBLE TEN
1960

Although Anne wasn't grateful to Mark Daschle, Moose was. Based on Mark Daschle's advice, Moose phoned the U.S. Marine Guard at the Consulate, the Marine phoned Tso Wai-yee, and she called Moose. He asked her to dinner and she said she was busy that evening, but she suggested meeting him for lunch at Jimmy's Kitchen.

Not a bad second-best.

"This restaurant has been here since before the war," she told him.

He didn't care if it was there before the Thousand Year War or was built this morning since today she was wearing a white cheong-sam with a high tight collar and a long slit, and she was with him. "What war?"

"The war. The Japanese occupation."

"Oh, of course. I thought maybe you meant the Korean War. It's nice here. I like it," he said. "I'm glad you suggested it. I hope you don't mind that I'm using the silverware. I can't operate chopsticks no matter how many people teach me."

"Eat the way you're the most comfortable." This was Moose's conclusive evidence that she was a magnificent human being worthy of sainthood. At a minimum that remark of "eat the way you're the most comfortable" was commensurate with "Do unto others as you would have others do unto you."

"You're very mature for being only 23 years old," Moose told her.

"Thank you." Thank you? She was appreciative. She was kind. She was thoughtful. Just like Mrs. Miniver. "But you know, I'm really younger than 23 by your calendar."

"You are?"

"I go by the Chinese calendar. Don't tell anyone, but it was easier to get the job at the Consulate that way. I would have been too young if I had given my age by your calendar when I came to work there. You see, in China when you are born you are already one year old, and your next birthday is on Everybody's Birthday."

"Everybody has the same birthday?"

"Yes. It's always the seventh day of the Lunar New Year." And then she almost whispered, "except for the people who live on boats. The Shui Sheung Yan." She looked around the restaurant and said even softer, "The Tanka. Their birthday is eight days later, fifteen days after the Lunar New Year."

"Why?"

"Tradition. A long time ago, being on the water meant they found out it was Everybody's Birthday eight days after it was over." She wrinkled her nose, what little there was of it. "They didn't know."

"Then how old are you, or do you even know, by my calendar?"

"I know. A horoscope is prepared for every newborn, so the Astrologer records the exact day and hour of birth because it guides you through life. By your calendar I'm 21 now."

"How did you jump two years rather than one?"

"I was born nine days before the Lunar New Year. So I was one year old when I was born and nine days later, when it was Everybody's Birthday, I was two. But I could have been three if I had been born in one of the years that has thirteen months."

"No kidding?"

"Sure. But we make up for it when we get older. When we get older we lie about our ages and add five or ten years. The older you are the more honor you are given. My grandfather said he was eighty when he was seventy-two. So when a Chinese tells you how old he is, you must understand that it may be a little different than you may think."

"You're only 21, Tso?"

"No. I'm 23. I am Chinese. I go by my people's calendar. Not only to get a job. I am Chinese."

If he offended her he was prepared to drown himself in the harbor. "Of course, Tso."

"Sure." And she looked at him and smiled. "And Moose, you call me by my family name. In China, our family name comes first. But my given name is Wai-yee. Or do you want me to call you Dunston?" She gave that cock of her head and smile.

"Oh, I'm sorry. I didn't know, or I didn't think."

"No, it happens often. It's just different. 'Wai' is the name of this generation's relatives, my cousins, uncles, and aunts, my father's cousins—and my sister, and it would be the same for my brother if I had one. The name that is mine alone is yee—Wai-yee."

"Uh-huh. I see."

"Do you?"

"No."

"It's different in the West."

"A little. It is. But, what does 'Wai-yee' mean?"

"It really depends on how it is written, not on how it is said. So you have to see the characters. But the way my name is written, Wai means 'greatest' and yee means 'virgin female'. So I am the greatest virgin female!" And she gave her wide smile. "Do you like it?"

Moose laughed. "Boy, that's some answer. I mean that's some name. Yes! I like it a lot! That's good."

"Sure. Do you like your food?"

"Yes. It's excellent. I like sweet and sour pork."

"But their specialty here is what I'm eating. Do you want some?"

He certainly didn't. She ordered her meal in Cantonese so he didn't know what it was going to be, and now that it was in front of her and she was eating it, it was probably best she didn't place the order in English. All he was certain of was that it was once alive in the sea somewhere and its appearance had not been altered before the kitchen presented it. "Oh, no, I'm getting full on this. It's delicious."

"This is so good. You can have some," she said.

"No, no thanks. I'm fine. I'm full."

"Moose?" she said, and it was wonderful to hear her say his name.

"Yes?"

"Where do you go from here? What do you do now?"

"To Saigon. On Tuesday I fly to Saigon. I'm training some of the South Vietnamese military. Administrative kinds of things. I'm not a soldier now, but I work for the Department of Defense as a civilian specializing in combating insurgency. The North Vietnamese have a heavy insurgent force in the South that they're directing, called the Viet Cong–Vietnamese communists. So it's pretty dicey for the South Vietnamese, and President Eisenhower has offered to help them out. That's where I come in. On this trip I think I'm going to meet their President, President Diem, so I'm looking forward to it."

"Is it dangerous?"

"Oh, no. I like the place. Good people. The only danger–the only thing I don't like about it is the heat, the humidity. It's terrible."

"Sure. It's bad here, too. Not now in October, but we have it in the summer. You get used to it."

"Wai-yee, do you get tired of men staring at you?"

"They don't stare at me."

"Are you kidding? Every man in this place keeps looking over at you."

"No, they don't. But you do. And I like it."

That was a surprise. He smiled. "Yes, I do stare at you, don't I?"

"Do you get tired of all these women staring at you?"

"Now, that's simply not true."

"I would stare at you if I wasn't at your table. After all, you are so big! But since I am at your table I can't be so rude."

This was working out very well. "If that's the case, maybe you ought to go to another table so I can get excited that you're looking at me."

She laughed and quickly put her hand in front of her mouth in that marvelous Asian feminine habit of hers, making her look guilty in her laughter. She looked down and only took quick glances up at him, just enough to be even more enticing. "Do you want me to go to another table?"

"Oh, no. Not for an instant."

For a while they ate in silence but exchanged quick glances and caught each other doing it. Then there were some glances that were not quick.

Eventually she asked, "Did you buy a lot of things here?"

He could hardly answer. He wanted the silence with the glances to go on longer. "No. What do you mean?"

"Shopping. Americans have to shop here. Or you get shot when you leave. When you leave, customs asks you what you bought. If you say nothing and you're an American, they kill you."

What a sense of humor, he thought. She was Jack Benny and Fred Allen and Bob Hope and Red Skelton put together. This woman–this girl–was Will Rogers in a skirt. "But I haven't bought anything."

"You must, then. You can get anything you want in Hong Kong if you have money."

He pushed aside his food, took out his pipe and tobacco pouch, he filled his big Dunhill, and he lit it. "What should I buy?"

"A suit."

Didn't she like the suit he was wearing? "Why?"

"I'll take you to a tailor where you can get a good suit for 30 dollars, American."

"Really? And it's good?"

"Oh, it's very good. And he'll deliver it to your hotel tomorrow, so you'll have it before you leave."

"But it's Sunday. Is he open on Sundays?"

"Sure. Hong Kong pays no attention to such things." She picked up the matches he had left on the table, and she read what it said on the matchbook cover. "Is this true?" she asked.

"Is what true?"

"What it says. It says, 'Don't say drug store, say Drug Fair.' Do you call them drug fairs now?"

Moose smiled and shook his head. "It's an ad. It's just a chain of drug stores in Washington."

She felt she had proved her ignorance about America. "You must buy a suit!" That was the way she ended the conversation about the matchbook cover.

Had she suggested that he buy Victoria Peak he would have done it somehow as long as it would keep her with him for a while longer.

He didn't have to buy Victoria Peak. All he had to do was go with her as she led the way to the shop of the tailor on Kimberley Road.

"His name is Hanson Hsu."

"Is Hanson his family name?"

"No. His Western name."

Moose decided to simply accept it without explanation.

"We have Western names, too. I don't," Wai-yee explained.

"Okay."

"He is an expert cutter."

"Good. That's what I want. An expert cutter."

She selected the material for the suit and she instructed Hanson Hsu in Cantonese, overseeing every movement of the intimidated tailor as he measured Moose. Everything he did seemed to be wrong by Wai-yee's standards. Wrong style, wrong fabric, wrong color, wrong shade, wrong measurements, all corrected by Wai-yee. When she became satisfied, the tailor told Moose it would be 595 Hong Kong dollars which Wai-yee quickly converted to be 34 American dollars. She started screaming at Hanson Hsu. He answered that 595 Hong Kong dollars was the same as 30 American dollars and she said no, and then told Moose, "you must not pay one cent more than 525 Hong Kong or he's a crook." Then she translated for Hanson Hsu who then brought the price down to what she instructed. In less than one minute they were in another fight. "Moose! He wants to deliver it the day after tomorrow! You'll be gone on that day! Let's leave! He gets nothing! We'll go somewhere else!" She said something sternly to Hanson Hsu in Cantonese. He answered softly and she nodded. She told Moose that "it will arrive at the Miramar tomorrow." Then she got into an argument with Hanson Hsu over a Certificate of Origin. She insisted he sign one so Moose could prove to U.S. Customs that the suit was not made in China. Hanson Hsu said no Certificate of Origin was needed for clothing. Wai-yee won. He said he would write a Certificate of Origin and deliver it with the suit. Wai-yee nodded and took Moose's hand. "Let's get out of here and go for a walk. I can't stand it in here any longer."

They went down one alleyway and small street and onto the main thoroughfare of Nathan Road, where she talked to every traffic policeman who stood in kiosks in the middle of the street, and they all appeared overjoyed to talk with her.

"What are you talking about to them?" Moose asked, re-lighting his pipe.

"I tell them they're not doing their work. There was a store on Hankow Road that was broken into last week and they didn't catch the man who did it. You have to tell them when they don't do their work or they get lazy." She was acting as though she owned Hong Kong. Joan of Arc.

They looked in window after window at pipes and electric razors and men's clothing, but she was careful not to stop at any window of a store that catered to women. She would not be suspected of hinting for anything from him.

Then there was the voyage on the ferry to Hong Kong Island where she took him to an open air market which was selling nothing but vegetables and fish with a smell and crowds that were nearly beyond his endurance. If there had been such a place at home, Moose would have tried to hide it from a visitor, but Wai-yee was so proud of it. "I want to show you all of Hong Kong," she said. "It is the most enchanting place in the world."

From the market she took him to Causeway Bay and to Shaukiwan and Aberdeen with masses of people that lived on sampans and some bigger boats.

"These are the people I told you about," she whispered as though she was in danger of being heard. "The Tanka. They celebrate their birthday eight days too late!" And she gave a guilty smile in a turtle-like gesture of injecting her head toward her chest.

Then a ride in a double decked red streetcar down Queen's Road, and back through Causeway Bay to Happy Valley where they walked toward the harbor on quieter streets as the sun was getting lower.

"Are you hungry?" he asked her.

"No." He was delighted that she wasn't hungry because he couldn't tolerate the smell of more fish which was undoubtedly what she would have wanted had she been hungry.

"What time do you have to be home?" He asked her.

She shrugged. "No certain time."

"Didn't you tell me you were busy tonight?"

"Sure. But I lied." She opened her eyes wide and smiled.

"Why?"

"I didn't know if I'd like you."

"And you do?"

"You're all right," and she laughed with her hand held to her lips again, then with her free hand, she took his. He held her hand very tight. "Besides I like the smell of your pipe. I never knew a man well who smoked a pipe."

"Do you want to just walk?" Holding hands with Wai-yee was more exciting and satisfying than making love to any other woman he had known.

"Sure."

And they continued their slow walk as though they had to walk to get from day to night.

"That man yesterday—Mr. Orr—did you like him?" Wai-yee asked.

"Yes. Why?"

"I liked him too, but I thought he was a strange man. Didn't you?"

"We talked a little. He seemed like a nice guy. I know what you mean though."

"I just thought he was strange."

"You know what's strange? That you mention him to me."

"Why?"

"It's just that he knew I was high on you. He was warning me not to fall too hard for you," and he quickly added, "or anyone."

"He didn't like me?"

"Oh, no. He was warning me about myself—just that I was falling."

"Falling?"

"For you. For Wai-yee."

"Was he right? And would that be bad?"

"He was right. And it's very good."

"You don't know much about me," Wai-yee said with some hesitancy.

"Everything I know I like—very much."

"You don't know me."

"I want to."

"Do you mind if we visit my sister?" she asked very unexpectedly. "Would you want to go with me to visit my sister?"

"Of course. Now? At this hour? Where is she?"

"She's at the Kowloon Ballroom. She works there. I told her I would try to see her some time this weekend. We don't have to but—"

"Of course. Wai-yee—whatever you'd like."

And so they went back on the ferry. Each ride was a glory of its own for anyone, but combining the rides with having Wai-yee sit with him was one of the great rewards of life. They saw Hong Kong Island become more distant, and at night with a black sky, the city became a pastel or painting rather than the sight of a moving city. That was because one of the few government regulations was that no electric sign was allowed to flash on and off or move at all or change colors, since Kai Tak Airport was too close and, for safety, the only moving lights could be those of that airport's landing strip. The end effect was a huge unmoving horizontal mural of the city.

And when they started walking the night streets of Kowloon, each corner turned was a new aisle-way of brilliantly colorful and stationary electric Chinese and English language characters.

The Kowloon Ballroom was immense. It was a dance floor surrounded by rows of small tables. He was the only Caucasian in the place. They sat at one of the small tables near the door. Wai-yee explained that "the ballroom caters to Chinese locals and in here the men customers pay for the company of a woman for a dance or a drink and most of the girls don't speak English. If the customer wants to take the girl out, he must pay the Kowloon Ballroom for whatever hours she misses at work. I know what you think—but this is very ordinary here in Hong Kong."

"I'm not thinking anything. It's fine."

"No, it isn't fine, but she's a good girl and she makes a lot of money here. There she is!"

Coming to them was someone who was so pretty that she could only be Wai-yee's sister. Moose and Wai-yee stood up, and Wai-yee and her sister kissed each other on the cheeks. Wai-yee introduced her sister to Moose.

"This is Winnie. She doesn't speak English."

"Hi, Wai-winnie," he said to her and there was only the response of a smile. He turned to Wai-yee. "Isn't it Wai-winnie?"

Wai-yee smiled as she sat down. "No. Winnie is her Western name. She has a Western name."

Moose and Winnie sat at the table while Moose was shaking his head. "Is Winnie your little sister or big sister?"

Wai-yee shrugged. "It depends on what calendar you use." She was kidding him but he knew he shouldn't have asked. Wai-yee went to Moose's ear. "Just don't fall for her," she whispered. "Remember, you're with me and I'll tell her you're an escaped murderer from Alcatraz if I see you look at her like you look at me."

"Sing-Sing."

"What's Sing-Sing?"

"A prison."

"No. Alcatraz. She heard of Alcatraz. It was in a movie, *The House Across the Bay* with Joan Bennett."

"It was?"

"Sure. Do you think Winnie is pretty?"

"I think you're both very homely. Not really ugly. Just homely."

She laughed, her hand quickly rising to her face. "Do you think she's prettier than me?"

"There isn't a woman in the world that pretty, Wai-yee."

"You think she's prettier than me!"

Winnie was paying no attention to them. She was roaming her eyes and smiling at men who were sitting at different tables.

"No, I don't think she's prettier than you. Please," Moose said.

"I'm glad she's pretty. But you don't need to look at her."

"I'm not."

"Now, let me talk to Winnie quickly. We can't stay long or they'll get mad. She's supposed to work."

For the next fifteen minutes, Wai-yee and Winnie were talking in Cantonese and Moose sat there without anything to say or do. But he enjoyed it only because the intensity of their conversation was so apparent in the volume of their voices, and their gestures. They seemed to forget where they were or who would hear them. The subject or subjects they covered could not have ever been discussed before by anyone with as much fervor. Then in an instant it was done. The abruptness of its termination was due to a customer who came over to Winnie and asked her to dance.

"Let's go," Wai-yee said. "She likes you."

"I can't blame her," Moose said. "We have so much in common, and we agree on everything."

It was late. They went to the Miramar for a drink and, on the pretense of wanting to talk, he took her to his room. But the pretense became reality. She sat on the edge of the bed and because she looked sad, he didn't sit next to her. He sat on a chair. He wanted her to feel as unsuspicious of his motives as she made him feel when she avoided the windows of stores that sold jewelry or women's clothes.

"Moose," she said. "May I tell you about me—and Winnie?"

"Please. You're very close to her, aren't you?"

"Sure. Winnie and I were able to leave China because my parents paid off smugglers to get us out. My father's a teacher. He is brilliant. He teaches mathematics. There is little pay for him from the government. He had to be very careful in working for money on the side. My mother keeps the cleanest house in Kiangchow and she works in the fields. My parents paid the smugglers everything they had—and more. Their parents, who are my grandparents, were executed by Mao's revolutionary court. I guess they had made some private statements against the revolution although I never really found out what it was that caused them to be—killed. That night was so ghastly when they were taken away. Before they took them away they did things to them in their own apartment that I cannot discuss. The torture was so brutal—and humiliating—that in honor of their memory I will not detail it. It is their life that I want to remember, not those hours of humiliation and torture in front of each other. They were already dying when they got to court. In China now, trials are held only after verdicts are given. If you are called for a trial, you are guilty. The trial lasted four minutes. The execution was in the back of their heads. Then they made my parents pay for the bullets that killed my grandparents.

"My parents wanted Winnie and me to have a decent chance in life, so they got us to Hong Kong at such great expense. Now it's our turn. We want to get our parents out of China. Kiangchow is a long distance away, near Peking. They can't even get to Canton without government permission. You can't go from city to city without government permission. We know who the smugglers are. The cost is very high, and when we have enough to get them out we want them to have a good life here. Do you understand so far?"

"Yes, I do."

"Winnie and I developed a plan. She makes a very good amount of money. Men pay a lot for her. I make fair money at the Consulate, but it's not anywhere near as high as Winnie. We pool our money in a fund to get our parents here. We don't know how long it will take. The people we deal with keep raising the price. After we get them here, we know how we will give our parents a good life. Winnie will not always be beautiful and when the years come when men will not pay for her, I will have the experience and reputation to have a job maybe in a high paying office. So for a while she makes the money and I make the reputation. When the time comes, I will make the money and Winnie can have a life without work. My parents will never have to work in Hong Kong between Winnie's work and my work, and then just when I work. Does that make sense to you?"

Moose gave a slow nod. "Yes, Wai-yee. It makes sense."

"Life is hard now. Not mine at the Consulate, it's a good job, but every day I think of my mother and father and what they are doing. They cannot write without authorities opening the mail in China. They are watched. When we arrange to get them out, the plan may fail. If they are caught trying to leave, they will be executed like my grandparents. I don't wish to complain to you but I want you to know what I am. If I could trade places with Winnie I would. I want you to know that. But Winnie can't do what I can do, she can't even speak English. I can do what Winnie can do and I would do it in a moment–but when the time comes that men would not pay for me, I would have no way to earn money. That is why we reached our agreement. She earns the money now. I earn the reputation now. But she is every bit as good as I am–and more so. She's better."

"What you are doing–I admire you, Wai-yee. And her."

"You are not through with me?"

Moose felt tears coming and he tried to keep them from swelling in his eyes, but he was unsuccessful. He waited a while so he would not talk through trembling lips. "I am not through with you."

She smiled at what he said and what she saw. "For such a big man, you are so gentle," she said.

"I don't normally get tears, Wai-yee. I don't normally do that."

"No. It's all right. A man may cry when he is sad or when he is glad. But a man must not cry when he is mad. You are sad at what I tell you?"

"I think it must be that I am so glad to be with you."

"You are gentle. You are a gentle man." She sat a little closer to the edge of the bed. "I must tell you everything."

"I want to know what ever you want me to know."

"I live in a very small room. Winnie and I don't live together because she needs to live alone in a nicer place for her customers. I don't want you to see my place. It's why I met you at Jimmy's Kitchen and why you must not see my home. At first Winnie and I lived in a squatter's hut without any water or any sanitation or any privacy. But we had some good times because we were together and we knew how to laugh. I made money by having a vegetable plot on the side of a hill, until someone ripped it out. Then the government here built resettlement buildings. They're all huge. You must have seen them when you came in from Kai Tak. They're big H-shaped seven story blocks—big housing blocks that hold over 2500 of us in small rooms. Families live together. I'm alone but it's only because people are good to me. Most of them have five people in a space that's 10 by 12 feet, American. But the rooms are as clean as we want to make them. Mine is clean. I'm always clean."

He nodded. "I know."

"I think that's important to always be clean."

"Yes it is."

"Almost every night I walk or go to the movies—alone. I like the movies. I like to get out of my room, and I enjoy the walks and the movies, particularly American movies. I know who all the movie stars are. And almost every weekend I spend most of Saturday and Sunday in a movie theater. Sometimes I see the same picture over and over again if it's good."

There was a knock on the door.

Moose yelled out, "Yes?"

A man's voice yelled back, "Mr. Dunston, you have a guest in your room. That is not allowed after 11 o'clock."

Moose looked at Wai-yee who gave a small closed-mouth smile. And she cocked her head in that feminine style that could knock him out. He smiled too, and nodded and yelled back at the voice behind the door, "All right. We'll be leaving in a moment."

"Room 19, leaving in a moment," the voice confirmed.

Moose hailed a taxi for Wai-yee and paid the driver in advance, much more than the prospective fare. "Wai-yee, will I see you again? Can I take you to dinner tomorrow night after you get off work?"

"There is no work tomorrow. It's a holiday. It's Double Ten, the tenth day of the tenth month, Nationalist Day, like your July the 4th, especially to the people on Formosa. But here, too."

"Oh, really? A day off? That's wonderful. May I see you? May I see you all day?"

She smiled and nodded. "I'll come by at nine in the morning. We'll have breakfast. Do you want to?"

"Oh, that's wonderful," he repeated. His vocabulary was diminishing the more he was with her.

The taxi drove off with her inside. He even admired the unknown taxi driver since the lucky stranger would be in her presence for a while.

As he walked back in the hotel he realized he had spent almost twelve hours with her, and he was crazy about her, and he hadn't even kissed her. He hadn't even come close to kissing her and it would have been such unimaginable bliss. It was all right that he hadn't.

His hand smelled of her perfume. That was enough.

On Double Ten, it was all day. In the morning he asked her what she wanted to do and she said, "I want to do anything. I want to do nothing. I want to do everything."

They did all three.

"We beat the Miramar at its own game, you know," he said.

"What do you mean?"

"We didn't have to care about eleven at night."

When it turned dark she told Moose that there was a new Debbie Reynolds picture at the Princess Theater just blocks away. "Tony Curtis is in it, too," she said, "and Jack Oakie. I like him."

"You want to go?"

She raised her eyebrows and nodded. "Can we? Is that all right with you?"

"Of course."

"Are you sure?"

"Yes. I'm sure."

"You see, there's a typhoon coming. A typhoon called Kit and I may not be able to go to the movies tomorrow night."

"Then you'll go tonight."

"It's called *Rat Race* and I want to see it." Then, with pride, she said, "Last week I saw *Summer of the 17th Doll* with Anne Baxter and Ernest Borgnine at the Princess, and *Let's Make Love* with Marilyn Monroe in Cinemascope at the Roxy, and *Song Without End* with Genevieve Page and Capucine and Dirk Bogarde in Cinemascope at the Royal." It was said as a series of accomplishments. "Do you like Cinemascope?"

He nodded with a smile. "I do."

When night came and they walked out of the Miramar, she paused near its outside entrance where there was a bronze plaque with the emblem of the hotel. She took Moose's hand and she raised their held hands to the plaque and she felt the plaque as though she was caressing the bronze. She said nothing. He felt the bronze, too. Their hands remained held with their fingers on the plaque. "The Miramar," she said with affection.

They sat in the back stalls section of the Princess Theater and she was eating popcorn that Moose thought was much too sweet, not like in the United States. Before the picture started he labored through one advertisement on the screen after another. Then a notice came on the screen saying, "Empty All Refuse Into Lorry" and then *The Rat Race* started.

She laughed, even at those things in the movie that were not funny. It was because she was happy. He loved watching her laugh.

It was late when they walked back toward the Miramar. It must have rained while they were in the theater as the streets were wet and glossy. It appeared as though the streets had been paved with waving fun-house mirrors reflecting brilliant electric signs. Firecrackers were going off in recognition of the holiday but neither Moose nor Wai-yee paid attention to them. She stopped when the Miramar came in view. "Always the Miramar. The Miramar is always in front of us. It's always there."

"I know." They both hesitated to walk to it since it was too late for them to be together there. "Will I see you again, Wai-yee?"

"I'll always be here in Hong Kong. Always."

"I'll be back. I'll be back if I have to borrow, cheat, or steal to be back."

"No. You would never borrow, cheat, or steal."

"But I'll be back."

"When?"

"When I can. As soon as I can. I promise."

"I promise I'll be here."

He wiped his eyes again. He did that more times since he met her than he had in decades.

They stared at each other. He held both of her hands. They stood like that for a long while. "I should go now, Moose."

He nodded but wouldn't let go of her hands. "I'll call a cab for you."

"No. I take a rickshaw." A rickshaw was right there and she broke from Moose and quickly sat in the rickshaw's bench-seat, saying something in Cantonese as an order to the rickshaw-man.

Moose stared at the man who quickly started his run down the glossy street with Wai-yee as his cargo. Moose felt paralyzed. He couldn't move while that rickshaw was in sight. Then the rickshaw made a U-turn and came back.

Wai-yee didn't get out. Apparently at her instruction, the rickshaw-man pulled her right next to Moose as he stood on the sidewalk. "Moose?" she said.

He whispered, "What, Wai-yee?"

"I love you."

If he said anything he would have sobbed and he didn't want her to see him do that.

But tears weren't done. They came again at the hotel when he opened the door of his room and saw the new suit with a Certificate of Origin on a hanger, hooked to the mirror. It had obviously been delivered by the tailor, just as Wai-yee had insisted.

SEVEN
IN SEARCH OF A SADHU
1960

The customs inspector at Dumdum Airport in Calcutta that night demanded that Anne Whitney open her luggage no matter how many gnats were eagerly waiting for it to be opened so they could fly inside. After the customs inspector's obvious enjoyment in handling her underwear and other feminine things in her luggage as though he was searching for something, and after examining and confiscating a State Department map of India that didn't have Kashmir designated as Indian territory, he closed her luggage, sealing either tens or hundreds of those flying gnats inside. Whether they would be alive or dead when she opened the luggage next was not uppermost on his mind. "Ah-chah," he said, moving his head side to side as though his head was a pendulum, which Anne assumed to be his seal of approval.

To both Anne and Calcutta's mutual delight, Anne was not going into the city, but rather to a connecting Indian Airlines flight to New Delhi where she was promised a U.S. Embassy official would meet her at Palam Ngurah Rai Airport despite the Embassy's knowledge that she was en route to Washington after being suspended from the U.S. Consulate in Hong Kong. There was still a sense of allegiance that she was "one of theirs," which she was. And she still held a maroon Official Passport, and that gave her some privileges.

"What do you want to do in India?" the U.S. Political Officer asked her while he drove her to her hotel through the night roads into Delhi's city center.

"See some things."

"The Taj Majhal? Fatehpur Sikri? The Red Fort? Like that?"

"I want a car or something. I want to meet some yogis."

He shook his head. "Oh, boy. Well, that's tough. Most of the yogis, and don't call them that here–they'll laugh or take you to the cleaners–the Sadhu's here, or at least 90 percent of them, are fakes. They're just beggars who found a better way to get money than pleading for bahksheesh. Bahksheesh means money, tips, handouts. Fake Sadhus go around from city to village and village to city, some with an elephant and they get free food and free lodging that way. Supposedly they are bound for Nirvana – that means heaven. A lot of people are scared not to help them just in case they're for real–but they generally don't have any more touch with Nirvana than you do." And, from what he already heard of her, she had very little.

"I want to see for myself."

"Okay. That's fine. You're entitled."

"What do I do?"

"Is this your first time to India?"

"Yes."

"Then get prepared for what we call 'culture shock.' This isn't a place you can understand in a few days, or a week–or even months. It takes years. This is a very tough place for someone used to the States."

"In what way? You mean poverty?"

"That, and a lot of other things."

"I've been to Appalachia. And I've been to the Deep South. Believe me, I've seen poverty."

"Those places are paradise compared to what you'll see here. You have to understand that."

"I've seen what we do to Negroes."

He nodded. "Did you ever hear of the caste system here?"

"Sure. Gandhi banned it. Nehru's against it, too. I know."

"Banned or not banned, it goes on. I just want to get you ready. You have to know. If a Harijan–an Untouchable–casts his shadow on you, you're expected to take a bath to de-pollute yourself. They're put so low, they aren't even considered a caste, and they're one-sixth of the population. They even have a caste system within a caste system. There are over six hundred sub-levels of Untouchability, so practically everyone can feel they're better than someone else. And do you know that widows of any caste are considered bad luck? They can't go to a wedding or a festival. They can't wear jewelry and their food is rationed from their village and their hair is shaved off. That is–that is the ones who didn't throw themselves on the cremation pyre of their husbands."

"Uh-huh. I didn't come here to criticize the Indians. We have problems of our own at home."

"We certainly do. I just want you to know. And I'm glad you know about our own injustices at home. That can help you here. It's just that this is so different than back home. I don't want you to think it doesn't take time to understand. I love India. Some people make up their minds too soon and they become critical. This is a wonderful country when you get to know it."

"How could you love it if you find so much wrong with it?"

"I understand it. And we're not doing enough. We've given India around three billion dollars worth of aid since independence thirteen years ago. Maybe that sounds like a lot but there are 500 million people here–so what is that then–six dollars a person? Or less than about one-half dollar a year?"

Anne shrugged. "We never do enough." But that was not her interest tonight. "I want to find an Indian teacher, a Hindu who has real wisdom."

"A Sadhu."

"Yes. I want to search for a Sadhu."

"Okay."

"So what do I do? I need to be able to get around and see things."

"I think we can get you a vehicle okay. Do you have an International Driver's License?"

"Yes." She reached in her purse and took out a small gray booklet and said, "I took care of all that."

"There's an American guy who's in Delhi from the International Communications Foundation and he's leasing or maybe he's even buying a Volkswagen Microbus, going all over India in it to make some documentary movie of some kind for the Foreign Service Institute. He's a friend of some of the staff, although I don't really know him. Anyway, he has this Microbus and he leaves it parked on the Embassy grounds when he's in Delhi—he packs it up with food from the commissary for when he goes out in the field. We let him have commissary privileges because that foundation is on a U.S. Government contract, and he buys the stuff; he can't digest Indian food. He got food poisoning when he ate in a village somewhere near Allahabad. So anyway, the car's on our grounds now, all loaded up. I think he's staying at Claridges, I don't know, but we can find out and you could probably make a deal with him to borrow it to go to Agra or somewhere, if he isn't using it when you want it. We could put you in touch with a bearer. You need a bearer. You want to be riding around with someone who knows the roads and the customs and the language. It's not good to be alone on the highway."

It was as though she was mad. "So how do I do that? I don't have a lot of time. I'm just here on my way to Washington. I had my choice to either go back to D.C. by the Pacific or this way. Hong Kong is exactly around the world from D.C. and I chose this way. So what do I do?"

"Oh, gee, come to the Embassy tomorrow morning, not now, and we'll see what we can do to help you. We'll set you up with Venki who's taking care of the Volkswagen for that guy. Venki Venkatarahan. He has the keys. You're staying—we made a reservation for you at the Ashoka. Sorry, but it's about nine American dollars a night, even for Embassy personnel, but I'm sure you want to be in a clean place. The Ashoka is run by the Indian Government and it's the best place around. You can walk to the Embassy from there in the morning. Weather's good. The monsoons are over. Walk out the door and turn left. You'll see us on the righthand side of the road called Shanti Path. We're right next door to the Soviet Embassy. We're just before you hit it."

"Do I see you in the morning?"

"Yeah, see me."

"How come you don't have your headlights on? Don't you think that would be a good idea?"

"No. No one does unless you're out in the country."

"Well how do you see?"

"I don't know, you just do. I don't even notice it anymore, I'm so used to it."

"Well, it doesn't make any sense."

"Wait till we stop for a signal and you'll really be surprised. You turn off the ignition here when you stop for a signal."

"That's dopey."

"They think it saves gasoline. Now I do it, too, so they don't think Americans waste gasoline. That's why you need a bearer when you drive. He can tell you what to do and not to do on the road, like being careful of cows. If you hit a human–stop. You can pay off the family as a rule. If you hit a cow–keep going–speed up. They'll kill you if they catch you."

"Are you the Embassy's spook?"

He turned to her sharply, and shook his head, "No. And if I was, do you think I'd tell you? You call them Spooks, already?"

"All right. Are you the Embassy's CIA Agent then? The Station Chief or whatever you call them? Is that putting it better? They usually are put in some weird-o position with a long job description that's nothing but mumble-jumble. What's your mumble-jumble?"

"I'm the Political Officer. If you have to see the spook," he said using her vocabulary but with a tone of sarcasm, "you better ask Ambassador Bunker to lead him to you. I don't even know who he is–if we have one."

"Oh for God's sake, please, I wasn't born yesterday."

"Did you know the spook in Hong Kong?"

She shook her head. "They never told me who he was because I'm just a J.O.T. If I stayed there a little while longer I could have figured it out. And I would have. I like looking for spooks."

That evening she sat out on the broad front lawn of the opulent Ashoka Hotel. A few feet away from her was a snake-charmer who was charming neither snakes nor tourists. He had a little basket with a snake in it and the snake was untalented and rarely peeped out of the basket, maybe because the charmer was playing one un-melodic theme after another on his hand-made woodwind instrument, the likes of which Anne had never seen before. Steps away from him was an old woman with a smooth, sad face, sitting cross-legged with a spread of costume jewelry on a blanket. The woman looked somewhat Chinese–but not quite. All that Anne knew for certain was that she wasn't Indian. She made no attempt to sell anyone anything.

Anne couldn't help but periodically look back at the woman, intrigued by her lack of sales ability and the lack of tourists who bought anything from her. Anne got up and walked over to the woman, and looked at the woman's display of bracelets and necklaces and rings and glass-like stones. The woman said nothing to Anne. This wasn't Times Square with the salesman saying, "Since you're the last customer of the night you can have it for 30 percent off."

"How much is this?" Anne asked, lifting a ring.

The woman rolled her head and said something beyond comprehension to Anne. A boy, maybe eighteen or nineteen years old, who wore a purple Ashoka uniform, saw the difficulty the two women were having in communicating. "May I help? You're a guest here, are you not?"

"Yes," Anne said, "Could you ask her how much this is?"

After all the translations were over, the ring was announced to cost what was converted to be less than seventy cents. Anne bought it.

"She's from Tibet," the boy said. "She's here every afternoon into the evening. She walked for four months across the Himalayan Mountains. The Chinese killed her husband and then she lost her son in the mountains. He was killed. He fell down in a snow-slide. None of them were professional mountain-climbers."

"How awful. But they shouldn't have left."

"She knew the Dalai Lama. She and her son left with him last year. The Chinese Communists had already killed thousands, some say one hundred thousand Tibetans, and the Chinese opened labor camps and they destroyed the monasteries. There were over six thousand monasteries when the Chinese invaded ten years ago. Now there are six. She told me about all this when she came here."

Anne shrugged. "Are you sure she's telling the truth?"

He nodded. "All the Tibetans tell the same stories. They all walked here across the mountains. They live all over our Hill Stations. I think there are more Tibetans in Dehra Dun and Dharamsala than us. The same in Darjeeling up in the northeast."

"She doesn't try to sell anything?"

"No. Tibetans aren't very aggressive people."

"The Chinese came into Tibet because it is Chinese territory, you know," Anne said as her explanation of what the boy had said.

"I don't know who owns it but I know the Tibetans minded their business for thousands of years. Mao Tse-tung said that Tibet was part of China, but he did promise them autonomy, you know. His government signed an agreement that the Tibetans could keep their way of life in a Special Autonomous Region. But the agreement was not kept. Now there is one soldier for every twelve Tibetans in Lhasa, the capital of Tibet. And anyone who prays publicly is imprisoned. Or executed."

"There must be more to it than that."

"Maybe," the boy said. "You asked me who she was. That's who she is."

"I didn't ask you who she was. Does everyone here have some cause or something?"

The U.S. Embassy staff continued their courtesy to Anne. Venki Venkatarahan showed her the Volkswagen Microbus. It was red and big and the only difficulty with it was that the steering wheel was on the correct side for driving in the United States but the wrong side for driving in India. Venki contacted the owner of the Volkswagen Microbus who said that as long as she has an Official Passport, Anne could borrow the car without paying him anything, but she must be back by the end of the week when he would be leaving to Jaipur, and she must pay his bearer 40 rupees, which was $8.40 for a week's time, even if she wouldn't use him all that time. She had to promise not only to pay the bearer no less—but no more, since if she gave him more he would then demand or expect that much from others. Further, she would have to pay for any food they used from the van's stockpile.

Her bearer was a small Bengali, Dhanilal Dass, who placed a narrow wreath of yellow and white flowers around her neck when he first sat beside her in the front passenger seat of the van, with her in the driver's seat. He called her "M'em Sahb" and she liked him calling her M'em Sahb.

He pretended to know all the places within a reasonable distance where she could find a "real Sadhu". "Not in Delhi," he told her. "We must go to the holy city of Varanasi at the Holy site of the Ganges, M'em Sahb."

"I never heard of it."

"You heard of Benares, M'em Sahb?"

"I don't know. I guess so."

"They are the same city. We call it Varanasi. You call it Benares."

"What do you mean 'you' call it Benares. I don't call it anything." Anne was on her usual defensive.

"The English call it Benares, M'em Sahb."

"I'm not English. I'm American."

"Yes, yes, M'em Sahb." This American was not going to be easy.

She was driving to Varanasi, Dhanilal by her side. Anne was getting used to the steering wheel being on the wrong side for India's roads, and she loved the attention caused by the big red van. Whenever villagers walked by the side of the road and saw her coming or going, they stopped and stared at the van as though it came from Mars rather than West Germany. What she didn't like was that shortly after they got out of Delhi, all the roads created so much brown dust as the Volkswagon rode over them, that she had to roll the windows up to prevent coughing, and her glasses became dirty only a moment after cleaning them, even with the windows up.

"Is Kennedy-ji going to win your election?" Dhanilal asked.

"I think so. It's Kennedy, not Kennedy-ji."

"No, M'em Sahb. 'Ji' is Hindi for an expression of respect. It's like saying 'sir' in English."

"Oh. Okay."

"Kennedy-ji is going to help India?"

"I'm sure he will."

"Eisenhower has not helped India." No addition of "ji" for Eisenhower. "We are not getting enough aid. Eisenhower likes Pakistan more than he likes India."

"Probably."

"The Soviet Union gives us power plants. Kennedy-ji must give us power plants. We must become an industrial nation, and he will help us do that. He needs to make the rupee strong and he must make it an international currency all over the world. India is the future. Do you know Kennedy-ji?"

"No."

"You will meet him though, Ah-chah?"

"I doubt it. I don't know. Dhanilal, what's that man doing to that blindfolded horse?"

"Oh," he laughed. "That horse is old and no good. He's trying to make it young," and he laughed again. "He has no money for a young horse."

"He's beating it."

"He's prodding it. It's a stick. It doesn't hurt."

"That stick has a nail on the end of it."

"He's trying to make the horse young, M'em Sahb." And he gave that 'everything is okay' laugh again.

"He's torturing it. It has wounds and blood spots all over it!" She stopped the car, got out and began shouting at the man. "You stop that! You're killing that horse!"

The man started rushing towards Anne with the stick. Anne quickly went back into the car and was able to drive off before he reached her.

"Oh, M'em Sahb! Oh, M'em Sahb!" Dhanilal was beginning to regret he accepted this assignment. "Don't stop the car unless you ask me, M'em Sahb. I'm responsible to your Embassy for your safety!"

"I can't stand to see an animal tortured. And I thought animals were considered to be sacred here."

"Oh, they are, M'em Sahb. They are sacred."

"Then that man was sacrilegious. And a monster."

"You must understand. There are times when a very poor man must make the animal do more. But they are sacred. You see the cows? They always have the right of way."

"They look pitiful. They look like they're starving. I was told that if I hit a person with a car I should stop and pay off the family, but if I hit one of those starving cows I can't stop or I'll be killed. Is that right?"

"I –I don't know."

Fortunately circumstances did not develop that allowed her to find out the accuracy of that advice regarding either humans or cows. "I don't get it. They beat animals but starve themselves rather than eat them. It doesn't make sense."

"Stop!" He yelled. "Stop!"

"Why?" as she screeched on the brakes.

"You see? Over there? A Sadhu-ji. Your Sadhu."

"Where?"

"M'em, Sahb, there!" He pointed to the horizon on the right. "You see?"

Dhanilal's eyes were very good. It was just an orange-gowned dot on the horizon but sure enough, it was a man—and soon over the horizon came what he was leading: a bigger dot that was an elephant. The man was leading it by a rope.

"Is he a real Sadhu?"

"Oh, yes, M'em Sahb."

"How do you know?"

"He's real, M'em Sahb. I know. Yes, I always know. He's a real Sadhu."

By this time some villagers gathered by the sides of the car peering in through the windows. Dhanilal opened the door on his passenger side and Anne opened her door with caution so as not to hit any of the villagers with the door. She was greeted with a pathetic, dirty young face. “Bahksheesh, M’em Sahib. Bahksheesh,” the boy said with an outstretched hand.

“I do it,” Dhanilal said. “I give him ten naya paise.”

“How much is that worth? I mean American.”

“I don’t know, M’em Sahb. A rupee is twenty-one cents and there are one hundred naya paise in one rupee so I gave him ten naya paise.”

“Good Lord! We have to give him more than that!”

“It’s enough. There are sixteen annas in a naya paise. So ten naya paise is 160 annas. That is good.”

Soon there were twenty or more children surrounding Anne asking for “Bahksheesh!” while the adults admired the Volkswagen Microbus.

Anne almost emptied her purse giving the children Hong Kong coins which they looked at in bewilderment, and when they were all given out, she gave them the few Indian coins she had, not knowing what they were worth.

“You watch the car for me,” she said to one small boy who nodded. “Here’s one rupee, a whole rupee to watch it.”

“Ah-chah,” he said with great joy as he nodded.

Anne and Dhanilal walked in the direction of the dot that was leading the bigger dot.

On the top of the hill, the Sadhu lit a fire despite the heat, and Anne, Dhanilal, and the Sadhu sat down on the ground around the burning wood. The Sadhu rubbed some ashes on Anne’s forehead, and then he rubbed them on Dhanilal’s forehead.

“Sadhu-ji,” Dhanilal said softly, and put the fingertips of his two hands against each other giving the sign of Namaste.

“Do you want to see a miracle?” The Sadhu asked Anne.

“No.”

“No miracles?”

“No.”

“Americans always want to see miracles.”

“I don’t.”

“Then what do you want to see?”

“I don’t want to see anything. I want to talk. I want you to tell me about life, about what you believe, about Nirvana, about death, about the truth.”

“Ahhhh! The truth.”

“Yes,” Dhanilal offered, “the truth, Sahdu-ji.”

“Ahhhh!” the Sadhu nodded.

There was silence.

“Well?” Anne asked fearing this was a fake and Dhanilal might be in on it.

“I am abstinent, you call it. Twelve years abstinence. All my power then remains inside. After twelve years of such potent male storage, I have been purified."

"Uh-huh," Anne said. "It's been twelve years?"

"I am strengthened by my inner male power that has not been released."

"You did it twelve years ago?"

He didn't answer.

"Why did you do it at all?"

He was not used to such questioning.

"What do you do with all that inner male power you have now?" she asked.

"I roll eyes back and see a flame in the center of my head."

"Then what?"

"I see the truth."

"Good. That's what I want to know. Now, tell me about it."

"I must roll my eyes back and wait for the flame in the center of my head."

"Go do it."

"It will take anywhere between one and two days until I finish."

"One or two days!?"

"You can not rush the truth. Americans always in a hurry. Would you rather see a miracle?"

"How long will a miracle take?"

"That is quick."

"What's the miracle?"

"I can pull your red automobile by connecting rope to my powerful male member and then walking backwards."

"What!?"

"I put rope on my powerful male member and I put other end of rope to the metal rod on the front of your car. I then walk backwards, pulling your car."

"Without the elephant?"

"No elephant. This is all done because of my inner power."

"Go ahead. This I got to see."

"May I have car if I do it?"

"Of course not!"

"Then no miracle. Americans only want to see miracles."

"Oh, God!" Anne said and she stood, dusting herself off. "Dhanilal, let's go. This isn't a real Sadhu. This is a real charlatan!"

Dhanilal was embarrassed and uneasy, trying to please both Anne and the Sadhu at the same time. "M'em Sahb, you must give him some money."

"For what?"

"For Sadhu's time with you."

"Who does he think he is, Mahatma Gandhi?"

"Gandhi-ji's dead, M'em Sahb."

"Oh, I know that. I won't give this jerk one cent."

"I give."

"No, Dhanilal. Here, I'll give him something. Wait. No. You give him one anna. I'll give it back to you."

"One anna?"

"Yes."

"M'em Sahb!"

"That's one-sixteenth of one one-hundredth of twenty-one cents, isn't that right?"

"Oh, M'em Sahb."

"That's all he gets." Anne started walking to the car and didn't look back to see if Dhanilal was or wasn't behind her.

The car had a large crowd around it now, and the boy to whom she had given a rupee to watch it, proudly extended his hand toward the car, as though he was the host of a presentation. It was his announcement that it was still operable because he did the job he was assigned. Anne reached in her purse and gave him another rupee. By the time she got in the car, Dhanilal, breathlessly, opened the door on the passenger side and he got in.

"To Benares, M'em Sahb," he said. "We go. No more Sadhu-ji here."

Under Dhanilal's direction they reached the Holy City and he instructed Anne to park the car about two blocks from the Ganges, and again she paid one rupee to a boy to watch the Microbus. Anne and Dhanilal walked down a narrow road toward the river.

The road was so narrow and congested with beggars and lepers and hawkers and cows and bullock-carts that it was difficult to be certain they were walking toward the river, which was obscured by all those things. But when the last obstructions on each side were finally left behind them, a mammoth spectacle was on display. It was an overpowering view of hundreds of people, some bathing in the Ganges, some praying in it, some cremating bodies by it, some putting ashes from the cremations into it, some getting rid of their bodily wastes in it, some washing their clothes in it. And some dying near it.

Anne Whitney was motionless, with her mouth open.

"The Ganges, M'em Sahb," Dhanilal announced without a sense of what was causing her immobility. "You see? They pray. It's sacred."

She didn't hear him or if she did, his words didn't register as being heard.

"Oh, no!" she said. "Oh, no! What is this? Where am I? Dhanilal! Did you know what this was?"

"Yes, M'em Sahb, yes. This is a sacred place. This is Varanasi. It is the confluence of five sacred rivers, M'em Sahb; the Ganges with the Sarswati, Gyana, Dhutpapa, and the Kirana."

"What are they doing over there? Over there with those woods burning?"

"That's the Jalaysayin Cremation Ghat, M'em Sahb."

"They're burning bodies?"

"Yes, M'em Sahb. The Untouchables prepare the dead and supply the flame for the pyre, then the ashes go to the sacred river."

"And there?"

"They're just bathing, that's all. The old woman in the sari is all wet now! Too wet!" And he laughed. "That's just a bathing place by that ghat."

"No, there! In the river. What are they doing? That smiling man is putting something in his pan. They are all holding pans."

"Oh," he looked embarrassed. "They are panning."

"For what?"

"They are poor. For gold teeth maybe. I don't know."

"From the cremations?"

Dhanilal nodded. "Maybe, M'em Sahb."

"What do you mean, 'maybe'? They either are or they aren't."

"Yes, M'em Sahb. And some poor people who can't afford the wood don't get cremated but they are put in Ganges. And children do not get cremated."

Anne put a hand to her forehead. "And there?"

"Washing clothes. They are dobes. They're washing clothes off that ghat."

"What's a ghat?"

"The stairways, M'em Sahb. The wide stone stairways, like this one."

"Look! Look! That man on the ground there waving his hand!" She was looking at a naked man laying on his back, one arm extended in the air moving his hand back and forth.

"He's sick, M'em Sahb. He has probably come here to die. I'm sure of it."

"Like you were sure the Sadhu was real? That man has come here to die?"

"You die here and you don't need to go through any more lives. You go straight to Heaven. That's why it is so crowded. This is the best place to die. I will die here some day if I am lucky."

"If he wants to die, why is he signaling with his hand?"

"His mind, M'em Sahb. He's probably out of his mind."

"I'm going over to him."

"No, M'em Sahb, don't do that. It's not good to do that," he said, but she was already on her way.

She knelt next to the naked man. He was no more than a living skeleton with a thin layer of skin. Flies were resting and crawling on his open, crusted lips and walking in and out of his mouth and nostrils, and they were buzzing around his eyes and clustered between the inner part of his upper legs, and he was making short moans.

"I'm here," Anne said to him. "I'm here. What can I do for you?"

He moaned.

"Are you hungry? Are you thirsty? Do you want food? Water?"

He moaned and murmured, "Khaanaa Laaiyee. Pawnee." He closed his mouth.

"Dhanilal!" she yelled.

He came over to her, "Yes, M'em Sahb."

"What is he saying?"

Dhanilal listened. Again the naked man murmured, "Khaanaa Laaiyee. Pawnee."

Dhanilal said nothing.

Anne glared at Dhanilal. "What is he saying?"

"He says something about food and water. He's out of his mind. I'll go to Ganges and bring sacred water in a leaf for him."

"You go to the car and you bring over a bottle of Coke and a lot of those canned little wiener things. And a can of beans, and a can of corn, too. Go get them now!"

"No, M'em Sahb, I can't do that."

"You do that or you're not going to get paid! Do you understand? And you'll never work for the Embassy again. Now go!"

"Yes, M'em Sahb." and he started walking from her.

"And don't forget our can opener. And the little bottle opener, too. And faster or he's going to die."

"Yes, yes. Ah-chah."

She tried to wave the flies away from the naked man's mouth and eyes, and they scattered, at least for a moment. She started wiping his forehead with her hand. "I'm here. I'm getting you some food and water. Just a few minutes. Just hang on." Again she waved the flies away who were much too persistent, and knew well their targets.

He moaned and said, "Pawnee. Pawnee." And when he opened his lips some flies tried to take advantage of the opening and two got inside his mouth.

Dhanilal came back with some cans, openers, and Coca-Cola.

"Open the wiener things," Anne ordered.

"He's a vegetarian, M'em Sahb. He should have a chapati. Indian food. It's better for him. He's a vegetarian."

"Not any more he isn't. Now be quiet and open the can! First, give me that bottle opener." He handed it to her and she opened the bottle of Coca-Cola. Then she propped up the head of the naked man and held the tip of the bottle to his lips and he gulped and swallowed and burped and gulped and swallowed and heaved.

Then she took one of the cans from Dhanilal. It was a can of Heinz beans. She opened it and put the can near the mouth of the naked man and she propped up his head further with her other hand. She tilted the can to his lips carefully, but the brown juice from the can ran down his chin. Anne lowered the man's head back down and she picked some of the beans from the can with her fingers and put them in the man's mouth, and the man's mouth sought them and he swallowed them.

She noticed from the corners of her eyes that legs were assembling near her and the naked man. She looked up to see that people were forming a circle and she and the naked man were the center of the circle. Others were coming to join the outer perimeter of the circle, and none of the faces she could see looked pleased at what she was doing. Dhanilal tried to lose himself in the crowd, standing near a mustached man with a knife strapped to his waist.

"Dhanilal!" she yelled. "You get over here. Bring me the wiener things that I asked for before, and the corn."

He walked over to her, shaking his head. "M'em Sahb, you must stop this. He came here to die. Maybe he came hundreds of miles to die here. You are defying the God Siva and Harishchandra-ji."

"I'm defying the Devil, you fool! Now you give me those cans. I won't have any of your arguments if you know what's good for you. He wouldn't eat if he wanted to die. He wants to live. Now get next to me with those cans."

"He's crazy, M'em Sahb, his mind is gone and he came here to die." She just glared at him again. He came to her side, squatting by her, and he handed her a can.

She started feeding the small weiners to the naked man. The crowd that surrounded the man and Anne and Dhanilal was now very large, large enough to cause a policeman to come over to see what was going on.

"What are you doing?" the policeman asked Anne.

"What does it look like I'm doing? I'm feeding a starving man and giving him drink before he dies, and these people won't lift a finger for him. They all ought to be in jail for complicity in a murder—for attempted murder."

"You see, M'em, this is—" but the policeman was interupted.

"I don't want any explanation. This man is ill. I want him brought to a hospital right away. I'm Anne Whitney and I work for Ambassador Bunker—Ambassador Ellsworth Bunker of the United States Embassy in New Delhi. Is that clear?" And she stood up and handed the policeman her Official Passport.

He studied it, opening it to see her picture. He looked back and forth at Anne and the picture. He closed the passport and looked at the gold lettering. "Ah-chah," he said. "We will get him to the hospital. The good hospital." He handed the passport back to her.

"When?"

"Soon, M'em Sahb."

"Now!" she ordered. "Not soon! Now!" And she took off her glasses in a sweep, once again proving her ability to make the putting on or removal of her glasses into a punctuation mark, this time turning a comma into an exclamation point.

"Ah-chah."

"What hospital?"

"Varanasi Hospital."

With the security of the policeman standing there, Dhanilal was less frightened of the crowd. Dhanilal said, "It's not far, M'em Sahb. I know it."

"Good," then she looked at the policeman. "Well, do it. Call for an ambulance and do it."

"M'em, we have our own ways. I assure you it will be done."

"Yes, it will," she said, now putting her glasses back on. "We have our ways, too. I'm going to the police station to visit your chief."

"Ah-chah," he said as he moved his head back and forth toward his left shoulder and his right shoulder in a roll. Her threat of going to his boss didn't frighten him.

She walked away and the crowd formed an aisle-way for her and Dhanilal.

Dhanilal looked down as he walked, not wanting the crowd to see his face.

"Dhanilal," she said, "get me to the police station."

There wasn't much of a conversation in the cold, stone office of the chief of police. He didn't speak English and Dhanilal did the best he could in translation, but the chief of police became impatient with the process and kept interrupting Dhanilal, not wishing to hear the entire translation of what Anne had to say. He was continually chewing beetle-nuts and spitting out the red juice of them on the stone floor, and there were red blotches all over the floor and walls that gave evidence of his habit. After only a couple minutes he asked if they would leave his office for a moment while he made an important phone call to check on the naked man. They went to the waiting room and within one minute he told them they could come back in. Anne smelled urine. Sure enough, he had obviously just urinated against the wall onto the stone floor of his office. The urine was running down the floor toward the corner. He made a lengthy statement that Dhanilal translated. "He says that you can assure Ambassador Bunker that the man will be treated in the hospital. And the man probably caught a cold on the ghat since he had no clothes, and that it is too bad, but he will be treated with good medicine. The staff of the hospital is as good as in New York," Dhanilal said knowing Anne was unconvinced.

"He's giving us the brush off," she told Dhanilal.

He did not translate that for the police chief but the police chief seemed to understand. Dhanilal translated the police chief's next statement which was, "This is, of course, very serious and you must let your Ambassador know we are grateful to you, his representative, for bringing this to our attention."

"You will take care of this now?" she asked.

Dhanilal translated and the police chief was nodding before he finished the translation.

"He says, 'Oh, yes,' M'em Sahb."

"Dhanilal, is there somewhere I can lie down in this city, other than in the car? I can't take any more of this."

"Yes, M'em Sahb. I know a place. They will rent out by the hour if you ask them."

Dhanilal took her to the Clark's Hotel and she fell asleep in a room with a revolving fan on the ceiling and a mosquito net protecting her while she slept.

Could hell be worse than today?

At her instruction that evening, Dhanilal took her to the Varanasi Hospital. She asked the attendant to let her visit with the man the police brought in from the ghats. The white smock the attendant wore was filthy and stained with red splotches that were either blood-stains or beetle-nut juice or both. The attendant nodded and took her down a dark hallway filled with patients laying and groaning on the hallway's floor. Hanging from the ceiling was a wire with occasional light bulbs, but not many of them. Walking down the hallway was a journey through an obstacle course of disabled humans. "Here," the attendant said, "This is the man your Ambassador Bunker was interested in."

She bent down to see a man covered in a white sheet that substituted for a blanket. Was it him? She couldn't tell. She looked at the man on the floor next to him. He looked just as likely to be the man she saw on the ghat. "Isn't there any light here?" she asked.

The attendant shook his head. "No, no. We have no more lights. Are you through?"

"Dhanilal," and she turned to her bearer. "Take me back to the Ganges. I want to see if this is him or—if he's still there."

If day by the Ganges was a spectacle of misery, the night was the ghost of that exhibition. In one field of vision she spotted at least a dozen naked men with their arms extended, waving their hands in the air. She went down on her knees in a fall. "It's hopeless! It's hopeless! This place is hopeless! What do I do now?"

Dhanilal watched her and said nothing.

She turned to him. "I want to go back. I want to drive back to Delhi tonight," she said to Dhanilal's great relief. "This is hopeless."

"Now?"

"Now."

He felt he had to warn her. "There are bandits on the highway at night, M'em Sahb. But we can do it if we get gasoline here. I know the station."

"We must. I can't stand this."

The night drive was spent in long silences as she avoided the cows and the bullock carts, and the lorries, and the bandits, driving through the night into the dawn, with the sun's first glimmer exhibiting women villagers walking by the side of the road with small pans of cow dung in their hands and bigger pans of cow dung balanced on their heads, the dung to supply fuel to burn and to build walls for their shelters.

Throughout the entire ride Anne would occasionally break the silence with only those two words: "It's hopeless."

By morning she was driving into the gateway of the U.S. Embassy back in New Delhi to drop off both Dhanilal and the Volkswagen Microbus. She paid Dhanilal for the agreed upon full week. She was eager to be done with both him and the car.

She walked in the Embassy Reception Room and showed the U.S. Marine Guard her passport and requested to see Ambassador Bunker's secretary. The U.S. Marine phoned the Ambassador's office. He received the okay after telling the secretary he saw Anne's Official Passport. He gave Anne the directions to the Ambassador's office and he pressed the buzzer for Anne's entrance.

Anne walked into the magnificent forecourt of the Embassy, the building forming an outdoor square with a wide open space in the center with a garden and fountain and pool. She went to the left walkway and to the last corner office.

She introduced herself to Ambassador Bunker's secretary and proceeded to tell her she took "Ambassador Bunker's name in vain. I acted as though I was the Ambassador's representative," and she told the whole story of what happened on the ghats and the police station. When she was done, Ambassador Bunker's secretary said she would tell the ambassador everything Anne had told her, and that she knew Ambassador Bunker would appreciate her telling his office what she did, before the authorities of Varanasi might say something to him.

Anne walked out of the Embassy grounds through the gateway on Shanti Path where something caught her eye. There was a man she recognized who was walking into the grounds of the Soviet Embassy next door. It was one of the men she met at the Consulate in Hong Kong on that morning of the second Kennedy-Nixon debate. She tried to think of his name and it came back to her:

Adam Orr.

"Oh, my God," she said to herself, certainly not loud enough to be heard by anyone except her. "Wouldn't the spook like to know about this one! Adam Orr! And he tries to act like he's Jack Armstrong, the All-American Boy! Adam Orr at the Soviet Embassy! Have fun with the Rooskies, Mr. Orr! And Mr. Daschle thinks Adam Orr is just great and that I'm the one who's a trouble-maker!"

Should she tell Ted Murphy? The thought came to mind, but Ted Murphy wasn't that receptive when he could have helped her, so why should she tell him? And, besides, knowing something others didn't know, gave her an inward sense of power.

All she wanted to do now was leave India and never search for a Sadhu again.

EIGHT
ALL THE TANYAS
1960

Now the aroma of Adam Orr's mission wasn't only something he was inhaling; his entire being was immersed in it.

He was the only American entering the Soviet Union's Aeroflot airliner at Delhi's Palam Ngurah Rai Airport. All the rest of the passengers who were taking their seats were Indians or Uzbekistanis or Russians. He had been assigned an aisle seat and that was unacceptable for his mission. He moved over to the window which sent a stewardess scurrying down the aisle to him to tell him to move back to his assigned seat. He did, but when the plane took off and no one was sitting next to him, he shifted back to the window seat. The stewardess stared at him, then walked into the pilot's cabin.

In a cloudless sky, just before the aircraft flew over what he figured to be the border of the Soviet Union, the airliner banked and headed in the opposite direction from where it had been going. Then there came the voice of the pilot saying there was bad weather and the plane must return to Delhi.

Back at the airport in Delhi he was given a boarding pass for the following morning with an aisle seat again assigned to him. He and the other passengers were taken on a bus to the Janpath Hotel for the evening.

The Janpath was not pleasant, devoid of upkeep. Once it might have been luxurious but no more, and its shabbiness added to the impatience of the night. He practiced the three-hundred rehearsed images of places from the U.S. Capitol Building to the Dai-ichi in Tokyo, and he practiced the rehearsed fifty-nine household objects from a toaster to a yardstick, before going to bed where he started doing it again before falling asleep.

He was up before dawn to wait for the bus that took him and the other passengers back to the airport, and the procedure of yesterday was repeated, but this time all the airliner's shades had been closed before they boarded. He took the window seat and rested his head against the shade and pretended to be asleep. A stewardess, not the same one as the day before, came down the aisle directly to him and told him to move to the seat. He looked up at her through half-opened eyes with an irritated expression on his face and said something in a language that didn't exist. Of course she didn't understand him and neither did he understand himself. She again told him to move and he repeated the same incomprehensible words, only this time louder and angrier. And then he tilted his head back against the drawn window shade and closed his eyes. She stood there for a while trying to figure out what language he was speaking and what she could do about his intransigence, and then she moved on.

He won. The plane took off and he was still in the seat he had given himself.

After the stewardess passed him by while she was handing out hard candies to the others, he raised the shade, just enough to see a bit of the outside, and again he pretended to be asleep.

There was cloud cover for three hours over India, Pakistan, and Afghanistan. The clouds lifted after he was confident he had passed over the border to Tajikistan in the Soviet Union. Every detail of time and place was being locked into his memory by associating all the new items to remember into the old ones already in his memory bank, creating fresh indelible images in his mind.

The documents in the brown envelope given to him in Wanchai by Happy Lee, that he had safely turned into ashes and flushed down the toilet of the Peninsula Hotel, had told him what to remember as well as what to do. His first instruction was to get his visa for the Soviet Union from the Soviet Embassy in India rather than apply for it in Hong Kong because he was too known in Hong Kong. The second instruction was to take particular flights. And there was a list of things to remember, while in the air and while on the ground. There were additional instructions on what he could tell Soviet authorities to entice them so his mission could be accomplished.

He landed in Tashkent in Uzbekistan of the Soviet Union where all the passengers from the flight were taken to a square room at the terminal. There was a long bench against each of the four walls. The former passengers sat on the benches for about fifteen minutes without anything happening. Then, out of the only doorway that interrupted the benches, came two women and one man, all three dressed in white gowns which, one assumed, was meant to convey that they were members of the medical profession. They came directly to Adam. Each of the two women were holding flasks of a white liquid.

"You must take this medicine," one of the women said. "It is for cholera."

"For cholera?" Adam asked. "I've already been vaccinated for cholera. Here—" and he reached in his jacket breast pocket for his leather secretary and pulled from it his yellow health card. "Here, here," he said as he hunted down the list of vaccinations and signatures of doctors and a record of dates.

"No, Mr. Orr," the same woman said. "You came from a very high risk area of cholera and you must take these medicines."

"Then we all did," he argued. "Then every passenger on the plane did. Everyone on these benches. We all came from India—from Delhi. The same airplane—the same everything."

"Mr. Orr," the man in white said, "disease will not be imported to Tashkent. Please take the medication or you will be sent back to Delhi on the next aircraft."

There was no question as to who was in authority and Adam wasn't even a competitor. He was about to say, "I live in a free country," but this wasn't the time or place to make a statement like that. "I'll only be in Tashkent a day, then I'm going on to Moscow." There was no response from the three figures in white, and so he did what he knew he had to do. As though he was quickly downing two flasks of barium, which is what it looked like, he swallowed the terrible-tasting liquids, one flask after the other.

That satisfied them. All three, almost as though they were one, walked back through the doorway and in seconds a stewardess appeared through the same doorway, escorting everyone through passport control, health certificate inspection, and customs, where his *Newsweek* magazine was confiscated.

In the pretense of explaining the confiscation, the customs inspector pointed to the printed message on the luggage ticket that read, "This is not the luggage ticket (baggage check) described by Article 4 of the Warsaw convention."

"So what?" Adam asked.

The customs inspector pointed to the message again.

"What's that got to do with anything? All luggage checks say that. I've never seen the luggage ticket that was described by Article 4 of the hare-brained Warsaw convention!"

That didn't prevent the customs inspector to point to it once more, then he closed Adam's luggage, and pushed the luggage to Adam. Adam grabbed it and walked to the doorway to the dark main terminal room, while shaking his head. "Article 4 of the Warsaw convention! Why do they waste such time, effort, and ink on every luggage check made to tell that 'this isn't it'? Is that supposed to mean your *Newsweek* can be taken away?"

Along with about half the passengers from the plane, Adam was escorted to a bus that was destined for the Hotel Tashkent across from the Opera House.

He knew it was going to happen and it did: when he walked off the bus at the hotel entrance he was met by a gorgeous young woman. Her name was dramatic enough–it was Tanya.

"I am your Intourist Guide," she said. "I will be escorting you throughout your stay in Tashkent. I have your vouchers for meals at your hotel," and she handed him a thin red booklet. "I will be available until you board your plane to Moscow tomorrow. If there is anything you need, please ask me. Now, we will go in the hotel." Her English was as flawless and accent-free as a Californian, but she was certainly not a Californian.

Since every Intourist Guide was either a member of the KGB or assigned by the KGB to write reports for them, there was no mystery as to why she was designated to be his escort. She was what the intelligence agencies called a "swallow," and he had been briefed that a "swallow" would surely be assigned to him, with all temptations planned. "Whatever temptations are realized can come back to haunt you," he was told, "years, even decades ahead–if and when it may serve their interests."

"I'm sure you'll find the hotel to be very comfortable," she said, and she smiled and blinked a long blink, as though she was trained by a mama-san in a Tokyo brothel.

No deal. He wouldn't even touch her elbow if she begged him.

They walked into the hotel. The lobby was much too ornate for its furniture that was falling apart. Turning in his passport to the man at the reception desk to be kept "just for a short while" was not an easy thing for him to do but he did it because he had to. "The hotel will return it to you soon," Tanya said, "at the latest tomorrow morning. Don't worry. Now, let me show you your room. It is comfortable. It's on the second floor."

The graying wallpaper in his room looked like it had been hung by some old Russian Tsar when the wallpaper was white. The chandelier looked like it was assembled by an assistant to Tom Edison. There was a small round table with two intricately sewn doilies on it. "It is nice," she said. "It has heat." Clearly that was a bonus.

He inspected the bathroom. The toilet had its hole to the plumbing in the wrong place; not at the bottom but at its back, too far up to perform well its intended purpose.

He walked back into the main room. In the drawer by the bed, there was, of course, no Bible. But he didn't expect to find what was there: a book in English entitled, *Overtake Iowa.* The pillows on the bed were so fluffy they took up half the wall space. "The bed, too, is comfortable," she said as if she would be glad to prove it to him.

"It looks just fine, Tanya," he said. "I think I'll take a shower and rest for a bit and then maybe take a walk around the city."

"Very well," she said. "I'll be in the lobby for you."

He didn't want her to be in the lobby or anywhere else for him, but he had quickly been turned into a servant who had to accept all orders. He was out of the decision-making business.

When Adam came out of the shower and back into the bedroom, a maid was looking through his luggage. She didn't apologize or even look bothered that she was discovered in her search, and caught at it by the naked man. She merely continued reorganizing his things in his open luggage, then she closed the luggage and said "pazhahlsta" and she left the room.

It was a marvelous sight: the lobby was devoid of Tanya. He quickly walked out the door afraid that she might reappear if he lingered. He walked across the street to the Opera House. There was a crowd standing around something he couldn't see because too many people were surrounding it. Was there a fight going on in the center of the crowd?

He walked up to the people and got to the front to see what was causing their attention. There it was: a rubber Mickey Mouse, or at least it looked like Mickey Mouse, about six feet tall, but its ears weren't as round as Mickey Mouse's ears. It was the kind of inflatable device he could buy at the A&P back home for less than five dollars. How could anyone be so transfixed by such a thing? It didn't move, it didn't talk, it didn't do anything except stand there. One man took out a camera and was taking pictures of it. Could life be this boring in Tashkent that this was actually interesting?

"It's not Mickey Mouse, you know." It sure wasn't. It was Tanya. "But it looks like him, doesn't it? The children love it." The adults seemed to love it even more than the children since there wasn't one child present.

"You found me," he said.

"Oh yes," she said and smiled. "Don't worry. You won't be lost." But that was not what was worrying him. He so much wanted to be lost. "Do you want to take a tour now? It's so delightful right now and you never know when the weather will change here, so this would be a good time for me to show you the city."

"All right."

"We have a car and driver."

He had no fear that she didn't have a car and driver.

And so the tour started. The black ZIM limousine had a great deal of space in the back seat with room to spare even if he stretched out his legs in full. Its floor-carpet appeared to be made of gray fur. The driver, whose hands wrapped around a gray fur covered steering wheel, passed by a large poster showing a Negro in chains with Uncle Sam clamping another chain on his ankles. Uncle Sam had an armband reading CWA, the Russian characters meaning U.S.A. Then there was a poster of what appeared to be Wall Street bankers in tuxedos with dollar signs on their jackets. They were depicted picking up torn and dirty dollars. Above them was the sun with a smiling face, labeled CCCP for the Union of Soviet Socialist Republics. Surrounding the sun were pictures of new rubles. Someone was taking a picture of the poster.

As Adam caught those sights, Tanya was telling him about Tashkent's history from Genghis Khan forward, and the achievements of the Soviets that, he was told, made Tashkent as marvelous as it is today.

They passed by a large building. He asked what it was.

"It's a plant."

"A plant?"

"Yes."

"What kind of a plant? It's big."

They were still driving by it. "A repair plant."

"A repair plant?"

"Yes."

"What do they repair?"

"All kinds of things. It's a repair plant."

"Like what? Vacuum cleaners? Radios? Cars? Stoves?" He didn't ask but he wanted to add, "Missiles? Bombs?"

"Oh, yes," she said.

Oh yes, what? No use asking. It was just a place where workers repair things.

Tanya was not only sitting by his side but she occasionally brushed his shoulder with her hair when she turned her face to the window or turned her face back from the window, and she didn't seem to care that her skirt was resting a little above her knees. He continually told himself that no matter how she might lure him, she was actually Boris Karloff in disguise.

When they arrived back at the Hotel Tashkent she got out of the car before he had a chance to get out and open the door for her. By the time he opened his door, she was nearly by his side. "Do you prefer dinner alone, Mr. Orr? Or do you want to ask me questions?" What a strange thing to ask.

"No, no," he said thinking as quickly as he could. "I'm tired and I don't want to take all your time. I'll just have a quick dinner and go to sleep. I'm going to have a pretty heavy schedule in Moscow and I want to be ready for it."

"Yes. Use your coupon. It says 'Dinner' on it in English as well as Russian, French, and German. Then in the morning use the Breakfast Coupon. You'll see they all say "Class Luke" which means you are special. After breakfast we will see the outskirts of the city and then I'll take you to the airport for your flight to Moscow, so please prepare your bags in the morning. Is that as you want?"

"Oh yes, that's exactly as I want."

"Goodnight, Mr. Orr."

"Goodnight, Tanya." He knew this would not be the end of Tanya tonight if he dared venture out of the hotel. He knew she would magically reappear, so he did what he said he would do: he went to the restaurant and handed the coupon to his waiter.

He waited 45 minutes for a menu and another hour before his soup arrived. The establishment was not worried that he would go elsewhere. There was no "elsewhere."

He went to the second floor and received his room key from the second floor maid. Once inside his room, he looked at his suitcase to see if it had been tampered with while he was gone. He could tell if it was or wasn't since this time he had arranged two of his shirts on top of his luggage at angles so he could detect movement. They were in total disarray. There was not even a pretense that his room, including the interior of his bags, hadn't been searched.

He knew enough not to talk out loud to himself in his memorization procedure. The chandelier was the likeliest suspect of a covered microphone but one could have been anywhere; behind a painting, in the telephone, anywhere. He locked the door and put a chair against it so he would be awakened if the maid tried to come in to take another look through his luggage in case she missed something earlier. He was also concerned that Tanya might make an appearance in a nightgown and a smile.

Upon the presentation of his morning coupon, he was given cucumbers for breakfast and, while eating them, he was given another lesson in Soviet achievements by Tanya. The only good news was that he was given back his passport. Then, filled with enough cucumbers to satisfy him for a couple of years, he sat beside Tanya in the back seat of the roomy car as they rode from one statue and monument to another, each of them erected for some great Soviet hero. Since the Soviet Union was only 43 years old, there appeared to be a hero for each day of its existence.

He found that he was looking forward to going to the bathroom, which is the epitome of boredom.

Tanya not only saw him to the airport but she escorted him from the terminal, across the tarmac, and to the plane. Being alone was made impossible for him. In his glee over the imminent end of his stay in Tashkent, he whistled on the walk to the plane.

"What's that?" Tanya asked.

"What's what?"

"What you're whistling. What is that song?"

"Oh. Oh. That's—that's—let's see, what was I whistling? That was 'Bess, You Is My Woman Now.' Gershwin. That was George Gershwin. That's from *Porgy and Bess*. Gershwin."

"Oh."

"Do you like Gershwin?"

There was a long pause as they walked. This was a difficult one for her. He knew he was putting her on the spot and that she would have to think of an appropriate, rather than an honest, answer. "I don't know," she said. That was an appropriate answer since Gershwin was an American composer and she didn't know whether Adam Orr worked for the CIA or the KGB. It's best, she must have thought, not to have an opinion on that one. "I hope you liked Tashkent. And I know you'll love Moscow. It will be colder there, but it will be beautiful."

That was a totally safe statement which could not be seen as subversive or suspect even if Adam was reporting what she said to Nikita Khrushchev, himself.

It was the same Aeroflot pattern as before for American passengers flying over the Soviet Union, or at least some American passengers flying over the Soviet Union: the aisle seat prescribed on the boarding pass, the closed shades, and the insistent stewardess. So Adam repeated his scenario of the sleepy foreigner who spoke and only understood some indefinable language. It worked again and this plane ride was totally successful. They landed in Samarkand, and instead of taking a chance on losing his seat by going into the terminal, he stayed inside, still pretending to sleep. He was going to be thought of as the sleepiest human ever to visit the Soviet Union. Not the best act but the only one available. Just as it was supposed to, the flight number was changed but the plane remained the same. It was now Aeroflot Flight 158 which was the one prescribed in the document given him by Happy Lee. Although he had more important things to do on the ground in Moscow, this was the most important leg of his mission in the air. If Flight 158 was going to remain true to its prescribed course, it would fly over, or at least very close to Tyuratam, the giant Soviet Missile Base in Baikonur, Kazakhstan, from which all Soviet Intercontinental Ballistic Missiles and all space probes were tested and launched.

By the time the plane was in the air for a half-hour, he was certain that below him was the western edge of Tyuratam. Every pattern, every site, every structure, every vehicle was being securely planted in his head, particularly the image of what was surely a launching pad.

Then the plane turned in a direction it shouldn't have turned, and it landed at an unannounced destination. He didn't know where he was and he wasn't told. But he knew where the sun was when the plane had turned, and where it was when they landed, and how long it took from the sudden turn to the unscheduled landing, and the number of landing-strip lights which told him the strip's length. He could figure out where they landed at a later time.

In an hour they were back in the air, going directly to Moscow.

Tanya was wrong. Moscow was not beautiful. It was massive and spellbinding, but not beautiful. Moscow was decaying. Photographers need not have wasted color film in Moscow as everything there was in black and white and grays. It wasn't that paints of different colors weren't used, it was that the paints of different colors that were used succumbed to the aura of the city, and any joyful representation of color they had was quickly granted immunity from exhibition. The sky even gave in to the massiveness and the grayness of the city that it was regretfully assigned to cover.

The darkness started in the airport's interior. He should have brought a flashlight.

If he thought the Aeroflot pattern from Tashkent to Samarkand to Moscow was the same as the Aeroflot scenario from Delhi to Tashkent, there should have been no surprise at more Soviet repetition: he was greeted at the dark and depressing airport in Moscow by another outrageously gorgeous young woman, this "swallow" even more beautiful than Tanya.

"Mr. Orr?"

"Yes."

"I am your Intourist Guide."

"I knew it when I saw you," he smiled. "What's your name?"

"Tanya," she said.

What? He just had a Tanya. "You're kidding!" he said.

She looked puzzled. "No. My name is Tanya. Why is that surprising?"

He shook his head, still smiling. When the KGB felt they had a good thing, they had to repeat it over and over again, but they never seemed to know that the repetition would, in itself, be suspect. If there was a successful Tanya in Tashkent, they would not take a chance on changing the script elsewhere. "Tanya was the name of my Intourist Guide in Tashkent. Is there also a Tanya in Leningrad and Stalingrad and Vladivostok?"

The second Tanya laughed. "Tanya is a very common name. It's like John in your country."

Well, not exactly. "Jane, maybe," he said. "Anyway, I have to call you something other than Tanya. It's too difficult to have two Tanya's on the same trip."

"You are permitted to do that. What would you like to call me?"

"I'll figure out something."

She seemed amused by him. "Come, I will take you to the hotel." He knew she would.

Better than Tashkent, a black ZIS limousine was waiting for them. "Tashkent only has ZIM's," Tanya Number Two said. "We have ZIS's here in Moscow. They are bigger and better." It was like a 1941 Packard. On the ride into the heart of the city, she pointed out the area the Nazis reached in their march toward Moscow, and she talked so much about the glories of the Kremlin that by the end of the ride he knew what he would call her.

"Tanya," he said. "I want to call you Kremlin-ette."

"I like that name!" she told him.

"It's both patriotic and feminine–just like you; Kremlin-ette."

"May I call you Adam?"

Oh, oh. She was much more forward than Tanya Number One.

"Of course," he said. "I'm an American. We're not noted for formality."

This time it was the Metropole Hotel just one block away from Red Square. Above the reception desk was a huge oil painting of Lenin and Stalin sitting at a kitchen table, talking with each other. Again, Adam's passport was handed over, this time under the eyes of Lenin, Stalin, and Tanya Number Two, making him more uncomfortable than when he turned it in only under the eyes of Tashkent's Tanya Number One.

Tanya Number Two, or Kremlin-ette, waited for him to get unpacked in his room that looked similar to the room in Tashkent. Again, a round table with two doilies, again a toilet in the bathroom that had its hole to the plumbing in the wrong place.

Kremlin-ette escorted him on the short walk to the very crowded GUM's Department Store that had an interior resembling a railroad station, where he bought a fur hat. It was a black beauty with ear-flaps for 700 rubles which were worth about seven American dollars. GUM's was crowded because by New Year's Day, 1961, all rubles were to be turned in and replaced with new rubles that would be worth $1.10. Therefore, Russians were buying like never before, so as not to present too many rubles to banks for conversion before New Years Day. They did not want to be questioned about having too many unexplained rubles.

GUM's was adjacent to Red Square which was the epitome of massiveness with nothing in it but space. Red Square was built on a slight hill, and its convex shape added to its appearance of importance and size.

Across Red Square from GUM's was the destination that Kremlin-ette dictated must be visited. He was to see the dead bodies of Lenin and Stalin, whether he wanted to see them or not. There was a line of people waiting to walk through the Lenin-Stalin Mausoleum and the line extended beyond Red Square. "I don't want to go in there," he said. "I'm not a mortician and dead bodies give me the willys, okay?"

"Oh, you must," she said. She meant it.

She took him to the head of the line since he was a foreigner, debunking the myth that there was no class criterion in the Soviet Union. The soldiers stationed there as honor guard, were goose-stepping. The hourly changing of the guard took place accompanied by bells ringing from the museum that had been St. Basil's Cathedral, the bells playing a short melody and three "bongs" for the hour. Adam and his Moscow companion walked in the somber dimly-lit room.

"They're dead all right," Adam whispered, the whisper meant to keep the solemnity of the place. She didn't think it was funny.

There the two bodies were, Lenin to the left, Stalin to the right, neither one looking very good. Stalin looked a little better than Lenin but, of course, he died more recently.

This was not a fun way to spend time. "Let's get out of this joint," he whispered to her in his most disturbing American style. She escorted him out back into the light and the cold where he put on his new Russian fur hat.

"There is something I want you to arrange for me, Etta." Now he was abbreviating Kremlin-ette; it was too long for him. She noticed that, but she didn't say anything about it.

"Yes, Adam, what would you like me to arrange?"

He wasn't going to ask for a ticket to the Bolshoi Ballet. "This may call for some work on your part—but I'm here for more than tourism."

She looked surprised at his volunteered statement, and she gave him an intense stare. "Yes?"

"I want to meet with your highest space exploration officer in Moscow."

"Who is that?"

"I don't know." He knew it was Vladimir Ponomaryov but if he said the name he would have appeared to know too much. Vladimir Ponomaryov had a history in the KGB before leading the space efforts at Tyuratam, so why wouldn't he want to meet with this American? The authorities suspected Adam enough to have Tanyas for him everywhere, and therefore he thought they would supply that top man to attempt to trap him, if nothing else. He was confident there would be a meeting and he wouldn't allow himself to be trapped. "I'm engaged in America's space effort and I want to discuss some ideas of mine with whomever would be the right person to see."

"You are engaged in America's space exploration?"

"Yes. I've been working at Cape Canaveral. Can you arrange an appointment? The big wheel in Moscow. I won't waste his time. I have some marvelous ideas that I think he will find interesting."

"That is difficult. I cannot do that today."

"You must try, Kremlin-ette."

"I cannot do that today."

"Then tomorrow. Please see if you can line that up for me, Tanya. I'll go back to the hotel now while you see what you can do, okay?"

She smiled. "Why did you call me Tanya instead of Kremlin-ette? I think I like Kremlin-ette better. Now you're too serious. Why so serious?"

"Because I'm here for business, Etta."

"All right. I'll walk you back to the hotel. When I get back from seeing what I can do to accommodate your request, I'll show you our subway stations. I think you'll be surprised at how grand they are."

"Not like New York?"

"Not like the New York subway or the Paris Metro or the tubes of London or any underground anywhere."

"I'll make a deal with you, Etta. You get me an appointment with the top man in space exploration here, and I'll go to every subway station you want. I'll extend my visit and we can ride the subway trains for the next five months–or years."

She laughed. "That won't be necessary."

Adam thought he was being taken to the Foreign Ministry but it was one of seven towering buildings that all looked exactly the same, the Foreign Ministry being only one of them. One or more of those seven identical buildings could be seen on the skyline from just about anywhere in Moscow. One success and they couldn't stop, just like their creation of Tanyas. But why this architectural horror was thought to be such a marvelous design that they wanted to build the same place seven times is still one of the great mysteries of civilization.

The reception room of the building was large, vacant, musty, and dark. It had sparse fluorescent lights on its distant ceiling; so sparse and distant that the illumination from the fluorescent tubes barely made it to the floor.

"Communism would be okay," Adam said to Tanya, "if you just knew how to light it."

She gave no response. She was different in the building than she was outside of it. Now she was official, devoid of any humor, almost as though he was a total stranger.

In the center of the floor two guards were sitting in a square-shaped enclosure. One of them nodded at Tanya, indicating she and her guest needn't check in with them. Like Tanya, neither of the guards had a trace of a smile.

"It's only on the next floor," Tanya said to Adam. "We needn't take the lift. We can take the stairs, unless you are tired."

"I'm not tired, Tanya."

"I will not go in with you. Mr. Ponomaryov speaks excellent English. I will be waiting for you when you come out."

"I'm sure of it."

The office's interior was spacious enough to match the massiveness of Moscow's exterior and, just like everything else in that city, there were so few things in the space provided that its size was exaggerated. There was only Mr. Ponomaryov's desk, his chair, one chair facing the desk where Adam was told to sit, and one chair off to the side where a man sat who was left without introduction, appearing as though he was a piece of furniture. He was writing in a notepad.

Vladimir Ponomaryov was not proficient in small-talk. "You have an offer, Mr. Orr?" He asked the question in a combination of Russian and English accents, since he learned English in London right after the war. That piece of knowledge was included in the information that was flushed down the Peninsula's toilet.

"Yes. I work at what we call AFMTC, the Air Force Missile Test Center at Cape Canaveral, which is, as I'm sure you know, also America's spaceport."

"Yes, of course."

"Pan American Airlines has a contract there to administer security. It's responsible for everything from the guards at the gates all the way to weeding out sabotage. It's security, just like you probably have at your spaceport. I'm an assistant director with Pan Am."

Vladimir Ponomaryov said nothing, he was just studying Adam's face.

"Now, RCA has a contract at the Cape for all the photography there, and a friend, a close friend, works for RCA at the Cape. He and I have gotten together on an idea. I think it's a good one. Between the two of us, we have thousands of pictures either taken by him or given to me since the first launch of an Atlas ICBM in June 1957. That's the bird that will eventually be used in the manned Mercury program." He knew what he was doing in bridging the missile program with space ventures. "That was Atlas Missile 4-A. It blew up. We have pictures of that and the interior of the missile's pods, the vernier rockets, all the components, and every motion that took place in the 20 minute hold of the countdown when they installed the destruct box." It was Adam's mission to be a powerhouse of information and act like a driven gambler. "As I'm sure you know, the destruct box perforates the bulkhead between the liquid oxygen and the fuel, destroying the missile if we want it destroyed. We have photos of everything."

After a long pause, Mr. Ponomaryov said, "And, Mr. Orr?"

"We also have photos of the components of the fully powered Atlas 3B and 4B. I have great pictures of their components–and good stuff of the Thor and the Thor-Able." He was hoping that at least one would do the trick. "More recently my RCA friend has been taking photos of the Titan ICBM and its components. Thousands of pictures, Mr. Ponomaryov, close-ups of every detail. Marvelous photos. I need them for the security staff. I even have photos of the miniatures they assembled for the Centaur, Saturn, and the Nova that will be built in the future, as well as every missile base in the country, every underground silo. And, Mr. Ponomaryov, I have pictures of every tracking site overseas. Every radar dish. Every console. Everything."

There was silence. They simply stared at one another. "Go on, Mr. Orr," Mr. Ponomaryov said.

Adam had no trouble in going on. "The photos of those underground silos in our bases–they're very good. I'm sure you know we'll have 132 Atlas' planted in them." Of course Mr. Ponomaryov knew that, but if this wouldn't escalate the dialogue, nothing would. "The stuff in Cheyenne is the best."

"Cheyenne?"

"That one's really coming along."

"Is it?" Mr. Ponomaryov asked.

"The negatives have been turned over to the U.S. Air Force, and more recently some of the space probe material has been turned over to NASA. You know what that is?"

Mr. Ponomaryov squinted and said nothing in response to the question.

"NASA is over at the Dolly Madison House in Washington. It's our new space agency that used to be the National Aeronautics Administration; now it's NASA, meaning the National Aeronautics and Space Administration. Before we turned over the material to NASA, and to the Air Force, my buddy and me–we kept prints of everything–and in some cases he's made inter-positives so that inter-negatives can be made from them."

There was silence again and then the expected, "And?"

"I want to trade with you, Mr. Ponomaryov."

The bottom-line had now been reached. Adam's rehearsed display of enthusiasm culminated by what appeared to be putting his cards face-up on the table in a sweep. Mr. Ponomaryov was, however, a gifted poker player who showed no hint of his own cards. There was not a moment of physical reaction. Nothing. Just another long silence and the continuing stare of Mr. Ponomaryov. He shouldn't have tried it with Adam. Adam returned the stare with equal intensity. It was like a game that two children play of staring at each other waiting to see who would laugh first. Mr. Ponomaryov broke the game. "Trade what for what, Mr. Orr?"

Adam acted like a victor who would be magnanimous. "A simple trade. Not photos for photos. What I want is permission to go to your space base to photograph whatever you allow. And in return I'll supply you photos of whatever you request at the Cape. I'm not a great photographer but my friend who is, doesn't want to come here. He's afraid of being fired and being put in prison or something. I'm not afraid, Mr. Ponomaryov. And I can use a camera. If I get in trouble in the States, I know where I can go to get out of there."

And then Mr. Ponomaryov stopped asking 'and?' exchanging that word for the most logical question that could be asked: "Why?"

Adam nodded. "I want to be paid, Mr. Ponomaryov. So does my friend. We want to be paid a lot because we will give a lot. In dollars from you, not rubles. And just so you understand, and it's no surprise, more money may come my way from some publications back home for what ever you allow me to photograph. I'm sure I can get paid from any number of publications and they'll promise anonymity—from *Life* magazine to *Aviation Week*. But I still want dollars from you. A lot of them. You see, Mr. Ponomaryov, I want to take advantage of my very rare access to places others can't visit—others can't penetrate." That word was important. "Of course you can have prints of everything I shoot at your spaceport, and I would expect to be accompanied and only allowed to photograph what you find acceptable for me to bring back home—for sale."

"Mr. Orr, if we wanted photographs of our spaceport in American magazines, why wouldn't we simply sell them directly?"

"Because you don't want to sell photographs. You don't need the money. But I do. And, in return, I would think you would like to have what I could supply."

"How many dollars do you want?"

"Fifty thousand American dollars. Nothing less."

Again there was the extended pause.

"Plus whatever costs I incur."

"How did you get your job in security?"

Adam acted almost nonchalant. "All by chance. By fate. I live in Cocoa Beach right next door to the Cape. I was there when they started turning the Cape into the Air Force Missile Test Center. I ran the Indoor-Outdoor Theater on Merritt Island there just a few miles from the Cape. Then I worked at the orange juice factory right outside Port Canaveral. When things started building up on the Cape in the mid-'50s I applied for a job, something with better pay than movie theaters and orange juice factories. I got accepted at Pan Am at the Cape for a low-level job in their communications department. But they liked me and I liked them. Then one night some FBI agents drove to the Cape to test security. One of them had a Cape badge pinned on him, but in the place for his photo on the badge, he had a photo of Hitler. The guy next to him in the car, another FBI agent, had a picture of Mickey Mouse on his badge. The guard wasn't paying attention. He let them in. He was fired, of course, but when I heard about it, I submitted the idea that all guards should have to rub the badge—feel the material with their fingers, rub the badge of everyone who enters the Cape, to check its authenticity and to insure they look at the photo and the face of the person. The Air Force loved the idea. Pan Am thought I was a genius. They adopted the idea—and me; I became an assistant director."

"So you want to go to Tyuratam?" Vladimir Ponomaryov knew what he was doing in saying that name. It was a marvelous ploy because both of them were aware that Tyuratam was supposed to be secret. Ponomaryov was taking a small risk for the possibility of a big revelation. Adam's reaction to that name could tell him everything.

"What's that?"

"What's what, Mr. Orr?"

"That word."

"Tyuratam?"

"Yeah."

"You mean you don't know that's where you want to go?"

"Sorry. But what difference does it make? All right, then that's where I want to go. Why? Is that supposed to be some secret?" Good work.

Vladimir Ponomaryov gave as much of a smile as he could, which was very little. "In fact it is."

"Then if you worked for me, I'd fire you." Even better. Suddenly Adam was showing authority.

"From what you're offering me, I think you would fire yourself."

Adam laughed.

"So you were there when Atlas 4-A blew up?"

"Sure was. What a day that was. Our only ICBM, and you were building them like there was no tomorrow."

"Do you know who else was there for that launch of yours?"

Adam shook his head. "What do you mean?"

"I'll tell you a secret. Your President was there. Did you know that?"

"No, he wasn't."

"Oh, but he was. You wouldn't have seen him. He was on a ship off shore. If the missile had been successful your government would have released the information he was there. But it failed, so there was no announcement that he was there."

"I didn't know that."

"Oh, yes."

Adam was now comfortable enough to be disturbed that Mr. Ponomaryov knew more than he did. "Anyway, with or without President Eisenhower, I have pictures of that bird's components before the launch and all the components that were found after it blew up, all put together as best as they could, laying on the floor of Hanger J. I suppose you know what that is."

"No."

Adam knew something Mr. Ponomaryov didn't know. Maybe.

"Well, you don't deserve to be told," Adam took a chance on joking again.

There was no laughter. "Your president was foolish. You know why you're so behind us in space? Your president. He wouldn't allow a military missile to be used for a satellite launch. Foolish. So you built Vanguards and they kept blowing up. Stupid. In the International Geophysical Year, you—America—had the assignment from the world's governments to put a satellite in orbit. Not us. You. But your Eisenhower had to have a new rocket to do it without using what he already had. Stupid. So we did it without the international assignment. We were able to do it and you couldn't with your Vanguards. Foolish president. Finally your German scientists talked him into using a military missile to launch a satellite. Too late. We did it first. And ours was a bigger satellite, and heavier, and better. Your Eisenhower was foolish. I don't admire fools, do you?"

Adam shook his head. "No. No, I don't, but he's no fool."

"Mr. Orr, do you have your passport with you?"
"Yes."
"May I see it?"
"Of course."
He took out his leather pocket secretary, pulled his passport from it and passed it to Mr. Ponomaryov.
"A tourist's passport?" he asked as he started flipping through the pages of visas.
"That's what I am."
Mr. Ponomaryov looked above the open passport that was in front of him, to Adam's eyes. "I see." He looked back through the passport. "I see you give your occupation as a Management Consultant."
"Yes."
"What does that mean?"
"Who knows? It's just what I call myself."
"You can make up an occupation for yourself on a passport?"
"I am what ever I say I am."
"What were you doing in Hong Kong, Mr. Orr?"
"In Hong Kong?" Adam smiled.
"In Hong Kong."
"Well, this is a little embarrassing but, in truth, I was messing around with some Chinese girls."
"That's all you did there?"
Adam's thoughts, of course, were on Happy Lee, but he believed Mr. Ponomaryov was simply testing his reactions. "No. It isn't all I did. I went to the U.S. Consulate there to hear the Kennedy-Nixon Debate. I didn't make out there. I don't like to mess around at Embassies and Consulates. That restraint is my form of patriotism."
"And India?"
"You mean why was I in India?"
"Yes. Why were you in India?"
"To get here. It's on the way. That's where I got my visa. Besides, I wanted to see the erotic carvings in Khajuraho. I heard that if they were looked at without feeling desire, I could go directly to heaven after death. I failed. Knowing I was going to hell, I thought I'd beat God to the punch and I went straight to your Embassy to get a visa to come here. I thought it would–"
"And Tashkent?"
Adam shook his head with a smile. "Boy, you really have my itinerary down pat."
"It's all in your passport, Mr. Orr. Why didn't you fly from New Delhi to Moscow direct? There were flights."
"I wanted to see Tashkent."
"Why Tashkent?"
"I like to go to places I've read about. Places most people don't go."
"Then to Samarkand?"
"A stopover."

"Didn't our Embassy in New Delhi tell you there was no Flight 158 anymore? How did you arrange to take it?"

That question was not a good sign, since that was the only commercial flight that flew anywhere near Tyuratam. Ponomaryov had obviously been informed of more than Adam wanted him to know about Adam from their Embassy in New Delhi. Adam had requested going from Delhi to Moscow on Flight 158. The Embassy official had told Adam Flight 158 had been discontinued. Adam had figured out that it still existed, taking off from Samarkand. "Is that on my passport, Mr. Ponomaryov? Show me the page."

"You took Flight 158 anyway?"

"When I got out of Tashkent, the flight went through Samarkand and to my surprise, it suddenly became Flight 158. What did your Embassy official do? Report every conversation to you?"

"He doesn't interest me. You interest me."

"Professional intuition, but a bad decision. You know, I think that guy at your Embassy in Delhi deserves your attention. He's going to defect to the U.S. Embassy one of these days. His name was Skryabin. Be careful of him. Remember I told you."

Mr. Ponomaryov gave him the Ponomaryov stare.

Adam returned the stare. The only difference between their expressions was that Adam had a trace of a smile. "Any other questions, Mr. Ponomaryov?"

With a sigh of futility, Mr. Ponomaryov handed the passport back to Adam. He opened the top drawer of his desk and pulled out a small, thin, blue and white cardboard box with a design of a horseman against snow-covered mountains. Then he closed the drawer. "Do you want a cigarette, Mr. Orr?" He opened the thin box and extended it toward Adam.

"No thanks. Not enough tobacco in them for me. I'll join you with one of mine. Want one?" It wasn't rude, it was almost gracious, since almost every Russian who smoked had access only to Russian cigarettes, but American cigarettes were considered a treasure. The Russian ones were long white hollow cardboard tubes with a small amount of tobacco on one end, equal only to the length of a filter of an American cigarette. Adam offered him a Marlboro.

Mr. Ponomaryov nodded, and took an extended one from the pack. "May I take two, one for later? They are better than my Cossacks." His entire demeanor had changed.

"Of course. Here," and Adam tossed the pack on his desk. "Take the whole pack. I have more in my room. Your customs agent in Tashkent didn't take them away from me—he only took away my *Newsweek* magazine. And your maids left my cigarettes intact—along with my pictures of my Hong Kong girlfriends—after looking through my luggage."

Mr. Ponomaryov gave a strained smile, not because he thought Adam said something amusing but rather he gave a smile out of glee that he was the recipient of almost a full pack of American cigarettes. He lit one of the Marlboros. "I'm afraid our customs agents are not our most polite public servants, but you know you were lucky. They usually make you sign a confession that you tried to smuggle in subversive material when you try and bring in one of your magazines. The customs agent you had was negligent. As for our maids—they are just maids. They like looking at American goods. We can't do anything about that." Then he held up the Marlboro box. "What are you doing to the packs now?" He examined it. "You have boxes now like we do?"

"A little different. They're called Marlboros and those are called Flip-Top Boxes. They're new. They just flip open and closed. All with one finger." Mr. Ponomaryov tried doing it with one finger and he succeeded at his top-flipping skill. "Philip Morris makes them. They didn't want to try out the box on Philip Morris itself, because if the box doesn't succeed, Philip Morris could go down with it. So they took one of their cigarettes that was a low-seller, a cigarette that was flopping, to try out the box."

"I like it. Now—how many days will you be staying in Moscow, Mr. Orr?"

"You tell me how long I need to stay to do what I want."

"There is nothing I can tell you. Nothing will be done during this trip of yours. I will discuss your offer with my colleagues, of course, and let you know some time in the near future."

"No. The mails are dangerous, Mr. Ponomaryov. I think any mail from Moscow to the States is read by our CIA or FBI or both. I would rather they wouldn't know about our meeting. In fact it could demolish the whole thing—and demolish me at the same time. I have a flight booked out of here to Vienna on Thursday. I'm sure you know the flight number."

Mr. Ponomaryov gave a very short smile. "So what do you want me to do between now and Thursday?"

"An answer. I want your sanction to take a future trip to your space center. If I have an answer and a date from you before leaving, I can then make my plans without any further contact with you. You simply tell your Embassy in some third country to issue me a visa. I'll pick it up on my way back here."

There was another long silence before Mr. Ponomaryov said, "Mr. Orr you are either a great fool or a—" and he stopped his sentence, then picked it up. "Or a desperate man."

"I am what I am."

"That's a foolish thing to say."

"That's what God said to Moses on Mount Sinai."

"Oh?"

"But maybe you're right. Maybe I'm both a fool and a desperate man."

Mr. Ponomaryov looked up at the ceiling, got up from his chair, took a long inhalation of his Marlboro, went to the window and looked out. Then he turned around. "Be here tomorrow afternoon, Mr. Orr. I may know nothing more than I know today—but maybe I'll have some information for you. Then you can leave as you planned the following day. Thursday."

"Thank you, Mr. Ponomaryov." Adam stood up, walked over to him, and extended his hand.

They shook hands and Vladimir Ponomaryov added, "There are no guarantees, you understand. I promise nothing."

"I understand. I'm grateful for whatever you can find out for me. If you want it, I'll bring you another pack of Marlboros tomorrow."

"That would be appreciated," and he smiled. "I will see you tomorrow at two o'clock."

Kremlin-ette was waiting outside the door. She probably heard everything. She probably took notes in case Vladimir Ponomaryov's tape recording didn't turn out well, or if the man in the office to whom he was never introduced didn't get everything down correctly on paper. She gave a wide smile. "All done?" She was back to normal now that the meeting was over.

"For today."

"Good. Now we can go to the subway stations."

"I can't wait." He was so pleased at the outcome of the meeting that he was ready for the subway stations.

"And I have a surprise for you," she said with a continuing glow as they walked down the stairs.

"What?"

"A third row ticket to tonight's performance of the Bolshoi Ballet."

Oh, no. "Etta, Etta, Tanya, Kremlin-ette, Tanya Two—how do you do it? You must know the right people in this town."

"I know Vladimir Ponomaryov well enough to call him Velodnya. That is how I got your appointment. And I know the man who was in charge of building the Franklin Delano Roosevelt subway station, and I know people at the Bolshoi, and that is how I got your ticket."

"Imagine—now to the subways and then the ballet. What more could any man want?" Now they were in the cold of outside walking toward the waiting limousine.

She said, "And in between the two I will show you the grave of John Reed. He is in the Kremlin Wall. He was an American communist, you know."

"One of my heroes."

She didn't know whether he was kidding her or being serious. She gave a confused expression, just like Tanya One gave when he whistled Gershwin. Tanyas always suspected that those they spied on were spying on them.

"And do you know who will accompany you to the Bolshoi?" she asked.

"Let me guess."

"All right."

"Velodnya?"

"No!"

"I think I got it."

"Your Kremlin-ette?"

"My Kremlin-ette!"

"You are right, Mr. Orr." And then she corrected herself. "You're right, Adam."

"I would be complimented by your presence. And I like it when you call me Adam."

"Do you? I thought perhaps since you called me Kremlin-ette I should call you General Pentagon."

In the middle of the *Swan Lake* ballet he noticed—noticed?—he was jolted by the sudden but soft feel of her lower leg against his lower leg. It was no accident and so she didn't move it back under her seat, and even as self disciplined as he was, he didn't move his leg away. Her eyes, however, were intent upon the dancers. She acted as though her leg-pressing was just something that happened involuntarily and she wasn't even conscious of it.

She was good. Tashkent's Tanya had a lot to learn from Moscow's Tanya. Moscow's Tanya must have been the pride of the KGB. No wonder she got a ZIS while Tanya Number One only got a ZIM.

"They are wonderful dancers, aren't they?" she asked him softly.

"Yes."

"Are enjoying it?"

"You or Tchaikovsky?"

"The ballet!"

"I like Tchaikovsky. I'm a simple man."

"No, you're not. And what do you mean by, 'you like Tchaikovsky?' You mean you don't like me?"

"I'm not afraid of Tchaikovsky."

"Shhhh! You're talking too loud. Does that mean you're afraid of me?"

"Petrified."

"What does that mean—petrified?"

"Scared stiff."

"Why? I'm harmless."

"That's what they said about Stalin."

"Are you comparing me to Stalin? He's not such a hero here any more, you know. Chairman Khrushchev revealed some terrible things about what Stalin did. Did you know that?"

"His picture's still up at the Metropole. And he's still sharing a bedroom with Lenin. Be careful, he may be resurrected some day."

"I don't have to be careful."

"Yes, you do, Tanya. And I'm not comparing you to Stalin."

"That's a relief."

"You don't have a mustache."

She turned her face away from the dancers and toward him. "No, I don't. See?" Their faces were very close, and she increased the pressure of her leg against his. She was very good. Their faces were so close it looked like she was inviting him to kiss her.

He didn't. He tried to regain his composure. "And you don't smoke a pipe," he said. "Stalin always smoked a pipe. You don't do that."

She smiled, her mouth slightly open. "How do you know what I do in private?"

"I guess I don't know. Maybe you do smoke a pipe."

"Can't you tell from my breath? Do I or don't I?" and she breathed out in a wisp of an exhale under his nose and on his lips. She was so good.

"Yeah," he lied. "You do."

"I do not!"

"Don't deny it. I like the scent of Russian pipe tobacco."

She continued looking at him and continued the pressure on his leg and she gave a heavier wisp of an exhale, this time much more centralized on his lips.

This was no way to celebrate the success of today's visit to Mr. Ponomaryov. The way to celebrate was to get rid of her, and to get rid of those instincts that were rising in him that could destroy all he hoped to accomplish. She closed her lips and, with affection, put her hand on his thigh as she looked back at the dancers on stage, and he was close to being a dead man.

She deserved the Medal of Honor or the Medal of Lenin or Hero of the Soviet Union or whatever they gave for whatever she was doing. Her hand was not motionless. She deserved to be written into his will.

"Tanya?" he said, recognizing that the aroma of his mission had disappeared under her spell, and her aroma had replaced it.

She looked back at him only briefly and then back at the stage. "Yes?"

"I don't really like Tchaikovsky."

"I told you that you weren't a simple man."

"I'm just a man."

She nodded. "Yes." She wouldn't look at him but kept her eyes straight ahead as though she was once again suddenly transfixed on the dancers, but she moved her hand that was on his thigh in a new direction and she said, even softer than her touch, "I know."

He knew the rules. He knew that not only was it probable that his room at the Metropole was wired for sound but that there could be a remote camera somewhere in the room clicking away when the KGB wanted it to click away. He knew. He knew. He knew. "Tanya," he said.

She looked at him with a cautious and smiling expectation. "Yes?"

"I know some day I'll regret this, but I have much studying to do and I want to go back to the hotel—and I need to be alone to study, Tanya."

The expectation left her face and her lips went straight and her leg moved away from his leg and her hand returned to her lap and she gathered the straps of her purse. "Let's leave now," she said. "I'll take you there and I'll drop you off at the reception desk."

He nodded. "I don't feel well," he said. He didn't.

Neither did she. She had failed.

He felt it the moment he woke up the following morning; something was wrong. It was in the air. Last night he was so elated at what he thought to be his success, but while he slept he felt that something had happened to that success.

When he went downstairs to have his breakfast she was waiting for him to deliver the confirmation of his defeat.

"Good morning, Mr. Orr," she said without a smile.

"Good morning, Tanya."

"I saw Mr. Ponomaryov just before coming over here, and he told me to tell you that the meeting the two of you had scheduled for today has been canceled."

"Until when?"

"He told me to give him your address in the States. I gave it to him. He will contact you some time in the near future by mail. He is very busy all this week. The meeting cannot be done now."

"Oh–I see."

"So what would you like to do today?"

Stay alive, he thought. *That's what I would like to do today. Getting out of the country might be my only victory.* "See if you can get me an earlier plane–please. I would appreciate that."

"I will." And for the first time that morning she smiled at him. There was, for that moment, a glimmer of affection.

It was possible that she admired him for his suppression of his desire for her the night before, even though it was a rejection. And it was possible that she even admired him for the mission she suspected was his. It was more probable that she didn't know whether or not she admired him for it because, under the conditions, she feared that even thinking of admiring his mission would place her at risk. Since she was a little girl, all the way to the present, she feared that her government might be able to read minds.

NINE
HUNGER IN FOGGY BOTTOM
1961

Anne Whitney was back in Washington, D.C. And so was Ambassador and Mrs. Fairbanks, Irene Goodpastor, and Cody Cooper.

And so was John Kennedy.

Boredom was prohibited in Washington, D.C. There simply wasn't enough room for it. In the 1960's there were too many autumn leaves and summer scandals and February snowstorms and angry demonstrators and humid nights and April parades and fresh flowers and July fireworks and afternoon showers and morning drivers and overcoated muggers and foreign visitors and varied lapel pins for even an idle walker to yield into a state of apathy. Boredom was somewhere beyond the District line. Maybe in Bethesda or Alexandria or Seabrook. For sure, those who sought boredom would never return to the District.

Washington, D.C. was trying to be something it couldn't be when 1961 began. It was trying to compete with major metropolitan cities of America, but it wasn't able to do that back then, although its act was often convincing. It had a number of methods for carrying out its pretense of being a city worthy of being in the competition. There was a Woodward and Lothrop Department Store affectionately called "Woodies" in the same way that Coca-Cola was called "Coke" but only suckers called it "Woodies." It didn't deserve a nickname. And there was the more luxurious department store called Julius Garfinkles. But how luxurious could Julius Garfinkles be if it was to have an ad campaign asking, "Have you Garfinkled today?" Would Bergdorf Goodman or Bullocks or Neiman Marcus do such a thing in their host cities? Of course not. They knew how to act. Julius Garfinkles didn't.

And there was something about the names of the streets. Wilshire Boulevard and State Street and Fifth Avenue were reasonable names for main shopping thoroughfares in other cities. But "F" Street? What kind of dirty joke was this? And how could *The Washington Post* and *The Evening Star* and the *Washington Daily News* be daily reading? They weren't like the *Trib* or *The Times* or *The Globe*. And the District's television newscasters didn't look like television newscasters. Where was Jerry Dunphy? And worse than all of that, there was a chain of drug stores called People's Drug Stores, a name to be expected in Moscow or Peking or East Berlin, but not in New York or Philadelphia or Boston. Why in D.C.?

D.C. did have a healthy mix of Hiltons, Sheratons, and Howard Johnsons, and with all these city accessories Washington said, "I am in the big league! Come on!"

But it wasn't.

What it was, was what it was meant to be: a city of temporary winners, to be eternally replaced by other temporary winners. In that way it was like Las Vegas with its winners staying until they lost. But unlike the casinos of Vegas, the District was set aside to house the ever-changing gamblers that ran the federal government. When it didn't try to be anything else, it was both magnificent and humble compared to other capital cities of the world. London, Paris, Rome, Tokyo, and most of the rest were incidental capitals within their significant cities. Washington was an incidental city within its significant capital. Government was its only industry and interest.

Pennsylvania Avenue was what held the District together. The Avenue's central area was its middle course which went from the Capitol to the White House. That was its site of glory which it handled like a professional without any rival. Although in other parts of the United States, Broadway beckoned with blinking lights and Bourbon Street blared with Dixieland and Beverly Drive boasted of movie stars, Pennsylvania Avenue had none of them and needed none of them. It knew its power. It was a proud host to eager crowds that came to view presidents and national heroes and leaders from around the world. The avenue wound around traffic circles and turned sharp corners at dead-ends where any other street would have given up. The obstacles were immense. If the avenue followed its diagonal course through the District without going around circles and across corners, it would have gone right through the Library of Congress, then the U. S. Capitol Building and, farther on its course, through the White House. But it was an avenue that knew how to reroute itself and survive for most of the journey. Borrowing a little of Fifteenth Street to continue to the White House and then beyond it, it acted as though it had an even more important destination ahead, but it didn't. Eventually it became trapped by M Street, which put a humiliating end to Pennsylvania Avenue. It was such an embarrassment. Pennsylvania Avenue should have stopped after passing the White House, and it had a marvelous opportunity to do it at Washington Circle where it should have generously yielded to another avenue but it didn't. It wanted too much and paid the price. The avenue, like so many defeated politicians, chose to ignore its own ending in the hope that it could go on forever.

South of Pennsylvania Avenue's middle-span, and within eyesight along most of its journey, loomed the Washington Monument: the tall obelisk which had become the symbol of the District much more than the symbol of the man for whom it was intended to memorialize. Surrounded by fifty state flags, the obelisk rose high above the city, and during the day it used the sun as a make-up artist to give it varying complexions: orange and pink, and later in the day an ominous gray; sometimes a blinding white, and when the sun was gone it used the black sky as a velvet backdrop. On its cone there were two red lights that blinked alternately, giving the impression that it was an antenna tuned to the world, receiving and transmitting secret messages.

Across the West Mall from the Washington Monument and across the Reflecting Pool was the Lincoln Memorial which had become a religious shrine rather than a statue housed in a building. It was a place for meditation and prayer. Although during the day there were busloads of entering and exiting tourists and waste baskets of flashbulbs and Polaroid film cartons, at night there were lonely figures who walked up those stairs and stood before the sitting statue of President Lincoln and talked to him. They confided their dreams, their worries, and their joys. And he listened. At some, he smiled.

President Jefferson's statue was too uninterested in casual visitors to engage in confidence. He was built standing up and he ignored the voices of those who came to see him. He was listening to something else. "Go see President Lincoln," he would say. But despite his rudeness he was magnificent in his domed housing that reflected itself in the distorted waves of the Tidal Basin. Even though he was wide awake at all hours, very few night visitors came by to see him, considering his attitude.

All those monuments and memorials made the White House look much less significant than it was. It wasn't visible from most horizons and in comparison with other Executive Mansions around the world, it looked unpretentious and humble.

It was the U.S. Capitol building down Pennsylvania Avenue that didn't understand the meaning of the word "humility." The Capitol Building housed the Senate Chamber and the Chamber for the House of Representatives in a grand majestic sweep of the eastern part of the mall. Against the night sky, its sprawl across the hill spread its triumph as far as it could reach, looking like a Gulliver washed up on the beach of Lilliput. Away from most of the monuments and memorials of the city, it stood egotistically alone.

Across the Arlington Memorial Bridge was the graveyard of heroes. But it was not gloomy or morbid. Rather, it held an aura of strength and inspiration. It was the podium of giants who kept an eternal watch over the capital city. The Washington worker was being observed by them. Only a fool would be corrupt with such worthy witnesses.

And there was something else on the horizon: the clock tower of the Old Post Office Building, always there, peering above every skyline to join, uninvited, the tall structures that commemorated heroes. But the Old Post Office Building had nothing to commemorate. Its clock did, however, announce the passage of Washington time, and that was very important.

With all these elements, it was impossible for anyone to be untouched. Washington was the drug, the addiction, and the cure for those with the passion to stand in the climate of purpose.

Every four years, before the inauguration of a president, it was the tradition for federal buildings to change their clothes. Some would be sandblasted or renovated or painted or just cleaned, but they would all be dressed up for the Inaugural Ceremonies. Changing the wardrobe of the U.S. Capitol Building was the most time-consuming of all, and over a year was spent in getting it ready for 1961. After its sandblast, its dome was red and it stayed that way for months until one coat of paint followed another, and in time for the inauguration of the new President it was more brilliantly white than it had ever been before.

On that bitterly cold winter morning of January the 20th, 1961, John F. Kennedy stood on the east portico of the U.S. Capitol Building with the central figures of the outgoing administration and many incoming appointees behind him, and the world in front of him. At the Constitutionally designated time of noon he was sworn in by United States Supreme Court Chief Justice Earl Warren. As soon as he said the final words of his oath, "so help me God," the military aide of President Eisenhower, Colonel Robert Schultz, handed a leather briefcase weighing some thirty pounds to the military aide of President Kennedy, General Chester Clifton. In that briefcase were the means and codes to be used in case a nuclear attack should ever be judged by the president to be necessary for the security of the United States. The briefcase was known as the "football" and would always remain within the proximity of the president until handed to the military aide of the succeeding president.

"The rights of man," the incoming president said, "come not from the generosity of the state, but from the hand of God." And he gave an unprecedented importance to the foreign policy of the United States by a statement that echoed around the world:

"Let every nation know, whether it wishes us well or ill, that we will pay any price, bear any burden, meet any hardship, support any friend, and oppose any foe, to assure the survival and the success of liberty."

No leader of any nation had ever said anything to equal the sweeping embodiment of that phrase. He was not simply stating that liberty of the United States was the quest, but the pursuit was liberty throughout the world, and the United States would take that effort on as its destiny, no matter its consequences.

Americans picked up other phrases in his speech to reprint and repeat and remember, but the people of other nations, from chiefs of state in palatial structures to well-digging villagers in dung-walled huts, heard in that phrase the promise and the warning of a new and generous mission of the United States of America. With that phrase, the light of the United States was brighter than ever expected.

In the eyes of the world, Washington, D.C., would never be the same.

Former Ambassador Gerald Fairbanks and his wife, Mary, were not invited to any of the inaugural events because a lot of Washingtonians, including John Kennedy's old senate staff and his old campaign staff and his current transition staff, knew that Ambassador Fairbanks had supported Lyndon Johnson for president before John Kennedy won the nomination. Ambassador Fairbanks had known Lyndon Johnson since the days when Fairbanks lived in Texas, and in later years he testified in front of him in Washington, always receiving a friendly reception from him. It was Gerald and Mary Fairbanks hope that Gerald could be appointed an Ambassador again, and Lyndon Johnson was their only hope. "You did great work as an ambassador," Lyndon Johnson used to tell Fairbanks at those Senate hearings, although Gerald Fairbanks hadn't had the opportunity to have done practically any work as an ambassador. He was very self conscious about that brevity of assignment and felt that the title of "Mister Ambassador," which he would have for life, was not truly deserved, and he wanted the opportunity to make it deserved.

John Kennedy didn't know him, and Kennedy's staff had a list of people who towered above Gerald Fairbanks for important assignments. Vice President Johnson's list for appointments was largely disregarded by the president's staff. At least Gerald Fairbanks wouldn't lose his top ranking position in the foreign service, since he was a careerist.

"It's better that you're known as a friend of Lyndon than a friend of Richard Nixon," Mary would tell Gerald.

"I'm not so sure," he would answer after a quick clearing of his throat. "Sometimes I think Kennedy likes Nixon more than he likes Johnson."

"Now don't be silly, Gerald," she would say. "We're going to be just fine."

"Don't expect invitations to the inaugural, my dear," he was telling her since the day after the election.

"I don't care about inaugurals," she would answer.

But being in the District without anywhere to go at a time when the city was in celebration was an ego-deflating experience. There was only one remedy: to be out of town.

Mary Fairbanks took care of being invisible by going to New York on Monday, not to come back until Friday. She was safe from the same fate she suffered when she was a senior in high school on New Year's Eve without a date, and was spotted at a local bowling alley with a girlfriend. Never again.

Gerald Fairbanks didn't have the luxury of invisibility by going with her since, other than inauguration day, he had to work during the week. And so when that world-watched Wednesday came, he locked himself inside their home and looked at the walls. It took forever for night to arrive.

"Two more inaugurals and I'll be retired and play golf all day," he said to himself with a sense of long-term relief. All he had to do in the short-term was to survive the night, not all ten years.

But he got hungry.

He never turned on a stove in his life other than to boil water, and he was even unsuccessful at that most of the time, as he couldn't remember if the small bubbles meant it was boiling or if he had to wait for the big bubbles. There was nothing in the refrigerator for making sandwiches. For hours he dismissed his hunger but his stomach starting making loud noises and he couldn't keep his mind from thinking of food. Chili. A bowl of chili. The kind of chili served at Hazel's Texas Chili Parlor on New York Avenue. *No. Can't. Don't even think of it.*

It would be best to go to sleep.

Go to sleep at eight o'clock? How could he go to sleep that early—especially when he was so hungry. For chili. Hazel's chili. Chili-Straight with crackers. *Chili-Straight, please,* he imagined himself saying. *Could you bring a little butter with those crackers, please?* It was as though he was rehearsing.

But he couldn't afford to be seen. And be seen there, of all places? It was in a decaying part of town, near the Greyhound and Trailways Bus Depots. But wait a minute. How could anyone see him in there unless they were in Hazel's themselves? And they wouldn't be in Hazel's themselves because they would be celebrating at some inaugural ball. Of course. Now his only problem was getting to Hazel's and back, unseen.

The phone rang.

He looked at it, almost in panic.

He didn't want to answer it. What was he doing home? But it could be Mrs. Fairbanks. He had to answer it.

"Hel-ll-ll-o," he said, putting his voice into a different pitch and rhythm from his usual tone, in case he wanted to pretend the caller had the wrong number.

A woman's voice was on the other end of the line. "Ambassador Fairbanks?"

Who was she? Maybe it was someone calling who was with Mrs. Fairbanks. But maybe it wasn't. He didn't know what to say. "Did you ask for an ambassador?" he asked the caller.

"Yes. Is Ambassador Fairbanks or Mrs. Fairbanks there?"

"Oh! I see. No. She isn't in now."

"Is this Ambassador Fairbanks?"

"Only for three months," he said, as though he was being tested for humility. "I was only an ambassador for three months."

"Then this is Ambassador Fairbanks?" the voice asked.

"Yes. In a way."

"In a way?"

"Yes, yes, that's right. I mean I'm here but just for a moment. I'm almost on my way out."

"Mister Ambassador, I'm sorry to bother you on a night like this but—this is Anne Whitney. We met in Hong Kong at the Consulate, remember? I got your number from the State Department. I'm back in D.C. Do you remember me?"

"Yes. Yes, of course, at the Consulate and up at the Peak with the whole group up there. Of course I remember. You work for the Consulate—for Daschle. Nice of you to call. You here on home leave?"

"No. I'm assigned here now. Could I see you and Mrs. Fairbanks as soon as possible? I've got a problem and there's no one I can discuss it with and—I remember how kind you were in Hong Kong and I—I trust the two of you."

"Well, that's nice." He cleared his throat. "Of course we'll see you."

"Oh, thank you. There's just something about the two of you that I—that I trust. I'm a little on the desperate side right now, as I think you can tell."

"When? When do you need to see us?"

"As soon as you can do it. I'd come over tonight if you could do it, but you're going out?"

"Mrs. Fairbanks isn't here at all. She's in New York and I was just going out to–to a–"

"Are you going to an inaugural thing?"

What could he say? "No. No, I don't like those things. They make me claustrophobic. Too many people. I try to get out of them. Mrs. Fairbanks isn't here and I was just going out to catch a bite."

"Could we meet?"

"Well, not now. I'm just going to bring some food back here."

"Can I bring some food over from a take-out place?"

"You mean pick up some food?"

"Yes. I have my own car and I could easily do that. I would like to, if you can."

He cleared his throat, this time not out of habit, but to give the impression that what she said didn't excite him as much as it did. "Where are you coming from?"

"Suitland. Where do you live, in Foggy Bottom isn't it?"

"Yes. 24th and G."

"It will take me about 45 minutes. Maybe an hour on a night like this–or a little more. Could I?"

"Well, all right. That would be all right. I'll tell you what–something to pick up–something to pick up." He made that noise again with his throat. "I know. There's a little place on New York Avenue. You'll probably be coming down New York Avenue won't you?"

"I can."

"That's where you'll come down. I know a place where it won't take any time for you to pick something up. It's not the best place in the world but it would be just fine. There's a little place near the bus depots–Hazel's Texas Chili Parlor it's called, do you know it?"

"No, I don't, but that doesn't make any difference. I'll find it."

"It's right on what will be your side of the street as you drive toward here. Right past the Greyhound place there. Just look to your right. Pick me up a bowl of–no, a couple bowls of their Chili-Straight it's called if I remember correctly." Of course, he knew he remembered correctly. "And a bunch of crackers and butter and that's all. You get whatever you want for yourself."

"All right. I'm not really hungry but I'll get something."

"Yes, that's fine. Come on over as soon as you can."

"Oh, thank you so much, Mr. Ambassador. I'll leave now."

"Chili Straight. If I remember right, it's called Chili-Straight. They have all kinds of chili but that's the one. And, of course, some crackers and butter. Ask them for some extra crackers and butter."

"It may be a little more than an hour, I don't know, but I'll leave right away. What's your address?"

"2409 G. It's right off 24th."

"I'll leave now and be right over."

"Yes. Leave now."

"I will."

"Two bowls."

There's something disturbing about seeing someone out of that person's element, in your element. It makes that person more of a stranger than the person may be in reality. Anne Whitney just didn't belong in the Foggy Bottom house of the Fairbanks' but there she was. And if it wasn't for her offer of picking up food for him, she wouldn't have been there.

It was worth it. Two big bowls of Chili-Straight and there must have been a dozen packets of soda crackers and plenty of butter. He had butter in the refrigerator, but he had forgotten all about it.

Even though his guest was a junior officer trainee and he was in his own home, he had put on his vest, and his pocket watch chain was dangling from pocket to pocket, and he looked very authoritative. By the time she took off her coat and scarf, he had set up two TV tables in the living room with a cup of coffee on each one. She was formal enough to have worn a business suit, and she was sporting a new pair of glasses much more reserved than the big round pair she wore in Hong Kong. She didn't bring anything to eat for herself, so her mouth was free to talk, and she didn't touch the coffee he brought in for her.

He was grateful that Anne had enough to say that he wouldn't have to respond all the way through his two bowls of chili. She told him about her disputes with Mark Daschle in Hong Kong, and that he told her to leave and go back to Washington, and that she stopped in India on the way home, and how she used Ambassador Bunker's name in India to the police in Benares without Ambassador Bunker's permission to do that, and that she came back to the Agency on November the First and has been there ever since with practically nothing to do, waiting for whatever her fate would be, and yesterday she was told her fate. She wouldn't be dismissed, she was allowed to stay with the Agency, but she would be posted in Washington for at least two years before going overseas again. By this time Ambassador Fairbanks was on his coffee. "Do you want your coffee heated up?" he asked Anne.

"No. I'm fine, thanks. Do you know who saved me?" she asked him.

"Saved you?"

"The one who went to bat for me so I wouldn't be fired?"

"Who?"

"I never would have expected it. Mr. Daschle."

"He's a very fine man. I've known him for years. We served together in Lagos. But I thought you said he was the one who was so angry, and was the one who sent you home."

"He was. He did. But I found out just today, and I was home today because of the inauguration–I got a call from a girlfriend at State who told me that Mr. Daschle sent a follow-up letter just before I got here on November the First telling the Agency to keep me, that I had promise, that our Embassy in Delhi had told him what I did in India, and he thought it was commendable. He wrote a lot about that. He rescinded his recommendation of my dismissal. I misjudged him."

"You did. What I think is that he was saying that he had misjudged you at first."

"No. He was right. I know that. I know that now and I think I probably knew it then."

"Really, Anne?"

"Wait. I still think Mao's a great revolutionary but I should learn when to shut up."

"I could argue with you on the first point but not on the second."

"I know. I'm just so surprised that Mr. Daschle saved me in the end. He thought my caring for the dying man in India was creditable and the fact that I used Ambassador Bunker's name was understandable under the circumstances. But he wasn't all complimentary. He also wrote that he advised I not be sent overseas for a couple years, that I should learn more, that it was too early to have me in an overseas post. I don't think I can stand two more years in D.C."

"You'll stand it. We all do."

"And there's a strong rumor that's been going on around this town for the past couple months that Kennedy is going to start Hubert Humphrey's idea of a Peace Corps with people like me, young people, going to places all over the world to teach the locals how to build schools and things. I want to do that and I want the Agency to recommend me, and I don't think they will."

"Realistically, I think you're right, I think they won't recommend you. Not now, anyway. I can't help you there."

"No, I don't want you to. I was just telling you. I want to be in the Peace Corps and I want to go to Tanganyika–or if not there, I have a list of preferred places."

"Now, what's your problem? What can I do for you? You acted as though you were in a panic and you had to have quick guidance from this old hand."

"I do. It got to me today when I heard Kennedy's speech. He was saying it's not what the country does for you but what you do for the country and–something like united we can do so much and divided we can't do anything–something like that, and it all got to me because I have three things–three things on my conscience, Ambassador Fairbanks. They're bad. The first one has been on my mind every day and night since October and I don't know what to do about it. But I can't just keep it inside thinking about it anymore. Ambassador Fairbanks, do you remember one of the people with us in Hong Kong that day was a man named Adam Orr?"

"Of course. Interesting man. I knew him from before, actually."

"The day I left the Embassy in Delhi I saw him walking–wait–do you know in Delhi the Soviet Embassy is right next door to ours?"

"I know."

"Well, I saw him walking into the Soviet Embassy."

At this he put down his coffee cup. "Adam Orr?"

"Yes."

"Are you sure?"

"I'm positive."

He was quiet for a while. "Well, that doesn't mean anything. We do business with them on some matters. We have diplomatic recognition. We have discussions."

"But he isn't with our government."

Again the quiet. "It's odd. I grant you it's odd but it doesn't mean anything. You can't jump to conclusions. There could be dozens of reasons."

"What do I do with the information?"

"You mean to whom do you report it?"

"Or if I should report it at all. I haven't. I don't snitch. I don't believe in snitching."

"That isn't snitching. It's—"

"Yes it is. And what if he gets in real trouble if I report him and what if he didn't do anything wrong, and I'd be getting him in trouble for something that didn't mean anything bad?"

"You want to know what I would do?"

"Yes. What would you do?"

"First, what I would have done—that's important. I would have reported it that day. If you work for the taxpayers, you work for them. If you don't, then quit. But don't go halfway."

"You sound like Mr. Daschle."

"I hope so."

"So what do I do now?"

"What you just did. Tell someone who can bring it to the proper place. You told me. Now get it off your mind. I'll take it from here."

"But shouldn't I tell my superior?"

"Who's that?"

"Oh, you don't know him. He's a GS-17. His name is Hugh Greenfield."

"I don't know him."

"Shouldn't I tell him?"

"Yes. If you have the courage. That's the correct protocol. That's what you should do. But by telling me what you saw, you got me involved. And I'm glad you did."

"Now they'll ask you why I waited three months."

"Yes, they will."

"What will you tell them?"

"The truth. You didn't want to. I'll tell them what you told me."

"I'm in enough trouble as it is."

"If you were moved by what Kennedy said, then you should do what's right, even if you get in more trouble."

"I guess so."

"Anne, you might just as well tell the Greenfield fellow, because you told me and I'm going to report it tomorrow to our friends across the river." Like most in the foreign affairs community, he didn't use the words or the initials of the Central Intelligence Agency. That agency was simply, "across the river." "So you might just as well report it too, because once I report it, it will all come back to you."

"I see."

"Anne, your problem is that you make trouble for yourself."

"I know."

"Now you said you had three things—three problems. What's the next one? Let's solve it."

"It's an apology, Mr. Ambassador. I was very rude to you in Hong Kong when we were on the Peak, when you talked about your plan for a new kind of world organization. I didn't know anything about what you were talking about, and I said something silly. I apologize."

Ambassador Fairbanks looked down at his coffee cup and rotated it on its saucer. "That's very kind of you, Anne. Don't worry about it. It's just an idea." Then he looked up at her. "You can't be in government as long as I have and not have some crazy ideas. That one is mine."

"Oh, it's not crazy, Mr. Ambassador! Mr. Daschle is very high on it."

He smiled and nodded. "He's been very encouraging through the years. That obsession of mine—it's just a way to—it's just an idea, and there are some weaknesses in it. It's something I'm working on."

"Do you accept my apology?"

"Of course. And I'm grateful. I'm grateful especially because you made no excuses—no defense of yourself; no justification. That's the way a big person apologizes. All accepted. Now, we've solved two of your three problems. What's the last one?"

"I found out something today. Nothing to do with the inaugural."

"What?"

"Ambassador Fairbanks, I came home through both Asia and Europe on my way to D.C. I met an American sailor in Germany. He's part of the occupation forces there. It was nothing serious. I mean I didn't fall in love or anything. I'm not even sure he gave me his right name. I didn't give him mine. He was just a sailor on leave and we met at the Hofbrau House—a big German eating and beer place. We had fun. You know what I mean?"

"Um-hmm. I'm afraid I do."

"So today I found out I'm going to have a baby in July. Do I report that? Do you think they'll let me stay with the Agency? I mean, not being married? Does that lower my chances of getting in the Peace Corps? I mean would that hurt the possibility of going to Tanganyika?"

Even though Gerald Fairbanks didn't go to any inaugural event that night, and all he wanted was some chili, he lived under the rules of the District of Columbia. Boredom was prohibited.

TEN
THE CHEFTLIN LUNCHEON GROUP
1961

Maybe it was only imagination but the White House seemed to change its exterior appearance with the presence of each new president. Without the movement of a brick or a change of landscape, every passerby received an instant impression of the character that inhabited the mansion at the time.

During the '40s and '50s, the White House had reflected the strength and warmth of President Roosevelt, then the courage and fire of President Truman, then the security and dignity of President Eisenhower, and now in the early '60s, the youth and vigor of President Kennedy.

Other than the president, most of the people who worked in the White House, didn't. They just said they did because it was easier to say that rather than to explain. What the world called the White House, the White House Staff called "The Mansion." The mansion was actually a small part of the Executive compound, serving as the living and entertaining quarters for the president and his family. The only government employees who worked there were those who maintained the house and cleaned and cooked and took care of the personal needs of the First Family.

To either side of the mansion were long and low structures which were enclosed hallways with rooms. The White House Theater and swimming pool and smaller rooms were located there. Each of those two structures led to a separate low building; on one side, the East Wing, which contained the working quarters of the First Lady, and on the other side, the West Wing, which contained the working quarters of the president. Most mornings the president would walk the ceilinged outdoor colonnade from the mansion to the outdoor entrance to the Oval Office in the West Wing.

Although the president's Oval Office was the main focus of the West Wing, the West Wing also included the Cabinet Room, the Fish Room named for FDR's aquariums, a reception room, the White House Mess, and other rooms including the offices of the president's closest aides. The rooms and offices of the West Wing were connected by narrow, plush-carpeted hallways and staircases. Framed photographs of the most recent activities of the president; a foreign trip or a White House party or inauguration or some other memorable event, decorated the corridors, the pictures often hung within hours after they were photographed, with older ones taken down to the White House archives.

The bulk and majority of the president's assistants could not fit into the office space of the West Wing, so they worked in a massive structure, the Executive Office Building, bigger by far than the mansion or the East Wing or the West Wing. The Executive Office Building was a very long, very wide, very tall gray gingerbread-style building across the private drive from the West Wing. It originally housed the State Department and the Headquarters of the Armed Forces. Its long halls were ornate and high-ceilinged, its floor laid with a checkerboard design, and its offices were some of the most formal in all of Washington.

Other than the president, his family, his staff, and visitors by appointment, there were four groups of almost-daily visitors within the compound: the tourists, the VIP guests, the White House Press Corps, and the fence-climbers.

The tourists came in at posted times through the East Wing and were escorted as far as the first floor of the mansion enabling them to view formal and lower state rooms. Earlier in the morning, before the flock of visitors were allowed in, there were VIPs who were given more personalized and longer tours and, depending on circumstances or the importance of the person who requested the tour, they were sometimes permitted to go into the West Wing.

Unlike other groups, the White House Press Corps was not transient. A select assemblage of Washington-based reporters were chosen by their news service or newspaper or magazine or network, as their representatives. They attended all the president's press conferences and the twice-a-day briefings of the president's press secretary, Pierre Salinger, in his office. They accompanied the president on his travels and attended any presidential function to which they were invited. They also attended more restricted events if they were able to coerce admittance from someone on the White House staff.

The Press Corps worked in the White House compound stationed within the West Wing lobby. A reporter's credential was authorized by Pierre Salinger, and that credential was an always-visible identification badge swinging in a celluloid covering on a thin-chained silver-colored necklace. With that identification, the Press Corps was allowed into the grounds at any time through the Northwest Gate "on their honor" to go only to the Press Quarters. With or without their honor, they couldn't have successfully gone anywhere else within the compound. There were posted guards outside and within the West Wing, the mansion, the East Wing, and the Executive Office Building.

There was another category of visitors that were rarely publicly discussed. They were the ones who climbed the fence or dug beneath it or rammed into it. They would crawl or roll or run until they were met by the arms of the Secret Service or the White House Protection Service. They came onto the grounds much more often than the world outside the White House was told. There was always someone who thought he or she could get away with it.

As a new appointee, Cody Cooper was glowing. He was surrounded by a city of unexcelled importance, and his new job was even more all-encompassing than he had imagined it would be. Like all those who had the privilege to work there, Cody Cooper would become a voluntary prisoner of history and, at times, a participant in it. His orientation was an immersion in sudden significance in world-changing events.

Three days after his appointment, he was given a very heavy magnetically stranded laminated card and was told that he always had to keep it on his person. It was his pass into Mount Weather in Virginia, a site that could only be reached by helicopter from the south lawn of the White House or from the Pentagon grounds. Mount Weather was the secret facility established as emergency headquarters for the president and selected members of the United States government in case of nuclear attack: the ones whose job would be to insure that the government would continue to exist. Family members were excluded.

On the fourth day Cody Cooper was given a tour of Mount Weather. At its base were huge steel doors, and beyond those doors were tunnels after tunnels that led to an underground city with offices, a hospital, twenty barracks, thousands of rations, a large eating room, as well as the president's private quarters.

On the fifth day, Cody Cooper was given his permanent office in the Executive Office Building. He inherited S. Sylvan Sullivan's grand office, and he also inherited S. Sylvan Sullivan's careerist secretary.

S. Sylvan Sullivan had worked for Robert Gray who worked for President Eisenhower, and he was bitter about the young Kennedy men who had invaded Washington. He was particularly bitter about the undesirable Kennedy man who had taken over his office and secretary, and as S. Sylvan Sullivan understood it from his former secretary, the new Kennedy man had his office repainted blue, and re-carpeted in yellow, and he even moved S. Sylvan Sullivan's desk away from the wall where it had been so comfortable for eight years. He put it next to the window.

Was there no limit to the excesses of the Kennedy people? S. Sylvan Sullivan thought.

Sullivan's former secretary used to impress him with her republicanism, and she cried when Vice President Nixon lost the election, so how could she have turned so fast? She was now a proud and happy representative of "The New Frontier" who phoned S. Sylvan Sullivan occasionally to tell him, "Mister Cooper would like to speak to you." She kept S. Sylvan Sullivan waiting for Cody Cooper to get on the line the way she used to keep others on the line waiting for S. Sylvan Sullivan.

Adding more insult to all this was that Mister Cooper sounded as though he was thirteen years old. "Hi, Sylvan," the broken voice said to S. Sylvan Sullivan. *As if both of us are men and equals,* S. Sylvan Sullivan thought, *when only one of us is a man and we are not equal.*

It was a bad time for the new Kennedy man to phone because the old Eisenhower man and his wife were packing plates in boxes in preparation for the move from Arlington back to Milwaukee. The old Eisenhower man imagined Cody Cooper sitting behind his desk which was now by the window of all places, and probably Cody Cooper had on a suit with a thin tie and was trying to look grown-up.

"How are you, Cody?" he conceded to ask.

"Adjusting, Sylvan," the kid who must be a Nazi said.

"Well, well," S. Sylvan Sullivan answered like the voice of experience. "Well, well," he repeated.

"I'll tell you why I phoned you, Sylvan," the pimple-faced killer finally said. "I need some guidance. The president's assignment for me, you know, is to be sort of a spokesman on his foreign policy initiatives."

"Oh, yes." He didn't know or care.

"So that's what I'm doing."

"That's smart."

"I talk to the public on foreign policy issues, y'know."

I know, I know, I know, I know. "That's very good. Well, what can I do for you, Cody?"

"Guidance on an audience. I have an invitation to speak before an organization called the Cheftlin Luncheon Group."

"Oh?"

"Yes. It's a group that meets in the Dining Room of the Albert Pick over on 12th and K every first Tuesday of the month for lunch. Know anything about it?"

"Yes, yes, of course." S. Sylvan Sullivan had never accepted one of their invitations since the Truman boys had tried to misguide him into speaking to them eight years ago. "Fine organization."

"Is it?"

"Oh, you bet."

"Is it important?"

"Influential. I wish we had had their support. We never had it."

"What does it do?"

"Well, they have speeches. They lobby—that's what they do. They lobby up on the Hill for various causes, various legislation. Worth your while. Don't refuse it, boy."

"What causes? What kind of legislation? I won't refuse it if you say it's important."

"Oh yes it is."

"They said I could talk about anything."

"You betcha."

"So what do they lobby for?"

"Well, Cody, I don't know what they're up to these days but, God knows, they'd like to speak to a real Kennedy man." *And see if they're human.*

"I think I'll talk about the Allianza, then. I've been to Latin America."

The what?

"Do you think that would be appropriate?"

"What was that, Cody?"

"The Allianza del Progresso."

Can't Kennedy men even speak English?

"You know, it's something that the president is trying to push."

The president? Eisenhower is the president, you cow-eyed communist. "Of course. Good subject."

"You think it's appropriate for the Cheftlin Luncheon Group, then?"

"You bet your bottom dollar it is."

"Well, I thank you, Sylvan."

"You tell them all about the Allianza. That's good."

"I can get into talking about Cuba that way. You know, and all the refugees in Miami."

"That's right."

"You think Cuba is too sensitive?"

"Oh, no."

"See? The president has a real interest in those refugees, and all refugees."

"That's a good topic. You do that."

"How about something on South Vietnam? There's an avalanche of refugees there coming from the North."

"Good. Good. That's good."

"I certainly thank you."

"You betcha. Glad to help."

The old Eisenhower man and the new Kennedy man both hung up and the old Eisenhower man went back to putting his old plaques and awards in boxes for shipment, and the new Kennedy man buzzed his secretary to tell her to accept the invitation of the Cheftlin Luncheon Group.

Chicken legs, green peas, sherbet, lukewarm coffee, an audience of fourteen ladies who were retirees, and two sleepy men who looked as though they were there only at their wives insistence, greeted Cody Cooper on the second floor dining room that was partitioned off to separate the Cheftlin Luncheon Group from the regular diners of the Albert Pick Motor Hotel.

Worst of all was the host, Harry Cheftlin. Although Cody Cooper had never met him before, Harry Cheftlin was acting as though the two of them had shared the better part of their lives together.

Harry Cheftlin rattled his spoon inside his coffee cup, and then inside his sherbet cup. The sherbet cup made a better tone. He had absolute quiet but that didn't stop him from rattling the spoon some more. He was the host and these moments only came once a month and he was going to broadcast his authority to the fourteen women and two men when he had the opportunity. "Thank ya. Thank y'all," he said. "Thank y'all for 'tendin'. My, my, my, my, we have got ourselves a house. Mrs. Somerset's here. Mrs. Somerset, ya want to stand up?"

Mrs. Somerset wanted to stand up and she received as much of an ovation as the small group could administer. Cody Cooper applauded too and he had no idea why. She smiled and sat down. Cody's habit of looking with interest at practically everything was working in overload. Today his interest was mixed with bewilderment.

"Thank ya, Mrs. Somerset." Harry Cheftlin wasn't even going to explain why she was asked to stand. "And Dolores!" Harry Cheftlin said. "Dolores Ann Wembley. We are so glad you're feelin' all well 'nuff now." Her name sounded as though she was Miss America, but she was not Miss America.

(Beauty queens and murderers always have three names.) They applauded again and so Cody, as before, joined in the applause with his mouth open as though he was fascinated with her recovery, although he had not known she had been sick. Dolores Ann Wembley received almost as much applause as Mrs. Somerset, but not quite. She didn't stand. There was a cane by her side. "We're gonna dispense with the minutes here, in honor of our guest," Harry Cheftlin announced, "but jes' wanna ask, ya all got yer tickets for the Potomac Cruise down to Mount Vernon?"

There were calls of "yes."

"Y'all raise yer hands if ya got the tickets."

Everyone raised their hands.

"Now, if ya don't have yer tickets, y'all call my office and talk to Betts. She's right on top of it. It'll be the event of the year. I guarantee ya that. Bring yer spouse or whoever," and he laughed as though he had just told the smuttiest, most sex-ridden, perverted joke in all recorded history. "Now, let's be serious," he said and his expression changed in an instant to one of a man before a firing squad. "Our guest of honor here at the Cheftlin Luncheon Group is a pa-tic-lar friend of mine who serves with Pres-dent John F. Kennedy. Now, Pres-dent Kennedy went and got him all the way from Dee-troit." He accented the "Dee." "He was on his way to being a doctor; an M.D. He was done with pre-med when the Pres-dent picked him out. Y'all heard him on the radio since being with the Pres-dent–and even seen him on TV. Oh, he's made the news, and he's got what it takes which is why Pres-dent Kennedy went and got him all the way from Dee-troit. So y'all better listen to him because I've been listenin' to him for a long time and I swear by him. Coop', here, has been a friend since longer 'n I care to remember–'least as I care to ad-mit." He accented the "ad." There were a few laughs at his rollicking sense of humor regarding his age.

"Here! Here!" some lady said.

"Now ya see, most folks don't care 'bout what this here country's comin' to. You folks do. God bless you folks. That's why you're im-poh-dant. Now let me give you my good friend, Cody Cooper, who came to Washington all the way from Dee-troit to help the Pres-dent. Have at 'em Coop'! An' don' mince no words for 'em. They can take it. They're all ears now. Have at 'em, Coop', like ya do! Take it away!"

Oh no.

And there was a round of tired applause. A little less than that received by Mrs. Somerset but a little more than the applause for Dolores Ann Wembley.

Cody Cooper was totally uninspired. But he had prepared a speech and he was going to give it. He talked about foreign policy in general and that it was not a matter of partisanship. He told them about the refugee's world-wide and accented Hong Kong. He spoke of FDR and the Good Neighbor Policy toward Latin America, and then he talked about the Alliance for Progress that President Kennedy was inaugurating, and the cooperation that was being received from Republicans. "It's a cooperative effort," he said, "not just in Washington. It is a cooperative effort in which all Americans from the entire Western Hemisphere will participate, and from that participation, they'll take pride."

He was even beginning to phrase his sentences like President Kennedy. "It will seek to destroy the age-old enemies of poverty, disease, hunger, and illiteracy through peaceful and democratic processes."

No one at the Cheftlin Luncheon Group understood what on earth he was talking about, and he knew they didn't, but there was something about the old and pure eyes of Dolores Ann Wembley with the cane. She really was listening. Maybe she didn't understand, but she was listening so intently. Those eyes of hers were so eager, so expectant, so hopeful, and Cody Cooper didn't want to disappoint her. He then addressed his speech in her direction and she nodded often after he had made one point or another and that made him glad. Dolores Ann Wembley caused him to do well.

"This isn't a hand-out to our friends, or even to the impoverished, but an agreement with them. The budget will be dependent upon how much money the countries of Latin America, international agencies, Western Europe, and private organizations are willing to put behind this program. The United States will match that sum, but only if the projects are those that we feel are vital for the people of those Latin American nations, for the entire Western Hemisphere including the United States, and in the long view, in the interest of the world. We plan on meeting with representatives of those nations at an Inter-American Economic and Social Conference later in the year.

"We believe that if we help to raise the standard of living across our borders, we will be encouraging the forces of peace and freedom in the face of heavy non-democratic influences from abroad, most particularly from the Soviet Union through Cuba. Fidel Castro is calling the president's plan an instrument of American imperialism. Just ask the Cuban refugees in Miami if he's right!

"While other nations are evaluating whether the forces of communism or the forces of democracy are the waves of the future in this hemisphere, the president is committed to encourage their understanding of what our system is all about. The president believes that one Cuba in Latin America is enough, and that some day Cuba's people will be free again."

They all applauded with Dolores Ann Wembley applauding very hard.

"Further, President Kennedy said that what was perceived, at first, as a Cuban revolution for freedom and democracy was perverted into a seizure for international communism. We are now committed to see to it that Castro's regime does not go on indefinitely. Now, you can interpret that in any way you choose. The president has said that we will not abandon the Cuban people to communism, and our patience with Castro is not inexhaustible."

Again, there was applause. Dolores Ann Wembley was nodding as she applauded.

"Now, before concluding, let me say just a few words about the president's policy in Southeast Asia, and particularly our pursuit of maintaining freedom in South Vietnam. The president has pledged that we will keep our commitments there, and he has clearly stated that it is a matter to which we must address our energy and attention to guarantee that those endangered are not overtaken by a repressive government that has caused millions to flee from North Vietnam to South Vietnam at risk of their lives.

"In short, President Kennedy is committed to freedom in our own country, our own hemisphere, and freedom for all those who live on this planet."

The applause was loud from all sixteen of them, led by Harry Cheftlin. Cody had come a long way through his very quick education in Washington. Although some advisors of the president had argued against hiring this young and eager campaigner, the president overruled them, and he chose wisely. Maybe, at this moment, it was only the Cheftlin Luncheon Group, but he did well with them.

Harry Cheftlin had to ruin it. "Y'all want to give him a big hand here?" he said after they had already given him a big hand. So in compliance to their host they did it again but this time fifteen of them didn't have the same enthusiasm as before only Dolores Ann Wembley maintained the impact of her hands from the first applause.

"Now y'all know what's happenin' down on Pennsylvania Avenue," Harry Cheftlin announced. "Ya got time for questions, Coop'? We have time for one, maybe two."

"Sure."

But there weren't any.

Dolores Ann Wembley was smiling at him but, apparently, she couldn't think of a question to ask him.

Harry Cheftlin ended the silence that permeated the room. "Now, tell me, Coop', what can we do to help?"

Cody nodded. "The president needs all our cooperation and support. The advance he's made so far is only a start. We need letters of support to the Congress."

"Y'all see? Y'all see?" Harry Cheftlin put his stamp of endorsement on Cody's answer. "That's what this here is all about. Our support. Now y'know. All right now, I promised y'all would be out of here by one-thirty 'n' Mr. Sheehe, my friend, the manager, wants us out of here, so let's get on and let's thank our guest once more."

Another requested applause and it was all over. Cody Cooper was looking forward to be done with Harry Cheftlin more than he normally looked forward to Christmas.

"Hey, Coop'," Harry Cheftlin said as the members of the Cheftlin Luncheon Group shuffled out, "Y'all want to come up to 'L' Street to my in-town office? It's not a whisper away and there's an 'in-desk' bar if ya know what I mean!" And he laughed. "Thought I'd ask you and ol' Mr. Sheehe, the manager here who's an ol' buddy; maybe he'd want to come and meet a Kennedy man."

"I have to get back to the White House, Harry," Cody Cooper said. "I didn't realize what time it was. I'm running a little late."

"'s only one-thirty. An 'in-desk' bar!"

"I have to see the president."

Harry Cheftlin's face changed back into the man in front of the firing squad. "Y'all get back there and do like ya do," Harry Cheftlin said. "Y'all keep up the good work for the pres-dent. We're with ya, Coop'. We're with ya all the way. Ya know it! Let the pres-dent know I'm with y'all."

Cody Cooper ran down the wide stairs to his waiting chauffeur-driven limousine on 12th Street.

He knew he had been given an intentional bum steer by S. Sylvan Sullivan, but seeing the eyes of Dolores Ann Wembley in reaction to Cody's words were worth the whole thing. She made him glad that S. Sylvan Sullivan had pulled one on him.

Cody Cooper had passed from boyhood to manhood, and there wasn't a quicker school in the world than representing the White House.

That night, in the Oval Office, Cody Cooper's memo regarding the Cheftlin Luncheon Group was the only item that brought a smile to the president. Cody wanted the president to know he had talked to sixteen people because he was told it was a good bet by S. Sylvan Sullivan, and he wanted the president to know what he had said in the president's name, including what he had said regarding Cuba, which was the only real area of controversy that Cody had touched on in his speech.

As soon as the president put the memo down on his desk, he picked up the manila folder next to it. In the folder were papers he had requested of CIA director Allen Dulles. It was a note and a transcript of the conversation between Dulles and the Chief of Nicaragua's army, Anastasio Somoza. Somoza had attended President Kennedy's inauguration and, after it was done, Somoza went to the CIA's headquarters in Langley, Virginia, at the invitation of the CIA director.

The note told the president that no one, other than Somoza and his brother, Luis, who was the president of Nicaragua, was willing to accommodate the United States by supplying a secret base for an invasion of Cuba by those who had escaped from Cuba. Since 1959, at the request of the Eisenhower Administration, Anastasio Somoza had cleared Puerto Cabezas in Nicaragua as the base to be used for a United States directed invasion by Cuban exiles. In the transcript of the post-inauguration conversation, Director of the CIA Dulles had asked the Nicaraguan what he wanted for all his government's help. Somoza responded that he wanted nothing. Somoza told Dulles that his secret base of Puerto Cabezas was ready and had been code-named "Happy Valley" which was the name of the race track in Hong Kong. The invasion site in Cuba would be Bahia de Cochinos, which was translated as the Bay of Pigs.

"Cody? Is this Cody Cooper?" but he pronounced it 'Coopuh', with the

New England accent that made his identity unmistakable on Cody's White House office phone.

"Yes, Mr. President."

"I—uh—I—uh—read your memo on that luncheon group speech, Cody, and it looks like you delivered the message to Garcia, all right, but Garcia was a little sparse (spahss)!"

"Yes, sir. I think I was given the business by one of our predecessors! As I wrote you, S. Sylvan Sullivan recommended I speak to them. There wasn't much of an audience."

"It's all right. Your message was good, particularly on the Alliance—and if there's one person who shows up to hear (hee-yuh) you—you give that person everything you have. In West Virginia one morning (mahwning) during the primary there (they-uh) I got up at three in the morning (mahwning) and I found myself talking to one man outside a coal mine there. (they-uh) But he deserved my attention—and he got it." President Kennedy's Boston accent was one of his most endearing personal characteristics, but not to Cody Cooper who simply had a rough time understanding him .

"Yes, sir."

"So, I—uh—I have an assignment for you to deliver a message. It—uh—it may not be as exciting as going to the Albert Pick Motor (Motah) Hotel but I need you to be a courier."

Unfortunately, Cody couldn't piece together that last word, the way the president pronounced it. "You need me to be a what, sir?"

"A courier."

"A Korea?"

"A courier."

"A career?"

"No, a courier, a messenger (messenguh)."

"Oh! Sure! Sure!"

"I have a message to go to a friend in Nicaragua and I'd like it to be taken there to him by a personal representative rather (rah-thuh) than some means that would be more (maw) impersonal. Will you do that for (faw) me?

"Yes, sir!"

"Bundy will get it to you. And you might read our National Security Action Memorandum 31. It's a little out of date but it'll give you some kind of sense of our (owuh) feelings regarding Cuba (Cu-ber) as you so well put in your talk today. It can't be quoted, but I want you to know my feelings, so when you talk, you know the seriousness of our commitment to the people of Cuba. (Cu-ber.)"

"I'll get that, sir."

"Mac—McGeorge Bundy will have it for you."

"When do you want me to make the trip, sir?"

"Right away. You just hand him the envelope when you get there (they-uh)—it's to be given to the president's brother (bro-thuh), the Chief of the Army (ahmy). Then you can turn right around and come home. Bundy will have it for you. On this one, Cody, I just want you to be my personal courier (Korea or career)," and then he added, "messenger (messenguh)," in case Cody didn't understand.

At least Cody had been able to understand Harry Cheftlin, of all people, who was from Savannah. It was so terrible having difficulty understanding the president of the United States. Cody, from Detroit, who had traveled a great deal of the world, did not have much experience traveling the United States. At this time he wished he had spent some time in New England.

He didn't know how lucky he was. It could have been a phone call from Vice President Johnson who was from Austin.

ELEVEN
TRACTORS FOR FREEDOM
1961

When Irene Goodpastor heard the radio announcement that Fidel Castro had declared complete victory over "the imperialist government of the United States" on the beaches of the Bay of Pigs, and that over 1,000 invaders had been captured, her instinct for political activism took one of its frequent leaps upward.

Last November she had gone to President-elect Kennedy's victory ball. In January she went to the inaugural ceremony and one of the inaugural balls. In February she went to a White House Tea hosted by Mrs. Jacqueline Kennedy who she did not like, and in March she had letters sent from friends and acquaintances encouraging the president to appoint Mrs. Goodpastor as Consul General to Hong Kong. Then she wrote a letter to Evelyn Lincoln, President Kennedy's personal secretary, with the "offer" of her availability. Her letter to Evelyn Lincoln was interspersed with all kinds of evidence of her expertise on Hong Kong, which she copied from the brochure written by Tso Wai-yee that she had picked up in Mark Daschle's conference room in Hong Kong last October.

She received carbon copies of twenty letters that were sent to the White House urging her appointment, and a letter she requested from the Consul General's Public Affairs Officer, Mark Daschle, who didn't urge her appointment, but verified her interest in Hong Kong. There was also a letter from Ambassador Fairbanks at the United States Information Agency, and Lieutenant Jonas Valadovich in Tokyo, testifying that they had met with her in Hong Kong, and knew of her concern regarding that Crown Colony.

When April came and there was still no response from President Kennedy, she phoned Cody Cooper at the White House, apologizing to him for not having invited him to her April Fools' Day Party, and requesting he put in a "good word" to the president regarding the Consul General's post in Hong Kong. He assured her he would bring up the subject to the president.

Four days later she received a handwritten letter from President Kennedy. He wrote that despite the fact that she would make a marvelous Consul General to Hong Kong, Mrs. Goodpastor was of more service to the United States and to him personally, "here in Washington."

That letter from the president was framed and now hung on her living room wall, or parlor as she called it, in her Georgetown home. It was hung among dozens and dozens of handwritten letters from chiefs of state and other international celebrities that spanned a good half-century. There was, in fact, some belief within the White House that Mrs. Goodpastor wanted that letter almost as much as she wanted the post of consul general.

They knew her well. All of Washington knew her well.

"David Wolper, in Hollywood, collects handwritten letters that were written to just anyone," she would tell guests that came into her house. "Who can't do that if you have enough money? The difference between me and Wolper," she said with unashamed pride, "is that every letter I have was written to me. I'm not Virginia Weidler in *The Youngest Profession* looking for autographs, like Wolper."

One of the framed handwritten documents that she displayed in her hallway was a piece of lined paper with the signatures of her Hong Kong acquaintances, along with their addresses, with the paper titled "To Be Together Again In Hong Kong in 1997." Above it was a picture taken from the Peak.

She hadn't told anyone, but she had written a letter of congratulations to Yuri Gagarin in the Soviet Union in recognition of being the first person to orbit the earth, and she had already arranged her framed letters in a pattern that would give his yet unreceived reply prominence, whenever it would arrive.

On a Sunday night in May while she was writing a letter to Alan Shepherd, she heard the news that a committee had been formed. A wonderful committee. She had to be on that committee.

That request was granted, giving credibility to President Kennedy's assurance that she would be of greater value to him if she was not sent overseas, but stayed in Washington.

Within the week she was sitting at the State Department with Eleanor Roosevelt, Walter Reuther, Dr. Milton Eisenhower, and lesser-knowns, accepting a fund-raising role with the objective of buying 500 tractors to send to Fidel Castro in return for 1,214 prisoners taken during the Bay of Pigs invasion.

In no time at all her parlor and breakfast room was established as a "command center" for the "Tractors for Freedom Committee," with dozens of Georgetown University girls sitting at rented typewriters, writing fund-raising letters. Mrs. Goodpastor conferred with farm machinery manufacturers, Eleanor Roosevelt, Cuban exiles, and Chester Bowles at the State Department.

She was in her glory.

President Kennedy was asking Americans to contribute to the effort. It was hard to tell if Mrs. Goodpastor was supporting him or he was supporting her.

She and the president were being credited by friendly members of the Congress, and also condemned by outraged members of the Congress who were calling the committee a scheme to collect ransom. But the attack only increased her passion for the project, and she wrote those critical members of the Congress angry responses. Her passion was doubly increased when people from all over the country wrote her that they wouldn't contribute to a blackmail effort, and she became convinced that it was an organized campaign against her committee when they all started saying the same thing: they wrote that all Castro would do if he received the tractors, would be to re-vamp them into bulldozers.

She would prove them wrong. She felt that nothing could diminish her effort.

But something did.

Castro.

He kept executing people and getting people in the United States upset.

That wasn't all of it. He sent a letter to the Tractors for Freedom Committee and it was typed. Not handwritten. Typed in Spanish. That made her mad enough, but even worse, it wasn't even addressed to her. It was addressed to Mrs. Roosevelt, Mr. Reuther, and Dr. Eisenhower. After the State Department translated it, she was informed that Castro didn't want 500 tractors anymore.

He wanted bulldozers.

"Girls!" she would yell at her troop of volunteers, "I don't want to see any more of those letters calling us ransom-payers and blackmail-answerers. They're written by the same people who are blaming the president for not providing air cover for the CIA! Letters like that are all written by General Walker and the John Birch Society and when you get them, you put them under the little blue lamp, and I'm bringing them all over to the White House to be traced and they'll all be put in jail where they belong. You understand?"

There was some murmuring in unison that sounded like a "Yes, Mrs. Goodpastor." Before long, the blue lamp was smothered in letters and there was no way to tell if the lamp was on or off.

Then Castro announced that if he could not get bulldozers, he wanted twice as many tractors as he had requested before, or in lieu of tractors he would accept money—but fewer prisoners would be set free than he had originally offered. The Tractors for Freedom Committee was going down the drain, and without one handwritten letter worth framing. She didn't even get one from Dr. Milton Eisenhower.

And so by the last week of June, the committee had been discredited and put out of business by Castro's demands. Irene Goodpastor was instructing her command center girls to help send back over 70,000 checks from donors.

So many defeats.

Adlai Stevenson.

An appointment as Consul General.

Yuri Gagarin.

Alan Shepherd.

Now Fidel Castro.

Were her days of victory all over? Was Washington seeing Mrs. Goodpastor in a new light? Were they even seeing her at all? Was she no longer a vital part of Washington life?

But it really didn't matter if Washington was seeing Mrs. Goodpastor in a new light because Mrs. Goodpastor was seeing Mrs. Goodpastor in a new light. She felt she was of diminishing value. Would anyone remember her life? She sat in her parlor alone on the second Tuesday morning of July. Practically every Washingtonian of prominence would be at Mount Vernon that evening attending the state dinner that President Kennedy was holding for President Ayub Khan of Pakistan.

A state dinner at Mount Vernon. It hadn't been done before. And Mrs. Goodpastor wasn't invited. The mailman came. It was the last delivery before the event. She looked hurriedly at each envelope. No invitation. An oversight, perhaps, but Mrs. Goodpastor wasn't used to oversights. And how did she know it was an oversight? Did President Kennedy, himself, say that she couldn't come? Or was it Jackie? Jealous. Jackie was jealous. Bess Truman was never jealous. Even Mamie, the Republican, was nice to Mrs. Goodpastor. Why did Jackie hate her if it wasn't jealousy? Mrs. Goodpastor got up from her chair to look in the mirror.

No, Jackie wasn't jealous.

She remembered that when she was a child she was uncomfortable around old people. Now she was one of them. That miserable man in Hong Kong said she would probably be dead in 1997. But inside she was still the same child. How could her looks not reflect that?

Those young Stevenson demonstrators at the Democratic National Convention just a year ago, had accepted her as one of their own. But she looked different one year ago. She looked different one month ago. Maybe one day ago.

She walked out of her house into the morning stickiness and walked and walked and walked. She found herself looking in the windows of the Eastern Airlines Office on K Street. There was a beautiful poster advertising a visit to Miami. But this wasn't the season. No one went to Miami in July.

She would. Just to get away. Maybe Washington would miss her. They would find out that Mrs. Goodpastor's phone would do nothing more than ring. Mrs. Goodpastor couldn't have gone to Mount Vernon even if she had been invited. She could say she was in Miami.

She called the airline, quickly packed, and taxied to National Airport with her destination of Miami.

She sat on the beach, she took a tour through the Everglades, she visited Seminole Indians, she spent an afternoon in Cypress Gardens, and she felt that Washington must be sick over her disappearance.

On the thirteenth day she flew to Tampa.

That flight was the miracle that transformed Mrs. Goodpastor back into the real Irene Goodpastor that she had known all her life.

"This is Captain Buchanan speaking," the voice came over the speaker. "I'm afraid that our flight has been diverted. One of our passengers, Mr. Oquendo is in the cabin with me and Mr. Oquendo has requested that your Eastern Airline Electra take a little side-trip to Cuba, and I've decided to accommodate him. My apologies for the delay this will cause all our other passengers." Captain Buchanan sounded very calm. A little like

Alan Shepherd with that astronaut-style to his voice. It was as though he was saying that everything was A-O.K. "No problem in the weather and so we should be landing at Havana International Airport in about forty-five minutes from now—thereabouts. From there we'll continue on to Tampa. Thank you."

You're welcome. Mrs. Goodpastor couldn't contain her glee. Her smile broke every wrinkle. And, as her wrinkles vanished, her eyes danced in excitement at what they would say about this when she got back to Washington.

The stewardess tried to calm the frightened passengers, Mrs. Goodpastor not at all among the frightened. She was searching through her purse for her Eastern Airline envelope that contained her boarding pass and her receipt for the ticket. She would have that envelope ready. *If Fidel is at the airport,* she thought, *he better put a note and his signature on it for the parlor wall. Will he recognize me?*

The little girl in her straightened her dress from beneath the seat belt and she excitedly looked out the window for her first glimpse of Cuba—and maybe Castro.

"Fidel, Fidel, Fidel, Fidel, Fidel," she whispered. "Maybe I can talk him into freeing some political prisoners. Let Jackie top that one—that jealous soft-voiced wench!" And then she even thought of a worse word.

Jackie Kennedy didn't know it, but there was a woman on a flight to Havana who was thinking of stealing away her husband. *I don't want to be "the other woman," she thought, but how can I control the president of the United States? It's up to him to think of his family and his position and not to be moved by lust. It's up to him, not me. That young man better control himself when he's around me.*

He would.

TWELVE
THE PADS OF COCOA BEACH
1962

There were many who predicted the end of the world, and they were not the usual group of fanatics who predicted such things with placards hanging around their necks as a call for others to become quick converts to some cult. In contrast to the eternal doomsday professionals, some of those who made such a prediction during October of 1962 were expert analysts of historical and current events.

Stores were quickly sold out of bottled water and canned food and flashlights and transistor radios. Batteries were nowhere to be found. The U.S. Office of Emergency Planning informed all local offices the location of bomb shelters within their areas and other places that could effectively be used for refuge in case of a nuclear attack. The local offices, in turn, told local media outlets.

The two places of the most imminent danger were Washington, D.C., and Cape Canaveral, the latter easily within range of Soviet missiles in Cuba.

On that Monday night in October, President Kennedy told the nation that unmistakable evidence had shown that a series of offensive missile sites had been spotted in Cuba as well as bombers capable of carrying nuclear weapons.

"I call on Chairman Khrushchev," President Kennedy said, "to halt and eliminate this clandestine, reckless and provocative threat to world peace and to stable relations between our two nations." President Kennedy invoked a search of all Soviet ships going to Cuba, and if any ship would be found to be carrying a cargo of offensive weapons, it would be turned back.

The phrase that captured the most attention of the world was the one in which the president stated that it would be the policy of the United States "to regard any nuclear missile launched from Cuba against any nation in the Western Hemisphere as an attack by the Soviet Union on the United States, requiring a full retaliatory response–upon the Soviet Union." His words and his delivery of those words mirrored the risk he knew had to be taken by the United States.

"Let no one doubt that this is a difficult and dangerous effort on which we have set out. No one can foresee precisely what course it will take, or what casualties may be incurred," he continued. "But the greatest danger of all would be to do nothing. The path we have chosen for the present is full of hazards, as all paths are. But it is the one most consistent with our character and courage as a nation. The cost of freedom is always high, but Americans have always paid it. And one path we shall never choose is the path of surrender or submission."

While he was still speaking, Highway A1A in Cocoa Beach, Florida, became filled with a procession of automobiles heading north to Cape Canaveral. In one of those automobiles was Adam Orr. Cape Canaveral and Tyuratam in the Soviet Union might well have been not only the most important places in the world, but the most important places in the universe, unless some beings of which were totally unknown on earth were also engaged in ventures into deep space. That destination gave the drive from Cocoa Beach to the Cape an ominous quality, with a chorus of chirping crickets acting as ushers in the night. Armadillos would creep across the road, sometimes drivers unable to swerve in time to avoid them. To the right was the ocean with its beach that had such hard-packed sand that cars would drive and park there. To the left were palmetto thickets and palms and swamp with an occasional water moccasin exposing itself, creating a quick tubular path from one thicket to the next. And further into the swamp off to the left were alligators who made quick motions and then stopped like statues, artfully camouflaged in their own designs.

That night, October mist hung above the car in slender horizontal columns that were gone under, like going under bridges, and then the mist disappeared to reveal the night sky of Florida in its fullness with so many thousands of stars that their clusters painted large areas of the sky silver, with little room for the black.

The concrete carpet of the straight highway suddenly made a sweep to the left so as to avoid smashing into the orange juice factory with its pungent odors, and the port just beyond it. The road now allowed no turnoffs, requiring the Cape-bound driver to go west for a mile, then north again for a mile, then east for a mile accomplishing a three-mile "U" to the main gate of Cape Canaveral.

There was the guard at the fence that separated the world from the way it had been for the past three billion years, to the way it could be for the next three billion years.

The guard with black pants and the symbol of Pan American Airlines on his white shirt and military type cap, bent down to the driver's window as it was lowered, and he fingered the badge worn by the driver, rubbing it as he looked at the photo on the badge, comparing it to the driver's face. "Mr. Orr," he said, "Good to see you this evening."

"Things okay, Al?"

"So far. I heard the president's speech. We're on high alert. We didn't need orders."

Adam nodded, "See you later." And the drive through Empyrean began.

The world thought of this Cape as a technological enterprise, but to those who knew it well it was a theological masterpiece. Without denomination it was the largest church or synagogue or mosque anywhere; the largest shrine of faith ever built.

After the gateway area, the road turned sharply north again and Adam passed the transmitter building and the liquid oxygen site, and there to the right of the road was the large sign that read "Safety Plan for Today" with numbers listed beneath the "Safety Plan" that had little to do with a safety plan, but instead supplied a code designating the missile-pads that were preparing for launch. To the left he passed Hangers "J" and "K" where new Atlas Missiles that just arrived from San Diego were laying down, resting before being taken to a pad from which they would be erected into a standing position and then launched to places where neither man nor machine had ever traveled. Then he passed the Central Control Building, made an oblique right, and headed toward the launching pads.

He parked near the Ready Room outside the concrete blockhouse of Pad 14. When he turned off the car's ignition and opened the door, surrendering his air conditioned comfort, the night humidity of the Cape enveloped him. Even that seemed important.

The presence of the heavens could not be ignored by anyone who was fortunate enough to be granted entrance to Cape Canaveral that defied cartographers, as its most significant dimension wasn't east to west, or north to south, but rather it was straight up.

Ahead of him, less than 800 feet away, was the giant red-and-white structure called the gantry which was the tower that would embrace and frame the next Atlas after the missile would be erected into place on the yellow iron launcher that rested on the concrete below.

The empty gantry seemed lonely. There was, in its emptiness, an obvious impatience for another space mission which would, like the space missions before it, combine the highest goals of human achievement all mixed together. The gantry had become a temporary meeting place for creativity, technology, medicine, endurance, discovery, invention, adventure, science, astronomy, and religion. With no craft or inspiration excluded, the mix of achievements could create a greater achievement than any of the ones from which it originated.

Adam didn't walk to that tower but went straight to the dome-shaped blockhouse. The walk was short, through another gate, passing the Coke machine, and the two adjoining thick doors to the blockhouse were open just wide enough to allow him to walk inside. If they weren't open he couldn't have opened them by himself since both sides of the concrete-thickness of the doors were enclosed and sealed in steel that could only be moved by cranks that re-set the door's ratchets.

Once inside, there was the rush of air conditioning. And there were the periscopes and walls and aisles of tall vertical computers and recorders and desks with easeled boards that had rows of colored buttons and switches on them, the room lit by fluorescent lights on the ceiling. Straight ahead were four television monitors serving outdoor static cameras aimed at the launching pad. Beneath the television monitors were four analog clocks that told standard time, countdown status, hold time, and zero launch time. That night only the standard time clock was operating.

The blockhouse was empty of human company except for one gray-haired man with a round face and very tired eyes who was sitting at a table facing a small digital countdown clock that was blinking twenty-seven, down to zero in quick red numbers, and then it would start over again, giving the appearance that it could not be turned off. The man turned from watching the clock to the doorway. "Adam!" he said and he stood up.

"Hello, Martin." They shook hands.

"How are you, Adam?"

"I'm all right. Were you waiting long?"

"Only minutes. I just got here."

"Did you have a good flight in?"

"Fine. Any plane that lands safely is a good flight as far as I'm concerned."

Adam gave a slight smile and sat down at the console next to him. "Did you hear the president?"

"I missed the first part, but I heard the end of his speech as soon as I left the airport. He did well from what I heard."

"Did you see any of the photos of the Cuban missile sites?"

He nodded. "All of them. We gave them to him. I briefed him and Sorenson again just before getting on the plane to Orlando."

"Did you? Are the Soviet missiles already on their launchers?"

"No. They better not be. But the launching pads are ready, and Castro has the missiles ready for deployment. And Soviet bombers are being uncrated there. Tomorrow Stevenson will show the pictures at the U.N., if we get a meeting of the Security Council."

"Are we continuing our surveillance?"

He nodded. "U-2s."

"You know, Martin, I feel like I failed you, failed the Agency a couple years ago in Tashkent and Moscow. I never heard from you after that until today."

Martin put his lips together and nodded. "We aren't the most sociable agency in government. It's our duty to be unsociable. Unless there's something to say with a good reason to say it, we don't say anything, even to our own and you know that. That's policy. No confirmation or denial. You know that you can't be sensitive in this business."

"It's not sensitivity. It's just that I know I bungled it, and I can't get it off my mind. Had I succeeded it could have been a real coup. Ponomaryov never contacted me, you know. I never heard from him after I left Moscow. No correspondence. No letter. Nothing."

"Oh, I know. But there's something you don't know. He didn't have time to contact you. Ponomaryov is dead."

Adam gave him a hard stare. "He's dead?"

"You should know this: your meeting with Vladimir Ponomaryov was more meaningful than any of us could have expected."

"Why?"

"Because you met with him on October the 18th. On November the 3rd, Pravda reported that he died of cancer on October the 15th."

"They said he died—before I saw him?"

"Then they reported deaths of a number of their other top people who we knew worked at Tyuratam. Cancer, heart, one car accident, a brain tumor for another, all kinds of things. Little by little, Pravda would have an item that one of them died on one day or another—over the span of a few months."

"What does that mean?"

"It didn't take too much time to put that together with some other pieces of information you gave us—combined with a lot of other things we received from a number of sources, and we recognized that he and many others were killed in an explosion at Tyuratam on the night of October 24th, six days after your meeting. I don't like to go against our 'Need to Know' policy, but in this case I'll change it to 'Deserve to Know.' Their missile blew, destroying the whole pad. The missile didn't get one inch off its launcher. We believe as many as one hundred people were killed in that explosion—including Vladimir Ponomaryov. You saw that pad earlier on your flight from Samarkand to Moscow, before it was a burnt-out ruin. So we have all those dates you gave us. Thanks, Adam. Strangely enough, the information you least expected to be of any use, was the most helpful—that you had a meeting with Vladimir Ponomaryov on October the 18th. And that particular piece of information didn't call for any of your tough memorization techniques. You can stop waiting for a letter from Ponomaryov. He's in no shape to write a letter."

"My heavens, Martin!"

"Feel better? You can stop thinking you failed. Frankly, even if you had worked out a deal with him for you to go to Tyuratam, we think they would have canceled you out after that blow-up."

"But since they knew I saw him when I did, how could they be so dumb as to report he died earlier?"

He shrugged. "That kind of thing is common. Who's 'they?' Their bureaucracy is even worse than ours—as hard as that may be to believe—so some one figuring out dates probably didn't know anything about your visit, or at least regarded it as being unimportant. But enough about that. Let me get to why I'm here."

Adam smiled. He had a great sense of relief from the discarded weight that had been on him for two years. "Shoot!"

"We're on the line here between the FBI and us. But Hoover's boys at the Bureau let us have this one because the domestic side is incidental to the international. There's a man named Guillermo Torrada who works for Central Control here at the Cape. Put someone on him tomorrow morning. Tight. He won't be on the Cape tonight because we've taken care of that, but we need someone with him here every minute starting tomorrow morning. He had a very clean record; a Cuban who's been here since well before Castro took over—during Batista. He's a U.S. citizen, cleared for secret, all of that. But today some of our Bay of Pigs boys told us some very disturbing things about him. They knew him in Cuba. We now have good reason to believe he's on the other side. We're going to get him out of here after this crisis is over, but it's in our interest to keep him here now. We want him monitored. He's working on Jupiter—on Explorer XV."

"That's scheduled for launch next Saturday."

"If there's no scrub. You get someone to be with him on some pretense, someone who knows every switch in Central Control. If he's going to do something for Castro, it may well be this week just to give us some trouble, causing us to go through every missile system. If we had to reappraise the Jupiter we'd be in a lot of trouble."

"Why the Jupiter?"

"You know what Jupiters are, don't you, Adam?

"Of course. They're nothing more than an IRBM, an Intermediate Range Ballistic Missile, with a space probe on top of them instead of a warhead."

"And those IRBMs would be the ones we'd have to use to hit Cuba. Can you see why this might be the time for him to move? We want him watched every second starting tomorrow morning. And the day of the launch–Saturday if it stays on schedule–we want Torrada's arms glued. As you know, all the way up to launch the bird will be controlled by the blockhouse, but right after launch, the power over the bird goes to Central Control and that's–"

"No problem," Adam interrupted. "I can get someone to stay with him and watch him with no problem at all. Where is he now?"

"At this moment?"

"Yes. Now."

"At the Starlite Motel Bar drinking Purple Label Rum. Potent!"

"With one of our Tanyas?"

"With Dee."

"Sharp move, Martin. He's had it. I wouldn't mind being in his shoes tonight."

"He's been trying to put the clamps on her for years. Tonight he scores–not really. But she'll make him believe he will. At Langley we say the difference between their 'swallows' and ours is that our 'swallows' don't swallow. Dee's perfect. She'll keep him on the string. And she's good at it."

"Being kept on the string with Dee would be fun."

"You should know, Adam!"

"No, no. She's a fine girl."

"The best. She can make a man feel the pads of the Cape are nothing compared to the hope of sharing a pad with her in Cocoa Beach. Now, one other thing. Don't stop that home Berlitz course in the Russian language."

"I already did."

"Start it again. There's plenty of time. There's no date set yet but we may want you to take a train ride. You like trains?"

"What's up?"

"Moscow has invited a promiment American to take a trip on the Trans-Siberian Railway. No westerner has ever done it. It goes from Moscow all the way to Vladivostok and passes very close to Tyuratam and a lot of other interesting places. Want to go with him?"

Adam closed his eyes and gave a slow nod. "You bet."

"We can try to work that out. That prominent American has a lot of obligations on his calendar and he doesn't know if their time and his time will coordinate. But he wants to accept the invitation. His trip may take place next year or even the year after that. The windows for him are very short, and you never know if the Soviets will close the windows if he waits forever. But if he goes, we have an interest in you being with him. There should be a lot of good scenery."

"Put me on."

"Some day soon all this will be unnecessary, Adam. We'll have satellites that will be able to see more than anyone's eyes—and remember more than anyone's mind. It won't be long, but we don't know when."

"Until it is, I'm on."

"That's it. Now I can ride back to Orlando and fly back to Langley. Tonight I was your Happy Lee—just a messenger." Martin stood up.

So did Adam. "I think I'll go to the Starlite."

Martin laughed. "Don't try to make a move on Dee. She'll be occupied."

"I can't wait to watch." Clearly Adam was rejuvenated.

"Since when have you been a voyeur?"

"Since about a half hour from now."

The night-drive back to Cocoa Beach had no competing traffic, all of the cars going in the opposite direction, toward the Cape. The marquee of the Polaris Motel that often congratulated successful space shoots and astronaut's recoveries, read, "We Support the president." Next to it was a sign that was always there: a picture of a happy mouse advertising the Polaris' lounge called The Mouse Trap, but tonight the picture of the happy mouse did not look appropriate up there. There was a line-up of stopped cars at the intersection of Highway 520 and A1A outside Bishop's Gulf Service Station, the car's owners waiting to fill their tanks with gasoline in case there had to be a quick getaway. Jake's Bowling Alley was transformed into a place for church services, something done in the past only on Sundays. Ramon's Restaurant and the White Caps seafood place were dark, either because it was felt they should close or because there were no customers to warrant staying open.

Dee Benning and Guillermo Torrada weren't in the Starlite Motel Lounge. And it was highly unusual for Dee to do anything different than a U.S. Government official asked her to do. Now Adam's interest in seeing Dee with Guillermo Torrada was more than curiosity; he was worried. Six years ago when Adam moved to Cocoa Beach, it would have been a cinch to conduct a search of likely public places in the city because there were so few of them. There was nothing more than the Starlite, and the bars at Bernard's Surf and Ramon's. Even if Dee had taken Guillermo Torrada to a motel room, which was most unlikely, she would only have had a choice of the Starlite, or two very small lounge-less places; the Sea Missile and the Sea-Aire. Now Highway A1A had been expanded into a four lane road that became a strip of motels on the beach side of the highway, all with lavish and jumping lounges that had flashing signs outside: there were neon satellites turning and imitation missiles going upwards and all kinds of space-related images in on-and-off lights serving as bright and colorful invitations to come in to the Vanguard and the Koko and the Polaris and the Astro Craft and the Satellite and the Holiday Inn.

To start looking for Dee and her companion, Adam drove the short distance from the Starlite where she wasn't, to the lounge of the Holiday Inn where the search quickly ended.

When Adam walked in, Helen, the organist started playing "Yellow Bird," as she always did when Adam came in. He smiled and nodded at Helen, and in the same glance he saw Dee and what had to be Guillermo Torrada sitting together at a small round table next to the unoccupied dance floor.

"Well, I'll be!" Dee said when she saw Adam. She was luminous, as she always was. And she smiled, as she always smiled with her lips parted, showing a perfect line of straight white teeth, and her blue eyes were flashing all over the lounge. She stood up, and as he came to her, she brushed her blond ponytail from her shoulder to behind her back. Then when he was next to her, she hugged him. "Adam! Sit down. I want you to meet my friend, Guillermo. I call him Guy, because he is one!"

"That's reason enough. How you doing, Guy?" Adam sat down with them. Guy shook hands with Adam, but from his expression, there was no question that Guillermo Torrada would rather have continued to be alone with Dee.

"You know what we're looking for?" Dee put her hand on Adam's forearm. "Maybe you can help us."

"What are you looking for, Dee?" Adam was used to Dee looking for something. She always was.

"Batteries. I went down to the U-Tote 'Em and they didn't have any left. Everyone bought them out in case—you know—in case the big 'it' happens."

Adam shook his head. "I don't think anything else is open now other than maybe Eckerd Drugs on Merritt Island or Winn Dixie or maybe Gaskin's near Patrick. But don't worry. I don't think the big 'it' is going to happen. What do you think, Guy?"

"Oh, I don't know," Guy answered. "Castro is nuts, you know, he's a nut. I come from Cuba, you know, and I know the mentality there." He said "mentality" very slowly since the Purple Label Rum was having some effect on his speech. "Castro, you know, is not only a nut, he's way out. So what does he gain? What does he get by all this?" Some of his words were slurred, especially when it came to a word with an "s."

"You come from Cuba?" Adam asked.

"A long time ago. I left. I couldn't take the mentality, you know, of those people there who were nuts about any nut who came along like a nut."

"Yeah, real nuts," Adam said to play along with Guillermo. Dee had really done her stuff with the rum. "What do you do now, Guy?"

"I'm at the Cape."

"Oh, he's a big man, Adam," Dee said quickly. "Tell him where you work there, Guy."

"I'm not a big man," Guillermo put on a shy look. "I just work at Central Control, that's all. I'm with the Cap-Com on manned flights."

"Oh, that's fine." Adam said.

Dee turned to Guillermo. "Adam is with Pan Am at the Cape."

"Uh-huh." Guillermo wasn't interested.

She turned to Adam. "Adam, you always miss the good nights. You should have been here a couple weeks ago after Wally Schirra's flight," she said flashing that intoxicating smile. "It was a lark. Not like this depression here tonight. Henri was buying champagne for everyone like he always does after an astronaut's flight, and Arthur Godfrey was here, Walter Cronkite was here, Martin was impersonating a German scientist—"

"Martin?" Adam interrupted with a start.

Dee gave a smile, and she winked at Adam. "Martin Caidin!" she explained and she accented the last name, knowing Adam was confusing Martin Caidin with their "secret Martin." "The author—the great author. Anyway, Martin Caidin was impersonating a German scientist, and he was so funny! McNabb was here, and Tom O'Malley, and Shorty Powers, and Jack Kirby were singing 'Hurrah for Schirra' and Alan Shepherd was sitting at the bar right over there, all alone and—"

"I'm surprised you weren't sitting with him," Adam interrupted her again.

"Now, come on. Come on, Adam. I was with Scott Carpenter."

"You were not! Come on, Dee, you weren't with Carpenter!"

"So I wasn't. So what? I was just telling Guy that I know all seven of the astronauts."

"She's telling the truth with that one, Guy. She's cleaned all their teeth. She works for a dentist—for Dr. Buck."

"No, I know them socially! I don't just clean their teeth! We're friends. Just think, I know the seven most famous men in the world! Adam, if they walked in that door right now they wouldn't even know who you are!"

"What difference does it make?"

"Well, it's just that all seven are friends of mine and you don't even know them! That's what! So I'm better than you are!"

"All right, all right, you're better than I am."

"You know, I can name all seven of the astronauts and I only know the name of one of the Wright Brothers: Orville. And I remember that because the young man who cleans out the swimming pool here at the Holiday is named Orville."

"I should have guessed that's how you would know!"

"Tell Guy what you do at the Cape for Pan Am," Dee instructed Adam.

"One of those boring jobs driving from pad to pad to pad to pad checking systems. But it gets me a paycheck and keeps a roof over my head, and food and booze. I even own some batteries. A lot of them."

Dee made a fist and hit Adam on the shoulder. "Then I want them!"

"Not a chance," Adam said to Dee. Adam was amused by her but Guy wasn't because he didn't like this interruption in his rendezvous. "Listen," Adam said, "I'm going to leave you two alone. I want to go up to the bar and see what's going on." He stood up.

"Well, aren't you nice?" Dee said with a frown. "We're going on, that's what's going on. Guy and I are going on, and this may be the last night of all of our lives. Don't you want to sit with us for a while?"

Now Guillermo jumped in, the Purple Label Rum causing him to look either angry or confused or both. "Oh, the last night of our lives! Who says, and what if it is? Look, when your number's up, your numbers up. You know. It's a number's up thing. If they don't do it, if Castro doesn't do it, look, we'd be, you know. So it's just a wait-and-see thing, and you can't. You know. It's a thing like that."

"That's what it is all right," Adam agreed. "It sure is. And the way I feel is that if my number's up at least I'll have some batteries when I go. That's what counts."

Dee laughed. "You!"

Adam ignored her laughter. "No one will say, 'and he didn't even have batteries.' I'm going to the bar."

Dee was still laughing, causing her blond ponytail to bob up and down. She was having fun with her assignment for the night. And she would have no trouble at all keeping her date occupied.

As Adam walked away, Guillermo whispered to Dee, "Are you a turtle, Dee-baby?"

She leaned over and whispered something in his ear, and they both burst out laughing.

All Adam was thinking as he walked to the bar was, *How the devil did this guy ever get a secret clearance?*

Adam stood by the bar, rejecting plenty of available stools. John, the bartender, came over to him. "Hey, Adam. How goes it on this awful night?"

"A-OK, John."

"What a night, huh? Did you hear the speech?"

"I heard it."

"I'll tell you, Adam, when he said if Castro hits anything in the western hemisphere we'd hit Moscow, I nearly hit the floor. But he was right."

"He sure was."

"It's the only way. Castro by himself couldn't threaten us. It's Khrushchev who's standing behind him directing this thing. Kennedy said it the way it is. What do you think will happen?"

"That's why I came here, John, to find out from you. You always know more than we do."

"No answers tonight. The only answer I have is that Dee's boyfriend there is getting drunk. I can't allow him to have any more drinks here."

"Yes, you can. Dee's no fool. She's driving."

"You sure?"

"Positive."

"Hey, Dee!" John, the bartender yelled. "Come here!"
"What do you want?" Dee yelled back from her table.
"Come here! We need you!"
"You, too? John, you're a married man, you don't need me. I'm going to tell Lucy!" But she excused herself from Guillermo Torrada and got up from the table to go to the bar. "Too bad that you need me, John. I have a date already."
"Hey, Dee, come close."
"Oh no, John, not the old 'come close' line!" But she came close.
He whispered, "That guy you're with is looped, Dee. I can't give him any more drinks unless I can have his car keys."
"You don't need them. He won't order any more because we're going. And we're going in my car with me driving. I'm getting hungry and we're going to Bernard's Surf. He can buy me a steak and I'll insist that he eat some of Bernard's chocolate covered grasshoppers and chocolate covered ants and he'll prove he's man enough to do it and he'll get sick. Then we'll go to the A&W Root Beer place on Merritt Island. Root Beer won't mix with the ants he's eaten. Then I'll insist we go to all night bowling at Satellite Beach or Indiatlantic. I've done all this before to turn off men. It works. Maybe by dawn he'll be all sobered up, sick, and angry. Then we'll come back here for him to pick up his car, and I'll go to work."
"Dee," Adam said while he shook his head, "You're something!"
"Adam," Dee said with her magic smile. "You're right!"
She stood on her toes to kiss Adam on the cheek and then she went back to an impatient Guillermo Torrada who craved both a seventh Purple Label Rum that he would not get, and his first Dee Benning that he had even less chance of getting.
What he would get would be a constant surveillance at the Cape for the next five days.

He was caught. But not while he was doing anything that could border on sabotage at Central Control. He did his job perfectly on Explorer XV on Saturday. What caught him was something he said to Dee Benning just hours after the launch. This time they were together at the Koko Lounge while, once again, he was under the spell of both Dee and Purple Label Rum. In a moment of showing off, he told her information that was known that evening only by President Kennedy, Nikita Khrushchev, Ambassador Dobrynin, Fidel Castro, a few intelligence agents and, mysteriously, Guillermo Torrada.
"Want to know a secret, Dee-baby?"
"Oh, Guy, I love secrets, but no one I know has any."
"I do. I know a big one."
"What, Guy? Tell me!"
"Just between you and me."
"Cross my heart and hope to die," she said with her fingers crossed, just like she was a little girl.
"You know those missiles down in Cuba?"

"Yes, of course. What about them?"

"As of two o'clock this afternoon, they're all ready to go. Deployed! They're ready to be launched! What do you think of that?"

"Oh, come on. How would you know? You're just trying to scare me!"

He shook his head. "I have friends in high places."

"In D.C.?"

"Higher places than D.C.!"

"Really? Wow! Where?"

"You know where Nipe Bay is?"

"Never heard of it."

"Cuba! Nipe Bay is in Cuba!"

"So what?"

"Some Soviet soldiers there shot down one of your U-2s!"

"Your?" Did he say "Your U-2's"? He didn't realize he had said it. She didn't comment on his error. Instead she looked very concerned and said in a soothing voice, "Did they? What do you think will happen?"

"This may be our last night, Dee-baby. Don't leave me tonight!"

She yelled, "Hey, you behind the bar! One more!" Then she went to the phone in the lobby and called Martin at Langley.

President Kennedy had his hands full, more so than any other night of the crisis, more than any other night of his life. His informal team of advisors on the crisis, which came to be known as ExCom, were beginning to fight among themselves, and all of them were worn out from exhaustion. The membership of ExCom had increased, then diminished in size as the days had gone on, and settled on some thirty men with most of them catching only a few hours of sleep in their offices each night. That Saturday night the president told them to go home for a break and spend the night with their families. The president said there wouldn't be a meeting until ten in the morning, and by then they could be reasonably refreshed.

In the morning, he planned to order air strikes against Cuba.

Before going home, some of the ExCom members continued talking to each other, discussing the assets and liabilities of making a deal with Khrushchev:

"If we want to avoid war we have to compromise. Stevenson is right. There has to be a compromise—a deal."

"Soviet missiles out of Cuba, and U.S. missiles out of Turkey—even out of Italy."

"And good-bye to NATO?"

"It won't kill NATO. Look. We already made a deal. The president wrote Krushchev today, giving assurances against an invasion of Cuba. Think he'll bite?"

"We might have to close down Guantanamo."

"You've got to give Khrushchev a way out. If he feels he's trapped into a corner, he'll go to war. You know how the president feels about the importance of giving Khrushchev a way to save face—that we shouldn't block all exits. He said we can't make a deal, but you always leave a path."

"By tomorrow morning we're going to be at war."

"If so, Cuba will be dust."

"Cuba will be a one-front war only for hours. Khrushchev won't let us choose the battleground. If there's no deal and we make war in Cuba, Khrushchev will make war in Berlin."

While they left the corridors of the White House that Saturday night, President Kennedy was walking in the colonnade to the White House theater with David Powers. The president's hands were in his jacket pockets, and he was slightly stooped. The burden was becoming visible. He heard footsteps on the pavement of the portico behind him and the president and Powers turned around to a lone figure walking to the East Wing. "Cody!" the president called to the youngest member of ExCom.

Cody Cooper turned around quickly. "Yes, sir."

"You don't have a family in the District, do you?"

"No, sir. My folks are in Detroit."

"Do you want to join Dave and me and see *Roman Holiday*?" Dave Powers quickly walked in the theater in case the president wanted to talk to Cody alone.

"Thank you, Mister President. I think I better get to sleep." To decline an invitation like that from the president was something Cody thought he would never do, but he was almost in a state of collapse. It would be better to fall asleep at home rather than in the theater with the president there.

"I think that's a good idea," the president said. Cody was always more conscious than others of the president's New England accent, and that accent seemed to get more pronounced when he was tense. "Idea" sounded more like "idear." "We just thought we'd rather think about Rome for a couple hours rather than Cuba." And "Cuba" sounded more like "Cuber." The president was trying to act as though he was calm and unworried. He took his right hand out of his jacket's side pocket and reached into his upper pocket to take out a cigar. He pointed the unlit cigar at Cody. "You go home, Cody. You get a good night's rest." He put the cigar in his mouth, then quickly took it out. "You smoke cigars? I've got some more here. (maw heah) They're good. They're Uppman's."

"No sir, thank you."

"These have been difficult days—and nights. You've been sleeping in your office, haven't you?"

"Yes, sir."

The president gave an assuring smile. "Don't worry, Cody. We—uh—we're going to have this behind us soon."

Cody nodded, but his nod was slow and seemed to lack meaning. "Thank you, sir."

The president smiled. "Do you doubt that, Cody?"

"No, sir. I don't."

"Did you ever hear this poem? Bullfight critics row on row crowded the enormous Plaza de Toros. But only one is there who knows, and he is the one who fights the bull."

Cody smiled.

Even at the height of crisis, the president was attempting to reassure a mid-staff assistant. "I have to fight the bull, but remember (re-membuh) that you have to give me a hand."

"Yes, sir. We all have great respect for all you've done, Mr. President."

"There is nothing I have done that you can't do. So you just–uh–you just get a good night's rest," the president said, "and we'll–we'll all take care of what needs to be taken care of, tomorrow."

"Yes, sir. Thank you. Good night, Mister President."

As the others left the White House Compound, the ExCom members who did have families were handed a sealed manila envelope by a Secret Service Agent. They were instructed to give it to their closest family member, and for that member to open it only in case of a national emergency. Inside the envelope were instructions of where the family members should go in a nuclear attack. It would not be the same place as the ones who brought the envelopes home.

"Cody?" the Secret Service Agent stopped Cody as he was leaving the West Wing.

"Yes?"

"You have your pass for Mount Weather on your person?"

"Yes. I always do."

"Can I see it?"

Cody nodded, and took it from his side pocket.

"Good. Just checking. Good night."

That was more than he learned from the president. Could it be that tomorrow he would be in the secret Virginia mountain facility as part of the surviving United States government, while around their shelter would be nuclear destruction?

At that moment, Attorney General Robert Kennedy was at the Justice Department with Soviet Ambassador Anatoli Dobrynin sitting across from him. When Ambassador Dobrynin asked what President Kennedy was willing to do about the U.S. missiles in Turkey, Attorney General Kennedy said he thought the president ordered them removed some time ago and they would be gone in four or five months after the crisis. The Attorney General further told the Ambassador that if the Soviets didn't commit to removing the Soviet missiles and bombers from Cuba as soon as they could load them onto ships, the United States would remove them.

Dobrynin contacted Chairman Khrushchev.

On Sunday morning, October the 28th, Chairman Nikita Khrushchev sent President Kennedy the message that the Soviet Union would have the missiles removed from the Cuban launching pads, and they would shortly be loaded on to ships which would be ordered to go back to the Soviet Union.

Six nights later President Kennedy had the confirmation that the procedure had started, and he announced that confirmation to the nation.

The morning sun rose without any barrier of haze between it and all of eastern Florida, and the sky was pure blue without a trace of a cloud. Cocoa Beach was glowing again, restored in a giant sigh of normality outside the motels, the homes, the offices, and the stores.

Outside the Polaris Motel, a man in plaid Bermuda shorts and a white T-shirt was standing on a ladder changing the letters of the motel's marquee with its letters of support for the president dangling sideways and upside down, and other letters were replacing them, the sign's new message still imperceptible. The picture of the happy mouse advertising the Polaris' lounge, The Mouse Trap, was more appropriate than it had been recently but it still seemed perverse, since signs advertising lounges should only be visible at night. Jack Bishop at Bishop's Gulf Service Station was gassing up one car without any line of cars waiting behind it. Jake's Bowling Alley was not closed for special church services, Ramon's Restaurant and the White Caps seafood restaurant displayed large signs announcing their normal opening times. And there were plenty of batteries delivered to the U Tote 'Em, but now no one was in a hurry to purchase them.

Adam was back to studying a Berlitz Russian language home course, Guillermo Torrada was in custody, and Dee Benning was cleaning teeth in Dr. Buck's office.

Cody Cooper and all the ExCom members received a small Tiffany silver calendar of October. The dates of 16 through 28 were engraved deeper than the rest. On the lower left of the one he gave Cody were the initials "C.C." and on the lower right were the initials, "J.F.K."

With nine words from the president, millions of people returned to the life they had feared would not be lived. "The Soviet missile bases in Cuba are being dismantled."

THIRTEEN
LET THEM COME TO BERLIN
1963

"I saw Hitler speak right there," the tall, blond driver said to Ted and Linda Murphy as they passed by what was left of the old Berlin Olympia Stadium. "I was there. I was only nine years old, but I saw him."

What was chilling was the driver's tone. There was sadness in it, and he was saying it with a sense of pride. In that one short statement he let it be known three times that he was in the presence of Hitler.

"That must be some memory," Linda Murphy said because she felt she had to say something or silence would linger, giving more emphasis to his statement.

"Oh, yes," the driver said, his eyes looking straight ahead at the road. "His bunker where he died is on the Reichskanzlei in the rubble of the bombing on the other side of the Wall. You can see it because you're Americans. I can't. I'm German. You can go through Checkpoint Charlie. His bunker is just steps away from there. I can't take you there. We—we West Germans can't get across to see it." Where "he died"? Or where he committed suicide? "You have to show them all the currency you bring in and they give your passport a long going-over, but you can get in. Not me—or they may keep me there."

Ted leaned forward toward the driver from the backseat where he and Linda were sitting. "You were in Berlin durin' the war?"

"I never left," and again he talked with a sense of pride. "Even during the heaviest bombing of your planes, my family stayed."

The Murphys didn't want to take a chance on exchanging a glance between them because the car's rear-view mirror would have captured that glance for the driver.

"Well, all that is done," Linda Murphy said. "The war has been over almost twenty years now."

"Eighteen," he corrected and then he became more precise. "Eighteen years and one-and-one-half months."

And then Ted Murphy blurted out what he couldn't hold in. "What did your family do durin' the war?"

He answered with immediacy. "My father was a ski instructor and my mother took care of the children." Another ski instructor? He was one of many they had met in Germany who said that in one way or another they had a connection with ski instruction during the war. Was it a nation of ski instructors during the war? Didn't anyone have anything to do with the Nazis?

"It must have been rough," Linda said.

"Look," the driver said pointing to the left through the driver's side window. "You can still see the bullet holes in those buildings."

"From the war?" Linda asked.

"Oh, yes. You'll find bullet holes all over buildings and houses. They are still in the walls of my family's home. Not just outside, but inside."

"How horrible."

"There is the Kempinski Hotel, straight ahead." he said. "It's better than the Hilton. You'll like it better. The Hilton isn't on the Kurfurstendamm, you know. The Kurfurstendamm is one of the great avenues of the world. There's nothing near the Hilton except Embassy Buildings bombed out by your planes."

Why mention the Hilton? To mention the bombing of embassies?

"Look behind you now. You see the Kaiser Wilhelm Church down there? That church was beautiful before the war. Now it's a bombed out skeleton of a church. We're going to leave it that way as a memorial, I think. It's good to do that. Let them see." *Who is "them" who should "see"?* "You are fortunate to have a room. Berlin is booked for your president's arrival tomorrow."

"It was booked for us a long time ago, really for Ted," Linda said. "Ted's a writer and he's doing an article on some of the stops on President Kennedy's trip, so the newspaper booked the hotels for us, and took care of everything—even the car—and getting you to be our driver throughout our trip here," and she gave a forced and uncomfortable laugh.

"The Kempinski is better," he said as though what she said was not worthy of attention. "It's ours." *What did that mean? Was the Hilton "theirs"?* "How do you like our Kudamm?"

"A Kudamm?" Linda asked.

"This. Where we are. The Kurfurstendamm. The avenue," as though she should have known. "We call it the Kudamm. Do you like it? Is it not beautiful? You can shop here or sit outside and have coffee and watch the day go by. You see?"

"It's beautiful."

"I like Americans," he lied, but it was almost the end of the ride and the beginning of the tip. "You saved our city from the Russians during the airlift," and he stopped in front of the Kempinski Hotel.

"Well, that wasn't my doin'," Ted Murphy said as he dug in his pocket for a tip. "I didn't bomb you in the war or save you after it."

Linda looked at Ted with surprise. "But we were all for the airlift," she explained in an attempt to repair Ted's remark. By her singling out the airlift she intentionally left the implication that maybe they weren't for the bombing. Ted and Linda Murphy were not typical Americans and their driver was not a typical German and all three deserved each other in their forced closeness.

Ted and Linda Murphy did what every American visitor did in the city. After they checked in, they went promptly out to see the Berlin Wall that surrounded West Berlin.

It was always easy to find, sometimes close and sometimes distant, but no matter the direction of travel, the Wall would come onto the horizon and seal the path of travel in a rude and horrible display of governmental perversity.

Seeing the Wall, particularly in the early days of its existence, before graffiti changed its appearance into a multi-colored teenage palette, was an experience that was dagger-like, piercing the viewer into revulsion and disbelief that this was not an historian's find or an archeological dig being moved to a museum. There was no tourist guide nearby talking about times past. This was part of now, with Soviets and East German soldiers making it taller each day, and each day there was new barbed wire being put on top of it, or new chips of glass being glued to the elevations where barbed wire couldn't be laid, or more windows being bricked up to become a section of it, or the emptiness of the no-man's land being widened, or higher watchtowers being erected to afford an easier site to catch and kill anyone trying to cross into the west. At night brilliant lights were spotted down from the towers just as the same kind of lights were used to shine from watchtowers into courtyards of prisons.

"Keep your distance from it," the Murphys were told by a West Berliner who was putting flowers on the cross for Peter Fechter, the placement of the flowers close to where Peter Fechter was murdered by East German guards in his attempt to cross the Wall into the west. "Touch that Wall and you are out of the western sector," they were told, "since it is built on their side of the zone, and those guards on the watchtowers sometimes pleasure in aiming their rifles at those on this side who feel or chip the Wall." They were later told that it was often playful aiming meant to intimidate, but there was no comedy in having a rifle aimed at your skull by a uniformed stranger, nor was their any comfort in knowing their bullets were largely reserved for East Germans who risked their lives in the attempt to go over or under the Wall or through the barriers leading to it. Recognition of that fact only served as proof of the primitive savagery of the builders and the overseers and the maintenance-keepers of that structure that circled the circumference of West Berlin and transformed the city into an island surrounded by, not shark-infested water, but shark-infested land.

There had never been anything like it. Never. Throughout the history of man, there had been many city walls constructed to keep invaders out, but never a city wall before this one, to keep its people in.

That depravity of government was fueled by quirks of both history and geography: When World War II was going into its final phases, an Allied conference was held in London to make preparations for a defeated Germany. The country was to be divided into zones of occupation by the Allies; the United States, Great Britain, France, and the Soviet Union. That division was to remain in effect until free elections could take place in Germany as a whole.

Berlin was in the Soviet Zone. But Berlin had been the capital and heart of all Germany before the war. Therefore it was decided that the city of Berlin would also be split into four occupying sectors; a U.S. Zone, a British Zone, a French Zone, and a Soviet Zone and, it was planned, when the occupation was done, Berlin would be the capital of a unified Germany, as it was before the war. In violation of the Four Powers Agreement, the Soviet Union made the sector of Berlin they occupied into a part of the Soviet Zone of the country. They called their zone of Germany the German Democratic Republic, with the sector of Berlin they held as its capital. That left the other three sectors of Berlin as a geographical and political unit surrounded by Soviet-occupied Germany.

In a kind of political shorthand, the Soviet sector of Germany was becoming referred to as East Germany, and because of Berlin's special status, the Soviet sector of that city was known as East Berlin.

The United States, Great Britain, and France jointly decided to establish a democratic state with free elections in the zones they occupied in Germany. They called this democratic state the Federal Republic of Germany with Bonn as its capital. Officially, Bonn was designated as a temporary capital until all of Germany could be united as one. In the new shorthand style, this was called West Germany. This entity could not, however, include any part of distant Berlin, so the U.S., British, and French zones of Berlin were accorded a separate status. Those three zones of that city would operate as one, officially not part of the Federal Republic of Germany, but enjoying an association with it in political and economic freedoms, with the United States, Great Britain, and France serving as its protectorates in the zones they occupied. It was referred to as West Berlin.

In June of 1948, a blockade was established by the Soviet Union so that West Berlin would be isolated from the outside world and literally starved to death. President Truman ordered an airlift which brought 2.3 million tons of supplies to West Berlin in airplanes landing within minutes of each other, day and night, at West Berlin's Tempelhof Airport. The corridor in the sky was never vacant, serving as a lifeline in the air. The Soviet Union thought the West would soon tire of providing the airlift, but there was no tiring. And so eleven months after invoking the blockade, the Soviet Union gave up on it.

There was fast becoming a marked contrast between the Soviet sector of Berlin with the other sectors of Berlin. Both politically and economically, the U.S., British, and French zones, operating as one, were free and active and construction was widespread with life markedly better than in East Berlin or any part of East Germany. The population of East Berlin was starting to dwindle as more and more East Berliners, along with other East Germans, crossed into the easily accessible West Berlin.

By 1961 some three million East Berliners and East Germans had left the East to go to or through West Berlin to freedom. The steady stream turned into a massive continuing exodus, and by August of 1961, over two thousand a day were leaving into West Berlin.

On August the 13th of that year, a wall started to be built by the Soviet and East German military; a wall encircling West Berlin. On Bernauer Strasse and other streets that bordered West and East, bricks were placed in the windows of the apartment buildings that were on the eastern side, overlooking the west. The Wall soon became sixty-seven miles of concrete, thirty-five miles of metal plates, five-and-one-half miles of bricked up windows in buildings, and three miles of barbed wire. And there were the guard dogs, the land mines, the self-firing machine guns, and there were guards in pairs, each ordered to shoot the other should one see the other make a motion towards fleeing to the West.

In June of 1963, the month of President Kennedy's visit, ninety East Germans succeeded in escaping and three were killed in their attempts.

On the morning of June the 26th, the Murphys were taken by their weird driver to Checkpoint Charlie for the president's arrival there. Most people were kept away from this more personal event, but the Murphys had a press pass that entitled them to witness the president's first look at the Wall.

President Kennedy, along with West Berlin Mayor Willy Brandt, walked up the wooden stairway on the riser near the checkpoint to look over the Wall into the East. Ted Murphy chipped at the Wall with his Swiss Army jackknife, showing no fear of the East German guard who had him in dead aim.

It would have taken an absolute fool to shoot Murphy across the Wall in the presence of the president of the United States. With pride in his ability to remain unintimidated, Ted put a small piece of the Wall in his pocket.

The president stared at the sight laid before him: the barren and desolate streets of East Berlin vacant of people and without a building in view that was constructed since the end of the war. In contrast to the excitement and vitality and modern sights of West Berlin, East Berlin appeared to be a ghost town or worse. A pall hung over it onto those streets. Its grayness was a carbon copy of Moscow. The president said no public words as he stood on that structure near Checkpoint Charlie, but there was a public statement written all over his face.

He walked down from the platform and passed right by Ted and Linda Murphy. "Good to see you, Mister President," Linda said but he didn't hear or didn't want to acknowledge any statement with a forced smile or a shake of the hand. Not at that moment.

"He didn't hear you," Ted said, feeling sorry for her in the wake of her being ignored by the president of the United States. "Look what I got!" He reached in his pocket, clenched something, raised his hand and opened the palm to show her his conquest. It was what appeared to her to be a very small stone, just slightly larger than a pebble.

"What's that?"

"A piece of the Wall."

"Hey, good for you. You chipped it off?"

He nodded. "Now, let's get back to the car. Let's get to the Square before he starts his speech."

"At least I saw him—and real close!"

"You were close. But the president didn't see you or he would have answered you. He might even have canceled the rest of his trip if he had to, to keep talkin' with you."

She smiled. "I don't think so. But I would have canceled the rest of mine to be with him."

Ted Murphy smiled because she was kidding.

Maybe.

It was not going to be easy to get from Checkpoint Charlie to the site of the president's major public address, since the motorcade of the president was preceding them, and there were blocked-off streets and there were crowds all over the place, but their driver was well accomplished in the art of maneuvering in West Berlin traffic.

"You know where we're supposed to go?" Ted Murphy asked.

"You will be there before the president," the driver assured him. "He's speaking outside the Schoneberger Rathaus, which is our Town Hall, in Rudolph Wilde Platz."

"Good. Just get us to the Platz in time," he instructed in words and a cadence that he borrowed from *My Fair Lady.*

"Don't worry, Ted," Linda said. "Kennedy's going to have lunch there first."

"No he isn't. He's going to have lunch there second. First he gives the speech and I got to catch that or the whole trip is a bust–a flop–the end –fini–no articles–no firsthand information to write about–exit–goodbye, ol' Ted Murphy."

"Mr. Murphy," the driver said. "Your trip will be successful if it rests on getting to the Rudolph Wilde Platz before your president speaks. Once an order is given, I know how to carry it out."

That was a remark that would have been better left unsaid.

"I have faith in you," Ted had to admit. "I'm just worried. Listen, you get us there in time and I'll give you fifty marks."

There was no response. In minutes, they magically arrived just three blocks away from the giant open-air plaza and the driver said it was as close as he was allowed to get. He said he would be there for them after the event. They walked the short distance and got there before the president made his appearance.

Their passes did them no good but one of the journalists recognized Ted and escorted him and Linda, pushing their way through a group of schoolboys in short leather pants with jumper straps criss-crossing their chests and backpacks with books mounted on each one of their backs. The Murphy's escort pushed and shoved and he and the Murphys managed to fight their way to the press section which the Murphys never would have found by themselves.

The setting was magnificent, like something out of ancient Rome before the entrance of Caesar. The crowd stretched well beyond the horizon where loudspeakers were mounted for those too distant to even see the newly constructed platform from which the president was going to speak, with huge red, white, and blue banners behind it, furling in the breeze.

When the president appeared there were thousands and thousands shouting in unison, "Ken-ne-dy! Ken-ne-dy!" Not even in a U.S. political convention had such emotional cheering been heard.

Then he gave a speech that could more accurately be defined as a piece of magnificent poetry rather than political rhetoric:

"There are many people in the world who really don't understand, or say they don't, what is the great issue between the free world and the communist world.

"Let them come to Berlin!

"There are some who say that communism is the wave of the future.

"Let them come to Berlin!

"And there are some who say in Europe and elsewhere that we can work with the communists.

"Let them come to Berlin!

"And there are even a few who say that it is true that communism is an evil system, but it permits us to make economic progress.

"*Lass' sie nach Berlin kommen!* Let them come to Berlin!"

And he concluded with, "All free men, wherever they may live, are citizens of Berlin, and, therefore, as a free man, I take pride in the words, *"Ich bin ein Berliner!"*

At that statement in which he announced that he was a Berliner, the crowd created a deafening chorus of cheers and applause and there were tears streaming down cheeks and there were the cries again of "Ken-ne-dy! Ken-ne-dy!"

The president walked to one side of the platform and shook hands with Mayor Brandt and then with West German chancellor Konrad Adenauer and U.S. Ambassador George McGhee. And then the president brushed his hair back that had gone all over his forehead from the breeze, and he looked ill-at-ease in trying to find a graceful exit.

His self-consciousness didn't last long as he was escorted toward the building's entrance where he was going to make another address for those attending lunch. On the way in, to the distress of the U.S. Secret Service and West German Security, he was swamped with people storming around him, including Ted and Linda Murphy.

That evening Ted Murphy stayed in their hotel room writing his "Murphy's Law" column for syndication in the United States. His column was destined to make him the hero of a very small but an emerging wing of the Democrats, with Ted Murphy writing, "the United States is going down a dark road in quest of enemies. George Washington asked us in his farewell address, 'Why quit our own, to stand upon foreign ground? Why, by interweaving our destiny with any part of Europe, entangle our peace and prosperity in the toils of European ambition, rivalship, interest, humor or caprice? 'Tis our true policy to steer clear of permanent alliances with any portion of the foreign world.'

"And even Dwight Eisenhower," Ted Murphy continued to write, "the military conqueror of the European Theater in World War II, told us in his farewell address three Januarys ago that 'in the councils of government, we must guard against the acquisition of unwarranted influence, whether sought or unsought, by the military-industrial complex. The potential for the disastrous rise of misplaced power exists and will persist.

"It is ironic that in having John Kennedy as president, who won his election with the help of this columnist's vote against Nixon, we find ourselves in the midst of Cold War threats that were raised to a new and more dangerous height today in Berlin. Eight months ago he took us to the brink of nuclear war over Cuba, of all places. Our president made the purchase of a nuclear shelter fashionable. We can be sure that Nixon would have done no better, but what we thought was the more sensible Kennedy, treated us last October, and again today, to fire-breathing oratory. Some president in the near future better deal with the realization that communism is not an enemy, but an idea. And if we are the country of ideas, we shouldn't perceive the Soviets or the East Germans as hostile forces. Our president should bite his lip before giving speeches with fancy phrases designed to elicit applause from foreigners. He should remember that the United States, with our system, is here to stay, and the Soviet Union, with its system, is here to stay. Co-existence and mutual respect is the only path to keep the peace."

Four days later, Pope Paul VI was coronated in Vatican Square to fill the vacancy left by the death of Pope John XXIII.

"Mister President," Cody Cooper said to the president aboard Air Force One as it was flying from England to Italy, "there were 200,000 people in the square for the Pope's coronation. You had 250,000 outside the City Hall in Berlin."

President Kennedy looked ill-at-ease with what might have been an irreverent comparison, but he said, "250,000, Cody?" The president smiled. Competitions with the Pope (if it was proper to call them that) were infrequent and rarely won.

On this trip there were a lot of winners. There was recognition by many that President Kennedy gave one of the best foreign policy speeches ever delivered by anyone, Linda Murphy at least came close to the president, and did it twice in one day, Ted Murphy wrote a column destined to enhance both his point of view and his name recognition, and best of all for him, he wasn't murdered by an East German guard at the Wall. And the Murphy's Nazi driver got a big tip for getting them to the Platz on time.

There was not good news for an unidentified man and woman who made an attempt to get from East Berlin to West Berlin that evening across the no-man's-land near Bernauer Strasse. In West Berlin gun shots could be heard from the other side of the Wall, and two East German guards were seen dragging two bodies away.

"There are many people in the world who really don't understand, or say they don't, what is the great issue between the free world and the communist world," President Kennedy had said. "Let them come to Berlin."

But the Murphys had come to Berlin, and they still didn't understand.

FOURTEEN
DRUMS
1963

Thursday, November 21, 1963 was the last full day in which the United States walked without a limp.

The next day there came the most incredible bullet. No matter what the Warren Commission Report would say, the bullet went in and out of President Kennedy, killing him and wounding every one else in the nation.

No one old enough to remember could ever forget what he or she was doing when the news was learned, because that was the moment when the bullet seared through their own flesh, never to be removed.

It was at the time seemingly impossible to have happened. Assassinations were far back in the American past in a different kind of world with a different kind of people. Assassinations were in costume. This tragedy had no place in the times of thin lapels and Chubby Checker, the twist, Andy Warhol, John Glenn, freedom marchers, Boeing 707s, Ingmar Johanson, hula hoops, open-heart surgery, Listerine mouthwash, and Kellogg's cereals. It was impossible. He would recover.

But Air Force One brought back his body, not his life.

There was no sound other than drums. To those who heard the drums, the sound was a continuing rhythm that repeated over and over inside of them.

With such a national wound, from that date forward, America was different:

U.S. military involvement in Vietnam, which was known to be an heroic effort on November the 21st with its Green Berets and other Americans fighting for the liberty of others, became perceived by the young as immoral and unjust as 1963 ended.

Drugs that were taboo on November the 21st became inviting and inhaled and injected before the end of 1963.

Sex acts that were only whispered about by the young on November the 21st became a challenge before the end of 1963.

The overwhelming quest was to do everything and to do it now because tomorrow, life may be gone. His was.

That morning in Fort Worth, Cody Cooper reminded the president that it was John Nance Garner's 95th birthday. John Nance Garner was President Franklin D. Roosevelt's first vice president. President Kennedy telephoned the former vice president to wish him a happy birthday. President Kennedy felt the former vice president did not have long to live. What, of course, was unknown was that the former vice president had four more years to live, while President Kennedy had less than four more hours. By the markers of life's end, President Kennedy was older than former vice president Garner.

As the news of the assassination of President Kennedy spread throughout the world, expressions of disbelief and grief started coming from everywhere.

At U.S. Embassies and Consulates from Paris to Ouagadougou, from Mexico City to Dar es Salaam, from Tokyo to Jiddah, there were lines of people entering to sign books of condolences. Never before had so many people of the world taken such a unified pause in the things they regularly did, and not because of a government directive, but because of individual expressions of grief.

The largest assemblage of world leaders in history came to Washington to attend his funeral. There were representatives from 92 nations including Prince Philip and Prime Minister Sir Alec Douglas-Home of Great Britain, Emperor Haile Selassie of Ethiopia, President Charles de Gaulle of France, Mayor Willy Brandt of West Berlin, the Shah of Iran, and Queen Frederika of Greece.

The door to Cody Cooper's office was closed. His head was resting in his hands and he didn't even have the strength to turn on the light. In front of him, on his desk, just in front of the Tiffany's silver calendar of October 1962, were the texts of the speeches President Kennedy had planned on delivering in Dallas and Austin.

"Above all, words alone are not enough," the unheard text read. "The United States is a peaceful nation, and where our strength and determination are clear, our words need merely to convey conviction, not belligerence. If we are strong, our strength will speak for itself. If we are weak, words will be of no help. It was not the Monroe Doctrine that kept all Europe away from this hemisphere–it was the strength of the British fleet and the width of the Atlantic Ocean. It was not General Marshall's speech at Harvard which kept communism out of Western Europe–it was the strength and stability made possible by our military and economic assistance. In this administration also it has been necessary at times to issue specific warnings–warnings that we could not stand by and watch the communists conquer Laos by force, or intervene in the Congo, or swallow West Berlin, or maintain offensive missiles in Cuba. But while our goals were at least temporarily obtained in these and other instances, our successful defense of freedom was due not to the words we used, but to the strength we stood ready to use on behalf of the principles we stand ready to defend....

"American military might should not and need not stand alone against the ambitions of international communism. Our security and strength, in the last analysis, directly depend on the security and strength of others, and that is why our military and economic assistance plays such a key role in enabling those who live on the periphery of the communist world to maintain their independence of choice. Our assistance to these nations can be painful, risky and costly, as is true in Southeast Asia today. But we dare not weary of the task....

"I pledged in 1960 to build a national defense which was second to none—a position I said, which is not 'first but,' not 'first if,' not 'first when' but first—period. The pledge has been fulfilled. In the past three years we have increased our defense budget by over 20 percent...doubled the number of nuclear weapons available in the strategic alert forces; increased the tactical nuclear forces deployed in Western Europe by 60 percent...and increased our special counter-insurgency forces by 600 percent.

"Almost everywhere we look, the story is the same. In Latin America, in Africa, in Asia, in the councils of the world and in the jungles of far-off nations, there is now renewed confidence in our country and our convictions....

"We in this country, in this generation, are—by destiny rather than choice—the watchmen on the walls of world freedom. We ask, therefore, that we may be worthy of our power and responsibility, that we may exercise our strength with wisdom and restraint, and that we may achieve in our time and for all time the ancient vision of 'peace on earth, good will toward men.' That must always be our goal, and the righteousness of our cause must underlie our strength. For as was written long ago: 'except the Lord keep the city, the watchman waketh but in vain.'"

"What are the rules?" Cody asked himself in the darkness of his office. "What are the rules on undelivered texts of a president; undelivered because of assassination? Do these speeches become part of history or am I supposed to destroy them?" Dallas and Austin would never be host to those words, as had been intended, but was their fate to be the wastebasket of Cody Cooper?

He put them aside and lowered his head back into his cupped hands.

Sunday night the center of the globe was the rotunda of the U.S. Capitol Building, which sheltered the remains of the former president.

Cody had stood by his flag-draped coffin the night before when it rested in the East Room of the White House. Now that the caisson had taken his body from the White House to the rotunda of the Capitol, Cody felt totally alone. The entire White House compound was, to him, an unimportant structure for the first time. The importance was the black crepe that hung over the north portico. The remains of the man who had become his inspiration had been taken in a horse-drawn caisson up Pennsylvania Avenue.

Through Sunday night and then into the morning, a quarter of a million people had walked past the president's bier in the U.S. Capitol.

"Why did this happen?" Captain Jonas Valadovich said that night, doubting the existence of God. After walking through the rotunda to be near the coffin, he paused outside the west exit and he leaned against the Capitol's exterior wall. A priest came over to him and said something and Captain Valadovich walked away.

Then Captain Valadovich walked around the building and went to the far end of the line to start through again because there was no other reasonable way to spend the time. Sleep was neither reasonable, nor even possible.

"Hello, Captain," the man ahead of him said. The man was holding hands with a small woman and they both were turned toward the captain.

"Good evening, sir," Captain Valadovich nodded.

The small woman shook her head. "No, it isn't a good evening, is it?" She wore a Kennedy-Johnson button on her coat. A tribute of sorts.

"No, it certainly isn't, ma'am," Captain Valadovich rethought.

"You from here?" the man asked.

"Yes, sir," the captain nodded. "I'm stationed up at the Pentagon right now and doing some work at Fort Myer, right across the bridge."

"We drove from Buffalo, New York. We just got here. We had to park a mile away."

Captain Valadovich nodded again. "You both must be tired."

"No, not now," the man said. "We had to be here."

"We want to be here," the woman said quickly, correcting him.

"I know," the captain said, "I know." He gestured his head toward the campaign button on her coat. "You were a big fan of his, ma'am?"

"No," she said. "No, but yes. I don't know what I was but I can't stand–this. This–thing." She couldn't say "his assassination" or "his murder" or "the killing" or "his death." She reached in her very large purse and pulled out a small bag of Fritos. "Do you want some Fritos?"

Captain Valadovich shook his head, "No thank you, ma'am."

Most people in the rear of the line were talking. Their voices assured each other that life was still going on, but as each person came closer to the Capitol the talking tapered off, and by the time they reached the steps they became mute. There was no sound there at all except for the shuffling of shoes. Something happened at the moment of the first step on that stairway. It happened to every one in that giant procession. The realities of the tragedy hit again just as though it was first heard. And, in spite of the long wait, most felt they didn't want to go up the steps and into the rotunda because that would be the confirmation of the horror. But it was still the only place in the world to be.

It was almost dawn when Captain Valadovich and his two companions from Buffalo entered the rotunda.

Stillness. Weeping. Four military men standing at attention by each corner of his flag-draped coffin. That's all there was to see–and it was too much.

When it was done, the captain and the couple walked slowly down the west stairway, facing the large expanse of Washington. The sun, low on the horizon behind them, had made its appearance while they were inside and now all the buildings to the west were visible.

"That's it," the man said because he couldn't think of anything else to say to the captain, but they couldn't just walk away from each other without saying anything.

"Do you want to have breakfast with us?" the woman offered.

"No thank you, ma'am," Captain Valadovich said. "I need to go back on duty pretty soon."

They shook hands and parted.

Their lives had interlocked that important night but he would never see the couple again. Captain Valadovich thought of that as he walked through the West Capitol grounds to the mall, and for the first time since Friday, he smiled. Life and death were not exactly as he had believed just the night before. Maybe it was the early hour and his tiredness that made him think differently, but thinking differently made more sense than the way he had thought before he entered the Capitol for the second time.

Who was dead? John Kennedy or the couple with whom he had just visited? He wouldn't see any of the three again. Surely, to Captain Valadovich, John Kennedy was the most alive of the three because he inhabited more of the captain's mind and would make his presence felt more often through the captain's life than the thought of the couple from Buffalo. For all intents and purposes, the couple from Buffalo would hardly be remembered.

He walked all the way to the Lincoln Memorial where his new thoughts were validated. There was President Lincoln whom he had been told was assassinated almost one hundred years ago, murdered long before the captain was born. But he knew more about President Lincoln than he knew about most people who were alive. The world had over three billion living people on this date, but most of them didn't exist at all for him. President Lincoln very much existed, and the shrine was full of him, not of most of the others that the census-takers said were living.

In fact, President Lincoln, to most people of the world, was more alive than the captain himself.

No one was there other than the current captain and the former president and a current park service officer. The officer was sitting in the small heated booth off to the corner, and was not paying attention to the captain or to the president.

Captain Valadovich looked away from President Lincoln's face and he walked to the south wall and read the words of the Gettysburg Address. He walked to the opposite side and read the words of the second inaugural address on the north wall. Then he walked back to the statue. As he walked, he noticed the sounds of his footsteps. He heard each footstep twice. The second sound echoed from the past, yet he heard it in the present. Somewhere that sound was still moving on. It didn't die.

President Lincoln looked down at the soldier. Captain Valadovich said to President Lincoln, "All I can remember of what the woman said was, 'Do you want some Fritos?'"

President Lincoln smiled at the captain.

"I don't know anything about them and I never will. I know so much about you."

The former president stared at him, but said nothing.

"And those echoes. Where do they stop? Or do they just keep traveling? Does anything really go away or is everything somewhere?"

The former president dared not nod but he wanted to.

The captain walked away down the wide stairway. President Lincoln watched him go down the steps and could see him walk around the circle toward Twenty-Third Street. The captain was finally out of the former president's view. President Lincoln was looking straight ahead at the Reflecting Pool and the Washington Monument. He heard the door of the heated booth open and close, and heard the footsteps of the park service officer, and in a few seconds the officer came within President Lincoln's scope of vision and both of them looked at the city together. After a while the park service officer felt a chill and walked back toward his heated booth out of the range of President Lincoln's vision.

President Lincoln heard the officer's footsteps and heard the door of the officer's booth open and close and heard the echo of the footsteps and heard the echo of the door opening and closing. President Lincoln was smiling again. The visit of Captain Valadovich had meant a great deal to him because the soldier understood what there was to understand, and most people didn't.

FIFTEEN
SUNSHINE ISLAND
1964

Four years had changed Hong Kong, as four years change all places and people. The skyline of Hong Kong Island had substituted a number of its colonial-style structures with high-rise buildings. Although there were still many junks in the harbor, there weren't as many of them as there were in 1960. There were now fewer rickshaws on the streets, and all sedan-chairs were gone. Fewer women were wearing cheong-sams, with more wearing western styles of clothing.

Some of the changes were sad and some were welcome, but beyond any argument was that the best change of all was that Hong Kong was in a transition from a society of the very many poor and the very few rich, to a society that had the very poor and the very rich acting as book-ends to an expanding shelf of those who were rising from the poor. Hong Kong was beginning to serve as an example to any current or future political entity of the success of liberty and hard work, mixed with patience. As too many other political entities had discovered in the past and other political entities would discover in the future, neither liberty, hard work, or patience would hold a reward without the other two. With the other two, the reward would be magnificent.

Tso Wai-yee had changed as her city did. Her soul and face were even more beautiful. Her hair was somewhat less beautiful as its length no longer reached down her back. It had been cut, its tips now resting on her shoulders. Unchanged was her loyalty to her family, and even unchanged was her loyalty to the man she had met four years back and hadn't seen since.

There was little visible change in Moose in his second visit to that city, but he was not devoid of change. His contractor status with the Department of Defense had been replaced with an appointment by President Johnson to the staff of the National Security Council in the White House. Although it was known that Moose had been an ardent supporter of Barry Goldwater in the presidential race, after the November election President Johnson was more secure in appointing Goldwater Republicans than he was with most Democrats for responsibilities in foreign affairs. Physically, Moose hadn't changed much except for a few strands of gray making appearances in his sideburns. And he had a new pipe. It was a Charatan; straight-grained, odd-shaped, big, and expensive. There was one more change, and it was invisible.

Wai-yee noticed the invisible but didn't say anything the first day of his reappearance in Hong Kong. They had sent and received letters from each other in a torrent that first year, and then there was more time between letters from him in the following years. She had asked him to come back to Hong Kong on his next trip to Saigon, but his next trip came and went and another trip to Saigon came and went and finally he said he would be able to come to Hong Kong on his way home from Saigon in December.

Wai-yee wrote him back immediately saying she would meet him at Kai Tak Airport and she would take care of reserving a hotel room for him. Although she had special sentiment attached to the Miramar, and every time she had passed it she had brushed her hand on the brass plaque emblems of the hotel that were on the hotel's outside wall, she did not reserve a room for him there. Along with her special sentiment was a special resentment that the Miramar kept guests of those registered from staying in rooms after 11:00 P.M. Her sister, Winnie, told her that the new Hilton Hotel that dominated the skyline with its 26 stories on Hong Kong Island, did not have such a policy. Winnie would know.

That was where Wai-yee booked a room for Moose for the three nights he had scheduled, and whether Moose would know it or not, she chose the $16 American single rather than the $12 American single, and she paid the difference in advance, insisting they give him a bill that had the lesser rate. She wanted the view of the harbor and Kowloon.

When he arrived at the airport that morning she embraced him and wouldn't let go for over a minute. Her face was a mixture of laughing and crying. He closed his eyes and held her as people passed them by on both sides. *How*, he asked himself, *did I ever postpone being near her?* Being near her was feeling everything he felt four years ago, all over again.

The Hilton provided a waiting car and driver, and they were taken from the airport through Kowloon, and the car went on to the Vehicular Star Ferry to take the two passengers to the hotel across the harbor.

Right after the bellman left their room, Wai-yee asked Moose, "May we go to the Peak? I have dreamt so long about us being there again, this time with no one else."

It wasn't what he had in mind. "Now?"

"May we go to the Peak?"

He nodded and smiled. "Yes. We may go to the Peak."

They sat on the mountain top far away from any of the tourists. They found a shaded place overlooking thousands of rooftops and the harbor and the distant mountains of China. He was sitting cross-legged, and she wrapped her arms around her raised knees and rested her chin against them.

"You love this place, don't you, Wai-yee?"

She nodded without lifting her head. "I wanted so much that you and I would some day be back here on the Peak, and alone, and let the whole city look up at us. I would be dead if it was not for Hong Kong, you know."

"I know, Wai-yee. Then I, too, am thankful for it."

"I cannot be up here and see the city and not pray in thanks for Hong Kong, and I pray that it will always be here for the Chinese. Do you understand? The devil took over so much of our land, and an angel created this small place for our escape. And now, each day, it is becoming more and more of a wonderland. Do you notice it has changed since we were up here together before? There are taller buildings now, there are fewer squatter huts on the rooftops, there are more clusters of housing units over there in Kowloon, there is more reclaimed land in the harbor, and the whole city has more of a gloss, a shine, a—a love."

Moose nodded. He didn't want to say anything because his voice would sound vacant in contrast to her passion as she talked of Hong Kong.

"Do you know," she asked, "that in the four years since I have seen you I have not let any man touch me? But I have still had an affair." She added quickly, "this city has been my affair."

It was even more inappropriate for him to say anything. She was, after all, confiding in him about another love, and the lover was present. There was silence for a long time. Wai-yee continued to stare at the city while Moose continued to stare at Wai-yee. "Tell me," he finally said softly, so as not to break the spell, "I want to know all about your lover."

She smiled. "You won't be jealous?"

"I might be."

"Oh, you should. My lover is older than you, more mature, but still very young. In fact, my lover is even younger than your country which always prides itself on how recently it was formed. This land on which we're sitting, and all of this land in front of us was barren, while your country was already a nation. Your Abraham Lincoln was 32 years old, practicing law when this island was given life. It was here before then, but only as a camping ground for pirates and a place for fishermen who were passing through and had either great courage or ignorance to think it was a safe place. At night, pirates would slit their throats for their catch of the day—right where we're sitting."

"Right here?" He only asked that to prove his interest in what she was saying. Her eyes sparkled at his question, and she nodded slowly. So he repeated the question. "Right here where we're sitting?"

"Right here!"

Moose was giving her passion for Hong Kong an escape valve. How much he would rather have embraced her and held her rather than listen to her, but she wanted to be heard and, after all, he had encouraged her to talk.

"This land was held by China, and China was trading with Britain. Neither government was any good. They both had a superiority complex. Queen Victoria thought we were unsophisticated, even uncivilized and primitive, and that we were devoted to ancient superstitions and myths. Our emperor Ching thought the British were corrupt, money-mad Europeans who were filled with the ambition of exploitation and they smelled of perfumes–or just smelled. Do you know who Emperor Ching was?"

"I know the name, but I don't know, really know, much about the guy."

"He was not a good Emperor. He said all westerners could only trade with us in a 'trading season' and only in one small area of China, in the factory area just outside of Canton–beyond those mountains there. He made very strict rules. The British were not allowed to bring their families into China. They had to drop their families off in Macau–in Portuguese Macau. And the British who wanted to trade with us were not allowed to learn or read or speak Chinese, and they weren't allowed to go out after dark. And to make things worse, no one was buying the things they brought to trade. The British had nothing any of us wanted. And we had little money to buy even what we might have wanted. But London women wanted our jade, our silks, our porcelain and our tea. Emperor Ching said the British couldn't trade their things for ours, they had to buy what they wanted with British silver.

"So the British were buying things to send home without selling anything. That is until they discovered there was one thing many Chinese people wanted to buy that the British could supply. Do you know what it was?"

"What?"

"Opium. There was plenty of opium in the Bengal area of East India which was another British colony. We Chinese, in those days, had a greater appetite for bad opium than the British had for good tea. The Emperor was infuriated. Opium addicts were replacing our supply of silver. Emperor Ching appointed a Special Commissioner whose job was to stop the British from selling opium to our people. The Special Commissioner he appointed was Lin Tse-hsu. Lin knew how to stop what Great Britain was doing. It was not very complicated–he simply cut off all food supplies to the British traders who were all together outside Canton, led by a man named Charles Elliot. When the traders became too weak from starving, some of them close to death, the British traders produced the chests of opium that had been hidden from the Commissioner. There were over 20,000 chests! And each chest weighed over 150 pounds! All that opium! And so Lin made a night-time ceremony of burning every chest, and he ordered the British out of China."

"To go where?"

"He didn't care. Just to get out. Now, you can understand that, can't you?"

"Yes."

"So they went to Macau, but that didn't work out. The Portuguese Governor there said he couldn't be responsible for their safety and that they should pick up their families they had already left in Macau, and he told them to go somewhere else. There wasn't any other land except China close by, so they stayed on British ships anchored right here–in the harbor right down there.

"The Emperor was told they were there and so, again, he had their food supply cut-off. In response, Queen Victoria had the British fleet come here to go northward to bombard our cities, one after the other. It was their Lord Palmerston who she put in charge. The Emperor's forces couldn't compete in a war against the British Navy, so the Emperor appointed a negotiator—a stupid man named Qishan. Qishan made up his own agreement without checking with the Emperor. He told the British that China would pay for all the opium they had burned and would allow the British traders back near Canton if they stopped their war against us."

"Why was that stupid?"

"You don't think so?"

Moose surely didn't want to fight over such a point. "Well, I don't know. I just want to know."

"Because the British, sensing our weakness, said that wasn't enough. They said they had to have a trade-treaty or a good-sized island where the British could camp permanently with their families, and be safe. Qishan said there would be no trade agreement, but the British could have Hong Kong Island.

"And so on January the 26th of 1841 the British flag was raised right down there—Possession Point. It's right there. You know who raised it? Charles Elliot, the one who brought in the opium in the first place and then had to surrender it all."

"And that's how Hong Kong began?"

Again Wai-yee nodded. "That's how it began. That's right. But the agreement made no one happy. The emperor had Qishan brought to Peking in chains for giving away even one inch of our territory. The British foreign secretary Palmerston was just as angry at Charles Elliot for accepting an agreement that didn't give the British a trade treaty and that only gave the Queen this barren island. Palmerston wanted a large island like Hainan. So both our emperor and the British Foreign Secretary punished their negotiators. Do you know what they did? The Emperor of China banished Qishan to Tibet, and the British Foreign Secretary sent Elliot to be Consul General—in your Texas."

Moose laughed. "That was a terrible punishment for the guy?"

She smiled. "Severe. Palmerston appointed a new commander, Sir Henry Pottinger, to take revenge on us because we hadn't offered Britain a trade-treaty. He blasted away at Canton, Xiamen, Ninbo, Shanghai, and then he even threatened Nanking. This time our emperor negotiated by himself. But he didn't have any leeway. Britain was so strong. He signed a trade-treaty. And he signed an agreement in his own name, giving Hong Kong Island to Great Britain—forever."

"Forever?"

"Forever! For all time to come! It was now a possession of Great Britain."

"But I thought you said Britain didn't want Hong Kong that much, that they didn't like it, that they sent that guy to Texas for having made a deal over it."

"Palmerston, who had been so upset about such a small island earlier was now out of the picture. His government in London had fallen during all of this, and the new Tory Government had replaced him with a Lord Aberdeen, who didn't care about our islands or whether they were big or small. Most of the British didn't care about this part of the world. In 1847 there was a book published in London titled *China* and the book had a chapter that told about the island that was given to Britain. The chapter was called 'Hong Kong–Its Position, Prospects, Character and Utter Worthlessness from Every Point of View to England.' That can tell you what the British thought of this place!"

Wai-yee's beauty became more and more pronounced as she spoke. Her entire face and body were filled with the subject that meant so much to her. Her eyes were at times laughing and at times sad, her nostrils flared when she spoke about the opium, her lips quivered a little when she mentioned the name of Qishan. She adjusted her position by outstretching her left leg, while her right leg was still kept bent at the knee with her chin near it. The way she was sitting, the slit in her yellow cheongsam reached clear to the top of her thigh, and with that unrehearsed pose, she was the ultimate of femininity.

"Then, way north of here, the emperor's navy captured a British ship called the *Arrow* and the emperor's navy put the crew in prison, saying the ship was in our waters and he said it was loaded with British pirates."

"Was it?"

"I don't know. The British said it wasn't in our waters, it was registered in Hong Kong, and it had no pirates. I think they were telling the truth, but I don't know. Almost at the same time the first British Envoy was traveling to be the First Colonial Secretary of Hong Kong and our navy fired on his ship on his way to present his credentials. That was not a good thing to do and that was the beginning of another war."

As much as Moose loved the United States, he didn't think he could give a recitation about it as Wai-yee was able to give about Hong Kong. It was imbedded in her. It was her.

"Of course the British won again. They were so powerful and this time they demanded the other side of this harbor–Kowloon–and over there–Stonecutter's Island, too. And they wanted a treaty that would give them that land forever, just like this island. Again, we had no choice. The treaty was signed. Kowloon and Stonecutter's Island–forever–forever British.

"Now we're in my grandparents times–and I suppose the times of your parents." What did she mean by that? Was she calling attention to the difference in age between Wai-yee and him? It probably wasn't intended as she was much too intent on her story, but it did come out. "It was near the end of the century when Japan attacked China. No one left us alone. This time Germany, France, and Russia came to our side, but they wanted something for what they did. They knew what Britain had received and they, too, wanted trade and treaties. The British knew those other Europeans well, and they thought a terrible European-Asian War was to break out, so they demanded more territory to protect Hong Kong and even to protect China itself. Britain said that China could use Hong Kong harbor for its warships against foreign powers, but the British had to have more territory here to back them up.

"We didn't want to give any more territory away to Britain, so we said this time they could use more land, but not forever. They could only have additional territory on lease. We said we'd give them a lease for 99 years and then they must give it back. And they would have to pay for it. We said they could have all the land up to the Sham Chun River for 99 years, as their new territories until 1997, when all the participants in the agreement would be dead."

"Aren't they dead now?"

"I haven't kept track of all of them. The emperor's dead. I don't think they're all dead, but the ones who are still living have to be very old. Then just two years before I was born, in 1937, Japan attacked China, and then when I was two years old, by your calendar, when the Japanese attacked your Pearl Harbor, they attacked Hong Kong as well. But they didn't just attack here, they invaded. Prime Minister Churchill gave the order for the British in Hong Kong to hold on. It was impossible to hold on, but the fight went on for eighteen days and nights through the New Territories, through Kowloon and finally through this island. On Christmas Day, Hong Kong fell. Governor Young had holed himself up at the Peninsula Hotel over there—and the Japanese found him and sent him off to Manchuria as a prisoner."

"Do you remember any of it?"

"I remember toward the end of it. But I wasn't here. I was in China. And I remember hearing about the atrocities committed here in Hong Kong by the Japanese. I cannot talk about them. Others will tell you. The Japanese here were sub-human. The Japanese lost their war 19 years ago and left. But just a little later, 15 years ago now, my country had another tragedy. That I remember so well. I was ten years old when Mao Tse-tung won his communist war in my country, and that's when my parents made sure Winnie and I would not have to live under him, and my mother and father had us smuggled out—here to Hong Kong. We weren't alone. Over 10,000 people were escaping into Hong Kong each week.

"While Winnie and I have been here, your nation started your embargo of goods from Communist China. You remember from when you were here before that your tourists have to have a Certificate of Origin on most goods they buy here, to make sure they aren't made across the border. That was good. It was good because we in Hong Kong pushed ourselves to make things, produce things, manufacture things that had only come from China before, and we have succeeded. That embargo of yours helped us become what we are today. Look—look what we are today. Look—left to right, right to left. We are Hong Kong!

"Can you see why I love this place? Even the British. I want you to know that China is my country and I want Hong Kong to be part of China, not England. But it must not go to China while China is ruled by communist dictators. The British were bad at the beginning but then they started governing here largely by not governing, and it's good because they leave us alone. They gave us our refuge and they leave us to be free. I will always be grateful for that refuge and that freedom. We were not able to get it anywhere else, from anyone else. At last, the Chinese people were free. Hong Kong is China without chains. And look what we have done." He was looking at her, not the city. "Please look. Look at this city. It is because we are free and we are Chinese. Do you understand why Hong Kong is my first love?"

"Yes. Yes, I do, Wai-yee."

He had never been jealous of a city before this day. How long would he have to live to accomplish what her lover did?

They went nowhere else throughout the day. They stayed on Victoria Peak until after the sun set over Hong Kong and the lights of the city came on in a flurry of spots igniting the new colors against the black palette that the sky provided for Hong Kong's light-makers.

Wai-yee spent the night with Moose at the Hilton and that night was, for Moose, life at its highest summit. He regretted, so much, that he hadn't come back to Hong Kong on previous trips to Saigon. For her, in great part, it was her dream of four years come true. But there was an invisible part of it that had not been dreamt.

They had breakfast brought in. As they sat at the assembled room service table she gathered the strength to say it. "Moose, it's different for you now, isn't it?"

His eyebrows went down and he shook his head. "Different? Of course not. It isn't different at all."

She nodded. "I think it is for you. Moose, have you married?"

He smiled as he shook his head. "Oh, no. No, no, no, no. Why do you ask that?"

She shrugged. "Then let me tell you what I think."

"Go ahead. Please go ahead."

"When you told me you were going to Saigon for a visit four years ago, I not only feared for your safety, I feared for your love. There are beautiful girls in Vietnam. Your type. I know your type. Moose, I think you met someone in Saigon. And I think you saw her on every trip there. And I think you lived with her on the last trip there."

She had it down right on the nose. "Oh, no, Wai-yee. Why do you say that—why do you think that?"

"Intuition—mixed with the fact that on your last trip you told me to write you at the U.S. Embassy rather than the Caravelle Hotel the way I did before on your other trips. Why didn't you want me to write you where you were staying? You didn't even tell me if you were still staying at the Caravelle."

"Oh, Wai-yee. I just wanted your letters delivered to where I was working so I would be sure and get them. When I went off to the Delta or up-country, the office would get the mail to me—there were Americans from the Embassy coming and going all the time. The hotel wouldn't do that. They'd just hold it."

"Moose, please tell me the truth. Are any of those things I just said, true?"

There was an uneasy moment of silence. It was only a couple seconds but those seconds were the confirmation she didn't want. "What do you mean, any of those things?"

"You don't need to answer." She lowered her head.

After thirty seconds of silence, she looked up at him. He nodded.

Her mouth was trembling.

"Wai-yee, I met a girl in Saigon. I'm not in love with her at all. I saw her when I went there. She's very nice and—and—that's all. It isn't the way it is with you at all. Not at all. It isn't the way you think, Wai-yee."

Wai-yee gave a brave smile but her lower lip was still trembling. She put her hand to her lips the way she did when she laughed, but this time it was meant to hide her sadness. She shook her head and put her hand down. "Sure. You have every right to do everything and anything you want to do. And I truly want your happiness, Moose. And you never told me that you loved me, so you are not bound by word. I said I loved you and I still do. I've never allowed one man to even touch me since I met you. Not once. Not a touch. I do love you, Moose, so much, but love doesn't mean possession." She lifted her hand to her lips again, just briefly. "I hate myself when I feel possessive about you and when I ask questions that are none of my business like I just did. Just to see you and hold you for a while and see you smile—and see you suck on that big pipe of yours," and she smiled even more, "is all that's important to me. Look, look what I have for you."

She stood and walked to her purse that she had left on a chair from the night before. She opened it and took out a small package that was gift-wrapped. She brought it to him at the breakfast table. She stood by him, waiting for his response. Moose said nothing. He couldn't. He untied the ribbon and ripped the paper and opened the dark brown box. It was a pipe.

"It's a Dunhill!" she said with her eyebrows up. "That's the kind you had before, but this is bigger, even than what you have now. The salesman said it's a special collector's model! Is it really? Do you like it, Moose?"

He put the box down on the table, and he stood and he held her as tight as any man could hold a woman without breaking her, but he broke himself. It happened again. Only with her. His eyes.

"Moose!"

It took him a while to say the words: "You're going to think I don't do anything but cry."

She smiled and backed away from him slightly, but his arms didn't leave her. "I wish that was all you did!" She made him smile. "Now, get ready. I have something I want to do today and I want you to help me. I have it all set up. Okay, Moose?"

He couldn't answer her with words for fear of breaking up. He just nodded with a clenched smile. Why he ever thought of another woman, was a question he couldn't answer. Why he ever admitted it to Wai-yee, was something he wished he could take back.

Wai-yee's quick regaining of her composure was perfect. Her self-control was a strength that appeared to be so inconsistent with her fragile physical frame. "Moose, I want nothing from you. If my love doesn't make you feel good, if it bothers you, then I will destroy it."

Now he had to regain control of himself. "Your love makes me feel like a giant, Wai-yee. I have never met a man who deserves you. There may not be one."

"Get ready, Moose! I made an appointment!"

At her direction they took a boat to Lantau Island, and from there Wai-yee hired an old woman who took them on the woman's sampan to a speck in the sea called Chau Kung To. The sampan was so small that Wai-yee had to practically sit on Moose which didn't bother either of them, and it made the old woman laugh. She spoke to Wai-yee in Cantonese. The only word Moose understood was when the woman said, very clearly in English, "Sunshine! Sunshine!"

Wai-yee explained to Moose that they were going to meet one of the finest men of the time, Gus Borgeest, who had won the Magsaysay Award three years ago for what he was doing for Chinese refugees. She told him that Gus Borgeest was an Englishman who was born in China and had escaped with his Chinese wife to Hong Kong after the Communist Revolution. They had two Hong Kong dollars between them when they arrived with their three adopted Chinese children who were orphans from Communist China. In his quest to help Chinese refugees, he leased Chau Kung To, a small, 160-acre uninhabited mountainous atoll that had active springs. The Hong Kong Government charged him only 180 Hong Kong dollars a year (U.S. $23.31). He brought groups of refugees to the island, which became known by the name he called it: Sunshine Island. On the island he trained the refugees to earn their own livelihoods, teaching them how to grow vegetables and fruits and teaching them crafts and how to arrange finances. Each family was given a thatched hut, gradually replaced with stone homes, with necessities provided, and each family was paid 50 Hong Kong dollars a month. He insisted there would be no hand-out, no charity, that self-respect was dependent on their ability to earn what they received. Then he helped them start a new life in Hong Kong or helped them for transport to foreign countries. The Hong Kong government gave those graduates who stayed two acres in the New Territories, plus a cow and farm tools and a small cash allowance. Gus Borgeest had graduated over 600 refugees by the time he won the Magsaysay Award. To earn money for his own family, he worked nights and weekends at Hertz Rent-a-Car in Kowloon.

"You will never meet his equal," Wai-yee told Moose as the sampan docked by the edge of the small atoll. "Everyone in Hong Kong has heard of him and admires him. He doesn't like to meet with people. He wants to do his work. I have not met him before, either. I told him on the telephone I would be coming with a man who works for President Johnson of the United States—you! I knew he wouldn't say 'no' to that! You see, I schemed!" She instructed the sampan woman to wait for them no matter the time, and they disembarked on the atoll.

Three huge German Shepherds ran down from the mountain towards them, barking as they ran, causing Wai-yee to almost back herself into the sea. Moose walked toward the oncoming dogs and knelt with his hands out to them. They stopped their barking, reached him, smelled his hands, wagged their tails, and Wai-yee came back from her near-suicide. The dogs ran around them, then showed them the way up the mountain, one running ahead and looking back to make sure Moose and Wai-yee were behind that lead dog, while the other two dogs continually changed positions with each other as they formed a guarded aisle on both sides of Moose and Wai-yee. There was no question but that they were a welcoming committee who would bring sanctioned guests to Gus Borgeest and his family, and keep away all others.

"You found our Sunshine Island all right?" Gus Borgeest asked with his hand extended to Wai-yee outside his rough stone cottage. Even the man with a reputation of sainthood was obviously taken with Tso Wai-yee, evident because as he saw them both he almost ignored the big Moose who accompanied Wai-yee. The tall and slender Gus Borgeest bent somewhat to shake her hand, and looking between her and Moose, he suddenly became conscious that he was wearing black shorts, a T-shirt and open thongs on his feet, and now he wished he had dressed better. Moose was in a business suit and a white tie-less shirt, and Wai-yee was wearing a green cheong-sam she had brought with her to the Hilton. After shaking Wai-yee's hand, Gus Borgeest put his right hand to his head and moved his hand back as though he was smoothing down something, but his 54 years had taken casualties including most of his hair. Since he was almost bald, he was simply rubbing his head, which served no objective.

"Sure," Wai-yee said. "We found your Sunshine Island. In fact our sampan woman knew that this was Sunshine Island and not Chau Kung To anymore. Mr. Borgeest, this is Moose Dunston from America. He works for President Johnson."

"Yes, I'm so glad to have you here," Gus Borgeest was controlling himself, forcing himself to shift his eyes to Moose from continuing to look at Wai-yee. "Wai-yee told me about you. Welcome to Sunshine Island." They shook hands. "Sit down please. Mona will be out in a moment with some tea. When the dogs told us you had arrived she went in to make some tea for us. I'm going to go in our 'Villa Borghese' for a moment and bring out the children so you can meet them. Please, sit down." Before they sat, he walked into the cottage.

The dogs had obviously interpreted Gus Borgeest's request of Wai-yee and Moose to sit, as an order that must be obeyed. All three of the dogs stared back and forth at Wai-yee and Moose waiting for them to do as Borgeest had instructed, and only after Wai-yee and Moose sat, did the dogs sit down next to them.

Gus Borgeest came back outside, accompanied by Naomi who was fourteen, Ruth who was five, and Angela who was three. They all seemed bored by the presence of the guests and wanted to get back to whatever they had been doing. Then came his wife, Mona, a small woman, not even five feet tall, wearing what looked to Moose like white pajamas but they weren't.

"Were it not for Mona," Gus Borgeest said, "there would be no Sunshine Island! Thank God for such a wife!" She gave a shy smile, and poured the tea, then went back inside with the children. And that was it. Mona and the children were seen by the two guests, then gone.

"You work for President Johnson?" Gus Borgeest asked Moose.

"Yes, sir. I'm on the staff of his National Security Council. Right now we're concentrating on this area of the world, particularly Vietnam."

"The North is getting supplies from both Red China and the Soviets, aren't they?"

"Yes, and the supplies are delivered to the Viet Cong in South Vietnam through Laos and Cambodia next door. Those transfers are difficult to stop."

"Will the United States be able to keep the communists out?"

Moose clenched his lips and nodded. "We better. 23,000 Americans are there now—most of them not in combat, but we do have some in combat with the ARVN troops—the army of South Vietnam. We're doing better now." Moose took a sip of his tea that had a few insects in it, but he knew enough to ignore them, to drink around them, and if he swallowed them he simply had to tolerate it.

"Good. That's good. I'm a great admirer of the United States. Your country always believed in victory rather than compromise until Korea, for which, I'm afraid, you will pay a steep price in the future. Your President Johnson must not aid South Vietnam in only a defensive war. It doesn't work. You must be on the offensive as well. I think that what Johnson should do is what Kennedy did when a proxy threatened countries of the Western Hemisphere. He threatened Moscow. What could Cuba have done without the supplies coming from the Soviet Union? And, similarly, the Viet Cong in the South gets its supplies from the North, and the North gets its supplies from the Soviets and Mao. You must always threaten the source. Kennedy did that. I believe that Johnson must do that. To hit the Viet Cong alone is worthless. He must hit Ho Chi Minh, and you must at least warn Mao and Kosygin that he will hit them if they continue to intervene."

"Believe me, Mr. Borgeest, this is under discussion every day. We recognize that's true." Moose took another sip of the tea. The insects were gone. Since they couldn't fly and had pretty well drowned when he first saw them, he knew where they must have gone. He tried not to think of it.

"Tell me, what happened to Khrushchev?" Gus Borgeest asked.

Moose nodded. "They dumped him a couple months ago. Their Politburo said his health was no good, but it wasn't that. They've been degrading him, saying he had built a personality cult, just as he had accused Stalin of doing. They said they wanted a return to Leninist philosophy of collective leadership. So Kosygin is now Premier but not First Secretary of the Communist Party, even though Khrushchev held both jobs. They gave the First Secretary post to a guy named Brezhnev. He was Chairman of the Presidium and it looks like Nikolai Podgorny will get that post. We'll see how long that collective 'troika' as they call it, lasts. One of them will tower over the others. A country never survives without one voice, particularly in foreign affairs."

"Yes, that's right, you're right."

Wai-yee said, "I wish you were running China, Mr. Borgeest, and I wish Moose was running the United States."

Gus Borgeest laughed. "I have no doubt of your friends capabilities, but I will be content to go back to China when anyone runs it who believes in the people's freedom. But now tell me, my young lady, you said over the phone that you wanted my help on something."

Wai-yee nodded and told him about her parents and then confided the most recent events. "We sent money, so much money to smugglers. They kept the money and our parents never got here. I don't even think an attempt was made to contact them. My parents write, and even though they would never write anything that would be too suspicious to the authorities, I can tell from what they write they didn't know about it. We have a code of sorts, and I can tell. The smugglers we sent the money to were probably nothing more than thieves."

Borgeest nodded. "It's that way so often. Remember, you can't trust a smuggler, my dear. They are not honorable. And they always ask for half in advance. Is that what they did?"

"Three-quarters in advance."

"Well, that's a new one but not surprising. Some of them would rather have whatever they can get and not even think about keeping their end of the bargain. Their end of the bargain is a risk to them. They would rather get less and not have any risk. They are not honorable."

"Mr. Borgeest, my sister and I are starting all over again to get them out. We could only cry so long about the wasted money. You are so involved in the cause of escapees—do you know anyone, any person on the other side of the border who can help us?"

"You mean a smuggler?"

"Yes."

Borgeest shook his head. "No. I don't know any smugglers. But there are people who have been here—refugees Mona and I have schooled—who were brought out by smugglers who at least kept their word. The refugees we now have here on the island—some 24 families—114 people, escaped all by themselves. What I can do is put you in contact with some of the ones we had here before who were smuggled out. They would know, of course, who got them out, and how to contact them, and how much it costs. But all of this is very risky."

"That would be so helpful. I know it's a risk. But the alternative is to just leave them there, and that neither Winnie nor I can do."

"Believe me, I understand. As long as you know the risk. The ultimate risk isn't losing your money as you've already done. In comparison with some others, you're lucky. The smugglers could have worked for Mao's government. Then they would have kept your money and turned your parents in, and you would never have heard from your parents again. It happens. Be careful. They could be waiting for your next step. And there's a further risk from the Hong Kong government itself. As I'm sure you know, in May two years ago, 70,000 dashed into Hong Kong. The Red Chinese government let them." Now he looked at Moose. "They opened the gates and looked the other way. They wanted to smother Hong Kong by causing a sudden cataclysm. It was the British government here that sent most of them back. It was terrible to see them do such a thing. Since then the smugglers have raised their rates, and now the smugglers bring refugees only over the water and at night." He looked back at Wai-yee. "It's a dangerous business from all sides."

"I know," Wai-yee said. "If my parents could have got to Canton they would have come with the others in 1962. They let us know through their little code that they were not permitted to leave Kiangchow. But you will give me some names of escapees you know who have been through it? Who succeeded?"

"Let me go in and get the records from Mona and a pad of paper. May I get you some more tea?"

Wai-yee nodded. "I would like that. Thank you."

Moose declined. "No, that was perfect. I'm in good shape now."

Borgeest went inside.

"Do you like him?" Wai-yee asked Moose.

"Of course. He's quite a man. There's nothing to dislike. Is Mona his wife's real name do you think?"

Wai-yee shrugged. "As real as any other name. Her Chinese name is Ho Pui-tsun. We can have both our Chinese and Western names on our birth certificate here in Hong Kong. But she was born in China so I suppose it's just what he calls her."

Moose shook his head. "I'm supposed to be an Asian expert. I'm an Asian amateur."

"If you listen to him enough you'll be an Asian expert."

"He doesn't say anything about himself. He asks questions."

"That's why he's so smart. He doesn't care what you know about him. He wants to learn more than he knew yesterday. I think he learned that trait from living in China, and from being a Quaker. He read a book written by an American about Quakers when he was a prisoner of the Japanese in China. When he came out he joined the Society of Friends."

From his inside jacket pocket, Moose took the pipe that Wai-yee had given him. He filled it carefully with tobacco from his pouch. "What a good feel!" he said. He lit it and gave a look of ecstasy. It couldn't have been that good. Not yet. It needed some breaking in.

"Do you like it? Does it smoke well?" Wai-yee asked excitedly.

"It's the best! What a great smoke!"

"Really? Is it really a special collector's model?"

"Oh, yes! I've never seen one like it! Or ever had a smoke like this!"

"And, Moose–" she was so outrageously girlish and virginal and plain cute when she said, "And, Moose." "Even governors of Hong Kong have praised his work, and even Royal Air Force men have come here on some weekends to help him. But you are so lucky to actually meet and talk with him because he doesn't want people who are nothing but visitors. You must ask him about himself or he will never tell you anything about what he has done."

Gus Borgeest came back out with Mona who was carrying a big ledger and a pad of paper. Borgeest carried with him the teapot and a small book with a red vinyl cover with some larger sheets hanging from its side. He told Wai-yee that Mona would go over the names with her and while they are doing that, "I want to show Mr. Dunston what the people of China have to accept as long as communism is their master. This book was just printed in Peking. It's the quotations of Mao, many of them never before heard in the west, or even Hong Kong, and it's being distributed all over China. I think this might be the first copy on this side of the border. A refugee family who escaped from Canton last Friday and is here now on Sunshine Island, gave it to me. Your president should read this book. Will you give it to him? It's in Chinese, but when I knew you would be coming with this lovely lady I translated for your president some key phrases. This is a very important book."

"I'll do what I can." Moose was being careful with his words. He was not so sure he wanted to give it to the president. He wanted to be courteous to Gus Borgeest, but without giving him a guarantee. Moose looked over at Wai-yee. She was busy with Mona.

"Let me read to you some phrases," Gus Borgeest said. He read from the translation pages he had inserted in the little red book. "Mao says this, 'People of the world, unite and defeat the U.S. aggressors and all their running dogs. People of the world, be courageous, dare to fight, defy difficulties and advance wave upon wave. Then the whole world will belong to the people. Monsters of all kinds shall be destroyed.'

"Now, this applies to Vietnam today, although he wrote it many years ago. 'This army is powerful because it has the people's self-defense corps and the militia–the vast armed organizations of the masses–fighting in coordination with it...' You see, what he calls the self-defense corps, is what has been organized in South Vietnam–today it's the Viet Cong and he writes that these civilian militias are as vital as the uniformed militia. Listen. He says, 'Without the cooperation of these armed forces of the masses it would be impossible to defeat the enemy. It is up to us to organize the people. As for the reactionaries in China, it is up to us to organize the people to overthrow them. Everything reactionary is the same; if you don't hit it, it won't fall. This is like sweeping the floor; as a rule, where the broom does not reach, the dust will not vanish of itself. The enemy will not perish of himself. Neither the Chinese reactionaries nor the aggressive forces of U.S. imperialism in China will step down from the stage of history of their own accord.'

"'The seizure of power by armed force, the settlement of the issue by war, is the central task and the highest form of revolution. This Marxist-Leninist principle of revolution holds good universally, for China and for all other countries.'

"'Every communist must grasp the truth, that power grows out of the barrel of a gun.' And then he says, 'Only with guns can the whole world be transformed.' 'First, we must be ruthless to our enemies, we must overpower and annihilate them.' Now, what does he plan for your country? He tells us. 'It is the Americans themselves who have put nooses round their own necks, handing the ends of the ropes to the Chinese people, the peoples of the Arab countries, and all the peoples of the world who love peace and oppose aggression. The longer the U.S. aggressors remain in those places, the tighter the nooses round their necks will become.'"

Moose said, "I will give the book and your sheets to the president." He meant it.

"Thank you. Every leader of the world should have read *Mein Kampf* but they didn't. The irony of totalitarians is that so often they publicly say what they plan—and no one who can do something to stop them read their words until the plan is well on its way to enactment."

"You are so right. That little red book is very revealing."

"Now, tell me, how long will you be in Hong Kong?"

"Only a couple more days, then back to Washington. That's quite a book, Mr. Borgeest."

"I'm glad you see its importance. I knew you would."

"Mr. Borgeest, has the British government been helpful to you here in your work?"

"That is not the issue. Allowing Chinese refugees in Hong Kong is good enough. They simply must stop sending any back. What happened in 1962 cannot be repeated. You see, the escapees want nothing from the British except to ignore them. I insist they work, and I pay them for their work here—not much, but I pay them. They must see the immediate reward for work. Welfare with the best intentions, subtly enslaves, which is why I pay them for their work here. When they leave, they have respect for themselves and for work. They send me letters after they leave. One wrote me, and I have memorized it, that 'owning one's own land, managing one's own affairs, does something to a man. Such,' he said, 'cannot be achieved or even understood by those who are content to let governments fill their rice bowls for them.'"

"That's wonderful."

"My dream is the day the entire world becomes a Sunshine Island. I believe that your nation is in the best position to make that Utopia come true."

"Perhaps we are."

"Will you tell your president that for me?"

Moose smiled haltingly. "I will do my best. Do you–"

"Now," and Gus Borgeest interrupted quickly. "You said you will only be in Hong Kong for a couple more days?"

"Yes, I must be back in Washington by Thursday."

"While you are here–now, I don't know if you're interested or not but you should talk to the people. Get to know them. Then tell your president about them. Tell him about Hong Kong. Tell him how Chinese people work when they are permitted to do as they choose. Tell your president that Hong Kong and America have the same principles–the same belief in freedom. You see?"

"Yes. I see."

"You will do this for Hong Kong?"

"Yes. I will."

On the sampan back to Lantau, and on the larger ferry back to Hong Kong Island, Moose had his arm around Wai-yee, her head on his shoulder and he kept his hand moving down her hair.

"Why do you do that?" she asked him when they were between Lantau and Hong Kong Island.

"I don't know. I like doing it. Your hair is so soft."

"Do you think it looks good this way? Since I cut it?"

"Oh, yes."

"Do you wish I left it longer?"

"I like it this way."

"But if you could have it any way, would you want it long or like it is now or even shorter than it is now?"

He shook his head. "Oh, I don't know."

"Tell the truth."

"I suppose long."

"Like it was?"

"I suppose so. But–"

"I knew it! The girls in Vietnam have their hair down to their feet! So will I! The next time you see me it will be longer than it was when we met! I promise!" Her face was less than an inch away, and the anger on her face at such a subject was as pretty as her affection. She seemed so physically small, yet was totally enrapturing him. "Why do men always like long hair?"

"Because–because we know it's trouble for you, but we like you to want to go through the trouble. It means you care about that. And there's something about knowing that your hair keeps brushing your cheeks–you must feel it all the time, and so you can't help but feel your femininity. The thought that you like to feel that way is very appealing to me. I think that's part of it."

She nodded and put her head back on his shoulder.

Moose added, "If women cut their hair and men let their hair swish against their cheeks, I think we'd have a nation of homosexuals in short time. Women would feel like men and men would feel like women."

"In Saigon you don't need to worry about that, do you?"

He couldn't allow that subject to dominate their time together. "Hey–I have an update for you on a couple of the people we met at the Consulate last time I was here." He was bringing the conversation to his terms.

"Oh?" She pretended interest.

"Yeah. Do you remember the Air Force guy up there? Nice looking Joe named Valadovich?"

"No, I don't."

"Jonas Valadovich. The only one in uniform. You remember."

"Oh, sure."

"I got to know him quite well since then. He came by the Pentagon all the time, working between the Pentagon and Fort Myer. That was before I got hitched to the White House. Good man. He's going to go far. Anyway, we've become good friends. I'll bet that some day he's going to be Chairman of the Joint Chiefs."

She didn't know what that was, nor did she care.

"And remember that young Kennedy supporter? Real young guy?"

"Sure," she said. She didn't.

"I haven't seen him since we were here last, but I know he was picked up by the Kennedy White House–and thrown out by the Johnson White House. Not really thrown out but they moved him from the White House to the State Department. They don't like those kind of ivy covered wall kids around them. LBJ is more of a folksy kind of guy. That kid was replaced by a Texan."

She nodded. "Oh?"

He knew she was totally disinterested. "Hey," he said, "Borgeest was great. Thanks for letting me in on that meeting. He's–"

"Moose," and she raised her head from his shoulder again and looked sharply into his eyes. "My hair will be so long the next time you see me that you will trip over it! And do you know who won't pick you up from the street with cars coming all over? Do you know who will just keep walking ahead while you're struggling to get off the street?"

"I'm afraid I know who that person is."

"Wai-yee!" Wai-yee said, suddenly speaking of herself in the third person. "Wai-yee will just keep walking. And you'll be bleeding all over!"

Moose forced a smile and shook his head slowly. "You wouldn't walk away. I couldn't imagine you walking away."

She looked very serious. "No. No, I wouldn't," and she thought for a moment and then said, "I would wipe the blood with my fingers. I would clean your wounds with my tongue–to make you clean again. I love you so much, Moose."

Everything in him surrendered. He said it softly, but he said it. "Wai-yee, I love you."

Neither of them felt like humans, if being humans felt the way they did all their lives before this moment.

The large, turbaned, bearded doorman of the Hilton opened the entrance door for them. "Good Evening, Mr. Singh," Wai-yee said to him.

The doorman smiled at her. "Good Evening!"

They walked inside and Moose asked, "You know him?"

"I never saw him before in my life."

"Then how do you know his name is Mr. Singh?"

"He's a Sikh. Their names are always Singh."

"All of them?"

"Sure. It makes it easy to call them by name, doesn't it? Singh means lion. And they all have to wear turbans, and they can't cut any of their hair—I guess you'd like that—and they all have to wear a dagger. There's something else they all have to do, but they don't reveal it. It's a secret."

"Really?"

"Sure. You know what secrets are."

"Wai-yee!"

"I'm sorry. I'm really sorry. Do you want to go down to the Opium Den? It isn't the real thing. Charles Elliot has been dead for a century. It's the name of their cocktail lounge downstairs."

"Yes. That sounds good. Let's go."

It was a delaying action by Wai-yee. She didn't want to go back to his hotel room with him yet. As much as she loved him, she felt she shouldn't be so willing to go there with him under the conditions that he had confirmed. Things were different, as they always are with the passage of time.

SIXTEEN
THE TUESDAY TABLE
1965

Nineteen sixty-five was not an easy year for those people engaged in the foreign policy of the United States: the secretary of defense testified that a missile attack could kill 122 million Americans and there was no defense from such an attack, the American flag was pulled from its staff in front of the U.S. Embassy in Uganda and torn to shreds, the Viet Cong executed two American prisoners, a bomb exploded at the U.S. Embassy in Saigon killing 13 and injuring 180, another bomb destroyed 22 planes at the American Air Base in Bienhoa, South Vietnam, 15,000 picketed the White House against President Johnson's Vietnam policy, East German police blockaded the Autobahn between West Berlin and West Germany, 21,000 U.S. Marines were sent to the Dominican Republic, Charles de Gaulle was making speeches to the French to keep France independent of the United States, India and Pakistan were on the brink of war, Mainland China exploded its second nuclear device with destructive power exceeding its first, Secretary of State Rusk was spat upon in Uruguay and Senator Robert Kennedy was spat upon in Chile. As if that wasn't enough, there was the continuing quagmire of deepening involvement in the war between the United States and Anne Whitney.

Ho Chi Minh at least did some things that the Johnson Administration could predict, but Anne Whitney's actions were beyond any forecast.

She worked hard and long hours at her assignment of writing the daily news for the Wireless File that was sent from Washington, D.C. to all U.S. embassies and consulates around the world. However she often inserted her own interpretation of the news, which required an editor to work overtime to identify and remove her editorializations of verified news events. Once a week she would include in the Wireless File a Ted Murphy column in which he condemned President Johnson for being in South Vietnam, or for being in the Dominican Republic, or for being in Texas. There was some evidence that Ted Murphy was using her as a "source" for his column that revealed policy guidance given to State Department and U.S. Information Agency officers. After the miscarriage of her baby, or at least that's what she claimed while many assumed it was aborted, she became very bitter, not only about the man who impregnated her whose name she did not know, but about all men, including Lyndon Johnson. She was seen demonstrating in front of the White House, although during most of the demonstration she was wearing a mask that had a painted skeleton's skull on it. There was also the unmistakable style of her writing in a letter published by *The Washington Post*, the letter advocating the unilateral destruction of all U.S. nuclear bombs and missiles, the letter signed by the name of Anna White. She regularly justified to Junior Officer Trainees, the policies of Kosygin, Brezhnev, Podgorny, Ho Chi Minh, and Mao Tse-tung.

"The First Amendment gives me the freedom of speech, of the press, and the right to assemble," she would tell her friends who were startled that she could get away with it.

"See if you could keep a job with the Ford Motor Company if you were advertising Chevrolet," she was told by a girlfriend who was impressed with Anne's ability to keep her job.

Anne simply answered, "I wouldn't work for the Ford Motor Company!"

"Where would you work?" she asked.

"For a place that believes in justice!" No matter the labyrinthine tunnel in which those who discussed all this with her found themselves, they endured an even worse penalty: simply taking on and off her glasses for emphasis was no longer enough for Anne. Her new habit was to shake her glasses by their edge, in front of the person's face. Now there was the hazard of having one of the glasses ear-stem tips ending up in some one's eye.

President Johnson's appointees at the Agency were particularly disappointed that so many top-ranking careerists were not only fond of Anne Whitney, they supported her against any criticism. The new Assistant Director of the Agency was both angry with her and fond of her. It was former Ambassador Gerald Fairbanks who was appointed by President Johnson to rise above his career position.

For the first few months at his new job he ignored doing anything about Anne Whitney. After all, she had once brought him two bowls of chili from Hazel's Texas Chili Parlor and had confided so completely in him. But time was passing and each time Anne created an incident, that incident became the foundation for another incident more difficult to ignore. There were some new ones that came to his attention near the end of a session at the Tuesday Table.

Perhaps the Table didn't even exist on any other day of the week. No one would have known because they only saw it on Tuesday mornings when they would file in the conference room a few minutes before eight-thirty and take their places around it, waiting for the entrance of the director. Every department and agency of the federal government had their own version of the Tuesday Table.

At the Agency, the director and his top staff of twenty-three people would sit at the Tuesday Table to hold their weekly staff meeting shortly after the director held his very early morning meeting with the secretary of state who, every one had assumed, had met with the president the preceding day. After the Tuesday Table was done, each one of the top staff would then go back to the section for which the particular officer was responsible and call a separate meeting of his or her own staff, and those staff members would then call meetings of their subordinates and so on down the line, until by the time the day came to a close, everything had filtered down to everyone in the federal bureaucracy.

At least that was the theory.

The attendees at the Tuesday Table had nothing at all in common except for their attendance around it. By habit, and not by rule, they sat in "their" chairs. There would be the man who would always sit in the chair on the far left on one side. Another man would always sit on the chair that was third from the right. A particular woman always sat second from the left on the other side. It was very neat and very organized and very ritualized until someone new entered the group and it presented a chair crisis which could be compared to a military coup in a third world country, but without any killing.

The new entry to the group would be ignorant of the ritual that entitled each participant to a favored chair so the new person would simply sit down on any chair that was vacant before everyone had arrived. The person who regularly sat in that chair would then enter and painfully sit somewhere else. In minutes, the whole table would be in silent turmoil, with people misplaced and no one wanting to talk about it.

The director always arrived last, walking in the door hurriedly without looking at anyone at the table, sit in his chair, (which no one had mistaken for his or her own) and started immediately to give a report. Everyone took notes because they wanted the director to think they cared about what he was talking about. Some shook their heads or nodded as they wrote. Never in the long history of Man has such undivided attention been bluffed as well as the exhibition held weekly at the Tuesday Table.

Then the participants of the Tuesday Table would, one by one, give a report on their particular area of expertise to the director and to the others assembled and they would speak in rotation starting from the director's left. They had brought themselves up-to-date just before entering the meeting by reading the cable traffic from U.S. Embassies, the Agency's Wireless File, and, more important, from reading *The New York Times* and *The Washington Post* which was how they found out about most secret government information.

Normally, to the left of the director would be Assistant Director Fairbanks.

To Ambassador Fairbanks' left would be the appointee who looked exactly like a new electric typewriter. He was immaculately groomed and dressed, his hair was trimmed in a 1942 style and he had some kind of hair tonic on it, maybe it was Vitalis, and everything he said came out of his mouth without one "uh" or hesitation. He never made a mistake of voice or said an incomplete sentence nor did one hair ever fall out of place. If, however, he had made a mistake or had said an incomplete sentence or if a hair was to have fallen out of place, there was no question at all that he would have broken and his gears would have fallen all over the table. That would have been the end of him unless he and all his pieces could have been quickly put in a paper bag and brought to an Olivetti repairman.

There was the cigar smoker who everyone at the Tuesday Table called Winston even though his name was Gregory. He once burned a small hole in the Tuesday Table when a large hot tobacco ash fell off his cigar. Every Tuesday he would come in very early, ahead of the other regulars, and lay a manila envelope in front of him, covering the hole. He would wait to be the last to leave. He considered the meeting to have been a success if no one had discovered the sole purpose of the manila envelope along with his early entrance and late departure. While others talked, he occasionally would lift the edge of the manila envelope just enough so that he alone could check the hole to see if it was as bad as he believed. It always looked as bad as he believed.

Then there was the woman who had smug confidence written all over her face. She knew, and everyone knew, that she had security. LBJ was trying to illustrate his rule of equality for women in government and women were going to hold more than secretarial positions. But did it have to be her? Surely there was some woman in the United States more qualified than "Lorna Liberated" who looked at each member of the Tuesday Table as if they were all animals in a zoo and she was the only one with her buttons on.

Sitting next to Lorna Liberated was the sniffer. He had an uncontrollable allergy that presented him with the problem of sniffing, which would have been all right except that he sniffed very loud and made a rumbling noise every time he did it. He never seemed to hear himself because he showed no sign that he was aware of the fact that he was disrupting the proceedings with that machine-gun noise that emanated from his nose, with no way for anyone to know when the next firing would take place.

There was the man with the small white beard who looked much too intensely at his peers as they gave their reports. He squinted his eyes at the speaker as if he was thinking deeply about every word that was said and then suddenly, while the speaker had yet to finish, he would snap his head from the stare and turn it to the director, nodding in approval, with his lower lip rising to cover his upper lip. By his actions he was saying, "It's true. It's true," but he generally didn't know what the speaker was talking about.

After each participant made his or her report, the director asked them questions. On the fourth Tuesday of November, the director was overseas and it fell to Ambassador Fairbanks to take over the Agency and, therefore, to officiate at the Tuesday Table.

He asked the young man who looked like an electric typewriter what the Agency did regarding the death of Henry Wallace.

"Anne Whitney wrote an obituary, sir," electric typewriter said. "It was picked up either in whole or in part by 34 major newspapers around the world and it played very well." He had no idea how many newspapers picked it up, but he talked with precision.

Ambassador Fairbanks cleared his throat. "Anne Whitney?"

"Yes, sir. She did a fine job."

"I'd like to see the obituary."

"Yes, sir. I'll have that to you this morning."

"Was it was published in 34 newspapers or 34 nations or both?"

"Thirty-four newspapers, sir, and they were in 26 different countries." That sounded good.

"I'd like to see them."

"Yes, sir. I'll have them for you. We'll get them together and I'll have them in your office this morning with her original text."

Lorna Liberated couldn't leave well enough alone. "Ms. Whitney also did a fine report, Gerry, on those five pacifists who burned their draft cards in New York."

It did not escape Ambassador Fairbanks that Anne Whitney was referred to as "Ms. Whitney" and he was referred to as "Gerry." But that was expected of Ms. Liberated. "I'd like to see that."

She nodded one nod, closing her eyes as she did it.

Gregory, who everyone called Winston, peered underneath his manila envelope and quickly snapped it back into position over the burn hole. "I have nothing to report, Gerry."

The sniffer sniffed loudly and said, "Every post asked for information on the east coast power blackout and we were able to get a kinescope of a CBS hour television show on it and we sent it all over the world, even to the Eastern European countries. It was a great success." And then he sniffed so loud that he frightened Ambassador Fairbanks.

"What purpose did that kinescope serve?" the Ambassador asked. "Where was the freight in that one?"

"Well, sir," the sniffer answered, "a lot of people around the world lost confidence in us when we had such a massive power failure. They didn't think that could happen in the United States."

"So what? What did the CBS film do to help us?"

"It explained it, sir."

"All right. All right. I hope we didn't spend a fortune on it."

"Less than one thousand dollars, sir, or we wouldn't have done it." He had no idea how much it cost.

Through all of this, the man with the small white beard was in bliss, squinting his eyes at one speaker after the other, alternating his look between the speaker and Ambassador Fairbanks, with a continuing nod as though he was the confirmation of all things.

It was easy to make lies come true in government. The electric typewriter asked his librarian for 34 obituaries of Henry Wallace from newspapers around the world, making sure eight of them were from duplicate countries, and he told her only a couple should be in English, and to be sure that some of the information that was written in the obituary was information that was also in Anne Whitney's text. That was a cinch.

Lorna Liberated re-read the Anne Whitney report on the burning of draft cards in New York and realized Ambassador Fairbanks might not like it, so she enclosed a memo saying "the other side" was also sent out, and enclosed a statement of Vice President Humphrey.

The sniffer found out the Agency spent $8,220 on the CBS television show on the power blackout, so he simply charged $7,500 to "Miscellaneous News Clips." The confirmation of the less than $1000 figure would go directly to Ambassador Fairbanks.

Ambassador Fairbanks was furious at the items that couldn't be covered up from him. The original text of the obituary of Henry Wallace made Wallace out to be a mix of George Washington, Mohandas Gandhi, and Albert Schweitzer, and there was a complimentary reference to Wallace's opposition to President Johnson's foreign policies.

The text she wrote about the draft card burners was in total support of what they did.

Ambassador Fairbanks pressed the intercom on his phone. "Get me Mark Daschle on the phone wherever he is in this God-blessed world. He's public affairs officer somewhere."

It was twenty minutes before his secretary buzzed him. "Mr. Daschle is in Brasilia, Ambassador Fairbanks."

"That's fine. I don't care where he is. Get him on the line for me–" and then realizing how rude he sounded, he added, "please."

"He's on the line, Ambassador Fairbanks. I was just telling you where he is. Pick up Line 2."

"Thank you. That's good. Thank you." He snapped the button. "Mark?"

"Hello, Mr. Ambassador," the very comforting voice of Mark Daschle greeted him.

"Mark! God bless you, Mark!"

"God bless me? To what do I owe all this devotion?"

"Just that you're a voice of sanity."

Mark laughed. "That's what you think. This place is driving me nuts."

"Brazil?"

"Brasilia. The country's magnificent, it's beautiful. But Brasilia–it's fine if you like living in Dulles Airport. That's what this city looks and feels like."

"That's what I heard."

"And we're in the middle of nowhere. They picked a devil of a place to build a new capital city. It's getting a little better. They're building some slums now, so it feels more like a city."

"Do you get to Rio or Sao Paulo?"

"Whenever I can. But I can't believe you called me to find out if I was happy. I'm just delighted about your appointment, Gerry. That's the best appointment the president has made. How's Mary?"

"Good. She's just fine." Ambassador Fairbanks cleared his throat. "Now, I have a problem, Mark. Mark, what am I supposed to do with Anne Whitney?"

"Oh! Anne!"

"Annc."

"Anne."

"Anne. Do you want me to go into detail?" Ambassador Fairbanks leaned back in his leather-backed chair.

"No. Please don't. I know Anne."

"You're the only one I can ask, Mark. You've worked with her. You had to send her home from Hong Kong. As it worked out—now I'm stuck with her."

"Have you thought of killing her?"

"That was my first thought, but I discounted it based on the prison term that could ruin my career."

"Give it more thought. It might be worth it."

"You want me to send her to Brasilia?"

"Don't even joke about that, Gerry. I'm not thinking of me. It's the U.S. relationship with Latin American countries. She'd organize the communists in Recife here, they'd stage a coup, President Branco would resign, then she'd attack Venezuela, knock down their democracy, and all of Latin America would be at war."

"What do I do, Mark?"

"Strangely enough, there's a lot of good in her, Gerry."

"I know there is."

"She has a good heart. But her head is all messed up. She resents any authority. Why don't you send her to some remote post? Send her to Nepal or Upper Volta."

"My first thought was to do something like that. She told me a long time ago that she wanted to go to Tanganyika, but I think she just liked its name. Ever since it merged with Zanzibar last year and became Tanzania, she hasn't expressed any interest in it to anyone around here. I still thought I'd send her there but Tanzania is getting in bed with Mainland China and you know where she'd come down on that one. You know, in thinking about sending her to some hardship post, any hardship post, I've finally come to the conclusion that it would be a mistake. She'd be getting hardship pay, she'd have servants, she'd live like a queen, and worse than anything is that the people there would think of her as 'the American', maybe the only American they'd ever meet. So I thought that what I should do is send her to some world center where they see so many Americans they wouldn't give her any importance. I started to lean toward that, toward Paris or Tokyo or Rome or London, but I'd be passing her over too many foreign service officers who have worked hard to be in one of those posts. I'm in a mess on this one."

"I'm not recommending it, but have you thought of just sending her out of the federal government entirely?"

"Oh, Mark. You know how hard it is to get rid of anyone in this bureaucracy. It would take years at best. She'd have so many appeals and God knows what she'd dream up as my motive for getting rid of her."

"Through her worst days in Hong Kong there was something I liked about Anne. Individuality, maybe. And then that little incident in India with the dying man showed her stuff. She knew she was risking a lot personally by the way she handled it, and it happened at a bad time for her, but she took that risk, just out of the goodness of her heart. She wasn't acting like so many of our officers would have acted under the same conditions. Good for her. I'm confident that in time she could be a real asset to the foreign service if she just knew enough about the world. She has great potential as a leader if she would stop thinking she already is one. Hey–I have it! I think I have it! I know I have it!"

"Go ahead, please."

"It just came to me. It's perfect. She can't possibly do any harm there. She'll learn more than she could learn anywhere else about what she needs to know. It's not some remote city no one ever heard of, and although it will be confining, it won't be us who would be confining her. She would learn so much."

"Where?"

"Hold on, Gerry, and don't react to my suggestion right away. Think about it."

"Where?"

Mark hesitated for a moment and then answered, "Moscow!"

Ambassador Fairbanks was silent. Then he cleared his throat. Then he cleared it again. He finally answered with a soft voice that seemed congested. "My God, Mark. You're a genius. You're an absolute genius."

"She doesn't like any establishment. Let her live under that one. What harm can she do in that place?"

"You're a genius."

"She'll be Ambassador Kohler's problem–and you know, I don't think she'll be a problem at all if he's just a little patient with her. She feels for people. She's going to feel for the Russian people, not their government."

"Genius!"

"You for it?"

"It's perfect. It's neither reward nor punishment. It will help us and it will help her."

"Good, Gerry."

"You really came through on this one. God bless you, Mark."

"Come on out to Brasilia some time, Gerry. We'd like to see you down here. It gets a little lonely. Even when congressional delegations come to Brazil they spend their time in Rio, not here. Imagine that–I even miss congressional delegations."

"You're a life-saver. Maybe a nation-saver. I'm going to move on that. Anne Whitney in Moscow! It makes sense."

Beyond the District that night in her Suitland, Maryland apartment, Anne's feet were high in the air, her legs were resting on the back of her couch, her head was almost on the floor, the phone's receiver was cradled between her left ear and her shoulder while her right hand was in perpetual motion between a bowl of popcorn and her mouth, and her glasses were giving magnified vision only to her forehead. "Guess where I'm going, Ted! Guess where I'm going!"

Ted Murphy was shocked when she told him it was Moscow; that she actually was being given a foreign post, and an important one. He called his wife, Linda, to the phone to congratulate Anne. Linda brought their crying infant boy to the phone, and it was difficult for Anne to hear anything but the crying.

"Wait," Linda said, "talk to Ted again. I have to take care of Tommy." Ted, happily, took the phone back and Linda and the baby went into the other room, and the crying dissolved into the background. Ted literally begged Anne to be a source from Moscow for his column. She didn't answer him, but kept him guessing. For once she was in a position of strength. When she asked him how his column was doing, he had to confess it was losing placement in newspapers.

"I can guess why, Ted. It's because they don't like your politics. You attack President Johnson on Vietnam and the Dominican Republic and all that, and those Goldwater-type publishers don't like it."

"Sorry, Anne. I'd like to be a martyr for the cause but that isn't it. It's television. It's that they're closin' up newspapers. The ones I've lost are ones that aren't in business anymore. They combine with other ones or they just close their doors entirely. TV is the place these days. That's where I want to go. I have a sharp agent who's talkin' to the networks for me. Hey, you can help me. C'mon, Annie, give me some good stories or some good leads from Moscow. A lot of the stuff you give me from the Agency and State is terrific, but from Moscow? Wow! Think about it, Annie. Between you and me we can change the world!"

"And me!" Linda yelled in from the other room where she had Tommy under control.

"And Linda," he added. "Linda wants to change the world, too."

"And Tommy!" Linda yelled back.

"The rev-o-loo-see-ohn!" Anne said. "Okay, Ted, this is your Moscow correspondent signing off. Got to go now. Do-svee-dah-nya!"

"Goodnight, Annie. Thanks for callin'. Tell Kosygin to call me any time he has a scoop! He doesn't have to go through you!"

"I'll do it. Bye-bye."

She hung up the phone which was resting next to her, then she went to the closet. She pushed the hangers from one side to the other and examined one dress after another. "I'll need a new wardrobe," she said to herself. "I'll need a fur coat." And then she corrected herself. "Oh, no. I shouldn't do that. I mustn't show wealth. I should live like the Russians!"

Ambassador Fairbanks could hardly wait until the next meeting at the Tuesday Table when he would tell the top staff that Anne Whitney was going to Moscow. By following Mark Daschle's advice, he was outsmarting them all.

"May God help Alexi Kosygin, Nikolai Podgorny, and Leonid Brezhnev," he said to himself.

SEVENTEEN
UNEVEN RHYTHMS
1966

"No dancing in the aisles," the train conductor said with a laugh when he saw Adam almost fall as he walked down the aisle. The train had given a quick jolt and was swaying from side to side in its rush—not rushing from Moscow to Vladivostok for which Adam had spent so much time preparing, but the train was rushing from New York City to Washington, D.C. Adam reached for the top of a seat with one hand and tightened his hold on the capped cardboard container of hot coffee with the other hand and he murmured a hostile sound.

"No swearing while you dance," the conductor said and laughed again, balancing himself perfectly without holding onto anything. The conductor flaunted his talent further by calmly walking down the aisle punching tickets of passengers, and making a show of the fact that he was unaffected by the jostling of the train. Of all the moments in Adam's life, this was not the appropriate one to bring to his attention anything that could be interpreted as an inadequacy in him.

"Big deal," Adam said beneath his breath to the conductor, not so he could be heard but so he could defend himself to himself. "If I spent my life walking in trains, I could balance myself, too." Adam sat down and uncapped his coffee while a quick sway of the train caused a small portion of the coffee to leap out of its container onto his right hand. "That does it! That does it!" And it was very hot.

The coffee that remained in the cup looked back at him with as pompous a stance as did the conductor. "That does what?" the coffee asked him.

"I don't know," Adam answered. "You win. You all win."

The coffee nodded as it settled down, content with the appeasement of the only spy that cup of coffee had ever met. Adam pulled his handkerchief out of his pocket to wipe his right hand. Now his handkerchief looked awful with its coffee stain, so he quickly stuffed it into his back pocket.

"In three minutes we will arrive in Bal-di-more. Bal-di-more," the conductor announced over the public address system. "Please check the seat pocket in front of you and the overhead rack for all your belongings. In three minutes, Bal-di-more."

That was Adam's golden opportunity and he knew it. "It's Bal-ti-more, you jerk, not Bal-di-more," which was a stunning, unheard victory. "Where did you go to school?" and he gave a slight tight-mouthed smile, then leaned contentedly back in his seat. But like a giant breaker surging forward unexpectedly, the thought of what he learned in New York about the cancellation of the trip on the Trans-Siberian Railway acted like a stab in his stomach that settled into nausea. The conductor and the coffee had been his friends after all, since they made him forget for a short time.

"I wonder, if that celebrity the Soviets invited knows?" he asked the coffee. "I wonder if he knows that as soon as my name was submitted to Moscow, they canceled the whole trip. I'm poison. They know what I'm up to and I won't be able to get back to the Soviet Union no matter what. It's done." He closed his eyes and rested his head against the train window, but the train shook so much that his head started rattling against the glass. He opened his eyes and took another sip of coffee. "I'm sick of failure."

In New York this morning he had met with Vladimir Suslov of the USSR's delegation to the United Nations, and Suslov gave little information except to say, "the travel will not take place, Mr. Orr. The trip is canceled indefinitely." And so all the studying of the Russian language was a total waste, as was his study of every city and place along the route of that distant railway which was to remain distant. To make matters worse, two trips he could have taken to Hong Kong had been passed by so he could continue his studies of the Soviet Union.

"Excuse me," the woman across the aisle leaned over, "but aren't you Senator Fulbright?"

"No," he said. He didn't want to talk.

"You look like someone."

"No," he said. "I'm no one."

"You look like someone. You're in politics, aren't you?"

"I'm not in anything."

"Are you that California governor? That Governor Brown?"

"I'm sorry. I do not govern things."

"Well, I'm glad you're not that Governor Brown."

"Good. Anything to make you happy."

"He executed Caryl Chessman out there, you know."

"Good. Good."

"It was lethal gas. It killed him."

"That'll do it every time."

"Are you sure you're not Governor Brown?"

"I don't think so. Maybe I am. I have a bad memory."

"Bal-di-more! Bal-di-more!" The conductor's voice came over the loudspeaker system and the view from the window became obscured by pillars and posts and a filthy interior station with stone stairways. "Please check the seat pocket in front of you and the overhead racks for all your belongings. This is our only stop in Bal-di-more." The station looked like something out of an old Warner Brothers movie that took place in France during World War I.

The train pulled out of the Baltimore station, which caused the rest of his coffee to spill all over the floor.

"Are you Governor Tawes?" That lady across the aisle hadn't taken her eyes off him.

"All right. You win. I'm Steve McQueen," he answered.

She moved her head backward slowly. "I don't believe you. You don't look anything like him."

"Then I'm Franklin Delano Roosevelt. I just don't remember."

"He's dead. That's not funny."

"Lady, there's no reason for you to care who I am. I don't care who you are. I don't care if you're Madame Curie or if you run a whorehouse. Can you just think of other things for a while? Surely there must be something of interest in your life other than trying to figure out who I am. Just, please force yourself to think of intriguing things that have happened in your ever-diminishing lifetime."

By the time the train passed the warehouse of the Hecht Company on Washington's New York Avenue, he came to the conclusion that he would get out of the intelligence business. He would be what others thought he already was: a security man with Pan American at Cape Canaveral. That would have to be good enough.

That isn't good enough. He closed his eyes and waited for the train conductor's final call for Union Station. *I'd go nuts if that's all I did,* he thought. *I won't do anything. I have enough money. I won't do anything. I'll find a cause. Some cause.*

"In three minutes we will arrive in Wash-ing-don," the train conductor announced over the public address system. "This is our last stop. Wash-ing-don, D.C. Please check the seat pocket in front of you and the overhead racks for all your belongings. In three minutes, Union Station in Wash-ing-don."

Now the conductor seemed to be a man of previously unrecognized virtue to Adam. After all, the conductor was functioning in his job in apparent contentment. He had no conscience because he wasn't doing something else.

And then the train conductor made a last appearance in the coach, checking the racks above the seats. He spotted a newspaper in the seat pocket in front of Adam. "Want your paper?"

Adam shook his head. "No, I don't want the paper. I'll leave it. That's fine."

The woman across the aisle said, "I'll take it." She was a scavenger.

"Fine," Adam said and the conductor took *The New York Times* from the seat pocket in front of Adam, and walked it over to her, and he performed that entire function while balancing himself perfectly without holding on to anything. He was good at what he did.

Between three minutes to Baltimore and three minutes to the District, the conductor became not only virtuous to Adam, but he gained Adam's intense admiration. "How does he do it?" Adam asked himself as he watched the conductor walking unbothered by uneven rhythms.

From Union Station, Adam rented a Dodge at Avis and drove to the Central Intelligence Agency Headquarters at Langley. He knew the way: he had to know the way because there were no signs, no maps, no confirmation to the public that it even existed off that unnoticed turn-off from the George Washington Parkway.

"Martin," Adam said, "I'm afraid I'm of no value to you anymore. I told you when you were at the Cape, it's no good. There comes a time to concede defeat and we stretched the time to its limits. Believe me, there's no one who regrets this more than I do. But I'm a realist. If I'm persona non grata in the Soviet Union, my value to you has to have gone somewhere down under the cracks."

He used to savor the scent he inhaled within that building, but now he smelled nothing. It was gone for him.

"Your only down-side to us, Adam, is your impatience. I think I told you before–beneath that thick-skinned exterior of yours, you're too sensitive. Any success we've had here comes after one hundred disappointments. Our success is our persistence. Let me put it this way–you know more about missiles and rockets than I'll ever know. Ask yourself, how many blew up on the launching pads there at the Cape before there was a clean launch? But even the blow-ups were successes in disguise because they demanded that you guys down there find out what went wrong. The only difference between the Cape and us at Langley is that the public at least knows when you have a success. We can't admit it when we have one. So the public thinks of us as the U-2 boys and the architects of the Bay of Pigs. That's all."

"Martin, I think the world of you guys, but I got to get on with my life. I'm not a kid, I'm a 55-year-old man. I want to help you in any way I can because I love the mission, I love the work, you're good guys. But the worst thing I can do is screw you up. You should have had some new guy on the Trans-Siberian Railway venture–some new guy without a history that creates suspicion by the Soviets. If some new guy had been given that assignment, the whole thing would probably have come through by now."

Martin shrugged. "But someone new wouldn't have had your outrageous memorization ability to recall so many hundreds of details without writing them down. And you know what things are important and what things aren't important. It was worth the risk. We knew it might not work. We've had bigger disappointments than this one. So the Soviet Union is out for you. Too bad. This one didn't work the way we wanted. Do you think we're all crying here? It's just another day."

"I'm not crying either. I just have to get on with life."

"I understand that. You speak Arabic?"

"Why? Now, what's this about?"

"I just want to know. You went to Morocco for us before I was here–that was a long time ago. Did you learn any Arabic?"

"A little."

"You still remember it?"

"A few words, at best. I was never proficient in it. I never learned the characters. I can't read anything or write anything in it. I could probably understand simple things but only if someone talks slow. What's this one, Martin?"

"You ever been to Egypt?"

"No."

"Saudi Arabia?"

"No."

"Syria?"

"No."

"Jordan?"

"Yes."

"Israel?"

"Yes."

"It's a great part of the world, Martin. Magnificent. No one should miss any of those countries. It's the Bible. It's all there. I'll tell you, Adam, I feel sorry for anyone who's reached the age of 55 or so and hasn't been in every one of those countries. Can you imagine anyone missing the cradle of our civilization? It's hard to believe that those with the opportunity wouldn't take advantage of it. But there actually are some of those people. Poor saps."

What was that aroma that suddenly seeped into the room? It was a comfortable, warm fragrance.

"What do I do about Pan Am? About the Cape?"

"Quit. Maybe a leave of absence. We can help on that. This one could be a long one."

"It isn't that easy. I'm very devoted to that place. It's home."

"You'll be back some day."

"And I have an efficiency there–in Cocoa Beach–a condo."

Martin shrugged. "Like the Arabs, one night you fold up your tent and silently steal away. Arabs have great wisdom. They accept life as a succession of caravans. Caravans leave. Caravans arrive. Sometimes when you see them coming or going on the horizon, those caravans move so slowly you can't even see the motion. But, sure enough, they're coming or they're going. There's no road. There's no path. If some sap constructed one it would only last hours because sand would cover it with one quick breeze. Their journeys are long and somehow they get where they want to go. They don't care about speed. Only the destination is important. Above all, they're unafraid to leave where they've been or to arrive where they've never been. We can all learn from such wisdom, Adam. You're just the man for this. And Moscow doesn't have to approve or disapprove."

Adam nodded slowly. "It sounds like the Mideast is to you, what Hong Kong is to me."

"I have memories there. But they won't be lived again. Now–back to you–I'm not suggesting you become the second Lawrence of Arabia, you know. The first Adam of America will do just fine."

Adam pressed his lips together, and he breathed in very deeply. Someone should have opened the window.

EIGHTEEN
JUMPING JAFFA
1967

President Gamal Abdel Nasser of Egypt made no secret of his intent. On Wednesday, May the 14th of 1967 he massed his troops into the Sinai Peninsula, and announced war was his objective.

By this time everyone who worked in the alleyway bazaars knew Adam Orr as Jonathan Steel, the American fountain pen merchant who handled the distribution of leading American fountain pen companies as well as distributing some of the best-known European brands. They knew he went from city to city within the Mideast, and that he somehow went into and out of Israel but never had an Israeli visa or entrance stamp in his passport. They guessed that through some act of pay-off, he held two U.S. passports. They were wrong. He held three. One of them had his real name, and the other two had his new name. One of those was to be used for Arab countries, another for Israel. Had there been an Israeli stamp of any kind in the passport submitted to airport authorities in an Arab country, entry would have been denied. The authorities weren't angry at his slick evasion of the law, they marveled at his assuredness.

Beyond the airports, through promises, dollars, and other acts of persuasion, he managed to entice one bureaucrat after another, going higher and higher on the bureaucracy's ladders until the top echelons of Mideast governments greeted him with at least temporary friendship. There were those close to kings, mullahs, emirs, sheiks, presidents, prime ministers, and generals, who knew him as a foolish but welcome American businessman who sold them sterling silver and gold pens and mechanical pencils for very low prices, and often at no cost at all, so they could give them as gifts. In exchange, he asked them to protect him if he got into trouble with either alcohol or loose women, both of which were highly restricted for the general population of most Arab nations.

"Ahhh," Adam would say while displaying his wares from an open, slender and wide black case to a government official. "Here we have a sterling silver Parker. And here's a rare Montblanc without its snowcap insignia that looks identical to a Star of David—it's gone—disappeared—magic. Wouldn't you say it's a Montblanc made to order for you? Or have you ever seen one of these old Eversharp pen and pencil sets? That's gold. It's a 'Command Performance' which came out right after the war. You can't get them any more. If I were you, I wouldn't give this to anyone—unless, of course, she gives you something just as valuable in return!"

Adam made sure that when in Arab governmental circles, he sounded like a total amateur in politics and government and war and peace, but he was often successful in turning the conversation to those subjects while acting bored by them. Between his tired looks and phony attempts to change the subject, he put into practice the camera and tape machine inside his head.

Cabinet members close to President Nasser of Egypt thought he was a corrupt capitalist.

Colonels that surrounded General Salah al-Jadid of Syria thought he was an alcoholic.

The Council of Notables under King Hussein of Jordan thought he was a pleasant man who, like so many, wanted to be on good terms with the government to impress others.

Arab Socialist Union Members of President Abdul Rahman Arif of Iraq thought he was a man who stole from America and Europe and turned his stolen goods into Mideast sales.

Family members of King Faisal of Saudi Arabia thought he was a crazy man who was probably a fugitive wanted by the police in the United States.

The dancer, Sabra Modai, who worked in Jaffa, Israel, dancing in a cage at the Jumping Jaffa, was the most mistaken of all. She thought he would be a likely catch.

Cabinet members of Israel and Prime Minister Levi Eshkol had no doubt that he was with the U.S. Central Intelligence Agency.

General Moshe Dayan of Israel knew him to be a friend.

From the end of April, Adam had been sending messages back to CIA Headquarters in Langley telling his superiors that Egypt was preparing for a war that would come within the next few months, that Nasser had been telling his cabinet that the war's objective would be to destroy Israel, and Syria's al Jahid had agreed to act under Nasser's orders. Further, Adam told Langley that it was probable that the Soviet Union would support Egypt and Syria, but someone else would have to find out how much support Premier Kosygin was willing to give. Pending anything beyond prediction, all that could hold back the war, Adam reported, was the United Nations Emergency Force that was in the Sinai and Gaza, whose job was to monitor and maintain the peace by preventing aggression from either side. Adam warned, however, that Nasser's top lieutenants and other Arab leaders were talking about the U.N.'s Secretary General U Thant as though he was under their control. "They wink when they mention him. From their remarks I would assume that either he is friendly to them and to the Soviets, or they simply scare him. I don't know what goes on in private between them, but it would be a mistake to count on U Thant to deter Egypt's plan for a war."

All of this he found out through the gifts of his fountain pens and the enticement of his personality.

Since the British Mandate of 1920 granted by the League of Nations and through the United Nations partition of 1947, the region was defined in maps of ever-changing boundaries. The League gave 78 percent of the territory for the creation of what became Jordan. The remaining 22 percent was partitioned by the U.N. between Israel and an Independent Arab State of Gaza, Judea and Samaria with Jerusalem as an international zone.

After partition, Egypt invaded and seized Gaza, and Jordan invaded and seized Judea and Samaria including eastern Jerusalem. Jordan called the territory they captured "The West Bank," meaning the west bank of the Kingdom of Jordan, a name that defined it as Jordanian territory, across the river from the rest of Jordan. All Jews who survived the Jordanian invasion were either killed or expelled. Their graveyards were all that were left of them and so they were destroyed, with the gravestones used as latrines. Christians who remained were mandated to send their children to schools to learn the Islamic religion.

For nineteen years following 1948, Jordan ruled Judea and Samaria, not allowing the discussion of an independent Arab state. Egypt retained jurisdiction of Gaza during the same nineteen years and, like Jordan, did not allow the discussion of an independent Arab State. And so it would have continued had not President Nasser massed his troops into the Sinai Desert that Wednesday in May of 1967.

On the following Sunday, May 18 of 1967, the Voice of the Arabs Radio announced, "The sole method we shall apply against Israel is a total war which will result in the extermination of Zionist existence."

On the same Sunday, President Nasser demanded that Secretary General U Thant of the United Nations organization get his United Nations Emergency Force out of the Sinai and Gaza.

On Monday, U Thant agreed to move the U.N.'s Emergency Force from its peace-keeping activities in the Sinai and Gaza, allowing invasion troops of Egypt to advance toward Israel.

On Tuesday, the U.N. began moving out as Nasser had demanded and U Thant had ordered.

On Wednesday, Egyptian tanks started coming en mass across the Sinai Desert toward the border of Israel, and Egyptian troops blockaded the Gulf of Aqaba in an attempt to isolate Israel from the rest of the world by preventing most shipments into and out of Israel.

Even the threat of war didn't stop the beaches of Tel Aviv from being lined with May sunbathers, and although the hotels were becoming absent of tourists, the lounges of the hotels were still occupied by Israeli residents. On Thursday afternoon General Moshe Dayan was at the bar of the Tel Aviv Sheraton sipping a cup of thick black coffee, and sitting next to him was his American friend with all the fountain pens, who was eating from a plate of scrambled eggs.

General Dayan, his eye-patch telling even a distant viewer who he was, gestured toward Adam's plate. "Scrambled! I have seen Americans in wealth, health, poverty, misery, away from their country in grand and deplorable conditions. Through it all, the thing of which they are the fussiest is the way their eggs are prepared! They say, 'Over easy!' Or 'Sunny-side up!' Or 'Scrambled!'"

Adam laughed. "I think you're right."

"And Nescafé. Every American carries Nescafé in case they don't like the local coffee!"

"General," Adam said, "When will the war start?" When in Israel, Adam did not make any pretense of being disinterested in politics and government and war and peace,

General Dayan nodded, his smile quickly disappearing. "Soon. It will be soon. The movement of their tanks and troops indicate they will attack soon."

"Do you wait for them?"

"Perhaps. It's a difficult decision. World opinion may go against us if we have a preemptive strike. But a preemptive strike might well save thousands of Israeli lives; civilians as well as military. We cannot allow the murder of Israeli lives for the sake of avoiding a hostile speech delivered against us in the United Nations organization. But right now there are too many variables to make a decision. We have time to appraise, but not much time."

"Couldn't victory be dependent on who strikes first?"

"It might, but at this moment at least, I believe we will win either way. The question to us is how many lives will be lost. We will win because Nasser's objective is expansion, while our objective is survival. We must win, and so we will. At this point nothing can be calculated with precision, not even on how many fronts we will have to fight."

"You know you'll have to fight on two fronts, don't you? In the west against Egypt, and the north against Syria."

"Our fear is three fronts," General Dayan corrected him. "Jordan will attack us from the east if Nasser gives the order to King Hussein."

"You sure?"

"No. In the Mideast nothing is for sure, but King Hussein is in a weak position in the Arab world. His own people would overthrow him if they had the chance. Many of his people are his worst enemies. We're not." General Dayan pushed his coffee cup aside and nodded to the bartender who came to him to refill it.

"Why not give him your word that when the war comes, you won't attack any of the territory he already holds if he doesn't attack any of yours? Neither of you will have anything to lose that way."

"That's logical enough but logic has no place in the Mideast, my friend. Don't you know the story of the scorpion who wanted to cross the Jordan River?"

"No. Not that one."

General Dayan started to play with his coffee cup, swirling the coffee dangerously near the brim of the cup. He liked to live close to the edge even on small things. "There was a scorpion who wanted to cross the Jordan River, and he saw—"

"Which direction? From Jordan to Israel or Israel to Jordan?"

"It doesn't make any difference. I don't know, that has nothing to do with it," and he stopped toying with his cup. "Listen to me. A scorpion wanted to cross the Jordan River and it saw a turtle that was heading to the river. The scorpion said, 'Turtle, please let me ride on your back. I want to get to the other side to see my relatives and I can't swim like you, but I can steady myself on your shell if you allow me to.'

"The turtle said, 'Oh, no. I know that you're a scorpion and we will get midway across the river and you'll bite me and I'll drown.'

"The scorpion laughed and said, 'Why would I do such a thing? If I did that and you drowned, I would drown, too. Think, turtle. I want to ride on your shell because I can't swim. My life will be dependent on your life.'

"The turtle thought over what the scorpion said and he nodded. 'All right, scorpion. Hop on my shell.'

"The scorpion hopped on the turtle's shell and they went in the river. About midway across, the scorpion crawled to the turtle's neck and bit it. The turtle turned his head toward the scorpion, totally perplexed. He started to feel the poison go from his neck to his head, to his feet, and then he couldn't move his feet and he started to drown. 'Why? Why did you do that, scorpion?' the turtle asked. 'It doesn't make sense. Now we will both die.'

"'Ahh,' the scorpion said, 'you forgot one thing, turtle.'

"'What?' the turtle gurgled.

"The scorpion answered, 'It doesn't have to make sense. You forgot—this is the Mideast.'"

Adam smiled and nodded. "A lot of truth there. That's very good."

"It's an old story. Arab and Jew alike know it, although everyone has their own version. Every version means the same thing: don't count on logic to have any bearing on decisions made in the Mideast. Now, on your idea of pledging to King Hussein that we won't touch his territorial claims if he doesn't touch ours, we've thought of all that. But you see, we can't talk to him. We have no diplomatic relations. He says we don't exist. You know the line."

"But would you give such a pledge?"

"Of course. If he would."

"I can talk to him."

"I do not mean to diminish your importance, my good friend, but Hussein isn't going to take the word of some unofficial messenger. He would need an emissary of my government, which is impossible, or your government which is possible but unlikely, to give him such a message from us. But I mean an official emissary, not a fountain pen salesman—or a CIA agent. I hope you're not offended, my friend. I like your pens," and the General laughed with a smile that erupted on one side of his face. The side with the eye-patch didn't move.

"Let me get a message off to our people in D.C. I'll walk over to the Embassy and get a message off. Would your government give a guarantee to our government that Israel would not attack Jordan if it didn't attack you?"

"As good as done. Get your message off if you want. Do it. It can't do any harm but I wouldn't count on your State Department agreeing to it."

"I can try."

General Dayan shrugged. "I like your Defense Department and your Intelligence Agency but your State Department is full of Arabists. They admit it. It's no secret. They say that the root of the problem in the Mideast is what they call the Palestinian Question. What kind of rot is that? What they call the question is, in reality, the answer for Arab chiefs of state in their quest of exhibiting some unity to the world. The only thing they can agree on is Palestine. Most Arab leaders know that the root of the Mideast's problem is their own leadership. Most of them want to expand their borders over each other's lands. Even if all of Israel ceased to exist, the government of Syria would still want to take over Lebanon and Jordan. The government of Libya would still want to take over Chad, the Sudan, and Egypt. The government of Iraq would still want to take over Iran, Kuwait, and Saudi Arabia. The governments of Somalia and Ethiopia would still want to take over each other. Yemen is splitting up and both halves want to take over the other half and then go after Oman. The only unifying force is that all those governments want to be done with Israel—throw us into the sea, as Nasser says, and then they can war among themselves over who takes the conquered territory. My friend, your State Department should understand that the quest of expansion by Arab leaders is the root of the problems in the Mideast."

"Our State Department knows the geopolitical realities here, but you know why they are Arabists, don't you?"

"They don't like us. They never have."

"Like and dislike has nothing to do with it. And it's not the American version of the turtle and the scorpion. This one has logic to it. Not morality, but logic."

"Then what is it?"

"Nothing more or less than human nature, General. They want to have a good time. State is full of foreign service officers who have a succession of foreign posts throughout their careers. With 21 Arab countries and another 20 other Islamic countries, 41 countries in all, the odds are that the average U.S. foreign service officer will serve in a lot of Islamic countries during a career. There's only one Israel and the odds are very low they'll even see this place. Life is easier for U.S. foreign service officers when they're serving in a friendly country whose citizens and government like us, rather than in an unfriendly country whose citizens and government are throwing rocks at us. It's that simple. They want to make life easy for themselves. They know the odds. 41 to one in which they'd be welcome."

"That's interesting."

"There's nothing more to it than that. But when it comes to war—they'll put their good life on the back burner. Believe me. They have no hatred of Israel. They're just weak. Let me walk down the beach to our Embassy and try sending a message on having a top-level emissary meet with Hussein."

"Be careful walking to your embassy, my friend. I don't want you to get blown up on your walk down there. These are ripe days for terrorists. It's all right if they blow you up on the way back, but don't let them blow you up on your way there." And he laughed, giving that one side of his face smile again.

One day later, President Johnson sent Under-Secretary of State Eugene Rostow to visit with King Hussein of Jordan. Rostow told the king that the government of Israel would make a pledge, guaranteed by the United States, that if Jordan would stay out of the war that was imminent, and not join Egypt and Syria, Israel would not touch any Jordanian-held territory, including Old Jerusalem and all the territory that Jordan referred to as its west bank. "There is a promise of absolute immunity," Under-Secretary Rostow told the king. King Hussein listened to the under-secretary, but made no commitment.

Unaware of the meeting that was going on at the time, Adam, with his case of pens, was making one of his increasingly frequent walks down the beach to the U.S. Embassy to beg Langley once more that such a meeting be held with King Hussein. As was the custom, he was the last to know if his requests had been accommodated.

"Orr! Orr! Adam Orr!"

Adam came to a quick stop when he heard the shout. Coming to a quick stop was a mistake and he realized it as soon as he did it. He was going under the name of Jonathan Steel, not that the Israeli government accepted that as his name. But the stop was done and there was nothing he could do to recover that quick period of time. After waiting much too long, he turned around. "Yes?"

"What the deuce are you doin' here, Orr?" It was not a terrorist but perhaps worse. It was the columnist, Ted Murphy.

"Hey there," Adam said. "Murphy, right? 'Murphy's Law.'"

"Ted Murphy." He approached Adam and they shook hands. "Remember? Hong Kong. We met in Hong Kong."

"I know." Adam put his thin black case down on the sand.

"You looked like I scared you!"

"You did."

"Sorry, Orr. Why be scared?"

"I didn't expect anyone to shout my name."

"Does that bother you?"

"Yes, Murphy, it does."

"Why?"

"Wouldn't it bother you—suddenly someone yelling your name?"

"It happens all the time. C'mon! C'mon! What's up? You froze!"

Adam hesitated, and then said, "Off the record?"

"Total. What's up?" Ted Murphy was sure he had something here.

"No one knows my name around this place. This is really off the record?"

"All the way. I don't cheat on that or I wouldn't have any sources."

"Good. I go by a fake name in these countries. I call myself Jonathan

Steel. Nice name, huh? I do it because I'm carrying more than one passport so I can be permitted entry to Arab countries. Get it?"

"Hey, that's sharp. How did you pull that one? I'd like to do that–but why did you do it?"

Adam smiled. "I didn't. It wasn't me. It was the company I work for. My distributorship worked it out so I could move around this part of the world. I don't doubt there was some money involved but I don't ask questions." Adam was looking right into the sun. He started moving in a small half-circle, causing Ted Murphy to instinctively move proportionately so Ted Murphy would be looking into the sun rather than him. "Those passports help me because I'm selling pens wherever anyone will buy them. And they buy them in this part of the world."

"You–what?"

"I sell pens. I keep them in that case." He gestured toward his thin black case, resting on the sand.

Ted Murphy used his hand to shield the sunlight. "I didn't know you were a salesman."

"Practically all my life."

"I see." Ted Murphy did not accept anything Adam was saying. "Where you headin'? To the Embassy?"

"No way. I stay away from government types. I was just walking. I carry the case because the pens are too valuable to leave in the hotel. What are you doing here?"

"Writin' from the scene of the crime. Waitin' for the war. You goin' to be around for it?" Now Murphy played the rotating game in the sun but Adam remained motionless no matter how close Ted Murphy came to him.

"I hope there isn't going to be any."

"There'll be one. I'm goin' to watch the beaches for the landing of our Marines. LBJ will send 'em. He wants to send 'em. He can't stay out of it anywhere. They'll be comin' after the Egyptians start takin' over this place. A U.S. liberation force LBJ will call it!"

"You think the Egyptians will take this place?"

"The Israelis will start it, and the Egyptians will end it. This place will be under the flag of the United Arab Republic, and then–" and he imitated a bugle call. "Enter John Wayne, alias Lyndon Baines Johnson."

"Well, I don't know. I don't keep up with politics. Government types bug me."

"Do they?"

"They're all the same. I don't care what country you're in. I stay away from them."

"Weren't you talking to Dayan last Wednesday at the Sheraton?"

He wasn't about to make the mistake he made when he stopped short at the sound of his name. "You been following me, Murphy?"

"I saw you there. I thought you said you stay away from government types."

"I do–unless they want what I'm selling."

"Is that what it was all about?"

"Off the record?"

"Off the record."

"He paid me 350 American dollars."

"For what?"

"For one of these." He picked up the black case and balanced it on one raised knee and then opened the case. He took out a gold Shaeffer, handed it to Ted Murphy, closed the case, then set it back down.

"For one of these?"

"It's worth it."

"It is?"

"Want to buy one?"

"I use a ball point, thanks."

"I have those, too. I have the first ones ever made. I have four genuine Reynolds. The first ones made. Want to buy one?"

"No. Can you talk on the record, Orr?"

"Sure. What do you want to know?"

"What the deuce are you doin' here?"

"Just like you, I'm waiting for the war. I don't want to sound mercenary, Murphy, but wars allow guys like me to make out pretty well. People buy. War makes them go in debt to buy. No one saves. I'm loaded with goods no one will be able to get when the war is on and when the war is over. I'll make a killing no matter who wins. I'll just throw away whichever passport becomes worthless."

"You stayin' at the Sheraton?"

Adam nodded. "Where are you staying?"

"The Dan. The whole U.S. Press Corps is there. When you feel like talkin', look me up there. You can trust me, Orr. I could use a good source here, and I think you're a prime candidate. If you want your message out, I'm your man. If you don't want it out, I'm your man too, because I'll find out what you don't want known and print it. I should be irresistible to you."

"Are you warning me, Murphy?"

"It's more than most of the others at the Dan would do."

"I'll remember that. Give my best to Linda."

"You remember her name?"

"I remember the names of all good looking women."

"I'll tell her. Orr?"

"What?"

"I swear I'm goin' to find out about you. I'm goin' to find out where you been and where you're goin' and what you're doin' wherever you go. I got sources all over the world, Orr. If you tell me nothin' it'll only be worse. I guarantee–I'm goin' to find out. I think I know who you work for."

"You have a rich imagination, Murphy. I think I like it."

"I think you hate it."

Adam messed up, but he knew enough not to let it dominate him. He knew that if he tried to fix it, he would only make things worse. To regain his concentration on those things that needed to be done, he had to forget Murphy and not mope about the incident. He knew what he would do. He would have dinner and then go to a destination that would make him forget that he messed up: The Jumping Jaffa.

There were hundreds of people on the dance floor. Some of them were high on something, and there were young men who couldn't dance very well who were with young women who were dancing very well, and there were teenaged girls dancing with middle-aged men, and women dancing with women, men dancing with men, transvestites dancing with men and women, and there were some people dancing by themselves.

War's potential seemed a million miles away, not advancing across the Sinai. But it wasn't just war that was being ignored. No one seemed to care about the heat and the smell of sweat in the place, the heat and smell feeding on each other. But there was one small area that didn't smell too bad, where there was some circulation. That was at the end of the bar where the air-conditioner was blasting down, which was the place Adam picked to sit and drink beer from a frosty mug as he tried to catch a view of Sabra Modai dancing in a large suspended bird-cage, but obscuring his view was a very close midget dancing with a fat woman in a wheel chair.

The midget was having a difficult time maintaining the rhythm as the wheelchair of the fat lady could not turn sideways each time he tried to make it move in that direction, and she was getting impatient with him. As soon as they finally danced and rolled past Adam, there was Sabra Modai in full view.

She was worth waiting for with her flowing shoulder-length red hair, her big, dark brown, innocent eyes, and her perfectly coordinated slender body dancing in the skimpiest of costumes lined with feathers in a vain attempt to make her look like a bird. At the end of the dance she opened the cage and jumped down and started walking among the customers. She caught Adam's eyes and came over to him.

Her job, between dances in the cage, was to find a victim and encourage him to buy her drinks that were so watered down that they were as intoxicating as tap water while being as expensive as liquid gold. The only way she differed from the world-wide routine was that she was so alluring that Roni, who managed the place and often acted as the bartender, let her get away with anything she wanted.

"Want some company?" she asked Adam, leaning all over him.

"Desperately."

"You were staring at me while I was dancing, weren't you?" And she blinked those big, brown eyes.

"Isn't that why you dance here? To be stared at? And then guys like me buy you drinks until they're broke?"

"That's the idea. Aren't you smart!" She leaned against him since there wasn't an available stool by him, or anywhere.

Adam stood up for her. "Sit down."

"No. You sit back down. I prefer to smother you." He sat down and she proceeded to smother him. "You're from America aren't you?"

"That's right."

"I can always tell."

"How?"

She shrugged. "I don't know. I can always tell. What state are you from?"

"Nebraska," he lied.

"Oh."

"Is that all right with you?"

"It's fine with me. How did you find this place?"

"It was the car that found the place. Not me. No matter where I am in the world, wherever I rent a car, it knows the way to these places and always takes me directly to one of them. Cars that are chosen by any of the better rental car agencies know where to go by themselves. There have been times when rental cars wouldn't take me where I wanted to go until after they took me to one of these places. They're all young cars who have only one thing on their minds."

She laughed. "You poor man. What do you do for a living?"

"I sell fountain pens."

Now her laughter turned into near hysteria.

"What's so funny?"

"That's a good lie!"

"Why do you think that's a lie?"

"Every man who comes in here who's middle-aged lies about everything. I never trust them. They lie about their name, they lie about whether or not they're married, they lie about what they do for a living, they lie about what they want. Last night one of them was pawing me all over, and he told me he was an Arab sheik looking for a wife."

"Maybe he was."

"Oh, please. A blond, blue-eyed sheik with a Scandinavian accent?"

"Would you have accepted his offer if he really was an Arab sheik looking for a wife?"

"If he paid me enough. And if he wouldn't war against Israel. What's wrong with that? As long as he could support me. What's wrong with that?"

"Nothing, I suppose—for a woman."

"For him, too. He'd get more than his money's worth."

"Until he's broke. Then you'd leave him for some jerk like me. And he'd still think you had married him because you loved him, when you never did."

"Ahhh! Men! Men! Men! Sure, I want to be taken care of, but men want war. Look at us. Here we are in a world run by men, and we're waiting for a war again. I don't like war. I like love."

"I don't like either war or love. They're the same things. The only difference is that war is a public death. Love is a private one."

"If you hate women so much what are you doing in a place like this?"

"I don't hate women. Just the opposite. It's just that they ask too much, so I don't stay with them when they raise the ante—and they always raise the ante."

"You mean you love sex, right?"

"Well, don't be so horrified by it. Your dancing isn't meant to make men think about museums."

She laughed again and swept back her red hair. "I suppose not. Will you buy me a drink?"

"You waited longer to ask than I expected. Yes."

"You see? I don't ask too much." And then she shouted so the bartender could hear her above the music. "Roni! Give me my regular!"

Adam shook his head. "What's your regular?"

"A Cherry Coke."

"At least you're not lying."

"It's the men who lie. Last night I was drinking with a member of the Knesset. He told me he sold light bulbs for General Electric."

"How do you know he was a member of the Knesset?"

"I recognized him. And he started drinking and he was telling me one secret after another. Light bulb salesmen don't know secrets." If Sabra wanted to do it, she could have been Israel's version of Dee who was America's version of the Soviet Union's Tanyas. She had the capabilities to fill that government-sought ability.

"What do you mean, secrets?"

"Secret secrets."

"You mean state secrets or personal secrets?"

"He said that just before Egypt attacks us, we are going to pretend we're going to attack Egypt from one place with all kinds of armaments and troops and get Egypt to protect itself from that site, and then we'll attack them from somewhere else where they have no defenses."

"Really? I wouldn't repeat that if I were you."

"Why not?"

"If it's the truth, you wouldn't want anyone to know, would you?"

"He was no boy. He was a middle-aged man. So he's lying."

"Where did he say Israel would pretend to launch an attack?"

"He didn't."

"I wouldn't repeat that one," he said again.

Roni brought her a very small glass of cherry coke.

She shrugged. "Only the young ones can be trusted to tell the truth. When they're young they're so innocent, they tell the truth. They don't know any better. They'll learn. I love your lie. It's so silly—that you sell fountain pens—that I could almost believe you."

"Thanks. I thought it was pretty good. What do you do when you're not here?"

"I go to other places to look for some man to support me. Someone rich. Are you rich?"

"Very."

"Can you support me?"
"Easily."
"Want to marry me?"
"I can't tonight. I have to get up early tomorrow. Next time."
"I may be married to someone else by the next time you come in."
"Then I'll have to wait until you get divorced. It's never long."
"I have to go dance again soon. Will you watch and wait for me?"
"No, but I'll be back. Maybe next week."
She downed her Cherry Coke in a couple quick gulps as though it was a shot of bourbon. "What's your name?"
"John."
"That's such a fake! Fountain pens were clever. John isn't. John what?"
"Jonathan Steele."
"Oh, my God! Please! Won't you watch me dance and wait? You only bought me one drink. It's not fair. Come on. Watch me. I'll make you think of the Louvre."
Now she made Adam laugh. "No, I can't stay. I saw your picture outside and couldn't resist coming in."
"One drink! That's all I got from you. I can stretch this break for one more. I don't think I can love you unless you're a lot more generous."
"I don't want you to love me."
"Then I'll hate you. Is that better?"
"It's safer."
"What's wrong with you?"
"Nothing. There used to be something wrong with me. But now I've lived long enough to know things I would never have guessed before."
"Like?"
"Being careful. I've learned that it's safer to sleep in the tent of my enemies than in the bed of a woman who says she loves me."
"You sound like an Arab. Maybe you're an Arab spy. Well, you don't need to worry about me. I could never love you."
"I appreciate that. But the real trouble is that I could fall for you. Any man could. That's what really frightens me. I won't allow that to happen. I'd be doomed. You see, I have pens to sell. And a man in love becomes miserably unhappy. I hope all my enemies fall in love."
"And get married?"
"That's only for my worst enemies."
"I hope some woman catches you and that you're miserable with her. And then you'll be sorry you didn't watch me dance again tonight."
"I'll watch you next week, if we're not at war by then."

On Saturday, May the 27th, President Nasser of Egypt announced that "our basic objective will be the destruction of Israel. The Arab people want to fight."
On Sunday, after one more conversation with General Dayan, Adam notified his headquarters at Langley that he believed Israel would launch a preemptive strike.

On Monday, Nasser said, "We have reached the stage of serious action and not declarations."

On Tuesday came the certainty of a third front. Under-Secretary Rostow's visit was not enough to dissuade King Hussein from agreeing to make a pledge to President Nasser of Egypt: he placed the army of the Kingdom of Jordan under Egypt's command. Minutes after the pledge was made, Nasser announced to the world that, "The armies of Egypt, Jordan, Syria, and Lebanon are poised on the borders of Israel."

On Tuesday night a film with Ted Murphy in Tel Aviv was on U.S. television, with Ted Murphy reporting that "there are those who are saying President Johnson wants the United States in the war." Ted Murphy was talking without his usual Chicago tough-guy accent. When the camera was on he was a different man; calm, articulate, and he appeared to be thoughtfully analytical. "Why do some say President Johnson wants the United States in the war? Because it would help him in what could otherwise be a difficult re-election next year." He made it appear to be a piece of news rather than an opinion-piece by saying, "there are those who are saying" and "some" without identifying "those" or "some." It was a common network news practice. "Those" and "some" could have been him and Linda–and were.

On Wednesday, President Johnson made it clear to Israel's Foreign Minister, Abba Eban, that the United States was totally opposed to an Israeli preemptive strike. The President said world opinion was important, and if Israel would strike first it would make it more difficult for United States support if needed. He said all parties should try to avoid war.

On Thursday, Adam notified his headquarters at Langley that even though Iraq, Kuwait, Saudi Arabia, Morocco, Algeria, the Sudan, and Lebanon either already had, or would publicly commit themselves to join Nasser's imminent attack against Israel, none of those governments were planning to risk troops in the military effort. It was only Egypt, Syria, and Jordan who would go that far.

On Friday, the headquarters at Langley notified Adam that the administration felt secure that Israel would wait to be attacked rather than stage a preemptive strike, and he was to verify this.

On Saturday, Adam notified Langley that he could not get any authoritative answer but he believed Washington had the wrong information. He also added, "In my opinion it would be naive to assume that a government would allow a potential enemy to set the time and place and amount of casualties of what could be a massive attack. I believe Israel's military leaders will judge a preemptive strike to be vital. A very unauthoritative source said that perhaps Israel will establish a decoy buildup to confuse Egyptian forces."

On Sunday morning a "Murphy's Law" column was published that said "the United States should stay out of the conflict and let events take their course between the parties, no matter their outcome. This place is crawling with the CIA."

On Sunday afternoon, Nasser received the public commitment of Iraq to join Egypt in the war, with President Aref saying, "Our goal is clear—to wipe Israel off the map."

Later that Sunday, Egypt's Intelligence Agency informed Nasser of its analysis that Israel was getting ready to launch an attack on Egypt, moving assault units and equipment to Eilat on the Gulf of Aqaba to stage that attack. They had observed that almost half of Israel's landing craft were being sent there.

In the early evening, Ted Murphy was standing in front of the Gulf of Aqaba, a 16 mm network cameraman filming him. "By the time you in the United States see this," Murphy said, "the Mideast might well be at war. If not, barring a miracle, it will be at war very soon. The Israeli military is preparing Eilat, which is just in front of me, as a staging ground. A staging ground for their military to go where? Over there," and he gestured to his right, "is Aqaba, in Jordan. It's about three miles to the east. And over there," and he gestured to his left, "is Taba in the Sinai of Egypt, around four miles to the west. Israel looks like it's setting itself up to go in either or both directions."

In response to the Egyptian intelligence report, now underlined by the Murphy television broadcast, Nasser ordered his combatants from the Mediterranean to reinforce Arab naval strength in the Gulf of Aqaba from a pending attack by Israel from Eilat.

Later that evening, Nasser rejected a plea from the United States and European nations to allow freedom of shipping in the Gulf of Aqaba, which could prevent war from breaking out.

On Monday, June the 5th, Israel launched a preemptive strike, not from Eilat on the Gulf of Aqaba where it had made a pretense of planning an attack, but on all of Egypt's airfields simultaneously, destroying almost the entire Air Force of Egypt. Within hours after the strikes on the Egyptian airfields, Israel went on to strike at Iraqi and Syrian military airfields, while Israeli ground units began moving into Gaza and into the Sinai, leaving Jordan and its "west bank" of Judea and Samaria alone. Hours later, King Hussein's troops of Jordan attacked Israel from Judea and Samaria and East Jerusalem, and Israel responded in moments by moving troops into Jordanian-held Janin, Nablus, and the Jordanian-held sector of Jerusalem.

On Tuesday morning, a loud alarm sounded in the Situation Room of the White House. For the first time since the Hot Line was installed, it was beckoning, not as a test, but as an urgent request from Premier Kosygin of the USSR to communicate with the president of the United States.

The Hot Line had become nothing more than a bore to those who sat in the White House Situation Room with the assignment of testing and waiting—and nothing more than testing and waiting for four years. Unlike what the public believed, the Hot Line was not a telephone but a teletype system.

Before becoming president, Senator John Kennedy had read an article by Jess Gorkin in the Sunday newspaper supplement, *Parade*. Gorkin suggested that there be an instant communication system established between the leadership of the United States and the leadership of the Soviet Union for quick personal contact in an emergency. John Kennedy clipped out the article and when he became president he offered Gorkin's idea to Chairman Khrushchev. Khrushchev didn't want any part of it. After the Cuban Missile Crisis when the world teetered on the brink of nuclear war, Khrushchev suddenly endorsed Gorkin's idea and told President Kennedy to go ahead. On August the 30th of 1963, less than three months before the assassination of President Kennedy, the Hot Line became operational. Every hour around the clock since then, something, anything, was transmitted back and forth as a test between translators in the White House and translators in the Kremlin. The messages were jokes and articles and poetry and lyrics of songs, for the sole hourly purpose of checking that the system was working. But this time the alarm didn't sound on the hour. It was 7:43 in the morning.

It was the first in a five day continuing series of direct communications without ambassadors, directly between Johnson and Kosygin through the Hot Line.

During those days Adam was going between Colonel Annon Resheff and General Yisrael Tal in Gaza, General Ariel Sharon in El Arish, General Uzi Narkiss in Jerusalem, and General David Elazar in Nablus, and even into the secret War Room outside Tel Aviv from which the Israeli military gave orders to its commanders on all fronts. With only a couple hours of sleep each night, Adam went between sites and back and forth to the United States Embassy communicating to headquarters in Langley with his appraisals of where the war was leading and what the United States would have to do if U.S. support was needed to do anything.

With Israeli advances on all three fronts, Premier Kosygin believed that Israel might go all the way from the Golan Heights to Damascus and take over the government of Syria. Through the Hot Line, Premier Kosygin communicated to President Johnson that if he didn't stop Israel from doing that, Kosygin would have no hesitancy to go to war with the United States.

President Johnson could have lost every bit of U.S. credibility if, as a result of the communications, he acted with any sign of weakness. Therefore, he ordered the Sixth Fleet to move close to the Syrian coast to show that the United States would not be intimidated by Premier Kosygin's threat.

Both the Voice of the Arabs Radio, and Ted Murphy reported the U.S. movement at sea was an exhibition of the eagerness of the United States to enter the war.

On Thursday, President Johnson told Premier Kosygin that an American ship was attacked off the coast of Sinai and that Johnson had ordered planes from the Sixth Fleet to get to that ship for a rescue operation.

On Saturday, the war was over. All parties in the Mideast agreed to a U.N. cease-fire. In those six days Israel had taken Gaza and the entire Sinai Desert up to the Suez Canal from Egypt, the Golan Heights from

Syria, and all of Judea and Samaria from Jordan, including the Jordanian-held sector of Jerusalem.

Israel was now four times the size it was six days earlier.

But war's casualties were high, going into the tens of thousands, including 34 Americans who, in an historical irony, were not killed by Egyptians or Syrians or Jordanians, but by Israelis who mistook the U.S. ship which was off the coast of Sinai, over 100 miles from the other ships of the U.S. Sixth Fleet, for a Soviet vessel aiding Egypt.

The losing governments of the war, too devastated to claim their loss was due to Israel's armed forces, chose to blame the more powerful United States for their defeat and, along with Arab nations that were not militarily involved in the war, severed diplomatic relations with the United States.

In the end, the United States gave no physical military assistance at all to Israel during the war. Its psychological assistance, however, was imperative because the Soviet Union was kept away by the Hot Line communications between President Johnson and Premier Kosygin, with President Johnson making clear to Premier Kosygin that the United States would not hesitate to retaliate against the Soviet Union should it become militarily involved in the conflict.

Ted Murphy did not prove to be prophetic, or even accurate, but he did prove to be a commanding personality on television. He had modified his coarseness, and even his fist-beaten nose had a certain visual allure. With the war done, he bid good-bye from Tel Aviv in front of a camera, and he ended his wrap-up by saying he would be reporting next week from Washington, D.C. on "the same channel you're watching tonight."

On the plane back home he was writing his farewell column of "Murphy's Law," thanking his readers for their loyalty, and that he hoped his readers would become his television viewers.

Adam had accomplished a priceless mission of supplying information. He couldn't resist giving himself a reward.

"You're back!" Sabra yelled from her suspended bird-cage, but no one could hear her because the music covered every sound with its madness. "Did you bring me a wedding ring this time?" she yelled.

When the break came she went straight over to him. "Johnny!" and she plopped down on his lap. "I have been thinking about you every minute since you were here last time."

"Have you really?"

"No. But I thought about you every once in a while. You're a strange man and I like strange men. But please understand that all I want from you is sex. I don't want you to get serious with me."

"Oh, nuts!" He said, "I hate sex. I want a home with a white picket fence. Maybe a dog. I want to rake leaves while my wife's baking an apple-pie. Can't I convince you?"

"Oh, you're like all men. All you want is marriage."

"I'm sorry."

"Are you going to be a sucker and buy me a lot of drinks?"

"That's why I'm here."

"You fool!" and she kissed him. "Roni!" she yelled to the bartender. "A bottle of champagne!"

"Who said I'd buy you a bottle of champagne?"

"Don't worry. I spit it out in the extra glass he brings me that you think is a chaser. It will just cost you a lot."

"Oh, that's fine then. I want to spend a lot of money, but I was worried you might get you drunk."

Roni came over to them with a big bottle of what looked like it might be champagne. Adam started to reach for his wallet. Sabra put her hand on his pocket, clutching his hand below the material. "Don't pay him now, Johnny. Run up a tab. In that way you won't realize how deeply you're getting in debt."

"Good idea," he said and nodded to the bartender to do as she said.

"All right," Roni said.

"You like this place, don't you?" she asked Adam.

"It's okay. But it's a little seedy."

"That's what I don't like about it. It's just a little seedy. I want it to be much seedier than it is. I want all normal people kept out. They can go somewhere else. There are plenty of places for them."

"There sure are. You should be in a much worse place."

"Please don't fall in love with me, Johnny."

"How can I help it? You look so great in that bird-cage that I want to free you and have you settle down with me."

"I want to be chained to the perch. They won't do it. They're prudes. They don't understand lust and eroticism."

"Why don't you just tell them off, and quit?"

"There's no place worse. If there was, I'd go there. I have to stay here if I want at least a little depravity."

"What a shame."

"You wouldn't understand. You just dream about a big wedding."

"I can't fool you."

"Johnny, can I ask you to make love to me?"

"No."

"Please?"

"No way. Marriage or nothing."

"Why don't we get out of here and go to the beach together?"

"At this hour? Why? What will we do?"

"What ever I want."

"I'll only go on one condition."

"What?"

"That we just talk. No fooling around. We'll talk about museums. I've been to the best ones in the world."

"I don't want to talk."

She won. They didn't say a word on the beach.

Now he had to plan the rest of his life. With a success behind him, he would feel justified in requesting that Martin send him to Vietnam, where he craved to go. He felt his request would be taken seriously since after all, every appraisal he made in the Mideast was correct and even his cover had worked. The only down side was Ted Murphy. But Murphy's suspicion did the mission no harm. Adam wrote to Martin a cryptic note. It said, "All in all, my pens were mightier than the sword, just the way we were taught in school."

NINETEEN
RED GUARDS
1967

The casualty figures of the Mideast War of 1967 were small compared to those on the other side of the world that year. Maybe Mao Tse-tung had gone crazy, but could so many Chinese people have also lost their sanity in the killing of their own neighbors?

That neighborhood was the entire mainland of China, with millions tortured and killed, while 300 Chinese soldiers were going farther, crossing the border into Hong Kong in the hope of bringing the Cultural Revolution to the British Crown Colony. The soldiers who crossed the border wore wide red bands on their left arms, waved little red books in the air, and carried automatic rifles on their shoulders.

On orders from the Crown, Governor David Trench had a plane waiting at Kai Tak Airport to take him and his family to safety should the revolutionaries be successful in a takeover of Hong Kong.

To make a public statement against the British jurisdiction of Hong Kong, the British Embassy in Peking was ransacked and then most of the Embassy was destroyed by those who were called Red Guards. Mao Tse-tung ordered all China's food shipments to Hong Kong stopped. Hong Kong's major water supply from China was turned off causing Hong Kong citizens to have no more than four hours of water from the tap every four days.

On the streets of Kowloon, mobs of students who supported the Red Guards stoned Europeans and Americans, and some buildings were set on fire. American naval personnel were sent back to their ships. Government House was surrounded by a mass of young students demonstrating their sympathy with the Cultural Revolution, singing "Unity is Strength" as they claimed they were members of the "Committee for Resisting British Oppression" and calling for an end to British "fascist atrocities."

It was almost two o'clock in the morning outside the Kowloon Ballroom where Tso Wai-yee was sitting in the back seat of a car, a driver keeping the motor running, both passenger and driver nervously looking at the doorway for the appearance of Wai-yee's sister, Winnie, hoping no mobs of Red Guard supporters would charge the street. The driver and the whole scheme of the evening had been arranged by friends recommended by Gus Borgeest, the refugee landlord of Sunshine Island. The journey for which the two young women had worked for years was scheduled to reach its destination within a few dangerous hours. But the long-planned objective had been cut in half. The rescue of their parents had become the rescue of their mother alone.

Since their father was a mathematics teacher, and teachers were considered by the Red Guards of the Cultural Revolution to be "revisionists" to be exterminated, in March he had been forced to kneel on broken glass and "confess his crimes." And then, unable to lift himself, he was lifted up by students, a wooden board was locked around his neck, a white dunce cap was put on his head, and he was paraded for two hours through the streets of Kiangchow while crowds threw rocks at him, on the way to his execution.

The principal of the school in which Wai-yee's father taught, had been beaten on a daily basis by the students, and when it became intolerable, he killed himself.

All this had started on May the 16th of the previous year, 1966, when Mao Tse-tung created his new revolution with his wife, Jiang Qing, designated as the Supreme Commander. The adult citizens of China were ordered to report their thoughts to students twice a day, and it was demanded that the adults had to participate in daily "Loyalty Dances." The objective of Mao's revolution was to be "closer to the masses than any leader in world history," by eliminating all those who existed between him and the people, which meant the persecution of those in the government itself, including State President Liu Shaoqi, and all teachers, academics, and artists. Most schools were closed and teachers were condemned, bureaucrats were accused of taking too much authority from the people, and beating them to death was encouraged. All students were told to be Red Guards and bring about the Cultural Revolution with Mao as their one and only father.

Wai-yee's mother was told that her husband had been buried, which was considered to be a kind gesture of the Red Guards since, in comparison, in Kwangsi-Chuang, over one hundred people were cannibalized, their organs boiled and served in cafeterias by the Red Guards.

Winnie rushed out of the doorway and into the back seat of the waiting car. Wai-yee embraced her and they started a ride of both agonizing and joyful tears, the lights of Nathan Street quickly being left behind them and replaced by the quiet road through northern Kowloon, then through the New Territories, their path lit only by the car's headlights and aided by a full moon. Their destination had been arranged by the driver, but unknown by Wai-yee and Winnie. After almost two hours of the drive, the car stopped on a grassy bank without a marker, where the sound of the sea was all that could be heard from the car. Their driver told them they were just south of Sha Tau Kok on the Hong Kong side of the border with China, directly off the South China Sea.

He instructed Wai-yee and Winnie to wait in the car and keep the door closed and locked unless he gave them a signal. He left the car, going to the edge of the bank that overlooked the sea. The moon gave enough light for him to be seen by the two passengers in the car. He was pacing on the bank with one hand kept on a revolver resting in his belt, and his other hand was holding a large unlit flashlight.

Since he was outside, he could hear three competing sounds, two of them very faint and distant: Beyond the sound of the close lapping of water against the land, there was the sound of Maoist propaganda coming from a loudspeaker on the mainland's side of the border, and there was the sound of a recording of Beatles music coming from the Hong Kong side of the border in a vain attempt to cover the Maoist messages.

It was an impatient hour-and-fifteen-minutes before there was a flash on the sea followed by black and then two flashes then black then five flashes. The man entrusted by Wai-yee and Winnie to be their driver, guide, and guard, turned on his flashlight in a dot-dot-dot-dash, Beethoven's Fifth Symphony victory pattern. The flashes from the sea were repeated, one, two, and five. He responded with his victory pattern, and the two signals repeated over and over again. The lights from a vessel on the sea and the flashlight on the bank were talking to each other.

The flashes coming from the vessel seemed to get larger and larger. Within one-half hour the dialogue of lights stopped and was replaced by the most welcome sound of the evening; the most welcome sound of decades to the sisters: the ship was bumping against the bank. Again there was a period of time when it seemed as though nothing was happening, and then twenty-two people emerged from the small boat that did not seem capable of holding more than five. The driver of Wai-yee and Winnie went directly to a small woman in black holding a piece of brown-splattered baggage made of blue fabric that was held together by a strap. He grabbed the baggage and helped her to the top of the bank, and then he escorted her quickly to the car.

He nodded at Wai-yee and she unlocked and opened the door, and the joyful weeping of her and Winnie and their mother could only be silenced outside by the driver quickly closing the door. He ran around the car to get to the driver's side, the sound of his footsteps competing with the rustling of those still walking from the boat to the bank overlooking the sea, and the three continuing sounds of Mao's propaganda, and the Beatles, and the lapping of the sea.

Where those other refugees would go was to remain a mystery, as the administrator of Wai-yee and Winnie's night turned on the ignition of the car and he headed back to Kowloon with his precious cargo of three.

The journey of so many years was done.

TWENTY
APRIL FOOLS
1968

There was a time when presidents and first ladies would instantly accept an invitation to the annual Irene Goodpastor evening April Fools' party. But as time passed and political figures came to Washington and went from Washington, the top echelon of her annual party went down a peg to the vice president, which was not at all bad.

She generally kept the invitation list non-partisan which meant ninety percent Democrats, ten percent Republicans. Since that was a higher ratio of Republicans than offered by the political breakdown of the District of Columbia, it was considered to be fair.

There was a very good reason why the District had such an over-population of Democrats. Republicans generally believed the federal government was largely responsible for many of the major problems of the nation and should be limited and not expand beyond the powers given it by the Founders of the nation. Democrats generally believed that the federal government could and should be heavily involved in the social adjustments and domestic problems of the nation, and should provide and regulate personal securities, creating what President Johnson called a Great Society. With those two conflicting beliefs regarding the role of the federal government, making a career out of government had a natural appeal to more Democrats than Republicans, and a natural distaste of more Republicans than Democrats. The population of the District of Columbia reflected the political passions of the people who worked there.

The District was also becoming a media center. Liberals generally gravitated to the arts, whether the art was composition or dance or the Broadway stage or the Hollywood motion picture industry—or the Washington news media. Conservatives generally gravitated to business. Therefore the celebrities of the Washington media were generally liberal and Democrats.

And so it was not Irene Goodpastor's own political involvement as a Democrat that made her parties tilt so heavily to Democrat invitees, it was that there was little choice. Her quest was to have important people at her parties from the administration, the Congress, the media, and the top layer of the career service, as well as personal friends. She was aware there were more Democrats than Republicans in all those 1968 categories, so she went out of her way to invite Republican members of the Congress where, at least, some prominent Republicans could be found.

Her Georgetown house was filled with guests for the April Fools' Party of 1968 with reporters and cameras and brilliant lights outside her home in anticipation of the entrance of the vice president and Muriel Humphrey. As of the night before, the vice president's importance had escalated to an unexpected height. The president, in an Oval Office address, told the nation that the bombing of North Vietnam would be greatly restricted in the hope that North Vietnam would agree to peace talks and "we assume that during those talks Hanoi will not take advantage of our restraint." But that piece of substance was not the end of his speech. In a move that surprised, even shocked the nation, he added that "I do not believe that I should devote an hour or a day of my time to any partisan causes or to any duties other than the awesome duties of this office—the presidency of your country. Accordingly, I shall not seek, and I will not accept the nomination of my party for another term as your president. But let men everywhere know, however, that a strong and a confident and a vigilant America stands ready tonight to seek an honorable peace, and stands ready tonight to defend an honored cause, whatever the price, whatever the burden, whatever the sacrifice that duty may require."

Vice President Humphrey wasn't talking, but he suddenly became a prime potential candidate to oppose Eugene McCarthy and Robert Kennedy in the quest for the Democrat's nomination for the presidency. With such a sudden turn of events, there was no wonder that the media centered themselves on the front lawn of Irene Goodpastor's home on the evening of April the First.

There were four copper pots for umbrellas by the inside of the front door. "I bought these at a bazaar in Izmir," Irene Goodpastor said, "while the Senator and I," she always referred to her late husband as the Senator, "were on a jaunt over there. Believe it or not, they only cost us four hundred lira each. Maybe a few kurus more. Can you imagine?" She knew that no one there knew the currency conversion of Turkey but no one would have the nerve—or the interest—to ask her how many dollars that would mean.

"Omar will take care of your coat, and drinks are right through there and to your left." Omar was a butler hired event-by-event who Irene Goodpastor instructed to give a slight bow to everyone as he removed their wet raincoats. He took the apparel to an out of view bedroom where they would soon be smothered under other wet coats.

Straight ahead and to the left was the small parlor that was filled with so many guests that those walking through had to walk sideways to get to the bar.

There were the expected jokes at the party that the president's declaration he would not run for re-election was an April Fools joke one night early to give added value to Mrs. Goodpastor's annual event. It certainly did that until the phone rang with the voice of Bess Abell at the White House telling Mrs. Goodpastor that "Vice President Humphrey and Muriel regret that because of urgent White House business they won't be able to attend your party tonight, and they were looking forward to it, so very much." There was apparently a public announcement of that as well, since almost simultaneous with her phone call the television lights went off outside her house and competing camera crews started talking to each other.

Mrs. Goodpastor put on a good front to disguise her disappointment by telling the guests, "the only way we would have a right to be disappointed would be if the vice president would come here, allowing his duties to suffer. Let's give our support to the president and the vice president during these important and difficult times for our nation. In addition to our support, I want you to have a good time tonight. If I told you there would be a pall over the rest of this party I would have to add, 'April Fools'!' Now, have fun and please help yourself to our buffet which is ready right now in the dining area. Without any courtesy to my honored guests, I'm going to be first in line!"

She was applauded, and the guests started to line up to enter the dining area. Just as Mrs. Goodpastor planned, while waiting and inching forward they couldn't help but look at the line-up of framed letters and signatures on the wall. Letters from presidents from Hoover to Johnson were there, vice presidents from Garner to Humphrey, foreign leaders from the Shah of Iran to Charles de Gaulle, movie stars from Katharine Hepburn to Gregory Peck, and a host of celebrities from all walks of life from George Foreman to John Glenn. She had given special prominence, including a wide red frame, to one from Sonny Bono who wrote above his signature, "I Got You, Babe!" Even though she did not get a signature from Fidel Castro, her story of being skyjacked to Cuba had been a success, having given her a renewal of Washington prestige. She bored everyone with it for years, adding new phony details at every retelling.

The line of guests extended through the hallways from one room to another. On the way back from the dining area buffet table, Mrs. Goodpastor passed by the line-up with her plate of vegetables and teriyaki sticks, and Congressman George Bush stopped her by saying, "Hey, Irene, what's this one about?" He was gesturing toward a framed piece of paper in the hallway, bearing eleven signatures and addresses, with the title "To Be Together Again in Hong Kong in 1997" with that picture above it, taken from Victoria Peak of Hong Kong.

Mrs. Goodpastor smiled and nodded. "That's my pride and joy," she said. "Look at the names, George. You'll recognize some of them."

He studied the document. "Yes, there's Gerry and Mary Fairbanks–sure, I know him. Barbara, you know him."

His wife nodded, "Of course."

"He's been in this town forever," Mrs. Goodpastor confirmed, nodding proudly.

"And, let's see. I don't know any other names here. Oh, my gosh, here's Ted Murphy. My lands! Ted Murphy! So, there's Fairbanks and Murphy. I don't know anyone else."

"We know him," Barbara Bush said, and she pointed to the signature of Moose Dunston.

"We do?"

"He's that big man who you liked so much. He testified before you on Vietnam. The Goldwater man who even Johnson likes so much."

"I don't remember."

"Yes, you do."

"So what's it about, Irene?" Congressman Bush asked Mrs. Goodpastor.

Mrs. Goodpastor told the story of meeting them all at the Consulate, and then going to the Peak, and she said it was her idea they should "all meet again as Red China takes over at least part of Hong Kong." She did not say, or maybe remember, that it was the idea of Tso Wai-yee. She further embellished the story by saying that the name of Orr that appeared on the letter was a man who tried to seduce her up on the Peak. "I keep in contact with all of them except him. They always tell me their new addresses so we can remain in touch for 1997. I invited every one of them except 'him' here for this party, but they're scattered all over the world."

She started scanning the letter for their names. "The man who had us all to the consulate there is now in Brazil and his little cute assistant is working at our embassy in Moscow; she's a dear. Lieutenant Jonas Valadovich, he's a captain now, is in Vietnam. Let's see. Dunston is here in Washington on the staff of the National Security Council. He couldn't come because they're working overtime tonight, as you can imagine with what the president said last night. He's the one Barbara said you know. And, let's see. This one is some Chinese girl who worked at the consulate. I guess she's still there unless she's working in some bar or something. Ted Murphy, as you know, goes all over the place, he's on TV every night. He and his wife were going to be here but he's doing a report tonight on President Johnson and what his decision means, and he told me to just turn on the television set and he'd be in my house. That signature there is the seducer. The Fairbanks called me today and said they couldn't—he's had to be at the Agency almost around the clock since the president's announcement. Cody Cooper is here. He was a great help to me when I wanted things done at the Kennedy White House. I don't know where he is right now, but he's here, I saw him when he came in."

"That's great, Irene," Congressman Bush said. "Gee, that's just great what you did in Hong Kong. What an idea to all go back at the same time. When is that goin' to be?"

Irene Goodpastor gave him a mystified look. "Well, what it says—1997."

"Well, that's just great. Hey, what does it take to get on your wall? Do you accept letters from lowly congressmen?"

"It depends on who they are."

"Don't I qualify, Irene?"

"Why, of course, George."

"I sent you a note after last year's party. It was all handwritten. Where is it, Irene?"

She thought quickly. "Being framed!"

"Oh sure, sure."

Despite the diversity of people at the party there were only three subjects that dominated every conversation: the president's decision not to run again, the Vietnam War, and mini-skirts. The last subject had to become a source of conversation since for the first time at one of these annual parties, three of the younger women guests were actually wearing them. D.C. was slower than the rest of the country in its acceptance of mini-skirts as it was slower than the rest of the country about almost everything. The eyes of others at the party, although trying to be inconspicuous, gravitated toward them.

"I like what New York's Mayor Lindsay said about those skirts," Mrs. Goodpastor said to a small group of careerists. "Did you hear him? He said, 'It's a functional thing. It enables young ladies to run faster. And because of those skirts, they may have to.'"

They laughed as though mini-skirts were a joke, although none of them thought of them as being funny. The men wanted to look at those three women without offending their wives who were wearing conservative Washingtonian clothes, and their wives were thinking of how they would look should they wear a mini-skirt, which was not, for all, a comforting thought. Mini-skirts became an enticement or a tragedy, depending on the wearer and the viewer.

The girl who entered with Cody Cooper was the most noticed of all. She had entered with an unbuttoned maxi-raincoat over a mini-skirt and refused to let Omar take the coat from her. She kept it on for a long time before recognizing that it was not raining in the house. She knew that it had an overwhelming effect as she walked. She would saunter with Cody from one spot to another, and with each step her unbuttoned long coat would reveal the totally unexpected—legs. Cody was the only man who could afford to be objective about her since he was going to be with her throughout the evening party and didn't have to rush a look. He could dwell on the subject of the president or Vietnam at the party.

"He did it because of Kennedy," he said to a circle of guests. "He could accept Eugene McCarthy trying to be the nominee, but not Robert Kennedy. If LBJ stayed in, Kennedy could win that nomination against him and LBJ couldn't stand to be rejected. Especially for another Kennedy."

"I take him at his word, Cody," a State Department careerist said to him. "He doesn't want to go through a campaign while trying to fight a war in Vietnam."

"It was Kennedy."

"Well, look, you worked for his brother."

"Yes, I did," he said proudly.

"Johnson took you out of the White House with the others, so—"

"I'm not mad or bitter about it," Cody interrupted. "That's not what I'm talking about. He has the right to have his own people with him. I have a fine job at State now. He took me out of a Schedule 'C' appointment at the White House that President Kennedy gave me, and made me a foreign service careerist. He could have just told me to go blow it and go back home to Detroit, but he gave me a good position over at State. So that's not why I'm saying what I just did. I'm convinced that RFK could have beat LBJ and that's why LBJ said he wouldn't run, that's all. So I don't blame Johnson for moving me, or bowing out."

"It wasn't because of Kennedy," Congressman Thaxton said slowly with a small smile. "It wasn't because of McCarthy. He did it because of the Tet offensive. It was a massive victory for the Viet Cong, let's face it."

Now Congressman Robert Dole jumped in. "The only ones who thought Tet was a victory for the Viet Cong were those in the press corps over there, Paul." Now he looked away from the other congressman and moved his gaze to others in the small crowd. "You have to read the casualty figures the Viet Cong suffered in that offensive to know how much of a failure it was for them. And then add to it that they didn't succeed at taking even one city in all the thirty-some cities they tried to take. Did you know that? No one told you that. Not our press corps. Not one city."

"They got into our Embassy grounds, Bob. You know that," Congressman Thaxton said with the same smile coming back to his lips.

"So what? There's someone getting onto the White House grounds every other night. The point is the Viet Cong didn't take the embassy. It was a suicide squad and they were killed. They failed at everything they attempted, except for killing themselves. And if the Viet Cong thought the South Vietnamese were going to stage an uprising in support of the North, they were terribly mistaken. That Tet offensive was an embarrassing defeat for the Viet Cong. The White House and the Department of Defense were cheering at the results. The only thing the Viet Cong had going for them was the reaction of those correspondents over there who were massed together at the Caravelle Hotel who misinformed this country. I'm not an LBJ man, I'm a Republican from Kansas, not a Democrat from Texas, but I feel for him on that one. The press gave it to him on that one. Even Cronkite. I don't see any excuse for that."

"So it's the fault of the press, congressman?" Congressman Thaxton asked with a shake of his head, retaining the smile.

"Misinforming the public was the fault of the press. Yes."

Cody's maxi-coated, mini-skirted companion grabbed and squeezed his hand as if to say, "I'm bored. Let's walk to another group where I can be seen better." He nodded in response to her squeeze of his hand.

Congressman Thaxton and Congressman Dole watched Cody's companion walk away to the other room with Cody. From the side, her legs were very visible as she walked. For a while two of the nation's best legislators, both passionate about Vietnam, were speechless in the spirit of non-partisanship.

Cody and his girlfriend found a corner in which to stand where she was on display and he could talk to her without being heard by anyone else. "Cathy–if Bobby Kennedy wins the nomination I'm thinking of quitting State and working for him."

"Uh-huh." It wasn't the kind of reaction he hoped for. No surprise. No enthusiasm. No encouragement. No anything.

"And if he can get that nomination, I think he'll win the presidency."

"Uh-huh."

"But I think Humphrey's going to get into it now. I still think Bobby will win but Humphrey will be tougher to beat than LBJ."

"Uh-huh."

"What do you think I should do, Cathy?"

"Oh. Well, what I think is that you should do what your heart tells you." *What your heart tells you?* "Always let your heart be your guide." *What kind of response was that?* He finally started to look grown-up, his voice wasn't cracking anymore, and there was no question but that he matured through the past years of experiences—but now he was with this girl who sounded like she was in the seventh grade.

"I know," he nodded. "Well, my heart tells me to work for him if he gets the nomination. The only thing is that if I quit State, and then Bobby Kennedy loses, I won't even have a job at State. I'd have to go back to school, back to medical school, I guess. I don't know what would be better then. I don't really like State. It's nothing like the White House. At the White House, President Kennedy gave us a lot of room to be on our own. He made you feel like you were running the place. If you thought of some creative ideas, he appreciated what you did, and you could work on your own a lot. At State it isn't anything like that. It will take me forever to get anywhere in that place."

Cathy lowered her eyebrows in deep thought. "But you never know what's around the next corner." Even her shapely legs didn't compensate for her empty head. Well, maybe they did.

"Cathy—I some times worry that I'm not up to it—that if I worked for Bobby Kennedy that I wouldn't be up to it, and I might do him more harm than good, and maybe I should just stay at State."

"Only you can decide," she said.

That confirmed it. Her legs were definitely not worth it.

"People! People!" Irene Goodpastor yelled out. Cody looked at his girlfriend and said, "Hey, let's go in the parlor."

"You never know what's around the next corner," she repeated in a growing sense of confidence in her ability to be profound.

"People! People! Are we all in here? I want you to hear this. The Congress is going to vote soon on a law moving Columbus Day, Washington's Birthday, Memorial Day, and Veteran's Day to Mondays starting in 1971 so that we have three-day holidays." There was applause mixed with some "No's." "Now, I want every member of the Congress who's here to vote against it! That's right, against it! We don't want Americans to think of those days as three-day holidays, but as important American events to commemorate. Are you with me?" There was applause mixed with "No's" again, except this time both sides were reversed and louder.

"All right," Mrs. Goodpastor reacted, "for those opposed, just think of this: did Columbus discover this country, did Washington become the father of our country, did veterans fight for it and die for it, so we could have a lot of three days off in a row? I have to disagree with some of my Democratic friends on this. But if there's no consensus on that, ask yourself this: should we move April Fools' Day to a Monday every year? Who's for keeping it on April the First?" There was unanimous applause and cheers.

"All right, then," she said. "Now, this is April Fools', and we do have a tradition here at these little annual get-togethers. Even though none of us are children, we play a little game to celebrate the event and get away from the troubles and crises of the world that all of you live with every day. Thank goodness the rain stopped, and for those of you who don't know or have never attended one of my April Fools' parties, we gather under the canopy we've put up in the yard and—"

Her voice was interrupted by a loud thud on the front door, followed by another one and another one as though someone was trying to smash the door down with a log. The three thuds were quickly followed by a chant that was yelled by a large chorus of voices: "1-2-3-4! We don't want your ******' war! 1-2-3-4! We don't want your ******' war!"

"What do we want?" one loud male voice yelled.

"Peace!" the chorus answered.

"When do we want it?" the single voice yelled again.

"Now!" the crowd yelled back.

It became impossible for Mrs. Goodpastor or anyone at the party to ignore what was happening outside.

"1,2,3,4!" the single voice yelled as though it was a question.

It was answered by the voices again, "We don't want your ******' war!"

Then the thumps on the door again.

Some of Mrs. Goodpastor's guests went to the windows. Cody Cooper went to the telephone to call the police. Mrs. Goodpastor went to the front door and opened it, and the chants were heard much louder. The outer side of the door was marked and chipped.

Members of the Congress and appointees accompanied her, forming a human wall around her for protection, which she did not want. Those in the crowd outside didn't even recognize them. Most of those in the crowd were very young and some carried Viet Cong flags. A few carried small U.S. flags that were mounted on their wooden staffs upside down. One of the boys carried a guitar. The television crews that had been dismantling their equipment were quickly putting their cameras back on their tripods, and the lights went on again. Irene Goodpastor pushed her way through her protection and went right into the middle of the crowd. "Does anyone here want to hear what I have to say?" She yelled.

"No! No! No! No!" they yelled back.

"Are you the only ones with the right to speak?" she yelled.

"**** your speech!" a girl no older then fifteen yelled back. "We've listened to your ******' talk; now listen to ours."

Then one chant followed another and another and another.

"What do you want from me?" Mrs. Goodpastor asked.

The girl closest to Mrs. Goodpastor said, "Peace, ol' lady. Make peace. I guess you want the ol' B-52s to bomb the gooks. Isn't that what you call them?"

Irene Goodpastor looked at the boy who was standing next to that girl. The boy was carrying a Viet Cong flag. In a shaking voice she asked him, "Do you want peace or do you want them to win?" and she pointed to his Viet Cong flag.

"Man, lady, this here is peace," he said pumping his flag up and down in the air by its staff. "The Cong is peace! America is war! This ol' dad is goin' to Canada when that ol' notice comes in the mail. You can't catch me up there! I don' want your ******' war, ol' lady!"

The girl said, "He ain't gonna be killed by your war when he's up in Canada!"

The boy added, "If I's on the battlefield, lady, you know what I'd do? I'd turn my rifle on my commander. That's what I'd do!"

The girl laughed almost maniacally and said, "Bang! Commander's dead! War's over!" and she shrugged her shoulders.

The boy with the guitar came forward. "When you gonna make love, lady? How come you like war? How come you gonna make war and not love?"

"Her?" the girl said. "Her? Make love? Frus-tra-ted. That's what she is. Frus-tra-ted. That's why she wants her war so much. She don't know what love feels like since she hasn't had it for a hundred years!"

The boys laughed.

"It feels gooood, ol' lady," the flag carrier said. "It feels real gooood."

"When's the last time, lady?" the girl said with a smirk.

Mrs. Goodpastor smacked her across her cheek. Very hard.

It was as though everything stopped. Even the chanting stopped. It was dead quiet.

The young girl put her hand to her cheek, and her eyes started filling with tears.

Mrs. Goodpastor opened her mouth in disbelief and shock at what she had done to the girl.

The guitar carrier broke the silence. "See? Their answer is always violence. They always got to be violent."

Mrs. Goodpastor was in a daze. "I'm very sorry," she said softly. "I'm very sorry, honey."

The girl started sobbing.

The guitar carrier gave a quick laugh and said, "She's like the ol' guy who sticks a bayonet in the other guys belly and then says, 'Oh, I'm so sorry! Please forgive me! I'm so sorry!' And the other guy's dead!"

Then some one threw a rock at the house but it landed in the shrubs, so another rock was thrown and it hit its target, smashing a window. The wailing sound of sirens could be heard in the distance. The television crews were walking through the bushes, climbing the trees, and one of the reporters was telling a demonstrator to wave the flag he was carrying and not look at the camera.

The sirens were becoming louder as the vehicles came closer, and in short time there were police and firemen surrounding the crowd. Some of the demonstrators yelled their chants, some laid down on the sidewalk, and some started pushing the police.

Then came the tear gas.

Ted Murphy finally made it to the party. He was late, but just in time to stand in front of Irene Goodpastor's house as police were taking away "young people who were exercising their constitutional right to peaceably assemble," Ted Murphy said to his audience, "to protest the war being waged by the United States government in Vietnam."

Mrs. Goodpastor couldn't stop trembling that night, despite all her public bravery. She never felt more alone than she did when all her guests and hired help had left. Maybe it was only the emotion of the time, and maybe it was the memory of what the kids had said to her and the ruined front lawn and shrubs and door and the broken window and the stench of tear-gas, maybe it was all of those things, but most of all it was the horror of the realization she had actually slapped a teenage girl. That made her decide, that night, to never again hold another April Fools' party.

TWENTY-ONE
GRADUATION DAY
1968

Gerald Fairbanks read about the Goodpastor party, and he was glad he was not there to witness its conclusion.

Its conclusion, however, was going to come to him. It would come to every one who lived in that city. It was an invading force of anarchy whose battle-lines would come across every road.

As Gerald Fairbanks drove across Key Bridge he went over a few parts of the text of his speech that lay beside him on the front seat, and he found some things with which he was dissatisfied. "Stop calling them kids," he said to himself. "They're young people. I was a kid. When I was a kid, I was on the defensive from adults. Now I'm an adult on the defensive from kids." He was rehearsing his commencement address he would give at Monroe High School in Virginia just across the Potomac. Both chauffeurs of the Agency were unavailable to take him there, and he had to drive himself in his old Chevrolet that had two hub-caps missing and a smashed grill. He quickly had it washed when he realized he would have to drive there himself, and was supposed to be greeted by the faculty of the high school.

His fears regarding his old Chevrolet were all for nothing. There was no reception committee, only a pencil-thin seventeen-year-old track star who escorted him to the principal's office.

The principal, Mr. Southard, stood up and smiled when Gerald Fairbanks walked in. Mr. Southard was a balding man with some hair left above his ears, his face was drawn and red and his expression was pained. The boy who looked like a pencil closed the door and left the two alone.

"I'm so glad that you accepted our invitation, Ambassador Fairbanks," Mr. Southard said. "Sit down. We have a couple of minutes."

Gerald Fairbanks sat down facing the principal at his desk. "Actually I was an Ambassador for just a few months some time back. Just call me Gerry. And it's an honor to speak to your graduates. I have always enjoyed talking to—young people."

"They can be challenging. They keep you on your toes."

"They do indeed."

"We were going to hold the ceremony outside but kept the auditorium ready in case it rained. When I heard it was going to be in the nineties, I re-scheduled it for the auditorium, rain or no rain."

There was silence for a while and then Mr. Southard came out with it. "We might have a little trouble, Ambassador Fairbanks," the principal warned him. "The graduates will be seated behind the speakers—behind you. A few of the boys and girls decided not to wear caps and gowns this year—they thought it was too 'establishment-oriented' as they call it. It's a form of protest and we said they didn't have to wear them if they didn't want to."

"That, sir, was a mistake, wasn't it?"

No answer. "And a few aren't going to come to graduation at all. We removed some of the seats so none of the seats will be vacant. We've also tried to arrange seating in such a way as to keep the real activists split up rather than in a group."

"Is all that really necessary?"

"I think it is. Also, some of them are not going to come when their names are called to receive their diplomas. That's not really your problem—it's mine, but I want you to know the mood. It's not exactly the kind of graduations that you and I had years back."

"Things are different now. I know."

"No comparison. We had some trouble in the school this year. Not very pleasant."

"What kind of trouble?"

"One of the boys was stabbed in the lavatory. He's all right. But it could have been very bad. Then only a couple months ago, some students called a strike. Only a handful of students came to school for a couple of days. Most of them were afraid to show up because the ones who organized the strike were pretty tough. It's been very difficult. We had three teachers resign. One of them was beaten up. The phys. ed. teacher."

Gerald Fairbanks nodded slowly.

"So I just want to tell you what the mood is like. I don't mean all of them. Ninety-five percent of the students are just fine. But—"

"You said that only a handful came to school for a couple of days. Why did they strike? Vietnam?"

"No, it wasn't Vietnam. Right after Martin Luther King was killed, the students went on a rampage. They took their cue from the District. They were smashing school property, looting, everything. It was like the District here. Then they wanted to run the school. They handed me a list of seventeen demands. I didn't give in."

"Good!"

"They wanted too much. I didn't allow that. They came back to school. But then a week after the strike, they broke into my office and ransacked it. Started a fire. You can still see that area over there," and he pointed to a charred portion of the wall which was a large black oval spot with wisps of brown on the top and on the bottom of the black spot.

"You're lucky you weren't hurt."

"I wasn't here. They did it at night. Then a couple of weeks ago when Robert Kennedy was killed, it was as though I was Sirhan Sirhan," Mr. Southard said. "Well, perhaps we better go to the auditorium."

Gerald Fairbanks pulled the text of his speech out of his inside jacket pocket and scribbled a few changes he thought of in the car, and other changes he thought of while listening to the principal.

The area for the audience in the auditorium was packed. Apparently the revised seating plan on stage didn't go as the principal had indicated, as there were empty seats scattered throughout the assemblage of graduates on stage, and groups of empty seats, and there were about a dozen students without caps and gowns seated together.

The valedictorian gave a long speech in which she gave a few negative remarks about United States policy in Southeast Asia and a few remarks about "changes that must be made in the basic fabric of the United States." After most politically-oriented statements there were some cheers from the clustered-together group of graduates without caps and gowns, and some applause from others.

After the valedictorian was through with her remarks, the president of the Class of Summer '68 introduced Gerald Fairbanks with no biographical information at all, except to say he worked for President Johnson.

There was some laughter and a few "boos" but there was also applause for him as he came to the podium. Not spirited but there was some applause. He didn't have long to wait for it to end.

"At another time, a graduation could not be considered an event of controversy," Gerald Fairbanks said, "but this is not another time." He read on about times that were changing and about the conformity that was taking place among so many of the "young people," a phrase over which he stumbled. The first five minutes of his speech seemed to go well. But then the mood of some of the students changed. He could hear some snickering behind him. He ignored it. "You will find, as your life continues, that you might well be inflicted with the uniquely American characteristic of impatience. Today we are impatient for a quick resolution to the Vietnam conflict–"

That was interrupted by applause. Then some students yelled in unison, "Hey! Hey! LBJ! How many kids did you kill today?" and it was followed by laughter. The chant came from the group without caps and gowns. They did it again. Gerald Fairbanks turned to them. They increased their volume. He turned back to the microphone and waited for their chant to subside. Mr. Southard was just looking down at the floor. He didn't do anything other than look down.

"We are equally impatient for our breakfast in the morning, we are impatient for our bill at a restaurant, and we are impatient for a cure for the common cold. In our large cities we buy Sunday newspapers on Saturdays. Around the country our magazines carry next week's or next month's date on their covers. The moment an election result is known, we speculate on what that result means in terms of the next election or the one after that. Every finish of a race is seen only as a new starting line."

There was more laughter from the same group.

"Now, as you graduate from compulsory education, you may find yourself impatient–and you may make a hurried decision in the areas which could have an affect on your entire life. Where will you find your career? Too many good people have simply passed by the idea of working in government, and that's where some of the best of other generations have been. There are, perhaps, more people in the last two centuries who have shared their greatness with the world from Washington than from any other city. You are fortunate to have that city and its people so close."

In unison, the same voices chanted "Stop the bombing! Stop the killing! Peace! Peace! Peace!" It had obviously been rehearsed. They stopped as quickly as they started. There was some snickering.

"You can see those people on any day in Washington. You can see them in marble and in flesh–in memorial and breath. There's an obelisk for Washington, a dome for Jefferson, pillars for Lincoln, and a flame for Kennedy. And there are others who work today in the White House and the Capitol and the Courts and some who are scattered throughout lesser-known buildings that stand between the Potomac and the Hill. Those in marble can expect a wreath. Those in the flesh can expect a demonstration."

He paused, expected booing or the chant at what he had just said, but there was only silence. When he realized there wasn't going to be any booing or chanting, he went on and knew he shouldn't have waited. "That's the way it always was and that's the way it will always be. Those who work with greatness in the cold climate of today do not have the luxury of having their work seen in retrospect. Memories take on a dreamlike quality of the 'good old days' with a beginning, a middle, and an end, while the present always seems unconnected, disorganized, and unsure.

"But some day these will be the olden days, and you and your generation will have families of your own and new students will study your time only for the purpose of passing a test. From the windows of their schoolrooms the fresh outdoors will beckon with their own springs and autumns, and their own springs and autumns will make their school book questions dull and boring: Where was the Gulf of Tonkin? In what city was Martin Luther King assassinated? Was Project Mercury a foreign aid program, a space program, or part of the War on Poverty? Select one.

"Will it come to that? Of course it will. The present always comes to that."

Someone started groaning very loudly.

"The leaders of today, along with all of us, will be neatly organized between pages 240 and 247 in a blue school history book. The names we all know so well like Lyndon Baines Johnson and Hubert Hum–" then it happened. He was interrupted by the chant, "Hey! Hey! LBJ! How many kids did you kill today?" Then it was repeated by that cluster of students who didn't wear caps and gowns. He looked back at them and tried to collect himself from the liability of impatience from which he had just told them to rise. Then they added a line that made no coherent sense at all, simply filled with profanities.

He repeated his last lines as the chants started to subside. "The names we all know so well like Lyndon Baines Johnson and Hubert Humphrey and Dean Rusk will be left to be spelled right and spelled wrong on three-holed blue-lined paper by another generation. And these days will take on a look we cannot yet imagine. In the meantime, we continue to write those pages ourselves. In our writings and actions, we should continue to be discontent with the world the way it is and try to make it better. But, as we do it, we should also appreciate what those before us and those with us have already accomplished for us, lest we lose all that has been gained."

Now it wasn't a chant, it was just disinterest. There were a lot of noises and talking.

"We are a nation not only impatient for incidentals, we are a nation impatient for Utopia. With loud voices of self-condemnation rather than self-confidence, with pessimism rather than optimism, we have become perversely interested in flagellating ourselves for not reaching Utopia, and congratulating others although they are even further from it." There were murmurs that were getting louder. "The advocates of that perversity have stood ready to flail the United States and its leaders for idealism and hard decisions." There were louder murmurs that turned into boos and hisses. "Simultaneously, they have eagerly justified and defended the actions of closed societies, shrouded in their curtained-off mystique, with the belief that what we don't know can only be better. Those messages were often applauded by the young. Even the U.N. caters to closed societies. Your generation must either revamp the U.N. or build a new world organization that will have the liberty of the peoples of the world as its objective." That was the line he hoped would have the strongest impact. Did they even hear it?

There was wild yelling and, again, the chant: "Hey! Hey! LBJ.! How many kids did you kill today?" There were some "shhh" noises but not enough to stop the boos and hisses and the chant. He looked at his text. There wasn't much left. He decided to continue even though he knew few could hear. The chant grew louder and more rhythmic with a heavy cadence. Mr. Southard acted oblivious to all this. He knew every scratch and mark on the floor as he continued staring at it.

Ambassador Fairbanks went on. One minute more. Twenty seconds more. Done. Unheard but done. He put his text back inside his jacket pocket. "Thank you and my congratulations to you." His victory was that he hadn't abbreviated his speech to satisfy those who yelled.

His speech was followed by the continuation of boos and hisses mixed with applause. Then his shoulder was hit by the edge of one of the square caps which was flung from behind him. The chant stopped. He went back to his seat and sat through the rest of the ceremony. But he didn't hear anything else that went on. He was drifting.

After the ceremony was done, some students and parents clustered around him and congratulated him. A number of students apologized for the discourtesy that was displayed by their classmates. One girl was crying, or so it seemed. He couldn't tell whether she was faking it or if she really was crying. There were no tears, just sobs. She said she was ashamed of the conduct of others. It was good of her, whether the crying was real or not. Ambassador Fairbanks thanked them all and told them he wasn't bothered by the outbursts. But of course he was.

He started back alone to his old Chevrolet. Mr. Southard was lost in the crowd of parents and students. The pencil-thin track star hadn't reappeared. The heat and humidity were intense and Gerald Fairbanks was perspiring. After a glimpse of his car, he stopped walking and he closed his eyes slowly and then, with great hesitancy, reopened them. Someone had drawn a swastika on his windshield with soap. "PEACE NOW" was written on the hood of the car in black paint or a black Magic Marker.

He reached the car, took his handkerchief from his back pocket and tried to wipe off the swastika but it just made a mess and the shape of the symbol could still be seen.

He opened the door of his car. There was an acrid odor inside. The front seat was wet. Gerald Fairbanks wiped his forehead with his hand and used his handkerchief again, this time to wipe the seat. He found a newspaper in a trash can and he placed it over the seat before sitting down.

When he arrived back at the Agency he didn't remember how he got there. The entire drive was lost in a trance that was devoid of all sense of time.

TWENTY-TWO
SALLY SAIGON
1968

Adjusting to Saigon in 1968 was an art. Thinking was a constant exercise in self-discipline. There were necessary rules about what you must dismiss from your mind; the possibility of the sudden end or slow end of your life being two of them. Friendships became vital, crowds were avoided, affairs became inevitable.

As the morning sun came up, Hondas were going in all directions, most of them driven by young women, the acceleration of those motorbikes making the women driver's long black hair furl behind their faces. They were wearing white, almost transparent pants with long, sheer flaps which were extensions of their blouses, but of such length that they hung beneath their knees, hanging in front of them and behind them. The rear white flaps, like the driver's black hair, were blowing back in the wind created by the Honda's forward motion. The transparency of their clothing proudly exhibited the outlines of their underwear. The apparel was called the ao-dai, and was an erotic fashion, enhanced by its high collar. Some, on their Hondas, wore yellow straw conical hats as though they were working in the rice-paddies. The attraction of their combined wardrobe was totally terminated that September morning by the sight on the sidewalk of a man's body without a head. The body was laying in front of a small bakery. Dried blood was on the sidewalk and into the road. His head was nearly a yard away from the rest of him. On the body, one of his shoes was so shiny it was like a black mirror. His other shoe was covered with gray dust. Some of the Honda drivers looked at him in passing, but only short glances.

Saigon had been a beautiful city in its mix of Vietnamese and French architecture and broad tree-lined avenues and traffic circles, but the occasional bodies, the barbed wire around buildings, the sandbags on corners and circles, the barriers creating detours on roads, made beauty a memory. The current was dominated by the tragic. That morning, a short distance from the decapitated man was a woman sitting on the ground in tears, loaves of French bread scattered on the sidewalk and into the road, where the Hondas skirted them as annoyances in their paths.

The humidity that enveloped the city long before the arrival of the sun, enhanced the smell of death from that sidewalk. The sputtering of the motors of the Hondas obscured any other sound, so if there were cries or yells or screams they were unheard.

A few feet from the bakery was a black shoe-shine kit, now in four large pieces, splinters of it close to the man's body. The boy who had been its owner had, by this time, mingled with the morning crowds, his Wednesday morning assignment having been successfully completed. He was likely on his way to pick up another shoe-shine kit with its bomb installed. His instructions were probably not to find a particular customer, but any customer other than a member of the Viet Cong since the objective was not particular deaths but death itself. Its grotesque abnormality was becoming the normal.

Another boy, no more than thirteen years old, passed by the decapitated body and then, as what must have been an afterthought, he walked back to it and with both hands he picked up the man's head. He walked it over to the body and set it down as though it was connected to the man's neck, and then the boy walked away.

The main avenue, TuDo Street, meaning "Street of Freedom," was as bustling as any Asian city's major boulevard at peace, with street-sellers having all kinds of foreign goods to sell, from cigarettes and lighters to candy bars and hi-fi's, and silk scarves and men's ties. TuDo started at JFK Square, then passed the Vietnam headquarters of *The New York Times* and *The Washington Post*, the Continental Hotel, the Caravelle Hotel, United Press International, then it ended at the Saigon River. In almost every direction there was something that reflected the war. At times soldiers with their rifles ready, while squatting behind a wall of sandbags, at times an explosive noise, at times a quickly built wooden barrier or iron gate blocking some building.

Since the new security measures were put in place shortly after the Tet offensive earlier in the year, the U.S. Embassy compound at the corner of Thong Nhoi and Mac Dinh Chi, took on the appearance of a military headquarters in a war-zone. The gun encampments and bunkers and barbed wire were not the stuff that any nation wanted to surround its embassy, but it was vital. Its workers went to their jobs a different way every morning so there would be no routine that could be learned by the Viet Cong.

There were a few offices in the U.S. Embassy that were set aside for visiting members of the Congress or from the administration when they came into Saigon and needed a desk and a phone and a place to hold meetings. One of those offices had been used before and was being used again as a temporary place for Moose Dunston of the National Security Council Staff. While in Saigon, Moose Dunston had three great fears: cockroaches, the press, and being killed, in that order. The last fear was one he knew he shouldn't even think about, but for the first time in his life he had his will written and left with a friend in Washington, and with another copy given to his frequent Saigon companion, Captain Jonas Valadovich.

The double bars of Jonas Valadovich's captain's insignia that were normally worn above his shoulders on his uniform weren't there that morning. Instead, the bars had been replaced with a gold-colored leaf on each shoulder. "Salute, Moose! A major just entered your office! Put down that pipe and show some respect!"

"Oh, no!" Moose said, setting down his pipe in compliance with the request. "What has happened to our military?" And then he broke into a big smile, stood up, walked around his desk and grabbed Jonas's hand, clutching Jonas's forearm with his other hand. "Congratulations, Big Wheel! Son of a gun, if they didn't give a promotion to the best man in the United States Air Force!"

"Thanks, Moose," Jonas said in his very deep voice, accompanied by a shy smile. "In that case, since you feel that way, you can smoke your old pipe."

Moose leaned against his desk and looked approvingly at the new identification of rank on his friend's uniform. "Hey, you get a raise in salary with that promotion, don't you? They still do that, don't they? They gave me more money when I went from a private to a PFC."

Jonas shrugged with a smile. "Just a little bit more. Not much."

"Don't give me that stuff! Tonight, you're buying the beer! As a captain you've put me in a poverty-zone because you were always broke!"

"All right, all right! The first glass, but that's it. Your stomach is too big. When you buy me a beer, it's a beer. When I buy you a beer, I have to fill a truck with that stuff!"

"Just the first thirty mugs, Jonas, that's all. For God's sake, Big Fella, you're a major now! Majors should always be generous to their friends. It's a service tradition."

"I never heard of that tradition."

"George Washington started it. If you want to end it, think of what you'll do to your country—but that's your choice." And then he smiled broadly again. "Congratulations, buddy! That's just great! God, you deserve it!"

There was a knock, more like a tap on the already open door, and not waiting for an invitation to enter, a small and very pretty young Vietnamese woman walked in wearing an ao-dai. "The morning report, Mr. Dunston." She handed him a sheet of paper and walked out as promptly as she walked in.

"I never get used to that," Moose said shaking his head, almost in disbelief that women like that walk in and out of offices here.

"It's a marvelous thing to get used to," Jonas said. "But what you have in your hand, isn't. Is that today's casualty report?"

Moose glanced at it, nodded, and then started to look it over. His expression changed into one of bitterness, clamping his lips together. "Body count."

"Bad?" Jonas asked.

"Yeah. Bad."

"What's up?"

"I never heard of it. A village called Aptrangdau—"

"Aptrangdau," Jonas interrupted. "I know that village. It's about maybe, I don't know, 25 miles from here. I've been there a couple times on quick visits. We're guarding Aptrangdau, forming an outside perimeter. The 101st Airborne is doing it. The V.C. kept slitting the throats of the elders and the teachers there, so we've been surrounding it to make sure the V.C. doesn't get back in."

Moose shook his head. "They got back in. They broke the perimeter and took women and kids and used them as shields. They killed thirty-three of our grunts—and almost wiped out the village. Aptrangdau isn't there any more. Here—" and he handed Jonas the paper.

Jonas slumped in the chair as he read through the report.

"Do you know any of them, Jonas?"

"I don't recognize the names. I don't know. I don't know the names."

"How about the injured? That's usually about midway through the report."

Jonas looked up. "Moose, what kind of advice do you give the National Security Council when you get home from one of these trips?"

"What I think."

"What do you think?"

"That every time we have a bombing pause the North Vietnamese interpret it as weakness, and they advance. You know why they interpret it as weakness? Because it is weakness. And I tell them if we fiddle around without absolute unconditional surrender as the objective, this won't be the only surrender. I tell them we should stop allowing privileged sanctuaries. Get them wherever they go—Laos, Cambodia, wherever they go or we'll never be done with this. I tell them that we should stop listening to kids in the street who haven't had any experience in anything except going to school. The next time I go home I'm going to tell them that the Soviets fought to win in Czechoslovakia last month. World opinion meant nothing to them. Nothing. And they won. There's a sick feeling in the world that when a power wants to take freedom away from people, it's regretted but accepted. But if a power wants to fight so a people won't be taken over—that power better quit."

"You do tell them that kind of thing?"

"Yes."

"What's the reaction when you say things like that?"

He shrugged. "It depends. Someone might say that popular opinion—or at least street opinion, can't be disregarded."

"You have a lot of arguments there?"

"Some times emotions run pretty high. There's one guy—he's no one particularly important—but he keeps saying it's an immoral war. I answer that I can't think of a higher morality in the world than to risk your life for the liberty of a stranger. I ask him, 'Can you?' and he doesn't answer."

Jonas shook his head. "Good question."

"Now, take a look at the wounded list. Anyone there you know?"

Jonas looked back at the report and started reading the names on the middle of the sheet. "No. I don't know them. Wait. Wait. What is an American civilian doing here? Yeah, I know him. So do you."

"Who?"

"Look at this second to the last name on the wounded list." He handed the report back to Moose.

Moose scanned it. "My God!" Moose said. "That strange son of a gun! He is a strange guy. Orr. Orr. A civilian. I have no idea what he's doing in Vietnam. Look, they got him. It says, "Left leg. Evacuated." Then he yelled, "An-Twit? An-Twit?"

The young woman in the ao-dai came rushing in. "Yes, Mr. Dunston?"

"Find out where this guy is, please. This guy." He walked to her and pointed down the sheet. She nodded and walked out.

"What's his game?" Jonas asked.

"I have no idea. All I know is, he's a loner. And apparently a wealthy guy as I remember. I don't know why I got that idea. Well, I do, too. When we were in Hong Kong he stayed at the Peninsula Hotel—not a cheap joint—the most expensive place there, and he said something to me about not worrying about money or something like that. I sort of liked the guy, but he's a strange duck."

"Why did you ask her to find out about him?"

"Curious. Just curious. I'm always curious when U.S. civilians are in places they shouldn't be. I suspect every one, you know. I've gotten paranoid."

"You mean of collaborating with the V.C.?"

"There are enough Americans these days who aren't on our side. Nine-tenths of the journalists here are friendlier to the V.C. than they are to us. You wait-and-see how this attack is reported. They won't say what the 101st was doing there. They won't report anything about the V.C. using women and kids as shields. They won't. I've been through this. I know. Do you think they'll report the village was wiped out?"

Jonas shrugged, then shook his head. "I don't talk to them."

"I don't either, but some people here have to. Barry Zorthian conducted a news conference every day for them and told them everything he could without endangering our grunts, and they called the conferences the Five O'clock Follies. They didn't want us to win. They still don't. I tell you, Jonas, I suspect every one who isn't directly involved in this war. If Roosevelt—if FDR had to fight at home at the same time he was fighting overseas, we'd have lost World War II."

"You don't agree with President Johnson at all, do you?"

"I believe you should fight the war, Jonas—you—the military should fight it. McNamara is a—is someone who doesn't know how to fight a war."

"I'm asking you if you agree with the president." Jonas tried again for an answer.

"His platform plank at the convention, what they called the Johnson-Humphrey Plank was better than the McCarthy-McGovern Plank. That's all I can say. That McCarthy-McGovern one called for an unconditional bombing halt. Unconditional. But the Johnson-Humphrey Plank wasn't that much better. Even that one said we should have a conditional bombing halt. As though that's the issue here. What's with this obsession with a bombing halt? Is that why we're here endangering our own lives? Yours more than mine. You think we're all here, all the troops are here to halt the bombing? We're here to win—or at least that's what I hope we're here for. But I'll tell you, Jonas, at home, a lot of people don't want leadership, they want follower-ship. Why don't we just elect George Gallup? Huh?"

Jonas didn't say anything.

"Let me turn around your question: how do you feel about it, Jonas? Do you like the way the president is handling all this? Is this why you joined the service and worked yourself into being a major? To stop the bombing?"

"He's my commander in chief."

"Look, the president is in a rough spot and I feel for him. When you're in the Oval Office it's different than when you're down the hall like I am, I know that. And I like Humphrey. He's a very decent guy. We get along great. But I'm not voting for him. I can't."

"If Nixon wins, maybe he won't keep you. Maybe he'll tell you to get out. New presidents have a habit of doing that to their predecessor's appointees, you know."

"Maybe. That's not the issue. The war is the issue."

Jonas nodded. "You're a good man, Moose."

An-Twit came back in. "I have all the information, Mr. Dunston. The man you asked about was writing a book on Vietnam. He was in a hand-to-hand with the V.C. during the attack. He killed three V.C. He's crippled, Mr. Dunston."

Moose and Jonas exchanged a glance. "He's on our side, Moose," Jonas said. "Don't suspect everybody. Just be cautious."

"Where is he?" Moose asked An-Twit.

"My Tho."

"My Tho? What's he doing all the way down there? There are better hospitals here, why is he there?" He was talking as though it was An-Twit's fault. He turned to Jonas. "Want to go with me, Jonas? I'm going to visit the guy."

"No, no. That's your business, Moose, not mine. I'd be going way out of bounds. You go ahead."

He looked at An-Twit. "Get me some way to be in My Tho today, please. Either a car, a jeep or a helicopter, or even a ferry. I want to be there and back today. Find out where I go to see him when I get there, please." He looked back at Jonas. "Our celebration—how about it being a little late tonight?"

Jonas nodded. "I'll be here. I'm not going anywhere."

"One more question, Jonas. What would you do if you were McNamara?"

Jonas sat silent for a while. There was no one listening other than Moose. "If I was McNamara I'd say to General Abrams, 'I'll get out of your hair. Now, win this thing in three months or you're in a Pentagon office until you retire. That's what I'd do if I was McNamara.'"

Unlike Saigon, My Tho wasn't losing its beauty since it never had any. It was a miserable city boasting one pagoda and one snake farm and one hotel, if a hotel is defined as a place where rooms are rented. And that was where Adam Orr was staying, not in a hospital.

The man at the hotel reception desk downstairs did not speak English well but was able to tell Adam over the house phone that there was a guest who wanted to see him.

"If it's Elizabeth Taylor send her up," the voice of Adam said through the phone.

The man at the desk asked Moose if he was Elizabeth Taylor. Moose smiled. "No, tell him I'm Jeannie Riley from the Harper Valley P.T.A."

"I heard that," Adam said. "That's even better. Get her up here quick. The door's open. I keep it that way so I'll be found in case I die."

The receptionist told Moose to go to Room 222.

He wasn't dying, but he wasn't in good enough shape to go for a walk. His room was very hot, and the revolving fan on the ceiling was hanging crooked and did nothing but make noise and blow the drapes back and forth. Adam was sitting in a chair with his left leg in a cast, propped up on another chair that had pillows on top of its cushion. He was holding an open bottle of beer. On Adam's lap was a little black cat with white feet and a white vest and her face had a triangular pattern of white with the upper point of the white triangle between her eyes, going down to both sides of her mouth. The cat was purring and lightly digging its front claws in and out of Adam's thighs in utter contentment as she opened and closed her eyes repeatedly, slowly and calmly.

"Pardon me for not standing up," Adam said as Moose entered the room. "You're a big man and you're taking up a lot of room in this place so don't breathe in and out while you're here, or you'll use up all the air and I'll die."

"If I don't breathe in an out, then I'll die."

"Do it out in the hall. You'll be taking up too much room in here, particularly if you fall dead with even some of you in here."

Moose smiled and came to Adam's chair and shook hands, while the little cat jumped up on Adam's right shoulder for protection. "It's been a long time since Hong Kong. Good to see you—but not like this." Moose gestured to the cat. "Who's that?"

"Sally."

Moose nodded. "Okay. She yours?"

"We argue a lot, but we're living together now. You know how it is with a woman. She picks on me."

Moose sat on the edge of the unmade bed, since it was the only piece of furniture unoccupied by Adam and his extended leg. Then Moose told Adam that he was now with the National Security Council staff of President Johnson, that he recognized Adam's name on the casualty list, and that he came to My Tho to find out if, as a non-governmental American civilian, Adam knew anything that would be of interest to the National Security Council. And, most of all, he wanted to know what happened in Aptrangdau.

Adam told Moose he was writing a book on Vietnam and he went to Aptrangdau because a Military Assistance Command Vietnam—MACV—helicopter was going there and he could hitch a ride and someone told him a lot of pretty girls lived in Aptrangdau. That's what he said, but when he used the name "Aptrangdau," he could hardly get it out of his mouth without choking up. "It's gone. The whole village is gone. A lot of people were slaughtered."

"What happened?"

"You probably know more about it than I do. I was asleep. Suddenly the V.C. were all over the place. I don't know how they got in there. Our guys had the place guarded. There were fifteen people, including me, in this big area covered with a makeshift metal roof. I ordered them to run, just as though I was a general. They did. All different directions. I stood there and I see this guy, this V.C., and he was like the others—in black pajamas and he had a knife the size of a samurai sword, or at least so it seemed—and he killed Sally's mother," gesturing with his shoulder to the cat who was now walking down Adam's chest back to her position on his lap. Adam pet her back over and over again. "And then he started to come to Sally. That's when it happened. We got in a fight over Sally. Can you believe it? The folks back home will say I did this over a cat. What can I say? I don't remember much after I went for his throat. I don't even remember him doing anything to me, nor was there any pain in my leg. The next thing I knew I was being carried off and I remember looking at bodies all over the ground from my stretcher and I was told what happened—which you already know. They told me I killed three of them. Maybe. Guess who was on the stretcher with me? Sally. There. That's your briefing. It's all I know."

"You're lucky you're alive."

"I knew I had more time on this planet. Let's not talk about Aptrangdau. Want to talk about women? Jeannie Riley. I thought you were Jeannie Riley. You said so. I thought maybe God heard my prayers. I don't pray about my leg. You hit it right—I pray about Jeannie Riley. Want a drink?"

"Anything. I'll drink anything. God, this room is hot."

"Well, I can't get up to get the beer for you. You'll have to get it yourself. You don't want this beer," and he nodded at the bottle he was holding. "I've been drinking it out of the bottle and you might catch a venereal disease. There's some fresh hot beer and an opener on the counter. It's all yours. There's nothing like it when beer's good and hot."

Moose walked over to a carton of Budweisers. "Where did you get the American beer?"

"I stole it from the V.C. I think they got it as a gift from some of our press corps. Probably a bribe."

Moose smiled, opened a beer, and sat back on the edge of the bed. "What does the doctor say?"

"He says to keep the leg elevated for about a month. Then he'll take the cast off and put on a lighter one and then—at worst—at worst, for a while I may walk with a limp. Just for a while. That's all. I'm okay."

"You in pain?"

"I'm taking some prescription stuff. It works good until my leg realizes I'm trying to sleep—then it acts up to remind me about that guy in the black pajamas. Did I tell you he was very ugly? He had a big mole on his cheek. If he was friendlier to Sally I would have recommended a plastic surgeon I know in Florida."

"How come you're staying here at the Grand Hotel? Shouldn't you be in a hospital?"

"They wouldn't let Sally in there so I told them to go shove their hospital. This is the best hotel in My Tho, believe it or not. I think it's the only one."

"Why didn't you go to Saigon? Hang Sanh Hospital was good enough for the Ambassador. Some one could take care of your cat. What's in My Tho for you?"

"My Tho has My Tho in it. I planned on seeing My Tho in September and I won't let the V.C. change my plans. It's September and I'm in My Tho."

"Why on earth does a man like you want to come to Vietnam at a time like this? You could go anywhere in the world you want, couldn't you?"

"Because this is now. I want to be where now is. Vietnam isn't going to be now forever. Some other place will be now, and I'll be there if I'm still alive."

"What's your book about? I mean I know it's about Vietnam but what's it say?"

"It's about Vietnamese women. It has nothing to do with the war. I've got about four hundred pages done, and I'm only down to their shoulders so far. It will be a big book."

Moose smiled and shook his head. "How long are you going to stay here?"

"Until the war's over. I take some breaks from it. I get to Hong Kong pretty often, which is the place I'm nuts about."

"Then why don't you live there?"

Adam shook his head. "Why ruin the mystique? You should never make a career out of your hobby, or make a wife out of your lover. There is no more certain way to lose passion than by familiarity. Keep your pleasures as pleasures. Keep them unique. Keep the passion. Keep the guilt. That's why I don't live there. So I'll stay here until the war's over, then back to Florida. After all, I don't want to miss the screwiest war in history. You have a half-million northerners coming south to get out of the north because they can't stand the government up there, and you have another half-million northerners coming south to kill southerners. Then you have a half-million American kids shouting to stop the bombing while another half-million American kids are here fighting for the southerners while there are a half million of the most beautiful women in the world riding on motorbikes. I wouldn't miss it. Imagine the dopes who are going to Canada and missing this."

"You have a rather unusual perspective, Orr."

"It's the only perspective. I'm not mad at the cowards who go to Canada because they're draft dodgers. I'm mad at them because they'd rather be alive than live. They don't know the difference. But they're kids. It's the adults who praise them that get me. Enough about the war. Let's get back to something important. Did you ever marry that gorgeous creature you fell in love with in Hong Kong?"

"No."

"Good for you. Do you still see her?"

"No. But we write. A lot. I went back once."

"Oh, oh. That was a mistake. Never try to re-live a memory, Dunston. Leave memories alone. If you try to re-live them you don't create new ones, you just mess up the old ones."

"The truth is I can't get her out of my mind. Every time I know I have a couple days off in Saigon I look at the airline schedules to Hong Kong."

"Don't do it. Leave her alone. Enjoy thinking about her. That's enough."

"We still write each other."

"You already said that. Repetition is a sign of alcoholism or love or age. You probably have all three. That's a shame. You're becoming a pitiful character."

"For a while I lived with a Vietnamese girl."

"Lived with one?"

"Yes. That was a mistake."

"A dangerous mistake. Look at me and Sally. We never argued before we started living together. Now she gets mad at me, then she kisses me, then she gets mad again. Women! Don't live with them. Look at these Vietnamese men. They live with them, they marry them, and they're all being led around by their noses by those women who look so frail you'd think you could blow them over by exhaling. They run the place, you know. So what happened, you don't live with her anymore?"

"I couldn't. You're right, she started giving orders. I took it for a while, but she drove me crazy. I might have taken it longer but the truth is, I love Wai-yee. I couldn't stay with some other girl while I love her."

"Who's Wai-yee?"

"The girl. The girl in Hong Kong."

"Her name is Wai-yee?"

"Yes."

"All I remember is that she was a doll and you were falling all over her. I'm disappointed that you call her by her name."

"What do you mean?"

"She's a woman. They're all Wai-yee's. All women are Wai-yee's and all Wai-yee's are women. It doesn't make any difference what you call them. You'll learn. Don't go back to Hong Kong."

"We signed a pledge to go back, remember?"

"Okay. Go back in 1997. You'll get over it by then, and think of how much happier you'll be. You'll still have the memories without all the grief. That is, you'll still have the memories if you haven't messed them up already by that second trip."

"You don't know. You don't know. She's special. You know how special? She got her mother out of China. It's all she worked for. She did it. She and her sister worked for years to get the money to get their parents out and give them a good home in Hong Kong. By the time they succeeded her father was dead, killed, but they did it. Wai-yee did it. She's a marvelous woman."

"Well, I'm a marvelous man but you aren't going to fall in love with me, are you? Not a chance. And I wouldn't think of living with you even if you just rescued a million people from a lava-flow of a volcano. I don't care how marvelous she is. That isn't what you love. Don't kid me. You love the womaness in her, that's all. Don't let anyone con you, and above all, don't let you con you. If she was an evil witch you'd still love her. Her femininity has you temporarily insane. That's what it is—temporary insanity."

"It's more than that."

"A permanent insanity?"

"No insanity. You're underplaying her goodness. You don't know her."

"Did you ever shake hands with a man, any man, and have him hold on to your hand after the handshake is done?"

"Yes."

"It's awful. It's sickening, isn't it?"

"Yes."

"Even if he found the cure to every disease, it would still be sickening, wouldn't it?"

"Yes."

"Did you ever shake hands with a woman—a total stranger—but a pretty woman, and have her hold on to your hand after the handshake is done?"

"Yes."

"Did you get sick?"

"No."

"If she was pretty enough, you kept your hand where it was, didn't you?"

"Yes."

"Did you do that because you knew that she did fine things for the helpless, or because she was a knock-out?"

"That has nothing to do with my feeling towards Wai-yee."

"It has everything to do with your feeling towards Wai-yee."

"Look, Orr, you're a crazy man and I worry about you."

"I'm the sane one. Sanity is a difficult thing to hold on to around pretty women, but I've done it."

"Sanity? Look at what you're doing in this room. You're crazy. You leave your door to this room open like that. I don't doubt some of the staff here are V.C.. They could take off your other leg while you're sleeping. You ought to come back to Saigon. There's better medical help there if you need it. There's nothing for you to see in My Tho and even if there was, you can't see it with your leg above your head. I have an Embassy car waiting and I don't want to spend too long here. Okay? The curfew in Saigon starts at ten tonight. The driver and I want to get there before then. We don't want to be on that road in the dark."

"You armed?"

"Of course. So is the driver. Want to come with us? I can get in the front seat with the driver and you can have the whole back seat with your leg up. We'll bring some pillows from this rat-trap."

"Can we take Sally?"

"We can take Sally."

"Sally," and he looked down at the purring cat. "You want to go to your namesake?" He scratched her under her chin. She closed and opened her eyes. Then Adam looked up at Moose. "Her full name is Sally Saigon."

"Is that where she's from originally?"

"I don't know."

"Then why is her last name 'Saigon'?"

"How do I know? It's just her name. Why is your last name Dunston? Did you come from Dunston?"

"Okay, fine. You and Sally Saigon. You can both come with me."

Adam thought for a while and then nodded. "I'll surprise you and do it. At least the Caravelle in Saigon has air conditioning."

"Is that where you stay there?"

"I'm holding a room. I never checked out."

"Orr, do you mind if I ask something that may not be any of my business? How do you make your living?"

"I don't. I have enough money to live the rest of my life without working. I don't have anyone counting on me for anything so I do what I want with my money."

"Was your family wealthy?"

"I made it all myself."

"Doing what?"

"When I was fourteen I started writing dirty books."

"Come on. I never know when you're serious or kidding. Let's get out of here."

"Sally has to get her toys together. I'm ready right now but it will take Sally a little while."

They made it to the Caravelle just after dark. The Caravelle was where the longest single battle of the war was being fought. It was the battle between the U.S. press corps, who stayed there, and the White House. It was a battle that was unprecedented in substance as well as length and, eventually, in its casualties.

Since every officer in the U.S. military was aware that the Caravelle was crawling with the U.S. press corps, they would go elsewhere on free time. The celebration for Jonas Valadovich's promotion took place at the crowded U.S. Army's Bachelor Officers' Quarters (BOQ). Its rooftop restaurant and bar, just like the Caravelle's rooftop restaurant and bar, provided the all too frequent sight of the rocket's red glare of war.

There were four chairs at their round table near the window at the

Bachelor Officers' Quarters; one chair for Jonas, one for Moose, one for Moose's guests, Adam Orr and Sally Saigon, and one for Adam's leg. The table was crowded with empty beer bottles, four semi-filled mugs, one open pack of Marlboros, and one open pack of Camels. A small Vietnamese waiter stood at the table with his note-pad.

Moose took the pipe from his mouth. It was the Dunhill that was a gift from Wai-yee. "We'll have some *cha-gio* with a little *nuoc-mam* and some *phong-tam* on the side–for the three of us," Moose said to the waiter without even looking at the menu, just as though Moose was a connoisseur of Vietnamese food.

Adam tossed his menu aside. "You can have that stuff, but not for me or Sally. Sally will have some tuna and a platter of milk. And for me, you got a Howard Johnson's 3-D hamburger?"

The small Vietnamese waiter smiled. "We can fix platter for the cat. And we can make you hamboogah."

"Yes! Yes! By all means! A hamburger!"

"You want moosetard on it?"

"A lot of moosetard! The works! Tomato, lettuce, ketchup, mayonnaise, and moosetard!"

"That sounds good," Jonas said. "Want to make me one, too?"

The waiter nodded and then repeated the order to make sure he had it right. "*Cha-gio, nuoc-mam, phong-tam,* all for one, some tuna, a platter with milk for cat, and two hamboogahs."

"That's it!" Adam said. "You test the milk first. She only drinks pasteurized."

The waiter looked confused but he nodded as though he understood.

Before the waiter came back with the food, they talked about the war, about Czechoslovakia, about the nominating conventions, and about political assassinations.

While they ate, they talked about the inability of anyone beyond the borders of the United States to make a good hamburger, that foreigners who make them mistakenly believe that if the meat is thick the hamburger is better, and they make the mistake of thinking that french bread must be superior to a good soft bun, and for some unknown reason, even the right condiments don't seem to work overseas.

Sally finished everything she was offered on the floor, except some of the milk, maybe because it wasn't pasteurized, and she jumped back on Adam's lap and started washing herself with one paw quickly going from her tongue to behind her right ear, back and forth. Then in a lurch, she started cleaning herself under the base of her tail.

"I haven't finished eating yet, Sally, please," Adam said to Sally. "Wait until everyone's done."

Sally continued her bath.

"She's a woman," Adam said. "She doesn't pay any attention to what I tell her."

When they were through eating, Adam lit a Marlboro with a wooden match and started playing nervously with the small square box of matches.

"Why so serious all the sudden?" Moose asked.

Adam kept toying with the box of matches, then looked up at Moose. "For the last number of nights I've been having nightmares. I wake up shaking, and I'm soaked in perspiration."

Moose and Jonas exchanged a glance. Nightmares in Vietnam had become an epidemic. "Since the attack on Aptrangdau?" Moose asked.

Adam nodded.

"It happens to me, too," Jonas said. "It happens to everyone here. We've found that talking about them eases them and, in a lot of cases, even makes them disappear. Do you want to tell us what you dream, sir?"

Adam shook his head. "It's pretty bad." There was a long silence while Adam just stared at his plate, not looking in their eyes. "It's something I don't like to talk about."

Moose nodded. "I know. But it really does help, Orr."

"Really?" And he looked up directly at Moose, and then at Jonas. "Does it? Do you think if I talk about it, the nightmares could really stop?"

Both of them nodded. "We've been through it," Jonas said. "It's nothing to be self-conscious about. In this place nightmares come naturally."

Moose asked, "Is it a repeating nightmare?"

Adam looked back at his plate. "It is."

Moose and Jonas both nodded. "They usually are," Jonas said and then he repeated his request, "Do you want to tell us about it, sir?"

Adam looked up again with a sharp glance at Moose and then at Jonas. "I keep dreaming that I'm married."

Jonas gave a confused look at Moose. Moose didn't look confused at all. He looked at Jonas and shook his head. "You don't know him, Jonas. This is what you can expect from this guy."

"How do I get rid of that dream, Major?" Adam asked.

"Don't answer him, Jonas," Moose injected quickly. "This guy's so anti-marriage he's ready to go to war against it."

"You have a girl, Major?" Adam asked sadly.

"I see a woman here, but there's nothing serious between us. She works at JUSPAO. She has a master's degree and now she's studying international law. She knows every treaty that's been signed between nations—treaties you and I haven't even heard of, sir."

"How are her legs?"

"Her legs?"

"The shape. Are they shapely?"

Jonas smiled. "Yes, sir. They sure are."

"Good. I'd like to meet her."

"Don't do it, Jonas!" Moose said, "He'll embarrass you and ruin everything between you and Lorraine."

"Lorraine?" Adam asked. "Is she an American?"

"Yes, sir," Jonas answered, still smiling. "She works for us here."

"Why? Why an American? You can do that at home. Look what you got here!"

"Orr," Moose said as he started packing his pipe with tobacco from his leather pouch, "Jonas likes this woman. They get along just fine. They have a good time together. Leave it alone."

"But America is full of Americans!" Adam said. "Almost everywhere you look in America you see Americans, and half of them are women. You're in Vietnam! Why look for an American woman here? Look at what there is in this country! Have you ever seen so many women that are so smooth and soft and who have such little feet in pointed shoes? God was in his best mood when he created them in this part of the world. It isn't that they don't have hair in their nostrils; they don't have nostrils! One of the great mysteries of this place is how women breathe with their mouths closed. I know how American women breathe with their mouths closed. They breathe through their noses! Right?"

Moose was laughing and even Jonas couldn't help but lose his composure by shaking his head with a smile.

"God gave them a different way to breathe, that's what I think," Adam continued. "The objective is–find it!"

"Orr," Moose said, "you're beyond hope," and he lit his pipe.

"You know, Major, you should always observe the 'Two Date Rule.' Never have a third date with any woman. That's perilous."

"I'll tell you, sir," Jonas said, "if this is the way you think while you're in pain, I don't know if I could take what you say when you're well."

This time Adam smiled. "I'm not in pain, major. And listen–don't call me 'sir'. I should be calling you 'sir'. I was a staff sergeant and to this day anyone I see who's an officer–I have to restrain myself not to salute. It's something you never get over. I don't care if you're half my age, Major, it's one of those things that will stay with me until the day I die. There is no issue of age when it comes to respect. If I saw my grammar school principal today at the age she was then, while I'm the age I am now, I'd still have the same feeling of respect I had for her when I was in the third grade. I'd even be afraid of her. And with your rank, you still have it all over me and you always will. So if I may ask, please don't call me 'sir,' Major."

Jonas smiled even broader and asked, "What do I call you, if you won't accept 'sir'?"

"Honest."

Moose nodded with a tight-mouthed smile. "That you are, Orr."

"You don't really have nightmares, do you?" Jonas asked Adam.

"No. Hey, look at Sally." Sally was putting her front and back paws extended out as far as they could go on Adam's lap.

"She's stretching," Moose said.

"She isn't stretching," Adam was shaking his head. "She's praying. Sally's a Muslim."

Moose shook his head. "How do you know?"

"She always prays in the direction of Mecca. See? She stretches out her front paws and lowers her head four times a day in the direction of Mecca. Just like she's doing now. It's the fourth time today. She's a good

Muslim, but it makes it tough for her here, you know. These are all Buddhists and Catholics, so she's in a tough spot."

"Yeah, I guess so," Moose said and continued to shake his head as he looked at Jonas. "His cat's a Muslim."

"Then, Mr. Orr," Jonas said to Adam, "you must make sure she makes a pilgrimage to Mecca. She must make the *hajj* while she is veiled from head to paws so that she appears the same as all others in the eyes of Allah."

Both Adam and Moose were stunned. Adam smiled and nodded. "Yes. And she must walk around the Black Stone of the Kaaba Shrine seven times, and kiss it."

"Built by Abraham and Ishmael," Jonas added. "Given to Mohammed by Gabriel."

"What's going on?" Moose asked. "Are you two guys nuts?"

Adam shook his head. "He knows Islam. The Major's more than a military man."

"I study theology, sir. The great religions are more interesting to me than anything in the world." The word "sir" was automatic no matter what he was told.

Adam nodded and looked at Moose. "This soldier is my kind of man," then he looked back at Jonas. "You and I have to talk, Major. I have thoughts of my own about religion based on absolute reality. I've been to the mid-point between life and—and heaven."

Jonas's eyes grew large, then squinted as he wondered whether or not this was another of Adam's jokes. "Where is that, sir?"

"Canaveral. Cape Canaveral." It was no joke. "It's why I live just miles away and go there every day when I'm home."

"You equate Cape Canaveral with the world's holy places?"

Adam nodded. "It is a holy place. It's the construction site of the stairway to God. You've never been there, Major?"

Jonas shook his head. "I haven't."

"You have to go. Some day or night when you have a few hours, I'll tell you about it."

"You name it. You say when," Jonas said.

Adam looked over at Moose. "You interested?"

Moose smiled and took a puff from his pipe. "A few hours? Count me out. Can't you tell him about the Cape in a few minutes? I can."

"I'm talking about God, not about some—"

His words were interrupted by a blinding flash and a loud blast from outside. Practically everyone in the place gave a lurch and Jonas had his hand on his gun in an instant, Moose quickly put his hand on his pipe so it wouldn't drop out of his mouth, and Adam looked like he was in pain since he jarred his leg in a quick motion. Sally jumped off his lap and went under Adam's chair.

It was lightning and thunder.

"Yes, sir," Adam said rubbing the cast on his leg. "There's no place in the world like Vietnam! Aren't you glad you're here? Where else in the world could one hundred educated adults in one dining room react to a thunderstorm by taking out their weapons?"

"Do you think maybe God wanted to see what we'd do?" Moose asked as he brushed the tobacco ashes off the table.

"Could be," Adam said. "If He did, He must be relieved to know that the biggest guy in the room thought fast enough to protect his pipe. I'm sure He admires such quick, selfless, and courageous thinking."

Sally jumped back on Adam's lap, looked up at him, closed and opened her eyes, and gave a quick meow.

"I know," Adam said to her. "Allah is great." Sally started purring.

TWENTY-THREE
THE ENDURA
1968

It became a habit. After Moose went back to D.C., Major Valadovich, Adam Orr, and Sally Saigon would sit at a table in the BOQ with beer, Marlboros, and Camels. Sometimes Sally Saigon would stay at the Caravelle. Some times Jonas would be on an air mission or at Lorraine's apartment, and Adam would sit at the BOQ alone. But, for sure, at least two nights a week Jonas, Adam, and Sally would be there, and generally on those nights Jonas and Adam would go on for hours about those things that put the war out of their minds for a while.

There was no talk of the missions of Jonas.

They were always given the same table near the window with one of the restaurant's metal ashtrays taken off the table and moved to the window ledge far from Sally Saigon. That was because when both Sally and the ashtray were on the table, Sally's tail would often find itself moving the ashtray to fall on the floor. As in most Asian countries, water was in the ashtrays to extinguish cigarettes, and one quick swish of Sally's tail, and she would create a mess on the floor of black and brown water, ashes, and cigarette butts. Sally enjoyed swishing her tail around to hit the ashtray onto the floor, and was very disappointed when it was taken off the table. She would look at it up on the ledge, trying to devise a way to knock it over as though it was accidental.

What was common among all the diners and drinkers at the BOQ were subjects far away from the war. What was uncommon was the subject matter of Jonas and Adam. Without the pragmatism of Moose there to keep them from the ethereal, they would talk about theology, one night devoted to Christianity, another to Judaism, another to Islam, another to Buddhism, another to Hinduism, and other nights devoted to religions less understood in the West, while often Adam would tell wondrous stories about Cape Canaveral. Nothing was petty.

"I have to see that place," Jonas said.

"It's a different life there. It's beyond life. There are no barriers there. When you're back in the States, I'll set up a tour of the place for you. When you see it the first time, it should be at night. The Cape grips the night. You'll understand when you see it. I'll work it out for you. I'll see, maybe I can give you the tour myself."

"I'll take you up on that one, Adam."

Sally jumped on the table and gingerly stepped over the salt and pepper shakers and beer cans and mugs, then with her right front paw, she hit Adam's Marlboro pack off the table.

Jonas bent down to pick it up for Adam, since picking it up would be a job for Adam with his injured leg. "Thanks, Major. You notice she hit my cigarettes off, not yours?" Adam asked Jonas. "She leaves your Camels alone."

"Why do you think she did that?"

"Mad. She's angry. She thinks we haven't devoted enough time to Islam, and that it's my fault. Sally always gives you the benefit of a doubt. I'm the guy she blames for everything. You know how it is. A guy like me does everything in the world for her, feeds her, shelters her, buys her toys and scratching pads, and she treats a guy like that–me–like dirt. Then some guy like you in a uniform comes along–someone who doesn't live with her, who doesn't pay that much attention to her, you give her one little piece of cheese from your dish and she drools all over you and thinks you're the greatest guy in the world. She knows the Camels are yours and the Marlboros are mine and I can't bend over. Only a woman would do something like that. A tom cat wouldn't. Look–look at her." Sally was rubbing her nose against Jonas' wrist.

Jonas was smiling. "She likes my watch."

"I have a Rolex! She's never complimented my watch!"

"Yours doesn't have world time. Sally has good taste."

"I never noticed it before." Adam was squinting his eyes looking at Jonas' watch. "Where did you get it?"

"The States. At a PX. It wasn't expensive but look, it tells the time everywhere in the world! Or almost everywhere. It's called an Endura." He unbuckled the brown leather strap, took it off his wrist, and handed it across Sally to Adam. "It doesn't have any city in India or Iran because they're on half-hour time."

Adam inspected the watch. "You turn the outside dial?"

"To any city it lists. There's twenty-four of them on that gold bezel. See those small letters? You rotate the bezel here, it just turns, and you set the name of the city you're in opposite the hour hand on the watch's face, and then you look for any city you want–if it's there–and you can tell what hour it is there–it's whatever number it's next to. You can't tell A.M. or P.M. but you can figure it out."

"Neat, Major!"

"I wish I understood it."

"It's easy. It's just a dial with the cities in their proper order, one hour apart. So you put–"

"I don't mean the watch," Jonas interrupted. "I mean time. I know it isn't what we think it is. But I'm not sure I understand its purpose."

Adam passed the watch back to him. "I understand it. It's a fake, Major. There is no such thing as time. Not in the real world–just in this one. That little cat doesn't care about time. She likes your watch only because it's yours. That's because Sally Saigon doesn't operate under the laws that were made for us. Do you think she cares if it's 1968 or 1868 or 2068? Do you think she cares what time it is in Paris or Los Angeles? She isn't trapped into the barrier of time. Give Sally your world-time watch, and she'll chew the strap. God made time for humans. Only for us while we're here. It's a trap, Major—the time-trap. Don't fall in it. He had to give us a beginning and an ending, so he cooked up something like your Endura watch. Round. Revolving, so we would have days and seasons to know how much of our life might be left. The trap is that we know the maximum but not the minimum. It makes us do things, doesn't it? It makes us hurry. You know what else He did with it? He made women pretty during their child-bearing years so we'd be maniacs over them at the right time, and keep the species going. Stay clear of it, Major."

"Why is it so important to have new humans all the time? Why not the same old ones? Why not immortality? Why didn't He arrange that?"

Adam laughed. "Are you asking why we don't live forever?"

"What would be wrong with that? Life wouldn't be as cruel."

"It's not cruel."

"Don't give me the answer you'd tell some kid with teen-aged angst. Adam, I can't be content without thinking these things through. I don't claim to be Einstein, but I can use him as a spring-board."

"Major, think what the world would be like if everyone lived forever. People wouldn't achieve very much, would they? Why would anyone write the poetry today or chisel the sculpture today or dance the dance today if every poet and every sculptor and every dancer knew they had a million years to create their art? Such lives would produce nothing more than justified procrastination. Sally here has no time-trap laid out for her because God isn't counting on her to do those things."

"What is your religion, Adam? I've never asked."

"My religion is one word. Honor. That's what's important in life. That's all that's important in life. The rest is somewhere beyond me. I'm not going to waste time trying to figure it out. Every once in a while I get a stab of what He's doing—just a quick insight. That's why I want you to go to the Cape. You can feel the rest, if not see it, at the Cape."

"And you don't fight time?"

"I ignore it. Time isn't my job. It's His. I respect the fact that He made the time-trap. Good idea. Great idea. I'm not against it. I just learned how to handle it without getting in its jaws. The way I do it is to concentrate on what I can control, and what I can control is my own honor. That's all. And that's enough."

"Adam, I told you that I had a strange experience when President Kennedy died. I felt a very, almost out-of-this-world experience with time. It was simple. I heard an echo, a sound I thought was gone, but then I heard it again. I thought it was dead, but that sound was still alive somewhere else. Do you know what I mean?"

Adam nodded. "You're a good man, Major. Let me think about what you're saying. We'll study it. You and I will study it and compare notes and come up with answers. Just imagine, Major. Think of all the women we could get if we founded a new religion! Even if we're wrong! We could be Elmer Gantry! Women would be all over us. We wouldn't accept any man—only women. We could have the world's first Women Only Religion, headed by two clear-minded men! I'll work out a plan and tell you all about it tomorrow night, if you don't have to go on some mission."

Jonas shook his head. "Adam, I may not be on any mission again very soon."

"What do you mean?"

"A report. It's just a rumor but it's pretty authoritative that President Johnson offered to accept North Vietnamese demands for an unconditional halt of the bombing, and in return Hanoi says that such a move would lead to peace. How's that for reciprocity? In short, there is no reciprocity. So, if it comes off, this will be the thirteenth bombing halt, and I'll just have to sit still and wait for Hanoi to build up the Viet Cong—and then go back on missions when they're more dangerous."

"Oh, Jonas! Major, I don't get it. This is the policy of postponement that we started with Korea. The idea is not to win anymore. Just negotiate. Make them sign something. Do you think those folks regard signatures the way we do?"

"Why is God allowing all this in Vietnam, Adam?"

Adam shook his head. "Don't blame God. Humans are in charge. Humans can fix it. We better win and do it quick or that time-trap will kill this nation—and us."

The waiter came over and reminded them of the time-trap of the evening. "Curfew starts in half-hour, so this is last call. More beer?"

"No," Jonas said. "More time."

TWENTY-FOUR
SORRY FOR THE INCONVENIENCE
1968–1969

The city of Washington, D.C., was not a happy place on the morning of Wednesday, November the 6th, 1968. People were tired from staying up all night and waiting for the squeaky outcome of the election which would not arrive until 9:30 that morning. More important, most of the thousands of people who filled the government buildings in that city hadn't voted for Richard Nixon.

Although they were tired and unhappy, they knew that as tired and unhappy as they were, they would have to work fast on a Washington tradition. For outgoing political appointees, Washington at transition time was like Christmas shopping on December 24. You better hurry.

And so all through that Wednesday, in the departments and agencies of government, there were small people in small meetings in small rooms. And, as a result of those meetings, the Wednesday in Washington that began in sadness, ended with a few smiles and winks.

With the coming of Thursday and Friday and the weekend, the smiles and winks increased in number until it seemed that it was a city of smilers and winkers.

The paperwork began, and the job shuffling began.

Many of the politically appointed jobs, called Schedule "C" Assignments, were moved into careerist spots, to GS-17s and FS-1s. One after another of the political appointees who were Democrats and who would have been replaced by new Republican political appointees, suddenly became Civil Service and Foreign Service careerists, and so they not only maintained employment in government, and an increasing pension, but they stepped into non-fireable jobs in which they assumed ranks at the top of the bureaucratic ladder, with positions over and above lower-level bureaucrats.

And that's where many lower level bureaucrats wanted them to be that November. It was better to have those who were politically sympathetic to them writing their performance-ratings and giving assignments and promotions and guiding their work. Better to keep the bureaucracy of government all in the family.

Then came the unavoidable horror of the invaders at the Tuesday Table: the transition team. They wouldn't sit at the table itself, but by the back or the sides of the room on one of the chairs against the wall. At senior staff meetings of each department and agency of government, one or two of them would be there, taking notes, with both sides having to maintain a forced courtesy to one another.

By mid-December, most of it was complete.

It was a relief for Washington to soon be done with 1968. It was a relief to the world. That year had started and ended with the deception that survival was its mission. At the beginning of it, a heart was transplanted from the dead to the living, and near the end of it there was the first visit of man into the heavens. On Christmas Eve there was an ethereal comfort. As Astronauts Frank Borman, James Lovell, and William Anders made the first manned flight around the moon, the voice of Astronaut Frank Borman beamed back to earth, "The crew of Apollo 8 has a message we would like to send to you: In the beginning God created the heaven and the earth. The earth was without form and void, and darkness was upon the face of the deep; and the Spirit of God was moving over the face of the waters. And God said, 'Let there be light'..." and he continued reading back to the earth from the first verses of Genesis. The Apollo 8 astronauts were preparing for a later Apollo mission when astronauts would land on the moon.

But the beginning of 1968 and the end of it was not all of it. Dr. Martin Luther King's voice would not be heard again by the masses standing at the sides of the reflecting pool. Senator Robert Kennedy would not be seen again on the Senate floor or at a political rally. The staff of the Czechoslovakian Embassy was gone, replaced by unfamiliar faces all authorized by the Soviet Union. Chicago had temporarily lost its reputation as a magnificent city, becoming a city of the convention conflict between the generations. And the District of Columbia had turned into an armed camp with long sections of 7th Street and 14th Street left in ashes from an April riot.

At last 1968 could be thrown away with the flattened wrappings and ribbons of Christmas parcels and replaced with the January hope that the worst events of 1968 were aberrations never to be repeated.

The first day of 1969 was so cold in D.C. that very few people were outdoors. The Ellipse was still decorated for Christmas but the fifty small pine trees, one for each state, would come down tomorrow, its visitors having come and gone during the last two and one half weeks. The carolers who sang in the cold there each night would not be back until next December. A huge dismantled statue of Juarez sat in wooden crates outside the Watergate, waiting to be assembled. A new star hung over the incomplete John F. Kennedy Center for the Performing Arts, a building which was to have been opened in time for the inauguration but would miss that schedule. Outside the White House, all construction on the half-completed Inaugural Reviewing Stand stopped for the day, leaving piles of wood and a sign apologizing to Pennsylvania Avenue walkers who weren't there: "SORRY FOR THE INCONVENIENCE BUT WE'RE MAKING WAY FOR ANOTHER GREAT MAN."

On the south side of the White House in a small triangular patch of grass by E Street there was a sign that read, "Please Do Not Disturb. Tulips Are Sleeping Here." Tulips were non-partisan in Washington. The tulips were planted during President Johnson's administration and they would bloom during President Nixon's administration, just like so many other things.

The inside of most Washington houses and apartment buildings were warm and secure, and particularly warm and secure for those suffering from the epidemic of the Hong Kong flu, which included the president, the vice president, and the president-elect. Television sets were broadcasting parades and football games, confirming that the world had endured 1968 since the new year was able to start as other years had. A bomb explosion or a demonstration or at least some sort of natural disaster would have been more appropriate, but there wasn't even a snowstorm. It was U.S.C. versus Ohio State, and an eighty-yard run by O.J. Simpson, and then Kansas vs. Pennsylvania State. Maybe there would be a violent protest at the end of one of the games. There wasn't. So maybe 1969 would be better than 1968.

There was a small Christmas tree lying down on the pavement of Massachusetts Avenue placed by someone who, like so many others, didn't like the old year and was in a hurry to be rid of the last physical reminder of it.

Even in the best of times no one in America knows what to do with New Year's Day. It is a day of scheduled bewilderment, most often appearing to be an additional Sunday thrown somewhere in the week without any duty attached. It is a holiday without gifts to buy or receive, without fireworks to explode or watch, without big dinners to prepare or eat. No one expects anything of anyone else or of themselves on New Year's Day.

Telephones generally don't ring on New Year's Day and if they do they sound twice as loud as normal. Moose lurched when he heard it in his Potomac Plaza apartment while he was making breakfast, dressed in only his undershorts. He grabbed the receiver of the phone as much to quiet it as to find out who was calling him. "Dunston here."

"Moose Dunston?"

"Speaking. What's up?"

"This is Richard Nixon."

Moose's first thought was to put on his pants.

From that moment forward, Moose Dunston's life made a dramatic change.

The reason for the phone call originated eleven weeks earlier when President Johnson announced he was offering another bombing pause to the North Vietnamese government. When the offer was announced, Moose Dunston resigned from the staff of the National Security Council. His resignation statement given to the press told of his "unyielding respect for President Johnson, but I have a disagreement over the consequences of bombing halts without guaranteed reciprocity. The consequences," Moose Dunston said, "I believe, can lead to catastrophic results." But that wasn't all Moose Dunston announced. At that hastily called news conference, a reporter asked him what he was going to do now that he didn't have a job. Moose answered, "I plan on joining the Nixon campaign as a volunteer during this last month before the election. I do this with great enthusiasm, but also with regret, as I admire Vice President Humphrey. I recognize that his agreement with President Johnson on this issue, indeed his advocacy of such a policy, is what he and the president believe to be in the best interests of the United States and South Vietnam. I don't. Despite my admiration and friendship for both the president and vice president Humphrey, I must make a decision based on policy considerations alone. Those policy considerations mean life or death to Americans, to the South Vietnamese, and perhaps to South Vietnam itself."

President-elect Nixon told Moose in that phone call on New Year's Day that he discussed staff with President Johnson when they met at the White House six days after the election, and President Johnson told the president-elect that although Moose's resignation "saddened me deeply," Moose was an exceptional staff member of the National Security Council through the years and that the president-elect would be well advised to have him in his administration as a close aide, since Moose shared the beliefs of the new president.

"I'm elevating the role of the National Security Council," the president-elect said to Moose, "not to compete with the State Department, you understand, but to compliment it inside the White House. Henry Kissinger or Dick Allen will be calling you sometime next week to see exactly where you can fit in there beyond the staff job you did for Lyndon. Not on the council itself, of course. There are only seven members, but a higher position than you had with Lyndon."

"I'm honored, Mr. President."

When Moose hung up the phone he sat in silence, repeating and repeating in his mind what the president-elect had said and what he had said in response. He called Richard Nixon "Mister President." Should he have said, "Mister President-elect"? *Oh, who cares!* After it all sunk in, he got up from his chair and with enough volume in his voice to be heard beyond the boundaries of Washington D.C., Virginia and Maryland, he yelled, "Ya-hoo!"

His next reaction was to tell someone. The person that came immediately to mind was Tso Wai-yee. It was a good time, nine o'clock at night in Hong Kong. As was Moose's habit, by impulse, he went even further than he expected to go. He had to add something to it. "Wai-yee," he said, "I want you to come here for the inauguration. I'm sure I'll be invited to the Inaugural Ball and all that. It's very exciting in Washington at inauguration-time and I want you here with me when it all happens...You just need to be here for a few days...I know the consulate will let you out of work for this...It's about two and one half weeks from now.... Be here on the 18th, Wai-yee, will you? I'll send you an airline ticket if you can do it. And I'll get you a hotel reservation to make it legitimate."

Wai-yee was thrilled, but she became immediately concerned with her clothes. She had nothing to wear that would be appropriate for an inauguration, and she had nothing to wear that would be appropriate for a Washington winter. She didn't know if she could do it, but she said, "Yes!"

She could do it.

And so could her mother.

The only other phone call he made was to the U.S. Embassy in Saigon, leaving a message for Major Jonas Valadovich. "Tell him Moose Dunston of the Nixon White House called to tell him to get his act together if he ever wants to be a colonel."

The rest of the day was spent in silent glory. He didn't go to bed until midnight, and he was awakened two hours later by the telephone. Could it be Kissinger or Allen? Not a chance. Even though he was awakened from sleep, he was still sensible enough to know they wouldn't be calling at this hour. In fact he was sensible enough to hope it was a wrong number because good news is rarely given by phone calls in the middle of the night.

"Yes. Yes. Dunston here."

"Mister Dunston, this is Mary at the White House switchboard."

"It is? Yes, Mary. Hi."

"I'm sorry to bother you at this hour at home but a woman named An-Twit who is with our Embassy in Saigon wants to get hold of you. I told her you were no longer with the White House. She knew that, but she didn't have your home phone, and she said it was urgent she talk with you. I didn't give her your home number. Do you want us to put her through?"

"Please, Mary. Yes, I do."

"Hang on."

"Thank you."

It took only a moment and there was as much clarity in the line as there would have been if An-Twit was in the next room.

"Hello," the soft woman's voice said.

"An-Twit?"

"Yes."

"Mister Dunston, I received the message you left for Major Valadovich when I came in this morning. Mister Dunston, I thought you knew. That message cannot be delivered. On October the 12th, Major Valadovich was confirmed as having been taken by the North Vietnamese as a prisoner of war."

Moose closed his eyes and his whole body seemed to settle in the pit of his stomach.

"Mister Dunston?"

"Yes."

"Did you hear me?"

"Yes."

"You did not know?"

"No. No one told me. What happened?"

"He was missing after being on a flight over Laos. A week went by, and then we got the word. He and five others were taken prisoner near Khamkeut."

There was a long pause before Moose said, "I don't know where that is."

"Laos. But the North Vietnamese got them."

"Is he hurt?"

"We don't think so. They said all the prisoners from that plane were in good health and are being well taken care of. They took them to Sontay in North Vietnam. They sent films of them. He looked as though he is all right. We told his next of kin who is his grandmother."

"I want to see those films."

"I can't do that, Mister Dunston."

"An-twit! I'll be back at the White House before the end of the month! You tell–I'll tell. Forget it. Listen. Listen to me. If you find out anything–anything at all, you phone me at home at any hour. Write this number down."

"All right."

Moose then gave her his home number. "You got it?"

"Yes," and she repeated it back to him.

"Yes. Or call me like you just did through the White House switchboard. But get hold of me! On anything–anything about Jonas." Even saying his name in connection with her message was difficult for him to do. "Anything. Every detail."

"All right."

"Anything else, An-Twit? Anything else that's known about him now? How about Lorraine? He used to date her."

"She doesn't work here any more. She's back in the States somewhere. Mr. Dunston, I don't know anything more. I don't think anyone does."

"Okay. Thank you, An-Twit. Call me. Any time, please."

Of course there was no way to even attempt to go back to sleep or to do anything that would take his mind from imagining Jonas in a North Vietnamese prison.

There was now an unimportance to the invitation he gave earlier in the day to Wai-yee, and an unimportance to her acceptance to come to the inauguration. At least he would be back at the White House after the inauguration and once again be privy to information; information about Jonas, if there was any.

In the weeks before the inauguration he talked to An-Twit every day. There was no news of Jonas.

He decided not to tell Wai-yee about Jonas. He had invited her to D.C. so she could have a good time and he didn't want her to think he was preoccupied. For those few days he would try to act as though she was the only thing on his mind.

To Moose, no one in the entire world looked more Chinese than Tso Wai-yee at Dulles Airport. He had absolutely not one bone of prejudice in his body but he was overwhelmed with how Chinese she looked, whereas in Hong Kong her Chinese appearance was totally incidental to him. They embraced, but it was only for a moment when they were interrupted by another person.

It was then he found out he was wrong. Wai-yee did not look more Chinese than anyone in the world. Her mother did.

Wai-yee was not only her mother's daughter, but now her mother's translator. As Moose drove from the airport to the District her mother could not stop asking questions about the large motorized van called the People Mover that transported the flight's passengers from the plane to the terminal without anyone going outside. She sat in the backseat of Moose's car while Wai-yee had shifted in her front passenger seat to look at her mother as she translated Moose's answers about the People Mover.

Did he make a mistake by asking Wai-yee to come to Washington? Or was the mistake in saying "yes" when Wai-yee asked if she could bring her mother with her? At this point Moose couldn't concentrate on his error because he had to concentrate on everything he could possibly say about the People Mover that he had always regarded as a Dulles Airport irritant rather than a conversation-piece. Occasionally, as he attempted to think about the workings of the People Mover, the warnings of Adam Orr regarding women came into his consciousness.

Adam Orr!

He might know something about Jonas. Those two had become close friends in Vietnam. Jonas had told Moose that while Adam was recovering from his leg wound, the two of them had met and talked endlessly night after night at the Bachelor Officers' Quarters about religion and life and death. Moose had to get hold of Adam, but he couldn't think about that now.

He pointed out the Washington Monument on the horizon which he mistakenly thought would interest Wai-yee's mother. He made another attempt to engage her interest by going across Memorial Bridge, telling them to look through the rear window to see the sparkling flame above the grave of President Kennedy. Then he circled around the Lincoln Memorial so his two guests could see Abraham Lincoln sitting there, but nothing could compete with that People Mover. Unlike her mother, Wai-yee was enthused about what Moose was pointing out, but she accommodated her mother's interest.

By the time he closed the door between Wai-yee's room and her mother's adjoining room at the Watergate Hotel, he was exhausted and tense with his thoughts of Jonas invading his mind, and he almost found it to be a relieving anger he had endured in the car during the translation process between sentences. The whole process kept his mind from concentrating only on Jonas during the drive.

"Mother will not be a problem," Wai-yee said in the recognition that Moose was not his old self as he sat on the edge of the room's bed with the luggage. "She knows she must be on her own most of the time while we're here."

"Oh, she's wonderful," Moose lied. And then he added a greater lie, "I'm glad you brought her."

"She's so thrilled, Moose. It was so good of you to allow her to come with me. She will be very comfortable here and she doesn't want to interfere with the two of us." She sat on the bed next to Moose, and she put her arm around him for their first embrace other than the weak and confused one at Dulles.

"I love your hair, Wai-yee."

"I told you I would never cut it again."

"I was taken by it the second I saw you get off the People Mover. You kept your word. It's longer than when I first met you. You look beautiful."

"What do you want to do?" she asked. That frail and soft femininity that came from that small figure was overpowering him again.

Moose smiled and he said to her what she had said to him on Double Ten nine years ago. "I want to do anything. I want to do nothing. I want to do everything."

She didn't remember it was her line. "Then that's what we'll do, honey." It was the first time she ever called him anything but "Moose." Although he knew she might have said it to overweigh his thoughts about her mother being there, he liked it. That new reference she used for him made Adam Orr's warnings about women vanish from his consciousness.

"We have a heavy schedule." He added, "We've been invited to everything."

"We have?"

"We have."

"What is everything?"

Moose reached to his breast pocket and pulled out a sheet of paper. "Listen to this, Wai-yee: The Young American's Inaugural Salute, the Inaugural All-American Gala, the Governor's Reception, the Reception Honoring the vice president-elect, the Inaugural Concert, the Inaugural Ceremony, the Inaugural Parade, one of the Inaugural Balls, there are six of them and we're going to the one at the Statler Hilton, and you've been invited to the Reception for Distinguished Ladies."

"Oh, my!" she said.

What he wasn't telling her was what he didn't know until he had received the invitations: they were not without cost. He had to pay for his and Wai-yee's attendance at most of the events. A lot.

"I don't know if I have enough clothes for all that!" Wai-yee said. "Now I'm scared. I didn't bring enough. I never want to embarrass you."

"You couldn't embarrass me even if you were to wear rags to

everything. Anyway, we won't go to all of them, but we'll go to the good ones that I think you'd like."

"What do you wear?"

"It's easy for me. One dark suit, and for a couple things it says 'Black Tie' which means a tuxedo. I rented one."

"Where do we start? What event is first?" she asked.

"The Reception for Inaugural Love-Making that's scheduled for this very room and we got here late," he said. "We must be on a very select invitation list. No one else is invited to that one."

"I can't wait for that one," she said. "What should I wear?"

Moose thought it over for a moment and then answered, "The invitation says 'Informal.' That means you're required to wear very little."

"Oh," she said, "then that makes it easy!"

No it didn't. The door between the rooms opened up and there, standing in the doorway, was Wai-yee's mother dressed to kill; dressed for Moose to do the killing. With an explanation made in Mandarin, she had somehow thought she was going with him and Wai-yee to some event, whatever it would be.

Moose controlled himself. The Reception for Inaugural Love-Making was put aside for the Reception for the vice president-elect at the Smithsonian, and Wai-yee's mother went with them.

It couldn't have been worse. That was because Wai-yee's mother fell in love with the small plastic tumblers that were used for the fruit drink in the punch bowl. The tumblers had the imprint of the seal of the vice president and the signature of Vice President-elect Spiro Agnew stamped beneath it. She told Wai-yee she wanted to keep her tumbler. There was no problem in that, but soon she wanted Wai-yee's tumbler too, which she gave her, and then she wanted Wai-yee to tell Moose that she wanted his tumbler. That wasn't enough. She went back to the table that held the punch bowl to get more tumblers. In short time Wai-yee's mother had fifteen tumblers all in a neat stack, one resting in another. No one other than Moose looked at what she was doing with shock. Instead, her addiction to the tumblers caught on. Wai-yee's mother was creating a precedent that quickly turned into an inaugural plague. In short time women dressed in thousands of dollars worth of formal wear and jewelry were holding their arms behind their backs, their hands clasped tightly to tall stacks of tumblers, each placed one inside the other. Men in tuxedoes were handed the stacks and became dedicated smugglers, heading out to the parking lot, running breathlessly to place the smuggled tumblers safely inside their cars before going back into the Smithsonian with expressions of innocent sophistication, while their wives or dates were busy collecting more tumblers for the next trip out to the car.

By the time the vice president and Mrs. Agnew arrived there were no tumblers left on the table, so the two people being honored couldn't have any fruit drink unless they wanted to dunk their heads in the punch bowl which, understandably, they did not want to do. Without their knowledge, the core of their problem came from the small Chinese woman who shook their hands and said something to them in Mandarin which the vice president-elect answered, "That's very kind. It's so good of you to be here." It was so good of Moose that he allowed her to be there. Moose was unable to shake hands with the vice president-elect because his hands were occupied behind his back after Wai-yee's mother quickly handed him her latest and final batch of tumblers.

As soon as they got in the hotel rooms that night Moose told Wai-yee he wanted to go back to the lobby to see if he could pick up some newspapers. He went to a lobby phone and asked the White House switchboard to get him Adam Orr at the Caravelle Hotel in Saigon right away. Luckily, he got hold of Mary at the White House who connected him to the Caravelle, and unluckily he found out Adam had checked out with no forwarding phone number. Moose knew he would have told the Embassy nothing about where he would be since he took pride in rarely reporting anything to anyone. Moose phoned Mary back at the White House and asked her to connect him to Greta, Ambassador Bunker's secretary in Saigon.

It was done with immediacy.

"Mr. Dunston," Greta said, "we know Mr. Orr well. He almost went—went berserk when he found out that Major Valadovich was captured. We only saw him once since then. That was the next day when he dropped his cat off here. He said he would be gone for a while and wanted us to take care of her. The Ambassador told him the cat could stay at his residence. We're worried about Mr. Orr. He left with us some envelopes for us to open 'if necessary', he said. We opened the ones addressed to the Ambassador. One was a will. We think he might be somewhere he shouldn't be."

"Like north of the 17th parallel? Is that what you mean?"

"Way up. The prison they took Major Valadovich to is in Sontay," Greta said.

"I know."

"You know Mr. Orr well, don't you?"

"Well enough."

"Mr. Dunston, Major Valadovich used to tell us that Mr. Orr would do anything to maintain what he called the root of his religion. He said that Mr. Orr told him the root is honor. Do you understand why we're worried? It's his whole nature."

"He would go up north, wouldn't he?"

"Yes. He would do such a thing."

After Wai-yee's mother made the beds the following morning, disbelieving it was the responsibility of the hotel maids, she said she would be too cold to attend the outside events of the Inaugural Ceremony and speech and parade, and she would rather watch those events on television in her hotel room. Before she could change her mind, Moose was grabbing Wai-yee's hand, heading to the door.

The sidewalks were filled with people walking to the U.S. Capitol and the streets were crowded with taxis and private cars and busses with signs above their exhaust pipes that read, "Farewell and Best Wishes, Lyndon B. Johnson," and "Welcome to Washington, Richard M. Nixon and Honored Inaugural Guests," and there were groups of kids standing with placards that read, "America Is Fascist," and "Peace Now," and "Dissent is American," and "Save America," and "Tell Us Why," and "Walter Hickle is a Tree," and "In-HOG-urate the Pig."

There were 8,000 members of the U.S. Youth International Party, or what were called the Yippies, who had come to demonstrate.

The drive that normally took twelve minutes from the Watergate to the U.S. Capitol took over an hour and then another half hour was spent walking from the car to the east side of the Capitol, but Moose and Wai-yee made it to the V.I.P. seats in time for the inauguration of the new president.

Moose pointed to Colonel Hayward Smith, the military aide of President Johnson, and told Wai-yee to keep her eyes on him when the new president would say, "So help me God" as Colonel Hayward would casually pass the "football" of nuclear war codes to Colonel James Hughes, the military aide of President Nixon. When it happened, Wai-yee screamed in delight that she actually saw it, causing people around them to think she was in pain.

President Nixon said, "In these difficult years America has suffered from a fever of words; from inflated rhetoric that promises more than it can deliver; from angry rhetoric that fans discontents into hatreds; from bombastic rhetoric that postures instead of persuading. We cannot learn from one another until we stop shouting at one another, until we speak quietly enough so that our words can be heard as well as our voices...Those who would be our adversaries we invite to a peaceful competition, not in conquering territory or extending dominion, but in enriching the life of man.... Only a few short weeks ago we shared the glory of man's first sight of the world as God sees it, as a single sphere reflecting light in the darkness. As Apollo astronauts flew over the moon's gray surface on Christmas Eve, they spoke to us of the beauty of the earth and in that voice so clear across the lunar distance we heard them invoke God's blessing on its goodness.... We have endured a long night of the American spirit. But as our eyes watch the dimness of the first rays of dawn, let us not curse the remaining dark. Let us gather the light."

When his speech was done and the ovation was over, Wai-yee said, "He should have mentioned that you are going to help him."

Moose couldn't help but laugh.

"Why are you laughing?" Wai-yee insisted. "He should have done that. That would reassure the country that everything will be all right."

Moose put his arm around her waist and held her tightly as they walked from the stand.

"Honey," Wai-yee said, "I don't want to watch the parade."

He turned to her quickly. "Are you okay?"

"Sure. Oh, yes. But we have the ball tonight and we won't have time just to be with each other alone. I want to be with you alone—not with thousands of people—and not even with you and my mother. Can we?"

That was an unexpected surprise. They went back to the Watergate and kept the door between Wai-yee's room and her mother's room closed and locked all the way through the afternoon and into the early evening, with Moose leaving Wai-yee only to get his rented tuxedo from his Potomac Plaza apartment, diagonally across the street. When he came back Wai-yee looked like a goddess in the formal cheong-sam she had designed and made herself in Hong Kong. It was a vision unlike any other. How could someone so small, who took such little room be so important? She was.

Wai-yee knocked on the door to the adjoining room with the intent of seeing if her mother needed anything, to tell her to call for room service for food, and to say good-bye for the evening. But there was no answer. She knocked again louder and longer. And then she stopped knocking, unlocked the door, and walked in.

Wai-yee and Moose would not leave the Watergate that night.

Wai-yee found her mother in bed with the quilt and blanket held tight above her head, and she was shaking. It was a long while before her mother was able to talk and when she did, it was slow and halting and mixed between crying, and Moose had to wait for a translation from Wai-yee to find out what she was saying.

Her mother confessed that earlier in the day when she had told them she didn't want to see the parade, it wasn't true, but she didn't want to infringe on Moose and Wai-yee being alone together. She waited until they left for the inaugural ceremony and then she got dressed and went to the lobby. The management, unable to understand her but knowing she wanted to see the parade, supplied her a scarf and hat and called and paid a taxi to take her as close as a taxi could get to a site on Pennsylvania Avenue near the Treasury Building.

She was very cold.

She walked along the parade route and ended up near a demonstration of dozens of kids, and they were holding placards and throwing rocks and bottles. Her mother thought they must be American Red Guards who were related to those who killed Wai-yee's father in China. Some were even wearing arm bands very much like the Red Guards wore. She became hysterical and pushed her way out of the crowd and ran as fast as she could. She got far enough away from the crowd to feel safe, but she didn't know the way back to the hotel. Somehow she found herself at a corner where there was a small gang of the kids and they yelled at her some chant she couldn't understand, and she ran away while they threw things in her direction yelling their chant. Eventually, she reached some street that was deserted other than for two policemen. They couldn't understand what she wanted until she showed them a matchbox from the Watergate Hotel. One of them pointed to the direction in which she should go. She got lost again, but through a series of people who read her matchbox, she found her way to the Watergate. By the time she arrived there, she was freezing cold and hysterical and went directly to her room. Without taking off any clothes she went under the blankets of her bed, and she put their ends over her head so the "Red Guards" wouldn't find her.

Wai-yee sat on the edge of the bed holding her mother's hand while Moose stood by the window. After her mother seemed to control herself and had stopped shaking, Wai-yee got up to go to the bathroom. She came back to find Moose sitting where she had been sitting, and he was holding her mother's hand.

Wai-yee stood there, spellbound.

Moose turned to Wai-yee. "You want to sit here with your mom, honey?"

Wai-yee shook her head, her eyes overflowing with tears. "No. I want to stand here and look at the most beautiful sight I have ever seen in my life." Then she whispered, "Thank you, Moose."

It was very late when her mother consented to have some tea and rice, if the hotel had some. The management got some, somewhere, and the three sat in the room with Wai-yee and her mother drinking tea and eating rice. Wai-yee helped her mother with her fork. Moose downed two large cheeseburgers, french fries, a Coke, and a pot of coffee, which was an easy order for the hotel to fill.

It was after two o'clock in the morning when Moose and Wai-yee, still in formal dress, left her mother and went back into the adjoining room. They sat on the edge of the bed. "I'm so sorry, honey," Wai-yee said. "I know you wanted to go to the ball."

"I didn't want to go to the ball for any reason other than to have everyone see you. But they couldn't have all seen you anyway, because with six balls, five-sixths of them would have missed you. The president probably wouldn't have seen you no matter what, because he just stays at each one of the balls for a few minutes. The most important thing to me, Wai-yee, is that I see you."

"You're the only one I want to see me."

It was time to confess and he knew it. "Honey, I want to tell you something. I know I haven't been myself while you've been on this trip, and—"

She interrupted, "You've been wonderful!"

"Wai-yee, I didn't want to tell you something because I wanted you to just have a good time, but it's been tough for you with or without knowing what I didn't tell you—and you'll be leaving tomorrow. The trip is almost done."

She was scared at what he might say. "What?"

"Wai-yee, it's my friend, Jonas. He was captured by the North Vietnamese."

"Oh, Moose!" She grabbed his hand and held it tightly. "Oh, Moose, I'm sorry."

"There's nothing anyone can do."

"When did that happen?"

"Over two months ago now, but I found out about it just a few weeks ago."

"I wish you told me, honey. Please don't keep things from me. I'm sorry. I want to know."

"I know–I just–I couldn't."

"Is he all right? I mean, is he wounded or anything?"

"They say he's in good health."

She squeezed his hand, then took her hand away to put her arms around him and embrace him as tight as she could, and they said nothing for a long while. The silence ended when Wai-yee said, "I love you, you know."

"I love you, Wai-yee."

She went to the radio that was built into the television set, turned it on and turned the station-knob until she found some slow music. "Will you ask me to dance with you, Moose?"

He smiled and nodded. "Will you dance with me, Wai-yee?"

"I would love to," she said. "Now there will be seven Inaugural Balls. Shall we invite the president?"

"No," Moose said.

And they danced and danced and danced in the room, long after all the guests had left the other six inaugural balls.

TWENTY-FIVE
MOON OVER MOSCOW
1969

"We are aware that you are in the propaganda business," Viktor Baskakov warned the U.S. Embassy's Cultural Attaché, Anne Whitney. "Your entry into our festival is nothing but propaganda for your Apollo. You are very clever." He was a tall man with a very serious and deadpan expression, and he looked at her with only his right eye, as the other one was either blinded or for some other reason, was looking upwards.

"Mr. Baskakov, when I first sent in our letter of submission to you for our film, *2001: A Space Odyssey* I did not know when Apollo 11 would be launched. It's just working out close to the time, okay?"

Mr. Baskakov grimaced.

"Or should I say A-OK?" she rubbed it in.

Mark Daschle's idea of sending Anne to Moscow, implemented by Ambassador Fairbanks, was not only a success, it went beyond the bounds of anything either of the two of them had imagined. Putting up with Anne was the most irritating and frustrating and hopeless endeavor of the powers in the Kremlin since Aleksandr Solzhenitsyn wrote *One Day in the Life of Ivan Denisovich*.

Her latest action was driving them nuts. She first asked for the night of Wednesday, July 16, for the exhibition of the official U.S. entry in the Sixth Moscow International Film Festival at the Kremlin's massive Palace of Congresses theater. After they granted her the date, she announced the film would be the new Stanley Kubrick film, *2001: A Space Odyssey*. It all "coincidentally worked out" that the night of the exhibition would be the night before three American astronauts would be launched aboard Apollo 11 from Cape Canaveral with the mission of landing the first man on the moon.

"You had this planned, Miss Whitney," Mr. Baskakov said. "You had all this planned when you first requested the date, and you did not tell us what you and your government conspired."

"My government had nothing to do with it," Anne said without a trace of being intimidated. "It was all my doing, Mr. Baskakov," and she winked at him, accenting his inability to use both his eyes. "And if you weren't so scared of your people finding out about our mission to the moon, you wouldn't care about what we were showing at your festival or when we were showing it. Live with it."

Anne's political metamorphosis was complete. It started very quickly after she arrived in Moscow. First, there was the USSR's prohibition of free speech, a freedom Anne had observed to its fullest extent in the United States, and in which she had excelled throughout her life.

Then there was *Pravda* and *Izvestia* as the nation's news organs with only the government lines in print, which got under her skin. It was unacceptable to her that all mimeograph machines were prohibited. Since anything that was written with nine copies was considered a publication that required government review, she regularly made ten copies of anything she wrote, just to see what would happen.

She never had much interest in religion so the Soviet prohibitions on religion didn't bother her personally, but it did bother her when Soviet citizens told her they had to hide their Bibles, and if the government authorities found out they had one, there would be severe consequences including losing their jobs or their apartments.

She had never understood economics but it hit her hard when she saw, on an everyday basis, old women sweeping streets with straw brooms, wearing miserable worn-out blue coats and gray rolled down socks and bending at the waist, their knees out-turned to pick up some piece of refuse, or after a rain, sweeping small puddles into one larger puddle and then into a sewer.

And there were the lines of people for everything. Life, itself, was a succession of episodes of standing in line, whether it was to eat something or see something or ride something. And purchasing anything meant shoving crowds, being pushed and pushing to view any display of shoddy unpackaged products for sale which were exhibited in dirty, dusty display cases made of glass that, invariably, was chipped. And there were the rows of machines that expelled a soft drink with pushing crowds in front of the machines, each person trying to be next to hold the one glass provided that was used by all, with a small faucet for the drinker to rinse it out.

Then there was the strangely composed huge oil painting above the reception desk of the Metropole. It was a painting of Lenin at a kitchen table talking to an empty chair. She was told that Stalin's image was once seated there on that chair of the painting, but he had been painted out in accord with his dismissal from history. The molestation of an artist's work did not go well with Anne.

And the city itself was a study in depression. Other than the Kremlin and some other complexes housing government bureaucracies, from stores to shops to the streets, things were in such disrepair that renovation would be impossible without demolition.

That absence of maintenance was secondary to the atmosphere of leaden weight. There were few if any smiles on those walking on the streets, much less than Anne had seen in the poverty-ridden paths of India where there was even laughter. Within the crowds of Moscow there was always silence. She could hear their feet shuffling, but rarely could she hear a voice.

It was apparent to anyone who came from a free country that here good people were treated as though they were bad animals—to be herded and grouped and worked and roofed and fed—and caged. The gift of life on earth was wasted for millions, by serving a system whose very foundation mandated that the quest of liberty was a crime.

Even within the U.S. Embassy there were nuisances with which Anne, along with the other Americans there, had great difficulty coping. Conversation in most places of the embassy was severely limited. The telephones in the embassy complex were heavy to lift with de-bugging devices in the receiver and cradle. All carbon paper, once used, even of non-security documents, had to be saved and given to a U.S. Marine guard to be placed in the burn barrel.

The only bits of life as she had known them from home were the American goods on the shelves of the embassy commissary and the little building in the compound known as "Uncle Sam's" where she could get hamburgers and hot dogs and potato chips and popcorn. And there was Kopp's Beer on tap there. On Tuesday nights she could sit on one of "Uncle Sam's" large cluster of kitchen-type wooden chairs and watch an American movie exhibited by an old 16mm Bell and Howell projector. The projector's sprocket-teeth wheels would, sporadically, miss the sprocket holes of the film, causing the images to jump and blur and cause the Marine who projected the film to stop the machine and turn the lights on for a quick repair of the film loop. But all that had to be accepted like other things in Moscow. With all its shortcomings, the U.S. Embassy's "Uncle Sam's" was comparative luxury.

To compound her frustrations and intensify her political and personal metamorphosis were the events that could not be justified: She heard about what the Red Guards were doing in China. There was the Soviet invasion of Czechoslovakia. It was as though Mao Tse-tung and Leonid Brezhnev had punched her in the stomach. And there were the posters all over Moscow that portrayed her country as a world evil.

The Kremlin's Palace of Congresses where meetings of the Supreme Soviet were held was filled on Wednesday night, not with the Supreme Soviet. Few in the audience of 6,000 knew that a U.S. moon mission was hours away from launch, or even existed at all. With Leonard Garment, who was assistant to President Nixon, Jacob Beam, who was the U.S. Ambassador to the Soviet Union, and former Vice President Hubert Humphrey sitting in the audience, the lights dimmed and the music of a Strauss waltz began the film, *2001: A Space Odyssey.* After one half-hour of the film, Anne, too nervous to sit still, went out into the lobby reception area.

Unfortunately, the lobby was filled with people who didn't seem to understand the film and were standing around talking about other things. Anne had spent weeks of work making sure the Russian subtitles were easily readable, and she was positive that she had the best translators for the five other languages that were coming through ear-phones posted at every seat, but there were those who just didn't understand what the film was all about.

Anne puffed on a cigarette and put it out half-smoked and then took out another one, lit it, puffed on it, put it out, and walked among the people as she tried to pick up bits of conversation, but she didn't know what most of them were saying.

She walked out of the Palace of Congresses and then out of the Kremlin walls and into Red Square where soldiers were goose-stepping, guarding the Lenin Mausoleum.

The bells were ringing from somewhere within the superstructure of painter's platforms that were surrounding St. Basil's Cathedral Museum. She looked directly above St. Basil's at the moon, which was only a sliver. "They're going to be on the way!" she said to herself. "Moon, wait until you see what we have planned! I wish I was going." While the destination of the astronauts would be the moon, her destination was the giant Rossia Hotel, the biggest hotel in the world with over 3,000 rooms. That night she would be at the hotel in the role of the U.S. Embassy's hostess of what she had planned as a magnificent party to follow the screening; a party to herald both the film and the coming Apollo mission. Almost everyone in Moscow's international community had been invited to the party at the Rossia; foreign ambassadors, other foreign embassy officials, American entertainment celebrities from Lillian Gish to Don De Fore to Mrs. Richard Rogers to John Phillip Law to Dimitri Tiomkin to King Vidor, and the American media would be there from Nancy Dickerson to Ted Murphy. He, of course, would not leave Anne alone. He begged her to give him a scoop about either the Soviets or the Americans. He had become a nuisance.

As Anne knew, a scoop wasn't all he wanted. He wanted Anne. In months prior to the festival he had repeatedly phoned Anne in Moscow, telling her that he and Linda had severe problems, that they were at each other's throat, and that Linda simply couldn't handle his fame as a television news personality. "It's you who are taken with your fame–Theodore," Anne would tell him.

Since the screening was still going on, the ballroom of the Rossia was vacant of guests. In preparation for their arrival, and under the instructions of Anne, waiters and waitresses were taping the U.S. Embassy's posters to the pillars; posters of American films interspersed with posters of the logo-insignia of Apollo 11. The writing on some posters were in English and others were in Russian.

"Tomorrow–we launch to the moon," Anne said to one of the waitresses, and Anne pointed to the picture of the moon on the Apollo poster, with its writing in Russian. The waitress looked confused and after Anne put her finger on the picture, the waitress nodded at Anne with a questioning look. Anne gave a very positive nod back and then flattened her hand and hit it against the picture of the moon. The waitress opened her mouth with a look of amazement. "Land on Monday!" Anne said. "Monday! Boom!" And she hit her hand against the picture of the moon again.

The waitress's mouth was still open and she said, "Monday?"

"Monday!"

The waitress shook her head, and then said, *"Nyet!"*

"Monday, *da!"* Anne answered.

And then with a smile the waitress said, "Moon Day!"

"Yes, yes," Anne said with a big smile. *"Da! Da!* Moon Day!"

The waitress scurried to the other waitresses and waiters to confirm what the posters indicated, and to tell them that Monday would be Moon Day.

Anne went to the elevator bank to go to the eleventh floor where the Embassy had a reserved room for the Embassy's staff to put their supplies, and to change their clothes for the Embassy events at the hotel. But she was told at the elevator bank that the entire wing of the hotel was off limits during a necessary short delay to fix the elevators. Anne, of course, knew that the delay was necessary because the "administrazia" was searching rooms.

"How long before the spies are done?" Anne asked the guard by the elevator-bank.

He pretended he didn't understand her.

"Hey, KGB Man," Anne said. "How long before I can get up there to change my clothes in the room my Embassy rented and paid for with American dollars?"

"Another twenty minutes," he said, but as he said it, the elevator door opened and a blue-coated elevator operator who looked like she was waiting for the cue, nodded and smiled at Anne and said, "*Pazhahlsta.*"

When Anne arrived on the eleventh floor, the floor maid who was standing behind her station had a look of fright, and she quickly put her right hand over her lapel. Her action prompted no mystery to Anne. The woman had undoubtedly taken an Apollo button from the box of 10,000 Apollo buttons in the Embassy room, and had pinned it to her lapel. Anne smiled. "I will bring you more," she said. The woman didn't understand but kept her hand tight against her lapel. *"Klyootch!"* Anne said, *"Klyootch. Ah-deen nat tsat, ah-deen nat tsat."* Anne was striving to speak enough Russian to ask for the key to the Embassy room. As the woman kept that hand over her lapel, she groped with her left hand, reaching under the counter of her station to get the key for Anne.

No need for a key. The door was open. But it wasn't the KGB that was waiting for her; it was Ted Murphy. "Annie, the door was open so I walked right in. These are comfortable digs! They gave me a room one quarter this size."

"Oh, God, Ted!"

"You got it right. It's God Ted."

"You better get out of here. I have to change my clothes and look like a hostess before the crowd comes in downstairs."

"Can I watch?" he said with a smile and a wink.

"Out! Out! Vah-moos!"

"Hey, Annie, you're tryin' to get rid of a big television star, do you realize that? One scoop from you and I'll be a good boy and leave. Come on, tell me somethin' I can use. You must know somethin' now that you have a black diplomatic passport and you've turncoated into a big emissary of our imperialist nation!"

Anne walked to the door, closed it, locked it, and then did something that was unexpected, totally out of context with the circumstances, and unbelievably erotic: she started taking off her clothes while she talked with a matter-of-fact tone, as though talking was all she was doing. How far would she go? Ted Murphy was spellbound, and with the visual placed in front of him, he had little interest in what she was saying.

"I'll tell you something that may be of interest, Ted. There is a provision in the rules of the festival that demands that no participating nation may offend any other participating nation within their films. Now, in conflict with their own rules, they showed a picture last night produced by what they called South Vietnam, meaning the Viet Cong. It was really made by North Vietnam and they called us aggressors and had an actor as an American captain. They found some big Vietnamese guy to play the role. He looked like he was six-and-a-half feet tall and he had on fatigues with a real big cloth nameplate sewn on his fatigues that said, 'Smith.' It was so phony. They had him shoot—kill a little boy who was screaming for his mother they had already killed, and it was very offensive. Now, do you know what I'm going to do about that, Ted? I'm not only going to protest, I'm going to warn Mr. Baskakov that I will recommend to our government that we won't allow the Soviet Union to participate in our San Francisco Film Festival and we won't participate in their next festival here unless they apologize from the stage of the Palace of Congresses tomorrow night and pledge that it will never happen again. Now, what do you think of that?" She unstrapped her slip and let it fall to the floor.

She was down to very sheer, small white garments, one on top and one on the bottom, and Ted's mind was being bombarded with her images, Anne moving in a nonchalance that far exceeded any design of a striptease artist, while making statements that had nothing to do with what she knew had to dominate his attention. It was like a banned film with the wrong soundtrack. She couldn't have planned a more seductive scenario.

"What do you think of that, Ted?"

"Well, Annie," and he tried to act as though his attention was on her words. "I think it doesn't sound like the Annie I used to know."

"Remember how we used to say not to trust anyone over thirty? This year I had my thirtieth birthday and I realize how little anyone under thirty knows. I can't wait until I'm sixty."

"You've turned into a Commie-hater! Boy, there's nothin' so extreme as a convert. I heard that all my life. Now you're the livin' proof!"

"I'm the same Annie you always knew except I didn't know how creepy these goons were. I've always been a Creep-hater." And with that she reached behind her back and unlatched the top white garment, took it off and gently put it on the floor. There was an innocence in it. She didn't let it fall off in a performance. She took it off with neatness. "So you can report what they did and what I'm going to do if you want, but only after I talk to Baskakov. There's an exclusive for you."

He nodded. He surely was having an exclusive. "But I don't know if that's the kind of thing I want. Tell me something really big, something earthshaking." He was so nervous that his voice was absent of the "I'm from the streets" accent, just as it disappeared when ever he was on television.

Anne nodded. "Do you know who Walter Stoessel is?"

"No."

She sat down, and as though she was on a forbidden stage, she literally squirmed her way out of the lower garment without speed. "Our Ambassador to Warsaw–to Poland." It was off.

Nothing was left but her glasses.

The glasses added to the eroticism.

"Yeah. So?" He pretended he cared.

"Come here," she said, and she stood up, and signaled with her finger for him to come next to her.

Nothing in his life had been more tempting. It was not that she was the most beautiful woman he had ever been with but, without contest, her style of the unexpected and unacknowledged of what she was doing had no match in his catalogue of previous encounters.

He walked to her with some fear in the few steps it took to get to her. Being so close to her in her nakedness was something he could not easily handle. She whispered to him. "He's been dealing with China–for us."

"What do you mean?" he could hardly get words out of his mouth.

"Nixon is having him deal with China. That's all I can tell you." And she walked to the closet and took out a formal black dress on a hanger. She put it across the top of the chair and then opened a drawer of the dresser, taking out black undergarments and dark stockings. She sat down again and as she slowly put on the stockings, the dressing was as uniquely intoxicating to Ted as the previous undressing.

"You mean we're having a dialogue with China? What about?"

"All I mean is that Nixon is talking to them–through Stoessel in Poland. That's all I can tell you, and you better never tell anyone where you got that one."

"It's not enough. I got to know more."

"It's enough. Now, do you want me to tell you about my meeting with Cardinal Mindszenty?"

"Wait a minute. Let me go back to China."

"No more. You want to know about Cardinal Mindszenty?"

He became obedient to what she was saying. With the show in front of him he let her have her way. "You met him?"

"I attended Mass in his room at the American Embassy in Budapest."

"You've got religion, now?"

"Do you want to hear?"

"Yeah, yeah." He didn't care at all about this one but the visuals of her in nothing but stockings that she was smoothing out against her legs made him want these moments to last as long as the planet.

"He's such a sweet man. If he walks out of the Embassy grounds he'll be arrested. The police are right outside the Embassy, waiting for him. They've been waiting out there to arrest him for thirteen years. He was released from prison thirteen years ago by the Hungarian Freedom Fighters while they were staging their attempted revolution back in 1956. When the revolution was failing because of the Soviet tanks, he ran to the Embassy and we gave him refuge—ever since. He just sits there in his room and conducts a Mass every Sunday for a few Americans at the Embassy. He has all his little Catholic things, his Rosary and things like that in a little wooden White Owl cigar box on his desk. And he walks outside in a walled-off compound. It's so small. Do you know what I brought him?"

"What?"

"I was told what he wanted. Do you know what he wanted?"

"I said, what?"

"Palmolive shaving cream. The old kind. The real green kind. He doesn't like the one Palmolive is putting out now. He says it's too light. He likes the real green kind. So I found some and got it for him."

"Good. Good. What else did you find out about him?"

"That he's a sweet man—a great man. You wouldn't understand. I think I'll be quiet."

"No, Annie, no."

She stood and put on her black undergarments and, in silence, the rest of her clothes, and when she was all done she put on earrings, an Apollo button near her left breast, and she started combing her hair. She looked not at all like the Annie he had known when she was younger. She was now truly a very good-looking woman. She had needed some age, and now she had it. Then she put a blue ribbon in her hair. She was an explosion of femininity.

Then, without saying anything, she put on her makeup, but not much of it. She turned to Ted. "Were you listening or looking?"

"Looking."

"Where's Linda?"

"Home. We're separated. We're really separated this time. It's bad between us, Annie."

"Does she know it's bad between you two? Or are you the only one who knows it's bad?"

"Of course she knows. We're separated."

"Does your little four-year-old son know you're separated?"

"Tommy knows that I'm not home at night."

"I'm sure."

"Don't you believe me that we're separated?"

"How could I not believe you?" she asked sarcastically. "Would you lie about such a thing? I know how it is. She just doesn't understand you."

"The trouble is, she does understand me."

"So do I. Now let's go downstairs." She took off her glasses and put them on the bureau table.

"Can you see?"

"Better than you."

The ballroom was packed. Anne found Mr. Baskakov. "Mr. Baskakov!"

"Miss Whitney. Thank you for the invitation," he said with no inflection in his voice and with his practiced deadpan face. He was looking at her with his right eye, his left eye aimed at the ceiling.

"Mr. Baskakov, we participated in this festival on the basis of your rules."

"I never questioned that. I questioned why you chose the film and the date. Yes. You obeyed the rules."

"Thank you. But when the festival started last week you showed a film that was slanderous, and I told you I didn't approve of the fact you broke your own rules of no film being allowed to offend a participating nation, and you told me it was not in the competition and so it didn't have to live under the rules. Well, last night you showed a film called *Fire* from North Vietnam and it was in the competition–and you knew even when we were talking earlier about the other film–you knew you were going to show an offending film in competition–and that was a deception."

"That was not from North Vietnam, it was from South Vietnam."

"Please!"

"And it should not have been offensive. It was an honest representation of your government, not about your people."

"Mr. Baskakov, our government is our people, and what you have done is very serious to the American delegation. We took great pains to make sure that the films we brought would not be offensive to any participating nation. I want you to apologize tomorrow night from the stage. And I want your guarantee that it will never happen again."

"Miss Whitney, Miss Whitney, we do not have speeches of delegates, we have films, and there is some misunderstanding of what would be offensive. Your nation brags about its freedoms. Do we not have the same freedom to exhibit what we choose?"

"If they're in accord with your announced rules. If you choose to say you obey your rules when you don't, then show what you want, Mr. Baskakov, but don't think we will participate again based on your lies!"

Baskakov started shouting at Anne in Russian.

"Ya ne paneemahyoo, ya ne paneemahyoo," Anne said in her very slight knowledge of the language, meaning she did not understand him. "Listen, Mr. Baskakov, would you participate in a festival in which the Soviets are called aggressors? You showed a film with actors–actors who played American soldiers–they were all North Vietnamese–and they said that we, the United States, want to destroy everything. A little boy screamed, 'Mother! Mother! Mother!' as an actor shoots the boy's mother, then the boy. And the narration said, 'Down with U.S. imperialism! Down with America! Yankees go home!' That, Mr. Baskakov, in my opinion, does not only ignore your rules but surely does not live up to the theme of this festival of 'Friendship Among Nations.' I know that the Soviet Union is planning on participating in our San Francisco Film Festival. I will

guarantee that if it works out that we invite you, no film in our festival will call the Soviets aggressors. No film will be on the screen there that shows Soviet war materials going to North Vietnam. No film will be shown of your invasion of Czechoslovakia."

His eye enlarged when she said the word, "Czechoslovakia," and he shouted at her louder than before. "Miss Whitney! Miss Whitney!"

She ignored the shouts. "We guarantee no offense to our guests. We should treat each other as guests and hosts. Now, either you apologize and guarantee this will not happen again and—I'll add something else—rewrite your rules for your next festival—do those three things or I will recommend to Secretary of State Rogers that we will not participate in your festivals and we will not invite you to ours. Get it?"

"Very well, Miss Whitney. You do as you choose."

"I will. You've made my choice for me. And your festival is going to lose every bit of international prestige without American participation and you know it. Good! It should. And I'm sending off that cable first thing in the morning!"

Anne started walking away from him, when he called her back. "Miss Whitney?"

She turned around. "Yes?"

"May I have an Apollo button?"

Could it be? Could it be that after all that, he could ask for an Apollo button? She took the button off her dress and gave it to him. It was not easy for her to admit it to herself, but now she knew that all through her entire speech he was thinking about getting her Apollo button.

She tried to forget about it, doing what she was supposed to do: mix with the guests and act the role of hostess as though she had done it hundreds of times before. She was superb.

She saw Ted at the appetizer table eating a Ritz cracker with a Kraft cheese dip while he was talking to some man she recognized. Then she saw Ted take out his small notepad and write in it. She wandered over to the appetizer table, shaking hands with different guests as she walked toward Ted. As soon as the man talking to Ted saw her, he disappeared in the crowd.

"Who was he?" she asked Ted.

"A friend."

"He's KGB, Ted."

"Who knows? Hey, this American food tastes good. Did you get it from the commissary at the Embassy?"

"Yes. You be careful, Ted. That man is KGB."

"I got to have more sources here than you, Annie. You don't produce."

"You be careful."

"I've been correspondin' with him for a long time. I finally had the opportunity to meet him tonight."

"Did he give you a scoop?"

Ted rolled his eyes and wiped his strange-shaped nose. "Yeah. He gave me a scoop about an old friend of ours."

"What do you mean?"

"I've been askin' him for over a year to find out about a guy I'm sure is CIA –that guy we met in Hong Kong and I met him again in Israel."

"Who are you talking about?" Anne knew exactly who he was talking about, and she was now glad she had never told him about seeing Adam Orr walk into the Soviet Embassy in New Delhi.

"It's my story, Annie. You'll find out. Anyway, I got a story."

"Well, I have a big one, too, and you can count on mine for accuracy."

"Shoot!"

"I did it, Ted."

"You did what?"

"I told Baskakov we won't participate any more. Just like what I told you I'd do. Even better. I really told him off, and I'm cabling Secretary Rogers tomorrow."

"You're a tough customer, Annie. What did he say?"

"He said he wanted my Apollo button! He's such a creep."

"I don't blame him for wantin' your button. So do I. All of them."

She smiled. "Do you?"

"That was some show you gave me, Annie. I can't get it out of my mind."

"Wasn't that enough for you?"

"It was like these–" and he gestured toward the table. "An appetizer."

She went back to her other interest, as only a woman can do. "Do you know who I can't wait to tell about what I did with Baskakov?"

"Who?"

"Daschle. He'll be proud of me. How I hated him in Hong Kong. But he'll be proud."

"You're becomin' more like Daschle than Daschle."

"Good for me. You might not approve because you're still a child, but do you remember the Chinese girl Daschle and I worked with in Hong Kong?"

"Yeah. How does that make me a child?"

"I'm not done. I sent her a letter of apology."

"For what?"

"For giving her a hard way to go about Mao when we worked together. It's been on my mind."

"God! You didn't!"

"She wrote me a beautiful letter back. All handwritten beautifully. It was like calligraphy."

"Isn't that sweet?"

"Cut that out!"

"Boy, did you ever get religion! Well, that's good. I can use you, Annie. Or you can use me."

"Oh?"

"That is if Daschle–your political guru, doesn't mind."

"Please!"

"Is he here?"

"In Moscow?"

"Yeah."

"He's in Latin America somewhere, I think."

Ted went back to the subject prominent on his mind. "Annie, why don't we go to my room when this thing is over?"

Her smile vanished. "Every room in this hotel is bugged. They might even have cameras. We'll go to the embassy."

"The embassy?" He wasn't about to say what he felt which was, "you mean you'll do it?"

"There are two rooms that are safe in the Embassy," she said. "There's the Tank or the Bubble, as we call it–it's a plastic bubble on the ninth floor with nothing touching the walls or anything. It's big."

"Wow! Can we be with each other in there?"

She shook her head. "I don't have a key. But I have a key to the other safe place."

"What is it?"

"Ambassador Beam's office. Wouldn't that be fun?"

It was.

And every night through the mission of Apollo 11, Anne and Ted went to the ambassador's office. While the astronauts were landing on the moon, and walking on the moon, and blasting off the moon, and docking with their parent spacecraft, and splashing down in the Pacific, and being recovered by the Hornet, and talking to the president, Anne and Ted rendez-voused in the evenings in Ambassador Beam's office.

On Friday night, as he embraced her on top of the ambassador's desk he said, "Houston? Tranquillity Base here, Annie. The Eagle has landed."

"It certainly has."

As he got up and started making himself presentable to the outside world he said, "Maybe these nights with you have been only one small step for Mankind, Annie, but I want you to know that it's been a giant leap for a man."

Anne stayed where she was on the desk. "Did you know the Soviets used to have a microphone behind that seal?" She gestured with her head toward the giant Seal of the United States on the wall behind the ambassador's desk.

Ted looked scared as he was buckling his belt. "A microphone?"

"Nothing to worry about. We took it out back in 1952. The office has been clean since then."

"Nothin' to worry about now? You sure?" he asked for assurance.

She turned around seductively to lie on her stomach. "Oh, Ted. Do you think I'd be here with you if I wasn't sure?"

"You better be right!"

"I am."

She wasn't.

All of this was being picked up by Soviet-placed microphones. And there was an occasional barely audible clicking noise that was coming from above the north-wall bookcase.

When Ted Murphy returned to his job in front of a television camera in Washington he said nothing to the national audience about the Moscow Film Festival but reported, instead, a "scoop" that he had been told as he stood at the appetizer table at the Rossia Hotel.

"Few Americans have heard the name Adam Orr," he said to the camera, "because he has been living a life of covert activities. His history is well known to this reporter. Most recently I have been reliably informed that he is now in Southeast Asia directing a secret war that the United States is conducting in Laos and Cambodia. He is involved with the CIA's secret air transport and supply network called 'Air America' operating out of Laos. Next week this reporter will have a series of exclusive reports on Air America and the shadows in which Agent Orr and the agency for which he works has been operating. This is Ted Murphy in Washington."

Two nights after Ted Murphy's announcement, Adam Orr's body was left at the front gate of the U.S. Embassy in Saigon.

Traffic went by his body in the usual roar of a Saigon morning. Hondas making their loud noises were being driven by slim women in white ao-dais who barely turned their eyes toward what remained of him.

A U.S. Marine guard came out of the gate, turned the body's head toward him and called for another Marine. The two of them carried his body inside the embassy grounds.

The 1960s were fast coming to an end. The fate of Adam Orr was known by very few; a cat, two U.S. Marines, Ambassador Beam, and the Viet Cong who had killed him. Others would not be told what happened to the man without a family until an investigation was complete. Ted Murphy, used by a KGB agent at a U.S. Embassy party at the Rossia Hotel, had been given calculated misinformation and it was repeated by him, as expected, to a television audience. Linda Murphy didn't know it, but her husband had no loyalty to anything, and she was a part of anything. Anne Whitney, who had gone through a transformation within the decade, received approval of Secretary of State Rogers to cancel U.S. official participation in the next Moscow Film Festival, and she received the scorn of her colleagues. Moose Dunston, in a stronger position than before at the White House, did not yet know what happened to Adam Orr. He was still unable to shake away the vision and aura of Tso Wai-yee, who with the patience of her heritage, waited for him to come to her in Hong Kong. Mark Daschle was to become a willing recipient of the temptations of middle age. Gerald and Mary Fairbanks were still posted in Washington, D.C., hoping for some plum foreign assignments before retirement. Cody Cooper had known a decade in which he had realized his dream to be at the White House under President Kennedy, and then felt the depression of having life turned upside down. Irene Goodpastor found it intolerable to have her respected status that she had known so long, diminish with a new generation that had little admiration of her. And Jonas Valadovich was in his eighth month locked in a five foot by three foot punishment cell in a prison in North Vietnam.

On New Year's Eve the windows of the restaurant on Victoria Peak in Hong Kong were covered with dew, drops of water running like tears down its outside surface, the city invisible. Hong Kong did not need to be told. It knew what happened to the man who had fallen in love with that city, and who had adopted it as his paradise, and who the city would not see again.

Outside the New York Times building in New York City, crowds cheered as an electric ball dropped to signal that the last year of the decade was done, *Life* magazine printed a double issue on all ten years, broadcaster Harry Reasoner made an analysis of them, band leader Lawrence Welk devoted an hour to their finale, and all of that was just as it should have been, for without it, no American could truly have felt the 1960s were done. It had been the first decade to be brought into the living rooms of millions of Americans by both image and sound and so, for the first time, millions of non-participants in historical events of their times felt part of them, beginning with the Kennedy-Nixon debates and ending with Man on the Moon. And for so many of those who participated in the international events of that decade and made it to the end, it was the beginning of a journey like no other Americans had lived before them.

PART TWO

THE 1970s

TWENTY-SIX
THE PROPOSAL
1970

"At last!" Adam's Last Will and Testament began, "I have a perfect excuse not to send out any more Christmas cards!" As a man without a family, he split his estate between Major Jonas Valadovich of the United States Air Force; Dee Benning of Cocoa Beach, Florida; Angel of the Hideout Bistro in Hong Kong; Ilka of the Cobenzi Bar in Vienna, Austria; Crystal of the 400 Club on The Block of Baltimore, Maryland; and Sally Saigon, cat of the U.S. Embassy in Saigon, South Vietnam. His condominium in Cocoa Beach was willed to Dee Benning with the proviso that she "give all my flashlight batteries to the Red Cross, keeping none for herself." Those people were now financially set for life, and Sally Saigon was set for the remaining eight of her nine lives.

There was a separate note: "As a veteran of World War II and the Korean War, I request to be buried at Arlington National Cemetery. Don't bother to attend my funeral. I attended very few and would not attend this one, but my attendance is unavoidable since no one would believe that I have other things to do. Please no flowers. I have never understood why they are given shortly after it's too late for the subject to smell them."

There were two separate envelopes, one for Dee Benning with the instruction for her to tell Martin of Langley, Virginia, "Obviously, I screwed up again."

The other envelope was addressed to Moose Dunston with an enclosure of ten thousand dollars in one hundred dollar bills, and a note telling Moose to "spend it all only on prostitutes. They're the most honest women I've known. With little exception, they're the only women who tell a man, in advance, what they'll do, and how much it will cost."

The envelopes were delivered, and Adam's will was released to his beneficiaries except for Jonas Valadovich who heard nothing but the shouting of guards and the threats of the smiling North Vietnamese officers who visited him with increasing frequency. Their visits were for the purpose of tightening ropes around him to non-endurance as he was bent, naked, over a bamboo pole, with both legs and arms wrapped around the pole until he was a ball. In that restraint he was beaten with rubber hoses by two guards, and usually he vomited and tried to refrain from screaming so fellow prisoners would not hear him. He was not always successful.

Ted Murphy was unrepentant, feeling no guilt over his television report in which he told what he believed to be Adam's CIA activities.

There was official quiet regarding the life of Adam Orr, and his planned funeral at Arlington National Cemetery was not publicly announced. The only indication that he had an out-of-uniform affiliation with the U.S.

government would be the Distinguished Service Medal pinned to his jacket at burial.

It was Moose who recommended the posthumous medal for Adam, the recommendation clearly not prescribed by Moose's duties as Chief of Contingency Planning, but the president was moved by Moose's plea. "There is yet to be an Unknown Soldier of this war, Mister President," Moose had said to President Nixon. Bob Haldeman was sitting by the side of the president's desk in the Oval Office taking notes of Moose's recommendation. "Unlike the unknown soldiers, his name is known, but his life isn't and may never be. Only his death is known. I have prepared for you a paper of his history–his history with the agency across the river. Everything he did was voluntary. At his own insistence, he was never paid a cent."

"I don't need to look at your paper, Moose. Can we get it done in time, Bob?"

Bob Haldeman nodded. "We can have it done in an hour. All it takes is your approval."

"Let's do it."

Moose smiled for the first time since he heard the news of Adam's murder. "Thank you, sir."

"Anything else, Moose?" the president asked.

"No, sir, except–unless you have any objections–I'm going to the funeral as your representative. No press announcement or anything. If anyone asks, I'll just say I was a friend of his."

"Of course. That's fine. Tell Ziegler you're going, though, so he'll be ready for it if anyone in the press asks. Now, when are you going on that Southeast Asia tour? Kissinger told me you were going tomorrow."

"I moved it to Friday, sir."

"That's good. I'll have some notes for you to give Thieu and Lon Nol and–you going to Thailand?"

"Yes, sir."

"I'll have a note for the king–King Bhumibol. He can move mountains in that country. There isn't anyone who doesn't have respect for Bhumibol. Also some notes for our ambassadors; Bunker, Godley, he's good–and the rest."

"Okay."

"The king, you know, he was born here in the United States. He's a friend, a good friend of the United States. Do you know all the protocol? They told you the protocol?"

"What do you mean, sir?"

"Remember, you have to bow when he walks in the room. Not a big bow. Americans aren't expected to give big bows. And you know, you never cross your legs there. You don't point your foot at the King. You don't do it to any Thai."

"I didn't know that."

"Oh, yeah. Believe me, I have to keep remembering. He'll extend his hand to you, and then when you shake hands with him you give a small bow again. Just a small one for Americans. He knows America and knows we don't know how to handle royalty. Only his right eye functions, you know. His left eye is glass. He was in an automobile accident in Switzerland and lost his eye; that was when he was a boy. He functions perfectly without it."

"I didn't know any of that."

"You'll like him. Young fellow; late 30s, early 40s maybe. Probably about your age. How old are you, Moose?"

"Forty-three, sir."

"That's right; he's about your age. Not as much brawn, though. He's a slender fellow. Glasses. Mild but strong. He's not an arrogant king, he's right at home with Americans, and he's a real gentleman. And listen, you buy some Thai silk when you're in Bangkok. Your wife will love it. It's the best in the world, you know."

"I'm not married, sir, but–" He almost started to tell the president about Wai-yee, but thought better of it and caught himself before telling a story the president did not invite and would surely not have time or interest to hear.

"Well, for a girlfriend then. You just can't help but score with Thai silk. What's your tour? What's your itinerary?"

"Thailand, Laos, Cambodia, Vietnam, and Hong Kong."

The president smiled. "Hong Kong?"

"Yes, sir."

He shook his head, still smiling. "Good. A wonderful city. Don't miss the Dragon Boat Bar or the Dragon Boat Restaurant or whatever it is, at the Hilton, you know."

Moose laughed. "I've been there, sir. If that's an order, I'll go there again."

"Oh, you bet. That's a presidential directive!"

"Not a bad order, Dunston," Bob Haldeman said. He hadn't been writing in his pad but was taking it all in. He looked back at the president. "We'll get your messages to the chiefs of state and our ambassadors when you have them ready, to go to Moose before he goes. I'll tell Kissinger what you discussed."

"Not everything! Not everything!" the president was shaking his head. "Although Henry probably knows more places than the Dragon Boat. That would be much too tame for Henry." The president looked back at Moose. "He may not look it, but Henry's a swinger, you know."

"I heard that. I've read the stories."

"Oh, I think he likes the stories. They're probably not true. You have someone there who you see in Hong Kong?"

"Yes, Mr. President."

"A beauty, I'll bet!"

"She is beautiful."

The tone of Moose's voice told the president that he hit on something. "Well, that's good. You saving Hong Kong for your last stop?"

"Yes, sir."

The president nodded. "Saving it for dessert. That's smart. I would too, if I were you."

The flag that was on Adam's coffin was folded by the honor guard and handed to Moose who requested its temporary custody. He accepted it in the hope that at a future date he would be able to give it to Jonas Valadovich.

Moose's new black passport identified him as a diplomat, and it had more advantages than allowing him to pass through customs of foreign nations with locked luggage. That passport made all phases of his travels far different than his previous visits to the fragile areas of Southeast Asia.

One of those differences was his invitation for dinner at the Grand Palace of the King of Thailand, (the nation that had been called Siam until 1939 and then briefly called Siam again after World War II). Without any lethargy, Moose accepted the invitation within minutes of its receipt. After all, he was not lethargic when he waited in line to see the movie, *Anna and the King of Siam* when he was a kid, nor was he lethargic when he paid a heavy fee to take a date to see Rodgers and Hammerstein's *The King and I* on Broadway when he was a young man. Now he was invited to be a participant at the palace rather than taking a seat in the audience to watch actors play king.

The compound of the Grand Palace was an ornate myriad of sculptured spires and green triangular roofs with orange borders and some with their colors reversed, and there were decorative bent sword-like rods jutting out from the corners of those roofs. And there were golden Buddhas and shrines scattered throughout the landscape of the palace grounds.

The king's bodyguards, with their white tops and blue ballooned pants, escorted Moose to the outdoor pool. He was told this was the prescribed location for the dinner and the entertainment, and Moose should wait on the guest's chair until the king and Queen Sirikit "come across." After Moose was seated, the bodyguards proceeded to fix the chairs for the king and queen, adjusting pillows, washing the floor around the chairs, and bringing the royal spittoon to the side of the king's chair, along with a small table with a golden ash tray.

Coming from the lighted throne room across from the pool was King Bhumibol Adulyadej, a slender man wearing horn rimmed glasses, dressed in a white short-sleeved turtleneck Tee-shirt, white full pants, white shoes, and he held a walkie-talkie in his hand. He stopped to talk to a guard who was not only bowing on his knees to the king, but then he lay prostrate as the king talked to him. The king spotted Moose in the guest's chair, and walked around the pool to him. Moose gave the customary slight bow that the president told him to give, the king extended his hand, and Moose said, "I thank you for having me here, Your Majesty." They shook hands, with Moose giving another slight bow.

"Mr. Dunston," the king said. "We are so pleased to have you here. We are to eat first; the dancers are not ready. And a fuse is out. You'll pardon me, please, as I must fix it or you will see nothing. The sun will be down in half an hour." With that he walked to the fuse box that was on a pillar near Moose. The king unscrewed one fuse and screwed in another without taking the walkie-talkie out of his other hand. He turned back to Moose. "Now, Mr. Dunston, you are with your president's National Security Council?"

"Yes, Your Majesty. Not the Council itself which is only the president, the vice president, the secretaries of state and defense, the director of emergency peparedness, the chief of our central intelligence, and Henry Kissinger who's the president's national security council director. I'm on the staff that works for them. My job is contingency planning."

"Yes, I am aware of your contingency assignment. You have contingency planning for Thailand should we be attacked from our eastern border?"

"Of course. This kingdom has always been our friend."

"I'm afraid not during World War II!" and he laughed.

Moose smiled but shook his head. "Your Majesty, when Thailand declared war on the United States back then, we rejected the declaration. We had never rejected such a declaration in our entire history. We could not regard Thailand as an enemy. And, unless my memory is not serving me well, it was not the royal family that made that declaration against the United States."

"Your memory serves you well, Mr. Dunston. It was Premier Pibul Sonngram who allowed the Japanese to occupy our country, and it was he who declared war against you and Britain. He was a war criminal. But that is done. Now to tonight. The orchestra will be accompanying the princess as she will be the—how do you call it? The star dancer. She is home on vacation from the Massachusetts Institute of Technology where she is studying."

"That's wonderful. One of the best schools in the world. And I understand you composed the music, Your Majesty."

"Yes. Music is the language of the soul and has no boundaries. The queen designed the set. It will be erected in moments. We are late. Everything is late. The fuse blew."

Young dancers were walking by and they bowed as they passed the king who didn't look at them. "I want to hear about President Nixon and what he plans to do to win the war."

"You should have his note to you." Moose reached in his inside breast pocket and gave the king a White House envelope. "He asked me to give this to you."

"Oh? What does he say?"

"I haven't read it, Your Majesty."

"I see."

"It's for you, not me."

After dinner there was the performance of the king's first daughter, Princess Ubol Ratana, who could easily have been a contender in any

Miss Universe contest—and could easily have won. There was a team of dancers and singers and a twenty-piece orchestra. The music was the king's unique and haunting mixture of Thai and rock.

Queen Sirikit went straight to her quarters after the performance while Moose and the king, holding tightly to his walkie-talkie as though it was part of his hand, sat under the canopy and talked about the war.

"What do you know about their treatment of prisoners of war, Your Majesty?" Moose asked the king.

"They do not obey the principles of the Geneva Convention on Prisoners of War. Inhumane. Inhumane. You have heard of the bamboo cages?"

"Yes. That's by the Viet Cong in South Vietnam. I mean in North Vietnam."

"There is no difference between the Viet Cong and the North Vietnamese. You Americans make a mistake in seeing them as separate, but they are not."

"They treat their prisoners the same to your knowledge?"

"You see, the North Vietnamese say their prisoners are not prisoners of war since there has been no declaration of war, therefore the captured are treated as common criminals. It is not that they know what a declaration of war means in your country. They know nothing about your constitutional processes. It is that they heard your demonstrators say it is not a declared war. Why are you asking, Mr. Dunston? Is it because they are your countrymen or do you know some men who are imprisoned?"

Moose nodded. "Both. And a very close friend is held prisoner there. He's in Sontay."

"I am sorry."

"In fact, Your Majesty, this is not any of my official business, but while I'm here in Southeast Asia, I am trying to seek information on how I can get my friend out."

"A rescue? An escape?"

"Yes. That's not official—that's me—what I want."

"Are you aware of the efforts of Ross Perot?"

"Yes. He's done a terrific job of keeping the prisoners in the spotlight of the world."

"I do not mean that. He has not made it public but he is engaged in trying to get some of your men out. A rescue operation."

Moose stared at the king and then slowly nodded.

"You must see him when you can. Tell him about your friend. He may be able to help more than you think."

"Thank you. That's good advice."

There was static and then a tone, and then a woman's voice came from his walkie-talkie. It was Queen Sirikit. He smiled, answered in Thai, and pressed one of its buttons when he was done. "The queen. She says it's time to come to bed. You are married, Mr. Dunston?"

"No, Your Majesty."

"Ahhh, you must. And you must have children."

"I have a—I have a girlfriend, a woman friend."
"Then you will be married soon?"
Moose gave a slight cock of his head, almost like the kind of movement that Wai-yee made. "I am seeing her on this trip, Your Majesty. She is in Hong Kong."
"She is Chinese?"
"Yes."
"I hope she is not a Communist."
Moose laughed. "The furthest thing from it."
"That is good. You must marry her."
"Just because she isn't a Communist?" Moose joked.
"Because you must get married. You must have children. Many children are good."
Moose nodded.
"A man is made to create. Without creation, life is pointless. And it is tragic not to create all you can while so many other men destroy. You must create."
"Is that why you write music?"
He nodded with a smile. "And have children. This woman in Hong Kong—how long have you known her?"
"Ten years, Your Majesty."
"Ten years?"
"Yes."
"That is too long. Ten months is too short. Ten years is too long. Why do you not marry her?"
"I can't answer that. I'm not even sure I know."
"You ask her. You tell her the King of Thailand insists on it!"
"I will! But I'm not sure that's the way to ask her, sir."
The king gave a wide smile. "It doesn't make any difference how a man asks a woman to marry. They will not say yes or no based on the way you ask them. What makes a difference is if you ask or don't ask. Now, tell me, Mr. Dunston, why is your president reducing troop strength here in Thailand?"
"We are reducing our troops everywhere in Southeast Asia. He's attempting to turn the war over to the South Vietnamese."
"It may be too soon. Premature."
"I understand your concern but we're doing good in our training of the South Vietnamese—with more modern weapons than they've ever had."
The king looked away from Moose as though he wanted to say something, but thought he shouldn't. The silence was too long and the king wanted to repair it. "I like your president. He knows the world well. But sometimes I think he gets too much advice. He should act on his own. Your government has too many agencies, too many interests of one bureau after another bureau. It is not good. The president does not have enough authority. Your country is run by bureaus."
"Our country is run by the people, Your Majesty. They vote."

"And once your people vote, then the people are through. It goes to the bureaus."

"Oh, no. It's still the people. The representatives of the people make the rules for the bureaus and there are elections every two years for our representatives, every four years for our president, and every six years for our senators, so the people can vote out or vote in who they choose with frequency."

"You can buy votes in America."

"I'm sorry, Your Majesty but I disagree with you."

"Oh, yes you can. I am sorry."

"No, sir. You can't. Nelson Rockefeller is one of the richest men in the world. He has tried to be nominated for the presidency. He has consistently failed even with all his money."

"What of John Kennedy's father?"

"He was rich. It is not illegal to have a rich father."

"Tell me, Mr. Dunston, what do you think of the Kennedys?"

"I voted for Nixon but I have great respect for John Kennedy's presidency. He was a remarkable man."

"You have great respect for all the Kennedys?"

"No."

"Ted Kennedy? Do you think he is fit to be president?"

"He won't be."

"Do you think he is fit to be a senator?"

"He is from Massachusetts. In Massachusetts the name of Kennedy is magic."

"You see, that incident–perhaps, at best, he was in shock. To administer world events, a man can not be susceptible to shock. And, anyway, a Kennedy should be special. They cannot do what he has done. If a man is great he should be different. Better than the ordinary. But Americans have a psychosis about being different. They do not want anyone to be different. It is a miracle that Nixon has won. He is different. But he allows too loud the voices of the sameness–the bureaus are the sameness. And now worse than the bureaus are the students. They are the sameness. They mass. They yell. They act as a herd. They give collective chants. They give orders."

"Not orders. Protests. It's our Constitution, Your Majesty. They have the freedom to protest."

"Protest, yes. Students here are not suppressed but they would not do what your students do, and your students are called intellects. They are not intellects. How can they be intellects with such little experience? They act in sameness. You need to define intellect in your country."

Again the walkie-talkie signaled with static and a tone and the same woman's voice. The king said something to her in Thai and smiled at Moose. "The queen is getting impatient. She likes to see to it that I get my rest."

"If I were you, Your Majesty, I would obey."

The king laughed. "Do you wish to have breakfast here tomorrow?"

"Thank you, Your Majesty. I would like that very much but I'm taking an early plane. I finished all the briefings today at the embassy and I'm off in the early morning."

"To Hong Kong?"

"Laos."

"Oh. Laos. Ah, Laos. The Land of a Million Elephants. That's what it is called, you know: Lanxiang."

Moose nodded. "I will have to have an early breakfast at your airport here before I leave."

"You will not like that."

"Why not?"

"We have lizards on the wall of the restaurant there. The big ones are Gekees. They make noises saying 'Gekee!' Americans sit and watch them and then the Americans can't eat."

"I've seen them! The first time I saw them I thought it was a design on the wallpaper. Then they moved."

The king laughed again. "Yes, they move. But that is good because they eat the insects, and that keeps the insects from getting in your food. I noticed you looked in your soup this evening. Were there insects there?"

"Oh, no. Not at all. None."

"I saw you look for them. Americans cannot tolerate insects in their food. There is a way you can get over that, that I must tell you."

Moose nodded. "Please. But it doesn't bother me."

"As soon as your food is placed before you, sprinkle it heavily with black pepper. Then you can't tell what is pepper and what is insect!"

Now Moose laughed. "I'll do it tomorrow morning at your airport."

"Instantly, when it is placed before you. Don't look at it beforehand. Now, you must tell me when you are coming back to Bangkok. And you must please give my very best to your president. When it is right, I would like to see your contingencies for Thailand. And I hope your friend who is imprisoned by the North Vietnamese is all right. What is his name?"

"Valadovich. Major Jonas Valadovich."

"Ah yes, all names are American names, aren't they?"

"You're right. Every name is an American name if the person wants it to be."

"That is different. There is no country like yours, Mr. Dunston. It is different. It must remain different. I appreciate its differences and its greatness. The people of the world appreciate your country."

"That is so good to hear from you, Your Majesty."

"That is—not all governments appreciate it—but the people appreciate it."

Ambassador Godley was slumped in his living room chair in one of the only residences that had air conditioning in Vientiane, the capital city of Laos. His cigar wasn't lit but it was amply chewed. He gave it one big chew, then took it out of his mouth, the tip of the cigar black and wet. "What's your contingency, Dunston, when we lose the war?"

"I don't have a contingency for that."

"Write one. The foreign service is coming out from under the covers. They tolerated LBJ because he was from the 'real' political party, as their brains believe, and they liked what he was doing domestically. But Nixon? They're screwing him. The most dangerous enemy isn't the Viet Cong next door to us from Vietnam, it isn't the V.C. across our border in Cambodia either, and it isn't the Pathet Lao here. They're chicken feed. It's our own foreign service people who are the tough ones. A press attaché here, Charles Mudge, a thirty-seven year old punk who thinks he knows more than the president about foreign affairs, is one of the foreign service officers I inherited. He came here just a little before I did from his last post that he screwed up in Casablanca."

"What does he do here?"

"Nothing now. He was our press attaché. Took care of the press. He isn't here any more. That's because he took care of the press and didn't take care of the United States. I'll give you an example, and it's just one example. Ted Murphy was coming here to poke around for television and I told Mudge I didn't want Murphy in our embassy. I told him our embassy is off-limits to that scum. That's the way I put it to Mudge. Mudge tells Murphy what I said and Murphy puts it on television as if I'm a tyrant who insults anyone who disagrees with what we're doing here. What Mudge didn't tell is why I called Murphy a scum. Murphy had said, on television, that an American civilian was waging a secret war here in Laos, involved with Air America. It was a lie. That civilian wasn't with Air America."

Moose was nodding with passion. "I know all about it. A lot about it."

"Was the guy CIA?"

Moose didn't answer, which was an answer. "He was a good man. I knew him well. A very dedicated man. He was trying to find a POW, in fact a POW who's a close friend. Mister Ambassador, in fact–" He was about to tell the Ambassador about his own pursuit to find Jonas, but he was interrupted.

"All right then, all right. Then you know well. And then you can see what kind of a man Murphy is. So I call Murphy a scum to Mudge. So now Senator Fulbright wants to have me in open hearings. Fulbright's angry. Mudge just resigned. But it's not good-riddance. It's what LBJ used to say; that it's better to have the enemy staying inside spitting out, rather than having him outside spitting in–he said something like that. Mudge is outside now, spitting in. He and his wife are staying in Vientiane and he's writing a book–against U.S. policy. He took all kinds of papers with him. He doesn't like me because I'm not a careerist, I'm an appointee. That's no good to him. He couldn't do more for the P.L. and the V.C. if he were working for them. If I were North Vietnam's General Giap, I'd put Mudge on the payroll."

"Before I forget, Mr. Ambassador, the president gave me a note to give you."

"He did?"

Moose took the envelope out of his breast pocket.

Ambassador Godley put the cigar back in his mouth and chewed it repeatedly as he opened the envelope and read the note. He didn't seem pleased by what he read. He took the cigar from his mouth. "Look, Dick Nixon's my friend. But I don't get what's going on here. There's something no one's telling me. The Red Chinese are building a road right into Laos; it will intersect with the one that goes from here to Dien Bien Phu. We should strike it, but he says we won't do that. I've been told before, when I pleaded with his boys to strike it, I've been told by Rogers and Kissinger and Laird that we don't want to provoke Peking. Why not? Do we want them to have a road directly in here? The Communists, the P.L.—the Pathet Lao, already holds two-thirds of the territory in this country—give Peking a completed road and they'll have the other third. In this note—Dick says we won't strike the road."

Moose felt he should try to explain the president's position but he didn't know exactly what the president wrote. He could now see the value in asking the president if he could read the messages he delivers for the president. "The president was very complimentary about you to me," Moose said to the ambassador.

"We're friends. He knows what he's doing, I don't doubt that. But something's funny here. Maybe he has some master plan with China that I don't know about. In the meantime the V.C. see the ARVN or the U.S. coming, and they run into Cambodia and we stop our troops from going in there and getting them. It doesn't make any sense. I'm glad we're finally bombing but we can't turn back on the ground forever. Do you know what they have in Fishhook—that Fishhook area of Cambodia? They have a facility there they call COSVN, meaning the Central Office for South Vietnam. It's a city. It's the North Vietnamese Headquarters. I'll tell you, if I were the North Vietnamese, if I was General Giap, you know what I'd do?" He put the cigar back in his mouth and this time he lit it. He took it back from his lips and examined its lit end admiringly. "I'd wait for that road from China to be completed, then I'd get out of Laos entirely. Take the P.L. out of here and have them mass on Cambodia and South Vietnam. Combine the forces of the P.L. and their own forces and screw us in Cambodia and South Vietnam. Then they could come back and take this place whenever they want."

"You mind if I write some of this down—to report what you're saying?"

"Go ahead. Figure out a contingency for that one. Dick knows how I feel. So do all his experts in Washington who play in the big boy's sandbox."

Moose made some fast notes on a folded piece of paper he took from his pants pocket.

"Is that your notebook, Dunston?"

"It's all right."

"Want a notebook?"

"No. No thanks, I'm fine."

"You smoke cee-gars?"

"No. No thanks. I smoke a pipe."

"Well, go ahead."

"No. I left it at the hotel. When I travel I have trouble carrying around all the pipe-smoking accessories—just too much stuff in my pockets, so I go without it at meetings and wait for the hotel."

"You should try cee-gars. This is the kind Churchill smoked some time. Partagas."

"Thanks. No thanks."

"What else can I tell you, Dunston?"

"How I get my friend out of a North Vietnam prison. Sontay. Someone in Bangkok told me to see Ross Perot."

"No. Don't do that. Perot's all right. He's on our side all right. But some say he's a loose cannon. Why don't you talk to some of the Air America boys? You know how we work Air America, don't you? We only hire civilians to fly those planes, so no one can say they're under military orders. Anyone can hire them to fly wherever they want to go. They'll jump. They'll rescue. Some of them will do anything if it will help our boys. It's our version of the French Foreign Legion except they're good guys. They're not mercenaries. They believe in something."

"Have they ever rescued prisoners? No one in D.C. gives me an answer to that."

"If you were a journalist they'd answer. Your problem is that you work for the president so no one tells you anything."

"Have they rescued anyone?"

"They've rescued, but not from North Vietnam. Look, your pilot tomorrow is a real daredevil. You can ask him. His name is Candy, believe it or not. He'll be your pilot on your flight tomorrow to Cambodia."

"Good."

"Don't expect an airliner with stewardesses. You'll be sitting with him, just like you're the co-pilot."

"That's fine."

"Not that the airliners here are much better. Royal Air Laos claim to luxury is that they pass out cotton to put in your ears. They're about twenty years behind the times. So since you won't be taking Royal Air Laos tomorrow, bring your own cotton. En route he's going to stop off in Samket. I've lined up a military briefing for you there. Standard stuff. You'll get the lay of the land. And then for the hairy stuff, you'll land near Long Tien in the Plain of Jars. Don't look for Long Tien on a map. We don't put it there because officially it doesn't exist. You know who runs it, don't you?"

"The Agency."

"You got it. Just north of there—I mean a couple kilometers north of there are the P.L. in caves. Thousands of them. And your plane will be dropping off some rice near the border. We do that every day. Not for the P.L. of course. We're feeding 250,000 refugees up there—refugees who got away from the P.L. Do you think that'll ever make the news back home? That's a story Murphy and his ilk have thrown away. They like exposing secret wars without thinking about why they're secret. They're not interested in secret humanitarian aid, are they?"

"You think the pilot can stage a rescue in North Vietnam?"

"No idea. You talk to Candy. If anyone can do it, he's your man. Look, have you seen the city here? You didn't bring your wife along did you?"

Again? "I'm not married, Mr. Ambassador."

"Too bad. In your line of work you should be. I'd go nuts here without my wife. Women can keep you from going nuts in a place like this. She finds Vientiane colorful. And she's more gung-ho than I am. She's wonderful. Did you see this city?"

"No. That's okay."

"You probably saw it and didn't know it. When you came here from the airport, you must have been looking the other way for fifteen seconds. Did you pass a Wat? One of those religious shrines?"

"I did. Three of them."

"That's it. That's the city. It's just a few blocks. It's like an Asian Dodge City except we have a couple of movie houses here. You been to your hotel yet?"

"Not yet."

"You'll love the hotel!" And he laughed. "I think the P.L. probably operates it, though, so be careful. But that's the way it is here."

At the Hotel Lane Xang there was an immense cockroach in the bathtub of Moose's bathroom. The people were small and friendly, the roaches were neither small nor friendly. It was much too big for Moose to kill with a shoe; he'd need a gun or a gallows or the electric chair. Moose let the cockroach have the bathroom. He turned off the bathroom light to make the cockroach happy, closed the door for its privacy, and he left the lights on in the main room so the cockroach wouldn't want to unlock the door, open it, and come in. In the morning Moose quickly dressed, grabbed his bags, and went to the bathroom at the Embassy to take a shower, never mind that the water came out purple, then turned pink. He brushed his teeth with bottled water.

Candy, the Air America pilot who looked nothing like someone who would be named Candy, said he wouldn't rescue anyone from the Sontay prison if he was given a million dollars, unless the president of the United States, himself, asked him to do it. "And even then," Candy said, "I would advice him against it. But if I couldn't talk him out of it—then, I'd say, 'yes sir,' and do it for nothing." He said that Ross Perot would be too risky for Moose to enlist or approach since Moose worked for the U.S. government. "Ross might do it, but if it failed, Nixon would have to answer for it, not you." Candy then went on to tell Moose about tortures beyond imagination that are routinely given to U.S. prisoners by the North Vietnamese.

When Moose reached Cambodia's capital city of Phnom Penh, he saw a city with wooden encampments with slits for the barrels of a gun on each street corner, and with cannons facing the river. Soldiers with guns and bayonets in position were everywhere. But worse than all that for Moose was that the U.S. Embassy had booked him into the Le Royal Hotel which was the headquarters of the U.S. Press Corps of 35 correspondents, and the U.S. Embassy had lined up a breakfast for him with Ted Murphy.

The breakfast room at the Le Royal was bright and pleasant and Moose observed the advice of King Bhumibol Adulyadej by pouring black pepper over his eggs quickly before looking at them. Unnecessary. The bug was in the coffee.

"You don't like me much, do you, Dunston?" Ted Murphy asked.

"It's closer to hatred."

"The business with Orr? I didn't kill him y'know."

"I can't talk, Murphy. I represent the president and whatever I say can be used against him. I know what you'll quote and won't quote on television, so I'm shutting up. Some day when I represent myself I'll tell you—or show you what I think of you. As a hint, I believe in an eye for an eye. Fair enough?"

"Fair enough, Dunston. You havin' a good time in Cambodia?"

"Great."

"Whatcha doin' here?"

"Eating eggs."

"Dump the First Amendment, huh? Don't tell the people nothin', huh? You're not a very good representative of the president the way you're treatin' freedom of the press as if it was some poison. If you don't like the First Amendment, you better let the people know."

"You guys think our founders gathered in Philadelphia to write the First Amendment alone, and then hurriedly dashed off the Preamble, seven articles and nine other amendments as some bothersome afterthoughts, don't you? Some day you ought to read the whole thing."

"I just thought I'd be a good guy and invite you to breakfast. I'm buyin'. I call it Operation Breakfast. You don't seem very appreciative."

Luckily Moose was looking down at his eggs thinking he saw one of the pieces of pepper move when Ted had used the expression, 'Operation Breakfast.' That was the Department of Defense's secret designation of the first bombing of the Viet Cong encampments in the eastern section of Cambodia.

Ted Murphy waited for a reaction and there wasn't any. All Murphy was doing was showing off that he knew the code. "Did ya hear what I said?"

"Yes, I heard you. Do you think I'm going to be appreciative for eggs and coffee? I'll pay for my own."

"And toast. Orange juice too, if you want it. That's just part of the menu, Dunston. It's a big menu here, ya know." "Menu" was the code name for the entire bombing policy of which "Operation Breakfast" was only the first part. Ted Murphy was continuing to let Moose know he was no amateur in investigative reporting.

"What kind of conversation is this, Murphy?"

"What's your plan, your contingency if the secret bombin' of this country doesn't work? You gonna invade this country?"

"No need for a contingency. The bombing did work."

"The secret bombin' you mean. Isn't that what it was–or is?"

"It was secret for good reason till you guys got hold of it."

"Till I got hold of it."

"What do you want, the credit or the blame?"

"The credit. I got it before *The New York Times* did. And I reported that even Rogers and Laird didn't want this place to be bombed. Why did Nixon do it? Off the record."

"No. On the record. I don't talk off the record. On the record, two years ago, before President Nixon was president, Prince Sihanouk wanted the North Vietnamese and the Viet Cong out of this place and asked LBJ to either chase them out of here in hot pursuit, or bomb their encampments. He wanted this place to be neutral, not a privileged sanctuary for the V.C. When we came in office there were 40,000 V.C. here in Cambodia in an area about ten or fifteen miles wide, right at the border where they'd run from Vietnam across the border and then they'd go back and forth. That was their safe haven here, a privileged sanctuary, because we wouldn't touch it. Well, now we touched it and since we bombed it we've saved thousands of American and South Vietnamese lives. But I don't expect you to report that."

"Why didn't you tell the American people you were bombin'?"

"There's no wall that separates the American people from the people of the world. If we told Americans, we'd have been telling Ho Chi Minh and Mao Tse-tung at the same time. Do you think Prince Sihanouk here would have wanted it made public? How do you think China would have reacted to him on that one? We couldn't put him on the spot. Anyway, Sihanouk is out of here now, so I don't care if everyone knows now. But we had to keep it secret then. Why we did it will remain a secret, not because we want it to be one, but because you and your cohorts won't let that one out to the American people."

"And you had to keep it secret from the Congress?"

"We told the leaders of the Senate Armed Services Committee–Richard Russell and John Stennis. Ask them. They said to do it. If we told the whole Congress it would have leaked in a minute. And it still leaked, anyway. Where did you get the leak, Murphy? From Laird?

"No comment, Dunston. You guys have secrets and I have secrets. But I do it to protect my sources. You do it to protect your rear end."

"The rear end of our troops. You want 150,000 V.C. able to re-arm and be safe in a privileged sanctuary? You guys get me."

"They're still there. Maybe you killed a few thousand, but the P.L. didn't run away. Don't you know they're at Fishhook and Parrot's Beak? You gonna invade? Is that what you're goin' to talk to Major Am Rong about today? Don't be late for your appointment, Dunston. I think this city needs a quick contingency plan for evacuation—from the Washington invaders."

"Can I answer your questions off the record?"

"Total. I promise."

Moose did something he hadn't done since high school. But it came as naturally as a habit of life. He gave a gesture with an extended middle finger of his right hand, and simultaneously said a phrase he rarely used.

When the U.S. Embassy briefings for Moose were done and the sun was down and Phnom Penh was quiet and dark and nervous, Moose lay awake not thinking at all about Murphy or about Phnom Penh or about tomorrow's visit to Saigon, but about his impatience for next Friday when he would once again be in Hong Kong. The thought kept him sane. As president Nixon had said, this would be the dessert. He sat up in bed before dawn on the day he would leave Phnom Penh to Saigon. Moose propped the pillow between the wall and his head and packed his pipe and lit it while planning the phone call he would make to Hong Kong from Saigon on the following day. He knew that Wai-yee always arrived at the Consulate in Hong Kong at eight o'clock in the morning. Tomorrow morning he would have the Embassy in Saigon connect him with Wai-yee at 8:45. That was the minute that Adam had told him was the only time for a man to propose marriage.

"Because," Adam had said, "you can think clearly then, unburdened by midnight and the tempting hours. If there was a law that men could only ask women to marry them at 8:45 in the morning there would hardly be any marriages. Men have their senses then."

Leaning his head on the pillow, Moose stared at the ceiling and said, "Adam, I'll have my senses then. And I'll do it. Good advice, my friend. See? What you said still makes a difference. You're the kind the king was taking about. You're different."

He flew to Saigon in the afternoon, attended Embassy briefings and heard more horror stories of Viet Cong atrocities. It was the first time he was there since the captivity of Jonas and the death of Adam, and now Saigon took on an atmosphere that was more painful than ever.

He couldn't look at the gate to the old Embassy where he knew Adam's body had been delivered.

There was a new plaque there that read, "In memory of the brave men who died January 31, 1968, defending this Embassy against the Viet Cong." He felt the presence of both Adam and Jonas everywhere. He couldn't bear to go to the Bachelor Officers' Quarters where he and Jonas had first hosted Adam and his cat. Now Adam was gone and Moose knew that somewhere north of here was Jonas in a cell.

He went to his room at the Majestic Hotel where he spent an evening of turning and tossing awaiting the morning.

He was at the Embassy embarrassingly early. With nervousness and anticipation, he called Wai-yee.

Wai-yee's voice was filled with excitement. "Oh, Moose, it won't be like before for you in Hong Kong. They know that you're very close to the president. You have an appointment with Consul General Osborn at ten o'clock, and lunch with Governor Trench, then meetings he's set up with a bunch of British officials, then a meeting with Run Run Shaw, and a reception and a party for you at the consul general's home. Everyone is very excited that you're coming here—and—and—I don't think you'll have any time to see me at all!"

"Honey, please cancel everything after the Run Run Shaw meeting. I don't want a reception and party and all that. I want to be with you."

"What do I tell them?"

"Tell them I'm tired. Tell them anything. Tell them I have syphilis." That isn't something he normally would have said. He felt more and more, that Adam was coaching him.

But not entirely. Could Adam possibly be coaching him to ask her to marry him? "Honey, it's 8:44 isn't it?"

There was a short silence. "No. It's 9:46."

"What?"

"It's 9:46, why?"

"I have 8:44."

"Oh, I see. That's because we're an hour ahead of Vietnam."

"You are?"

"Sure."

"Well, you're not an hour and two minutes ahead of Vietnam!"

"One of us is two minutes wrong, that's all. I think my watch is a little fast. Why is that important, honey?"

"It isn't. It isn't. I was just wondering." He couldn't think fast enough to establish whether he should propose when it's 8:45 his time or her time. Of course it was his time but he couldn't think it out in his frenzy. "Look, I'll meet you tomorrow morning on the Peak at eight o'clock in the morning, is that okay?" It would be better to ask her in person, anyway.

"Sure. I have to be at the consulate at eight o'clock but I'm sure I can get off—to see you. You're very important now! But can't I pick you up at Kai Tak tonight?"

"No. I'm going to be in too late. It'll be after midnight. I have to fly from here back to Bangkok and then to Hong Kong and I'm going to have to sit around the Bangkok airport for hours. It will be very late, I'm supposed to get in at 12:35."

"The consulate booked you at the Hilton you know."

"I know."

"We have a suite this time."

"Really?" *Did she say* we *have a suite?*

"Moose, I don't want to wait until the morning. Do you?"

"You want to meet me at the hotel?"

"I want to meet you at Kai Tak."

"And wait around that airport all night if the plane's late?"

"Sure I do."

"If you really want to."

"I really want."

"Okay, that's—that's great. I'll give you the flight number and all of that. Wait a minute."

"I have it. I have as much information about your travel as you do. Washington sent us your itinerary. You're very important now to everyone here, not just to me anymore. You have a black passport now, don't you?"

"I do."

"That's why I like you!"

"That's the reason?"

"Sure." And she giggled and he could imagine her cocking her head and putting her hand in front of her mouth, and her long black hair falling over one shoulder from the cocking of her head. "Oh, maybe there are some other things about you, but I can't think of any. No, honey. It's the black passport."

One more day—then Hong Kong.

Adam was having the time of his life or, more accurately, of his death. He was absolutely ecstatic watching Moose and Wai-yee in Hong Kong. First, as a Peeping Tom he couldn't have been more excited if he was alive as he watched the two of them that night at the suite in the Hilton. But the prize of all was what happened the next morning on the Peak.

Following Adam's advice, at exactly 8:45 in the morning Moose asked Wai-yee to marry him. But then came the unexpected for which Moose was totally unprepared. After they embraced and kissed, with tears from her eyes running on his shoulders and tears from his eyes running on her shoulders, she said, "No, Moose. I have waited for that for ten years. But we cannot."

Adam was never happier. Fortunately, as a dead man, his laughter couldn't be heard.

Wai-yee, who was as mature as anyone three times her age, said she couldn't marry him because she would never abandon Hong Kong and she wouldn't expect him to leave the United States for her, yet there was no reason they couldn't continue to love each other, and distance could not take that love away. "This is not your typical woman," Adam whispered to Moose.

"I am Chinese," she said, "and my hope is to see a free China when Mao dies. And if the British leave in 1997 and the Government of a free China takes over, Hong Kong will be home again—as free as it is now, and as Chinese as it should be. I must be part of that. And if it works out poorly, if China still has the same kind of government it has today, then there is even more reason why I must be here. When I needed Hong Kong as a little girl, it was here for me. As a woman, I must be here for Hong Kong if it needs me. I cannot abandon. And you, Moose, must stay with your president who has faith in you, and you must always think of your country first as I do mine."

Adam loved it. He was rolling on the clouds, or whatever he was rolling on.

Adam watched them throughout the trip as they made conversation, as she explained again and again why they couldn't marry, and as they made love.

And then when Moose was flying back to Washington, Adam nudged him from his sleep. "Hey, Man," Adam said, "you couldn't ask for anything better. You asked her and she said 'no,' and you still have her love and sex and all that. I never would have had such luck, man. Congratulations!"

Moose closed his eyes again. He didn't know what woke him. But he was smiling.

TWENTY-SEVEN
CRISIS MORNING
1970

No one has to announce anything.

There is something in the air unrecognized by visitors, but familiar to every Washington resident.

A White House spokesman behind the Press Room podium can only confirm or deny or head off speculation by spelling it out, but the air itself is the press secretary of crisis, and its podium is the city.

That spring morning in 1970, the air announced it before dawn and that was when a lone figure came down the block to the black iron fence on the Pennsylvania Avenue side of the White House, and he stood there waiting. A few minutes later there was a young man with a girl, both in cut-off Levi's. Then there was another young man and then another. By five-thirty in the morning, there were nine people standing and waiting, unsure of what they were waiting for, but it was important. The vigil had begun.

In the past, the vigil-keepers had stood even in snow and even in heat waiting; just waiting for nothing in particular. At least this Thursday morning at the end of April the weather was good. Like other times, it didn't matter that there was nothing to see. They had stood out there during the Cuban Missile Crisis, and they stood out there after President Kennedy was assassinated. There was a blind man standing out there most of the Saturday night on which President Kennedy's body was in the East Room of the White House. The blind man was at the black-spoked fence, those sightless eyes piercing the mansion. He just wanted to be there the same way a person would want to be near a friend when the friend was in need. And there were those who stood out there every time there was a new chapter in the Vietnam war.

The tenth figure of the morning came carrying a placard. He was not there only to touch importance but to take part in it. Instead of standing by the fence, he stood closer to the edge of the sidewalk by the avenue and held his placard to face the oncoming automobiles. "Honk Twice If You Want Him Impeached" it read. There wasn't much traffic yet, just stray cars. But one of them honked twice and the man by the edge of the sidewalk raised and lowered his placard in a signal of acknowledgment.

President Nixon had changed the designation of the "mansion" to the "residence," and the Executive Office Building of the White House Compound was now called the Old Executive Office Building since a new one had been built across Pennsylvania Avenue, up 17th Street. A lot of things were changing in Washington.

Inside the Old Executive Office Building that Thursday morning, the long palatial hallways were barren except for a small figure making loud echoing footsteps on the black and white checkered horizonless floor. The figure was that of a middle-aged woman holding papers in her hands. She walked the long stretch of the east hall from her office and then she disappeared beneath the polished brown banister of the winding staircase to the basement. She was en route to the West Wing. Minutes later she reappeared above the banister without the papers, going back toward her office which adjoined the office of her boss, the president's chief speech writer.

S. Sylvan Sullivan was on his way back from the men's room when he saw her in the hallway returning to her office. He had already seen the figures at the fence and he was an expert on the meaning of vigil-keepers. "Hi, early-riser!"

"Hi, Sy." She was an old-timer who felt comfortable in calling him by a name that was reserved only for the use of those who had been in service with him during the Eisenhower Administration.

"You're here awful early, Margaret."

"You mean late!"

"Oh, really? You've been working all night?"

She nodded. "You're here early, Sy."

"I had some work to do."

She gave her confidential smile. "Busy times."

"Not talking, huh?"

"Busy. Just busy." No one ever got much out of her.

"A big one?"

"My fingers just type the letters, Sy. They don't think. Q-W-E-R-T-Y-U-I-O-P."

"I read you, Margaret!" S. Sylvan Sullivan knew enough not to prod her further.

She entered her office and then came back out again while he was still walking down the hall.

"Sy?" she called after him.

He turned around quickly. "Yes?"

"I can tell you one thing."

"What?"

"It has nothing to do with Sherman Adams." That was a reminder of how long they had known each other throughout the years of Ike.

"Yeah," he answered. "Thanks for the information." He walked into his office. And it was truly his office. He had refurbished it to look exactly as it did when he was there during the Eisenhower Administration, with no evidence of the eight-year intermission that started with the takeover by Cody Cooper.

S. Sylvan Sullivan was confident that whatever Margaret had been typing for the president from the longhand notes of her boss, would set the record straight and the White House would get back to normal.

Moose, back from his Southeast Asian tour, was sitting at a table in the

White House Mess with Dick Moore very early in the morning, while all the other tables were vacant.

Dick Moore was the White House sage. That wasn't his title. His official position was special counsel to the president but that title wasn't worthy of the unofficial wisdom that he provided. He was a few years younger than the president but looked like he could be his father. For that matter, he looked like he could be everyone's father or grandfather, it was the way God made him; age had nothing to do with it. He had gray hair, generally in a crew-cut, or at least very short. He was big and lumbering and took up a lot of room, jostling side–to–side when he walked. His face was generally red, filled with humor even in bad times, and his kind, Irish eyes always sparkled beneath drooping eyelids. He had an old man's habit of often stumbling over his words when he was thinking deeply, but that was because he was thinking so hard that the words had difficulty keeping up with those things his mind was imagining. Dick Moore was the man every assistant to the president would visit for advice. Too bad that some of them didn't accept his advice, once given.

His reputation had been confirmed almost six months ago by an act that other Nixon aides at the White House would not perform. That act emblazoned his bravery forever within the White House. During the first week of the Nixon administration, the White House archivist presented President Nixon a book that listed White House possessions he could use as president. One of the items in storage in the sub-basement of the White House was the Wilson Desk. As an admirer of Woodrow Wilson, he asked to see it. When he saw it, he asked for it to be placed in the Oval Office as his desk rather than the one he inherited from LBJ. It was done immediately. Later, when the archivist learned that President Nixon thought it was Woodrow Wilson's desk, he told a small number of people on the president's staff that it was not the desk of President Woodrow Wilson, but the desk of Vice President Henry Wilson during President Ulysses S. Grant's second term.

Some of President Nixon's aides didn't tell him because they were scared to do it, and others didn't tell him because they thought he should simply enjoy it and his error in identification didn't make any difference. Ten months later, in his most important televised speech to the nation given to that date (November 3, 1969) when he publicly announced the policy of replacing American troops in Vietnam with trained and supplied South Vietnamese, (Vietnamization) and he first used the phrase "the Silent Majority," he added, "Fifty years ago, in this room and at this very desk, President Woodrow Wilson spoke words which caught the imagination of a war-weary world. He said, 'This is the war to end all wars.'" It was Dick Moore who, the next morning, felt the president's false identity of the desk could not go on, and he had the unprecedented courage to tell the president that he was mistaken about the desk, and that it was used only by Vice President Henry Wilson.

The president was not pleased.

Dick Moore changed the subject quickly to the effectiveness of the president's speech. But the president was thinking, *Henry Wilson?*

Dick Moore became the White House hero as well as the White House sage.

"When you walked in," Moose said, "did I see right? Are you wearing new shoes?"

"Yes," Dick Moore answered. "That's the good news."

Moose laughed.

One of the Philippine stewards dressed in a maroon jacket emblazoned with the presidential seal approached Dick Moore and Moose. "You're here early, gentlemen."

"I'm not awake yet," Dick said, and Moose grunted.

"You want coffee?" the steward asked.

"Please. Right away for both of us," Moose said.

"Pronto," the steward nodded and in no time he came back with two coffees and two small blue menus, each with a gold-colored tassel hanging down its stapled side. "Menus, gentlemen?"

"Not for me," Moose said. "Scrambled eggs and bacon."

Dick said, "The same, Ernesto, and make my bacon crisp, please if you would. Just burn it black, I don't care."

"Yes, sir. It's too early for you, sir." The steward was hoping one of them would volunteer some explanation of why they were at work that early, but he wouldn't think of asking. "Awful early, gentlemen."

After the steward disappeared into the kitchen, Dick leaned over toward Moose. "The president didn't get any sleep last night, you know."

"I know. Neither did I. Who else did he call? Do you know?"

"I don't know, but I know what he's going to say tonight."

Moose nodded. "Same here. And I'm all for it."

Dick nodded. "I knew you'd agree with it. You probably recommended it." And he laughed.

"We got to do this. This will be the most important speech since last November when you told him about the Wilson desk."

Dick threw back his head and laughed. Then he shook his head. The laughing was done. "Did you see the demonstrators out there already? And they don't even know what he's going to say yet. Wait until tomorrow. Just wait," and he shook his head again. "There will be a demonstration ten times as big."

"I hope you're wrong, Dick, but I think you're right. I didn't give any thought to what the reaction of the kids would be and the reaction of the press. Maybe I should have. I was agreeing with him, thinking solely about winning this war."

"That's what we have to do, you don't make policy to please students, or the press."

"We could. We could surrender."

Dick gave a "Hrumph," and then said, "I just wish that the president—I wish he—" and he paused, hesitant to continue his sentence.

"What?"

"I wish he could be on television the way he is when he's with you or me, one-on-one. But he gets that–when he's on television he feels he's talking to 200 million Americans instead of one American. See? Kennedy was good at looking at that camera and seeing it as just one person. FDR did it on the radio with his voice. One American, that's all. One at a time. I wish he could just imagine he's talking to Julie or Tricia."

"Did you ever suggest that to him? To have Julie or Tricia next to the camera?"

Dick nodded. "He looked away from me. You know how he does that. He doesn't want to hear it. You know, he never looks at a tape of himself on television. Never. He has yet to see the debates he did with Kennedy. He–he–you develop habits when you're on television that you can only correct if you watch yourself. He won't do it. You know what he does on television? Instead of moving his head, he moves his eyes, and that looks shifty. He's in a big close-up on that television screen and if he moves his eyes from left to right or right to left, his eyeballs sweep across the whole screen. You got to move your head if you want to look around on television. I wish he'd just watch himself sometime. He's just the opposite of LBJ. He always watched himself. You could only photograph him from his left side. Even when he talked to a joint session of the Congress he faked it so the cameras got his left side. RN doesn't care how you photograph him. But both of them thought of an audience of millions. That doesn't work with the people."

"So what do we do about it?"

"Oh, we take it. I'm just worried about–about tonight's speech. I'm not worried about what he'll say tonight, I'm worried about the presentation. JFK could be in that Oval Office and give a speech saying we're going to use the bomb on Moscow and Peking and Havana and Hanoi and East Berlin–and–and Acapulco, and people at home would be applauding. He knew that camera was one person."

Another change at the White House was that President Nixon had given the White House press corps a place of their own rather than the West Wing Reception Room where they used to wait for a briefing in the press secretary's office. Their new privacy, with a large room for briefings and small nooks for each of them, was constructed over what used to be the White House swimming pool. That Thursday morning their new room was quickly becoming filled with the members of the White House press corps who weren't supposed to be there until hours later. No one had asked them to come this early but they had felt it, just like so many others in D.C.

"What do you hear?" the correspondent from a mid-west syndicate asked the open-vested fat man with a big black cigar who represented an eastern newspaper. He was slouched down on his chair.

"I hear the president jumped off the top of the Washington Monument with three Pakistani children and a dog on his shoulders. You can have the story. I'm not using it. I'm holding out for better stuff."

"Come on, come on. What do you hear?"

"I'm not kidding."

"How can you smoke one of those smelly things for breakfast?"

"I don't like the smell of Corn Flakes."

"You know that NBC is setting up on the North Lawn for a stand-up?"

"That don't mean a piece of fudge. They'll get their slick-haired Mister Charming out there telling the whole world that he's standing outside the White House waiting. That Mister Pretty-Boy can make a three-minute story out of the fact that he doesn't know anything."

"I think NBC does know something."

"The TV boys know less than we know. You know who's the only bright one? Murphy. And that's because he was a print journalist—and he's not a pretty boy. And he's getting the good assignments. He's in Southeast Asia now where the real story is. The story isn't here anymore."

"It's here. There's a rumor that Nixon's going to give a speech."

"Rumor? Of course he's going to give a speech. When the light in his EOB office is on all night and that chick toddles back and forth across West Executive Avenue all morning, then Mr. Big is going to give a speech."

"You've been watching the building all night?"

"When you see that red-headed kid come out of the EOB rolling a moth-eaten blue curtain to go behind the president's head, you know he's going to give a speech."

"Then you do know."

"Know what? So the president is going to give a speech. Big deal. It's probably Tricky Dick saying we've invaded Cambodia. Big deal. We heard that days ago from our buddies in Saigon. So Mr. Tricky's going to tell us and ask for support. Big Deal. So what?"

"He better not wait until prime-time to do it or we'll be up the whole night writing about it."

"Ziegler may give us an advance. Then we can write our stories early and get out of here."

"Take a look out there," the correspondent said, moving his head toward the window.

"What's out there?"

"There must be twenty or more people standing out there by the fence."

"They have placards?"

"Some do. Take a look."

"What do they say? Get out of Vietnam or get out of NATO or get out of Puerto Rico? Or is that nut still out there who's parading around who knows 'the truth' about the Kennedy assassination?"

"I can't read them from here. They're facing the street."

"They probably say: Make marijuana legal. Investigate the assassination of Lincoln. Stop capital punishment. Free Rudolf Hess. That's it. Good causes!"

"My cause is to get a good story."

"Get Nixon out of here—that's my cause."

It was hard to tell if he was kidding or not.

Sixteen men on high-backed leather chairs sat around the great mahogany table in the windowless Roosevelt Room of the White House, while a bust of Franklin Delano Roosevelt stared across the room at a painting of Theodore Roosevelt who was looking at the live participants who were engaged in small talk, waiting to find out why they were called together earlier than usual.

During World War II the room was occupied solely by the fish of President Franklin Delano Roosevelt, swimming in a complex of aquariums, and it was called the Fish Room. Not only presidents, but fish leave the White House when their time is up, and the fish left the White House. The room was then reserved for meetings of the president's senior staff. When President Johnson came to the White House, he adorned the room with paintings and busts of FDR, because FDR was his hero of the presidency. When President Nixon came into office he had a Roosevelt who was a hero, too, but it wasn't FDR, it was Theodore, or T.R. as President Nixon called him. He had paintings and busts of Theodore Roosevelt put into the room, keeping one bust of FDR on a desk, and he called it The Roosevelt Room, honoring both Roosevelts. If there would ever be a third President Roosevelt, no one would know what to do, because the room would have an unequal balance of political parties represented, and so they would probably put the fish in there again.

The door opened and the chief of staff, Bob Haldeman, walked in. Those at the table quickly dispensed the small talk in mid-sentences. Even the grandfather clock against the wall seemed to stop ticking so it could hear what Bob Haldeman was going to say. Bob Haldeman took his place at the head of the table.

He gave them the contents of the president's Address to come, and readied them for the dissent that was sure to follow.

"Tonight," the president said to the nation, "American and South Vietnamese units will attack the headquarters for the entire Communist military operation in South Vietnam." He then went on to say that Cambodian sanctuaries in the Fishhook area, about 70 miles from Saigon, and the Parrot's Beak area, about 33 miles from Saigon, were "completely occupied and controlled by North Vietnamese forces...a vast enemy staging area and a springboard for attacks on South Vietnam...We will not allow American men by the thousands, to be killed by an enemy from a privileged sanctuary."

Within hours the protests started, and they lasted into and beyond the weekend: students from the University of Wisconsin staged a raid on a Selective Service Office; students of Stanford University in California set their buildings on fire with the work of ten visiting scholars destroyed;

the University of Maryland's R.O.T.C. building was ransacked; Yale University called a strike against all studies and urged other universities to do the same. Soon over 400 universities and colleges across the nation went on strike.

The president said, "You see these bums, you know, blowing up the campuses. Listen, the boys that are on the college campuses today are the luckiest people in the world, going to the greatest universities, and here they are burning up the books."

Ted Murphy was interviewing U.S. troops of Alpha Company in South Vietnam who were about to cross the border into Cambodia. He asked them four questions: "What are you going to do?...Do you realize what can happen to you?...Are you scared?...Do you say the morale is pretty low in Alpha Company?"

Robert Dole, who had risen from congressman to be the first-term Senator from Kansas stood in the chamber of the U.S. Senate and said, "Does freedom of the press include the right to incite mutiny?...I believe a reporter has become perilously close to attempting to incite mutiny by playing on the emotions of soldiers just before they were to go into battle...I can think of no other war in our history where this sort of thing would have been permitted."

The greatest campus tragedy took place at Kent State University in Ohio. After the R.O.T.C. building was burned down on the campus, and rocks and chunks of concrete were thrown at National Guardsmen, some guardsmen fired into the crowd.

Four students were killed.

The president had his head in his hands in his private office in the Old EOB. Kent State was the worst news of all. Was this to be the result of his decision to go into Cambodia? Death at home? The military against students? Violence? Civil war?

To the president and to many others who lived In Washington, D.C., nights and mornings were no longer divisions between going to sleep and waking up.

For the first time since he accepted the assignment, Moose doubted his own ability, with students at home having been killed. He was cursing himself for not having considered that something like this could happen. Why didn't he warn that some fool would pull a trigger at home? His job, after all, was to think "what if?"

The clock on the tower of the Old Post Office looked down at the city, knowing that it was being watched by more residents than usual at this hour. Against the night sky it was exhibiting that it was two-thirty. That was when Moose walked from his Potomac Plaza apartment to the Old Executive Office Building. Once he got there, he was as restless as he was in his apartment.

Moose stood in his high-ceilinged, blue-draped office, looking out that giant window, and he could see a few people gathering against the Pennsylvania Avenue fence to the White House grounds, even at this late or early hour. He walked from the window and sat behind his desk. On his desk was a large square of cellophane, and on top of the square of cellophane were two small stacks of tobacco. He mixed the two stacks together, just to keep himself occupied. Near his telephone was a round wooden pipe-stand with pipes in every one of the dozen slots. He grabbed the big Dunhill.

Behind him was a glass door framed by more blue drapes looking out on a balcony. The view from his office and the balcony promised more in the winter months than it revealed now in the spring. The trees were so thick with leaves that they obscured much of the North Portico of the White House. That view still gave this office one of the best outlooks in the Old EOB, and made it one of the most sought-after plums of presidential assistants in each administration.

He started stuffing the pipe bowl with small wads of mixed tobacco, and he tamped each wad into the bowl carefully and tightly with his index finger. Then he lit his pipe and puffed a few times, causing the flame to rise and lower and rise and lower and when he seemed confident that the lighting was evenly accomplished, and that enough tobacco had been caught by the fire, he shook the match out, tossed it into his brown executive ashtray and leaned back in his chair, closing his eyes. The difference between his apartment and his office was that here he was surrounded by walls and fixtures and furniture that seemed to shout at him with their experience. They had seen other days and nights of crisis and they were packed with more information than he had at his command. They were the incumbents of history and he was a new temporary inhabitant among them. He felt they knew what to do. Adam Orr's respect for the inanimate was creeping into Moose's consciousness.

Moose walked in and out of his office and in and out again and he walked through the empty hallways and then outside between the Old Executive Office Building and the West Wing. He walked on the south lawn and saw the light was on in the residence's Lincoln Sitting Room. It had to be the president who was there at what was now four o'clock in the morning.

The president looked through the window of the Lincoln Sitting Room overlooking the Washington Monument. He saw Moose pacing the lawn, and he saw some young people walking on the Ellipse beyond the White House. He turned on the phonograph and played Beethoven's Violin Concerto, very softly. Manolo Sanchez, the president's valet, hearing the music, quickly dressed and came in the Lincoln Sitting Room to see if the president was okay or wanted anything.

"Thank you, Manolo. I'm fine. Thank you for checking."

"May I get you anything, Mr. President?"

"No thank you, Manolo. I don't need anything." He walked back to the window. "The city is so beautiful, particularly at this hour. You know, the most beautiful sight in this city is the Lincoln Memorial at night, right across there. That's where the kids are going, I think."

Manolo nodded.

"You can see it right over there, but you can't feel it from here. You can't see Lincoln sitting there from here. There's a feeling inside that memorial that you can't get anywhere else. Especially at night. Don't you think so?"

Manolo looked at the president uneasily. "I have never been there at night, Mister President."

The president kept staring at the distant memorial. "You should. Let's go there now," the president said.

They did.

TWENTY-EIGHT
THE VIEW FROM DACOR HOUSE
1970

On Saturday morning, May the 9th, 1970, the streets of D.C. were filled with young people walking in groups of demonstration, which was no longer unusual for a Saturday. Some demonstrators were at Lafayette Park, some were on the Ellipse, some were outside the Justice Department, and some were walking up and down Connecticut Avenue and through the alphabetized streets.

Totally out of context with the current was a small building on H Street that was resting between a shoe store and a pizza parlor. It was an old four-level red brick building called Dacor House that had been renovated into a private club for U.S. diplomats and consular officers and for retired foreign service officers to come and pass the day with friends from other times. Long ago it had been a private residence, but that was when there were cobblers instead of shoe stores and when no one heard of pizza, and when students studied. Dacor House had largely refused to change with the times, with only the air-conditioning units that jutted out between its green shutters as its compromise with 1970.

There were two entrances, one almost underneath the other, neither one precisely at street level. The main entrance for guests required walking up a small semi-circle of stairs and the other, for members, was down an old straight stairwell of some half dozen steps which led to a musty interior corridor. It was there that the members of Dacor House kept their private lockers which housed their private bottles.

Toward the front of that downstairs area was a small parlor whose windows looked out onto H Street. Since it was a little below street level, only the legs of the passer-bys could be seen through the window, and cars could be seen passing at eye level.

For hours, each midday, Former Ambassador Gerald Fairbanks sat by the H Street window of Dacor House and watched those half-bodies pass by. His interest in the half-bodies, and his concentration on things that had never interested him in the past, came out of necessity. Those things that were truly of world interest were no longer interested in Ambassador Fairbanks.

"A marvelous sound," he would say to himself when he moved his drink back and forth. "Those ice cubes clicking and jiggling. The sound of a cold transparency!" He had become a connoisseur of details in his retirement. "Look over there!" And across the room there would be smoke swirling above another former ambassador's cigarette, the smoke in a shaft of light. "Look at the designs," he told himself. "Isn't that something?"

There would be those idle moments when he could be heard singing to himself, "You've got a lot to live while Pepsi's got a lot to give!" It was from a television commercial. "Details! See through this pane of glass? It's a window that shows all kinds of people's legs walk by and you can imagine any chest and face you want on them. They're all busy. They're all doing something. They're all going somewhere. I don't know why. But there they are moving in both directions and some are driving to get somewhere. To get where? Where is everyone going all the time? To get where the others have been."

Then, on this Saturday, there were no people at all. The street seemed vacant. There were no cars or legs passing the window. There was absolute silence that accompanied the vacancy of movement. That signaled that the police had cleared the street for a large group of demonstrators. From the distance came a chant becoming louder and louder yelled by what at least seemed to be hundreds of young voices. "Im-peach-ment! Im-peachment! Impeach Nixon! Impeach Nixon! Im-peach-ment! Im-peach-ment!" A lone voice yelled, "Do you want the U.S. in Cambodia?" The crowd yelled back, "No!" The lone voice yelled, "When do you want the U.S. out?" And the crowd answered, "Now!" "Who do we want in Cambodia?" the lone voice asked and was answered with a chorus of "Cambodians!" And then the impeachment chant started over again, either louder than before or it just appeared that way because they were closer to Dacor House.

Legs came into sight again, this time hundreds and hundreds of marching legs from right to left. They were dragging dozens of black-shrouded coffins. The chants continued, very loud. There was a sudden distant explosion that rocked the window of Dacor House, not causing it to shatter, but causing it to vibrate back and forth. The procession went on for over one half-hour. And then the legs were gone and the chant became distant.

The traffic started again and so did occasional legs walking in both directions. A pair of woman's legs stopped in front of the window, then walked a little to the left and then to the right as though she was searching for an entrance. "Here she is! Here comes Anne! That crazy girl!" Ambassador Fairbanks said to himself.

He tightened his tie, pressed down his hair, flicked his mustache, cleared his throat a couple times, and put his drink a distance away from him on the coffee table, to appear as though it wasn't his, and he quickly picked up the Washington Post to give the impression that he had been reading.

"Ambassador Fairbanks!" Anne Whitney said as she entered and she walked over to him as he stood up. She stood on her toes and kissed him on the cheek.

"Hello, Anne," he said with a weak but broad smile. "It's so good to see you." With or without the weak smile, his eyes were welcoming her.

"I'm sorry I'm late," she said, "they blocked off the street for those creeps."

"I know. It's all right. I have nothing but time."

"They bombed the National Guard Association headquarters, you know."

"Is that what the explosion was? Was anyone hurt?"

"I don't know. But the streets were closed. I'm sorry. I don't like to be late. And I know you hate excuses but, honest, the streets were blocked off."

"You don't need an excuse, Anne. To have you here means so much to me–and I have nowhere to go!"

"Well, you've retired! And I remember how much you were looking forward to it!"

Ambassador Fairbanks nodded. "I might have retired just in time. This city is going mad. Sometimes I think the world is going mad."

"I know."

"Sit down. Sit down."

They both sat facing each other, the small coffee table between them with the drink at its corner. "How's Mary?" Anne asked.

His lips lowered and he sat for a while hunting for words, and then he shook his head. "No," he said. "Mary's–gone."

"Oh, no! You mean–"

He nodded, and he cleared his throat a couple times. "She went very fast. All of it took three months. That's what it took." His eyes clouded.

"When?"

"December the Second."

"Oh, Mr. Ambassador. I'm so sorry." She leaned across the table and took both of his hands in hers.

Feeling her hands on his felt good. He closed his eyes. When he opened them, the clouded eyes had turned wet. He gave a helpless shrug. "Some times I'm all right, and then someone who doesn't know comes along–and I cave in. I don't expect it."

"I'm sorry, Mr. Ambassador. I'm sorry I did that to you."

"Oh, no. No. How could you have known? It's me that's the problem, not you. I'm lost without her, Anne."

"Oh, I know. She was so wonderful. Even to me at my worst she was so wonderful."

"I can't get a grip on things." He closed his eyes again.

"Oh, Mr. Ambassador!"

He opened his eyes and gave a forced smile. "Do you want a drink? A Coke or juice or something?"

She nodded. "Yes. A Coke. Will you have one?"

"Yes. I'll have some tomato juice. I'll get it."

"I'll get it."

"No, you can't. You have to be a member here. They have rules."

He released her hands and left to get the drinks and she sat there trying to think of some way to comfort him and she didn't know how to do it. Should she talk about Mary or talk about something else? Something else. He didn't volunteer how it happened so she wouldn't ask him. She decided to try and get his attention, at least temporarily, on something else. But when he came back with the drinks and sat down, he said, "It's life, isn't it? December the Second. Our anniversary was just one month earlier; the Second of November. It was our 45th anniversary. It used to be, when I was a boy, there were only a couple dates a year that meant anything to me. My birthday and Christmas. That was about it. The older you get, the more dates have meaning. Happy times are remembered like birthdays and anniversaries and other–happy times–the date one thing or another happened in 1958, the date that another thing happened in 1962. And there are the tragic times like–like that. If you live long enough, every date has a meaning."

"Yes. It's happening already to me, Mr. Ambassador."

"No," and he shook his head. "You've filled in just a bit of the calendar, but not so much."

There was a chant from outside. It was a chant with some words Ambassador Fairbanks was embarrassed to hear in the presence of Anne. "Can you imagine, Anne? Some day that generation out there will be running the country. I fear that day. They could destroy so much. They have no sense of morality or loyalty."

Anne nodded. "Then are you–can you–what are you doing now in your retirement? You were looking so forward to it. Are you playing golf or anything?" And she quickly realized how unimportant the word "golf" sounded. She felt she should have said "going around the world," or "meeting with foreign leaders" or even "seeing old friends," but she didn't think quick enough.

"Golf? I sit here, Anne. Mary and I dreamed of my retirement. But I get up and I get cleaned up and dressed and I come here."

"Oh, you have to do more than that! You have so much inside of you. Travel, foreign leaders, old friends." She got it in.

He shook his head, dismissing those suggestions as easily as he dismissed golf. "And you Anne? Are you the same little rebel?"

She smiled. "Oh, yes. But this time I'm not a rebel without a cause, I'm a rebel with a cause!"

"I'm afraid to ask. What's the cause this time?" She got his attention on something other than his grief.

"It's not Mao Tse-tung," she said with a laugh.

"Thank God."

"Thanks to you. You were so good in sending me to Moscow."

"I heard you did an exceptional job there, Anne."

She nodded without any modesty.

"All right then. What's the cause?"

"The president."

"Nixon?"

"No. Whitney!"

"What do you mean?"

"President Whitney, Mr. Ambassador. It won't be one of those creeps outside! It will be me! And if you're good, I'll make you my National Security Advisor! And I'll see to it that you have Hazel's Texas Chili every night!"

He laughed, a real laugh. It felt so good to laugh. It was the first laugh he had since December the Second. "Oh, my God. What does all this mean?"

"Don't panic. I'm not going to run in '72 or '76, but some day. I'm going to stay with the foreign service for a few more overseas posts, then I'm going home to Pennsylvania and run for some city office there, and then for the House of Representatives, and then for the Governor's Office or the Senate, and then I'm going to be president!"

Ambassador Fairbanks was happily surprised. "Well," he said, and he cleared his throat. "That's very good. You have a plan. I think you'll make it, Anne. I'm all for it! The first woman president of the United States!"

"I don't care about that. I want to be the best president of the United States."

"Good. Good. You're right. The best president of the United States."

"Will you be my National Security Advisor?"

He smiled and nodded. "Yes. I'll be your National Security Advisor. But why not Secretary of State?"

"I want you at the White House with me."

"All right, then."

"Besides, Mark Daschle is going to be my Secretary of State."

"Oh, that's very good. We work very well together."

"I didn't ask him yet. You're not mad, are you?—I mean that you won't be Secretary of State?"

"No. I think it's a wise choice. We'd make a good team for President Whitney! I'm pleased as punch, as ol' Hubert Humphrey would say!"

"And you know—I've been thinking. Do you know what I want you to do as my National Security Advisor?"

"What do you want me to do, Madame President?"

"I want you to help me create your idea for a new world organization of democracies!"

His tired eyes had a new warmth. "Anne!"

"The one you mentioned at the Peak in Hong Kong that I didn't understand. I've been thinking about it a lot."

"Anne! Anne! You are a wonderful girl."

"No!" This time there was a modesty. "It's your idea, not mine. Have you written anything about your idea?"

"Reams! Reams of papers. I showed them to Dag Hammarskjold and—"

"I know!"

"And U Thant. Hammarskjold seemed interested. U Thant wasn't. But you don't need any papers. I can tell you the basis of it in a few sentences. Just imagine a world organization where the only way you, as a government, can be a member is to have the rule of law in a free society—to be elected in a democratic election, to have free, fair, and frequent elections with all the institutions of a democracy: a separate judiciary, civilian control of the military, checks and balances between the executive and the legislative branches, a free press. All of it. Don't you see? The U.N. would fade into nothing because there would be no prestige in being in it. This would be a real forum for the people of the world, with no non-democratic governments invited or allowed."

"I think it's spectacular."

"There are weaknesses. Mark knows all the weaknesses. The main weakness is that there are so few democracies to begin with. Of course the idea is to give nations incentive to become democracies, but there are so few to start it off. Right now the U.N., with its membership of 126 nations, has no more than a couple dozen democracies. And we have friends—a lot of them—friendly governments that were not democratically elected. What do we do with them? We have to exclude them, don't we?"

Anne nodded. "Yes, we do." She was not as interested in what he was saying as she was in that he was saying something with enthusiasm. To see some animation in his face, and hear him talk about world affairs, was something she wanted to extend. "Like who would we exclude that you're worried about?"

"Iran, the Philippines, Practically all the Latin American states. How many are there? Thirty-five? Only four of them are democracies. Our non-democratic friends aren't totalitarians, but they aren't democracies; they're authoritarians. They permit free emigration, they even encourage it, and they aren't expansionist, those are the major differences between them and totalitarian states. Take the country you know so well—the Soviet Union—that's a totalitarianism—they keep people in, they have expansion as their policy. So you see, there are weaknesses in my idea that excludes and gives no recognition between different kinds of non-democracies. Yet you can't have some in and some out. They all must stay out. Mark thinks my idea might not work unless we have a kind of junior membership for those who promise democracy and have concrete plans for democratic institutions in, say, four or five years. If not, Mark thinks it could only work if the day comes when there are a majority of democracies in the world. You see?" He cleared his throat.

"Then we need to work on that, don't we?"

"Yes. I admire Wilson for his League of Nations. But it had totalitarians and other weaknesses. The U.N. is worse. This must have no weaknesses. In truth, the U.N. has now become a force for the Soviet Union. U Thant, as Secretary General, sponsored a symposium on Lenin, calling Lenin a man with ideals of peace and widespread international acceptance. U Thant said that Lenin's ideals were in line with the aims of the U.N. Charter! The U.N. is becoming a joke, except that it's serious. The Third World Nations are supporting the Soviets in the U.N., not because they're in love with them, but because they're afraid of them. They're not afraid of us. So with their fear and with U Thant's seal of approval of the Soviet Union, they vote with the Soviets. The U.N. has become a forum to blast away at us."

"Why doesn't Nixon make you his U.N. representative?"

Ambassador Fairbanks gave a smile, a shake of his head, and moved his left hand in the air. "No. No. Charlie Yost is fine. And Mark is there you know, not our representative, but part of the U.S. Mission there, and he fills me in. Nixon isn't going to appoint me as anything."

"Mr. Daschle is there?"

"Oh, yes."

"I didn't know, but I don't keep up with where the officers go."

"He fills me in."

"Well, just wait until I'm president and you're my N.S.C. Advisor. We're going to make your idea work!"

"I think we will!"

"Now I have to work on the rest of my Cabinet."

"Before you do that, what's your next post?"

"Oh, that. Well, I've requested to work in Africa, but I think they want me in some communist country. That's all right. I'm not fussy. I remember when I was stuck in D.C. forever! So I'll be grateful for whatever I get."

"You're a good girl, Anne. You're an exceptional girl. You're an original."

She smiled. "And I've been invited to attend next Tuesday's Director's meeting and give a report to him and all the assistant directors on the Public Affairs Officers' Conference we held in Osaka that I attended when Expo '70 opened."

Ambassador Fairbanks showed surprise. "Good for you, Anne. I didn't know you went. Will the Director, Frank Shakespeare be there?"

"I think so."

"Good. You'll like him. He's a giant. He knows more about the world and international affairs than Bill Rogers and Henry Kissinger and Mel Laird put together. You'll like him. And he likes originals. He'll like you. Now, I didn't know you went to the Expo in Osaka!"

"It was a good thing to do. I learned a lot when I was there. But they're going to learn a lot more from me when I give the report. I'm not shy, you know."

That had never been her problem. "I realize that. Mary and I were sure of that when we first met you. And that's good. Shy people don't make it to the White House, you know."

"Now, it's going to take a long time, Mr. Ambassador, before I become president I mean, so tell me what you're going to do before you come to work for me."

He smiled and shook his head. "I don't know. All through my life, my second greatest fear was growing old. Now it's come."

"No, you're not! What was your first greatest fear?"

"Not growing old!"

Anne laughed.

"You are a perfect straight-man—or straight-woman."

"So what are you going to do?"

"I just don't know."

"Well, then you have to find something you like."

"I'm too old to find something. I've passed all that."

"Ambassador Fairbanks! You're not too old for anything!"

"Oh, I am. I feel the signs."

"What signs?"

"I'll tell you one of them: when I walk down the street and I smile at a pretty woman, now she smiles back. She has no anger and no fear. They used to be angry or scared or both—and now I realize how wonderful that was. They know that now I'm harmless. I want them to walk away fast again."

Anne laughed again. "Oh, I'd be afraid of you if I saw you on a dark street! But I wouldn't walk too fast. I think I'd want you to catch me!"

"Anne, you've never been afraid of anything."

"Do you really just come here every day? You must do something else."

"Anne," and his face lost the smile, "I lost everything. It's a new life for me. It's like I died and I was reborn at this age and I have no strength for it. I have no ambition, no energy, no—no Mary. I died with her. Then all I had left was the job. At least it filled the daytime hours. The weekends were the worst. But at least the job filled the daytime hours of five days of the week and the work got me tired. That was good. I was tired enough to sleep at night. Then, even the job was taken from me. Even that. There's nothing but here—Dacor House. I go home at night. But I sit. I'm not tired enough to fall asleep. And I can't watch television anymore. Every show that's on, I used to see with Mary. I want a new television season to come so much so there will be some new shows. Anne, I'm living beyond my time, and I know it. All I do is study details."

"What do you mean?"

"I notice the things I never noticed. The details have become important. This window has become important. The people walking, the colors of their clothes. The new cars. The other morning I caught myself staring at the sink—and being fascinated with it. How did they do this? How does the whole plumbing system work? I turn a faucet and water comes out that I can drink. And I turn it the other way and it stops. I never realized how many things have been done. Nature is wonderful, but look what Man has done. There is so much. So many things. And the radio, and now television. Do you know that I have no idea how those things work? Then the simple things. Your necklace is so pretty, Anne. I like it. Someone designed that necklace and made it. Do you know what I mean?"

Anne didn't know how to respond and so she nodded and just sat there looking at him.

"I like the ribbon in your hair."

"Thank you. I always wear one now. It's my trademark!" she said proudly.

"And you don't wear glasses anymore, Anne. How come? Can you see?"

"Oh, I have contacts now!"

"Even that! Can you see as good as you did with glasses?"

"Oh, yes. I can see perfectly. They're a nuisance and they hurt sometimes, but I like them. I'm going to get the new soft kind."

"Isn't that something?"

Again, Anne simply didn't know what to talk about. Out of desperation to make him feel good she said, "you are so terribly missed by everyone. I know that."

He shook his head. "No, Anne. I'm not. I knew it at the party. They give everyone a party, you know, a going-away party. They had the party in Room 1100. There must have been one hundred or more people there. They had the room decorated with red, white, and blue crepe paper with streamers hanging from the light fixtures and from the scaffolds. In the center of the room there was a table covered with small sandwiches and red punch in a big bowl. They had a tape machine waiting to catch and preserve all my words for purposes unknown. They never play back those things. No matter. I hadn't prepared anything.

"In recognition of my thirty-four years of government service they gave me a bronze plaque with twenty-two signatures engraved on it and they gave me a painting of the Alamo. You know, Mary and I were from Texas. I didn't care for the plaque or the painting or the party. They took pictures of me holding the plaque and the painting. For a while it seemed like a celebration. But they all came up to me and told me they'd miss me. But I knew the truth—that the next morning someone else would put his initials at the bottom of memos and on out-going cables and when someone else would receive them, maybe that person would notice that there was a 'D.S.' written on them instead of a 'G.F.' That's all. In a few days they wouldn't even notice that.

"You know, Anne, I didn't feel any older, but maybe they were right and I'm too old. Now I feel it. Every day now I read the morning Post and, although I never did before, I pass up the front section because there's no reason to waste time to learn what's going on in a world in which I am no longer a contributing member.

"Instead, I turn to Section 'D' and try to get interested in nonsense. I can't, but maybe I can learn to get interested."

She leaned across the table again and clasped both his hands again. "Mr. Ambassador, you have to stop this. Do you know what you're doing to yourself?"

He looked in her eyes as though she was a teacher and he was a young child. He shook his head.

"You're feeling sorry for yourself, Mr. Ambassador, and I won't allow it. Yes, you are reborn, and you're reborn with so much knowledge and so much ability and you can contribute so much. Isn't that good to be reborn?"

He gave a slow nod.

"See? Now, what you have to do is think of all the people you could teach. You taught me things in one evening. There's something about you that is so very authoritative and credible. You could do so many things. Things that would be so valuable."

His eyes were wandering. He was looking around the room as though he was searching for something. She lost his concentration and she wanted to regain it quickly.

"If it wasn't for you and Mr. Daschle I'd be out there with those creeps. Honest, I know I would because I wouldn't know any better, but you could say one sentence to me—just one sentence, and I understood. I knew you were an honest man who was telling me things for my own good, and it meant so much. You've had such an impact with so few words. You teach without preaching. Don't you see how you could take young people and teach them about all kinds—"

An explosion interrupted what she was saying. Anne half-jumped out of her chair, but Ambassador Fairbanks gave no sign that he heard the explosion or saw Anne's reaction. He was too occupied in staring at the ice cubes in Anne's Coca-Cola.

Anne knew she would not see Ambassador Fairbanks again. Dacor House was too much like a luxurious version of the ghat that led to the Ganges in India, and the Ambassador was too much like a dressed duplicate of the naked man on the ground who extended his arm in the air, waving for help. Both had come to a place where they had chosen to die, and although both had second thoughts, neither one had the strength or the time to reverse the decision they had set in motion.

TWENTY-NINE
A GUEST AT THE TUESDAY TABLE
1970

Anne had never been invited to the Tuesday Table before. She was instructed by the director of policy not to sit at the table itself but, rather, to sit on one of the chairs against the wall.

Anne was nervous, and she had little experience with nervousness. She knew that what she was about to do was unprecedented, and that most of those who sat at the Tuesday Table would turn on her after hearing what she was about to say. She wore a trim gray suit looking very businesslike. The gray ribbon in her hair was pushed back to hardly be visible.

She repeated to herself three statements that would keep her from modifying those things she hoped she would be strong enough to say:

In the U.S. Consulate in Hong Kong, Mark Daschle had told her he didn't give one hoot who "loves or hates Anne Whitney—or Mark Daschle. I want them to understand and respect U.S. policy. Do you get it?"

At his home in Foggy Bottom, Ambassador Fairbanks had told her, "If you work for the taxpayers, you work for them. If you don't, then quit. But don't go half-way."

Behind a podium on the east side of the U.S. Capitol Building, President Kennedy had said, "Ask not what your country can do for you. Ask what you can do for your country."

She had considered giving a private report to the director, Frank Shakespeare, but she decided that it would be cowardly to do that without the presence of those who would oppose her.

Deputy Director Henry Loomis took the director's chair at the Tuesday Table, and announced that "Director Shakespeare is in a meeting at the White House with the president and Secretary of State Rogers, so I'll be officiating this morning." She was disappointed that Frank Shakespeare wasn't there.

The Area Director for the Far East introduced Anne, although practically everyone at the table knew her or certainly knew about her. They loved her in the old days, but most of them had heard she had become a convert of late. "Anne attended Expo '70," he said, "but she isn't here to discuss the exposition. She was in Osaka to attend a world-wide conference of our Public Affairs Officers and some of their Deputies, Information Officers, and Cultural Affairs Officers. We're delighted to have you visit us, Anne. Here—come over here." He gestured toward the chair next to Henry Loomis; the chair on which Henry Loomis normally sat when Frank Shakespeare was there.

"Thank you," she said, and that would be the high-mark of her courtesy for the day. Holding on to her black purse and a yellow folder, she rose and went to the designated chair of higher prestige, and put her purse and folder on the sacred Tuesday Table itself.

"For some time I have had the suspicion that this agency, and perhaps other agencies and departments in our government have what I now call an Invisible Monarchy."

There were some smiles and light laughter, with no one understanding what she was talking about or where she was going with it.

"What I mean by that term," she continued, answering the unasked question, "is that the highest ranking foreign service and civil service careerists make more of a difference to the bureaucracy beneath them—to people like me—than the president of the United States or the appointed head of the Agency. We, in the lower-level bureaucracy recognize that the president and his appointees are temporary figures, whereas you in the Invisible Monarchy—most of you at this table—stay and stay and stay, and train princes and princesses in your own mold. The performance reports you write about the job we're doing are what counts towards the future of everyone's career here. Mr. Shakesp—" and then she stopped herself in recognition that she had to change the name she had rehearsed. "Mr. Loomis can write a glowing report on my work, but it will mean nothing when a new administration comes in. What will mean something is the performance report you give me, Mr. Bixley, or you, Miss Wexler, or you, Mr. Hardy. Now I have had that suspicion confirm—"

"Anne," the Far East area director said, "we want to hear your report on the P.A.O. Conference in Osaka. Your complaints are interesting, honey, but there are proper procedures for grievances."

"If you'll allow me to continue, Mr. Bixley, I had my suspicions confirmed when I was in Osaka. For the first time in the eleven years I've been with this Agency, I had the opportunity to meet with our top officers from dozens and dozens of our embassies and consulates all over the world."

Ned Bixley nodded. "That's good, Anne. Get to your central point, please."

Even Henry Loomis was nodding. "Please do get to your point, Anne."

"Mr. Loomis," and she turned her head to look directly at him from only inches away. "You are being given a very big snow job as a representative of the president of the United States. You know what these people around the table think of you? That you're an amateur in their business. They look at you as a temporary nuisance that interferes with their expertise. They'll act loyal as can be while they're in a meeting with you, but wait until they get in the elevator and the elevator doors close. In that sound-proof enclosure they laugh at the way they conned you at these meetings. I've been in those elevators."

There was absolute silence at the Tuesday Table.

Henry Loomis broke the silence. "Anne, Ned's right. This isn't the appropriate forum for something like this."

"Then is it the appropriate forum for something like this?" She opened the yellow folder she had put on the Tuesday Table. "I want to quote—precisely quote, what our officers are saying overseas. I want to read to you some of my notes from top foreign service officers I met at that P.A.O. Conference in Osaka." And she looked around the table. "Ready? Here goes!" She had the rare ability to be a very articulate woman at one moment, and a little girl the next moment. She never did the expected.

"There was the man who was posted at our embassy in Dar es Salaam who told me, 'Do you know what I tell the Tanzanians? I tell them we call him Tricky Dick. They laugh. There was a demonstration against Nixon around the Embassy last month. Some of our Peace Corps young people were in that demonstration. I told them I was with them and I wore black that day to identify to the Tanzanians that I was with the demonstrators.' That's what he told me.

"I met a woman who serves in the U.S. Embassy in Caracas. We met at a reception in Osaka with a lot of foreigners. She found a Venezuelan and said, 'I think of Nixon what you think of your President Caldera. Neither one of us knows what a true democracy is. But we can see what our governments do to our countries. I'm not spreading any of that anti-Castro propaganda I get from Washington. Castro might be better for his country than Caldera is for your country or Nixon is for mine.'

"There was the man who's in the U.S. consulate in Nairobi, Kenya, who told me, 'When a visitor comes from Washington I put the picture of Nixon right-side up. When he leaves, I hang it back upside down. Those students from Kenyatta College laugh when they see it upside down. I relate to them. They're the coming leaders of the African continent. They aren't as with-the-times as our students back home, but they're learning. I recommended to the Agency and State that we put a U.N. flag on the moon, not our flag.'

"There was the man in his second tour in Pakistan, first in Karachi and now in Islamabad. He said, 'I never mention Vietnam here unless someone asks me. And then I just tell them the truth: it's a civil war and we have no business being there.'

"There was the man who has a very couchy job in Rome at our Embassy. He said, 'I served in Rome before; back in 1961 I saw big red banners saying *Vota Communista.* I was surprised, but then I learned why they had those banners. This country still has the biggest communist party in Western Europe. And it isn't all a protest vote like everyone in Washington wants you to think. Communism might well be the only thing that could stabilize this country and end the fragmentation of strikes and political and social chaos. If they ask my opinion about politics I just say I have no comment. They know what that means. And when they ask what's going on in America, I tell them the best man can't always win in our system.'

"I met one of our officers who's in Ibadan, Nigeria, who joined an Anti-American demonstration last November on Vietnam Mobilization Day. He told me, 'When Nixon gave that Silent Majority speech I thought I'd barf. I didn't tell the locals here that Humphrey supported Nixon on that. I wanted to give the people some hope about America."

Ned Bixley interrupted her. "I think that's enough, Anne. You're making these charges and it's very difficult for me to believe that you're quoting our officers accurately. Are we to believe that you wrote down all these very detailed statements and got them right?"

The jaw of the man who looked like an electric typewriter was pulsating which appeared to be his space bar being pressed repeatedly. The eyes of the woman who thought she was the proof of women's superiority, were piercing at Anne's eyes. The sniffer had his mouth open, so he had no need to sniff. The man with the white beard who generally squinted his eyes with intensity at whomever was speaking, was squinting at neither Anne nor the Deputy Director but, rather, at the wall. The cigar smoker who generally flipped the manila envelope that covered the hole he burned in the Tuesday Table a long time ago, was rubbing his Zippo lighter.

Anne looked over at Deputy Director Loomis. "Mr. Loomis," she said, "before leaving for Japan I went to the Norelco Service Center on 11th Street and picked up a cassette tape machine. I don't know if you've ever seen them but they use real small tapes and I was able to record what different U.S. foreign service officers said, and then I transcribed them to these notes." She reached in her purse and pulled out a small tape cassette. "Here," she said, and put the tape down on the Tuesday Table in front of Henry Loomis. "Here's the tape. Maybe they confided these things to me, or in front of me because they thought I'd still be in sympathy with them. Thanks to other people at this agency, some marvelous people at this agency, I grew up while those people I just quoted didn't, and they're a lot older than I am—in years. Mr. Loomis, I don't want to give the impression that there aren't marvelous people in the Agency. There are. But there's a sickness, as well. I would identify by name those marvelous foreign service officers but if I did it at this table, it would only hurt their careers."

Anne was now considered to be a traitor by most of the participants around the Tuesday Table, but not by Deputy Director Loomis.

"Thank you, Anne," he said. "I don't need the tape. But I want a more detailed report from you with everything you said put into writing, and with names. I appreciate your—" and he paused for a while and then used the word he knew was accurate, "courage."

Anne closed her yellow folder and slid it on the table to him. "Here. The report is already written. But may I say something else, Mr. Loomis?"

"Yes, you can."

"Many of our careerists I met with were from African and Latin American posts. They said that they don't talk about Vietnam to the locals because the people there aren't interested in Vietnam. I asked them, Mr. Loomis, if they would talk about our Apollo missions if the locals there weren't interested in it. They all said 'yes, of course.' They had to admit they talked about Apollo because they were so proud of it. 'And Vietnam?' I asked. They would smile or laugh or something like that. That illustrated the whole problem with this agency. Apollo is easy to sell. Vietnam isn't, so they choose not to do it. That sends a message to everyone in the host country, doesn't it? By the silence of our own officers, they haven't built up a reservoir of understanding about Vietnam overseas. All they hear about it is from the other side. One of our officers, the one in Dar es Salaam told me to tell Mr. Shakespeare to tell President Nixon that Vietnam makes his job difficult. I told him that the president doesn't work for him, that he works for the president. But that's the way they think—that the president was elected to make their jobs easier, not that their job is to make his job easier. Do you understand what I mean? Mr. Loomis, some of the careerists are sick. I used to be an upcoming princess in the Invisible Monarchy. No more. I don't want to be part of the royalty. Do you know what I mean?"

He nodded. "Thank you, Anne." He knew what she meant.

The rest of those at the Tuesday Table were as motionless and speechless and empty as the hole in the Tuesday Table.

THIRTY
MIXTURE 18
1970

It was that strange time that comes between Halloween and Thanksgiving. The beauty of fall is gone and it's too early to start preparing for Christmas and New Year's, and it gets dark early, and there's a new cold in the air, and no one knows exactly what to wear. It is an uneasy time.

Each year in that limbo of three weeks or so, there is the thought that the coming Christmas could be terrible. It might be wonderful, but this is the time to worry about it. "It certainly can't be as good as that other Christmas was, and it might be the worst of my life–I wish it was over."

That early dark of a November sky made the people on Fourteenth Street move a little faster to get home for Saturday night. Five o'clock seemed more like eight o'clock and the new coldness in the air made the warmth of home even more inviting than usual.

But there was a temptation on Fourteenth Street–a pipe shop window with a golden glow that would delay going home a while longer. A soft bell rang as the door opened and the inside emanated with a comfortable warmth mixed with the secure smell of latakia and perique. The golden glow seen from outside was no hoax.

The small shop was built to hold no more than four customers at a time but there were twice that number, and all that was not needed was the entrance of the frequent Saturday customer from the White House, Moose Dunston, but at five o'clock he opened the door, the soft bell rang, and the other customers had to move to even more confining areas to allow his big frame enough space. He was, as usual, smoking his thick-walled Dunhill Special Collector's pipe which was burning a distinctive mixture, and that warm aroma was at least some compensation for his presence to the other customers. He took quick looks at those other customers, knowing he smoked the best pipe of anyone there. It was one of those small victories of life.

Other than when he was going on a trip or just back from one, his Saturday habit was to buy three small cans of Mixture 18, one for himself and two for the president. This Saturday he was going to buy enough to be safe for a while, just in case the next few weeks would keep him from another visit to the golden place on Fourteenth Street.

If everything would work out as Moose had hoped, this night would be the beginning of the end of Jonas's imprisonment, and Moose had been an influence in the rescue operation that was being planned.

"The regular, Mr. Dunston?" the tobacconist asked. His name was Mr. Weathersby. No one addressed Mr. Weathersby by his first name. The prefix of "Mister" was used in the manner of "Ambassador" or "Senator" or "Congressman." A tobacconist was regarded as a man of rank. He was standing in his usual position behind his glass counter looking as knowledgeable as a combination of Aristotle and Houdini. With his arms spread out and his hands resting on the glass top, he was ready for consultation; not just a simple sale of tobacco.

To the discomfort of the other customers, Moose was going to wait in the store for a man who planned on meeting him there, and who had not yet arrived. "Nine cans of Mixture 18 this time, Mr. Weathersby." Moose said. "And take a look at this." He took the pipe out of his mouth. "Can you buff the edge of the stem here? It's getting that acid-white look."

Nothing was an insurmountable problem to Mr. Weathersby, and every regular customer knew he would come to their rescue. If it wasn't a needed buff, there would be a stem chewed up here, a pipe that bit there, the tobacco that needed to be stronger or milder. How there could be so many problems regarding a simple implement remained the mystery of pipe smokers, but it dictated that the tobacconist had to be hired by the shop not for his sales ability, but for his wisdom. He could only be a salesman to the woman who would come in for a gift–or to the young student who would want a pipe because he thought it made him look good. But both of them were pests. Mr. Weathersby would rather talk about the secret he shared with the White House–and Moose was his connection with that secret.

"See what I mean?" Moose said. "That white stain there just looks awful."

"Dunhill's always do that with their vulcanite stems. It's from the normal acid of your saliva. I'll buff it for you, but it will happen again, so just bring it in when it gets to the point that it bothers you." Mr. Weathersby turned to the small shelf behind him and turned on its buffer and Moose backed up a little forcing a tall, thin man who had been looking at the most expensive handmade pipes to bend on his knees to continue to see all of them in the lower glass case.

"Take your time, Mr. Weathersby," Moose said. "I'm in no hurry." The other customers had hoped he was. He flipped through the latest edition of *Pipe World* magazine, picked up a brochure for a new pipe line from Denmark, then picked up a meerschaum pipe with a sculpture of President Nixon's face as its bowl.

"When did you get this one?" he asked Mr. Weathersby, who turned away from the buffer to look at what Moose was talking about..

"It's been there a long time. Do you think he'd like it?"

Moose shook his head. "No. I don't think so."

The door opened, the soft bell rang, and a cold breeze came in with a middle-aged crusty-faced man in uniform, most of the uniform covered by a black overcoat. Now it was nearly impossible to move in that store. The newcomer took a quick scan around the shop at the customers. With the small amount of room in the shop there was no way to make the scan more than quick. "Mmmmm," the man said, "that smells good! What is it?"

"It's the shop's own Mixture 18," Moose answered.

"I'll take some of that," the stranger to the shop said to Mr. Weathersby who was turning around again from the buffer. "Just a small one."

"You bet," Mr. Weathersby said. Then he turned to Moose, "How's this?" He gave Moose's Dunhill back to him. The stain was gone.

"Perfect!" Moose said. "How much do I owe you?"

"Nothing for the buff, Mr. Dunston. And I'll just add the cans of 18 to your bill." Then he turned to the man who had just entered, and Mr. Weathersby put some of the magic mixture in a plastic envelope. "No charge," he said. "Give it a try."

"How do you make any money here?" the military man asked him.

Mr. Weathersby laughed. "When you want to buy a pipe like Mr. Dunston has there, just make sure you buy it here!" He gave Moose a black bag containing his cans of tobacco. Moose shook Mr. Weathersby's hand and walked outside, then waited for the uniformed man in the overcoat to leave and meet him outside the shop.

With Moose's departure, the shop breathed again. Mr. Weathersby said in a voice loud enough to be heard easily by everyone in the shop, "You know who he picked up that tobacco for?" He spread his arms even wider apart than usual, his fingers tapping on the counter. "Do you know who he bought those cans for?"

No one answered.

Mr. Weathersby acted as though he was taking a cautious look around the shop, pretending he, somehow, wanted no one to hear what he was almost yelling. "The president." Then he made a clicking noise with his tongue against the top of the inside of his mouth. "Up the street."

"Really?" the tall thin man asked, now standing up again from his kneeling position that Moose's presence had previously demanded. "I didn't know Nixon smokes a pipe."

"It's a secret. He smokes a pipe with our Mixture 18. It's how he relaxes. That man comes in from the White House. He comes in and buys a number of them and walks out, just like he did just then. The president loves a pipe. He loves our mixture. I don't normally let people know, even though it would bring customers in. Let them go to Bertrands. I don't care."

One by one, the customers buttoned up their topcoats, put their collars up, and left with a black paper bag that sheltered a new tobacco or a cheap Dr. Grabow pipe or a new hundred-dollar Charatan. Most tried to leave with something as a confirmation of that aroma and time. Even a ten-cent box of Duke filters. They were on their way home this night to a wife or parents or a girlfriend, and the wives or parents or girlfriends would not have known that moment. Out of the corner of their eyes they would catch him, fiddling with something—maybe examining a label on a tobacco tin or quickly smelling a black leather pouch or putting a small filter inside the stem of a pipe, and there would be a strange, content, and almost guilty look on the smoker's face. In an uneasy season, to some it could be a good Saturday after all.

The middle-aged man in uniform and overcoat didn't go to a home.

Right after he walked out of the tobacco shop he made a few short steps to Moose who was looking in the window of the jewelry shop next door. "You're Dunston?" the uniformed man in the overcoat asked.

Moose turned from looking in the window. "Hello, Colonel. I was getting a little worried about you showing up in there." They shook hands.

"You picked a kooky place to meet. Why couldn't we have met in your office, for blaze's sake?"

"The press was all over the place today. If they saw you coming in the White House, they might have put two and two together. That's why I called you to meet me here. It used to be that they weren't around on Saturdays, but lately they've been coming in. They don't want to miss anything."

"Well, where are we going now?"

"We're going there, but I have to see if it's all clear first. Just before I left to come here, I told Zeigler to tell the press corps nothing more would be cooking today. Besides, I had to come here this afternoon to pick up the president's tobacco and it will only take us minutes to get to the White House."

They started walking toward the White House. "Will I be seeing the president?"

"Yes. I'm sorry but I'll ask you to allow me to go into the EOB first and just make sure we're all clear–that the press isn't watching. You might have to just stroll around the avenue for a while. I hope not long. Then I'll come back out and walk into the EOB with you. Do you think things are pretty much in order, Colonel?"

"They will be on our end. It's up to the president."

"I'm sorry for the weather, Colonel. It's a little wintry tonight."

The colonel ignored his comment, probably because the weather was inconsequential to a man who lived regularly in more peril than cold gusts of wind. "You work every weekend, Dunston?"

"Almost. It's very rare that any of us get away for a weekend."

"That makes it pretty rough for your wife and family, doesn't it?"

"I'm not married, sir."

"That figures. This is a messy town for keeping a marriage together. Everyone is off working at all kinds of hours in this town. I don't think that's good. I think they forget what it's like to be part of a normal American family. That's how Washington loses touch. People in this town begin to think they're more important than the average American; that if they stop working the whole country will fall apart."

"Maybe so. But you work for the country, too, so we're doing the same thing, aren't we?" The brilliantly lit White House was on the near horizon to their left. "Aren't we doing that? It's Saturday night."

"Get married and have a family when you get out of this town, Dunston. Potomac Fever is fatal."

They passed the White House residence, going the short distance to the Northwest Gate. Moose left the colonel on Pennsylvania Avenue while

Moose took a quick tour of the Press Room. It was empty. When that was done, he went across West Executive Avenue to the president's office in the Old Executive Office Building. He told Rose Mary Woods the colonel was waiting. Moose went back to Pennsylvania Avenue and gave the colonel the all-clear, then ushered him into the EOB.

They hung up their coats in Moose's office and Moose looked at his wall clock. "We still have some time. Rose Mary said it would be about five, maybe ten minutes. He's just down the hall."

"We're not going to the Oval Office?"

Moose shook his head. "No. Just down the hall."

The colonel saw the picture of Wai-yee on Moose's desk. "Well, she's a beauty. Who's she?"

"I was going to marry her once. I keep the picture there to make sure I don't accept any less than her."

"That's going to be a tough goal to reach. She's a beauty. Good for you. Did she dump you or were you crazy enough to dump her?"

"She dumped me. In a very nice way, Colonel. She didn't tell me to go to the devil or anything like that. There was no third party or anything like that. Whatever it was, it didn't work out."

"There's always a third person, Dunston. When someone says there isn't one—don't believe it, even if you're the one who's saying it. You're either lying about yourself or you're fooling yourself about her. And since you don't impress me as a liar, she has another boy. Sorry, Dunston, but I'm a military man and I can't afford to mess around with things that aren't true. She's got someone else, Dunston. You lost a beauty."

That was a thought that had never occurred to Moose before. Wai-yee with someone else?

The phone rang. It was Rose Mary Woods. The president wanted to see the colonel.

The president's suite in the Old Executive Office Building was warmer than the Oval Office. There were personal knickknacks all over the place including one small replica of an elephant after another. There were framed political cartoons on the wall—many of them ridiculing him. The president was sitting in his soft lounge chair by the side of his desk, his legs resting on its matching ottoman, and he was puffing on his pipe. Moose and the colonel were seated in other soft lounge chairs facing him. King Timahoe, the president's big, red Irish Setter was sleeping on the floor next to a large alabaster elephant.

"When do you think you'll be able to do it, Colonel?" the president asked the colonel.

"If everything goes as I expect, Mr. president, it will be two weeks from tonight. You need to know, sir, General Manor wants a little wiggle room in there. There are a lot of factors that could go wrong. Sontay Prison is not an easy place to stage a rescue. But we'll do it, and we're aiming at two weeks from tonight."

The president nodded slowly. "Are your boys fully prepared?"

"We have a secure corner of Eglin AFB in Florida where they've been training for over two months now. But they haven't been told what they're training for."

"I thought these were volunteers. They have to be volunteers, you know."

"They are. But they haven't been told the operation. They've been told it's dangerous and they may never come home, and they could even be tortured to death. They still volunteered. We had so many volunteers we could be selective in who were chosen. Some three hundred Green Berets said they wanted to do whatever was needed. We have some good men, Mr. President. The best. But we can't afford a leak on this or they'll be dead for sure."

"How many are you going to send?"

"Seventy."

"When do you plan on telling them where they're going?"

"After they get to a base we have right at the eastern edge of Thailand. Within about three hours from when they're told, they'll be at Sontay. It's a helicopter ride of a little over three hours. It's dangerous territory, Mr. President. It's only twenty-three miles west of Hanoi."

"I know where it is. I was there a long time ago. Mrs. Nixon and I visited Sontay in 1953 when that site was a refugee camp."

"I didn't know that," Moose said.

The president continued. "What are the odds on this one, Colonel? Don't lean to optimism. I want the real odds."

"I don't know. We could all be killed as soon as we hit the ground. And it's even possible they may have moved the Americans out of there if they got any wind of what we've been training for in Florida. We don't know. But if those Americans are still there, we can't let them rot in cells under continual punishment. Twenty-eight of them have died of torture, sir. The kind of torture we thought we were through with when the Nazis and the Japs surrendered. They do unthinkable things to them, Mr. President. We can't allow that to continue. They're our boys. If there's one chance in ten that we can take out one prisoner, it's worth trying."

"Let's not give them any new ones. What's the plan?"

"Ten helicopters. Some of them will be empty in the hope we can rescue somewhere between seventy to one hundred Americans and bring them back with us. We're going to be escorted by fighter planes, F-105's, to do whatever they may have to do. In addition we're going to have some planes take off from carriers in the Gulf of Tonkin as decoys so the NV think we're going to attack them from the coast."

"Mr. President?" Moose said.

The president looked over at him.

"I know I've been a strong advocate of this raid, sir, but—"

"A strong advocate?" The president interrupted. "You never stopped. I know your friend is there."

"Yes sir, but my job here for you is contingencies. And I want you to be aware before you give the final go-ahead that I emphasize to you not only the risk to those Green Berets who stage the raid, but also of what can happen here at home. If it fails, we better be aware of what can happen. Chaos. The streets. Your imagination is as good—or better than mine on that."

The president nodded. "I can't let that influence this. There are a lot of good men in that camp: Ellis, Swindle, Crayton, Fisher, your friend, Valadovich. We can't abandon them because of what some students here at home are going to do in the streets."

Moose was stunned that he knew names of those imprisoned, but the president said them as naturally as he would have recited the names of his closest friends. "Most of those kids, those demonstrators, don't know they're being used." He reached in the top drawer of his desk. "Here—here. Read this out loud," and the president passed a piece of paper to Moose, and the president looked at the colonel. "It's what North Vietnam's Premiere Pham Van Dong said on Radio Hanoi last October. Go ahead, Moose."

Moose nodded and read, "'This fall, large sectors of the U.S. people, encouraged and supported by many peace and justice-loving American personages, are launching a broad and powerful offensive throughout the United States to demand that the Nixon Administration put an end to the Vietnam aggressive war and immediately bring all American troops home...We are firmly confident that with the solidarity and bravery of the peoples of our two countries and with the approval and support of peace-loving people in the world, the struggle of the Vietnamese people and U.S. progressive people against U.S. aggression will certainly be crowned with total victory. May your fall offensive succeed splendidly.'"

"What can we do?" the president asked.

No one answered.

"What can we do about that?"

Moose answered, but not very well. "Somehow, we have to let kids know they're helping the enemy when they do—what they've been doing."

The colonel shook his head. "They know. We have to live with it."

"Colonel," the president said, "you have to succeed at this. You pay the same price for doing something completely as you do half-way, so do it completely."

"You might also consider, Mr. President," Moose said, "who in the Congress you want to tell in advance. Senator Fulbright will probably be asking for your impeachment if you do it and don't tell him before it can be stopped."

The president put his pipe in the large ashtray on the table by his chair, he shoved the ottoman aside with one foot, and then he stood up. "I know." He started pacing and he looked through the window at the brilliantly lit West Wing and residence. He turned around to them. "Do it, Colonel. Tell your men for me that I—that as the president of the United States, I have no words that can in any way express our nation's thanks. Our country—their country will forever be in their debt."

"I will tell them that, sir."

"Colonel?"
"Yes, sir?"
"I want them to have Thanksgiving dinner here—here at the White House. It will definitely be all over by then, won't it?""
"Yes, sir."
"What do we call this raid, Moose?" the president asked.
"I've been calling it Mixture 18, sir."
The president nodded. Then he did what he frequently did to keep things from getting too heavy. "How's that Chinese girlfriend of yours in Hong Kong, Moose?"
Moose smiled and nodded. "Okay, sir. She's all right."
"You ought to marry that girl, you know."
"It's too late," the Colonel offered. "He muffed it."
"You did?" he asked Moose.
"The colonel's right. I muffed it."
The president shook his head with a smile bigger than the smile of Moose. "What kind of a staff do I have?"

Two weeks later, in a small border area of Thailand, Colonel Arthur Bull Simons received the final go-ahead from the White House. Within minutes Colonel Simons told his Green Berets what they would be doing in three hours and fifteen minutes from that moment, and he told them the risk. After a period of stone silence they all stood; seventy men standing as one, and they loudly applauded.

Somehow, the North Vietnamese had known to move the prisoners out of Sontay long before the Green Berets had arrived. No one was rescued.
The Green Berets got into the camp, killed thirty-some North Vietnamese soldiers, searched the cell blocks in their entirety, and managed to get back to their helicopters without any casualties, but without any rescued prisoners.
After it was done, word of the attempt reached American prisoners throughout the prison camps in North Vietnam. Their captors told them they had killed the potential rescuers, but that was doubted by the prisoners, and there was now the knowledge among them that they had not been forgotten by their nation, which some had feared. Now it was known that the United States was willing to risk lives for their lives. That was the saving grace.

On the day before Thanksgiving, President Nixon presented the Distinguished Service Cross to Colonel Arthur Bull Simons and three others for action beyond the call of duty in the raid on Sontay.

Moose was in a state of depression. He knew that with the disappointing results of the raid on Sontay, there would be no second attempt. That depression turned each day into an agonizingly long series of hours. No. Each minute was agonizingly long.

He finally snapped out of it on the crisp, clear, and very cold night of December the 16th. That night the president lit the nation's Christmas tree on the Ellipse, and with it he also signaled the turning on of the new lights of Washington that poured intense white illumination onto the memorials and monuments and federal buildings and some of the streets throughout the city. Some had been lit before but not as brilliantly, and some had been left in the dark before this night. With the city's skyline looking so optimistic, Moose felt guilty in retaining his depression. He walked with the president from the podium that had been erected on the Ellipse to the limousine that would take the president across the street to the White House. They were surrounded by a moving circle of Secret Service agents.

"Those lights make a difference, don't they Moose?"

"Yes, sir, they do."

"They'll probably say we're wasting energy."

Moose gave a short laugh. "Probably."

"I think it gives the city energy." He looked sharply at Moose. "I hope it gives you some."

Moose was surprised by that remark. He didn't know his mood of the last weeks had been that apparent. The president added, "There are some things we can't change as quickly as we want them to be changed, but if we give up, they'll never be changed. We're going to keep at it. It's going to take a while but we're going to make the future as bright as those new lights, aren't we?"

Moose was looking down as he walked. He felt his eyes would give him away. "Yes, sir." Then he looked briefly at the president. "Mr. President, how did the North Vietnamese know we were going to make that raid?"

The president tightened his lips against each other, and shook his head. "There is no such thing as a secret in this city. Nothing. We might as well tell everything we're going to do in an East Room ceremony."

"Maybe we should. Maybe that's the way. Then they'd ignore it."

"Keep your spirits, Moose. When your spirits are down, you lose, you know. Why don't you walk through this city and let me know how it looks tonight with those new lights. That's what I'd do, if I could." And he gestured toward the Secret Service agents.

Moose took his advice, and for the first time since the raid, and in the brilliantly lit streets of D.C. he felt there was something new in the air.

After being dropped off at the residence, the president walked across West Executive Avenue to his EOB suite. He sat on his cushioned chair and put his legs on the chair's matching ottoman, then picked up his pipe from the small table and moved the ashtray closer to him. He hit the back of his pipe-bowl over the ash tray, and the ashes of Mixture 18 fell out.

THIRTY-ONE
REVELATIONS
1971

Winter was welcome in Washington because it was too cold for demonstrations. Through the window of Dacor House that cut off the horizon above street-level, the lower parts of a large black car could be seen. It had been parked there and then it drove into the street spewing white and gray slush from beneath its tires. Within minutes a woman's legs beneath a short white fur coat were passing by in high heeled white boots, intentionally stepping on the snow near the curb to avoid the ice on the center of the sidewalk. She was holding some large shopping bags that dangled in front of the window from unseen arms above the window's view. Tires of passing cars came by and spewed slush haphazardly and the legs moved over to the ice. She was walking to the upper door of Dacor House.

The upper door of Dacor House opened and closed. Anne was greeted near the doorway off the main room by a middle-aged woman in a black dress.

"I'm a friend of Ambassador Fairbanks," Anne Whitney said.

There was some silence, and then the other woman said with a very soft voice, "Who told you?"

"Who told me what?"

"Oh, my," the woman said. "Oh, my."

Anne closed her eyes in comprehension. She opened them when she felt the woman's hand on her arm. "When?" Anne asked with total resignation.

"This morning," the woman answered. "Ten-twenty this morning or very close to it. Gawlers Mortuary just picked—just picked him up."

Anne closed her eyes again and shook her head.

There was a silence that was very long. Then the woman said, "You just came and—you didn't know?"

Anne continued shaking her head.

"He's had such few guests. Why did you decide to come today?"

Anne closed her eyes again. "I think I knew. I must have." Anne was almost whispering her words and they came very slowly.

"Please, take off your coat and sit down."

Anne didn't do it. She didn't want to be there now that he was gone. "Maybe I was being told. I think some voice must have told me. I don't know."

"I think that's true."

There was another long silence. Then Anne said in a soft voice, "When I woke up I planned on coming this morning. But since I was coming, I thought I'd go to some stores around here. So I came here, downtown, and did some silly things," she raised and lowered her shopping bags to indicate their presence, "and didn't get here until now."

"It must be fate," the woman asked Anne.

"I should have come earlier. I knew it." She didn't cry. She just shook her head back and forth. "I'm too late. Just–at 10:20?"

The woman nodded. "Are you a close friend?"

"Yes." There was silence again until Anne asked, "Did he suffer?"

"No. He was sitting in his chair looking through the window. And he died there without a sound. There were others in the room. They thought he was asleep at first. He often fell asleep that way but usually not that early. He told us, so often, that he didn't want to go on any more. I think he died when Mrs. Fairbanks died. He said he was just existing since then. Please, don't you want to sit down?"

"No. I want to leave." Now Anne's voice was strong. "I hate this place."

"Who are you?"

"I'm Anne Whitney."

"Oh," the woman said with a slow nod and a kind smile. "You're the little rebel Anne that he talked about."

"Did he?" Anne asked.

"He said you were the little rebel with a cause."

Anne gave a trembling smile. "Did he?"

"Just last week he said that to me. He talked about death so often, and he said that if you should come by some day and he isn't here, to tell you that he's sorry he simply doesn't have the time to be able to accept that job you offered him, but that he will be anxiously waiting for you to get to that position you told him about. He said to tell you, if he isn't here, that he's so proud of you. That was just last week. He said, 'Tell Anne that.'"

Anne bit her lip. She turned away and left Dacor House.

The evening services for Ambassador Fairbanks were held at the Washington Cathedral one week after his death so as to leave time for foreign service officers to arrive from wherever in the world they might have been. His burial would then be held in Austin, Texas, next to Mary. At the Washington services there were banks of flowers and two large wreaths, one from former president and Mrs. Johnson, and one from president and Mrs. Nixon.

Anne was sitting next to Mark Daschle who had flown down from New York. He had taken a taxi directly from Washington National Airport to the cathedral, posting his luggage in the cloak room.

The crowd of foreign service officers listened to the eulogies and Anne, who hadn't cried once since she heard the news, suddenly started sobbing when one of those giving a eulogy talked of the dignity of Ambassador Fairbanks. It wasn't anywhere near as sad as so many of the things that had been said about him just before that but, somehow, that word hit her hard, and Anne made a quick noise as she choked up. Mark grabbed for her hand and she responded by holding his hand tightly and crying even more audibly. The feel of his hand made all restraint disappear.

"I want to go," she said to Mark as soon as she could get the words out.

"I'll go with you," he said and they took their coats and left into the rain and the cold.

He had forgotten that he didn't have a car in Washington and couldn't take her anywhere; she had to take him. He quickly remembered his luggage was in the cloak room of the cathedral. He ran back into the cathedral and grabbed the bags. Anne drove him to the Key Bridge Marriott where the Agency had booked him at his request.

She had never thought of him as a man before—first he was a boss to her, then he was a tyrant to her, then he was a father figure to her, and tonight all of those roles were gone. He was a man to her—like other men.

He had never thought of her as a woman before—first she was an employee, then a burden he couldn't tolerate, then he heard she had become an admirable young woman, and tonight all of those roles were gone. And she was pretty. She wasn't pretty before.

Neither of them felt the kind of affection toward the other that ignites a fire. That kind of thing just wasn't there. But both of them felt a question being asked from wherever questions of sparks begin in human beings. Was there something, anything, that could ignite? The outward signal was that he wanted to have dinner with her that night and she wanted to have dinner with him that night and neither one of them were hungry.

And more indicative was what he found himself doing. He took her to dinner, not in the ground-level coffee shop of the hotel, but up on the top-story Chaparral Restaurant of the hotel. Why was he doing that? He thought he knew why: he wanted to be kind, particularly when she was feeling so sad. But he realized that didn't explain why he gave the Maitre'd ten dollars to give them a window table.

"This is nice, Mr. Daschle," Anne said as she was seated by the Maitre'd. "Thank you."

It was nice for people who liked to see a giant view of gray. "What a shame that it's raining!" Mark said. "This is generally a beautiful view. Have you ever been up here?"

"Never," she said. "I'm usually taken to the Golden Buttery on Seventeenth Street. Not up here."

"Anne, this is an incredible view. Right there—you can't see it right now—is the Washington Monument." His finger was pointing to a rain drop on the other side of the glass pane of the window. Before it could drip down he moved his finger a little. "The Capitol Building is right there almost behind it. The Jefferson Memorial is way over here, see? I think. Well, it has to be. The Kennedy Center is right there. Directly down there." He was giving a magnificent tour of the invisible. "I wish we could see it."

"Oh, that's all right," she said. "I can tell. It must be beautiful."

The waiter was standing by their table. "Can I get you something from the bar before dinner?" he asked.

Mark nodded and asked Anne, "What would you like to drink?"

"I think a daiquiri."

"Okay, that's good. A daiquiri for her, and a glass of red wine for me. Cabernet. Your house wine."

"Thank you," the waiter nodded and disappeared.

"Anne," Mark said, "I heard you did a marvelous job in Moscow. You made Gerry very proud, you know. He told me all abut your Moscow post and how you handled it."

She nodded. "I know he was proud."

He tried to quickly think of something else to talk about. "Right around the corner here is the Iwo Jima statue, and I don't understand—they have the soldiers holding a fifty-star flag. Well, as you know, it was forty-eight stars back then when they raised the flag there on Mount Suribachi. It would be like a painting of Washington crossing the Delaware with a fifty-star flag."

"Yes," she smiled. "You're right."

They were both ill at ease together in this unexpected setting. "I'm at the U.N. now, you know," he said. "Imagine, I'm in the foreign service and the foreign country they send me to is New York!"

She gave a short, forced laugh. "Is it all right?"

He shrugged. "It's okay when you get used to all the protocol. No complaint, but I want to go back overseas." Mark inhaled a faint trace of her perfume mixed with her scent and he remembered that mixed fragrance from when she was in the consulate in Hong Kong. But it didn't have any allure to him in Hong Kong. At the Chaparral the same soft mixture was very pleasant.

And she noticed that he wasn't wearing any of those bow ties she despised that he used to wear every day in Hong Kong. He was wearing a straight tie, and she liked it.

Mark asked, "You heard about Adam Orr, didn't you?"

She nodded. "It comes in threes, doesn't it? Doesn't it always? Have you noticed movie stars always die in three's? And now, three people are gone who were with us up on the Peak, and they were gone almost right after each other. I hate to bring up that day but now there are only nine."

"I don't believe that 'three's' thing. It just seems that way at times. I know times when it was just one or sometimes four or five."

She shook her head. "It comes in three's."

He wanted to be done with that. "Anne, did you ever imagine, could you ever think that one of them would cause the death of one of the others?"

She looked up abruptly. "What do you mean?"

"Murphy."

"What do you mean, 'Murphy'?" She could feel her stomach twist.

"You know how Orr was killed don't you? And why?"

"Well, I heard what some people said. I know he was killed by the North Vietnamese but I don't know that—"

"Oh, Anne. Murphy goes on television and says Orr is CIA and the next thing we know, Orr is dead. Of course that was why."

Anne's voice got loud. "I don't believe that, Mr. Daschle! That's very unfair to say!" The New Anne was suddenly the Old Anne.

Mark nodded. He realized she was still capable of talking like a little girl and the two of them were still capable of confrontation with each other, and he remembered the tension that went along with that confrontation. He didn't want that again. She was defending Ted Murphy of all people. Or did that quick but passionate statement of defense mean that something was going on between her and Murphy? He remembered the wink Murphy gave her at that conference table so long ago. How did he remember that? Did he feel something for her then that planted that in his head? Then he did it. "Do you ever see him?"

She shook her head, and she was nervous. "No. I saw him in Moscow. He was there. He always wanted a Moscow source," she said with a spurt of a laugh which was given to take attention away from the arrows she knew she had thrown in her defense of him. And she surely didn't want to give one gesture that would indicate what happened between her and Ted Murphy in Moscow. "He was after a source, but I don't do that. I'm a very confidential person. But, boy, did he bother me with questions! He's funny."

The waiter returned with the drinks and large, red, velvet covered menus.

"Thanks," Mark said.

Anne picked up the menu in front of her and she started to look at the choices, studying them and reading the same items again and again as a means of keeping occupied without saying anything. Then she examined the paper napkin that had a printed drawing of the sights that she was supposed to be seeing from the window. She looked back and forth from the napkin to the view of gray as though she was comparing them to judge the napkin's accuracy. Then she went back to the menu.

"I recommend everything," Mark said. "I don't mean that I've had everything on the menu, but I've never been disappointed here."

She looked up from the menu. "Have you been here very often?" *With other women?* she didn't ask but she meant.

"When they just built it. That was before my divorce. Betty and I came here, and some times some of the guys and I would come here. I've been up here maybe a half dozen times, something like that."

Something was happening. She showed signs of jealousy as well as being ill-at-ease. He liked that. Or was all this his imagination? "What's a Steak Diane?" she asked.

"Oh, that one I do know. It's good. It's where they put it on fire right in front of you. They have a big fire right here at the table."

"I want that! May I?" There was something very cute about her asking, 'May I?' Her question was particularly welcome because the New Soft Anne had once again replaced the Old Adversarial Anne.

He smiled. "Of course."

They both had Steak Dianes but neither one of them ate much of them. Over dinner he told her that "when my post is over at the U.N. I'm going to request to be sent to Hong Kong again. It was the best post I ever had."

Then he told her that she made a lot of new enemies at the Agency after her courageous report at the Tuesday Table.

She said she's "glad not to have creeps like that as friends," and she confided that she had told Ambassador Fairbanks that she was going to run for office some day and that "if I ever reach the top, I told him, I want you to be my secretary of state and I told him I wanted him to be my national security advisor. And he left a message for me that he was sorry he wouldn't have the time to do that."

"Anne, it's so good that you told him that. He must have loved what you said." Then he paused and added, "I do."

"Do you? Do you think I'm being silly?"

"I think you're being visionary. And I would be proud to serve with you, as I know he would have been. And I'll campaign for you, Anne. You're serious, aren't you?"

"Oh, yes. I'm very serious. I know everything I want to do."

"I'm sure you do. And I'm sure you'll—do it all. You'll go all the way."

"I will, Mr. Daschle."

When they got up to leave, she examined the table and hurriedly picked up the swizzle sticks lying on the tablecloth. Then she picked up the small paper napkin that had the printed illustration of the view she didn't see. She put them in her purse without looking at him, while her face, which was held low, had an expression of defiance.

"Anne?"

She quickly looked up at him, and her expression of defiance changed to a look of fear, as if he was going to condemn her for her act of thievery. "What?"

"It's so good to see you again, Anne."

She smiled. She was pleased that he had said that. Her eyebrows lifted, both of them forming the shapes of upside-down 'v's', and she said, "I collect swizzle sticks—from all over the world."

That statement told him enough to cause a glow inside of him. That was because her justification for the pilferage of the evening's swizzle sticks from the table at the Chaparral did not explain her confiscation of the napkin.

He knew she was preserving a memory.

Irene Goodpastor informed the others who she had met in Hong Kong about Mary and now Gerald Fairbanks, and she had previously written them about the imprisonment of Jonas Valadovich. But she hadn't sent a letter that informed her select recipients about Adam because she had yet to be told anything about him.

She was called to the State Department by one of those who received her regular letters of information: Cody Cooper.

He was sitting at his desk and Mrs. Goodpastor, wearing a large plastic-covered visitor's badge, was sitting across from him. He handed her a piece of paper that he had asked his secretary to bring in to him. "When I received your letter about Ambassador and Mrs. Fairbanks, I realized you didn't know what happened to Adam Orr, Mrs. Goodpastor," Cody said. "I not only want you to know, but I'm sure you want to inform the others."

She read the cable he had given her which had the notification of Adam Orr's death. With her free hand, Mrs. Goodpastor took a handkerchief from her purse. She sobbed and re-positioned her handkerchief and sobbed some more. Then she blurted out, "We were in love!"

"You and Mr. Orr?" Cody asked in amazement.

Mrs. Goodpastor looked up at the ceiling and nodded. "No one knew. It started in Hong Kong. I don't want to go into all that, but we were–in love."

Adam, more than ever, wished that he was once again alive when he heard that one. How could she lie like that?

"Were you going to get married to each other?" Cody asked.

Mrs. Goodpastor nodded again, and she put her handkerchief to her nose. "Let's not talk about it. I have a ring," she added.

Adam couldn't help it. He turned the electricity off and then on again. Cody's desk light and the air conditioner made a jolt.

"What was that?" Mrs. Goodpastor asked as she rolled her handkerchief into a loose ball.

"Probably the storm," Cody said. "It probably did something to the electricity, but we have a generator here."

She put her rolled up handkerchief on her lap and Adam blew it off. She bent down to pick it up. "Will there be services when they return the body, Cody?" she asked.

"Oh, he's been buried, Mrs. Goodpastor. I'm sorry you didn't know at the time. He's buried at Arlington."

She nodded. "Oh, yes. He was a veteran. He was in the battle of Tarawa."

"I wasn't in Tarawa!" Adam said, but of course he couldn't be heard. "I was in the Battle of the Bulge, you old battle-ax!"

"Oh, I thought he was in the Korean War," Cody said.

"I was!" Adam said, "I was there, too."

"No," she said. "It was just World War II. Tarawa."

"What on earth do you know?" Adam asked.

"I'll write the others," she said.

"Don't!" Adam almost yelled.

There was the sound of a fleet of sirens outside. Cody got up from his desk and went to the window. "It's a procession on Twenty-Third Street. I guess the president is going somewhere. When he goes somewhere with all those cars behind him, it looks like a funeral."

"Please don't talk about funerals, Cody."

"Oh, I'm sorry. I didn't mean anything."

"I know. I know." Then she gave what she hoped appeared to be a brave smile. "How about you, Cody? Is there a love in your life?"

"No one in particular. But I'm seeing someone."

"Isn't it wonderful?" And she put the handkerchief to her nose again.

"It's not like you and Mr. Orr. There's nothing serious between us."

"Adam and I didn't know each other before we sat across the conference table in Hong Kong. It wasn't love at first sight. At least not for me." Adam was beside himself. Mrs. Goodpastor continued. "It took time. Love takes a while. Is yours anyone I know? And remember, I know just about everyone in this city." Her grief over the man she claimed was her fiance, seemed to be under control.

"No. And we're not in love."

Mrs. Goodpastor nodded with satisfaction. She looked around the office. "What do you do here, Cody?"

"North Africa. I was on Latin America and now they put me on the North African Desk."

"Do you like it?"

"I'm just learning it. It's okay. It's just that I can't get anywhere here. You learn one thing and you get transferred to another. You never get any higher. Just lateral changes."

"You'll have your moment, Cody."

A button on his telephone panel lit and there was a buzz. He picked up the receiver. "Yes, Traci?"

The voice said, "Mr. Sullivan at the White House on nine-three."

"I'll take it." He cupped his hand over the receiver and looked over at Mrs. Goodpastor. "I need to take this."

"Do you want me to leave, Cody?"

"Oh, no, no. Stay here."

She nodded. While he talked on the phone, she walked to the window to watch the procession. It had already gone across Arlington Memorial Bridge. She walked away from the window and looked at the plaques and photos on the wall including one in color of Cody with President Kennedy taken in the Oval Office. It had a slight green cast to it as the sunlight coming in through Cody's windows had caused the photo's colors to fade. There was a signature on the matte of the photo and Mrs. Goodpastor recognized the signature as authentic.

When Cody got off the phone, she sat down facing him again and he said, "You know who that was?"

"Who?"

"Sullivan at the White House."

"Oh?"

"He has my old office there."

"Does he?"

"It's actually his old office. He had it under Ike. I got it under Kennedy. Now Nixon gave it back to him. You know what Sullivan wanted?"

"What?"

"He wanted to know if I could send him over copies of all President Kennedy's statements on Southeast Asia; that Nixon would be interested in seeing them." Cody was smiling. "I think they see me as sort of a Kennedy expert."

"Well, you are. That's good, Cody."

"I have all the material. They always phone me with Kennedy questions."

"Good for you. Well, you were with him. You know more than they do about him."

"Yeah." He looked self-satisfied.

"The only thing you have to be careful of is that you don't spend a lifetime as an expert on Kennedy. Some day you have to be an expert on Cody Cooper."

"Huh!" He nodded.

"Do you follow me?" she asked.

"Yeah."

"And some day people should call you, not to find out what Kennedy would have thought, but what you think. Isn't that right?"

He shrugged his shoulders. "I'm not an expert on anything else yet. I'm still learning."

"You have no duties here on Vietnam? I thought everyone did."

"Just that phone call from Sullivan. That's all, thank goodness."

"You surely must have feelings about it."

"No, I don't. That's not my field."

"You don't even know how you feel about what the whole nation is talking about every day? If I were you I would prepare myself."

He stared at Mrs. Goodpastor, thinking about what she said. "I don't know. I just haven't studied it. My friends are on different sides. And it's a very sensitive subject here at State."

Mrs. Goodpastor shook her head. "President Kennedy wouldn't be happy about that, Cody. I knew him very well and I think you remember that he liked his people to think for themselves."

He nodded.

"Don't you want to think for yourself, Cody?"

"There are some things I don't care about anymore, that's all. That big demonstration last November—the big one. My friends came to Washington to protest and I didn't demonstrate or anything with them, but I was walking down Fourteenth Street with them when it just got dark, that's all, but they starting throwing rocks at windows. They broke the windows of Garfinkles and the American Express Office, and the police were coming at us, and I got scared when the police were coming and I separated from them. The next thing I knew there was tear gas all over the place and I thought I was going to gag. It was like a real sharpness in my throat and nose. My skin around my eyes was burning. I felt like I was a criminal and I didn't do anything. I hid for a while near the Western Union office, and then I started running and I went to E Street. There were busses parked real close to each other, forming a wall so I couldn't get through. It was real dark. I heard that Peter, Paul, and Mary were going to sing at the Washington Monument, so I started to go there thinking I could get lost in the crowd, but they turned the light off the Washington Monument and I thought I shouldn't go there because they turned the light off and it was over. It was funny. It all felt funny. There was all this tear gas all the time and sirens and things, and there was a lot of shouting. Chants and things like that. Then something happened. I saw a glove in the street, it was on G Street, and I felt like crying, not from the tear gas, but crying because someone had lost a glove. Someone probably wanted to find that glove. I didn't know whether to pick it up or just leave it there in case some one was looking for it, and they may trace their steps or something. So I left it there. But I couldn't stop thinking about the glove."

"Your friends—did they get arrested?"

"No. But see, they're friends. I don't want to get mad at them or anything, but I can't do that kind of thing like they did. I don't know. They were having a lot of fun, and I think they think I'm real square. I mean I work for State and all that and I ran away from being with them. I just don't want to get involved in any of this—on either side. I just don't care about all that."

She stood up and walked to the picture of him and President Kennedy. Then she turned toward Cody. "Cody, this picture is fading. Look at you on this picture. It's like you were when we first met when you were such an ambitious, enthused, eager, and opinionated young man. You gave up your education in medicine to be a volunteer for Kennedy. Now you just don't seem to be interested in anything. What happened?"

Cody looked down at his desk, then straight at her. "Dallas."

"You can't hitch your wagon to a star, Cody. Stars die. It's the way it always is. You have to hitch your wagon to your head. I know you loved President Kennedy and it must have been so marvelous to work for him, but nothing is forever."

"Mrs. Goodpastor, if it wasn't for me, President Kennedy would be alive today!"

Her mouth opened. After a moment of total bewilderment, she asked, "What are you saying, Cody?"

"I didn't know."

Mrs. Goodpastor went back to the chair facing his desk and sat down again. "You didn't know what?"

"I didn't know anything about motorcades and things like that."

"Cody, you're not making sense to me."

"I went to an Advance Team meeting early that week. Kenneth O'Donnell was in charge of the whole thing. It was in the EOB. The president was going to go to San Antonio, then Houston, then Fort Worth, then Dallas, then—then Austin, and everything was already planned. I've gone over this in my mind a million times; Roy Kellerman, Winston Lawson, and some guy I didn't know from the Dallas office of the Secret Service were all there. I was given a big map of downtown Dallas and we were discussing the route of his and Vice President Johnson's ride, and the vehicles in the motorcade, and where Governor Connally and Senator Yarborough would be, and everything. They said the cars had to get from Love Field to the Trade Mart. On the map I drew a big red line to trace what they said was the route. We wanted crowds. I went to my office and I called the *Dallas Times-Herald* with the map in front of me and I told them the whole route. They printed it in the next morning's edition. That's what I wanted, Mrs. Goodpastor."

"And so you think that Oswald—"

"I told the newspaper the whole route! They printed it!"

"But how else would you have had crowds if people didn't know where the motorcade was going to be? You were doing your job, weren't you?"

"No one told me to do that. I just did that. It wasn't my job. But I was invited to the meeting. When you're in a meeting—you participate—or you feel funny. Then there was a discussion there about the bubble-top, too. Even if it was on, it wasn't bullet-proof or anything but—I said I thought it should be off if the weather was okay. I wasn't the only one or anything, but I was for it."

"Oh, Cody. How could anyone know?"

"I shouldn't have called the newspaper. And I should have said it's crazy to take off the bubble-top even if the president wants it off. That's what I should have done. I was one of those who said, 'yes,' to everything about that trip. Everything."

"Do you know how many people who worked in your White House think they could have prevented what happened? You have to stop that. You all have to stop that."

"Mrs. Goodpastor," and he looked at her with his eyes open very wide. "For a while I thought I'd work for Bobby Kennedy if he got the nomination. Then they killed him, too, and I was so—destroyed. But I was glad that I had nothing to do with that night. I wasn't on his campaign. I didn't tell him to have his headquarters that night at the Ambassador Hotel! I was glad I didn't have any role in that campaign! At least I didn't do it to him!"

"I'm telling you, Cody, the way you talk—do you know who you're disappointing? The one you're disappointing isn't me or even you—or the State Department. You're disappointing President Kennedy. He thought enough of you to have you with him at the White House. You must be what he knew you were. Now, you live up to that, Mr. Cooper! You owe that to him."

He stared at her.

"Now is that what you want? To disappoint the man who had such belief in you?"

He shook his head slowly.

She stood up. "Now, I must be going."

Cody stood up. "Mrs. Goodpastor, I think you're right."

"You know I'm right."

He nodded.

She smiled and came to his side of the desk and attempted to kiss his cheek but her lips only reached the side of his chin.

"And Mrs. Goodpastor, I'm sorry to be the one to tell you about Mr. Orr. I didn't know how close you were."

She gave a look of pain. "It still hasn't registered with me, Cody. But I'm glad you were the one to tell me. I'm going to Arlington. I'm going to get some flowers and take them to him."

The door to Cody's office swept open but no one was standing there. Adam shook his head, "Don't bother, you moth-bitten dwarf!"

"Your moment will come, Cody," Mrs. Goodpastor said. "Be ready for it."

On the first Sunday night of May, Cody was watching television when he received a phone call with an unusual directive. So did Anne Whitney. So did Moose Dunston. So did hundreds of others who worked in Washington, D.C., from top and high-level policy positions to those who had emergency responsibility in the United States government. They were told to be at their desks by five o'clock in the morning since protesters of U.S. policy in Vietnam were going to attempt to stop the government from operating by putting human barricades and roadblocks across bridges and traffic circles. Two-hundred thousand young people were expected to participate in the attempt to close down the federal government.

Within one hour of the phone calls, the secret time told by private phone calls was revealed publicly by Washington television newscasters.

But most of the protesters weren't watching television that Sunday night. They were at rest by that time in both East and West Potomac Parks, massing in what appeared to be thousands upon thousands of dark heaps lying scattered from one end of the parks to the other, lit only by a quarter moon; some with sleeping bags, some with blankets, some with fires, some alone, some couples, some in clusters, some asleep, some strumming guitars, some with tape machines blaring loud rock music. Some on a high, some on a low, some drunk. Some with American flags upside down, some with Viet Cong flags right side up. Some making love. A hundred odors, one odor replacing another with each few steps taken, like the changing sounds from a radio when the tuning dial is turned non-stop. And there were placards lying between people wherever there was a clear place of ground.

Most of those in government who received the directive over the phone made it to their desks before the chief obstructions began the following morning. Cody Cooper didn't make it at all, not because of an obstruction across Key Bridge, but because of an obstruction of his nature. Shortly after nine in the morning, he called his office to say he had a cold.

He told his friends who were demonstrators the same thing.

Anne had arrived at work at four in the morning.

Moose had gone to the White House shortly after he received the phone call, and slept the night in his office at the White House.

When the sun came up, it brought a day of anarchy on all the arteries leading to, and within the city. Once inside a government building that day the worker was stuck there, unable to walk outside since crowds of demonstrators prevented exit or re-entry by lying on the outside stairways and blocking the doorways.

That day of anarchy in the streets and parks and bridges became an overture to a larger anarchy: the anarchy of national security revelations.

The Pentagon Papers, (actually a study of seven million words in 47 volumes titled, *The History of U.S. Decision-Making Process on Vietnam,* commissioned by former Secretary of Defense Robert McNamara when he wasn't "former") were in front of the world's eyes. It included a collection of government memos including secret and top secret documents relating to the Vietnam conflict. The publication in *The New York Times* created a crisis throughout the world.

The political people at the White House weren't bothered by it because the papers were disclosures about the Kennedy and Johnson Administrations, not the Nixon Administration.

The policy people at the White House were greatly bothered by it because too many of the revelations were bound to have effect on current events. Their concern was confirmed by President Kennedy's and President Johnson's Secretary of State, Dean Rusk, who said the release of the papers, even at this time, served the interests of the Soviet Union and North Vietnam.

The intelligence agencies were more than upset about it because many of the memos revealed current code-breaking information, allowing the Soviet Union and North Vietnam to instantly read thousands of cables between Washington and Saigon. Further, there was information about CIA agents and informants whose lives could be endangered.

The National Security Council recognized that the entire Southeast Asian effort was put in jeopardy. Because of acclaim from so many, the revelations served as an invitation to others in the bureaucracy to leak other secret documents.

Foreign chiefs of state were fearful that their own administrations were in jeopardy because many foreign leaders were revealed as being implicated in helping the United States.

President Nixon wanted the publication of the documents brought to court since, at a minimum, those papers were stolen, and theft was illegal in the United States. Most important to the president, the papers included national security information.

Moose Dunston was particularly upset because the papers divulged contingency plans that were still in effect from the previous administration's recommendations.

All of this became even more serious when the president was told that the Embassy of the Soviet Union had been given The Pentagon Papers prior to the time they were printed in *The New York Times*.

Moose was ready to resign after he read a memo signed by "HAK," (Henry A. Kissinger,) that told Moose that he no longer had responsibilities on Vietnam contingencies. "Hold on," Adam advised him. "You resigned when you were working for LBJ. It's not a card you can play with frequency. What principle is involved here? That you're angry? There's no principle this time. Don't even think of threatening to resign. Henry Kissinger, himself, has threatened to resign so many times that threats must be a common, frustrating bore to the president. Every other day he threatens to resign. All the president needs is a threat from you."

When Steve Bull, the president's personal aide, phoned Moose to tell him the president wanted to see him right away, Moose hurried to the West Wing, rehearsing in his head the resignation speech he would use. Or was he to be fired before he could resign?

There was neither a firing nor a resignation. There was, instead, a new assignment.

Moose was asked by the president to prepare a paper of hypothesis: What would happen in Taipei, in Moscow, in Eastern Europe, in other places of the world, and what would happen in the United Nations organization, "if I were to visit Peking? China."

"*Red China*?"

The president nodded. "We've been working on this almost since we took office. No one knows now but you, Henry, and Stoessel in Warsaw, of course. A couple others. We have to hold this one as close to the chest as anything we've ever done before. The international implications are—are enormous, as you can imagine."

"Yes, they sure are."

"You start imagining those implications, Moose. Good, bad, pro, con, Brezhnev, Chiang Kai-shek, the whole ball of wax. Now I want you to know my thinking on this, Moose. What we gain, if we do it, is a triangular lead. Us, the Soviets, and Red China form the triangle. Brezhnev will have to soften up or he'll think he'll be out in the cold. He'll worry about what we and China can do together. It's the right time. You see, some president is going to have to do this some day, anyway, and it's best for us to do it now—before China becomes a powerful world force, rather than wait until they already are a world force. They have 750 million people there. On the political side, Hubert couldn't do it. It would have been politically impossible. They'd impeach him. We can. No one doubts our anti-communism. You put together a list for me, Moose. Now, I don't need the paper tomorrow. Not even next week. I want you to give this your best thinking. I don't want an option paper, I just want every possibility of reaction. We use a code name for it—'Marco Polo.'"

"Does Henry know I'm on this?"

"I'll tell him. Don't worry about Henry. He's high on you. And you'll have carte blanche."

Moose didn't write a paper, he wrote a book. He wrote about implications from domestic media applause, to shock and dismay from Chang Kai-chek, all the way to risking the alliance between the Republic of China on Taiwan with the United States, to some nations taking such a U.S. presidential visit as a signal to vote for the expulsion of the Republic of China on Taiwan from the United Nations organization and to admit the Mao Tse-tung government of the mainland. "Last November Mao got 51 votes, while 49 voted on Chiang's side, with 25 abstentions. We demanded that the issue be considered what the U.N. calls 'an important question' calling for a two-thirds majority for such a change. If we hold to that we might be able to keep the status quo at the U.N. Keep in mind there have been enough abstentions and wavering countries to top even our two-thirds criterion. We have to show them that we're not wavering in our support to keep the Republic on Taiwan in the U.N. Our advocacy of a Two Chinas Policy with both Chinas in the U.N. can't work because, as you know, that concept is rejected by 'both Chinas.' In short, should you visit with the Mainland government, we should be prepared for the U.N. to expel our friend, and at the same time, give Mao veto power over everything that ever comes up in the Security Council in the future.

"I recognize, Mr. President, that you asked for a paper of implications and not options or recommendations, but I can't help but add that I believe there are inherent dangers that outweigh the advantages in making such a trip to Peking."

On July 15 President Nixon made a world-shaking announcement. His televised Oval Office address lasted little more than three minutes. He announced that Henry Kissinger had been to Peking during his recent world tour, and that the government of the People's Republic of China, being told of the president's expressed desire, had invited him to come there prior to May of 1972. He said he had accepted the invitation with pleasure.

The only part of the short address that Moose liked was the president saying, "in anticipation of the inevitable speculation which will follow this announcement, I want to put our policy in the clearest possible context. Our action in seeking a new relationship with the People's Republic of China will not be at the expense of our old friends."

But he didn't specify the old friends.

That evening Moose received the first phone call from Wai-yee in eight months. She was screaming with anger. "Did you advise this treason?" she asked Moose.

"Honey, I advised against it. He's doing what he thinks is right."

"Right? Right? He's a traitor!"

"No, Wai-yee, he isn't a traitor."

"Do you know what this means? He even called it the People's Republic of China! Since when have we ever used that name? We haven't here at the Consulate! Did you get that?"

"Yes, I did. That's what we call it as of tonight."

"Are you going to resign?"

"No, honey. I'm not going to resign. What good would that do?"

Wai-yee hung up—very loudly.

It was even a shorter conversation than the president's speech.

"See?" Adam asked Moose. "Aren't you glad she said 'no' when you asked her to marry you? Told you."

THIRTY-TWO
SEIZE THE MOMENT
1971

Cody Cooper's moment arrived at his office on a Monday morning while he wasn't there. Without his knowledge, the phone in his sixth-floor office had been ringing while he sat sipping coffee in the first-floor snack bar, watching the procession of mini-skirted office secretaries waiting in line to pick up other coffees. *So many of them!* he thought. *How could there be so many of them looking so different?* He would have stopped looking had he known what was going on six floors above, but as tired as he was and as diverted as he was, he remained in the snack bar until a few minutes past nine.

As soon as he walked into the reception room of his office, everything changed. "Oh, Mr. Cooper," his secretary said, "the under secretary called and I have a whole list of people who want to talk to you. The phone has been ringing constantly since I walked in. There's been a coup in the Sudan."

Cody Cooper didn't recognize this as his moment, but he could feel the news reverberating through him. First, the under secretary had never called him before and, second, very few people at State had called him before. Third, he knew he better find out everything he could about the coup in the Sudan since he was supposed to be the expert this week, while the real expert was on vacation. And fourth, why did he spend so much time in the snack bar thinking of unimportant things?

"Get the under secretary back. While I'm talking to him, see if you can get Blaine up here and then call back everyone else who phoned me and tell them I'm in a meeting or they'll think I'm late to work."

From the top drawer of his desk, he took out his Crisis Sheet. It was prepared long before Cody had come to the State Department, written by a nameless foreign service officer to be used in case some crisis occurred about which the reader knew nothing. The text worked for almost anything.

His secretary buzzed. "The under secretary is coming on nine-three."

He pressed the phone button. "Yes, sir?"

A woman's voice answered, "Just a moment for the under secretary." An announcement. Not even his name. Just his title. During the pause, Cody looked over his Crisis Sheet.

"Mr. Coogan?" A very deep voice came on the line. It had to be the under secretary.

"Yes, sir. Cooper," he corrected.

"Tell me what's going on in the Sudan, Coogan."

"It's a fast developing situation, sir. The reports have been coming in all night, but they're incomplete and things are changing minute by minute." That answer was right at the top of the Crisis Sheet.

"How does it stand now, Coogan?"

"Cooper. It's not good, Mr. Secretary. We have conflicting reports. Some say there was a great deal of turmoil, and others say that things are within government control. It was a complete surprise, except there were a few who had warned that something like this was going to happen, as I mentioned to others earlier. They had not predicted it this soon. I've been with this all night, Mr. Secretary, and it would be irresponsible for me to speculate, but things don't look very good. I'm supposed to be getting an update at nine-thirty–our time, of course–and that update should be complete. Also, I have appointed a committee to come up with plans and operations. That meeting is set up for ten o'clock, sir."

"Good, Coogan, good. Have we heard any word on al-Nimeiry?"

"Al-Nimeiry?"

"Yes, is he alive or dead?"

Cody was on his own on that one. The Crisis Sheet didn't say a word about al-Nimeiry, but he kept scanning the paper as he talked. "No one seems to know at this moment, sir, but I have requested that information a number of hours ago. It must have been about three o'clock in the morning–our time, of course." There it was on the paper–the whereabouts of a chief of state: "Some mentioned that he sought asylum," Cody Cooper said to the under secretary, "but that's been denied. The truth should be coming in with the nine-thirty report if we know it by then."

"Asylum, where?"

Here there were some options: "A car which appeared to be his was seen heading towards the airport. I repeat it appeared to be his car." He accented the word, 'appeared.' "We have no confirmation regarding where he was going, if it was his car, and if, in fact, he was going to a friendly country for asylum. We are on top of it, though." He looked at the map on his wall. "He might be going to–to–Ethiopia!"

"Ethiopia?"

Was that wrong to say? "It's certainly unexpected, sir, but that's where some have speculated. There's no way to know for sure, sir. We should take no action until we know more and have some confirmations. We can't act on rumors, sir."

"Coogan, I was going to have a staff meeting at nine-thirty. We'll hold it off until eleven to have the benefit of your update and your committee meeting. I want you at our staff meeting with a complete report and your recommendations. You can bring anyone else that you want. The information you gave me is useful in the meantime. Stay on top of it, Coogan."

"Yes, sir. Cooper. I'll see you then, sir."

The under secretary hung up and Cody hung up, sighed, and put his Crisis Sheet back in the top drawer. He buzzed his secretary. "Get our policy sheet on the Sudan, get every UPI and AP story on the coup in here, get this morning's *Post* and *The New York Times*. See if there's any traffic on it over the wire. Schedule a staff meeting in twenty minutes. I have to be at the under secretary's at eleven o'clock, and what's the capital of the Sudan?"

"Khartoum."

"Get Khartoum on the phone. I'll talk to anyone at the embassy from the ambassador to the marine guard. Has Blaine come in yet?"

"He's waiting for you, Mr. Cooper."

"Send him in."

Blaine came in with a big smile and his hand extended. "Congratulations, Cody. This is it, you know."

"This is what?"

"This is it! A coup! Just think of it! A coup! And you're the man this week. It's like being an understudy and having the lead sick while all the critics are out there. This is your time, Cody!"

"The under secretary called."

"Of course he called. Did you handle it all right?"

"I had the Crisis Sheet. It worked fine, but I felt terrible using it. I didn't know what else to do."

"There wasn't anything else you could do. Now, handle this well, Cody. This could be the turning point of your career. It's a communist coup, you know."

"No, I didn't know."

"This could be their first real entrenchment on the African continent. It could make Tanzania look like peanuts. It could be bigger than Castro in Latin America."

"Really?"

"Let me tell you what I know. There's a guy named Mahgoub. He used to run the country, but was ousted a couple of years ago. Since then, he's been running the Communist Party there. He's been in cahoots with the military, working with a guy named al-Ata. It looks like the two of them pulled off the coup. al-Ata's a general or a colonel or something. I'll find out. The prime minister is al-Nimeiry—he's the guy who ousted Mahgoub before. He's been hard on Mahgoub and the communists. He just made the Communist Party illegal."

"Al-Nimeiry! That's right! The under secretary mentioned his name."

"So, I guess this is the repercussion of al-Nimeiry making the party illegal. Mahgoub's a sharp boy."

"Al-Nimeiry—is he alive or dead? "

"I don't know. See if you can get through to Khartoum."

"I already placed a call."

"Now, when you see the under secretary are you going to be alone?"

"No. It's a staff meeting."

"Good! Couldn't be better! The seventh floor! You've got to shine!"

"Give me some advice."

"First, know everything. Get your staff together and find out everything. Don't bring anyone with you to the under secretary's meeting. You have to be the expert. You can't look like you've brought someone from this office because they'll think you brought him because he knows more than you do. Before anything else, read the wires, study them. They're better than our traffic."

"I've arranged for that."

"Memorize all the names. Talk about them as though they're your personal friends. Memorize a few facts that have nothing to do with the coup, but make it just flow like second nature. Just a few facts will do it. Get the *World Almanac*. See, you can say things like, 'Of course, Khartoum with only 92,200 people, is like taking over Bethesda.' Find a city in the United States with about the same population. You'll sound very knowledgeable. Make it just roll out. Always give odd numbers. If the population of Khartoum is 90,000, make it 92,200; it's better.

"Then say that 'the populace isn't really concerned about communism and democracy. It's a country that lives off the land. If it weren't for their mineral exports'—and find out what they are—'it would be purely agricultural.' I mean, check this out but it's easy to get that data. Get the *World Almanac*. Say, 'They don't know the difference between communism and democracy but we know what that will mean to the whole continent.' And don't worry about the under secretary. He doesn't make any difference. Address yourself to him, but you're really talking to the careerists there. They're all 'us.' Jeff Richardson will be there and Morton Barlow and Tom Keely. Do you realize that? They can skyrocket your career if they're impressed. Now that doesn't mean you ignore the under secretary; the staff likes you to look at him and they'll understand if you sound very concerned and very worried about this whole communism business. They know this administration is paranoid about it. This could be the best thing that ever happened to you, Cody. Now get busy."

"Blaine—I don't know."

"What do you mean you don't know?"

"I don't like to do this. I don't know. It's—what if I do some damage here?"

"Damage where?"

"Here. I mean damage in the Sudan. What if I don't know enough and say the wrong thing? Lives and deaths are involved in all this, aren't they? I didn't know what I was talking about to the under secretary."

"But no one knows anything right now. We don't have any information, so no one could do any better. At this moment that's your bottom line. We don't know, but that won't last. You'll be the man who knows everything. All I'm doing is giving you techniques. I don't want to see you do everything else right but have the wrong techniques. Don't you get it?"

"I guess so."

"No guessing, Cody! This is your moment! You don't want to stay at this desk all your life. Some one has to take charge of this and you're the one. This is the way people get ahead in this place. They have the right assignment at the right time. If it doesn't come, they can rot here. So this is your future. Think of it! You'll be on the seventh floor! I know you've worked at the White House, but you're a careerist now; an F.S.O., and this is the seventh floor! Don't mess it up!"

By eleven o'clock, Cody Cooper was the leading Washington expert on the coup in the Sudan. He found out everything there was to find out. He had read the morning papers and the wire services, he could authoritatively say he couldn't get a phone line through to Khartoum, he already had a staff meeting, and to enhance his techniques, he memorized seven unimportant facts from the *World Almanac,* and the names al-Nimeiry, al-Ata, and Mahgoub rolled out of his mouth as if he had been talking about them every day for years. In addition, he had a speech prepared about the threat the coup presented to the interests of the United States. It was accurate. What he didn't know was that Blaine was going to send up a sealed envelope with a piece of paper in it that would tell Cody something–anything that could appear to be confidential, telling the under secretary's receptionist that Cody had to have it immediately.

It worked.

Everything worked.

Cody retained perfect composure at the meeting, highly disturbed that there should be a communist stronghold on the African continent, yet very cool and knowledgeable on how it occurred, with recommendations regarding the safety of Americans and a list of implications for Egypt, Ethiopia, Kenya, and Chad. When a secretary came in with a piece of paper for Cody, it was a knock-out. He was the man of the meeting. Even the under secretary was impressed, not that it made any difference. Cody received handshakes in the halls. He was a hero.

He had the department wired so that every piece of information regarding the Sudan came to him, and he was the only one who could assimilate it and make sense out of the jig-sawed facts.

Tuesday he didn't go to the snack bar. His secretary brought him his coffee. Three or four buttons were always alight on his phone panel. He had left word with his secretary to be discriminate in who she put through. And he didn't have to refer to his Crisis Sheet anymore. Blaine was right. No harm had been done.

By Wednesday, in the late afternoon, he had a report of 72 pages with color-coded index tabs, full of facts and assessments. This time he called the under secretary and the under secretary got on the line right away.

"Mr. Secretary, I think it's vital that we have a meeting tomorrow morning with the staff. I will have completed a thorough analysis and I would like everyone to be abreast of the facts, implications, and some recommendations of mine."

"What time, Cooper?"

Cooper? It happened. He got his name right. "At your convenience, sir. I'll be done by midnight."

"I have a meeting at the White House the first thing in the morning. Can I see it before then?"

"Yes, sir. I'll send you an advance copy. But the whole staff should be informed."

"Very good. Have it delivered to my house whenever it's complete. We'll schedule a staff meeting for when I get back–say, at 10:30 in the morning."

"Very good, sir. I think it vital for the whole staff to be there."

"We'll get everyone together."

"Goodbye, sir."

"Goodbye, Cody."

Cody? Cody? He would buy a new suit at Raleighs and, tailored or not, he would have it for the morning meeting. Wide lapels and everything. Perfect.

When he arrived at his office in the morning in his new suit, Blaine was waiting for him. He did not look happy. "It's all over," Blaine said.

"What do you mean, it's all over?"

"The coup."

"How could the coup be over?" Cody walked cautiously to his desk, as though it was rigged to trap him.

"There was another coup."

"In the Sudan?"

"I'm sorry. There was a counter-coup."

Cody couldn't sit. He looked at his phone panel. None of the lights were on. "What happened? Isn't this counter-coup interesting to anyone?"

"Well, it's just all over, Cody."

"This is good, then. Doesn't anyone want to know this?"

"They know. It's simple. Al-Nimeiry is president again. That's all there is to it."

"And al-Ata and Mahgoub?

"You can forget their names. They think al-Ata has been shot. Mahgoub is to be hanged."

Cody looked back at the phone panel and its series of unblinking lights.

"I know how you feel, Cody."

Cody Cooper banged his fist on the desk. "So everything's the way it was before the coup?" Everything except for his new suit. He looked down at his lapels.

"It was a very short coup," Blaine said.

"I've never heard of anything like this."

"It was a lousy coup, Cody."

"Look, I know everything there is to know about al-Ata and Mahgoub. It seems to me that–"

"It was the worst coup I can remember."

"What a week. What a week. Not even. Three days."

"It was your best, Cody. It was your best. Honest to God, no one could have done better."

"Let's go down to the snack bar and get some coffee."

There were still some secretaries in mini-skirts standing in line.

THIRTY-THREE
THE VICTORS OF HOA LO
1972

"If you understood what communism was, you would hope, you would pray on your knees that we would some day become communist," the movie actress, Jane Fonda, had said to 2,000 students at the University of Michigan. At Duke University in North Carolina she repeated what she had said in Michigan, adding, "I, a socialist, think that we should strive toward a socialist society, all the way to communism." Both pieces of news were repeatedly announced to American prisoners in North Vietnam.

Jonas had been brought from Sontay to Hoa Lo Prison in Hanoi. Because of his refusal to sign a "confession as a criminal acting against the Vietnamese people" and his refusal to tell the names of those American officers "in charge" of other American prisoners, the torture cell was a daily ordeal. In the evenings when he was brought back to his own cell he was ordered to stand at attention for six hours. His laughing guard took great joy when Jonas, involuntarily, emitted bodily functions including vomit, which Jonas was forced to wipe up from the floor with his bare hands, then beaten with a rubber hose for having to take time from standing at attention. At uneven intervals, that guard put the point of his ball point pen into the side of Jonas's eyes as Jonas tried to remain silent. Those procedures were not reserved for Jonas and he knew it, since with frequency he would hear the screams from other cells, and at the sound, his own guard would laugh.

Rear Admiral James Stockdale disfigured himself to avoid any exploitation by North Vietnamese propagandists. When they demanded information from him regarding other prisoners, he wounded himself again in a horrible way, thus proving to his captors that he would sooner die than implicate other prisoners for what he was told they said or did.

Jonas, as well as other prisoners, was given a constant stream of announcements of demonstrations in the United States, along with the repetition of the lines that Jane Fonda had told her audiences. Now they were adding to that repetition that she was coming to Hanoi to support the North Vietnamese efforts against South Vietnam and the United States, and she was going to visit the American prisoners. They were ordered to meet with her.

Some did. Some wouldn't.

Before the prisoners were given that order, they heard the recordings she made for their captors for replay on Radio Hanoi:

"I'm very honored to be a guest in your country, and I loudly condemn the crimes that have been committed by the U.S. government in the name of the American people against your country. A growing number of people in the United States not only demand an end to the war, an end to the bombing, a withdrawal of all U.S. troops, and an end to the support of the Thieu clique, but we identify with the struggle of your people. We have understood that we have a common enemy: U.S. imperialism....

"I want to publicly accuse Nixon of being a new-type Hitler whose crimes are being unveiled. I want to publicly charge that while waging the war of aggression in Vietnam, he has betrayed everything the American people have at heart. The tragedy is for the United States and not for the Vietnamese people, because the Vietnamese people will soon regain their independence and freedom...

"To the U.S. servicemen who are stationed on the aircraft carriers in the Gulf of Tonkin, those of you who load the bombs on the planes should know that those weapons are illegal, and the use of those bombs or condoning the use of those bombs, makes one a war criminal.

"I'm not a pacifist. I understand why the Vietnamese are fighting...against a white man's racist aggression. We know what U.S. imperialism has done to our country, so we know what lies in store for any Third World country that could have the misfortune of falling into the hands of a country such as the United States and becoming a colony.... You know that when Nixon says the war is winding down, that he's lying."

The order of the North Vietnamese for the prisoners to visit with her was made with threats of additional torture should there be denial of their demand. For refusing to meet with her, a navy commander was beaten daily while in a three foot by five foot windowless cell, for four months. A lieutenant commander was hung by his broken arm attached to a rope, then dropped by the end of the rope time after time, as the table he stood on was kicked out from under him. A captain was hung under his elbows from rounded hooks on his cell wall and beaten into unconsciousness with bamboo sticks. Jonas was locked in ankle irons while naked, forced to lie on his stomach while one guard stood on the back of his neck, and jumped, and another guard beat him from shoulders to feet, with a rubber hose.

Each prisoner in North Vietnam who did not bend to their captors had his own system of endurance. For Jonas it was hearing the voice of Adam saying over and over again, "Honor. That's what's important in life. That's all that's important in life." And Jonas kept thinking of all their conversations in Saigon about God, religion, and time. His watch had been taken from him and the loss of any guidepost of time was another means of psychological torture. In the place of the loss of time measurement, Jonas reminded himself of that walk on the mall after passing by the bier of President Kennedy, and then his visit with President Lincoln, and hearing an echo.

He looked forward to the quiet of what he could only assume were late nights when he would tell himself that "time does not exist except as an illusion. No matter what happens to my body, I must remember that the pain is not happening now, because there is no now. Time is an illusion." When beaten he would think of the moments to come when he could take out the folded small papers which he had hidden in narrow spaces between slabs of concrete in his cell and, with a ball point pen, he would write his religious beliefs in lettering so small that the words could barely be read. Blank paper was treasured, and his writing would start at the tip of the upper left corner down to the lower right corner without a millimeter of space left without writing. Luxury, which was once a car or a vacation, was now the making of a margin.

"It is so difficult," he wrote, "to recognize that pain to the body is irrelevant, but that is our task. We must always remind ourselves that every moment when we are allowed to sleep and dream, we know what it is like to be without body, time, and space. That is what we must always keep in mind when we wake and face our captors. We have been given bodies only to serve us as a means to have an earth-bound part of our journey. What is in us cannot be injured or touched. Only honor can be injured or touched. Pain to our bodies must be inconsequential."

Three weeks after the Jane Fonda visit, penalties were increased for those who also refused to meet with Hanoi's new visitor, former Attorney General Ramsey Clark who, like Fonda, made a propaganda broadcast over Radio Hanoi. He went there with a Swedish group to "reveal U.S. Crimes in Indochina."

The prisoners endured the torture. The refusal to see the visitors and the endurance of the consequences were considered by the prisoners to be their victory.

"They are the best treated prisoners in history," Jane Fonda said after she returned to the United States.

Ramsey Clark confirmed her testimony by saying the American prisoners "were unquestionably humanely treated; well treated," and their living conditions "could not be better." The health of the American prisoners are "better than mine, and I am a healthy man."

THIRTY-FOUR
THE TAXI
1972

"How long will Dunston last?" Ted Murphy asked the president's press secretary, Ron Ziegler, at the White House news briefing that was packed with the White House press corps.

"The president has full confidence in Moose Dunston, Ted. That question is off base."

"Does Kissinger have full faith in him, Ron?" Murphy wouldn't let the subject drop.

"The National Security Advisor has full confidence in everyone on the N.S.C. staff." He nodded at Helen Thomas who had her hand up. "Helen?"

Ted Murphy walked out of the briefing to his partitioned space in the press room and took from his desk drawer a folder marked, "Dunston." He knew he had a story, but it was incomplete. What he did know was that Moose had been opposed to the president going to China and when the president went to China, Moose wasn't on the trip. He knew that some people at the White House were treating Moose like a pariah, particularly since that trip to China that Moose had opposed, received both domestic and world approval.

Ted Murphy wanted to add more to the story. He had sources in the State Department bureaucracy who would nod when Murphy gave a fictitious accusation about Moose, allowing Murphy to say "it was confirmed by a State Department source."

He reported that Moose's contingency paper on what became the "China Decision" did Moose in with both Kissinger and the President and the rapport between him and Kissinger became magnified during the war between India and Pakistan, when a leak from the Washington Special Action Group that had been put together by the National Security Council, was revealed in the press by columnist, Jack Anderson. The revelation was ruinous to U.S.-India relations since the leak was nothing less than precise minutes of three secret meetings of that group in which Kissinger had told its members that the United States was "tilting" toward Pakistan rather than maintaining a policy of neutrality between the two governments. Murphy reported that Moose was high on the list of suspects as the one who had given that information to Jack Anderson.

Moose was keeping a low profile, which was easy for him to do since he had not been given a new assignment. He would sit in his office without anyone expecting anything from him.

To relieve his boredom and to relieve his conscience while remaining on the job without assignment, Moose wrote an unrequested paper on the civil war in the African country of Burundi, in which Moose concluded that the United States foreign policy in Africa was unjustifiably following the lead of the U.S. media rather than reality: that the United States was only taking tacit interest in 200,000 being killed in a genocide between Hutus and Tutsis in Burundi. He wrote, "Please note that in South Africa three black men are killed by a white man, which causes worldwide horror, while in Burundi hundreds of thousands of blacks are killed, with the media and, in fact, most of the world yawning because the killers aren't white–they're black. What have we done for Burundi? Nothing, except substitute our ambassador for another one there. Do we care about the murdered, or is our interest limited by the color of the murderers?" Moose received a memo back from Kissinger saying he had sent Moose's report to Secretary Rogers over at the State Department.

"The State Department will kill it," Moose said to himself.

One month followed another without an assignment.

The question continued: "Let me try it again, Ron: how long will Dunston last?" Ted Murphy asked Ron Ziegler again, as he did at practically every Press Briefing.

"Nothing has changed, Ted. You're wasting your time–and the time of your colleagues–and mine."

"What's his assignment, Ron? What's he doing?"

"Ted, you know that we don't comment on the daily assignments of the National Security Council staff. You'll notice that the middle initial of N.S.C. stands for 'security,' as unhappy as that may make you."

Ted Murphy wouldn't give up. His folder labeled "Dunston" was beginning to bulge. He even had papers in that folder on who Moose was dating.

From his partition in the White House press room, Ted Murphy dialed Moose's private extension.

"Dunston here," Moose answered.

"Hey, ol' buddy," Ted said. "You still workin' here?"

"Who's this?"

"Ted. Ted Murphy."

There was a long silence then a very quiet, slow statement, "I thought you were still in Southeast Asia somewhere."

"You don't watch TV, ol' buddy. I'll be goin' back to 'nam in a couple months. I needed the rest and relaxation of the White House."

"What do you want?"

"Jeez, you're a friendly sort."

"What do you want, Murphy?"

"I want to know why you leak to Jack Anderson and not to me? Wouldn't you rather have your stuff on TV rather than leaked to a has-been columnist?"

"You're the one who started this Anderson thing. There isn't a person in this complex who pays attention to your stuff. I don't leak to anyone, but if I did you'd be the last one on the list unless I was leaking ...leaking ****."

"You know we protect our sources, Dunston. Anderson doesn't tell–and neither do I. But I hear rumor that Kissinger thinks you're the leaker, and he's sending the Plumbers after you." Murphy was using his old device of saying a word that would indicate he had an inside story.

"Cool it, Murphy."

"Well, some one's spreading the story that Henry's gonna have your head."

"It's obvious who's spreading the story."

"I didn't start it. Maybe it's Henry. He's the one who would know. For all I know, he's the leaker. He's a more likely suspect than you. He leaks as much as Mel Laird, but Laird has more loyalty–he only leaks to Evans and Novak."

"Get off it, Murphy. Go get your stories somewhere else."

"Listen, Dunston, give this one thought: if you really care about the folks in Africa, give me a copy of your report and I can get the entire world to care about those folks. I can make a 'three-parter' out of it and call it 'The Dunston Report.' 'The Secret Papers of the Dunston Report.' You'd be all over the map. It would be good TV. Good for you, good for me."

How he knew about the report on Burundi was a total mystery. Moose didn't answer him.

"This'll do you good. You're the only guy in the whole town who seems to care about Africa. You know that Henry isn't goin' to do anything with your report. I'm in the position of bein' able to go above his head directly to the people–and I'm givin' you that opportunity, ol' buddy. That is, if you really care about those folks in Africa."

Moose retained his silence.

"Hey, 'ol buddy. Maybe you better vote for McGovern!"

Moose hung the receiver back on its cradle.

President Nixon won re-election 49 states to one, more states than had ever been won in U.S. history. Only Massachusetts and, as expected, the District of Columbia, voted against him. Since the opposing candidate, George McGovern, wanted America to get out of Vietnam, with the theme of "Come Home, America," the election was not only a victory for the President, it was a victory for U.S. policy in Vietnam. That landslide of opinion had the potential of stopping the North Vietnamese government from its perpetual habit of leaving the Southeast Asian Peace Talks convening in Paris, then coming back, then leaving again. If the North Vietnamese government perceived the election as U.S. unity on the war, the President believed that peace might be very close.

The morning after the election, there was a memo on Moose's desk: "All members of the White House Staff are expected to submit a pro forma letter of resignation to become effective at the pleasure of the President. Please include with your resignation letter the attached confidential memorandum indicating your personal plans and preferences for the next term. These should be submitted to the Staff Secretary by Friday, November 10.

"The purpose of the resignations is to give the president a free hand to strengthen the structure of government as he begins his second term.

"While it is recognized that this period will necessarily be a time of some uncertainty, this will be dispelled as quickly as possible....This is not a vacation period."

Unlike many of his colleagues, Moose was delighted with the memo. The attached instructions and form gave him the opportunity to do exactly what he had been hesitant to do in the past for fear it would have seemed that he was a resignation-addict or appear to be disloyal. He wrote a letter of resignation as requested, along with filling out the form, writing he would stay only if he could work on Vietnam policy and develop contingencies for the return of American Prisoners of War.

The following Saturday morning there was another memo on his desk. It was a scribbled handwritten note that read, "MD—TP in KB enthusiastic re your memo. Start re POWs now. HAK approves. You're on. I'm glad, Moose. HRH." MD was Moose Dunston, TP was The President, KB was Key Biscayne, POWs were Prisoners of War, HAK was Henry Kissinger, and HRH was Bob Haldeman.

"H.D.!" Moose said to himself. H.D. was Hot Dog. Then he looked through his window at the deep blue autumn sky above the White House residence. "Did you read that memo, Adam? POWs! That includes Jonas, too! Not bad, huh? Or did you have a hand in all this, A.O.?"

The flag above the residence was tight against the silver pole, and then it furled out just for a moment and quickly went back against the pole in the breezeless Saturday morning.

He started his work that day. Where should the former prisoners be brought? Where do their families go to meet them? How long before they go home? Where should the former prisoners be brought for a physical exam? Will they need psychiatric help? What de-briefings should take place? How long before the media should be able to interview them? What if they condemn U.S. policy? What if they have lapsed into the Stockholm Syndrome and praise their captors? If they condemn their captors, does it endanger those prisoners Hanoi might still be holding? What should the president's personal participation be in all this? By Saturday night he had a list of eighty questions, and all that was left to do was to think of every option to all eighty questions and give eighty recommendations.

The next week was spent going between the White House, the Department of Defense, the State Department, and talking on the phone to former American Prisoners of War who had been held in enemy territory during World War II and the Korean War. Generally, the few known to have been freed from North Vietnam were of no value. Most were the ones who, mid-war, had bent to the demands of their captors and came back home giving the lines the North Vietnamese demanded in return for their freedom.

"Where to, chum?" the cab driver asked Moose at dusk as the driver leaned toward the window of the passenger side of his taxi outside the State Department. "I'm going downtown," the driver continued, "so if you are, then come on in."

"The White House," Moose said. "Northwest gate."

"Jump in!"

"Thanks." Moose went in the cab.

"You mean the Red House, don't you?" The taxi driver had his own designations of Washington buildings and institutions.

"What do you mean?" Moose slammed the door closed.

"Hey! Dump the pipe!"

Taking a taxi in Washington was one of the horrors of that city. Drivers regularly told the passengers where they were going, not willing to go out of their way for the prospective passenger. The customer was never right. If the cab driver didn't smoke, he wouldn't let his passenger smoke. If the cab driver wanted to listen to the radio, his passenger would have to listen to the radio, and with the cab driver's choice of station and volume. The cab drivers were fussy and left stranded anyone they wanted to leave stranded. When it rained they ignored everyone except those standing in groups of four or more. They never cared if their cab's top-light was on or off to indicate whether the cab was occupied or unoccupied, therefore it was usually off and everyone who wanted a cab at night had to wave at all oncoming automobiles in the hope one would be a vacant taxi. None of the District cabs had meters, as they operated on a zone system found nowhere else in the world. Each crossing of a zone brought a pre-determined higher charge. The zones were marked on unintelligible maps covered with ripped, yellowed celluloid, posted on the back of the front seat of every taxi. To add to the confusion, there were metered cabs from Maryland and Virginia that would drop off their passengers in the District but would be legally unable to pick up anyone in D.C. And there were the special airport-only cabs, whose drivers would stop for a frantic, waving person, the cab driver mouthing the word "Airport?" through a sealed window, and then speed on before the frantic person could answer. It was worth thinking over whether or not to attempt to get a cab. It was often wiser to walk and spare the tension.

"What are you going to do at the Red House, chum?" the taxi driver asked.

"Okay, okay. What do you mean the Red House?" Moose asked.

"Haven't you heard, Mac?"

"Haven't I heard what?"

"The China thing. It's the Red House now. Who are you going to see over there, pal? Nixon or Mao?"

"Neither."

"Charlie Chan?"

Moose didn't answer him.

"Why don't you go to the Hecht Company instead?"

"I want to go to the White House."

"There's a sale at the Hecht Company."

"Some other time."

The cab driver braked to a stop at a corner where a woman stood holding two large bundles. "Where to, hon'?"

"Crystal City. Is that okay?"

His answer was his foot on the accelerator. It was not okay.

"When I think what I did for Nixon in '68. I didn't do it this year for him."

"You worked for him in '68?"

"Hey! I know who you are!" He was looking at Moose through the rear-view mirror. "Hey, pal, I know who you are!"

"You do?"

"You were on TV last night!"

Moose shook his head. "Sorry. Not me."

"Oh, yes it was. I have a good memory for faces. That was you."

"What was I doing?"

"On the news. You're one of those Watergate guys. You know, you're in the Watergate thing."

"What are you talking about?"

"You working for Charlie Chan?"

"I work for President Nixon."

"See? You were on TV. You're in the Watergate thing."

"Just exactly what is it you saw?"

"You, chum. It was on the news. Ted Murphy was giving a report on Watergate. I don't remember what he said, but your picture was there and he talked about you."

"Okay. I think you have me confused with someone else."

"I don't confuse. I never confuse."

They rode in silence for a while with the cab driver looking periodically through the rear-view mirror at Moose's face. "It was you, chum."

"It wasn't me."

"You know what I did for your boss in '68? You want to know what I did for him?"

"What?"

"I told everyone of my passengers if they didn't vote for him I'd drop them off on 14th and U. And if they gave me any lip, I did it. You should have seen them tremble with the Black Panthers all around them. I watched them through the rear-view mirror after I dumped them. I won that election for him. Now I wish I did it for Humphrey. He wouldn't have done that China thing. I don't know, if you vote for an anti-commie, you get a commie. If you vote for a commie, you get an anti-commie. You know what I did this time? I voted for Norman Thomas as a write-in."

"He's dead."

"Not if he won. I voted for him because he's a dead socialist. That means he'd come back to life and drop the bomb on Moscow."

"I don't think you'd like that. Think that one over."

"You want to go to the Northwest gate of the Red House or the corner of 14th and U?"

"The Red House," Moose conceded.

"Hey, is that pipe still burning? I have asthma, Mac."

"Sorry. It doesn't go out right away. I'll put the ashes in the ashtray, here, and that will stop it."

"Don't put them in the ashtray! I like to keep it clean. And don't put the ashes on the floor; this isn't New York. Open the window and dump out the ashes."

Moose lowered the window and held his pipe outside, then turned it upside down so the ashes fell to the street.

"It was you."

"It wasn't me," Moose answered quietly.

"If it wasn't you, you sure look like whoever it was. I say it's you but you guys all look the same. Every one of you guys come to Washington looking different from each other and you leave looking like each other. It happened with the Kennedy boys and the Johnson boys, too, so it isn't just you guys. This town once had five hundred Ted Sorenson's and then it had a thousand George Reedy's. You end up looking like the other people in the administration. You Nixon guys all look like Ken Clawson. And I'll tell you–you go tell your President you don't like the China thing and you'll look like you did when you came to this town. You looked better then."

"You didn't see me when I came to Washington."

"You looked like yourself." The taxi pulled up in front of the Northwest gate of the White House. "That'll be $1.10. We crossed over the zone line. You should have walked to 21st Street before you hailed a cab. You could have saved 50 cents if you caught me at 21st. You'll learn when it's time to leave this town. That's when they all learn. And you couldn't have looked this way when you came here."

"What way?"

"The way you look now. One dollar-ten and don't slam the door like you did when you came in. I have a headache. It comes with the asthma."

The first thing Moose did when he got inside the West Wing of the White House was to go to the men's room to look in the mirror. He didn't look like Ken Clawson. Maybe a little.

After picking up a cheeseburger-to-go in the White House Mess, he went to his office in the EOB. His secretary was gone. On his desk was a pile of papers that arrived through the day. He rapidly looked through it and found a manila envelope with the words THE WHITE HOUSE on the upper left, recognizing it as his daily copy of the President's News Summary.

He sat at his desk and flipped through it, and then found evidence that the cab-driver did have a good memory for faces:

On Page Six of the News Summary was the paragraph, "Ted Murphy reported that 'As if President Richard Milhous Nixon needed any more trouble, his foreign policy team is in disarray. National Security Advisor Henry Kissinger is in a bitter rift with criticism coming from this man, Moose Dunston, a middle-level staff member who has battled with Kissinger on every topic from China to Vietnam to the Soviet Union to African policy. In secret papers called The Dunston Report, he accused Kissinger of a racist African policy. There are those in the White House who say Dunston is on his way out.'"

Moose was sick. He read it again. And then again.

He threw the cold cheeseburger in the waste basket, then picked up the phone receiver and asked the White House Operator, "Give me Signal, please, Mary Ellen."

He waited until a voice announced, "Signal."

"Dunston here. I want you to run last night's 6:30 News, Channel 9. Can you do it?...When?...Great. I'll turn the set on." He punched the button of his television set and sat through a replay of last night's news. And that's when he discovered why the cab driver associated him with the Watergate break-in. Ted Murphy was giving a report on "political dirty tricks" and behind his left shoulder was a huge chromo-keyed picture of the Watergate complex. Murphy changed subjects to "As if President Richard Milhous Nixon needed any more trouble..." but the picture of the Watergate complex sustained throughout the entire narrative about Moose, with the picture of Moose fading in on the other side of the screen.

Moose picked up the receiver of the phone again and punched the "I.O.", the Inter-Office button which by-passed secretaries, then dialed 500.

"Henry?...Moose Dunston. May I see you?...Whenever you have time.... Thanks...I'll be right over."

Henry Kissinger couldn't have been more understanding. If this was the way he was negotiating with Le Duc Tho in Paris, Kissinger would get an agreement on Vietnam beyond anyone's imagination. He said that he recognized Ted Murphy was attempting to attack the administration, and that he and the president had full confidence in Moose. "Your loyalty is unquestioned. As for the paper on Burundi, both the president and I want you to keep writing exactly as you have been; frank and thoughtful. Neither the president nor I want yes-men around, and your insights and recommendations remain valuable. Don't worry about the media or the rumors. If we worried about those things here, this administration wouldn't have lasted one day. Ignore Murphy and keep your eye on our goals. I'll see Ziegler so he knows how to answer these things, and if necessary I'll talk to the press about it. I'm glad you're working on Prisoner of War return contingencies. It's my hope that we can put them to use very soon. Peace is at hand, Moose."

As Moose walked from Kissinger's office back to his own office he didn't know if he was a beneficiary or victim of Henry Kissinger's genius of diplomacy. But no one did. That was part of the genius.

When he got back to his own office he requested Signal to re-run the Murphy segment of last night's newscast. When it was done and Moose clicked off the television monitor, he couldn't help but think of the cab driver. who thought Moose took part in the Watergate break-in, or as he called it, the Watergate Thing. The visuals on the television screen justified that thought.

Moose felt he had to get out of there for a while. He felt confined with too many things on his mind.

He walked out of his office, out of the EOB, and all the way to L Street where he rented a car at Hertz. He had no idea where he was going to drive. He drove straight and L Street turned into New York Avenue and New York Avenue turned into the Washington-Baltimore Parkway and the Washington-Baltimore Parkway turned into Paca Street in Baltimore. Adam must have been guiding the car. Moose turned right and ended up at a place he had never seen before. It was filled with one club after another, each lit by a bright neon sign. It was "The Block."

"Park your car right over there, Moose. Your dates in D.C. have been so dull they drive me nuts. Spend some money on something valuable for a change. Buy some drinks for these poor, deprived women. Hey, there's some new clubs since I've been here!"

Moose didn't even want to run the risk of being seen in a car on "The Block." He whisked around the corner.

"Ah, you chicken! I can't go in alone, you know," Adam said.

THIRTY-FIVE
NEW YORK SNOW
1972

There was snow in New York and what was dingy had turned into a Currier and Ives lithograph. There were ice-skaters in Rockefeller Center and Christmas decorations were going up in Fifth Avenue store windows and when night came even Times Square looked clean because there was so much white on the sidewalks. The streets, unable to retain the white, were wet and reflecting the lights from the signs of Times Square, the reflections creating psychedelic splotches of greens and reds and quick ons and offs. Then, as a traffic signal acted as a starting gate, there was a flood of taxis rushing down that triangle where Broadway and Seventh Avenue converged and those taxis appeared to be choreographed in a well-rehearsed ballet of yellows.

New York was an experienced wench who used snow as makeup to look like a lady. She was totally successful. The makeup would soon run and reveal the truth, but while it was fresh, she flaunted a false virginity. The snow had another assignment: it was not only an effective makeup but a powerful deodorant. Gone was the usual street smell that combined pizza and dust, replaced with the freshness of Lifebuoy soap.

One of the many people in Times Square that night said, "I'm here!" To her, snow was an aphrodisiac. She was standing in a three-sided Times Square sidewalk phone booth with ripped pages of a phone book on the small metal floor of the booth, the pages wet from melted snow topped with cigarette butts and there was some gray slush packed tight to the metal floor's edges. She was wearing her short, white fur coat and her white boots, and her hair and white bow-ribbon was wet with sparkles of snow that had not yet turned to water.

"I beg your pardon?" the voice on the other end of the line asked.

"I'm here!" The white sparkles in her hair and on the ribbon were quickly disappearing as they turned into small cold drops that ran down her cheeks and she liked the feeling.

"Who's 'I'm' and where is 'here'?"

"Is this Mr. Daschle?"

"Yes. Mark Daschle.""

"'I'm' is Anne and 'here' is New York!"

"Anne Whitney?"

"I'm in New York, Mr. Daschle!"

The aphrodisiac was pouring its way in feminine spurts through the New York phone wires from the booth in Times Square to Mark Daschle's apartment on the East Side. He could feel it. "What are you doing here?"

"I'll tell you when I see you."

"When?"

"I'm not on duty tonight, just in transit. Will you buy me a drink?"

"Yes. When?" How could he get so excited about Anne Whitney? It couldn't have happened when she was in Hong Kong on his staff, but there was some excitement when he was with her in the Chaparral overlooking Washington, and he thought of that often since that night.

"How long will it take you to get to the roof of the RCA Building?" she asked him.

"The roof?"

"Mmm-hmm."

"In this weather?"

"Yes! We can go in the bar of the Rainbow Room up there and have a drink. How long will it take for you to get there?"

He paused and then said, "An hour."

"That long?"

"I have a couple of things to do first, so it will take an hour. Maybe even a little longer, Anne." The couple things were taking a shower, putting on a different suit, and giving his apartment a quick cleaning, just in case.

"I'll be waiting for you—the RCA Building roof," she said slower than she talked before during the phone call. She looked up at the large animated Accutron sign with hundreds of light bulbs showing a cartoon of a little man running up one stairway, then another to change the hands of Big Ben to match the time on his own Accutron watch. It was 9:32. "I'll see you at 10:32," Anne said.

The spurts of the aphrodisiac coming through the phone were becoming more enticing. "Okay. Good."

He didn't have to look for her. She was the only figure on the roof of the building, proud of her endurance to withstand the powerful and continual gusts of wind. She was facing away from the interior, looking at the diffuse view of the Empire State Building and lower Manhattan, so she didn't see him come out to the roof.

He had to stand close behind her to be heard above those furious gusts of wind. "Hello," he said.

She turned quickly to him, and with a smile she looked up at his face. "Hello."

Although it would have been totally unnatural for the two of them to have kissed in the thirteen years they had known each other, at this moment it would have been totally unnatural for them not to kiss. The night on the roof was so cold, so windy, their clothes were so heavy and their faces, particularly hers, so red, and their lips so close, that it would not simply have been unnatural, it would have been impossible for them not to do what they did—embrace tightly, pressing against each other with their coats an unwelcome but warm shield. They kissed with enough passion to make up for the thirteen years without it.

They were in a mutual trance. When the kiss was done, the embrace wasn't. They looked at each other, both thinking the same silent question,

"How did this happen, and there is something unworldly going on between us." The look between them couldn't last long because the magnetic pull was too powerful and they had to put their lips together again and this time they kept moving against each other in their embrace.

The amount of kisses became beyond count and the taste of each other overpowered the cold. Even the wind lost the competition against her soft scent. What side was God on?

"I don't want to sit and drink," she said with her lips so close to his that he could feel their movement on his lips. "I want what you want," she said, then she paused, her eyes taking a quick tour of his face, and then she added, "like I have never wanted anything before." They stared at each other, her lips were trembling, his breath was fast, they kissed again, and she almost screamed as they did it this time. He had never heard a woman do that while kissing and nothing else. She backed her face away, her mouth open, and then she said loudly, "Mark!" She had never called him by his first name and she did it without thinking about it, in a total immersion in the moment. And then she said a series of "Oh!"'s, the first one loud, with each one a little softer than the preceding one. When the "Oh"'s got too soft for him to hear, he kissed her again for that wonderful taste and feel, and this time her "Oh" was suddenly loud, so loud that the sweeping sound of the wind became frightened as it was momentarily obscured.

Miraculously, with all the shields of heavy clothing between them, he felt a passion that obscured all else.

The taxi ride to his apartment building was a fantasy in itself. All bundled up in their heavy clothing, they sat with their arms around each other, their faces and lips continually brushing, kissing, licking, and whispering incoherent words.

To them, the driver was invisible, no more than a part of the car who had been built and installed at some factory and implanted behind the steering wheel, that was taking them where they wanted to go.

Mark breathed in the soft aroma of her hair as a man dying of thirst would drink water.

Anne whispered, "Are we getting close?"

Mark nodded.

Another kiss, and there was her close sigh that created a short, high-pitched sound.

"Anne!"

"What happened? How did this happen?" she whispered.

"I don't know."

"What do you think of the name NOLA?"

What was she talking about? "NOLA?"

"Yes," and she kissed him again.

"It's a nice name." What was she trying to tell him?

"That's what I think I'm going to call Ambassador Fairbanks' plan."

Mark looked confused. What did all this have to do with what they were feeling for each other?

What it had to do with it was Anne's brilliance in exhibiting that she could think of something else, making him even more anxious for her than before, if it was possible. She knew every feminine trick. Whether it was instinct or learned was unimportant. She always accurately assumed that a man might lose interest if he knew her surrender had been achieved.

"What plan?"

"His world organization. He never told me if he had a name for it. Did he tell you?"

At this particular moment, Mark was in no mood to go through his memory bank to try and recall whether or not Ambassador Fairbanks ever told him a name for his plan. "I don't think so."

"It has to have a name, and it has to have an acronym. What do you think of The Nations of Liberty Alliance? NOLA?"

Mark forced himself to think about it. Her face was so near. It was very difficult to think of anything other than her as a woman, certainly not as a foreign service officer. But this was what she was asking, and so he thought about it to prove that he too, could think of other things. He smiled and nodded. "I like it."

"Do you?"

"It's very good."

Anne nodded. "I thought of it."

"Very inventive. It works. It's just what I'll bet Gerry would want it to be named."

"That's what I'm going to call it when I'm president," and like an animal, she licked his lips.

Anne was never one to be content with the moment. There was always more.

He was glad he had taken time to straighten things in his apartment before he had left it earlier. As soon as they walked in she said, "Don't turn on the lights, Mr. Daschle." She turned toward him. "I like calling you Mr. Daschle." She knew there was a certain submissiveness inherent in her referring to him that way rather than by "Mark" which she did when that name just spurted out.

There was enough light coming in from the 26th floor picture window to see the outlines and silhouettes and even some of the detail of the apartment's interior. He took off his coat and opened the closet to put it inside while she walked to the large window where she could see through the turned out venetian blinds to see other buildings, and just a tip of the United Nations organization building and the East River. She stood there looking out for a long time.

"Anne? Do you want to take off your coat?"

"Come here, Mr. Daschle," she said.

He came to her side.

"Look," she said. "There's a man sitting at his desk in that building."

"Where?"

"There."

"Yes. I see him. He's working late, isn't he? You know what that's like."

She grabbed the draw-rope by the side of the venetian blinds and in one strong pull she opened the venetian blinds all the way up to the top. "Mr. Daschle," she said, putting aside the rope and looking at him. "Turn on the light switch, please."

"You want the lights on?"

"Yes."

He walked to the wall and turned on the light while she continued to stand by the window looking out.

"Now, turn it off.... Now on.... Now off.... Keep on, Mr. Daschle, on and off, on.... There. He's looking here now. It caught his attention. Now he sees me. Don't come near me, Mr. Daschle. Leave the light on. Stay off to the side by the wall, please. I want him to think I'm alone. He's looking right at me."

She had gone from submissiveness to taking charge, as only Anne could. Mark watched her, and so did the man in the office building. Anne opened her coat, but didn't take it off.

Time passed and Mark had no idea what she was doing. With her back facing him and her coat remaining in place, what she was doing was just between her and the stranger.

"Oh, Mr. Daschle! I wish you could see his reaction, but I don't want you to be seen, so don't you dare! He doesn't even know I see him. I'm keeping the poor man from working!"

"His reaction to what?"

"To me!"

Mark remained standing by the wall. "Anne, what are you doing?"

"You'll never know! That's the idea! I don't want you to know! Maybe nothing. Maybe he sees more of me than you've ever seen of me."

"You haven't taken anything off!"

"Oh?" Then it appeared as though she might be doing exactly that. "You wouldn't know. You can imagine what ever you want to imagine, or what ever you don't want to imagine. It's snowing! Oh, he has to look at me between the snow flakes! Are you imagining what he sees, Mr. Daschle?"

Mark hesitated, then answered, "I'm worried."

"I didn't ask if you were worried. Are you imagining what he sees and you don't?"

"I don't know."

"I think you know."

"Anne! Come over here."

"Not yet. This is too much fun. You're Mister 1950s and I'm Miss 1970s, and I'm going to bring you into the times. You can always ask me to leave, you know."

Mark was silent.

"Do you want me to leave?"

"No."

"Oh, Mr. Daschle! You should see him. You should see me! Oh, I love it. He's going crazy!"

"Anne, please come here—or, at least, turn to face me."

"Or did you see more of me than I know?"

"What are you talking about?"

"Did you ever try to take a peek at me in Hong Kong?"

"A peek!? Of course not. I don't do that kind of thing."

"Mr. Daschle, didn't you ever try to sneak a look at me when I was sitting in your office for a staff meeting with the others? While we were all talking? You know what I mean. It's only human. Men do it all the time. I like it. Did you ever try to see more of me than you were supposed to?"

"Oh, Anne. You are something."

"Have you?"

"No. Never."

"Not even for a moment? When I wasn't looking?"

"Never."

"You're lying, aren't you?"

"No. It was never a thought."

"Oh, I think it was."

"Never."

"I saw you look once where you shouldn't have been looking. I let you, you know."

"I don't know what you're talking about."

"Too bad you're not in that building across the way. Then you could look out the window and see me. I feel safe this way. He can't touch me. He can't even talk to me. There isn't any contact. There are panes of glass and space and falling snow between us. It's just like when I let you look that one time in Hong Kong. I was safe, because you would never do anything. You were too 1950s. But I saw you looking. It excited me because it was Mr. Daschle of all people! I was having fun with you and you didn't even know it. I knew if I could do it to you, I could do it to anyone. I let Curly Kwang see once. Remember Curly? You should have seen his eyes! I thought he was going to explode into a million pieces right in front of everyone! I pretended I wasn't looking at him, but I kept passing glances. He didn't know I knew. For once he was looking at me and not at Wai-yee. Did you think Wai-yee was pretty?"

"I didn't notice."

"Oh! What a liar! Did you ever have anything going with her?"

"Of course not!"

"She was beautiful, wasn't she?"

"Her beauty was of no interest to me. She was a good worker."

"Oh yes. That's what interested you about her. The funny thing is, I even believe you. Oh, look at that man now! He hasn't taken his eyes off me for a moment. Not a moment. He's so excited!"

"Have you ever done this at a window before?"

"Oh, yes! But never while it's been snowing. Oh, I love it! I love driving men crazy! What power I have by doing so little. They just look, and I own them. I wonder what he should be doing that he isn't doing because he wants to look at me."

"I–I–"

"He doesn't even know if I see him–yet. But now I want him to know that I see him. Do you know what I'm going to do?"

"I never know what you're going to do."

"I'm going to be sure he knows I see him. I'm going to look directly at him. I want him to see me looking at him, and let him know that I want him to see me, that this is no mistake of mine. And then do you know what, Mr. Daschle?"

Mark shook his head. "No."

"I'm letting him know that I know. He sees. He loves it. Oh, this is such fun. You don't know! I'm driving two men crazy at once. But I'm going to be more careful with you than him, because there's no glass between you and what you want. You love this, don't you, Mr. Daschle?"

He didn't answer.

"You can't answer, can you? If you said 'yes', you would be confessing. If you said 'no', you would be lying. And so I'm not afraid of you any more. Don't come near me. Mr. Daschle, turn off the light now. I've done what I wanted to do to him." To the stranger or to Mark Daschle? She had created his confusion, anger, jealousy, and intoxication all at once. She gave motions to imply she was organizing herself beneath the coat. "I'm going to lower and then close the blinds so there will be no light coming in and nothing for you to see. That's your punishment. Turn off the light."

He turned off the light. "You didn't let him see anything, did you?"

"Is that what you think?" She pulled the draw-rope that lowered the blinds and then she turned the adjoining ropes until the blinds were closed tight. The room was black. "Think what you want."

Then she turned to him and walked to him.

There was only the intoxication of her scent.

The window was Anne's overture to the rest of the evening.

"Mr. Daschle?" she whispered and he felt her soft breath on the side of his cheek.

And just when everything was about to happen, she whispered, "I love the name of NOLA, don't you? Isn't that a good name for an international organization? Do you remember what it stands for?"

He remembered.

It was her way of remaining in charge and causing him, once again, to think that she didn't have as much lust for him as he had for her. Her faked change of mood did what she wanted; to turn his passion into desperation. He craved her.

This lust for her needed no logical explanation. All he knew was that it was something he had never felt for anyone before this unexpected evening.

THIRTY-SIX
NEGOTIATIONS
1972–1973

Mark was of no value to the world. Not the next day. He was so worn, so tired, so dry, his stomach seemed like it was folded, his muscles so strained, his mind so deadened, that being in a suit and tie and pretending he was concerned about the U.N. General Assembly's last session for the year was a deception he couldn't possibly pull off. Anne. Anne, of all women. "She did this to me. No, no. I did this to me."

While he had been in the world of Anne during the night of December the 18th, the other world; the one that had a lot of countries in it, was not having an adventure of eroticism but, rather, was having a new and intense dispute among its leading inhabitants. Mark tried to grasp what he had missed: last night the United States started bombing Hanoi and Haiphong in retaliation for the North Vietnamese leaving the negotiating table again, and for starting a massive buildup in preparation for an offensive against South Vietnam. The Soviet Union was threatening the United States for the bombing, warning that "the governing circles of the Soviet Union are giving the most serious consideration to the situation." Mark's boss at his post of USUN, which was short for United States, United Nations, was George Bush, who President Nixon had appointed as the United States Ambassador to the United Nations. While Mark was attempting to rehabilitate himself in the reality of unwelcome daylight, Ambassador Bush was called in to U.N. Headquarters across the street to see the Secretary General of the U.N., Kurt Waldheim. Secretary General Waldheim was not pleased about what the United States was doing. Ambassador Bush came back from the meeting and called in Mark.

"Mark, that man just doesn't get it. You know Waldheim. Sometimes I think he has a screw loose. He's a scary sort. He knows why we're bombing but he acts like he thinks we're doing this for fun. We'll end the war by this—the NV will start negotiating, you can count on it. But, golly, we have a PR problem that you and your people have to get on top of. Before all these people across the street go home from this session we better get a policy paper on all their desks that will give it to them straight."

"Bush, not Anne! Bush, not Anne!" Mark told himself. Now he was angry about the night before. He unsuccessfully tried to evaluate his feelings about Anne. *Think! Get your sanity back! This could be the turning point of the war in our favor and here I am, like a fool, trying to figure out whether or not I should have been with Anne last night! Bush! Vietnam!*

Happily, Mark's staff was professional enough to have already started drafting what Ambassador Bush was ordering before they were told he wanted it done. Mark read over their papers through blurred eyes and nodded. "Yes. Good. Very good. Get this to Ambassador Bush's office for his clearance, and let's get this out before the session's done. We only have a couple hours." Then he said, but only to himself, "Thank God the session's going to be over in a couple hours or I'd have to be working all night here. I have to get some sleep."

But it didn't take long for his passion to win its war against his tired body and mind, and in his passion's victory there was a tremendous re-ignition of all he felt the night before. Once a couple hours at work passed and the paper his staff had prepared was released, he was no longer evaluating his feelings about Anne. He craved her.

Back across the street in the General Assembly, its president, Stanislaw Trepczynski, closed the year's session by "deploring U.S. actions in Vietnam." Before the sun was down, the U.N.'s delegates were heading toward JFK Airport to go back to their respective capital cities, and with the chamber vacant, Mark Daschle was free to leave for the day.

The doorman of the apartment building greeted him, Mark went to the elevator, he took it up to the 26th floor all in hope that he would open his apartment door and Anne would still be there. If she would be gone, how would he find her? The night before, they had not talked about why she was in New York. He didn't know where she was staying, or where she was going from New York, and in the morning there was only a kiss between them while she was still in his bed, and she turned to go back to sleep when he left to USUN.

Now he was back in the hallway outside his door and it looked like it had never looked before. Before, it was the door to his apartment. Now it was the door that might be protecting her.

He turned the key and opened the door that knew more than he did. His stomach sunk. His apartment never looked more vacant. The blinds of the window were still closed which at least was a physical memory of last night. Some daylight was seeping in through them, but not much. He turned on the light rather than upset the physical memory. But the apartment looked so empty. So was he. "Anne?" he called out. "Anne? Are you here?"

He went to the bedroom. Not there. She had made the bed, and she made it better than he ever did. He walked slowly back into the living room and to the window, just to be near it because she was near it last night. He inhaled heavily and there was still a touch of her soft aroma. Just a touch, but it was unmistakable and wonderful.

There was one thin ray of sunlight coming from the blinds in a horizontal glow, beaming close to a letter left on his work table. The handwriting was unmistakable. He remembered it from Hong Kong. She wrote with a very hurried scrawl, but it was still easy enough to read because her letters were made large:

"Dear Mr. Daschle:" the note started. Those words were crossed out and replaced with "Dear Mark," and that was crossed out and replaced with

"My Dear Secretary of State: The Agency booked me at The Taft Hotel and it's creepy. I'll be checking out at noon and then to the airport on the shuttle back to Washington. I came to New York only to see you. I'm coming back on Valentine's Day. I need to have a meeting with my secretary of state that night. He owes me a pair of stockings. I ripped mine and I don't know how, but it's his fault. He better have a pair for me that night. I can't wait, Mr. Secretary. I made such a mistake in looking for my Sadhu in India, when, although I didn't realize it, I had been working for him in Hong Kong. I hurt. Love, the president." She had perfumed the note. His stomach stopped hurting. In one quick moment he was in virtual celebration.

He went back to the bedroom and plopped down on the bed. He had plenty of time to sleep, but now he wasn't sleepy. And her aroma was all over the pillow. Lying there awake with one night behind him and a night scheduled to come, was better than sleep. He wanted to dream while he was awake.

In Building 8 at Hoa Lo Prison, Jonas heard the bombs dropping—very close to the prison. All the American prisoners of war there heard them. The walls were shaking with the explosions and roars, and chunks of the ceiling's plaster were falling all over the floors. The prisoners of war cheered and kept cheering. In Building 2 where a number of prisoners were together at the time, John Dramesi, Larry Guarino, Jim Kasler, Bob Schweitzer, and Ray Vohden not only cheered, but they danced. The guards did nothing to stop the celebration, as they were ordered to run for cover.

There was a celebration at every prison camp in North Vietnam where the American prisoners could hear the bombs.

"Moose, I think your contingencies for the return of our prisoners of war are going to be used very quickly," the president said. "Keep it under your hat."

"You do, Mr. President? You think they'll be released?"

The president nodded. "You can't count on the North Vietnamese, you know, but now they know we're serious. They didn't think we'd bomb again. They thought we'd be frightened off by the demonstrators. They're going to find out we're not going to be protested into giving up. We won't stop until they come back to the table in Paris." Then he gave a slight gesture with his left hand. "One exception, just so you have it straight. Even if they don't go back to the table in the next two days I'll suspend the bombing for Christmas. Some of our people disagree on that—maybe you do—but I'm suspending it. We can't bomb on Christmas. We'll stop at six Sunday night—the night before Christmas and we'll warn them that if they don't come back to the negotiating table, we'll start it up again after Christmas is over. Now, I read what you wrote, and I can't agree with you on one particular thing you recommended: I'm not going to

Clark Field when the prisoners land there from Hanoi. That would just be grandstanding."

"I thought you wouldn't want to do that. How about when they refuel in Hawaii at Hickam, or in San Francisco at Travis?"

He shook his head. "No. They've been going through hell. This is going to be their time. But you have some good thoughts in those papers. We have to be prepared to take whatever they say when they get home. That's up to them. If they curse us—then—they curse us. And you're right in changing the name those Pentagon boys want to use—whatever it is they want to name the prisoner's return. What gets into them with that bureaucratic talk? What do they want to call it?"

"They want to call it Operation Egress Recap."

"Not on your life. Our men return from going through hell and we're not going to call their return any Egress Recap."

"Mr. President, when they come back, would it be proper if I were there?"

"Where?"

"Clark Field. The Philippines."

"You better be there. You bet. You see to it that things come off well for them."

Very softly Moose said, "I will."

"I hope your friend is on that first plane. Valadovich, isn't that who he is?"

"Yes, sir."

In his usual change of subject before a meeting ended, he made the mood lighter. "How about that Chinese girl, Moose? You ever get back with her?"

"No, sir."

"Too bad. You should have married that girl."

It didn't make much difference what channel was being watched in the living room of the nation's homes:

"It's the Christmas Bombing," Ted Murphy told his audience. "This is carpet bombing, 65 bombs at a time."

Dan Rather of CBS told his audience that the United States "has embarked on a large-scale terror bombing."

Harry Reasoner of ABC told his audience that "Dr. Kissinger's boss had broken Dr. Kissinger's word. It's very hard to swallow."

Eric Sevareid of CBS told his audience, "In most areas of the government, the feeling is one of dismay, tinged with shame that the United States is again resorting to mass killing in an effort to end the killing."

Walter Cronkite, anchorman of The CBS Evening News, told his audience that the "Soviet News Agency Tass said hundreds of U.S. bombers destroyed thousands of homes, most of them in the Hanoi-Haiphong area.... Hanoi Radio said the bombings indicate President Nixon has taken leave of his senses." He let the quote stand.

And the nation's major printed press were consistent with the television reports:

James Reston of *The New York Times* wrote, "This is war by tantrum."

Anthony Lewis, also of *The New York Times,* wrote, "Even with sympathy for the men who fly American planes, and for their families, one has to recognize the greater courage of the North Vietnamese people...The elected leader of the greatest democracy acts like a maddened tyrant...It was the response of a man so overwhelmed by his sense of inadequacy and frustration that he had to strike out, punish, destroy."

Syndicated columnist Joseph Kraft wrote, "Mr. Nixon called on the bombers–an action, in my judgment, of senseless terror which stains the good name of America."

A *Washington Post* editorial said, "He has conducted a bombing policy...so ruthless and so difficult to fathom politically, as to cause millions of Americans to cringe in shame and to wonder at their president's very sanity."

Ted and Linda Murphy sat in their living room watching a televised tape of Ted condemning the raids and, once again, calling those raids "the Christmas Bombing." Ted was nodding in approval of everything that the on-screen Ted was saying.

"Ted, aren't you going to get in trouble? I thought you told me he had a cease-fire for Christmas."

"Baby, If I'm shootin' ya one day and stop another and then start again, what difference does it make? Merry Christmas? I'm still goin' to kill ya tomorrow. We're all callin' it the Christmas bombin'. All of us are."

"I see," she said. "Honey, did you ever think you'd be part of history?"

"You bet I did. And it's gonna get better. Ziegler called me disloyal. Can you imagine him callin' me disloyal? Him callin' me disloyal, when he works for a man who's turnin' this country into an imperialist power that will bomb anyone that gets in his way."

"No one believes Ron Ziegler, honey. You're the most loyal man I know. That's one thing I know about you. It's why I never worry about what you're doing when you're away. You're a loyalist."

"Love ya, baby."

When Irene Goodpastor received a large white envelope with her name and address written by hand in calligraphy, she thought it had to be an invitation to the president's second inaugural events, and she hurriedly opened it.

There was the usual large envelope inside the larger envelope and then the large card. In bold printed italics it announced that she was invited to the wedding and reception of Gloria Eagleton. "Who's she? Senator Eagleton's daughter? I never heard of her." She wasn't Senator Eagleton's daughter. And the word "Honorable" was nowhere to be found on the invitation. This was not an invitation of Potomac prestige. When Irene Goodpastor looked further down the large card, she found out why she was invited to the wedding of a stranger. Gloria Eagleton's husband-to-be was Cody Cooper.

That invitation did not bring Mrs. Goodpastor joy. Not only because it wasn't from a president or a senator or a congressman; her mailbox had learned to accept the absence of their correspondence. Very simply, she didn't want Cody Cooper to be married. Despite the fact they were a generation apart, she thought he was enamored with her, or at the very least she believed he thought of himself as a kind of an adopted son of hers, or an adopted something who confided personal things to her. Surely, he should have sought her advice on love and if, somehow, he was swept away by someone close to his age, he should have introduced her to the Eagleton girl before going this far.

She put the invitation down beneath her small blue lamp on her parlor table, and she phoned the State Department office of Cody Cooper.

"Congratulations, Cody!" she said with fake excitement. "I received the invitation, and that's such wonderful news! I didn't know this was going on!"

"She's a marvelous girl, Mrs. Goodpastor. Will you come?"

"I wish I could, Cody. It's on the 18th, just two days before the inaugural, and the Foreign Minister of Italy is coming to Washington just to take me to the events and the events are going on practically all week. Are you and–Gloria–going to one of the inaugural balls?"

"No."

"Why not, Cody? Wouldn't it be nice to ask Gloria to go to an Inaugural Ball with you? It should be quite a celebration. The war may be over by then."

"We'll be on our honeymoon on the 20th. We're going to Jamaica!"

"Oh, what a shame. I mean that you'll miss the balls. But you'll love Jamaica. It's a perfect place for a honeymoon. But tell me–who is Gloria Eagleton?"

"She's an R.N., Mrs. Goodpastor. She's a registered nurse."

"Well, isn't that–important –I mean isn't that good."

"She's a nurse who works here at State."

"A nurse who works at the State Department? I didn't know you had nurses there."

"Yes, we have some nurses. She's wonderful. She campaigned for President Kennedy, too. I want you to meet her. She's very smart–like you."

"Good for you, Cody. I'm sure she's smart."

"Mrs. Goodpastor?"

"Yes, Cody?"

"Those things you told me in my office that time–I want you to know that I never forgot them, and one of the reasons I love Gloria so much is because at times she says the same kind of things to me that you did–she's very encouraging–and she reminds me of you."

"Of me?"

"Yes. Very much, Mrs. Goodpastor. She's both smart and pretty, and she's kind. She's like you."

Now she liked Gloria. She liked Gloria a lot. Cody was making a wise choice. Too bad she had lied about the Foreign Minister of Italy coming to Washington to take her to inaugural events. Going to Cody's wedding might have been more fun than she originally thought. It would surely be more fun than what she would be doing: nothing.

But this was no time to worry about it. Since it was Wednesday, tonight she would have something to do that had become her Wednesday night habit. She would get all dressed up, pour a glass of red wine for herself, put it and a can of Planters cashews on a TV table in front of the television set, and watch the "Sonny and Cher Show." She didn't like Cher, and could not understand what Sonny Bono saw in her. But she certainly understood what Cher saw in him. "Some day, Mr. Bono," she would say. "Some day!"

U.S. Consul General David Osborn in Hong Kong, called his staff together in the Conference Room. "It's over!" he said. "The North Vietnamese signed the accords in Paris! The bombing worked! It's over! All the prisoners are going to be released within the next sixty days, according to the agreement. What a year this is going to be! Too bad it wasn't a few days earlier, in time for President Nixon to have announced it at his inaugural, and in time for LBJ to have lived to see it. But it's over!"

There was applause and cheering around the table. "We're getting a copy of the accords over the Wireless File. I want them out to every one in the Hong Kong press, moments after we get them! Give the whole text to the *South China Morning Post* and the *Standard* and we'll want it in every Chinese language newspaper in the colony. So Wai-yee, get ready to translate."

Curley Kwang raised his hand. "Mr. Consul General?"

"Yes, Curley?"

"What do the accords say, sir?"

"Free elections. All the people in South Vietnam will have their freedoms guaranteed–speech, press, belief–all of them. The North Vietnamese signed it."

Wai-yee raised her hand. "Mr. Consul General?"

"Yes, Wai-yee?"

"Is there any estimated date of the prisoners release? Is anyone talking about a particular date?"

"Not yet, but we know it won't be long. It's part of the accords that all the prisoners will be released. I don't think it will be before Chinese New Year. Maybe a little after Everybody's Birthday on the 3rd. Based on what I was told, the N.V. could–if they choose–wait through the sixty day limit in March."

"Will they be coming here?"

"No. Clark Air Force Base in the Philippines. But don't let that one out yet. We'll let the White House release all those details."

"Mr. Consul General?" Wai-yee had her hand up again.

"Yes?"

"Will we, our Consulate, have some delegates there at Clark?"

He smiled. "Yes. I think so. I don't know how many. I'll have to check with State when the details come down."

Even though Wai-yee opened her mouth to say something again, no words came out.

Consul General Osborn nodded. "Unless we don't send any at all, you'll be a prime candidate, Wai-yee."

She gave that cock of her head with her smile. That gesture always caused whoever received it to be influenced, even under the most serious conditions in which a woman's smile should receive little attention.

There was a message from Anne on Mark's apartment answering machine. "It's exactly one week before the night of Valentine's Day when you see me." It was her style to put it that way: not before she would see him but before he would see her. "Go to bed early each night, Mr. Daschle. Don't plan anything for us that night because I have plans. But don't forget the stockings you owe me. I'll let you know where and what time to meet. If you can't do it, I'll find someone else on Valentine's Day night and I'll appoint him as my secretary of state, not you." There was a pause and then, "Mark?" There was a longer pause. "I can't wait. Oh, I just can't wait!"

THIRTY-SEVEN
LIBERTY
1973

During the evening of March the 11th, Jonas Valadovich, along with other American prisoners of war, were brought to an interrogation session in which the group was told by North Vietnamese officers that when they get back to the United States they must not reveal their treatment or any other information about their internment at Hoa Lo. Consequences were unspecified but imagined. The prisoners agreed to nothing. The warning was interpreted by the prisoners as the way in which the North Vietnamese were letting them know they were all going home, and no definition of happiness could have been worthy enough to describe the feelings of the prisoners that night. Before the night was done, the confirmation came that of the 591 known American prisoners of war, Jonas would be included in the first group to be released. That confirmation came by civilian clothing being issued to him and he was told that he could put those clothes on when the sun rises. As shoddy as the clothing was, to Jonas it looked like the wardrobe of a king. Still the confirmation was suspect.

No prisoner in Hoa Lo slept that night.

When the brilliant morning of March the12th began, Jonas was told to get in a line with 115 other prisoners, and they were ushered to busses. The busses left the gates.

Hoa Lo was behind them.

There was instinctive apprehension that the bus would stop and make a U-turn and take them back to Hoa Lo.

It didn't happen. They were on the road to Hanoi's Gia Lam Airport.

On the tarmac were three U.S. Air Force C-141 Jetstar medical evacuation planes. If his clothes were fit for a king, then the planes were the gates of Heaven.

The prisoners stood in formation and U.S. officers who seemed to be the delegates of God, escorted them aboard the aircraft. They were told their first destination would be Clark Air Force Base outside Manila in the Philippines.

Once the wheels of the first C-141 raised above the take-off strip and were no longer touching the land of North Vietnam, the plane-load of former prisoners erupted in sheer joy. Dr. Roger Shields and his team of nurses couldn't subdue them.

President Nixon had phoned Lady Bird Johnson to ask her if she had any objection if he cut short the 30-day period of national mourning for her late husband, so as to put the flags of the United States at full-staff nine days early, allowing the returned prisoners of war to see them at the top of the poles on their landing. Mrs. Johnson said that her husband would want the first United States flags that the returned prisoners of war would see on their return, to be at full staff.

Clark Air Force Base had never been host to a crowd like this one. When the first plane landed, a red carpet was rolled out to meet its passengers. There was an army of television cameras and movie cameras and microphones and reporters and still photographers and officials on the tarmac. The first words of the returnees were as eagerly awaited as the words of Neil Armstrong three-and-one-half years earlier, broadcast from the moon.

During the preceding years, the small amount of prisoners who had been returned were those that largely cursed U.S. policy. There were those in the United States who said all the prisoners felt that way.

The first passenger walked out, and the world held its collective breath. It was Captain Jeremiah Denton who had been imprisoned by the North Vietnamese for nearly eight years. Captain Denton walked down the stairwell from the plane and went directly to the microphones. He scanned the crowd. His voice was filled with emotion, yet steady and strong. "We are honored to have had the opportunity to serve our country under difficult circumstances," he said. "We are profoundly grateful to our commander in chief and to our nation for this day. God bless America!"

One followed another, many repeating "God bless America," some kissing the ground, and some on stretchers unable to kiss the ground but kissing the air.

The 23rd man off the plane was Major Jonas Valadovich who, like so many others, kneeled on the ground and he said a silent prayer. Then he stood, and in a voice loud enough to be picked up by the microphones, he said, "May God bless all those who supported us, and above all, who supported our mission to bring freedom to those whose freedom was challenged."

He looked at the crowd of strangers and saw the one man who was not a stranger. Moose broke all the rules; the rules that he helped create. His small blue pin on his lapel, given to him by the Secret Service, allowed him to break those rules. He went to Jonas and no protocol could prevent them from a strong and emotional embrace. Moose said, "God love you, man. And so do I."

"You son of a gun, Moose. Somehow I knew you would be here. How did you do it?"

"Your Grandma is going to meet you at Travis in San Francisco. She's fine. She's so happy. I told her I would call her tonight."

"She's okay?"

"Couldn't be better."

"Moose, you're a saint."

"I can't stay with you, Jonas. They're taking you and the others to a hospital here for a few days to make sure you're okay, then you're going to be flown home. First to Hickam Field in Hawaii and then to Travis in San Francisco, and then home. Then it's up to you and the U.S. Air Force."

"I'm okay. I've never been better. What bureaucrat said we had to go to a hospital for a few days?"

Moose gave a smile. "This one."

"You?"

"Take care, Jonas. I'll see you tomorrow at the hospital. That is, if they let me in."

"How do you rate in–" and he gestured to the crowd, "in all this, Moose?"

"I'll tell you tomorrow. I'll just let you know now that I am a representative of your commander in chief. So don't give me any guff!"

"You are incredible!"

"And even though you don't know it, you're Colonel Jonas Valadovich now. No more 'Major' stuff. That's by orders of your commander in chief. I'll see you tomorrow, Colonel–and bring you up to date."

"You son of a gun, Moose. You son of a gun."

"See you, man. You better get with the others. I'll see you tomorrow."

"Saint Moose."

Moose recognized that so many in the crowd were staring at him because he had gone next to the aircraft where they were not permitted to go. He went toward the crowd, where an unexpected beautiful face framed in shoulder-length black hair was standing just behind the yellow barrier that was separating the officials from the field. Her sparkling eyes were staring at him.

"Moose," she said softly, almost in a whisper.

He stopped in his path.

"Hello, Moose." She had a slight smile.

That picture on his desk at the White House didn't capture the totality of her. Why wasn't every man in the world in love with her?

Wai-yee was looking down at her tea cup, and nervously rubbing its small handle. The staff of the coffee shop of the Savoy Philippines was between serving meals and there were very few people there.

"Did he? The president of the United States thinks you should have married me?" she asked him.

"I don't want to be a name-dropper, but so did the King of Siam."

"Not Queen Elizabeth?"

"I'm sure she would have, but she hasn't said anything to me about it–or anything else."

"Did you tell the president and the king that I love you?"

"No."

"Why not?"

"In truth, it's not the business of the president or the king, only you and me."

She looked up from her cup. "I didn't refuse your proposal because I didn't want to be your wife, Moose. They should know that."

"I know. Hong Kong had to come first."

"And America–for you."

"And America–for me." He wanted to change the subject. "Is your mother all right?"

"Sure. She's fine. She loves Hong Kong. It took a while but she loves it now."

"I'm so glad. And Winnie? Is she okay?"

"She's in Bangkok. She's at a club there and she's doing better there than in Hong Kong. But she hates the weather. It's very hot all the time, even worse than here in Manila. She writes that it's sticky all the time. At least we have relief in Hong Kong."

"Wai-yee, your beauty increases every time I see you."

She smiled. "Thank you. But I cut my hair. I only had it so long for you."

"I noticed. You'd be beautiful if you were bald."

"It's not really short. See?" She fingered some of the strands of hair near her shoulder. "It goes to my shoulders and curls down."

"You look so beautiful. Hey, you know Kissinger will arrive in Hong Kong tomorrow. He's going to stay there for a while for some R and R between being in Hanoi and going to Peking. Be careful. He's a swinger."

She gave a smile. "I'm not worried about that. I know he's coming. I have to be at the consulate when he arrives so I have to get right back to Hong Kong tonight. I just came for the arrival of the prisoners. I'm so glad about Major Valadovich. I know he means a lot to you."

"Then I won't see you tonight?"

She looked down at the cup again and shook her head. "Oh, no." Her tone was unmistakable. She was saying something much more significant than that she was going back to Hong Kong. She didn't say, "I'm sick that I can't be with you tonight," or "No, I can't," or even just "No." She said, "Oh, no."

Moose had to do it: "Wai-yee, have you found someone?"

She wanted to keep looking at the cup before answering but she knew it would be an act of cowardice, so she looked straight into his eyes. "Yes."

Moose felt his stomach collapse. He knew it was possible. What did he expect? What was she to do? Wait? Wait for what? For either one of them to give up their roots? "I see," Moose said.

Then silence, and the silence was terrible.

"I see," he repeated.

"Moose, I'm 35 years old."

Moose nodded, knowing his eyes were becoming clouded. He gave a closed-mouth smile. "No, you're not. You're 33."

She smiled back. "You remember the difference in our calendars?"

"I remember everything."

"We had good times, didn't we Moose?"

"Yes."

"They are good memories for you, too?"

"The best. They'll never come back, will they?"

"But they're part of us. They will never come back, but they will never leave, either."

They said nothing again. The waiter came over, asking if they wanted something. "Want more tea?" Moose asked Wai-yee.

She shook her head. "No."

"A little more coffee for me," Moose told the waiter.

The waiter walked away.

"You married, Wai-yee? Did you marry him?"

"Moose, I'm married and I have a daughter."

He closed his eyes. More terrible silence. The pain in his stomach was churning into nausea. "I see." The waiter came back and filled Moose's cup with coffee, then walked away again. Moose asked what he knew he shouldn't ask but he had to ask. "Do you love him, Wai-yee?"

"Yes, Moose, I do. He's a wonderful man. He escaped from China. He's a lot older than I am. He's older than you. He loves me very much and he treats me very well."

"I'm glad. I'm glad of that, Wai-yee. I know you wouldn't accept any less."

"You would like him. And he's so good to my mother. He treats me like gold."

"He should. You are."

"You'd like him."

He took his cue from what she had been doing before: he looked at his cup as though the cup was important. "What's his name?"

"Yeung Chi-shing. Dr. Yeung Chi-shing. He's a medical doctor."

"And your daughter? What's her name?"

"Liberty!" She said it with pride, lifting her chin as she said it, and saying it very loudly.

"That's a beautiful name." He looked up from his coffee. "That's her Western name?"

"That's her Chinese name!" Now her pride turned into defiance. "That is her only name on her birth certificate. Her name is Liberty!"

Moose nodded.

"She's the most beautiful child in the world!"

"With you as her mother, of course."

"You'd love her, Moose."

"I'm sure of it." He looked back at the coffee.

"You would love what you and I created."

Moose's head lifted quickly. "What?"

Wai-yee nodded.

His eyebrows became a single arch while his forehead became a mass of horizontal stripes.

"Moose, don't look that way." She reached her hand across the table and put her hand on his. "I want you to be glad. I am."

"I'm just shocked. I never thought that—"

"Last December the 16th was her second birthday by your calendar.

She is three now, by ours. It was Everybody's Birthday last month, February the 9th."

Moose put his hand to his forehead and wiped it. "I'm her father?"

"No."

"No?"

"No."

He didn't have the time to figure out if he wanted to be the father or wanted someone else to be the father. "Wai-yee, I don't understand."

"You and I created her together and I love you for that as well as for so many other things. But Chi-shing is her father. He takes care of her. He loves her. He was there at her birth. He loves her very much. He likes you very much. I told him all about you. There are no secrets between us. I want Liberty to always think of Chi-shing as her father because he deserves that, and so does she. I want no conflict—ever. When she becomes older I will tell her that you and I created her, but that Chi-shing is her father. I expect her to understand. Do you understand?"

Moose nodded slowly.

"And I know you, Moose. You're going to ask to help her with money, or something. No. I provide for her. Chi-shing provides for her. That is the way it should be. That is the way I want it for her. Do you understand?" She almost said it with anger.

Moose couldn't nod or shake his head.

"After I tell her, then I want her to meet you," she said. "Will you?"

"Oh, yes. Yes. I want to. I'll be there any time you want. Any time. Now."

"Later. After I tell her. I don't want to introduce the two of you as though you're just a friend. That would be a lie by omission. I want to tell her that before I met her father, the love between you and I created her. And I'll tell her that you want to meet her, and her father and I want her to meet you. That you are a very great man."

"Wai-yee, I—I—"

She saw the emotion all over his face and so she smiled and cocked her head and said, "She better not become as big as you, Moose!"

Moose struggled to make himself smile. He was unsuccessful.

"Really, Moose! Oh, how I feared that she would be as big as you!" She put her hand in front of her mouth as she always did when she laughed or even smiled broadly. "I feared that until just lately, when I could see she's keeping a small delicate, feminine frame. Chi-shing says she will have a small frame like me. Since he's a doctor, he can tell. We're lucky, you and me. She has my frame and your sensitivity. You know that you're more sensitive than I am, don't you?"

Moose gave a short shake of his head. "No."

"Sure. I love you for that. With all your brawn, I think I'm stronger than you. But you are wiser than I am. She will get your wisdom, I promise you. You owe her nothing, Moose. I want you to know that. She owes you because you gave her life. And you owe me nothing. I owe you everything because you gave me her. You gave me Liberty."

Rubber tubes were resting on top of Jonas's chest and the nurse was wiping off the Vaseline from him, and putting suction cups away. Then she gathered and folded the long strip of electrocardiograph paper.

"How does his heart look?" Moose asked her.

"I can't read these papers. The doctor will do it, Mr. Dunston, but he seems fine."

"Fine?" Jonas said. "I'm better than fine, I never felt so good in my life. But I don't want to go from one prison to another. When do I get out of here, Moose? I'm feeling great!"

"You can put on your shirt, Colonel." The nurse walked away, rolling off her chrome wagon of supplies.

"You'll be out of here in no time, Jonas," Moose predicted. "When you feel like talking I want to know about Hanoi. There'll be a de-briefing you know. I know it was beyond my imagination."

"It was a piece of cake. It was the Hanoi Hilton. Other than the de-briefing, I don't want to talk about it yet, Moose. We'll have plenty of time for that. Bring me up to date. You tell me what's been going on. In Hanoi, they weren't very conscientious about telling me what was going on at home. I know the big stuff. I know the president was re-elected, I know there was a baseball strike, I know Oakland won the World Series over the Reds. I wanted the Reds to lose. I want anything named Reds to lose. I know the P.L.O. killed the Israelis at the Olympics. I know the Weathermen exploded part of the Pentagon with a bomb. I know cigarettes can't advertise on TV anymore in the States. I know Truman died." Then he shook his head. "On the plane from Hanoi they told us Johnson died, too. What else did I miss?"

"Not much. But there are some more–more personal things."

"What kind of personal things?"

"You don't know about Adam, do you?"

Jonas nodded. "I know about Adam."

Moose had a mixture of relief and regret. He didn't want to be the one to tell him, but he didn't want him to have learned about Adam from his captors. "They told you?"

"They told me first on my birthday. They said that was my birthday gift. And they told me again every night for months. Every horrible detail. They went over it again and again every night. They wanted me to memorize every word they said and then repeat it to them. I memorized it because they repeated the telling of what they did to him so many times. I never said it back. Not ever. But Adam was my salvation. In so many ways, he kept me going – I remembered all the talks we had about important things. I might have died without those conversations I had with him. Or I might have folded."

"I know you really hit it off."

"He was looking for me, wasn't he, Moose?"

Moose hesitated. But it was a direct question. "Yes."

"I knew."

"He left you some—some trinkets, Jonas." He wouldn't tell him that Adam left a great inheritance to Jonas. He wanted that message to come from his grandmother.

"Did he?"

"Your grandma has them."

"Moose, we, at the prison, gave an oath to each other. We're not going to talk publicly about what they did to us. Not until the others are out. We know they'll take it out on the ones left if we talk too early."

"Okay. I understand that, Jonas. That makes sense."

"Now, tell me about yourself. Tell me how you can be working for another of my commanders in chief? You always work for my commander in chief, whether it's LBJ or Nixon! And tell me about Wai-yee. Did you marry her yet? If you did, whisper, so Adam won't hear."

"No, but I have a lot to tell you, Colonel."

"Hey, where's my new silver cluster?"

"Oh, no. It's no silver cluster. I didn't say lieutenant colonel. I said colonel! You skipped a rank, buddy. Your commander in chief insisted that you have eagles on your shoulders! I argued that he shouldn't do that, but commanders in chief win!"

After the former prisoners were told that all the known Prisoners of War were freed, press conferences were held throughout the United States with the former prisoners telling what happened in the North Vietnamese prisons.

Jane Fonda also made a public statement about the former prisoners: "They are liars and hypocrites, and history will judge them severely."

THIRTY-EIGHT
THE MASK
1973

Anne took advantage of her unique ability to dress like a prostitute and still look like an angel. Angels were not known to wear high-heeled shoes, certainly not that high; or short black skirts, certainly not that short; or white low blouses, certainly not that low; but angels had faces like hers—even when she wore a Lone Ranger mask that matched the red of her shoes. And tonight the ribbon in her hair was also red. Maybe angels wear red ribbons, but there's no scientific evidence of that.

Every one who entered the New York nightclub had to wear a mask. The club offered a choice between Nixon masks and McGovern masks and George Wallace masks and Ted Kennedy masks and Ho Chi Minh masks and Marlon Brando masks, but most people selected the Lone Ranger style that only covered their eyes. Since it was the evening of Saint Valentine's Day, the Lone Ranger eye guards given out were shaped like hearts. All this anonymity made sense because the nightclub was called Somebody Else, with the hiding of identity mandated. Patrons could bring their own masks if they wanted to, but if they didn't have one, the club would accommodate them. If someone didn't wear a mask, either brought in or given before passing the entrance desk, that person wouldn't get any further.

And so the place, which was much bigger inside than it appeared from outside, was filled with men and women who, by the rules, could not reveal their faces, and they were doing in public what most of them would not do without masks, even in private. Strangers were embracing one another and dancing in ways that professional choreographers did not originate. The bar area was filled with drinkers and smokers so close that barstools were on the floor in heaps to make room for more people to stand at the bar, and on top of the bar there were unhired dancers. The music was so loud that it acted as an additional mask; an audible one covering any voices so they couldn't be heard.

Anne had entered Somebody Else at 11:00 o'clock that night and had told Mark to meet her there at 11:30, giving herself the time she wanted to prepare for his first sight of her. It was important for her to make that sight indelible.

The timing was precise. Mark's eyes, bordered by the black Lone Ranger mask he was handed at the door, were immediately drawn to her. That was easy since she was dancing on top of the bar, dancing with her eyes moving as quick as her feet framed by those very high heels. Men, and even some women, were looking up at her to whatever the swirling skirt would reveal of her. And some men reached out for her ankles and calves.

She didn't seem to object or at least she didn't dance away from them quickly.

Mark was spellbound. Every dream he had of Anne's presence since he saw her last was granted in the very first moment at Somebody Else. This woman was a painting of excitement. She glanced at him, and there was only her quick smile and an almost-wink. His presence didn't stop her, it only encouraged her to be even more enticing in her dance.

Mark was almost knocked over by others walking with drinks and hugging others as they walked from one part of the club to the other while he remained motionless, staring at Anne.

Others got up on the bar and danced, all of them dancing solo, and none of them could compete with Anne. It wasn't that she or the others on top of the bar could stop dancing when the music stopped because it wasn't about to stop. Finally, she sat on the bar between two men and she put her hands behind her and using them as braces, she jumped down from the bar as hands reached out. She smiled at those doing it, but avoided them, and walked to Mark. She had to yell to be heard by him, with the music still overpowering all other sounds. "I have a place for us and the drinks are waiting there!" He could read her lips easier than hear her voice.

The club did not have booths or tables. It had mats and pillows of different colors, all over the floor. It was like a giant living room without furniture other than the mats and pillows.

"We'll be comfortable!" she yelled at Mark, leading him by the hand to a blue mat with red pillows by the wall. "Isn't this something?"

"Is this place legal?"

"Sit down!"

Mark didn't look at ease as he knelt down awkwardly to get into a position to sit.

"Mark! This is the 1970s!" And she plopped down without any difficulty, paying no attention at all to being graceful or careful or prudent or demure.

"These people are on dope!" Mark yelled as he sat down, not quite knowing what to do with his legs.

"Shhhhh! I'm not on dope and you're not on dope! They're fools to need it! I'm high enough without it! Isn't this great? We're anonymous! Have you ever?!"

"Ever what?"

She leaned over and kissed him. "Ever, ever, ever!"

There was an uncorked bottle of champagne by the wall. Mark picked it up. "What do we do with this?" he yelled. "There are no glasses. I don't think I can call for a—"

Anne stopped his voice by putting her hand on his cheek and giving him a deep and long kiss. Then she took the bottle of champagne and kissed him again.

Another couple sat down beside them. They were laughing, holding two bottles of beer and glasses. The man was wearing an Elvis mask, and the woman was wearing the same kind of red, heart-shaped Lone Ranger-style mask that surrounded Anne's eyes.

The couple was very close to Anne and Mark, the young man's arm brushing against the side of Anne's shoulder.

"Hey!" Anne shouted. "Can we have one of your glasses?"

The man in the Elvis mask looked over at her. "Huh?"

"We have no glasses!" Anne yelled. "Can we have one of yours? You can have some of our champagne. You two can share one glass, and we'll share the other one! Okay?"

He looked confused, then nodded and yelled, "I'll trade glasses with you!"

"We don't have any to trade!" Anne explained.

"Yes, you do!" He leaned forward toward her in his sitting position, and he took one of Anne's red shoes from her foot. Then he said, "Gimme!" He reached for the bottle of champagne from Anne. In no time, he poured champagne into her shoe. Then he drank from it. "Mmmmm," he said, and he handed the shoe to his girlfriend, who drank the remainder of the champagne left in the shoe.

Anne was smiling. Mark wasn't.

"Isn't this decadent?" Anne turned to Mark. "Isn't this wonderful?" She looked directly at Mark's face and saw his discomfort. "You're anonymous!" she reminded him. "Do anything you want here! Here," and she reached way over to a foot of the other woman. "Let's be even!" she said to the woman. Anne took the woman's shoe from her foot. "Now pour me some champagne in your shoe!"

She did, with a laugh.

Anne looked over at Mark. "Want some?"

Mark shook his head.

"Prude! Did you bring my stockings?"

Mark reached in his jacket pocket and pulled out a cellophane package. "I hope it's the right size. I got this thing at Newberrys."

"Let's see!"

He gave her the package, she studied it, nodded, then opened it with her teeth. With a total absence of modesty, she did what he feared she would do, although his fear was mixed with an intense feeling that spread from her eroticism. She took off her remaining shoe, then she took off her one-piece stockings. She had extreme patience as she adjusted the new one, and then put it around her feet and slowly put on the new one-piece stockings. She knew what she was doing.

There was scattered applause from some others, including from their new companions.

"Thank you for the stockings," she said to Mark. "They're the right size. You did good!"

The woman who was still holding Anne's shoe asked, "May I have your old ones?"

Anne made a ball of her old one-piece stockings and passed them to her. In turn, the woman gave them to her date who seemed very pleased for the gift.

"Wwwww!" Anne said.

Mark was terribly ill at ease, and his only salvation was in pretending he didn't see any of it, or at least wasn't bothered by it.

Anne kissed him. "Want to dance?"

He shook his head even more emphatically than before. "Anne, of course not. I can't dance to any of this. This isn't my kind of music. I'm a two-step man." He was glad she gave him an opportunity to avoid talking about her stockings episode.

"Oh, it's easy. You'll see."

"I can't do that."

"Who cares? No one knows or cares what anyone else is doing and besides, we have on masks. It's a perfect way to learn." She got up from the mat, gave the woman's shoe back to her, and extended her hand to Mark. He grabbed it, putting his other arm behind him to use as a support as he stood, trying to at least appear agile.

Mark didn't know why he did it, but he was on the crowded dance-floor with Anne, leaving the two strangers on the mat with their champagne. Shoeless Anne was dancing like a teenager with Mark, who was pretending he was doing some kind of dance. Anne was right. No one cared. No one was looking at him. The dance floor was so crowded that no one was even looking at Anne or anyone else. Then Anne stopped dancing like a teenager and embraced him in a new dance that had nothing to do with the beat of the music.

Mark didn't know if he wanted to stay forever or leave immediately. Did the generations really make this much difference? Would he be entirely different had he been born a generation later?

By the time the dance went on for ten more minutes, everyone on the dance floor was bathed in perspiration with any number of them holding hands with people they didn't know when the dance began.

Anne and Mark walked back to the blue mat with the red pillows. The other couple was gone, and so was the champagne, and so were Anne's shoes.

"Let's get out of here," Mark yelled above the music.

Shoeless Anne had to adjust to Duffy's Doughnuts, which had nothing in common with Somebody Else. Duffy's Doughnuts was an L-shaped counter with twelve wooden stools, each one covered with torn purple imitation leather. The only employee was a guy named Sol who sobered up the unsobered with coffee and his frost-covered twisted crullers. "I know it's tacky," Mark said. "I come here often in the morning when I don't have time for breakfast. That's when Duffy is here." Duffy was Mark's kind of guy. Duffy never drank champagne from a red shoe. For that matter, neither did Sol.

Both Mark and Anne were having coffee and crullers. "Anne, how—or why—do you come up with these schemes, these adventures?"

"Because I always want you to be surprised by me. Because I always want to keep your interest in me. Because I don't want you to know what's next. I've seen men get tired of women. I never want you to get tired of me."

Mark felt so good not to have to yell to be heard. "I'm flattered."

"When you sent me back from Hong Kong and I had to stay in Washington for all those years of boredom, I wrote a story almost every day or night or both—stories that would fulfill me. By the time I was sent to Moscow I had a volume done and I called it '2002 Nights.' I plan on living 1001 of them—with you. Tonight is only Number Two. Just wait until we get to the higher numbers! You'll live through things you never thought of, and no one ever thought of—but me. Some of them will be insufferable for you but, in the end, you'll crave another just like it—and there will never be another just like it. All of them will be different."

"And the other 1001 nights?"

"Without you! But I'll tell you about them—and watch your reactions. See? When an adventure without you is over—it won't be over, because I'll plan on how to tell you about it, knowing you won't be able to stand it. They might be lies! They might not! You'll never know! You'll be furious but you'll be so bursting with thoughts of me that you'll be driven crazy."

"You're incredible."

"There isn't any one like me!"

"I'm sure of it."

"I want to live! And you're going to be my catch! I'll admit it!"

Why? Whether Anne was his greatest fortune or his worst diversion, why him? If God wanted Mark to enjoy life, He certainly was giving Mark an opportunity. If, however, God wanted Mark to prove his strength so as to continue doing those things he had practiced for so many previous years, God couldn't have provided a greater temptation.

"Somebody Else wasn't good for you yet," Anne said. "You weren't ready for it. You were too uncomfortable. With the way you felt, I couldn't do what I really wanted to do there."

"What did you really want to do?"

"Uh-uh. I won't tell, because I'll save it for some other time when you've shaken the 1950s out of you. Now, do you know what we're going to do tonight?"

"I'm scared to ask."

"I plan on going to your apartment tonight to reward you for doing such a good job at the U.N. with the war being signed away and the prisoners having been returned from North Vietnam. Ambassador Bush told me to reward you!"

"He did not. You don't even know Ambassador Bush!"

"George? He said, 'Anne, I don't know how to thank Mark enough for his good work. What you have to do is be very inventive and make him a happy man! It's for your country!' That's what Georgie said."

"Anne, you're lying to me."

"If you don't believe me, then you're leaving me without a reason to reward you."

Mark took a sip of coffee. "I believe you."

"I knew you would! Now, finish your silly doughnut or whatever it is, and let's get out of here. Tonight you get the nation's thanks!"

"Well, that's very nice."

"And something even better! Secretary General Waldheim told me to thank you for the entire world! It's a big responsibility for me! Oh, wow! I have to thank you for all 135 nations! That's such a big job, but I accepted the responsibility! Tonight's the night!"

Mark took a final bite of his cruller. She was right about Somebody Else. It was not for him. He didn't want to be with anyone else but Anne. He couldn't stop looking at her, and smelling that light fragrance of her. And along with all her 1960's and 70's ideas, there was that red ribbon in her hair. Didn't she know it came from the 1950s? Probably even the 1930s.

THIRTY-NINE
THE 405, ANDROMEDA, AND LOT'S WIFE
1973

Los Angeles' personality was that it didn't have one. As the only major city in the United States without a center, it didn't seek to dominate. Its charm was that it would accommodate the resident or the visitor and bend itself to whatever the individual wanted of it. To the actor, the city would say, "Perfect! This is the place!" To the young family, the city would say, "You couldn't have made a better choice!" To the night prowler, the city would say, "Of course! You name it! It's here!" To the conscientious worker, the city would say, "You hit it! This city was made for hard work!" To those who wanted to do nothing at all, the city would say, "Fine! Doing nothing is L.A.'s purpose!"

From an airliner, Los Angeles was a massive carpet of structures and swimming pools that had no visual intermission. At night the carpet turned into a field of lights stretching to every horizon no matter how high the aircraft.

It was difficult to remember exactly when particular events happened in Los Angeles because there was so little natural evidence of time moving on. It was the autumn of 1973 but the weather was just like the winter of '72, and the summer of '71, and the spring of '70. Shovels, rakes, and overcoats were foreigners, and even the rare local umbrellas were bored, since no true Los Angeles resident remembered how to open or close those things, nor did they know where to put an umbrella when it was wet. It was easier to leave them in the closet forever.

The single rule of residency was that the people of Los Angeles were required to lie about distance. All residents had to tell others that their house or apartment was perfectly located and, amazingly, nothing would take longer than fifteen minutes to reach from wherever they lived: fifteen minutes to get to the airport, to get to Hollywood, to get downtown, to go to Santa Monica, to Beverly Hills; only fifteen minutes to drive every place in the general Los Angeles area. It wasn't true, but everyone understood that lying about distance was not only understandable, it was essential.

When visiting others, the traditional compliment was to tell them, "Why, it's like living out in the country here, but you're so close to the freeway!"

The residents would always nod with a smile, even though it wasn't like living out in the country and it was difficult to get to the freeway through the traffic.

"Hey, buddy, how are you going to get from Vandenberg to L.A.?" Moose asked Jonas over the phone. "You flying down or driving?"

"Driving. I'm looking forward to it."

"Well, when you get close to L.A., get on the 405 South and just keep going until it turns back into the 5."

"I know the way to San Clemente, Moose. I was born in L.A. I could drive to San Clemente blindfolded. I was driving there before there was a 405 or a 5 or anything but the Pacific Coast Highway and 101. Are you in San Clemente right now?"

"I'm in L.A. I didn't leave with the president's party from D.C. I'm going down to San Clemente tomorrow. Your appointment's for Saturday afternoon at 4:30."

"What are you doing in L.A.?"

"I'm just here, man!"

"Where exactly are you?"

"I'm calling from a place called Gale's Coffee Shop that's attached to a big drug store across from a little corner park that has a merry-go-round and horses."

"You're on La Cienega and Beverly Boulevard. That's where—"

"That's right! La Cienega and Beverly Boulevard! That's what they told me. Very good! You really do know this town!"

"That little park is where divorced men take their children on weekend visits. Loaded with divorced men and their kids. What are you doing at that place?"

"I'm not in the park. I'm in Gales. I came here to go to the drug store."

"All the way there? What for?"

"I wanted to buy some after-shave lotion. Jeez, do I have to defend that? I may even buy some toothpaste! Is that okay?"

"Okay, okay, okay. I'm just asking. I didn't know you knew L.A."

"I don't know L.A. I can't figure it out. This is the strangest city in the universe. I was looking for a drug store. I asked some guy on the street where I should go and he told me this was the largest drug store in the world. It took me three hours to get here."

"From where?"

"From the airport."

"From the airport?"

"Yes."

"Moose, I hate to tell you but it should have taken you fifteen minutes. And there are much closer drug stores to the airport than that one. That's far. You must have passed all kinds of places that had after-shave and toothpaste."

"I know. Okay. That's what every one in the drug store told me. I got lost, that's all. The guy I talked to said it was on the way downtown. It got to be a challenge. I want to get out of this city but I don't think there's a way out. I think once you get here, you're here for life."

Jonas laughed. "Hey, I thought, or I hoped that maybe you might have a date there tonight with some young movie starlet."

"No way. I'm getting out of this drug store and go to the Biltmore Hotel and I'm going to bed."

"The Biltmore? Why are you going way out there?"

"I don't know. I don't know. That's where they booked me. Is there something wrong with it?"

"No. It's a good hotel, it's just way out of the way. It's downtown."

"I know. How far away is it?"

"If you get on the Santa Monica Freeway, probably about fifteen minutes."

"I'm nowhere around Santa Monica, am I?"

"No. That's just what it's called. You take it the opposite way. It's really the 10. Get off before it turns into the San Bernardino Freeway."

"Does anyone understand the design of this city?"

"I don't think so. That's never been an important consideration in L.A."

"Okay. Listen, on Saturday I'll meet you at the San Clemente Inn around 3:45. You know where it is, right?"

"Of course. Off Interstate 5 at the Calafia turnoff."

"Fine. We'll have time for a cup of coffee together, then we'll drive to the Western White House together in a staff car. It's just a few minutes away. Okay, Jonas?"

"Sounds good, buddy."

"Listen, Jonas, you have to know that when I take someone in to see him, I generally look at my watch in about eight minutes and tell the president he has another appointment waiting. You get it? It's so he doesn't have to be rude. You sort of have to condense your thoughts; get them in your mind ahead of time."

"No problem."

"He's looking forward to seeing you, Jonas. So am I. But right now I'm looking forward to anything I can find without getting lost."

It wasn't the ideal time to visit President Nixon, but he wouldn't reject a request by one of the former prisoners of war. The president and his entire staff was spending more and more time on answering questions regarding Watergate, and were being bombarded with one crisis after another, with the word "impeachment" beginning to be part of the daily vocabulary.

Even for Moose, who was totally involved in foreign policy, walking into the White House each morning or the Western White House in San Clemente was like walking in a mine field. If someone said something to him that would hint of an unreported revelation, he was well aware that he could be considered guilty of an obstruction of justice if he didn't run to the special prosecutor (which he wouldn't do) and reveal the conversation he heard. Moreover, Moose was becoming a figure the press viewed with suspicion, and no matter what he recommended or planned as a secret foreign policy contingency, the press had word of it in short time, reporting it in association with the image of Watergate.

The White House press corps was as mobile as the president. If Air Force One or, as the president called it, The Spirit of '76, (the idea of Dick

Moore,) went across the country so the president could be in San Clemente, the White House press corps went there, too.

They were there at the San Clemente Inn Saturday afternoon. And they flooded around Moose as soon as they saw him walk in the door to the reception room of the Inn. "Why did the president appoint Ford as his Veep when we hear he really wanted Connally, Moose?"

"I wasn't involved in any of that. I have no idea what went on."

"Were you with the president during the 'Saturday Night Massacre'?"

"Get off it, will you? There was no massacre! What do you think we're doing? Playing cowboys and indians? And I'm strictly foreign policy, so you're wasting your time talking to me about these kind of things."

"Do you talk to the president about the Mideast?"

"Yes."

"Did you ever stop to think that the alert he called might have been ordered to save his presidency rather than to save Israel?"

"You guys are a bunch of sharks. And you missed the biggest story of all with that alert because you wanted it to be something it wasn't. You," and he looked over at a CBS correspondent, "had a special on television called 'The Mysterious Alert' as though the alert was a trick. Jeez, what a shark. *The Washington Post* did the same kind of analysis—as though the alert was a diversion. There we were, on the brink of World War III and all you guys missed it. The Soviets were behind Egypt's and Syria's surprise attack. Brezhnev was airlifting weapons. He did it through Hungary while you were trying to find the Watergate complex in all of that. We tried to tell you guys, but you didn't care. Brezhnev sent over 30 transports, the big ones, the AN-22s to Egypt and another 20 of them to Syria—transports loaded with tanks and ground-to-air missiles and all kinds of ammunition, and those transports of theirs were big enough to have planes inside of the planes. Besides all that, they put three Soviet divisions on alert and threatened to intervene. They launched a satellite to monitor the area. Do you think the president could put his head in the sand because you guys would accuse him of some diversion from the things you're interested in?"

"OPEC is cutting off our oil for what the president did, Moose."

"Tough. We'll survive. Israel wouldn't have survived if we didn't do what the president ordered. Golda Mier said that, not me. The president used the Hot Line more than it's ever been used in its history while what you called 'The Mysterious Alert' was going on. Now, if you'll excuse me—" and he edged his way to the coffee shop, but the press followed him shouting questions about tapes, about the courts, about Archibald Cox, and about things of which Moose never heard. Jonas heard the yelling voices as Moose and the following press corps walked toward the coffee shop door.

Moose and Jonas didn't sit together there. Moose saw Jonas waiting, and gestured with his head toward the parking lot.

"You go through this all the time?" Jonas asked in the car, with Moose driving north to the western White House.

"It's become a way of life, so I don't go out much. I can't even get a sandwich at Drug Fair in Washington anymore. I stay home and make a sandwich for myself. And it's worse for some of the other guys."

"Moose, it's not as bad as your problems but you should see what I go through in this uniform in some places in California, particularly San Francisco. I've been called every name in the book. Not by everyone. Some people are wonderful but–some just–I have to watch my temper because I can't haul off and slug someone while I'm wearing this uniform."

"Yeah. I know. God, that's depressing to hear."

"Listen, Moose. Don't worry about me taking much time with the president. I'll be very brief. I rehearsed myself."

Moose looked over at Jonas and smiled as they pulled off to the roadway on the right, heading to a metal mesh fence. "Welcome to Casa Pacifica, Jonas. It's not much, but I call it home!"

"Hello, Moose," the president stood up from behind his desk in his light and airy office, as Moose and Jonas came in. "Hello, Colonel." Behind the president was a large window overlooking the Pacific Ocean, the view framed by the flag of the United States to the window's left and the flag of the presidency to the window's right. Like the Oval Office, against the right wall were the four flags of the armed services.

Yesterday Moose had prepared and had given to the president a "Talking Points" paper that told the president a summary of Jonas's background and service record. Moose went through the customary introductions and the president asked them to sit down. "You're here on a beautiful day," the president said as he sat down. "I'm glad you could come here, Colonel. We missed you at the P.O.W. party at the White House. I finally had an opportunity to meet your friends. We had over 300, you know, and it was a real honor for Mrs. Nixon and me. It isn't that often that we have an opportunity to meet so many heroes."

"They appreciated it very much, Mr. President. I heard from so many of them. I had a cold, something like the flu. It's strange. I didn't have one cold in prison, and thanks to you, I got out of there, and after all that, I couldn't fly to Washington for your party, with my temperature."

"You all right now?"

"Oh, perfect. It was nothing."

"Well, we missed you. Bob Hope was there, John Wayne, you know, Sammy Davis, Jr. They were all there. Irving Berlin was there. He's way up there, I don't know, he has to be in his upper 80's. He sang 'God Bless America.' How's your grandmother?" Moose had written on the "Talking Points" paper that Jonas's parents were killed in an automobile accident when Jonas was an infant, and his grandmother brought him up.

"She's in perfect health, sir."

"Is her first name Paola?"

"Yes, sir."

Moose looked surprised. That wasn't on the "Talking Points" paper.

"Valadovich isn't a common name," the president said, "and I remember Paola. Everyone pronounced it Paula and that was wrong. It was Paola, a beautiful name. You know, she was a volunteer for me in my first congressional campaign."

"I do know that. It's amazing you remember, sir."

"She did a real job, a real job. Give her my best, Colonel. I'm grateful to her. She worked like a tiger." He picked up a newspaper from the top of his desk, "Moose, take a look at this. What do you think of this?"

Moose nodded, got up, and took the newspaper back to his chair.

"You'll get a kick out of this, Colonel," the president said. "They're really at it back in Washington. I tried to get away for a while and I can't even take Mrs. Nixon out to dinner here any more. Read it out loud, Moose." Then he looked back at Jonas. "It's *The Washington Post.*"

Moose started reading: "The headline of the article says, 'President Exceeds Gas Limit.'" Moose shook his head. "What's this about?"

"Read it out loud," the president repeated.

"It says, 'President Nixon and his entourage have used at least 170 gallons of gasoline for pleasure driving during the president's 18-day stay in southern California. A compilation based on the president's announced travel and on a conservative estimate of his drive on unannounced trips with C.G. Bebe Rebozo shows that Mr. Nixon himself has driven about 500 miles in his late-model Lincoln limousine. According to figures of the Environmental Protection Agency, Lincoln limousines get 7.9 miles to the gallon. This would mean that the presidential car has consumed 62 gallons in his drives around Southern California. Mr. Nixon has been accompanied on all of his drives by Secret Service agents in a late-model station wagon, which also gets about eight miles to the gallon." Moose looked up from the newspaper, shaking his head.

"Well, I'm as good as under house arrest here," the president said. "One foot out the door and I've given them a new reason to attack. Even here I'm imprisoned. Not like you had to endure, Colonel. This is a very pleasant prison, but I think you know what I mean by that." "It's unbelievable, Mr. President."

"No. Nothing is unbelievable. I take that back. Different subject, but what is unbelievable to me is that *The New York Times* finally corrected themselves on something more important. They finally ran an article that said a Hanoi film showed there wasn't any carpet bombing by us, after all. The *Times* called it carpet bombing last December. You know, in what they called the Christmas bombing. A little late, but better than nothing."

Jonas nodded. "Sir, I don't want to take your time. In fact, I wouldn't even have told Moose I wanted to meet with you unless I felt it was valuable. First, I want to thank you for these eagles," and Jonas touched the silver eagle on his left shoulder, "but I'm here because I put together some statements made by my fellow former prisoners that I believe are important for you to know, not so much to review the past, but to serve as a piece of information for the future. Do you mind if I refer to my paper, sir?" He unfolded a piece of paper from his uniform's jacket side pocket.

"No, no. Not at all. Go ahead."

"I talk to my buddies all the time, sir. I told them I wanted to put some of their thoughts together, and here are some quotes that I wrote down:

"Colonel James Kasler said that those prisoners meeting with delegations who came to Hanoi were handed the questions and answers, and the prisoners had to go in and perform. He said the prisoners were tortured to rehearse what should be answered. He said that many times the prisoners were tortured again, just to show the others what would happen to them if they failed at the conference.

"Commander John Fellows said, 'I personally hope that the people who came to Hanoi representing the dissident groups in our country can some day be brought to trial on this or forced to answer for this. I feel that I personally stayed two extra years because of the groups that kept pressing and pressing for a split in our country.'

"Captain James Mulligan said, 'If I had my way, I would personally like to see them tried, convicted, and sentenced for what they did to me and my friends in Hanoi. They tried to use my family against my country, and tried to deprive me of my legal rights under the Geneva Convention. And the media–why do you think we're so disturbed by *The New York Times*? While Harrison Salisbury was sitting in Hanoi, me and other guys were being tortured. And I know that he knew nothing about it. He was completely duped.'

"Captain Harry Jenkins said, 'Probably the press is partly to blame for this–the items that were covered, that were talked about. Americans are an impetuous people. We haven't the patience of an Oriental, for example.'

"Lieutenant Commander John McCain said, 'These people, Ramsey Clark, Tom Hayden, and Jane Fonda, were on the side of the North Vietnamese. I think she only saw eight selected prisoners. I was beaten unmercifully for refusing to meet with the visitors.'

"Major Harold Kushner said, 'I think the purposes of Fonda and Clark were to hurt the United States, to radicalize our young people, and to undermine our authority.'

"Major Norman McDaniel said, 'I think that the division on the war, what ever amount of it existed, did in fact prolong our stay there.'

"Major Jon Reynolds said, 'I have always maintained that the anti-war movement in the United States lengthened our stay. It was a source of strength to the North Vietnamese.'

"Colonel Robinson Risner said, 'I feel beyond any doubt that those people kept us in prison an extra year or two. Not just the people demonstrating, but the people who were downing or bad-mouthing our government and our policies. There is no doubt in my mind, and it was very evident to all of us, that the communist's spirit or morale went up and down along with the amount of demonstrations, protests, and anti-war movement back in the States. I could not see stopping aid to the countries I knew needed the aid. I could not see abandoning our friends and allies.'

"Colonel Alan Brunstrom said, 'We felt that any Westerners who showed up in Hanoi were on the other side. They gave aid and comfort to the enemy, and as far as I'm concerned, they were traitors.'

"Mr. President, my own experiences were similar. My conclusions are similar. What is important is that Vietnam was probably not the last conflict in which we will be called to defend others. This paper may prove valuable to you and to all forthcoming presidents of the United States."

The president was spellbound as Jonas talked. He said nothing for a while, then said very softly, "Thank you, Colonel. I regret it's too late for what you've been through, and all the others."

Jonas stood up. "Thank you, Mr. President. I'll leave the paper with Moose. I thank you for your time, sir." He was initiating the end of the meeting. Visitors rarely initiated the end of a meeting with the president.

"Sit down, Colonel. Sit down," President Nixon said, waving his left hand in a downward direction.

Moose interrupted. "Mr. President, you do have an appointment and you're a little late for it."

"Cancel it," the president said quickly.

Moose looked confused. "Yes, sir." Now what should he do? Walk out of the room to cancel an appointment that didn't exist? The president knew he had no appointment waiting. Jonas knew it. Moose knew it. Yet Moose still had to give the appearance of credibility so, without fooling anyone, he walked out of the room as though he was doing what the president requested.

"You know, Colonel–"

"Please sir, call me Jonas." And Jonas smiled, "You do out-rank me, sir, even with the promotion you gave me."

"All right, Jonas. Jonas, I'm being pressed to give amnesty to the draft-dodgers. I'm not going to do it. No way. You know, there's never been an unconditional amnesty of draft-dodgers following any American war. We can look at them one by one, but no mass amnesty."

"I agree, sir."

"You men served, a lot of you are dead, wounded, missing. Should the run aways come home scot-free? And it would set a dangerous precedent that might convince some young men, in future engagements, not to risk anything. They'd feel they'd be let off. Ducking out. I won't do it. I won't allow it. Amnesty means forgiveness. You paid a price for serving; they have to pay a price for disobeying the law. I want to ask you something, Colonel." The president swerved his chair a bit on its rotator, and he put his hands together, fingers to fingers, then put those extended hands under his chin, not looking at Jonas. "Colonel–Jonas–how did you do it?" And then he shifted his weight to turn the chair back in Jonas's direction. "How did you keep yourself from saying things you were under orders not to say? How did you take all that physical and psychological pain? How did you keep yourself sane?"

Jonas nodded. "I had to develop a whole ritual, a whole new way of thinking."

"What was it? What did you do? Listen, do you want to have a cup of coffee?"

"Are you having one, sir?"

"Yes, I am. I make it here. They don't know how to make a cup of coffee here."

"If you have coffee, I would like one."

The president got up and went to the east side of the office and to the coffee pot. "I hope you like it strong."

"Yes, sir, I do."

"Good. Good." He continued to prepare it and Jonas couldn't help but think of how incredible this was. Could this be? Could the president of the United States be making him a cup of coffee? "It will be ready in a few minutes, Colonel." The president didn't go back behind his desk. He went to the lounge chair by the side of his desk and put his feet on its ottoman. "Here, swing your chair around, Colonel. Now, tell me, tell me how you handled it in Hanoi."

"The short answer, sir, is 'God.'"

The president nodded. "I'm sure of it. Risner told me that. So did Singleton and Jeffrey—your compatriots. So many of them told me that. You know who told me that, too? Sadat. Anwar Sadat, the president of Egypt. He was in prison, you know. He was tortured and all that. A lot of isolation and all that. He said that because the Creator was his friend, he couldn't possibly be afraid of men."

"Did he?"

The president repeated it. "Because the Creator was his friend, he couldn't possibly be afraid of men."

"That's very good. It's very true."

"Now, you told me God was the short answer for you. Give me the long answer."

Moose came back in the office, having waited an appropriate amount of time for him to have canceled an appointment if one had existed. "Sit down, Moose. Sit down. Want coffee?"

"No sir, I'm all right." Moose had long ago been victim to the president's coffee and he didn't want to go through that again.

Jonas, hearing Moose's response, felt that maybe he did the wrong thing in accepting the president's offer of coffee.

"Now, go ahead," the president said to Jonas. "I've been asking him, Moose, what he did to survive in Hanoi."

Moose nodded.

"Mr. President," Jonas said, "I had a friend in Saigon, before I was captured. Moose introduced me to him. An exceptional man and we would meet a few times a week and discuss theology. He prepared me for what neither he nor I knew was ahead. I'll tell you what we arrived at together—in just a moment. I want you to know first that he was killed trying to rescue me."

"You're talking about Orr?"

"Yes, sir."

"Moose here, he went to bat for him. He wouldn't leave me alone about your friend. We gave him the Distinguished Service Medal, you know."

"I do know."

"He was CIA, you know."

"I never asked. I guessed he was, but I never asked. He couldn't tell me anyway."

"Oh, he was working for Dick Helms. Before that for Raborn. He's been at it for a long time, even when I was vice president. He worked for Allen Dulles. He was CIA."

"He was also a writer."

"Was that his cover? I didn't know what his cover was."

"No, I mean he was a good writer. And a deep thinker. He wrote novels about space exploration under a pen-name. He had a lot of experience at Cape Canaveral; very knowledgeable about space. Anyway, Mr. President, as we batted things back and forth, he told me that honor was the most important element of life. And we arrived at the conclusion that time, that time—minutes, hours, days—time was simply made as an invention for Man, and that it's not real. Once you grasp those things you can withstand almost anything, because you realize that the present—the present torture, if that's what you have to endure—is just a—a bleep that is memory, nothing more than that. And don't let time interfere with honor."

The president was just staring at him without a signal of approval or disapproval. Jonas caught the look on the president's face and he guessed that the president was asking such questions because he was preparing to endure his own untenable future.

Moose was ill-at-ease and didn't know if Jonas should be going into all this, but he would have had no credibility in saying there was another appointment for the president.

"Keep going, Colonel," the president said. "I'll get the coffee. Keep going." The president walked across the office again.

"Yes, sir. It may sound funny. I just—"

"After what you've been through I would expect it to be something unusual. You go ahead."

"Adam, my friend—the CIA man who knew so much about space, said that we could look up at the sky and see a particular constellation up there with our bare eyes. It's the constellation of Andromeda. But what he said was that we see it as it existed two million, two-hundred thousand years ago. That's how far away it is. Then he told me that if someone on a planet in Andromeda had a telescope that was strong enough to see our planet through that scope, he would see the Earth as it existed two million, two-hundred thousand years ago."

"Einstein. That's Einstein. It's called the space-time continuum. Am I right?"

Jonas nodded, but the president didn't see him since he was pouring the coffee. "Go on," the president said. "Do you use cream or sugar?"

"No, sir. Just black is fine. I think I can prove—or at least this was Adam's proof that time doesn't really exist: Imagine that it's night in New York City and you see a strange red and green flash of lightning hit the top of the Empire State Building. Then, after the lightning has struck, you see a giant red and green light hitting the moon. Do you follow me, sir?"

"Yes, yes." The president was carrying back two cups of coffee. He set one on the small table next to Jonas, and he carried the other back to his lounge chair. "Go on."

"Now imagine Neil Armstrong, or some other astronaut, is on the moon when all this happens. He's looking through his telescope—a powerful one—at New York City. Through his peripheral vision he sees the flash on the moon right next to him, and then he sees the lightning hit the Empire State Building. To you, on Earth, the lightning hit the Empire State Building first and then the flash went off on the moon. To Armstrong, there was a flash on the moon before lightning hit the Empire State Building. You think the flash on the earth caused the flash on the moon, and Armstrong thinks that the flash on the moon caused the flash on the earth. Which one really came first? Both and neither."

"That's Einstein."

"Yes, sir. Now imagine you're on that planet in Andromeda again. To you on the planet in Andromeda, there was no flash on either the building or the moon, and neither will happen until 2,200,000 years in the future."

"That's right."

"Now, another thing to think about; if you were leaving the earth on top of a Saturn rocket that could go faster than the speed of light, and if you could see inside the White House as you went up and up, you would see the White House's occupants in reverse. First you'd see you in there, then President Johnson, then President Kennedy, then President Eisenhower, and so on, all the way to George Washington."

"Fascinating, Colonel. But, just so you know, Washington didn't live in the White House and, as I recall, Einstein said we could never travel faster than the speed of light."

"Yes, sir, but that isn't the point. If we could, that's what time would become. So time is just an illusion. It doesn't exist as we think it does. So we have to think of life, and what we're going through, without being obsessed with its punishment, if punishment is what we're enduring. This man, this friend, Adam had his own religion. It was a belief in God, of course, but a belief in honor and distance. He used to say, 'When you go far enough away, you're on your way back.'"

"Your friend, Orr, and Anwar Sadat would have gotten along fine. Anwar says the same kind of things. He said that he was able to move beyond the borders of time and space when he was imprisoned. He said that he really didn't live in a four-walled cell, but in the entire universe.

He said that time didn't exist. He learned that in prison. You should meet him."

"I would like that."

"That can be worked out. Go on. Go on with what you were saying."

"I just thought over and over again, this isn't happening now because there is no now. I thought all the torture was nothing more than something that would be the past. Everything is a quick moment that will soon be the past. Both glory and grief are temporary. Run a clock faster and the present disappears quicker. How many times have you heard, or said, 'The year is over already? Why, it seems as though it just began!' I think I know why. As you get older, years have to go faster. The only way we can judge time is from how much of it we have spent. When you're five years old it takes another one-fifth of your life before a year is over, but when you're fifty, it's only a fiftieth of your life. We all measure time by our own internal clock, no one else's."

The president walked to the window facing the Pacific Ocean, his back to Jonas and Moose. "Fascinating. But you said you imagined life without time. How did you do that, Colonel? Life without time is impossible to imagine."

"It's easy to imagine because we go through life without time every night. If you didn't have a clock you might think you were asleep for minutes when it's been hours, or hours when it's only been minutes. I don't know about you, sir, but in my dreams I talk with people who I know have died, and sometimes I talk with them without even thinking that they died. There is no time in sleep. My grandmother appears in my dreams as she looked when she was in her 30s, even though I'm older than that myself now. I'm 40. And even though I see her in her 30s, I still look at her as being older than I am. Do you know what I mean?"

The president continued looking through the window at the ocean. "You have an interesting concept there, Colonel."

Moose never witnessed anything like this. He was involved in countless visits of the president with strangers, and the president always did the talking. Sometimes the visitors were so silent and so awed that they would phone Moose afterwards and ask what happened in the Oval Office because they didn't remember. Jonas was talking to the president rather than being a nodding listener, and the president had encouraged it.

"I'm sure, Mr. President, that in your dreams you change locales and times in an instant without even questioning the rapidity of the changes. I dream I'm still in school. In the next split second, I'm climbing a mountain in Switzerland. Nothing takes me from one place to another or from one time to another. Our body plays no meaningful role in dreams. So it's just a tool, Mr. President, while we're awake. So pain isn't what we think it is. When I was being tortured, I kept imagining myself on a planet in Andromeda watching my own torture—but that was 2,200,000 years ago. I put myself on the planet in Andromeda, not Hanoi on the Earth."

The president turned away from the window and looked at Jonas. "You have a very powerful ability to discipline your mind, Colonel."

"I worked on it, sir. But it saved me."

"You're to be complimented. I don't know if I could do that." He went back to his desk.

"Neither did I when Adam told me his beliefs. Strangely enough, I had hints of it before. When President Kennedy was assassinated I went to the Lincoln Memorial and I remember hearing my footsteps echo, going somewhere. I thought then that everything is somewhere—everything quickly moves somewhere else. At least its sight and sound moves somewhere else. For us, God made a time for everything."

"Ecclesiastes."

"Yes, sir."

"That's Ecclesiastes. 'A time to be born and a time to die, a time to plant and a time to uproot, a time to kill and a time to heal, a time to weep and a time to laugh, a time to mourn and a time to dance, a time to embrace and a time to refrain, a time to be silent and a time to speak.'"

There was a long silence. His recitation and memory of the words was unexpected by his guests.

Jonas reached for his coffee cup and took a swallow and did everything in his power not to spit it out. It was the strongest coffee he ever tasted. Since there was a time to embrace and a time to refrain, he said, "It's good, sir."

"It's real coffee. No one else knows how to make coffee around here. Colonel, if you aren't busy, do you want to have dinner with Mrs. Nixon, Julie, and me tonight?"

Jonas looked over at Moose for a cue on how to answer, but Moose looked as confused as Jonas, so Jonas looked back at the president. "Yes, sir. I would be honored."

"You too, Moose," the president said. "Mrs. Nixon likes you. She thinks you're the biggest man she ever saw. She thinks I gave you the wrong offer—that I should have asked you to be my bodyguard. And Julie—I know you've become a good friend of Julie and David. Julie would be mad if you didn't see her while you're here. Can you boys do it?"

"Yes, sir, Mr. President," Moose said. "That sounds good."

"Go over to the residence, Moose. Show the Colonel around. You can walk there or take a golf cart over there. We're having Mexican food tonight. Moose, tell Manolo to call El Adobe and tell them to make it for five. You like Mexican food, Jonas?"

"I love it, sir."

"El Adobe sends it over. You ever eaten there?"

"No, sir."

"You'll like it."

He had to like it more than the coffee.

At dinner it was different. Moose had told Jonas to let the president talk. The president and Mrs. Nixon talked about their family and Julie talked about the pre-presidential years, and then the president started talking about the North Vietnamese violations of the Paris Peace Accords, and that South Vietnam was in increased danger again, particularly because of the Congress' passage of the War Powers Resolution, and the Congress' subsequent override of the president's veto of the Resolution. The president said that executive authority over military engagements was being eroded, and the acts of the Congress would cause him and forthcoming presidents to surrender much of their foreign affairs jurisdiction given to them by the Constitution.

"Should we have signed those peace accords, Mr. President?" Jonas asked.

"They got you and your friends home, Jonas," the president answered.

"I know, sir. But now that you know they're violating the accords, should we have done it, even if we'd still be back there?"

"I never look back, Colonel. You're a theologian. You know the story of Lot's wife, don't you?"

"Yes, sir."

"She looked back, and she turned into a pillar of salt. I don't look back. You have some marvelous ideas about time, and Andromeda was your friend when you needed one. I may have to use Andromeda, too. But for now I turn to Lot's wife."

FORTY
THE HAREM OF ERFOUD
1973-1974

Animals were running in every direction; zebras to the south, rhinoceroses to the west, a giraffe and her baby following the rhinoceroses, even two impalas stopped attempting to kill each other, so as to scurry away to the northern horizon. A herd of impalas were jumping in thirty foot leaps, rising ten feet straight up in each jump. They were followed by running baboons and waterbucks and gazelles. One lone elephant looked confused but started lumbering to the east. Even falcons and sunbirds and harrier hawks resting on the branches of flat-topped African thorn trees started flying away, turning parts of the deep blue sky into moving blankets of black. Maybe from their elevations the birds could see what this was all about, but there was no sight or sound that gave reason for this panic of the animals. They knew from something other than sight or sound that a threat was coming. That threat emerged on a cleared stage: from what seemed to be out of nowhere, a pride of eight lions slowly walked onto the expanse of land that had just been vacated. All lions, except one, rested under what they pre-selected as their tree.

"How majestic they are! How beautiful!" Anne said to Taita, the driver of a dust-covered Land Rover. "I can't believe I'm actually seeing all this!"

"But you are," Taita said with a broad, toothy smile. Taita was a young and strong man with a bushy mustache, short hair, and very bloodshot eyes, who was wearing about twenty red necklaces. "They don't always run like that. I've seen hippos stay and walk right up to them. I think they just followed the leader today. Some run so they all run," Taita said as the lion who hadn't rested under the tree started coming directly to the car. "It's a male. Simba. That's a good boy. Too bad you don't have a camera, Miss Whitney."

"I don't want to see the world at f 8, looking through a viewfinder. I want to see it with nothing between my eyes and the world. Is the simba tame, do you think?"

"Oh, no. But he won't attack us here in the car. He could," he shrugged, "but he won't. They only eat every three days or so."

"What day is this?"

"Number three," he said and he laughed.

The lion rubbed his chin against the front tire on the driver's side, just as a domesticated cat would kiss a piece of furniture. Then Anne lost sight of him. "Can I roll the window down just a little?" She asked Taita.

"Oh, no. Not now. He's too close."

"It's so hot!"

"Better hot than dead, yes? That's an old Kikuyu proverb."

"It is not!"

Taita gave his lackadaisical shrug. "Everything is an old Kikuyu proverb."

"Where did the simba go? I can't see him."

"Lying down."

"Where?"

"The simba likes the tire. He's lying in front of it."

"Which one?"

"The one on my side."

"Now what?"

He shrugged and gave the toothy smile again. "We wait."

"How long?"

"Until the simba goes back to the pride."

"But what if he takes forever?"

"Then we go in reverse."

Anne turned around to look through the rear window. It looked clear. "Shall we do it now?"

"He's moving. We wait."

"I want to see him!"

"So do I, but I'm afraid neither one of us can right now. He just walked behind the front tire rather than in front of it."

"What does that mean?"

"We stay for a while. We would now hit him by going forward or reverse. That would not be good."

"Would we kill him?"

Taita laughed with his bloodshot eyes sparkling. "We would make him angry. That is not good. If he uses his strength against us, he would kill us. He would eat us alive. And the pride would help him do it! Best we sit."

Anne had arrived in Nairobi, Kenya, yesterday en route to tomorrow's scheduled arrival at her new post in Bujumbura, Burundi. The U.S. Embassy Charge d'Affaires in Nairobi picked her up at Embakasi Airport and she immediately met the officers of the Embassy. Next was lunch with Ambassador McIlvaine in his palatial residence, and in the afternoon she was taken to visit the Voice of Kenya Radio studios to meet their officials, then to Kenyatta High School to talk with students about life in the United States. The day was complete after three briefings at the embassy by the political officer, the public affairs officer, and the cultural affairs officer. By the time she reached the Intercontinental Nairobi Hotel at night, she was exhausted, and her notebook was filled with briefing papers.

Today was to be one of leisure before going on to Burundi. She could walk the city or shop or tour, or whatever she wanted.

"Animals!" she had said to the cultural affairs officer. "I want to see wild animals!" When he told her that a local who worked for the Embassy would take her just five miles away to Nairobi National Park, she protested. "I want the real thing!"

"But the National Park is the real thing. An animal is an animal. They're all there," he told her.

"I don't want to go to anything that's called a National Park!"

"It just means it's preserved and maintained in its raw state. It's huge; 44 square miles."

"No! I want what isn't preserved and maintained! I want it really raw. not advertised raw!"

The cultural affairs officer learned quickly what others took too long to learn. It was easier to surrender to Anne. He nodded. "Okay. It won't be our driver, then. He doesn't know the country. There's someone we can put you in touch with. Taita is from up country. He's a driver that we sometimes contract–" and he hesitated but said it, "in difficult cases. He'll find a place you'll like."

Taita found a place she liked. But what heat! Since now the windows had to be closed in the presence of wild animals, the heat was almost untenable. But Anne's insatiable inventiveness in how to make an erotic adventure out of any unusual circumstance saved her from both the discomfort of the heat and any fear of lions. And Taita, who had started the day in the belief he would be bored by having to assume his role of being a tour-guide was about to consider himself the most fortunate man on the African continent.

They sat with little to say, waiting for the lion to move and it wasn't moving.

"Taita?" Anne said as a question.

"Yes?"

"Are you married?"

"Oh, yes. I have four wives."

Anne gave a look of amazement. She had expected him to say "yes" or "no" but not give a number.

"Oh, yes," he said with nonchalance in answer to her expression. "I would have more if I had more money. But it's all I can afford."

"Do they all know that you have more than one?"

"Oh, yes. It is part of our culture. Each wife has her own hut, right across from the others. Most Kikuyu men have two wives, but it depends on what they can afford. I knew a man–he's dead now–he had fifty-six wives. He was very rich and very happy. I am not that rich and not that happy," and he laughed. "But I am not poor and not unhappy. So far, I have four wives. I hope to have ten. That will make me happy enough." He laughed again.

"Aren't they jealous of each other?"

"No, no. There's no jealousy. It is our way. You have your way. We have our way."

Anne blinked like a total innocent. "Are any of your wives white?"

His big, toothy smile took over the moment. "Oh, no, Miss Whitney. They are all Kikuyu like me!"

For a while she said nothing. Then it came to her. "Taita?" she said again as a question.

"Yes?"

"I am very hot. I want you to turn your head away. I need to unbutton my shirt or I'll die. Will you turn away?"

"Yes," he said with some confusion. "Of course. I look at the pride." He looked to the left at the lions under the tree as Anne unbuttoned her white blouse, leaving it on but opened. Beneath it was a white brassiere. She untucked the bottom of her blouse from her khaki slacks. Anne hadn't worn slacks in years; not since she was the Old Anne, but when she dressed this morning she wanted to be in harmony with the surroundings of a semi-safari.

"Taita?" He was still looking away from her, staring at the pride beneath the tree.

"Yes?"

"Why are your eyes so bloodshot? I saw so many just like that yesterday, too. So many bloodshot eyes."

"It is common. It is Apollo Eleven disease."

"Apollo Eleven?"

"Yes. They brought it back from the moon."

Anne laughed. "They did not!"

"Oh, yes. We all got it after Apollo Eleven."

"Let me see!"

"You want to see my eyes?"

"It's all right. I'm decent. I forgot what I was wearing at first. I'm more decent than I am at the beach. Let me see your eyes."

He looked at her with a sudden sweep of his eyes from the window. And he looked at what he had missed. Even though she was very decent, it was still an erotic sight. Her blouse was open, revealing a white brassiere.

"Oh, your eyes are so red!" Anne said.

"Apollo Eleven, Miss Whitney."

"No! And you have some sleep in the corners of your eyes."

"Sleep?"

"Stuff. Stuff from the sandman. Now, maybe that's from Apollo Twelve, I suppose. Here." And she took her index finger of her right hand, causing her to twist a little in her seat, and she dabbed her finger in the corner of his left eye slowly, gathering the "sand", and then she wiped her finger on her slacks. "There."

"Thank you," he said.

"I'm not done." And then she repeated the procedure on the corner of his right eye. She heard his breathing getting faster. She was taking a great deal of time to do it. Then she wiped her finger on her slacks again.

"Thank you," Taita said.

"I'm not done."

He didn't have a third eye.

"You have something else. I don't know what it is—by the corner of your lips."

At this, his lips were lightly trembling.

"I think this one has to be from Apollo Seventeen. I'm sure of it." This time she used her middle finger, allowing her index finger to stroke the bottom of his nose and mustache very lightly, and her other fingers to stroke his chin with the same lightness; first the right side of his lips, then the left side. He allowed his mouth to open a little, and she put her middle finger, very slightly, between his lips. "There's more," she said. There was more. But nothing she could remove from his lips, or his mouth. The more that was left was Anne's creativity. "Do you taste my finger?"

"Yes." He was now breathing very heavily.

"Does it taste good?" And she gave a short laugh.

He nodded. "Oh, yes. It tastes very good."

"Have you never tasted white skin before?"

"Never."

"What a shame! I've never tasted black skin. Give me your hand."

He more than willingly was receptive to her request. He lifted his left hand to her lips. While her finger was still exploring his lips, she licked his index finger and then put it between her lips and closed her lips around his finger, sweeping her tongue around it.

His mouth opened wider, taking three of her fingers between his lips and she swept them from one side of his mouth to the other.

"Wwwww," she said and allowed his finger some freedom while she talked. "I like the taste of black skin! Wwwww! It's good food for me to eat if the simba decides to stay here and I get hungry!" And she clamped her lips around his finger again. Then she released it. "You're perspiring," she said. She took her fingers from his lips with the same slowness she was doing everything.

"Yes," he said. "Now I, too, am hot."

"It's intolerable," she said. "Turn your eyes away again."

He turned his head toward his window in unbearable anticipation, but just then the lion walked by his window. "He's moved!" Taita said because it was much too obvious to pretend nothing was happening, with the lion obscuring the sunlight coming through his window. The lion seemed bored, walking slowly toward the pride.

"Then we can leave and lower the windows," she said.

Taita was not a happy man. If he had a gun the lion would have been lying in a pool of blood for having moved from the tire.

When they arrived back in Nairobi, she had to behave. And she would have to behave for a long time. There would be little opportunity in Burundi to steal away with someone other than Embassy personnel and that she wouldn't do. She had some limits. After Taita left her at her hotel, she had little time before packing and waiting for the Embassy driver to take her to the airport for her flight to Burundi. The intense heat dictated that all flights were at night while airports sizzled in abandonment during the day.

The Sabena flight that had been reserved for her was a direct one to Bujumbura, Burundi, but once in the air, the captain announced that the plane was going to land at Kampala's Entebbe National Airport in Uganda for a twenty minute stop. Under ordinary circumstances that would not have bothered her, but Uganda was not an ordinary circumstance. Only weeks earlier the U.S. Embassy had closed its doors and diplomatic relations were broken with the government of Idi Amin Dada. Last July he had detained 112 U.S. Peace Corps volunteers for two days, accusing them of being mercenaries and Zionists, while they were sitting at Entebbe Airport en route to Burundi and Zaire. Then, in October, President Amin warned that he would imprison all Americans in Uganda if the United States helped Israel in the Yom Kippur War. That warning included the U.S. Embassy staff, with President Amin calling them all spies. He expelled the U.S. Marine guards of the embassy. That was the last straw. The embassy lowered its flag. Its staff left the country.

After the airliner stopped on the tarmac of Entebbe, four soldiers in fatigues entered the aircraft and walked the aisles, requesting to see every passenger's passport. Every passenger accommodated, except for Anne.

"No dice!" she said.

"Passport, please, Miss. Passport!"

"Not a chance," she said. "I didn't want to land in Uganda. I don't want to be here. I'm going to Burundi."

"I'm afraid we need to see your passport, Miss."

"I'm afraid you're not going to, sir. I'm a diplomat and I don't want you touching my passport."

"You are American?"

"Yes. I am an American diplomat en route from Nairobi to Bujumbura."

"We must see your passport or we will have to hold up the flight."

"Get Idi Amin here. I'll show it to him!"

The soldier walked to the other soldiers, they had a short discussion and then they walked out of the plane.

An hour passed. Not one passenger spoke to Anne while they waited, although some gave her angry looks knowing that she was responsible for the delay. One of the passengers requested that the air conditioner be turned on, and asked for the No Smoking sign to be extinguished. Both requests were granted.

The four soldiers reentered and all of them walked to Anne as a group. "You may hold on to your passport. But we need to see it. Hold it for us."

She opened her purse and held it in the air with both hands clutching it. The black cover with the word DIPLOMATIC told them she was telling the truth. Again they walked out of the aircraft, and within a minute they walked back in. "Either we take the passport for a few minutes or you come into the transit lounge with us."

Anne nodded and got up. "I'm staying with my passport."

The transit lounge was empty of passengers except for Anne.

"Sit down," one of the soldiers said.

She sat holding her purse tightly. "This is a very famous waiting room, isn't it?" Anne asked. "Isn't this where the two Roman Catholic priests were killed? Is it right where I'm sitting?" She moved her hands in the crease between the cushion and the back of the ripped brown leather seat, until she felt a cluster of small things. She turned her head to see what they were. They were dead bugs. She lifted her hands quickly and looked under her nails at the evidence.

"What priests?" A soldier asked Anne.

"Two years ago, when your president staged his coup. They were killed in this waiting room, weren't they? On one of these seats? Was it this one?"

The soldier jumped up quickly as something caught his eye from the open doorway. "Stand up, please."

President Idi Amin Dada walked in the room escorted by a circle of armed soldiers in battle fatigues. The soldiers looked like they had been picked off the streets. Idi Amin walked directly over to Anne. She stood in acknowledgment of his presence.

He was a big man with his face seemingly as big as the rest of him. He extended his hand to her. In one split-second her mind raced through the rules of protocol as well as her own instincts. The hand he extended was the hand of a murderer and the hand of a government with whom the United States had broken diplomatic relations.

Instead of shaking his hand, she shook her head. "I understand our embassy has closed its doors, Mr. President. We no longer recognize your government. Your officials came aboard the aircraft en route to Burundi and demanded the passports of the passengers. I am a United States diplomat and I will not surrender my passport to any government that we do not recognize. Not even for a moment. I believe you know the international code."

Idi Amin gave a smile, but his eyes were not smiling. Like Taita in Kenya, his eyes were bloodshot. "You know Nixon?"

"President Nixon," she corrected. "No, I do not know him. But I do work for him. I am going to be with our embassy in Bujumbura."

"He is an imperialist who is a tool of the Zionists. You work for an aggressor for the Zionists who occupy Tel Aviv, and your Nixon leads the puppet regime in Saigon. The Palestinians and the Viet Cong will win over your Nixon. And so will the Cambodians who he bombs in preparation for his global war to destroy Asia and Africa."

"I think you're behind the news. Now, may I get back on the aircraft, please, and will you allow it to go on to Bujumbura?"

He laughed. "Of course I allow. I have no will to prevent your flight. May I see your passport?"

"No. I landed here out of necessity, not desire."

Again he laughed. "I need to see your passport. I won't keep it. I want to see if you are a diplomat or not." Even Idi Amin mellowed in the presence of Anne.

She opened her purse and again took out her passport. He nodded when he saw the black cover. He took it from her hand without a pull and she allowed him to do it. He looked through each page of visas but his eyes did not travel across the pages. Anne knew he was illiterate and surely couldn't read English. He was not reading anything. He handed it back to her.

She could not resist to go a step further than necessary. "What did you read, Mr. President? What did it say? Did you even read my name?"

His smile changed to lips that tightened into a straight line. "My eyes are very bad. Nixon's Apollo Eleven brought back germs from the moon to infect all African's eyes."

"That's only what happens at first, Mr. President. It eventually takes off your nose."

He stared at her and she at him. "Then your penis falls off." She wiped her passport on her skirt to cleanse it after his handling of it.

He laughed. "You don't like Africans?"

"I like Africans as much or as little as I like other people. Which of the two of us have ever killed an African? You or me? How many shoes of Africans have been placed by the side of the road? Eighty thousand pair, am I right?"

She was referring to the custom of putting the shoes of the dead by the side of the road, as Amin's habit was to order the removal of the shoes of those to be executed before stuffing the person into the trunk of a car that would take the victim to the place of execution.

"And how many slaves do you have?" President Amin asked.

"Oh, a few hundred on my plantation!"

"You are a daring young woman, aren't you?"

"You do not scare me, Idi Amin."

"President Amin," he corrected by plagiarizing her sign of respect for her president.

"President Amin. I stand corrected–although it escapes me to recall when there was an election in Uganda that elected you President of anything."

He nodded, agreeing with her. He made no apology or explanation. Instead he said, "If I wanted your Nixon to win his war against Asia and Africa, I would write him a letter to tell him you should lead his army!"

The compliment was not returned. "You wouldn't write him, Mr. President. You would have it written."

Again, his lips went straight. He started walking out of the lounge as his entourage quickly assembled around him and walked, almost bumping into each other.

She thought of something she should have said earlier, so she went ahead and did it now. "Mr. President!" she called after him.

He turned around quickly and the entourage shuffled to a stop. "Yes?"

"We have Asians in our country. Why did you kick out or kill every Asian who was in your country? Fifty thousand, am I right?"

President Amin 's face looked as though it was ready to explode. "Even Asians can be spies for your Nixon, Miss! Don't over step my courtesy to you! I wish you well in Burundi. I promise you, you will wish you were here in Uganda!"

In Bujumbura, the capital city of Burundi, Anne was becoming everything she thought she was in Hong Kong, but wasn't. Thirteen years ago she thought the people of Hong Kong loved her, and they didn't. Now she didn't care what the people of Bujumbura thought of her, but they did love her. She was admired by both of the warring tribes of that country to the point that they would visit her in the U.S. Embassy to discuss the horrible, the unbelievable, the unthinkable atrocities that were being done to one tribe by the other tribe. And if they said one word against the United States, the look in her eyes was enough to stop them in mid-sentence.

Anne, who long ago had abdicated from being a princess of the Invisible Monarchy of the bureaucracy, was now the unofficial Queen of Bujumbura.

Those two tribes, the Bahutus and the Watutsis—one short, one tall—one an overwhelming 85 percent majority, the other a 14 percent minority that ruled the country—were not simply at war, they were both killing and being killed in primitive and torturous massacres that took 200,000 lives in the year before Anne arrived. The Watutsis, some who measured over seven feet, were the minority but dominated the smaller Bahutus and slaughtered them, targeting the educated and the elite, and the smaller Bahutus would often cut off the legs of the taller Watutsis to even the heights between the tribes. Atrocities were known in most of the African countries, and minority governments were not, in any sense, unusual. 47 of the 51 African nations had minority governments of one kind or another with nations ruled by minority tribes or by presidents-for-life or unelected kings or governments taken over by military coups. Only the four countries of Senegal, Gambia, Mauritius, and Botswana had freely elected governments.

Through all the massacres that continued into 1973, something was happening to Anne that was not easy for her to explain to herself. Just as the people became devoted to her, she became devoted to Bujumbura. She became attached to Burundi. And she wondered if she were to have gone to India for the first time while she was this age, with the experiences she had since 1960, would she have had affection for India rather than hatred? She knew she would have seen it differently than she did thirteen years ago. The cultural shocks that jolted through her in 1960 were no longer culturally shocking. Now the memories of India were not only the horrors she had seen and heard and smelled and felt there, but something else beyond definition that made her want to see India again. She didn't know if she had greater wisdom then, or greater wisdom now. Was it a form of understanding that she had acquired through the years or was it a dismissal of human misery by getting used to it, or even by some perverse nostalgia? There was something that was deep inside of her that made her love the similarities she found between Benares and Bujumbura, rather than the hatred she might have felt for this African city had she come as naively as she had come to India while she was so young.

She also wrestled with two other conflicting passions: the love she felt for Mark, and an insatiable appetite for feminine adventure that had nothing to do with love. She made sure those passions remained fantasies not to be lived while she was on duty in Bujumbura. Later.

Bujumbura was a hardship post and so the U.S. government gave her increased pay, and provided her with housing that could well be described as a mansion by Burundi's standards, complete with servants and maids. Not once did she treat them as servants or maids because she knew she was perceived as a nation, not a person. Even though it was customary to slap hands together twice to call a servant, she wouldn't do that.

When the government of Burundi gave most-favored nation trading status to the Soviet Union, Anne drafted a message for Ambassador Yost to send to Burundi's President Micombero, the message threatening that the United States was contemplating a break in diplomatic relations. He didn't send the message.

As famine followed massacres, Anne was on the streets and fields feeding and nursing the starving. Like Benares. "I'll leave Bujumbura if I can't do this," she told David Mark, who suffered from being the third U.S. Ambassador in two years. "I want to stay and do the work assigned to me," she said, "but at night and weekends, on my own time, there is no rule that demands I must be with the Peace Corps or A.I.D. to do what is necessary to do here." And that was how Anne became the unofficial Queen of Bujumbura among both Bahutus and Watutsis.

And then came the vacation.

"Maybe I'll just stay home and putter around," she told the Embassy staff. That was half-true. She didn't stay home but she did plan on puttering around.

Her plans were made without the involvement of the Embassy Travel Office. Her destination was anonymity. And the place of anonymity was one she had imagined since dreaming of 2002 Nights. Not Saudi Arabia. Not any of the Arab Nations north of Burundi. She wanted to go to the western edge of the African Continent to a city whose name was irresistible to every romanticist–Marrakesh.

It was where she had read that all the buildings were pink and the city was walled and Churchill had gone there and painted pictures in one of the rooms of the Mamounia Hotel. And just a short distance away was the romance of Humphrey Bogart and Ingrid Bergman in the painted white city of Casablanca. All of this in Morocco, a country that was friendly to the United States and better yet, as long as she did it on her own, there would be no Embassy car at the airport, no Embassy reservation at the hotel, no Embassy briefings during the day or Embassy receptions at night. She would be a woman representing no one but herself again, just for a week.

"Who is that man?" Anne asked the concierge of the Mamounia Hotel, as she gestured toward a golden-skinned middle-aged man who towered above the others in the lobby. He was neither brawny or slender, but he was very tall, and he was wearing a white headdress. She had to find out who he was since the man looked like a figure out of Sigmund Romberg's *The Desert Song*. When his gaze drifted passed Anne, it quickly jolted back, and he stroked his chin as he looked her up and down. Anne, of course, was a stand-out with her blond hair topped by a wide-rimmed straw hat instead of her customary ribbon, and there was her pretty face and her below-the-knees skirt that was still too short for an Arab country. She was in her glory, which she hadn't been for a long time.

In that one quick moment, Anne knew this vacation would not be a waste.

Her planned week of anonymity was already on a visible path.

"That is Abdelikamel Rahal," the concierge answered her. "Quite an imposing figure isn't he, madam?"

"Yes, he is."

"They call him the Sultan. He isn't really a sultan. We call him the Sultan because he has carte blanche here. Anything he wants he gets. And he pays. He is rich. Very rich. Our bellmen make more in carrying one of his bags to his suite than they normally make in a week. He's from Saudi Arabia–part of the royal family there, and he spends a lot of time here in Morocco. He goes between Rabat and the desert and he stops off here. He is a personal friend of King Hassan. He goes into the sands with many weapons for our troops in liberating the Sahara."

"He is an arms dealer?"

"He is an every kind of dealer."

Anne walked to the main door to go outside into the brilliant daylight of Marrakesh knowing, with absolute certainty, that the man they called the Sultan would not let her get away that fast, if at all.

"Madame!" He was right behind her. He had to have followed her out. She knew what she was doing.

She didn't turn around. Not on the first call.

"Madame!" He called again.

Now she turned around. Her vision was obscured by his white tunic on his chest. He was so close and so tall that she had to look almost straight up to see his face. "Yes?"

"I am Abdelikamel Rahal. Who are you?"

"I am Anne–Anne Smith." For all her imagination, she didn't do very well in inventing a quick name.

"You are American?"

"Canadian."

"A wonderful country. Where in Canada?"

"Saskatoon."

"Good. And where are you off to this morning?"
"Shopping."
"You are touring then? You are on holiday?"
"Yes. I am a teacher on vacation."
"Where do you shop?"
"I'll look for a bazaar."
"No. There are no bazaars here. What you want are called Mendeenuhs. And they will fleece you. You must have an escort. I am going to be gone for a few days. While I am gone you must use my car and driver. It is much safer for you."
He wasn't slow. But neither was Anne.
His eyes were bloodshot. Oh, no. It couldn't be that he, too, would blame the Apollo Eleven astronauts.
"Your eyes," she said. "Have they been hurt? They are red."
"It comes from the sand and the dirt. It's called Hahmatahn."
At last. Neil Armstrong and Buzz Aldrin had nothing to do with it.
"So you take my car and you take my driver," he said. "Maybe you want to go to Casablanca or up-country. My driver's name is Hahmidoo. He waits right over there for me when I stay here. The hotel gives him that spot. I will tell him that now he waits for you until Thursday at dusk when you and he will pick me up in Mhamid. I am being taken there by others, so you may have him now. Until Thursday at sunset he will take you where ever you may want to go."
He didn't ask her, he told her. And she liked it. She accepted his order.
"And if he touches you–his arm will be cut off. I will tell him. And, Madame, if you touch him–you are a woman and I would not cut off your arm–but you will wish your arm had been cut off." And at that he smiled. Somehow, he had her pegged, or was taking a chance on pegging her that way.
She loved it.

For three days, Hahmidoo took her everywhere. She saw much more of Morocco than she had planned when she had prepared this trip. Hahmidoo drove her from Marrakesh to Casablanca to Tangier by the Straits of Gibraltar and back to Marrakesh. The only city she didn't visit was Rabat. It was too close to the flagpole: the flagpole on top of the U. S. Embassy.
Thursday at sunset by the desert's edge she waited in the limousine staring at the dunes of the Sahara as they changed from white to gold to red as the sun went further and further down. While they were violently red, men on camels appeared, walking in a procession coming over the horizon toward the place of civilization where Hahmidoo and Anne waited on pavement. In front of the procession was a man so much taller than the others.
"The Sultan is on time! He always is!" Hahmidoo said.
"Did he travel by camel?"
"There's no other way. They are the best vehicles for the Great Sahara. Thcy can travel 60 miles a day, and they can go for a month without

water if they can simply munch on bushes and acacia. You see? He made his trek safely."

The Sultan got in the back seat with Anne but hardly acknowledged her presence. Sand was all over his face and all over his clothes and his black boots. He took out a handkerchief and wiped his face.

He talked to Hahmidoo in French.

"Excuse me," Anne said softly, feeling like a total outsider.

They kept on talking in French.

"Excuse me. *Excuse moi,*" she said like a child.

They kept on talking.

Anne interrupted them by submissively saying, "Thank you, Sultan Whatever-your-name is. I had a wonderful time. I spent a day in Casablanca!"

He continued his conversation in French with Hahmidoo, then turned to her. "That's good," he said. "Hahmidoo took you where you wanted to go?"

"Oh, yes. He was a superb guide."

"Hahmidoo will now take you back to Marrakesh."

"And you?"

"I will go from there to Erfoud."

"You are not staying in Marrakesh?"

"Not tonight. I wish to go to Erfoud."

"Why?"

"That is where my harem is located. Just outside the city."

Anne's eyes opened so wide, they hurt. "You have a real harem?"

"Yes, of course. Why not?"

"With women and everything?"

"Yes, Madame. What else would be in a harem?"

"I want to see it!"

He smiled and once again brushed his forehead with his handkerchief. "That cannot be done. I am taking you back to the hotel in Marrakesh. I wanted you to be safe with a good driver and an escort, that's all."

"But I want to see your harem!"

"There are no tours."

She was hunting for words that could make him change his mind. "Just to see?" she asked very softly, even more submissive than before.

"There is only one way a woman can see it, Madame."

"What? How?"

"To be a part of it."

"You mean—"

"That is the only way."

"Are you asking me to be a part of it?"

"I am telling you how a woman may see it. I did not bring this up."

"You mean for a night? Is that what you're saying?"

"My dear Anne, I am a businessman. I am not a boy who steals a kiss in a movie house. One year as a minimum. I will pay you five million dirhams, which is one million American dollars. You will be expected to stay for a year and I will have an option to keep you for another year at a cost of another five million dirhams."

Anne's mouth was open. For the first time in decades, she was speechless.

"And," he said, "that's all there is to that."

"Are you serious!?"

"Why not?"

"And what would I be expected to do for a year?"

"Wait for me. And when I call for you, you do as I say. That is the way of all my women."

"You must be putting me on! My God, what are you saying?"

"I don't, as you say, 'put on'."

"Why on earth do you think I would do that? You think I would do that for a million dollars? Do you think that I'm that hungry for money?"

"I don't care why you would do it. It is my guess that you would do it to satisfy your urges for excitement. The five million dirhams are to remind you that you are mine, that's all. The payment is to keep you under constant humiliation. You must receive the money to be a reminder to you that you have sold yourself to me."

"What would you do if I—if anyone would protest what you want?" Anne was melting in her seat, and he saw her attitude. "Will you beat me?"

"Of course."

"Well, isn't that inviting!"

"You will become an animal—if you're not already." He yelled to Hahmidoo in the front seat, "Isn't she an animal to be tamed?"

"You want me to be a prostitute, don't you?" Anne asked before Hahmidoo had a chance to answer.

"I do not want you to be a prostitute. Who needs some woman to rent for an hour? There's nothing in that for me. I only work in leases. A one year lease. 'Yes' or 'no.' Any more questions from you and I will interpret that as a 'yes' or you would stop your talking. Say 'no' and that will mean you do not want to hear any more about it, and I will drop you off in Marrakesh. I always keep my word. So say 'no' and we'll be done with this."

There was an intoxicating silence.

"Let me visit your harem," she said very softly. "Just a visit. Please."

"I told you there are no visitors."

"But I want to see it. Tonight."

"As a participant?"

Again that silence. Then, "I want to see it. Just to look. I don't want any dirhams. I just want to see it."

"I have a compromise."

"Oh?"

"You may see it. But for you to walk on its premises, you must pay me!"

"You are outrageous! Now you want money from me?"

"It's the only way I can think of, Madame. I will bend the rules to allow you a tour. I am a reasonable man, so I will allow it, but only if you pay me the price for your humiliation."

"How much?"

"One dirham."

She made a quick mental currency conversion. "Twenty cents?"

"Yes."

"Take me to Erfoud. I am humiliated."

"Now! Pay me now!"

Anne took a dirham from her purse.

He ripped it in half, rolled down the window and threw its two pieces outside, then rolled the window back up. "It would be me who would be humiliated if I kept it. Now it's you who is doubly humiliated because I rejected your offering. You are an animal. That's all you are, Madame. Now sit back. It is a long ride to Erfoud. No more talk. You must use this time to think—and worry as a wild animal would worry after capture, not knowing where the animal is to be taken or what the animal will encounter, once there."

Anne closed her eyes. Could this be happening? It was. The uncertainty of all this was driving her exhilaration more than anything else. And, somehow, she trusted him.

Most of the women wore silk tunics that were very loose, and the tunics had embroidery of gold on them. Below the tunics they wore loose, filmy, ballooning pants that went all the way from the waist to the ankles. Others were wearing filmy silk robes over whatever else they were wearing. There was nothing that was revealing. They were all beautiful.

One very young woman with black flowing hair came up to the Sultan and gave a mixture between a bow and a curtsy. He nodded at her, then gestured towards Anne. "This is a tourist. Nothing more. She paid to have the privilege of seeing our rooms and grounds, and I granted it. She will not be rewarded with spending time with me. Take her to all the rooms into which you are allowed. Say nothing to her other than giving her orders, and accept no words from her. She is not entitled to explanations of any kind. Before her tour begins, and as long as she is on the premises I want her to be dressed accordingly. No foquia or kaftans or anything of beauty. She does not deserve anything like that. Dress her in a haik so that all of her is covered except for her eyes. You must bathe her before dressing her. She has been in a car all day and she was sweating. If she protests anything you do, you may force her to obey. If she protests any of that, you let Hahmidoo know, and he will drive her to a hotel in Erfoud, and that's all we'll see of her here—her tour will be done. If she decides to stay until morning, give her comfortable quarters for the night, and then at seven in the morning take her to Hahmidoo and she can go back to Marrakesh where she came from."

That young woman, with two other women took her to a huge room that had mosaic paintings inlaid in the floor. The paintings were life-sized figures of unclothed men and women. At the far end of the room was a huge square shell. The shell was adorned with modern plumbing fixtures. One of the women turned a golden knob and water flowed into the square tub. As it poured, the other woman started taking off Anne's clothes. Anne started taking them off herself, but her hand was whisked away by the other women's hands. They were in charge, and they completed the shedding of all her clothing and they lifted her into the tub.

Sitting on the rim of the square shell, they scrubbed her with their soaped hands from her shoulders to her feet. And then a long drying before they dressed her as they were instructed, with Anne covered in totality except for her eyes. Then the tour began with two other women walking beside her, each holding one of Anne's hands. Each room; some big, some small, had different colored pillows all over the floor, just like Somebody Else in New York. But here there were also blankets of different colors, and slabs of concrete. The women explained nothing. There were doors they passed that they did not enter. And in each room whose door they opened, there were other women sitting on the floors; some were eating, some were talking, but they stopped whatever they were doing when the tour-guides walked in with Anne. She was brought to face every woman, and every woman looked her over with intense interest.

It was not Anne on tour of the harem, it was the harem on tour of Anne. She viewed sixteen rooms, and the tour lasted over one hour, although the walk-through could have taken no more than five minutes.

By the time she was brought to her bedroom, she was totally worn out. They took her clothes off and put her on her bed. There were no covers. The room was not in absolute darkness. There were small candles flickering on the tables and there was some light from the moon through the window. They put a white gauze over her eyes and she could only see their hazy images. They fanned her with large white fans, and she was invited to sleep, which they knew would be impossible for her. They continued fanning and staring at her, and through the gauze she watched them stare.

She did not know that all of this was only a preamble.

She was covered with sweat after two hours, and they took her from the bed, to have a second bath.

Again, they walked her to the big room with the paintings on the floor and the tank. The repeat of the atmosphere and procedure and her acknowledgment of it were now so effective that she wanted it to continue on and on, but they were the time-keepers.

The bedroom was even more impossible for sleep than before. She never felt more naked. This time it was men who put the white gauze over her eyes and fanned and watched her. They blew out the candles. Through the gauze she saw the figures stand over her. And then, one by one, they left, leaving one who went to her.

At seven in the morning, Hahmidoo drove her to her hotel in Marrakesh.

"Did you have a good time?" he asked back to Anne from the front seat.

She almost trembled in her answer, which was a very slow "yes."

"I'm sure that the Sultan is glad you had a good time."

"He disappeared after he brought me in."

"Are you sure?"

"I'm sure."

Hahmidoo smiled. "You do not know Sultan Abdelikamel Rahal."

"Oh?"

"Who did you see last night?"

"His—his employees."

"One of them was the employer."

"No. Not once."

"The Sultan Abdelikamel Rahal is no idiot."

"I only went on a tour. You know that he bent the rules for me."

"The Sultan Abdelikamel Rahal gives tours for many, many women. Giving tours is his highest pleasure."

Anne looked at Hahmidoo with a pained expression. "There have been other tours?"

Hahmidoo nodded and glanced over his shoulder at her quickly, and then he looked back at the road. "Do not feel bad. I am assigned to tell you. It is the procedure. But do not feel that he left you only with others. I know how he conducts the tours and by this time he wants you to know. In the end he was with you."

Anne closed her eyes. Finally she was sleepy, and although she knew she had been deceived by the man they called the Sultan, she was content in knowing that he did not leave her alone and that it was him who was with her when all the others left.

"How was your vacation?" Mark asked Anne over the phone when she was back at the Embassy in Bujumbura.

"Wonderful! I went to Morocco without anyone here even knowing."

"Really? Did you have a good time?"

"What do you think?"

"I shouldn't have asked," Mark said. "I know you."

"I'll tell you when I see you."

"Eat any of that good French food they have there?"

"I didn't go out to restaurants much. Just a little, but I think I might have caught something."

"You mean food poisoning?"

"Oh, no. My eyes. They're bloodshot. But I'm sure it will go away."

FORTY-ONE
THE AUGUST STAIRWAY
1974

"The Old Man," which was the way Ken Clawson referred to the president, "has had it. The ship of state is sinking." Ken Clawson, the president's director of communications, had hastily invited Moose, Dick Moore, and Larry Higby (who had been known as "Haldeman's Haldeman") to leave the White House Mess on Monday, August the 5th, and have lunch at Trader Vic's where they could eat in a booth where no one would hear them. "Loyalty is no longer expected."

There was a pall at the table.

Dick Moore took his thin cigarette-sized cigar out of his mouth and stomped it out in the ash tray. "Is he going to resign, Ken? Is that what you're saying?"

"He's wavering. Last Thursday he pretty well decided to do it, but now he's wavering. Today he's going to release a tape that Haig, Buzhardt, and St. Clair call 'The Smoking Gun.' If we jump, if we all jump, you can count on it—he'll resign."

"What's the tape?" Larry Higby asked.

"June 23, '72, with your former boss," Ken was referring to Bob Haldeman. "It's the Old Man and Bob talking. We can defend it, but aside from what's said on the tape, there's another factor here that can make it the end of the road."

They waited to hear the other factor but Clawson hesitated before he explained himself. "It's a surprising factor." Then he looked at each of his invited guests around the table, stopping his gaze at one, then another, then another. "Mutiny."

No one responded except for the looks of confusion on their faces.

"It's not Charles Laughton and Clark Gable," Ken Clawson said, making his parallel to *Mutiny on the Bounty*, "It's the Old Man and Al."

"Haig?" Higby asked.

"Al Haig. The Old Man's replacement for your boss, Higby. If you don't believe me, go to Haig's meeting with the staff at three-thirty this afternoon in Room 450. I think he wants the Old Man out. Although the transcript can be defended, Al won't accept any defense. He's going to give orders for none of us to appear on TV or radio, to refuse all interviews, and no conversation with the print press. He's trying to make sure the Old Man doesn't decide to hang on."

"Al's doing that?" Moose asked with some disbelief.

"Al's doing that, Moose. I'm just giving you guys a little advance. It's going to be up to you. You can either work for Al or you can work for the Old Man—but you can't work for both."

"Maybe Haig's just following the president's directive," Higby offered. "Maybe the president told Al to squash any defense."

Clawson shook his head. "No. That's not what's going on. Let me tell you what happened. Up at Camp David yesterday, James St. Clair said he would resign as the president's lawyer unless the president released a transcript of that tape. And then St. Clair told the others up there that now that they knew about the tape, they'd all be guilty of obstruction of justice if they were silent about it—that is, if the president decides not to release it. And so they all advised the president to release it. No one actually saw the president up there except Haig, Ziegler, and St. Clair but the rest all gave Haig their votes for him to tell the president that he should release it and—he should resign."

"Who were the other ones at Camp David?" Higby asked.

"It's not important now." Ken Clawson had picked up the president's habit of changing the subject when it suited his convenience. "You know we're sitting in the Old Man's booth? This is where they always seat him and Mrs. Nixon. And, if you've ever been here with him—he walks out and passes the people here and stops at some table that has a woman at it—he always does—and says, 'Is this a Mai Tai? Be careful with it. They sneak up on you, you know.' And the woman laughs and her date laughs and they're so excited and amazed that the president is here and would do that with the Mai Tai!"

"You have the transcript?" Dick Moore asked Ken.

He took it out of his brief case by the side of the table, and slid the stapled papers across the table to Dick Moore who nodded and he read them slowly. He looked up at Ken Clawson and shook his head. "It's a piece of cake. It's no smoking gun."

"May I see it please?" Moose asked.

Dick Moore took out his small tin of cigarette-sized cigars, opened it, took out a fresh one, and lit it. "Moose," he said, "You'd be smart to stay out of this one. You report to Kissinger, not Haig. Your job is foreign policy. Keep it that way or you're going to get into quicksand like the rest of us."

"If he's in trouble, then his foreign policy is going to be in trouble. Let me see the transcript, Dick," Moose said.

Dick Moore looked over at Ken Clawson and Ken nodded. "Shoot it to him. It's his choice."

"Here," Dick Moore pushed it over to Moose. "Don't read it. You'll be up for an obstruction of justice if the president doesn't release it today. You have to stay clean. I wouldn't get involved in this thing if I were you."

"Yes, you would if you were me, Dick, or if you were you. You've never been on a lifeboat in your life, and neither have I. I'm not going to get in one now any more than you are."

Dick nodded. Then he gave a slight click of approval with his tongue by the side of his mouth, as he nodded.

Ken looked between them and said, "Even if you guys wanted a lifeboat

I don't think there are any left. I think they took them all to Camp David over the weekend and used them." Then Clawson picked up the big brown menu of Trader Vic's. "Let's have some Cho Cho. It's the Old Man's favorite. They're little sticks of teriyaki meat and you dip it in hot sauce. He bathes the meat in it. That's what I'm having."

"Gosh!" Dick Moore shook his head. "When I think that I told John Dean to tell the president there was a cancer growing on his presidency. Little did I know what John would do with my line—what it would all turn out to be—what John would turn out to be."

"Suddenly, I'm not hungry," Moose said, putting the papers on the table. "I could defend this stuff easy."

"I think you ought to have a Mai Tai," Dick Moore said. "But be careful of them, Moose. They sneak up on you, you know. Just like getting involved in this mess can sneak up on you."

On Tuesday, August the 6th, a common practice turned into a revelation that would stay with Moose for the rest of his life. He regularly opened his private office door to the east hallway of the Old Executive Building and he would slowly walk its length, and then back again, with no one being able to tell he had a repeated destination. The length of that hallway with its checkered floor and high ceiling and prestigious aura acted as a narcotic that allowed him to think with clarity, just as a forest does for a naturalist, or a view of the ocean does for lovers. The only ones who were familiar with Moose's habit were the four secret service agents who stood in the hallway outside the president's EOB Office, who noticed everything that took place in the east hallway.

On that Tuesday, while on that walk, Moose saw one of the highest-ranking assistants of the president running up the wide north-east semi-circular stairway of the EOB to the second floor, two steps at a time, his mouth open, his gaze straight ahead, a gaze that almost looked insane. He was oblivious to any one or any thing other than getting up those stairs unimpeded. He didn't answer Moose's, "Hi!" There was no question as to where he was going or why he was going there. The second floor was where the vice president and his staff had their offices. That run up the stairway was repeated again and again throughout the day by others on the president's staff as they embraced Gerald Ford, making their pitch of why they should stay to serve the new president, should president Nixon resign. They were no longer using their talents for the president when those talents were needed the most, but instead, were using their talents to influence the vice president to keep them on staff. Ken Clawson was wrong: the lifeboats were not all accounted for at Camp David. The sinking ship of state had an upper-deck on the second floor of the EOB where other lifeboats were sheltered, and that shelter was the place to be for those in the president's crew who were more interested in saving themselves than anything else. Moose was spellbound by the sight. It hit him harder than yesterday's conversation at Trader Vic's, and it hit him harder than yesterday afternoon's staff meeting with Alexander Haig where things Ken Clawson had told him earlier were confirmed.

Moose walked back to his office, almost shaking from that sight of the running up on the semi-circular staircase. As he entered his office, his phone was buzzing on the intercom line from his secretary's office. "Yes, Ruth?"

"There's a Cody Cooper on the line from the State Department. He said that it's urgent that he talk with you."

"Thanks." he snapped the button. "Hello?"

"Mr. Dunston?"

"Yes."

"This is Cody Cooper. We met many years ago. I worked for President Kennedy, but we met even before then. It was so long ago that it was before that election. We met in Hong Kong at the time of–"

"I remember you, Cody. Of course. And I receive those Irene Goodpastor letters that keep me up-to-date on everyone who was there. Good to hear from you. What can I do for you, Cody?"

"Nothing. It's what you can do for yourself, if not your country, Mr. Dunston. Your president is heading towards his Dallas. I don't mean assassination, but his end. A tragedy. Mr. Dunston, I don't want to go into the whole story but I could have prevented what happened in Dallas, and so could a lot of people who worked for the president. We didn't think. We just didn't think of all the possibilities that could happen in Dallas."

Moose didn't answer.

"Do you know what I mean?" Cody asked.

"Yes. I know what you mean."

"And Mr. Dunston, you have an advantage we didn't have eleven years ago. You can see it coming, can't you?"

"Yes."

"If you don't do everything you can to prevent it, your conscience will never leave you alone."

Again, Moose didn't answer him.

"Do you know what I mean?"

"What is it you suggest I do, Cody?"

"I don't know. I can't suggest anything. I don't know all the things that are going on there these days. All I know is what I read in the wires here, and the cable-traffic, and in *The Washington Post.* And I know what's coming. And my old boss, President Kennedy–he liked your boss. I don't know how close you are to President Nixon. I don't know what the system is over there now. I don't know anything about you guys. I don't know what you can do, but you have to do everything you can to prevent your Dallas."

"You're a good man, Mr. Cooper."

Cody didn't know what to say.

"My God, you're a good man. President Kennedy would be proud of you."

"I wish I could help you, Mr. Dunston. But I don't have any clout with your president or really with anyone. I'm just a bureaucrat over here, that's all I am now. I just want you to know that every moment is important and you have to help your president. You have to," and he gave a quick swallow. "You have to seize the moment, or it will be gone."

Moose was nodding. "I will."

"Good. That's all I wanted to say to you."

"I'm very grateful to you, Mr. Cooper. I hope, very much, to talk to you again."

"If not before, I'll see you in Hong Kong in 1997, Mr. Dunston."

King Timahoe, that big, red Irish Setter of the president, walked in Moose's office through the open door from the hallway, with a look of desperation. He was panting and he looked at Moose as though he was pleading for Moose to do something about all this. Moose sat with King Timahoe for a quarter of an hour, scratching his chin and petting him. But King Timahoe wanted much more than that. His eyes were saying, "Please!"

The president didn't know it, but he was under house arrest again, even more extreme than when he was in San Clemente. This time many on his own staff were the wardens of the house arrest. The mutineers had placed the president off-limits to those on the president's staff who were not involved in the mutiny. It became common dialogue in the White House that the leader of the mutineers had already talked to Senator Goldwater, Senator Scott, and Congressman Rhodes, to brief them on the psychology to use to make the president resign. The two senators and one congressman who were to meet with the president the next day were told that within the meeting they shouldn't mention the word "resignation," but they should tell him that the votes in the House and the Senate were not there for him to avoid impeachment and likely removal—but not to say anything more, because it would raise his instinct to fight.

The phone call from Cody Cooper and the visit of King Timahoe were not easily dismissed by Moose Dunston.

Moose tried to think of what he could say to convince the president not to resign—to let the Constitution work. Moose walked back and forth in that hallway, in and out of the West Wing, back and forth across the north lawn, then to the south lawn, then to the East Wing, then to the residence, then to the West Wing again, then back to the EOB, then to Pennsylvania Avenue and across the street to Lafayette Park, then back into the long hallways, thinking of what could be said to the president.

He found himself putting his hands together and talking to Adam, as in prayer, and then talking to Jonas on the phone, and then preparing what he would say to the president, with every word absorbed in his memory.

For the first time since he came to the White House, Moose's request for a meeting with the president was denied. Alexander Haig said "No" with finality. David Parker, the president's appointment secretary, said "No" with sadness. "I can't, Moose. I've been ordered, no appointments with the president unless Haig allows it, and he isn't allowing it." Only Rose Mary Woods and the president's family wanted Moose to meet with the president, and even they were unable to break the barriers of his house arrest. Julie Nixon Eisenhower said she wouldn't give up trying to reach her father.

Moose didn't sleep at all that night. That image of presidential assistants running up that stairway kept reappearing in his mind over and over again.

On Wednesday, August the 7th, Julie sat in Moose's office, where she attempted to call her father, but the mutineers refused to put her calls through. "Leave me alone here for a moment please, Moose. I have an idea." Moose walked out of his office and sat in his secretary's reception room while Julie wrote her father a letter appealing to him to visit with Moose, in the hope no one would destroy it before he could read it. She repeatedly used the phone in attempts to get through to her father, while writing that letter. Then, in impatience, she walked into the hallway from Moose's office through his private door without going through his reception room. She was on her way to her father's EOB office, four doors down the hall.

Only a minute passed before Moose, still sitting in his secretary's reception room, heard the private door of his office open. Then he heard the ripping of paper. Julie opened the door between the office and the reception room. "He'll see you, Moose, right now. Don't even take the time to comb your hair."

"You saw him? They weren't able to stop you? You got through?"

She smiled and nodded.

"Not the Oval Office?"

She shook her head. "He's down the hall."

The president was sitting in his soft lounge chair by the side of his desk in his EOB office, with his left leg extended in front of him resting on the ottoman. He was puffing his pipe. "Come in, Moose. Come on over here."

"Thanks for your time, Mr. President."

"Sit down, Moose. Sit down."

"Mr. President I recognize that many here are—"

"You don't need to start at the beginning. I know why you're here. Julie told me."

Moose made his speech to the president. He had tried to cut it but he did a poor job of that. It was long.

The president gave no indication of which way he was leaning until he answered Moose's appeal with, "It's my instinct to fight and not quit. I'd fall on the sword. That's my instinct. But let me tell you the way it is. Later on this afternoon a delegation's coming here. Congressional delegation, you know. They're going to give me the count in the House and the Senate. Goldwater, Scott, and Rhodes." He extended his arms with the palms of his hands facing the floor, and he gave a swift wave downward. "I know what they'll say. I know the count. And then tomorrow another delegation."

"Barry Goldwater, Hugh Scott, and John Rhodes are men, Mr. President. Only men. I'm talking about something much bigger than men. Don't think of it in terms of mathematics and head counts and what one man is going to do and another man is going to do. Don't look at it as a man would look at it. Even if they tell you the House members votes will be 435 to zero, and the senators will vote 100 to zero. They're the stuff of the common. You remember what my friend, Valadovich, told you how he survived in Hanoi's prison? You seemed so interested in what he said, so consumed by it. Please think about it now. You've always taken the long view, and you've always fought. Some kid, one hundred years from now, has to know that you didn't quit. There's a higher plateau than your naysayers. There's a higher plateau than all this; it's foreign affairs. You have to get up there again. You've been there before."

The president's response made Moose unsure that his words were getting through. "Then I'll write my book in jail."

"What?"

"Then I'll write my book in jail."

"Yes. Perhaps."

"It's all right. I don't even mind that. Sadat said there were eight months of his prison term that was the happiest period of his life. I asked him about that—two months ago when I was in Egypt—I asked him why. He said it was the solitude. You see? The happiest period of his life. He said that he doesn't hold the presidency to be of greater value than himself. Anwar was Anwar whether in jail or in the president's office. It's not the public's acclaim. It's what you know you are."

Moose didn't respond to that.

"So I can write a book in prison if that's what it is. It doesn't make any difference. It doesn't make any difference. I can do that. But I'm not guilty of anything. I didn't remember what I said when—you know I talk—or what it would sound like on tape years later, separate from everything else. They'll drain these things out little by little. Every time I think it's over, there are more things in those tapes that they'll make something out of. Then we'll continue to be on the defensive. And you can't do anything when you're just defending and trying to remember what you meant when you said something years ago, and weren't even paying any attention to what it would sound like if someone wanted to make something of it. So you can count on it. There will be more and more. It will just go on. It's time to stop this agony from becoming the nation's daily exercise. That's what it will become if I stay."

"Whether you resign or stick it out, it's going to go on and on. Little men are longing to participate in a public autopsy, Mr. President. They savor tragedy. They take joy in your tragedy."

"But then I won't be president, so it won't make any difference to the country. It's better that I let them destroy me rather than bring about the destruction of our foreign policy—the destruction of the presidency."

"Staying in office won't destroy the presidency."

"It could. And it could bring down our institutions. Can you imagine our country's place in the world if they bring down our ability to gather intelligence? They wouldn't stop. Look what they've done already. The press isn't composed of Horace Greeley's anymore, you know. I have a choice right now to make it worse for me or make it worse for the whole country."

"Mr. President, in truth, I'm not thinking about you as much as I'm thinking about what this will mean in terms of war and peace, or to say it with the kind of precision that you prefer—the difference between liberty and slavery. We all know what's going on now in Vietnam, Cambodia, and Laos. The North Vietnamese are spitting on the Peace Accords they signed. Ford can't handle this. He doesn't know foreign policy. If the North Vietnamese mount another offensive, the Congress will let them get away with it. The Congress doesn't care about the signatures on the Paris Accords. They've passed the War Powers Resolution. Do you think Gerald Ford's going to fight them on that and bomb Hanoi again if it's necessary to prevent the North Vietnamese from taking over Saigon? All the lives that have been lost there, all the way since Eisenhower was president, will be in vain."

"Not in vain. Don't say that. Not in vain. But I know what you mean. I know that, Moose. But whether I'm in the White House or out of it, there may be no way out for Vietnam with this Congress or the next one. They don't want to save the Vietnamese. But they may be more sensible if I leave. If I fight it out, foreign policy will be in shambles. This thing can go on and on and Brezhnev can take advantage of it. Why not? Why shouldn't he? I would if I were him. Brezhnev will know that the president of the United States is in a weakened position, a president without teeth. It's likely that he'll take advantage of it. He wouldn't be a leader if he didn't. He's likely to mount another crisis in the Mideast. Look what happened last October when I called the alert. They thought—the press thought—they thought I did it to divert attention from Watergate. Everything I need to do will be suspect. As president I won't be able to do anything. You see, I can't govern and he'll know it. No one will be governing. They won't let me do anything. They'll stop everything. If I stay, you have to realize all three branches of the government will be wrapped up in this thing—and not just for three or four months. It could go on for two years. All three branches paralyzed by this. If I was Brezhnev and saw this weakness going on and on—no, no, no. And I'm the only one who can end it—quickly, and be done with it. And they'll have Jerry Ford."

"But there's another way to end it. The American people are very fair and if they knew what we know about the wiretaps and taping system of LBJ and for that matter, JFK—and of all those things the Washington journalists and the JFK and LBJ staffs just haven't told the American people—those things the Washington journalists keep sacred—the American people would then be able to put all this in context. Journalists in this town have had the code of not talking or writing about those things—the information has never gone west of the Potomac. They changed the rules in the case of your Administration. The journalists themselves were the ones guilty of one cover-up after another over the years. We all know the hidden chapters, but the rest of the country doesn't. If we would simply reveal that information to the American people, they would be able to put all this in its whole fabric."

The president barely allowed the words to conclude when he started shaking his head. "Don't ever attack a former president to defend me, Moose. Don't do that. Lady Bird Johnson is alive, and she's—" and he hunted for words. "—she's a lovely woman. I don't want her to be hurt. Nor Mrs. Kennedy. She's been through hell. Our predecessors did good jobs. Even the ones we fought against. Don't use that argument to keep me in office."

"It's not speaking badly about JFK or LBJ, but look, Mr. President, this is one of the few times in U.S. history when there isn't one former president living, and I'm sure they'd come forward if one or more of them was still around. But their staffs are around and they're silent about tapes. It's infuriating. Now, as long as the press and your other opponents are vivisecting every conversation you ever had, the people have to be able to put things in context or they're going to come to the wrong conclusions."

"No. Don't do that. That's out. Enough good people have been hurt in all this."

Then the argument shifted back to foreign affairs when Moose said that the country had withstood longer periods of time in greater crisis and came out stronger than ever. He said that if foreign powers wanted to create havoc for the United States during the coming period, the Congress would have to put their partisan instincts away. The president agreed that if they perceived an international emergency they would do just that, but it would be their judgment of the foreign powers, and their world view, which few had, that would become paramount. "They could misjudge and mistakenly believe there was no emergency," the president said.

Finally, Moose used the ace card—the supremacy of the Constitution and to "let the U.S. Constitution work and have the Senate trial."

The president answered, "Time for the nation's best interests isn't on the side of those long Constitutional processes. The Constitution, as you know, does not prohibit resignation. Its authors assumed it might happen."

"So you're going to quit, Mr. President?"

"I'll listen to that delegation coming here. Well, maybe I won't. Scott! Can you imagine? I'll think. I'll think. I'm having dinner with Henry tonight. That's your turf. That's my turf. That's foreign affairs. I'll listen to him. I moved him to secretary of state because he knows diplomacy and he knows what affects world leaders. This will affect them. Then I'll think by myself about what's best. Ray—Ray Price dropped off a suggested speech for me to make. It's—"

"A resignation speech?"

The president nodded. "It's good. Ray's a good man. I requested it from him. I even told Ray what Goldwater, Scott, and Rhodes will tell me, so he could include it in the draft. I know what they'll tell me. It's just a draft. Just a contingency. You know about contingencies. Just if I think it's best, it has to be ready. Foreign affairs are the important things. I'll talk to Henry tonight."

"Don't think in human terms. He's only a man. They're all only men." Adam put those words in Moose's mouth, and he knew it.

The president stared at Moose, then after a long silence he puffed on his pipe and it didn't respond. It was out.

Moose repeated, "They're only men, sir."

The stare of the president continued in silence until he said, "But so am I. That's what we are."

The morning of Thursday, August the 8th, the president's News Summary that was on the desk of the president, with copies on the desk of his aides, was bulging with speculation and with painful reading for the president:

"The question in D.C. shifted from whether or not RN would resign to how and when, led Chancellor. The capital was seized by resignation fever, began Mudd. Rumors of RN's imminent resignation swept DC and the world, led ABC. Hill was seething w/rumors, speculation and gossip that RN was to resign, said NBC. Al Haig and VP Ford were responsible for much of the confusion, said CBS.

"Goldwater on all nets in lead stories said he, Scott and Rhodes were 'extremely impressed' at session to which RN invited them w/RN's putting best interests of U.S. uppermost in his mind. RN's made no decision yet and they didn't suggest resignation—neither that nor immunity came up. They told him Hill situation's 'gloomy' and 'very distressing.'

"UPI leads earlier: 'Squelching reports that he'd resign before the day was out, RN told 3 Hill leaders he hasn't decided whether to quit or submit to impeachment and trial.' CBS noted HAK (Kissinger) came to WH in evening and that RN's family was w/him during the day...CBS cited RN's seclusion as adding to the resignation fever.... RN was shifting, by CBS w/reconsideration of options.

"CBS said Al Haig told VP to prepare for the transition of power...2 close VP friends who saw him Wed. say resignation's expected, but not for several days as the departure needs to be arranged w/grace and ceremony.

"Top E. Eur. countries have gone to USSR for meetings w/Brezhnev to discuss relations w/west notably w/US. Fate of RN has been assigned key role in discussions, according to diplomats, adding 'at best, detente will be slowed down or frozen. At worst may peter out.' (UPI) Soviet press for first time faced up to looming impeachment and told readers RN could be removed.

"Communist's took Da Nang offensive to besieged town of Duc Duc following capture of nearby district capital and destruction of its entire 500 man defense forces. North Vietnamese have alerted some of its 6 home based divisions amid ominous signs of a possible countrywide Communist offensive in South Vietnam, U.S. officials report in AP story. These officials are more concerned than at any time since ceasefire was supposed to end the war. Some analysts suggested Hanoi may regard Admin turmoil as opportunity to strike hard in South Vietnam. Officials denied expressions of worry were intended to influence Senate to restore $300 million cut in aid.

"Brokaw said he wouldn't go so far as to describe WH mood as one of crisis, but it's clear these are grave times and no one knows what RN's going to do. It's clear he'll make the decision and he's now 'agonizing' over it. Physically, he appeared fine, said Brokaw who added RN gave 'small, deliberate smile' to press on way to WH from EOB and he's said to be serene. Reflecting his thesis that WH has come to halt, Brokaw noted that as he gave his report, Clawson and staff were watching him from their balcony to see what he was saying.

"In addition to resignation as virtually accepted fact, in reports cited above, Ted Murphy had 3 other stories not on other nets that emphasized public desire that RN go. Murphy said, 'But RN's a stubborn, self-confident man w/enormous capacity to deceive public, deceive Capitol Hill and deceive family, so odds aren't prohibitive. Everybody wants RN to resign and besides his own stubbornness, secret, informal negotiations are probably holding things up.'

"CBS 60 Minutes has scrapped next Sunday's show for possible resignation. 'Everyone's in a state of alert,' CBS spokesman said."

The front page of *The Washington Post* had a picture of the president and Julie in an embrace. That picture was so loud that the newspaper could not be put in the corner without its siren penetrating every thought.

That early morning the president wanted to walk alone without the Secret Service, without anyone, from his EOB Office to the West Wing of the White House. It took over an hour of preparation.

The entire area of Pennsylvania Avenue where his walk could be seen from the street had to be barricaded from passerbys, and the growing crowd outside the fence had to temporarily be moved to the eastern edge of the corner. The simplest things became mammoth undertakings.

It was around nine in the morning when the covered typewriter was wheeled from the Old Executive Office Building to the West Wing. A maintenance man wheeled it. To those who knew why it was going there and knew the text that would be typed by it and wanted his presidency to continue, it looked like the wheeling of a gurney to gather the tragedy.

It was to be the last afternoon. Not many knew for sure how close it was to the end, but it was guessed.

Pennsylvania Avenue was packed again with those who wanted to be close to importance, straining against the black iron fence. It was as though they expected a shroud to be put around some one's head and tied at the neck for a hanging or, more accurately, it was as though they were watching someone on the brink of jumping from a building as they yelled, "Jump! Jump!"

In Room 345 of the Old Executive Office Building, phone lines and tables had been set-up, and volunteers under the supervision of Ann Higgins were given space there to answer the thousands of telephone calls coming into the White House from those around the country literally begging, many crying, beseeching the volunteers to tell the president not to resign. Helen Thomas, of United Press International, was there, invited to answer phones herself to hear what people around the country were saying. She was invited to pick up any ringing phone at random.

Ken Clawson's assistant, Don Risko was in the hallway. "How do you think things look, Moose? Huh? Huh?" He was shifting his weight from one foot to the other with his hands in his pockets. "Huh?" He had asked that question and given that pendulum-type pose for months on end. A very decent man, he was intoxicated with the disease of frustration. "Do you think it's as bad as they say? Huh? Huh?"

Clay Whitehead, Brian Lamb, Laurence Lynn, and Jonathan Moore were meeting together. They had secretly been preparing a "just in case" transition from Nixon to Ford since last May, under orders of Philip Buchen who was Gerald Ford's close confidant. It had to be done.

When the secret transition team returned from their meeting, Vice President Ford was handed a thick notebook of issue papers with a one-page index itemizing quick decisions to be made, should President Nixon resign.

Then two men wheeled the blue television-background curtain from the EOB to the West Wing. It only took one man, but there were two.

Then the public announcement. President Nixon would speak to the nation from the Oval Office at 9 o'clock in the evening.

Within minutes CBS made the decision to start its coverage very early for a 9 o'clock speech—they would start it at 6:30 P.M. and continue through 1:00 A.M. It was clear what was going to happen.

Then the hallways were "swept" to see that only White House people were in the White House complex, from the East Wing through the Old Executive Office Building. Everyone else had to leave and stay out, and every White House person who was in, had to stay in. There would be no entrance or exits until the speech was done.

There was a three o'clock rain. A quick one but a heavy one.

The afternoon hallways were strangely quiet. Every once in a while someone would walk in the east hall heading to the wire-room which was packed with staff people. That was the room in which there was a Xerox machine. The staff people were standing in line to copy their memos from years back, to take and keep them—as the originals, by orders, were going to the office of the special prosecutor. Was it legal to make copies to take out of the White House? No one asked. No one wanted to ask.

About one hour before the speech began, Moose received a phone call from Jonas. He told Moose that a number of his former colleagues at Hoa Lo prison tried to talk to the president, and the White House operator said she couldn't put them through.

Moose called the White House operators and told them if any caller identified himself as a former prisoner of war, they should put the call through to him. Within one minute one of the former prisoners was on the line. He was crying. He said, "I have never traded before on my incarceration–never–but I must now–to the president–I've got to talk to the president. He mustn't do this."

"I wish I could put the call through to him," Moose said. "He wants to be with his family and not have any calls.... He has made that clear to us. I can't get through to him myself. I just want to tell you on behalf of the president–"

"I know you guys are there to keep him from folks like me," the voice interrupted.

"No. That's not true. I can't get through to him myself. But I'll do my best to see if I can for you. I can't promise anything. I'll call you back."

King Timahoe walked out of Moose's office into the hallway. He walked slowly, his head down.

The former prisoner gave his phone number and said, "I'll wait all night."

There was no need to wait all night. The president made his speech in which "I shall resign the presidency effective at noon tomorrow. Vice President Ford will be sworn in as president at that hour...."

Among others, Moose called back that former prisoner of war. All Moose could say was, "I'm sorry." All the former prisoner of war could say was, "It's a mistake." His voice was quavering.

Even at the time of crisis, the smallest matters can invade a human mind and rest there. The thought occurred to Moose that his secret missions to the tobacco shop on Fourteenth Street were over and done. How will the president get his tobacco?

A couple dozen members of the staff had come to Ken Clawson's office so as not to be alone after watching that evening speech. There was a lot of drinking and a lot of helplessness going on.

After the evening speech, every television channel had analysis. One of the local D.C. news persons said "Richard Nixon becomes the first president to resign in disgrace." Ted Murphy heard it, and he said it on television as though it was an original Murphy statement. So did others hear it, and then they said it until the word "Nixon" was said as a middle name with his last name being "Whoresignedindisgrace." Those six syllables, said as one word, brought nods from much of the nation's newsrooms. It was picked up with unashamed plagiarism by those who wanted to use a new negative catch phrase.

The president's staff stayed together for hours after the speech. It was after midnight. If they left, it would have been the confirmation that it was over. Staying seemed to be a thread that extended his presidency.

Then a memo was dropped at every staff office, inviting the recipients to come to the East Room the following morning at 9:30 A.M. for the president's goodbye to his staff. The memo went on to read that the president would be departing by helicopter from the South Lawn right after that.

No emotion on the paper.

Just before midnight Dick Moore told Moose that he was hungry and Moose must be, too, and they should get out of there and have something to eat. Moose agreed. Dick Moore phoned the Madison Hotel and the hotel operator rang the dining room, but there was no answer. Dick hung up, dialed the hotel again and this time the hotel didn't answer. He dialed Washington Information and Washington Information didn't answer.

"Dick, I'm going to the men's room," Moose said.

"I hope it isn't locked. This isn't our night."

Moose walked out of Clawson's office into the massive empty east hallway of the Old Executive Office Building. As always, its length and majesty were overwhelming. His footsteps echoed from that checkered horizonless floor. There was a White House Protective Service Man sitting at the small wooden desk in the hall outside President Nixon's EOB office. The Secret Service agents weren't standing there, which meant he wasn't in that office. They wouldn't be standing there again.

Moose walked to the men's room and Dick Moore was right. It was locked. As Dick said, it wasn't their night.

There was another men's room downstairs, so he walked down the massive semi-circular stairway letting his hand run over the polished wooden banister for one more feel of it. He reached the basement and walked down the hallway where there were two plainclothesmen from the FBI and one White House Protective Service Man standing outside the room next to the men's room. That was where the White House Tapes were being kept.

Moose went in the men's room and as he stood there, he once again thought what he often thought when he stood in that men's room. "I should have drilled a hole in the wall and taken all those tapes out of there and destroyed them."

Then, because he knew he may never see them again, he walked down other hallways of the building. He opened the door of Room 127 which was reserved for the putting together of the president's Daily News Summary. Normally it would be busy at this hour with a maze of people writing, duplicating, and stapling the next morning's summary. But no one was in the room. It looked like a firetrap. Stacks of magazines, newspapers, bulletins, and television transcripts were spilling from every table, desk, and across most of the floor. Large brown White House envelopes, pre-labeled with the names of the president's aides who were normally to have them on their desks by seven-thirty in the morning, were in a stack.

Everything and every place in the building, other than Clawson's office, was so barren of people.

By the time Moose got back to Ken Clawson's office, Dick Moore had found an eating place that was open. "We can go to the Carriage House in Georgetown. They closed at midnight but they're still there, and they said they'll wait for us. They said they'd make us whatever we want. And there won't be any cost. Believe it or not, a Kennedy man owns the place, and he feels sorry for us."

"I believe it," Moose said.

Moose and Dick walked that corridor of the EOB toward the Pennsylvania Avenue exit. The silence of the giant building was interrupted by the two sets of footsteps, and then another two sets echoing up on the ceiling and the walls, and then down again to the floor.

Moose and Dick Moore passed the water fountain that was barely attached to the wall. It had been hanging there and hadn't worked for months. Would the Ford people have it fixed? What a worthless thought. Who cares?

Moose nodded at the guard behind the desk facing the Avenue. The guard pressed the buzzer and Moose opened the small mid-sectioned gate as he had done hundreds and hundreds of times, and then he and Dick Moore walked through the foyer and Moose opened the door to Pennsylvania Avenue. This time, like no other time before it, the noise from the street was ear-shattering. The noise was music and happy screaming and laughing and people were holding up the morning edition of *The Washington Post*, its large headline inescapable: "NIXON RESIGNS." There was dancing in the street.

Pennsylvania Avenue had been roped off by the police. No automobile traffic. Just happy people. People stacked together filling the Avenue like New Year's Eve in Times Square, celebrating. And there was Ted Murphy rushing up to Moose and Dick with a crew and mini-cam and portable lights, with other correspondents and crews with portable lights running behind him. But what was there to say? Murphy wouldn't understand. None of them would. How could they? They were on the same street as Moose and Dick, but the crowd was in heaven and Moose and Dick and others leaving the White House Compound that night were in hell.

They walked no more than a few steps to West Executive Avenue between the EOB and the West Wing, and got in Dick Moore's car.

As they drove from the White House compound, Moose said, "If it wasn't for you, Dick, Rehnquist wouldn't be in the Supreme Court. You did a real service in that place. You're the one who knew him and recommended him. That's how much the president trusted you."

Dick Moore was lost in his own thoughts. He said, "On the first inauguration night, the president was making speeches at all the inaugural balls, you know the way he did that. There were so many balls, and the last line he used at the last ball was that he had a key to the door of the White House in his pocket, and he said, 'I think I'll go over there and see if it works.' Everyone applauded and cheered. It was a great line." And Dick looked over at Moose and smiled and winked. "I wrote it!" Then his smile faded. "Now it's his last night to use that key."

Then Dick Moore did something that was as dramatic in its simplicity as anything that was done that evening. For no apparent reason, as he was driving to the restaurant in Georgetown he said, "George Washington–John Adams–Thomas Jefferson–James Madison–" and from memory he went through the entire list of presidents as though he was in a trance. And then he came near the end of the list: "Dwight Eisenhower–John Kennedy–Lyndon Johnson–Richard Nixon" and he gave a pause that was longer than the ones he had used in the cadence he had established, and in a softer voice he added, "Gerald Ford."

Then came the dreaded morning of Friday, August the 9th. There was another quick rain that hit ferociously and ended quickly. In the lobby of the Old Executive Office Building all the color photos of President Nixon had been taken down by an unknown "they." Just the small, naked picture hangers were sticking from the walls.

That morning, for the first non-holiday Friday since the Administration began, there was no president's News Summary on the desks of those in the staff who had always received them.

The South Lawn could be seen in full view through the windows on the walk to the East Room. There on the South Lawn was Army One, the helicopter that had just landed, its giant propeller still spinning after the landing. It would wait for the president.

By this time "they" had put quick black and white photos of Gerald Ford on West Wing walls.

The Marine Band was playing in the reception area of the residence just as it always did for presidential events, but this was not the time for music, surely not what they were playing: a medley of songs from *The Sound of Music*. It was simply that no one told them not to.

And then the president bid goodbye to the staff.

Unlike the death of a president, the flags were not lowered to half-staff, nor were bridges quickly renamed, nor were plaques engraved, nor were chisels in sculptors' hands hurrying to make his likeness in blocks of stone.

But like the death of a president, the Administration was over in mid-term, and grieved people were crying in the East Room, and the South Lawn seemed like Arlington Cemetery. Not a casket to go beneath ground but a helicopter to rise above ground, to scatter the grass, to move into the gray sky as viewers strained to follow what fast became no more than a dot lost behind a mass of trees on the lawn.

The assemblage silently walked back to their offices out of a need of a place to go rather than a sense of purpose. On their desks were piles of work they had once planned to accomplish, but instead, many of those piles were to be packed in boxes to become another part of futility.

Television lights that were still hot from illuminating his last presidential speech were turned off and cooled in the East Room before being turned on again for the next ceremony.

The cameras self-consciously waited.

President Nixon's staff, back in their offices, watched that next ceremony on their television sets. It was an unworldly feeling when Chief Justice Burger announced, "Ladies and gentlemen, the president of the United States" and it was Gerald Ford.

In each office the duty was simple. Just like the unknown "they" who had already removed the color pictures of President Nixon from the hallways, it was up to each individual to take down the pictures of President Nixon from their respective offices. Quick, without thinking about it.

There were holes left in the walls of Moose's office. But they would be repaired. Whoever took over the office would call for them to be puttied and the walls would be repainted.

There was lightning and a loud clap of thunder at 4:28 P.M. Then another tremendously bright lightning and a sear of thunder occurred simultaneously, meaning it had hit the White House grounds, or very close.

The morning of Saturday, August the 10th, was reserved for isolation. Moose sat behind his desk which was barren of things that needed doing. Like most Saturdays, his secretary was not there. He put a sheet of paper in his typewriter and typed a letter addressed to President Ford.

"I recognize and appreciate that you have asked everyone here at the White House to stay, but you must have room for your own appointees, and if all of us stay you will not have that needed opportunity. Therefore, with great respect and belief that you will have a very successful administration, I hereby resign."

He signed it and put an envelope in the typewriter and typed the name "President Gerald Ford" on it, enclosed the memo in it, then walked in his quiet secretaryless outer office and opened his secretary's top desk-drawer. He started poking around the pencils and paper-clips and small cellophane packages of Kleenex and those other things his secretary used daily in her work, and the aroma of the desk-drawer wood had a smell of efficiency. "Now where does she keep them?...Here they are." Moose picked up an envelope marked "Red Tags," opened it, and pulled out a one-inch square piece of red cardboard. With a piece of translucent tape, he attached the small cardboard square to the envelope. It indicated that the contents were important. He put the envelope in his breast pocket.

He picked up the telephone's receiver and, as usual, without dialing anything, the White House operator asked him whom he wanted to call. "Can you get me the American Consulate in Hong Kong, Dorothy?...Charge it to me, it's a personal call.... The Marine Guard is fine. It's almost ten o'clock at night there, he's probably the only one there. But tell him it's me at the White House.... Thanks." He hung up. In a few minutes there was the bing-bong, bing-bong ringing sound that did not sound like a telephone ring, but it was the way the White House phones rang during the Nixon Administration. Moose grabbed the receiver.

"Yes?...Is this the Marine Guard?...This is Moose Dunston at the White House.... Can you connect me to Tso Wai-yee at her home?...That's right, the pretty one.... Please.... Yes, I'll wait."

It was less than a minute when he heard her all familiar and beautiful voice come on the line.

"Hello, Wai-yee.... Yes, I know you heard.... I'm okay.... Yes, honest.... I'm fine. It's a rough time.... Thanks.... I know, Wai-yee. I just called to hear your voice. Apologize to your husband for me. Is he all right?...Is Liberty all right?...I needed to hear your voice...a friend.... Honest, I'm fine.... Yes.... Thanks."

He walked out of the office into the massive empty hallway of the Old Executive Office Building. Again, his footsteps echoed. The little table for the use of the Secret Service and the White House Protective Service outside what was President Nixon's EOB Office, was gone. It was really done. That was the confirmation, if he needed another confirmation. He walked the hall's length, then downstairs to the basement, and then down another flight to the subterranean basement, and to the White House Telephone Operator's Room. But to get to the room required stooping as he walked so his head wouldn't hit the pipes hanging from the very low ceiling of the subterranean basement.

The operators were there. All of them were there, plugging in wires and unplugging them and saying, "White House," and writing notes in their sharpened grease pencils on the plastic slabs under colored buttons, and red lights everywhere on their boards seemed to be flashing.

Because the operators so rarely had visitors in their "dungeon," Moose wanted to thank them. Their voices were so much more familiar than their faces. Their faces filled with glee just to see anyone down there who was a visitor, but it wasn't an appropriate time to visit as they were busy this Saturday morning. While he was talking to them, under Number 595 a red light blinked. It was the number of the president's elevator. Dorothy plugged in a wire and said, "Yes, Mr. President?" It was, of course, Gerald Ford talking to her from the president's elevator. That did it. Moose wanted to leave.

He went back upstairs from the subterranean basement to the upper basement, then out the door to the guarded driveway ramp across West Executive Avenue to the basement entrance of the West Wing. A White House policeman nodded at him and he went to the small elevator that ran between the basement and the upper floors of the West Wing. He pressed the button for the first floor.

He exited in one of the narrow gold-carpeted hallways, this one leading to Alexander Haig's office. He was in. He was staying as President Ford's chief of staff. Moose then passed the closed door of the Oval Office and went into the adjoining room. No one was there. He reached in his breast pocket for the envelope with the red square and put the envelope on the desk. He walked out into the West Wing Reception Room, and then outside.

When he stopped at the Northwest gate of the White House this time, he handed his White House Identification Badge to the White House policeman who looked confused by that action.

"Why are you leaving the badge, Moose?"

Moose shrugged. "I won't be back, Ned."

Ned swallowed hard. "Moose, can't you stay?"

"The president I worked for is–isn't here anymore, is he?"

Ned was searching for something to say. "Well, hang onto the badge, Moose. Stick it out. Anyway–anyway–I think, if you leave, you go through security or something like that, anyway. Don't just leave it off. I can't accept it. Maybe you'll come back on Monday. Why don't you come back on Monday? Don't you think so?"

Moose shook his head. "Come back where? This is a different place than it was, and it has to be that way now. The place to come back to, is gone."

FORTY-TWO
WHITE FLAGS
1975

From that August to the next April, the restaurants and bars of Le Royal Hotel in Phnom Penh, Cambodia, and Hotel Lane Xiang in Vientiane, Laos, and the Caravelle in Saigon, South Vietnam, were filled with the U.S. press corps, waiting for the inevitable. The inevitability was created when the 94th Congress of the United States, in violation of the signed agreements of the Paris Peace Accords, stopped all aid to the governments of Cambodia, Laos, and South Vietnam. With the hollowness of the economic pipeline, a massive avalanche of supplies went to the Viet Cong and the Pathet Lao from the Soviet Union and to the Khmer Rouge from the People's Republic of China.

There were billows of black and gray smoke on the horizon of Phnom Penh, Cambodia, and there were quick glimmers of flames and an occasional thud of an explosion from the north along Route 5 and the south from Takhman. Cambodia's Premier, Long Beret, came from Takhman into the city: "We have no more material means. We feel completely abandoned."

Shortly after dawn, eggs and waffles were being served in the restaurant of Le Royal, where Ted Murphy was holding court at a round table with six other members of the U.S. press corps. Sidney Schanberg from *The New York Times* was sitting to Ted's left. "I've seen the Khmer Rouge and they aren't killing anyone," Schanberg said. "It's difficult to imagine how the lives of Cambodians could be anything but better with Americans gone. Anthony Lewis wrote a great column for my paper. He wrote it clear as could be, in simple words. He asked, what could be more terrible than the reality of today's Cambodia? Today's Cambodia, not tomorrow's Cambodia. He puts down the right wingers who are predicting a bloodbath, but good."

"Tell us, Sidney," Philip McComb, the correspondent from *The Washington Post* said. "What's going to happen when the Khmer Rouge come into Phnom Penh and this place surrenders?"

Sidney Schanberg shrugged. "Sometimes certain people are executed by victors, but it would be tendentious to forecast such abnormal behavior as a national policy under a communist government once the war is over. My bosses at the *Times* had it right in their editorial when they said that further aid from the United States to Cambodia would only extend this nation's misery."

McComb took the last soft chew of his eggs. "Did you see my paper, Sidney?" referring to *The Washington Post.*

"I don't get it here, Fred," Ted Murphy answered for Schanberg, with a smile. "Somehow my subscription just isn't delivered the way it used to be back home. I think Sidney's *Washington Post*'s paper-boy is lost, too."

"The *Post* is bursting," McComb said. "Joe Kraft wrote a column asking if it really matters whether or not Cambodia goes communist. He said that if getting rid of Nixon meant letting go in Cambodia and the rest of Southeast Asia, then the price was small. And Tom Wicker wrote a piece for the *Post* saying there isn't much moral difference between the government here and the Khmer Rouge."

Ted Murphy pushed his empty plate aside. "But there are still some bozos back home sayin' the Khmer Rouge are a bunch of commies who are killers, and there'll be all kinds of atrocities committed here unless we give the government more supplies. They're sayin' the Khmer Rouge'll turn this place into a bloodbath." He took a sip of his coffee. "They'll see." He turned to Sidney Schanberg. "You gonna stay to watch the Khmer Rouge's liberation? Not me. I'm heading to Bangkok and from there to Saigon. I don't want to miss that surrender for this surrender. You gotta make a choice. Ford and Kissinger are tryin' to pump some quick aid into this place, but it ain't gonna happen. McGovern, Mansfield, and Dodd are sayin' no way, no deal, McNeil! Listen to this. They said this stuff when they cut the aid. It's good stuff."

Ted Murphy pulled a small gray cardboard covered spiral notebook from his back pocket. "McGovern said, 'Cambodians would be better off if we stopped all aid to them and let them work things out in their own way.' Mansfield, said, 'The cut-off of aid is in the best interest of Cambodians.' Chris Dodd said, 'The greatest gift our country can give to the Cambodian people is not guns but peace, and the best way to accomplish that goal is by ending military aid now.' Right on. So it's a done deal. Ford and Kissinger are whistlin' Dixie."

"Let me have a lead," Schanberg said. "Tell me something I don't know, Ted."

"I know that our Ambassador, Ambassador Dean, told the Cambodian big-boy, General Marak, he'll give him refuge and get him out of here before the Khmer Rouge come into Phnom Penh."

"Is Marak going to do it?"

"He said, 'No thanks. Thanks, but no thanks.' He said he's a Cambodian and he's gonna stay in Cambodia. And he said the United States didn't keep its word on aid. He said his error was in believing the United States."

It was their last breakfast together at Le Royal.

On April the 17th it was over. The Khmer Rouge came into Phnom Penh and ordered its immediate evacuation, as well as ordering the evacuation of all other urban areas of Cambodia. Within that one day, three million people were herded to march into the countryside at risk of death if they stopped walking. Surgeries in progress at hospitals were ordered stopped and the doctors, nurses, and patients, were ordered from the hospital's surgery rooms and patient's rooms and hallways to the pathways to the fields. In the largest hospital of Phnom Penh, over one hundred patients were murdered by the Khmer Rouge in their beds. On the trek to the fields, it was a capital offense to complain about the food. It was a capital offense to talk with each other.

The next day, all married couples were separated, their children taken away, and all family names were changed with those names forbidden from use, so that no one could locate other members of their families after their forced separations. Public executions were held all over the country, and starvation was rampant. All of those found to have served in the previous government were executed, as were their wives or husbands. The designation, "S-21" became a more dreaded designation than death. It was quickly known throughout the country as the name of the Khmer Rouge's torture chamber in Phnom Penh. "S-21" had previously been a high school called Tuol Sleng.

Pin Yathay, a civil engineer who escaped through the western border into Thailand revealed his last experience in Cambodia: "A teacher ate the flesh of her own sister who had died in her arms. The teacher was caught and beaten from morning to night until she died in front of the whole village as an example, and her child was crying beside her."

All street signs were whitewashed. All money was declared illegal, with rice as the only currency. All medical facilities, religious temples, postal, telegraph and telephone communications were destroyed. Atheism was the new official creed with the practices of Buddhism and Catholicism punishable by death. Death was the sentence for listening to the radio or dozing at work. Flirting was considered to be promiscuity punishable by death. All books published before August 17, 1975 were ordered to be burned.

Only eight remaining foreign embassy's were allowed to function: The People's Republic of China, North Korea, Cuba, Albania, Laos, Romania, Yugoslavia, and Egypt.

Ted Murphy, by this time, was landing at Tan Son Nhut Airport in Saigon, South Vietnam.

As were all Americans in South Vietnam, Ted Murphy was told the secret contingency plans to inform them of imminent danger, and he was told the plans for quick evacuation should it prove necessary.

Too late. *Time* magazine had put the contingency plans into world view: "The Pentagon made contingency plans for an all too conceivable eventuality: the closing of Tan Son Nhut by Communist troops or the lethal SA-2 and SA-7 missiles that were being positioned near the airfield. This operation—known as Phase Two—would be carried out by more than 60 giant CH-46 and CH-53 helicopters. The choppers would whirl in from the decks of the U.S. aircraft carriers *Hancock*, *Okinawa*, and *Midway*, now standing off South Vietnam as part of a veritable armada of more than 40 vessels, including two other carriers.

"All Americans in Saigon were advised last week that the Mayday signal for Phase Two would be a weather report for Saigon of '105 and rising' broadcast over the American Radio Service, followed by the playing of several bars of 'White Christmas' at 15-minute intervals. That message would send the last Americans still in Saigon streaming toward 13 'LZs,' or landing zones, situated throughout the downtown district, all atop U.S. owned or operated buildings...."

The morning of Tuesday, April the 29th, began at a very early hour for all residents and visitors in Saigon. It was four o'clock in the morning when the explosions were heard. To those who turned their radios to the U.S. Embassy's Security Network, they heard the call of "Whiskey Joe" in the U.S. Defense Attaché Office Compound at Tan Son Nhut Airport. The call of "Whiskey Joe" meant the airport was under attack. Then there was the report that two Marine Guards were dead. Soon there were fires at Tan Son Nhut.

The U.S. evacuation plan was no longer credible since its publication had been revealed in *Time*.

Ted Murphy, in nothing but underwear shorts, stood on the roof of the Caravelle Hotel and watched the fall of Saigon.

New evacuation plans were to be discussed at the Embassy at 8:00 A.M, but fifteen minutes before the meeting began, the Counselor was asking U.S. Ambassador Graham Martin to get to Ton Son Nhut Airport. The streets of Saigon were filled with people scurrying in all directions by motorbike and by foot, some with bags and luggage and roped together boxes, all this during a disobeyed 24 hour curfew. Outside the U.S. Embassy were throngs of Vietnamese banging on its walls and fences. Streaming from the Embassy's roof were thin straws of paper that were once documents, but now shredded into strings.

The embassy staff was leaving from the helipad that was on top of its small structure on the rooftop of the Embassy with a long stairway leading up to it. The Embassy staff was joined by a pouring of Vietnamese who wanted to get out with them. One helicopter after another took off from, and landed on, that helipad and the helicopters poured their human cargo on the U.S.S. *Blue Ridge* off the coast of the South China Sea. Soon the quantity of helicopters became unmanageable on the deck of the ship and one helicopter after another had to be dumped at sea immediately after being evacuated, to make room for the latest incoming ones.

But all of South Vietnam couldn't fit on them, and so that very day the phenomenon of the Boat People began; Vietnamese, on the seas, searching for refuge.

The morning after the evacuation of the embassy staff, a tank smashed down the gates of the presidential Palace, and South Vietnam as a country, as a separate political entity, was no more.

Dinh Ba Thi, the representative of North Vietnam in Paris, expressed his "warm thanks to all socialist countries of national independence and all peace and justice-loving peoples, including the American people who have supported and helped our people in its just struggle. The victory gained today is also theirs."

The colonel of the North Vietnamese army, Bui Tin, who demanded and received the unconditional surrender of South Vietnam on April 30, later said, "Every day our leadership would listen to world news over the radio at 9:00 A.M. to follow the growth of the American anti-war movement. Visits to Hanoi by people like Jane Fonda and former Attorney General Ramsey Clark and ministers gave us confidence that we should hold on in the face of battlefield reverses. We were elated when Jane Fonda, wearing a red Vietnamese dress, said at a press conference that she was ashamed of American actions in the war, and that she would struggle along with us.

"When Nixon stepped down because of Watergate we knew we would win. Pham Dan Dong (prime minister of North Vietnam) said of Gerald Ford, the new president, 'He's the weakest president in U.S. history; the people didn't elect him; even if you gave him candy, he doesn't dare to intervene in Vietnam again.' We tested Ford's resolve by attacking Phuoc Long in January. When Ford kept American B-52's in their hangers, our leadership decided on a big offensive against South Vietnam."

The Paris Peace Accords were nothing more than a relic for which Le Duc Tho and Henry Kissinger had received Nobel Peace Prizes. Those Paris Accords contained the provisions which were the very reason U.S. military involvement had ended two and one quarter years earlier: "The South Vietnamese people shall decide themselves the political future of South Vietnam through genuinely free and democratic elections under international supervision" and guaranteed were "democratic liberties of the people; personal freedom, freedom of speech, freedom of the press, freedom of meeting, freedom of organization, freedom of political activities, freedom of belief, freedom of movement, freedom of residence, freedom of work, right to property ownership and right to free enterprise."

North Vietnam's General Van Tien Dung, while admitting with pride his government's blatant violations of the Paris Peace Accords, said that due to the cutoff of U.S. aid, President Thieu of South Vietnam "was forced to fight a poor man's war."

NBC's Jack Perkins watched Saigon's War Memorial being toppled into the street by North Vietnamese soldiers, and he said to his American television audience that the statue had been "an excess of what money and bad taste accomplish. I don't know if you call it the fall of Saigon or the liberation of Saigon."

Peter Kalisher of CBS said to his American audience, "For better or worse the war is over, and how could it be for worse?"

May began, and Saigon's name was changed to Ho Chi Minh City. The American Embassy was totally ransacked and left in ruins. Estimates of up to one million residents of what was Saigon, were moved to the countryside. New Economic Zones (NEZ's) and Re-Education Camps were established for "undesirable elements." In the cities, typewriters were outlawed, everyone was required to submit to the authorities a list of books they owned, and were required to report to the authorities "all private conversations deemed contrary to the spirit of the revolution."

Next door, by year's end, Laos had more political prisoners per capita than any other country in the world, including Vietnam and Cambodia. Following the pattern of Vietnam, "Reeducation Camps" were established for the undesirables. To be sent to the dreaded Phong Saly meant to never be heard from again. Two-hundred thousand Laotians managed to escape to Thailand. On December the Second, the nation's name was changed to the Lao People's Democratic Republic.

Estimates of escapees on unworthy vessels by Boat People were to reach one million, with 600,000 of them lost beneath the South China Sea.

It was long remembered that back on that night of the white flags, April the 30th of 1975, former Senator J. William Fulbright had announced that he was "no more depressed than I would be about Arkansas losing a football game to Texas."

FORTY-THREE
PRIVATE RESCUES
1975

Among those first thousands of escapees was a cat named Sally Saigon who had managed to get on the last helicopter from the Embassy's helipad. She was too frightened to let anyone know she was on that helicopter until it landed on the U.S.S. *Blue Ridge* when she made a jump from the helicopter to the deck of the carrier. U.S. Ambassador Graham Martin gave his approval for her to be with the group that was going to Guam and then on to the United States where she would have to be quarantined. He knew well the history of Sally Saigon and the provisions for her life that the cat inherited from a murdered American hero named Adam Orr, who came to Vietnam before the ambassador arrived.

While Sally Saigon was in quarantine, Adam's will was once more read to find someone who would be a logical candidate to care for her. The prime candidate was Colonel Jonas Valadovich who had bought a condominium in Los Angeles where he spent weekends away from Vandenberg Air Force Base. He eagerly accepted the adoption of Sally Saigon.

Jonas was a psychological mess since the U.S. Congress had refused any economic or military aid to Cambodia, Laos, and South Vietnam. And after that, with the surrenders of April, he sunk into a depression with less hope and strength than he maintained throughout his imprisonment in Hoa Lo. Jonas was 42 years old and because he had enlisted when he was so young, he now had served enough time in the U.S. Air Force to retire, and although he had no need of a paycheck since he was armed with all the cash, stocks, and bonds left him by Adam, he had no thought of retirement from the military, until the April surrenders. Then the thought took root. He was being tempted to stay with the carrot of replacing the eagle on each shoulder with a star on each shoulder.

But he had to do something radical to adjust to the new realities of world events in which he had been so involved. The leadership of the United States had changed, the governments of South Vietnam, Cambodia, and Laos had changed, and the foreign policy quests of the United States had changed. So many goals, long pursued, were nothing more than the unattained. Radical changes were the only cure in the private lives of thousands of Americans so as to rescue themselves from the changes of the public life of the nation. In early May, Jonas wrote and handed in his papers for retirement from active duty, retaining service in the U.S. Air Force Reserve. By autumn he left Vandenberg Air Force Base with his discharge papers.

Anne Whitney physically ripped the calendars in her Bujumbura home and her office, and threw them away. She wrote appointments down on blank paper. She didn't want to look at anything with the marker of 1975. "I'm glad," she told herself, "that Ambassador and Mary Fairbanks didn't have to deal with this." She was already scheduled to leave her Burundi assignment, and in order to look forward to years ahead, she made the decision to serve in only one more foreign post, and then run for public office. That would bring her candidacy for some office to either the elections of 1978 or 1980.

Mark Daschle had his own method of erasing from his mind the horrors of Southeast Asia that he read about every day on the Wireless File in his first days at his new post in Athens, Greece. He substituted those thoughts of a surrendered Cambodia and South Vietnam with the only other subject he found could occupy his mind; Anne. Thinking of her had the rare effect of obscuring pain.

Ted and Linda Murphy had an unusual adjustment to make. They weren't attempting to rescue themselves from defeat, but from victory, and the emptiness they felt without a cause. President Ford wasn't worth hounding, and his foreign policy couldn't be condemned because no one, at the time, knew what it was. Linda had to additionally adjust to a husband who now came home every night without a crisis to cover, and had no excuse to stay away from her and their young son. That left Ted with the burden of trying to find a new justification to be gone, and left Linda with the hope he would find one.

The saleswoman at Louise's Les Champs Carpet Gallery in the Watergate asked the small, gray-haired woman for identification before accepting her check for the rug. To most people, that would have been a customary request. For Irene Goodpastor, it was an insult.

"Dear," Mrs. Goodpastor said, "are you new to Washington?"

The saleswoman shook her head. "No."

"I'm Irene Goodpastor, dear."

"Our policy is to have identification. Ma'am, could I see your driver's license?"

Mrs. Goodpastor knew she had to surrender to this young saleswoman. She reached in her purse and produced an American Express card. "I don't drive. Will this do?"

"You don't have a driver's license?"

"I don't drive," Mrs. Goodpastor said softly, restraining herself.

The saleswoman looked like she didn't know what to do. "Well, it doesn't have an address on it. We need an address."

"Jean Louis at the cleaners in the mall knows me very well. Please call him. He cleans all my clothes."

The saleswoman called for the manager to come to the counter.

If the manager of the Carpet Gallery hadn't known who she was, and if he hadn't acted so honored to have her there and said he would deliver it himself, she would have walked out without the purchase. Less and less people knew the name of Irene Goodpastor. She hadn't had a party since 1968. Even the haters didn't hate her any more. They forgot about her.

Mrs. Goodpastor walked across Virginia Avenue, very slowly, to the orange-roofed Howard Johnson's Motor Lodge before going home. She walked past the reception desk of Howard Johnson's and into the motor lodge's restaurant. She sat at the counter. She hadn't sat at a counter since she was a college girl. She hadn't gone to a restaurant alone since she was a college girl. Even when she was traveling, she would call room service rather than eat in a restaurant alone. This afternoon she was eating alone in public because she didn't want to go back home yet, where she had so much of nothing to do. There were too many hours left before she could watch Eyewitness News and Johnny Carson. It was Wednesday, but Wednesdays didn't have the same meaning since the "Sonny and Cher Show" wasn't on any more. Her depression over the show's demise was eased, in fact brought some delight to her, by what brought about the end of their show: Sonny and Cher split from each other.

The waitress came over to her, setting down a glass of water. Irene Goodpastor asked for a grilled cheese sandwich.

And then something quite unexpected happened. She didn't know how to wait.

Should she just sit there and read the posters advertising different hotplates? Should she look at the napkin container? Should she look at the customers? Well, what? Her inexperience at what others considered the ordinary was a challenging experience. She wished she had brought something to read but she hadn't. And so she read the menu from cover to cover without caring what it said. Ten minutes passed and still the grilled cheese sandwich didn't arrive. It was her unfortunate choice, but Howard Johnson's on Virginia Avenue that had a world-wide reputation as being the lookout for those who had burglarized the Democratic National Committee at the Watergate, had a more important reputation for those who lived in the neighborhood: it had the worst service of any restaurant this side of the Berlin Wall.

"Mrs. Goodpastor!" A voice yelled out. Those words were a godsend to her. She looked behind her, then to her left, then to her right.

"Mrs. Goodpastor! Here!" It was a voice from a booth.

Not President Ford. Not Vice-President Rockefeller. Not a senator. Not a member of the House of Representatives. Not an Ambassador. Not a *Washington Post* columnist. But it was a face that made her smile. "Cody!"

"Come on over and join us!" It was a more welcome invitation than one for an evening at an embassy reception. Cody's face was always welcome, and there was the added benefit of being rescued from the counter where she didn't know what to do.

Cody and the woman he was with had apparently already eaten, as their dishes had little more than small pieces of hamburger bun on them and spots of catsup and a few french fries. "You must be Gloria!" Mrs.

Goodpastor said as she sat down next to the woman at the booth, opposite Cody. "Gloria the nurse!"

Gloria nodded with a warm smile. "I'm Gloria the nurse all right! And I'm Gloria the wife of Cody." She was a little older than Cody and a lot younger than Irene Goodpastor. She was neither glamorous or homely, her brown hair was in a bun, but her most distinguishing feature was that she looked like she was in her twelfth month of pregnancy. "And pretty soon I'll be Gloria, the mother."

"Oh?" Mrs. Goodpastor acted as though she hadn't yet noticed Gloria was pregnant. "Well, yes, you are expecting aren't you?"

Gloria nodded with a smile. Cody was smiling, too.

"Cody told me so much about you, dear," Mrs. Goodpastor said. "He told me that you're very special."

"He's very special, Mrs. Goodpastor."

"Oh, I know that."

"She's pregnant," Cody said quickly, as if it needed a further announcement.

"Isn't that wonderful!" Mrs. Goodpaster said.

Cody gave an uneasy smile. "I never saw you here before. What a great surprise."

Mrs. Goodpastor nodded at the waitress to let her know she had moved to the booth. The waitress displayed no interest in Mrs. Goodpastor's signal to her.

"Mrs. Goodpastor," Cody said with some excitement in his voice, "Let me tell you what we've decided to do."

"Yes, yes. Please."

Cody caught himself, recognizing his lack of courtesy in not displaying any real interest in Mrs. Goodpastor's life. "How are you?" That just came out of Cody from nowhere and, of course, it would have been much more appropriate for him to have asked her that when she sat down, rather than now.

Mrs. Goodpastor acted as though it was normal. "Fine, thank you."

"Good. That's good, Mrs. Goodpastor."

"Now, let me hear about you!"

"Well," and Cody nodded with some impatience. "I've had it with the State Department. I never liked them and, candidly, they never liked me. I got there through a fluke because LBJ was kind enough not to leave me out in the cold, but I don't want to spend the rest of my life in a place that thinks I'm an obligation to them. And the kind of remarks I was hearing at State when Cambodia and Vietnam fell, made me sick."

"Did you say anything to them, Cody?" Mrs. Goodpastor asked.

"No."

Gloria wanted to explain. "He's not a confrontationalist, Mrs. Goodpastor. State took away all that from him with all their–their emphasis on diplomacy. But, Mrs. Goodpastor, Cody has very deep feelings. He expresses himself in his own ways."

Mrs. Goodpastor nodded.

Cody wanted to add to that. "See, I don't have any authority there. It doesn't make any difference to them what I think. But it gets me so frustrated because I know how dedicated President Kennedy was to the people of Southeast Asia. He would have fired all those people at State if he was still alive. Every day I would read the refugee reports on the wireless file. They're not secret. They're not even confidential or limited official use—but no one picked them up. No one said anything. Anyway, if I told them about what I think President Kennedy would do, they would probably have just walked away—or maybe they'd tell me what they think he would have done. You're the one who made it clear to me, Mrs. Goodpastor, that I couldn't just stand in President Kennedy's shadow. Gloria agrees. Gloria encouraged me to do what I'm going to do—and to do it right after our baby comes," which seemed to be an event that could happen right then and there at Howard Johnsons.

"What are you going to do? Tell me!"

"There's a charity called the World Refugee Mission that does good work overseas in places where they're needed. It isn't religious or anything even though it sounds that way. They take care of refugees wherever they may be in need. Camps, water, medical needs, language training, vocational help, things like that. Gloria talked to them about me, and then they talked to me a couple weeks later and even though most of the people they recruit are volunteers with no pay, they offered to hire the two of us with our backgrounds and experience and things like that. It didn't take us long to tell them we would."

"Both of you?"

"Both of us," he said.

Gloria said, "He always had an interest in refugees."

"You'll both be going overseas?" Mrs. Goodpastor asked.

"Yes."

"But what about your baby?"

Gloria interjected. "That's the point. The baby can come with us."

"An infant?"

Gloria gave a short nod. "Not right away. For a while just Cody will go. Then I'll join him as soon as the doctor says the baby can travel. That won't be long."

"You work at State, too, don't you, dear?" Mrs. Goodpastor asked Gloria.

"Not anymore. I'm on maternity leave, and I'm not going back. We have to be together. I'm going with him. It's going to work out good for both of us—for all three of us. Mrs. Goodpastor, Cody can do great things. He already did when he was at the White House. But he dreads getting up in the morning to go to the State Department. He's doing better since he's made the decision to leave. But it was just killing him. He became a shell of what he could be—of what he used to be, from everything I had heard about him. He should do what makes him happy. Then I'll be happy, too."

"Gloria," Mrs. Goodpastor was shaking her head, "you're the best thing that ever happened to him."

"She is," Cody said.

The waitress came over with Mrs. Goodpastor's grilled cheese sandwich. "One check? Two checks? Three checks?"

"One!" Mrs. Goodpastor said quickly.

"No, no, please," Cody said.

"Let me. Cody. This is all so wonderful. I'm so proud of both of you. It's very brave, very courageous. Do you know where you'll be going?"

Cody shook his head. "No. Not yet. The point is that we'll be going somewhere where we're really needed or they won't send us—and thanks for the—the food."

"Well!" Mrs. Goodpastor said. "You do have news, don't you?" She took a bite of her sandwich.

"And there's something else in all this, Mrs. Goodpastor," Cody said. "Gloria had a very close friend—a Cambodian girl. She was a nurse. She was here in the States for a couple years for training and she and Gloria hit it off when she was at State. I didn't know her. She went back home and was in Phnom Penh when it fell. Gloria hasn't heard from her since, and she used to write all the time. The letters went back and forth through the diplomatic pouch up to mid-April. We know what the Khmer Rouge did to the people at the hospitals when they took over that day last April, and that's where she would have been."

"Oh, how terrible. I'm so sorry," Mrs. Goodpastor said.

Cody put his hand across the table to hold Gloria's hand, then he released it and looked back at Mrs. Goodpastor. "I know you've had your own tragedies in the war, Mrs. Goodpastor. I told Gloria about you and Adam."

She put down her sandwich. "About me and—" she was going to ask, 'who?' when she caught herself. "Adam. Yes. Yes. I try," and she looked at the ceiling and then back down, "I try not to talk about it."

"Of course," Cody said sympathetically. "Are you okay, Mrs. Goodpastor?"

"Oh, yes. Maybe some day, if the right president gets in office, you'll find that I'm the U.S. ambassador to wherever you'll be living! You never know!"

"Really?"

"I've had a number of offers through the years, but I wanted to stay here. Maybe the right time is coming. If Hong Kong comes up again I'll take it, even though it isn't an ambassadorial post—just Consul General. You know about that one, Cody."

"Gee!" Cody's eyes widened the way they used to.

"Presidents have offered you ambassadorial appointments?" Gloria asked.

"Yes. All the way since Truman. Nothing really that good from Ford. But I shouldn't talk about offers. It's not right to tell people what you've refused, you know. Particularly not from presidents."

"Isn't that great!" Gloria was smart enough to know that Mrs. Goodpastor was not being totally honest, but Gloria didn't mind it. She felt that she and Cody were complimented that a woman of Mrs. Goodpastor's prestige wanted them to be even more impressed with her. "I'm not surprised about the presidents," Gloria added. "But you're so right in not just taking any appointment. You hold out for what could really excite you, Mrs. Goodpastor. Just because presidents offer you something, doesn't mean you need to accept. It's your life, not theirs."

Mrs. Goodpastor gave a hesitant, almost humble nod. "That's what Eleanor Roosevelt told me before she died."

"Wow!" Cody said. "Before she died?"

"Well, of course," Gloria said. "You know what she means." Gloria always fixed things up.

Jonas Valadovich's condominium on a Hollywood hill above Sunset Boulevard overlooked the sweep of Los Angeles, providing the same kind of view seen from airliners landing at LAX. The city was spread before him in a panorama through the condominium's floor to ceiling windows. Opposite one of the walls of windows were white bookcases that sheltered his increasing collection of books on Einstein, time, space, and the world's great religions.

Sally Saigon was particularly welcome in his condominium not only because she was Adam's cat, which was certainly enough, but because her personality, or catality, helped him in the rescue from the depression that he allowed no human to witness. Sally would see him sitting at his reading desk with his elbows bent and his head resting on his cupped hands, and she would quickly jump to the desk and bring her nose to his nose and she would stare at his eyes which were less than an inch away, which would make him laugh. They understood each other ever since the night they met in Saigon. Since then they both had suffered through their own Southeast Asian traumas.

"Do you remember Moose?" he asked Sally as she sat on his desk looking at him.

She gave a look of total disinterest. She scratched her cheek with her paw.

"That real big guy. You remember. Moose. Moose Dunston."

Sally gave Jonas a quick look, then continued her scratching.

"He's going to come over here tonight, all the way from Washington, Sally, and I want you to give him a nice welcome, will you? He feels just as bad as we do about everything that happened in Vietnam, believe me. And to make things worse, he doesn't even have a job. I only hope he'll let me help him. He's a proud son of a gun, and I have to be careful about how I do it. You know what I mean?"

Sally was pretending she didn't understand English. She did that whenever she felt like not responding to him.

"I think I'll invite Dawn and Roberta over from down the hall. You like them, don't you?" That caught her attention. "It will be a double date. I'll fix Moose up. A double date with you as a chaperone. What do you think, Sally? Good idea?"

Sally's eyes showed great interest, but she was in no mood to let him think he could fool her into believing he was trying to please her, rather than simply trying to please himself. She started cleaning the paw she had just used to scratch herself.

"Good idea, Sally?"

She jumped from the desk and walked slowly into the other room. It was her way of saying he was boring her.

It was different when Moose arrived just before sunset. Sally was as excited to see Moose as was Jonas. And Moose was excited to see Sally Saigon who hadn't aged a bit in six years.

To Moose, no one looked more inappropriately "civilian" than Jonas.

The three of them were survivors.

"Man, this is plush stuff you got here, Colonel!" Moose said looking at the place in absolute awe. "What a view! What a pad! Wow! I didn't know officers in the U.S.A.F. got stuff like this!"

"They don't. I thank Adam for this. He bought it for me, didn't he?"

"God, do I feel his presence in this room."

"That's because he's here, all right. It's like old times, Moose!" Jonas said. Jonas sat down on a plush, heavily cushioned brown leather lounge chair. "Sit down, friend."

Moose sat on the couch, his weight causing the end he was sitting on to dip toward the floor. Sally Saigon spread out on the rug between them. "I know that we should be grateful that we made it," Moose said, "and particularly that you're out of there, Jonas, and I have more gladness than I can ever express. But every morning lately I wake up with a stab in my stomach, knowing it's another day of hell for An-Twit and Nguyen and Vu and Hoang and Tran—if they're alive—and so many other friends in Saigon—and this time there won't be a rescue."

Jonas was silent, almost relieved to see that he wasn't alone in his depression.

"Unless, Jonas, they can somehow get to the land's edge, and then risk a voyage to wherever they can get."

"Moose, I feel guilty every morning." Jonas was tapping his fingers on the soft arm of the lounge chair. "Every morning. And then I just try to think of other things. And then I even feel guilty when I realize I've been successful at thinking of other things."

"You? Guilty?"

"Yes. I'm alive. I wake up in comfort. This place is so—so comfortable. Even the temperature is perfect when I wake up. I have a thermostat. And I get out of bed and I brush my teeth, and I take a shower and get in decent clothes and I make coffee for myself and I get in a car and drive where I want to drive. I have all that—all that liberty and—and life with such luxury."

"You deserve it, buddy. You deserve this place. You deserve everything. What do you think you're supposed to do, live on the streets?"

"No. Look, I can't spend the rest of my life looking out this window at the city. I appreciate it so much, I never want to give it up, but I have to do something that means something. I'm a retired man already. I'm staying in the Reserves, so it's not a complete departure. But I'm out of active duty. You know why, don't you, Moose? I retired because I didn't know what our mission was anymore. Even in Hoa Lo I had a mission, a purpose. By surviving I was proving something. Surviving by itself was like spitting in the NV's face. It was a valuable purpose. Now, I don't know what we're supposed to do in the Air Force. See? I just said 'we.' It's not 'we' anymore, it's 'them' but I can't get out of the habit. I guess I don't want to get out of the habit. Well, I'm in the Reserves so I guess it's okay to say 'we.'"

"I know how you feel. That's normal. Don't go nuts. Did you get that silver star yet?"

Jonas shook his head. "They'll give it to me. It's one of the enticements in staying in the reserves. They promised it."

"Then you'll be a general!"

"It looks that way. I think I'm going to absorb myself, Moose, in the study of theology and time. Those are the things that fill me with some hope. I went to Zurich to meet with Aleksandr Solzhenitsyn and it was one of the greatest days of my life. He is a giant. He was in the Gulag Archipelago –the Soviet's prison system, and when he was there he learned about God, as I did when I was in Sontay and Hoa Lo. We plan on meeting again. I'm learning more, Moose. That's what I want to do. I want to learn more about important things."

"That's marvelous." Moose recognized that he had little to offer Jonas on the subject that interested him most.

"Adam used to say that the only subject that's logical–is God. And he said the only place that made sense to him was Cape Canaveral. He spoke about it continually, and told me to go there."

"Have you gone?"

"Not yet, but I will. Adam used to compare Cape Canaveral with Hong Kong. Hong Kong, Adam said, was the ultimate of what Man could build in earthly things, whereas the Cape was Man crossing the line into the heavens reaching to God."

"All he ever talked to me about was women."

Jonas smiled. "He did his share of that, all right. He wanted to have the rich, full life, and he did it. He really did it. You know, it doesn't bother me that he died young because he did everything there was to do. He lived more in his years than most guys live if they turn into withered, old men. Their fantasies were his realities. What gnaws at me is that he died while trying to rescue me–so I have to be worthy of the rescue. And worthy of all he left me."

"Jonas, you don't need me to tell you–but he wanted you to have the rich, full life like he did. Do it."

Jonas nodded. "The rich, full life is different for different people."

"How's your grandma?"

"In Paris."

"Paris? She's in Paris–France?"

"Yes, sir. She always wanted to see Europe. She's with a girlfriend." Then he thought of what he just said. "A girlfriend! I think Sadie's in her eighties!"

"You took care of the trip?"

Jonas gave a modest smile. Then he nodded, "That was one of my greatest pleasures–when I gave her the tickets. Moose, what are you up to? You're not working yourself these days, are you?"

Moose took his pipe pouch out of his breast pocket and started the ritual of the pouch and the tobacco; those things that gave him great comfort. "I'll be working again as of next Monday."

"You will?"

"I sure will. I got a good one. Maybe not as good as the last one, but it's a good one."

"What's going on?"

"Did you ever hear of Hanson Alpert?"

"I know who he is. Rich guy. A C.E.O. of something. A lot of overseas ventures. Isn't that it?"

Moose nodded. "He's starting an Asian magazine. It's like our *Time* and *Newsweek*. It's going to be called *Asia World Weekly* with headquarters in Hong Kong. He wants me to write foreign policy and defense stories and analysis for the magazine."

"Great, Moose! Wai-yee have anything to do with this?"

"No. Not Wai-yee."

"How did it happen?"

"He just wrote me, that's all. I don't know. I think Nixon talked to him. I don't know for sure, but the president knows I'm out of a job. He knows I love Hong Kong. He knows, or he thinks I have something going on with Wai-yee. I never told him about her being married or about Liberty. And he knows Alpert. So I suspect him. When I phoned him and told him about it, he was glad all right but I know him pretty well and I don't think he was really surprised. He just said it was smart of Alpert to get me. Right after I got the letter from Alpert, I sent back a wire accepting, and I've been in touch with his office ever since. Next Monday his guy gives me my first assignments. I'll stay in D.C., writing. Then when Alpert gives the word I go to Hong Kong. I have yet to actually talk to Alpert."

"That's just great, Moose. I'm so glad. So what are you doing here?"

"Seeing Nixon. I want to know some stuff on a few foreign policy articles I have in mind."

"That's terrific! Does Wai-yee at least know about it?"

"I called her. I talked to her, and for the first time I talked to her husband. It seems strange to use that word in talking about her. But I talked with him. He seems like a nice guy. They both said they want to see me whenever I get there. They said, depending on when it is—I could see Liberty."

"Do you still love Wai-yee, Moose?"

Moose looked at the floor, glared at his pipe for a moment, bit his lip, and nodded. "How can't I? God, Jonas, what a woman!"

Jonas didn't want to encourage Moose's passion for Wai-yee. "How old is Liberty now?"

Moose thought for a moment. "She has to be about four. Yeah, I guess four. She was two years old when Wai-yee told me about her on the day you were freed—when we saw each other in the Philippines. So I figure she's got to be four."

"Do you know her birthday?"

"I think she told me, but I was too flustered to let it sink in. But don't ever ask anyone who's Chinese when their birthday is. They have a Western birthday and a Chinese birthday and an Everybody's Birthday and God knows how many other birthdays. They're young or old, that's all. The rest is too hard to figure out and be accurate."

Jonas stood up and rubbed his hands together. "Hey, buddy. I got a surprise for you. You know what's going to happen here in about—in about," and he looked at his replacement for his Endura watch, this one doing nothing more than telling the time, "in an hour?"

"What?"

"Pizza is going to be delivered. It's from a great place that makes real New York Pizza. Thin crust. Lots of cheese. It's just like you get in the worst places in New York that have the best pizza. I think this place here has the water shipped in from New York for it. And then two beautiful women are going to walk in that door! They live down the hall, and they're dying to meet you. They take care of Sally Saigon when I go away. And when I say gorgeous—I mean gorgeous."

"You didn't!"

"Actresses. Starlets. Well, I don't think you've ever seen them in movies or TV unless you looked pretty quick—but tonight they just want to meet you. Roberta is a brunette. Big eyes. Big—everything. Dawn is a little blonde. Really cute. I'll be a sport, a sacrificial sport, and you can take Roberta."

"In other words, you like the other one."

"Dawn."

"Yeah. Dawn. Bring 'em on!"

Sally Saigon's ears perked back at those words, and she stretched out on the carpet, her front paws straight ahead, her feet way out behind her, in her third prayer of the day to Allah.

After the delivered pizza was eaten by Jonas, Moose, Dawn, Roberta, and Sally, the conversation turned to Washington, D.C. and to Ford and Nixon and Johnson and Kennedy.

"I was ten when my teacher told the class that President Kennedy was killed. We were all called in from recess," Roberta said.

Dawn showed off. "I was nine."

With that said, the two gorgeous women in Jonas' condominium lost some of their gorgeousness. Ten? Nine? They could easily be Jonas's and Moose's children. Only Sally Saigon seemed unbothered by the remarks. She rubbed herself against the foot and leg of Roberta and then of Dawn, as they sat on the couch facing both Jonas on his leather chair and Moose on a wooden kitchen chair. The two men were separated from the women by Jonas' glass-topped coffee table.

"Don't trust Sally Saigon's opinion of these women," Adam whispered to Moose. "I've been trying to tell Jonas, but he won't believe me: Sally Saigon wants Jonas to marry one of those girls. Sally is a woman. She thinks every man should be married."

Jonas said sharply, "Stop, Sally!" But Sally continued the rubbing against Dawn's leg.

"Oh, that's okay, Jonas. Let her," Dawn said.

"No, don't let her," Roberta tried to wave off Sally from her rubbing. "She's in heat!"

Dawn smiled. "Well, I'm glad no one stops me when I'm in heat!"

Jonas looked quickly at Moose at that remark but both of them felt uneasy after hearing how old Roberta and Dawn were when Kennedy was killed. This wasn't going to work.

Roberta couldn't have prepared a worse follow-up: "Do you want to play Yahtzee? I have the board and the cards and dice and everything in our place down the hall."

That did it. It was better than an offer to play hop-scotch, but not much better.

Jonas stood up. "Oh, we can't," he said. "I don't know about you, but I have to get up early tomorrow. I have to go all the way to Vandenberg to pick up some stuff. And I'm having breakfast with some of my buddies up there. I'm leaving here at 4:30."

The two young women looked over at each other, then Roberta looked at Moose. "Moose," she said, "why don't you come down the hall to our condo and we'll have a drink while Jonas, here, goes night-night like a good little boy."

Moose had to think quick. "No thanks. I'm worse off than Jonas. I'm not driving in the morning–I have to drive tonight."

"To where?" Roberta asked.

"The San Clemente Inn."

"Tonight?"

"Yep."

"You're both party-poopers!"

She had a point. Of the three hosts; Jonas, Moose, and Sally Saigon, only Sally Saigon wanted to party.

"Oh, God," Moose said to Jonas after the young women walked down the hall and the door was closed behind them, "They weren't even born when Eisenhower became president! Not even born! They think Truman's in the same historical league that we think of—of John Adams! Jonas, are women getting younger or are we getting old?" Moose submerged himself on the couch while Jonas went back to his leather chair.

"We're getting old, Moose. I thought I'd fix you up. You got to admit, they're pretty. But you're right. Nine years old when Kennedy was killed!"

"They're just so young. I like my women—to be women."

"I wanted to take your mind off—and my mind off all the—the stuff."

"Thanks for the effort, Jonas. It was good thinking, but the only thing that will help is the passage of time."

Jonas gave a short smile. "Yes." He nodded. "That's why time was invented."

Moose didn't get it. "I feel like it's one long April 30th that doesn't end."

"Moose, you're beginning to look like a pillar of salt."

At that, Sally Saigon jumped up on Moose's lap, and rubbed her chin against Moose's cheek.

"You know, Moose, Adam is contagious, isn't he?"

"What do you mean?"

"I think we've both become injected with those things that are making you and me more like him. Maybe in different ways, but we're both becoming more and more like Adam. Neither one of us is hot on getting hitched, right? He's living through us, isn't he?"

"Maybe."

"Do you know what I mean?"

"Yeah." There was a short silence. "Jonas, I have the flag that was on his coffin at Arlington. When you were in prison in Hanoi, I hoped I would be able to give it to you some day—and I haven't. I've been putting it off because it's just—I don't know."

"Keep it. I don't want the relics of his death. Only his life. Thanks, Moose, but keep it. Some times I think I'm a relic of his death. He died for me. I inherited his riches. Moose, I want to be a relic of his life."

"Are you trying to be like him?"

"No. It's just happening."

"You're not going to get married—ever, are you, Jonas?

Jonas shook his head. "No. I want to be free. I want to be able to see whatever woman I want to see. And I want to keep my time as my own. You? You going to stay single?"

"I don't know. It's not Adam's influence. It's Wai-yee. No one compares with her. I still crave her. So—I mean, y'know."

"I'm telling you, Moose, Adam changed both of us."

Moose shook his head. "He would have been in bed with both of them tonight. Not us. See? We think they're too young, and he wouldn't have cared. So we aren't exactly like him. For us, they have to remember FDR."

Jonas thought it over. "Truman's okay."

It was different than it used to be. On the metal-mesh fence there was a sign warning that no sightseers should stop there, but the warning had little teeth since the fence had no gate, only a space wide enough for any car to drive through. But there was a barrier a short distance from there: a second fence, this one with a closed gate and a phone. Moose announced himself, the gate opened, and he drove onto the grounds of Casa Pacifica, a place that was now bathed in unaccustomed quiet.

Nora, who used to be the secretary of Ken Clawson during the White House days, was sitting behind the desk where Rose Mary Woods used to sit when she had flown in with the president for short visits away from Washington. But that was when Casa Pacifica was the Western White House.

Nora embraced Moose. Embracing became a habit of those who had worked in the Nixon White House when they saw each other again. They had lived through too much together not to embrace each other.

Manolo Sanchez, the president's former White House valet was there, too. Manolo was still working for him. His embrace came right after Nora's. Manolo still wore his red jacket with its presidential seal, but it didn't fit as well as it used to. There was too much room in it as Manolo had lost weight. "Hey, Manolo. Isn't Fina feeding you anymore?"

"Too much. She feeds me too good. I still want to lose about ten more pounds. Then I'll be down to your weight!" he joked.

Retired Marine Colonel Jack Brennan, who was now former President Nixon's Chief of Staff, walked in from the president's office. He gave his usual big, warm smile on his sun-tanned face. Another embrace, this one a bear-hug of two who had been through the wars. "The president's waiting for you, Moose," Jack said.

"Come in, Moose. Come in." President Nixon's legs were extended straight ahead of him, resting on his ottoman. It still looked like the president's office: the four flags of the armed services still stood against the north wall, and the flag of the United States and the president's flag still framed his window, which today exhibited the fog almost obscuring the view of the beach and the Pacific Ocean. Untypically, the former president didn't get up from his lounge chair to greet Moose, but it was obvious why.

"Good to see you, Mr. President." Moose walked over to him, they shook hands, and Moose gave a gesture to the former president's left leg. "Is that okay?"

President Nixon nodded. "No pain. Phlebitis is like that and that's not a sign of it getting better or worse. But it's fine. I just have to keep it up. The doctors say I'll be able to play golf before you know it. Sit down, sit down, Moose. I want to hear all about your new job—joining the media. If you can't fight them, join them! And what have you got there?" He nodded toward the large black bag Moose was carrying in his left hand.

"Mixture 18, Mr. President, from your friends on Fourteenth Street. I told them I'd be coming by."

The former president smiled as Moose handed it to him. "Hey. That was good of them!" He looked in the bag. "How many are in here?"

"It'll hold you for a while."

He handled some of the tobacco cans and gave a nod. "I'll write them a note. That was good of them. Now, you didn't buy all this, did you?"

"No, sir. It was a gift from them."

"Well, isn't that good." He set it down on the small lamp stand next to him. "Now, tell me about what's going on with you and Hanson Alpert."

Moose told him that he didn't know very much about his new assignment other than he would be writing about foreign policy and defense, highlighting Asian issues, he was glad about it, and that he suspected the president had something to do with it.

President Nixon laughed and denied it with a "No, no," and then quickly changed the subject, asking Moose what he thought about President Ford's administration and "Who has the clout now in the White House?"

"Rumsfeld, I believe."

"Hartmann's out now, isn't he?"

"He isn't out, but I understand he isn't in the inner circle anymore."

"He's out."

"Look, I'm no source. I'm no expert on what's going on in the Ford White House. I have a few friends who are still there, but we don't talk much about the in's and out's and who has what office."

"Yeah. Yeah. You talk foreign policy. That's good. Stay out of that power-play stuff. You know why I try to stay interested?"

"Well, sure. It's what's going on."

"It's because I don't want to think about what happened. Because it's done. Southeast Asia's gone. Moose, it's over. Our doctrine is over. You know what those Paris Peace Accords said that Henry and Le Duc Tho signed, don't you?"

"Yes. Of course."

"We guaranteed that we'd replace any of South Vietnam's armaments one-for-one. They lose a bullet, we give them a bullet. They lose a helicopter, they get a helicopter. You know, replace. One-for-one. The Soviets could do the same for the North. So the Soviets gave the North four-to-one while we kept our word and gave the South one-to-one. Then the Congress enters the picture and votes to give them nothing—against what we agreed: no military aid, no economic aid. That meant defeat. Then the North acts like they didn't sign Article Nine that promised the South's self-determination would be honored by all, and the South would have free and democratic elections under international supervision. That was all part of an agreed upon cease-fire and, as we wrote, to avoid all armed conflict.

"You know what we should have done? I'll tell you. Ford should have had a massive airlift to Cambodia last February and March when there was time to save it. Massive. Then the same for Vietnam if necessary, but it wouldn't have been necessary if we did it for Cambodia. After Cambodia, they knew we wouldn't do anything to protect South Vietnam. They had carte blanche and they knew it. It was theirs for the asking. They knew we'd turn our backs. They saw those guys like Mansfield in the Senate. Did he care about China's guns shooting Cambodians? If he did, I never heard him say it—or wanting to do anything about it. Our days as a world power could be over, Moose, if we just keep looking inward. Look at what happened to Rome and Athens—even London when they started looking inward. It was over. Over."

"Maybe. Maybe we'll change direction."

"With that Congress? With the press we have? Maybe someone will come along. It could be. But there has to be a big change. Maybe Reagan. He'd be a change, all right, but it has to be someone who can change the congress. Maybe he could bring that about. See, but the media will rip him up. They'll make him look like a lightweight, like a mental midget, like a kook, and he's not any of those things. You know, he's smart. Reasonable. Now, Reagan doesn't have broad international experience but he has tough international instincts. You know, he'd probably agree with you on things. And Reagan is good on television. He's good. Rockefeller is terrible on television. You seen him on television lately?"

"Yes."

"He does have international experience, but he can't project anything. He's not going to be president unless Jerry pulls an LBJ; you know, and then Nelson can have the office that way, but I don't expect that. I expect Jerry to run again. He won't give up. And if he wants the nomination he'll get it. Reagan, the others, will have to wait. But the prime thing is that we have to have someone who has a global view. You know what John Kennedy told me? He had just been president, I don't know, maybe two or three months and he had me over to the White House and we talked for a good long time about Vietnam, about Laos, about Cuba, about Berlin. We went all over the world together in that conversation and when it was done he said, 'It really is true that foreign affairs is the only important issue for a president to handle, isn't it?' You see, he knew his Constitution. He knew what the Congress should do and what he should do. Then he said, 'I mean, who cares if the minimum wage is $1.15 or $1.25, in comparison to all this?' See, he didn't mean all that didn't make a difference, he meant—and he was right—that it isn't the stuff of presidents.

"Then you look at who the Democrats have now, other than Hubert—and he isn't going to run. So look what you have: you have Bentsen and Carter and Church and Jackson, and don't write off Kennedy. Bentsen and Jackson have knowledge of the world, Jackson particularly—but neither of those two are going to get the nomination. They can write that off. Carter's an unknown. He doesn't know anything about foreign policy. He could screw things up. But can you imagine Church or Kennedy? Ted's not John, you know. And Church—can you imagine? He's killing our intelligence agencies at those hearings of his. And Colby is the worst CIA director we've ever had. He nods his head at Church like a fool and he waives the contract agreement of all the CIA's employees. He tells them they can reveal secrets. They're announcing names of agents. My God! Now Church wants to be president. If he ever gets there, just let him try to get intelligence from what he's ruined. The agents he'd need will have been killed."

"Are you going to make any statements on '76?"

"You mean to the press or go to the convention or something?"

"Yes."

"No way. No way. I'm sitting it out right here. Goldwater is already saying I want to be ambassador to China. God, where does he get his information? I wouldn't accept ambassador to the moon. I'll tell you, this is going to be the first election since 1946 that I'll be sitting out. Look, if anyone asks you what my plans are on supporting candidates and things like that, tell them I'm writing my book and that's that—and I'm sorry, I regret—I'm sorry about the whole Watergate—all of that." There was a tap at the door. "Yeah! Yeah! Come in!" the president said loudly.

Nora opened the door. "Mr. President, it's blood pressure time."

"Yeah. Yeah. Fine. Send in Dunn." Bob Dunn was already walking in, right behind Nora.

Moose stood up.

The former president said, "You knew Bob Dunn. He's become an expert on this."

"Hi, Moose," Bob Dunn said.

"Hey, Bob."

"Sit down, sit down," the former president said to Moose. He sat, and Nora walked to the president's desk and straightened some folders.

Moose asked, "What do you do, Bob, if the president's blood pressure is high or low or something?"

Bob Dunn smiled at Moose. "I call Dr. Lungren. But the president's doing real well." He rolled over a small blood pressure unit that was by the side of the president's desk. The president stood to take off his jacket, then rolled up his shirt sleeve, sat down again, and Bob Dunn wrapped the unit's cloth around the president's left arm, pumped up the pressure, watched the gauge as he allowed the air out, then announced that his blood pressure was "a healthy 143 over 72."

"And your pill, Mr. President," Nora said handing him a pill. She poured some water from a small pitcher into a glass on the lamp desk.

"We sure fooled them, didn't we?" and he rolled his sleeve back down and attached his cuff link.

"Fooled who?" Nora asked.

"Everyone." And he gestured toward his left leg as he stood, put his jacket back on, and then sat down again. "They didn't know it. We went to the Mideast and to Moscow and they didn't know a thing about the leg. We fooled them, didn't we?"

"Frankly, Dr. Tkach said he thought you were killing yourself," Nora said.

"No way."

Nora nodded. "I wasn't on those trips, Mr. President, so I don't know what you were doing."

"Fooling them all, except for Walter Tkach." Bob Dunn rolled the unit back to the side of the desk while President Nixon lit his pipe. "Thank you, Bob. Thanks, Nora."

They walked out of the office. The president shifted in his chair. "Moose–tell me–how's your friend, Valadovich?"

"Okay. He's fine. I saw him last night. He's retired from active duty now."

"Retired? He's a young man. Why did he do that?"

"Vietnam."

"He had his hands full in that prison?"

"No. His hands got full in the surrender."

He nodded. "Disgusted?"

Moose nodded. "I don't know what he's going to do, but he's very serious about the study of religion."

"What's he want to do? Be a priest or something?"

"Oh, no. I don't think so. A theologian. The study of religion."

"What is he, Catholic?"

"That's funny. I never even asked him. I think so, though."

"Look what he went through at Hoa Lo. Theology calls for strength, you know. He has it. Faith calls for courage. He has it. Good for him. You know Billy Graham?"

"We met. I don't really know him."

"Strong man. He's been good to us."

"I know."

"You ought to line up Valadovich with Graham."

"Good idea. Jonas visited with Solzhenitsyn to talk to him about–things."

"He did? Good for him. Solzhenitsyn is a recluse. He doesn't see many people. Listen, call Graham. Tell him I'd like him to meet Valadovich."

"I will."

"Sadat, too, if Valadovich ever wants to go to Cairo. I told him that."

"I'll remind him. He's staying in the reserve. They're going to make him a brigadier general."

"We promoted him, didn't we?"

"Yes, sir. From major to full colonel."

"We should have made him a general. Well, maybe it would have been too much then. It's all right. As long as he stays in the reserves he'll probably have a couple silver stars before he knows it. That is if Rumsfeld knows enough about Valadovich, over there at Defense." The president shifted in his chair with some visible discomfort. "You know what worries me?"

"What?"

"Those tapes." He had such ease in moving subjects. "There's more to come."

"What do you think you said that you're worried about at this point, Mr. President?"

"A couple of conversations. You know all your contingency papers?"

"Sure."

"Well, you know, in private we used to bat contingencies off the walls in the Oval Office."

"I know. So what?"

"Wait until they hear the tapes about the bomb. I think you know it was a contingency–twice. You wrote them, I think. Maybe not. I gave the bomb a lot of thought and I was ready to use it if necessary–twice. Once in '71–you know, the war between India and Pakistan. If the Soviets or the Chinese did something, we could have had World War III. I had to weigh the possibility of the bomb. But you know how things like that sound on tape."

"The second time was during the Yom Kippur war, right?"

President Nixon nodded. "Two years ago. If Brezhnev went any further–I weighed the possibility–the probability, I'll correct myself–the probability of using the bomb. I wasn't about to let Israel go down the tubes. But you know how that's going to sound on tape? Everything sounds horrible on tape."

"Have you heard those particular tapes played back?"

He shook his head. "I can't listen to those things any more. I went through enough of that in the EOB. They're hard listening. The coffee cups are louder than the voices. They're terrible recordings, you know."

"Yes. I heard a lot of them."

"Aren't they awful?"

"They're tough listening."

"They're God-awful. Better than Lyndon's but they're awful. You know, Lyndon thought he might use the bomb once, too. And we know Kennedy was ready. Cuba. And Ike was ready in Korea. But it's different when we talk about it, you know. And I swore. You know how we do that. I listened to some of those tapes and I was swearing, so it sounds even worse. What do they call them, the swearing?"

"Expletives."

"Expletives, yeah. I went through a lifetime never swearing in public and now I sound like–I don't know what."

"So what? I've never heard you swear in public or even in private in front of a woman or a child. The obscenity isn't what you said in private in front of men, the obscenity was done by others when they released them to the public."

"You know who swore more than anyone I've ever heard?"

"Who?"

"I mean a president."

"Truman?"

"Oh, God no. He was a piker. Not Truman. Ike."

"Really?"

"Well, he was a professional soldier, you know. He swore like you wouldn't believe. That didn't make him a bad president, did it? The press knows it. They know it. Some of those in the White House Press Corps knew Ike. Well, that's all over with. You can't look back, you know. Do you know the story of Lot's wife?"

Moose smiled. "You told me."

"Don't ever forget it."

"I won't. Hey, Mr. President, I want you to know that Woodstein keeps phoning."

"Woodstein?"

"Oh. That's what we call them. Bob Woodward and Carl Bernstein."

"They've been calling you?"

"Woodward calls at least once a week. They want to meet with me. He and Bernstein are writing another book about your administration and he found out I had a meeting with you just before you resigned."

"What do you tell him?"

"I tell him, 'No.' You know, they can quote me wrong or they can mess up what I could tell them, and I don't want to take that chance. Then they say to everyone they talk to that we're sources of credibility. That's what they did with the first book, isn't it?"

"See them."

"You want me to?"

"What harm can it do at this stage? Do what you want, but as far as I'm concerned, do it. But let me warn you, if you do, I've been told how they work. They play 'good cop, bad cop.' You'll hate Bernstein. You'll like Woodward. That's how they try to get what they want. Bernstein excuses himself to go to the can or something and Woodward will act like he doesn't like Bernstein and he'll tell you things that make you think Woodward is your best friend. That's the act. But as long as you know, it might be good for us for you to see them."

"How do you know that's what they do?"

"They've been interviewing a lot of our friends. They all tell me the same thing."

"Good to know."

"But if you don't tell them I was acting crazy, clawing the walls, they won't print what you say."

"No. They'll have to print it. Woodward's been bugging me so much about it."

"Believe me, they won't. But go see them. It can't do any harm. See them and then forget it. There's only one way to rescue yourself from all the pits of the past. Fill in what you can fill in, and then leave it all behind. I'm filling in the pits right now, but it won't last long. The book I'm writing on all that will be done and that will be that. Gannon's helping me, and Diane—Diane Sawyer's here, and Khachigian. You know Ken, don't you? Ken Khachigian?"

"Of course."

"He's a good man, Khachigian."

"I know."

"But when the book is done, that's it. That will fill the old pits. Then we have to look ahead or there won't be anything ahead. Build a new road. And I'll tell you, when you do that you drive your opponents right up the wall. They want you to spend your time hating them, and to dwell on the past until the day you turn into salt. When you do, all they do is give a blow of their breath and you don't exist at all. Salt scatters. So let's forget about all that. We have a Bicentennial coming. Two-hundred years. In the history of civilization, Moose, there's nothing to equal this nation. I thought I'd be president when we turn 200 but I was wrong. So, somebody else will. Jerry will. He'll do fine. My concern is what happens to our place in the world."

"That's really why I'm here, Mr. President. I want to know about the leaders in Asia. I haven't met most of them or negotiated with any of them. I need that background."

The former president gave long narratives on one leader after another from Chou En-lai to Indira Gandhi to the differences between Yahya Khan and Ali Bhutto and on and on going from one nation to the other with descriptions of their beliefs, their successes and failures, all the way to their mannerisms and appearances down to their cuff-links, if they wore them, or if they had their clothes pressed for a meeting.

Every time the subject got to what one world leader or another said about the former president's departure from office, President Nixon said, "Let's not talk about that," but in short time he would return to the subject himself.

"You know, Mr. President," Moose said, "this is one of the few times in a long time that you haven't told me I should have married that girl in Hong Kong."

"That Chinese girl?"

"Yes."

The president smiled. "Well, you should have." And he laughed. "Do I do that a lot?"

Moose nodded and he stood up, ready to leave.

"Well, it's good advice!" the president said. "Listen, do you want to stay for dinner? Some Mexican food? Pat would love to see you. Did I tell you she thinks you should have been my bodyguard?"

Moose nodded and clenched his lips. "I'd like that, but I can't. I have a plane to catch back to D.C."

The president shoved his ottoman aside, and stood up, then slowly and carefully walked to the window. He stood there with his back to Moose. "Fog," he said.

"What?"

President Nixon turned away from the window and toward Moose. "There's a heavy fog now. Be careful when you drive up the coast. You're driving, aren't you?"

"To LAX."

"Well, be careful. Maybe the fog will lift in an hour, or two hours, maybe not until tomorrow. Weeks, months, years, but it's going to lift."

"I know."

"Nothing lasts forever, you know."

"Valadovich would have something to say about that if he were here."

"Except this country. It's got to last forever. We have to stop looking inward or we'll be lost in that fog."

FORTY-FOUR
WHEN THE TALL SHIPS SAILED
1976

Bands played, fireworks soared, uniformed groups marched down city streets, pretty girls twirled batons, flags unfurled, bells rang, and tall ships sailed.

The United States was 200 years old, and the nation had endured. Six million people gathered at New York harbor and along the Hudson River to watch the sixteen tall ships and two hundred other vessels from around the world, with 10,000 small U.S. boats escorting them.

In Philadelphia, facing a crowd of one million people, President Ford said, "Liberty is a living flame to be fed, not dead ashes to be revered, even in a Bicentennial year.... The world may or may not follow, but we must lead because our whole history says we must." The Liberty Bell was carefully tapped with a rubber mallet, the tap very light so as not to cause another crack, and that tap signaled bells to ring in all fifty states.

In Washington, thousands of people were on the Mall, with kids dunking their feet in the long reflecting pool between the Lincoln Memorial and the Washington Monument. It seemed as though everyone was taking pictures with thin, black Kodak pocket 110 cameras, to enter in *Life* magazine's Bicentennial Photo Contest.

Around the world at U.S. embassies and consulates there were parties with hot dogs and hamburgers and Coca-Colas and Pepsi-Colas and Nescafé.

In Hong Kong, at the insistence of their highest ranking local employee, Yeung Tso Wai-yee, the U.S. Consulate did not hold their party in the Consulate Building, but went just one hundred feet below Victoria Peak, away from tourists, but still commanding the high view of the city.

Governor Sir Crawford Murray MacLehose was there, as were other government officials from Great Britain, officials of many other countries, and a healthy amount of Hong Kong dignitaries and their families.

Wai-yee brought her five year old daughter, Liberty, who was outrageously cute, and Wai-yee also brought her husband who was not only old enough to be Wai-yee's father, but old enough to be her grandfather.

With all the competition of speakers, from Hong Kong's Governor MacLehose, to U.S. Consul General Charles Cross, the speech that garnered the most attentiveness in the crowd was the one given by Wai-yee: "With all respect, may I please have your silence?"

The crowd quickly became silent. Even the children.

"Mr. Consul General, thirteen years ago, your President John F. Kennedy was in West Berlin and he said, 'All free men, wherever they may live, are citizens of Berlin, and therefore, as a free man, I take pride in the words, I am a Berliner.' I am a free woman, and along with every person in the world who lives in freedom, I take pride in the words, I am an

American. No, not by law am I a citizen of the United States, but as your president meant in Berlin, the free have a bond. He was a Berliner, but still an American. In the same way, I am an American and also British, but still Chinese.

"I am Chinese by birth and some day I will be Chinese in death.

"Governor MacLehose, with all the criticisms and complaints I have personally leveled against your government of Great Britain, I bend on my knees in thanks to you and your countrymen for giving us refuge, and for allowing us to retain the freedom with which we were born, but which our own government of China took from us. Governor MacLehose, your queen is going to be in the United States in two days to celebrate," and she looked at the Consul General, "your nation's Bicentennial, Mr. Counsul General. She will bring a gift of a bell cast at the same foundry as the Liberty Bell. She is celebrating what has become of a former colony, lost by her nation, in war.

"We, too, in 1997, will possibly become a former British colony. Beyond the New Territories, even Kowloon and this island may be under the jurisdiction of China, not Great Britain anymore. I hope so—but only if the government of China, by that time, believes in liberty. It is my hope that we, like Americans, will then host a visit by the royalty of Great Britain who will celebrate our freedom. But as long as China is governed by communists, stay here, Great Britain.

"Governor MacLehose, Prime Minister Churchill's mother was American and his statue outside your Embassy in Washington has one foot on the British soil of your Embassy's grounds, and one foot on American soil.

"With much pride of her mother, my daughter also has American blood. And her name is Liberty.

"Your Statue of Liberty, Mr. Consul General, holds a lamp that lights Hong Kong's way. That lamp's torch is held by Hong Kong people every moment. It ignited and welded all the irons that have built the city you see here at the base of this mountain.

"If it was not for the inspiration of the United States of America, we would not have known that real freedom was possible. And we saw what you did after World War II when you could have had the world as your taxpayers, but instead, you gave to them rather than took from them. And so today, Hong Kong people celebrate your Bicentennial. This is not a congratulation made out of courtesy or diplomacy, but out of love and passion for the freedoms your nation taught the world was a birthright. We learned that those are the things that are worth living for, and if necessary—worth dying for.

"Therefore, on behalf of the people of Hong Kong—and on behalf of those Chinese above the border who cannot speak out—Happy Birthday."

FORTY-FIVE
A JOURNEY TO FOREVER
1977

A mosquito was waiting for Jonas Valadovich in Orlando. As soon as that little insect saw Jonas walk out of the aircraft, he bit him on the back of his hand and then flew to his ankle for another quick bite. Jonas also received the "Welcome to Florida" gift of savaging humidity. But just as Adam had told Jonas years ago, mosquitoes and humidity were part of the romance he would find in Florida, along with the sky that was unlike any other sky in the world in its blueness and pillowed clouds and expanse above the flatland.

It was eight-thirty at night and so Jonas couldn't judge the sky's blueness or clouds or expanse but he could judge the mosquitoes and humidity. He had slept on the plane so that he could stay awake without difficulty on this first night in Florida. That was in compliance with Adam's advice that his first visit to Cape Canaveral should be at night.

Once inside the airport's terminal, Jonas went directly to the Men's Room at the terminal, as he knew he had an hour's drive ahead of him. There were two Men's Rooms next to each other, and across from them, there were two Women's Rooms. Jonas knew why. Adam had told him that when he moved to Florida in the 1950s and for years thereafter, the Orlando airport had one restroom for "White Men," one for "Colored Men," one for "White Women," and one for "Colored Women." When the 1964 Civil Rights Act became law, the signs were taken down, but a lot of public places were stuck with four restrooms, as well as two drinking fountains. Plumbing renovations waited even longer than justice.

He was given a Sunoco map of Florida at the Avis Rent-a-Car counter, and the attendant had marked the route of the "Bee Line Highway" that Jonas should take to get to Cocoa Beach, but he didn't need the map. Jonas felt confident that if he got lost, Adam would guide him to find his way.

As he started his eastward journey across Highway 50 there was an "Evacuation Route" sign giving a visible signal that World War III was not out of the question.

The crickets were louder than the car's motor, and there was nothing to see on either side of the road. There were miles and miles of darkness as the car passed unseen swamps and palmetto and probably millions of mosquitoes hoping Jonas would have to park and walk outside.

Adam nudged him to take the separation road to Highway 520 and still there was the nothingness until a sign advertising the upcoming "Barnett National Bank" was by the side of the road exhibiting a signal of civilization, and then a sign advertising "The Missile Lounge" ahead in Cocoa Beach. There was really going to be civilization ahead somewhere. Then there were the thump-thumps of the car's tires going over metal rods in a causeway, then the metallic hum as the car's tires passed over the drawbridge across the Indian River. Back to thump-thumps again with fishermen and women fishing as they hung over the bridge, miraculously content to be out there in the humidity without being frightened by mosquitoes, and balancing themselves from falling in the river or falling the other way and getting run over. At least there were human beings in this part of the world, but why were they out there fishing? Was it all worth it? Don't they have enough money to just buy some fish if they want them?

There, by the right side of the road was Merritt Island's Indoor-Outdoor Theater where Adam once worked, and off to the distant left–there was the glow of Cape Canaveral with its beckoning lights; as important, as mysterious, as sublime, as inviting as Adam had described. Then another draw bridge with its thumps and hums across the Banana River.

Jonas passed the last intersection before the end of the road at the Vanguard Hotel with only the beach of the Atlantic Ocean a few feet from him. Adam had told him that cars drove on the beach and hundreds of people would park there to watch the missile launches, and at night lovers would be in their cars parked haphazardly on the beach. But there was a barrier straight ahead with a sign that read, "Motor Vehicles Prohibited On Beach. Ordinance #310." The fence's doors, however, had been moved aside, and Jonas could see cars parked on the beach. He drove straight ahead, his headlights aiming at the oncoming breakers of the Atlantic, his tires riding on the hard-packed sands.

Very close by his left side was a cluster of cars in a circle, with their headlights aimed at each other. In the center of the cluster of cars were people standing in a smaller circle.

Jonas parked and got out of his car and walked to the circle of people. There, in the circle's center, was a man performing artificial respiration on another man who was totally drenched, dressed in a soaked yellow shirt and brown cotton slacks. "He just appeared," a woman told Jonas. "He came in with the tide–perhaps a tourist gone out too far in the ocean, perhaps a resident who wanted to commit suicide, perhaps a spy. He's dead. He can't be revived."

Jonas looked up from the dead man to view the distant Cape. Some of its lights were steady, some were blinking. He looked back down at the dead man, then back at the Cape where one searchlight after another was going on to center on a rocket launching site there. An intense and eerie feeling overtook Jonas who, with no more than a movement of his eyes, could see headlights of cars lighting a dead man, and searchlights of the Cape lighting a rocket. Both were going to unknown destinations.

It was a ghastly, and yet a uniquely appropriate prologue to Jonas's visit to Cape Canaveral.

Jonas's friends at Vandenberg Air Force Base in California had taken care of all the credentials necessary, including his car-pass and badge for the Cape so that he wouldn't have to go through the long daytime procedure that he would otherwise need to go through at Patrick Air Force Base on the other side of Cocoa Beach.

Jonas's credentials allowed him entrance beyond the gate, where the guard rubbed his badge, looking between his badge and his face. Jonas drove to the lighthouse at the tip of the Cape as Adam had instructed, and from there he could see the length of both sides of the Cape and practically every launching site. He left the car and now the humidity didn't bother him, nor did the mosquitoes come to him. The moment was creating an immunity from earthly things for Jonas. The launching pad that was bathed in the beams of searchlights was Pad 12, the second pad down the line from his view. It was an Atlas, mission unknown, but its nose cone, a large Centaur, indicated this was a space probe whose destination would be very far away.

The large red-and-white magnificent gantry; a tower that sheltered the rocket, started raising its twelve stories of doors from their centers to reveal the fullness of the rocket it had been embracing. The doors raised and raised until the doors were invisible in hinged vertical positions hugging nothing, just standing by the sides of the red and white gantry. Then, almost imperceptibly, the gantry started moving backwards until the Atlas-Centaur was standing unsheltered and isolated with only a thin umbilical cord on a slender adjoining tower acting as its breathing device in a slim connection with earth. The gantry continued its motion backwards and then went off to the side in the direction of the ocean into darkness, like a performer on stage that knew it had a supporting role. At the appropriate time it had to be in the wings, leaving the major performer center-stage for its triumphal moment. There was, perhaps, some jealousy but it was professionally contained by the gantry who was much better wardrobed in red and white, but still uncompetitive with the silver performer who needed no clothes at all to give it importance.

Then came the chorus: like a thousand high-pitched women's voices screaming in unison, the liquid oxygen at a temperature of minus 287 degrees Fahrenheit started flowing through the rocket's pipes to freeze and contract, causing those deafening screams, its voices accompanying a plume of white that was jutting out near the top of the rocket.

Through loudspeakers came the voices of the conductor of the performance, and his chief assistants who answered his check-off:

"Dovap status?"

"Go."

"Beacon status?"

"Beacon status, go."

"G.E. systems?"

"Go."

"Range telemetry ready?"

"Go."

"Azusa status?"

"Azusa status, go."

"Telemetering quality?"

"Go."

The rocket acted as if it heard nothing, too focused on its own purpose and performance. It had no sense of nervousness, but was reveling in its flurry of justified exhibitionism.

At its base, near the bottom of its thrust section were the arms of a strong, iron, yellow launcher holding tight to its possession of the rocket while an avalanche of water started flowing from the back base of the launcher at a rate of 20,000 gallons a minute, bringing water to the skirt level of the rocket.

Again, through the loudspeakers, the conductor and his assistants gave a final check of systems:

"Range safety armed light on?"

"Affirmative."

"Range ready?"

"Affirmative."

"Water system ready?"

"Affirmative."

"Preparation complete? Light green?"

"Affirmative."

"T minus 27 seconds and holding."

"T minus 27 seconds and holding."

The rocket knew what that magic number of 27 meant. Unless there was something that needed to be corrected, T minus 27 meant that with one more push of a button, nothing more would be needed to be done by humans through the rocket's launch. It was all programmed to be automatic.

"We will pick up the count at 27 seconds on my mark. Mark. T minus 27 seconds and counting. All recorders to fast. Vernier start."

The last button had been pushed, and all else would take care of itself. The rocket, the umbilical tower, and the launcher were all on their own. The two pods at the sides of the rocket were spewing white flames from their bases.

The sound from the loudspeakers seemed to be in a state of suspended animation. The suspension went on for 17 seconds and then, "Minus 10, 9, 8, 7, 6, 5, 4–"

There came a furious brilliant explosive expanse of fire jutting out from the dual chambered boosters of the thrust section of the rocket, with a complimentary roar exceeding the volume of any thunder heard on earth. The ground was shaking the entire Cape. Jonas held on to the lighthouse. The rest of the countdown could no longer be heard. The force of the flame was keeping the water at just under the saturation point of the thrust section of the rocket as the water flow was increased by almost a doubling in force. The yellow launcher was straining with all its strength to hold the rocket from leaving the pad with its powerhouse of thrust, until the programmed second of release.

The umbilical tower ejected its cord from the top of the rocket and the yellow launcher opened its iron arms in a moment of tremendous relief, allowing the massive bird to be free and rise; allowed to go on its own into the heavens.

It seemed to move slowly, up, up, up with ice falling off its sides, and a massive flame from its boosters poured back toward the vacant launcher that was looking up at its departed lover, still with its arms opened, and water frothing from its mouth.

Where the applause came from was unknown, but applause of the audience seemed to come from all over the Cape, and there was cheering and yelling, although there were no people visible to Jonas.

The rocket's speed increased in its freedom, going up and up, faster and faster into the black, and lighting the entire Cape and Cocoa Beach with the flames from its boosters. Higher and higher it went, until it was just a yellow spot of light as the roar was becoming a distant rumble and the beaches were becoming dark again.

It was minutes before the yellow light was so far away that it disappeared from view behind some clouds, but it was so brilliant that it lit those clouds for a moment.

The searchlights still lit the launcher and there was still water, like giant tears, flowing down its sides.

The searchlights were turned off.

Jonas was immobile. It was impossible for one earthly thought to enter his mind.

Where was the space-probe going? Jupiter? Saturn? Uranus? Pluto? Or was it going on a journey to forever? On earth this night, Jonas was witness to a sight, a sound, a feel that was the definition of importance. The race for space against the Soviet Union as an international pursuit was extending to its logical end: intergalactic pursuits. "My friend," Adam said to Jonas as Jonas stood leaning against the lighthouse of Cape Canaveral, "there is no end to the journey."

The crickets could be heard again, there was sweat from the evening's humidity on Jonas's forehead, and a mosquito gave a quick bite on the back of his hand. Now the sky gave no visual or audible evidence of its newest guest in the heavens, and Jonas was back on earth.

When he returned to Cocoa Beach, the dead man was no longer lying on the sand, nor were the cars there. The fence to the beach had its doors closed, and Jonas parked by it and he walked to the other side of it where there was only ocean and beach and black sky and way off to the north, the Cape. There were no searchlights coming from the Cape now. But there were small red lights that were going on and off on the top of its gantrys.

There was nothing that was trivial. Nothing. It was why he decided to stay on the beach. Getting a room at a motel, even the thought of it, would have put him back into triviality. He would wait until morning to see those things in Cocoa Beach that Adam had told him he should see after going to the Cape. Not now. By simply leaving things as they were, everything within sight of Jonas that night was important.

FORTY-SIX
ALL QUIET ON THE EASTERN FRONT
1978

There was a wall of soldiers, each participant in the wall standing fifteen feet from another, their rifles with bayonets mounted, pointing toward the Pacific Ocean, guarding the summer home of Nicaragua's president Anastasio Somoza near Masachapa, Nicaragua. On the veranda, overlooking both the tennis court and the ocean, was President Somoza with former U.S. Ambassador Turner Shelton, sipping orange juice. Between their chairs was a square glass-topped table that held an ash tray, two black telephones and one green one, with cords going all the way into the house, and between the ash tray and the phones was an issue of *Playboy* magazine.

"I don't know whether to praise him or condemn him," President Somoza said pointing to the issue of *Playboy*. "Geraldo Rivera took the cork out of the bottle in this *Playboy* interview. I admire his honesty, and even his personality, but the sins to which he confesses to *Playboy* are, in my view, unforgivable."

Ambassador Shelton picked up the issue of the magazine he had brought to President Somoza. "I hope no one saw me buy this at the airport. No one would believe I bought it because I wanted the president of Nicaragua to read its interview with Geraldo Rivera. That's rather far-fetched, isn't it? I think we better make this look a little more respectable in case the Sandinistas invade in the next few minutes! Better they kill us than embarrass us!"

President Somoza laughed as Ambassador Shelton flipped the inside back cover over the rest of the magazine so as to hide the scantily clad Monique St. Pierre on the cover while exhibiting, instead, a picture of O.J. Simpson advertising leather shoes.

"So, Turner," President Somoza said, "tell me about this man who will phone me."

"If he gets the call through, he'll call you some time within the next fifteen minutes, or close to it. That's the way we had it timed, anyway. He's a humorless, intense fellow named Cody Cooper–but a very nice man, a very dedicated man who met with me on my Asian trip."

"Cody Cooper. That name rings a chord."

"It should. He worked for President Kennedy. He said he came to Managua back then to give you a letter from Kennedy."

Anastasio Somoza smiled and nodded. "Yes, yes, I remember. A thin man. Very young. Very thin. I remember. That was when Kennedy accepted my offer for allowing Puerto Cabezas as a base for his Bay of Pigs invasion. And his man–this Cooper fellow–kept raving about Kennedy's Alliance for Progress. I was bored silly but he was a very likable fellow.

I told Kennedy he had a good man there. Very thin, though. And very young. He doesn't work for Carter now, does he?"

"I wouldn't inflict that on you. No. He's working with refugees from Vietnam. He seemed like talking to you was a matter of life and death. I told him I'd be visiting you this week and I told him to go to the U.S. Embassy in K. L. and they'd get you on the line."

"What's K.L.?"

"Excuse me. That's my State Department orientation coming back. Kuala Lumpur. Cooper is in Malaysia. He and his wife and his kid, a little kid, are in some Godforsaken place on the east coast of Malaysia at some refugee camp there, but he said he'd go to Kuala Lumpur to call you. Let him tell you what it's about, I'd screw it up. He's all right. He's a little frantic but nice. He went through such trouble to meet with me, I feel sorry for him. He knew I had been U.S. Ambassador to Nicaragua in earlier years and he heard or read somewhere that I was on an Asian tour. He went down to Singapore to meet with me and literally begged me to arrange a meeting or at least a phone call with you."

"You know why I remember his name? Gary Cooper. His name sounded like Gary Cooper."

"He told me he met you before you had a mustache."

President Somoza laughed.

"He confidentially told me that he thinks you look more like a Latin American dictator with the mustache."

Now President Somoza burst out laughing. "He's right! I do look that way now, don't I?" He laughed again and the laughter was penetrated by the ring of the telephone. It was his secretary telling him the U.S. Embassy in Kuala Lumpur, Malaysia, was on the line. The president nodded at Ambassador Shelton. "Pick up that phone—listen in," and by the movement of his head, the president indicated the black phone closest to Turner Shelton, while the president was on the green one, pressing a button beneath it. "Hello?"

"President Somoza?" the voice said.

"Yes."

"Hello, Mr. President."

"Yes. Hello. Go on."

"Mr. President, this is Cody Cooper. I met you many years ago when I worked for President Kennedy, and—"

"Yes, Mr. Cooper, I remember you well. You came to Managua. Now I understand that you are with refugees. I was told that by Ambassador Shelton who is sitting right here."

"Oh, good. Yes. I am with the World Refugee Mission."

"I don't know what that is. What is that? Is that attached to the U.N. High Commissioner for Refugees?"

"No. It is an independent, non-profit organization. We take care of refugees. My wife and I are working with boat people from Vietnam. And I believe you can do something for us and we can do something for you."

"I'm not sure anyone can do anything for me at this stage. Tell me, what can I do for you?"

"Right now the Western countries, including the United States, have great guilt over the fate of the boat people from Vietnam. The United States has been good. Hong Kong has been good. Malaysia has been good. Some other countries have been good. But most haven't been good enough. Most nations want the refugees out of their countries, and there are around 200,000 still at sea. That's comparable to more than half the population of Managua." He drew on the old technique of population comparison that he learned in the State Department.

"Yes. It is tragic."

"Then let them into Nicaragua. Accept the ones that other nations deny. The perception of you would be turned around in a moment. As you know, the perception of you in the United States is terrible. The press is all over you every day. Since no one expects anything of you, and the boat people have not directed a request to you, the world would be quieted, stunned, shocked, and silenced if you would do what no country is willing to do. And you would prove you care about human rights. You would be doing a great thing, and in doing it, the world would have another view of you. Take them in."

"Mr. Cooper, I am horrified by what is happening to the Vietnamese. But it is nothing new, Mr. Cooper. All that is new is that they use the sea, but that's because there is now no choice for them. They were escaping every day from North Vietnam to South Vietnam by land. Now with North Vietnam the victor, the refugees continue, but they can't flow by land to freedom any more, because there is no land left there uncontrolled by the communists. So they go to the only other exit that exists—the sea."

"Will you take them in?"

"Mr. Cooper, I understand your concern, and I respect your pursuit, but in the end, the Vietnamese were deserted by your government, by your Congress. The consequences are severe, but the battlefield has shifted. The war is now here, Mr. Cooper, and I have to put Nicaraguans first. There was a time I could have handled what you are bringing up to me, and it is so worthy I would have done it, but now it is impossible. My country is paying a very dear price for our friendship with the United States. My predicament here—Nicaragua's predicament, Mr. Cooper, is a direct result of what I did back in the days when you delivered that message from your president. You know that, don't you?"

"No, sir, I don't."

"I'm sure you know what was in that letter you delivered to me from your president."

"Yes."

"The United States and Nicaragua became partners in that invasion attempt of Cuba, didn't we? After the invasion's failure and the exposure of my role, Fidel Castro called me a puppet of Kennedy's, and I would live to regret my affiliation. Now he is making good on that threat. What I don't understand is Carter. I support the United States in every controversy—on every vote in every international organization. When you have a handful of votes in the U.N., one is always mine. You talk of the Vietnamese boat people. My feeling for them is real. I was the only Western Hemisphere Chief of State who offered to send troops to Vietnam to fight beside your troops. The offer was declined, but gratitude was expressed from both Johnson and Nixon. Now the tables have turned and now my country is at war against the communists. And what side does Carter choose? He sides with the communists. Your embassy in Managua has been told to disengage themselves from me, you know."

"I'm sorry. I didn't know that."

"Oh, yes. Your government mystifies me. Listen to the irony: if I oppose a communist takeover here, I incur the wrath of both the Soviet Union and the United States. If I support the Soviet Union's proxies, then I win the support of both the Soviet Union and the United States. Your President Carter does not understand the world, least of all Latin America, and he surely doesn't understand what the alternative here would mean to the United States. The only military support I'm getting is from Israel. They have a world view. They understand the word 'survive.' I may, indeed, be a dictator, Mr. Cooper, if that is the way your Carter wants to define my administration. But then how does he define most Latin American governments? And I am a rather unique dictator, aren't I, who encourages opposition parties? What a unique dictatorship this is since we have a totally free press with a history of criticizing me. I am a dictator in a nation who insures that the people have the freedom to dissent, to strike, to leave if they want, and I invite the Red Cross and the press to visit my prisons. Compare all that with most other Latin American nations."

"Mr. President, I am not talking about reality. I am talking about the perception of you—of Nicaragua."

"But you must know these things, Mr. Cooper. You must understand what is happening here to understand what I can and cannot do. You—and Carter—you want to do things, without the patience to figure out how to do them. You worked for my friend, President Kennedy, and so I will not be cryptic with you. Your Carter is like you. He doesn't listen. Maybe I am being too harsh on your Carter. I have to admit that he launched an international human rights campaign that had a magnificent purpose. Who could fault him? Not me. His purpose was to bring human rights to the people of the world. President Carter has a deeply passionate belief in human rights, and his presidency of your country had great potential with his belief.

"But the implementation of his human rights campaign went to your Department of State."

"Yes, sir. I know the State Department well and—"

President Somoza interrupted him. "They planned to use his objectives for their own goals. As an incoming president without foreign policy experience, I suppose their expertise was difficult for Carter to challenge. So he took their advice. Do you know what it was?"

"No, sir."

"That the first three most prominent targets on the rather extensive list of governments that violated human rights were to be U.S. allies, not foes: The Shah of Iran, Romero of El Salvador, and me.

"Castro was ecstatic. Brezhnev was ecstatic. Had Carter gone the other way–had he first targeted the countries threatening our countries–we could have eased our political restraints that he did not understand, as our countries were trying to survive. Had he gone the other way, the threats would have been gone for our countries. You would assume your Carter would think again when the Sandinistas and the Palestine Liberation Organization announced their intention to 'join forces and wage war on the State of Israel, Nicaragua, and U.S. imperialism.' But, under the guidance of your State Department, he ignored all of that."

"In all respect, Mr. President, that isn't what I'm talking about." Cody didn't know, or forgot, that presidents can talk about whatever they want.

"Your Carter cut off all our aid–all of it including nutritional assistance and rural education. He sent us his new U.S. ambassador, Lawrence Pezzullo. Pezzullo visited with me and told me that President Carter and Secretary of State Vance wanted me to resign and leave Nicaragua. That would have left the road open for the Sandinistas supplied by Castro."

"Mr. President, sir, I–"

"Of course I was shocked. I told Pezzullo that I would not do that. He then insisted that an election in Nicaragua take place immediately, in advance of our constitutionally prescribed election which is to take place in 1981. That would be like foreigners insisting that you hold an election in advance of your constitutional prescription. Further, he insisted that an international body, not Nicaraguans, take-over, supervise, and conduct campaigns and perform the media work and polling and everything. Nothing in the hands of Nicaraguans. He added that the electoral districts must be re-defined as the Sandinistas wanted them, and that registration of voters be eliminated. I wanted normal registration so foreigners could not cross into our country to vote. He also insisted that my family and I must leave the country before the election, not allowing me to campaign, and if I should lose the election then he insisted that my family and I be banished from Nicaragua and live somewhere else in exile. Would any chief of state agree to such demands?"

"No, sir."

"I said that what I would do is have an immediate plebiscite on my continuation in office with international observers and monitors and the international press present, and if I lost that vote, I would leave. Pezzullo did not accept that suggestion. I told him I could not go along with the absurd demands that he made, rejecting them as outright insults."

"Yes, sir."

"Then, Mr. Cooper, your government smuggled weapons to our foes. They came from New Jersey and Florida to the Sandinistas through Venezuela, Costa Rica, and Panama.

"Mr. Cooper, I do not think that accepting Vietnam refugees into my country is going to be very good for the refugees or for Nicaragua. You see why I refuse what you so earnestly request of me?"

"Mr. President, I am not engaged in politics anymore. I work for refugees. The World Refugee Mission does not engage in politics, only in humanitarianism."

President Somoza laughed. "Your Mission does not engage in politics, but only humanitarianism? To talk of humanitarianism without talking about politics is impossible. You are still an innocent, Mr. Cooper."

"You disagree that if you were to do it, it would help your situation with the press, and the world powers would treat you better?"

"That is naive. You must be aware that whatever I do, your press will be against me. If I was able to take in every Vietnamese boat person, and did it—they would say I was doing it to deceive the world. Then what? Spending our treasury on the Vietnamese and ignoring our own very pressing needs, the Sandinistas would take over in a snap and send the refugees back—or find some other penalty for them. Now, you expect the press to be unbiased? Mr. Cooper, do you read *Playboy*?"

There was silence for a while. "*Playboy*?" How did the president of Nicaragua find out?

"*Playboy*."

"No, Mr. President. I mean I've seen it but I don't buy it. I mean maybe once or twice I did. Not in a long time." There was a pause. "Really."

"Get it. Get the current issue. Ambassador Shelton and I have been going over it. It will tell you about the workings of your press."

"Okay."

"You will read it?"

"I don't know if they allow it here in Malaysia."

President Somoza reached for the issue of *Playboy* and skimmed through the pages until he stopped at the one that had a bent corner. "Do you know who Geraldo Rivera is?"

"Yes. He's on TV at home—in the United States."

"He's the correspondent for the ABC Network here in Central America. He was in Panama during this year's debates on President Carter's treaties on the Canal. The polls changed dramatically in your country from opposition to Carter's treaties, to support for his treaties. They suddenly wanted to give up the Canal and give Carter his treaties. Do you know how that happened? Let me read to you what Rivera and others in the U.S. press corps did, just months ago, to influence your people's opinion. It has great bearing on us, here in Nicaragua. Rivera says this:

"'I am very appreciative of the power of the media. The media definitely influence events, even if people don't admit it. They're not benign observers. Let me give you an example. In my coverage of Panama, I reported every point of view, and toward the end, I was clearly in favor of the treaty. I felt that, regardless of my own personal or political feelings, or the identity I felt with the students or the Panamanian left or with the whole sense of Panamanian nationalism versus U.S. imperialism, the treaty was the best possible compromise.'

"He goes on to tell about an incident that occurred there that, if revealed to people in your country, could influence them against the Carter treaties. So Rivera said he downplayed it, because, he says—and I'm quoting again: 'That was the day I decided that I had to be very careful about what I said, because I could defeat the very thing I wanted to achieve. Later I had dinner with some people from *The New York Times* and *The Washington Post*, and we all felt the same way.' Mr. Cooper, he was admitting that he and his colleagues would be careful not to tell the news that would harm the chances of the passage of the treaties, because they wanted the treaties to pass."

Cody could never have predicted that one day the president of Nicaragua would be reading from *Playboy* magazine to him.

"Then Rivera says, 'It was tremendous, if you think about it. There was ABC News, the *Times* and the *Post* having dinner together. You don't have to be a real student of the media to understand that that is a lot of power.' Now, listen to this—again I quote: 'It happened in Nicaragua, too. I was talking to a group of radicals and I said, listen, I'm just here to cover what is going on, but if every time I get out of my car, people are going to shoot bullets in the air, then your story is not going to get on American television. The only story that is going to get on is General Somoza's, and if that is what you want, fine, I'll go back to the hotel.' The *Playboy* interviewer then makes a very intelligent comment: 'It would seem you were giving them a crash course in the proper use of the media.' Rivera agrees. He calls himself an educator. So ABC and *The New York Times* and *The Washington Post* correspondents agreed on what they would accent or downplay. Mr. Cooper, that's called conspiracy.

"You must read his confessions, Mr. Cooper, so that you become more realistic about your press."

"I'll read the interview, Mr. President, if I can get it here, since you make that request of me, but will you consider what I requested of you?"

"I will consider it, Mr. Cooper, out of respect for how we met—for the fact that you once worked for President Kennedy. He was young and made mistakes in his first year, but he was a good man and he caught on quickly. But there is no excuse for the kind of betrayal President Carter is inflicting on your country's friends around the world. He should know that if the Sandinistas are successful here, you will see a wider war in Central America. Once evil wins, as it did in Vietnam and Cambodia, it means evil will seek more battlefields. And now the battlefield is here. With enough help of Brezhnev, Castro will get his way and have Daniel Ortega sitting on this patio. If that happens, you can be sure that the Sandinistas non-elected takeover will be applauded by your President Carter. And it won't stop at the borders of Nicaragua. El Salvador is next. You think you will be in Malaysia long?"

"Yes, sir, as long as the Southeast Asian refugees are in need."

"Don't count on staying, Mr. Cooper. With your government abandoning one friend after another, you will have your choice of refugee centers where you can work. If the Sanidnistas win here, you will have plenty of refugee centers in Central America. That's not far from your home. Should that happen, take care of my people well, Mr. Cooper. Please do that. And do not plan on the press telling your nation who the victims are and who the aggressors are. The Sandinistas will be their heroes. They already are."

"Will you think about taking in the Vietnamese, Mr. President?"

"I will think, Mr. Cooper, if there is time left to think beyond our nation's survival."

The moon was the only source of light, and had there been a switch on the moon that could turn itself on and off, it would have turned itself off rather than view the eastern shore of Kuala Terengganu, Malaysia. It wasn't a refugee camp that it lit, it was a refugee horror. There were thousands upon thousands of Vietnamese, and there were no shelters and there was no sanitation and there was nothing but a vast field of sand for them to occupy for a while. At least they were no longer endangered by the whims of the South China Sea, and no longer endangered by pirates who had an appetite for whatever possessions may be aboard, and appetites for Vietnamese women after throwing the men and children overboard.

Cody and Gloria made their nightly ritual which they named the "R and B Rounds" which stood for rice and bandages, although sometimes the Mission supplied them with some medications and miscellaneous "treats" that stretched the definition of the word. Among the refugees, Cody and Gloria were seen as holy figures for being where they were, and doing what they did.

That night, a small black, wooden vessel crammed with dozens of closely standing refugees, found its way to the shore line. Along with the Vietnamese who went to welcome the boat's occupants, some Malaysians who were sick of all this, joined them, but they threw rocks at the boat and at the refugees on shore who were attempting to help those on board to get to the beach. And some Malaysians started pushing the boat back to sea while it was still half-filled. There was a Malaysian naval patrol boat close by with a tow line, but the rope was not taut. It was doing nothing to usher in the craft.

Cody and Gloria ran to the refugee's boat and yelled at the rock-throwers and at those pushing the boat away, but the holy couple were not obeyed.

Cody and Gloria managed to get aboard the boat, and as they were helping some to get off, those pushing the boat from the shore became successful. The naval patrol boat went to the north, admitting its tow line was unattached to the refugee's vessel.

Cody and Gloria jumped off, an old woman on Cody's back, and a child clutched to one of Gloria's paddling arms.

When they got to the shore, they released their human cargoes to safety.

The refugees' boat, without any power to fight for itself, started drifting with its load of Vietnamese refugees. The boat became a slave to the current that chose to slowly carry it away. Those who had earlier managed to get off were screaming from the beach for those who were still aboard, to jump. The refugee's boat was getting more distant as it was bouncing and listing from side to side. Many jumped. Some made it to shore. Many more didn't.

And then Cody felt himself to be super-human, beyond the bounds he had known all his life. He went back into the sea. And not once, not twice, but three times, Cody went back and forth to the teetering black vessel that was moving further away from the shore. On each turn-around he delivered to the shore another rescue; first one more woman, then two more children, then one woman and child, and then he fell on the beach.

A large, wide, black cloud came between Kuala Terengganu and the moon, and the light was masked. The moon had seen enough. When the cloud had finished its journey and the moon's light shone down again, Cody was standing, Gloria embracing his waist with both of her arms, and the boat with the rest of its human cargo was not visible. After more screams and sobbing of the Vietnamese from the shore, the beach became quiet. The cloud that had obscured the moon was now far away and those on the beach strained their eyes to scan, again and again, for something on the bobbing sea.

Cody and Gloria were the last to stare at the sea, having to accept that the boat was no longer a part of Kuala Terengganu. That boat, with its human cargo, was never seen or heard from again.

What Cody Cooper did that night was talked about throughout Malaysia, and then throughout Southeast Asia, and then the story spread overseas. That night Cody Cooper had seized the moment, oblivious to his life-held weaknesses and limitations. Like the black, wooden vessel, his weaknesses and limitations were part of the past.

FORTY-SEVEN
OF HAWKS AND DOVES
1978

Miss Red Socks lived on the fourth floor of Potomac Plaza, down the hall from Moose Dunston. Everyone who lived in the building called her Miss Red Socks because she always wore them and they were so apparent pulled up tight against her shapeless calves above her saddle shoes. She had come to rest at an indefinable age when she looked like an old woman or at least beyond middle age, and it was difficult to imagine that she was once younger or that she would some day be older. She was stuck at this age.

Miss Red Socks had no particular prejudices. It was true that she did not like black people but she did not like white people either. She disliked Jews, Protestants, and Catholics with equal fervor. She didn't like the Republicans or the Democrats or conservatives or liberals or presidents or the Congress or the Supreme Court, nor did she like the sound of a typewriter from an apartment down the hall. The only things that she seemed to like were red socks and talking, which she wore and accomplished on a daily basis.

She also liked nodding. She always nodded when she talked.

It was a Friday afternoon in mid-December when Miss Red Socks stood in the small cubicle between the double-doored entrance to Potomac Plaza talking to Raymond, the uniformed doorman, who was the only person who could tolerate her intolerance.

Raymond had another unique talent; an extraordinary memory from which, at will, he could draw the name, face, and resumé of every person who lived not only in Potomac Plaza, but across the street at both the Watergate and Columbia Plaza. He was a living biographical encyclopedia of the District's area known as Foggy Bottom.

"Well," Miss Red Socks nodded, "they're open on Sundays, you know."

"Who's that?" Raymond asked, not sure that he had heard her correctly.

Her nodding became very emphatic. "The Safeway grocery!"

"Well, that's nice for people here in Foggy Bottom."

"On Sundays?"

"Isn't that when you said?"

"They don't make enough money on Saturdays, I suppose? Or Fridays?" Then she went backwards through the days of the week without a flaw. "Even God rested on Sunday, but not the Safeway."

"I see what you mean," Raymond agreed in capitulation.

A taxi pulled up with a passenger inside and Raymond left his protected cubicle, letting the cold in and himself out. Miss Red Socks called him back, "Don't open it for him."

Raymond pretended that he didn't hear her through the glass and he opened the taxi door. Moose Dunston paid the driver, came out of the cab, thanked Raymond, the taxi whizzed on, and Raymond opened the door to Potomac Plaza for him. Moose walked past Miss Red Socks, greeting her with a "good afternoon." He opened the inner glass door before Raymond had an opportunity to open it for him. Then he went to the elevator.

"He's a bum," Miss Red Socks nodded.

"No, he isn't. He's a writer. He worked at the White House once."

"He's still a bum. Some young tramp walked out of his apartment at three-thirty in the morning last Tuesday. She was all made up like you know what, Raymond. I thought she was Fanny Fox all dolled up that way."

"You saw her at three-thirty in the morning?"

"I was taking out the garbage. How could I sleep with all that racket going on down the hall? No one could sleep. And after she left he was typing all night. I think he only does it to keep everyone awake. I read some of it he put in the garbage once. It's all about missiles and bombs and all about China."

"He writes for an Asian magazine. He seems to be an expert on that part of the world. He's no bum."

"Well, you can't get any sleep on the fourth floor."

"Everyone works at different hours."

"That magazine pays him or he volunteers?"

"I'm sure they pay him. He wouldn't be doing it for free."

"See what I mean? He just thinks of himself. I'm sure he got paid for working at the White House. Taxpayer's money."

"That's the way it works."

"Well, no wonder, then. With all the money they waste on the likes of him, it's no wonder our taxes are so high. Think if all that money taxpayer's gave him went to the Red Cross? We should be giving to the Red Cross rather than the likes of him." And then she thought over what she was saying. She didn't mean to praise the Red Cross. "Except you don't get a button anymore when you make a contribution. People like you and me give and give and they don't send us a button anymore. They used to give buttons and now they don't give you the time of day."

"Well, life goes on," Raymond said with no apparent meaning.

"I'm going over to the Safeway," she nodded with great determination as though she would show them!

Raymond knew that she wouldn't come back with groceries. She was making her trip to count the items of customers in the express lane to make sure that no one had more than nine items, as the sign above the lane directed. She always caught one or two who had more.

He opened the door for her and he watched the red socks beneath the infuriated woman, walk across the street.

In half an hour, the red socks returned. The face on the top of the body whose feet they protected, was as red as they were.

"Raymond!" she ordered, "Is that bum in?"

"Mr. Dunston?"

"You've learned. Is he in?"

"I think he's still in. I haven't seen him walk out unless he went through the garage."

"Wait until he hears what I heard," and she pushed the inner glass door as she nodded. She stormed over to the elevators.

Within a minute she was pounding on Moose Dunston's door.

"One second," the voice from inside yelled. "Be there in a second."

"Oh, I have time," she said back to him as though it was a warning that she wouldn't go away.

He opened the door, his hair disheveled and his tie loose around an open collar. "Why, hello, Miss–Miss–" he didn't know her name.

"Never mind. I have some information that I think you'll be most interested in hearing. What is–What is–" and she unfolded a small piece of paper with her handwriting on it. "What is the Mutual Defense Treaty of 1954?"

He looked confused at her question. He knew the answer but it seemed totally out of character for her to care, and to care so much that she would pound on his door to find out. "Why that's–listen; come on in. It's a little messy in here right now–I've been doing some writing, but come on in."

She did and she took one disgusted look around his apartment and plopped down on his sofa, her red socks adding a new brilliance to the drab colors of his old furniture the building had provided.

She read her note again. "Well, Mr. Expert," she was mad, "The Mutual Defense Treaty of 1954. Do you or do you not know what it is?"

"That's the treaty between us and the Republic of China on Taiwan. Why do you ask?"

"Because. Because. Do you know that we're going to rip it up?"

"What do you mean?"

"That's right."

"What do you mean, we're going to rip it up?"

"I know," she said. "Do you know what's going to happen tonight?"

He thought for a while and nodded. "The president's going to make a speech. Is that what you mean?"

She nodded and looked down at her scrawled note. "That's right. And do you know what he's going to say?" She stared at Moose while she nodded.

He shook his head slowly. "No. No, I don't."

"That we're going to–" and she looked back at her scrawled note, "recognize the PRC. What's that?"

Moose had a look of amazement. "Where did you hear this?"

"Never mind. What's the PRC?"

He answered very slowly. "The People's Republic of China. The mainland. Red China." He felt as though he was letting her in on a secret when, in fact, indeed she was letting him in on a secret.

"All right," and she looked at her paper, "We're going to recognize the

PRC and that means—so I understand—that he accepted all the conditions set by the PRC." She continued reading her note, "including the breaking of the Mutual Defense Treaty of 1954 with the ROC. What does the ROC mean?"

"The Republic of China. The one on Taiwan. The mainland calls itself the People's Republic, not just the Republic. Did you write that piece of paper?"

"I did. I wrote down exactly what I heard. How does that strike you?"

He sat down on a wooden chair opposite her. "I don't believe it."

"How's that for the latest?"

"I believe that you misinterpreted something—some conversation that perhaps you didn't understand."

Her lips tightened, her eyes inflamed, and her voice became very harsh as she nodded, looking at her note. "We're going to recognize the PRC and we accept all the conditions set by the PRC including our troops out, breaking of relations with the ROC, and the breaking of the" and she added a word, "big Mutual Defense Treaty of 19—" and she looked at him "and 54 with the ROC."

"Ma'am," he said as he got up and started pacing the floor. "Please tell me where you heard that."

She raised her head and jutting out her chin she said, "The Safeway!" There was a tone of victorious authority.

Moose looked confused. "The Safeway? The grocery? Are they making policy over there now?"

"That's right."

"The Safeway?"

"Standing in the express lane; they were there."

"Who was there?"

"Never mind. I've said too much. They had just come from a meeting in the West Wing, they said. And that, Mr. Expert, is the end of your big Mutual Defense Treaty of 19 and 54!"

It wasn't really his treaty, it was Ike's, but that wasn't the point. "You're quoting what you heard?"

She nodded slowly.

He slumped in a cushioned chair, his arms on each arm of the chair, his legs spread and extended as far as they would go without splitting off from the rest of his body. "That's unbelievable that President Carter would do that."

"Just remember where you heard it," she nodded.

"We can't do that."

"Just remember who found it out for you."

"Good Lord, I hope that you're wrong. I know what to do—" and he went to the phone and dialed quickly. "Is Dan there? This is Moose Dunston....Okay.... Okay.... Yeah, good, Merry Christmas to you, too, Eileen. Yes, I'll hold."

Miss Red Socks kept nodding at Moose as though to say, "You'll see that I know what I'm talking about!"

He cupped his hand over the mouthpiece and looked over at Miss Red Socks. "He'd know. He would know, believe me, and I'm sure that what you heard was just some idle conversation and misguided speculation."

"No need to ask him." Her nodding was becoming a constant vertical pendulum.

"He'd know."

"He doesn't know. They know. I know. You could know, Mr. Expert."

"But I certainly thank you for telling me what you heard."

"You'll see. You'll see," she said. She got up, she opened the door for herself, and while still nodding, she slammed the door shut behind her.

By that time Moose's contact had come to the phone.

"Hi, Dan. Listen, I heard a rumor. It sounds pretty far-fetched to me but I wanted to verify that it's not true. Could it be that President Carter's going to recognize the PRC?.... I know, I know.... No, I don't think so either.... No, that wouldn't be possible, but I heard a rumor.... Sure.... Well, okay.... Sure, I'll wait...."

Moose's contact said there was a policy meeting going on across the hall and that he'd walk in, find out if they were talking about the president's speech, and come back to the phone.

Minutes passed.

"Yes, I'm still here," Moose said as Dan returned to his end of the phone line. "You mean it?...Really?...Really?...No, I won't...I know, I know...God! Can you believe it?...I know.... Okay.... That's something.... Yes.... Okay.... Good-bye.... Yeah.... Okay.... You too have a great Christmas, Dan.... Thanks.... Thanks.... Bye."

Miss Red Socks overheard very accurate information.

Moose reached for the phone again, this time calling San Clemente. President Nixon did not find what Moose was saying as credible. He had assumed that should this decision have been made by President Carter, that President Carter would have sought President Nixon's advice, or at least President Nixon would have been informed by President Carter. President Nixon questioned Moose about his source. Moose did not mention Miss Red Socks or the express lane at the Safeway or the president would have thought he was crazy—but he did tell him about Dan, and that Moose had absolute confidence in Dan's reliability.

President Nixon sounded noticeably shook.

After the televised speech from the Oval Office in the evening, President Carter leaned back in his chair and joyfully said, "Applause throughout the nation!"

At the same time, Miss Red Socks walked with hard, firm, determined steps down the fourth floor hallway of the Potomac Plaza. Moose Dunston was already opening his door, knowing she would be there.

"Well, Mr. Expert, what now?"

"Wow!" he said.

"He didn't break the big treaty, but don't think for a minute that I didn't hear right."

He shook his head. "You heard right. They weren't wrong about the big treaty. He just didn't mention it because he didn't want to say what concessions he gave the PRC. He gave them everything they wanted, with no reciprocity."

"We're breaking the big treaty?"

"From what he said, we had to agree to everything and we got nothing. We're breaking it. Our troops will leave. We'll break diplomatic relations with the ROC. That's what he said by everything he didn't say. He referred to the Republic as 'Taiwan.' According to what he said, it's no more than a piece of geography, that's all."

"So you see?"

"I see. You were right."

That night Moose decided to spend less time at the White House, the State Department, the Pentagon, and Capitol Hill, and more time wandering around the Safeway, especially near the express lane.

Jonas was in Cavendish, Vermont, the new home of Aleksandr Solzhenitsyn. Unlike when he met Solzhenitsyn in Zurich, in Cavendish he had two homes. His family lived in one home and down a walking path there was another structure where the imposing, bearded and kind-eyed Solzhenitsyn was authoring a new book. After lunch in Home Number One, Jonas was escorted on the short walkway through the snow to Home Number Two where Solzhenitsyn and Jonas exchanged what they learned from those torturous prison experiences both had endured. When Jonas told him about his beliefs regarding time and distance and honor, Solzhenitsyn smiled.

"Honor! Honor! That is all there is! We have come to the same conclusions from our experiences! Do you know how I kept from signing an absurd confession the Soviets demanded I sign? My dear Colonel Valadovich, they sat me in a barren room at a wooden table with two uniformed men hovering over me. On the table were documents they had prepared for me, and a pen for me to sign those documents. From the next room there was the sound of a woman screaming. I knew it was a common technique. They would do it to get signatures from prisoners. They would say it was your wife or your mother or your sister, and they would say they would stop the torture when the prisoner signed the statement. Maybe it was who they said it was, maybe it was an actress, maybe it was a recording, but the prisoner didn't know. I didn't know."

"How did you keep from signing?"

"I pretended that everyone I loved had been in a train wreck. A horrible train wreck in which all of them were killed. Too bad. Too bad, but it happens. So all I had left in the world was my honor. That's all that was left. If that were to be gone, there would be nothing."

"Then we have come to the same conclusion, haven't we?"

The telephone rang, and Solzhenitsyn walked quickly to it. "It must be important," he said. "They do not interrupt me for small things."

Solzhenitsyn said practically nothing more than "I see. I see. I see," as he listened over the receiver. He hung up and looked over at Jonas. "It is so very foolish! Fools!"

"What happened?"

"China. Your weak, your very weak President Carter is giving them diplomatic recognition."

"What?"

"You Americans throw away friends like pits of a pear!"

"What did he say about Taiwan?"

"Nothing. It is, to him, another pit, down your garbage disposals in your kitchens!"

At noon on Tuesday, the Hawk and the Dove Restaurant, a few blocks from the U.S. Capitol Building, was filled with Representatives and Senators who had quickly come back to Washington from vacation, all discussing the surprising China decision of President Carter. There was only one booth in which the customers were not discussing China. Ted Murphy was unsuccessfully reaching for Anne's knee under the table. "Annie, I got a proposition for you."

"I don't accept propositions, Murph'," she answered, drawing herself away from him in the booth.

Ted withdrew his hand with a laugh. "You don't even know what I'm goin' to propose!" He put his hand on the table, his fingers spread to exhibit they were going nowhere.

"That's better," Anne said. "I can imagine what you want from me. That's why I insisted on lunch instead of dinner with you. You can't be trusted when the sun goes down."

Ted shrugged. "I can't be trusted when the sun is up, either. The sun and the moon have no influence on my conduct with my victims!"

"What do you want from me, something straight or kinky? You're not going to get either, you know."

"What I want is so straight you'll think I've lost my virility."

"What virility?"

"Hey, what do you mean? You loved my virility in Moscow, Annie, honey!"

"I would have made love with Peter Pan in Moscow, as long as it was on the ambassador's desk."

"All right, all right, enough insults. Now, hear me out."

"Before you begin, I assume that you and Linda are divorced and you're seeing Tommy every weekend and paying for his support, right?"

Ted looked down at the table. "Almost."

"Almost? Have you and Linda left each other?"

"In a way."

"Ted, please. There is no 'almost' and there is no 'in a way.' I wasn't born yesterday."

"Are you gonna listen to me, or what?"

"I'm all ears, Ted, even though I don't remember my ears being the part of me that interests you most."

"Okay. Here's my proposition—"

"Murph', I said that I don't want to hear a proposition, and I mean it."

"It's one word."

"A four letter word, if I know you."

He started counting on his fingers by tapping one finger at a time on the table. "Hey, it is! It is four letters! But it's not what you think."

"Go ahead. What's the word?"

Ted gave a smile and put his hand on hers. "Iran."

Anne drew her hand away and gave a confused expression. "Iran?"

Ted gave a gesture with his right hand, opening and closing his fingers against his thumb. "These folks here are all jabberin' about the wrong story. They're talkin' about China. What's to talk about? They can't undo what the president did. They just like to think they can. Annie, the story is Iran." Then he counted on his fingers again, this time against the air. "I'll give you another four letter word: Shah."

"What are you talking about, Ted?"

He was persistent enough to put his hand on top of hers again. "The Shah's gonna be a dead man. He's had it right. You know about what's goin' on in Iran?"

"A little. I haven't followed it." She withdrew her hand again.

"His kingdom or shahdom or whatever you call it is goin' to the dogs. The students are riotin' every day and he's frantically tryin' to keep things in check and he's lost his grip. There's a holy man waitin' in the wings. A man like Gandhi or Martin Luther King. He was exiled from Iran, then placed under house arrest in Iraq, and now he's in Paris. Annie, this guy is goin' to run Iran. He's like Christ, man. He has disciples, followers, the whole shootin' match. A holy man."

"Huh!"

"And it won't be long. They'll hang the Shah by his feet like the Italians did to Mussolini."

"Who's the holy man?"

"I can't pronounce his name. Ay Yahtuh Luh Somethin'."

"I just don't know enough about all that. I've been concentrating on other parts of the world. So what do you want me to do about it?"

"Okay. Okay. Here's the stuff. Now don't get excited. Hear me out and think about this. I'm doin' a show—a very important TV show. It's an exposé of the crimes of some of the folks our government does business with. And I'm focusin' on the Shah. That guy has secret police and all kinds of prisons and beatin's and tortures, and if I can get the goods on him—we can get the whole American public on the side of the holy man and change that part of the world! You with me?"

"So what do you want from me?"

"Get to Iran. You have seniority. You're waitin' for a post assignment and they got to pay attention to what you request as a post, right?"

"No, you're wrong. They don't have to do anything."

"But you got that seniority."

"It doesn't make any difference. They don't like me. They'll send me to some cuckoo place or keep me in D.C. Anyway, I've already requested Europe."

"Europe? What do you know about Europe?"

"Not very much, so I've been studying. I want to learn about it."

"Well, you don't know about Iran either, and that should be the same thing then. That's reason to want to go there—to learn about it."

"What do you want me to do if I get there? Why don't you go?"

"I'm gonna go. I'm goin', gal. I got my reservations at the Teheran Hilton with the rest of the press corps. I'm goin'."

"So you want to have me in bed every night in Teheran?"

"That's entered my mind. But that isn't all of it. You have a black passport and I don't."

"So what?"

"You have access to the diplomatic pouch. You can send things out of your post without goin' through their inspectors and customs. That's all I need. A few tapes sent back to the good ol' U.S.A. through the diplomatic pouch for me. That's all. Easy. No big deal. And maybe you can find out things I can't—at the embassy, you know. You with me?"

Anne drew herself away from him, while shaking her head back and forth. "You have such nerve!"

"That's what you like about me, Annie!"

"That's what I hate about you, Theodore. This TV show your planning, this project of yours. Do you show the torture in the Gulag of the Soviet Union? Do you show what goes on in Cuba? Or Czechoslovakia? Or is this one of your 'hate the U.S.' shows?"

"Boy, you've come 180 degrees to become Miss Yankee Doodle Dandy. Get off it and remember when life was fun, Annie."

"Grow up, Murph'. You've never grown up. You've never learned anything."

"You know how much I make, Annie? You know what I got goin'?"

"I don't care if you make a billion—a trillion dollars a minute. You'd do anything, wouldn't you?"

"What I'm doin' is a service, skirts!"

"A service for Theodore Murphy. God, I can't wait to get to Europe—if they give it to me."

"Oh, give me the word with your big morality. You're goin' to Europe because it's Daschle-land. Who do you think you're foolin'?"

Anne backed herself away from him, all the way to the edge of the booth. "What do you mean?"

"Annie, I got sources. You and Daschle. I know it. That's no state secret, you know. So he's in Greece and you want to be near him so you can mess around with him. I understand that. But don't give me the story that you want to learn about Europe as though it's such a learnin' thing. You're at the age when your juices are flowin' and Daschle's the lucky man. So good for him."

"You creep!"

Anne took a taxi back to the Agency. There was a message waiting on her desk to report to personnel right away.

David Scudder, the personnel director, stood up from behind his desk and extended his hand to her as she walked in his office. "Congratulations, Anne. You've been assigned a plum! An important one! We have some good news for you on your next post."

She very excitedly asked, "In Europe?"

"Better than any place in Europe at this time of history!"

"China? Do you mean China?"

"More important than China right now."

"Where?"

"Iran!"

Mark was more emphatic than Anne had ever heard him. "Don't!" He yelled over the phone from Athens. "Please, Anne, don't! Just refuse! They can't do anything to you. Just refuse! Please!"

"Mark, from Teheran I can come to Athens every once in a while. It isn't that far. It can work out."

"It's very far. But that isn't the question right now. Iran is a dangerous place, Anne. It's falling apart. The Shah is holding on by the skin of his teeth. Anything can happen there. I don't want you there."

"I'll be able to buy a Persian rug there. I left mine behind in Hong Kong and you'll remember that it was your fault."

There was no response from Mark.

"Mark, I'm getting real complete briefings before I go. I'll be fine." There was still no response. "Mark, are you listening to me?"

"I'm listening."

"All kinds of briefings: political, economic, diplomatic, historical. I'm taking a quick course in Farsi at the Foreign Service Institute. I'll be all right. You know me. I can take care of myself, Mark. I can take care of myself," she repeated, but this time she didn't say 'Mark'. This time, with an ultra-feminine sway to her voice, she said, "Mr. Daschle."

"Well, you should get a briefing from me."

"That sounds like fun."

"It isn't fun. You know what Carter ought to do with Iran right now? Right now he should be calling an emergency meeting of NATO and CENTO. World leaders flying to Brussels for an emergency meeting like that would signal the National Front in Iran that we'll guard Iran's security, and that we won't allow that country to be taken over by fanatics who want to bring about a fundamentalist revolution. If we don't, the Shah can fall. And I don't want you there when that happens."

"Mark, you're still more of a hawk than I am. I really don't know much about all those things."

"It's not a question of being a hawk or a dove. Nothing but disaster is ahead. Anne, if you accept that post, then I'm going to go to Teheran and take you out of there."

"Wwwww! You'll kidnap me?"

"Yes."

"Do you promise? Handcuffs? A blindfold?"

"Whatever it takes."

"Then the only thing I can do is give you the 999 nights left that I owe you. I can wear my new dress! You'll love it!"

"Anne, don't do this now. Don't make light of this. I don't want you there. You don't know what can happen there, and neither do I. The Agency isn't doing you any favors. Believe me, they know what they're doing. Say you won't do it. Anne, I just want you to be safe."

There was a long silence. Then, "Mr. Daschle?"

"Yes?"

There was another long silence and a very soft, "I love what you're saying. I love that you care." They listened to each other breathe for a while. "Mr. Daschle?"

"Yes?"

"I won't disappoint you."

"Well, you were right, Moose," President Nixon said to Moose over the phone the following Tuesday. "You had good sources."

The Safeway express lane? "Mr. President, aside from the depression I felt regarding President Carter's speech, it was worse when I heard on Saturday morning—I heard it on the radio, that you and President Ford applauded President Carter's decision on China."

"And Kissinger, too, they said."

"I recognize that no statement came directly from you, but those I talk to have extreme bitterness about what they heard you said. A lot of what was left of your constituency is off the bandwagon again."

"Off the bandwagon again, yeah."

"Now, without being presumptuous, I want to make a suggestion—a statement you should make."

"Sure."

"This is your voice—I believe you should say, 'I started the process in the hope of bringing about full diplomatic relations with the People's Republic of China at such time as they rescinded their three demands upon the United States.' Period. That's it. You wouldn't be offending anyone. It's saying you wouldn't have done it this way, but without saying it in those words. It would be a statement that you wouldn't agree to abrogating the Mutual Defense Treaty or taking our troops out of the ROC or breaking diplomatic relations with the ROC. Now, I don't care about your reaction over the phone. I'm suggesting it to you because of the whole principle of the thing. I'm not alone on this. Your constituency is dwindling."

"Yeah, I know. The difficulty, of course, here, is that neither Henry nor I did anything of the sort of what they said. We didn't do that. Both of us said we were going to study the thing and we were not going to make any public comment at this point. That's what we both said. We've been in touch, of course, all the way through. And this statement about Ford, Kissinger and me agreeing with Carter is something that they just put out. It wasn't put out by Carter, it was put out by the White House, whatever that means. So I've been in touch with Henry. In fact we're going to talk again this afternoon, and see just about what line we can take. But I agree with him. This is all just for your own information and should not go any further at this point, not now, but we're trying to think of a way to see to it that we don't get in some shouting match with the White House, you know—that sort of thing. We're trying to think of a way to handle the situation and we frankly haven't come up with it yet. But, as a matter of fact, this ticked Henry off for having been quoted as having endorsed it. You see what I mean? So there isn't any question on where we both stand on it. It's just a question—that they put something out like this."

"The term I heard was 'applauded.' That you applauded."

"We both had exactly the same conversation: that we would study the matter but that we would not make a statement at this point."

"As long as no statement of denial or a correction is made, people believe the White House release to be true—that you're for Carter's decision."

"Sure, I understand."

"I mean, you could have had the same deal with the PRC when you went there in '72, but you didn't accept that deal. They gave you the same three preconditions and you rejected them: abrogate the treaty, get our troops off Taiwan, and break relations with Chiang."

"You're saying just what Henry said. That's correct. That's absolutely correct."

"You said, 'No.' When Ford became president, he said, 'No.' The great breakthrough of Friday night was simply Carter saying, 'Yes.'"

"That's right. That's right. Now, a line that you might use in your articles is this. You might say, 'I notice that the media, as you might expect, is saying that this is a very courageous decision. When does it become courageous to cave?' That's all there is to it, I mean—nothing else. Just one of those things. They just caved in."

"Yes."

"But it's a fait accompli now and we've got to find a way—it can't be rescinded, you know. Unfortunately all this jazz about whether he had the legal right to terminate the treaty and so forth and so on. They—it just—"

"It's not going to work to fight him legally?"

"No, no, there's no way, Moose. I checked that out already."

"It's done?"

"It's done. And presidents do have the right. They can rescind treaties."

"Even though a treaty is made with the advice and consent of the Senate? You don't need the advice and consent to rescind?"

"Apparently not. Although that issue's going to be made, you see. And really that is where the next round has to go. It has to go to the Congress. You may get a resolution, you may get some sort of a thing which some of the boys are working on now, of which I'm aware. I'm quite aware of this. It isn't going to work."

"But regardless of what Congress does—regarding a statement from you—"

"It's just a question of how to handle it in a way that's firm but not necessarily belligerent. You know what I mean? I don't want to say, 'you lied about that,' you know what I mean? But they did."

"I know they did and I know you won't say that. But—"

"Let me talk to Henry about it. In this case he and I should go along together. We're in a perfect position to do so, because he feels exactly as I do. If anything—he feels even stronger than I do because he feels that—you know, he's sensitive about being misquoted. I'm used to it. Henry's in New York today. We'll talk before the end of the day and get out something, probably not before tomorrow. But we'll get out something, I can assure you. Moose, you keep hitting 'em. Now, when are you going to Asia? Or are you just going to keep writing from your perch in Washington there?"

"In my perch. Until I'm told otherwise."

"You like working for Hanson Alpert?"

"He's fine. He leaves me alone. My opinion is my opinion. I don't have to check anything."

"Well, I know you like that. Should I ask? I haven't asked you recently. How about that Chinese girl?"

"Yeah. Well, I can imagine how she feels about what Carter did Friday night."

"Pretty bad? They feel pretty bad over there in Hong Kong?"

"I haven't talked to her. But I can just imagine. I don't remember if I told you, but she was ready to kill me in '71 when you said you were going to Peking."

"She was?"

"She sure was."

"Well—you can tell her, very honestly, that you were against it. I remember that, all right. That should get you off the hook with her."

"I know how they feel in Taiwan. I don't know if you heard, but this morning President Chiang said that the United States made a horrible move, and that we never severed relations with a friendly country before; that this is the first time. And he said that we've repeatedly reaffirmed our intentions to retain our diplomatic relations with the ROC and to honor our treaty commitments and now they're all broken. The United States, he said, can't be expected to have the confidence of any free nation in the future. And the People's Republic's statement says that the reunification of Taiwan is entirely China's internal affair, without any pledge not to use force. You know, they referred to your Shanghai Communiqué, but they didn't refer to the complete U.S. position in that communiqué, including that we want a peaceful resolution. Worse than that, they suggested that you wrote in the communiqué that the United States maintained there was one China and Taiwan was part of it, rather than what you did write–that the Chinese on both sides of the strait maintained that position–not us–you didn't write us, you wrote them. Mister President, at least Carter could have made his recognition of their government conditional on the PRC pledging not to use force to take over Taiwan and he didn't even do that. Not even that. And he could have demanded some guarantees on Hong Kong come 1997. But nothing. And think of what the people of China think–the millions–the billion who would like to be free."

"It's a fait accompli, Moose. It's done. Don't look back. Look forward. There's a new year ahead: the last year of the decade. Remember how it started. We were both at the White House, weren't we?"

"Yes, Mr. President. I'm glad you asked me to be there with you. I'm very grateful for that."

"Well, in a couple weeks it will be ten years, won't it? Make the best of the next ten, Moose. Make them as good as the way the last ten started."

FORTY-EIGHT
MARG BAR SHAH! MARG BAR AMRIKA!
1979

In 1979 the dissolve from Europe to Asia began in Greece where, at times, there was a quick smell of urine, but then it was gone. It was where one boy in the city square would sit in a crouched squat position balancing his behind one half-inch from the ground, but it would only be one boy there doing that. It was where the written language had few similarities to English, but there were some. It was where "As" began to sound like "Ahs" but not all of them. It was where men and beasts carried some heavy loads, but rolled most of them. It was where there were thick, unpatterned crowds in the streets at night, but they didn't wail.

Across the Aegean Sea in Turkey, the dissolve was over. The smell of urine was not just quick anymore. There were dozens and dozens of crouched boys and men in the city center. The written language had no similarity to English. The "As" were pronounced as "Ahs." The loads were equal to or heavier than their animal or human carriers. There were bazaars thick with wailing crowds and beggars, and small running rats were common colleagues.

At least once a month and often once a week, Mark Daschle went between those two nations representing United States mediation in the Cyprus conflict. At times he would stay in Turkey's capital city of Ankara, but most of the time he was at his post in Athens, Greece.

When he looked at his desk calendar and saw that large number 14 of February, his thoughts immediately went back to that February the 14th in New York with Anne. He didn't want to appear to be overly sentimental about an anniversary of sorts, particularly St. Valentine's Day, but he had an irresistible urge to phone her at her Teheran post to let her know he was thinking about her. He didn't have to.

"An Anne Whitney is on the phone, Mr. Daschle," his secretary told him over the intercom line. "She says she's with our embassy in Iran."

"Yes!" he said. "She is! Put her on!"

And then came a click and Anne's voice. "Hello, Mr. Daschle!"

His face was one large smile. "Hello, Miss Whitney."

"Oh, don't call me that. I won't report you if you call me Anne. I just phoned to wish you a happy anniversary of a wild Valentine's Night. Wild for you. Tame for me."

"Happy anniversary!" He did it. "Are you okay?"

"I'm fine."

"How are things in Teheran?"

"I don't know. They were all right when I left."

"When you left? Where are you?"

"Now?"

"Yes, now!"

"In your reception room."

Only Anne.

He hung up the phone and walked toward his closed office door while he quickly straightened both his hair and his tie with two quick sweeps. He didn't need to open the door. She did. She looked more seductive than any sight he had witnessed since the last time he saw her. Of all things, she was in a short and wispy dress although the weather was a good 20 degrees too cold for such sheerness.

Mark's secretary was looking at some papers in an effort to pretend disinterest in both the guest, and the reaction of the host. The devil with his secretary's presence, Mark kissed Anne without any hesitancy and without any let-up. Anne looked over at Mark's secretary, then took a deep breath and yelled, "Rape!"

Mark's secretary smiled. "I don't think so."

He sat at his desk, and asked her to sit down. Anne, of course, sat on his desk facing him.

"You don't like the chairs in here, Anne?"

"They're for men to sit on."

"Anne, you can drive me crazy when you're so close."

"That's the idea. What are you doing tonight, Mr. Daschle?"

"I have no plans."

"I do."

"Anne, first let me ask you what I want to know. I want to know about Teheran, about your job, your safety, your–"

"Teheran is in anarchy, my job is good, and I stay safe."

"You shouldn't be there and no American should be there. If President Carter and Secretary Vance didn't know that last year, they certainly should have known it when the Shah left, what is that, a month ago? Almost a month ago. And then when the Ayatollah Khomeini came back and started acting like the chief of state, they should have closed the embassy. Do you know what Andrew Young, our Ambassador to the U.N. said last week?" And then he answered his own question, "That Khomeini will be somewhat of a saint when we get over the panic. Don't they get what's going on? Anne, get out of there."

"I don't want to talk about it, Mr. Daschle. I want to talk about tonight."

"Have you seen Ted Murphy in Teheran? He's there, you know, giving reports on television to back home." He had never gotten rid of his fear that Ted was in her life.

"He calls me every day begging to see me. I haven't seen him once and I'm not going to. He wants me to be a source. I'll take my chances with Khomeini before Murphy."

His face suddenly became free of every line, and his smile was like that of a joyous boy. "When did you get into Athens?"

"Last night. Very late."

"Have you seen anything here yet?"

"Nothing. Just the Hilton, and now you."

"I want to show you Athens. How long will you be here?"

"Just today and tonight. I've never really liked Europe."

"You haven't!? Why not?"

"The hotel keys are too heavy. They make them so heavy that you can't keep them with you—you always have to turn them in at the desk when you go out anywhere. I don't like that. And when you try to unlock your door you never know which way to turn them. They have to do something about the keys."

"That's an unusual reason not to like Europe! Athens is a wonderful place. I'll show it to you tonight."

"I told you—I already have our plans for tonight."

"All right! What's your plan?"

"The Plaka! It's a very swinging district!"

"How do you know about the Plaka if you've never been to Athens before?"

"I know all things that other women either don't know, or do know and pretend not to like." And she leaned down from the desk-top perch so her lips were almost touching his.

"You are something!" Mark said.

"I know."

"Anne, I have a meeting with Ambassador McCloskey. Stay here. I shouldn't be long. But let me get up, please."

"That depends. Will you give the ambassador a message for me?"

"What?"

She gave him a kiss that was beyond the experience of most men or beasts.

"No," he said as he got up. "I won't give the ambassador that message."

She, of course, used the time alone to adjust herself on the couch in a position that would entice him, but when he came in, his expression told her this was not the time for a seduction. "Sit up," he said and she did.

He pulled up a chair opposite her. "Thank God you came here, Anne."

"Why?"

"And I don't want you to go back to Teheran."

"What's up?"

"Your embassy has been taken over."

Anne opened her mouth but no words came out. She shook her head.

"Your embassy's been taken over, and you can't go back."

"What happened?"

"Your ambassador's office, Ambassador Sullivan's office was hit with automatic weapon fire. A lot of it. All the windows were blown out and bullets kept coming into the office. Some of the staff was in his office but he was down the hall at the time—in the communications vault. You know where that is?"

She nodded slowly. "Who was hurt?"

"His staff hit the floor. Bullets were flying all over."

"Is anyone dead?"

"I don't know yet. Listen. Whoever was doing it, the revolutionaries –they knew where the Ambassador's office was. There were revolutionaries all over rooftops shooting in. Then the revolutionaries came over the embassy wall, shooting in every direction. They stormed the embassy up to the second floor, up to Ambassador Sullivan's office. But, as I said, he was in the communications vault and when he was told what was happening he started shredding documents. He ordered the Marine Guards not to fire anything but tear gas at the invaders. The embassy was surrounded and he felt he was in an embassy war he couldn't win. Practically everyone on staff went to the vault and they were all shredding documents. By this time the revolutionaries had taken over most of the Chancery Building. They won. The ambassador left the vault to go to his office and he had told the others to leave the vault as well, and to surrender the building. The revolutionaries lined everyone up–maybe twenty or so of the staff there–they lined them up in the reception room of the Ambassador's office. The revolutionaries ordered them to take everything out of their pockets and purses. They were all frisked and searched. The revolutionaries asked some of them if they were Moslems. If they said no, they beat them. The ambassador tried to reason with them, but there was no reasoning. And that's the way it stands."

"Oh, my God! Do you know how everyone is?"

"No. I don't know. All of this just happened. Ambassador McCloskey got the word from State while I was with him just now. I excused myself as quick as I could to get back here to tell you. You appear and disappear so quickly and I never know where you are, so I wanted to get back here before you took off somewhere, like back to Teheran. I never know what you're going to do. You can't go back."

"Mark–I want to know how everyone is. I have good friends there."

"I don't know, Anne. I told you everything I know."

"Please find out. Go back to McCloskey's office. Please!"

"You promise me. You promise me that you'll be here in this office when I get back?"

"I promise."

He nodded. "I'll find out everything I can. Just wait for me."

"I promise."

"And I'm telling him you're here."

"Fine. Okay. Please!"

From the ambassador's office, Mark called his secretary and said he would be a long time, to cancel all meetings that had been scheduled, and he asked her to take Anne to the commissary to eat.

After lunch he called Anne from the ambassador's office. "Everything's okay, Anne. They're okay. No one's hurt and they're all safe. Listen, I'm still going to be a while. I'm finding out all the details. I'll have an embassy car take you to your hotel and I'll meet you there when I get done."

They sat on the outside balcony of her room at the Hilton facing the Acropolis across the city, the Parthenon imposing on its hilltop as the sun was going down. They had food and drink brought in from room service.

"And so," Mark said, "it ended as weirdly as it began. Somehow, a counter-attack took place with orders from the Provisional Government–Khomeini–for the revolutionaries to get out of the embassy."

"They all got out?"

"Yes."

"And no one, not even one person was hurt, Mark?"

"As far as we know, every American is okay. That's what State says, anyway."

"And the locals? The locals who work for us?"

"They're okay. Some revolutionaries got killed by their own fire. One idiot aimed his machine gun at the Marine Guard in the booth at the main door, but the glass in front of the guard was bulletproof. He fired at the marine, and the machine gun bullets ricocheted and hit the idiot who was shooting. Killed him."

Anne said nothing.

"I can't tell you, Anne, how glad I am that you were here, instead of being in all of that. What a miracle. It's just–I'm so glad this was the anniversary."

"Happy Valentine's Day!"

"I found out today what you must have been going through since Khomeini came back to Iran a couple weeks ago."

Anne nodded. "It's been pretty bad. The streets are full of what they call the 'komitehs', it means 'committees.' They patrol the streets and they arrest and kill people whenever they feel like it. A lot of them are kids. It's like the Red Guards were in '67 in China. Since the Shah left last month you can't go outside with any safety. Thousands of people have been killed. No one can do anything about it. The government doesn't want to do anything about it. I'm surprised Khomeini stopped the takeover of the embassy today."

"We ought to close that embassy. Just get out of there. Get every American out of there. Enough is enough. And if Washington is dumb enough to keep it open, I don't want you there."

"I'm okay. I live in an apartment building just across the alley from the embassy. It's filled with embassy staff people. It's safe. I'll call Barry Rosen at the embassy tomorrow–or if I can't get through, I'll call Washington–Reinhardt or Olekswi at the Agency, and see what they want me to do."

"Anne, you're not going back to Teheran."

"Mark–I'll call and find out. Mark–I'll see. Mark–it's my career."

"Anne–it's my love."

That stunned her. They stared at each other and her eyes were becoming misty. "Do you mean that?"

He hesitated, having been unprepared for the words that had just come out of his own mouth.

She got up from her chair and kneeled down by him, and she kissed him. "Do you love me, Mark? Is that what you meant by that?"

He nodded.

She smiled. "It is? It is what you meant by that?" She wanted him to say the words. "Mr. Daschle, whether you do or you don't, I think you better know that I love you so much."

He swallowed very hard.

Then there was a piece of magic on that balcony facing the Acropolis. Their faces were so close and they were so stirred by their own words and thoughts that studying each other's face was a kind of nakedness. What could have been considered some small physical flaw on someone else was a beautiful feature. Every characteristic, every expression, every movement, was a treasure given by God. This studying of each other's face became an ecstasy.

It took a while but it came. "I love you, Anne, and I think I always did."

It was such a relief for her to hear the words that she didn't want to over-emphasize their importance, risking he would take them away. She simply gave the softest kiss. "Even when you hated me?"

"I never hated you."

"But you love me?"

"I love you, Anne."

"Then we can go to the Plaka?" It was her way.

"Let's just stay here. I'm worn out from today. We don't need to have an adventure every night we're together."

"Yes we do, Mr. Daschle. Oh, yes we do. I'm not going to ever let down on that. I can't wait to tell you what I did in Morocco! Every night will be a different adventure for you—and me. Not one night will be the same as the other. I don't want you to be bored by me. I don't want me to be bored by me. I will not allow you or me to feel a lack of excitement. Not ever. I'm not going to allow either of us to think of me in one way. There will be no routine. Ever. Routine is what kills marriages, isn't it? It's not going to kill ours."

"Our—" and he stopped.

"You have 999 nights coming. After tonight you'll have 998 nights left and then I'll think of more and more to last a lifetime. And if you want them, then you'll have to marry me." Moving fast. "I'm sorry, Mr. Daschle, but there are no negotiations on this. Tonight is your last free sample!"

"You're unbelievable."

"Yes. I am. And I'm irresistible, too, aren't I?"

"Yes. You are."

They walked through the Plaka district like two young lovers in a journey of surrealism. The most proper man in the foreign service who dealt with diplomats from around the world and attended receptions in tuxedoes and listened and even gave the most appropriate toasts to heads of state was, this Saint Valentine's night, walking streets that had no interest in embassies and consulates and world affairs; only private ones. There was a powerful feeling of intoxication from the holding of Anne's small hand as she led the way to their destination, and he let her be the usher because it added to the inappropriateness of the night. He continually looked around him to search for those who might recognize him as a representative of the U.S. Embassy, while they both knew that with one tighter clasp of his hand he could lead them both out of this area. He was enjoying himself too much to do that.

Anne led him from the brilliant streets to a barren dark alleyway. "There!" she said as she gave a short movement of her hand that held his. "Up those stairs!" She was gesturing to a long diagonal wooden stairway built by the side of a dilapidated building. The stairway looked like an after-thought, leading to a second-floor door serving what appeared to be an entrance to a storehouse loft.

Maybe that's what it once was, but it had been transformed to a club of sorts without much embellishment from earlier days. The bar was host to only three men with empty bar stools between them, all three looking totally absorbed in nothing. There should have been a sign outside advertizing "Place of Men's Unhappiness." Mark felt secure that there was no one in this hovel who would recognize him as being from the embassy. There were six small, round wooden tables with two of them occupied with pretty young women sitting around them. They were talking with each other and laughing, and one group of three women was playing cards. If the men had come to the bar for the company of women, they either didn't have the money to keep the drinks flowing for them, or they didn't have the courage to approach them. The women who were paid on commission by the club to interest any unescorted man who entered, seemed much happier playing cards and talking among themselves rather than performing any acts of entrapment.

But not Anne. She was more professional than the professionals. She led Mark to the bar and she sat on a stool to the right of one of the three unhappy men, leaving a stool to her right side for Mark. The man she chose to sit beside had a stubble of what was not yet a beard, and he looked as though he had a bad day, or a bad week, or a bad life. Anne made sure she brushed against him as she sat down and, as though it was totally unintentional, her skirt went up to her thighs as she sat, to the delight of this otherwise wretched, sorrowful, glum figure. That exhibition was meant as an exciting reminder to Mark of how she behaved in any surrounding in which she could get away with a display of her late-found femininity.

"Hey, Anne," Mark said, giving a short gesture with his head, his eyes looking at her skirt resting on her thighs.

"What, Mr. Daschle?"

"You know what." Then he whispered, "Watch your skirt!"

"Oh," and she looked down at her lap. "This? Oh, of course. I can take care of that." She did. She raised it higher.

"Anne!"

The man to her other side had his mouth open. *Then there is a God,* he was thinking.

Anne leaned over to Mark. "Don't get excited, Mark. It's less than he'd see on the beach if I was wearing a bathing suit." She always used that line to excuse herself.

"But you're not on the beach in a bathing suit."

"That's what makes it so much better for him—and for me. How about a daiquiri?"

Mark nodded, and ordered the daiquiri for her and a scotch and water for himself. After the drinks were brought to them, Mark clicked his glass with hers. "To another Valentine's Day."

She took a quick gulp, then set the glass down. "Will you excuse me for a moment?"

"Sure."

She got up from the stool to the dismay of her other bar-stool companion, who accepted her departure as life's injustices coming back. Anne walked over to the table where the three young women were playing cards. To the surprise of Mark, who thought he had built an immunity from being surprised by Anne, she pulled up a wooden chair and joined the card players. They accepted her immediately and dealt her a hand of casino, and they all talked and laughed together.

Mark and the man who sat two stools away from him glanced at each other. Although the stranger didn't say a word, his expression showed satisfaction that Mark had been left alone, since her departure gave some evidence that there was someone else in the world who was disappointed.

One of the women playing cards with Anne called the four women over from the next table. They came running over and there was more talking and smiling and laughing—and then a lot of nodding.

Anne returned to the bar with all the women who were there. "Happy Valentine's Day, Lucky!" Anne said to Mark. Now Mark was neither Mr. Daschle nor Mark; he was Lucky, which was very appropriate for the moment. "These seven girls are your Valentine's Day gift from me! And they would like to join you and me, Lucky! They think you're the best looking thing that ever came to Athens! Girls, this is Lucky Smith!"

"Good to meet you," Mark or Lucky said hesitantly as he nodded his head at one and then the others.

"They don't speak English real well, but don't worry, Lucky! There isn't much reason to talk!"

"Anne, I'm not sure we should be doing this."

"You won't accept my gifts to you? What kind of a man are you?"

"I—I—"

Her new companions seemed happy enough about being the presents for him. Whether or not Anne was paying them, which he suspected, was not a question he was going to ask. A few of them were laughing and one of them leaned over and put her hand on the back of Mark's neck as another put her hand on his knee.

"You—you?" Anne asked parroting Mark's hesitancy.

"Oh, Anne!"

"In Morocco I had countless men at one time. I can't live with that memory knowing you wouldn't have something comparable. See what my conscience can do for you?"

"Anne!" He simply couldn't say anything other than her name. There were too many gorgeous faces for him to think of any dialogue.

"You know where we're going?" Anne asked without waiting for an answer. "The Acropolis! Have you ever spent the night with eight women at the Parthenon, Lucky?"

Lucky shook his head. It was not a difficult question. He didn't have to search his memory.

Anne had a broad smile. Her new companions were laughing. "Anastasia here knows a way we can avoid the guards! She's experienced up there! She knows the secret road the restorers are using! Imagine—just the eight of us with Athens at our feet and sculptures of Greek gods watching us!"

Mark never paid a bill to a bartender with more impatience. The man who was sitting a couple barstools down from Lucky watched the crowd of eight leave. He was an atheist again.

The ride was in a small taxi with Anastasia telling the driver her secret route up the Acropolis. The driver was having fun of his own with this load. It was difficult to know who was sitting on what lap but, of course, Anne made sure she was snuggled close to the driver. One girl was sitting next to her and another was on her lap. Mark, in the back seat, was being smothered by the other five.

When the top of the brilliantly lit Acropolis was reached, Anastasia asked how much they owed the driver. He replied in Greek but no one needed to understand the language to understand his reply, with its accompanying gestures which meant: "Nothing, if I can go with you."

Anne nodded. It was a deal.

There were a couple security men in the Parthenon so Anastasia led the group for a very short walk to the neighboring Erecthelon with five huge Greek gods looking down at them, and looking down at the city beneath them. Those Greek gods hadn't so closely witnessed a more bacchanalian evening since 400 B.C.

Mark wanted the dawn held back but it came in a brilliance that lit the beauty of the women that Anne had brought there, and the beauty of the city at their feet. Even with all that, Mark couldn't take his eyes off Anne who was more beautiful than any of the other women, and more beautiful than the city.

The taxi driver took the seven women back to the Plaka, and took Anne to her hotel, and took Mark to a corner not far from where he lived. He would walk the short distance because he didn't want his living quarters revealed.

In an hour and a half, Mark and Anne were seeing each other again at the embassy, both still filled with the breaths of last night. Even their toothpastes were unsuccessful in pretending last night was done.

Instead of Anne phoning, it was Mark who called the embassy in Teheran. He wanted to hear the instructions for her first-hand. He couldn't get through. He called the Agency in Washington.

"Tell her to get ready to come home, Mark," he was told. "We can get through to Ambassador Sullivan and we can ask him, but you can bet he'll say she shouldn't go back to Teheran right now. I talked to him this morning and he told me two U.S. Marine Guards are missing. He knows they were taken prisoner—by the revolutionaries. Khomeini isn't intervening."

"I didn't know that."

"We haven't made a release on that yet."

"Okay. What does Anne do right now?"

"Have her stand by the cable desk for her instructions."

"Okay."

"And Mark—you heard what happened to Dubbs yesterday, didn't you?"

"Who?"

"Ambassador Dubbs in Kabul, Afghanistan. Our ambassador there."

"No. What about him?"

"His car was abducted by some extremists there in Kabul. They brought him to a hotel and—and they murdered him."

Mark was silent, biting his lip.

"So we had a rough day yesterday, Mark. Things are unraveling. Look, I'll talk to Sullivan and we'll cable Whitney her orders in minutes."

Mark rode with her in the backseat of the embassy car to Athens Hellinikon Airport. Her head was on his shoulder, his arm embracing her, and he was kissing the top of her head, her hair, her ribbon.

Before kissing her good-bye at the waiting room of the gate at the airport, he told her that her next post would be with him; that the State Department allows and even encourages married couples to work together overseas.

"Do you know what you just said?"

He knew. He nodded.

"You're not even going to formally ask me?" It didn't make any difference to her. It was done.

"It would be unnecessary conversation. We have no time for that."

"Then we're engaged?"

He thought for a moment, and he nodded again.

"Sucker!" she said. And she laughed.

"I'm not a sucker. I'm the most fortunate man in the world."

"I'll make sure that's true!"

And again came the studying of each other's face. And then, as though they discovered kissing as something a man and woman could do, they did it from the softest to the most uncontrolled. Their conduct couldn't help but be watched by others in the waiting room of the gate. It didn't bother Mark, although something like this was unimaginable for him to have done publicly before. And it certainly didn't bother her. Being watched delighted Anne.

Washington, D.C. was becoming more alien to Anne than a foreign country. She decided to behave and be the "good little bureaucrat" for fear if she wasn't, that her conduct would be taken out on Mark when ever they found out Mark and Anne were to be married.

And so she said nothing when officials of the State Department showed little interest in a communist coup in the Caribbean island-nation of Grenada. She said nothing when she saw the State Department in virtual celebration when President Somoza left Nicaragua, under threat from the United States had he stayed. Two days later the Sandinistas took over the government of Nicaragua and she heard her colleagues saying to one another that human rights would now be restored. It was the same conversations she heard at the U.S. Embassy in Iran when the Ayatollah Khomeini was emerging in the distance as Iran's "savior."

She couldn't wait to get out of Washington. Anywhere. Preferably Greece, but she knew it wouldn't be Greece.

She knew where it was likely to be, and it was.

Anne was asked if she would go back to Teheran, the request put in the framework of it being voluntary but that "everything is returning to normal there, and it's important that we, as a nation, don't act as though we're intimidated. What happened in February was an aberration, with even some pluses to it, as it told us that the provisional government of Khomeini was sophisticated and knowledgeable enough to get the militants out of there right away. Khomeini's people felt as bad as we did about it. Those marines who were taken as prisoners have been freed. We're even going to allow the dependents of the staff to go back to Teheran very soon. Anne, you already have such a feel for the Persians, and you know so much of the language. But, of course, it's up to you."

Anne agreed to go back.

As a foreign service officer, she had to fly with a United States airline as first choice, even if the flight wasn't direct, and so she flew PanAm from Washington to New York to London to Teheran for an evening landing. On the last leg of the trip it became apparent that among the airliner's passengers, there was fear of the destination. One by one, the women on the airplane who were dressed in Western clothes, went to the plane's restrooms, emerging back to their seats in black chadors. They were covered in black with only their eyes exposed. Anne had no chador with her, but she did have a long gray coat, and when the "No Smoking" light went on and the announcement was made, she put on the coat and buttoned it up. A woman, now in a head to toe black abaya with a shoulder-length head scarf, who sat across the aisle bent over to Anne. "Remove your lipstick from your lips, or they may remove it themselves. They will put a razor blade in a handkerchief and then wipe your lips very hard. It has happened." She handed Anne a packet of Kleenex. Anne took the packet and wiped her lips as clean as she could get them.

Her black passport was of no consequence to the official at Teheran's Mehrabad Airport who wore fatigues and didn't look anything like an airport official. He rummaged through everything in her luggage and everything in her purse. The customs official took her small bottle of perfume from her purse and he threw the bottle in the waste basket by his side, the basket crammed with articles, some on the floor. He took a tube of lipstick from her purse.

"You use this?"

She didn't answer.

"You use this on your lips?"

"I write with it. I always write in red."

"It writes?"

"Yes."

He took a piece of paper, uncapped the top of the tube and made a long red mark going from the top to the bottom of the paper. He capped the lipstick and put it in his pocket. "You use it on your lips?"

"No."

"You are an American diplomat?"

"Yes."

"You are a friend of Shah?"

"I never met the Shah."

"Where is Shah now?"

"I don't know."

"I know where he is. He's in Cuernavaca, Mexico. First to Egypt, then Morocco, then Bahamas. He is a man without country. We will get him back and handle him. Or maybe he will die soon and the world will celebrate. You will celebrate?"

"I don't celebrate anyone's death."

"You are a friend of Shah?"

"I told you I never met him."

He stared at her and she stared back. For over a quarter minute there was nothing but the stares between the two. Then he asked, "Are you here for business or pleasure?"

"Are you kidding!?" She took a chance on being audacious. "You'd have to be crazy to come here for pleasure."

He laughed and in a wide sweep of his arm, he stamped her passport. "Welcome to Teheran, American diplomat!"

With relief she walked through the narrow aisleway by his booth.

"Miss Diplomat?" he called after her.

She felt a catch in her breath. "Yes?" she stopped but didn't turn around to face him.

"I know what you did with that red tube. You painted your lips, didn't you?"

She turned to face him. "Try it, if that's what you want to do. It's yours now."

"Those customs people are all new, Miss Whitney," the U.S. Marine driver told Anne, outside the airport. "They are all Revolutionary Guards." It wasn't the usual embassy car for the forty-five minute ride; it was a van with bullet-proof windows. The U.S. Marine opened the back door for her, slammed it, it gave a number of clicks and he got in the front and drove off with her.

The night streets were vacant except for occasional men walking with different colored arm bands and rifles and submachine guns. As the embassy car entered the city limits, Anne saw clubs and bars shuttered with scrawled, spray-painted, unreadable writing on the walls. She recognized one scrawl as "La Illah Illallah" which translated to "There is no God but Allah."

"They closed all the clubs?"

"Oh, yes. Ma'am, didn't they do that before you left?"

"Some of them, I guess. I didn't pay attention. Is Baccara still open?"

"Oh, no."

"Cave d'Argent?"

"No."

"Vanak?" She knew the clubs.

"None of them. They tried and executed the owners and some of the employees. Men and women both. Women in this country are back to where they were a thousand years ago, so you must be very careful. Trials last minutes."

"I know."

"Do you know that you don't live off Roosevelt Avenue anymore?"

"What do you mean?"

"The building–Bijon Apartments is still there, don't get me wrong, but the name of the avenue has been changed."

"To what?"

"Mobaracen."

"What does that mean?"

"I don't know, Miss Whitney."

"I should know. I took Farsi."

"And Shah Reza Avenue is now Revolution Avenue."

"Oh, I know that one. They did that before I left."

She kept looking through the darkened window. "God, this place is desolate. Is it the tint of the window?"

"It's the tint of Teheran."

"It's so dark."

"And dangerous, Miss Whitney. You have to be very careful."

"I was told things were getting under control."

The marine shrugged.

"What's the atmosphere like at the embassy?"

"You get used to things. The ambassador's gone, you know; Sullivan. His bosses at the State Department felt he had been too close to the shah. President Carter named Walter Cutler to take his place and Khomeini said 'no' to him. We let Khomeini have his way. I'm afraid we're taking orders from him. So the D.C.M. runs the place now."

"Bruce Laingen?"

"Yes."

"He's our ambassador now?"

"He's taking the place of the ambassador. Not official yet. Everything in this place is up in the air. Listen, Miss Whitney, just so you know what we're going to do when we get to Bijon. I'm going to walk you to the door where another marine, Sergeant Lopez, will be waiting for you."

"Is it that dangerous?"

"It is. And we can't shoot, that's our orders, unless it's clear-cut defense. So you have to keep that in mind, Miss Whitney. You know that Sergeant Kraus and Kassebuh were taken prisoner, you know."

"Yes."

"They're free now. But it was hell for them. Every day here is a time-bomb. At least this van is bullet proof. I was told to pick you up in this one. That should tell you how dangerous it is, Miss Whitney."

"I've never been in one of these things before."

"Don't go out any more on your own—just from the Bijon Apartments to the embassy grounds, and a marine will accompany you even for that short walk. We have thirteen of us here now. Don't go anywhere alone."

There was a grenade blast that went off close to the car.

The marine turned briefly to Anne. "It's okay. You get used to it. It didn't hit us."

"Why did they tell me things were normal?"

"Maybe they're right. It's just that this is the new normality, ma'am."

When they arrived in the alley between the embassy compound and the Bijon Apartments, she attempted to open the car door as the marine got out from his front seat. It didn't open. She unlocked it but it still didn't open.

By that time the U.S. Marine driver was outside her door. He opened it with effort. He smiled at her. "Don't try to open the door of this vehicle yourself, you'll never be able to."

"Why?"

"This car is armor-plated. The doors are filled with steel, they're very heavy. Besides, it's my job to open doors, not yours."

Her room at the Bijon apartment building was just as she left it, except now there were bars on the windows and there were sandbags between most of the glass and the bars. The apartment seemed smaller that way. It almost seemed like a cell, except for the cheerful knickknacks and books and other things that she had left there that were untouched.

Anne was awakened early by loud chants coming from Razmavaran Avenue: "Marg Bar Amrika! Marg Bar Amrika! Marg Bar Shah! Marg Bar Shah! Marg Bar Amrika! Marg Bar Amrika!" Anne didn't need to have taken Farsi to know that they were calling for "Death to the United States" and for "Death to the Shah."

A marine guard walked her across the alley to the embassy compound. The grounds were a horror to Anne who had known it before St. Valentine's Day:

Furniture and other possessions of embassy staff people and dependents who left hurriedly, were laying all over the outdoor compound, around the drained swimming pool, and inside it. There were hundreds of couches and chairs and tables and all kinds of smaller things scattered on top of each other without any sense of order. And the athletic field was now a continuation of the parking lot that had been separated by a garden pathway. Now the athletic field and the parking lot and the garden pathway between were filled with dozens of abandoned cars.

In Anne's office, the file cabinet was gone, the furniture was rearranged, there were bullet holes in the wall and, like her apartment, there were bars on the windows. Her only view was of sandbags, instead of the garden that had faced what had once been called Roosevelt Avenue.

Anne was greeted by the security officer, Al Golacinski, who told her to go to Room 112 of the small office building across from the commissary, for a security briefing from an anti-terrorist expert who was visiting from Washington.

"If things are getting back to normal, why did they bring in some anti-terrorist expert, Al?"

He didn't answer.

The expert, Richard Caruthers, looked back and forth from a Defense Department document as he spoke to her. The first four pieces of his advice were not ones that indicated great optimism of coming events:

"First, Anne, update your will and have several conformed copies made. Put the original in a safe repository and send copies to the executor and your lawyer. Second, we advice you have your Treasury Department paychecks sent to a U.S. bank account rather than to the post here. Third, make sure all insurance policies are up to date. And fourth, be sure that you carry no classified information or information that could conceivably be damaging to the security of the United States, remembering that information might be misinterpreted or misconstrued to be something that it is not."

"Wow!"

"Keep in mind anniversary dates of the government and militant organizations here. Many groups have been known to undertake operations on or near dates that have some special significance to them."

"Is that my job or yours?"

"Everything is all of our jobs when it comes to anti-terrorism. Now, let's stay with precautions here: always carry a card that indicates your blood type and any special conditions that may exist, and be sure you carry, on your person at all times, a supply of medications that you require.

"Now, when you leave Bijon Apartments, or any other places you may visit regularly, use different doors and gates and times when you leave and arrive. For that reason, your hours are not going to be regular. Do you have a car here?"

"No."

"That's good. Then we can skip a lot here. If you're being driven and if there's shooting, lower yourself in the vehicle so that you present less of a target to whomever is firing. Remember, most rounds will pass through the body of an unarmored vehicle. On the bright side, they may be deflected and their velocity and penetrating power will be reduced. If your vehicle is armored, it's different—but know the capabilities and limitations of the armor. It's not totally safe.

"I'm going to give you this booklet on surveillance, hostage survival, and interrogation—but I need to tell you, orally, a few of the most important points to remember."

"Mr. Caruthers, why don't we just break diplomatic relations with this government and get every American out of here if it's this bad?"

"That's not the best judgment of the president or the Secretary. We have friendly relations and we want to maintain them."

"Friendly relations?"

"Yes. That's what we want to maintain."

"Someone's dreaming. Or this briefing is outrageous. These warnings you're giving me are so ominous. We don't have diplomatic relations with a lot of countries. Why the hold-out here?"

"This is a very strategically important country. We're on the Soviet border. And the oil is important, as well. This is not a place we can just throw away. But none of that is my field, Miss Whitney. I'm here to give you the best precautions and advice I can."

"Go ahead. Shoot if you have more."

He looked back at his document. "The moment at which a person is captured, no matter where that capture may occur—in your apartment, in an automobile, or in your office—is a very psychologically traumatic moment."

"No kidding!"

"You may suddenly be transferred from a relaxed or complacent frame of mind to a state of absolute terror. Some freeze, while others automatically put up resistance. Stay as relaxed as you can."

"Oh, sure!"

"Any sudden or misinterpreted movement of yours could be very dangerous. Don't make any. If you're captured, the captors are undoubtedly hostile toward you and the United States. They have not had the opportunity to get to know you as an individual, so they will feel no compunction about killing you if they think it serves their purposes. At this point of the attack, except in a case of hijacking, the perpetrators always have the option of simply assassinating their victims and escaping if things seem to be going wrong. This option may suit their purposes nearly as well as hostage-taking. Naturally, it is in your interest to ensure that they do not see this option as the most attractive. Above all, do not make yourself appear threatening.

"Fortunately, most of us are able to cope with much more than we had ever expected. If you're transported by captors, you will probably be blindfolded, bound, and gagged, and likely be forced into a position that may be awkward or painful, and placed in a very confining space such as in a shipping trunk, the floor of the back of a car under the feet of your captors, the trunk of a car, or even in a sack. It is important to remember that this confinement is temporary and it is important that you use this time to gain whatever information you can through a very active use of whichever senses you still have available to you."

"You mean I'm even expected to work at a time like that?"

For the first time during the meeting, Richard Caruthers smiled. "What you do is listen for tire sounds that may indicate what type of road surface you're traveling on; listen for outside noises like factory sounds, traffic noises, or aircraft; for voices that may enable you to subsequently identify your kidnappers; and for distinctive motor or other vehicle sounds. Note unusual odors that might indicate certain types of manufacturing activities, a fishing industry, the nearness of the sea or other body of water.

"When you get to where they take you, keep your mind active. Read anything offered you to read, and although they may take your watch and leave you in the dark and attempt to remove your sense of time, detect temperatures that are associated with day or night, observe the patterns in which meals are served, detect any noises that may occur at particular times, observe guards who may appear more sleepy and less active; that may mean it's night—all so you can keep a sense of time. That's important for your own well being. Some hostages have been so effective at this that they were only a few hours off in their calculations after months of captivity. Plan for a long captivity by establishing a calendar of at least 30 or 60 days and then extending it if necessary, rather than having unrealistic expectations of a short stay that could be dashed.

"Finally and most important, do everything you can to retain your own self-respect and dignity no matter the conditions and possible torture. Make it known you have no information that would be useful for them. If you can't do that, if others have already provided information about you or classified documents have been compromised, use idiomatic language and unusual words to make yourself difficult to understand. Be vague and indefinite, be misleading and inaccurate, and digress into irrelevancies. If they see they are not going to obtain useful information from you, they may leave you alone.

"Now, here's the booklet, Miss Whitney. There are a lot more details in it than I covered, and they are all important."

Mark was right. She should never have come back.

Since it was overcast, there was little sunlight coming in her apartment's bedroom from the slit of visibility above the sandbags that were behind the bars of her window. She turned off the clock's alarm and went back to sleep. That decision was a more important one than she could have envisioned when she closed her eyes for a short while more.

It was a half hour later when her sleep was again interrupted, this time not by a clock's alarm. She awoke to loud chants of "Marg Bar Amrika!" but they didn't seem to be coming from the avenue. She pushed a chair to her window and stood on top of it to see above the sandbags. The view provided an expanse of the embassy compound with its huge grounds across the alley from the apartment building. The compound, that was comparable to twenty city blocks, was now filled with running and chanting young Iranian men with huge banners and pictures of the Ayatollah Khomeini strapped around their necks and covering their chests. Most of them had submachine guns and they were waving them. She could see more men with banners and pictures of the Ayatollah Khomeini jumping over the ten foot high compound walls. From her vantage point she couldn't see the main gate, but there was such a stream of militants coming from that direction that it was obvious they had stormed the gate and now the compound was a free-for-all of Revolutionary Guards.

This, she remembered, was November the 4th, the anniversary of when Khomeini was exiled to Turkey in 1964, and the one-year anniversary of an anti-Shah demonstration in which some Iranians were killed outside Teheran University. It was also an anniversary in reverse—one year forward would be the election for the next president in the United States. These were past and future events that could have served as a warning to her and others, but did not.

Within one minute of the start of her viewing, she saw the flag of the United States being set on fire in the center of the compound. As it burned, the two-storied Ambassador's residence was being stormed by screaming young men waving their banners. Then she saw four U.S. Marine Guards who were bound, being brought to the center of the compound.

Suddenly the overcast turned into a rainstorm. It was pouring as the invaders charged in one embassy doorway after another, shooting their submachine guns in the air and shouting their chant, "Marg Bar Amrika!"

They had not yet thought to cross the alley-way to the Bijon Apartment Building. Anne rushed to her closet, put on a chador, grabbed her purse, ran down the staircase, then went outside into the alley. The rain was a God-send to her because she could run and might be thought by others to be running to get out of the rain. She ran to Razmavaran Avenue, the main street leading away from the embassy, and it was vacant and quiet.

She ducked through alleys and cross-streets, not having any sense of direction or destination.

The rain stopped as suddenly as it began. She slowed down, not because she was running out of breath; she had more staying power than she ever thought she was capable of maintaining. She slowed down because she knew that without rain, a woman running through a residential area would cause attention. Further, any attention drawn to her might cause an observer to look at the lightness of her skin that was revealed around her eyes.

She became an unhurried walker out on a stroll.

There was a middle-aged, dark-haired mustached man who was coming from behind the fence of his home, and he had a garden spade in his hand. On seeing him, she thought she should turn the other way and run before she would reach him, but good sense dictated that she continue her walk and look undisturbed. He knelt down, and with his free hand he started pulling weeds from the dirt near his plants and flowers. When she got closer, he stopped his gardening to stare at her.

Anne saw him stand, but she wouldn't allow her eyes to rest on him. A few more seconds of her walk seemed like an eternity as she became directly parallel with him, and then beyond him. "Miss," he said in English. She kept on walking. In a soft but audible voice he added, "Long Live America."

She stopped short. Was this a trick? Should she walk on? Should she run? This had not been covered in the security briefing. Whether it was smart or falling for a trap, she turned to face him. He tossed the spade from his hand to the ground. He nodded to her. His eyes looked as though he was pleading. He repeated, "Long Live America." There was only a slight accent. They stood, a distance apart, and she simply didn't know what to do, recognizing that her decision of saying something or moving on or just standing there could mean her life or death. Did he throw down the spade to indicate he had no want of a weapon?

He reached his strong hand out as though he wanted her to take it or shake hands, but there was too much distance between them for that. His hand was covered with dirt from the earth. He looked at his hand and cleaned it by rubbing it on his khaki pants and then he extended it again. "Long Live America. Long Live Shah."

Since he didn't know her, he was taking a great risk of his life. She felt that if this was not a deception, she must return his risk. She walked to him slowly. When they were only steps apart she literally threw herself at him, and as though they were brother and sister, she put her arms around him and sobbed uncontrollably. The mustached man put his arms lightly around her. "You must come in our home. You are welcome here. Let us move fast so you will not be seen."

Mohammad and Maryam Azimi soon called it "Anne's Room." It was on the second floor in the back of the house, and only rarely, and with the shades and drapes drawn in all rooms and hallways, did Anne venture out of that room. There were times Anne Whitney felt as though she was Anne Frank.

"I have never felt more at home at any time in my life," she told the Azimis when the first week was done. "I feel so much at home that I often forget that you are endangering your lives for someone you don't even know."

Mohammad Azimi took a draw of his cigarette. "Your country is not a stranger, and you have confirmed all we thought of it through so many years. You, Anne, have restored our belief in the United States, and that belief had been in decline." Anne was sitting on the edge of her bed, and the Azimis were sitting across from each other on plastic chairs at a small desk they had brought upstairs for her from their kitchenette.

"I don't even know if I want to leave," Anne said. "I'm happy here. You have done that for me."

Maryam Azimi laughed. She was a beautiful woman in her early thirties, with black hair that reached her shoulders and she had large brown eyes. This was a striking couple. Both of them had been educated in Great Britain and both of them were scholars as well as people of courage. Maryam reached over to touch Anne's arm. "I don't think we want you to leave. But the time will come. When it can be done with safety. Only then."

"Let me correct something," Mohammad said. "Our lives are no more endangered with you here than they have been since the first day of February when Khomeini came back to Iran. He ordered the execution of all those who had either worked for Shah or were friends of Shah. I worked for him at different times, and both Maryam and I are friends of Shah. Now I am an electrician. I have always known carpentry and I worked as an electrician when I was a young man. I learned it from my father. So all those things, and gardening have been known by me. Now being an electrician is my profession, as long as Maryam and I are not found out. So far it seems no one has turned us in. That is a miracle that cannot last forever. Our only hope is that Khomeini will be overthrown."

"Do you think there will be a counter-revolution soon?"

"No. He is showing his power now. He is holding your whole nation hostage. That precludes a counter-revolution. If he scares America, he scares any counter-revolutionary. He calls your nation the Great Satan. He said that all of you at the embassy were engaged in espionage and therefore you are not diplomats, you see, but you are all criminals and you must be tried and punished. He has gone against all international law in taking over your property. An embassy is as much your territory as your nation itself. He is a crazy man—crazy with his own objectives. Your leaders should not have let this happen. I am sorry but your government should never have demanded Shah free prisoners. Shah had faith in whatever Carter said. Shah had no reason to doubt Carter's advice since six American presidents before Carter befriended Shah. So Shah freed the prisoners as Carter demanded, and it was his undoing—they are the revolutionaries—they are the ones who rallied for Khomeini. Carter sends his Chief of U.S. Forces in Europe, General Huyser here, to tell our generals not to back Shah—to back Bakhtiar who was calling for Shah to get out. Now Shah is gone. And Iran is gone."

"And now," Maryam said, "Shah is dying, isn't he?"

"President Carter allowed him into the country, Mrs. Azimi," Anne said. "He is at a hospital in New York. At Cornell. The medical center there. That was good of President Carter to let the Shah in."

Maryam Azimi nodded. "You are a loyalist, Anne. I like that."

"Mrs. Azimi," Anne added, "because President Carter let him in our country, that's why they took over our embassy."

"No, Anne," Mr. Azimi said. "You may defend your president but never justify evil. Khomeini and his militants who took over your embassy did it because they are evil. He does not see your captured friends as humans. He sees them as weapons. They have become his arsenal. There are no excuses for such things. Once you start giving excuses for evil, evil is the victor."

Anne did not want to argue with her saviors. "Do you think this will go on for a long time?"

"You must adjust yourself to that," Mr. Azimi said.

"I have adjusted myself to being here. I told you, and I mean it, that this has become home in such a short period of time. What happens to you if I'm found here? And what happens to me? What happens then? I worry about being away from the embassy. What if there is a rescue attempt? What if it is successful and I'm not there? Should I go to the embassy?"

"I am disappointed. Do not show such fear, Anne. You are at risk here with us, and certainly at risk at the embassy. Now, if there should be a rescue of the hostages at the embassy and you are here, then I am afraid you may become Dora Bloch and you should know that."

"Who is Dora Bloch?" Anne asked. "Her name is familiar."

Mrs. Azimi said, "When the Israeli commandos rescued 103 of their countrymen who were held hostage at Entebbe Airport in Uganda by Idi Amin's cut-throats, one of the hostages was not there. She was at a hospital. After the 103 hostages were rescued—the Ugandans killed Dora Bloch."

Mr. Azimi took over, "I know we sound cruel, Anne, but you must know all truths and be ready for anything here. Maryam and I are ready. There must be no hiding of any truths between us."

Anne nodded. "I met Idi Amin. We had words. We had real words between us. I would be proud to be Dora Bloch, Mr. Azimi."

Mohammad Azimi nodded. "I believe that. You are quite a woman. Do you know that before you were born, your President Roosevelt said, 'the only thing we have to fear is fear itself—nameless, unreasoning, unjustified terror which paralyzes needed efforts to convert retreat into advance."

"Yes, of course. That first part is a very famous phrase from his first inaugural. I didn't know the whole thing but we all know the first part."

"In truth, Anne, he would have been more precise had he said 'the only thing we have to fear is the exhibition of fear' because there can be no courage without fear. There can be stupidity, but not courage."

Mrs. Azimi said, "There is, Anne, much to fear by being in this house. Anything can happen at any moment. The door can be blasted open before this very minute is done. Do I seem frightened to you, Anne?"

"No, Mrs. Azimi, you don't."

"Then I am a good liar. Let me confide to you that I am scared to death—for the fate of him, for the fate of you, for the fate of me. To ignore such possible fates with a shrug is impossible. To ignore such possibilities would be unrealistic. So how do I feel? I am very frightened, Anne."

"But," Mr. Azimi added to his wife's confession, "that is the last you'll hear of it, you see. We must always know that we can rise above it, and that courage is our only salvation. I want courage, not ignorance. Fear is the only creator of courage. Are you afraid, Anne?"

"No."

"Are you lying?"

"Yes."

"That's good. You must even lie to me and to Maryam. Are you lying when you say you are unafraid?"

"No."

"That's better. You lie well. You are courageous. We are blessed to have you here. You are the reason, I think, that God made humans rather than just more animals."

With each day there was more discouraging news heard over the large radio in Anne's room. The Ayatollah Khomeini said that "Even if the Shah is extradited, only as a sign of goodwill or as a special gesture would we consider releasing the Americans, because they are spies...If they are tried, Carter knows what will happen."

Then, surprisingly, thirteen hostages were released, all were women and black American men, although two women, it was said, remained as well as one black American. "Islam has a special respect for women," the Ayatollah said, "and blacks, who have spent ages under American pressure and tyranny, may have come to Iran under pressure, therefore Islam mitigates their cases if it is proved that they have not committed acts of espionage." Some of the freed hostages spoke well of their captors even though they said they were tied most of the time and not allowed to communicate with each other in the embassy. One released American said, "I got a different look at American imperialism."

Then there was the news that the U.S. Embassy in Pakistan was stormed, with two Americans killed; Corporal Steven Crowley and Army Chief Warrant Officer Brian Ellise. And the embassy there was set on fire.

Then the Shah's nephew was assassinated in Paris.

The Shah was sent from the United States to Panama.

Anne pleaded that somehow Mr. Azimi get word to Mark, that she was safe. Her pleas were denied. "There are three people in the world who know you are here: you and Maryam and me. Any person who knows, I don't care who it may be, adds a new risk. How can I tell him? By phone? I wouldn't even tell him in person even though he is your fiance. At present your State Department has not released a list of names. That is smart. Your man just assumes you are being held hostage in the embassy. Let him. It is better that way."

On Christmas Eve, Maryam brought a meal of turkey to Anne's room and the three of them celebrated the coming of both Christmas and the Islamic holiday of Al-Ashura.

They could hear the chants of "Marg Bar Amrika!" up and down the block, at times, right outside the Azimi's home. They could hear a helicopter overhead with repeated swooping down near their home. They made no comment on any of the sounds. They kept eating without looking at eachother.

When the sounds disappeared, Maryam said, "This is truly your home now, Anne. We only apologize for the terror outside and the danger inside, and we apologize for your confinement. I do that on behalf of Persia—of Iran. I want you to always remember you are not confined by the people but by this government that confines us all. The Persians and the Americans are both victims of this terror, and we must win. Anne, you and your nation are family."

Anne's nation, in this decade, had lost many members of its international family.

PART THREE

The 1980s

FORTY-NINE
THE KOWLOON SIDE
1980

As should always be expected, nothing was as expected.

When 1980 started, 58 days had passed since the American embassy and its staff were held hostage in Teheran. In Afghanistan, five days had passed since the invasion by the Soviet Union. In Nicaragua, the new Sandinista Government had increased its number of political prisoners to 7800, while Former President Anastasio Somoza was in exile in Paraguay. In Thailand, 200,000 land refugees were sheltered after the invasion of Cambodia by Vietnam. In the South China Sea, 70 men who were South Vietnamese Boat People were thrown overboard by Thai pirates, with 62 women aboard the boat taken to the Thai city of Ko Kha and raped. In Hong Kong, old camps that had held British prisoners during the Japanese occupation of World War II were being renovated to give shelter for South Vietnamese Boat People.

To Moose Dunston, who arrived on New Year's Day of 1980 to assume residence for *Asia World Weekly*, the entire city was unexpected. He had not seen Hong Kong in ten years. Now, with the exception of a few colonial structures, the skyline had changed so dramatically that it looked as though the island had been excavated and used as a site for tall buildings, one more unique than the other. And there were streets where once there was a larger harbor, and some of the streets were unable to be crossed without going up and down steep stairways and across escalated walkways and pedestrian bridges, or by going through new pedestrian underground tunnels. And there was a massive tunnel between Kowloon and Hong Kong Island for automobiles.

Now there were hardly any junks with canvas sails in the harbor, and hardly any women were wearing cheong-sams and there were only 15 rickshaws left in Kowloon and 15 left on Hong Kong Island and no local residents took them, and even tourists weren't taking them, only posing by them for pictures to show back home. It became doubtful that any of the ones who hawked for passengers would even have the strength to pull them more than a few steps.

But the most unexpected of all was the husband of Wai-yee. Moose was not looking forward to meeting him, but it was unavoidable if he was to meet Liberty, and to see Wai-yee again. He would much rather have met Liberty with Wai-yee at some place other than their residence, so it would just be the three of them, but he couldn't possibly request that. Honor would dictate that he meet Dr. Yeung Chi-shing. He had imagined the elderly doctor she had married to be quiet, stern and, probably, courteous but resentful of Moose—with valid reason. Could he look the doctor straight in the eyes without feeling like an enemy, like a rival who had made love to this man's wife, and who had fathered, or as Wai-yee would say, helped create Liberty? He feared the meeting for years and now on the evening of the first day of the new decade, it was only minutes away as the taxi brought him up the winding Kung Lok Road on Crocodile Hill. The driver slowed down the taxi, looking in the dark for the address of the apartment complex. Moose had expected them to live in government block housing, but this wealthy area of apartment buildings was not provided by government. Would Wai-yee answer the door? Would Liberty be standing next to her? Or would Dr. Yeung be standing with Wai-yee, ready to shoot their guest? Or did the Chinese prefer the use of a knife? "Look," Moose rehearsed in a low murmur, "this wasn't adultery, you know. She didn't even know you then. I mean, so what?"

Would Wai-yee have to translate? Would she cry? Wai-yee didn't usually cry. But this could do it. "'You're a lucky man to be married to Wai-yee,'" he would tell Dr. Yeung. *Oh, no, that's too ordinary, too expected. That doesn't mean anything,* Moose thought. *Of course he's lucky to be married to her. That's out. I could say,* Look, you old duffer, you lucked out, that's all, but I'll bet you fall down in the love-making department! *No! I can't even think of things like that. Just be yourself and take what comes. Did she tell him I asked her to marry me? Well, that ought to make him feel good. She said,* No, *to me and she said,* Yes, *to him. But does he know why? If he was going to leave Hong Kong she'd have dumped him, too. Oh, cut it out!* Moose couldn't even agree with himself. *Above all, you're going to meet your daughter–* and then he added, *–of all things! Oh, God! How did all this happen?*

The driver stopped. The apartment complex was right there. The driver's very big American passenger paid the driver, having a little difficulty in getting out through the small doorway of the taxi. He walked to the series of four doors right off the street. There was the one with the gold plate marked Number Four. He wanted some difficulty in finding the place so as to postpone the moment, but there was no difficulty. It was all seconds away. There was the bell. There was his index finger. "The idea," he said, talking to himself, "is to bring the finger to the little round button there–and push. That's what I guess the idea is."

He clenched his teeth, opened his mouth, closed his eyes, and let his finger push. "Hello, Wai-yee," he murmured to himself in final rehearsal. "I was so much looking forward to this. I can't wait to meet the doctor. He's such a lucky man." Why was he rehearsing everything he didn't want to say?

The door swung open.

"Mr. Dunston?" The tall, thin, elderly man stood alone at the doorway, and he had a wide and warm smile.

"Yes, sir, Moose Dunston. You're Dr. Yeung?"

Dr. Yeung's smile became even wider as he nodded. "Ahh, so good! Please call me Chi-shing." He extended his hand, and his grip was strong. Dr. Yeung put his other hand on Moose's shoulder, as though they were old friends seeing each other after a long absence. "I'm the man who is so handsome," Dr. Yeung said with a twinkle in his eyes and an attempt to hide his smile and block his laughter. "And I am so well constructed, and such a magnificent lover, that any woman, including Wai-yee, easily would choose me over you! In fact, she told me you were disabled as a lover! Some kind of a problem. Come in!"

Moose roared with laughter, and even Dr. Yeung could not help but laugh at his own remarks. Dr. Yeung had done the undoable. He put Moose at ease, and took away all concern that two men normally face when they both have loved the same woman.

Dr. Yeung had to be in his middle 70's, and his sense of humor was magnified because of his age, because he was Chinese, because he spoke perfect English, because he was a doctor, and because he was a man of such considerable stature. He ushered Moose into their living room which looked unexpectedly western rather than Chinese, except for the colors. There was plush, modern furniture, all of it either red or black or transparent, and the main wall was dominated by a huge framed colored photograph of John Travolta.

"This is so nice," Moose said. "This is beautiful. And—do you know John Travolta?"

"Oh, no. Wai-yee bought that monstrosity. She'd give me up and give you up—both of us put together for one night with John Travolta! Sit down. She's movie-crazy, you know."

"Is she?" Of course Moose knew, but he wisely thought it best not to voice any memories. As soon as he sat down, he stood up. Wai-yee walked in the room. It was not courtesy that made him stand. It was awe. How could God do it? Why did God allow her to defy all the rules and make her more and more glamorous with the passing of years? That wasn't normal. Not like this. And still, rejecting all the changes of Hong Kong style, Wai-yee was wearing a cheong-sam. Yellow. Slit. High collar. God!

"Moose!" She gave her sparkling smile, walked quickly to him and when she got very close she seemed not to know exactly what to do, so she extended her hand.

"Oh, for Heaven's sake," Dr. Yeung said. "Kiss the big ox. Don't be sensitive because I'm here. I could never be jealous of anyone who looks like that!" Again, Dr. Yeung commanded the moment. Both Moose and Wai-yee had to laugh and the laughter prevented an awkward kiss—or any kiss.

But there was the way she laughed; the hand up to her mouth and the cocking of her head. "Chi-shing! You are impossible! Moose, it's so good to see you! Please, sit down, ho—" she started to say 'honey,' and Moose caught it and Dr. Yeung caught it.

Dr. Yeung gave a comforting smile. "Please sit softly, Mr. Dunston. Don't break the chair." He wanted to act as though he didn't hear, or at least catch, Wai-yee's error.

Wai-yee should have dropped it, but she was thinking of any word that would have the sound of 'ho' that she could say as a substitute for "honey," as though she had started another word. She came out with, "Ho–Ho–How are you?"

"Fine, Wai-yee. I'm just fine," Moose answered.

"He's fi–fi–fine," Dr. Yeung said, mimicking what she did. He was smiling as he stood in front of the picture of John Travolta. Then he turned to Moose. "She still can't speak English after living in Hong Kong since she was a little girl and after having worked at the American Consulate forever."

"Chi-shing! I speak perfect English!" She sat opposite Moose. "I quit the consulate, you know. I've been gone a year."

Moose was taken by surprise. "You did? You quit?"

"After President Carter gave his speech recognizing the communist government–" and she motioned with her head toward the north wall of the apartment, "across the border. That was a betrayal."

"You quit?"

"That was the last straw."

"After all those years?"

"Sure. I couldn't stay. If I stayed it would be as though I forgot what they did to my father."

Moose nodded. "What are you doing now–any job or–"

"She quit on me," Dr. Yeung said with melancholy. "I demanded that she still earn some money, so she's turned to prostitution."

"Oh, I did not! Chi-shing, you've got to stop! He'll believe you!" And she turned back to Moose. "Liberty is a job! But, yes, I go to work, too. I do a few things part-time. I help a teacher. His name is Szeto Wah and he is a friend of Chi-shing. It's not every day, but I help him grade papers and things he doesn't like to do. Sometimes I even teach his students a little English. He can't speak good English. On other days I help another friend of Chi-shing, an Englishman, Jack Edwards, who was a prisoner of war of the Japanese in Taiwan. He's running the Royal British Legion here. I help him in trying to get money for the former British prisoners of war here, and for their widows. And I work for his best friend, Arthur May, too. He was a prisoner of war of the Japanese here in Hong Kong."

"You sound busier than before," Moose said. "I can't get over it–that you quit the consulate. What does your Mom think?"

Wai-yee looked down. "Mother's gone," she said.

Then that terrible silence as her words sunk in to Moose, and it was a terrible silence to Wai-yee, having heard her own words.

"Oh, Wai-yee! I'm sorry."

Dr. Yeung nodded. "It's been a year now. She was ill for some time. It was difficult. It still is difficult for Wai-yee, and Wai-yee's sister, Winnie, and me. It happened in Bangkok while she was visiting Winnie. But she was in a coma for over a week–eight days–and then–we expected it. It had to happen."

Wai-yee looked up with a forced smile, wanting to change the mood back to what it was. "Winnie is married to a banker there. Winnie likes Bangkok and she's very happy there. It's so different than here. It's always so hot. I visit her maybe twice a year or so, or she comes to visit us with her husband."

"I'm sorry about your mom, Wai-yee." Moose said. "She was such a kind woman." Saying "was" rather than "is" acted as a confirmation she was gone.

Wai-yee nodded with a small smile, then expanded it in another effort to go on with something else. "Winnie has been married now for three years. Can you imagine, Winnie married?"

"Is he a good man? Do you like him?"

Wai-yee nodded. "He loves her. He's a Thai. Yes, he's a nice man." She said it without much enthusiasm. "Winnie speaks of going to China some day. But that's out. We thought maybe things would be better in China with Hua Guofgeng and Deng Xiaoping. Deng is now like the others. You heard what he did to Democracy Wall?"

"Yes, of course."

"So those poor students who were told they could put their posters up have been put in prison. For what? Is it a crime to want democracy? I answer my own question. It's a crime–" and she again gave a gesture towards the north wall of the apartment, "–across the border. Nothing changes there."

"Democracy Wall's existence was too good to be true."

"It's done," Dr. Yeung said. "And I differ with Wai-yee. One thing has changed there. The language. They've changed the pronunciation and spelling of Chinese names for all those languages that have a Roman alphabet. It's called the Pinyin system. It's idiotic. They should have called it the Pinhead system. Peking is now called Beijing. And Canton is now called Guangzhou. Wait until you see the new spelling of Mao Tse-tung and Chou En-lai. Do you know how China is spelled now? Z-H-O-U-N-G-H-U-A. Of all things they could have changed, they chose spelling. But no, there is no Democracy Wall or Xidin Wall anymore. Imagine when you look at the world as a whole–the wrong wall came down, didn't it? The Berlin Wall stands, and the Democracy Wall is through."

Wai-yee nodded with her usual degree of passion. "One of those posters on Democracy Wall called on Carter to pay attention to human rights in China. The boy who put that up is in prison. They say he's a counterrevolutionary. Anyone saying a word they don't like is called a counterrevolutionary. And you've heard the other new policy? Those couples who have a third child have their salaries reduced until the child is fourteen years old, and the child will have no education or medical attention. That's law. Yes, I quit the consulate when Carter recognized such a government."

Dr. Yeung retained his standing position with John Travolta looking over his shoulder. "Now tell us what you're doing, Mr. Dunston."

"Writing. My boss at *Asia World Weekly* finally demanded I come to the scene. No more Asia-watching from Washington. For my first one from here I thought I'd do an editorial on China or maybe Hong Kong, but I can't. I'll be doing one on Afghanistan. I can't ignore Afghanistan this week."

"I should say not," Dr. Yeung said.

Wai-yee looked disturbed. "You're not going there, are you?" There was the same feeling she had felt almost twenty years ago when he said he was going to Saigon.

"Oh, no. I'll be based here. They got me an apartment on the Hong Kong side. It will be ready in a week. In the meantime I'll be at—at a hotel." The Hilton. He wouldn't say it. "A hotel near the office—on the Hong Kong side."

Wai-yee's eyes opened wide. "You should see what they're building on the Kowloon side! A big new hotel called The Regent that's supposed to be the most luxurious hotel in the world, overlooking the harbor! They're building it here on the Kowloon side!"

"The Kowloon side! The Hong Kong side!" Dr. Yeung said. "There is something crazy here in Hong Kong. I wonder how many millions of days have been wasted if we put them all together in telling what side of the harbor is being talked about. Every day someone asks me what side I live on, as though the two sides are at war. I say, 'the Kowloon side,' and they nod. I think we should wear uniforms—red or blue—depending on what side we live on!"

Wai-yee nodded and smiled at Moose. "You know, he's right? Now—do you want to meet Liberty?"

"Oh, yes!"

"I'll get her, dear," Dr. Yeung said.

Wai-yee turned to him. "Thank you!" Then she turned back to Moose "You know, she's nine years old now."

"I know." As soon as Dr. Yeung left the room, he added, "Or ten or eleven or whatever your calendar says." He felt a tinge of guilt by saying anything he wouldn't have said in the presence of Dr. Yeung. As soon as he said it he wished he hadn't.

Wai-yee smiled and said softly, "You remember! It isn't that complicated!"

"I still have trouble with it. Wai-yee?"

"Yes?"

"Wai-yee, he's really something. I had thought I might tell him how lucky he is to have you—and he is. But you picked wisely, too. This must be tough for him with me here, but he won't let any hurt intrude. And he wants me to be comfortable."

Wai-yee looked solemn. "He's a wonderful man. I'm so glad you like him."

Moose nodded with his lips pressed together. Being alone with her, even for this quick moment, created a new feeling in the room—a new feeling that was the old feeling of the consulate, the Peak, Jimmy's Kitchen, the Miramar, the Princess Theater, Sunshine Island, the Hilton, the Watergate, Manila. He had to resist the impulse to reach out for her. She felt it, too. In a strange way, he wished Dr. Yeung had not left the room.

"I like him very much, Wai-yee," he almost whispered. "I'm glad he came along for you. The best deserves the best." He was beginning to choke up. He craved to embrace her.

"Moose—you are still so gentle!"

Then they said nothing. She stroked her hair so it would fall evenly behind her shoulders. Of course he noticed it was long again, just the way he liked it, but it was not appropriate to mention it without seeming to use the moment while Dr. Yeung was out of the room, and he wouldn't do that.

"Here she is!" Dr. Yeung's voice yelled loudly from the hallway. "Get ready! Here she comes! Here comes Liberty!" It was as though he was giving them a warning, not only for Liberty's entrance, but for his re-entrance.

And in ran—not walked, but ran—a beautiful miniature Wai-yee, with her arms and hands flying haphazardly in all directions to announce herself with pomp and pride and immense importance and she was even wearing a tee-shirt that read, "Here I come!" Before her grand entrance was done, she did a pirouette to show Moose the back of her Tee-shirt which read, "There I go!"

Liberty was stunned by Moose's size. She had never seen a man that big, and she made no secret of her amazement. "You're Smoky the Bear!"

"Liberty!" Wai-yee said.

"He is, Ma! He is! Aren't you Smoky the Bear?" she asked Moose.

Moose gave a short shake of his head. "We just look alike. We're very good friends."

"See, Ma?"

Liberty took to Moose as quickly as Moose had taken to Dr. Yeung. She danced and sang Chinese and American songs for him, as she played a number of records she had placed on the record changer of the stereo set. She was very good.

Dr. Yeung beat cadence with his hand on his knee and nodded with the same cadence to exhibit his approval of Liberty's performance. When each song was done the audience of three applauded and, during the pause between records, Liberty would bow and then stand with her eyes closed in preparation for the next song. "Wait," she would say. "Wait."

Wai-yee was bursting with happiness at the scene.

"Now," Dr. Yeung said to Liberty. "You must show Mr. Dunston how you dance on your ears!"

"Oh, Pa! I don't dance on my ears!"

"You don't?"

"No! No one dances on their ears!"

"Are you sure?"

"Oh, Pa!"

Dr. Yeung looked at Moose with a look of bewilderment. "Don't people dance on their ears any more? The world has gone mad! It used to be that dance halls were filled with people dancing on their ears." And then he looked back at Liberty. "A long time ago, before I met your mother, I won the ear-dancing championship."

"Oh, you did not!" Liberty laughed and gave a fist and socked the air in his direction.

"Oh, yes I did. But, of course, I did not win the prize all on my own. I was dancing with a beautiful girl who had already won many ear-dancing contests before we danced together. She was very good, probably because she had seven ears and at the time, I only had three. As you know, now I'm down to two, but that happens as you get older."

"Pa! Every one has only two ears! I only have two! Ma only has two! Mr. Moose, the Bear, only has two!"

"Are you sure?"

"Yes! Count them!"

"Everyone only has two these days?"

"Yes!"

"Well then, the competition shouldn't be very difficult now. I didn't know that. I thought I could never win a prize again. But since no one has more than two any more, I think I'll enter some contests again."

"Pa! Ma, is he telling the truth?"

Wai-yee closed her eyes with her now-constant smile. "Liberty! You know your father. He's just kidding you. He didn't win an ear dancing contest!"

"But is there such a thing as ear dancing?"

"Now, what do you think?"

"You'll see," Dr. Yeung said. "You'll both see when I come home with the prize! Then the two of you will be standing in a line to apologize to me. Mr. Dunston, these two women are both the same! They conspire against me–the two of them! Mr. Dunston, I'm sure you have gone ear dancing!"

"Yes, of course."

"You see?" He looked at Liberty, then at Wai-yee, then back at Moose. "Did you ever win a prize?"

"No. I wasn't very good at it."

"What a shame. Now, if you or I were John Travolta they would believe us."

Liberty's eyes were open wide. "Do you know John Travolta?" she asked Moose.

Moose shook his head. "I'm sorry. I don't."

"But you live in America," she said assuming such proximity must mean the two knew each other.

"I don't know everyone in America. It's very big."

Wai-yee couldn't stay on the sidelines of this subject. "Did you see *Saturday Night Fever*?"

"I missed it."

"I didn't," Dr. Yeung said. "I didn't see it but I didn't miss it. I have no interest in being entertained anymore. I don't go to the movies any more no matter how much these two women try to talk me into it. At my age

I don't have the patience to sit for hours in a dark auditorium. And I don't have the bladder for it, either."

"What's a bladder?" Liberty asked.

"I'll tell you tomorrow," Wai-yee nodded, and quickly turned from Liberty to Moose. "I saw *Saturday Night Fever* four times."

"Five," Dr. Yeung corrected.

"Five," she admitted. "Anyone hungry?" And she looked at Moose. "I know you love raw fish!" She knew he hated it, and she didn't hesitate to indicate her memory of his appetite. "Wait until you see it! I left the eyes for you! The best part!"

This was the fourth time in his life when Moose felt like an accredited adult. No one really leaves their childhood, but there are those moments. The first time he felt like an adult was when his barber didn't need to put a wooden board on the arms of the barber's chair for Moose to sit for a haircut. The second time was when Moose was issued his uniform in the army. The third time was when he called his dentist by his first name, (the sure sign of adulthood.) And now he was sitting at a dinner table with Wai-yee, Dr. Yeung, and Liberty. This was a family that never knew him when he was a child. Life had moved to place and time where that little girl was his child.

Wai-yee had prepared a steak for Moose while everyone else had the eternal fish. After dinner but still at the table, Dr. Yeung offered a cigarette to Moose, but Moose took out his pipe. It was the one Wai-yee had given him just before they went to Sunshine Island. Wai-yee glanced at it, then at his eyes, and then she looked at the table, then at Liberty to have a point of focus.

"Bed!" Wai-yee said to Liberty. "Into your pajamas!"

"*Ma*!"

"Bed!"

"I don't want to!"

"Liberty!"

Liberty promptly went running off to her room, the "There I Go!" message on the back of her tee-shirt vindicated by the moment.

"And brush your teeth and then potty," Wai-yee called after her, "and then call me when you're in bed!"

Dr. Yeung said to Moose, "Each night when I put Liberty to bed, and before Wai-yee comes in her room to sing her to sleep, I teach Liberty all about K'ung Fu-tze, who you call Confucius. And each night I tell her at least one of those truths that K'ung Fu-tze left to us. When I can, I pick out one of his truths that applies to the current day or night. And tonight, Mr. Dunston, I will tell her why I enjoy having you in our house—that tonight I have accommodated the wisdom of K'ung Fu-tze in contracting friendship with you, because the wise K'ung Fu-tze said: 'Never contract friendship with a man that is not better than thyself.'"

Wai-yee looked down at her tea cup and slowly shook her head in joy. She couldn't look at Moose because she knew that he, too, was affected, and if they caught each other's glances, there could be tears. Probably his.

After Dr. Yeung went into and came out of Liberty's room, and after Wai-yee sang to Liberty, Wai-yee said Liberty was not yet asleep, and she asked Moose if he wanted to say goodnight to her.

Moose walked in the dark room with just enough light from the open doorway coming into the room for Moose to see the whiteness of the walls and the cleanliness of its many shelves with Liberty's collection of Chinese dolls, and models and pictures of Disney characters, and a small statue of Smoky the Bear. The purity of her room almost matched the purity of her face.

"My father said that I should be grateful to you," Liberty said to Moose.

"For what?"

"He said that without you I would not have been created."

"Did he?"

"Yes. Thank you."

Moose clenched his lips together, which was becoming a habit. He nodded.

"My father always tells me the truth."

"You can count on that. He's an honest man."

Liberty nodded with pride. "My mother told me that you and she created me—but my father is my father."

"Liberty?"

"Yes?"

"You have such marvelous parents."

"I know." She closed her eyes.

Moose stared at her as sleep was coming over her, and he tried to imagine what she was thinking. What could she dream? With such short and innocent knowledge of life, how many images could she envision? Did she understand what she had been told? Was she only thinking of Disney characters or Chinese dancers or Smoky the Bear? The life and innocence in this little replica of Wai-yee overpowered the room, causing Moose to regret the events and actions beyond Crocodile Hill that some day would be familiar to her. Reality would surely invade her in coming years, and Moose wanted it held off.

"He who merely knows right principles is not equal to him who loves them."

"Confucius?"

Dr. Yeung nodded. There was a night breeze on the patio, almost a wind. The two men were seated on bamboo chairs at a small bamboo table, looking toward a garden of the apartment complex. It wasn't like sitting on a patio in the United States. There was an aroma of Hong Kong in the air. It was a humid aroma even though there was no humidity. Wai-yee came out to the patio holding a tray with a plate of grapes and cheeses. "Liberty's asleep," she said and she placed the tray on the table.

"We are discussing principle, Wai-yee," Dr. Yeung said as Wai-yee sat on the chair between them at the table. "Your favorite subject. I told him that he who merely knows right principles is not equal to him who loves them—and I was about to tell him that you love them."

"You needn't tell me that, Dr. Yeung," Moose said. "I know she is a woman of principle."

"Let me tell you what she does now. She minimized it to you. On Mondays and Fridays she works for Szeto Wah, as she told you, he is a teacher like her father. Wah is a friend of mine. Both of us were in China together during the Japanese occupation of Hong Kong. He was like a son to me. A marvelous man. On Tuesdays she works for Jack Edwards, and Wednesdays for Arthur May, both good friends of mine who were prisoners of war. They're both British and best friends. We're all in the same generation. We're all gray-haired old fossils. Jack Edwards is a little younger than I am, Arthur May is about my age. Maybe four or five years older. Do you know who he is?"

"No, I don't."

"He was a prisoner here of the Japanese. He saved Hong Kong single-handedly. I'll explain afterwards. Wai-yee used to work for another great man before Liberty was born. A man of Italian descent, but he was born in China—in Shanghai. He was taking care of refugees here from China. Maybe he still is. We haven't kept up with him. His name is Gus Borgeest. He and his family live on an island he leased from the British to take care of refugees. That's where Wai-yee went to teach them English and she helped them with the land. It's called Sunshine Island. She always says she'll go back some day. I'm sure she will, when there's enough time in her schedule to help him again, if he's still there."

Moose felt a stab. He couldn't help but look at Wai-yee at that one. It was obvious from the way Dr. Yeung spoke that he knew nothing about Wai-yee bringing Moose to Sunshine Island so many years ago. A memory she hadn't shared with Dr. Yeung.

Wai-yee looked totally at ease, although she brushed her hair back for no reason since it was already in back of her shoulders. "He takes care of refugees on a little island." She was confirming to Moose that she had not told Chi-shing anything about their visit.

"That's nice," Moose said, trying not to exhibit any nervousness. "That's a good thing to do. Refugees. That's good. That's good to help a man who does that."

"We are all refugees," Dr. Yeung said. "That is what Hong Kong is all about. Who lives here who is not a refugee? Very few."

"I guess that's right," Moose agreed.

"I'll tell you one man who isn't. The man she works for on Wednesdays. Arthur May. Do you want to hear an amazing story?"

"Yes. Yes, of course."

"Chi-shing loves to tell this story!" Wai-yee said with relief that Sunshine Island was no longer Chi-shing's subject of interest. "Wait until you hear! What a movie it would make! As Chi-shing talks, imagine Arthur May is being played by William Holden!"

"Wai-yee, he looks nothing like William Holden! You know that," Dr. Yeung said.

"Maybe not now! He showed me pictures of how he looked during the war! Just like William Holden!"

"He never looked anything like William Holden!" He turned from Wai-yee to Moose. "She never says I looked like William Holden when I was younger, and she saw pictures of me!"

"Handsomer!" Wai-yee said. "You are still much handsomer! And brilliant! And you talk, talk, talk!"

"Ahhh! Handsomer! And brilliant! Mr. Dunston, I look like an old man. And that's because I am an old man. I talk a lot now. I admit it. But I talk a lot because just like children should be seen and not heard, the elderly should be heard and not seen."

Moose smiled. "Confucius?"

Wai-yee shook her head and answered, "Not Confucius. It is Yeung!" Then she turned to Dr. Yeung. "Now tell him about Arthur!" And she turned just as quickly back to Moose. "This is such an amazing story! And he loves to tell it! But you must imagine William Holden!"

Dr. Yeung leaned toward Moose. "While I was in China during the war, Arthur May was a prisoner of war of the Japanese here in Hong Kong. He was a British citizen here, a civil engineer. He was in his mid-thirties like I was when the war broke out, and he lived with his parents. Now, listen to what he did: On Christmas Day of 1941, while the Japanese were taking over Hong Kong, he was getting water and electricity supplies in an old bombed out building to bring to hospitals before the Japanese got to him. In that building he found a flag there—the Union Jack, the flag of Great Britain. He folded it and—he doesn't know exactly why he did it, probably it was an act of sentiment and patriotism, but he hid it beneath a cushion of the couch in his parent's living room. He felt it was safe there because the Japanese said they would imprison all the British in Hong Kong except the old and sick, and his parents were old and sick.

"The Japanese soldiers found him and took him off to prison. It was the worst one, the one in Shamshuipo on Argyle Street in Kowloon. That's where he was put. It's still there, being readied for Vietnamese refugees now.

"One of the prisoners taken that day was Franklin Gimson who had been the Number Two Man to Governor Mark Young. They took Governor Young to Manchuria as a prisoner, so Gimson was the highest ranking Englishman left in Hong Kong. Both Gimson and Arthur became friends, with Gimson taking covert charge of the prisoners, continually giving them hope that the future would be theirs. Arthur was acting in the service of Gimson—in a sense, his deputy. So it went through the early 1940s. At the beginning of 1945, Gimson and Arthur had heard that President Roosevelt wanted Chiang Kai-shek of China to take Hong Kong when the war was over rather than having Hong Kong revert back to Great Britain.

The United States was giving the orders in the Pacific Theater and if that's what Roosevelt wanted, that's what Roosevelt would get at the end of the war. What could Churchill do? You know, Roosevelt was very anti-colonial since he was a child. He was sixteen years old at the time the New Territories were leased to Great Britain and he didn't like it even then.

"But President Roosevelt died in April and the war was still not won. President Truman didn't care whether colonialism survived or didn't survive. He said that when the war ended, as far as he was concerned, whichever of the two powers got to Hong Kong first, could take it. After all, both Churchill and Chang Kai-shek were allies of your country.

"Of course China had every advantage to get here first. China was across the border whereas Great Britain was across the globe. And so Arthur and Franklin Gimson devised a plan; a plan that, as it worked out, did what even they could never have envisioned:

"Just before dawn of August the 18th of 1945, Arthur and a few other prisoners were sent to chop rocks at Kai Tak. When the chains were off their ankles so they could chop, they gave each other the signal and ran like the devil to a triple layer fence. There was barbed wire, then a link fence, then an electrified fence. Arthur and the others were so thin by this time of their imprisonment that they were able to get under those fences. Arthur had gone from 175 pounds to 97 pounds. They escaped and they kept on running. Arthur led the small group of escapees to his parent's home and rescued the flag that was placed beneath the cushion on the couch back on Christmas Day almost four years earlier. They took it, then they crossed the harbor on a junk and went on to Victoria Peak, high above the city, where Arthur raised the flag of Great Britain for all to see. A small group of Japanese soldiers rushed to him and his friends, but Arthur told the soldiers that Japan had surrendered and he was reclaiming the city for the Crown.

"The Japanese government had not yet officially used the word 'surrender,' although on the 14th they had de facto surrendered. The Japanese soldiers in Hong Kong didn't know what was true, and what wasn't true and the ones on the Peak were afraid that if they disallowed the flag to remain up there the British would take revenge on them—kill them or something, they didn't know. When Franklin Gimson, at the prison camp, saw the distant flag above the Peak, he immediately took the oath of office as Acting Governor representing His Majesty King George VI, and he told the Japanese officers to get out of the prison encampment. With the same fear as the Japanese on the Peak, they obeyed.

"Well, it took twelve more days until the British ships of Rear Admiral Sir Cecil Harcourt got to Hong Kong to accept the formal surrender of the occupying Japanese—twelve days that beyond any doubt would have brought the forces of China to simply cross the border and claim Hong Kong as theirs if Great Britain's flag had not already been planted and the territory re-claimed.

"What no one could have known, not Arthur or Franklin Gimson or King George the Sixth or Chiang Kai-shek or President Truman, was that

Arthur and Gimson were saving Hong Kong from a fate that was far different than they thought. Four years forward, in 1949, Chiang Kai-shek would lose the entire mainland of China to the communist rule of Mao Tse-tung, and Mao would then have included Hong Kong as part of his captured territory from Chiang Kai-shek.

"The flag of Arthur May saved Hong Kong for the British. But more than that, he saved Hong Kong from a communist government that was to come into power in 1949. Franklin Gimson was soon Sir Franklin Gimson, and the Governor's Office was handed back to the freed prisoner, Governor Mark Young, reassuming the Governorship that he had begun before the Japanese attacked.

"So, Mr. Dunston, had that flag not been saved and hidden on Christmas Day of 1941, and then raised almost four years later by Arthur May, the miracle of today's Hong Kong would have never come to be."

"What a story!"

"Arthur still has the flag," Wai-yee said. "I've touched it. I help him on his correspondence and writings."

"That's what Wai-yee does on Wednesdays," Dr. Yeung said with pride. "She takes Liberty with her. Wai-yee doesn't waste a moment. That's principle. That's love of principle. You see that he who merely knows right principles is not equal to Wai-yee who loves right principles. Now, let me tell you about what she did on Sunshine Island to help that man named Gus Borgee—"

"Oh, no, Chi-shing," Wai-yee interrupted. "He's heard enough. Talk, talk, talk. Let's go inside, it's getting cold."

"I better go," Moose said, to insure the subject of Sunshine Island would be shelved. "I start my first day of work in Hong Kong tomorrow and I better be rested. If it's okay with you, I'll call a cab. It's been a wonderful evening."

It had been.

Moose asked the taxi driver to drop him off on Nathan Road so he could walk in Kowloon and then take the ferry to Hong Kong Island.

Nathan Road was brighter than he had seen it before. More lights. No police kiosks in the streets any more. Some railings had been placed adjacent to the sidewalks to prevent jay-walking. With all its changes, it was still paradise.

The Miramar was still there at the corner of Kimberley Road, but it had been enlarged. Moose went inside. It was difficult for Moose to figure out where the old reception desk and bell captain's desk and elevators were—but he found them in the old wing that was being prepared for renovation. How he longed to see Room 19, but he resisted the impulse to ask if it was occupied. "Always the Miramar," he remembered Wai-yee saying on the last night of the trip in which they met. He went back outside the hotel and there were the old plaques with their "Miramar" emblems on them. Which was the one they had raised their hands to caress? That one. He felt it again.

The ferry ride to the Hong Kong side was vacant without Wai-yee beside him. The soft noise of the sea lapping against the side of the 'Twinkling Star' ferry was like a beautiful song. Those buildings! So high, so many of them, so magnificent and so beautifully lit for the Christmas and New Year season.

Once on the Hong Kong side, he walked for over an hour up and down Queen's Road Central, just to breathe it in. Now there was even a McDonalds. So many changes. So many things, unexpected.

Finally he went to his destination of the Hilton, where Liberty had been created. Now Liberty was a living, breathing human being; a beautiful little girl who lived on the Kowloon side.

FIFTY
THE FOURTH OPTION
1980

Almost every night since November the 4th, Mohammad and Maryam Azimi went up to Anne's Room. bringing dinner with them. It was Saturday, January the 26th, the 84th night since their guest arrived.

Anne had never allowed herself, or her room, to be unkempt. She kept herself looking as though she was going to attend a public event. She was clean and put on cosmetics, and after taking care of herself every morning, she made her bed, and cleaned the room. There was not a scrap of paper out of place. There was a psychology of well-being to maintain for her hosts, and for herself.

On that 84th night, Mohammad was late. He ran up the stairs after being away all day, and he was literally bursting to talk. Maryam was knitting, talking with Anne when he knocked on the room's door and said, "It's me. It's me."

Maryam opened the door, they gave a short kiss and he almost ran in the room. "Anne, I don't know if I have put my thoughts in an orderly fashion, so forgive me if I ramble, but everything I have to say is important."

"Slow down, Mohammad," Maryam said.

"Tell me, Anne, do you know a married couple, the Staffords, and another married couple, the Lijeks, and do you know a Robert Anders and Lee Schatz?"

Anne's eyes seemed twice their normal size. "Yes! All of them! Why?"

"You know them well?"

"Very well. They all work for the Embassy. Are they okay?"

Mohammad nodded. "They're fine," and he sat down at his usual place at the dinner table Maryam had set in Anne's room.

"We waited for you for dinner. I'll make it," Maryam said.

Mohammad shook his head. "Later."

Anne said, "Lee Schatz is the agricultural attaché, and all the others you mentioned work for the consular section at the embassy. Bob Anders runs the consular office, Joe and Kathy Stafford process visas there, and Mark Lijek is the consular attaché. I don't know his wife very well. Her name is Cora and she just got here recently. She's a clerk there, I think. How do you know all their names?"

"Never mind. Four of them ran like you did when the embassy was invaded. They were on the second floor of the consulate building when the militants stormed into the compound. You may remember, the first floor had just been re-painted in the last number of days before the takeover, so the militants who invaded walked into the first floor, and they thought the building was deserted because it was all fresh wet paint. They got out of that building, and they didn't go back in and go up to the second floor until a number of hours later. So Anders, the Staffords and the Lijeks had time to get out when they realized what was happening. Shatz happened to be at some other Embassy and he went to a friend's house."

"Where did the others go?"

"They ran, just like you. Schatz went to some friend's place, the other five got to Anders' apartment and he took a chance and phoned a friend who works for the Canadian embassy, John Sheardown. He's the chief immigration officer there. Anders told Sheardown what was happening at the American Embassy and told him that he and four others needed a place to hide. His apartment would be overridden in short time and he knew it. Sheardown offered to take them in, then he went to his Ambassador, Kenneth Taylor, and they agreed to split them up between the Ambassador and Sheardown. The Ambassador cabled his superiors in Canada and got instant approval for the Canadians to shelter the Americans, no matter the risks. The Staffords moved in with Ambassador Taylor, the other three remained with Sheardown and his wife. Later, Shatz joined the group. They're all still at the Taylors and the Sheardowns."

"Wow! How do you know all this?"

"I'll get to that in a moment. You see, the American people, the public, have never been told a precise number of those held hostage. One day the White House will say they think one number, maybe fifty, maybe fifty-two, then the next day they give another number. There's been one sharp journalist who's caught on–Jean Pelletier, but he's not revealed anything. He's been conscientious. You see, you're not the only one who ran that morning."

"Mr. Azimi, how do you know all this?"

Mrs. Azimi looked uneasy. "Tell her, please."

He nodded. "I do more than electrical work, Anne."

"The CIA?" Anne asked. "For our CIA?"

"At times. I know this city's western diplomatic community very well. Ambassador Taylor phoned me this morning and said his electricity needed some repairs at his residence. I knew what that meant. I went over there with my equipment just as though I was going to do some electrical work."

"Then he told you all this?"

"He told me because he wants my assistance. Assistance I will give. While I was there an embassy courier delivered a diplomatic pouch from Canada–the hand carried type with 'Privileged' marked in red. He spilled its contents on the Ambassador's table. It was what he requested: With the cooperation of his government and your CIA there were six Canadian passports with the signatures and pictures of the six Americans, all the passports showing some wear, all with different visas from previous trips, visas stamped from different countries, and all kinds of identification for them. Fake. There were fake credit cards, driver's licenses, union cards, health cards, business cards, all kinds of things they'd be expected to carry. Works of art. It's as if they were members of a business delegation visiting Iran and staying with members of the Canadian Embassy staff while they were here.

"And plane tickets—for Monday morning—the day after tomorrow—to get out of here—six Swissair tickets to Frankfurt with a stopover in Zurich. As backup, in case the flight is canceled or something happens, there was a packet of tickets to get out on K.L.M., Air France, and British Airways to all different places in Europe on Monday. It is very daring of the Canadians. Our Mehrabad Airport is where I come in. A number of us—people the Canadians trust—CIA locals, as you would say, will be standing around inside the airport—that's all. If something goes wrong, we know how to distract the attention of inspectors through diversions. They call us the 'Mother Hens.' As one of the 'Mother Hens,' I'm going to be fixing some of the electrical circuits near the departure lounge—and changing some bulbs. I can do anything, if need be, from dropping a bulb and creating a minor explosion, to something much more devastating."

"Ohhh, Mr. Azimi! That is so dangerous! Will you be safe?"

He nodded.

Mrs. Azimi shook her head. "There is no use talking about safety with him. I have given up using that word to him."

Mohammad Azimi ignored the remark. "My regret, my dear Anne, is that I did not know anything about all this until today. Had I known earlier I would have told Ambassador Taylor about you, and there would be seven 'Canadians' at Mehrabad Airport the day after tomorrow, not six. But that was not to be. I am sorry. All the preparation and documents are done. And the ambassador is worried that some one knows about the Americans at his residence. The other day there was a phone call and Mrs. Taylor answered it. A man's voice asked for Joe or Kathy Stafford. Mrs. Taylor played it very well even though she was scared to death. She said she didn't know who the caller was talking about. The caller said he knew they were there, staying with the Taylors. He demanded one of them be put on the phone. She told the caller to talk to her husband at the embassy because she knew nothing about what he was talking about. And she hung up and then she called the ambassador to tell him.

"She was going to leave Teheran today but because of the snow, she can't. She will go tomorrow. The weather looks like it will be all right. The Taylors are amazing and courageous people. You realize that they are taking their lives in their hands? And the Canadian Government, Prime Minister Clark and Foreign Minister Flora MacDonald gave their okay in a snap of the fingers. This is all unprecedented."

"It's such a risk! Will it work?"

"Tonight, probably right now at this moment, your six friends are going through a practice interrogation of their Canadian rebirths; of where in Canada they were born, where they were raised, the schools they went to, their jobs, their bosses, their entire backgrounds. Yes, it is very risky."

"Will the ambassador go with them on Monday?"

"He is going to leave on Monday too, on a later plane than the six

Americans, but before word gets out of what he did—and they come for him. The Canadian embassy will be closed. No one will be there."

"Did you tell the ambassador about you and Maryam sheltering me?"

"No. In one way I wanted to, very much, but I knew it was too late and there would be nothing he could do at this point because all the arrangements had already been made. And I also knew that he would have no choice but to tell the American authorities where you are when he gets out of here. If he knew about you and told your Secretary of State, it would not be good. I do not trust your government. It talks too much. Look what they have done to other intelligence information. Other than a few friends, I am one of the last in this country who still will do work for the CIA. Some of the names of my friends have been revealed at your Congress' hearings. Some have been revealed in your nation's press. As of this moment, no one knows you are here except Maryam and me, and so far, we have not had any problems. But I know it can't go on forever. Anne, this all made me realize we must develop a plan very quickly, for your escape."

Anne was silent.

Mrs. Azimi asked, "How?"

"The ambassador had three plans for those six Americans. The first one was for the six Americans to go north by road all the way to Tabriz, then have a helicopter take them to Turkey across the border. He called it 'The Turkish Option.' The problem was that it would take over two months to set up. They'd need safe houses along the way. It would be a very complicated drive, and, too, it would be complicated to set it up with the Turks. The second option was to drive west to Khorramshahr near the Iraqi border. From Khorramshahr they would go down a short waterway to the Persian Gulf. But that ride from Teheran to Khorramshahr is very long and very dangerous. So the third option was the one they chose—fly out through Mehrabad Airport.

"Unless either of you two very intelligent ladies can think of a fourth option, I am considering Option Number Two: the drive to Khorramshahr, with all its dangers."

It was after midnight when Anne, in her nightgown, knocked on the bedroom door of the Azimis.

Mohammad Azimi got out of bed and, pajama-clad, he opened the door just a crack. When he saw Anne he opened it all the way. "Come in! Is everything all right?"

"Yes. I'm sorry to bother you at this hour, but the time is so short before the Americans and Ambassador Taylor leave Teheran. I have an idea. Is Mrs. Azimi awake?"

"Now she is. Come in."

Anne sat on the bed. Maryam raised the pillow on the bedpost and propped her head against it. "Are you all right, Anne?"

"Yes. I'm fine. I have an idea. A fourth option."

Mohammad turned on the lamp and sat on a small chair near the bed. "Go ahead, Anne."

"After the Staffords and the Lijeks and Bob and Lee get out–after the plane leaves–and the ambassador leaves–there will still be backup tickets left on other airlines, right–for later flights that day?"

"Yes. K.L.M., Air France, British Airways, if they don't have to use them."

"They are already in someone's possession?"

"The ambassador has them."

"Okay. If you tell the ambassador about me tomorrow–could he furnish a blank Canadian passport? I don't mean as well as what was done for the others, but just put my name in it, and my picture from my U.S. passport or one of the picture's dupes. I have them. I'll take my chances–after the rest leave. I don't need all the other identification. I can say I lost my wallet but I kept my passport and tickets separately. I really do that, anyway."

"You mean get the passport all fixed up in a day? Here in Teheran?"

"Yes. As best as can be done. Maybe one of the talented 'Mother Hens' could fix it up. And I'll take one of the backup tickets that aren't used. Someone can give it to me at the airport."

"I don't think so."

"Will you think about it?"

"It seems unrealistic and much too dangerous."

"Is it any more dangerous than driving to Khorramshahr?"

After Anne left their room, Mohammad and Maryam talked it over before going back to sleep, and they decided against it.

Their decision changed in the early morning when their phone rang and Maryam answered it to hear a man's voice on the other end ask, "Is Anne Whitney there, please?"

"What? Who?"

"Anne Whitney, please. It's very important."

Maryam handled it well, having been told about the incident at the Taylor's residence. "There is no one here by that name."

"I know that she is there, staying with you. Please put Anne Whitney on. Is she still in the second story bedroom?"

"You are drunk. Please annoy someone else. I am not well."

Within an hour, Mohammad Azimi went back to the Canadian Embassy grounds, holding on to his metal box with all kinds of electric gear.

He did not come home until nine o'clock at night. Maryam had been pacing by the door and from time to time moving the drapes slightly to see outside. When she saw his car drive up, she opened the door for him, she kissed his cheek and she said, "we were so worried." He came in and closed the door.

"I know. I couldn't help it."

"Anne and I ate but there's plenty left over."

"Good. Don't worry. Let's go up to Anne's room."

Anne sighed in relief after the bedroom door opened and she saw them both together. "I was so worried! You are so late, Mr. Azimi! Maryam and I were so worried! Are you all right?"

"Yes, of course," he said calmly. "I was out shopping."

"Shopping?"

"Yes. I bought you a gift from Maryam and me. Now, close your eyes."

"I can't close my eyes. I'm so glad to have my eyes see you."

"Please. Like a little girl. Close your eyes. I will tell you when to open them."

She closed her eyes, as ordered.

"It's a book, Anne. I brought you a very good book. I'll read the beginning of it aloud."

Maryam smiled when he took the small booklet out of his jacket pocket.

He started reading: "The Secretary of State for External Affairs of Canada requests in the name of her Majesty the Queen, all those whom it may concern to allow the bearer to pass freely without let or hindrance, and to afford the bearer such assistance and protection as may be necessary."

At 4:30 Monday morning Mohammad Azimi was at Mehrabad Airport for the beginning of the succession of escapes. Most of the time he was on a ladder near the departure lounge with wires hanging from the ceiling as he attached one to another to another and took them apart and put them together again.

Two Canadian Embassy cars arrived at 6:20 A.M., one with the Staffords, and the other with the Lijeks, Lee Schatz and Bob Anders.

Other than a twenty minute delay for some mechanical problem with the Swissair plane, there were no hitches in the departure of the six Americans. The plane lifted above the ground, and it was on its way beyond view from Mehrabad.

Later came the next departure, for which no problem was expected or encountered. The Ambassador waved good-bye to Iran. Unseen by anyone at the airport was his nation's flag, neatly folded in his briefcase, leaving with him.

No backup airline tickets had been needed.

After the British Airways flight left with Ambassador Taylor aboard, the same Canadian embassy car went back into central Teheran and picked up a woman dressed in a black chador on a corner, a block away from

Razmavaran Avenue. The car then drove back to Mehrabad Airport, this time with the new passenger.

At the first checkpoint, it was easy. The Revolutionary Guards looked through her luggage, snapped it shut and that was all there was to it.

She went to the K.L.M. counter and received her boarding pass.

At the second checkpoint she showed her passport and there was no problem. Not even one question.

At the third and last checkpoint before entering the departure lounge, she had her choice of lines in which to stand before coming to the Revolutionary Guard Immigration Authorities. Mohammad Azimi was on a ladder near the doorway to the departure lounge fooling with something behind a panel hanging from the ceiling.

The passenger line in which Anne stood was long but it moved fast. When she was only two people away from the immigration officer she saw who he was: the same Revolutionary Guard who gave her a difficult time about her tube of lipstick when she entered the country the last time—as an American, not as a Canadian. She almost let out a yelp, but caught herself. It was not that long ago that they had talked, and she had been so haughty and feisty toward him, and he had paid such attention to her as an American diplomat.

She busily started looking through her purse, her face held down, as though she was unable to find something. She took one thing out after another and then got out of line, looking confused, as though she had to find something left behind.

She went back almost as far as Checkpoint Number Two, still looking through her purse. Then, as though she discovered whatever it was she had lost, she returned to the area of lines of Checkpoint Number Three. She chose the line closest to the wall and three lines away from the recognized Revolutionary Guardsman official.

This line was slow while the other lines were proceeding with speed. When once again she was two passengers away from the immigration officer, he got up from his chair, left his booth, and walked to the man she wanted most to avoid. The two of them talked and looked over to the line in which Anne was standing. She quickly turned around and again delved in her purse with her back facing them. She knew they could have been talking about anything, and not to panic. To her knowledge, the Revolutionary Guard Immigration Officer she was trying to avoid did not see her face. After a couple minutes of waiting for the immigration officer to come back to the booth, Anne looked up at the place where Mohammad Azimi pretended to be working. He took brief glances down and saw Anne looking at him. He quickly looked away toward his work.

The immigration officer came back to his booth, the dialogue between the other officer unknown to Anne. She stayed in the same line. The two passengers ahead of her went through the checkpoint and then Anne put her passport in front of the man. "How long have you been in Iran?" he asked in English.

"Three weeks. Close to three weeks, anyway," she said with a casual tone.

"Purpose of visit?"

"Tourism, I guess you'd call it. I wanted to see the Revolution for myself."

"Where did you go?"

"Everywhere I could. It is even better than I imagined. My girlfriend works in the Canadian embassy and she told me to come visit her if I wanted to see the revolution first hand. It was like being a part of history. So I went to their embassy, and stayed in her apartment. I tried every day to see the Ayatollah. He is a saint. But he was so busy he could not see me. I am going to see him some day when he travels the world, or else I will be back to see him—and I will be glad if I can just touch his gown."

"You are a Moslem?"

"No. I am a Christian. But I can recognize a God-like man when I see one whether he is a Christian or a Moslem. Someday I will touch his gown."

The immigration officer nodded with a large smile. "Good luck," he said and he stamped her passport. She walked into the Departure Lounge.

Her flight was called. There was another line, but no check point procedure other than giving the boarding pass to the guard at the gate. She went aboard, and the doors were closed. In minutes the airliner started out of the gate, down the take off strip, and the flight took off. It was like flying away from a grave that had been dug for her.

After the K.L.M. flight was nothing more than a far off speck in the sky, three Revolutionary Guardsmen came to the base of the ladder on which Mohammad Azimi was standing.

He looked down at them.

They surrounded the base of his ladder, looking up at him.

"Yes?" He asked. "What do you want?"

One of them answered, "How is your work proceeding, Mr. Azimi?"

They shouldn't have known his name. "Fine. Fine. I'm almost through."

"You are through now, Mr. Azimi. Your wife is in our car waiting for you. The Islamic Fundamentalist Revolutionary Court is anxious to see both of you today." One of the other two guards started shaking the ladder back and forth and then sideways, tilting it further and further until Mohammad Azimi fell to the floor, his equipment falling with him. He lay as though he was a puddle. The three Revolutionary Guards picked him up, one by each foot, and one under the arms, and they carried him out to the waiting automobile.

FIFTY-ONE
DIFFERENT CHANNELS
1980

The television series "Three's Company," "The Jeffersons," "Charlie's Angels," and "Dallas" had serious competition. It was the image of an angry President Carter.

"At this time in Iran, 50 Americans are still held captive; innocent victims of terrorism and anarchy. Also, at this moment, massive Soviet troops are attempting to subjugate the fiercely independent and deeply religious people of Afghanistan. These two acts—one of international terrorism and one of military aggression—present a serious challenge to the United States of America and indeed to all the nations of the world. Together, we will meet those threats to peace.

"If the American hostages are harmed, a severe price will be paid. We will never rest until every one of the hostages is released. But we now face a broader and more fundamental challenge in this region because of the recent military action of the Soviet Union.

"The Soviet Union must pay a concrete price for their aggression. While this invasion continues, we and the other nations of the world cannot continue business as usual with the Soviet Union."

Another channel: Ted Murphy looked foolish wearing a poorly wrapped headdress, standing against a mountainous background. "This week I'm reporting from somewhere in Afghanistan," he told his audience. It was true, except 'somewhere' could easily have been revealed, although it would have lost the audience's perception of danger if he had acknowledged that he was standing exactly three steps across the border from Pakistan.

"Let me read the president's statement to you," Ted Murphy said to the camera. "These are the president's words: 'The implications of the Soviet invasion of Afghanistan could pose the most serious threat to the peace since the Second World War.... The situation demands careful thought, steady nerves and resolute action—not only for this year, but for many years to come.... Meeting this challenge will take national will, diplomatic and political wisdom, economic sacrifice and, of course, military capability. We must call on the best that is in us to preserve the security of this crucial region. Let our position be absolutely clear. An attempt by any outside force to gain control of the Persian Gulf region will be regarded as an assault on the vital interests of the United States of America. And such an assault will be repelled by any means necessary, including military force.'

"Clearly President Carter is not going to stop at imposing economic punishments and boycotting the Moscow Olympics, although many argue that those measures are already going too far. They say it isn't the Russian people or our American athletes who have created this conflict, yet they will be the ones who will suffer from the president's actions. There are also those I've talked to here who say that if any conflict is a local one that has no bearing on the United States, this is one of them. As for the Soviet Union being in Afghanistan, it was pointed out to me that they have been here politically, long before their troops arrived. Many wonder what the United States would do if, perhaps, one of the governments in the Western Hemisphere was a government of which we disapproved. Most people I've talked to know what we would do, and that it would not be much different than the Soviets are doing." Murphy paused and gave a short smile. "Does anyone remember the Bay of Pigs? This is Ted Murphy, somewhere in Afghanistan."

"Good one!" the cameraman yelled out.

Ted Murphy quickly took off the headdress, walked three steps back into Pakistan, and got in the waiting automobile. He ordered his Pakistani driver to take him back to the Khyber Intercontinental Hotel in Peshawar.

Another channel: Iran's Foreign Minister Sadegh Ghotbzadeh was standing outside the American Embassy in Teheran with a crowd in the background who were shaking their fists at the camera while two men behind Ghotbzadeh carried a banner that read, "U.S. The Great Satan. Death to Amrika and Canada"

"Sooner or later," Ghotbzadeh said, "somewhere in the world, Canada will pay for their illegal forging of passports, their illegal forging of the stamps, and illegally taking out of Teheran the Americans they had harbored in their Embassy in clear violation of international law. Because of what they have done here, the Canadian government will be directly responsible for any harsh treatment we mete out against the 50 American spies."

Another channel: Cody and Gloria Cooper, as the most prominent refugee advocates, were being interviewed from the departure lounge of Subang Airport in Kuala Lumpur. Their sound-asleep five year old son's head rested on Gloria's shoulder. "We're leaving," a bearded Cody Cooper said, who looked much more distinguished than he used to look clean-shaven. There were even touches of gray in his beard, adding to his dignity. "There's nothing more we can do here."

Gloria had increased her visual credibility as well, looking more matronly and authoritative than before with no makeup at all, her hair still tied into a bun but it was more visible behind her head, and a skirt that brushed the floor as she sat. She told the interviewer, "Last year the Pope visited the remains of Auschwitz, the Nazi Concentration Camp, and he said that it's necessary to ask with fear, how far can cruelty go? The very morning after that, at 6:00 A.M. there was an answer to his question, half the world away from him. Cody and I saw it and couldn't stop it–110 empty buses arrived at Aranyaprathet in Thailand. Cambodian refugees were put aboard those buses without being told where they were going. But some had a premonition and they tried to escape the soldiers who were administering the boarding process. Those people were clubbed, beaten, and forced back onto the buses. The soldiers told them that they had their orders. Sound familiar? The buses headed for the Cambodian border full, came back empty, went toward the border while they were full again, came back empty, and on and on the process went, until 43,000 people had disappeared from Thailand. Those people had once risked their lives to get to freedom. To be sent back to Cambodia was certain death. I had heard their stories. I was trying to find out what happened to a friend of mine who was a nurse when the Khmer Rouge took over. I found out. She had been murdered by them on April 17, 1975, when they massacred those in the hospitals. So if they did that back then—just because she was a nurse—what do you suppose was the fate of refugees sent back from Malaysia?

"A week after they were sent back, the government here in Kuala Lumpur—here in Malaysia—announced they would send 76,000 Vietnamese refugees to the open sea; that they would leave them to isolation in international waters, and they would shoot on sight any Boat People found trying to enter Malaysia.

"At one time Malaysia was a refugee haven—that's when Cody and I came here. But we saw it change. That's when Cody did—did what he did, which is now so well known—when he rescued so many Vietnamese refugees from a boat that was sent back to sea. There are few refugees left here now from either Cambodia or Vietnam, and the government would rather we would leave. And so we will leave, and we'll go to where we are wanted. The World Refugee Mission is sending us to El Salvador where the refugees are escaping from Nicaragua and becoming more than El Salvador can handle. They asked for us."

Cody started speaking and the camera panned to the left to get him in frame. "A person I knew once in Nicaragua told me that there is no separation from humanitarianism and politics, and it's true. Neither the World Refugee Mission nor I enter into taking sides in political conflicts, but it is undeniable that the refugees all over the world are victims of the political decisions of the governments they flee: they are the governments of Cambodia, Laos, Vietnam, Angola, Mozambique, Ethiopia, South Yemen, Iran, Afghanistan, Guyana, and Nicaragua. We cannot point fingers if we refuse those refugees a safe haven on our own shores. I would hope that the president and the Congress join together to save the lives of those men and women and children without a country. Please, politicians, read that tablet on the pedestal of the Statue of Liberty. It has Emma Lazarus's poem that offers world wide welcome that was probably the greeting received by most of your parents or grandparents—or maybe even you. It says, 'Give me your tired, your poor, your huddled masses yearning to breathe free, the wretched refuse of your teeming shore. Send these, the homeless, tempest-tossed to me, I lift my lamp beside the golden door!'

To the president and the Congress, would you have taken down that tablet generations back and prevented your own heritage from coming here? Don't take it down now. And don't turn away from it.

"As you know, I worked for President Kennedy. On the first day of his administration, he said, 'Let every nation know, whether it wishes us well or ill, that we shall pay any price, bear any burden, meet any hardship, support any friend, oppose any foe, in order to assure the survival and the success of liberty.' But now we say, 'Let every nation know, whether it wishes us well or ill, that we will pay no more cost, bear no burden, meet no hardship, betray a friend, befriend a foe, in order to assure the survival and the success of apathy.'

"I just told you what President Kennedy said on the first day of his administration. On the last day of his administration President Kennedy said, 'Without the United States, South Vietnam would collapse overnight. Without the United States, the SEATO Alliance would collapse overnight. Without the United States the CENTO Alliance would collapse overnight. Without the United States there would be no NATO.' That's what he said and now NATO is all that's left. We deserted the others, and South Vietnam collapsed, the SEATO Alliance collapsed, and the CENTO Alliance collapsed. We have an obligation to pick up the pieces. And the pieces are human beings."

Another channel: President Carter was talking about the Soviet presence in Afghanistan and the threat that presence might portend to the Persian Gulf. "I don't think it would be accurate for me to claim that at this time or in the future we expect to have enough military strength and enough military presence there to defend the region unilaterally."

Retired Brigadier General Jonas Valadovich nodded. "You and the Congress did it—emasculated the military," he said to the image on the television monitor.

Sally Saigon, resting on Jonas' lap, slowly closed then opened her eyes, along with spreading her claws, then tightening them, showing solid agreement with Jonas' appraisal of the president's statements. Jonas wanted to reward her for agreeing with him, so he turned the power-off button on the remote, and the president's image and voice disappeared into a vanishing dot in the middle of the tube.

Sally started purring, but the purring stopped and her eyes opened wide when she heard the telephone. She knew that meant she would be dumped from his lap.

"Pardon me, Sally," Jonas said as he lifted her off his lap and set her on the coffee table. She jumped off the table and like any woman, she walked out of the room as if she had more important things to do than sit with him, anyway.

Jonas picked up the phone. "Hello?"

"General?"

"Yes sir."

"Congratulations on your silver star, General. It's good to call you General. How are you, Jonas?"

"Thank you, but who is this?"

"This is Dan–Dan Graham. General Daniel Graham."

"Oh, for God's sake! Hey, General! I'm fine. Fine. This is a surprise. How are you?"

"Good! Did you hear the president?"

"Yes, sir."

"Listen. I'm doing some advisory work for Ronald Reagan. I told him I'd call some of the best military thinkers in the country and get the best opinions. That's why I'm calling you. What do you think of what Carter said?"

"You're working for Reagan?"

"Just helping him. He's high on defense, you know, and I want to help him in his presidential campaign."

"You pressing him on your High Frontier?"

"You bet I am. I gave him the works on that. I told him if we don't have a High Frontier program with the ability to knock out incoming missiles, we're not providing the nation with the common defense demanded of the government by the Constitution. But that's not why I called. I want your thoughts. I need them for Reagan. What do you think of what Carter's saying?"

"President Carter admitted what you and I already knew, didn't he–that we've short-changed our military capabilities. Maybe this will wake up the country. I have my list of D.O.D. requirements, and I'm sure you have yours in addition to your High Frontier Missile Defense System. The president's statement ought to get Secretary of Defense Brown to make some urgent requests of the Congress for defense now."

"You have a list?"

"I do."

"Send me your list, will you?"

"You bet."

"And how about his policy towards Iran–the hostages?"

"There is no policy in existence other than fear of Khomeini. Carter should recognize an Iranian Government in Exile and load it with economic and military aid–anything and everything they need. My only hesitation on that is I think Khomeini killed all the generals and colonels who would have been able to lead an effort like that. But if that's true, then we have to recruit the right people. It wouldn't have to be in exile if Carter had just left things alone in Iran. Khomeini wouldn't even be in Iran."

"I assume you're saying that you don't think the hostages will be released soon by using economic and diplomatic sanctions. Am I right?"

"Khomeini will only release the hostages if he should fear for himself, and President Carter is not a man to fear. And so our whole nation becomes afraid."

"How about U.S. ground troops?"

"Absolutely, if it becomes necessary. No hesitation."

"You're a tough customer, Jonas!"

"I'm like you, Dan. When you have to do something–do it. Dan, if Carter didn't abandon the Shah, he would have prevented the first Islamic Fundamentalist Revolutionary Government from taking power. Now there are other Islamic governments that are going to plagiarize what the Ayatollah got away with. What if it spreads throughout the Mideast, and even to Islamic countries beyond the Mideast?"

"I'm with you. What about Afghanistan and Nicaragua?

"We're going to have to use surrogates. Both places. If we don't, the Soviets will use Afghanistan to get to the Persian Gulf, and use Nicaragua to take over El Salvador and beyond. But I don't know if we have the means even for supplying surrogates adequately–or the will. But we better have the means and the will, and if we don't–we better get them back quick."

"I'm sorry you're not Secretary of Defense."

"No, thanks."

"Maybe that opportunity will come, if Reagan becomes president."

"I don't want it. I'm beginning to like the life I have now."

"What are you doing, anyway?"

"I'm giving advice on the military when anyone wants it, like I'm doing right now, so maybe I can be an influence that way. And I'm studying religion–every day."

Sally Saigon appeared at the doorway to the living room and gave a dirty look at Jonas as if to say, "Are you still on the phone? You're wasting time you could be spending with me."

"Religion?" General Graham asked.

"Yes, sir."

"Good for you! But what brought you to that?"

"What is it George Mallory said when he was asked why he wanted to climb Mount Everest? He said, 'Because it's there.'"

Sally walked out on him again.

"I'm with you. Good for you. So–any other thoughts? Any other way to go than what you already said?"

"There is another way, President Carter's way. President Carter's way is to follow Khomeini's lead."

"Send me any thoughts you have, will you?"

"You think Reagan can win?"

"I think he'll get the nomination. It will be tough but I think he can get it. And then we'll work to see he gets the presidency. And, unless I mess up, he's going to give our nation a defense against missiles. And, unless you don't want it, I think you can be a big part of that effort. It's going to be a great journey!"

Anne Whitney wasn't watching television. It was television that wanted to watch her. The producers of "CBS Morning News," "Good Morning, America," "Today," "Meet the Press," "Face the Nation," and "Issues and

Answers" all asked for television interviews with any of the Americans who received the aid of Canada in escaping, since a Montreal newspaper, *La Presse,* had leaked the story of the Canadians involvement in the escape of Americans, and the story was confirmed by all three governments; Canada, the United States, and Iran.

There were no interviews, on orders from the State Department to all the American escapees. Anne didn't care as much about that as she cared about the Azimis. She knew she would find out nothing about them. She couldn't. There was no one to ask. She didn't even tell the Agency their names in recognition that she would have to be as secret about the Azimis as the Azimis were about her. Trust would be a risk.

Even if the media knew of Anne Whitney's return to the United States, they wouldn't have known where to look for her. It was one of the few places in the world to which she was a stranger: Las Vegas, Nevada, at the Little White Wedding Chapel on the Strip.

"Do you want pictures of the ceremony?" the Justice of the Peace asked Mark. Anne gave a quick, "No," before Mark had an opportunity to even think about it.

"Do you want a recording of it?"

"No."

"Flowers?"

"No."

"Anything?"

"Just ask me if I want him and he wants me. Don't make a production out of it. If we wanted a production we'd be in Saint Patrick's Cathedral."

The Justice of the Peace nodded. There would be no supplementary profits to make off this couple. All they wanted was to have the ceremony done and get to their hotel room.

Their room at the Desert Inn was a mess. Clothes had been thrown and left to lie where ever they happened to land, and there was open luggage on the chairs and Pepsi cans were on the tables, the top of the television set, and the floor. Mark and Anne had taken immediate and absolute possession of the bed with the rest of the room being well beyond their interest, as was the magic city that was surrounding them.

"The last two months were absolute hell," Mark whispered to her. Anne's face was too close on the same pillow to speak in anything but a whisper. "It was every moment," he continued. "I was on the phone at least three times a day to the State Department, and three times a day I was told they were sure you were all right, but they couldn't confirm anything. I knew they were guessing. Anne, I didn't know if I would ever see you again. I didn't even know if you were alive. I don't ever want to let you out of my sight again."

Anne closed her eyes in contentment.

"For one moment this morning, when you did nothing more than went to the restroom at the Chapel–I became scared all over again. I thought, what if you don't come out?"

"Mark, don't." She raised one of her hands from under the covers and she brushed her hand through his hair. "I won't leave your sight."

"How did I waste all these years without you? It's not only that I love you more and more. I like you more and more."

"Mark?"

"Yes?"

"Don't like me more and more. This is the most dangerous time of all, more dangerous than when I was in Teheran. I want you to love me, but you won't crave me if you like me too much. Once you think of me as a person rather than a wench, all the excitement will be gone. I don't want to be your best friend, you know."

Mark smiled. "How did you get so smart?"

"What's smart is knowing how to keep this feeling. We can't stop the adventures!"

"Oh, yes we can—because we must."

Anne raised her head from the pillow. "What do you mean?"

"Anne, were you kidding Ambassador Fairbanks, and me, when you said that some day you were going to be the president of the United States?"

She stared at Mark's face. "No. I was very serious."

"Then your kind of adventures—your kind—have to stop. And you also have to make some very important decisions very soon—this week."

"What decisions?"

"Right now you can be the hottest piece of news in the country, but that opportunity won't last long. You can become a celebrity in an instant."

"So?"

"So that's what you'd need for a congressional race."

She leaned on her elbow. "I can't go on those shows. The State Department has nixed them. They're worried that something I could say would endanger the hostages left behind. But I don't know anything. I wasn't in the embassy. The only thing I know is who took me in, and I'll never reveal that. I'd die first."

"Anne, don't let this time slip by."

"What should I do?"

"Quit the Agency right away and go on every show you can. And aim for a congressional race in '82. It's already too late for you to run this year. We're going to shop for a place to live. After my post ends in Athens next year I'll be back in D.C., and we should get a residence in a Maryland or Virginia district where there won't be an incumbent in '82. I'll research it. And you have to have an organization. You have to have a professional campaign manager. There's a lot that goes into a campaign. I know a lot of members of the Congress who could be helpful. Campaigns are a career in themselves. Money. A lot of money. You have to know what you're doing. Are you up on all the issues?"

Anne shook her head.

"You better be. This is your time—if you want to have a time. Look how everything points to you. Iran. You were there. The invasion of Afghanistan by the Soviet Union. You were posted in Moscow. And you were good. You were very good."

Anne sat up in bed, not even looking at him now. "Oh, Mark. I'm scared."

"That's all right. Let it scare you. It's a big decision."

She turned to him. "I'm not scared of running for office. I'm scared of losing you. You like me too much. You're not excited by me now. You can't be, if you're thinking of all this. I want you to be excited by me every moment."

"Anne, stop worrying about that!"

"I can't help it."

"Excitement doesn't have to be every moment! Quit the Agency! Then go with me when I go back to Athens, and before we go—you become a celebrity. It's the right time. You can become a celebrity—tomorrow! Tomorrow night you could be on national television—and then a winning landslide!"

Anne rested beside him again. "No more adventures?"

"Not the ones you invent. They're too wild. You put away that '2002 Nights' book of yours."

"All that's over?"

"It's your choice."

"When do I need to make a decision?"

Mark looked up at the ceiling, and squinted as he thought about it. "Tomorrow. But not the day after tomorrow. Tomorrow."

"Then today and tonight I don't need to think about it?"

"That's right."

Anne raised her eyebrows. "Then there's still time for an adventure?"

Mark shook his head. "No. Not if you want to be a celebrity. You have to go public as the expert on foreign policy—and you are. You have to be the expert on Brezhnev, and you have to be the woman who challenged Idi Amin and fooled Khomeini. You are, you know!"

"But what would I say in those interviews? I know less than the average American knows about what's going on in Iran at the Embassy. I've been isolated."

"It isn't what you say about it that makes a difference. It's what you are. It's your presence—how you come across. You get on television! Let every one see you!"

Anne thought for a while, and then laid down again, this time not next to him, but on top of him with her face looking straight down at his face. She smiled with a sparkle in her eyes. "I got it! I can be naked on TV, can't I? That would make me a celebrity very quickly, wouldn't it?" She extended her hands and put them on his cheeks and kissed him long and deep. "Isn't this better than friendship?" Anne whispered.

He had to agree. "I guess I can always find a friend."

"So don't like me too much. Okay?"

"Anne, whether you know it or not, you've never had an adventure like the one ahead!"

"Wwww!"

"I'm talking about a political campaign."

"I'm not."

For the first time at 11:30 at night, Irene Goodpastor chose to watch Ted Koppel rather than Johnny Carson. She had read in the morning's *Washington Post* that Anne Whitney would be Ted Koppel's guest on "America Held Hostage" and Mrs. Goodpastor felt it must be the same Anne Whitney who was the outspoken girl she had met long ago at the U.S. Consulate in Hong Kong. "Escaped from Iran under the cloak of Canada's Embassy" the synopsis read beneath her name in the *Post*.

Viewing television had become either the godsend or the curse of Mrs. Goodpastor's evenings. Without a dream to pursue, the programs she watched became a new pattern of life. She was transported back into the world of people who were doing things. Television viewing became the chief diversion from her fear that she had a terminal illness, periodically thinking she had a new one. "What's that?" she asked herself with each new pain or symptom of something or nothing. Every week seemed to bring a new pill to take, and an old pleasure to abandon.

Nothing was simple any more. Inconvenience even became changing the television set's channel selector. She generally kept it on "Four". She simply dismissed television shows on other channels. It made life a little easier. Anne Whitney didn't know it, but Irene Goodpastor was expressing a mammoth interest in her by doing something so many others did with little thought: turning to Channel Seven.

It was worth it. For the first time Mrs. Goodpastor saw Anne as a woman. And what a woman. She handled herself masterfully, and she was so pretty now–a woman who exhibited authority without minimizing her femininity–the blue suit with a red trim accented her authority, but there was the red ribbon in her hair that put down proclaimed-feminists who might hope she was one of them.

"In an age when cowardice is expected and excused," Anne told Ted Koppel, "the Canadians were out of step with the trend. They were brave. How unfashionable, isn't it? Can we even imagine the penalty that Ambassador Taylor and his staff would have suffered had they been found out? We were given the greatest gift any nation can receive from another nation–being taken in. You see, real friendship among nations requires no treaty, no ceremony, no legal and binding contract, no threats for non-compliance. Their Minister of External Affairs, that's like our Secretary of State, Flora MacDonald, said her government never had a second thought, never a thought of not doing it. Canada's Prime Minister Joe Clark is the definition of being a friend. Yet he didn't even know us."

"And what do you think, Miss Whitney, of our policy, of President Carter's response to Iran regarding Canada's actions? Iran's Foreign Minister, Sadegh Ghotbzadeh, has said that Canada will pay for that, and he warned of harsh treatment to the American hostages because of it. Do you feel that President Carter has acted appropriately?"

"I do not have the information the president has, nor do I have his responsibilities, so that question is not one I can answer." It was a smart and diplomatic answer that no one could denounce.

Ted Koppel tried again. "I know you had to have heard the criticism of President Carter given from so many quarters. They say he should threaten Iran by saying that any action taken against Canada or Canadians would be regarded as an attack on the United States. Would you agree with that?"

Anne, with the aid of Mark, had rehearsed an answer, should Koppel put it that way. "I have to repeat, Mr. Koppel, that I am not in a position to offer suggestions of policy to the president. If you are asking what I would do if I were president—knowing only what I know today—I would warn the Ayatollah Khomeini that if there was any action taken against Canada or Canadians for what they did—I would, without hesitancy, wage war against his government using every means available to us to win that war quickly and completely. Canada didn't think twice, and neither should we. Further, Mr. Koppel, the actions already taken against our own diplomats, I believe would warrant such a response as I've suggested. But I offer this not as criticism of the president. With all the criticism that has been leveled against him, we shouldn't forget that he has responsibilities all over the world. What he did at Camp David in bringing peace between Egypt and Israel is something that is unequaled in the history of the Mideast. There is a tendency in the United States to be focused on one place at a time and to forget all things that interfere with the most dominant news. The president has the job of keeping his eyes all over the world at all times." She had become a skilled ambassador.

"Miss Whitney, can you give us a feel of what the hostages are going through at this time?"

"No. I'm not with them."

"From your previous vantage point?"

"I have nothing to offer on that." Again, perfect.

"During the president's State of the Union Address, the president said that, 'If the American hostages are harmed, a severe price will be paid.' I imagine that you agree with that. But what kind of price should that be?"

"But I don't agree with that." This was what she wanted to be asked, although what she planned on saying would undo any fondness for Anne from the president and his foreign policy advisers. "A severe price should be paid now, even while the hostages are being held. President Carter's error is that he's focusing his attention on my friends—our diplomats. Once our foes know they can hold our nation hostage by kidnapping a few, then those foes become our leaders, and those who we think are our leaders become nothing more than followers."

"Miss Whitney, are you saying you believe the diplomats lives are expendable?"

"No American is expendable, but it's visionless to think primarily of those held hostage now. The whole world counts each day. Your program tonight is one of a series entitled "America Held Hostage." On Day Number Two the president should have bombed the Khomeini Government out of existence, even if it placed me and the other diplomats at risk from the bombs, or from retaliation from Khomeini's thugs. He's right in pledging this nation will never yield to blackmail, but we are yielding to blackmail when he considers the lives of the diplomats above all. He should retaliate now."

"And you think your fellow diplomats would agree with you?"

"Do you remember, Mr. Koppel, what the P.O.W.s said when they got out of Hanoi? They said they had celebrated because we bombed the guts out of Hanoi, and whether or not the bombs hit the prisons, with them inside of them, was almost immaterial to every P.O.W., they were so glad that our nation wasn't resting in passivity."

"Miss Whitney, do you believe it would be the same for hostages?"

"I emphasize this because I must be clear: even if the retaliation does harm to our diplomats, it must be done so that hostage-taking of diplomats would be known throughout the world as having no value. Who would seize American hostages for no reward, but rather for guaranteed punishment? The reward for an enemy now is seeing our nation suffer. Americans must be able to go anywhere in the world without fear, and they would be able to do that if the message of our government was clear to all chiefs of state that if they touch one hair of our countrymen–if they touch one hair in hostility–that their reign will be through. It's always easier to talk about current hostages without thinking of future hostages, because we don't know who among us they will be. We better think of that. One could be you–or anyone watching this program."

"We thank you, Miss Whitney. And we're so glad to have you safe and unharmed, back home from Iran." Koppel was genuinely warm.

"Thank you. I do want to correct something you couldn't possibly have known. I'm no longer Miss Whitney," and she gave a smile. "I'm Mrs. Mark Daschle."

Mrs. Goodpastor didn't even hear the next line of Ted Koppel. Anne's remark caused Mrs. Goodpastor to hear nothing at all after the words "Mrs. Mark Daschle." Mark Daschle? How could that be? He and Anne were going at each other's throats back in Hong Kong! Or was something going on between them even then? Was it just a lover's quarrel she witnessed between them in Hong Kong? Was there a secret affair going on at that Consulate? "Mark Daschle!"

She was so shocked that she turned off the television set.

All of this made her feel even older than before she had turned on the television set. Marriage! Anne had to be in her early forties and looked like she was in her twenties. Mrs. Goodpastor was in her seventies, but she felt that she was in her nineties. Anne's skin was flawless. Mrs. Goodpastor was finding new age spots on her face and hands with alarming frequency. And Anne's teeth were so white and even. Some of

Mrs. Goodpastor's teeth were removable. And Anne was so smart and articulate and handled herself so well, and Mrs. Goodpastor felt she wouldn't come across that way to the public. Worse yet, it didn't matter. No one was asking her to appear on television. No one was asking her for an interview. No one was asking her what she thought of the president's policies.

When she was young she rarely thought of death. Now she thought of that subject every day. Of course she could live a long time to come, but no matter what she did, she asked herself if this was the last time she would be doing it. Moreover, her age had a disadvantage she hadn't thought of in earlier life: in her good fortune of living to this age there was the commensurate misfortune of seeing the death of so many others for whom she cared. It was, she learned, one or the other: do it or see it, there was no way to avoid both.

It would be unfair and inaccurate to say that watching television was her only habit. The rituals of getting up in the morning and going to bed at night became more than automatic, continually getting longer. It was not just the bath and the brushing of teeth and putting on makeup any more, "Which is all that dear Anne Whitney has to do! Just look at her!" It became all sorts of things that extended the post-sleeping and pre-sleeping rituals into enumerated procedures that had to be counted to insure none were forgotten.

"These aren't the Golden Years," she said to herself. "They're the Scotch-Tape Years—they're spent just trying to hold things together.

"I must remember to write Anne, and tell her how good she was on TV. And I must congratulate Mark Daschle! I think I should leave them something or other in my will. I'll leave her some jewelry. She'd like that. Those earrings she had on TV were fakes." That was another dominant thought: leaving someone something or other, or leaving someone nothing. Changing her will with codicils had become a monthly routine, as some of the people she liked became disliked, and some of the disliked became liked, and some of the liked died. Every first of the month was greeted by sitting at the parlor table in preparation of changing dollar amounts, or beneficiaries. Some times she would change the whole thing, then she would rip her previous will into vertical shreds and she would cut the shreds horizontally with a scissors, into minute thin squares of paper. Who would have an interest in reading one of her old wills was unclear, even to her. Nevertheless, all this was a way to greet each new month.

The rewriting of her will would always be followed by a notarization process which would at least get her out of the house for a while, walking to Rigg's Bank and back, with the walk providing her with the appropriate atmosphere to review her life in terms of accomplishments. Had she done enough? How would she be ranked by God and by those left behind and by those she would meet in heaven? It would be heaven, wouldn't it? Was it too late to accomplish more? Or was she, plainly, too tired to accomplish more? Her conscience troubled her that she had not done enough with life. Her memories and possessions were not enough. "And I'll write down instructions for Anne and Mark on how to throw a successful Washington party!"

Her worst malady was an unconscious one for which there was no doctor's prescription to minimize. It was the conceit that so often comes with advanced age of those who were once celebrated, and is somewhat like other diseases that can come with age, this one's chief symptoms being that all past accomplishments become central. That conceit creates a desire in the afflicted to talk about those past accomplishments, even to tell strangers, even to tell the cashier at the bank, even to tell the mailman, if only the stranger would have the patience to hear them. It was an appeal for continued prominence.

At this time Mrs. Goodpastor didn't believe that another glowing chapter of life could be ahead. She did not know that every age could have its advantages as well as disadvantages.

She turned on the television set again. It was still on Channel Seven. She switched the channel selector to Four. That took effort. But it was worth it. Johnny Carson was still on.

"That's Anne!" Wai-yee shrieked. "That's Anne!" All she saw was the last couple sentences of Koppel and Anne, as Wai-yee had turned on the television just before Anne was going off. It was a Hong Kong channel's replay.

Dr. Yeung put the South China Morning Post down from his reading position. "Shhhh! You'll wake Liberty."

Wai-yee turned down the volume. "That was Anne!"

Dr. Yeung turned his head to look at Wai-yee by his side on the couch. "Who's Anne?"

"On TV! Did you see her?"

"I was reading."

"She worked with me at the consulate when I just got the job there. And that was her saying she married Mr. Daschle!"

"Who's Mr. Daschle?"

"The P.A.O., the Public Affairs Officer we both worked for in those days! Can you imagine? She married him! And she's beautiful! She's changed!"

"Did you like her?"

"I hated her! She was in love with Mao Zedong in those days!"

"She was a Communist?"

"Just fooled. She didn't know much in those days."

"That's all right. It's an old Chinese proverb said by K'ung Fu-tze, that if you're 20 and aren't a socialist you have no heart, but if you're still one at 30 you have no head."

"That's not an old Chinese proverb by K'ung Fu-tze, Chi-shing. Churchill said that. And I wasn't a socialist when I was 20, and I had a heart."

"I'm wrong on both things then." He picked up the newspaper and started reading again. "I take defeat well."

Wai-yee ignored what he said. "Can you imagine? Anne Whitney married Mr. Daschle! I can't wait to tell Moose! He'd remember both of them!"

"Moose knew them?"

"He met them. We were all together the same day. He knows who they are. I can't wait to tell him! The next time he calls, remind me!"

"I'll tell him," Dr. Yeung said in his usual light manner of taking charge. He picked up the phone.

"You'll tell him?" Wai-yee looked confused. "Why do you want to tell him?'

Dr. Yeung dialed Moose's number. "It saves time."

"Dunston, here," came the voice on the other end.

"Dunston where?" Dr. Yeung asked.

There was some silence, then, "This is Moose Dunston."

"This is Yeung Chi-shing."

"Oh, Doctor Yeung! Hello!" It was not an expected phone call. "Is everything okay? Wai-yee okay? Liberty okay? You okay?"

"Everything is fine. I just want you to know that Anne Whitney loved Mao Zedong but now that old Mao is dead, she married Daschle."

This time the silence lasted longer. "What?"

"That's all." And he hung up. He looked at Wai-yee. "I told him," and he went back to his newspaper.

"Oh, Chi-shing! He can't have known what you were talking about!"

"If you told him, it would have taken you an hour. You don't know how to lay out the facts. I told him everything you wanted him to know."

Wai-yee shook her head with a resigned smile and she turned up the volume on the television set. Ted Koppel was talking to Iran's Sadegh Ghotbzadeh in a split-screen interview. Wai-yee looked over at Chi-shing who was immersed in reading the newspaper. "Chi-shing?"

"Hmmm?"

"If you had it to do all over again, would you marry me?"

"Either you or Julie Andrews. One of the two," he said without taking his eyes off the newspaper.

"Oh?"

Dr. Yeung looked up from the newspaper at her, and put the newspaper down. "But in time, I suppose I would have been bored with Julie Andrews. How many times could I listen to her sing, 'My Favorite Things'? In time it would have driven me to violence, I'm afraid. So I suppose I'd choose you again."

"And if she didn't sing 'My Favorite Things'?"

"Then I would have chosen her, of course. Now, what else is on television?"

FIFTY-TWO
THE WORRY DAY
1980

At the base of Temple Street in Kowloon there were stalls set-up with wooden tables and wooden chairs, and a lot of noodle-eating, tea-drinking, and fortune-telling. Those stalls, called *dai pai dongs*, were setup every night unless rain was heavy.

It became a ritual that on Tuesday nights, Dr. Yeung Chi-shing would sit there with Jack Edwards and Arthur May to talk and eat noodles.

"Arthur, I told Moose Dunston about the flag you raised on the Peak in 1945, and the way that saved Hong Kong," Dr. Yeung said between trapping noodles with his chopsticks. "Mr. Dunston was fascinated, and I'm sure he'll write an article about it for *Asia World Weekly*."

Arthur May smiled. He was eating his noodles with a plastic fork. "That's good of Dunston. You know that Jack has the flag right now. We made a pact that whomever dies first leaves the flag to the other, so it will be on top of both of our caskets."

Dr. Yeung put his free hand on the forearm of Arthur May. "That's such a pleasant thought! I can't wait to attend both events! Rush it up, will you?"

Arthur May and Jack Edwards both laughed. "How is it, Chi-shing," Jack Edwards asked, "that you never seem to worry about anything? I have never seen you in a bad mood." He pushed aside what was left of his noodles, and poured some tea from its enameled pitcher into a cup.

"How could I be in a bad mood?" Dr. Yeung asked. "Would you be in a bad mood if every night you slept with this?" Dr. Yeung reached for his wallet and exhibited a picture of Wai-yee. "My difficulty, of course, is that at my age, I actually sleep. Wai-yee probably thanks God for that."

Arthur May said, "You never do complain, Doctor. Don't you worry about anything?"

"Once a month. I reserve one day a month for what I call the Worry Day. During any other day when a worry comes into my mind, unless it's something under my control, I dismiss it quickly by writing it down on the list of things to worry about on the next Worry Day. Then, when the day comes on the new moon, I take out the list and worry about all of the worries I've listed through the month, but most of them are not worth worrying about anymore. You would be surprised how many take care of themselves. If they still linger, and I can't solve them, I put them on next month's Worry Day."

"Is that true?" Jack Edwards asked.

"Oh, yes. My father did it before me. And his father before him. Like both of them, I lock myself up alone when I do that, so my worries bother no one but myself. And they only bother me one day a month."

Arthur May brought up the obvious. "Do you worry about 1997?"

"Every Worry Day. It's something that moves from list to list, one month to the next, but each month I try to do something that will ease that time, should the government in China take us over, as we believe it will."

"What can you do to ease that time?"

"Last Worry Day I decided to give a message to the British Broadcasting Company and Voice of America, and every other radio service that gets short-wave through to China."

"What's the message?"

"It's an old Chinese story, but I don't know if this generation of Chinese ever heard it, and the leadership may have forgotten it. So the old Chinese story goes, an old woman wanted to sell her teapot in the marketplace of Yixin. A traveler came by and, at her invitation he drank tea she poured from the teapot. It was the best tea he had ever tasted and he offered to buy the teapot from her for a sum she never expected to be offered. While he went away to get the cash to pay her, she became conscious of the used appearance of the teapot. She was embarrassed. Because the traveler offered her so much money for it, she scrubbed the teapot inside and out, not realizing that by removing the dross accumulated from years and years of tea leaves used in the pot, that she was removing what made every cup of tea as wonderful as it was. She destroyed the very reason he wanted it.

"1997's Yixin teapot will be Hong Kong. It cannot be fooled with carelessly, or it will be destroyed."

"You are distributing the story?" Now Arthur May concluded the eating, leaving Dr. Yeung as the only one going to the bottom of the bowl.

"By radio. It is not so much that I want to reach the people of China as I want to reach the government there. They must know the consequences that come with what they perceive as their inheritance of Hong Kong. Now, what do you worry about? I will either solve your worry or put it on my list for the next new moon."

Jack Edwards nodded. "Solve this one. I worry about the men who fought here and were taken prisoners by the Japs during those years."

"Japanese," Arthur May corrected. "We don't call them Japs anymore."

"Japs. The ones who took me prisoner and who took you prisoner are Japs. They're the ones I'm taking about–the torturers. The inhumane torturers. The others are Japanese. I've been waging a campaign to have the former defenders of Hong Kong, whether they be British or Chinese, the prisoners of war, whether they may be British or Chinese, and their wives, whether they be British or Chinese, recognized with British passports, medical treatment, and pensions. And the same tributes should be paid to the widows of those whose husbands were killed or died since their service here. It is outrageous that London hasn't done that through all these years since the end of the war."

"You are right, Jack," Dr. Yeung said. "You prove what K'ung Fu-tze, Confucious, said that 'he who wishes to secure the good of others, has already secured his own.' What does Governor MacLehose say about all this?"

"It's not his decision. I have appealed and continue to appeal through London's winding, incredibly stupid bureaucracy."

"Write Prime Minister Thatcher."

"I have."

"Write the queen."

"I have."

"Then I'll worry about it next month. Don't think about it until then. Anything I can solve for you, Arthur?"

"I'm getting old."

"There's only one solution for that."

"That's true."

"You have been blessed with a solution, not a problem. I won't even put that on my list of worries."

Jack added, "One more for you, Chi-shing. If this place goes to the blokes on the mainland in '97, how do I get the old flag Arthur put up on the Peak in '45 flown again—officially up the flagpole on the last day of British rule?"

"That's easy. The governor, whoever he is when the time comes, will do it. Simply ask him. Why should that be something to worry about?"

"Because I know all about the London bureaucracy. By the time they give an answer it will be 2097."

Dr. Yeung thought for a while, then took his chopsticks to lift the last noodle to his mouth. After chewing it and lifting a small paper napkin to clean his lips he said, "Then there is yet another easy solution. Have you ever been to China?"

"To Canton."

"Did you see that everyone, man or woman, boy or girl wears blue jackets, blue pants, and blue caps?"

"Yes. Everyone. I went there early this year. There was nothing but a mass of blue that was moving as one big blob pushing its way into the doorway of Colonel Sanders Kentucky Fried Chicken."

"Get an outfit just like theirs. On the last day of British rule go to Government House in your blue jacket, blue pants, and blue cap, and put the flag up yourself. Everyone, including the governor, will think you're from the mainland performing some kind of official act, one day early. You'll be doing what Arthur did in '45,—with the same flag. They won't know until they see it furling at the top of the pole, that it's the Union Jack. Everyone will be so confused they won't know what to do. They'll think someone surrendered." Then Dr. Yeung took a small package of M&M's from his shirt pocket, ripped it open and put two M&M's in his mouth. "Do you want some?"

Both Jack Edwards and Arthur May took some .

"I have a packet a day," Dr. Yeung said. "It beats any fancy dessert." Not that there were many fancy desserts served in the stalls of Temple Street.

An old Chinese woman with a deck of cards in her hand, came to stand by their table. She talked in Cantonese to Dr. Yeung, ignoring the other two men. They engaged in back-and-forth conversation, and she walked away.

"What did she want, Chi-Shing?" Jack Edwards asked.

"She's a fortune teller. She wanted to tell my fortune."

"What did you say?"

"I said I know my fortune. I said I will die. She said, 'Ahh, but do you know when?' I said I know exactly when. She asked me, 'When?' and I said 'If you are a fortune-teller, you know when. Why do you ask? Why, in fact, do you care? You don't know me.' She said she cares about me and my friends, and that she charges one hundred Hong Kong dollars for fortune telling because she is so good. I said I charge exactly the same amount, but I will tell her fortune for only eighty Hong Kong dollars, out of professional courtesy. That was when she walked away."

"Are you a fortune teller, Dr. Yeung?" Arthur May asked.

"No. That was not good of me. It bothers me that I still make errors of judgment at my age. I will worry about that at the next new moon."

"You're serious, Chi-shing?" Jack Edwards asked.

"I'm very serious."

Arthur May leaned toward Dr. Yeung. "What is at the top of your list, Dr. Yeung?"

"Iran and Afghanistan. The world needs a leader. I thank God for Margaret Thatcher, but she's practically all there is. And, with respect to you, Arthur and Jack, Great Britain does not have the power and authority all of us remember it had before the war. The United States has acquired that role in such a short period of time. If the United States allows itself to drift with amateur leadership that doesn't have a global view, the United States will, in time, lose that role. Who would have thought before last year that Iran and Afghanistan would be added to the list of nations that have become quick skeletons of what they were? Unless the United States gets hold of itself, Iran and Afghanistan will simply be names located somewhere in the middle of the list that will be unsolvable one Worry Day after another."

FIFTY-THREE
WATERMELONS
1980

If Iran and Afghanistan weren't enough, a war was being fought less than two thousand miles from Washington, D.C. Armed guerrillas supplied by the Soviet Union, Cuba, and the new government of Nicaragua, were fighting to take over the government of El Salvador.

Usually, war breeds refugees streaming across borders out of the country, but in this case refugees were not streaming out, they were streaming in. The refugees were coming from Nicaragua, either through Honduras or in boats crossing the Gulf of Fonseca to escape the revolutionaries who had taken over Nicaragua ten months earlier, even if they had to seek refuge in a country at war.

There was only a barely visible sliver of moonlight the Sunday night of May 11, 1980, and the line of refugees at the camp were standing single file in the dark, waiting to have audience with the bearded man and the woman who wore her hair in a bun, whose reputations had followed them from Southeast Asia. Their reputations had been greatly enhanced because of an incident that occurred one month previous to this evening. That was when, in Havana, six Cubans crashed a bus through the gates of the Embassy of Peru in a quest for asylum at the embassy. In retaliation, Castro took away all guards from around the embassy of Peru, but his retaliation backfired. Within a week there were 7000 Cubans on those embassy grounds, wanting refuge from the Castro Government. There were births and deaths on the embassy grounds, so crowded that some people were living in trees. That was when Cody Cooper publicly appealed to President Carter to take them into the United States.

President Carter announced 3500 would be taken in.

Cody made another appeal. "It's not enough. What if," Cody publicly argued, "Rosalynn Carter was Number 3501? And Amy Carter was Number 3502? President Carter is a moral man. I beg him to think of people, no matter the advice of his political advisors."

President Carter said the United States would take in more.

Refugees all over the world had increasing respect for Cody and Gloria Cooper. And so for a refugee to see and talk with them at the refugee camp outside of San Salvador, was a sought-for experience. The fact that Cody and Gloria Cooper had a five-year-old son named John Fitzgerald Cooper only added to the aura they cast.

Gloria was apprehensive of the adulation. "Don't let them think we can work miracles," she would tell Cody.

That night the line of refugees moved slowly outside the wooden building with the tin roof where Cody and Gloria saw their evening visitors one by one, and some would walk in the darker room where their son was sleeping. When one woman said that Gloria reminded her of the Virgin Mary, Gloria responded that "our son was born from the same act that created your child. This is San Salvador in 1980, not Bethlehem one thousand, nine-hundred and eighty years ago."

The last in line that night was an old woman who walked with the help of a cane. "I want Mr. Cooper to heal my leg," she said when she sat opposite Cody and Gloria, with her hand tight on the handle of her cane. She moved her gaze between Cody and Gloria, then settled on Cody's eyes. "I know you can."

"What's wrong with your leg, ma'am?" Cody asked.

She shrugged. "Shot. I was shot near El Tanque leaving Nicaragua."

"Is the bullet still in your leg?" Gloria asked.

The woman turned to Gloria, and shook her head. "It was never in my leg. It went in and out."

"Let me look at your leg," Gloria said.

The woman gave a look of appeal to Cody. "Can you just heal me?"

"No, ma'am, I can't."

"Look," she said and she put her free hand inside her blouse, and drew a number of small pictures from where they had nested near her heart. She handed the small stack to Cody. He looked at each picture and, one by one, he passed them on to Gloria. One of the pictures was of Jesus, the next of Mary, the next of the Pope, the next of President Kennedy, and the last one was of Cody and Gloria.

"We are flattered," Gloria said. "You put us in company in which we do not and can not put ourselves. Please don't ask more of us than we can give." She knelt down to the woman's leg, and then looked up at her. "You are very fortunate to still have a leg. You have already had it treated. I can tell it was recent. There is nothing more we can do. You'll be all right."

"But when I walk there is pain and I have to limp."

"You must give it time," Gloria said in a comforting tone.

The old woman smiled. "Just being with the two of you will cure me." She kissed the hand of Gloria, and then kissed the hand of Cody.

It was not an unusual evening at the refugee camp.

But it was a very unusual evening a short distance away, outside the residence of the U.S. Ambassador to El Salvador. A crowd of 5000 surrounded the building yelling in both Spanish and English, "Ambassador Robert White–Go back to Cuba!" "Ambassador Robert White–what United States do you represent? The United States of America or the United States of the Sandinistas?" "Ambassador Robert White–Stop embracing Brezhnev and Castro!" "Telephone the U.S. Embassy and Jam the Switchboard! Demand Free Trials: 26-7100! 26-7100!"

Inside was U.S. Ambassador Robert White with an uneaten dessert of vanilla ice cream, now melted in its plate in front of him. His guest, Ted Murphy, was sitting across from him and had finished his dessert. Both of them had to speak louder than normal to be heard by the other over the chants of the crowd outside.

"You're doin' a good job, Bob," Ted Murphy said. "Don't let them get to ya."

"What?"

"Don't let them get to ya."

"Believe me, I won't."

It was not just unique, it was bizarre. The messages chanted by the demonstrators were so different than the chants that were so often yelled outside U.S. facilities in foreign countries. Not only that, but Ted Murphy was known to be traditionally opposed to U.S. policy, not supportive. All of these changes were due to U.S. policy regarding El Salvador being different than U.S. policy toward communist expansion in other countries under other presidents.

"Are you putting this demonstration on U.S. television?" the Ambassador asked in a very loud voice.

"Nah!" Ted Murphy was talking as loud as he could. "My camera crew is at the hotel, at El Camino Real. This isn't worth coverin'."

"Good!"

Ted got up from his chair and walked over to Ambassador White so he could be heard without shouting. With some discomfort, Ted bent down to the ambassador. "I was in the Senate Hearing Room when you went through your confirmation hearings and what you're doin' is what they told you to do, Bob. I remember Senator Javits sayin' that while theoretically you may be an ambassador, you are a proconsul as far as he and his fellow senators were concerned. He said that you have to be an activist in this country, that bein' an ambassador isn't enough—that you have to take the step to be a proconsul. You know, I didn't know what a proconsul was until I looked it up that night. I remember bein' surprised when I found out it meant an administrator of an occupied territory, governing that territory as its conqueror."

"That's what Senator Javits said. You're right."

"So you had your marchin' orders, and you're settin' this place straight. You're a courageous man, and I got to hand it to ya. Ten months ago next door in Nicaragua, a lot of people thought we could never get rid of Somoza there. He's somewhere in Paraguay now and the Sandinistas are finally in charge of Nicaragua. If our Ambassador there, Larry Pezzullo could do it, then you can get rid of the right wing here, Bob. You'll do it. Bob, I got to get goin'." Ted straightened up. "I have to do a lot of home work at the hotel—writin' and all kinds of things. I got to get movin' out of this country. My bosses don't like me to spend too long in one place."

"Don't you ever get tired of traveling all the time?"

"It's gettin' that way. I just go from one place to another, where ever there's news. My bosses have nothin' but money, and they keep me movin'. Next week I can be in Paris or Timbuktu just dependin' on what happens in the world. What a job, huh? I have a passport that looks like an accordion! The Passport Office had to put in accordion pages for all the visas! Since the new year began, I haven't been home for more than five days. I miss home."

"I'll give you a car and a driver and a bodyguard to get you out of here—Atilio is good. He'll take you out the back. It's dangerous out there with those right-wingers who would scalp me if they get inside."

"I'll take the bodyguard, but I have a car and driver of my own waitin'. My car has regular plates. I don't want to be in a vehicle with diplomat's plates. Besides, I want to talk to the demonstrators."

"They're dangerous."

Ted shrugged. "It's my job. I got to talk to them."

Driving out the gate in a private car wasn't much better than driving out in an embassy car. Part of the crowd surrounded it as soon as the car was out of the gate, and the driver wasn't able to move the car faster than a crawl without killing someone. In the back seat, Ted looked to the front seat at Atilio, the provided bodyguard, and said, "Wan' to go out there with me?"

"You want to get out?"

"Yeah. You comin' with me?"

Atilio nodded. "I'll go with you."

When they got out, Atilio's size and his easily visible gun in its holster were imposing, but the crowd was not intimidated. It took only seconds for Ted and Atilio to be in the center of a circle of shouting men and women. Ted tried to assure them that he did not work for the Ambassador, but was a member of the U.S. press corps, a credential that didn't do him much good in this crowd. "Reporter!" Ted yelled. "Press*! No habla Español! No habla Español!"*

"I speak English!" a man near the front of the crowd said. "I can translate for you." He turned around to the crowd and told them he would translate. Ted was certain this was not his best night.

The translation process began with a question from the middle of the crowd. "Do you know what your great United States, the captain of capitalism is doing?"

Ted nodded. "You bet! I know we're tryin' to bring land reform here. I know that we want the poor to have an equal chance so that your country is no longer ruled by fourteen families!"

The translator said it in Spanish and the crowd roared with jeers and some with laughter. One man yelled out in English, not needing a translator. "Ambassador White, the watermelon, must have told you that. He gives the orders to the other watermelon, President Duarte."

"What do you mean by watermelons?"

"You don't know? They are watermelons! Green on the outside, red on the inside!"

The circle of people around Ted and the bodyguard was tightening. The bodyguard was yelling for them to back up. "*Detente!* Back up! *Detente!*"

"What is it you want?" Ted asked to no one in particular.

"To be left alone!" a woman answered in English. Much of the crowd seemed to understand her, because they cheered.

Ted tried to talk but he couldn't be heard.

The translator yelled out to the crowd, "*Dejarlos Hablar!* Let him talk! Let him talk!"

"I'm a reporter! You talk to me and I'll tell the world."

Three men who were together pushed their way toward Ted. "We speak English!" They were neatly dressed, the speaker in pressed black slacks and a yellow tee-shirt that left no question as to his political party. Over his heart was the name of the party, "Arena." "You are Ted Murphy, aren't you?"

Ted didn't know whether or not to answer "yes," but his ego won. "Yes."

"I go to Miami and New Orleans often. I see you on television."

"Good! Then tell these folks I'm not on the ambassador's payroll!"

He nodded and turned to the crowd. "*El esta en* American television. He's on American television. *El es reportero para los Estados.* He is a reporter for the States." Then he turned back to Ted. "Do you want to know why we are angry?"

"I'll put it on television. Just let me know. Your message will get through." Ted took out his small gray spiral notebook from his shirt pocket, along with a ballpoint pen.

"You please listen to me, Señor Murphy. We're angry because one month after the inauguration of Carter in the States, we had an election here. The ruling party, the National Conciliation Party, won the election, and the new President was General Carlos Humberto Romero. You know this?"

"Yes. I know that. We reported that."

"As all our presidents had been, he was anticommunist and supported your country. Carter accused the party of vote fraud."

"And wasn't there?"

The man shrugged. "There's always been vote fraud in this country. But whatever fraud there was in that election was not enough to change the results. We were doing good under the National Conciliation Party. We were self-sufficient in food, we spent very little on the military, we were doing much better than most of Latin America—much better than Mexico or even Venezuela with all its oil."

"But fraud is fraud and I remember there were demonstrations against Romero's victory! Big ones—and some of those demonstrators were killed. Am I right?"

"Yes. Forty people were killed. Carter said the National Guard did it. But now, with the penalties for all this by your country, 30,000 people have been killed. Your country's policies sent an invitation to the guerrillas to wage war. Humberto Romero's government fell just three months after Somoza's government in Nicaragua fell—but in the case of Romero, he did not fall by a takeover from guerrillas. They didn't have the strength of the Sandinistas across the Gulf. Our country was taken over by a coup—a junta. Carter appointed Robert White to come here, and behind the scenes he was the overseer of the Junta, bringing this country to socialism."

"Socialism or land reform, my friend?" Ted asked.

"Socialism. Two months ago, on March the 5th, detachments of soldiers in battle dress came through the roads in trucks, jeeps, and troop carriers. They seized 376 farms, over one-third of Nicaragua's farmland, and the most productive private enterprises in the country. They seized our homes with all our personal possessions. We couldn't even go in to get our clothes. They said they would give the farms to the workers on the farms, the peasants—for land reform. But do you know who owns them now? The government. Those peasants now work for the state!"

One of the man's two friends, this one in light slacks and a black jacket said, "I'm a banker. I used to be a partner in a bank. While the government was seizing farms, all the top officers of our banks, savings and loans, and all other financial institutions were called by government officials to attend a meeting, so we went. While we were there, detachments of soldiers in battledress, some in armored cars, surrounded all the banks and seized them for the state."

"You know who did all this?" the man in the black slacks and the Arena tee-shirt asked.

"President Duarte," Ted acknowledged.

"He followed orders by your country. It is common knowledge here that Ambassador White gave him the orders. Your State Department's 1979 Report on Human Rights said that there should be changes made in El Salvador's socio-economic structure. That report said that El Salvador's economic orientation is strongly capitalistic. So your country changed all that."

Now it was the third man's turn. He wore Levi's and a white shirt. "President Duarte announced with pride that what was done was more profound than anything the communists were doing. Then he said, 'Our revolutionary process has shattered all the models not only advocated here but in all Latin America. For example, there's not a single country in Latin America where all the foreign commerce and the banking system have been totally nationalized, as in ours.'"

The man with the Tee-shirt was nodding. "He admitted what he was. You see? A watermelon."

"Then there was a tragedy," the man with the black jacket and light slacks added. "Our Arch-Bishop Oscar Romero was assassinated. To this day no one knows who killed him, but your Ambassador White blamed the anti-Communists and said that Roberto D'Abuisson was chiefly responsible. D'Abuisson is the head of the anti-communist force. He leads the Arena political party. Without trial, D'Abuisson was jailed under the charge that he was trying to topple the junta. We believe that White gave the orders to Colonel Majano to put him in prison. He did it. He put him in prison—along with thirteen others White didn't like. That's why we're demonstrating. Let there be trials! Will you put all that on television?"

"I need pictures, my friend."

"Pictures?" the man in the Levi's and white shirt said. "You people are too selective in the pictures you take. There were plenty of pictures to have been taken in March when the soldiers took over our farms, our homes, our institutions. There were plenty of pictures to have been taken when D'Aubuisson was hauled off to jail. Where are your cameras tonight?"

Ted nodded. "I'll go back to the hotel and get the camera crew out here–if I can find them."

"What hotel?"

"El Camino Real."

The man with the slacks and black jacket laughed and nodded. "Hotel Watermelon, we call it! That's where all the American press stays. You will really get the cameras?"

"Yes."

"And we'll talk to your cameras?"

"Yes. Of course. I'll go get them now."

The man who thought he was going to translate yelled out, "*Dejenlo salir!* Let him through! Let him through!"

After Ted Murphy and Atilio the bodyguard drove off, the man in the tee-shirt with Arena stitched on it, shook his head. "He will not be back. We will not see his cameras. His cameras will not see the thousands of us around his ambassador's residence."

When Ted got back to the El Camino Real he phoned the rooms of his camera crew and none of them were in. He went to the bar. They weren't there either. "You seen m' boys?" Ted asked the bartender.

"They were here maybe an hour ago. They said you gave them the night off. They met some girls here who were hungry, so they went to La Curbina for dinner."

Ted nodded. It was enough. He had made his attempts. He wouldn't bother them at La Curbina. After all, they had met some girls.

"What do you want to drink?" the bartender asked Ted.

"Nothin'. I'm turnin' in."

Ted walked out of the bar to the hotel's reception desk. He asked for a wakeup call the following morning.

"We have an envelope for you, Señor Murphy," the receptionist said. "It was left for you by a messenger."

"Oh?"

The receptionist took a square white envelope from the drawer in front of him and gave it to Ted.

Ted opened the envelope in the privacy of his room.

It was an invitation for him and Mrs. Murphy to be a guest at the "First Anniversary of the Sandinista Revolution in Managua, Nicaragua on July the 19th."

With excitement, Ted picked up the phone and put a call in to the

United States. Within minutes the operator called back with the number ringing.

"Hello?"

"Annie! Annie! Annie! You divorced yet?"

"Who is this?"

"Murph'!"

There was a short silence. "Ted Murphy! You want to talk to me or to my husband?"

"Get off!"

"You have a nice way of saying congratulations!"

"Congratulations. Is Mark there?"

"Yes. You want to speak to him?"

"No! I mean can he hear you right now?"

"He's in the other room. I can get him."

"No, Anne. Listen, Annie, I'm in El Salvador."

"I should have known!"

"Don't you watch me on television?"

"No."

"Thanks."

"Your welcome."

"Well, I'll tell you why I'm callin'. How would you like to go to the biggest celebration in Latin American history?"

"Are they going to hang you? I'll be there!"

"Even better. I've been invited next door to Nicaragua, for their government's first anniversary celebration in July! I'm invited as a guest of honor! I think Castro's gonna be there."

"I don't doubt it. Good for you. Good for Fidel. What's that got to do with me?"

"I can't go as a guest. You know—someone would make somethin' over it—a conflict of interest—stuff like that. But I'm goin'. I'll go as a correspondent. But they invited me to bring a guest, so I'd like you to come—you know, as my guest."

"Are you kidding?"

"No kiddin'! Wouldn't that be fun?"

"Ted, you're outrageous! I'm a married woman."

"Will you still be married in July?"

"Ted! I'll be married to Mark until the day I die! Besides, I wouldn't go with you even if I wasn't married! And I wouldn't go to Nicaragua on a bet."

"Then give me an exclusive about what you did in Iran. It's Day Number 189 of the hostages. A week from Thursday is Day Number 200 and I want to have a special report. I need an exclusive—and you're exclusive."

"Not a chance!"

"Come on, Annie!"

"Ted, no way! Get it? No way! Go to your celebration and get an exclusive from your new friend, Fidel!"

"You think not? You think I won't? You think your ol' Murph' couldn't pull it off?"

"Oh, I think he'd be delighted to speak to you either in Nicaragua or El Salvador."

"You won't go with me? Annie, we could have fun like the old days in Moscow."

"Forget about the old days. I have."

The night before the celebration, at an official reception, Fidel Castro praised the Carter administration's "more intelligent and constructive policy" toward Nicaragua. It was the first public compliment of U.S. policy that Castro had given since coming to power during the administration of President Eisenhower.

By this time, according to Human Rights activists, the Sandinistas had executed over one thousand people, with one hundred executions admitted by the government. Also admitted was the uprooting of 8,400 Indians from their homes. The government had additionally forced the Jews of Nicaragua into exile and confiscated their property, taking over the country's Jewish synagogue in Managua.

By this time, over one million Nicaraguans had fled their homes.

By this time, four Nicaraguan journalists, Melvin Wallace, Carlos Cuadra, Juan Alberto Enriquez, and Isidro Tellez, were sentenced to two years at hard labor for articles the government said "damaged the interests and conquests" of the Sandinista revolution.

By this time, the Sandinistas had praised the Soviet Union for their invasion of Afghanistan and condemned the United States for interfering in Afghanistan.

By this time, free elections for Nicaragua had been postponed from the constitutionally prescribed time of 1981 to 1985.

By this time, the Sandinistas had nationalized the banks, the radio and television stations, cotton, coffee, meat, sugar, shell-fish, and 60 percent of the farmland.

By this time, Daniel Ortega of the ninemember Sandinista Directorate praised Castro's Cuba as "the first liberated territory of the subcontinent" and called the governments of Iran and Cambodia, "beautiful victories."

By this time, the Nicaraguan National Anthem was changed to include a lyric claiming the United States is 'the enemy of mankind.'

By this time, the government had admitted they had taken 7,800 political prisoners, 3,000 of whom were incarcerated for having collaborated with the "previous pro-US regime of Anastasio Somoza."

By this time, over 600 tons of weapons, ammunition, communications equipment, medicines, and uniforms had arrived in Nicaragua from pipelines originating in the Soviet Union and Bulgaria, Hungary, Czechoslovakia, East Germany, the PLO, Vietnam, and Ethiopia, and from Nicaragua the material had been transported to the guerillas in El Salvador.

The response, after all this, was the endorsement of President Carter and the United States Congress to send 75 million dollars in aid to

Nicaragua. U.S. aid had been stopped since April of 1977 when Anastasio Somoza was President until, as President Carter put it, "it becomes clear that the human rights situation has improved." That was before the 18-month war had started and left 45,000 dead and 100,000 wounded.

The week after the U.S. aid was approved, Sandinista leaders flew to Moscow to sign a trade agreement.

In the days before the celebration, police rounded up and arrested 900 more Nicaraguans accused of being anti-social elements. Sandinista Police Chief Enrique Schmidt said 200 policemen were involved in the operation which began with house-to-house searches.

The one year anniversary celebration drew a crowd of 200,000 to whom the Guest of Honor, Fidel Castro, praised "the wisdom of the Sandinista leadership...What unites us all today, even the United States and us, is our tribute to, and recognition of, the heroic people of Nicaragua."

Ted Murphy was not the only U.S. celebrity invited to the Sandinista anniversary celebration. Jane Fonda was invited but she didn't go. Ted went as a correspondent, and Linda Murphy went as a guest of the government, having no idea that Ted had offered the invitation to Anne before he extended it to her.

Sitting in the stadium one row in front of Linda Murphy, was Donald McHenry, U.S. Ambassador to the United Nations. Sitting with him was Lawrence Pezzullo, U.S. Ambassador to Nicaragua, and William Bowdler, Assistant Secretary of State for Inter-American Affairs. Pezullo and Bowdler had played major roles in demanding Somoza leave Nicaragua, clearing the way for the Sandinistas to take over the country.

Each of the official guests, including Linda, was holding on to a program, and a packet of invitations for the forthcoming events of celebration.

Ted was walking through the stands, interviewing Nicaraguans who told him how much better their lives were now. Between interviews he was talking to members of the Sandinista Directorate in an attempt to arrange an exclusive interview with Fidel Castro. "How about Arafat instead of Castro?" Daniel Ortega answered.

"Yasir Arafat? Is he here?"

"He arrives Monday. Tuesday we're having the ceremony establishing diplomatic relations with the P.L.O."

"I can't stay till Monday. I got to get goin'. I want Castro. I need him today."

"How about Maurice Bishop?"

"Who?"

"Maurice Bishop. The Prime Minister of Grenada. He's here now for our celebration. You can interview him."

Ted looked confused. "Why would I want to interview him?"

"He's very important. You'll like him. He's very interesting. He is a friend of ours. He and Castro are very close."

Ted shook his head. "I want to interview the big man himself."

"No. I can't ask him. He's our Guest of Honor. We don't want to ask him to do any more than he has already done for us. He wants to get back to Havana. You should talk to Maurice Bishop."

"Castro!"

"I will mention your request, Mr. Murphy, but there will be no pressure from us for him to accommodate you."

It was a cameraman's nightmare: Ted Murphy and Fidel Castro standing outside, facing each other. Standing next to Fidel Castro, Ted appeared to be a circus midget. There he was with a strange bent nose and a yellow sport-shirt, next to the massive and tall Fidel Castro with a full beard, wearing green army battle fatigues. Ted was placed on top of a black box that had been used to house one of the light stands for the camera crew, which made him look taller than he was or made Castro look smaller than he was, but the scene still looked odd. There was a question of brawn. Castro looked like he could have knocked Ted out with one touch of his hand.

Daniel Ortega, who arranged the interview, stood just inside camera-range. "Out!" the cameraman yelled. "You! Back up five steps!" Ortega backed up five steps.

After some adjustments, the cameraman said, "We're rolling."

Ted nodded and said to the camera, "I'm standing here under the bright Managua, Nicargua sun on this beautiful July day, with Fidel Castro, President of Cuba, at the First Anniversary celebration of the Sandinista Revolution. President Castro has consented to an exclusive interview," and he moved his gaze to Castro as the camera zoomed back for a two-shot. "And we thank you for that, Mister President."

Castro gave a bothered nod.

"President Castro," Ted continued, "if Ronald Reagan should become President of the United States, how do you feel that would affect your nation?"

"Reagan is a threat to peace. He is a cowboy, not a President. He would support genocidal regimes in Latin America. He would cut aid to Nicaragua. Now, Carter, as I have so often said, has an intelligent and constructive policy towards the new Government of Nicaragua."

"But then how do you feel about Carter's boycott of the Olympics in Moscow because of the Soviet's invasion of Afghanistan?"

"Carter was wrong. He remains wrong about Afghanistan. Cuba totally supports the Soviet Union in Afghanistan."

"And Carter continues the trade embargo against your nation. Surely you do not feel any improvement has come from President Carter on that."

"None. He is continuing the faulty embargo of your Presidents since Eisenhower, and there is no justification for it. Who told the United States that the peoples of Latin America can't choose socialism? The trade embargo is a criminal attempt at the strangulation and economic genocide of our people."

"President Carter has accused your government of harboring a Combat Brigade of two to three thousand Soviets, and he says that brigade represents a threat to the Western Hemisphere."

"There is no Soviet Combat Brigade in Cuba, and on that issue Carter is dishonest, insincere, and immoral. What your country calls a brigade is a training center."

"And he has accused your government of having over 100,000 troops in Angola and Ethiopia."

"Yes. We are proud of them. We will always have outright support for revolutionary movements in the world. For each reversal, for each step backward, for each desertion, revolutionary victories will multiply."

"Do you see a time when Cuba and the United States can be friends?"

"When the United States changes its policies towards our people and towards other peoples of the world. You are on the right track now with Nicaragua. But the United States has been a rotten pseudo-democracy, discriminating against blacks, prostituting women, sexually exploiting children, and permitting violence, drug addiction, and crime."

"But I mean in the future. What is it that the United States needs to do to have your nation's friendship?"

"As I tell you, it is not just your nation's policies against Cuba. It is the poor of the world that are victims of United States imperialism. As example, the United States must refrain from its repressive maneuvers to perpetuate Puerto Rico's colonial status. You must stop your puppet-state, Israel, whose actions duplicate the genocide that the Nazis once visited on the Hebrew people. And worldwide, wealth is still concentrated in the hands of your nation and a few other powers, whose wasteful economies are maintained by the exploitation of the labor, as well as the transfer and plunder of the national and other resources of the peoples of Africa, Latin America, Asia and other regions of the world. There is a moral obligation of those who benefit from the plunder of our wealth and the exploitation of men and women for decades and for centuries. Your nation and wealthy imperialists should pay $300 billion to developing countries in the next ten years. This is an absolute necessity. This should start with $25 billion in the first year."

"Do you think the United States and other industrial nations will agree to your request?"

"With no resources for development, there will be no peace. I will conclude this interview, Mr. Murphy, with the same words I used to the United Nations organization last October: I address myself to the rich, asking them to contribute. I address myself to the poor countries, asking them to distribute."

Castro knew how to indicate the interview was over. He walked off.

Ted jumped from the light-stand box.

Daniel Ortega escorted Fidel Castro away into the stadium and then came back to Ted Murphy as his camera crew was dismantling the equipment. "Did you like the interview?" Daniel Ortega asked.

"Wonderful! Wonderful! Thank you for gettin' him for me."

Daniel Ortega shrugged. "What he said to you is nothing new. He said those things before either to the United Nations organization or to the Conference of the Non-Aligned Nations, or to others. It was nothing new."

"I didn't expect anything new. He was good. He was good. And now he said it for our cameras."

Daniel Ortega shook his head. "You should have chosen Maurice Bishop for news."

Linda was drunk at the evening cocktail party of the Sandinistas, held at the pyramid-shaped Intercontinental Hotel.

"This hotel has one thing in common with you," Luis Angel Cajina of the Sandinistas told her as they stood in a corner of the crowded suite. "The hotel is a national treasure, as you must be in your country."

Linda blushed. "I'm afraid not, Señor Cajina." The word 'señor' didn't come easy, nor was it pronounced well.

"Call me Luis, please," he said.

"Call me Linda, please. No one heard of me in my country–Luis." She tried it out. Saying "Luis" in the manner she said it, immediately brought her back to her high school days. She hadn't flirted with anyone but Ted since then. "Only my friends know who I am. I am no national treasure."

"Then it is a national tragedy!" he said.

She looked up at him through blurred eyes, the martini lapping against the side of its glass with occasional spills. "You know who you look like, Luis?"

"I look like someone?"

"You look just like Errol Flynn."

He laughed. "I remember him!"

"He was very handsome and dashing like you, and your thin mustache is just like his was. When I was a little girl I kept a scrapbook of his pictures."

"Had he seen you, he would have had a scrapbook of your pictures, I am sure. Would you like another drink?" Since most of her martini had been taking leaps and was on the floor, her glass was worthy of refilling. "Señor!" he yelled to one of the strolling waiters.

And that started it. In short time she was leaning against him, then they were arm-in-arm, then they were walking out on the balcony together.

"I notice your ring," Luis said. "You are married?"

She looked down at her left hand, as though the ring was a surprise to her. "Not tonight," she answered as she took it off and put the ring on her right index finger.

"Ahhh! That's good. Is–he is not here with you?"

"He's at the funny hotel across the street from the airport. We're not staying together. I'm staying here. I'm a guest of the government!" she said with hoped-for stature.

He dropped the issue since there was obviously no reason to discuss it. "Would you like to see where Howard Hughes lived before the earthquake?"

"Oh, yes," she said. Then she gave a loud hiccup. "Where is it?"

Luis discreetly pretended he hadn't heard the hiccup. "Here, in this hotel. He had the whole seventh floor. A bunch of Russians are up there now, but I know a secret room he had that isn't occupied."

She nodded with an expectant look on her face. "That would be—" and she had a rough time making it to the end of her sentence. The hiccup was very loud again. "—fun."

It sure was fun.

Her inexperience was unique to Luis, and his experience was unique to Linda. Ted had turned into a total bore, and anyone would have been better. Luis loved her reactions because they came from instincts. All of this would have been even more fun for both of them if she didn't have to throw up twice. But few things are perfect.

Aside from that, it was thrilling until some hours later when they walked back into the party holding hands and Ted was there.

"Ted!" she said. No one in the history of the world looked guiltier than Linda.

Luis knew how to handle it without a blink. He let go of her hand and quickly extended his now-free hand to Ted. "Ahhh, good," he said with a smile of confidence. "She was looking for you, Señor. She got quite sick. Something she ate—or drank. She seems to be a little better now—after I took her to the —you know—the toilet."

"Yes!" the inexperienced Linda agreed. "He took me to the ladies room. Thank you! Thank you!"

Ted looked back and forth at them. He looked confused, and suspicious. The first confirmation of his suspicion was the speed at which Luis disappeared into the crowd.

The next confirmation was even more certain. It was later in the evening when they were walking through the crowded room from group to group and he held her hand—her right hand—and he felt her wedding ring—where it shouldn't have been.

He said nothing.

He wanted to have something on her. He quickly planned to save the confrontation to a time when it would do him the most good. All Ted talked about that evening was his interview with Castro. She was gushing with pretended interest.

Two months later at the refugee center outside of San Salvador, Gloria was taking care of Cody rather than the refugees. Whatever he had contracted had caused him to lose eleven pounds, and she had him on intravenous as well as medication. He couldn't eat or drink anything, and she was putting ice cubes on his lips.

Outside the wooden room with the tin roof there were dozens of refugees who were praying.

There was no certain diagnosis. He had bites all over him, some from his stay in Southeast Asia and some newer ones from El Salvador. But Gloria had bites, too, and she wasn't ill.

No one would dare tell Cody the news of the day. Anastasio Somoza had been assassinated in Asuncion, Paraguay. The official United States reaction came from the State Department through its spokesman: "Of course we deplore violent death, no matter where it occurs and to whom it occurs. But," he added, "it is not really our affair."

"Who did it? Who murdered our President?" one of the refugee women asked another outside the encampment where Gloria was treating Cody.

The other woman hesitated, and then answered, "Watermelons."

FIFTY-FOUR
A DISTANT MIRROR
1980

Three days after the dozens of refugees had assembled outside the quarters of Cody and Gloria Cooper, their numbers had expanded to hundreds. Whether it was a lifewatch or a deathwatch was then unknown.

It was 9:30 in the morning when Gloria opened the door and walked out a few steps and stopped. She slowly scanned the crowd with her eyes, and then the nod of her head told them all they had dreaded.

That was followed by gasps and loud weeping, and the entire assemblage knelt as one.

She tried to speak, but her lower lip was trembling and even after standing there for minutes, she was unable to say anything.

And then one man near the front of the crowd stood up from his kneel and walked to her and kissed her hand. He was shaking. And then three children stood and waited behind him, and then others stood until the entire crowd was standing, forming a line behind those in front of her.

Throughout the spontaneous procedure, not one word was said by anyone.

Some twenty minutes passed before a woman who reached the head of the line gave a gesture with her head toward the dwelling with the open door. By that small movement, she was asking Gloria if she wanted to be done with the greetings. Gloria gave a confirming nod, and the woman took her arm and accompanied her inside.

Throughout the remainder of the day people came from all over El Salvador to stand there and kneel and pray, and then stand around the dwelling as though they were protecting it.

The sun went down and up again and down again and up again and Gloria and John Fitzgerald Cooper buried Cody near the refugee center while thousands came to stand by their sides, and where messages from around the world were read.

The death of Cody, like his idol, President John Kennedy, was ultimately responsible for strangers standing together in grief. "There is nothing that I have done, that you can't do," President Kennedy had told Cody eighteen years ago.

FIFTY-FIVE
TRIBUTES
1980

"Dear Gloria," the letter started in perfect slanted handwriting. It had to have been written by some one who was old, who had learned handwriting at a time when handwriting was strictly taught in school:

"There are no words that can express my sorrow since I heard the tragic news about Cody. He was so special, and so are you, dear Gloria. You filled him with such joy. I never saw him as happy as he was with you, or even when he was talking about you. You brought out the best in him. You gave him respect for himself.

"I tried to do that and failed. You tried and succeeded.

"I am late in writing this to you only because the news paralyzed my thoughts for these weeks. If you ever need help, I offer whatever that need may be. I now carry little if any influence in this city, but I know that never affected Cody's friendship toward me, in contrast to so many here. I wish I had influence, if for no other reason, to be of some help to you.

"I think Cody had three great loves. First, the love for you, and second, the love for John, and third, the love he had for President Kennedy. Those are the only three people in the world that made his face light up when he talked about them. As long as I live, Gloria, your son has a home here in Washington if he wants one. And so do you.

"Love, Irene Goodpastor."

The letter whose envelope had a stamp with Queen Elizabeth's profile, was from Moose Dunston:

"When things were very rough for President Nixon and very rough for all of us who worked for him, I received a phone call from Cody that took me by surprise. His affection for his own President, President Kennedy, did not make him a partisan unable to have empathy for President Nixon and for our staff. I have thought of that phone call so often during the years. His compassion at a difficult time taught me a great deal. I believe I have been more thoughtful of others since then, because of Cody's example. He touched more lives than he ever realized.

"You don't know me, Mrs. Cooper, but I met Cody 20 years ago in the place I live now; Hong Kong. I have been asked by one of those who met him at the same time I did, to extend her sympathy to you, and to tell you that she has fond memories of that day she met Cody. She's Yeung Tso Wai-yee, who worked at the American Consulate in those days. She asked me to tell you that the Vietnamese refugees in the refugee centers here put their flags of South Vietnam at half-staff for three days in memory of Cody. Their respect for you is equally high.

"Sincerely, Moose Dunston."

Ted Murphy gave a tribute to Cody on television, and Linda Murphy sent a videotape of it to Gloria. "Cody Cooper wanted nothing more or less than to bring help to the unfortunate," Ted said to his television audience. "His courage is well known throughout the world. At least once, and probably more times than once, he risked his life for those who had been ignored by others."

Mark and Anne Daschle sent Gloria a letter in which Anne wrote, "We hope you have some comfort in the love Cody displayed for human rights, and the more personal love for you. During his short life he made so many lives longer than they would have been without him. He left great gifts for our times, and great moral lessons for all time."

"He was a patriot and a humanitarian," General Jonas Valadovich wrote in his letter, enclosing a small handkerchief-sized flag of the United States made out of small patches of cloth and threads. "The enclosed flag, secretly assembled by my fellow Prisoners of War in Vietnam, should be yours, as it reflects the same dedication to liberty that led Cody to save so many Vietnamese and other oppressed peoples. When some of my friends found out that I had once met Cody Cooper, I was asked his religion. My answer came very quickly, 'He worked for God. Does that religion have one name?'"

FIFTY-SIX
THE PORTRAIT AT THE SEMIRAMIS
1980-1981

Mark's plan for Anne worked as though it had been charted by the best political campaign experts. Without a single dollar spent, she had immediate public name recognition. Better yet, the name recognition was all positive; even heroic. Unfortunately the name that was recognized was Anne Whitney, not Anne Daschle, despite her revelation to Ted Koppel. Since all the State Department records, including her biography, public documents on her Moscow, Burundi, and Iran posts, and her resignation letter, were recorded as "Anne Whitney," the press more often referred to her by that name. She got so sick of correcting it, that she didn't. In the end, her campaign chairman and her campaign manager advised that she use "Anne Whitney" as a professional name throughout the campaign. "There are those who will support you just because they recognize your name. Sorry, but that's the way name recognition works in a political campaign. This is the time to use the name they know, and no time to introduce a new name." Although both Anne and Mark fought it at the outset, they finally agreed to use the dreaded Ms. designation preceding her name.

It could well have been that Anne would have made enemies when she quit working for the United States government and started accepting the attention of the media, but under Mark's guidance and Anne's expertise, she walked on the edge of risk without a mis step. In most of her appearances, the State Department was proud of Anne. So was President Carter. So was candidate Reagan. So was Canada's Prime Minister Clark and Foreign Minister MacDonald. Other than those in the Islamic Fundamentalist Revolution, the Soviet Union and other unfriendly governments to the United States, the only one who was disappointed in her was Ted Murphy because she was unwilling to give him any exclusive information on her stay in Teheran, and because she married Mark Daschle. Two good reasons.

To no avail, Ted had phoned Anne countless times while she was in Washington, D.C., and he had phoned her again after she and Mark were back at Mark's post in Athens.

"Please, no calls from you! Please! Enough!" Anne was shouting into the phone. "There is not a chance I would meet with you here, there, or anywhere! I am a married woman, Ted! And in case you don't remember, you're a married man!"

"Linda is off in the Caribbean shackin' up somewhere with some guy."

"What do you mean?"

"She met this joker in Nicaragua. I don't know where she is right now. They meet in one of those Caribbean Islands. They're down in Barbados or Trinidad or Grenada or somewhere with palm trees and blue seas and all that jazz."

"I'm sorry." Anne felt he deserved it, but she wouldn't say that.

"Don't be sorry. I'm glad. She doesn't know I know, but I found out. I got friends. She tells me she's always visiting some girlfriend named Louise who's a travel agent. It's a boyfriend whose named Luis and he isn't a travel agent, he's a buddy of Daniel Ortega, the guy who's now President of Nicaragua. So, see? I told you a long time ago that our marriage was on the rocks. Now can I see you?"

"Ted, your problems don't change the fact that I'm a happily married woman!"

"Little Annie Loyal! Do you remember Lew Loyal, the comic strip and radio character durin' World War II? Well, you're his daughter I guess. Just my luck–you're Little Annie Loyal!"

"You bet I am!" Anne was feeling good about herself.

"That's okay! Hey, that's okay, Annie! But loyalty is such a tiring thing. I read about you, and I notice they call you Anne Whitney. Good for you. You're makin' a good step by keepin' the ol' unmarried name. It makes it easier when you get a divorce. When you've had enough of the marriage bit, you know where to find me–even before you get a divorce. I'm not fussy. You can always find me in the city that makes the day's headlines, whatever city it may be. You know, I have everything a man could ask for; a great salary, travel, the TV camera, people listenin' to me, new women in every city, I even have an AFTRA pension that's addin' up–and with all that, I don't have what I really want. You know what I really crave more than anything else?" He didn't wait for her to guess. "Little Annie Loyal!"

"You crave what scoops I can give you, that's what you crave. And I know what else you crave. I know you, Murph'."

"Annie, I want to see you even if you seal your mouth with tape! Don' cha feel sorry for me? A fella like me alone while his wife is in the Caribbean with some joker? I'm lonely. I'm cryin'. Why can't I see you?"

"Never! Not ever!"

"No wife waitin' at home. I just go from crisis to crisis and right now there's so many of them I don't know where I'll be tomorrow. I'm high-risk, gal! My life is fragile! Don' cha feel sorry for me? I've been goin' back and forth between wars–wars at home and wars all over the globe. Right now I'm in yer old hauntin' ground–Teheran. I'm at the Semiramis Hotel. But that wouldn't stop me from comin' to Athens for some R and R. You name it and I'll be there."

"What are you doing in Teheran again?"

"They love me here. I've been stickin' around since I've been here with my new buddy, the Ram."

"What's the Ram?"

"Ramsey Clark."

"Oh, my God!"

"Guts, huh?"

"I would expect that of you. It's not guts, it's treason."

"Get off! My buddy, the Ram! Imagine me havin' a buddy who was once attorney general of the U.S. of A.? Would you believe it?" Ted gave a short laugh.

"I'd believe you and that particular attorney general would get along. God! After what he did in Hanoi during the war, don't you know what he is? He screwed up those American prisoners there and now he's screwing up the American hostages in Teheran. Murphy–the hostages are my friends!"

"Hey, he asked for their release! He said he'd trade places with them!"

"Oh, please! If they wouldn't take Mohammed Ali's offer to take their place, they wouldn't take his. He knows what he's doing. Come on, do you believe him? That isn't why he's in Teheran. Please!"

"Hey, it's a free country, isn't it? The Ram was here for a conference on 'Crimes of America.' And get this one, Annie–I met Khomeini. I went to his house with the Ram. There I was sittin' on the floor with my legs crossed!"

"Why didn't you do the world a favor and while you were there, kill him?"

"I'm a journalist, not a murderer. Besides, how many people get to go to somethin' like that? No women there, though. That's a tough one. But Khomeini was real good to me. See? If you stayed in Teheran and didn't go out as a Canadian, I could have talked to him and have gotten your release! That's as long as you didn't pull the Little Annie Loyal stuff. He said that you U.S. government folks are 'worse than animals from the wilderness.'"

Anne was disgusted and was becoming more and more angry. "And you just sat there and took that kind of thing?"

"I'm a journalist! I sat there with my notebook. The Ram did the talkin' with Khomeini. The Ram said Carter's screwed up rescue attempt, what Carter called 'Operation Eagle Claw,' was a lawless act and–don't get in a tizzy–he says our hostages should be freed but that takin' them was understandable in human terms."

"God! Understandable? And you just sat there and let him say that to Khomeini?"

"What do you want me to do, stand up and jump? Listen to this one–the Ram said that Nixon and Kissinger are the real enemies, and although he would take the place of any of the hostages who are being held now, it might be different if they had Nixon and Kissinger. How do you like them potatoes?"

"President Carter has a travel ban there, you know. What Ramsey Clark is doing is against the law–against a lot of laws."

"He makes the point that he's exercising his constitutional right to travel."

"He was the attorney general and he doesn't even know that travel isn't mentioned in the Constitution?"

"It isn't?"

"It isn't."

"Okay. Then it isn't. I'll tell him."

"Is this call being tapped?"

"Probably. I don't care. Who cares?"

"Are you reporting all these things he said?"

"That's how I got where I am. Now all I want to report is the other side—that not everyone agrees with the Ram. See? I'm fair. Don't you feel committed to give me the other side?"

"I think the president is giving the other side."

This time he gave it a sing-song cadence. "Little Annie Loyal! Hey—Can I come to Athens and buy you a dinner?"

"You don't give up! Yes, you can have dinner with Mark and me."

"Is that the only way you'd do it?"

"Murph'—Mark would bust you in your already busted nose. In truth, I wouldn't have dinner with you even if I had Mark and the entire NATO force to protect me. Can I please ask you not to call me anymore?"

"You can ask, but I'll still call. What are you doin'? Just sittin' aroun' while Mark is off at the embassy?"

"I love it."

"You'll get tired of it. I know you, Annie. You got to be doin' somethin'. You're gonna get sick of sittin' around. You're not the marryin' type. Hey—whatcha wearin' right now? Let me imagine you."

"None of your business."

"I'm imaginin' you the way I used to see you."

Bang! She put down the receiver so loud that the vibration reverberated all the way from his listening ear to the ear on the other side of his head.

Ted looked up at the picture of the Ayatollah Khomeini that was hanging on his hotel room wall. It was difficult to find a place in Teheran where there wasn't a picture of the Ayatollah Khomeini. Ted nodded at it. "Don't get upset at me, ol' man. Haven't you ever heard of the First Amendment? I can say what I want to her."

There was a lot to dislike about the Ayatollah but, to Ted, nothing exceeded the outrageous policies of making liquor so inaccessible, and covering up the women with some of them even wearing veils and hoods, so only their eyes were visible. But whenever Ted looked at their eyes and their eyes looked at his eyes at the same time, which was in violation of law, it was as intriguing as seeing a woman in a mini-skirt and a low blouse sitting at a bar. The streets of Teheran gave evidence that as little or as much of whatever a woman makes visible, is of little ultimate importance. The intrigue is in what ever is hidden, and the possibility—even if it's a distant possibility—of some visibility.

Intoxicated by having heard Anne's voice, Ted left his room at the Semiramis Hotel to walk around the block in search for a woman who would give him an exchange of glances.

There was something both so horrible and so inviting in seeing those women in black who would not look at him. He managed to get around three fourths of the block when one woman in a chador, veil and hood, did look at him, but only for a moment, and then she quickly looked down as she continued walking toward him. When they were close to passing each other, Ted said, "Hi, baby." Her eyes quickly looked even further downwards. Then, in a total surprise, she looked up, back at his eyes. He wasn't prepared for it, but he thought quickly and gave a toss of his head as though to say, "follow me." She gave the slightest nod. What did she mean by that gesture?

He kept walking. Would she turn around so as to follow him to wherever he would lead? Is that what she meant by that nod?

Ted circled the block in full, and he was back at the entrance to the Semiramis. He felt his heartbeats that seemed to be coming from his stomach. He wanted to look and see if she was behind him, but why look? She either was behind him or she wasn't. Why find out now? He walked into the hotel, practically yelled his room number to the receptionist, in the hope she was behind him and would hear him. He received his key, and he walked to the bank of two elevators. Then he decided against an elevator. In case she didn't hear him give the receptionist the room number, he wanted to remain in sight. There was a semi-circular stairway and his room was only one flight up. He walked up slowly, he went to his room, and went inside. He closed the door and waited. In a moment there was a soft knock on the door. Could this be?

Ted opened the door; and there she was, her eyes looking straight into his eyes. That forbidden act was the signal of an arousing feast waiting for him. He said nothing since he didn't know what to say. He opened the door wider for her to enter. She walked in, and he looked down both sides of the hallway to insure no one was watching all this. The hallway was vacant. He closed the door behind the two of them.

"Do you speak English?" he asked.

She didn't answer.

"I don't speak Farsi," he said. That did not seem to be an issue.

There was just that stare of hers and her breathing was breaking the silence. Those loud breaths were either from fear or lust or both. Ted walked over to her, trying to avoid looking at the portrait of the Ayatollah Khomeini who he knew was giving him a look of intense disapproval. Ted reached for the black veil that rested on top of her nose hiding most of her face.

She reached for his hand so as to prevent the removal of the veil from her face. Her grip was light but certain. Now she was holding his hand, and she lowered his hand, and with more surprise than he could ever have hoped, she put his hand on her chador at her waist. How could this be acceptable to her, while it was unacceptable for him to see her face?

With one swift movement of his other hand, he pulled down the veil that had shielded her face. His action was too fast for her to stop him. The revelation of that face was another surprise. This woman was young and beautiful with wisps of flowing black hair falling from beneath her hood. He removed the hood.

Her mouth was open to allow her deep breathing to escape with greater ease. And that breathing became even more intense. Her hand did not release his hand. Instead she clutched it, insuring that he brought it to wherever she wanted it to go.

He tried to move her to the bed but she wouldn't go in that direction. She wanted to continue standing.

Again, he tried to move her to the bed, but she continued to resist. She wanted to remain standing, and finally allowing the lifting of her chador, she wanted to do things usually done in other positions. This was all so illicit and dangerous under the laws, that it increased the passion to the almost unendurable.

And when it was done, it was done. She pushed down her chador and straightened it, lifted her veil back to the upper part of her nose, pushed back her long flowing hair into invisibility as she replaced her black hood, and then in the consistency of her silence, she simply walked out of the hotel room.

It was as though she had been shopping, and now her shopping was done and it was time to go home.

Of course there was really nothing that she could have said or he could have said, since neither one spoke the language of the other. What a magnificent blessing between a man and a woman.

Now Ted was brave enough to look at the picture of the Ayatollah Khomeini. This time Ted didn't mention the First Amendment to the picture since, if travel wasn't mentioned in the U.S. Constitution, he assumed that his latest activity probably wasn't mentioned in the U.S. Constitution either.

"Haig!" Moose said with alarm over the phone to President Nixon. Is the *South China Morning Post* right? It says that you endorse Haig to be Reagan's secretary of state."

"You calling from Hong Kong?"

"Yeah."

"Well, you heard the news right. I think it's a good choice. Don't you?"

"No. Mr. President. The last week of your administration, from Monday forward, he was leading the White House mutiny. Don't you remember that, Mister President?"

"Moose, what do you want? Revenge? Al felt—"

"Al felt he wanted Al to survive," Moose interrupted. "If he truly thought it was better for the country if you resigned, he could have made that happen ethically, rather than as a mutiny. All he had to do was resign himself, and then say whatever he wanted to say. You wouldn't have survived the week. At the time, remember, we were worried that James St. Clair would resign, who was a minor figure compared to Al. We thought if St. Clair resigned you'd have to. But Al didn't do it the right way. And it's clear why. He didn't want to leave. If he had done it ethically, he wouldn't have been chief of staff to Ford, and he wouldn't have been supreme commander of NATO. He would have had to have given up that pedestal from which to rise higher."

"He didn't know he'd be kept by Jerry. He didn't know he'd still be chief of staff and that, in time, he'd be supreme commander of NATO. Moose, he kept that position under Carter after Jerry left. Do you think he knew that was going to happen with Jerry and in the Carter administration, too? You're using what you know now to accuse him of what Al didn't know then. Now, when you go back to our administration, the point is, Moose, that in that last week, you ought to have in mind that he was, of course, pretty shaken, of course, like everybody else—about all the uproar about the famous June 23rd tape and all that sort of thing. You see, that was Monday that you're talking about."

"Exactly."

"And so under the circumstances I think that up to that point there was no question Al wanted the administration to survive. But beyond that point he didn't think it was possible, and I think that's what happened. Now, there may have been another way to do it but I don't think that the other alternative was even suggested to him. He probably didn't even think of it."

"Why not think of it?"

"Well, he didn't. You know. That was a pretty hectic week. We got to understand, too, in all fairness that it was not just Haig. Let's face it. It was people in the Cabinet. You know that. You know the people I'm talking about."

"So what if many were against you? Even in the Cabinet. But your chief of staff?"

"Well, it's past, and no purpose would be served by you getting angry. Now we have to rally against those clowns like Pell and the rest who are against Al. They're after him because he's a hawk. Let's face it. Because he was for the bombing. Because he was for a tough line on Vietnam, you remember. Because he wanted to kick Allende out of Chile. Now, when they go after that kind of stuff, that tells you who the enemy is. Now, did you hear the Dragon Lady is over in your part of the world? She went over to Beijing."

"What?"

"Oh, you know, the Dragon Lady. You know who I mean—Anna Chennault."

"Mister President, we were talking about Al." Moose didn't want to change the subject but the president did and that was that.

"Well, that's what we were talking about. But I want to know if you heard about Anna Chennault in China."

"Yes, I did."

"You going to be writing about it?"

"I hadn't thought about it."

"It would be a good subject. Wouldn't it?"

"Yes."

"I think so."

"Yes."

There was some silence. "It would be a good subject. I don't think anyone's writing about it. What did you think of her comments?"

Moose knew it was time to stop an unwinnable argument. Maybe not soon enough, but at least he caught on. "Some of her comments are surprising to me. Is she changing sides? Do you make sense out of what she's doing? She's been such a big supporter of the Republic on Taiwan. Is she changing sides?"

The president seemed to be relieved that Moose caught on and was being courteous if nothing else. "She's just diddling around, trying to get in. But what's more significant is that Deng saw her for two hours. And she's going to Taiwan to report on it. Very interesting. That's the point. That he would see her–to me, was surprising. He doesn't even see senators, but he saw her."

"But didn't it surprise you that what she said to the press, that those things believed in 1950 are not necessarily true in 1980?"

"Yeah. Particularly when you consider that in her book she attacked me for even going there."

"I wonder what kind of reception she'll get when she gets to Taiwan."

"I wonder. I wonder. Look, Moose, I'm sorry if I'm tough on what you said. I know how you feel. You should know that I want Al to be Secretary of State. You know, Moose, I can't think of an international policy on which you'd disagree with him. He's a tough guy, you know."

"I know."

"You got some international policy disagreements with him?"

"I can't think of any. He's great on policy but that isn't–"

"Good," the president interrupted. "That's the important thing. Now, how are you doing, Moose?"

"Okay."

"Send me your articles, will you?"

"Sure. I will."

"How's Hong Kong treating you?"

"I like it. I always have."

"Oh, I know. You ever get over to the Dragon Boat Bar or Restaurant or what ever it is at the Hilton?"

"No. Not yet."

"They have another great little restaurant too, you know. The Den I think it's called. It's right there as you walk out that side entrance as if you're going to the consulate."

"I'll try it."

"You ever see that girl you–you cared for over there?"

"Yes. I've seen her–and her husband–and her–and her daughter. I see all three of them very often."

"Oh. I see." Then he was silent. It was the first time Moose mentioned anything about what happened to her. "Well, you know. Things don't always work out the way we think–or want."

"No, sir. They sure don't."

At 12 o'clock noon on the 444th day of the Iranian hostage crisis, Ronald Reagan was inaugurated president of the United States. Thirty-three minutes later, the first of two airliners lifted up from Mehrabad Airport in Teheran, Iran, with all the U.S. hostages aboard, their ordeal over.

As they boarded the plane they were kicked by Islamic Revolutionary Guards. The chants of "Death to America" and "Death to Reagan" in both Farsi and English, became a chorus.

Former Deputy Secretary of State Warren Christopher had negotiated a deal with Iran during the closing days of the Carter Administration, although the term "negotiations" was not used since the world had been told by President Carter that the United States would not negotiate with terrorists. The Algerian Government was used as a conduit, as a middle-source in which the United States agreed to revoke all trade sanctions and withdraw all claims against Iran, as well as bar and preclude prosecution against Iran of any pending or future claims of the United States or of U.S. nationals rising out of the hostage crisis. Another provision in the agreement was that the United States would freeze all the U.S. assets of the late Shah and any close relative, with the United States ordering all persons within U.S. jurisdiction to report to the U.S. Treasury any information known to them regarding such property and assets. Additionally, "the United States pledges that it is, and from now on will be, the policy of the United States not to intervene, directly or indirectly, politically or militarily, in Iran's internal affairs."

It was a deal Khomeini could not refuse since there was the fear of the unknown in President Reagan who was entering office and might just do what had heretofore been undone–retaliate.

The Ayatollah Khomeini, not wanting to give President Carter the pleasure of being president when the hostages were freed, waited until those 33 minutes after he left office.

President Reagan then immediately appointed President Carter to be his official representative in greeting the returned hostages when they landed in Wiesbaden, Germany, after a stop in Athens, Greece, where they were met by under secretary Christopher and other U.S. representatives from Washington, D.C., as well as representatives from the U.S. Embassy in Athens. The bulk of the media were rushing to Wiesbaden, so the Athens stopover was relatively private. Only the U.S. Embassy was given enough warning from Washington.

At Hellinikon Airport in Athens, Anne shook hands with every returned hostage and embraced and kissed some of them she knew well, while Mark stood behind her as part of the U.S. official delegation. As Mark's wife, as an "alumna" of the official U.S. family, and as someone who was part of that Embassy Staff in Iran at the time of the Embassy's takeover, her presence was more than appropriate.

There was a photographer standing next to Mark. The photographer was snapping pictures of Anne with every hug and kiss, with every shake of hands. Mark had hired him to "preserve the moments for official purposes," but there was an unofficial purpose that Mark also had in mind: an upcoming congressional election.

"Oh, no you don't!" Anne said when it was all over, as they walked to the embassy car from the airfield. "That's taxpayer's money. Does that sound familiar? Do you remember who used to say that to me? Mark, my sense of what is right and wrong comes from you. Don't disappoint me."

That got to him. He nodded. "Then we won't have prints made for ourselves."

"You promise?"

"Yes."

"Say it." She grabbed his hand and pressed it tightly.

"I promise."

"Honest to God?"

"Anne, I don't say that about anything."

"Yes, you do." She clasped his hand even tighter. Her hand was making a statement. "Honest to God?"

"Honest to God."

"Okay, then."

"You satisfied?"

"Mark, I want you to know something."

"What?"

"You want me to win an election because you love me, right?"

"Of course. And I know you'll do such a remarkably good job."

"I want to win because I know what I want to do in office. And to get there I'm not going to take any short-cut that might be smart politically but 'if-ee' on the straight and narrow. I don't want to do that. If I win this I don't want to look back at the campaign and think I got it by some trick, or some smarty-pants move. I want to win it because the people who vote for me are able to appraise me correctly. They're the ones who will pay my salary, you know. I don't want them to regret it. Is that asking too much?"

"It's asking too little."

"It's what I want. And I'm the candidate."

"Next time I marry a candidate I'm going to be sure she isn't so sold on standards."

Anne smiled. "You know I learned it all from you, Mr. Daschle."

The student had exceeded the teacher.

Nothing against the hostages, but Linda Murphy wished that Khomeini had kept those Americans in captivity. "If all the hostages have been released, that means Ted will be coming home again," she said to Luis Angel Cajina who she still thought looked like Errol Flynn.

Luis Angel Cajina kept applying the suntan oil to the back of her shoulders as she lay on her stomach on a blanket by the pool of Barbados' Sandy Lane Hotel underneath a brilliant sun. "And you must go home, too, Linda?"

"I have to be there when he walks in the door," she said with her eyes closed, her chin resting on the back of her two clasped hands.

"You see?" Luis said. "You see what Reagan has done? His inauguration is bad news for everyone in the world except for 52 hostages. Reagan even makes you leave me. I so much wanted you to go to Grenada with me. It is the most beautiful island in the Caribbean."

"I'm sorry, Luis. I was looking forward to it."

"Prime Minister Bishop, himself, had offered us his home."

"Is that where you'll stay?" Linda turned to face him while she held the unstrapped top of her bathing suit to insure it wouldn't fall.

"Yes—now I must stay there hopelessly alone." Luis put the bottle of suntan oil down on the blanket which rested on the concrete. "Reagan! He scared Khomeini. He scares you. He does not scare Castro. He does not scare Ortega. He does not scare Bishop. He does not scare me."

"I'm not scared. It's just that I should be home when Ted gets there." Linda tied the top of her bathing suit.

"Why not let him suffer without you?"

"I can't imagine what he would do if he knew that I've been with you."

"Must we always hide?"

Linda nodded.

"Then we will always hide and search for places to meet?"

"Ted and I have been married 20 years, and neither one of us has even touched another person. Well, I have—with you. He would kill himself if he knew. Luis, please understand. I can't let him find out. Loyalty is like a religion to him."

Ted Murphy, who had made so many trips to Iran during the hostage crisis, was leaving for good. Once Day 444 was done there wasn't any meaning to Day 445 except to pack bags and leave.

He gave a final salute to the portrait of Khomeini on the wall of the room at the Semiramis, and he grabbed his bags. This trip was so short he didn't even have time to look for the woman in the black chador who had so brightened an earlier and surprisingly wonderful day in Teheran.

FIFTY-SEVEN
PROCESSION IN EGYPT
1981

There are two events more certain than others to bring about reunions of old friends and even old chance-acquaintances: political campaigns and funerals. October had both.

When Anne announced her candidacy for the House of Representatives five months ahead of the primary election and thirteen months ahead of the general election, she received letters and phone calls from those she knew in school; even grammar school, all the way to retired foreign service officers.

Most of those who supported her did it because she was Anne, but more than most candidates, she drew support from those who respected her experiences around the world and believed in the foreign policy objectives she wanted to accomplish in office:

"The Nations of Liberty Alliance," she announced at her first fund-raising event in the backyard of some couple she didn't know but who had offered their residence for her use. "I call it NOLA and it will be my long-range goal—to end the international influence of totalitarian and terrorist states." She looked up at the sky and winked at Ambassador Fairbanks. "NOLA will cause the United Nations organization to die by its own weight. No longer will the United States taxpayers be charged for 25% of that organization's bills, while the same organization invariably bows to those who oppose us."

There was applause among the seventy people who stood on the autumn lawn who were eating cheese and fruit and drinking punch. Anne kept her eyes wandering over the afternoon crowd as she spoke, but she couldn't help but continually look back at the large, handsome man in his late forties, maybe five years older than Anne, who was standing next to Mark. He was smiling and nodding with affirmation as she spoke.

"To be a member of NOLA, a nation must have free, fair, and frequent scheduled elections, the rule of law, and all the institutions of democracy. There will be what I call NOLA Associates who will be non-voting members for those nations who have a reasonable transition to full democracy planned, but not yet completed.

"Number two on my list is defense. President Reagan will have no trouble with me. Defense is the only budget item that has to be a guess because it's the only budget item that depends on the intention of other nations. In addition, we never know what's going to happen tomorrow—what chief of state will die, or what revolution will take place, or what power will combine in an axis with another power. If we budget our defenses too high, then we'll waste a lot of money. But if we budget our defenses too low, we'll waste the United States. I will vote for a budget that may be too high—I'm warning you of that—but I'll never support a budget that takes a chance on allocating too little."

Again, there was applause. The man next to Mark applauded with strength and his nodding was even more emphatic than before.

"Third is terrorism, a subject of which I have had personal experience, as you know. I'm going to encourage President Reagan to ask the Congress for a declaration of war against terrorism. You heard right! A declaration of war. Look, terrorism has already declared war against the United States and has often captured our most prized property—our citizens. Our declaration should regard terrorism as a sovereign state—as a nation in itself. The Nation of Terrorism is a chain of non-contiguous bases, training camps, safe-houses, and other facilities that dot portions of the globe, going into and out of other sovereign states, with the sanction of the leaders of those other sovereign states acting as shields for them. That shield must be a thing of the past! Our declaration of war will not mean a declaration of war against the surrounding state or states, but against the bases of terrorism within those countries, as long as those surrounding states permit such bases to exist on their territory. And those bases will be eliminated."

Again, applause. And, again, the man next to Mark accompanied his applause with long, strong nods.

"And finally, fourth and immediate—El Salvador. Am I afraid of 'Another Vietnam' in El Salvador as critics continually warn? My only fear is that we will do nothing—that the current Congress, the 97th Congress, will continue to cut aid for El Salvador, repeating the error of the 94th Congress when it stopped all aid to Vietnam. That's my fear. Such a policy will invite the continuation of the expansion of hostile forces. 'Another Vietnam' has become the rejection of American involvement anywhere.

"I suppose that if Hitler rose to prominence and started crossing borders, not in the late 1930s, but in the early 1980s, we would be warned by many political observers that we better not become involved in 'Another Vietnam' We speak now of either 'peace' or 'Another Vietnam' as though there is nothing else.

"To those who argue that the Marxist guerrillas fighting to take over the government of El Salvador are simply part of a local uprising, let me ask a question. Where do they get their weapons and ammunition? Those arms didn't grow on the trees of El Salvador's forests.

"The 97th Congress wants to ignore all that. I assure you, should I win this coming election, the 98th Congress will cut off the tentacles of those from abroad who choose to rule in the Western Hemisphere."

Along with the applause were chants of her name. She noticed that the man next to Mark cupped his hands and held them above his head in approval.

With her speech done, like a professional, she walked among the crowd shaking hands and making small talk. This was what she was told she would have to do for the months ahead: "work the room, even if there is no room, wherever you are," Mark had instructed. She was able to call the guests by name since all the guests had paper stickers on their jackets or shirts or blouses with the printed message, "I'm for Anne. I'm–" and then the first name that had been entered in a Magic Marker's black ink by one of the two women who had sat at a card table on the driveway to the house, the two women having greeted every person who entered, and having insured they paid their twenty-five dollars.

"Thank you for coming, Louise!" she would say to an absolute stranger. "I'm so glad you're here, Tommy!" Or did it say Tammy? It was a woman. "So good to see you, Fran-cis-co!"

She went through the whole procedure, planning her walk to gradually come to Mark and whoever the man was who was standing next to him. When she got to them she stood on her toes and Mark bent down, and they gave a quick kiss. "Hi, honey!" she said.

"Great speech, Anne! Good going! Too bad there's no press here!"

"They'll never be around when I'm any good. But I'll bet that every newspaper and television station will be here if I trip or drop the mike!"

Mark and the man laughed. She looked over at the man and glanced as quick as she could at the name tag. As the candidate, it had to be quick, since too long a stare at the sticker would indicate she didn't really "remember" the person's name. "Good to see you, Jonas!"

"Do you know who he is, Anne?" Mark asked.

"Jonas! He's Jonas! Of course!"

"But Jonas who?" Was Mark trying to trap her?

Jonas gave a broad smile as he extended his hand. "Jonas Valadovich, ma'am. We met twenty-one years ago overseas." For a moment she was scared. Overseas? Did she have an affair with him or something? Does he have a venereal disease he wants to tell her about? "I'm on my way to Cairo from California, ma'am. Mark wrote me about your campaign and he enclosed newspaper articles that told how you feel about defense. I wrote Mark back to offer some help, and he asked me to stop by when I'd be on the East Coast. This was the time. I stopped in D.C."

"How good!" She decided to take a chance. "Where did we meet overseas?" She was relying on his discretion, if it was called for.

"I met you and Mark at the Consulate in Hong Kong. I was a little younger then," and he laughed. "You and Mark seemed to have stayed the same age. I was in uniform then–at the meeting Mark put together to hear the Kennedy-Nixon debate."

"Oh, my God!" And she gave a wide smile. "Of course I remember!" Although she didn't remember his face, which had changed in twenty-one years, she now remembered his unique low voice, which had changed not a bit.

"He did rather well since then, honey," Mark said. "He's retired now–a retired general–and he contributed the maximum to your campaign."

"Really? Thank you, General!"

Mark continued. "General Valadovich is willing to offer his help on defense. He knows every side of it–procurement, troop strength, weapons systems–everything."

"That's wonderful! Thanks! That would be wonderful."

"When it comes to a defense issue, he could be a great spokesman for you—a surrogate."

"Oh, boy!" Anne said like a little girl. "That's so good of you!"

Jonas shook his head. "It's not good of me. I agree with what you're saying. But if I recall correctly, you were a little different twenty-one years ago—I mean politically. Am I right?"

She laughed. "Big time!"

"Look," Jonas said. "I'll give you what time I can, but it's somewhat limited. I live in L.A. and, believe it or not, I'm back at school—U.S.C. courses on theology. And I'm spending a lot of time working with General Graham and Buzz Aldrin," and he looked over at Mark, "that's Dan Graham, working on High Frontier, a missile defense system idea of his."

Mark nodded. "How about Reagan? You doing anything for the president?"

"Nothing much. Occasionally I do some advisory work for the staff at the White House. There's a colonel over there, Oliver North, with the National Security Council, who I work with at times. I just saw him today. But I come to D.C. as infrequently as possible. There's something about it that doesn't appeal to me, so I do work by phone and mail." He looked back at Anne. "But what I can do for you is write up some military policy papers, and maybe I can come back here for a couple fund-raising events closer to election time—or brief you before debates." And he quickly added, "if you want."

"I want!"

"El Salvador is going to be increasingly important. You can take the lead on that subject, easily. I'm impressed with what you've been saying about Central America. You've been studying. But the one thing that prompted me to support you, more than anything else, is that you have grasped the only reason anyone should run for an important office."

Anne smiled and shook her head, "What is that?"

"Saying what you believe. When you're running, people care what you say. Every thought of yours on policy becomes important. Those thoughts even make the news. Win or lose, you have influence during this period of time. You're taking advantage of it. A lot of candidates run for office and take polls to find out what others think, and they say whatever is popular. They aren't worthy of holding office because they want to win to be someone, not to do something. You're good, Anne. You may lose the election, no one knows, but in your candidacy, you're taking advantage of this time by saying what you think. People care. It's a time that may never come back. But, frankly, I think you're going to win, and then what you say will always be influential."

Anne smiled even wider, her face giving a slight blush, which was rare for Anne. "Thank you!" In an attempt to lose the blush, she asked, "Did you say you were going to Cairo, General?"

"I am."

"Why Cairo?"

"Former President Nixon arranged for me to meet with President Anwar Sadat," he said with some hesitancy, almost with embarrassment because he felt like a name-dropper. But she asked.

"Oh, wow!"

"Anne—may I call you Anne?"

"Please!"

"Anne, I promise you I will never give you unsolicited advice. You'll get much too much of that. So if you want any advice, you'll have to ask. That is, with one exception, only because I think it's so valuable."

"What?"

"If you win, and I believe you will, you must do something that will go against all your instincts. From the moment of your victory you must pretend you have died and have been re-born. In this new life your only duties are to the nation and its ideals. You can't do anything to harm those duties. You can't have anyone on your staff simply because they're friends. You have to tell everyone you hire or appoint that if they want to do something parting from your goals, they must first resign. In fact, in this new life, you have no friends, and shouldn't seek them. Tell those who were your friends that you'll see them in two, four, six, or eight years, when ever your job is done. Then, when your time in office is over, you can go back to the old life, picking up where you left off, if you want. But not while you're in office. Remember, Anne, you must pretend you died. Gone. And then, like a reincarnation, you are alive again, but this time you were born into a very unique and important position."

There was a powerful silence between the three of them. Even the noise of the crowd seemed to be subdued.

Jonas waited for some reaction beyond the silence, but it didn't come. And so he added, "If you are not prepared to do that, then you are not prepared to be a member of the Congress."

Anne asked, very softly, "Is that what the members of the Congress do?"

Jonas shook his head. "Maybe a few."

Mark nodded. "Good advice. Great advice. Thank you."

"Now, no more of that," Jonas said. "No more unsolicited advice, I promise. How many of these fundraising events are you going to have?"

Anne couldn't answer, she was still thinking of what Jonas had said about dying and being re-born. Mark answered, "A lot of them. Got to. We hope to make about $2,000 tonight. That's nothing. So we got to have plenty of these so we can pay for direct mail and radio ads, and yard-signs, bumper stickers, maybe some TV, and all kinds of things. So it will be a lot of fundraising events."

"I don't envy you that."

"It'll be worth it!" Mark said. "Anne's going to make it!"

"You're right," Jonas nodded. "I know she will."

Jonas left from Dulles International Airport to go to Cairo for his scheduled meeting with President Sadat. He attended, instead, President Sadat's funeral.

By the time he landed on October the 6th, Sadat was dead, assassinated by men in Egyptian army uniforms who were on a truck in the military parade President Sadat was watching from a reviewing stand. As President Sadat and most of the others at the event were looking upwards at Mirage jets flying in exhibition, a truck in the parade stopped in front of the reviewing stand and six uniformed men ran to the stand, opening fire. Along with Sadat, seven others were killed.

There would be a mourning period of forty days. All public assembly was banned other than the funeral procession, and a State of Emergency was invoked for one year.

With the personal letter of introduction Jonas held from President Nixon to President Sadat, the U.S. Embassy invited Jonas to be part of the American delegation for the funeral. That meant he would be in the procession in Nasr City (Victory City) and be given a room at the El Aram Hotel. The entire hotel had been vacated to make it an American encampment with its own U.S. security force, including the Secret Service. There was good reason. The Egyptian security forces could give no guarantees of security.

There was no real beginning or end to the unstructured funeral procession of walkers, only a middle. The American delegation waited in the intense heat under a mammoth tent, with cold water served by tuxedoed waiters. After a horse drawn hearse with President Sadat's casket passed the tent, the Americans joined those already walking, in no particular order or place. There was justified fear of the very military that were providing security to the visiting dignitaries. That fear was so pronounced that the U.S. Secret Service had successfully warned President Reagan and Vice President Bush not to attend.

Representing President Reagan were former U.S. presidents Nixon, Ford, and Carter, who joined the procession, sometimes with each other, some times distances apart, often in idle conversation with Prime Minister Begin of Israel or President François Mitterrand or former president Giscard d'Estaing of France, or whoever happened to be near. Even Great Britain's Prince Charles was walking unaccompanied and talking to whomever happened to walk by his side during the processional. Like the former U.S. Presidents, he had his own security forces although others didn't know who they were.

For those accustomed to the strict ceremonials of state funerals, this was an unconventional, almost bizarre, procession of informality, every guest walking at their own pace, almost in a casual stroll.

Occasionally Henry Kissinger would be talking to one former U.S. president or another as they walked, and some times he would be walking alone or with Secretary of State Alexander Haig.

"Jonas! You made it!" President Nixon said.

"Yes, sir."

"Too late."

"How I regret it, sir."

The president said nothing for a while as they walked in the assemblage.

"I should have come sooner," Jonas said. "I wish I knew him. I am impressed with the number of heads of state who are here."

"I'm disappointed. But I didn't expect to be impressed. I'm saddened by those who aren't here."

Jonas looked sharply at the former president. "Who are the ones who aren't here?"

"Waldheim isn't here. He rejected the invitation. He sent his Chief of Protocol who said that the Secretary General would not attend since there has been no established rule for the Secretary General of the U.N. to attend 'funerals, weddings, christenings,' or any of those. That's bunk, you know. Secretary General U Thant went to Kennedy's funeral. He was there. And Secretary General Waldheim, himself, was at Pompidou's funeral. So you see, he didn't want to be here for Sadat. Then you don't see some of our Arab friends. They aren't here. You know who's here from the Arab Nations? Only three delegations. The rest, you know, cut diplomatic relations with Egypt over Anwar's negotiations with Israel. And when Anwar allowed the Shah to live in Cairo, they were done with him. He gave the Shah a state funeral. So Khadaffi and the rest are having their revenge on him. Did you hear about the celebrations in some of those countries?"

"No, I didn't."

"Oh, sure. They celebrated Anwar's assassination. In Libya, Iraq, Syria, and Lebanon there were celebrations in the streets. Did you hear what Yasir Arafat's spokesman said?"

"No."

"He said, 'We shake the hand that fired the bullets. It was inevitable that the ruler of Egypt should receive his due.' Can you believe that?"

"Is that public?"

"It's public. I'm going off on a private trip after I get out of Cairo today. On my own. Jerry and Carter are flying back home together. Nick and I are going on to Jordan, Saudi Arabia, Tunisia, and Morocco. We'll see Hussein, Khalid, Bourguiba, Hassan. They all got it right," and the former president gave a smile. "They're kings and presidents for life."

Seemingly from out of nowhere, King Baudouin of Belgium greeted the former president. Jonas had never before been interrupted by a King, let alone one who happened to walk up from behind. So he separated himself from the King and the former President by picking up his step.

In less than a minute Jonas was joined again, this time by a stranger. "Are you General Valadovich?" It was an American with an ear piece.

"Yes, sir."

The man, so obviously a member of the Secret Service, adjusted his ear piece which was hurting his ear; one of the occupation's more common, but comparatively minor hazards. "An Arab gentleman from a foreign delegation that flew in last night would like to see you, sir. He's just behind us, so you might slow down a little if you would like to walk with him."

"Who is he?"

"I can't pronounce his name, sir. Just slow down a little, sir."

Jonas stopped walking and turned around. Former President Nixon and King Baudouin passed him. A short distance away, just in front of President Carter and Henry Kissinger, was a man in a white Arab headdress walking in quick step toward him. Jonas nodded at him, and started walking again as soon as the man was by his side.

"General Valadovich?" the man in the Arab headdress asked.

"Yes, sir."

The man introduced himself and the nation he represented, then he said, "I understand you came here to Cairo with the intent of meeting with Anwar." Saying President Sadat's first name was the intentional signal that the man had some importance.

"I did."

"What a tragedy! I'm sure you didn't plan on anything like this. What a tragedy! Anwar was a great man."

"I know he was. But I didn't know him. What can I do for you, sir?" Jonas asked in American impatience.

"General, I hear very good things about you. I understand you are a military and policy expert–and you are trustworthy."

"I don't know about the word 'expert.'"

"Did you come to Cairo to give Anwar military advice?"

"Oh, no. I asked to come here. He didn't ask me. And it was not to discuss military affairs. I wanted to discuss God."

The man said nothing for a moment and then asked, "You are a believer in Islam?"

"I believe in God. I was told by a very good source that President Sadat had a marvelous and unique religious philosophy in his Islamic beliefs. We were both prisoners in different places and different times, and we both benefited from the experiences. I wanted to talk about those things with him. I wanted to discuss theology."

"I see. Yes, yes. His Cell 54. He's talked of it to all of us. He often referred to himself as 2151. That was his prisoner number. So that was the reason for your visit here?"

"Yes, sir."

"General, my interest in you, unfortunately, is not to discuss theology or prisons, but to discuss strategy and advice–military strategy and advice."

"Oh?"

"When most of our brothers deserted your nation, we did not. And we supported Anwar when he went to Israel, as your nation did. Our brothers kicked him–kicked Egypt out of the Arab League, the Arab Monetary Fund, the Organization of Arab Petroleum Exporting Countries–and cut all diplomatic ties to leave Egypt hanging as a pariah. Only a few of us stayed with him. We argued to our other brothers to support Anwar, and to have friendly relations with the United States."

"I know. Our nation is grateful for that."

"Now, let me get to the point as long as you know that background. We believe that Khomeini is a threat to all of us, particularly in the Arabian Peninsula. Additionally, we are not naive regarding Brezhnev's ambitions here. Anwar had to expel the Soviets here. The Soviet Union is involved in an overall plan to encircle the Arabian Peninsula, and they want to cut the oil routes to Western Europe, Japan and the United States. All of that oil, which is two-thirds of the world's ocean-shipped oil, must pass through the Strait of Hormuz. Iran is on one side of the Strait, General. So we see need for protection from both Iran and the Soviet Union. Then there is a third threat to our stability and well-being, and that is Yasir Arafat."

"Arafat?"

"That one surprises you?"

"Coming from a representative of an Arab state, yes."

"General, that should not surprise you. Do you think all Arab leaders want Arafat to have an independent Palestinian state?"

"That's the impression that's given."

He shook his head with a slight smile. "Do not be fooled by necessary public statements. Other than the idiots, all of us hope the United States never agrees with Arafat to have an independent Palestinian state. 'The Forgotten War' was now some ten years ago, when King Hussein of Jordan fought Arafat–a war. Arafat's guerrilla's wanted to take over Jordan. There was a bloody war. King Hussein's forces defended Jordan and Arafat went into Lebanon, where now he has formed a state within a state. We do not remind the world of the war, as the world's forgetfulness is in our interest. But we remember, and we do not trust Arafat. The truth of our feelings was almost given away by Anwar when he was in your country two Septembers ago. He was on one of your television interview shows and was asked if Arab leaders really want an independent Palestinian state. Anwar was taken by surprise by the question. He hesitated and then answered, 'It is a family business and I choose better to abstain.' His honesty was frightful. Your State Department was very unhappy with him for that, but it caused no press and no one made anything of it."

"What has all this to do with what you want from me?"

"So you see, we face many dangers: Khomeini, Brezhnev, Arafat. We have faith in Reagan if we need the United States, but we had faith in Carter, too, and he allowed Khomeini to take over Iran and threaten all of us. And so we must be able to defend ourselves. We need the best advice. We need to make plans, both defensive, and offensive if necessary. No secrets. Just advice. You know who our friends are. You know who our enemies are. You come highly recommended. Would you be willing, for just compensation, of course, to give us your best strategic thinking,

General, before leaving Egypt? Perhaps all day tomorrow. Can you do it?"

"For just compensation?"

"Yes, of course. I have been given authority to offer, shall we say, a generous amount of Swiss francs or English pounds, should that be preferable. We can work out the details."

"No. I do not want that kind of compensation."

"Then we can arrange American dollars."

"I will be glad to spend the day in discussion, but not for any financial compensation. I do not want to be a foreign agent in my country. But I would want compensation."

"Yes, of course. What would that be?"

"Information. I need to know what I came to Cairo to find out. Everything—everything Sadat believed. Everything that changed him into a man of God. I don't care about politics when it comes to Sadat. I want to know everything he knew about God. There must be those with whom he confided. I found his writing inspiring, but not detailed enough. He was a private man, and I want to be included in his privacy."

"You ask for something unusual."

"Try. Your compensation to me will be your efforts. That is what I ask."

The man walked without saying anything for a while, but Jonas knew this was only a hesitation for effect. "It is agreed. We will work out the details as best we can."

Suddenly some of the Egyptian armed forces on a wall raised their rifles and aimed down, directly at the procession. The two stopped short, and were almost bumped by former President Carter and Henry Kissinger, behind them.

"I hope they're just pretending," President Carter said to Henry Kissinger.

The rifles went back across the soldier's shoulders. Then the procession seemed to get congested as no one moved.

Henry Kissinger looked baffled. "What do we do now?"

President Carter looked around him. "I think it's over."

"What's over?" Kissinger asked.

"This procession. This is the end of it."

"We will not attend the services, the eulogies, the entombment?"

President Carter shook his head. "It's all only for those of the Islamic faith. Private."

"Then now what?"

President Carter shrugged. "I don't know. I'm not sure."

Jody Powell walked up to them. "To the airport, Mr. President. Just you and Ford. Nixon's not coming. Your bags are in the car. The vehicles are over there behind the stand."

Henry Kissinger expressed the opinion of so many of the Americans. "I do not feel as though I attended a funeral."

After dinner at the hotel, U.S. officials sat together in an informal semi-circle in the inner reception room, smoking their cigars and pipes and cigarettes and talking about their memories of Anwar Sadat.

"I was with him after the Shah's arrival here in Cairo," one of the delegates said, and he reminded the others of how the Shah had been forced to leave Iran, then to leave Morocco, the Bahamas, Mexico, the United States, Panama, and only Anwar Sadat of Egypt would accept the Shah. "And I said to President Sadat, 'Tell me, Mister President, it must have been a very difficult decision for you to invite the Shah, knowing that it might cause some real repercussions.'

"President Sadat was very indignant at my suggestion, and he answered me by saying, 'Difficult? Why should it be difficult to decide how to treat a friend? For me there was no difficulty.'"

Jonas shifted in his seat. He had not said a word during the discussion until now. He said, "Your story is intriguing. It says a great deal about him–and a great deal about you representing our country through that question of yours. The story should mean that Sadat was an ordinary man and you, a fool. But, unfortunately, in today's world, the story means that Sadat was a giant and you were an ordinary man, whose fear of integrity has now become the expected. And that is why today mankind is so very far from being civilized."

To the delegation's relief, Jonas left the room to visit the Pyramids of Giza. He wanted to go back 4,600 years.

The next day, that inner reception room of the hotel was vacant except for two people, Jonas and his Arab friend who took notes on a yellow legal pad as Jonas spoke. They spent the morning and most of the afternoon discussing every aspect of a defense structure, until most pages of the yellow legal pad was filled. Then it was Jonas' turn. "Now, on Sadat."

The man nodded, and reached down to his attaché case, from which he lifted another yellow legal pad, this one with notes already written on its top pages. "I talked with others by phone last night, and wrote this down for you.

"First let me give you a summary of his thoughts regarding the Cold War, because it connects to your interest, and then I will get to what you asked for directly–about God and Sadat. He said that if you in America do not again take up your responsibilities as a superpower of the world, all of us are doomed. He said if you don't do that, we shall see the Soviet Union putting their puppets everywhere. Sadat said he knows what it means to be a puppet of the Soviet Union, and they foreclose people's dreams and cancel out all logic. He says that they, themselves, are robots, with only the head of the party who can act. His advice is to put them in check. He said he dealt with the Soviet Union for a long time, and only if you put them in check will they pull back."

Jonas nodded. "He's right. He speaks and writes very clearly. I believe that President Reagan believes as he does."

"Now that connects to his beliefs of which you asked about–those things of your personal interest that did not come about because of the Cold War, but from which he said he learned so much:

"Where Anwar was confined, in Cell 54, there was no bed, no table, no chair, no lamp. There was nothing except a palm-fiber mat, hardly big enough to sleep on, and an unbelievably dirty blanket. In the winter, water oozed from the cell walls, and in the summer huge armies of bugs marched up and down those walls. Anwar wondered how bugs could live in that perpetually wet place. That is where he lived for eighteen months.

"But then came God. In time, Anwar was able to transcend the confines of time and place. He said that spatially, he did not live in a four-walled cell but in the entire universe. Time, he said, ceased to exist once his heart was taken over by the love of the Lord of all Creation. He said he came to feel very close to Him. That's what he learned in Cell 54. He said that everything in existence became an object of love, for, like him, it was made and existed through God's love for it and its love for God.

"And Sadat spoke often about what he considered to be success and failure in life. He said that inner success is a source of permanent and absolute power, independent of external factors, while outward success fluctuates in response to changing circumstances and is therefore of a purely relative value. He wrote that most people are fascinated by outward success—their social position, financial gain, power or, in a word, their image in the eyes of others. If their external image is, for any reason, shaken, they are inevitably shaken and may even collapse. They lack fortitude because they are neither true to themselves nor honest with others, and that a man should maintain conscious communion with all existence. Without such communion he will be left with nothing beyond ephemeral success or failure. He will be reduced to a slave to time and place, and his being becomes quite simply unreal.

"Sadat believed that we have been created to bear the responsibility of which God has entrusted us. Though different, each man should fulfill his specific vocation and shoulder his individual responsibility. To do this he should first recognize and be loyal to his real entity within, regardless of any external factors; for it is this alone which will enable him to belong and owe allegiance to that Entity which is greater, vaster, and more permanent than his individual self.

"In Cell 54 this belief of his began to assume the proportions of a real faith and came to constitute an integral part of his very being. If a day passed without his having done something worthy of belonging in that greater and all-embracing Entity, he took himself to task for failing to honor his responsibility through a whole day.

"He believed that two places in this world make it impossible for a man to escape from himself: a battlefield and a prison cell. Freedom, he said, is the most beautiful, holy, and precious fruit of our culture. An individual should never be made to feel that he is at the mercy of any force of coercion or that his will is subordinated to those of others. You see how all this connects to his belief about the United States and the Cold War, and why your country must live up to its prescribed destiny?

"Sadat even went further. He said that Man can conquer time and space. He believed that the majority of people do not know this."

Even though Jonas was too late to visit with Anwar Sadat, he fulfilled the purpose for which he came to Egypt: knowledge.

Before he left Egypt, Jonas bought a new gold-toned Seiko watch at a small Cairo shop. Like his old Endura, this new watch told time around the world, but this one was digital, and had a map of the world that blinked the time zone to which it was set. Jonas stared at it at the airport. It was a reminder of what he had confirmed regarding time and space from the words of Sadat, as told to him by a stranger.

FIFTY-EIGHT
HOSTAGE TO FAME
1982

Anne liked her new hostage status. She was a hostage to fame, and what she said made a difference and was even quoted in local newspapers. Because of her national celebrity status, sometimes she was even quoted outside of her district. What was printed was not always accurate, but how she felt about policies and what she believed became important to an expanding amount of people. As Jonas had told her, that was its own reward.

She wouldn't ask anyone for money, yet she knew she had to raise a campaign chest. And so almost everyday, sometimes twice a day, she would be driven to a fund-raising event, where she didn't need to ask for funds, but received them since there was a charge for the people to attend and see her. Usually those events took place just as the first one did, in someone's home. Repetitiously, the driver taking her there would slow the car as she would see the red, white, and blue balloons on a driveway to some house. Gradually the outdoor decorations would become more professional. There would often be a big poster clipped or taped to a garage door, the poster with a now all-too-familiar picture of her with the diagonal writing across it that read: "Anne Whitney: Experience, Knowledge, and Back Home—for You!" That was Mark's idea, to subtlety remind the voter that Anne had been in Teheran during the hostage crisis.

One accessory that didn't change was the card table that was always on the drive if the weather was good, or just inside the door, if the weather was not good, with two women always sitting behind the card table passing out those paper badges that would be given out when the admission fee was received. Anne was getting tired of all that, although deeply appreciative that volunteers would do that work to bring about her victory. Then she felt guilty when she didn't enjoy the fundraisers. She didn't like seeing the posters of herself. And she was sick of the small talk: "How was the ride over here?" "Did you get caught in the rain?" Did they really care? Was it really interesting? But when she gave a speech, and everyone was listening to what she said and reporters were taking notes, and what she said would be printed, it was different. Maybe people might be influenced to believe as she did.

The weather was very cold, and the event was inside. "I want to thank the McCoy's for opening their beautiful home for us—and thanks, too, Ben and Sarah, for those marvelous appetizers!" And there was applause. Then from the makeshift podium that had been put together by up-ending one apple-cart on top of another, and then covered with a sheet, Anne got to her real interest. As was her style, she tried to intrigue her audience into thinking about a subject of which they might not have had much interest before:

"Have you ever noticed that every September, when a television season begins, there's a bunch of new shows, but somehow most of them seem to be the same as other series that you've seen before? In one of them, the detective's office has changed but that's all that has changed. In another, the cowboy's face has changed but that's all that has changed. In another, the couple living in a New York apartment look different, but it seems just like that very successful series last season, about a couple living in a Hollywood apartment. Well, there's an odd remake this season and it's playing every night on the network news, and it's unbelievable that they'd want to re-make this series, but they do.

"I'll tell you the plot in just a few sentences. It's about a country that's being overtaken. And the Congress of the United States eventually cuts off all aid to the side that's friendly to us. And when our aid stops, the opposition wins the war and takes over, and the show ends with extreme violations of human rights, more than the country has ever suffered before. In addition, the United States would get an enemy in power instead of the friend that was in power before. The old series were entitled 'Vietnam' and 'Laos' and 'Cambodia' and 'Ethiopia' and 'Angola' and 'Nicaragua' and 'Iran,' and the new series is entitled 'El Salvador.'

"Don't think the new series doesn't have big name actors in it. It does. Ed Asner, Mike Farrell, and Martin Sheen are in it. And there's a cameo appearance by a former attorney general, Ramsey Clark. And there are a lot of members of the U.S. Congress joining them. Pretty good cast, isn't it?

"This series is being run on all three networks! It does sound familiar doesn't it? An old idea for a new series! Well, I want that series to fail! And if I get into the 98th Congress of the United States I'm going to do everything I can to see we don't have another Castro and Ortega taking over a country in this hemisphere. I want El Salvador's capital city of San Salvador to be the capital of a free state."

There was much applause and then chants of "Anne! Anne! Anne! Anne! If Anne Can't Do It, No One Can!"

Then there was the traditional question and answer session, and Anne would always call first on whomever was from the press. "Anne, you have advocated an organization of countries that are democracies only, to take the place of the U.N., and you also advocate that we support the current government of El Salvador. Under your criteria, would that current government be admitted to the international organization of democracies? And would the Shah have qualified? Would Somoza have qualified?"

There was not a moment of hesitation from Anne. "No. None of them were qualified. You're talking about the proposed organization I call NOLA, the Nations of Liberty Alliance. Since the qualifications would demand that every member-state would have all the institutions of democracy, they would not have qualified, but it would have been a marvelous incentive for those governments to establish those institutions–to join their friends, the democracies of the world. Now, maybe they wouldn't. I don't pretend to know what they would have done or would do. But I do know that the alternative governments were worse for their own people, for their neighbors, for the United States, and for the world. We should always know the choices, not imaginary ones, before we say the chief of state has to go.

"In Cuba, the choice wasn't between Fulgencio Batista and Alexander Hamilton. It was between Fulgencio Batista and Fidel Castro.

"In Vietnam, the choice wasn't between Nguyen Van Thieu and Thomas Jefferson. It was between Nguyen Van Thieu and Phan Van Dong.

"In Cambodia, the choice wasn't between Lon Nol and James Madison. It was between Lon Nol and Pol Pot.

"In Ethiopia, the choice wasn't between Haile Selassie and Abraham Lincoln. It was between Haile Selassie and Mengistu Haile-Marium.

"In Angola, the choice wasn't between Jonas Savimbi and Theodore Roosevelt. It was between Jonas Savimbi and Agostino Neto.

"In Iran, the choice wasn't between the Shah and Dwight Eisenhower. It was between the Shah and the Ayatollah Khomeini.

"In Nicaragua, the choice wasn't between Anastasio Somoza and John Kennedy. It was between Anastasio Somoza and Daniel Ortega.

"And in weeks from now, there will be an election in El Salvador. Do we support those who want elections, or do we support the Marxist guerrillas?"

She had thought it out more completely than the inventor of NOLA; the late Ambassador Fairbanks.

"I want you to understand that NOLA is my long-range plan for the future. The current is short-range, and dictates that we do not support the worst of the alternatives that fragile countries offer."

She quickly added, "As it stands right now we can count on the United Nations organization to support the worst of alternatives. Yes, I want the U.N. to be replaced by NOLA."

"Ms. Daschle," a reporter from a local radio station called out, "are you thinking beyond 1982–do you want to use this congressional seat as a springboard to the U.S. Senate?"

Of course the traditional answer would have been a firm denial and an expressed interest only in being a representative of the district. But Anne didn't give traditional answers. "I have no plans on wasting my time going for the Senate. I plan on going right from the House of Representatives to the Presidency." She was smiling.

The reporter didn't know if she was kidding or not, but the crowd of supporters were delighted with her answer, and cheered and applauded.

After all the questions were done, Anne walked from behind the makeshift podium into the crowd and shook hands and talked and once again "worked the room," something she was beginning to despise, but she pretended to enjoy it. She kept a smile–until the campaign's pollster, Earl Miller, came to her with a filled cloth-bound notebook in his left hand.

"Can I see you a second, Anne?"

"Right now. Go ahead. Shoot."

"Well," and he looked around uncomfortably. There were people around them. "When you get done."

"Get Mark. The three of us will go off together into some private room."

When her shaking of hands was done, Anne and Mark walked with Earl to the kitchen.

"Anne," Earl said, "you have to talk more about jobs and wages and taxes and crime. You have to mention those topics in every speech! Stay on message! They don't care about El Salvador. You're wasting yourself on all that. Look, here's a new poll that has it all in black and white." He extended the filled cloth-bound notebook for her to take from him. "Last weekend we phoned 2,500 people. You know where El Salvador is in terms of interest? Number 17! And the ones who disagree with you on El Salvador are eight to two."

She didn't take the extended notebook. "But you heard the reaction here!"

"Other than the press here who disagrees with you, these are your supporters. I'm telling you—we took a poll."

She still wouldn't take the book from him.

He put his hand that was holding the book, back down.

"What did your polls say about my Nations of Liberty Alliance?"

"So low it doesn't have a number. Very few even know what you're talking about. It's not a subject of interest, Anne."

"I don't care about your polls. Keep the book. You know, every time you give me a poll about what people think, I never read them."

"You don't care about what people want you to do?"

"I don't. I want them to care about what I want to do. There are plenty of candidates who can follow polls. I'm going to lead."

"You know, Anne, if you would just bend a bit, and do what the polls indicate you should do, you'd win—and then—then you can do what ever you want when you get in—you can do your thing."

"I don't want to win by acting as though I'll do one thing when I plan to do another. And besides, Earl, once you bend, you never stand up straight again—and you know it. If I get in office doing what you say, then you'd just advise me to keep obeying the polls so I can win re-election—so keep your polls."

Mark put his hand around the back of Anne's waist. "She's right, Earl. Hey, she just confirmed my idea for a slogan for her: 'Leadership, not Followership!' How's that?"

Anne looked up at him with a big smile. "I love it."

"Good," Earl said. "That's a good slogan for a loser."

But she wasn't losing. Even though she didn't read polls on issues, she read the polls that told who was ahead and behind in her congressional race. She had gone from nine points behind to two points ahead. There was little question that her time spent in Washington, Hong Kong, Moscow, and especially Iran, were paying off in votes. And her opposition made a mistake by calling her "Anne Salvador." Rather than be intimidated and tame down her interest in foreign affairs and world trouble spots, she accented it. She decided to take time off the campaign, cancel some fundraisers, and make a trip to El Salvador's capital, San Salvador, in the week before El Salvador's election for its Constituent Assembly on Sunday, March 28.

She didn't know how much of a name she had until she arrived at Hopango International Airport in San Salvador. She didn't even have to go through the terminal. She was met on the tarmac by U.S. Ambassador Deane Hinton, along with the ambassador's bullet proof limousine. She was, after all, the famous woman who had been confined to a Teheran secret place during the first months of the Iranian hostage crisis. Even without her old black passport, she was treated as though she had one. She was told that her bags would be taken care of by some unseen member of the Embassy staff and brought to the Ambassador's residence where she would be staying. Soon she was being driven through the streets with two small flags waving in the wind on either side of the car's hood—the flag of the United States and the flag of El Salvador.

On the ride out of the airport grounds, through rural areas where any number of raids had occurred, she thanked the Ambassador for all his courtesy, and she added, "I read the list of your embassy staff assigned here, and I know some of them. Some of them are real creeps!"

The ambassador laughed. "They're diverse all right! But no creeps!"

"Diverse!? Creeps! Do you want to know which ones?"

Ambassador Hinton was still smiling and shook his head. "No thanks. Listen, Ms. Whitney, tonight there's going to be a party at my residence—and I hope you know who the guest of honor is going to be!"

"Me?"

"You, of course. And you can see some of the friends you used to know—and probably some new ones!"

Ambassador Hinton's residence was lined outside by the El Salvadoran military for good reason: the U.S. Embassy had been attacked five times since the beginning of last year. The Marxist guerrillas were now threatening to kill all U.S. diplomats.

At least, Anne thought, there were no balloons on his driveway, and no guilt about a card table with two women behind it handing out name badges, and no big poster of Anne's face, and no room to "work."

The Ambassador's living room was filled with prominent El Salvadorans, plus a good deal of the U.S. Press Corps. Although some of the Embassy staff was there, none of the embassy "creeps" showed up, all giving different excuses for not being there.

The members of the press were crowded around Anne, asking one question after another about her stay in Teheran, which was of much more interest to them than her congressional campaign.

Anne continually shifted the conversation from what she knew about Iran to what they knew about El Salvador. "Tell me about the election for the Constituent Assembly next Sunday," she asked. "That must be very exciting!"

A small, balding man with glasses answered her. "It's exciting, but it may not tell us very much. After all, the most popular political element isn't represented in the election."

"What element is that?"

"The F.M.L.N.."

"What's that?" Anne knew, but the advantage in playing dumb was that the press corps might be more candid, not expecting any challenge.

"The Farabundo Marti National Liberation Front."

"Oh, those are the guerrillas, aren't they?"

"Yes. That's right."

"Are they the most popular?"

"Oh, yes."

"And they won't be allowed to enter candidates in the election? How terrible!"

"They're allowed. They're boycotting it."

Ambassador Hinton overheard the conversation and walked over to the group that was surrounding Anne. "They're boycotting it because they know they won't win," the ambassador said.

"Mr. Ambassador," the small man said, "they're afraid the right wing will assassinate them if they start campaigning publicly here."

"No. That isn't it. They've been offered guaranteed protection, not only by the government here, but by the United States as well. I've written them personally on behalf of our government. As another option, we have suggested that the F.M.L.N., the guerrillas, could even make television spots in Mexico City for protection, and those TV spots would be used on El Salvador television without cutting or comment. The government here has agreed. What more can be done for them? Finally, if, as the F.M.L.N. claims, the people really want them to take over the leadership of this country, then you would have to assume the people would vote for them with or without a campaign–if their names were simply on the ballots–and the guerrillas won't allow their names on the ballots. They want to take the country by force, by violence, because they know they're not the people's choice."

"We talk to the people every day," a woman near the back of the group said.

Ambassador Hinton nodded. "I know you do. We'll find out on election day if they vote at all which, if they don't, would prove your point, or if they vote for the junta, which is moderate, or if they vote for the Arena Party, or some of the others that, like Arena, are furthest away from the politics of the guerrillas. We'll find out, won't we?"

"I'm not so sure we'll find anything out, Mr. Ambassador," a tall thin journalist in a half-unbuttoned white shirt said. "Maybe that's what you and Ronald Reagan keep saying, but I am not at all convinced that this election is going to be free and fair. And there are a lot of members of the U.S. Congress who share my concern."

"The election will be internationally monitored," Ambassador Hinton said. "And no one can vote twice. When they vote they will be thumb-printed in ink that can be seen in black light, and their thumbs will be checked at every voting place."

A man with a dark suntan in a sport shirt that had "Rock City" written on it said, "Ambassador Hinton, would you deny that this country is run by an oligarchy—by the 14 families?"

"That's a line on Radio Moscow every day. We'll see the accuracy of that on election day, when the people from every family can vote. Let me leave you now with Anne." He smiled at Anne. "I think you're more interesting than I am, Anne, and you're the reason everyone is here. After all, they can talk to me any time they want."

As soon as the Ambassador walked away, Anne said, almost in a whisper, "Wow! He's a real Reaganaut, isn't he?" She was playing her game.

"We've heard you are, too, aren't you?" the small, bald man with horn-rimmed glasses asked.

"I'm my own woman," Anne answered quickly. "I've worked under the administrations of six presidents; Eisenhower, Kennedy, Johnson, Nixon, Ford, and Carter, so I can think for myself."

"You've been around that long?" the man with the unbuttoned shirt asked. "What did you do, start when you were a child?"

"Thanks, but I'm 44 years old. I'm no spring chicken!"

The woman with the pencil in her hair said, "We don't blame Hinton. He has to be a Reaganaut. Reagan appointed him. The ambassador that was here before was much closer to the people—Robert White. He understood what was going on. He was very good."

"Now, tell me," Anne said, again almost whispering. "Now that the Ambassador isn't around, what's going on in this country? And what would be best for the people?"

"It's very simple," a seated woman correspondent who previously had looked bored said. "There are six political parties in the election. The one the United States is backing is Duarte's party, the Christian Democrats—that's the ruling junta. The other five parties are all extreme right wing, including the National Republican Alliance—that's called Arena, which is the most right-wing party of all. They don't want to negotiate with the guerrillas; they want to defeat them in the war. So, of all the choices on the ballot, the best on the ballot would be to keep the status quo of Duarte's junta. But the one that isn't on the ballot, the F.M.L.N.—the guerrillas—they are the will of the people."

"Too bad you can't advocate that position in your news stories going back home, but I know you have to be careful about appearing to take a side," Anne said like a totally naive non-sophisticate.

And she scored. Robin Carpenter of *Newsweek* magazine smiled. "I advocate my position in my articles. *Newsweek* approves. I believe in advocacy journalism and *Newsweek* does take a side. What's wrong with that?"

"Really!?"

"Our readers have an average mentality of a seventh grader," Robin Carpenter added. "Guiding them is no sin."

"So what do you tell them? What do you write?"

"It depends. But I have an attraction toward the guerrillas. They're the underdogs. They're young–my age. They have their act all together–the government here doesn't."

The man in the unbuttoned shirt asked Anne, "Do you know who Meg Knowles is?"

"Of course. I don't know her but I know who she is. She's a journalist who covered the Sandinista Revolution in Nicaragua."

"She said, 'Most journalists now, most Western journalists at least, are very eager to seek out guerrilla groups, leftist groups, because you assume they must be the good guys.' Those are her exact words. So no one's trying to hide anything."

"Is she right? Do all your colleagues feel the same?"

"We're all journalists–professional journalists," the seated woman answered. "But it's fair to say that we'd all like to see a political solution here–not a war solution."

Anne finally couldn't hold back any more, now that she had heard the confession she wanted. "A political solution is such an imprecise phrase. What do you mean by a political solution?"

That seated woman's voice was getting stronger. "Negotiations! Why can't there be negotiations between the government and the guerrillas? Why can't the government agree to that?"

"To arrive at what?" Anne asked with calm.

The seated woman stood up. "Compromise! Put some of the guerrillas in government. Give them a voice. Wouldn't that be better than more killing?"

Anne's voice now matched the strength of the woman who just stood up. "What if we had warring guerrillas fighting to take over our government back home in the United States, and the guerrillas were getting their arms from the Soviet Union, Nicaragua, Vietnam, Ethiopia, and the P.L.O.? Would we negotiate with them? Would we agree to give them an office in government? Would we give them a share of executive or legislative power? Can you imagine?"

"That's apples and oranges," the woman said as she sat back down, shaking her head.

"No it isn't. You want the guerrillas in power, that's all–and you're going to help them gain that power through influencing the United States public–that's all. And you, Robin," and she turned to the correspondent from *Newsweek*. "If you say your magazine's readers have a seventh grade mentality, isn't that more reason to give them the news straight? If you work for a magazine that claims it tells news, don't you have a responsibility to do that?"

"Oh, please!"

The man from *The New York Times* said, "I want you to know that we don't all feel exactly the same. *The New York Times* doesn't believe in advocacy journalism. The only advocacy is on the editorial page where it belongs."

Ambassador Hinton was close by again and he felt it was his time to intervene. He heard the latter part of the conversation. "Not true. Your news stories are slanted. As for the editorials, they can say what they want. My gripe is that the articles always seem to advocate the position of anti-American guerrillas in Third World countries. At least the editorials make no bones about it."

"Only when there are guerrilla movements that are worthy," another correspondent added.

Anne's celebrity status was officially confirmed the following morning when, at breakfast at the ambassador's residence, he gave her a piece of paper with her schedule for the day neatly typed, the piece of paper enclosed in celluloid. In other years she had passed out those celluloid-covered schedules to visiting officials from the Congress or the Administration. And to make it even better, two of the scheduled briefings were to be conducted at the U.S. Embassy by those she thought of as "creeps." She knew what they thought of her, but the more she knew they resented her, the more she looked forward to the briefing.

Before breakfast was done, Ambassador Hinton told her, "whoever wins next Sunday's election should negotiate with the guerrillas. That must be done."

"Et tu, Brute?" she asked.

He laughed.

She didn't.

The only meeting without an embassy official or a government official was at 4:30 in the afternoon with a correspondent from the United States who requested a meeting with Anne at the Sheraton Hotel. Even though it was scheduled as an interview, it turned out to be something different than an interview.

He was waiting for her in a corner of the coffee shop, drinking hot chocolate, and he stood up when she entered. He was a somewhat overweight man with gray hair and a weathered face who she recognized from seeing him in the crowd the previous night at the party.

"Hello again, Ms. Whitney," he stood up with a smile. "We didn't talk but I was standing in the back of that group last night at the party."

"I know," she said. "I saw you. You didn't say anything." She sat down and he nodded as he sat.

"No, I didn't say anything. It was best not to. Do you want some coffee or something to eat? Hot chocolate?"

"No thank you," she said. "I've been drinking coffee all day."

"Briefings at the embassy?"

"Briefings, briefings, briefings!"

"Ms. Whitney, I requested to see you alone because I want you to know what's going on here. I can tell you don't understand why the journalists feel the way they do."

"You're right. I don't."

"I've been around war zones a long time, Ms. Whitney. The reason I've asked to meet with you here at the Sheraton is because no other journalist will be around and see us. They don't come here. They're all staying at the El Camino Real, and that's the problem."

"What do you mean?"

"Something has developed that takes place every time the United States gets involved in a foreign conflict. It's very destructive. I call it 'Hotel Journalism.'"

"That's an intriguing name. What is it?"

"The journalists live together in one hotel. I understand its roots were planted in the Dan Hotel in Tel Aviv during the '67 war when for the first time the U.S. press corps stayed together at one hotel during a war and formed a closeness. That camaraderie was born of fear of being alone, but it spread to be a camaraderie of ideas when the Dan in Tel Aviv moved to the Caravelle in Saigon. The war in the Mideast was too short and had no U.S. armed forces to materialize into what it became at the Caravelle. I was part of it there. My newspaper booked me a room at the Caravelle Hotel. In Phnom Penh, Cambodia it was Le Royal. In Teheran, Iran before you got there, when the Shah was in trouble, it was the Hilton. In Managua, Nicaragua, it was the Intercontinental. In Beirut, Lebanon right now, it's the Commodore. And here it's the El Camino Real."

"What's the harm of that?"

"The journalists form a tight circle there—what I'd call a Mini-Government in Residence. In the mornings you can see them in a tight circle as they meet in the hotel's restaurant for breakfast together. In the late afternoons they meet in the bar for drinks, and later in the evening they meet for dinner. Then later on at night, they meet again at the bar. Although it isn't formal, they almost have a president and a vice president, and a Cabinet. The president is usually some big-time TV guy—the Ted Murphys of America."

Anne's head jarred when she heard the name. She covered it up with a nod.

"And if some kid journalist comes to town, fresh from a small news outfit in Podunk—or even an old timer like me from a bigger city—that newcomer is out—unless that newcomer proves that he or she thinks and acts and writes like they do. If not, that correspondent won't get the benefit of their contacts and tips and leads. And he'll be eating and drinking alone.

"That person runs the risk of becoming an outcast, and that means the others have the stories, and he doesn't. The result of Hotel Journalism is that the news stories, the analysis, the articles, the reports from those on the scene, read and sound as though they all had the same author with the same emphasis. They draw the reader or the listener to the same conclusions. It's the outcome of Hotel Journalism. It has to be. We have to get stories, we have to meet deadlines, we want to get tips and leads on which to follow-up, and often the sources are each other. That's the way it is."

"Has Ted Murphy been here?"

"He's made periodic trips here. He doesn't stay long. He does a couple reports and goes somewhere else. He isn't here now. He'll be here for election day. One hundred sixty-nine of the U.S. press corps will be here for that - for next Sunday. You know him?"

"I met him."

"That's all we need here is Murphy."

Anne didn't want to show too much interest in what he was saying about Ted. "What are your stories like here?"

"They're okay—but I miss a lot. They beat me to press all the time with the hot stuff. For one thing, I don't have any insights to the guerrillas. They don't meet with me. And my colleagues keep me in the dark when they know something."

"Did you ever become tempted to be part of that mini-government?"

"Not here. Not now. I was part of that mini-government in Saigon at the Caravelle. And, Ms. Whitney, what a difference there is to be part of it. Not only for the tips and leads, which is enough, but because of the psychological security the mini-government offers in a place where you can be blown up. In a way, being a part of it is like being in the military, and that camaraderie I talk about gives you a feeling of safety. In the Caravelle I could walk in the halls and see my friends—not my enemies. And you know if anything should happen, they'd be with you. So other than the most courageous of journalists, any originality of thought was given a quick self-erasure. The penalty for not employing that self-erasure, was to have no tips, no leads, and be alone at war."

"Why did you stop being one of them?"

"After Vietnam fell, I was a mess. Besides the agony of it, I had a conscience. I had told misleading stories when I was there. I wasn't alone in that, Ms. Whitney. Peter Braestrup, who had been in Saigon for *The Washington Post*, was much more courageous than I was. I just stopped being a part of it. He went further than I did. He wrote a giant book—two big volumes called *Big Story* about the Tet offensive. He concluded that reporters there, at best, wrote overwrought instant analysis - and, at worst, they participated in a vengeful exploitation of a crisis that proved unfounded. That reporting about the Tet offensive was central to turning around American opinion to be opposed to U.S. involvement in the war."

"I never heard of the book."

"Who did? It came out maybe five years ago now. Very quietly." He wiped his lips with his napkin. "Now let me get to the El Camino Real here in San Salvador. That hotel affords the Marxist guerrillas a quick access. It's a convenient place to infiltrate. They have a massive campaign to influence—not to influence the El Salvadorans—they can't do that—but to influence the U.S. press corps. It's no secret. The press knows that the Marxists have a blueprint to influence them, but they fall for it. In truth, they're flattered by it." He tossed the napkin on the table. "Last night at the party I was very taken with that conversation you had."

"I couldn't get over some of the things they said."

"Where do you think most of those journalists you met last night went after the party?"

"Where?"

"To the El Camino Real where a van picked them up—a van of guerrillas who took them out in the mountains to one of their headquarters. They gave them a tour."

"Last night?"

"Right after the party. Didn't you notice that they left the party fairly early?"

"Did you go with them?"

"I wasn't invited. I'm never invited."

"Why don't you write for your newspaper, all you just told me? That's a real story!"

"I did. I thought if Peter Braestrup had the guts to tell the truth about Vietnam, I could do it about other places. So I did."

"When?"

"I wrote it three times. From Nicaragua, from Iran, and from here."

"And?"

"I'm still waiting to have those articles printed." There was an uneasy quiet.

"How long are you staying here?"

"I'm going back home right after the election here. And if I were you, Ms. Whitney, I'd get out of this place before then. This place doesn't tend to be kind to people who feel as you do. And you're a famous person."

"I'm leaving Saturday. I have a fundraiser on Monday that I can't cancel."

"Good. Before then, go out to some of the rural areas and look at the posters along the way. Do you read Spanish?"

"No. A little, but not much."

"There are posters all over that say, 'Vote in the morning and be dead in the afternoon.' That's what the guerrillas are posting."

"Do they mean it?"

"They mean it. They've already blown up 196 busses with passengers aboard. Murder is not unique for them. There are even bullet holes in this hotel, the Sheraton. Two Americans were killed here. There is, however, a privileged sanctuary. There are no bullet holes, no casualties at the El Camino Real."

Sunday throughout El Salvador was a day unlike any El Salvador had ever seen in its history. Despite repeated warnings by the F.M.L.N., there were long lines of voters in intense heat, waiting for hours to go into the nation's voting stations.

Ted Murphy stood outside the *Gymnasium Nacionale* where lines of people waited their turn to vote. He waited for James Wooten to be done with his analysis for the ABC network.

"Good morning, David, on the kind of glorious Sunday Salvadorans usually call *undia hermosa,* which translated means it's a great day for the beach. But first things first today. Politics above pleasure: voting—which is what all these people have come here to do today. To vote in an election, curiously enough, that probably means more to Ronald Reagan and to Alexander Haig than it does to them.

"That's because they're not voting in a vacuum. This election has a context, a context so bloody and so blighted that it reduces the election itself to something significantly less than a milestone in El Salvador's troubled history.

"It is a lush and lovely land, but its beauty is deceptive. Most of the people are poor. Most don't get enough to eat. Most live and work on land they do not own, producing profits and privilege for those who do; that minority of families that is El Salvador's ruling class.

"Nobody here can remember when it wasn't that way. Nobody can remember when the government wasn't trying to keep it that way, using the army to work its right wing will on a nearly feudal society—for fifty years an unbroken chain of generals and colonels commanding the country. Until, in the later 1970s, something happened. Almost overnight, El Salvador's green hills gave birth to *Los Muchachos,* the boys. A tiny, tiny core of working-class youngsters with Marxist, socialist, and communist leanings. Kids mainly, drawn to the left by their homegrown experience with the right. Inspired by Nicaragua's Sandinista Revolution, they launched one of their own, with weapons from Havana, from Managua, from any place they could get them. El Salvador was at war with its children, with itself....

"The army, even with millions of dollars of U.S. weaponry, couldn't cope with *Los Muchachos....*"

"This voting, all these people coming here to the *Gymnasium Nacionale* probably won't be a significant chapter in El Salvadoran history. A paragraph perhaps, but nothing much more than that...David?"

By the end of the day, Ted Murphy was on a plane going back home, trying to think of a way to justify what he had said publicly earlier in the day. Sunset brought the news that more than one million of the 1.3 million eligible voters cast a ballot, which was not just a massive turnout, but a higher percentage of people than ever voted in a national election in the United States. The vote counting was revealing that the ruling junta won 41 percent of the vote, while the five anti-communist parties won a total of 59 percent among them, putting them in position to put together a coalition led by Roberto D'Aubuisson of the Arena party. He would easily be their leader as Arena had won 29 percent of the vote, the highest percentage of the five anti-communist parties.

When Anne came home, her celebrity-status had increased by virtue of the fact that she had gone to El Salvador in the middle of her campaign. Her first fund-raiser after that trip was not only filled with guests who paid to attend, and local television, radio, and newspaper correspondents, but there were some national journalists from across the Potomac in Washington, D.C.

Mark introduced her as, "the candidate who doesn't wait to be told the news—she's part of it! From Hong Kong to Moscow to Bujumbura to Teheran to San Salvador please welcome your candidate, who is even more than that to me—Anne Whitney Daschle!"

There was the usual wild applause for her, but this time there were cameras with motors whirring, microphones registering, and dozens of notebooks open and ready.

"The significance of what happened yesterday cannot be exaggerated," Anne said to the crowd. "There was an election to decide the members of El Salvador's Constituent Assembly. That's like our Congress or more like a parliamentary system, where those legislators choose their country's leader.

"Even the Americans who were plainly against what they called the right-wing parties are admitting that the election was free and fair. Speaker of the House Jim Wright, who led the U.S. monitors and who had been outspoken against the anti-communist political parties of El Salvador said, 'The unprecedented numbers participating in yesterday's election surely must prove beyond any doubt that the terrorists and guerrillas do not speak for the nation, and that democracy can be made to work if given half a chance.'

"Theodore Hesburgh said, 'We saw people threatened with death if they voted and they went ahead, literally stepping over bodies to go to the polls.' And there were bodies.

"And here's something—the newspaper *La Prensa* in Nicaragua of all places, had the headline, 'Citizens Line Up to Vote Despite the Danger. The Vote Wins in El Salvador.' The censors, however, immediately eliminated the headline and cut out more than half the front page, and *La Prensa*'s publication was then stopped by the Nicaraguan Sandinista government.

"Now, what does yesterday's election tell us? That democracy can win no matter the challenge, that those who said the people of El Salvador would choose not to vote to show their support of the guerrillas were wrong, that our own government's position of backing the junta was wrong. Who were the ones who were right? Those who said the people of El Salvador would choose a government that would reject Moscow, Havana, and Managua.

"Not everyone in our government is willing to bend to the choice of the people of El Salvador. Senator Pell had said that if the right wing would win, that we ought to cut off our aid immediately. Congressman Long had said if D'Aubuisson should win we should just pull right out. Congressman Murtha had said he is not willing to continue aid unless the election would go to Duarte.

"My pledge to you is that if you elect me to the 98th Congress, I will never bend to those who demand free elections but are unwilling to abide by them if proven anti-communists win.

"To those government officials I knew in the Kremlin—if you hated me when I was posted in Moscow, you'll hate me even more if I get to the United States Congress!"

There was the heaviest applause of all and the shouts of "Anne! Anne! Anne!" and much of her speech and its reaction made national news on television, radio, and the press.

Four days later, Anne received a stuffed manila envelope in the mail at her and Mark's apartment. The envelope did not have a return address. It was postmarked from Washington D.C., and before opening it she shook it in her very uncertain test to see if it was a bomb. With some hesitancy, she opened it.

There was no letter enclosed. It contained a dozen 8x10 pictures of her. Not portraits. They were photographs of her and Ted Murphy on top of the U.S. Ambassador's desk in Moscow. There was also a reel of audio tape that she did not play.

Anne asked that her name be taken off the ballot for reasons of health. The unspent contributions were returned.

Her campaign was over.

FIFTY-NINE
THE TRUTH ACROSS THE RIVER
1982

Every morning that week, Anne woke with what felt like a twisted stomach. Not in the first few seconds. It took that long to remember that life was now different. The dreams of night had blocked out the ache. Sleeping was the way it used to be when awake, and waking was the return to the nightmare.

Worse than that, what had been a reason for being, was now part of the past. "I was good, wasn't I?" She hadn't even looked over at Mark's side of the bed to see if he was awake.

Mark turned toward her to see her eyes wide open, looking at the ceiling. His voice was very quiet. "Yes."

"The phone isn't ringing, is it?"

He didn't answer.

"The press doesn't call anymore, do they?"

He didn't answer.

"They don't care any more about how I feel about all the issues, do they?"

He didn't answer.

"The quiet is so overbearing, isn't it?"

He didn't answer.

"Do you hear? Do you hear all that quiet?"

"I think there's a good side to having some quiet," he said.

She turned to him. "Do you still love me, Mark?"

"What do you think? Of course I love you."

"Still?"

"Always, Anne. I just want you to get better. If these doctors can't find anything, then we'll go to the Mayo Clinic."

"Oh, Mark. I'll be okay. I just tired myself out. It was all too much. The campaign, topped by El Salvador, all those fundraising events and just everything. I didn't know what I was doing to myself. I have to rest, that's all. I can't campaign, but I can still make love!"

"We're going to find out if it's only because you're tired. I'm worried about you, Anne."

Anne almost whispered. "I'm worried about other things. I'm worried about us. I've been worried about us since we married, but all this has brought us to the edge. I feared right from the beginning that we would get to know each other so well and like each other so much that—that any passion would seem like incest, and so we'd lose the passion. Mark, I'm neither your sister or your best friend. I told you, Mark, I'm your lover. I'm your plaything. I'm your wench!"

He moved closer to her and put his arm around her. She lifted her head a little to allow for his arm, and she pressed against him. But nothing happened.

"Mark?"

"Yes?"

"I would rather lose the Congress, I would rather lose anything, than lose you."

"You can't lose me—even if you try." Then, out of the blue, he said, "Do you know that some of your friends who the Canadians took out from Iran, Mark and Cora Lijek, are posted in Hong Kong now?"

She nodded, but she was biting her lower lip to prevent tears. He did not want romance. When she felt she could talk without her voice trembling she said, "Let's have breakfast." Having breakfast, she felt, would get them out of a useless morning bed.

They sat at the breakfast room table with coffee and toast in front of them. Sitting there trying to do the normal was a chore. Mark was pretending that nothing had changed between them while he knew that she had put into words a terrible truth.

On the far end of the kitchen table were two piles of papers. One of them was a few hundred leftover press releases that explained that her health was affected by a "female problem." The other pile was a stack of letters and telegrams and phone notes. There was the letter from President Reagan saying that he and Nancy were wishing her recovered health and that he appreciated what he considered to be a great and courageous campaign that she had waged. There was a handwritten card from Vice President Bush telling her he hoped she would run for the Congress again when she feels better, and that he was wishing the best for her and Mark. There were letters from strangers and there was a letter of regret from Jonas, and a letter from Mrs. Goodpastor inviting her to meet with her when she feels better, and there were two cables from Hong Kong, one from Moose and another one from Wai-yee, both telling her that they had read about her campaign and admired her, and hoped her health would soon be back to normal.

To Anne, the stacks of paper looked like week-old eulogies while she was still alive.

It was Ambassador Fairbanks who taught her that waiting is wrong. So she took the envelope of pictures from a locked metal box in her closet, she put the envelope in her largest purse, and she went across the river.

The CIA agent was so young that he looked like he was skipping a class at Georgetown University to sit behind the desk in the building off the turnoff from the George Washington Parkway. But the office wasn't at the CIA Headquarters. It was at a near-by brown-bricked building used for purposes of talking to "guests." She didn't like the idea that she was not invited to go into Headquarters. And since when did a CIA man have long hair, put in a braid? The brown suit and tie gave her some evidence that, at least, he was trying to be grown-up.

Under the conditions of what she wanted to give the agency, she would have been given an appointment with a female agent, but when she requested to see an agent, Anne didn't indicate what it was about. "It's so good to see you, Ms. Whitney," Jeffrey Stempka stood behind his desk. "I was all for you in the election. I hope you're feeling better. Sit down. Are you doing all right?"

Anne sat. "I was never sick."

He looked confused as he sat back down. "I beg your pardon?"

"I was never sick."

"But I'm talking about why you had to drop out of the congressional race."

"It was a lie. I wasn't sick. I'm here to tell about the lie. I wore these gloves here so I wouldn't get any more fingerprints over it." She put the envelope on his desk, and then took off her white gloves.

He didn't pick it up. He shook his head with a lowered-eyebrows look of discomfort. "What's it all about, Ms. Whitney?"

"1969," she answered, and then she told him. Everything.

This was the most unexpectedly exciting morning Jeffrey Stempka had since he started at the CIA. Without one interruption from him, Anne took a full quarter of an hour to go through the chronology of events that ended in the Ambassador's office at the U. S. Embassy in Moscow. The expression on Jeffrey Stempka's face told Anne that he had the stimulation that Mark didn't have that morning. But how couldn't he? He was trying his best to remain professional. "Ms. Whitney, I think it would be best if perhaps we gave this to Mrs. Amherst who—"

"No!" Anne said. "I don't want to go through this again! You look at them!" Anne had the unrestrained impulse to become Anne. "You look at them," she repeated in a softer voice, and she put her gloves back on, stood, and reached over for the envelope, opened it, took the pictures out, and she put the pile of photos on his desk in front of him. She sat back down. "I didn't even tell my husband. He knows nothing about this." She reached in her purse and took out a reel of tape, then put it down on his desk. "And a tape. They recorded Mr. Murphy and me as well as taking pictures of us."

Jeffrey Stempka was the epitome of professionalism. He didn't glance down at the photo on top of the others. He shook his head. "Mrs. Amherst is the one," he said looking straight at her without even a blink.

What he didn't know was that this was what Anne reveled in: a challenge, and a challenge that brought back passions she hadn't felt since the campaign began. All at once she realized her political advocacy and her sexuality had tapped different flames of the same fire that was always glowing within her. While one flame was leaping, the other had subsided. There was no need for both, but there was always need for one or the other. "Look at them, Mr. Stempka! I will sign a paper saying I instructed you to do that if you're worried about this." And then she justified her statement. "I want to be done with it."

He looked around the office uneasily. Anne knew she had a victory and that it would only be seconds before his surrender to the temptation of the photos. He looked back at her eyes, and nodded. "That won't be necessary," and then he looked down at the top photo. There was no hurry. He took his time looking at it. Then he looked at the next one, and the next and the next, until he saw every one of the dozen pictures.

If he was excited he didn't reveal it, except for a lot of swallowing.

"What do you think, Mr. Stempka?" It was Anne's spirit coming back, calling such a young man by his last name.

"We'll have to analyze these for wherever the cameras were located and try to find out who sent this material to you, and—and this must be very difficult for you, which we appreciate. We appreciate what you're doing."

Anne stood up and came to his side of the desk as she looked down at the pictures in front of him. "Look at this one," she said and flipped through the photos and put one of them from the middle of the pile, to the top of the pile. She knew she was so close to him that he had to be uncomfortable. She could hear his breathing. She knew he could inhale her scent. "Look," she said. "Now look at this one," and she put another picture next to it. "I think these were taken with two different cameras, don't you?"

"No, I don't think so."

"But look at the change of position."

He didn't know quite how to say it, but it was obvious that the change of position from one photo to the other had nothing to do with the camera but with the positions of her and Ted Murphy.

"You see?" she asked. "Look there—and then here."

Now he knew how to say it with some dignity. "Well, these weren't snapped like a movie. There was time between the frames. You can see by the background that it's the same camera that took both of them. The backgrounds are both exactly the same. You can tell by the edges. They're exactly the same."

"Oh!" and she reached for other photos, setting them down in front of him in a neat row. "You're right! You're so right, Mr. Stempka."

"So—"

"I was foolish back then. I was old enough to know better."

He wanted to say something, or his silence would reveal his uneasiness with her direct reference to herself on the pictures. All he could think of saying was, "1969?"

"I was 31 then. Now I'm 44, you know. How old are you? You're just a boy, aren't you, to have such a job? I mean to be a spook?"

"I'm 32."

"I thought you were even younger."

He could feel her breath on his cheek. "No. I'm 32," he said, trying to keep a steady voice. "I've been at the Agency five years now." She knew by his difficulty in getting out the words that she had an affect on him. After all, he was looking at totally revealing pictures with the model standing by his side.

"Really?"

"Almost six years now."

"You're still a boy." And she laughed and walked away from him to the other side of the desk.

"So we'll keep these under lock and key, Mrs. Daschle." He intentionally called her by her married name. "You can be sure of absolute confidentiality, you know." It was just to say something.

"I trust you."

"It was very courageous of you to bring them here."

"But you're the one with courage—just working here!" Anne was at it.

"Believe me, they will be safeguarded. You'll hear from us. Probably from Mrs. Amherst."

She knew she wouldn't hear from Mrs. Amherst but, rather, that she would hear from Jeffrey Stempka. What she didn't expect was that it would be so soon after her visit. There were questions he had to ask her, he told her on the phone at 9:00 o'clock the next morning. He told her he had to come into D.C. and he would be sitting on a park bench in Farragut Square eating lunch from a brown-bag at 11:45 in the morning and she should sit next to him, as though he was a stranger. She was not only glad that he called so quickly, but also because the park-bench instruction was just the way she thought spies should operate.

The weather even made it more exciting. It was one of those first post-winter mornings of Washington, very bright and filled with the stagnant smell of early humidity and saturated with the fresh aroma of grass breaking through loose soil when, no matter the events of the world, Washington politicians and bureaucrats and shopkeepers talked about how nice it was outside. Before the lunch hour, linings were zipped out of coats, most coats abandoned altogether and then, like an unscheduled, spontaneous Easter Parade, Pennsylvania Avenue and Connecticut Avenue and K Street and all the small parks of the city became filled with people, and the small shops who didn't have revolving doors, had their doors open, which meant the heaters were turned off and put away.

On the south lawn of the White House that morning there were specks of green emerging on the branches, and those white things—were those small cherry blossoms on that one tree? Or were they dogwood? It was the same question every year. By late morning, government workers were assembled, sitting on the grass and park benches while Lafayette Park and Farragut Square turned into Dufy canvases, rich with the color of spring life. The government workers sat and promenaded, making the visual statement that winter is done, that they recognize it, and that they were already doing something about it. No Washingtonian learns, but they should, that within a short period of time, maybe tomorrow, with much embarrassment, coats may well be taken back from the racks, linings re-zipped inside the coats, heaters taken out again in the small shops, and streets at lunch-time could become sparse with only bent figures, heads against the wind and hands clutched to the uppermost buttons of those coats.

And so on this day they didn't remember how the weather works in Washington, and there were women in red and yellow blouses and dresses with designs all over them to announce there would be no wind and no rain, and men were walking holding their jackets over a shoulder with one finger propped in the neckbands so that their jackets dangled behind their backs.

Jeffrey Stempka was one of them, and he draped his jacket over the back of the park bench, sat down, opened his brown bag, and pulled out a paper-wrapped sandwich. He loosened his tie. Maybe he should have loosened his hair from its braid.

Just as dependable as the second hand on a clock, Anne, showing no sign of recognition, looked at him sitting on the bench at 11:45. He was moved by what she looked like this morning. Gone was the dowdy dress she had the day before in Langley, replaced with a short, filmy yellow skirt revealing her very shapely legs, and a white blouse with a blue flowered design on it. She was carrying a small white purse, and covering her eyes were very large white plastic-rimmed sunglasses.

She sat down only inches from him and put her head way back, as though gathering the sun, her legs extended in front of her. She knew what she was doing. Her intoxication quotient was back to its normal setting.

"It's a beautiful day, isn't it, Miss?" Jeffrey Stempka asked.

"Oh, it's gorgeous. Spring has sprung!"

"It has. We can talk, Ms. Whitney." He was back to using her professional name rather than her married name. A good sign. "No one is paying attention, although we have to remember that some people will recognize you."

"My goggles help. That's why I'm wearing them. It isn't the sun." Now she sat up straight.

"Yes. That's good."

"But why are we here? I would have gone to Langley again to see you, and I want to see your headquarters."

"I have an appointment in an hour right across the street on 17th. This is perfect for me."

"What can I help you with, Mr. Stempka?" She loved playing subservient to him.

"You never told your husband, Mr. Daschle, about the—the incident?"

"Are you kidding? He'd kill me. With Ted Murphy? He'd just kill me. Are the pictures and tape safe?"

"Of course. They're totally secure. Mr. Daschle, obviously then, doesn't know about you seeing me?"

"I should say not. I keep secrets very well. I was cleared for Top Secret, you know. I was even cleared for 'Q'."

"Yes, I do know that."

"If I'm ordered by a superior, I keep my lips sealed," she said with a healthy ounce of flirtatiousness.

"Is there any possibility that he saw them between the time you received them and when you came to us yesterday?"

"Oh, no. I received the mail and I put the envelope in a strong box in my closet way behind my shoes. It has old love letters in it, and I have the only key. He doesn't even know I have a box like that."

"I see."

"I keep secrets well."

"We know. Has Mr. Daschle been given a new post yet?"

"No. Not yet. We expect he'll get one soon. Although you never know what the higher-ups are going to do. They could keep him in D.C. forever if they want to, I suppose. Why?"

"I think I can give you some information on that."

"Oh?"

"We understand that Vice President Bush has recommended your husband to Jeane Kirkpatrick at the U.N."

Anne looked confused. "Really? I didn't know that. He doesn't know that, unless he hasn't told me. And I can't imagine that."

"I think within the next week or so he will be asked. I was just afraid that maybe the U.S.I.A. might have asked him to go elsewhere in the meantime."

"Bush did that?"

"Yes."

"How do you know?" Her mood had quickly changed from being flirtatious to being interested in what he was saying.

He laughed. "Where I work, it's our business to know. Would he want to go back to the U.N.?"

"He liked working for Bush. I don't think he knows Kirkpatrick. He didn't like New York. And he didn't like the U.N. He wants to go overseas. He's a foreign service officer."

"Would you go with him wherever he goes?"

"Of course. I'm his wife. I was a foreign service officer, too. I know the life."

"I just wanted you to know about the possible return to the U.N. You've been very good to us, Ms. Whitney. Giving us that material yesterday took courage. We want to be kind to you, or at least as much as we can. Would it be comfortable for you if he goes back to the U.N.?"

"Could you stop it if I didn't feel comfortable about it?"

"We could have an affect."

"No. The U.N. is fine." Anne nodded, "We adapt."

"Well, that's good then."

"Is that all?"

He looked uneasy.

"Or did you just want to see me?"

Two women were passing by and one of them was staring at her. "Anne Whitney?" The women stopped at the bench.

"Yes."

"Oh, it's so good to see you. We were going to vote for you. I wish you were still in the race. My parents just love you!"

"Well, thank you!"

Jeffrey Stempka went back to his sandwich. Both of the women standing by the bench were smiling broadly. The one who did the talking asked, "Can I have your autograph? I mean I know that's frumpy, but I would love it for my mother!"

"Of course, I'd be delighted."

Jeffrey Stempka deposited the paper that had been around his sandwich into his brown paper bag. With a sudden motion, he stood and walked away. Anne looked after him for a moment and then back at the women. "I think I have a pen in my purse and—and—" she dug in her purse, took out a small piece of paper and a pen. "What's your Mom's name?"

"Joanne. You're going to personalize it? Thank you! With two 'n's' and an 'e'."

When the procedure was done and the women walked away, Anne looked for wherever Jeffrey Stempka might have gone. She saw him by the corner waiting for the light to turn to green. There was something about all this that made Anne uncomfortable, but she didn't know what it was. "What was all that about?" she asked herself.

There was a breeze. Then another one and this one was more like a gust of wind. No matter, it seemed. Just a quick one.

And then there was a heavier gust of wind and then a heavier one than the ones before it. The branches of the trees in Farragut Square were swaying, then jolting almost as though they were ready to break and fall.

Anne got up and huddled herself in her arms as she walked toward the street among others who were walking and even running. Jeffrey Stempka was gone.

The winds were full of chill and then, of all things, hail started and it was hitting and even smashing on trees and sidewalks and glass windows and on Anne.

The park was quickly barren.

The doors of the small shops were being shut. Their heaters were carried to the front of the shops and plugged in.

The trees on the south lawn of the White House were naked and swaying. There was no dogwood or cherry blossoms or whatever they weren't.

The seasons played their annual hoax on Washingtonians.

Just like every year before and every year after this one, Washingtonians were led to believe spring had arrived, while winter laughed and re-emerged.

That night, with a howling wind outside, Jeffrey Stempka turned in his report: "Ms. Whitney insists she did not show the pictures to Mr. Daschle, but Mr. Daschle's fingerprints are on all of them. He is now under continued surveillance. We will insure he will not be posted overseas. Without drawing any conclusions, the most obvious possibilities are:

"1. Ms. Whitney is lying.

"2. Mr. Daschle did not tell her he saw the pictures so as to protect their marriage while not bending to Soviet blackmail, but also not reporting to us.

"3. Mr. Daschle did not tell her that he is a Soviet-employed sleeper."

SIXTY
SAVIORS
1982

With a smile, a tilt of his head, and a quick nod, President Reagan said, "Well, you know–" and he paused and swallowed. "I asked the little boy how many brothers and sisters he had, and he answered that he had eleven of them. 'Well, My Heavens,' I said, 'that must be very expensive!' And the little boy said, 'No,' and the President drew out the word 'No' and tilted his head again. 'We don't buy 'em, we raise 'em!'"

A president's jokes are always funny, whether the jokes were President Lincoln's or President Roosevelt's or President Reagan's, and President Reagan's cabinet members all laughed loudly as they sat around the great mahogany table beneath two gold chandeliers in the West Wing's Cabinet Room at the White House. There were others who weren't cabinet members who were seated on chairs against the walls and they laughed too, but not as loud since it wasn't their place.

President Reagan had an open manila folder in front of him as he sat in his chair, the back of the president's chair constructed slightly higher than the chairs of others around the table that all had an even height. Traditionally, he sat on one side of the table, not the head of it. Behind the president, on the south side of the Cabinet Room were two flags to either side of the green-draped window; the flag of the United States on the left, the flag of the presidency on the right.

No one knew what to do next because they didn't know if the president was going to say something more, or if he was waiting for one of them to talk. It was a frequent problem in the Cabinet Room. President Reagan glanced back over his shoulder at the flag of the presidency and said, "You know, children usually have it right. When I came to the White House back in January last year, a nine-year-old wrote me a letter that told me what to do. That nine year old wrote, 'Now get to the Oval Office and get to work!' And so that's what I better do!" And they laughed again.

The president closed his folder and put his hands on the edge of the table starting to rise, when Secretary of State Schultz said, "Mister President," and the president quickly sat comfortably again as he looked around the table, not knowing exactly who called for his attention.

"Yes?" he asked.

"Mister President," the Secretary said louder than his usual soft tone, and the president turned to him. "It might be of interest to all of those here to mention that this afternoon you're going to meet with Gloria Cooper of the W.R.M., the World Refugee Mission, and present her with a posthumous Medal of Freedom for her late husband. Mister President, besides your obvious concern for Mrs. Cooper and your depth of feeling for what her husband accomplished in the field of human rights, by the presentation of that medal, you're giving a message to the peoples of the world about our concern, our nation's concern, for all those who have been displaced by hostile forces—hostile forces who have used their might for expansionist purposes, leaving human misery in their paths."

The president tightened his lips together and nodded. "George," he said softly, "one of the great benefits of this office is the opportunity I have to meet the real heroes of this country." The cabinet members nodded as a chorus. "I have here—" and he opened his manila folder and looked through the top sheets. "Here—here—I have these Talking Points that Bud prepared for me for my meeting with Mrs. Cooper. She's such an exceptional woman, and her husband was an exceptional man. He saved so many. Did you know," and he looked around the table, "that he worked here, in the White House, for President Kennedy?"

There were a number of soft "yes" and "no" responses as well as nodding and shaking heads.

The president continued. "He and his wife—they weren't married at the time—they both worked on John Kennedy's 1960 campaign, and Cody Cooper worked here throughout—right to the assassination—to Dallas. Then he went into trying to do something for refugees."

"Between the two, he worked for the Department, he worked at State," Secretary Schultz corrected. "After working here, he was a foreign service officer at State. And he met his wife, who's going to be visiting you—he met her at State, too. She was working there. A nurse there."

The president scanned the paper in front of him. "Yes. Yes, you're right, George. The White House, then to the State Department. Yes, there it all is. You're right. Then to the World Refugee Mission, where he did that exceptional act of valor—real bravery—saving those Vietnamese refugees from the sea. You know, you know I should have invited Mrs. Cooper to be with Jeremiah Denton and Lenny Skutnik at the State of the Union last year—last January. She's worth citing to the people. I could have cited her and have her stand. I should have thought of that."

Since no one had thought of it at the time, and since the president was blaming himself rather than anyone else, Ed Meese, counselor to the president, quickly said, "I should have thought of that," but it wasn't really his responsibility. "We'll have a photo op when you're with her today in the Oval Office and at least give her that recognition. At least some pictures can make the networks and papers."

"Well, you work that out, Ed. Tell Larry. Let's give more recognition to the heroes in this country, not just at the State of the Union address, but throughout the year whenever we can. So if you know of anything that comes to your department's attention," and he looked around the table, "just let us know. We can use more inspiration for the country. There's no shortage of heroes in the United States, there's just a shortage of people hearing about them." Then he tilted his head and gave a broad smile. "Now, I better get to work." He got up and so did everyone else.

Michael Evans, the president's personal photographer took some pictures of the president giving Gloria Cooper the Medal of Freedom while they stood in front of the flags in the Oval Office, and then the press was invited in for their photo opportunity. When the press left, the president asked Gloria to sit down on one of the plush yellow cushioned chairs. She couldn't help but notice the sign on his desk that read, "There is no limit to what a man can do or where he can go, if he doesn't mind who gets the credit." Near it was a large glass with beer mug handles, filled with jelly beans.

"Where are you off to now?" the president asked Gloria. "I hope we're taking good care of you here in Washington."

"Oh, yes sir," she said. "I'm sitting in your box tonight at the Kennedy Center–but I don't think you're going to be there, are you?"

He gave one of his long "No's, and added, "Nancy and I can't make it over there, but you'll like it. They have champagne up there and you can just be comfortable up there. It's the best seat in the house! What's the play tonight?"

"I don't even know. It will just be thrilling to go there and sit in your box. Cody and I used to sit way in the back of that theater when we went. We could hardly see the stage."

"Just think, if I didn't get into politics, I might be performing there tonight!"

They both laughed.

"Well, you have a good time," the president said. "Now, what's ahead for you? I mean regarding refugees?"

"Hong Kong. Their refugee centers are loaded. Hong Kong has been wonderful to the Vietnamese boat people, taking them in. Tomorrow morning I'm leaving from here in Washington to Hong Kong."

"Well, that's Prime Minister Thatcher's decision. She's a great leader. You know, people say that conservative's have no heart–well, they've never heard of Margaret Thatcher, I guess. You be careful there. Where is your son?"

"He's in Hong Kong already. He has to be in school."

"Well, I'd like to meet him when he gets to Washington."

"I'll make sure that happens, Mister President."

"We're proud of you, and we cherish the memory of your husband. The country is proud of both of you."

She clutched onto the boxed Medal of Freedom he had given her, and she left the Oval Office.

While Gloria was leaving the White House, Prime Minister Margaret Thatcher was leaving the Imperial Palace in Beijing after having discussed the "Coming 1997 problem." The rumor going around the world was that Deng Xiaoping had won the day over Prime Minister Thatcher and that China would take Hong Kong Island, Kowloon, and the New Territories come 1997 no matter Prime Minister Thatcher's appeals.

Before going back home to London, Prime Minister Thatcher stopped off in Hong Kong. Waiting at Kai Tak Airport for her arrival at night was a huge crowd of Hong Kong's reporters, photographers, and others. Near the front of the crowd, just behind the photographers, was a very big man holding the hand of an eleven year old girl.

"Will she be here soon?" the little girl asked the big man.

"You getting tired, honey?"

She shrugged. "I'm okay."

"This is historical, honey. I want you to be here. And maybe, just maybe, she'll answer some questions. She'll be here any minute." Just as he said that, men started coming in through the gate, and in a blaze of flashbulbs the Prime Minister appeared. She looked around the crowd, and the person who caught her eyes, as she always caught people's eyes, was the little eleven year old girl. Prime Minister Thatcher walked right to her as the flash bulbs went off and reporters were yelling questions at her that were difficult to understand as their voices were simultaneous.

"I'm so glad you're here to greet me, dear! What's your name?"

"Liberty!"

"Liberty? Is it?" For confirmation of her unusual name, the Prime Minister looked up at Moose who was holding Liberty's hand.

"I'm Liberty!" Liberty answered for herself.

"That's the most beautiful name I've ever heard! How old are you?"

"Eleven and three quarters. What's your name?" Liberty asked her.

"Margaret."

Moose interjected at this surprising meeting. "Honey, this is Prime Minister Margaret Thatcher! The person we've come to welcome to Hong Kong!"

"You're Prime Minister Thatcher?" Liberty asked.

"Yes, Liberty, I am. I live in London. Do you live here in this magnificent city of Hong Kong?"

Liberty ignored the question. "Ma is mad at you!"

Moose looked startled and clenched his hand tighter around Liberty's hand. "Liberty!"

"Who, dear?"

"Ma! My mother."

"Oh?" the prime minister asked.

Liberty repeated her statement casually. "She's very mad at you."

"Why, dear?"

"She said you're going to give away Hong Kong. Why are you going to give away our home? We don't want Hong Kong to be given away to bad men."

By ignoring the press and coming over to Liberty, the prime minister made an error. Liberty, in her innocence was more direct and tenacious than any of the press waiting for her.

"My dear," the prime minister said, "My country, Great Britain, has a moral responsibility here in Hong Kong, and we take that responsibility very, very seriously."

Prime Minister Thatcher moved on through the crowd.

The giant frame and the knowledge of Moose was nothing to fear compared to the smallness and inexperience of Liberty. Liberty was the formidable force who challenged the Iron Lady.

"You didn't!" Wai-yee said to Liberty, and it was the first time Moose saw Wai-yee leave her mouth open for an extended period of time without covering it with her hand. "You said that to the Prime Minister of Great Britain?"

Liberty lowered her head, the gesture exhibiting her shame. But Dr. Yeung was laughing. "Good for Liberty! Liberty is Chinese, and K'ung Fu-tze, Confucius," and he looked at Moose, "Confucius as you call him—would be proud of her! K'ung Fu-tze said, 'To see what is right and not do it, is lack of courage or lack of principle.' Liberty has no lack of either. Good for Liberty! No offense to your friends, Moose, but Liberty has the spirit of China in her, not the reluctance of the West!"

With Dr. Yeung's approval of Liberty's actions, Wai-yee smiled. It was permission for Wai-yee to be comfortable with her daughter's boldness, and permission for Liberty to raise her head, and permission for John Travolta's picture to give a look of relief. "Moose," Wai-yee said, "I read your article in the *Asia World Weekly* and you said even worse, didn't you? If I recall correctly, you ended it, 'Stay home, Maggie!'"

Moose nodded. "I did. I did. But I didn't do it to her face. I suppose I should have, tonight. Doctor, you're right, we have a certain reluctance, don't we? We think of it as diplomatic courtesy but, indeed, it's a reluctance."

"What did you write?" Dr. Yeung asked. "I didn't see it."

"I wrote it before she left to Beijing. It was a cover story called 'The Melt-Down of the Iron Lady.' I wrote that China isn't the Falkland Islands, and now she isn't challenging with Leopoldo Galtieri of Argentina, she's challenging Deng Xiaoping of China."

Wai-yee added, "But then you wrote just what Liberty was getting at! You said that the meeting in Beijing has little to do with the future of Margaret Thatcher; rather it has everything to do with the future of all Hong Kong people. Didn't you?"

"I wrote something like that."

"Then you must praise Liberty," Wai-yee said to Moose.

Moose looked confused. "I thought you were the one who was unhappy about what she said!"

"Well, she didn't have to tell Margaret Thatcher that I was mad at her. I mean what does the Prime Minister of Great Britain care about what I think of her?"

Dr. Yeung shook his head with a smile. "That isn't what bothers you, dear. If Liberty had said 'my Mother admires you,' you wouldn't be unhappy with what Liberty said. You were unhappy because Liberty told Margaret Thatcher what you really thought. So you see, when you tell us that the Prime Minister doesn't care what you think of her, you're fibbing, my dear. You care about what got back to the Prime Minister, which was nothing less or more than the truth."

Wai-yee looked back and forth between Dr. Yeung and Moose. "My fault! My fault! Everything is my fault! What is this?"

Getting Wai-yee angry was not a good idea and Moose felt his usual western reluctance. "That isn't what the Doctor was saying, Wai-yee."

"Yes it is!"

"This time Wai-yee is right," Dr. Yeung said calmly. "You see, my dear, I am coming to your side. You are absolutely right. Everything is your fault."

There was something about Dr. Yeung's style that caused Wai-yee to smile. "Everything?"

"Perhaps not everything. You had nothing to do with the rise of Hitler."

Wai-yee gave a sigh of futility.

Moose, who learned how to change a subject from the master of changing subjects, Richard Nixon, said, "I can't wait to find out what happened in Beijing between Thatcher and Deng. I'm going to the consulate, the U.S. consulate tomorrow to find out whatever they know. Anyone want to come with me?"

"Me!" Liberty said.

Dr. Yeung put his arm around her. "Not you, Liberty. We are not prepared to go to war with America."

Consul General Burton Levin, sitting behind his desk with the flag of the United States behind him, shook his head at Moose. He got up from behind his desk to sit on a chair facing Moose who, as usual, had caused one side of the Consul General's couch to slope toward the floor under his weight.

"Thatcher did a good job, but she couldn't have won, Moose. It's like you wrote in that article last week. Deng held all the cards."

"Should she have gone to Beijing at all?"

"She had to. That was a false charge against her—the one you wrote that she should have stayed home. That wasn't fair of you, Moose. Do you think Deng would have forgot all about 1997 if she had stayed home? She went while she held a position of strength. She won the Falklands War just three months ago. She was victorious. So she went in strength, and also necessity."

"What was the necessity?"

"Great Britain has been giving fifteen year leases to whomever wanted property in the New Territories. Now, add it up. It's 1982, right? And 1982 plus 15 is 1997. How could her nation give leases to anyone if there was some mystery of whether or not Great Britain would be the land-holder before any new leases are up?"

"So what happened in Beijing between her and Deng?"

"There's no transcript, but I talked to Governor Youde. He was with her in Beijing. They aren't going to release any of the dialogue but you can quote me, Moose. Deng's taking all of Hong Kong on July 1 of '97. The date is set. Everything goes; the island, Kowloon and, of course, the New Territories. Everything. Thatcher lost. They didn't like that she had been saying that Hong Kong's prosperity had been achieved under British jurisdiction. They couldn't deny it, but they didn't like it. So they weren't in a good mood. Not that they ever are about Hong Kong. Now, this is just for background. All right?"

"Go ahead."

"She argued that the treaty for the island and the treaty for the Kowloon peninsula were in perpetuity. She said it was only the third treaty, the one for the New Territories, that was a lease, and she wanted to extend that lease another fifty years. Deng said the first two treaties were 'unequal' and that China is not bound by 'unequal' treaties and that the whole of the Hong Kong area will be recovered. Thatcher argued that 'if a country will not stand by one treaty, it will not stand by another,' and that abrogating the perpetuity clauses of those two of the three treaties would be very serious. 'Very serious, indeed,' she said. But he didn't bend. Deng said 'I could send the troops in this afternoon should you not agree.'

"Prime Minister Thatcher told Deng, 'Yes, you could and there is nothing I could do to stop you because you have only to go over the border. but the world would know what China was like, and how she dealt with the affair."

"That's it then, Burt?"

"They're going to negotiate through diplomatic channels some kind of a joint agreement that will spell out the transitional arrangements and spell out what will happen in 1997. Here, Thatcher won a large point. She might have been our savior. They apparently agreed to a guarantee that Hong Kong's prosperity and stability will continue. That's good. Don't ask me what the spell-out will be, but Britain and China are supposed to work out the arrangements for a joint declaration."

"When will they have that done?"

"No deadline. It'll take a while. Months. Years. Who knows? They'll appoint some kind of a committee, I suppose, to work out all the arrangements."

"Will Hong Kong people have any voice in all this?"

The consul general looked down at the desk. "It's between the Brits and the Chinese."

Moose got up and paced around the consul general's office. "July 1, the whole thing?"

"July 1, 1997, the whole thing."

Moose continued his pacing.

"Hey, Moose, is your magazine doing a story on what's going on down on Argyle Street today?"

Moose shook his head. "What's on Argyle Street?"

"Gloria Cooper. She's arriving at the Vietnamese Refugee Center there. It's quite an event for the boat people."

Moose smiled. "Gloria Cooper! I met her husband in this very building twenty-some years ago. He was a marvelous guy. He helped me out once when I needed some help. I don't really know her. Just some correspondence."

"You met Cody Cooper right here?"

"I sure did. Quite a guy. When will she be over at Argyle?"

"She's supposed to arrive at 11:00 o'clock this morning. It's a good story. It would be a good column for you. It might keep you from blasting Thatcher in your next issue."

Moose shook his head. "Maybe. Let me finish with this. Did Thatcher tell Deng about the polls on how the Hong Kong people feel about a handover to China?"

"I'm sure she didn't. But so what?"

"Ninety-five percent of Hong Kong people want the status quo to remain, for the British to stay. And 86 percent of those said the most important reason they wanted the status quo to continue was because they value freedom. That says something."

"Do you think polls of Hong Kong people would have influenced Deng? He doesn't care. What good would that have done? What do you think he's going to do, call for a plebiscite?"

"The Hong Kong people are not going to take this lying down."

"And just what can they do about it?"

Moose groped for an answer and couldn't think of any. "Nothing, Mr. Consul General."

Across the harbor and on the other side of Kai Tak Airport in Shamshuipo was that compound that had been a prison for British officers during the occupation of Japan. The prison was closed 37 years ago and opened again as a refugee center for Vietnamese boat people. This November there was gaiety in the compound. Hanging from one tree to another, near the camp's entrance, was a white cloth banner with a message painted in yellow that read, "WELCOME GLORIA COOPER" with the word, "WELCOME" in three languages; Vietnamese, Chinese, and English. Throughout the camp were flags that once flew over South Vietnam, and hundreds of the refugees were clustered inside the entrance off Argyle Street.

When the car drove up, they started applauding. When the car door was opened by the tall British Administrator of the camp who had been waiting for her outside the gate, the crowd of Vietnamese on the other side of the gate cheered with expectant, almost tearful expressions. Gloria came out of the car. Some didn't cheer but, instead, went to their knees.

"I'm Hanson Ambrose, Mrs. Cooper. On behalf of Governor Youde, we are so glad to have you here. As you can see, we are all waiting for you."

She extended her hand. "It's so good to meet you."

"I do say, Mrs. Cooper," the tall man said, "you are looked upon as a kind of savior here, actually." They walked in through the opened gate and the tall man ducked to avoid the center of the cloth banner that was hanging low. "Mind your head, now."

She reached for one extended hand of a refugee after another.

"Come along," he said. "I'll show you the camp and the clinic and your quarters. The clinic is quite good, actually. We can get most of the supplies you need if you find it wanting."

"Hello! Hello!" so many of the refugees yelled out to her with pride in knowing how to say the word. "Hello!" And then some small Vietnamese boy said, "Good Morning!"

Gloria was smiling broadly. "Good morning!" she answered. "Hello! Hello!" She and the tall man quickly became immersed in the crowd with him yelling to the refugees, "Stay clear, now! Stay clear!"

"No," she said, "let me greet them."

"Yes, of course."

"Queen Gloria!" another young boy yelled.

Gloria smiled and shook her head. "I'm not a queen," she said. And for twenty minutes she walked among them, smiling at them, shaking their hands, bending to some children who had no idea who she was.

"I want to see how they live," she said, getting up from a kneel.

"Yes. Of course. You know, we take them all. We have never sent one away that has reached Hong Kong. This year alone we've had 263 boats arrive with over 7,000 refugees. The height of the avalanche came three years ago in 1979 when near 70,000 Vietnamese came here."

"All on boats?"

"Most. Most. It all started right after the surrender of Saigon. One boat, the *Clara Maersk*, had over 3,500 on it, actually. That started it."

"Do all the refugees that make it come here to this center?"

"Oh, no. We have many centers, actually. Jubilee was a nice one but we closed it last year, and some were sent here from Jubilee, so it's a bit crowded. They must stay here until we process them into countries of settlement."

"May I see inside there?" She gestured toward a door to a wooden building.

"Anywhere. Yes, of course. Then I'll show you where you'll be working; the clinic, actually."

As they started toward the door of the building, an out of breath Moose Dunston rushed from the entrance to them. "Gloria Cooper?"

She turned around and had to look quite far up to see his face. "Yes?"

"Hi! I'm Moose Dunston. I was a friend of Cody. I'm here writing for *Asia World Weekly*. Do you mind if I tag along with you?"

"Of course you can. You knew Cody?"

"Not real well, but I met him here in Hong Kong when he was here for the first time, and since then we've—we've talked. He was very good to me."

"How nice." And then she looked far-off, thinking. "I remember. You wrote me about Cody. You wrote me that he contacted you at the Nixon White House."

"You have a remarkable memory."

"It was a remarkable letter."

The British administrator extended his hand. "Hanson Ambrose, Mr. Dunston. I'm the administrator here."

"Oh, fine. Good to meet you. Okay with you if I stick around? I'm with *Asia World Weekly*."

"I read your articles every week, Mr. Dunston. You're very good." He probably didn't read 'The Melt-Down of the Iron Lady.' "And any friend of Mrs. Copper is a friend of ours. Come along."

It was a vast room full of three layers of shelves. Each shelf was a row of "homes" of sorts. Some of the shelves had curtains, some had wash hanging. Each shelf "home" was no wider than five feet with a height of three feet. Their depth was six feet. One, two, even three people lived on each shelf, each numbered by white paint on their black metal rods that separated the "homes." The curtains were opened and the refugees stared at her, some with their hands in a position of prayer, some were kneeling. Shoes were lined up in a neat row on the concrete floor.

Gloria and the tall, thin, British administrator, and the big, massive Moose walked slowly, with Gloria reaching out to each refugee who extended a hand. There was a stench but it wasn't bad because it was combined with the smell of some kind of disinfectant spray that muted its natural state.

A young woman's voice stopped Moose from following Gloria and the British administrator. "You are not British. You are American, aren't you?" He had to look quickly at the shelves to find who was talking to him. "Me," she said, "I'm over here." The voice came from one of the middle shelves, labeled Number 42B. Being on a middle shelf, she was on eye-level with Moose.

She was gorgeous. She was sitting with her legs tucked beneath the rest of her. Whereas the others were dressed shabbily, some of the men in underwear tops and shorts, and some with no tops at all, and the women in pants and men's shirts, this young woman dressed as though she was going to the Governor's Ball, dressed in a white Vietnamese ao-dai. "I'm Lo An," she said. Her black hair was like a silk garment that went from her forehead down her back. His type. "And you are from America. Aren't you?"

Moose could hardly get a sound to come from his throat. "Yes," he said softly. "I am."

For a while they just stared at one another. It happened. That spark. That thing. Could it happen at his age? Again? That crazy, illogical magnetism that pulls in an instant. Just like that, there it was.

"I'm Vietnamese," she said. Her voice was so little and so soft.

"Yes, I thought so." And then he thought what a dumb thing that was for him to say. He thought so? Everyone in this terrible place was Vietnamese. But why did he care if it was a dumb thing to say? He wouldn't have cared if he said it to one of those other people sitting on shelves. "I was in Vietnam many times—during the war." It was another dumb thing to say. Was he trying to show off his knowledge of Vietnam to her? And, of course it was during the war. Would anyone imagine the government would have allowed him in there after the war?

"You know Saigon?"

Moose nodded. "Yes."

"I still call it Saigon," she said softly. "Do you call it Ho Chi Minh City?"

"No. Never."

By this time Gloria and that tall man were far down the line of shelves. "You must go with your friends?"

"No," he said. "I'm alone."

"Do you know Mrs. Cooper?"

"Yes. Yes, I do. Very well." No, he didn't. He just met her.

None of that made any difference. Lo An knew what he was feeling. It was all over his face.

"TuDo Street. I always liked walking on TuDo Street," Moose said as he was getting more and more disgusted with his silly comments but he simply couldn't think quick enough or well enough to say anything that had any merit.

"It was so nice," she said. "They changed it to Dong Khoi Street, but we still call it TuDo when they can't hear us."

How old was this pretty thing? In her twenties? She was in bloom. This was her time. This wasn't his time, but he felt as though it was. Maybe there is no time for things like this.

"Are you here alone?" he asked her. A reasonably intelligent question.

"I have this bunk alone. I'm here with my parents. We're Boat People."

"A long voyage?" Well, of course. Was Vietnam to Hong Kong a shorter voyage for her than for others? Did the South China Sea compress for her?

"Yes. You know they have other kinds of boat people here in Hong Kong. There are over 3000 of them who live on boats in Aberdeen and they're Chinese."

"I know." What a powerhouse of knowledge he was. Wai-yee had told him about them years ago.

"They're Tanka. A lot of Chinese reject them even though they're their own. They are really 'Egg People'. Did you know that?"

"No. Egg People?" Wai-yee hadn't told him that, or if she did, he forgot.

"They used to pay their taxes in eggs. It's all they had to pay with."

"I didn't know that."

She smiled.

What was there to talk about next? "Are you married?" he asked. At last, a question with a destination.

She smiled and shook her head. "No."

"You speak beautiful English."

"I think in Vietnamese, but I know English very well. My father worked for the Americans in Saigon."

"Did he!? What a good man. At the Embassy? I was there often."

"No. At JUSPAO."

"Are you going to America?"

"Will you take me?" She gave a broad smile. She had total command over this meeting.

He moved his head around between a nod and a shake of the head in a gesture that had no meaning at all. "I'd like to!"

"Let's go!"

He laughed. But it wasn't funny. He tried to move his eyes off her, but that was difficult. "I'm a writer. I'm going to do a story on refugees. I will be back here. Maybe then we can talk."

"All right."

"Goodbye, then–Lo An."

She smiled and extended her hand. He took it and it was so small and fresh and smooth and yielding like that of a baby. He couldn't shake it. It wasn't a shaking kind of hand. He just held it.

She asked, "When will you be back to interview me?"

He thought for no more than a second. "I don't know."

By this time Gloria Cooper and the British administrator were out of sight.

On his way to catch up with Gloria and the Englishman, he made a quick decision not to come back. *Leave her be*, he thought. He didn't need to flirt with love again. And there was something else: he would feel as though he was cheating on Wai-yee. Even by the flirtation he felt disloyal. It wasn't that he hadn't flirted with other women, he had, and even made love to them, but this time he felt the spark. And that seemed like an act of disloyalty, even though Wai-yee was married. There was still a psychological connection he was incapable of destroying.

Mark wasn't Mark. His mind had been invaded by discontent, and now the invaders were being replaced by even worse elements; hopelessness and fear of weakening manliness, and even hate. The only thing he liked about being back in New York at the U.N. was that Anne was often in Washington for one excuse or another, and so she would not have as much evidence of his inadequacy. He never questioned her excuses to be in Washington because he wanted her to be there.

He would not watch television, out of fear that Ted Murphy would be on the screen with that punched-in nose and sick smile. For once, Mark felt he was capable of using violence. It was the first time he felt the pain and sickness of jealousy since he was in high school. Yet he didn't want to be with Anne. His mind was ill.

At night, he would walk down bad streets. Mark was looking for something, having no idea what that instinctive and uncontrollable search was all about. On those walks, he would make quick looks behind him, assuming every stranger was watching him.

Mark felt he had to prove to himself that he was still alive, and prove he was capable of something. Anything. Anything other than being lost.

Mrs. Goodpastor used to write letters by the dozens every day, and enjoyed it. Now, writing one was an effort, which was followed by looking for the right-sized envelope which she never seemed to have, and trying to remember where she put stamps. But today she wrote letters to Mark and

Anne Daschle, Ted and Linda Murphy, General Jonas Valadovich, Moose Dunston, and Tso Wai-yee. She wrote them, "I am sure you have read that the future of Hong Kong has been established. Now we can set the date for our reunion. I look forward to seeing you on the Peak at twelve o'clock noon on June 30, 1997, the last day of Hong Kong as a British Crown Colony. God willing, I will see you fifteen years from now. I will make reservations for a block of rooms at the Hong Kong Hilton for June the 28th through July the 4th, 1997."

She wrote a special letter to Gloria and John Fitzgerald Cooper telling them that "I know it seems a long way off, but reserve the dates. Cody was part of the pledge when we met twenty-two years ago in 1960, and we would be honored for you to join the reunion."

General Daniel Graham was looking for a red one in the jug of jelly beans. He was sitting in the Oval Office facing the president who was sitting at his desk.

"You know," the president said, "in those days Warner Brothers was making a lot of war pictures. Black and white. Warner Brothers hardly made anything in color then. You remember *Yankee Doodle Dandy* with Cagney?"

"One of the best."

"You remember Cagney dancing down the steps of the White House residence?"

"Yes, sir."

"I think about that when I use the stairway of the residence. He had that meeting with FDR, and he danced down the steps. That was right near the end of the picture. Cagney was great! Dan, did you hear about the two old-time actors who were seated next to each other at the Academy Awards?"

"No, sir."

"One looked at the other with surprise and he said, 'That's funny! I thought we were both dead!"

The president and General Graham laughed, the president's face almost red.

"But listen, Dan, I don't want to take your time with all these Hollywood stories. I asked you here because I need to hear more about your missile defense idea—your High Frontier. Last July the 4th I mentioned that there were defensive possibilities in space. Did you hear that address?"

"I sure did, Mister President. I hoped you were referring to High Frontier."

"I was just planting a seed. You know, most people think we could knock down an enemy missile. They don't know that we have nothing to do it with. They don't know we'd just have to let them hit us."

"We'd have 32 minutes—to pray. That's all we could do," General Graham said.

"And atheists would have 32 minutes to convert!" The President laughed.

"That's right!"

"Now, tell me—you say there's no nuclear blast with your High Frontier?"

"That's right. Mister President, there's nothing. The idea is for 432 satellites, consistently in position above hostile territory to spot any missile launch. Within the first eight minutes after an enemy launch, one of those satellites loaded with non-nuclear heat seeking rockets would hone in on the fire trails of the missile and knock it out of its trajectory. The missile is knocked out by simply hitting it with pellets. Kinetic energy. There's not even an explosion. Any stone—anything—an ice cube could do it. We could have that stage of High Frontier in place by 1988. In case any missiles get through, you have another layer of satellites that will do the same thing prior to the time the warhead re-enters the atmosphere. That could be in place by 1992. In the void during these years while we're deploying all this, you have a third layer placed at our missile silos to protect our missiles. They could destroy an incoming warhead as close as 3,000 feet away. Radar would trigger them at that late stage while decoys would already have burned up during re-entry. That stage could be ready in two to three years to fill the void. 1984 or 1985. Mister President, it has the potential to save the nation."

"How much would it cost?"

"Twenty-six billion dollars. It's a lot. But we're talking about saving the nation."

"Colonel Aldrin is with you on this?"

"You bet. He's a great supporter. So is General Valadovich. They've been through every detail with me. It will work."

"I used your word—frontier—last July the 4th, you know. I said defensive possibilities in the ultimate frontier of space."

"I know, sir. What was the reaction?"

"I don't think anyone picked up on it."

There was a beep on the president's intercom. He picked up the white phone nearest him. "Yes?"

The president was listening for a long while with his mouth slightly open. "For Heaven's sake! For Heaven's sake! All right. Tell them across the hall. No. I'll tell them." He hung up the receiver and looked at General Graham coldly. "Brezhnev. He's dead."

President Reagan walked in the Roosevelt Room, causing everyone sitting around the big mahogany table to stand up. This was not a normal appearance at their senior staff meeting. President Reagan put his hands in front of him, moving them sideways as a signal to tell them to sit down. "No, no. Please go on. Sit down. I'll just be a moment. I don't know what you're discussing but you should know that Leonid Brezhnev died. A heart attack."

There was silence at the table broken only by a few surprised, "Uuuuhh's."

"I'm going back across the hall. I'm with General Graham. Please continue." And the president left, leaving the participants looking toward the head of the table at Chief of Staff James Baker, who was quickly trying to gather his thoughts.

"Who's the next president there, Bill? Who's the next in line?" James Baker asked Bill Clark, the National Security Advisor.

Judge Clark shook his head. "There is no line. Maybe Chernenko. Maybe Yuri Andropov. He ran the KGB. Brezhnev was, at least, the devil we knew. The sign of who it will be, will come when we hear who's going to lead the funeral."

"Jim?" a man near the end of the table said.

"Yes?"

"It can't be the president who goes to the funeral. It's got to be Bush."

"Now, wait a minute. The president ought to go to this one," a man who wanted the president to do everything said.

"Let's not get ahead of ourselves," James Baker said. "We don't even know if it will be a public funeral or anything."

"We need a list," the man who always made lists said. "We need to find out who went to what funeral in the past."

The man who never forgot anything said, "We don't need a list. Khrushchev didn't go to Kennedy's funeral. And Brezhnev didn't go to Ike's, Hoover's, Truman's, Johnson's. There's your list. So that's how they regard our Presidents."

"Those were different," the man who wanted the president to do everything answered. "Kennedy was killed and the others weren't president when they died. President Reagan should go."

"You're making excuses for them," the man who never forgot anything said. "vice presidents are meant to be saviors for their presidents. They keep them from having to attend funerals. That's their purpose. Bush. It's got to be Bush. You remember what Rockefeller said when he was appointed vice president by Ford, and was asked if he was going to be traveling a lot overseas? He said it would depend on how many chiefs of state die."

James Baker ignored all that. "Let's get a letter of condolences drafted, let's find out whether they're going to have public services or what, or who's going to be invited to Moscow –or wherever it's going to be–and what the date will be, and see what we have to cancel and all that. Even if the vice president goes, you can't have the president at some happy event here while a funeral is going on for Brezhnev."

"So we have arrived at Bush then?" a man who always looked confused asked.

Then it was a free-for-all. "On that letter of condolences, it's got to be very sensitive. Someone ought to call Khachigian to draft something for the president. We need a craftsman."

"We can handle it here. Have some faith in us. We can handle it."

"It's important that we be as respectful as we can throughout all this."

"Let's not go overboard. Just a week or so ago Brezhnev was rallying against the president for being opposed to a nuclear freeze. He was saying we're all imperialists and aggressors and all that. He said we're raising our military too high, trying for military superiority, and that we're trying to ruin the Soviet Union's economy. All those kind of things."

"Sounds right on to me!" The man who never forgot anything said. "The president is against the freeze, we do want military superiority, and we are trying to ruin the Soviet Union's economy. What's wrong with that? Maybe the president should say we'll miss Brezhnev's insight."

"Then is it Bush?"

SIXTY-ONE
CROSSED SWORDS
1983

It was difficult for anyone in the television audience to take their eyes off Anne in her guest appearance on "Crossed Swords." She had a sensuality and gregariousness that integrated perfectly on television, now that she wasn't trying to be as proper as she was during her congressional campaign. What was invisible was the information and military statistics tucked in her brain after being on the phone with Jonas Valadovich for two hours that day.

The young man who was the host obviously had a session with a hairblower, and his makeup made him look as tanned as a Hawaiian surfrider. "Good evening," he said to the television camera, "and welcome to 'Crossed Swords.' Just hours ago, President Reagan called for American scientists to turn their talents to the development of an antiballistic missile system capable of destroying the warheads of an enemy's missiles before they reach their targets. He said that he is—and I'm quoting now—'directing a comprehensive and intensive effort to define a long term research and development program to begin to achieve our ultimate goal of eliminating the threat posed by strategic nuclear missiles.' And he asked, 'Wouldn't it be better to save lives than to avenge them?'

"Listening carefully to the president were our two guests who will be crossing swords over the president's initiative. They are Senator Crayton Lewis who is opposed to the president's proposal and has been a longtime supporter of a nuclear freeze, and Anne Whitney, the former congressional candidate, who believes the nation should support the president's idea, and who opposes a nuclear freeze. Let me go first to you, Senator. Why are you opposed to the president's initiative?"

"I'll echo the words of my colleague, Senator Kennedy, who tonight accused the president of misleading the nation through red scare tactics and reckless Star War schemes. I think Senator Kennedy hit it right on the nose. Let me add to that some of the statements of my other colleagues. Senator Cranston called the president's initiative 'a nightmare,' Senator Hart, with his grand tongue-in-cheek humor, said, 'Once upon a time there was an evil empire that threatened us with terrible weapons. But then one day our side discovered a magic invisible shield. When we stretched it across our country, no missiles could penetrate it. From that day on, we stopped worrying about nuclear war and lived happily ever after.' And even on the Republican side of the aisle, Senator Hatfield said, 'The president's advisors must be called to account for these terrifying proposals.' Now, let me put it in my own words. It's time we stopped this madness of adding one weapon system on top of another, increasing and expanding the arms race. The president is trying to usher us into just what Senator Kennedy said—an era of Star Wars."

"And Anne Whitney, isn't what the Senator said true? Isn't President Reagan expanding the arms race, and isn't this new weapon system something akin to a Star Wars scheme?"

Anne quickly asked, "Why do you call it a weapon system? It can't kill a moth. It's meant to stop a warhead sent by a missile after it's launched. Is a bullet-proof vest a weapon? I don't understand how anyone can oppose that. Now listen to me; would we rather be hit by a nuclear warhead than have a system that could stop it before hitting us? I didn't know that tonight Senator Kennedy called it a Star Wars scheme. It isn't meant to start a war but to prevent one before there's any destruction—before there's any killing."

The senator looked frustrated. "There is a much more practical and less costly way of stopping the nuclear threat that hangs over all the peoples of the world. The way to do that is for an immediate freeze on building or deploying nuclear weapons on both sides. That's what my colleagues and I have been arguing for, but the president simply won't listen."

Anne didn't hesitate for a moment. "If we agree to a nuclear freeze of both sides, we will be freezing the Soviets into superiority. It's that simple. The Soviet Union has 351 intermediate range ballistic missiles deployed in Eastern Europe aimed at Western European targets. Senator, how many intermediate range ballistic missiles do we have in Western Europe aimed at Eastern Europe targets? None. None, Senator."

"Ms. Whitney, aren't you forgetting that we have, not in Europe, but here at home, enough Intercontinental Ballistic Missiles to blow up the world?"

"Of course, and so does the Soviet Union have even more Intercontinental Ballistic Missiles than we have. That isn't what I asked. Since you didn't care to answer, I will. We have no response to the Soviets SS-20s, their Intermediate Range Ballistic Missiles. The ratio between us is 351 to zero. Now, if the Soviet Union launched their missiles at Western Europe and we would have to respond by launching our Intercontinental Ballistic Missiles from here to protect Western Europe, we would have nothing left to protect our own country. The Soviet Union knows that. They, on the other hand, would still have their massive amount of Intercontinental Ballistic Missiles intact that could fire at the United States."

"Then do we just continue this mad arms race, or does some responsibility take hold and bring this craziness to a close?"

"I would rather be in a race than invoke a surrender."

"Peace is not surrender." The senator was shaking his head with a smile.

"That depends on whether you hold peace higher than liberty, or hold liberty higher than peace." Anne was passionate. She was prepared to take him on. "President Lincoln could have had peace and spared the states the agony of war and the death of over one-half million Americans on the battlefield. He could have done that by removing the Union's troops from Fort Sumter and by allowing the secession of South Carolina and allowing the other states that sought confederation to become independent of the Union. There would be two nations. One free, one slave. And there would have been peace.

"In the second decade of this century, France and Great Britain and the United States could have avoided World War I by refusing to pick up arms. And there would have been peace.

"President Roosevelt could have brought about peace for the United States by standing before that joint session of the Congress on Monday, December the 8th of 1941 to request of the Congress, not a declaration of war to return fire for fire but, instead, a declaration of accommodation. And there would have been peace.

"Surrender, senator, brings about peace, and neutrality brings about peace—the peace of the palace for those in authority, the peace of subjugation for the many who are timid, and the peace of the prison-cell for the rest. But there is peace.

"Peace without liberty is surrender."

"Ms. Whitney, in a quest for peace, someone has to make the first step. I simply propose we make that step."

"It's amazing to me that when we did hold superiority you and your colleagues wanted to 'Ban the Bomb,' unilateral disarmament—destroying all our bombs unilaterally, not a freeze. Now that the Soviets hold superiority, you want a freeze. Senator, the Nuclear Freeze Movement started in Moscow under the direction of Leonid Brezhnev, and Yuri Andropov continued it after Brezhnev died last year."

The host interjected, "Senator, is that true?"

The senator shook his head again. "No, it isn't true. President Carter was the first to suggest it, and it really originated in the hearts and minds of all those who oppose war. There are demonstrations for a Nuclear Freeze all over Europe, and the International Physicians for Prevention of Nuclear War have endorsed it without reservation."

Anne was biting her lip but stopped very quickly. "I said Brezhnev originated the movement, not the idea. It was the idea of President Carter, and you're proving my point, not yours. That was in 1979 when he met with Brezhnev in Vienna for the signing of the SALT II Agreement. Brezhnev rejected it because the Soviet Union didn't hold superiority at that time. Then two years later, after Brezhnev deployed 351 SS-20 Intermediate Range Ballistic Missiles aimed at Western Europe, each with three independently targeted warheads on them, he wanted the freeze. As I said, we had zero missiles in Europe aiming at the Soviet Union and we still have zero. And also in those two intervening years, Ronald Reagan was elected president of the United States, pledging a buildup in our defense efforts. So after the threat of Reagan, and after Brezhnev had his 351 SS-20s, then, and only then, did Brezhnev advocate a freeze, and then, and only then, did he call for his front groups in Western Europe to start advocating a nuclear freeze. My history is correct, Senator. We can't afford such a freeze, we need our own missiles deployed, and we need a missile defense system—the president's Strategic Defense Initiative."

There was that shaking head of the senator again. "Again, Anne, you're only perspective is from one side. If we continue this madness of building missiles and putting nuclear warheads on them, we increase the possibility of nuclear war by error. That is, perhaps, the greatest threat to the peoples of the world through such proliferation. It's not that the president of the United States or the president of the Soviet Union will order their launch, but as more and more are built and more and more are deployed, the factor of error becomes more and more likely."

"You're right. I am only looking at it from the perspective of one side. Ours. And I would rather take a chance on nuclear war by error, than U.S. destruction by Soviet design and our appeasement. May I quote a hero of mine, Senator?"

The senator smiled. "Genghis Khan?"

"This quote is by a hero of mine; President Kennedy. He said, 'There can only be one defense policy for the United States and that is summed up in the word 'first.' I do not mean first 'but,' I do not mean first 'when,' I do not mean first 'if.' I mean first 'period.' Only then can we stop the next war before it starts. Only then can we prevent war by preparing for it.' And I have another quote. This one by General MacArthur. He said this before Pearl Harbor: 'The history of failure in war can be summed up in two words: Too late. Too late in comprehending the deadly purpose of a potential enemy. Too late in realizing the mortal danger. Too late in preparedness. Too late in uniting all possible forces for resistance. Too late in standing with ones friends.' Now, put the general and the president together. General MacArthur summed up the failure of defense in two words: 'Too late.' President Kennedy summed up the success of defense in one word: 'First.'"

When Anne walked out of the studio, someone was waiting in the reception room. "Ms. Whitney–hello." It was a man with a long blond braid hanging down his back. "Congratulations!" Jeffrey Stempka said. "You did a marvelous job. I was watching you here on the monitor," and he gestured to the television set hanging on a bracket above the desk where the guard sat.

"Mr. Stempka!"

"I heard you were going to be a guest on the show tonight, and I came right over. They didn't let me in the studio but set me down here. I'm glad they at least have a television set here. If I had to guess, I'd say they'll ask you to be on again–permanently."

"You're a pretty good prophet, Mr. Stempka. I'll pay attention to what you say. You were right about the offer Mark received."

"How does he like working for Jeane Kirkpatrick?"

"He likes her a lot. But he still doesn't like the U.N. I don't think even Jeane Kirkpatrick really likes the U.N. that much. And Mark still doesn't like living in New York. He wants to go overseas."

"Can I take you for a bite to eat, or a drink?"

She hesitated and then gave an enthusiastic, "Yes! I'm not hungry, but

I would like to just relax and have a drink. I'm still on a high! And I'm sure you didn't just happen to be in the neighborhood. You must have something on your mind."

He nodded with one of his quick and rare smiles. "You're right, Ms. Whitney."

"I have my own car. I'll meet you somewhere."

"Nathan's in Georgetown. M Street." Very firm. Very well-rehearsed. He didn't ask her if it was all right. Good spy.

She chose to drink her old favorite, daiquiris in the rounded booth of Nathan's. And she went back to her old habit of too many of them. "Did I skunk him?"

"You trounced the senator, Mrs. Daschle. You did." It was clear that Jeffrey Stempka wanted Anne to know he was on her side. "You won that debate hands down."

"Hands down!" And she put her hands in front of her, and thumped them down on the table.

He had no reaction. "Tell me, how is your husband enjoying his stay in New York?"

"You asked me that already. I told you. It's okay."

"And you?"

Anne shrugged. "I like excitement. I have to do something–something like the show tonight. I don't only like excitement, I need it. New York is exciting but it isn't the same kind of excitement I get here in D.C. This excitement is about important things. And I'm alone a lot in New York. Mark is working too many long hours, and he's working too hard. But he does that no matter where he works. He's a workaholic."

"What exactly is his job there?" He faked ignorance.

"Public information. What all Public Affairs Officers do for the United States Information Agency."

"Ms. Whitney, I'm sure you know that U.S.I.A. people aren't allowed to do any work for us–for the CIA, because if some U.S.I.A. person does do work for us, and is ever found out, the whole credibility of the U.S.I.A. goes through the cracks. Just think of what would happen to the U.S.I.A. and all its officers overseas if foreign nations thought U.S.I.A. personnel could be American spies. We never ask the U.S.I.A. to do anything for us. That's smart policy. I've been ordered to keep to it."

"I know the policy."

"That's why I'm coming to you, and not to him. I must ask you not to tell your husband about this meeting with me."

"Good! I'm ready! If I can't be in the Congress, I want to be a spook!"

"Then I have a request for you tonight."

She moved closer so her arm was pressing against his arm. "Wwww!"

Jeffrey Stempka smiled. "The request is business, unfortunately for me, not pleasure."

Anne moved back to her original position. "What a disappointment! At least, I hope it's about those pictures."

Jeffrey Stempka was surprised at her reference to the pictures. He smiled and shook his head. "It's not about the pictures. It's about what you can do for us. Let me tell you. The Soviet Union has the biggest U.N. delegation of any nation, more than the U.S. and China put together. They have 275 people there—and they're all KGB. The U.N. has become a Soviet spy den. Ms. Whitney, do you know any members of the Soviet delegation there?"

"Oh, yes. There have been parties, just receptions and parties. I met some of the Rooskies at those things, but they know I'm not a 'friendly,' so other than a couple of them, two of them who flirt with me, they don't have much to do with me."

"How about Mark? Does he know a lot of them?"

"Probably. Oh, I know he does. He knows people from every delegation, I think. I don't think he knows the Iranians or Cubans or Libyans, or delegates from other governments we don't recognize. We don't go to their parties, they don't get invites to ours. You know how it works. But Rooskies? Oh, yes. We recognize their government so, as little as they mix, they go to our things. You know, there's almost a party by some delegation or other every night. Every country has its National Day or some silly reason for a party. I don't like them anymore."

"So who are the two who have become friendly with you? The ones who flirt."

"I'm not sure of their last names. Mark would know, I'm sure. But I know their first names. Sergey and Nikolay. They're at everything."

"Have they ever asked you to do anything that might be an attempt to find out classified information?"

"No. They seem to have other interests in me! They're flirts with all the women." And she came closer to him again. "Do you want me to be a 'swallow'?'"

Jeffrey Stempka tried to ignore her vamping of him. "Oh, no! We do not want that. But I see you know the term. Let me be direct. We want to know who their 'sleepers' are. Do you know what I mean by that?"

"The ones they sleep with?"

"No. You don't know that term?"

Anne shook her head.

"'Sleepers' are their espionage agents here in the United States—there are over a thousand of them in the U.S. who are working for the Soviets and their satellites. We call them 'sleepers' because they don't do anything until they're asked—until they're 'awakened', and then they perform."

"For money?"

"Some do it for money. Some do it for a woman—or a man. Some do it because they simply believe in the Soviet system. Some do it because they're mad at this country for one reason or another. Some do it because they're blackmailed."

"How do I fit in?"

"Ms. Whitney we know that many of the 275 Soviet delegates at the U.N. have employed 'sleepers.' If you have access to the delegates, and you're observant, it may make a difference. We usually find out who the 'sleepers' are through some error made in conversation or some thoughtless action. Don't think of these Soviet delegates as a bunch of James Bonds. They're human, and some of them aren't very bright."

"What exactly do you want me to do?"

"Who do they talk to at the parties, who is around them, who do they mention to you and to Mark, what do they talk about? That kind of thing. That's all. Don't try to get anything out of them. Just be observant. We'll take it from there."

"That's all?"

"It would be very helpful to us."

"I'll do it."

"Great. Nothing obvious. Just be observant, that's all. Just get to know them."

"Mr. Stempka, may I ask you something? Two things?"

"Of course."

"One business. One pleasure."

"All right."

"First, business. Why does the Soviet Union have so many delegates here? Why don't we just insist they have as many as we do, or China, or something?"

"Good question. The answer is one conversation between Stalin, Roosevelt, and Churchill at Yalta. Stalin came out of Yalta with three delegations in the U.N. In fact, to this day they have three votes in the General Assembly and everyone else, including us, has only one. What happened was that at the Yalta Conference, when those three leaders were forming the U.N., Stalin wanted sixteen votes in the General Assembly, one for each of his republics at the time. He said he deserved them because Great Britain's Commonwealths of India and Australia and Canada and Nigeria and all the 62 British Commonwealth countries would each have a vote, so his republics should each have a vote, too. Churchill tried to explain to him that the British Commonwealth was composed of totally sovereign nations, not under his control, while Stalin had jurisdiction over all his republics. Roosevelt laughed about the whole thing, and said if Stalin wanted that, then the United States should have 48 votes, one for each state. There was finally a compromise, giving Stalin three votes, the ones Stalin said suffered the most in World War II; the Ukraine, Byelorussia, and one for the rest of the Soviet Union including Russia. Roosevelt agreed, saying he would retain the right at a later time to have two more for the United States, maybe one for Texas and one for New York. Of course we never did that. That's why the Soviet Union has three votes, and three delegations."

"Oh, you're such a historian!" She took a long gulp of her daiquiri. It had been so long since she had been in a bar with a man. She looked at his face directly. He was so young. And that excited her. "Now my second question."

"Please."

"First, if I was a candidate I couldn't do this." And she took another swallow of the daiquiri leaving an empty glass. "Not in public. Not even in private. May I have another one?"

"Of course."

He called the waiter and ordered the drink for her and while they waited for it there was nothing but silence between them. It was what she wanted. Silence took away from the aura of business. She wanted to throw away everything that had interfered with the simplicity of him and her sitting close together.

After the drink arrived and the waiter walked away, she said, "Tell me. Did you ever look at those pictures again?"

He made no comment.

"Did you?"

"Yes."

"Why?"

He shook his head. "No reason."

She gave a laugh. "I can think of a reason."

"Oh?"

"Which one do you like best?"

"I don't know."

"Yes, you do, Mr. Stempka. You have a favorite don't you?"

He wouldn't look at her, but rather at the drink in front of him, and then alternating between looking at the table, and looking far off.

"Which one?"

"Do you want me to describe it to you?" Now he looked at her.

"Yes, I want you to describe the one you look at–at night when you get home. There is one, isn't there?"

Again, he didn't answer.

"Describe it to me." And then she added, "or else."

"Or else what?"

"Or else I'll make you suffer with frustration."

"And how do you propose to do that, Mrs. Daschle?"

"I did that in your office, didn't I?"

"In a way."

"I can make it one hundred times worse."

"And how do you propose to do that?"

Anne smiled. "That's something you won't be told. But I know I can because I saw how excited you were by nothing more than a black and white glossy. You should be ashamed of yourself. You're nothing but a boy looking at pictures–and playing spy."

"Mrs. Daschle, you're a married woman."

"I use the name Whitney–Now, what's being married got to do with it?"

"A lot, considering what you're saying."

"I haven't said very much except you're a boy and I know how to make you suffer–and you deserve it."

"You might know what you're talking about, but I don't."

"Tell me which picture you look at the most. Describe it to me."

His words were staggered. "There's one–I suppose–there's the one where–it's where–" and then he thought of a way to identify it without saying too much. "It's the one where you can't see Mr. Murphy at all. There was only one like that. It must have been the first one the camera took."

"I knew that was the one."

"Did you?"

"Yes. What am I doing on the picture?"

"You're not really doing anything."

"What do you like about it?"

"You know."

"Close your eyes."

"Close my eyes?"

"Close your eyes." She reached over and put her hand over his eyes and passed them down as though she was shutting them. They were closed when she took her hand down. "Now keep them shut."

He waited for perhaps a half-minute in an expectant black. "When may I open them, Mrs. Daschle?"

"When I tell you, Mr. Stempka."

The black continued. He tried listening for a sound of what she was doing but there was no sound. "How long do you want me to keep my eyes closed?"

Suddenly he felt her hand on his cheek. Then he felt her other hand on his other cheek. Her hands were barely touching him. She moved them around his face with lightness. That's all she did. It was all so light. When she was confident he was moved by that, she said, "Open your eyes."

He did.

"Did you like that, Mr. Stempka?"

He nodded. "You haven't changed much from the way you were in 1969 have you, Mrs. Daschle?"

"I've changed a lot. I've gotten better. Any girl–just a girl could do what I did on that desk in the Embassy. No girl and very few women could do what I just did. And that, Mr. Stempka, is all you'll get. Now go home. Other than me, every date you have will just be with young and inexperienced girls who will leave you with nothing to think about no matter what they allow. But they wouldn't even think of doing what I just did. It's why you'll think of me, Mr. Stempka. And that makes me glad, because I'll only think of you when I want to, which will be rare."

It was the first time she didn't tell Mark about an escapade. She couldn't, or she would have violated the word she had given to Jeffrey Stempka. But she could have just said she met a man and had drinks with him. She would have done that if it would have made him jealous. She would have done that if it would have made him excited. She would have done that if it would have made him angry. But she didn't say a word, because she feared there would be no reaction.

Anne had no concern of Mark having another woman because if he did, she could win over another woman. But indifference was something she could not challenge. She attempted to deny the confirmation of indifference, while the signals seared at her stomach.

Maybe she could make him jealous by paying attention to Sergey and Nikolay. If she failed in making Mark jealous, at least her attempt would be patriotic.

"There was a party tonight," Anne told Jeffrey Stempka, over the phone. Her voice was filled with excitement. "It was given by the Nigerian delegation. Sergey and Nikolay were there. I walked them out to their limousine. Sergey asked me if I still see Ted Murphy. Do you get that? Still see Ted Murphy! I asked him how he knew that I ever saw Ted Murphy, and he laughed and said he guessed. It was his way of telling me he saw the pictures or at least knew about–you know–without putting it into words. I think he was telling me he had one on me, and I better be accommodating to him. He never saw me so friendly as I became. Then he asked me if I would help him. I didn't find out who his 'sleepers' are, but he recruited me as a 'sleeper.' He almost sounded like you–he said to be observant–except, unlike you, he offered me something in return."

"Where are you calling me from?"

"A phone booth."

"What did he offer you?"

"Fifty thousand dollars."

After a pause, Jeffrey Stempka asked. "What did you say?"

"I acted as though I cared about the money. You should have seen my eyes! I was good! I said I needed money, but it would depend on what he wanted me to find out–through observation."

"Good! Good! Did he tell you?"

"He wanted to know if I knew, or could find out, what we planned on doing about the airport that's being built in Grenada by the Cubans. He wanted to know if we were going to bomb it, or if we were planning to stage a coup. He was not very kind to Reagan. He said Reagan wants a nuclear war, and the Soviets want peace, and all that."

"What did you say?"

"Seventy-five thousand dollars."

Jeffrey Stempka laughed. "What did he say?"

"He said it was too much."

"And what did you say?"

"I said seventy-thousand dollars and in addition, I wanted his promise to never mention anything about Ted Murphy and me. I said it was my final offer."

"What did he say?"

"He kissed me."

Jeffrey Stempka was silent again, and then asked, "And then what?"

"I can't tell you, Mr. Stempka. But we have a deal."

"Was Nikolay there when you discussed all this with Sergey?"

"Right next to him. The three of us were standing outside their limousine."

"Did Nikolay say anything during all this?"

"Nothing. But he did kiss me between kisses from Sergey. That was before the three of us got in the back seat of the limousine."

There was no response.

"Mr. Stempka? Are you there?"

"I see."

"You see?"

"Did you drive anywhere?"

"Oh, no. Mr. Stempka. What do I do now?"

"Nothing. Do nothing."

"They'll contact me. What do I say?"

"Say you're finding out the information. That's all. Say you're finding it out. Avoid seeing them. Catch a cold or something. We'll see that the period of time you have to stay away doesn't last too long."

"I can't tell Mark?"

"No! No! You can't get him involved in any way. You know that."

"All right."

"You can't tell anyone. That's what security is all about."

"I promise. I'll be good. But I have to think of a reason for not going to parties with Mark."

"It won't be long."

"I'm making it more difficult than it is. He doesn't ask me that often."

Two weeks later, Sergey and Nikolay were expelled from the United States. Under guards from the F.B.I. they were escorted to John F. Kennedy International Airport and seen off on an Aeroflot flight to Moscow.

Anne wasn't a congresswoman, but she was the next best thing. At long last, she was a real spook.

SIXTY-TWO
YANKEE, GO HOME; YANKEE, PLEASE STAY
1983-1984

The U.S. invasion of Grenada brought demonstrators outside United Nations headquarters and Mark had a difficult time passing through them to get in. He was a beaten man, not by the demonstrators, but beaten by what his life had become since Anne's candidacy had ended. He and Anne were now living two separate lives held together by a chain of two rusting links: memories and legalities. A third link of hope had dropped somewhere out of sight. During the half-year between the expulsion of Sergey and Nikolay in April, and the invasion of Grenada in October, Mark and Anne became strangers.

On paper, they lived in a New York apartment. But Anne was there only for an occasional weekend. "Crossed Swords" had offered her a contract to be on air five days a week with part of the contract calling for the provision of an apartment in D.C. She had accepted.

It wasn't geography that was drawing them apart. New York and Washington, D.C. were closer than the distance between Athens and Teheran when they were their closest. Geography was a phony in providing distance between people, as it always is.

The demonstrators outside the United Nations headquarters held signs that read: "U.S. Out of Grenada," "Leave Caribbean Nations Alone," and someone who was way behind the times had a sign that said "U.S. Out of Vietnam." Just an old sign taken out of a garage somewhere.

Mark was greeted in his office by Charles Lichenstein, one of Jeane Kirkpatrick's chief delegates, whose weathered face looked grim. "Here we go again, Mark. Another day, another condemnation."

"Moscow condemning us?"

"Let's see. I've lost count of the governments that are writing their own versions of condemnation. Leading them is the Soviet Union and Cuba and Nicaragua and right behind is every one of the Group of 77. They're all saying, 'Yankee, Go Home.' Practically all we have with us are the eleven Caribbean nations who joined us in the invasion, who were begging us to take military action. Those are the members of the Organization of Eastern Caribbean States. But we don't have many other friends on this one."

"Give me the details, Chuck."

"We'll win. But on the down side is that there's a band of U.S. reporters waiting in Barbados in the hope of getting to Grenada, and they're fit to be tied because we won't let them get there. They don't understand why they weren't invited to the invasion. They think that wars are fought to be reported, not won."

"How many of the press are waiting?

"Between the ones already in Barbados and the ones en route, there must be somewhere over one hundred of them."

"Big names among them?"

"Yep."

"How angry are they?"

"If they get any angrier, we'll have to invade Barbados."

The palm trees were swaying, an afternoon rain was done, rum-loaded drinks were being poured into tall glasses, the sea was green, and the white beaches of the island-nation of Barbados were feeling the bare feet of the U.S. press corps. "This is a lot better than Afghanistan," Ted Murphy winked at the assemblage of eight of his peers wearing cut-off shorts and open sport-shirts and one had a straw hat. In their attempt to look like they belonged, they revealed they didn't. "I wonder if we could find some joker who would rent us a boat, any kind of boat, and take us to Grenada," Ted said. He was sitting crossed legged, while his friends were lying back on the sand with their eyes closed, each one of them with a satchel beside them.

"By the time we get there, the war will be over," a correspondent said, his face totally covered by his straw hat.

Ted nodded. "That's the order of Reagan and Company. I'll bet Reagan got the idea from Thatcher. She didn't let the press into her war in the Falklands and I'll just bet she told Ronnie that's how she won the war there. Kill 'em when no one's lookin'."

"Does anyone understand why we're in Grenada? Who ever even heard of it before all this?" It was a correspondent drinking a rum swizzle.

Ted was sure he understood. "I understand exactly why we're there. It's what's called a diversionary tactic. Invade Grenada and everyone forgets that we just lost over 200 marines in Lebanon. And I'll bet the count gets higher."

"What's this jazz Reagan's been saying about this invasion being a rescue operation of American kids in a medical school there?" the correspondent drinking a rum swizzle asked. "I thought it was over the airport they're building for military jets. Isn't that what Reagan was mad about?"

"It's all jazz," Ted answered. "It isn't about the airport. And he'd go in there even if there were no American kids in Grenada. The only person that he better rescue is Luis Angel Cajina. He's my great white hope. If we rescue him, I'm home free. Linda will divorce me and marry him and I'm out of there. No alimony, no nothin'."

The correspondent with the straw hat over his face laughed as he took his hat from over his face and put his forearm on the sand, lifting himself into a semi-seated position. "Who is he? A Grenadan?"

"A Nicaraguan. She doesn't know I know, and that's okay with me. I want her to spring it on me. But the bozo was a friend of Maurice Bishop. He helped Bishop stage the coup in Grenada back in '79. And I don't know what's goin' to happen to him—or what already happened to him. I just wish we knew what was goin' on, on that island."

"You think our troops will kill him?"

"I think the new government of Grenada will kill him. Maybe they already have. When they killed Bishop last week, they killed a bunch of his friends. The guy who led the coup was Bishop's own general of his People's Revolutionary Army."

"General Austin? Hudson Austin?"

"Yeah."

"I thought Reagan wanted to get rid of Bishop. You'd think he'd be thanking Austin for staging a coup, rather than invading Grenada to get rid of Austin."

"Austin's even closer to Moscow, Havana, and Managua than Bishop was. He thought Bishop was movin' too slow. He doesn't like the old friends of Bishop, so my wife's lover might be a dead duck."

"I never heard of anything like that!"

"What? One commie killing another commie? Happens all the time. It was the history of Afghanistan's leaders. Daoud. Boom. Dead. Taraki. Boom. Dead. Amin. Boom. Dead."

"That isn't what I'm talking about. I'm talking about you—hoping your wife's lover is safe. I never heard of anything like that."

"It's my free pass. He's rich. He's a big man in Managua, and in Havana, and he's a buddy of Arafat. He's got more money than Ben Bradlee and Bill Paley and all of us put together. She'll leave me alone if they get married."

"I just never heard of anything like that."

"That's because you're too young to understand."

"And how about your son?"

"He's fine. He'll be okay. He's a big boy."

"You'll still have to pay child support, you know."

"Nah! No mas! Tommy's eighteen years old and out of the house. He's livin' with a doll."

"So let me get this straight. You want Linda to tell you she wants a divorce and wants to marry this guy?"

"You got it. I'll cry and all that. Y'know. I'll make it look like I'm sad and all that and tell her I'll give her anything she wants and all that jazz. And she'll feel guilty and say she doesn't want anything—because she won't need anything when she has Cajina. So I'll cry some more and beg her to stay with me and then, in the end, I'll give in and tell her I hope she has a happy life. Cajina's my boy! I love 'im!"

"You really got this thing down pat," the correspondent with the straw hat said as he lit a cigarette.

"I just hope the son of a gun is alive! I'll rescue him, myself, if I can get to Grenada! Hey—watcha smokin'?"

"A Camel. Want one?"

"A Camel? I got my own stuff." Ted took a small plastic envelope and a packet of thin paper from the sack next to him. He lifted out one of the thin papers. Ted started to pour some of the contents of the envelope onto one of the thin papers. He said, "If Cajina's okay, I'll be on a high for the rest of my life!"

On the day of the end of hostilities in Grenada, eight days after the invasion began, Ted Murphy was one of four members of the press testifying to the House Subcommittee on Civil Liberties. It was 9:30 A.M. on November the Second in Room 2141 of the Rayburn House Office Building in Washington, D.C. Facing the Subcommittee, while seated in a row behind a long table with a green covering and four microphones, was Ted Murphy, Edward Joyce, who was the president of CBS News, John Chancellor, who was a Senior Commentator of NBC News, and David Brinkley, who was a Senior Correspondent of ABC News.

Presiding was the chairman of the cubcommittee, Congressman Robert M. Kastenmeier. "Mr. Joyce, we are most pleased to have the benefit of your testimony this morning. Mr. Joyce, you may proceed."

Ed Joyce leaned in to the microphone in front of him. "Whatever the rationale, the public, which received firsthand information from the press in Vietnam, Korea and in World War II, was denied firsthand reporting from Grenada. I submit that is intolerable. I want to emphasize that the American press is a responsible press. We are not seeking to report military secrets. We are not seeking to jeopardize lives. But those interests could have been protected without resorting to the unprecedented censorship that the president imposed in Grenada....

"One CBS News correspondent was told by two colonels at the Pentagon that, 'We learned a lesson from the British in the Falklands.' Well, that lesson was censorship. CBS News protested that action in a letter to the Secretary of Defense on October 25. There has been no reply.

"On the third day of the invasion, the Pentagon began to release its own film, which clearly represented what the Government wanted the public to see and believe. It may have been an accurate portrayal. Without the presence in Grenada of a free and independent press, America will never really know.

"When the press was finally admitted to Grenada, for several days it was compelled to operate in the most limited and restricted fashion. We saw what our Government wanted us to see, when our Government wanted us to see it, for as long as our Government deemed appropriate. It was not until the sixth day of the invasion that the press was allowed to cover Grenada in a more meaningful fashion.

"We at CBS News are concerned, frustrated, and saddened by the press restrictions of the past week. We are concerned by the repressive actions of the government toward the press. We are frustrated because we were not able to do the reporting job the public expects of us and we expect of ourselves. And we are saddened to bear witness to this new, unchecked censorship leading to an off-the-record war.

"Thank you, Mr. Chairman."

"Thank you, Mr. Joyce. Mr. Chancellor?"

John Chancellor nodded. "There are American troops in combat, fighting against Cubans, putting Russians into custody—and not a single member of the American press allowed to observe.

"The government is doing whatever it wants to in Grenada without any representative of the American public watching what it's doing. No stories in your newspapers or magazines; no pictures in your living room....

"In Grenada, the Reagan administration has produced a bureaucrat's dream: do anything, no one is watching....

"It doesn't consult the Congress, only informed it, and it ducked the serious parts of the War Powers Act....

"The Secretary of Defense explains American casualties in Grenada by saying, 'The price of freedom is high.'

"What freedom? The freedom of the American people to know what their government is doing?

"This Administration clearly doesn't believe in that.... We are told that the decision to keep the press out was a purely military decision. That is hard to believe. There is a long and honorable tradition of cooperation between the American military and the American press. Never before has the press been excluded from a military operation of this size. The decision to keep the reporters away got into the area of politics. If there is one thing sure about life in America it is that the military doesn't make political decisions on its own....

"Thank you."

"Thank you, Mr. Chancellor. And now David Brinkley."

"Mr. Chairman and members of the committee, speaking for ABC News, I would like to thank you for allowing us to appear....

"Reporters could have been taken ashore an hour or so after the operation began and when it was no longer a secret....

"We place great responsibility upon our military leaders and demand of them a very high level of performance in difficult circumstances. And in that light, their attitude may, to some extent, be understandable. But in my view, it is still bad policy, since any military operation is carried on in behalf of the American people. And if military leaders are to have, as they must have, the support of the American people then they must know what it is they are asked to support.

"There is nowhere they can learn that but from us. And they cannot learn it from us if we are not allowed to go there....

"Thank you."

"Thank you, Mr. Brinkley. Mr. Murphy?"

"Thank you, Mr. Chairman." He was in his public mode, and the microphone made him automatically lose the accent of the streets that he used at more candid times. "I would like the committee to re-read the First Amendment which guarantees freedom of the press. How can the press be free when it is shackled to the island of Barbados as U.S. forces invade Grenada? Walter Cronkite said, 'Now we will never know what happened in those first three days.' Those three days are now over, but our purpose in being here is to see there are never three more days like those. The First Amendment is the guiding light under which the American people live and this administration, the Reagan administration, has walked all over the First Amendment to impose its military might wherever it wants to seize control. The Administration is saying it had to rescue American students at St. George's University Medical School on the island. That is absurd. Those students were not in danger. U.S. troops seized the government of Grenada and lives were lost because Grenada's government was not one that pleased Ronald Reagan. His experiences in the make-believe world of Hollywood have become reality in the hard consequences of the real world since he came to Washington, D.C.

"Thank you, Mr. Chairman."

"Thank you, Mr. Murphy. The chair would now like to yield to the gentleman from California, Mr. Moorhead."

"Thank you, Mr. Chairman," Congressman Moorehead said. "Usually we have opening statements on both sides in this kind of hearing. I must admit that I find it more than a bit alarming that we are meeting this morning to discuss, in part, freedom of the press and sharing of information, and yet it was not until yesterday morning that we in the minority found out that there was going to be such a hearing stressing the Reagan Administration's handling of press coverage in Grenada...."

Ted Murphy quickly leaned into the desk microphone. "Well, Mr. Congressman, we will have plenty of the other side. In fact all the public has been getting is the other side. And the other side will continue to be well represented. Tonight I will be in a televised debate with Anne Whitney on 'Crossed Swords' where you can bet the nation will hear both sides."

Congressman Moorehead shook his head. "No need to advertise, Mr. Murphy. I'm talking about having the other side in these hearings. Let me present some facts for your comment: This was a rescue mission utilizing commando tactics against an enemy that wore civilian clothes and drove civilian vehicles. There was no clear battle line. In other rescue missions in recent memory, such as the Israeli raid on Entebbe and the attempted Carter rescue mission in Iran, the need for secrecy was recognized as paramount. And the press was excluded. Yet the American public was provided a full accounting of the events after the need for secrecy had passed. By denying access to the press, the American commander on Grenada ensured the safety of his men and the people he was sent to rescue. We are all aware that the first amendment to the Constitution recognizes the right of free speech and the right of the press to print anything it wants. However, there seems to be some who fail to recognize that it does not guarantee access to information which would jeopardize the safety of Americans....In World War II, you had a system of war correspondents who actually wore uniforms, were given the courtesy rank of an officer, and were subjected to censorship."

Ted Murphy gave a smile. "Well, when it came to Grenada, we were certainly subjected to censorship, Mr. Congressman, but we weren't given uniforms or given ranks of officers!"

Ed Joyce of CBS was nodding. "If I could add to that, I think there are a host of questions for which we do not have independently verifiable answers, such as who fired first. The Cubans are saying that they gave word to their troops not to fire first. How stiff was the Cuban opposition? Over 600 prisoners out of a total fighting force of between 700 and 800 does not give the impression of having fought to the last man. What happened to the Grenadan Army? There are no reporters who can really answer that for us."

"Mr. Congressman," Ted Murphy added, "A very good friend of mine was killed in Grenada. I don't know who killed him. I have my suspicions but I don't know who did it. How can I find out now?"

"A journalist?" Congressman Moorehead asked.

"No sir, a friend."

"An American?"

"No, sir."

"A Grenadan?"

"No, sir."

"A Cuban?"

"A Nicaraguan."

Congressman Glickman said, "I'm sorry for the loss of your friend. Let me ask; in any of the modern memory of the folks sitting at the table today, have the media ever been restricted before in the same way that you are restricted in Grenada?"

All four of the representatives of the media were shaking their heads. "Not to my knowledge," David Brinkley said.

Ed Joyce agreed. "Not to my knowledge. I can't recall exclusion from a total area of conflict."

Ted Murphy said, "Never."

John Chancellor added, "I think the answer is that the United States sent a task force of 15,000 people to invade a sovereign country. No military operation of that size, in my experience and in my reading of American history, has ever been done without the accompaniment of the American press."

Congressman Glickman nodded. "Okay, one final question. The Secretary of Defense and others seem to imply that there is some danger in taking the press into their confidence. Is there any such danger?"

Again there was a row of shaking heads. David Brinkley said, "There is nothing in the record to suggest it, Congressman. As I have said, in military operations in the past, including many a great deal bigger than this, the press has been taken into the military's confidence in advance, and there have been no leaks."

John Chancellor had something to add: "In the last year or two we have seen three of the world's most notable democracies bottle up information going to their people. The Israelis, one of the world's most respected democracies, in their invasion of Lebanon, used political censorship early in that conflict. The British, the mother of Parliaments, used political censorship and actually deliberately misled its own pool reporters, the British reporters, in the invasion of the Falklands. That was censorship. And now we find in a major and historic moment in American history, the press was denied access when it was most needed by the United States..."

Ted Murphy was nodding. "The public can only win when it knows what's going on. Otherwise the public loses. Now, I'm not saying that the public always likes what it hears. In fact, candidly, my mail is running against me. John here, John Chancellor, gave a commentary the night before last—Monday—pretty much what he's saying here, and he told me his mail is running eight to one against him."

Congressman Sawyer picked up on that. "Well, having listened to Mr. Chancellor's diatribe on Monday night, I am delighted to hear that your mail is running eight to one against you." There was laughter in the committee room. The congressman continued, "Now I am not a letter-writer, but I came awfully close to writing one on that, and it is refreshing that the public responds well.

"We didn't have any media along on the Iranian rescue attempt, did we?"

John Chancellor shook his head. "No, sir; but the fact is that the press did not complain that it wasn't asked on that mission. That is a very key point."

"Well, that was a rescue mission, wasn't it?"

"That is right."

"And that is what the Administration says that this was as far as the students were concerned. I mean, you may disagree with that, but that was their position on it, as I understand it."

David Brinkley added, "Well, the Iranian rescue attempt was very small and brief. It was all over in a few hours."

"Well, that is because it was bungled."

"Well, okay," David Brinkley agreed.

"It may have been quite an extended operation if it had not run into the disaster."

"But it was small," Brinkley added.

Ed Joyce felt he should explain it better to Congressman Sawyer than David Brinkley was doing. "I don't think, sir, with all respect, it was projected as an extended mission. I don't think there was any thought of holding Teheran or holding a section of Teheran."

"Is it the size that governs, then, whether the media ought to be present or not?"

"I think a number of us did make the point that none of us sitting here today is saying that there cannot be secrecy, but that we object to a concept of military secrecy."

"But where is the size cutoff? I mean, how big a group, before all of a sudden you need the media, and how small a one so that you don't need them?"

David Brinkley answered. "I don't think it is a question of size, Congressman."

"Well, I thought that was the point somebody made, that the Iranian thing was small."

Ed Joyce said, "Small and of short duration."

Chairman Kastenmier looked to both sides and when he saw there were no more questions, he looked at the witnesses and said, "I would like to thank you, Mr. Joyce, Mr. Chancellor, Mr. Brinkley, and Mr. Murphy, for your contributions today. The committee is indebted to you. Thank you very much. And Mr. Murphy, we'll be watching you tonight for your appearance on 'Crossed Swords' where you promise a representation of both sides!"

"Thank you, sir," Ted Murphy was smiling.

Anne Daschle wasn't smiling. When she called Mark and told him she would be debating Ted Murphy, there was no level of understanding. Mark was pained and angry. She explained that for once, Ted Murphy was a newsmaker who testified on Capitol Hill rather than simply a journalist, so this was a once-only engagement. Mark asked her not to do it. But Anne had the strength to push his reaction into a corner of her brain and let it sleep there, so she could make her television appearance without conscience.

Ted repeated on "Crossed Swords" what he had said to the committee about the importance of the First Amendment and he added, "We have to live by that, and as journalists, we are the custodians of the First Amendment and the people's right to know."

"Get off it, Ted," Anne said. "Don't act as though journalists are a ragtag band of pipe, flute, and drum players. I'm sorry to reveal this, but journalists do not work as non-profit philanthropists to keep the nation informed. Nor would you do it without pay, Ted. From your testimony this morning the public is led to believe you are pathetic public servants who volunteered to sacrifice yourselves so as to champion our constitutional rights in the quest of information for our 'misinformed citizenry'. I wish I heard someone this morning at the Congressional Subcommittee Hearings tell the truth and say, 'Look, I get paid for what I do. It's a terrific job, and the more information I can get the better I can do my job. If I do it good enough, I can even get a raise.' That would be honest. No one should believe that you or other journalists would be hitting the beaches of Grenada with crews and cameras and notepads in hand, for free. You're not public volunteers locked in a dreaded career. When contract negotiations are going on between you and management, the words, 'First Amendment' and 'The People's Right to Know' don't come up, do they? You know very well that those words would be greeted with laughter. I've been in those rooms and what comes up is how much your salary will be, how long it will be paid, what authority you'll have, the minimum amount of raises that will be given between the signing of the contract and its expiration date, and what perquisites–frills–go with the salary. Usually an agent or manager enters the picture and gets a cut. Nothing wrong in all that. It's fine. But there's no reference to the Constitution! Don't give us this stuff about you being the great representatives of the people, Mr. Murphy!"

"Nothing wrong in what you said, Annie. Sure, I get paid. The journalists during World War II got paid, too. But they were trusted. They were with our troops throughout the entire war. No one told them to be quiet! Reagan simply isn't FDR."

"But during World War II the military didn't have to worry that some of the U.S. journalists might be on the side of Hitler."

"What are you talking about?"

"The modern journalists are either neutral or, more often, on the side of whomever is fighting against the United States. You know that. During World War II, American journalists were on our side and wouldn't reveal information that could endanger the GI's as they were called. There's only one purpose of a nation at war: to win. And to win with as little loss of life as possible."

"Do you think we in the media would endanger our troops? We work for the public's right to know, and if I can quote Walter Cronkite –"

"Don't bother. I heard you quote him this morning. He said that we'll never know what happened in the first three days of the invasion. That was the ultimate of arrogance! Does he think the Grenadans can't talk? They were there! You don't have to have a press-card to talk! Go ask them what happened! Do you think everyone there is dead?"

"Annie, you have to be a trained journalist if you want to dig for information. That's what we do. What do you want? A country where the government tells you what's going on, and you just have to take it because you don't have any independent source?"

"Aren't you listening? So go there and talk to the Grenadans. I want a responsible press, and recently too many in the national press corps feel that they should be the ones to make the decisions on what should and shouldn't be kept secret. The Code of Ethics and Restraint, if you can even call it that anymore, no way resembles what it used to be. There are three sides to this: the side of those in government who say 'No press at the outset of a military engagement,' there's your side that says, 'We should be there because of the people's right to know,' and there's a third side. That's the side of those in the armed forces whose lives are at risk. Do they want their commanding officers to be in charge of worldwide knowledge of what could or could not put them in jeopardy, or do they want the press corps to be in charge of that? It's a reasonable question."

"They want to know what they're fighting for, and if you ask me, they'd rather be fighting for the people's right to know than they would for the government's demand to keep it quiet!"

"How do you know? I didn't see you in the armed forces. Weren't you about the right age during Korea?"

"Dirty pool, Annie. I was a beginning journalist. But I suppose you'd rather there wouldn't be any."

"The president is the Commander in Chief. He has the duty to protect those Americans fighting in combat. I would hope that duty is never overridden by those who are unelected."

"I would hope a free press is never overridden."

"Just remember, Ted Murphy, when you pat yourself on the back for the testimony you gave this morning, just remember those who were not giving testimony: the imprisoned people of Vietnam, Cambodia, Laos, Angola, Iran, and Nicaragua, who wished that much of the press had stayed home in earlier years. Ted, there will be free elections in Grenada now. Did you see the pictures of the graffiti the Grenadans are writing on the walls? They're writing, 'God Bless U.S.', 'Long Live U.S.', 'Thank You, Reagan', 'Yankee, Please Stay.' You people in the media showed no anger at liberty lost, but great anger in liberty restored."

Mark didn't watch her that evening. He didn't even want to think about the show on television. While she was debating, he was saying a quick goodnight to the guard at the USUN and then he walked to a street that was getting to know him.

In Washington, Anne went back to her empty apartment.

Ted Murphy wished he went to an empty apartment. He went home to Linda. She was in secret mourning over the death of Luis Angel Cajina. Ted was also in secret mourning over the death of Luis Angel Cajina. They both had to hide their mournings from each other, neither one saying one word that would tell the other of their sadness that Luis Angel Cajina was no more.

"Yuri Andropov is no more," President Reagan said to the staff that assembled in the Roosevelt Room. "He's dead. You know," and he cocked his head, and gave it a slow shake back and forth. "I'd go to a summit but their presidents keep dying."

President Reagan walked across the hall back to the Oval Office, leaving his senior staff to work out the details.

"Send Bush," the man who always wanted Vice President Bush to go to funerals, said. "He did just fine at Brezhnev's funeral. Now he'll know everybody there."

National Security Advisor Bud McFarlane said with his usual calm, "This time Chernenko will probably make it. Who else is there?"

"We'll have to wait and see," the man who always looked confused said.

"We need a great statement. Someone get hold of Khachigian," the man who always wanted a great statement, said.

"All we have to do is fiddle around with the Brezhnev statement. That was good."

"No. No. You can't do that."

"I can't wait to hear Bush's reaction when he finds out!"

SIXTY-THREE
AFTER THE NINTH LIFE
1985

It was not just Leonid Brezhnev, Maurice Bishop, Luis Angel Cajina, and Yuri Andropov who were no more. In January of 1985, it was Sally Saigon.

Unlike Leonid Brezhnev, Maurice Bishop, Luis Angel Cajina, and Yuri Andropov, there was no evil in the little cat who had been a political refugee. There was nothing but innocence in her.

For a cat, seventeen years was a long life, and in those seventeen years she had seen more history first-hand than most cats who lived their full nine lives or, for that matter, more than most humans had seen, no matter the amount of years lived.

Jonas was shattered. On Wednesday, January the 16th, he took her small, furry remains to the Los Angeles Pet Memorial Park in Calabasas, where he had picked a site on top of one of its grassy hills, and he gave her an Islamic service and entombment.

For Jonas, the world was now a different place. After days of hesitation, he put Sally Saigon's milk bowl and scratching pads and blankets and balls and toys in the closet. He couldn't throw them away. He would keep her favorite toy where she left it against the wall in the living room: a thoroughly ripped-apart hand puppet of Krazy Kat that she had batted all over the place. She had knocked it there the morning of the day she was to die.

That was while Jonas was on the phone, talking to Bud McFarlane, the national security advisor of President Reagan, with Jonas suggesting to him that the president introduce a new name for the Strategic Defense Initiative. "In his second inaugural, the president should call it the Space Shield," Jonas said. "Maybe if he gives it that good short-hand name, they'll stop calling it Star Wars."

"How about Security Shield?"

"No. Space Shield."

"You don't like Security Shield?"

"It's better than Strategic Defense Initiative. But Space Shield would be the best."

"Want to come here to that inaugural, General? I know the president would like to have you here."

Jonas hesitated. "Thanks. He'll have enough people there, I'm sure. Let me pass on that, Bud. I try to stay out of D.C."

Then he looked over at Sally Saigon who was motionless. She was often motionless, but in one second, he knew. He quickly ended the phone call and went to her lifeless body.

The weather of Washington, D.C. was so freezing cold on Monday, January 21, that the president canceled the parade, and the inaugural ceremonies for his second inaugural were moved from outside the U.S. Capitol Building to inside, beneath the dome of the Rotunda.

"I have approved a research program to find, if we can," the president said, "a Security Shield that will destroy nuclear missiles before they reach their target. It wouldn't kill people, it would destroy weapons. It wouldn't militarize space, it would demilitarize the arsenals of Earth. It would render nuclear weapons obsolete."

Anne was one of the one thousand guests allowed into the Rotunda to witness the proceedings. Twenty-four years ago, on President Kennedy's inauguration day, she had no possibility of receiving an invitation to an inaugural. She was a rebellious bureaucrat hoping to meet with Ambassador Gerald Fairbanks that night to seek his advice. Now she was a celebrity in her public life, the defeated candidate for Congress who had risen to prominence as a television debater on "Crossed Swords," while in private life she was the defeated wife, planning a divorce.

"One people under God," the president concluded, "dedicated to the dream of freedom that He has placed in the human heart, called upon now to pass that dream on to a waiting and a hopeful world."

And there was applause, and then people went to afternoon parties and prepared for evening balls in the cold.

Anne was walking toward the east door of the Capitol while putting on her coat, when she felt its collar being raised slightly so her arms could easily find the arms of the coat. Anne turned around quickly and saw that her helper was the man with the braid. She gave a wide smile. "Mr. Stempka!"

"May I talk with you?"

Instead of going outside, they walked over to the quiet area by the statue of Will Rogers in the Capitol Building's Statuary Hall. Jeffrey Stempka wasted no time with small talk. "Are you getting a divorce?"

Anne was surprised. "Is this a question for official purposes?"

He tightened his lips together, then shook his head. "No."

"Is it personal?" Anne couldn't help but give a flirtatious smile. It was part of her nature. She had to.

"Not really, Ms. Whitney. It's that you ought to know some things that–that you ought to know."

"I ought to know what I ought to know?"

"There are things you should know. That's what I meant to say."

"Do I fluster you?"

"Perhaps. I don't like talking about this in public."

"You can come over to my apartment. That's where I'm going. Give me an hour, and then come by." She looked at her watch. "Two o'clock okay?"

"Where is it?"

"You mean you don't know? I expect you to know those things."

He admitted it. "Columbia Plaza. Ambassador Building. Ninth Floor. The west end of the hall. A-903."

Anne nodded. "That's what I would expect."

At two o'clock, Jeffrey Stempka walked down the west end of the hall on the ninth floor of the Ambassador Building in Columbia Plaza, and he pushed the black button on the door beneath the magnification viewer.

She opened the door. She had changed into a bathrobe. "Sorry. I just got out of the shower."

"It's beautiful," he said.

"What?"

"The apartment. The furniture."

Anne shrugged. "The station took care of it all. I get all this for being on 'Crossed Swords.' Sit down."

It was a large living room, with modern furnishings and paintings and a wall-length south window between the room and an outside balcony. To the left of the entrance to the apartment was the kitchen and across from the living room was a small hallway to the bathroom and bedroom.

She had the place prepared. On the coffee table in front of the sofa were two glasses of red wine, and a bottle of the rest of it waiting between the two glasses.

"Sit down on the couch, Mr. Stempka," she said again.

He did, but she didn't. She looked down at him as she stood between him and the coffee table, so close to him there was little room for her to hand him the glass of wine, but she accomplished it.

"Will you sit down too, Mrs. Daschle?" He was giving her the Mrs. Daschle treatment again.

She let it go. "I prefer to stand."

"It makes it a little awkward to talk this way, Mrs. Daschle."

"That depends on the subject we talk about, doesn't it?"

"I need to talk to you about something serious."

"You are such a boy, Mr. Stempka. You are such a boy. I like boys. When I was a girl I liked men. Now I'm a woman and I like boys. I'm tired of men. They have no stamina. They think too much. Boys don't think too much. I'll bet you have great stamina."

"I'm not a boy."

"Oh, yes you are."

"Mrs. Daschle, this is awkward."

"Why don't you be quiet, and just look. Mr. Stempka, don't lie to me. I can see that you enjoy looking."

Jeffrey Stempka was trained to resist. He stood up. Now his eyes were free. "I have something important to talk to you about."

Feeling rejection was becoming Anne's habit. She nodded. "Sit back down. I will, too," she said as a statement of concession.

He sat and she sat next to him, but not too close. She lifted her wine glass for a toast. "To a serious conversation." She wanted to retain her frivolity so as not to reveal her hurt.

He nodded, and lifted his glass. "Mrs. Daschle, do you know what a false-flag operation is?"

"No. What is it? You've become my teacher in spookism."

"It means you cast the impression you're working for one government, but you're working for another. It's used by intelligence services of any country. Let us say the Soviets suspect some Muscovite of being a spy for us. So they establish a false-flag operation. They assign one of their KGB agents to act as though he's CIA, and he offers the suspect some money for some Soviet secrets. You'd be surprised how often it's worked. Or, let's say we set up a false-flag operation here, suspecting someone, we'll say, of working for the Soviets. And so we have one of our own operatives pose as a Soviet agent and he offers that someone some money or something else of value, in return for some U.S. secrets. You see?"

"Yes. You give him bait. If he takes it, you've got your man." She was talking with resignation, still hurt at her failure to entice.

"That's right. Now, if he takes that bait and then comes to us to tell us about it, it's something else again. But he must come to us either way, whether that person accommodates or doesn't accommodate. Remember how you came to us with the information about Sergey and Nikolay? There was no need for a false-flag operation to be put on you."

"But even if you did, could Sergey and Nikolay have been a false flag operation for us?"

"They could have been. But they weren't. Sergey and Nikolay were the real things, as you know. And your loyalty is unquestioned. But sometimes there are people who will spy for anyone—if the price is right. They'll spy for Americans, they'll spy for the Soviets, they'll spy for anyone. Soldiers of fortune without uniforms or guns."

"Why are you telling me all this?"

"Because we established a false-flag operation on your husband."

Anne's mouth was open. She shook her head. "On Mark?"

"Yes."

"—And?"

"Mrs. Daschle, do you know where your husband is right now?"

She shook her head.

"He's in Geneva."

"Oh?"

"He didn't tell you?"

"We haven't talked recently." Anne's words were untypically very slow. "He goes back and forth to Geneva often. There's always some U.N. conference going on there on something. What's that got to do with it?"

"He isn't scheduled to attend a U.N. conference. He isn't going to be in Geneva long."

Again, a silence and then a slow, "What do you mean?"

"He's coming back to the United States. Maybe he's en route now. We have some men from the Bureau taking him back. He should be escorted back from Geneva on a plane from there to Dulles."

Anne was shaking her head. "I can't believe that! Mark would never do anything against this country! There has to be a mistake–a terrible, tragic mistake!"

Jeffrey nodded. "I'm not saying he did a thing against this country. Mrs. Daschle, your husband came to us a long time ago with information on Soviet, Ukrainian, and Byelorussian staff members at the U.N. who were after our security information. We told him not to turn them off, we told him what to give them so that he could get further information from them. In short, he posed as an informer. It was very dicey because he's U.S.I.A.. You know our policy. But there was no choice. He had information we needed. They gave him money, and at our instructions, he opened an account for himself in Geneva where he deposited the money he received from them. He reported to us continually. He was invaluable. In truth, with the help of Mr. Daschle, we now have enough information to prove a lot of those Soviet, Ukrainian and Byelorussian staff members are espionage agents. By a lot, I mean more than one hundred.

"But something happened simultaneous with all that. You came to us with those pictures–the pictures that had been taken in 1969 in Ambassador Beam's office in Moscow–the pictures with you and Mr. Murphy. There was only one set of fingerprints on them, other than yours. Mr. Daschle had handled all of those pictures."

"He saw them!?"

"Yes. All of them. It was why I pressed you to tell me if, perhaps, you had showed them to him."

"I didn't."

"Or he found them."

"He couldn't have."

"If all that is true, and we have no reason to doubt it, that means he reviewed them when someone else showed them to him before you received them–undoubtedly some Soviet agent at the U.N. who had cleaned the pictures of any prints prior to showing them to Mr. Daschle. We assume he was being blackmailed in the hope he would get you out of your Congressional race. He, apparently, couldn't be blackmailed. So they sent the pictures to you, knowing his fingerprints were on them. They knew it would be enough to get you out of the race, no matter how you handled it. And if you came to us, we would know that Mr. Daschle saw the pictures. It all suggests that they wanted us to think he was an informer. The great difficulty in all this is that Mr. Daschle never came to us about those pictures, he never reported all this. That was probably to protect you–he didn't want to have that knowledge about you in the hands of the agency. That may be understandable, but not acceptable. That was very serious. Someone was attempting blackmail, Mr. Daschle knew who it was, and didn't tell us. That's when we tried a false flag on him. He didn't bite. That should make you feel good. But he didn't report that, either. And that's very serious."

"Why are you telling me all this?"

"Because this morning in Geneva, he told us to tell you anything and everything."

"He did?"

"He did. Everything. He said he couldn't tell you. He said, 'I want Anne to know everything that's going on. By the time I get home I want her to know everything you know and everything you think. He said he can't live with secrets from you anymore. He was very clear about that. He took out a pen and said he wanted to sign a statement giving us permission to tell you everything. Mrs. Daschle, we were glad he said that to us. We don't like having secrets from you. You've been very good to us."

"What else do you know?"

"He started seeing a member of the Soviet Delegation of the U.N."

"Who?"

"A woman."

For a while she said nothing. Then, just a short, "Oh?"

"She wasn't a false-flag. She was a Soviet. He bought her things. A lot of things. Jewelry, a watch, a coat, a good coat, a lot of expensive things. Apparently, they were having an—an—a fling. That combined with the pictures he saw but didn't tell us anything makes a messy situation. Naturally, we're a little concerned when he starts to see a woman from Moscow. That kind of a thing between a U.S. government official and a Soviet without telling us is suspect. He told us to tell you."

Anne felt limp.

"I'm sorry," Jeffrey Stempka said.

"Who is she? The woman."

"That's not important."

"It is to me."

"I don't know much about her."

"Is she pretty?"

"I don't know."

"You know. Is she young?"

"I don't know."

"Is she thin?"

"Thin!?"

"Yes."

"I never saw her. I don't know. I never asked."

"I don't blame him. We were—we started living like a brother and sister. I don't blame him for her. But—all this—the whole thing, the fact that she was a Soviet. That doesn't mean anything." Now her words were fast and loud. "Don't you see that doesn't mean anything? Believe me, he would never do anything against this country. He fell for some—some woman, that's all. This is a nightmare!"

"Is he going to go to prison?"

I don't think so but I don't know. To my knowledge there's the possibility he could be charged under Title 18, US Code, Section 794. That's used for espionage and conspiracy to commit espionage by passing classified CIA documents to agents of the KGB. But the circumstances do not necessarily indicate that, they do not conform to the usual. All of this is not my area of expertise, but from what I know, I believe he'll tell us everything he knows under interrogation and, as long as he does, there would be some leniency. After all, he has a very good record prior to all this. That isn't up to me however. It's out of my field entirely." Then Anne started crying and the crying turned into weeping and the weeping turned into uncontrollable sobs.

Jeffrey Stempka put his arm around her. "I'm sorry."

Through her tears, she looked up at his eyes. "You don't know him! Men are men. They fall for a pretty woman who knows how to do it."

There was no more said. They sat in that position, with her sobbing on and off for at least an hour, and then he fell asleep. She was in a wide-awake nightmare.

The sun had gone down while they remained motionless. Then there was a ringing of the phone. She ran into the kitchen to answer it.

Jeffrey Stempka wiped his eyes and walked into the bathroom. He turned on the light, opened the medicine cabinet, and couldn't find what he wanted there. He opened the cabinet under the sink. There was a bottle of Lavoris. He took a swig from it and spit it into the sink.

When he walked back in the dark living room, Anne was still on the phone. He could hear her final remarks. "I know. I believe you. I love you, honey."

She walked into the living room and there were tears in her eyes and on her cheeks.

Jeffrey Stempka was standing in the middle of the room. "Was it Mr. Daschle?"

She nodded. "They landed at Kennedy. New York, not here. Not at Dulles the way you said." It was a rather small victory. "And he doesn't want me to see him now. He doesn't want me to go there. He said he saw another woman, but that's all. That's all. He said he'll tell me everything later. I told him I believe him."

"Will you be all right, Mrs. Daschle?"

She almost screamed her answer. "No! No! I won't be all right!" And she sobbed and made fists and she punched their edges on his chest while she wept.

Hesitantly, he put his arms around her. "I'm sorry about all this, Mrs. Daschle. I'm truly sorry."

She was uncontrollable in her weeping. "This can't be happening! Why did you do this to him?"

"Mrs. Daschle—"

"Why did I come to you? Why did I ever come to you with something that happened a hundred years ago!?"

He said nothing.

"Why did I report the pictures? Why did I do that?"

"Because you couldn't do anything else. Because, Mrs. Daschle, you're an honorable woman."

"Honorable! It's because I gallivant around and flirt around and go to bed with—"

"It's because you are an honorable woman."

In her weeping she clutched his shoulders, her fingernails digging into them. "It's because I believed Ambassador Fairbanks!" Her voice was painfully slow again. "It's because of him!"

"Do you want to be alone, Mrs. Daschle?"

"Yes! Leave me alone!"

He tried walking from her but her hands still clutched his shoulders.

"Do you want me to leave?"

"No! Stay! I can't be alone!"

They stood standing there for minutes.

"No," she said softly. "I don't mean like that. I just can't be alone. Stay here, on the couch."

He nodded. "All right. I won't leave."

"Jeffrey Stempka is staying," she said as though she was giving a narrative. She walked in the small hallway that led to the bathroom and her bedroom. She went in her bedroom and closed the door.

As the night went on, Jeffrey Stempka lay on the couch in the living room, listening to the sound of her crying through the closed door.

He left before she awoke.

"General Valadovich is mad at us. He wanted it to be called Space Shield, not Security Shield," Bud McFarlane said at the Senior Staff Meeting. "Not that it makes much difference. The media are still calling it Star Wars."

The president stuck his head in the door. "Wait till you hear this one!" the president said with his head tilted, moving it from side to side. "You won't believe it. Chernenko is dead." The president shook his head even more and left the doorway.

Luckily, Vice President Bush was in Geneva at a U.N. Conference on African Famine Relief, already wearing the black suit which he had worn to the funerals of Brezhnev and Andropov, so he wouldn't have to have it sent from Washington.

There was little conversation about this at the senior staff meeting in the Roosevelt Room. They had been through it so many times that no one needed to say, "Send Bush," or "Get hold of Khachigian." The man who always looked confused didn't even look confused. Most of them just looked at each other and nodded.

"Right."

"I will."

But they were answering questions no one had asked.

And so the list of those who were no more, was increased; Leonid Brezhnev, Maurice Bishop, Luis Angel Cajina, Yuri Andropov, Sally Saigon, Konstantin Chernenko, and a breathing Mark Daschle who, despite his active vital signs, was a member of the group.

SIXTY-FOUR
DETENTE
1985

Anne didn't stop the divorce, she delayed it until Mark's troubles were settled. Then the divorce was accomplished with neither Anne nor Mark asking the other for anything. "I love him," Anne would say to anyone who asked, "but it just didn't work out. It's probably my fault. You know me–I have to get all involved in politics and causes, and I made things very rough for him. He took a chance marrying me, and he lost."

In view of Mark's career and accomplishments, the United States Government treated him with leniency. Before the revelations, he had played a significant role in gaining information that allowed National Security Advisor Bud McFarlane to make an unprecedented recommendation to the president. With a stack of evidence, Bud McFarlane proposed that some 170 staff members of the Soviet, Ukranian, and Byelorussian missions to the U.N., be sent home, as their continued presence would pose a risk to the national security of the United States. Although more confirmation was requested by the State Department, it was now just a matter of time until it would be done. Bud McFarlane vouched for the importance of those things Mark Daschle did to bring that about.

All the money Mark had banked in Geneva was unspent and given back to the agency, as expected. He answered every question to the satisfaction of his interrogators, and they had every reason to believe that he had given no information to any Soviet agent, even the woman from the U.N. The affection he had for her ended abruptly. Further, he took an early retirement from the U.S.I.A., an offer he made before it was demanded, a demand that was sure to come. Fortunately, the story of what brought about his end of service, did not leak.

Anne didn't know if President Reagan had been told the full story regarding Mark, but he and his staff seemed to go out of their way to be kind to her. Maybe it was just because of the President's sympathy for her due to the divorce, which was public news. She received a letter of thanks from the president after her televised debates in which she blasted the House of Representatives for rejecting $14 billion of nonmilitary aid to the Contras who were fighting the Sandinista Government of Nicaragua, and another letter from the president explaining why he disagreed with her on her opposition to arms talks with the Soviets, and she was an invited guest at the president's state dinner for King Hussein of Jordan. The president, himself, phoned her to give her "an advance" that "things look good" for "that Summit we've been hoping for" with Mikhail Gorbachev, "and we've agreed on Geneva."

"Is that public, Mister President?"

"It is now."

"Do you know when?"

"November. You've been so supportive on most things, and so influential on television and, you know, I wanted to give someone in the press this tip who just got a friendly divorce, and the only other candidate was Carl Bernstein. So you won."

Anne laughed. "Mr. President, may I ask you something?" Not the usual way to phrase a question to the president of the United States.

"Well," and he elongated that word, "Yes. Of course."

"Are you going to negotiate on arms in Geneva?"

"Well, we don't know yet, Anne. This is a get-to-know-each-other meeting and we don't have an agenda yet."

"I just want to mention that everyone says they want a mutual and verifiable treaty but–"

"That's right. You know, there's an old Russian proverb that I live by. It's *Doveryai no proveryai.* That means, 'Trust but verify!'"

"Yes, Mr. President but you can't verify. Their mobile missiles can be anywhere all ready to launch! They can be put under bridges, in tunnels in railroad cars, anywhere. It's not like the 1950s, '60s, even most of the '70s, now that they have so many mobile missiles that don't have to be launched from silos."

"We do have satellite photos, you know."

"But you can't have satellite photos that see under roofs. Right now, a satellite can see the roof of the White House, but it can't see what you're doing in there. You can't see in Gorbachev's bedroom!"

"I hope not! You have a good point, Anne."

"And one thing I want to point out, if I may. I know that if you don't sign an arms agreement, you're going to have to face some pretty harsh questions from the press. You and your staff knows that the press isn't going to condemn you for getting an arms agreement, but they will condemn you for walking away from one."

"You're so right."

"You see? A good press means enacting the kind of policies that the press endorses. I know they may say nice things about you as a man, but they're selective on what policies they'll endorse, and what policies they'll slaughter."

"I don't disagree with you. As much as they loathed President Nixon, and smeared him for his Supreme Court nominees, or his Cambodian incursion, or his proposed abolition of the Office of Economic Opportunity, they weren't adversarial at all or critical–they were complimentary when he enacted liberal policies–when it came to his trip to China, or his appropriations for the Arts and Humanities, or his proposed Family Assistance Plan."

"Or signing SALT I with President Brezhnev," Anne added. "You can look at any other recent administration the same way. It's policy. Wouldn't it be good, but it won't happen, but wouldn't it be good if the White House Press Corps dismissed its own political philosophy and became as adversarial toward a liberal decision of a president as it is toward those that are more conservative? The press, and in particular the White House press corps credits itself as being a watchdog. But is it a watchdog for all Americans, or only for those who share their political view?"

"Well, you're right there. And I'm not going to do anything for the purpose of getting a good press."

"It seems to me that Strategic Arms Treaties with the Soviet Union make us the first free nation in history to seek permission of an adversary before building weapons to defend ourselves from that adversary. So I just want you to know that I'm for any treaty with the Soviet Union as long as we give up nothing, and I'm opposed to any treaty with the Soviet Union that stipulates we give up anything."

"'*Doveryai no proveryai.* Trust but verify!'"

"Oh, Mr. President!"

The president's phone call inspired Anne to develop a plan that only she could devise: a plan that would make Mark proud.

"I don't want this reported, but President Reagan phoned me." she told the news director. "We had a long, long, long conversation. Take me off 'Crossed Swords' for a few days while the summit is being held, and let me do commentaries from Geneva for the news. I'm certain I'll have an inside track that you wouldn't be able to get from any reporter."

"Sold! You're on!"

"But do me a favor. Where are the major media going to stay?"

"The International Hilton. That's where most of the satellite feeds will originate."

"I don't want to stay there. Put me somewhere else. I want to be independent."

"Okay. We can do that."

"Find out where the Soviets are staying. That's where I want to be."

It was the Hotel Epsom. It was miserable. But she asked for it. It was small. It was old. Never renovated. There was one elevator, a very small elevator with those old-fashioned collapsing gate-grill doors that had to be opened and closed by sliding it from side to side, with the assumption that every passenger had experience as an elevator operator with a white glove in the 1940s.

And just as she requested, the Epsom was a hotel filled with Soviets. Somehow, they found, liked, and booked this antiquated building.

The first morning after the first night, there were all kinds of large-shaped envelopes that had been slipped under the door of her room. The envelopes contained invitations from both sides of the summit; invitations to receptions, meetings, speeches, briefings by National Security Advisor Bud McFarlane, briefings by Georgi Arbatov of the Soviet Communist Party Central Committee, news conferences with White House spokesman, Larry Speakes, and all kinds of things. Waking up to such a flurry of invitations under the door seemed to be more like being a delegate to a political convention in the United States than being a guest at a Summit in Switzerland.

There was one invitation more intriguing than all the others. In calligraphy that was so fancy it was almost unreadable, was a request for her to attend a party that night at 8:00 P.M. in a suite on the top floor of the hotel, with the invitation signed by Mr. Viktor Baskakov. Under his signature was the message, "This is meant to return your courtesy for inviting me to your film festival party sixteen years ago at the Rossia, and for the thoughtful gift of the Apollo button you gave me."

Surely in all this time, he could have learned to smile, but he didn't. His lips went straight from corner to corner. Surely in all this time, he could have had some cosmetic work done on his left eye or wear an eye-patch, but he didn't. It was looking upward while his right eye looked straight ahead at Anne. "We have followed your career since you left Moscow, and you have done very well for yourself. You are now quite a celebrity in your country, am I right?"

"I am the Queen of Sheba."

"I beg your pardon?"

"I am bigger than Stalin, Khrushchev, Brezhnev, Andropov, Chernenko, and Gorbachev put together."

Mr. Baskakov nodded. "Congratulations." Did he believe her? There was no sign that he didn't. But that was his style.

"And you, Mr. Baskakov. Are you still with the KGB?"

"I was never with the KGB. I am still in cultural affairs." A waiter holding a tray of drinks was walking by them through the crowd. Mr. Baskakov took two drinks from the tray. "Have some vodka, Miss Whitney."

"I'll take yours. You take mine. Switch them."

He pretended to look confused.

"It's my way of saying I don't have any trust in cultural affairs officers." She smiled.

He just wouldn't smile.

The room was crowded and musty and to make matters worse, a string quartet started playing.

It took only a short time before Anne was the seated center of a semicircle of vodka-drinking Soviets. There was concern of Anne as to who all these people were. She had enough experience to know they all had an affiliation of some sort with the KGB or they wouldn't be here, but there were the greater questions: who knew what about her? Who had seen the pictures, or knew of their existence? Who knew about the limousine incident with Sergey and Nikolay outside the New York party of the Nigerian delegation? Who knew she turned them in for their expulsion from the United States? Most of all, who knew about Mark's more recent troubles? Who knew she and Mark were divorced? She had been trained to assume they all knew everything about what she didn't want them to know. She was also trained to know that at an event like this, there was one among them who was the 'head spook.' She knew she could seek him out.

"It's so good to be here!" she said to the semi-circle of Soviet strangers. "A real summit!"

"Have you seen your president's son?" one of the men asked her.

"Ron, Jr.?"

"Yes. He's here, you know. He was with Sam Donaldson today."

"I haven't seen him. Not yet."

"He's at the Hotel de Bergues. You ought to contact him. Tell him we would like to meet him. He's a dancer, you know, and we have some dancers here."

"What are dancers doing here?"

"When we found out the president's son was coming, we thought it would be in his interest to have some dancers. We brought some members of the Bolshoi."

"I'll tell him when I see him."

"Tell me, Miss Whitney, what do you think the summit will bring?"

"Nothing. This is the fifteenth summit since they began in Teheran. Your leaders have never kept their word regarding anything that's been agreed and signed at summits. I'm talking about since Stalin went to them. So the only thing we can hope for is that our president keeps the cap on his pen, and comes back home with everything in his pockets that he had in them before this summit."

"Miss Whitney, a direct question. Does your president want peace?"

"Now, what do you think? Do you think I'm going to say he wants war? Yes, he wants peace. He wants to discuss arms control, regional issues, bilateral issues, and human rights. The problem is that he has those four topics with 26 subdivisions. It's too neat. It's our silly State Department. We come here with a list and your leader has a bulls-eye to aim for–only one objective. He wants us to stop the Strategic Defense Initiative."

"Star Wars! Why does Reagan insist on such space-strike weapons?"

"Because he wants your missiles to be as impotent as all of you." It was fun to no longer have to be a diplomat. It was even more fun to try and enrage them.

"Miss Whitney, your nation and our nation are the two great superpowers of the world. It is unfair for just one of us to have such a system to make war in space. We want peace on earth and peace in space."

"You have to admit, your nation is hardly a superpower industrially, hardly a superpower agriculturally, hardly a superpower economically, politically, spiritually, morally. What makes your nation a superpower is only your military with its nuclear weapons and missile delivery systems." Somewhere in the back of Anne's mind was something she heard from Jonas Valadovich when he said, "The greatest weapon in the world, bar none, is fear." The memory of that line pushed its way to the foreground of Anne's brain. "That's the legacy of Leonid Brezhnev," Anne said. "It's an investment in making others afraid. Since President Reagan made his commitment to the Strategic Defense Initiative, you see the possibility of losing your superpower status. If your ICBMs can't reach their targets, you'll become a third-rate, Third World nation. You'll go broke trying to keep up with the SDI, and you'll crumble under your own weight. Pufffff! There goes the C.C.C.P., there goes the Soviet Union!"

She had gone too far for most of them, just as she had planned. One of them walked away from her, followed by the others except for a short, fat man who stayed near her. She had been successful at the isolation of the one she sought.

"You have become a harsh critic, Miss Whitney," the 'head spook' said. "But I have to admit, as much as I find what you say untenable, you are charming."

"Am I?"

"I'm Nikolai Guzhenko. With Novosti."

"Yes, the news agency. Background and feature stories, right?"

"That's what we do at Novosti, but I am not a writer. I am an administrator." Fat chance. "Tell me, Miss Whitney, do you work directly for President Reagan?"

She looked at the ceiling, squinted her eyes, looked side to side, and then nodded. She was ready to lie. "How did you know that?"

"I didn't know. That's why I asked you."

"I don't know if you'd call it working for him, exactly. Ron and Nancy and I have been very close." She lied well.

"I want you to know I have great respect for him." No question about it, he had to be the 'head spook' of this group. "I never thought of him as a cowboy like some of my colleagues. They don't understand him. I think of him as a leader in the mold of FDR."

"Exactly!"

"Now, tell me if I'm right or wrong. I believe that he and Secretary Gorbachev have a great deal in common. We have here, two reasonable men who want the best for their people."

"You have it right."

"You know where I believe most of the trouble starts?"

"Where?"

"Not with your president or with Secretary Gorbachev. The trouble starts in your profession because you have a number of people who get on television and cause suspicion and mistrust. Sometimes your leaders are blamed for what independent journalists say. We have never understood how your leaders can permit such things. We have journalists, too, but they work in the interests of the people. Now tell me, what do you think of Peter Jennings and Tom Brokaw and Dan Rather? They are paid millions of dollars, aren't they? I mean is that fair to a talent like you who works as hard as they do, or even harder? You surely have the talent, but you cannot get the millions of dollars."

"That's because they bring in the ratings. They've all been around for a long time and have a certain star quality, so they have big audiences. That's capitalism. I'm a newcomer to all this. If I succeed, I'll get the millions, too."

"You are too kind. Isn't some of your lower status—compared to them that is—because you're a woman?"

"Barbara Walters is a woman. So is Jane Pauley. So is Diane Sawyer."

"Yes. That's right. You are a good defender of your system. I admire that. Now tell me, what do you think of what we might call the second tier of your television; Garrick Utley, Sam Donaldson, Ted Murphy?"

There it was. It was the question he had been leading to. In that one instant, she was sure that he knew everything, including what happened on the 1969 desk of Ambassador Beam and in the 1983 limousine of Sergey and Nikolay.

"I don't know Garrick and Sam well, but I know Ted Murphy–oh, very well! In fact I know him very, very well! In fact–do you know what I mean?"

"I'm afraid not."

"We've made love!"

He was astonished, with more astonishment coming.

"On the desk of Ambassador Beam! Jacob Beam was our ambassador when we did it. That was a while back, though. Sixteen years ago."

He was totally unprepared for this.

"Surely you've seen the pictures, haven't you?"

"The pictures?"

"The pictures your automatic camera shot in the Ambassador's office. They were good. Of course I was a lot younger then, but I've kept my figure pretty good, don't you think? I work out."

He slowly nodded.

"I'll send you a copy of the pictures if you give me your address."

He slowly shook his head. "I–uh, I–"

"They were wild pictures. That is, if you like that sort of thing, and I do. Don't you? Your government sent me prints but they waited so long after taking them! I was getting worried. I thought maybe they didn't turn out and they were embarrassed to tell me."

"I know nothing of all this."

"Aren't you the head spook in this group?"

"The what?"

"KGB. Aren't you the highest ranking KGB here?"

"I work for Novosti. I told you that."

"But that's just a cover. Look, I was stationed in Moscow. I know the way all that works. Now, do you want to know some secrets?"

"Secrets?"

"Yes. Don't you want to know our secrets? I'm close to Ron and Nancy. I don't want my wastebaskets gone through and all that. I'll just tell you and save your people the trouble, and save me the anger–unless you're not interested."

"I am not interested."

"Okay. Then what do you want to talk about?"

He was baffled by all this and didn't know how to respond.

"I'll go back to Baskakov, then. Maybe he wants to know some secrets. Then he can tell your superiors the secrets I tell him, and they'll wonder why he was so effective and you weren't. You'll love the Gulag!"

She started walking through the crowd looking for Mr. Baskakov while Nikolai Guzhenko was at a loss of what to do. He followed her for a few seconds and then stopped. She found Mr. Baskakov talking to two men about some Mexican diplomat who was murdered in Moscow. It was not a story of urgency to Anne. "Mr. Baskakov," she interrupted. "May I see you for a moment?"

"Yes. Pardon me, Mr. Tarasov. Pardon me, Grigori," and he moved aside with her. "Yes, Miss Whitney. What can I do for you?"

"I have three secrets to tell you, Mr. Baskakov."

"What is this?"

"I said I have three secrets to tell you."

"Secrets?" His eye was drilling through her.

"Yes. Three of them."

"What are they, Miss Whitney?"

"I don't want to tell you here. Let's get out of here."

"I can't leave the party. I'm the host."

"Let's go in the elevator and take a quick ride. It's the only place I can trust without observation or recordings or cameras. Don't you want credit?"

Once inside the small elevator, and after she pulled the grill sideways, she pressed the button for the ground floor.

"What is it you want to say?" Mr. Baskakov asked.

"You know I always say what I think, don't you?"

He nodded. "I am positive of that."

"Then listen to me. Mr. Baskakov. You're just like me in your own way. You are honest. I know where you're coming from and you know where I'm coming from. No con from either of us. Am I right?"

"On that you are right."

"Then let us hold the Elevator Summit."

"Very well."

"And as the world watches Reagan and Gorbachev, let us have a detente."

"I agree."

"It's my move. I told you I would tell you three secrets. Secret One is that Nikolai Guzhenko should be watched. I think he is a false-flag. Do you know what that is?"

"No, I don't."

"Well, maybe you call them something else. But false-flags give the impression that they're working for one government when, in fact, they're working for another government."

"And Nikolai is one of those?"

"I would check him out if I were you. I have reason to believe he's working for the Mossad of Israel."

The elevator reached the ground floor and Anne immediately pressed the top button which started the elevator going back up.

"The Mossad!?"

"That's right. I have very good information on that."

"What's your information?"

"I can't go any further than that."

"That would be very hard to believe. Nikolai has always been a devout patriot."

"Those things are always hard to believe. Your allies in the Mideast should at least be told to keep their eyes open." Then she felt conscious of the fact she had pluralized the word, 'eye,' but what could she have said?

"For Nikolai?"

"For Nikolai."

"I'll do that. Yes. Yes. What else?"

"Secret Number Two?"

"Yes."

"President Reagan."

"Yes? What about President Reagan?"

"President Reagan—"

"What?"

"You should never for a moment think he'll back down on the SDI. I talk with him, you know."

"Oh?"

"No matter what. No matter what, he's going to stick to it. You know what he told me?"

"What?"

The elevator reached the top floor and Anne pressed the button to go to the ground floor again.

"He said, 'If everyone in the Congress, if everyone in the country, if everyone in the world, wants me to give up the SDI, Anne,' he said, 'we are going to go ahead with it.' And," now she started whispering. "Come here." He came close, not that there was more than an inch in which to come closer, and not that anyone could hear them in the elevator if they were yelling. "The SDI has gone much further than everyone thinks."

He hesitated, then asked, "How much further?"

"Much, much further. Let me put it this way. It's 'on the road' as we say in the trade. It won't be long before it's a reality. Now, I've said too much. So I'll go to Number Three. No more on Number Two."

"Wait. Tell me—"

The elevator came to the lobby and she pressed the button to go back up.

"No waiting. I'm done on Number Two."

She had certainly captured his interest. In futility, Viktor Baskakov asked, "What is Number Three?"

"Ted Murphy." Anne had taken her time to think out this one. "Ted Murphy is a great journalist. He's recognized as a talent even by those who don't like him. Although I disagree with his politics, all of his life isn't politics. As you know, we have something special going between us." She winked. "As far as you're concerned, he is totally trustworthy—for your side. He was on your side on every major issue through seven presidents: he was against our U2 flights, he was for Khrushchev's peaceful coexistence, he said publicly that Kennedy was a Cold-Warrior, he was against what we were doing in Vietnam and Cambodia and Laos, he endorsed your nuclear moratorium, he opposed our neutron warhead, he was on your side in Angola, he endorsed your nuclear freeze, he was against our invasion of Grenada, he was against Reagan's Strategic Defense Initiative, he wanted us to spend less on the military, he was against the Contras, he was against our putting missiles in Western Europe, he took your side in foreign policy from Eisenhower to Reagan. That's guts, isn't it? That's integrity, isn't it? I think, Mr. Baskakov, you ought to reward him. You Russians do not understand Americans. We like to see appreciation, no matter what."

"What do you suggest?"

"What I would suggest is something you won't do. I suggest you give him the Order of Lenin. Give him a medal."

He was as amazed at the suggestion as she was bold in making it. "Miss Whitney, are you telling me he would even want something like that?"

The elevator reached the top floor and she pressed the button to send it back down.

"You bet. I know him very well—you know how well I know him. He'd love it. What an honor! He thinks he's unappreciated and it bothers him. Surely you can think of something. Don't ignore him is what I'm telling you. Give him some public acclaim—maybe as a peace-maker. Who could be against peace? Just imagine Secretary Gorbachev giving him some symbol of recognition that Ted Murphy has been a peace-maker in a dangerous world."

"This is extraordinary."

"Think about it. I believe that, just like anyone, if he doesn't get some kind of recognition, he'll go to where he can get it. And I wouldn't blame him."

"I'll think about it."

"Good! Just don't ignore him."

"And why are you being so friendly these days, Miss Whitney?"

"I'm telling you all this because I've had a very rough time. I want a new life. My husband and I are divorced. My political campaign ended in disaster. I can't go on like I did before. Have I ever told you anything just to give an impression?"

"No."

"Do you remember when I said I was going to recommend to our secretary of state that we stop participating in your film festival?"

"Yes."

"And what happened?"

"Your government didn't participate."

"I don't ever, ever lie," she lied. The elevator reached the ground floor, and this time she pulled the grill-gate aside and opened the door to the lobby.

"That still doesn't explain why you are telling me all this."

"Because I want a detente and I want you to trust me—and, in that way, maybe you'll give me what I most want in return."

"And what is it that you want in return?"

"I want very little in return for all this. I want you to recommend to

Gorbachev that when he wants a fair interview to be presented to the people of the United States, I should be the one to interview him. Wouldn't it be nice if he did it with a woman? Wouldn't that say something nice about the Soviet state?" Anne wanted a news-making coup, and the other element in her request was that she wanted to top Ted Murphy who had interviewed Fidel Castro.

"I can recommend that. I don't know if Secretary Gorbachev will do it, but I'd like to cooperate with you."

"That's all I want in return. Now I'll leave."

"You are not coming back to the party?"

"I'm going to the lake. I have to do a stand-up in front of that big spurt of water they call Le Jet d'Eau in the lake. I have to stand in front of that silly thing in the cold and talk to the television camera."

Anne was shivering in front of that high spout of water leaping from the lake, even though her coat had a fur collar to protect her from the cold. But when the lights went on and the crew was ready, the magic of the lights and the use of the camera made her forget the temperature. And also making her forget the temperature was the audience of a dozen passers-by who stopped to watch her perform.

"If you think all is mellow and filled with the atmosphere of detente, think again! I'm sorry to tell you but earlier in the month Secretary of State Schultz and National Security Advisor Bud McFarlane were in Moscow talking to Secretary Gorbachev and Foreign Minister Shevardnadze about the upcoming Summit here, and that meeting was no picnic. Generally after a meeting between their side and our side, our State Department issues a statement saying, 'it was a useful and constructive meeting in which a wide range of subjects were discussed.' That's what the State Department usually says. 'Useful and constructive' means nothing of any importance happened, and 'a wide range of subjects were discussed' means the two sides got rid of all the junk they felt they had to tell their people back home they discussed, and then they harped on one subject.

"This time the State Department said that the meeting was 'frank and businesslike.' 'frank' means it was just short of a screaming-match, and 'businesslike' means well, maybe they had a fist-fight, but no one was knocked out. I've been told that Secretary Gorbachev interrupted Secretary Schultz a number of times and then Secretary Schultz did the same with Secretary Gorbachev, so the whole meeting turned out to be very 'frank and businesslike.'

"I was also told that Secretary Gorbachev didn't know the details of the arms proposal that our side had presented. He didn't seem to understand our presentation nor was he interested in it. In fact, Secretary Gorbachev didn't even seem to know enough about the proposals that the Soviet Union had made! And here our side has been studying every word, counting missiles, warheads, bombers, and checking one count against another count, and all those weapons and counts don't mean anything! Gorbachev just wants to stop the president's SDI. That's the only reason he's here in Geneva.

"The rest of their proposals are nothing more than mathematical funny-stuff to make us think they're serious about arms reduction. So Secretary Gorbachev's lack of knowledge at the meeting certainly makes sense. We should be glad the meeting was 'frank and businesslike.' It would have been terrible if it was 'useful and constructive.'

"This is Anne Whitney at the Summit in Geneva."

"Hold it! Hold it! Hold it!" the Assistant Director yelled out. "Don't take off the mike. Just stand there and smile. Hold it! Okay! You're free!"

Some of the onlookers applauded since they didn't know what else to do. One of them not only applauded but whistled. The lights blinded her from seeing more than silhouettes but she knew who it was. "Little Annie Loyal did it again! If it isn't the girl from Shamshuipo who's now the woman who rules the summit! Ronnie will love what you said!"

She ignored him, going straight to the limousine that was waiting for her with the driver behind the wheel, the motor running, and the heat on. As soon as she entered the backseat of the car and closed the door, the driver started driving off. She lowered the window and yelled out, "Go home, Murph'! Go home!"

"Back to the Epsom?" the driver asked her.

"As quick as you can."

There was a note from Mr. Baskakov in her mail box at the reception desk. "If you are back before midnight, please come back up to the suite. The party will still be going on and I would like to see you."

It was very much going on. In her absence, the room had filled with cigarette and cigar smoke, and vodka had apparently flowed with greater intensity than the water spout on the lake had flowed with water. Mr. Baskakov wasn't drunk and neither was Nikolai Guzhenko, but they were the exceptions. As soon as Anne walked in the room, Nikolai Guzhenko walked to a far corner of the room away from her. Mr. Baskakov greeted her. "I'm glad you came back." He still didn't know how to smile. "Come with me. There is someone here who wanted to meet you, and was sorry you didn't return earlier. He said he noticed you from across the room." He led her to a man who looked like a heavyweight champion in a suit, although not a very good suit, and a face that had the look of a movie actor, although not a very good actor.

"This is Anne Whitney," Mr. Baskakov said. "Miss Whitney, this is Valentin Vladychenko."

Anne turned to Mr. Baskakov. "Is he KGB?"

Valentin Vladychenko smiled. "I am not KGB."

Anne looked at him suspiciously. "Then I'll bet someone in the KGB asked you to try and seduce me."

He shrugged with a wide smile. "It was no one's idea but my own."

Now she smiled. "You win. In that case, you can seduce me." She turned to Mr. Baskakov. "Do you want to watch?" Then she turned back to Valentin Vladychenko. "Where do you want to seduce me?"

"Your choice."

Anne was having fun in her new acting role. "Every room in this place has probably been wired by your government. I've been burned once." Anne had found out the secret combination for not being blackmailed: simply make sure it was understood that she didn't care what they knew about her.

Mr. Baskakov was standing like a statue, not knowing how to behave.

"I got it," Anne said. "Why don't we go in the elevator? Mr. Baskakov and I talked in there with privacy. You and I could fool around with each other in the elevator with privacy just as easily. I think it sounds exciting in an elevator. We can push the emergency stop button."

"The elevator here is very small."

"How much room do you need?" There was an uneasy silence. She turned around to Mr. Baskakov again. "Mr. Baskakov, I was right wasn't I? There is no camera in the elevator, is there?"

Mr. Baskakov closed his eye in a long blink. "Miss Whitney, this is not part of my job. Mr. Vladychenko asked to meet you. May I see you alone for a moment? Do you mind, Valentin?"

"I mind very much, Viktor," Valentin Vladychenko said, "but that's all right as long as you don't keep her away from me too long."

Mr. Baskakov gestured to Anne. They walked just a few steps and Mr. Baskakov said softly, "Miss Whitney, I am not a procurer for Mr. Vladychenko, and no one here is on assignment for the KGB. I would be very much relieved if you would realize that. What you do is your own business and I am not influencing you in any way."

"I want to thank you, Mr. Baskakov. I'm looking forward to the seduction. It makes me feel so young again. Now, I don't want you to be disappointed. No matter what he does and no matter what I do, I will not tell him how I know Nikolai Guzhenko is part of the Mossad, or everything President Reagan told me, or how Gorbachev should honor Ted Murphy. So you see? Your government will not find out anything from the impending love-making. Okay? But I might tell you more—and only you—if you get me that interview with Gorbachev!"

Anne was glad that Mr. Baskakov was not present the following day at a briefing by the president's spokesman, Larry Speakes, who told the audience of correspondents, "Don't try to get leaks from your sources. Those who talk don't know. Those who know don't talk."

SIXTY-FIVE
HOLD FRAMES
1986-1987

It wasn't that Jonas wanted heaven on earth. He just wanted bad things to stop.

"I know it's hard to understand that sometimes painful things like this happen," President Reagan said to the nation. "It's all part of the process of exploration and discovery. It's all part of taking a chance and expanding man's horizons. The future doesn't belong to the faint-hearted. It belongs to the brave. The Challenger crew was pulling us into the future and we will continue to follow them.... We will never forget them nor the last time we saw them this morning as they prepared for their journey and waved goodbye and 'slipped the surly bonds of earth to touch the face of God.'"

Maybe it was a dozen times, maybe more, but on that horror-filled January 28, Jonas watched the constant television replays of the launch of Challenger with seven Astronauts aboard, the camera following it through the seventy-fourth second when the explosion ended all seven lives in the Florida sky.

Watching the replays that day was like watching the Zapruder film of the assassination of President Kennedy. The conclusion was already known, yet each time it was seen there was a bizarre, unrealistic hope that on this replay, it wouldn't happen.

"They had a hunger to explore the universe and discover its truths. They wished to serve, and they did. They served all of us," the president said.

Jonas did what some would have called crazy. He had made a videotape of the flight, and then he had an idea: he stopped the playback just before the explosion on the seventy-third second, and he stared at the image of hold-frame. He felt as though he was engaged in combat against time, and in the suspension of its image he had an opportunity to cause its retreat.

But what an opposing army! Time laughed at Jonas in its willingness to be perceived as motionless.

And there was another replay of that day. There was the repeated shot of the seven astronauts as they had walked from the hanger to the van that would take them to the launching pad, and they were smiling. Just like watching president and Mrs. Kennedy at Love Field in Dallas, smiling. All Jonas was able to do was preserve moments of hope, knowing, but trying not to admit that the preservation was nothing more than visual myth. "God?" Jonas looked through his window at the sky above Los Angeles. "I'm still mystified. Finally we waged a war against the barriers of time. Now seven have died for it. Knowing the American people, the tragedy will create another tragedy. The quest will be postponed. Is victory futile?"

To Jonas it was connected: On April the 5th there was a terrorist attack on La Belle, a West Berlin discotheque with 230 people wounded, including 50 U.S. soldiers. Two were killed, one of them U.S. Sergeant Kenneth Ford. "Time!" Jonas said on the phone to Oliver North of the National Security Council staff at the White House, "You can't allow time to pass. Whether you folks in the White House know it or not, you always have more than one enemy, and one of them is time. You have to outfox it, beat it, kill it. In this case, retaliate quickly, or our attack will be seen as aggression rather than retaliation. Retaliatory efforts have to come right after the crime. Hit, and hit hard!"

"General, you're talking to the marine who already recommended that to Poindexter," Colonel North answered. "The NSC is divided. Poindexter is for it, Vice president Bush is for it, Schultz is for it. The other side isn't opposed but they say that we don't have enough evidence to know with certainty who was behind that attack. We believe it to be Qaddafi, but we need more confirmation. It's like that TWA blast last Wednesday, sir. That might have been Qaddafi, but some group called the Arab Revolutionary Cells said they did it, they took responsibility. We don't know whether or not they did anything. They put these groups together overnight, sir. We don't know if they have one member or one thousand, or if they plan to take hostages, or just scare us, or blow up buildings."

"Forget confirmation! Hit! It's the only way! What's lost if you kill the wrong terrorists? All the world would lose would be terrorists!"

"I'm with you, General. I'm for it."

"It isn't a question of being for it. It's for doing it quick. Will you tell that to your boss, to Admiral Poindexter?"

"Yes, sir."

"The terrorist attack in West Berlin was Saturday. Today is Tuesday. Four days. Do it quick or more Americans are going to be killed somewhere else."

"I'm with you."

"Okay. Good to talk to you, Colonel."

"Semper Fi!"

On Monday, April the 14th, Jonas was phoned by Oliver North to tell him that the United States had just bombed terrorist headquarters and facilities in Tripoli and Benghazi, Libya. "Eighteen F-111s left Britain at 12:13 A.M., sir. It was successful. General, we'd like you to come to Washington to talk. We hit our targets but we might have had some collateral damage as well. Outside of Margaret Thatcher we have practically zero foreign support. The French wouldn't even let us overfly their territory to make the raid."

"But you did it! Congratulations, Ollie."

"The president did the right thing, but we may be in trouble."

"First, don't say 'collateral damage.' It sounds like it's entered in a ledger. Spell it out in human terms. Say that some innocent people might have been killed."

"Point well taken, sir. Listen, sir, there are some other things."

"What do you mean, there are some other things?"

"Can you come to Washington?"

"Not if I can help it."

"We could sure use you for a consultation."

"What are the other things?"

"You know who Abu Nidal is?"

"Of course. He leads a Palestinian terrorist group."

"His real name is Sabry al-Banna. We think he's in Libya. But his group is headquartered in Syria, in Damascus. He–uh–he–he's been–"

"Go ahead, Colonel."

"He's sending out death threats because of our retaliation."

"Death threats against who?"

"Me."

Jonas was silent and so was Oliver North. Jonas gave an unseen nod. "That's a kind of award, Colonel. See how important you are?"

"That's not much consolation, sir, but I'll keep that in mind. He's also threatening death to General John Singlaub, who's been advising us–like you have. And Abu Nidal's threatening a third man, Edward Luttwak. I don't think you know him. He's at Georgetown University, he consults with us too, and he's fairly public. He does a lot of television commentaries here in Washington. General, what I want to do is let you know that Abu Nidal doesn't like us, or our frequent consultants–and he knows who they are. He could add your name to that list at any moment. In fact, I don't doubt you're on it already."

"Okay. I appreciate the warning."

"He has followers. Around 500 of them. They've killed 181 persons of which we know. So keep looking through your rear view window when you're on those freeways out there in Hollywood."

"I'll remember that."

"See, our little team has been pretty successful. Last year we've foiled 126 terrorist missions."

"That many?"

"That many."

"Great, Colonel! Now, tell me what I can do to be of help this time around, from the West Coast?"

"You don't have a secure phone so I can't talk freely. It's why I want you to come here for a day or so."

"Not now."

"I can tell you this on the phone; these Mideast terrorists who keep on taking Americans hostages in Lebanon are driving the president nuts. You know the president is a soft touch, and families of the hostages visit with him in the Oval Office and he darn near weeps. I mean he's so concerned about the way those families feel. He's drained."

"I can understand that."

"I wish he wouldn't visit with them. I'm proposing that. Maybe you could help."

"Not me. I don't see how. You have more clout than I do. What's the other subject?"

"The one I've been on for a long, long time."

"Nicaragua? The Contras?"

"Yes. The Nicaraguan resistance–they're losing because of those crazy laws made by the Congress–those crazy Boland Amendments written by Congressman Boland that prohibit any intelligence agency of ours from giving aid to the Contras. When one of those amendments is in effect, our hands are tied. The Sandinistas are going to kill the Contras off, or push them out of Nicaragua into Honduras. We have some ideas we'd like to talk about with you."

"Ollie, I know what you're up to. Some things, anyway. Are these ideas you've already enacted, or ideas you're thinking about?"

"A little of the former and a lot of the latter. Can you come to D.C., sir?"

"No. You do well enough without me. The president has the right instincts. He does what's right."

"I can't talk you into it?"

"You can't."

"You don't like our little city here, do you, General?"

"Washington isn't a city, Colonel. It's a disease. I keep as far away from it as I can. You ought to get out of there before you get contaminated."

"Yes, sir."

"You can phone me at any time. In fact, you can come here at any time. My time is yours as long as I don't have to cross the Potomac."

But Jonas crossed the Potomac. All it took was one quick phone call from President Reagan. "General, I hope we can still count on you from time to time, so some of us here can absorb some of your wisdom. I understand you don't like the District, right?"

"D.C. would be magnificent, Mr. President, if it was just memorials and monuments. It's some of the people there that ruin it."

The president laughed. "We'll try to keep them from you! We'd like to see you for a couple days, and I'll tell the staff to make sure you only see the monuments! No people! Two days here and then you'll be back to God's Country!"

Those few sentences from President Reagan did it. Dawn dropped Jonas off at American Airlines at LAX.

No one knew it at the time, least of all Jonas, but his consultations in D.C. would last eighteen months.

There was something very pleasant about walking into Room 302 on the third floor of the Old Executive Office Building. It wasn't just that Ollie North was there. It was that Fawn Hall, his secretary, was there. With long, flowing red-brown hair, a beautiful face, a gorgeous smile, a perfect figure, any man who didn't enjoy walking into Room 302 had to be a homosexual.

Since life is unfair, she rushed Jonas out of her office and into the office of Colonel North who quickly stood up behind his desk in the corner of his office.

"Hey, General!"

"Hi, Ollie."

"Good to see you, Jonas!" They exchanged a handshake and Ollie motioned to chairs around a conference table to the left of his desk. The table was filled with documents. "Sit down, General!"

They sat at the table, facing each other.

"You're looking good, Ollie. What's up?"

"I take it you want the truth, the whole truth and nothing but the truth, General?"

"As long as you can tell it all and I can still get to Dulles in time for the 5:45 back to L.A."

"General, it's a devastating experience to meet with a wife, daughter, mother, or the son of a hostage and see the anguish in their eyes, and know your government isn't doing anything. As I told you on the phone, having met with the families myself, I don't want the president to meet them. Do you understand? In fact, we had set up a program by which the vice president would meet with the families, not that the vice president is more callous, but that the ultimate decision on things to be done regarding the hostages, wouldn't be his. It would have to be the president's. But the president meets with them. I don't mean this in any way to be critical of our political process in the White House, but I think that places an unfair burden on the heart of our president. The president feels deeply about it. And I am willing to admit that that may have colored my decision or my recommendations, or even his decisions.

"There were several events that moved the president—very deeply: the murder of Robert Stethem by hijackers who took TWA 847 was one of them. He went to Arlington to bury him—and there was the murder of the Marines in El Salvador by terrorists, and two other American citizens were killed along with them. And there was the murder of Leon Klinghoffer—all of those affected, I think, all Americans and certainly the president."

"What's the point of telling me all this, Ollie? I know how the president feels. We've all been through it."

"But we haven't all been through the decision-making process of what we do about it, General. You and I obey our commander in chief. He has to make the decisions that we obey."

"Of course."

"General, please stay with me. Then there was William Buckley—you know, I don't mean the writer, I mean the CIA station chief in Beirut. He was an expert on terrorism, and he was involved in another program of enormous, really enormous and extraordinary sensitivity. He was healthy when he was taken hostage in Beirut. But after he was taken, he was beaten severely. Mr. Buckley probably died of the complications of pulmonary edema–and that is that he'd been kicked so brutally in his kidneys that his lungs filled up with fluid, and he basically suffocated. We have never recovered the body of Mr. Buckley. General, the president knew about this as it was going on through CIA reports that came down with the PDB, the president's Daily Brief and the like. They were contained in reports that I sent up to the president.

"And then we saw photographs and videotapes–and by 'we' I mean Bud McFarlane, Admiral Poindexter, the president, and myself–we saw pictures that we were able to obtain of Bill Buckley as he died, over time. We saw him slowly but surely being wasted away. We were able to obtain, through intelligence sources, those pictures with the assistance of a European who worked with us in this activity. And they were awful."

"You mentioned a proposal to try to remove the president a step from the burden. You didn't want him to visit with hostage families. Did anything ever come of that or will come of that?"

"No." Colonel North looked down and it was apparent that he was struggling with a thought.

"Ollie, what are you trying to tell me?"

"I went to Iran, Jonas–General."

"What?!"

"Twice. I went to Iran with General Secord. And with Bud McFarlane and–"

"Oh, my God!" Jonas closed his eyes and shook his head.

"And we made a deal. Arms."

"Oh, my God!"

Colonel North nodded.

It was a strange scene. Colonel North nodding while General Valadovich was shaking his head. "First, first, first, they could have taken you and Bud hostage! Then what? You guys work directly for the president!"

"The trips were so black, so hidden, that we used non-U.S. government assets throughout. We used European or Middle Eastern airlines, no U.S. air registration. We knew we might never be heard from again. The government would disavow the entire thing. And Bill Casey, Director Casey said he wouldn't let us go unless we were prepared to deal with the issue of torture. We knew by then that Bill Buckley was probably dead, and that he had been tortured. We knew that under torture–the severest torture - we had reason to believe he might have given as much as a 400 page confession that we were making every effort to recover. And Director Casey told me that he would not concur in my going on the advance trip unless I took with me the means by which I could take my own life. I didn't tell Betsy, my wife–my best friend, Betsy. She still doesn't know. I don't ever want her to know."

"So we traded weapons for the hostages?"

"Yes, through third parties–other countries that helped. The money to get the arms came from private sources."

"Did Iran want the weapons to use against Iraq? And what were the weapons?"

"Yes, to use against Iraq. And the weapons were Hawk missiles, one thousand TOW missiles, SA-7's—"

"God!"

"Yes, sir."

"Did it at least work? Did they release hostages in Beirut?"

"They're out. Three hostages out and no new ones taken. You see, Iran dictates to the terrorists in Beirut."

"Ollie, I don't need to tell you, but the president said we'd never negotiate with terrorists."

Ollie North nodded. "This isn't the end of the story, General."

"God! What's the end of the story?"

"The Iranians paid for the weapons. That gave us some funds."

Jonas hesitated, then asked, "Did anyone profit?"

"No. No individuals profited."

"What did you do with the money?"

"It went to the Nicaraguan Resistance."

There was a great quiet that engulfed Room 302. The quiet was so massive that it felt like it was going through the entire Old Executive Office Building. "The profits went to the Contras?"

"Yes, General. To the Nicaraguan Resistance—what's called the Contras."

Jonas sat there for a while trying to put the pieces together in his mind. "Does the president know that?"

"I thought he did. But he didn't. My superiors didn't tell him."

"Deniability?"

"Maybe. My superiors tell me to do something and I salute smartly and charge up the hill. That's what lieutenant colonels are supposed to do. I have no problem with that. I'm not in the habit of questioning my superiors about whether or not they told their superior. Admiral Poindexter never told me that he met with the president on the issue of using residuals from the Iranian sales to support the Nicaraguan Resistance or that he got the president's specific approval. But I believed the president had authorized it. I was wrong."

"Well, who did know? I mean who ordered all this? You?"

"Admiral Poindexter. I work for him."

"And he didn't tell the president?"

"I believe now that that's right, sir."

"I take it, you were for the funds going to the Contras?"

"I saw the idea of using the Ayatollah Khomeini's money to support the Nicaraguan Resistance as a good one. I still do. I don't think it was wrong. I think it was a neat idea. I advocated that. And we did it. We did it on three occasions. Those three occasions were February, May, and October. And in each one of those occasions, as a consequence of that whole process, we succeeded. It was a good idea because we weren't using the taxpayers' money, we were using the Ayatollah's money. And it went to support the Nicaraguan Resistance."

"Isn't giving money to the Contras–to the Nicaraguan Resistance illegal under the Boland Amendments?"

"No, sir. That's the crux of it. The Boland Amendments prohibit our intelligence agencies to give them federal money. I did not view, nor did my superiors view, that the National Security Council staff was covered by the Boland Amendments. The NSC isn't an intelligence agency. There were people who were concerned about that, and we sought and obtained legal advice to the effect that it was legal. The Boland Amendments were not intended to control the conduct of private citizens either. There is nothing in the Boland–any of the Boland Amendments that refer to them. And see? There are times a Boland Amendment isn't even in effect. Ed Boland keeps putting them in other bills, and they expire. And see–in terms of private money, none of those amendments of his prevent private citizens from raising money or contributing money to the Contras. We set up outside entities, and raised non-U.S. government moneys by which the Nicaraguan Resistance could be supported, too."

"What does the Congress say about all this?"

"They don't know about it–yet. And I'm not sure how to handle it with the Congress. We have had incredible leaks from closed committees of the Congress. As you know, I was part of the coordination for the mining of the harbors in Nicaragua. When that one leaked, there were American lives at stake, and it leaked from a member of one of the congressional committees, who eventually admitted it. When there was a leak on the sensitive intelligence methods that we used to help capture the *Achille Lauro* terrorists, it almost wiped out that whole channel of communications.

"On that raid we just had on Libya, General–we had a secret briefing for some members of the Congress here in the EOB, before the raid. The president told them what was to come, told them the sensitivity of it, and told them that lives of Americans were at risk. When the briefing was over at about 5 o'clock or 5:30, two members of the Congress proceeded immediately to microphones and said the president was going to make a heretofore unannounced address to the nation on Libya. I'll tell you, General, the volume of fire over the Libyan capital was immense that evening, and two American airmen died as a consequence of that anti-aircraft fire. In my military experience and yours–we know that nobody keeps that volume of ammunition sitting around in their guns. They needed a half hour or an hour to break it out, to get ready. Our strategic surprise was sacrificed by the comments of those congressmen.

"Now to today, and to the funds we've been getting from foreign leaders. I promised them absolute discretion, that we wouldn't reveal what support they were providing. And the reason we promised them that was because they would be in jeopardy of reprisals some from the Sandinistas and reprisals from their own internal political dissidents. We told them, 'Don't worry, we won't divulge it.' I told them that on instruction."

"Why did they provide the help with all those dangers?"

"A head of state of a foreign country said to me, 'You must understand,

Colonel, that we are in the mouth of the lion. And you Americans hold the lion's tail.' Some of those chiefs of state saw the totalitarian regime in Managua as a disastrous threat to their own safety, the security of their people, and the opportunity for economic development. And I didn't have to push these people. All I had to do was nod and say we would be grateful. And indeed, I believe we should be. General, it certainly didn't take prodding."

"You have a mess on your hands, buddy."

"General, listen," and Colonel North pushed a piece of paper from the side of the desk, to rest in front of him. "Listen to what President Washington said. 'The nature of foreign negotiations requires caution, and their success must often depend on secrecy. And even when brought to a conclusion, a full disclosure of all of the measures, demands, or eventual concessions which may have been proposed or contemplated would be extremely impolitic, for this might have a pernicious influence on future negotiations or produce immediate inconveniences, perhaps danger and mischief, in relation to other powers. The necessity of such caution and secrecy was one cogent reason for vesting the power of making treaties, etceteras, with the president.'"

"And what is it you want from me, Ollie?"

"Advice."

"You have George Washington's advice. Do you really need mine?"

"That's why I asked you to come here."

"I think going to Teheran wasn't worth the risk. I have no problem with funds going to the Resistance, but the whole Iran business should have been avoided. As for now, you better 'fess up. You phone those chiefs of state, let them know you have to tell the Congress, but that you won't reveal the names of the countries to the Congress."

"And what do I say when the Congress asks the names?"

"Fall on the sword, Colonel. Kill the lion first, while you're still holding its tail. Then, I'm afraid you have to use the sword on yourself."

"What do you mean by that, sir?"

"You made an oath not to tell a secret. You can't take a conflicting oath to tell the whole truth. You made an additional oath to friends overseas who were helping us that you would never reveal their names. Too many oaths, too many conflicting promises. In the shortest time possible you should request a closed congressional hearing, not a public one. You tell the Congress only those things that don't conflict with other oaths you took. Tell them that. You'll come to a point when they'll insist you break your previous oaths. They may even do it publicly. Closed or public, that's when you have to fall on the sword. There will be a lot of pain. Prison is painful. But if it comes to that, it won't be as bad a prison as Solzhenitsyn endured, or Sadat endured, or for that matter, even I endured. But it will hurt. I'm sorry, Ollie. You just have to pretend you're on the battlefield. You were ready to fall on the sword in Vietnam. Do it in Washington. All you'll have left, my friend, is your honor."

"Agreed, sir."

"If I were you I wouldn't even take the oath to tell the whole truth. I would tell them that you can't do it without breaking a previous oath to the United States and previous promises to friends of the United States who will be put in grave danger. Then, Colonel, you must take the consequences. Just like you were willing to take the consequences with that little pill you had with you in Teheran—the one your wife doesn't know about."

"Yes, sir."

"So I agree with George Washington."

Fawn Hall said goodnight to Jonas, and suddenly he forgot about everything except Fawn Hall. "Adam," Jonas whispered, "Come on. I can't do that. I'm involved in things much too important for that. But what hair!"

Without Sally Saigon to come home to, and with Dawn who kept shipping Jonas more and more of his clothes to the Madison Hotel, and then shipping more and more of his personal properties to keep him happy, Jonas had an unwelcome second home in Washington.

One of his most unwelcome items was the television set in his hotel room, where he was regularly greeted by Ted Murphy staring at him out of the tube. "It wasn't just dumb," Ted Murphy said. "It was a deception of the American people. First, the president tells the world we will never negotiate with terrorists. Then he says we didn't make a deal to free the hostages from terrorists but he gives four reasons why we gave them arms and one of the four reasons was to effect the safe return of hostages. If this makes sense to you, please explain it in twenty-five words or less, send in what you wrote with a Kellogg's box-top, and claim your prize!"

The congressional hearings were not closed. They were public, and on live television. An agreement had been reached between the White House and Congress to keep the names of supporting nations secret. To accomplish that, a plan was devised to refer to each nation by a number: Country Number One and Two and Three, and so on, rather than names. The numbering system was revealed by the press, who figured it out within hours.

"Israel! Brunei! Saudi Arabia!" Ted Murphy said to his audience. "There were at least eight other countries. I'll have all the other names soon for you. Now, let me ask if it was a sheer coincidence that suddenly the Prime Minister of Israel and the King of Saudi Arabia and the Sultan of Brunei all decided to do this? Was it some simultaneous act of charity? Or do you think they did it at the request of the White House?" He paused while he listened to a voice from the newsroom coming over his earphone. He nodded while looking at the camera. "Add Singapore and South Korea to the list. Wait!" He listened again through his earphone while he nodded.

"Portugal, El Salvador, Taiwan, Honduras, Guatemala, Costa Rica. If there are any more, we'll let you know!"

Jonas watched the hearings at the White House, most often in the Roosevelt Room with members of the senior staff. He rarely said anything, maintaining his ethic to never give unsolicited advice.

"What do you think, General?" the man who always looked confused asked.

"About what?"

"The whole thing. What do you think?" That was a solicitation.

"It was too risky. The way to stop terrorism is to retaliate, not negotiate. Once you retaliate, you scare them as the president did with Libya. Once you start negotiating, you never stop, the way the president did with Iran. The president might have been too empathetic with those families of the hostages, but it can't excuse a policy that drove against his own philosophy.

"And just from a practical point of view, what if they killed Bud? Or killed Ollie? What if they held them hostage? We could have been at war over any of that. They weren't members of some covert team the president could have disowned, nor could he have pled ignorance. They were members of the president's staff! Now, on the Contra-connection, can you imagine not telling the president? That was much too important for Admiral Poindexter to have done without the president's approval. Deniability can go too far. Now, maybe he did tell the president and he's trying to protect the president, I don't know. But I believe John when he says he didn't tell him. As for Ollie, he's a great soldier. The best of the Marines. He's risked his life for this country so many times I can't count them. Now look what might happen. We're going to make heroes out of the Ted Murphy's of the world."

One positive event on which Jonas did not count on, happened. The testimony of Colonel Oliver North was a smash throughout the country. He gave an unexcelled performance. The networks had made a decision to televise his testimony without interruption, assuming it would kill him. It made him.

A new word was added to the American vocabulary of 1987; "Olliemania."

It was night when Jonas walked out the Northwest gate of the White House, and as soon as the black fence was behind him and he was on Pennsylvania Avenue, a brilliant white light aimed at his face. "General Valadovich," a woman's silhouette asked as she stood against that white light. "Are you advising the president on the Iran-Contra scandal?" All Jonas could see clearly was the microphone coming closer to his mouth.

Jonas looked confused. "I can't even see you. I'd like to know who I'm talking to."

"I'm sorry. Kitty Argyle. Eyewitness News. Are you advising President Reagan on the Iran-Contra scandal, General Valadovich?"

"Ma'am, that's no one's business."

She wasn't prepared for an answer like that. "It isn't?"

"That's right, ma'am. Unless you have the credentials of the United States Air Force, the FBI, the CIA, and the police, you're out of luck."

"General, I don't know if you've been able to watch Colonel North's testimony on the Hill today, but–"

"A little. Not all of it. What I saw was spectacular. He did quite well. I heard that in my home town, the Hollywood sign was changed to read 'Olliewood.' Can you imagine? What did you think of how he did today?"

Kitty Argyle gave a nervous laugh. "Well, I'm not being interviewed."

"Yes you are. I can interview, too. Anyone can. He did well, didn't he?"

Kitty Argyle's laugh changed from being one created from nervousness, to one that became genuine. "Yes," she conceded. "He's doing well in public relations, but there are those on the Hill who seem to think he acted against the law."

"I know. I saw parts of the hearings. But they're wrong. Now, Miss Argyle, if you'll excuse me."

She turned to the cameraman. "Cut it!" She lowered her microphone and turned back to Jonas. "General, that was the worst interview I ever conducted! You are tough!"

This time Jonas laughed. "I'm sorry, ma'am. I don't mean to be unfriendly. I just treat private conversations as private conversations."

"I understand. Where are you going?"

"To the Lincoln Memorial."

"Really?"

"Really."

"May I go with you?"

"I'm walking. It's a long walk."

"In this heat?"

"In this heat."

"We have an air-conditioned car. Can we take you?"

"I want to walk."

"Can I meet you there?"

The lights went out, and the crew started dismantling the equipment. For the first time Jonas could see her face clearly without the lights aiming at him. Kitty Argyle had short black hair with bangs down to her eyebrows. Big brown eyes. A wide smile. Very young. Not Fawn Hall, but not bad. Different.

"Of course you can meet me there."

She was sitting on the top step of the memorial, waiting for him. President Lincoln was sitting even higher, on that pedestal above the top step, waiting for him. She stood when she saw Jonas starting the stairway. President Lincoln didn't stand, but he smiled.

She met him on the top step. "It was a long walk, wasn't it?"

Jonas nodded.

"While I was waiting for you, I thought that maybe you would want to be alone here."

"It's impossible to be alone here." He gave a motion with his head toward President Lincoln.

"I mean alone with him."

"Yes, I do. Do you mind?"

"No. I want to read the two speeches on the walls."

Jonas walked to the base of the podium and Kitty Argyle walked to his left to read the Gettysburg Address.

There was the echo of the footsteps again, just like so many years ago. She read the Gettysburg Address twice and then walked over to the wall across from it, to read President Lincoln's Second Inaugural Address three times. She did that much reading to give President Abraham Lincoln and General Jonas Valadovich enough time to have their conversation. They had a lot to say in bringing each other up to date.

Then Jonas looked over at Kitty Argyle who was still standing by the north wall. He gave her a short nod.

She walked over to him. "I guess I was asking the wrong question about you advising President Reagan. I should have asked if you were receiving advice from President Lincoln."

Jonas smiled. "I would have answered that one."

"Are you—are you all through?"

He nodded. "But first I want to go to the far side, behind the Memorial."

She walked with him around the Lincoln Memorial and she understood why he wanted to walk there as soon as they arrived at his destination. There was the view of the twinkling and sparkling flame at the Kennedy gravesite across the Potomac River.

"Sometimes," Jonas said, "I can't see it and so I get alarmed and think it's out. But it's just the wind or fog or something that obscures it for a short while, and then it comes back into view. It's such a comfort to see it." She didn't say anything. He stared at it for a while, then turned to her. "I'll go now."

"Where are you going?"

"The Madison."

"Our studio's practically around the corner from there, on LaSalles. The car and the crew are parked just around the circle. Here. We used to be able to park right out front, but they don't allow cars in front of the Memorial now. Something about the environment. Everything used to be so easy. Now you can't drive anywhere like before. But the car isn't far—and it is cooler than walking. Want a lift?"

Jonas got a great lift. He sat at the bar of the Madison Hotel with Kitty Argyle for hours. She was smart enough not to mention another word about Iran and a Contra connection. She just gave him her blinking eyes as she asked all sorts of things that had nothing at all to do with the day's events. She even said she liked his watch with the little map on it, and wanted to know how it worked. He took it off, and while in the middle of allowing her to press the buttons to see the appearing and disappearing map, and the appearing and disappearing illumination she said, "Look at the time! I want to see the Ten O'clock News. I'm on it."

"Not with my interview!"

"Oh, no. There was nothing to run. But I always look at myself. I have some interviews on the Hill I think they'll run."

"Is it ten already?"

"Mmm-hmm. In three minutes."

"Where can we see it?"

"Your room must have a TV. Doesn't it?"

"Sure. Of course."

She gave back his watch, and he clipped its clasp around his wrist as they walked to the bank of elevators.

That night while the United States was filled with Olliemania, Jonas was in his twenties again. The timepiece of his life had reversed. Since he remembered how his feelings for Dawn were destroyed when he found out she was only nine years old when President Kennedy was killed, he made sure he didn't ask Kitty Argyle what presidents she remembered while they were in office.

Even those who weren't fanatical about the passage of time as he was, might think too much of it had passed between his year of birth and hers. For one night, the devil with it.

He was inheriting even more of Adam.

It was such a good night that he forgot all else for a while. He knew that, of course, it would end. And so, like other times, he tried to create a hold-frame, this one not to prevent a tragedy but to extend an ecstasy. It didn't work. In the dark she pressed the button on his watch that illuminated the digital display. Each time she did it, they saw the numbers advance. He considered removing the battery, but that would have been cheating on the rules of life.

SIXTY-SIX
DOVERYAI NO PROVERYAI
1987

Viktor Baskakov welcomed Anne at the Connecticut Avenue entrance of Washington's Mayflower Hotel. "Secretary Gorbachev is on his way."

"You kept your word, Mr. Baskakov. I appreciate it."

"Come with me." He escorted her in, and they started walking through the long, opulent, glass-chandeliered lobby which was more like an indoor street than a hotel reception area, stretching all the way to a distant exit on 17th Street. The walls were lined with paintings of the founding of the United States and early presidents. "Your camera crew is setting up in the Grand Ballroom," Mr. Baskakov informed Anne. She took off her fur-collared black coat and Mr. Baskakov helped its release from her arms. "There's a coat room down here across from the Grand Ballroom."

"I could have come to see Secretary Gorbachev at your embassy, Mr. Baskakov. You needn't have gone through the trouble of doing it here."

"We liked the ballroom here as background for your television. It looks Russian. Most of our staff is staying at the Madison but it is not appropriate for pictures. At this time of day there is no event in the ballroom, and the hotel offered it to us without charge after we inspected it for appropriateness."

"I'm glad."

"I regret that Secretary Gorbachev gave Tom Brokaw the first interview, but that was in Moscow before this summit. You will have the first one in the United States now that our U.S. summit is done. And you did request that you meet with him when he comes to the United States. Secretary Gorbachev left the White House from the final session of the summit with President Reagan just hours ago."

"I'm very pleased. Thank you."

They reached the Coat Room and Mr. Baskakov gave Anne's coat to the woman behind the counter, accepting the ticket from her. "Ms. Whitney, before we go in, let me speak to you, just between the two of us."

"Of course," and they moved from the counter.

"You gave us accurate information, Ms. Whitney."

Anne looked startled and was about to say, "I did?" but she caught herself. "Yes," she said. "I know I was accurate when I told you those things. I don't lie. You know that."

"Comrade Nikolai Guzhenko has been transferred from his position at Novosti. He has no more contacts with Zionists. And you were quite right regarding what you told us about your president. He does not budge on Star Wars." She wanted him to go on to her third "revelation" regarding

Ted Murphy, but he didn't. "Regard this interview as a symbol of our gratitude for your candor."

She nodded and repeated, "Now we're even. Has Secretary Gorbachev enjoyed this first stay of his in Washington?"

They moved to the entrance of the Grand Ballroom. "Oh, yes. You ask him for yourself. But you did hear what he did on your Connecticut Avenue this morning, right at the corner here, did you not?"

"What did he do?"

"He and your vice president were in a motorcade going to the White House. Secretary Gorbachev asked his driver to stop, and he got out of our limousine–and he greeted the people. It was a sight. There was quite a crowd that gathered around him. Your people welcomed him warmly. Secretary Gorbachev didn't want to stop shaking hands."

"I didn't know that happened!"

"Oh, yes. I think he could run for the president here when Mr. Reagan's presidency is done." In a rare instance since Anne had first met Mr. Baskakov, she saw a trace–just a trace–of a smile. "Then your vice president got out of the limousine, too, and I don't know if anyone even recognized him. I think they thought he was a member of the Secret Service you provided for Secretary Gorbachev."

They entered the Grand Ballroom and Mr. Baskakov was right. It looked like a room in the Kremlin. There were six half-circled balconies on each side of the room, and beneath them were white panels with gold frills. On the ceiling were three glass chandeliers. Cables were all over the floor, two cameras were set up on blonde-wood tripods, brilliant white lights were mounted on aluminum stands, and they were positioned around two plush armchairs facing each other.

"Are we all ready?" Anne asked the crew. All four members of the crew nodded and the director answered, "Whenever you say 'go'."

Mr. Baskakov introduced Anne to the interpreter, then she was seated opposite an empty chair while someone in the crew acted as a stand-in for Gorbachev as the lighting was adjusted. The door opened and Secretary Gorbachev entered in a fast walk.

There was no question that this was a man of prominence. Everything in his manner reeked of self-importance. He gave quick smiles and handshakes to those to whom he was introduced, and a long hand holding with Anne, along with a smile that lingered longer than those he gave to the crew. Whether he had a tan or he was already made-up was unknown, but it added to his aura. The stand-in left the chair, and Secretary Gorbachev sat there quickly. He then professionally counted to ten in Russian to give the sound technician a level. The interpreter sat on a wooden chair off-camera. Anne received the signal to start the interview. "We're rolling!" the director said.

"Mr. Secretary, I understand you left your car this morning and caused quite a stir out on Connecticut Avenue. Did you enjoy it?"

"Yes! Your people were very kind to me. In fact I enjoyed it so much that I was late to my last meeting with President Reagan. When I finally arrived your president said he thought that perhaps I had gone home without saying goodbye to him!"

"You get along well with each other?"

"I call him Ron. He calls me Mikhail."

"That's a good sign. As you know, he is our president because he was elected." Secretary Gorbachev nodded. "Do you see the day when the Soviet Union can have free elections—that is, with more than candidates from the Communist Party?"

Secretary Gorbachev was not the least disturbed by the question. "In our society there is no need for any other party. That is the view of our people."

"Really?" Asking "Really?" was not an expected question from an interviewer.

"Really!"

"How come last month Boris Yeltsin was kicked out of his position as Communist Party Chief of Moscow?"

"For good reason. He did some good work, and actually made changes for the better, but he moved too fast on changes of economic reform, and when his work was not improving, and even worsened in some respects, he tried to blame his own shortcomings on others. Some of his comments were totally absurd causing perplexity and indignation in the Central Committee. He has been given another post. He is now Deputy Chairman of the State Committee for Construction. And he has not been well, his health has not been good. His heart has given him trouble. And he is very emotional."

"He is not on the 'outs' with you?"

"I do not understand."

"You are still friendly?"

"Yes."

Anne nodded. "That's good. Now, you and our president signed quite an agreement Tuesday, on Intermediate Nuclear Forces; medium and short-range missiles. I'm sure you know that there is a lot of controversy here in the United States regarding that agreement. For a long while you and many members of our Congress wanted a nuclear freeze. In the end, we did not have a nuclear freeze and NATO deployed Pershing and Cruise Missiles in Western Europe. Now you are negotiating the mutual removal of the missiles—ours and your SS-20s, since our Pershings and Cruises are in place, although still not as many as your SS-20s. Since you wouldn't have done that before our missiles were there, doesn't that prove the nuclear freeze would have been a mistake?"

Mikhail Gorbachev gave a wide smile. "For you, maybe, but not for us, and not for world peace."

"But isn't it true that we are now negotiating while your nation still holds the advantage in those missiles in Europe, and this imbeds that advantage?"

"There is some asymmetry in all agreements. But our objective is peace, and we are not planning on attacking anyone."

"Nor are we. But if I may get to some of the specifics of the agreement, Mr. Secretary: According to the agreement, we are to have no Pershings and Cruise missiles in Western Europe, and you will remove all your SS-20 missiles from Eastern Europe."

"That is correct."

"But you retain all your SS-11s, 13s, 16s, 17s, 18s, 19s, 24s, and 25s."

Again, he was not disturbed by the question and answered as soon as the translation was done. "We agreed on medium range missiles. What you call 11s and 13s are short-range, the others you mention are intercontinental. What this agreement does is eliminate your medium range missiles and our medium range missiles from Western and Eastern Europe. You see? After all, you have intercontinental missiles in your country as we have in ours."

Her 'Crossed Swords' briefings by Jonas came back to her in a flash. But this time it wasn't Anne against Senator Crayton Lewis, it was Anne against Secretary Gorbachev. *Give him the whole works*, she said to herself. *No prisoners.*

"Yes, but if we use them to defend Europe, you know that we would have none left to defend ourselves. On the other hand you can hit Western Europe with short range and intercontinental range missiles, and still have plenty of ICBMs left. It's geography here that makes a difference. You are close to Western Europe. We are across the ocean. Your SS-18 missiles alone have ten nuclear warheads each, and you have 308 of those missiles. On those alone, that makes 3,080 nuclear warheads."

"Perhaps you should be a negotiator rather than a television personality, Ms. Whitney! And, like you, I hope we move to a real agreement on intercontinental, not just intermediate, but intercontinental ballistic missiles."

"Not me! I don't hope that!"

"You see, as soon as we make a step forward to meet the United States position, the United States takes a step back from it. Instead of wasting the next ten to fifteen years by developing new weapons in space, allegedly designed to make nuclear arms useless, would it not be more sensible to eliminate those arms and bring them down to zero? As far as we are concerned, the elimination of all remaining nuclear weapons will be completed by the end of 1999, and there will be no nuclear weapons on earth. Now let me observe that you are turning this into a debate rather than an interview." He had a smile. "We should see to it, we must see to it, that neither side holds an advantage in space-strike weapons. My responsibility is to insure there is peace. If your president wants to continue with research on such a system, he may do that—not deployment, but research—as long as there is no violation of the Anti-Ballistic Missile Treaty that was signed by General Secretary Brezhnev and President Nixon in 1972—that was when you were posted in Moscow, wasn't it?"

He knew she was in Moscow? Gorbachev knew? Who told him? Baskakov, of course. This was a savvy politician. "I didn't attend that summit. I left by '72." She didn't attend any summit except Geneva as a commentator. "But Mr. Secretary, we have any number of records of violations of the ABM Treaty by your side, and if we stick to it, you must stick to it, too."

"Name the violations!"

"Krasnoyarsk! What is your radar dish doing there? And you moved two radar's from Shary Shagan to Gomel, where they are not permitted by the ABM treaty."

"False! Those radars were disassembled. We do not violate agreements. Those charges are entirely false. Let me see your evidence!" He was angry.

"Do you think I have the radars in my purse? How can I give you the evidence? But we have evidence. We have satellite photos. And I believe you know that we detected between 80 and 103 SS-20 missile launchers located in areas that are prohibited by the new agreement you signed on Tuesday. Will they be removed?"

"If they are in prohibited areas, they will be removed!"

"That's reasonable. I understand, but you say you now have 650 SS-20s. Our Defense Intelligence Agency says you have 1,200."

"Your Defense Intelligence Agency is wrong!"

She didn't want him to get too angry at her or he might be tempted to walk off. "I understand the president said that he lives by an old Russian proverb: *Doveryai no proveryai.* Trust but verify."

"He says that at every meeting!"

"But doesn't verification–if it could be done–make sense?"

"We are willing to have effective verification. Verification is no problem as far as we are concerned. There are on-site inspections in our agreement."

"But what sites? You can store mobile missiles anywhere."

"We cannot have peace if the United States accuses us falsely with such unbridled propaganda!"

"Mr. Secretary, there is no peace in Afghanistan. Your troops invaded and they are not getting out."

"A new subject now?"

"Yes. Afghanistan."

"The government of Afghanistan asked us to come in."

"But you had the president there killed! Daoud asked you to come in, and you killed him? That doesn't make sense. You had him roped up, forced to watch the one-by-one torture and execution of his family including his young grandchildren and then he was killed. You replaced him with Taraki and then he was killed and replaced with Amin, and he and his family were killed and you put in Babrak Karmal. I don't know if he's still alive, I guess so, but you replaced him with Najibullah. Which government invited you?"

On this one the translation process took prominence, including a short conversation between the interpreter and Secretary Gorbachev. "Ms. Whitney, the records of those periods of time are clear and you are covering a lot of ground in years with Brezhnev and Andropov and Chernenko and me. Now, regarding current problems, I told your president what I'll tell you. We want to return our troops back home. There is nothing I want more. And we will do that over a twelve month period if your country will stop providing the rebels there with arms. We cannot leave until we have such assurances. Your president did not provide those assurances to us during our meetings."

"You said 'over a twelve month period.' When do the twelve months begin?"

"When your aid stops."

"That would mean you win. But may I turn to Nicaragua?"

"I would welcome that. Now, go to Nicaragua."

"The president's national security advisor, General Colin Powell has said that your buildup in Nicaragua is a direct threat to El Salvador, Honduras, and Costa Rica. Why don't you permit free elections in Nicaragua? Why are you planning on supplying the Sandinistas there with MIGs and missiles? You have built them up already to a military force that exceeds all of Central America. You are using Cuba as a conduit between you and Nicaragua, aren't you—and supplying the El Salvadoran communists with arms to take over El Salvador? I mean—that is beyond any doubt. May I ask—what's up?"

"What's up is your imagination. The United States spreads a multitude of fantastic stories regarding the Soviet Union and Cuba to justify the escalation of the military venture against Nicaragua. If it were not for American interference in the affairs of other states, regional conflicts would be on the wane and be solved in far simpler and in more just ways. Ms. Whitney, my visit to the United States has been a very good one in terms of relations between our two nations. Better than Geneva, and much better than Reykjavik. Your president and I signed a treaty that reduces the threats of war. We still have disagreements, but I hope we can continue a frank and business-like dialogue as we have conducted in the last few days. We would like to see your nation and our nation live in peace with each other, with a growing mutual respect."

"If all the missiles and all the nuclear warheads are destroyed on both sides, that would mean a reliance on conventional forces, right?"

"That's right."

"But it's no contest! You're way ahead in conventional forces. You have four tanks to each one of ours. Our own Defense Department has said NATO couldn't survive more than two weeks."

"If that's true, Ms. Whitney, then I suppose you will increase your conventional forces. But at least the world would no longer have to worry about nuclear war. And we do have Mutual Balanced Force Reduction Talks going on in Vienna."

"Those talks have been going on for fourteen years. They aren't going anywhere since you won't settle for parity."

"We prefer to talk for fourteen years or fourteen hundred years, rather than make war in any year."

"Mr. Secretary, I should congratulate you for being successful in your campaign to stop us from being able to stop your tanks should they invade Western Europe."

"Stop our tanks?"

"With our neutron warhead."

"Oh, yes. President Carter used good sense in stopping the bomb that kills people and leaves property intact."

"I recognize that phrase was used in your propaganda campaign and it was picked up by your front organizations in Western Europe, and finally by our own media at home. Popular opinion stopped it from being deployed—all because of your nation's campaign that it was 'the bomb that kills people and saves buildings.'"

"And what Leonid Brezhnev said was accurate. Can you deny that?"

"It was a device to give some sort of deterrent to any invasion of a Western European country by your tanks, as your leaders did in Eastern Europe—in Hungary and Czechoslovakia. If you invaded a Western European country, our neutron warhead was meant to destroy the invading tanks and, in their destruction, not destroy the people or structures of the invaded western city your tanks would be occupying. Therefore, it was a device of pinpoint accuracy with as little surrounding fall-out as possible. With your history and your massive amount of tanks at the borders it was a perfect solution for prevention of invasion. After President Carter surrendered its assembly, your campaign was referred to by the Chief of the International Department of the Hungarian Communist Party as 'the most significant and successful political campaign since World War II,' and the American Bar Association revealed that your government had spent over one-hundred million dollars on that propaganda campaign. You had even changed the name from the 'neutron warhead' to the 'neutron bomb.' That was more potent-sounding and it was a name that masked its purpose. If we had all those tanks near the borders of your allies, you'd do something to deter them too, wouldn't you?"

"I know nothing of what you're saying and, at any rate, you're accusing my predecessors, not me. I was not in authority in those days, as you know. Now, Ms. Whitney, I have been very cooperative with you. You may have one last question."

Anne nodded. "Your embassy here. Both of them. You're in the old one on Sixteenth Street and you're building a new one. And we're doing the same in Moscow."

"That is correct. We started those negotiations under Khrushchev and Kennedy, and we completed the arrangements under Brezhnev and Nixon."

"And your current embassy on Sixteenth Street has more antennas on the roof than any place I've ever seen. And they aren't for television reception, are they?"

He smiled at her. "They're to watch you on television, Ms. Whitney."

"And your new embassy is on the highest ground in all Washington on Mount Alto. And the antennas are going up there, too! And it's not just a chancery and Ambassador's residence. It's a city with restaurants, a car wash, a car repair facility, a greenhouse, an apartment building with 160 units, 20 more units that are suites for visitors, parking lots for 147 cars, a school with eight classrooms, a gymnasium, a swimming pool, a theater and a health club. It's a city of Moscow's on the highest hill of Washington!"

"You seem to know more about it than I do."

"Under our agreement you can only use one of those embassies, but you're using both of them."

"No. Only the old one. We would like to use the new one. It's been completed now since 1980–seven years ago, waiting for you to move into your new embassy and allow us to move in our new embassy."

"Mr. Secretary, your people have been working in there for two years now. You're using both of them. And we have discovered that both of our embassies in Moscow are filled with listening devices. We've discovered that our old one, the one we've been using since 1952, has been fully compromised, fully penetrated. The new one is so bad, so honeycombed with bugging devices that our Senate Intelligence Committee has recommended we demolish it."

"Then demolish it! We are not spying! You, on the other hand, have all kinds of devices in our embassy. We live with it. Demolish it if you want! I think some of your people are just trying to divert attention from your embassy marines who have, themselves, been found to be guilty of some security breeches!"

"From your swallow, if you know what that means! They weren't spying for us, you know. The particular U.S. Marines were aiding your swallow who was spying for you!"

Secretary Gorbachev laughed. "Spies! Spies! Spies! You are obsessed with spies here! Now I thank you for your courtesy. I enjoyed our conversation."

"Thank you, Mr. Secretary!"

"I liked him," Anne said to Mr. Baskakov as they walked the long hallway of the Mayflower Hotel after getting her coat from the coat room. "He's very charming."

"You were very confrontational, Ms. Whitney."

"That's what interviews are like in the United States."

"That was too confrontational."

"I don't throw softballs."

"Too confrontational."

"Do you think he would do it again with me in the future?"

"Do you have more information for us?"

"Maybe. We'll see."

"If so, and if there is another interview, it cannot be so confrontational. We must have mutual assurances between us of stricter ground rules."

"Mutual and verifiable?"

"That is correct."

"Trust but verify?"

"That is correct."

"Doveryai no proveryai!"

Mr. Baskakov's eye gave her a sharp look.

SIXTY-SEVEN
A LESSER NEW YORK
1988

It was worse than the Hotel Epsom. To see Mark living in a miserable, windowless loft in Greenwich Village was more than Anne could accept, and more than Mark wanted Anne to see. It was a room that was a perfect square with three gray walls and one wall that had been painted a glossy black. The room had a cot, a sink, a toilet, and one metal chair covered with chipped brown paint. There was an out of context gray, metal bookcase, but nothing was in it. Mark had never told her where he lived, but she appealed to Jeffrey Stempka to locate him for her, and it wasn't difficult for Jeffrey Stempka.

"I want you out of here, Mark." She felt more like his current mother than his former wife.

"How did you find me?" He sat on the edge of the bed.

She stood. "Never mind. Let's get you out of here."

"It's all right, Anne. It's okay," he said. "I don't need more than this."

"You need to get out of here."

This was the man who was accustomed to having a purpose, and living in New York and in foreign cities in prestige and luxury. And now he was living in not much more than a box. And he looked awful, his face drawn, his glance vacant, his clothes unkempt. She felt guilty in knowing she looked good and pretty and clean. He looked at that good and pretty and clean face and said, "I don't deserve to get out of here, Anne. This place is what I deserve. It's why I'm here."

"Mark, come to Washington and live with me until you get sorted out. The station gave me an apartment that's big enough. It's a one-bedroom, but the living room is big, and you can be comfortable there."

"Anne, I'm fine."

"Why are you here? Mark, you saved money, didn't you?"

He nodded slowly. "I saved. But I spent it. I finally spent it. Don't ask me how, or what I have to show for it. I threw it away. I threw it all away. I bought things. I just bought things."

"Where are they? Where are the things you bought?"

"They're gone."

"Things for that woman?"

"She's gone with the things. She's long gone. That was nothing."

"Do you love her?"

He gave a spurt of laughter. "God, no."

"Did you?"

"Not a moment. It was a fling. A stupid thing. I couldn't love anyone like I loved you. No, like I love you."

She looked down at the floor. It was the first time she noticed it. It was decaying wood. "Remember how you wanted to some day go back to Hong Kong and live there? On the Peak, wasn't it, Mark?"

"I was the P.A.O. there. You worked for me."

"Mark, I know that. I'm talking about the future, not the past. Don't get loco on me."

"I'm not going to be anything in the future."

"Mark, you can go back to where you were–and beyond. I can help you. I'm making money."

"No, you don't understand, Anne. I'm living in a prison, and I don't mean this place, I mean this body, this soul. I'm in a prison and I can't get out."

"I have the key! Take it!"

"I don't deserve your key. I never deserved you."

"Don't ever say that! Don't ever think that!"

"How one mistake can ruin everything!"

"Will you go with me, Mark, please? To Washington?"

His lips were parted, and he shook his head. "No. I've ruined enough. I just want to know that you have everything you want. I think you do, if I stay out of your life."

"Mark?"

"What?"

She walked to him and kneeled down by him. "Be what you were."

He said nothing for a while, and then answered her. "No one is what they were," and he put his hand on her cheek. "Some get better, some get worse, but no one is what they were. You're better than what you were. Get better yet, Anne. I'm a man who was good and gave it up."

"You're a man who is and will be great!"

"Please leave, Anne. I love you too much to have you stay."

Anne put her forehead on Mark's knees, and they stayed that way for a long while.

And then Anne left, just as he wisely asked her to do.

SIXTY-EIGHT
THE PLUM BOOK
1989

There was a room on the third floor of the White House that was the most comfortable and brightest room of the residence and it had yellow drapes and yellow chairs and yellow all over, particularly the yellow coming through the large windows when the sun was out, and it appeared to be totally oblivious to the troubles of the world. Since on the first floor there was the Red Room and the Green Room and the Blue Room, it would have been consistent to call it the Yellow Room but it was called the Solarium.

It overlooked the South Lawn, the Ellipse, the Washington Monument, and beyond to the Tidal Basin and the Jefferson Memorial. It was the attic when Abraham Lincoln was president, and during President Wilson's administration it was turned into a bedroom for visitors. President Coolidge turned it into the Solarium, calling it his "Sky Parlor."

On the day following his inauguration, the new president, George Bush and his wife, Barbara, sat at the Solarium's glass-topped table, with the corner of the table between them, coffee cups in front of them, and a bowl of fruit ignored by both of them. The stewards didn't yet know their eating habits that well. The sun was flushing the room in yellow brightness. They had just come upstairs from a reception for tourists, which hadn't been done since President Taft was inaugurated.

"That was fun!" President Bush said.

"It's a first!"

"Well, golly, that's good. We set a precedent already," the new president said.

Barbara Bush looked out the large window at the expanse of Washington laid out like a blanket with monuments rising from that blanket. "Isn't it nice to just sit for a while and enjoy the day?"

"It won't last long. I still have a list of phone calls to make from Gorbachev to Mubarak to Thatcher to Kohl to Takashita, and a bunch more of them. They gave me a list here, somewhere. Got to phone them when the time is right in their cities, so—so I won't get eight hours straight of sleep until Monday night. And I got a raft of positions that we better fill right away. You've seen the Plum Book with the list of positions for me to appoint? It's a volume! We still have most of it to go. The transition period didn't take care of a tenth of it–I don't know, even a twentieth."

"Don't get excited, George. Don't get impatient. One at a time. I'm sure that won't be any trouble. Everyone will be giving you a list of people who want jobs."

"They already have. The trouble is in not taking them all. This isn't like taking over from a Democrat president where you just say goodbye to his appointees and wish them well and they're out, and you bring in your people to fill the vacancies. A lot of the people that Ron appointed want to stay—and they're good—they're friends. But y'know, you can't keep them all. Then there are those we just want with us, that's all. So you have to have a slot for them and—I'll tell you someone I'm going to take care of right away. You know who?"

"Dick?"

"You bet. He's one guy who hasn't made a pitch for anything. Dick Moore. He's going to be Ambassador to Ireland."

"I knew you were going to give him that post! Does he know?"

"I think he has an idea."

"You know, George, there's someone I think it would be nice to appoint to something. Everyone seems to have forgotten her."

"Who?"

"Irene Goodpastor."

The name was too long ago for an instant reaction but then he remembered. "Oh, golly, no!" And he shook his head.

"She was always so nice to us. She was so nice to everybody. And such a diplomat! She's Washington's forgotten woman. Wouldn't she make a good diplomat somewhere?"

"I thought she was dead. You sure she isn't dead?"

Now Mrs. Bush shook her head. "A recluse."

"Did she campaign for us or anything? She's a Democrat, isn't she?"

"Of course she's a Democrat. I'm sure she didn't campaign for you—but I'll bet she didn't campaign for Dukakis, either. She's just a woman who thinks she's all through and deserted. Do you remember how prominent she used to be? She was the Grand Dame of Washington. She'd make a marvelous representative of the country, somewhere."

"I don't know where she'd fit in."

"An ambassador."

"Oh, golly!" The new president squirmed in his chair.

"It would be a wonderful appointment. And I think it's better that she's a Democrat. It would be a nice non-partisan surprise. You need to do something like that. And she'd be confirmed by the Senate in an instant. Can you imagine George Mitchell saying 'No' to Irene Goodpastor? To an Institution?"

"Maybe to some small post somewhere."

"Is Hong Kong a small post?"

"Hong Kong? That's a big post. Not in size. I mean it's an important one. Why Hong Kong?"

"It was so well known she asked Kennedy to be the Ambassador there. She always talked about how much she loved it. Don't you remember?"

He shook his head. "And that's not an Ambassadorial post. It's not a country."

"Well, something, then. George, why don't I call her for a tea and just talk to her?"

"Yeah. Yeah, fine. A tea is fine. That's good."

"I'll feel her out, George." That wasn't exactly what the president said.

"Feel her out, but don't mention anything. A tea is fine."

When Irene Goodpastor walked in the Northwest gate of the White House, years of her age were left behind on Pennsylvania Avenue. They just dropped off as a rush went through her; the same kind of rush she never thought she would feel again. She had almost forgotten how it felt to be alive, and now she felt she was more alive than anyone.

One week later, she dropped even more years when the results of her afternoon tea with Mrs. Bush was a phone call from the president telling her that there was a position available at the U.S. Consulate in Hong Kong.

"It's not the Consul General, Irene. That one usually goes to a careerist and Don Anderson is in there—he's a good man, but there's an important job that's freeing up; the D.C.M."

"Really?" She had no idea what he was talking about, but she didn't want to admit it.

As though he read her mind he said, "Deputy Chief of Mission. Pardon me, you get caught up in all the initials. It's open. That makes you the Number Two Man—Woman."

"You want me—you want—in Hong Kong?" She wasn't being as articulate as she would like to have been.

"You'd do a bang-up job there, Irene! A bang-up job! You go there all the time, don't you?"

"Well, I—I—" Once. A long time ago. "I do know it quite well."

"Give it some thought. Get back to me."

"I will, Mr. President."

Irene Goodpastor didn't need to give it any thought.

Her rebirth was surely a miracle, and awaiting her was another miracle: It was the sight of what Hong Kong had become in 29 years. Could it be the same city? Its changes might not have been as apparent if she had been a frequent visitor, but sometime in those 29 years it won the competition for the most magnificent skyline in the world—with Hong Kong's skyline of 1989 filled with masses of buildings of such varied sizes and shapes that on every block there appeared to be one building that could only have been blueprinted by Howard Roark in *The Fountainhead*, standing next to a building that even Roark wouldn't have had the imagination to design.

The welcoming party for Irene Goodpastor was held three quarters of the way up Victoria Peak at Consul General Donald Anderson's residence, the home provided by the United States government, its picture windows providing a sweeping view of the city beneath the Peak.

The living room was filled with the diplomatic community, the consulate's staff, local businessmen, and Hong Kong's social and political celebrities. "It isn't often," Consul General Anderson said in his toast with his lifted wine glass, "that Hong Kong has the opportunity to welcome a new resident with the reputation and prominence of Irene Goodpastor. This city is honored to have you here, Irene."

There were calls of "Here, Here," and the clinking of glasses and the toast was done.

Then there was a toast to two people who were not present, the president of the United States, George Bush, and the Governor of Hong Kong, Sir David Wilson. When that was done, Consul General Anderson lifted his glass in a toast to the two people standing to either side of Irene Goodpastor, both of whom Irene Goodpastor hugged at the waist. "And all of us proudly toast Gloria Cooper and her 14-year-old son, John Fitzgerald Cooper, for the magnificent work you are doing here in Hong Kong for the thousands who have escaped from Vietnam."

A lot of those present didn't know Gloria and her son were there, but they all knew who they were. There was a very quiet and respectful, "Here, Here," and "To Gloria. To John."

As all conversations did in those days, small talk quickly turned into tall-talk about the event to come in eight years when Hong Kong would be taken over by the People's Republic of China. And as always, the Hong Kong businessmen were optimistic and echoed the constant phrase, "It is the biggest non-event in history!" The democracy advocates disagreed, and they talked about their concern for human rights and freedoms that could be at risk. The U.S. Consulate staff members were careful not to put themselves on any side, giving only slight movements of their heads or a shrug at almost all comments, and they talked about hope rather than prophecy.

Mrs. Goodpastor was taking her cue from the staff of the consulate. She gave small movements of her head and shrugged when they gave small movements of their heads or shrugged. Gloria did not nod or shrug, but talked with the candor of one who was indebted to none. "To you in the business world here in Hong Kong–think of who you are." She said it to just a few people around her, but her tone and manner was so different from the others that it made clusters of guests quiet down and pay attention to her.

In short time other people weren't talking at all. It was all Gloria. "With the success that the freedom of this place gave you, you have done so well that you now downplay the enslavement of those who didn't make it here. Why do you do this? Why are you so friendly with your old wardens? Do you think they'll put their arms around you? Is it money that moves you? You are the world's only refugees who grab the bait of worms from the hooks of those from whom you fled."

John Fitzgerald Cooper added more than his fourteen years of life would have indicated he would say. "Come to my mother's and my house some night at the refugee camp and see what you once were."

Gloria nodded. "The only difference is that they're Vietnamese and you are Chinese. It holds 2,600 of them. It's even called a Detention Centre of all things–the Kai Tak V.B.P.D.C.–the Vietnamese Boat People Detention Centre. And you can find those centers all over Hong Kong if you care enough to find them. There are sixteen of them. How many of you have been to one? Detention Centres! But all of the people in them would rather be imprisoned in Hong Kong than walking the streets of Ho Chi Minh City, just as you or your parents would have chosen that to walking the streets of any Chinese city above the border. You should visit us at the Kai Tak V.B.P.D.C."

There was quiet at the party. Not even the sound of a cough, and not even a motion of any of the guests. Not even a swallow of the wine, or a bite or a chew of one of the small sandwiches that some held in their hands.

"I would like to go!" Irene Goodpastor said, surprising even herself.

Gloria gave a sealed lips smile, and closed her eyes for a moment. Then she said, "You can come any time you want, Irene. John and I will introduce you to the refugees, and we will show you everything. We would love to have you there. But the fact that you want to go–and no one else spoke out–indicates that you are the only one here who does not need that experience."

Again, there was quiet at the party.

Then, in a very soft voice, Irene Goodpastor said, "I'd still like to go, Gloria."

This time the consulate staff took their cue from her. They nodded and one said, "I'd like to go, too." There was a lot of nodding and then another said, "We'd all like to go, Mrs. Cooper."

The Hong Kong businessmen started sipping wine and biting and chewing the small sandwiches that some held in their hands. The ones that didn't hold a small sandwich, reached for one. It gave them something to do without making a statement.

SIXTY-NINE
THE GODDESS OF DEMOCRACY
1989

Why is it that capital cities in countries that have totalitarian governments find it to be so much fun to have an immense city square with so little in it? Are they showing off that they have room to spare? Even a fountain would be nice in the center, or how about a tree or two, or maybe a little pond with some ducks? But they just won't do it. Usually they're happy with some statue near one of its edges or maybe some piece of granite signifying something or other or, more likely, a grisly tomb at one end of the square, and that's it. Sometimes they even have a large picture in the square of whomever's embalmed body is in the tomb. The rest is a testimonial to emptiness.

Before the communist revolution of 1949, Tiananmen Square in Beijing (then spelled Peking) was just a normal-sized city plaza. But Mao Zedong (then spelled Mao Tse-tung) had the square enlarged to be four times as big. With that enlargement it looked just right for a totalitarian-governed state, even bigger than Red Square in Moscow. They did put a granite obelisk there with Mao's own handwriting embedded in it (an idea they probably got from Grauman's Chinese in Hollywood) reading "Eternal glory to the people's heroes." All the square needed now was a swell mausoleum. But only one person was considered worthy of that honor and, unfortunately, he was alive.

Not forever. In 1976 he died, and they fixed him up and built the Mao Tse-tung Memorial Hall and put him in there. The mausoleum's main competition, located in Moscow, was outdone. Like the square itself, the mausoleum in Beijing was bigger than the mausoleum in Moscow, even though the one in Moscow had once been used to shelter two fellows; both Lenin and Stalin.

Twelve and one half years passed since the death of Mao, and it was April the 15th of 1989 when the former Communist Party General Secretary, Hu Yaobang, died. His death became more important than the death of Mao. Hu, of course, was not destined to be put in a mausoleum in Tiananmen Square. Mao certainly wouldn't share his abode with Hu, of all people, since little more than two years before Hu died he had issued a statement condemning Mao's Cultural Revolution. Worse, he talked about problems in China in the field of democracy and human rights. Even if the dead Mao would have forgiven him, Hu would still have been in trouble because his statements were interpreted as meaning that Deng Xiaoping wasn't his choice of a great leader. Deng Xiaoping fired him. Deng said that Hu failed to defend the People's Republic against the "sugar-coated bullets of the bourgeoisie." Deng announced that Hu "resigned" his position of Communist Party General Secretary after confessing to having "made mistakes on major issues of political principles."

Hu still stayed in the Politburo where he talked often and long about the need for ending government corruption and nepotism. He advocated that the people be given their rights as prescribed in the Constitution. At an early April 1989 meeting of the Politburo, while his colleagues taunted his repeated criticisms of the government, Hu declared, "We have failed the people and the nation!" As soon as he got the words out, he collapsed in a heap and was carried out to a hospital. Within a week, he was dead.

The news of Hu's death traveled quickly by way of what was called "Small Lane News," the greatest communication device of China; the traveling whisper through the streets and narrow, age-old alleyways called hutongs. That method of communication was so effective that by the time his death was publicly announced the next day, it was already well known among the population of Beijing.

Particularly saddened were students of Beijing University. They had regarded Hu Yaobang as their champion, and he had suffered severely for his championship. The students went to Tiananmen Square on April the 17th, holding posters requesting that the government reappraise Hu's life, stating that he was a hero, not a villain. Posters read: "When You Were Deprived of your Post, Why Didn't We Stand Up?' "We Feel Remorseful. Our Conscience Bleeds." "Those Who Should Die Still Live. Those Who Should Live Have Died." "Deng is Still Healthy at the Age of 84. Hu, Only 73, Has Died First." By day's end some five hundred students were in the square. These were the greatest acts of political courage since students had hung posters on Democracy Wall a decade earlier. Some of those students were still imprisoned for the posting of those messages.

Day by day the demonstrations in Tiananmen Square enlarged. On April the 18th, the 500 grew to 2,000, and the next day to 10,000, and that night to 40,000. Two days later there were 100,000 in Tiananmen Square. The original demonstrators from Beijing University had been joined by those from People's University, the Central Institute of Nationalities, the Central Drama Academy, Beijing Agricultural University, and Qinghua University. Hu was no longer the major subject of their placards and slogans. The major subjects became an end to government corruption, the advocacy of an independent judiciary, a free press, freedom of expression, and the right to choose their own jobs and careers. There were cries of "Deng Xiaoping and Li Peng; Hear Our Grievances!"

By the beginning of May, there were students from thirty of Beijing's colleges and universities, and young people from other provinces of China and even from Hong Kong came to Tiananmen Square. There appeared to be some safety in numbers, even more safety with President Mikhail Gorbachev of the Soviet Union scheduled to come to Beijing and become the first Soviet leader to visit China in thirty years, to be accompanied by one thousand journalists from all over the world with the ability to witness events taking place in Beijing.

President Gorbachev was not taken to Tiananmen Square. Had he been, he would have seen one million Chinese in demonstration. It was likely a record number of people for any demonstration, anywhere.

That great city square, known for holding vast emptiness, had little emptiness left. To the great displeasure of Deng Xiaoping, Li Peng, and Mikhail Gorbachev, even the historical announcement of normalization of relations between the Soviet Union and the People's Republic of China took a backseat to the world's interest in the crowds of Tiananmen Square. The meetings and statements of the two leaders became a side-show to the story that was taking place in the square. Gorbachev called the demonstrators "hot-heads." On his way back to Moscow he lashed out at the government of the People's Republic of China for not containing the demonstrators.

In a small courtyard of Beijing's Central Academy of Fine Arts, a beautiful eighteen-year-old girl named Liberty, who had come from the University of Hong Kong one week earlier to join the demonstrators, was posing in a long robe for twenty art students who were secretly working with plaster and styrofoam over a wooden frame, to create a giant thirty-three foot statue called the Goddess of Democracy. The statue was being made in three parts with plans of having the sections wheeled to Tiananmen Square on three tricycle carts.

As she posed for the artists, Liberty's right arm was extended upward, holding a long, thick stick, her left hand also extended, to grasp the lower part of the stick. As the student artists' recreated her likeness, the stick was reproduced as a torch, and Liberty was posing in a posture that was, intentionally, very much like the most well known statue in the world.

"I'm posing for a magnificent statue, Ma!" she said to her mother in Hong Kong from a telephone in one of the many abandoned offices in the University of Beijing. "A Statue of Liberty! You gave me a name to live up to, Ma!"

"Is it safe there?"

"Oh, yes. There's nothing to worry about. How is father?"

"Worried about you. But he is all right."

"Are you seeing him every morning?"

"I think the staff of Queen Elizabeth Hospital thinks I work there. Your father deplores being a patient. Of course I go every morning. I wouldn't miss one. Moose sees him every night."

"How's Moose? Has he been over?"

"He told us we shouldn't have let you go there. He thinks there might be trouble."

"No, there won't be. There are people from the Western press all over the Square. The government can't afford to do anything. And, Ma, you know that even if there is trouble–it is right what we are doing. And you always preached to me about doing what is right no matter the obstacles."

There was no response.

"Didn't you, Ma? Didn't you and father both say that to me?"

There was a very quiet, "Yes."

"I knew you would let me come here because of that. Don't ask me to come home yet. We are changing China, Ma! We will all be able to live anywhere we want in China when Wang Dan wins! All of China will be as free as we have been in Hong Kong!"

"Who is Wang Dan?"

"He's the student leading all this. A thin boy with glasses. He's leading along with a beautiful and wonderful girl, Chi-ling, from the University. Haven't you seen their pictures?"

"No, I haven't."

"They are marvelous! Wang Dan is what father must have been like when he was young. Our only fault here is that none of us are as logical as father. We are all short of specifics. We want freedom and democracy but we have no concrete plan. But Wang Dan is a marvelous leader."

"Are the two of you in love?" Wai-yee was always suspect. No girl as pretty as Liberty could avoid the interests of any young man. And Liberty inherited the natural flirtatiousness of her mother.

"Wang Dan? Oh, no, Ma! I am in love with his mission. I love him but I love every student here."

Again there was quiet on Wai-yee's end of the line.

"Ma?"

"Yes?"

"I know you're worried, but every policy expert in the world says the government here will not clamp down—that it would ruin their economy and that it wouldn't be in their own interest. They just plan on wearing us out—but we won't wear out!"

"Moose is a foreign policy expert. He doesn't agree with the others. Szeto Wah is an expert. He agrees with Moose. Jack Edwards agrees with Moose. Please stay safe."

"I am safe. I'm not staying in the Square with most of the others. I go there often but I'm staying at the University. And when I go to pose for the statue, that's a mile and a half from the Square. I'm very safe. What did Moose say exactly, about me being here?"

"He pretended he wasn't worried about you at first, just like we all pretended. But then he just—exploded yesterday. He suddenly became so emotional. You know that he adores you. He wants you to come back to Hong Kong."

"I can't. I must be here. You know that, don't you, Ma?"

Again there was the quiet.

"You know that, don't you, Ma?"

"Liberty—"

"I can be reached at the University number, and I'll phone you when I can. Ma, I want you to be proud of me."

"Oh, Liberty! How could I not be proud of you? We are all proud of you. You are everything."

On May the 18th it wasn't only Moose who became emotional over the events in China, it was Hong Kong itself. The city that hardly knew how or why to have a protest of any kind, became a sea of demonstrators marching through Central in support of the students in Beijing, with the demonstration led by Szeto Wah, with Jack Edwards behind him in the procession.

With Gorbachev back in Moscow, Deng Xiaoping met with the man who he had selected to replace Hu Yaobang as Communist Party General Secretary; Zhao Ziyang. Deng had been displeased to hear that Zhao had told Gorbachev, "Political reform and economic reform should be synchronized. It won't do to lag behind in political reform." This was not what Deng wanted his Communist Party General Secretary to say either publicly or privately. Deng had a charming way of warning Zhao: "I have three million troops behind me!"

Zhao is said to have answered, "I have all the people of China behind me."

"You have nothing!" was Deng's reported reply. There was little question that Zhao, like Hu before him, would not have a long tenure as Communist Party General Secretary.

At the dawn of May the 19th, Zhao went to Tiananmen Square to express his sympathy with the protestors, particularly some 3,000 hunger-strikers with whom he sat and talked. With tears he said to the demonstrators, "I came too late, too late. We deserve your criticism but we are not here to ask your forgiveness." He asked them to end the hunger strike and he signed his name on student's clothing.

On Saturday, May the 20th, Prime Minister Li Peng went on television to decree martial law in Beijing. The demonstrators were ordered to leave Tiananmen Square or face twenty years imprisonment. The reaction of the demonstrators was to change their chants and posters to "Li Peng, Resign!" "Down with Li Peng!"

Before the day was done the government announced that units of the People's Liberation Army would enter Beijing to restore order. After the directive was given, the Square's crowd became larger than before the decree.

On the outskirts of the city, residents assembled on the main roads that could be used by the army, so as to block them if they entered. When vehicles filled with soldiers came, those who stopped the troops gave them steamed buns, candies, and cigarettes. They read newspapers to them, and told them to "love the people." There were embraces between the people and the troops. Many wept, and the troops turned back.

Now those in the square were not only students. The people assembling were all ages and from all walks of life. The news from Tiananmen Square in Beijing created an epidemic of protest, with thirty-four other cities in China expressing their solidarity with the students in Beijing and joining them in demonstration with the advocacy of democracy.

On the same Saturday there was a second demonstration in Central of Hong Kong, despite a tremendous downpour of rain and gale-force winds as Typhoon Brenda hit the Crown Colony. In the worst weather, some 40,000 Hong Kong people marched from Central to the Xinhua News

Agency, which was the de facto Embassy of the People's Republic of China.

The following day, Sunday, May the 21st, the Hong Kong demonstrators swelled to over one half million, with Szeto Wah and his followers calling for Li Peng to resign. Behind Szeto Wah, as usual, was Jack Edwards. Again the march went from Central to the Xinhua News Agency, but the crowd was so large that it spilled through dozens of streets and the Royal Hong Kong Jockey Club opened the doors to the Happy Valley Racetrack for the demonstrators, providing them with an arena. Then the participants did more than demonstrate. They took collections of money to send to the protestors in Beijing.

There was great difficulty in phoning anyone in Beijing from Hong Kong and Wai-yee could not get through to Beijing University. Each morning she lied to Chi-shing in his hospital room and told him she talked to Liberty each day. And she didn't tell him any of the news from Beijing or anything about the demonstrations in Hong Kong. She would rush home from the hospital to check her answering machine.

When she came home from the morning visit to Queen Elizabeth Hospital that Sunday, the machine's red button was blinking.

It was not Liberty's voice. "Hi, Wai-yee. It's me—Moose. Call me, please. After I visit the doctor tonight, I want to stop by. Call me here at the office and let me know if it's all right. I'll be at the demonstration with Szeto Wah and Jack Edwards, and then back at the office, writing all day, then to the hospital."

It was the first time Moose was in the home on Crocodile Hill without Dr. Yeung and Liberty in it. Wai-yee brought him coffee along with tea for herself, and they sat across from each other in the living room, with the picture of John Travolta acting as a watchful chaperon.

"I'm going, Wai-yee. I'm going to Beijing. I'm going to find Liberty. I can't take this any more. I told my editor I'd either take time off or I'd bring him back a story from Beijing—from Tiananmen Square. Either way, I'm going."

Wai-yee closed her eyes. "Thank God."

"I'm going to bring her home, Wai-yee."

Wai-yee nodded and repeated, "Thank God." And then she smiled and said, "Chi-shing told me that whenever he failed in curing one of his patient's ailments, they would blame him—and whenever he was successful, they thanked God." Her smile became wider. "I suppose I'm guilty of that now. Thank you, Moose."

"There's nothing to thank me for."

"I wish I could go with you."

Moose shook his head. "That's not good. One of us is enough. You stay here or the doctor will worry. I told him tonight that I have to go to Macau for a few days, that the magazine wants a story there."

"What did he say?"

Moose shrugged. "He smiled. I don't know. I don't know what registers with him. Sometimes he doesn't react much, but at least I told him I was going to Macau, so just stick to the story when you see him tomorrow."

"Are you going tomorrow?"

"Tonight."

"Tonight?"

"From here I'm going to Kai Tak. I have the bags in the car."

"No wonder you wanted to see me tonight."

"The plane leaves at 9:40. I'll be staying at the Great Wall Sheraton. Or the Sheraton Great Wall. I think it's the Great Wall Sheraton. I have the phone number here for you." He took a folded piece of paper out of his shirt pocket and unfolded it. "5005-566. Here," and he reached over to hand it to her.

She looked at the paper and nodded. "Why did you decide to do it all of a sudden? Did anything happen?"

"No. Nothing special. But yesterday, you know, the government there declared martial law. You know that, don't you?"

"Sure. But they didn't enforce it, did they?"

"No. I called Irene–Mrs. Goodpastor at the consulate, and she told me that today China started jamming Voice of America. It's the first time they've done that in ten, eleven years. That was when they cracked down on the Democracy Wall kids."

"You know that Liberty said she doesn't stay in the Square. She says she stays at the University. I don't know whether to believe her or not. Not that she'd lie but she'd want to make me feel good. Do you think she's okay?"

"Yes, I do. She's okay. I'm sure she's okay but she's been there long enough and I don't know–I don't know."

"What else?"

"Irene read me some of the official stuff from Washington. She quoted a statement from Secretary of State Baker. The statement supported the aims of the students but he called for restraint on both sides. I don't know. The statement sounded like a neutral or something. I mean he's doing what Bush wants him to do. Why say restraint on both sides? Brent Scowcroft, he has the job Kissinger used to have, you know, National Security Advisor–he's been saying the same thing about restraint on both sides. What should the students restrain, anyway? There is no equivalence between the sides. You know what I mean?"

"Yes."

"We have to show some strength here if we want that government to act responsibly. Bush should warn Deng Xiaoping and Li Peng that if they–they–you know, use force in the square–that the United States will retaliate by cutting off all trade and those cultural exchanges and technology transfers, and if necessary we'll act militarily. The timidity of the administration is an invitation to Deng. You have these American corporations doing business there, making the Chinese government prosper. There's Chrysler, Pepsico, Beatrice Foods, PPG Industries, Occidental Petroleum, ARCO—why doesn't Bush tell the PRC he'll tell them to all get out if one kid is hurt? What's he going to do, wait until there's some crackdown? Until some kids are—" and then he hesitated. "Until some kids get in trouble or something?"

Wai-yee knew what Moose was going to say and didn't. "Will you call me as soon as you're with Liberty?"

"Yes, but don't worry, don't count on a phone call right away. The phone lines are awful and I don't know how the embassy works in Beijing. Now, you know where I'll be and I'll try to contact Irene here at the consulate if you're not home. Just don't worry. Contact Irene whenever you want. Well, you know all the consulate people."

"Moose, how did you get all the papers and everything so quick to be able to go to Beijing? That isn't easy, is it?"

"I had the magazine put in for it the day Liberty left, just in case I wanted to get there."

"You did?"

He nodded. "Just in case. And my Nixon connection helped with the PRC. I used his name. I wrote all over their applications that I had worked with him at the White House. That's the golden word there, you know. I got my visa faster than anyone at the consulate said I could."

"You be careful, Moose."

Moose smiled. "I called Nixon today and told him I'm going to Beijing and I told him why. He said if Liberty gets in trouble he'll go to Beijing himself to get her out of there."

"Did he really?"

"Really."

Wai-yee closed her eyes again. "Thank God."

"You just can't do it, can you?"

She opened her eyes and looked alarmed. "Do what?"

"Remember what the doctor told you about thanking God?"

Wai-yee gave that wide smile. "You mean I have to thank Nixon?"

"It might be nice."

"If he helps Liberty—I'll thank him, I'll hug him, I'll kiss him, I'll—"

"Maybe it's best that you thank God."

Walking through Tiananmen Square that first night in Beijing wasn't what he thought it would be. Hearing about the gathering of hundreds of thousands of people was far different than being among them. There was a presence that bathed the crowd in something far different than any demonstration Moose had seen before. This was a demonstration of so many who had not known freedom and were gathered to attempt to have it. This was not Potomac Park with the smell of marijuana and the crowded sleeping bags, as strangers searched for physical pleasures, nor was it an arena for cowardice to be justified by slogans of false innocence. This was something different. The only similarities to those crowds in Washington were the smells of unchanged clothes and the noises and disorder, but all of that paled in minutes, and it even seemed welcome and good because there was something that permeated the Square that reeked of an ageless and timeless importance. Despite the quantity of young faces, this group had assembled before, centuries ago. One placard had the words, "Let My People Go" in both Chinese and English.

Searching for any particular person in the Square was hopeless. There was no starting point or ending point and even if everyone stood still it would have taken a great deal longer than a single night to look at every face, and they didn't stand still. Moose stayed the night, although he had already checked in to the Great Wall Sheraton and a clean and quiet room waited for him there. Like Jonas staying on the beach near Cape Canaveral, Moose felt he had to stay in the square since the Great Wall Sheraton was nothing more than a hotel, and the square reeked of the most serious quest of Man.

At dawn, on the narrow and winding back streets of Beijing there was the smell of ashes outside the small businesses, as there was in the narrow streets of most cities in underdeveloped countries. It always seemed as though something was burning, because generally something was.

After dawn but in the early morning, the lobby of the Great Wall Sheraton had a smell very much like the ashes of the narrow streets, but most hotel lobbies of underdeveloped countries had that smell.

There was someone waiting for Moose at the Great Wall Sheraton when he arrived just after dawn. Sleeping on a chair near the reception desk was Liberty. She had bent her legs so her feet were tucked beneath the rest of her. She was dressed in the baggiest pants imaginable and her blouse or top or whatever it was, was adorned with a flag of Hong Kong. She was too beautiful and seemed to be too much at peace to be awakened.

He stared at her and felt totally justified in thanking God.

He knelt down and, very softly, kissed her forehead.

In the hotel's dining room used for breakfast, there appeared to be one hundred waiters for each customer, yet to catch the attention of even one of them was an achievement. That was true in most hotel dining rooms used for breakfast in underdeveloped countries.

"I called Ma last night," Liberty said at the table lit by the skylight above a seven-story atrium. "And for a change I got through. She told me you were going to check in here."

"I'm so glad! It would have taken me forever to find you. Did your mother tell you why I came here?"

Liberty smiled. "Oh, she didn't have to. I told her. I know you. I know Ma. If you didn't come, I'll bet she would have. Moose, I belong here. You're so good to care as much as you do, but I must stay here until it's over."

"The question is, how will it end?"

"We're going to win! That's how it's going to end! We're going to win!"

"What do I do, Liberty? What do I do? Just leave you here? Go back to Hong Kong without you? Your father asks about you every night. Your mother is worried sick. So am I. We all admire you so much, honey—so much, but I can't just leave you here with that government that's capable of anything. You know what they can do."

Liberty looked down at her tea cup just the way her mother would look down at something on a coffee table when she didn't want to look in Moose's eyes. "But what do you want me to do, Moose? Just give up?" Then she looked up at him. "I'm posing for a statue, you know, that they're going to put up in the Square, and I organized a lot of the Hong Kong students to take care of bringing food and water and all kinds of supplies to the people in the Square. I'm part of all this now—and I want to be. Do you think I would be happy—or I would be right in just coming home? Maybe I'm exaggerating my importance, but I feel as though I'm needed here. And I need to be part of the Square. What should I do?"

Now Moose copied her and looked down at his coffee cup. "I don't know." He put one elbow on the table and his hand on his forehead. His other hand was resting on the table. Then he felt her hand on his.

"Compromise," she said. "Do I hear a vote for compromise?"

Moose looked up with a smile. "What's the compromise?"

"A time limit. We'll have a time limit. I'll report to the U.S. Embassy every day if you want me to, so you can go home, and I'll come back home by a certain date."

"One week."

"Three weeks."

"One week!"

"Three! I know we can win in three weeks!"

"One week, Liberty!"

"Two weeks! That's a good compromise. See how I compromise?"

"And I'm staying for those two weeks. And I always want to know where you are. See how I compromise?"

Liberty gave a Wai-yee smile, and nodded. "We'll phone Ma and tell her! Let's see if we can get through!"

More and more threats were being given by the government through radio and television messages. Throughout the week employers were told to tell their employees that if they missed any work they would lose their jobs. Two hundred thousand troops were now surrounding Beijing. Those protestors in the square were being worn out, and for the first time demonstrators were leaving Tiananmen Square.

There almost seemed to be a reversal between Central in Hong Kong and Tiananmen Square in Beijing. On May the 28th, the streets of Central were filled with 800,000 people supporting the demonstrators in Tiananmen Square. But Tiananmen Square was not filled anymore. It was beginning to look like a squatter's camp that was becoming deserted.

Then something happened in the very late hours of May the 29th. Students from Beijing's Central Academy of Arts wheeled in the three sections of the Goddess of Democracy. At first it was difficult to make out what these huge packages were. As the statue was erected, first the base, then the robe-encased legs, then the top section of chest, head, arms, and hands holding the torch, the square became crowded again. Although it seemed illogical, as the crowd became larger, the crowd became quieter.

By the early hours of May the 30th, the Goddess of Democracy stood without its surrounding wooden scaffolds. Then there was noise: there was cheering and what was despair became a celebration and a revitalization. Throughout the day the crowds kept increasing to see the statue that faced north toward the portrait of Mao Zedong, in challenge.

The government was enraged at the statue and threatened the demonstrators either to tear her down or face unspecified and severe punishments. The demonstrators didn't touch her except to lay flowers at her base, and students from Hong Kong surrounded the statue with small tents and brilliant flags from colleges and universities.

"It's you!" Moose said to Liberty, his arm around her back, his hand on her shoulder as they both stood near the pup tents, craning their necks back to see the face of the Goddess.

"Do I really look like that, Moose?"

"It is you, Liberty! It's the statue of Liberty!"

"They cut my hair too short, and I don't think my neck is that thick, is it?"

"That's called artistic license. I don't think we'll complain!"

"Wait until Ma and Father see pictures of it! Now I'm sorry I told Ma I was posing for it. I would rather Ma and Father would be surprised in seeing it. Do you think they would recognize me if I didn't tell Ma?"

Moose tightened his grip on the back of her shoulder. "They'd recognize you!"

"Now aren't you glad I didn't go home?"

"Yes!" And then he said somewhat softer, "One more week."

"We'll have won by then!"

"Want something to eat?"

They walked from the Square to East Changan Avenue, but it was blockaded. "What's up?" Moose asked a policeman. The policeman didn't answer. Liberty asked the same question in Cantonese, and then in Mandarin. She translated his answer to Moose. "The street is closed, he said."

In the distance they saw why. And they stood watching.

A procession of tanks was advancing on East Changan Avenue toward the Square. The rumbling procession looked and sounded like Unter den Linden in East Berlin in 1953, and Parizska Street in Prague in 1968, and TuDo Street in Saigon in 1975. It was the most imposing and ominous signal since the students came to Tiananmen Square in April.

East Changan Avenue had been cleared of auto and pedestrian traffic other than those who were in the area before the barricades went up. The tanks for which the avenue was cleared were met by the most unlikely obstacle: one man, a young slender student in a white shirt, dark slacks, holding onto a small dufflebag and jacket, obviously not having prepared for this moment. With his right hand he signaled for the tanks to halt. If they didn't, they would run him over.

"He's crazy!" Moose said.

"He's a saint!" Liberty answered. "There's an aura about him. The tanks will stop."

The tanks stopped.

Then the drivers of the tank started again but tried to maneuver around him.

The slender man moved into their path, no matter their maneuver.

He climbed on the lead tank, and others on the sidewalks that were fearful of his fate, ran to him and grabbed him and took him from the street.

"Who is he, Liberty?" Moose asked. "Can you see who he is?"

"I think I know him. He's so far away but I think I know who he is."

"Do you know his name?"

"Yes."

Moose looked away from the street to look at Liberty. "What is it?"

"I'll spell it for you. W-A-N-G, W-A-I-L-I-N."

"Wang Wai-lin?"

"I think it's pronounced Patrick Henry."

Moose nodded. "You're right. You know him."

Liberty nodded slowly. "'Is life so dear, or peace so sweet, as to be purchased at the price of chains and slavery? Forbid it, Almighty God! I know not what course others may take; but as for me, Give me Liberty, or Give me Death!'"

Unknown to the government, on a balcony of the Beijing Hotel overlooking East Changan Avenue was Tony Wasserman of NBC who videotaped the young man facing the tanks. The young man's back was to the camera, the procession of tanks facing him. The videotape and stills made from the videotape went around the world, and the power of that image obscured any words of the government of the People's Republic of China.

On Thursday, June the 1st, the government prohibited coverage of any demonstrations in Beijing, banning photographs, videotapes, and press coverage of any army troops acting in the enforcement of martial law.

On June the 2nd, the army took up ten positions around Beijing, surrounding the city with troops. The news went all over the world despite the banning of press coverage.

"I am going to Bangkok to see Winnie," Wai-yee told Dr. Yeung. "She's having a big party for the bank, and she asked me to help her. It should be fun. I'll be back in a couple days."

Dr. Yeung nodded. It was doubtful that he understood what she said, and it was better he didn't because she was not telling him the truth. She was off to Kai Tak to fly to Beijing. She could no longer wait for phone calls. The arrangements were made by the American Consulate. Like Moose, she used the name of Nixon as a reference for the PRC.

In the pre-dawn hours of June the 3rd, on East Changan Avenue toward Tiananmen Square came five thousand troops marching five abreast. There was another equal mass of troops coming down West Changan Avenue toward Tiananmen Square, and a third equal amount of troops marching up Qianmen Street, the three masses forming a "T" converging on the square. Citizens of Beijing, along with some demonstrators from the square, rushed to the center of the "T" to stop them, forming a human obstacle before the soldiers could enter the square. From all directions, the marching of the soldiers stopped as they listened to the people, talked with them, and some soldiers embraced the people. There was little appetite among those troops to go into the square and put down the demonstration.

Then one soldier-filled jeep went right into the human barricade with total abandon. Three people were knocked down by the speeding jeep. They were killed. The three masses of soldiers seemed as shocked and saddened as the civilians. They did not advance on the square.

The "Small Lane News" reaching the square was that Deng Xiaoping directed that the People's Liberation Army must "recover the square at any cost."

The authenticity of the order was not confirmed, but throughout the day some demonstrators were beaten and some soldiers were hurt as well, and it was a standoff. More than the independent acts of fighting, there was a tension in the air that was undeniable. That tension was felt, even by the least sensitive. It was like a silent countdown to catastrophe, and no one seemed to know what the count was.

Then came hell.

After sunset of June the 3rd, radio and television announced "Do not come into the streets. Do not go to Tiananmen Square. Stay at home to safeguard your life."

Moose and Liberty were already there at the Hong Kong Material Supply Station, a large group of tents and quickly constructed tables on the Square to serve the Beijing demonstrators with food and drink and medical supplies.

Unseen by them, on West Changan Avenue, a woman was kicked by five policemen, until she fell. Then, as one held her hair, she was beaten with truncheons. A few feet from her, a man was being beaten for over one minute. The police went away as the woman lay there and the man staggered away with blood coming from gashes in his face and chest.

Before midnight, troops arrived in the city in greater mass than before and this time they were not as young and inexperienced as the ones who were marching there during the day. These were not soldiers of the 38th Army who were residents of Beijing, but professionals from the 27th Army from outside Beijing, arriving in armored vehicles that would not stop for those shouting at them. They fired their assault rifles into the crowds as they advanced toward, and finally into, the northern area of Tiananmen Square.

The citizens outside the square threw fire-bombs at them. One of the military's vehicles caught on fire and the crowd killed a soldier. Other citizens grabbed crowbars and bricks and rocks and bottles and anything else that could be used as a weapon as they heard that 350,000 soldiers were just outside Beijing from the 16th, 17th, 28th, 65th, and 69th Armies.

Outside of Tiananmen Square, soldiers were beating all those who stood in their paths. Crowds started throwing their bricks and rocks and bottles at them, and the soldiers fired back with AK-47s. People who lived in apartment buildings on Changan Avenue had to lie on the floor for safety since bullets from the AK-47s were firing in all directions. At the Minzu Hotel a soldier killed a civilian in the lobby while other soldiers went to the occupant's balconies and shot down those on the street.

Casualties were lying over one street after another, many in pools of blood, their insides on the streets.

The Voice of America was now joined by the BBC in being jammed. That left Radio Beijing. The listeners to the English language service of Radio Beijing heard the most surprising commentary:

"This is Radio Beijing. Please remember June 3, 1989. The most tragic event happened in the Chinese capital, Beijing. Thousands of people, most of them innocent civilians, were killed by fully armed soldiers when they forced their way into the city. Among the killed are our colleagues at Radio Beijing. The soldiers were riding on armored vehicles and used machine guns against thousands of local residents and students who tried to block their way. When the army convoys made a breakthrough, soldiers continued to spray their bullets indiscriminately at crowds in the street. Eyewitnesses say some armored vehicles even crushed foot soldiers who hesitated in front of the resisting civilians. Radio Beijing English Department deeply mourns those who died in the tragic incident and appeals to all its listeners to join our protest for the gross violation of human rights and the most barbarous suppression of the people. Because of this abnormal situation here in Beijing, there is no other news we could bring you. We sincerely ask for your understanding and thank you for joining us at this most tragic moment." (The unidentified voice was never heard from again.)

Then, as though a scene from one movie was spliced onto a film of another, Prime Minister Li Peng gave a radio and state television speech on the environment. He was talking about clean air and pollution, as though he was a member of Greenpeace, his image painted by Salvador Dali.

Midnight passed and the massacre of the streets was soon to become the massacre of Tiananmen Square, beginning in a fury as troops moved into the square from all directions.

Tanks and other Armored Personnel Carriers ran over tents in Tiananmen Square although it was known that students were in the tents. The soldiers poured gasoline over the demolished tents and over the flattened bodies, and then they put flames to the poured gasoline.

At least thirty-three carts, each carrying three dead bodies, were wheeled away shortly after the Army opened fire.

Bayonets were becoming as frequent as bullets.

Doctors attempting to heal the wounded were killed. Hospitals were instructed by the government not to reveal how many had been brought to their doors, or how many the hospitals listed as dead. The bodies were not allowed to be given to their families.

Some students in the square linked their arms together to form a wall in front of advancing soldiers. The soldiers stopped to kneel and spray the crowd with live bullets. The line of students fell to the ground from left to right.

Bodies were everywhere, and on the pavement there were long patterns of blood from where bodies had been dragged away.

"Liberty! Liberty! Liberty! Liberty!" Wai-yee was moving slowly and frantically through the Square yelling the name of her daughter.

"Miss," one young Englishwoman she was passing, stopped her. "Miss, that is terribly dangerous to yell that word. I wouldn't take that chance if I were you. It won't do any good, you know. That is very dangerous."

"That's my daughter!"

"What's your daughter?"

"Liberty! That's her name! That's her statue!"

The English girl thought she was talking to a madwoman. "It's not the Statue of Liberty, Miss. That's the Goddess of Democracy."

"It's my daughter!"

"All right then, have it your way, Miss, but be quiet about it or you'll be killed yelling that word like that."

And the Englishwoman's prophecy was accurate. There was a splash of gunfire that seemed to come out of nowhere and both the Englishwoman and Wai-yee were on the pavement with blood streaming so heavily between them that their blood mixed in ever-increasing puddles and there was not a movement of either of them. The Englishwoman's eyes were closed. Wai-yee's eyes were open, left looking up at the statue.

Somehow, with no memory of how they got there, Moose and Liberty were kneeling beside her, Wai-yee's head resting on Moose's chest, Liberty kissing her lips. The English woman was being dragged off by soldiers.

"Ma! Ma!" Liberty's face was drowned in tears.

Moose had his eyes closed, pasted by his own tears. "I love you, Wai-yee. I love you more than anything in the world."

Moose carried her body in his arms out of the Square, and he and his most valuable cargo, and Liberty, walked all the way to the Central

Academy of Arts where immediate plans with the students were made for a cremation.

Sunrise was not sunrise. The sun was invisible behind the gray and the smoke. Bodies were strewn throughout the Square. As bodies were picked up by those daring enough to remain in the Square, many of the rescuers were shot by soldiers and became motionless bodies themselves.

It was just a little past five o'clock in that gray morning when one tank headed directly to the Goddess of Democracy and smashed the giant statue to the ground.

SEVENTY
PROOF
1989

It took the most superhuman strength to witness. Students from Beijing's Central Academy of Fine Arts were all dressed in white, the traditional color of mourning. They had meticulously made a paper model of a large and intricate house with miniature furniture and a miniature model of an air conditioner and even paper servants inside the miniature house. Other students made a red paper car, and other students made a paper boat, and other students made a paper clock, and other students made other things of paper, and all those things were burned, to accompany Wai-yee's spirit in heaven.

Neither Liberty nor Moose felt alive on the flight back to Hong Kong. This was a new and horrible existence that had to be endured because there was no choice. On Liberty's lap was a closed white box with the filled urn inside it. Liberty was motionless, sitting erect almost soldier-like, her eyes straight ahead, her hands never leaving the closed white box for an instant. Moose's arm was around Liberty, his mind in total disarray. When he felt the surge of a sob that couldn't be stopped, he turned away from her in the hope Liberty wouldn't know he was beyond control. But there was the sound of it.

Just like her mother, it was Liberty who comforted him. "Moose," she said, "Moose. Ma is here. Ma is here with us. She loves you, you know."

He nodded quickly, doing his best, which was not good enough to control his tears.

All of this was an unreal hell.

"Ma is here," she repeated. Moose didn't know if Liberty was looking at him or still looking straight ahead. He didn't want to find out. He didn't want her to see his face. He wanted to run. He wanted to stop thinking. He wanted to stop living. He didn't even know he was saying out loud what he was thinking. "What kind of a God are You?" he said to God.

Liberty answered, "He's a good God, Moose. He made Ma. He let us know her and be with her. He let her carry me and sing to me and love me. He made Ma and He made you and He made Father. He is taking care of Ma now. He is a good God."

She was so much her mother's daughter.

How could Hong Kong still be going on? The lights. The people. Some of them laughing. Life going on as it was before he left. How could that be? And tomorrow the sun would come up again? And there would be new days and nights and weekends and holidays and seasons changing and all those things? How could that be? They'll cancel July the 4th, won't they? And Thanksgiving and Christmas? Things can't go on as before. Everyone has to stop those things.

"Jonas, I must see you." Moose was trying to keep from breaking down on the phone. "Please come to Hong Kong. Jonas, there is no God. There's nothing. Jonas, please. There is no God."

In little more than a day, Jonas was in Hong Kong. Had it taken him any longer, Moose was not at all sure he could have survived. He was nothing more than a maze of terrible thoughts without intermission between the thoughts. Seeing Jonas provided a continuity link with previous days when even at worst, there was sanity.

It was an unusual sight at Kai Tak that night. Two grown, very mature men, in an embrace, with one of them, the largest of the two, murmuring. "Jonas. Jonas. Jonas. Thank you!"

"Where is Liberty now?" Jonas asked as they walked out of the terminal to the taxi area.

"Home. A girlfriend is staying with her. And Wai-yee's sister who lives in Thailand is coming here I think on Wednesday to be with her for a few days."

"God, Moose, I'm so sorry."

"I know you are. We haven't told Dr. Yeung. Liberty and I went to see him and he's–he's so bad off. Now he goes in and out of consciousness. He doesn't know what people are saying. I don't think he recognized me. Liberty held his hand for an hour and he didn't say anything. We couldn't tell him. Why should we? What good would it do?"

"Maybe the state he's in is a godsend for him."

"If he goes, Jonas, what will Liberty have? No mother–then no father? How much can Liberty take? But can she take him like he is now? Either way, what does she have? She has nothing."

"She has you."

Moose shook his head, then changed it to a nod. "Yeah. A fine thing that is for her. I can't even think. Wai-yee was – was...Jonas, I've lost the ability to think. Do you know what that's like?"

"Yes."

"You do?" And then he remembered what Jonas had been through for four years. He had forgotten something of such importance. "Yes, of course. Of course you know."

The taxi was passing the government housing blocks with laundry hanging out of windows in the heat of the night.

"I got you a room at the Shangri-La. It's good. It's on this side, the Kowloon side."

"Thanks."

"The driver," Moose said. "He must be in his twenties, isn't he?"

Jonas was bothered by the question. Why was that of any interest to Moose. "I suppose so."

"I get angry at any person I see who's younger than Wai-yee was. I'm mad that they're alive and she isn't."

"I understand."

"I'm glad he didn't smile when he took the bags. If they smile, I could slug them."

"Do you get mad at Liberty? She's younger."

"Oh, no. Never. She's everything. She's unbelievable. But if there's a God why would he say that Wai-yee has to go? Why does he allow Liberty to suffer? Why does He do what He does? Wai-yee has to die while all these people live, some of them so wretched. Why would God do such a thing?"

"I don't know, Moose."

Moose nodded with righteousness. Then the nod stopped and the look of righteousness was gone. "You're honest. I was afraid you might start to preach to me with a bunch of stuff from the Bible. You're honest. You say you don't know. I appreciate that. But you study all these kinds of things. You've given this sort of thing more thought than any person I've ever met. And you don't know."

"If I knew then I'd be God, wouldn't I?"

"Jonas, I know how to answer my questions. The answer is, there is no God! How can you believe there is? Wai-yee's dead but Deng Xiaoping lives and Li Peng lives and Idi Amin lives and the Ayatollah Khomeini lives and Pol Pot lives and Muammar Khadafy lives. Yeah, I'm not going to waste my time praising God."

Jonas, for the first time this night, gave a short smile. "I'm sure it doesn't mean much to you but Khomeini died."

"No, he didn't."

"He did. I'm sure you haven't heard any news since all of this, but he died while the Tiananmen Square Massacre was going on."

Moose gave a grunt. "Why didn't he die when he was twenty? It would have saved so many good lives. What's that, some kind of balance? Khomeini for Wai-yee? And Wai-yee is going to Heaven and Khomeini's going to Hell? Is that what I'm supposed to believe? Is that what you believe?"

"I don't concern myself much with what happens after death anymore. I used to. Too much time is spent on that when it's the only thing we're all going to find out whether we want to or not. And if we don't find out then, for sure, it's not worth thinking about. I think about life. I know what that is."

"So do I. I'm finding out what it is. What kind of an evil, sorrowful scheme is life?"

"Do you talk to Liberty this way?"

"No, of course I don't talk to Liberty this way. She wouldn't listen to me on this, anyway. She has as much belief in God as you do. She's like a rock. But see? You can't answer, Jonas. Why not just admit there is no God? Do you remember, I don't know how many years ago, but do you remember that cover of *Time*? It was a black cover and it said 'God Is

Dead.' I think that's what it said. I got mad when I saw it. I was mad at *Time* magazine. But they were almost right. Almost. It should have said that God Never Lived."

"Are we to believe no one created us? Moose, I don't believe in God because I have faith. I believe in God because the alternative is too illogical. But I admit it's a belief. Like you, like everyone, I want proof, too."

"After we drop the bags off at the hotel and you check in and all that, I want to show you something. It's on the other side. I want to show you what I believe in."

Jonas didn't want to say it, because he knew that nothing was on Moose's mind other than the suffering of the tragedy, but when Jonas saw the skyline of Hong Kong Island, he was awed. But that wasn't what Moose wanted to show him. What he wanted to show him was in Victoria Park.

There were one million people holding candles. It was more than one sixth of the entire population of the entire Hong Kong territory, standing there in silence. At the center of the massive crowd was a giant replica of the Goddess of Democracy, taller than the original that had stood in Tiananmen Square.

"That's Liberty," Moose said to Jonas. "That, Jonas, is my daughter. She's what I believe in."

Then Szeto Wah stood at the base of the statue and spoke to the crowd through what seemed to be hundreds of loudspeakers. Neither Moose nor Jonas could understand what he was saying because he spoke in Cantonese.

Some of the organizers were passing out pieces of paper. When one of the organizers saw Moose and Jonas, the organizer nodded and reached to the bottom of the stack. "We have English," he said and he handed each of them a paper.

The paper told that troops had mopped up Tiananmen Square by burning and removing bodies, and in the absence of more targets in the Square, the killing had expanded on the surrounding streets. The paper said that Beijing hospitals had verified 700 deaths in the massacre while Amnesty International estimated that the number was a minimum of one thousand and the Red Cross gave the figure of 2,600 until the Red Cross was ordered by the government of the People's Republic to deny their report. Other estimates were as high as 10,000. The paper said that precise figures were unknown since so many of the corpses were burned on the spot, while others were put on helicopters to be taken to locations unknown, and the living were warned to remain silent.

The bottom of the paper had a statement of U.S. President Bush from Kennebunkport, Maine: "I deeply deplore the decision to use force against peaceful demonstrators and the consequent loss of life. We have been urging and continue to urge non-violence, restraint and dialogue. Tragically, another course has been chosen. Again, I urge a return to nonviolent means for dealing with the current situation."

"Moose, may I meet Liberty?" Jonas asked.

Moose nodded. "Yes. Tomorrow." He dreaded going to that home. How could he look again at those things that were Wai-yee's? How could he look at that picture of John Travolta that she had hung on the wall. He wanted to phone John Travolta wherever he was, to thank him for giving Wai-yee some pleasure in life. But how he dreaded seeing the picture of him hanging there.

Tomorrow came and the house on Crocodile Hill was filled with students. Filled. This was not a place of grief. "I won't let this house be sad," Liberty said to Moose and Jonas. "This was always a place of happiness, and that's the way it's going to remain. Father once told me an old Chinese proverb, 'That the birds of worry and care fly over your head, this you cannot change. But that they build nests in your hair, this you can prevent.' This house has always been a place where we made plans. So my friends and I are making plans. Ma didn't teach me how to cry. Ma taught me how to laugh." And she walked away into a small circle of students.

Jonas said, "You don't need me, Moose. You need her. In all my years of studying religion and probing the philosophy of Solzhenitsyn and Sadat and reading about every great thinker of our times—she's the answer, isn't she? I came to Hong Kong to try and be of some help to you, if I could. I didn't expect to receive help, myself. Moose, I don't care whether or not you believe in God. Do as you choose. That young woman just proved Him to me. My search for proof has ended."

SEVENTY-ONE
THE LAST GEISELA
1989

When he wasn't on camera he was either drinking, or he was taking drugs by mouth, or nose, or injection, or he was doing something else that he had to hide. His wife, Linda, was no longer naive. She was resigned to it all. Ted's trips away from her were more eagerly awaited by Linda than ever before.

Ted was supposed to be in Berlin, and had he made the flight from Hamburg to Berlin, he would have covered the collapse of the Berlin Wall. But he didn't know it was going to come down.

His assignment, for which he was running late, was to get to Berlin because, little by little and then a lot by a lot, Eastern Europe was shifting to the politics of Western Europe. That transition became an avalanche in the five months following Tiananmen Square, starting with Poland having an unprecedented free election and, as expected, it brought about a rejection of communism and the victory of Tadeusk Mazowiecki as Premier, who was the closest advisor to Lech Walesa of the Solidarity movement. That gave courage to others. Hungary allowed thousands of East Germans to go through Hungary to enter West Germany via Austria. Hungary was soon not alone in providing an aisle-way for the exodus of East Germans. Czechoslovakia was next, with a more direct route from East Germany through Czechoslovakia to West Germany. Fifty thousand East Germans took advantage of the opening by leaving their homes. By mid-October the staunch follower of the Soviet Union, Eric Honecker, was ousted as East Germany's leader by his own Politburo. Within days Hungary proclaimed itself as a free republic and officially commemorated the 1954 unsuccessful attempt for freedom from the Soviet Union. On November the 9th, East Germany's new leader, Egon Krentz, announced that he would ease restrictions on the travel of East Germans to the west.

And so Berlin was a very logical place for Ted Murphy to give his reports. But why not interview people in Hamburg first? He could do it on that Thursday until the sun went down. That would leave Hamburg's Reeperbahn for when the moon came up. He could go to Berlin tomorrow.

It was a very sad disguise of a mustache and glasses that he put on at the Hotel Vier Jahreszeiten. True, he didn't give the instant appearance of Ted Murphy any more, but that nose was a real giveaway if anyone studied him enough.

No one would study him that much where he was going.

Because a hotel doorman hailed the taxi for him and the doorman asked him where he was going, he went to the train station, which was certainly a respectable destination. Then he took another taxi from there to the Reeperbahn, which was not a respectable destination.

The Reeperbahn was a wide avenue in the St. Pauli district with a lot of establishments that catered to the more prurient interests of tourists.

Ted Murphy, with his silly mustache and glasses, went from bar to bar, and at one of them he befriended the bartender, who introduced himself as Heinrich, who could get Ted anything he wanted in Hamburg.

"You mean anything?" Ted asked with an inappropriate and phony innocence, which would even have been unbecoming for a teenager.

"Yah! Anything!"

In short time, Ted was the proud possessor of a folded piece of paper with an address that was "the best in St. Pauli! No! The best in all Hamburg! Only for special people!" The Reeperbahn was filled with one place after another that had bartenders who gave folded pieces of paper with addresses that "were the best" because their customers were always "special people."

Ted, in a casual gesture, put the folded piece of paper in his shirt pocket and thanked his new buddy, Heinrich. He didn't want to use it right away. He wanted to have some restraint, so he went on to another bar and to another, getting himself deeper and deeper in the mood.

By two o'clock in the morning the mood was as intense as it was going to get. "Okee-dokey," he said to himself. "I'm a-comin'. This doll better be good!"

The streets were very quiet once the Reeperbahn was behind him. Not a bird chirp, not a dog bark, not a leaf falling. All the doors to the houses looked too low, as though they were built only for the entrance and exit of children. Something was wrong with all the doors.

As he walked, he kept comparing every street sign to the street whose name was spelled on the folded piece of paper with twenty-two letters, seventeen of them being vowels. It took him many back and forth looks to compare the street signs with the writing on the piece of paper, but there it was. And there was the designated number.

The door was unlocked because it didn't allow entrance to anything more than a stairway. He was supposed to go four flights up. No elevator. Each staircase ended by a too-small door with a gold name plate nailed to each one. He felt like a Nazi Storm Trooper going to get someone in the middle of the night. Maybe Paul Lukas picking up an Englishman who sat by a big shortwave radio. Or did Paul Lukas play someone in the underground? Oh, what difference did it make? This girl was supposed to be the best.

His legs hurt from too much walking up stairs. He knocked on the door. He heard the rustle behind the door. A woman's voice yelled out something in German that sounded like a short question and, he assumed it must have been "Who's there?"

"Heinrich told me to stop by," Ted yelled back.

"Goot! Goot!" No mistake. This was the right place.

She opened the door.

This was the wrong place. Unless Heinrich had pulled one on him. And of course he did.

"Zzzoh!" the not-pretty and very overweight, over made-up, over-blonde in the under-doorway said to him.

"Zzzoh!" he answered her. He'd go in, anyway. It had been too much trouble to find the place to just walk out. Besides, his legs hurt and he had to wait before going down the stairs.

"Come in, American."

She was terrible but so was he. It didn't work. He should have known. When he realized he was failing, he said he really didn't want to do what he wanted to do, and she pretended she was disappointed. It was awful. And he didn't have enough German marks. "American dollars are as good as marks," she said as though she was giving a tribute to the United States.

"How much?"

"One hundred is fine. You didn't take that much time with me."

I'll say. He nodded.

"You must call me when you're back in town. You can phone me direct because I like you." What a compliment. "Then it will be cheaper than going through Heinrich. I want to see you again."

"Same," he said. Never. He wanted a drink. But not here.

"I'll give you my number," and she shrugged. "Save some money." She took out a pencil and pad from a desk drawer and started scrawling on it. "Here."

He looked at what she wrote. There were too many digits in the telephone number just like there were too many of all things in Hamburg. "All those numbers?"

"I added the code from the States." As if he was going to call her from the United States to make sure she could schedule him. "I wrote my name, too." He hadn't even asked her name. Nor did she ask his.

"Geisela," he read.

"It was a name that was popular during the war. But my parents still liked it when I was born. No one is named Geisela anymore."

"Well, I'll see ya."

"I'm the last Geisela."

He hoped so.

She opened the door for him. Then she added another "Zzzoh!"

When he got to the street he stood there waiting for a taxi to come by. After a wait of about five minutes, a vehicle was coming towards him and it had a dome light and he waved his arms with such passion that it appeared he was signaling a helicopter while on the Sahara Desert after weeks without water. It was a police car. The police stopped for him. "Sorry," Ted said. "I didn't mean you. I was signalin' a taxi." They didn't understand English, but it didn't make any difference. They zoomed off.

He started walking. He found his way back to the still brightly lit Reeperbahn and went into the first bar he came to, had a drink, and then went to another bar. Then he wanted something to get him even higher and that was back at the hotel. He couldn't walk very well, but he didn't need to. On this street there was a line of taxis waiting to take away the depressed who had a tough time walking after hours on the Reeperbahn.

The too-ornate-for-Americans lobby of the Hotel Vier Jahreszeiten was ominously still and the night-clerk wore a tuxedo of all things to be wearing at four in the morning. An elderly woman was mopping the floor near the reception desk. That, too, was in keeping with the stillness because neither her mop nor her soft shoes made much noise. Ted had already taken off his fake moustache and glasses, and had straightened his tie and had brushed his hair back before making his grand appearance before the night-clerk.

"Good evening," Ted Murphy said in his loudest I'm-not-trying-to-hide-anything voice, but the tuxedoed night-clerk answered back "Good morning" which had a very definite you-are-too-trying-to-hide-something tone.

"Zweihundertzweiunddreissig," Ted gave his room number in perfect and very loud German.

"Two Thirty Two," the obnoxious night-clerk translated into English as he took the key off its hook above the mailbox. He refused to be outdone in anything.

When Ted got to his room he turned on the television set to see if anything was being broadcast at this hour. Something was. It was the continual coverage of the Berlin Wall coming down. East and West Germans were dancing on top of the Wall at the Brandenburg Gate. There was chopping of the wall by Germans and tourists. Mallets were hitting chisels, driving holes in the Wall, and large chunks of it fell. Then bulldozers pulled down entire slabs of it.

Under the conditions, Ted put Geisela in a drawer of his mind that was packed with incidents that he would swear, even to himself, never happened. He reached in his suitcase and took out a small packet. With what he had in the packet combined with what he had in the bars, he was going to be a different man, or at least in a different world. He drifted into unconsciousness, and before everything started spinning, he noticed there was a painting of the Eiffel Tower on the wall directly above the television set. That didn't make sense. This wasn't Paris. If he was in Paris would his hotel room have a painting of something in Hamburg? Maybe a painting of the last Geisela.

For one month, the whereabouts of Ted Murphy were unknown. He had checked out of the Hotel Vier Jahreszeiten on November the 10th for an untold journey. "On assignment" was the only excuse for his absence that was given on television. On December the 12th he showed up at work in Washington, D.C., where he immediately collapsed.

At 7:25 in the morning, every seat was taken on the two long sides of the mahogany conference table in the Roosevelt Room of the White House's West Wing. The chairs at the head and foot of the table were still vacant, waiting for Chief of Staff, John Sununu, to occupy the head chair, and the Director of the Office of Management and Budget, Richard Darman, to be at the foot.

Before those two seats were occupied, the Senior Staff Meeting of the Bush White House was very much like a classroom before the teacher walked in. The only difference was no spit-balls.

"Pardon me for not crying because he's sick," the man who always slumped in his chair said. "Besides—do you really believe Murphy had a heart attack?"

"Let it be that way," the man who always jutted out his chin like FDR said. "That's not our concern. Our only concern about Murphy is what the president should do if—if the fellow—if Murphy should die."

"What do you mean, what should the President do?" the man who hated to establish precedents asked.

"I mean, does he go to the funeral?" the man who always jutted out his chin like FDR answered.

"If Murphy dies, he might as well," the man who was always disgusted with everything offered. "He went to the funerals of Brezhnev, Andropov, and Chernenko. He might as well complete the cycle with Murphy. At least this funeral won't be in Moscow."

"Now, now, now," the man who never wanted to make waves said.

"He's already sent a telegram to Mrs. Murphy expressing his hope Murphy gets well quick," the man who was secretly writing a book on President Bush said. "That's enough. If Murphy doesn't come out of this, going to the services is too sticky. It isn't like some chief of state died. Let's not treat it that way."

"I agree," the man who hated to establish precedents said. "You got it. Let's not elevate the importance of a television newscaster."

"He isn't just a television newscaster," the man who appointed himself to make sure this was a kinder and gentler president said. "You have to remember that Murphy's been around a long time and there are a lot more Americans who care about him dying than any of those Soviet leaders."

The man who always wrote out lists brought his right hand in front of his face and he raised one finger at a time. "First, the Wall has come down. Second, Lebanon's President Moawad has been assassinated. Third, communism is falling apart all over Eastern Europe. Fourth, Noriega says Panama is at war with us as long as we continue economic sanctions. And here we are worrying about whether or not the president should go to the funeral of Ted Murphy—and he isn't even dead! Come on. Let's assume he dies. With everything else going on, if the president goes, I think the people would ask what kind of priorities he has."

"High priorities," the man who appointed himself to make sure this was a kinder and gentler president said. "They'll appreciate that he takes the time to go."

"Send Quayle," the man who always said, "Send Quayle" said. "That's what vice presidents are for, aren't they?"

"Dan shouldn't go. No one should," the man who wished Bush was Reagan said.

"I agree," the man who wished Reagan was Bush uniquely agreed with the man who wished Bush was Reagan. "Look–Murphy has been dumping all over the president since the president was a Congressman. Let's knock all this off. He already sent a telegram to Mrs. Murphy. Enough is enough. No president, no Veep, no anyone."

"Now, wait a minute. Let's just wait a minute." It was the man who always started his suggestion with "Now, wait a minute. Let's just wait a minute," and silence always followed for a few seconds as though he was about to reveal the wisest thoughts of mankind. "You know, Murphy was a very respected and idolized figure for decades, no matter what we might think of him. The president recognizes everyone's contributions and so this–" and he grasped for words, "–journalistic giant can't go ignored by the president." That was it. That was his offering.

The man who always acted as though he knew the president better than anyone else said, "No. I don't want my president honoring someone who has done more harm to the world, to say nothing of this country, than any citizen who hasn't been locked up in the pokey for years."

"I want to interject something," the man who always monitored the news said. "That telegram he sent to Mrs. Murphy made the wires, and most of the papers picked it up. The nets ran with it. The reaction is good this morning and he ought to keep it up."

The man who appointed himself to make sure this was a kinder and gentler president added, "And the fact that Murphy was against the president is reason enough for the president to go. If Murphy supported him I may think differently, but going to the funeral of a known political opponent would show what a big man the president really is."

"Or what a fool he is," the man who wished Bush was Reagan said. "Where's the moral balance in all this? Are you suggesting that you don't go to the funeral of your friends but you go to the funeral of your enemies? What logic!"

"Send Quayle!" the man who always said "Send Quayle" said.

"Before we go on," the man who always made out lists said. "Does anyone have a list of all the funerals he's been to since the inauguration, and then we can compare it with how many Reagan went to?"

"Good idea," the man who never had an idea of his own said. "We should get a list."

The man who always slumped down in his chair said. "Oh, let's get off that. We don't need a list. We can think for ourselves. We can set our own precedents."

"Can I say something?" The man who rarely said anything said. Since he asked no one in particular, no one answered. He went on, anyway. "If Murphy dies, then the president should go to the funeral, which would probably be in New York, so the president should have something else to do there, so it isn't the only reason he makes the trip."

"Like what?" the man who never wanted to make waves said.

"Anything. Couldn't he see Governor Cuomo? He's been requesting to see the president. Or even Mayor Koch for that matter. It won't do any harm."

The man who never wanted to establish precedents said, "Would another president have gone to a newscaster's funeral? Let's think for a minute. Let's go back to the beginning. JFK was the first real television president. Would he have done it for a television newscaster?"

"Who cares what JFK would have done?" the man who always slumped down in his chair said.

"He wouldn't have gone. That's my point, and I don't want to see any more honors heaped on Murphy. He's told eight presidents to go shove it and he's told them time and time again what to do, and he's been wrong every time, but he always acted as though he was right, even after he was proven wrong. Still, the public believes he was always right. Making a hero out of this guy is just going to encourage others to do what he did. Let's knock it off before they start naming bridges and monuments after him. We can set all sort of precedents and patterns by this."

"Quayle, please," the man who always said, "Send Quayle" said very softly.

The west door from the hall flung open and Chief of Staff Sununu walked in briskly with papers under his arm. Instant quiet. "Good morning," John Sununu said. The teacher was here.

There was a quiet chorus of "Good morning, Governor."

Then Richard Darman walked in the west door, looking angry. But he often looked angry.

"In case anyone in this room cares," John Sununu said, "Ted Murphy is up and walking. He should be out of the hospital next week and recover just fine so he can tell us off on television for years to come. And get this–he received a get-well letter from Gorbachev! Now, have you been talking about what our response should be to Noriega's comments on our Panama sanctions?"

"Yes, Governor," the man who never wanted to make waves said.

SEVENTY-TWO
YOU BETTER NOT POUT, I'M TELLING YOU WHY
1989

Batman collaborated with the high-rise New World Centre, to wish nighttime onlookers a Merry Christmas and a Happy New Year in animated lights. Batman enjoyed the prominence of his logo beautifully lit on practically the entire side of the building. In an effort to illuminate everything possible, even the TM, which stood for "trade-mark" was in brilliant neon. That was not to suggest that Batman and his accessories glowed alone. Almost every high-rise building on both sides of Hong Kong's Victoria Harbor was brilliantly lit in colored spectacle, each building trying to outdo the spectacular clothing of the others.

To the visitor, Hong Kong, lit unlike any other city for the holidays, was in a dazzling celebration. Too bad, but it was an electric mask. Voltage was covering-up the worst Hong Kong Christmas season since World War II. That was because here on the South China Sea, the Tiananmen Square Massacre was not just a matter of last June, it was a matter of life and death.

A very changed Moose Dunston turned his head away from the lights because it was a Christmas season that Wai-yee wouldn't witness, at least from a platform on earth.

It had continued to be a nightly ritual for Moose to go to Queen Elizabeth Hospital and sit by the bed of Dr. Yeung. Liberty would go there in the day between classes at the University of Hong Kong. A couple times a week she would meet Moose there at night and she would put her hand on Dr. Yeung's forehead and brush it back over and over again, while Moose would sit quietly, some time holding Liberty's hand, some time holding the hand of Dr. Yeung. The visits were down to only about ten or fifteen minutes, since there was no audible communication with Dr. Yeung. No one had told him about Wai-yee, but both Moose and Liberty were confident that, somehow, he knew.

The only bright note of this Christmas season was that Liberty had a boyfriend from the University, Andrew Fung Kai-hung, who idolized her and had, at least temporarily, passed the rigid tests of both Moose and Jonas who had let him know that unless he treated Liberty as the goddess she was, he would be a dead Andrew Fung Kai-hung.

Nine nights before Christmas it was Liberty's nineteenth birthday and, because of that, Queen Elizabeth Hospital was host to a visiting delegation to Dr. Yeung's room: Liberty, Moose, Jonas and Andrew all entered together against hospital rules, but hospital rules were always dismissed when it came to the room of Dr. Yeung. When the visit was done, the three men took Liberty to Lai Ching Heen Restaurant at the Regent Hotel and then to the hotel's cocktail lounge.

Getting to the Regent through the streets of Kowloon was not easy. The streets were roped off and Moose had to park his car blocks away. They had to walk with the greatest care so as not to trip over hundreds of extended tripods with cameras mounted on them. It was the annual Christmas season rite of Hong Kong people taking pictures of each other in front of brilliantly lit buildings, and pictures of the buildings without anyone in front of them.

"Jonas," Liberty asked as she and Andrew sat on two heavily upholstered purple chairs next to each other in the cocktail lounge, with Moose and Jonas on the same type of chairs opposite them. "Will father ever be as he was? Is there any chance?"

Jonas hesitated before he answered because he knew the answer. "I'm not a doctor, Liberty. You know as much as I do."

"Jonas, I'm asking you because you believe in the power of faith."

"I do. But, Liberty, I'm not a prophet."

She turned her eyes to Moose. "Moose?"

"Yes?" He was hoping she wouldn't ask him the same question.

"May I have a real drink? A real one?" It was the first time she asked him permission to do anything, as a daughter would ask her father.

What a relief, and what a marvelous feeling. "You bet. It's your birthday. You're a woman, not a girl now. But don't make a habit of it. This isn't going to be the start of something." He heard himself sound like a father, and liked it.

Andrew put his hand on Liberty's hand, then quickly drew it back when that action caught the quick attention of both Moose and Jonas. "What would you like to drink, Liberty?"

Liberty inherited the gesture of her mother; she tilted her head down and cocked it and put her hand in front of her mouth while looking up at Andrew, even though she wasn't laughing. "What tastes good?"

"Tomato juice!" Moose said simultaneously with Jonas who said, "A Coke!"

"No!" Liberty smiled wider, and put down her hand.

"All right," Moose nodded. "How about champagne? We'll get a bottle and we'll all have some."

Liberty nodded, and she started to stand. "I'm going to the restroom."

Moose and Jonas stood up immediately and a perplexed Andrew followed suit.

When she walked away to the restroom, Moose and Jonas sat again but Andrew didn't do it until Moose and Jonas were seated. Now Andrew was left alone in the intimidating company of the elder protectors of Liberty.

"I'll tell you, Andrew m'boy," Moose said. "If you're ever with her and some other guy, and he doesn't stand up for her, or if he doesn't open the door for her, you have my permission to slug him in the gut."

"Yes, sir."

"Flatten him. If you get put in jail I'll bail you out."

"Yes, sir."

"I spent many years of my life dealing with contingencies. You know what that means?"

"Yes, sir."

"Those are contingencies. You never know who she'll meet. If anyone ever gives her a tough time—if they don't give her the respect she deserves and, God forbid, if any man ever tries to touch her—you do everything short of murder. Jonas or I will finish him off with a gun or a knife. We know how."

"Thank you, sir."

Jonas was nodding through the catalogue of violence.

"Mr. Dunston?" Andrew said uneasily.

"Yes, Andrew?"

"I know how fortunate I am that Liberty spends time with me. I know what she is. I worship her, Mr. Dunston."

Moose smiled. "So do I."

Jonas agreed. "That's a good phrase, Andrew. 'Worship her' is exactly right."

Moose leaned over to Andrew. "Andrew, let me ask you something."

"Yes, sir."

"There are times when I phone Liberty at night and she isn't in—that happens often. I never want to spy on her, ever. I have absolute trust in her. But when I talk to her the next day and ask her where she was, she always gives the same answer that tells me nothing. She says that she has 'things to do.' If she's with you, that's fine, I have no problem with that. I know you respect her, but it's that she seems to be secretive about where she is. I worry about her. I can't help worrying about her."

Andrew pursed his lips together. "I know," he said.

"You know what?"

"It happens to me too, sir. I ask her if she was studying at the library, or went to a movie or something. She's very honest. She will never lie. She answers that she had so much to do, and she gets an angry tone, so I don't question her further. I think she's telling me it's none of my business."

Jonas said, "Do you think she's out with someone else?"

"No. No, I don't. She would tell me if she was."

Moose shook his head. "Then what do you think?"

"I don't know, sir."

Moose and Jonas exchanged a glance, then Moose looked back at Andrew. "I want you to know that I trust her, Andrew. You have to trust her, too. I just don't want her to be endangered in any way."

"Yes, sir. Last week she gave me a different answer when I told her I called her until a little after midnight and I was concerned about her."

Moose leaned further to Andrew. "What? What did she say?"

"She said, 'Andrew, I take after Ma.'"

"What do you think she meant by that?"

"I don't know, sir. And there's something else I don't understand about her."

"What?"

"She never seems to have any money. I know that her mother left her a trust fund. I know that you have been very kind to her. But I never see her spend any money. She never seems to have any."

Liberty came back from the restroom and sat back down next to Andrew, and she started talking immediately. "There were two young girls in the bathroom," she said, "and they were singing. Do you know what they were singing?"

"No," Andrew said while Moose and Jonas shook their heads.

"Listen to this," and she started singing to the melody of 'Santa Claus is Coming to Town.' "'You better watch out, you better not cry. You better not pout, I'm telling you why. Deng Xiaoping is coming to town!' They were laughing. It's not funny. It's true. Do you know what I hate?"

There was no answer.

"I hate the way some Hong Kong people accept it. They accept it. I don't accept it. Do you know who I love?"

"Who?"

"That woman you both knew who works at Ma's Consulate now." Liberty called the American Consulate, 'Ma's Consulate.' "Irene Goodpastor. I never met her, but she put a picture of Ma in the reception room. I went there just to see it. I asked the Marine Guard who did that, and he said Irene Goodpastor asked the Consul General, Donald Anderson, and he agreed right away. They loved Ma there. She quit, but they still love her. See? They knew she had principle." It looked for a moment as if Liberty was ready to cry, but she smiled. "And so they have her picture up. Everyone–everyone sees her now. No one can go there without seeing Ma. Did you know that?"

The next morning Moose was in the American Consulate Building standing in front of the black-framed photograph with a black ribbon above it. As was true with every photograph of Wai-yee, she looked like a movie star. Beneath her picture was the inscription, "Yeung Tso Wai-yee who served the American Consulate with distinction from 1959 through 1978." It was on the wall across from the photographs of President Bush and Vice President Quayle.

After the U.S. Marine Guard gave him a badge, Moose went through the reception room to the elevator to the fourth floor office of Irene Goodpastor. They had reversed their responsibilities from years back. Now it was Irene who had an American flag behind her desk in a U.S. facility. Moose had to wear a visitor's badge when in a U.S. facility. He thanked her for putting up the picture of Wai-yee, but then it was not a conversation of thanks.

"My God, Irene, what the devil are we doing as a nation? What is President Bush doing? Kowtowing to those murderers who run China?"

Irene swallowed hard. She respected Moose and she knew that he was not a man who made a habit of striking out at his own government. And Moose, too, had respect for Irene. She had been an observer of government most of her life and now she was in the position of representing the government as an appointee of the president. Moose knew that, out of loyalty, it was entirely probable that Irene would defend what she wouldn't believe was worthy of defense. He was right. "President Bush has been very tough with China, Moose. The day after Tiananmen Square the president announced sanctions against China with a suspension of military equipment, a suspension of government-to-government trade, and he said Chinese students in the United States could apply to extend their visas. I hope you know that three days later he said that our country couldn't have normal relations with the PRC until the PRC would agree to recognize the validity of the democracy movement there, and–"

Moose interrupted her. "Irene, I love you, but what you're saying is the line. I know the drill. I know what he said. I know the whole thing. But so do you know the whole thing. I'm talking about what we've been doing, not saying." There was a toughness and anger in the tone of his voice that was new since last June.

"What is it you want to know?" Irene asked quietly.

"I want to know what the president's National Security Advisor and Deputy Secretary of State were doing in Beijing last week–when in June the president told the nation that all top-level meetings were banned."

"Brent Scowcroft and Larry Eagleburger went to Beijing last week to tell Deng Xiaoping and Li Peng what happened at the Malta meeting between President Bush and President Gorbachev. Now, it's vital they know, so they don't think there's some conspiracy being planned between our country and President Gorbachev. That's why Brent Scowcroft and Larry Eagleburger went to Beijing."

"Does it take ten hours of talking to tell the Chinese leaders what happened in eight hours of talks between Bush and Gorbachev? And we could easily have used our Embassy in Beijing to tell the Chinese leaders what Bush and Gorbachev said. No. I simply don't believe it. That subject might have taken a few minutes of discussions in China but I grant you, Irene, there was a lot more to that meeting than what Bush told Gorbachev in Malta."

"What is it that you suspect?"

"It's easy to figure out. They told Deng Xiaoping and Li Peng not to worry, that our bilateral relations are more important than these–" and Moose struggled with the remaining words, "with these–atrocities–that we don't approve of what they've done, that our country is enraged, but–but I'll bet they told them that, 'We know these are your internal affairs.' Want to bet?"

Mrs. Goodpastor was biting her lip. "Well, I don't know what they said."

"God, Irene–God, look what Deng and Li Peng did since Tiananmen Square. Within ten days they arrested over one thousand kids. Remember the kid, Wang Wai-lin, who stood in front of the tanks? Remember him? My magazine found out that he was executed on June 18."

"I heard that, too. I don't know."

"There's one captured demonstrator after another paraded on television with a bowed head and their hands cuffed behind their backs appearing before a 'court.' These are the kids we all praised as heroes before June the 4th. Now they're on television as criminals. And you know, Irene, because you get the reports from State, that there have been house to house searches since Tiananmen–asking every household in Beijing where everyone was and what they were doing in April, May, and June. The government has been urging everyone to snitch on others as a patriotic duty, including turning in members of their own families. Our magazine found out there have been telephone hot lines instituted for informers who want to be anonymous. Every workplace has to have new committees that investigate everyone else at work, and other committees investigate the primary committees. Neighborhoods have them, too. In time everyone will be signing statements, filling in forms that reveal where they were and who they saw. So no one knows what anyone else is going to write or say. Do you know what Document Number Three is?" He didn't wait for her answer. "It's a directive issued by the Communist Party Central Committee there. It says that the number of people imprisoned and executed will not be published anymore; that only a small number will be revealed so as to serve as an example. In other words they're attempting to tell the world little, while still causing fear in their own citizens."

Irene nodded.

"You're nodding, Irene. You know it's true. Where is our response? Scowcroft and Eagleburger toasting Deng and Li?"

"*Your* president went there too, you know, just two months ago. Nixon."

"I know. I don't defend that. I told him I was against it. What can I do? At least he wasn't official. He's a private citizen now. He doesn't represent the government. Eagleburger and Scowcroft represent President Bush."

"What do you think is our motive, Moose? What is your mind dreaming up as President Bush's motive?"

"Oh, I know the motive. He truly believes we have to get along, and there's the business interests in our country. There's trade. The business interests think of one billion customers–not one billion human beings. Imports. Exports. Wallets. Do you know what Deng said? A dozen days after Tiananmen, Deng said that once he's stabilized the political situation and has the economy going again, the foreigners are going to be back knocking on his door. Bush has made Deng honest. It's true. We're back. It's a half year and we're back."

"What do you want me to do, Moose?"

"Tell your president he's wrong. Bush appointed you. You know him. He respects you, Irene. Don't be a 'Yes-Man' or a 'Yes-Woman.' Tell him. As for what I'm going to do, every article I write will condemn our policy. I'm writing one now about the Scowcroft -Eagleburger trip of last week."

"Moose," and Irene Goodpastor looked like she was about to cry. "You keep saying the Scowcroft-Eagleburger trip of last week and–"

"Yes. Last week."

"Moose, there's something you should know."

"What?"

"This isn't Brent Scowcroft and Larry Eagleburger's first trip to Beijing since Tiananmen Square."

"What do you mean?"

"The White House has confirmed–the news will be out tomorrow–that this is their second trip to Beijing since Tiananmen Square."

"When was their first?"

"July."

There was a long silence as Moose stared at her. "July? Tiananmen was June."

"Yes."

"July?"

"Yes."

"Do you mean right after Bush said there would be no high-level meetings–there were high-level meetings?–that the National Security Advisor and Assistant Secretary of State were sent to Beijing?"

Irene didn't answer.

Moose stood up and started pacing the office. "Why are you telling me, Irene?"

"CNN had the report–they found out–and by the time it's morning in the United States, the White House is going to confirm it. We got word from State. State is saying he sent Brent and Larry to accent our shock and our concern over what happened."

"My God! July!" He was looking out the window.

"Moose?"

He turned back to Irene. "Is there something else?"

"The Commerce Department is going to announce that they've approved the sale of three communications satellites to Beijing, and that Commerce won't impose the sanctions against China that Congress voted for. It's an executive decision."

Moose sat down opposite her again. His voice was very low. She could hardly hear him. "Trade. Money. I'm a free trader, Irene, but not with tyrannies. There are thousands of kids imprisoned in Beijing who are making products for export to the United States. That's what they have to do. I remember when you couldn't even bring anything into the United States from Hong Kong unless you had a certificate of origin proving it wasn't made in China. You remember that, too. Now we buy products made by kids who are prisoners in the Laogai, the Chinese version of the Soviet's Gulag Archipelago. Why are they there? Because they want a democratic government."

Irene couldn't say anything.

"Some change, huh, Irene?"

Irene went back to giving the side of the president. "Maybe trade is the way for China to become more democratic, for the government to give more civil liberties, to grant more human rights."

"Do you believe that, Irene? You've seen a lot of history. Is that the way it works? Did it work that way back in the late 1930s with Germany? Did our trade change them? How much have all our recent economic agreements accomplished with China? For that we got Tiananmen. The tragedy of our trade with China is that human nature at the end of the 1980s is the same as it was at the end of the 1930s."

"I don't have any power, Moose."

"We still live in a democracy. We all have power. You more than most. Will you write a memorandum of our meeting?"

"Of course. In fact, I have to. But you know that the president isn't going to see it. I go through the Consul General and he goes through State."

"Through Eagleburger!"

"Well, I suppose. Officially it's through Secretary Baker, but I suppose it's Eagleburger."

"I'll write an article. Maybe someone will read it. Anyone."

Three nights before Christmas, Liberty was by the side of an elderly driver in a black van going northeast through the New Territories, and beyond.

The van stopped on a grassy bank without a marker, where the sound of the sea was all that could be heard. They were just south of Sha Tau Kok on the Hong Kong side of the border with China, directly off the South China Sea.

The driver and Liberty got out of the black van, and they went to the edge of the bank that overlooked the sea. Liberty held a flashlight.

After flashing signals, there were responding flashes from the sea. In a short time a black wooden vessel bumped against the bank, and some twenty people went from the boat to the bank, and they were hurriedly crammed into the van.

On the ride back there was just the murmuring and whispering in Cantonese, from the passengers. With four in the front seat, Liberty was pushed against the elderly driver. In the back, the seats had been removed for those who were packed tight together.

"Any word from Gus Borgeest?" Liberty asked the driver.

"No, Madame Yeung. He just disappeared. No one knows what happened to him. Sunshine Island is deserted."

"Are you getting afraid in doing this, Wing-fai?"

He shrugged. "Are you?"

Liberty shook her head. "No."

"We're both doing something against the laws of both China and Hong Kong, Madame Yeung."

"The laws are wrong. And if I'm found out I will confess and take whatever consequences are imposed by Hong Kong."

"Where to tonight, Madame Yeung?"

"When we get to Kowloon I'll tell you the way. It's an old warehouse just the other side of Boundary Street."

He nodded. "You never let them out in the New Territories, do you?"

"Never. I adhere to the old 'Touch Base' policy. Once over Boundary Street into Kowloon, they're safe."

"How much have you paid smugglers in China in the past few months?"

Liberty shook her head. "Everything I haven't paid you."

"They are reliable, aren't they?"

"I met the smugglers when I was in Beijing. I took a chance on their reliability. It worked."

"How long will you continue to do this?"

"Which ever comes first–until China is free–or until I go to prison–or until Deng Xiaoping comes to town."

SEVENTY-THREE
"AULD LANG SYNE"
1989-1990

Most people don't know what the lyrics mean, yet whether the year was good or bad, when the song is heard, there is emotion. Unlike some other classics that are heard at any time of the year, and unlike Christmas classics that are heard throughout a season, "Auld Lang Syne" is heard but once a year; at the moment of a new year's entrance. That melody, those lyrics, put everything known into the past, and the performance of it draws a distinct line that is being crossed into an unknown. People are so aware of what happened in the year that just ended and all they know is the four-digit title of the year that is starting.

And so there were tears at the goodness of the year that just ended in Europe, where chunks of the Berlin Wall were being sold as souvenirs, and there were tears at the horror of the year that just ended in Asia, where Beijing became the scene of a massacre. For Europe, could 1990 be any better? For Asia, could 1990 be any worse?

There could have been no greater drama that occurred that night in Luk Yu Tea House. It was packed with people. A number of tables were put together to form an extended table for fourteen of the leading democracy advocates of Hong Kong. Szeto Wah was there, and Martin Lee was there, and Jack Edwards was there, and seven other leaders of the movement were there, along with Liberty, Andrew, Moose, and Jonas. Those at other tables continually looked over at those Hong Kong celebrities.

Then it happened: when the countdown reached midnight, the orchestra started playing "Auld Lang Syne." Most who were part of the large crowd in the restaurant were wearing paper and aluminum-foil hats provided by the restaurant near each place-setting. The people were blowing the provided whistles, and they were churning provided noise-makers, and they were kissing each other, and many of them were singing. But at the prime table of fourteen all of that was substituted by other things.

As Auld Lang Syne continued to reverberate throughout the restaurant, Szeto Wah raised his glass, and then the entire table of thirteen others raised their glasses and Szeto Wah gave a toast to Liberty's mother, Yeung Tso Wai-yee. That was followed by Martin Lee giving a toast to the eternal liberty of Hong Kong. And then a group of them around the table lifted Liberty, in her white cheong-sam, to stand on the center of the table. And once there, all the noise-makers of the people at other tables stopped, and so did the blowing of whistles, and so did the kissing, and so did the singing.

The orchestra continued the playing of the song as Liberty raised her right arm. Martin Lee, who was taller than most, briefly stood on the table with her and lowered her right arm to place a paper replica of a torch in her hand. Then he knelt down to give a short jump off the table, and Liberty raised her right arm again, this time with the paper replica of the torch. She clasped her left hand on her right wrist. The orchestra repeated the song with a new strength and everyone in the restaurant raised their glasses to toast the Goddess of Democracy.

PART FOUR

THE 1990s

SEVENTY-FOUR
THE NIGHT OF LYUDMILA
1990–1991

Wang Wai-lin, the man who stood in front of tanks on East Changan Avenue, did not change China, but in thirty seconds he helped to dismember the Soviet Union. It was the repeated dialogue among those who rose up against the Soviet Union that if "that young man could do it, so could we." The impact of that man who did what seventy-two years of world leaders struggled to do, cannot be over-estimated. There was merit in being photographed from behind since in his spontaneous, unprepared act, his face remained a mystery, and it could have been anyone's face if anyone else had as much courage.

It would surely be appropriate to have a parade, or at least a presidential proclamation every year to commemorate the anniversary of the end of the Cold War. But unlike the 11th Hour of the 11th Day of the 11th Month, or V-E Day, or V-J Day, the end of the Cold War had no date. Maybe it was November 9, 1989, when the Berlin Wall came down. Maybe it was July 6, 1990, when NATO announced that the Soviet Union was no longer an adversary. Maybe it was one of those days in late August of 1990, when one republic of the USSR after another declared independence. Maybe it was March 31, 1991, when the Warsaw Pact military alliance disbanded. Maybe it was August 24, 1991, with the official independence of Russia. Maybe it was December 18, 1991, when the Confederation of Independent States was inaugurated. Maybe it was December 26, 1991, when the U.S.S.R. was formally dissolved. With all its witnesses, no one was sure exactly when it could be said it was over. For that matter, no one knew the exact date it started, so the Cold War was ending in the same fuzzy way in which it began.

In the absence of a precise date, no one knew quite how to handle a dying nation.

Red Square looked different than it had looked for the past seventy-three years, although there was no excavation or construction there. Somehow, the ominous majestic and frightening spaciousness of the square and its bordering Kremlin didn't look so ominous or majestic or frightening. Not even as spacious, although nothing had diminished its physical size. The early 1990s Red Square looked like a movie set built to resemble Red Square when communism reigned supreme, but the art director didn't do a very good job. And to make it as it used to be, more extras would be needed to stand in line outside Lenin's mausoleum.

Anne was in Moscow giving commentary on the day-by-day changes, and she also had the futile hope that she would be granted another interview with Mikhail Gorbachev. He, however, would have nothing more to do with her.

Anne, at the age of 52, had become age-conscious. She was still a beautiful woman, but she didn't think so. A turtleneck sweater was a frequent part of her wardrobe to hide her neck that was not as smooth as it used to be. Mirrors were not her friends anymore. They had turned against her, showing her what no one else could see, while telling her that whatever she didn't like was all anyone could see.

Nights she would have spent in other ways were now spent either in conversation with government officials or alone in her room. One of the positive changes in Russia was a negative change for Anne—the women were much prettier than they had been under communism. They even shaved their legs which, of course, rivaled the importance of the end of communism.

Anne was certain that Russian women were younger now. She finally concluded that women throughout the world were younger now.

On screen left was Senator Conklin with the U.S. Capitol against the bright daylight sky behind him. "What are you Reaganauts going to do now that you don't have the Soviet Union to kick around anymore?"

On screen right was Anne at night with Saint Basil's Cathedral behind her. "We are going to congratulate each other! The question is, what are you McGovernites going to do now that you have to justify your past?"

"Justify doing what in the past?" Senator Conklin asked. "You talk in generalities. Be specific, Anne. It was the liberals, not the conservatives, who were pursuing a peaceful resolution of the Cold War."

"Some pursuit! You wanted Khrushchevian co-existence, which would have sustained the Soviet Union forever. I'll be specific. No generalities. It was the conservatives who wanted to build U.S. military forces to a position so strong that the Soviet Union would go broke trying to keep up with us. Opposing those efforts were Brezhnev, Andropov, Chernenko, and the leadership of the liberals.

"It was the conservatives who opposed a nuclear moratorium that would have guaranteed superiority of nuclear forces by the Soviet Union. Endorsing a nuclear moratorium were Brezhnev, Andropov, Chernenko, and the leadership of the liberals.

"It was the conservatives who advocated military escorts of ships going through the Persian Gulf in the mid-1980s. Opposing U.S. military escorts through the Persian Gulf were Brezhnev, Andropov, Chernenko, and the leadership of the liberals.

"It was the conservatives who wanted the neutron warhead deployed in Western Europe. Opposing the neutron warhead were Brezhnev, Andropov, Chernenko, and the leadership of the liberals.

"It was the conservatives who supported the liberation of Grenada that brought about free elections in that island nation. Endorsing the communist imposed government were Brezhnev, Andropov, Chernenko, and the leadership of the liberals.

"It was the conservatives who backed Jonas Savimbi in Angola in his quest to end the communist dictatorship of that nation. Opposing aid to Jonas Savimbi were Brezhnev, Andropov, Chernenko, and the leadership of the liberals.

"It was the conservatives who advocated the deployment of Pershing Missiles for the protection of Western Europe. Endorsing a nuclear freeze that would have prevented such deployment were Brezhnev, Andropov, Chernenko, and the leadership of the liberals.

"It was the conservatives who supported a reinterpretation of the Anti-Ballistic Missile Treaty. Opposing such a reinterpretation were Brezhnev, Andropov, Chernenko, and the leadership of the liberals.

"It was the conservatives who accused the Soviet Union of violating arms treaties. Denying the violations were Brezhnev, Andropov, Chernenko, and the leadership of the liberals.

"It was the conservatives who wanted to develop a Strategic Defense Initiative to guard the nation and make an enemy's ICBMs worthless. Opposing such a defensive system for the United States were Brezhnev, Andropov, Chernenko, and the leadership of the liberals.

"It was the conservatives who wanted to bring down the Sandinistas of Nicaragua under Daniel Ortega who was expanding communism in Central America, and it was the conservatives, not the liberals, who supported aid to the Nicaraguan resistance so that a Soviet satellite wouldn't be permanently implanted on the mainland of the Western Hemisphere. Embracing Daniel Ortega and opposing the Nicaraguan resistance were Brezhnev, Andropov, Chernenko, and the leadership of the liberals.

"And it was a conservative President, Ronald Reagan, who accurately called the Soviet Union and its hold of satellite nations, an Evil Empire. Ask those who are overpowering that empire today, if it was so funny. Ridiculing the president's phrase were Brezhnev, Andropov, Chernenko, and the leadership of the liberals."

After that performance Anne was too wide-awake to go to her room. She went to the dismal bar of the gloomy Belgrade One Hotel. (In the Soviet way of duplicating things that worked, there was a Belgrade Two Hotel.) The bar of the Belgrade One Hotel smelled of stale Russian cigarettes. She was alone there having a drink that was supposed to be a daiquiri but tasted like rubbing alcohol mixed with lime juice. An attractive tall brunette who was somewhere in her forties came in, looked around, and sat next to Anne. "American?" she asked. At least Anne was attracting the only other customer in Belgrade One's bar. But did it have to be a woman?

"Yes! Amerikanski!" Anne answered with pride.

"I speak English. You speak Russian?"

"After this drink I won't even be able to speak English!"

"Our drinks aren't as good as they used to be. Everything is changing. Some things are better, some things are worse. You are an American so you needn't worry about what's happening to us."

"Are you a lesbian?"

The woman laughed. "Oh, no! Are you offended that I talk to you?"

"I'm not offended. It's just that I know Moscow very well. It used to be if a woman came up to me in a bar she was either KGB or a lesbian. And now the KGB is falling apart, so I thought you must be a lesbian, unless they're falling apart, too."

The woman laughed again. "Those were the only two possibilities before, but now there's another probability. Loneliness. I'm just lonely. I was never lonely, but I am now, because all the changes scare me."

"You don't like the changes?"

The woman shrugged. "I don't know yet. This transition is frightening. I feel like a child thrown out of the house of my parents who had been strict disciplinarians. Suddenly the yellings are done, the beatings are over, and the fear of them are gone. But in their place there is no one who will give me shelter and food and drink and wipe my nose, and take care of me when I'm ill. I had always hoped that some day I would be free, but now that I am, I'm as frightened of liberty as I had been of those who told me what I could and couldn't do."

Anne nodded. "I understand that. But don't you feel that a world of opportunity is opening to you? Maybe it will be so new that it will be hard to adjust at first, but all new things are hard at first, aren't they?"

"To some. I think to me, known hardships are easier to accept than unknown hardships."

"I hope you stick with the changes. As an American I can tell you that once you live in freedom on a daily basis, doing what you want to do, you'll never want to give it up."

The woman gave a cautious smile. "If America becomes a dictatorship I may visit you there and assure you that once you live with security all your life you'll never want to give it up. There are times I want things here to be as they were. It's what I know."

"What's your name?"

"Lyudmila," she answered. And then she thought for a while. "Those things that I told you are not only my thoughts. My name is Lyudmila, but my name might as well be Russia."

"The Soviet Union is writhing on the other side of the New Year and there is no need to let it in," Moose wrote in *Asia World Weekly* in its first issue of 1990. "There are many thanks to give to Pope John Paul II, Former President Ronald Reagan, Prime Minister Margaret Thatcher, and President Mikhail Gorbachev for bringing this about. And there are others from Lech Walesa to Wang Wai-lin. But all free people of the world, including the newly free, must not assume that the terminal illness of the Soviet Union and its empire is synonymous with world liberty. There are still tyrannies who are not writhing, but increasing: Islamic Fundamentalism, North Korea's military, and the pending super-power status of the People's Republic of China. They're all under the covers. There should be no 'Peace Dividend' in the United States budget. Since this decade began we have been cutting our military virtually in half. The number of army divisions are being reduced from 18 to nine. The navy is shrinking from 546 ships to 300. The number of air wings is declining from 36 to 18. To cut defenses is the guarantee they will be needed."

Moose became both a mother and father in very short time. Dr. Yeung had passed out of life one night in his sleep, without pain, after holding on to life longer than everyone on the staff of the Queen Elizabeth Hospital had expected. It was pneumonia that was written on his death certificate, but what it said was unimportant. He had also suffered from what might have been Alzheimer's disease or something with the same symptoms.

Jonas kept putting his departure from Hong Kong back to Los Angeles aside one more week, two more weeks, one more month, always a time when he would leave, but always the time more distant. He had become a wanderer with any number of temporary homes. The Regent Hotel in Kowloon was the most difficult temporary home to leave than any of them. Only Cape Canaveral was a temptation for a new temporary home, but he felt that area was too untouchable; that it was God's place, and it would be irreverent for him to take temporary residence there.

His latest excuse for staying in Hong Kong was that with Liberty parentless, he should help Moose become a father to her. But that excuse was invalid, and he knew it. Moose needed no help. Liberty needed no help. It was Jonas that needed help in seeking a more reasonable justification to stay. To make sure he didn't leave, he accepted future speaking engagements at the Hong Kong Policy Institute, the Chamber of Commerce, the Kiwanis, the Rotary, and all kinds of groups. His speeches were always about the decaying empire of the Soviet Union, and the questions were always about the coming superpower status of the People's Republic of China.

But he was discontent in staying where he felt he wasn't needed.

In most early evenings, Liberty would walk with her boyfriend, Andrew Fung Kai-hung, on the Promenade Harbor Walk while the lights across the harbor were turning on, one after the other. "You have inherited your mother's goodness, strength, and beauty," Andrew said. "And you have inherited your father's stability, wisdom, and gentleness. They left you a great Chinese inheritance. What is so good is that you are worthy of it, Liberty. Those gifts from them are so much a part of you that even a stranger who glimpses you is aware of them."

"I hope what you're saying is true. I want Ma and Father and God to feel they didn't waste their time on me. I want Moose to feel that way too, and you, Andrew."

"You are so much the daughter of your parents."

"You could say nothing that could please me more."

Now came the tough part. Andrew summoned all his courage to take issue with her on a subject she didn't want discussed. "Liberty, may I please make one request of you? The only one I ask?"

She looked at him cautiously. "What?" Through her look at him, she made it apparent that he was in danger of igniting her anger.

"I want you to stop those trips to the border to pick up refugees. It is dangerous, and even if it wasn't, it is against the law of both sides."

Liberty ignored what he said. "Ma died so quickly and so unexpectedly. Father died so slowly that he died before he died. Do you understand? Didn't you feel that? That disease—Alzheimer's—you die before you die. I know the date Ma died so indelibly that it's a marker that I will never be able to shake out of my memory. But I have to think to recall the date Father died—I know the date when it was final, but that isn't really the date he died, was it?"

"No, it wasn't."

They held hands walking toward the Clock Tower of Kowloon.

"Liberty? Will you stay safe for me?"

Again, she avoided the subject. "You know, the Soviet Union has Alzheimer's disease, doesn't it? It's dying—maybe it's dead already. It doesn't make much difference, because its life is over. Now, isn't it ironic? While so many nations of the world stage revolutions in rejection of communist governments, our little Hong Kong is in reversal of the world. We wait for it to come to us."

"There is nothing we can do to prevent it. We can only hope they will provide us with the rights under which we live now."

"Give us those rights? Living free is a birthright, not a government-given right, Kai-hung. Governments should not be created to provide rights, but simply to insure they are not taken away."

Irene Goodpastor had successfully made a transition from a tired and bored old woman who was obsessed with her advancing age, into a totally engaged stateswoman who had become an effective representative of the United States in Hong Kong. "We are correctly perceived here as being the victors in the Cold War," she wrote to Secretary of State Baker. "It is regarded as a wonderful victory, but absorbing the interest of the people here, more than the end of the Soviet Union, is the beginning of China's jurisdiction that is on its way in this decade, not far away. The Basic Law Drafting Committee is done with its work, and has published what will become Hong Kong's 'mini-constitution' for the fifty years of 1997 through 2047. Many Hong Kong people are not calling it 'The Basic Law,' but calling it 'The Basic Flaw,' having found repeated violations from the original Joint Declaration between Great Britain and the People's Republic. The future here is one big question mark. It would be worthwhile for you to come here to state United States policy."

For the first time in many years, Mrs. Goodpastor was thinking of the future in relation to herself. Although her major public concern was what would happen to Hong Kong in 1997, she wondered what would happen to her if President Bush should lose re-election in 1992. She knew she would then have to leave Hong Kong and leave the diplomatic service. "I can never go back to watching television and looking at the walls and thinking of my maladies. I have to do something. But he'll win." Because she was taking part in the current, she allowed herself to think of a future.

Gloria Cooper argued that the dismemberment of the Soviet Union was diverting attention from the sin of Phoenix House, an old factory that had been converted into a way-station for sending screened-out refugees back to Vietnam. Just before 1990 began, at 3:00 A.M. one morning, nine Vietnamese men, sixteen Vietnamese women, and twenty-six Vietnamese children had been awakened, loaded into buses and driven to Kai Tak Airport and brought to a waiting Cathay Pacific Airways Tri-Star. On their journey to Kai Tak, journalists who had been patrolling in shifts along the route to Kai Tak, saw the buses with Vietnamese passengers crying, wailing, and a scrawled handwritten sign through the bus window that read, "We would rather die than go back to Vietnam."

Out of sight of the journalists, the Vietnamese were ushered aboard the plane and at 5:00 A.M., before Kai Tak was normally allowed to open, the plane took off to Hanoi.

Vietnamese refugees in ten camps located throughout Hong Kong demonstrated against the new policy. Six thousand had been scheduled to follow as "economic migrants to be repatriated to Vietnam," with thousands more awaiting screening. There were suicide attempts, including one self-immolation at the Chimawan Detention Camp after 48 Vietnamese were forcibly transferred from Chimawan to Phoenix House to await their forced repatriation.

There were few days that Governor David Wilson did not receive a written appeal from Gloria to stop the repatriation, or a letter from her fifteen year old son, John Fitzgerald Cooper, pleading for the Vietnamese refugees to be treated as though they were members of the Governor's family. He went to the American Embassy at least once a week to appeal to Irene Goodpastor for the Consulate to use the influence of the United States to stop Hong Kong's repatriation policy.

John Fitzgerald Cooper was having a problem of his own. Since he had a sense of values, he knew his problem was minor, but it bothered him. He wanted to be referred to as J.F.C. in recognition of being named after J.F.K. It didn't work. No one called him J.F.C. They called him John, no matter how many times he corrected them. It was as though there was a conspiracy of everyone in the world not to honor his rather simple request.

Mrs. Goodpastor called John Fitzgerald Cooper to the Consulate to deliver the good news that Secretary of State James Baker met with British Prime Minister Margaret Thatcher and Foreign Minister Douglas Hurd to object to the Hong Kong policy of returning Vietnamese. The White House issued a statement that the policy was "odious" and the United States was "unalterably opposed to forced repatriation to Vietnam unless and until dramatic improvements occur in that country's economic, political and social life." The spokesman for the U.S. Department of State, Richard Boucher said, "We believe British authorities should continue to grant asylum to all those persons from Vietnam who seek it."

John Fitzgerald Cooper thanked Irene Goodpastor, assuming, or at least wanting to believe that she told President Bush, James Baker, and Richard Boucher what to say.

"You're just like your father, John," Irene Goodpastor told him.

"J.F.C., Mrs. Goodpastor," he corrected.

"Yes, of course, John. I was saying that you're just like your father, always giving credit to others, and always courageous in what he did." He was? Always? Cody was always courageous?

"I know."

"Did your mother ever tell you about what your father did during the Vietnam War?" Mrs. Goodpastor gave a small smile.

"Yes. He was in the State Department."

"Do you know why he wasn't in the military?" Her eyebrows raised.

"Because he was working in the State Department."

"Oh, I knew him during those years, even before your mother knew him. He wanted to go into the military and tried and tried," she lied. "First the Marines, then the Air Force, then the Navy, then the Army. He tried and tried and tried. They wouldn't do it. They wouldn't do it, John, because Secretary Rusk—he was Secretary of State at the time—wouldn't allow any of the armed services to take your father away from the State Department. He was much too valuable to Secretary Rusk."

"Dean Rusk?"

"Dean Rusk!"

"Wasn't Dad at the White House then?"

"Oh, yes, at the beginning when President Kennedy was there. He appointed Dean Rusk. But then after President Kennedy was killed, Mr. Rusk wanted your father with him! That's why your father went to the State Department in the first place. That's before he even met your mother. I don't know if your mother was ever told the whole story. Your father was a very modest man, you know."

"How did you know that about Secretary Rusk and Dad?"

Irene gave a small laugh. "I can't tell you everything, dear. But Dean and I were—well, just let's say we were very close."

"You mean like—"

"All I mean is that we were very close. No questions, John."

"J.F.C."

With the Soviet Union dismembering, and so many battles surrendered, Ted Murphy was becoming a less important figure and, worse than that, there were less places of foreign intrigue to be sent.

Since West Germany, he had only been sent to two places; Panama and a second trip to Nicaragua. He was sent to Panama to cover U.S. troops going into Panama to find and take General Manuel Noriega into custody after having been indicted by a federal grand jury in the United States for drug trafficking, and Ted was sent to Nicaragua for the inauguration of Violetta Chamorro. They were both brief trips and both of them reduced Ted's credibility at home.

Ted had told his audience that Panamanians were opposed to the United States troops, but every piece of footage taken by his cameramen and those of all others, showed Panamanians hugging and embracing the U.S. troops, and yelling chants against Noriega. Noriega had previously proclaimed a state of war against the United States, with Panamanians who opposed him under government threat. There were wild celebrations after Noriega was captured, but Ted did not cover the celebrations. Instead, he covered Ramsey Clark's visit to Panama in which the former attorney general condemned the United States.

Worse than the success of the intervention in Panama for Ted's credibility was the inauguration of Violetta Chamorro in Nicaragua. Ted Murphy, along with others in the national media, had predicted that if an election were held, there would be a landslide victory for the Sandinistas. Those predictions led Daniel Ortega to allow an election.

Ted Murphy said, "The electoral victory of the Sandinistas will be the worst day for Bush, and a bad omen for Reagan's place in history."

Ted Koppel of ABC said, "Almost certainly the Sandinistas will win."

Ed Rabel on NBC said, "The topic of the day is how will a freely elected Sandinista Government be treated by the United States?"

Peter Jennings of ABC said, "For the Bush Administration and the Reagan Administration before it, the polls hint at a simple truth: after years of trying to get rid of the Sandinistas, there is not much to show for their efforts."

The night before the election, John Dancey of NBC said, "Reagan's dogged support for the Contras forever marked and ultimately scarred his foreign policy.... It has been one of the longest and most traumatic chapters in U.S. history in Latin America, and tonight it seems to be ending, and ending in a way Ronald Reagan never could have imagined."

But it ended in a way the U.S. newscasters never imagined. The Sandinistas lost by a large margin. The Contras were in celebration. And the Contras were overtly applauded.

The inauguration of the new president was no fun for Ted Murphy. When the preceding president, Daniel Ortega, came into the hot, outdoor sports-arena used for the inaugural, Nicaraguans yelled, "Assassino! Assassino!" while Vice President Quayle received the greatest ovation of any foreign representative.

The defeat of the Sandinistas in Nicaragua combined with the failure of the Soviet Union, the expanding rejection of communism by its republics and by its Eastern European satellites, gave Ted little choice. To retain some credibility, Ted Murphy, following the example of so many of his colleagues in the media, suddenly became anti-Communist, as if he always was. Recognizing the short memories of Americans, much of the media knew they could get away with it.

Mark wrote Anne one of his few letters to her since their divorce. It was handwritten and Anne didn't know if it was because he didn't own a word processor or a typewriter, or if he handwrote it to be personal. "Now is the time for you," he wrote. "With the world changing so radically, and the Third World no longer fearing and often joining the side of the Soviet Union, this is the time for your Nations of Liberty Alliance–your NOLA, Anne. Gerry's problem, and yours, was that we couldn't have an organization limited to democracies while friendly non-democracies opposed the expansion of the Soviet Union. We are now at a mammoth crossroad of history, and so much will depend on what we do at this crossroad. Do it now, Anne. You aren't in Congress but you have a pedestal on television, and people listen to you. This is the time for your NOLA." He signed it, "Love, As Always, Mark."

She handwrote her response in her big-lettered scrawl. "I'll do it, Mark," she wrote from Moscow. "You're right, but first I'm trying to set the record straight before it becomes forgotten, and then distorted. From what you call my pedestal, I have an opportunity to remind my audience who are the victors, and who were the quislings in America; the ones who wouldn't fight in the Cold War, or fought on the other side. When I'm through correcting the ones who don't have the guts to apologize to the country, I'm going to do exactly what you say. I miss you, Mark."

Anne walked to the villainous mirror in her room at Belgrade One. In the reflection she didn't see the end of the Soviet Union or the correction of revisionists or the beginning of NOLA or the coming superpower status of China or any of the changes of the world. She saw wrinkles.

But her desires weren't wrinkled. They didn't subside at all. While she was in Moscow she felt she had to discover some secrets to tell Jeffrey Stempka, and then with that as an excuse, arrange to meet him at the darkest place she could find in Washington. A place so dark that what caused the mirror to laugh at her, would be invisible to him.

Maybe it was a difference between men and women: Anne was scared she might become more and more like Irene Goodpastor, while neither Jonas nor Moose had no hesitancy to become more and more like Adam, and Ted Murphy hoped to become more and more like Walter Cronkite.

Anne walked from the mirror. She wanted, so much, to be what she used to be and do those things that she had done for so many years. Then she had the frightening thought that maybe her name was Lyudmila, too.

SEVENTY-FIVE
YELLOW RIBBONS
1991

Saddam Hussein did one thing that not even Mother Theresa could do. Saddam Hussein gave Ted Murphy a justification for getting away from Linda. Mother Theresa never even thought of invading Kuwait.

Saddam Hussein did. He not only invaded Kuwait, he took it in six and one half hours, declaring Kuwait to be the nineteenth province of Iraq. Kuwait's leader, the Emir Sheik Jabir al-Ahmad Al Sabah, sought refuge in Jordan, and his brother, Sheik Fahd al-Ahmad Al Sabah, was killed by the strafing of Iraqi jets. With Kuwait in the hands of Iraq, 100,000 Iraqi troops next massed near the border with Saudi Arabia.

Ted Murphy would have been content to go to Saudi Arabia with the rest of the press corps who were sent there for Desert Shield, but Saddam Hussein allowed a few U.S. journalists to report directly from Baghdad, Iraq, and among those few was Ted Murphy.

In no time, Ted was out the door with Linda close behind to drive him to the airport. When she dropped him off, it was not exactly like Humphrey Bogart and Ingrid Bergman. "See ya," Ted said to Linda. "Take it easy," Linda answered.

President Bush was organizing a coalition of 29 nations to defend Saudi Arabia and other Gulf states. That military protection, called Desert Shield, came at the request of King Fahd of Saudi Arabia, meant to prevent Iraqi troops from going further than Kuwait, conquering other nations on the Persian Gulf.

Desert Shield then became Desert Storm. In contrast to the Shield, the Storm was not simply to protect nations from the invasion of Saddam Hussein's troops, but to liberate Kuwait that had already been conquered. The Storm meant there would be bombardment of Iraq all the way to its capital city, Baghdad, prior to a land incursion into Kuwait.

Baghdad's night was filled with air-raid sirens, the black of the sky interrupted with the brightness of what appeared to be hundreds of slow rising files of shooting stars that were not celestial but were Iraqi tracer bullets. On the horizon were blasts from the U.S. and coalition bombardment, accompanied by the constant exploding of Iraqi anti-aircraft shells.

In the basement of the Al Rashid Hotel in downtown Baghdad was a bomb shelter where most of the press corps gathered for safety through the evening bombardments.

Not Ted or his crew. They met each evening in the cameraman's room at the Al Rashid, since the cameraman's hotel window had the best view of the evening spectacles. It was there that Ted reported his comments, with the war periodically visible over his shoulders. Night after night, Ted Murphy talked about the killing of Iraqi civilians in U.S. bombing raids on Baghdad, his reports echoing the official line of Iraq's government.

In contrast, Antonia Radios, an Australian TV journalist in Baghdad reported, "We have been seeing every day civilian casualties, but sometimes we have to travel three hundred or four hundred kilometers to see them. So we were just wondering, some of my colleagues and I, why do we have to go so far if the Iraqi government says the main target is civilians? I think what is important is that Baghdad today is a town which is basically not destroyed."

Such commentaries didn't last long. Saddam Hussein ordered most western members of the media to get out of Iraq. The order was not given to Ted Murphy.

Ted's daytime itineraries were directed by the Iraqi government, including a tour of a residential neighborhood which Ted reported to have been heavily damaged by U.S. bombs. Then he reported that the United States had bombed a facility producing baby formula.

Ted Murphy was amassing a unique coalition of U.S. supporters. In this first post-Cold War military confrontation, Ted and others known as doves during the Cold War, retained their consistency in being opposed to U.S. military involvement, but surprisingly they were now joined in that opposition by some of those who were the most prominent hawks during the Cold War. This unlikely coalition warned their U.S. audiences of thousands of body bags that would come back with the remains of Americans.

"Fools!" Anne almost shouted on television. "Those few particular veteran conservatives are turning their backs on their own philosophy that has been so successful! All these years I thought all my friends were anti-totalitarians, but a few, I now find out, were only against those totalitarians who were communists. Now that Soviet Communism is dead, they've shed the wings of hawks for the chirps of doves. Beyond my expectations, they have adopted the McGovern slogan of 1972, 'Come Home, America.' Not me! I'm not with them in joining the Ted Murphys of the world! I'm anti-communist, anti-fascist, anti-Khadafy, anti-Saddam, anti-any totalitarian."

Anne was wearing a dark-blue turtleneck sweater with a bright yellow bow over her heart, as well as a yellow ribbon in her hair. She pointed to the one over her heart. "Put these on your blouses, your shirts, your jackets, your coats, your front doors, and wrap yellow ribbons around trees! It's showing your solidarity with our troops!"

"Hey," Ted yelled into the large Inmarsat phone in his Al Rashid hotel room, "can you hear me on this thing you guys gave me?"

"You're coming in loud and clear, Ted," his producer yelled back from Washington.

"Good! Listen, Hugh! Tell Anne Daschle that my buddy, Saddam, thinks she looks jazzy with her yellow ribbon, and he wants her to put a little Iraqi flag in her hair to give both sides equal time! And tell her that she's gettin' too hot under the collar and ol' Saddam doesn't like what she's sayin' about me and my new buddies! Tell her to get her sweet, shakin' rear end to Baghdad where the action is!"

The producer became an unwilling messenger of communications between Ted Murphy and Anne Whitney. Anne told the producer to "tell Murph' that Hitler's posthumous regret is that Ted was born too late to report from Berlin during World War II."

"Tell Anne that I'll vote for Bush's reelection if he promises to put her in the White House durin' his second term and get her off the airwaves!"

"Tell Murph' that I told Bush to bomb the Al Rashid."

Although Ted Murphy was the only American journalist left in Iraq, he was not the only American there. Just like in Panama, former Attorney General Ramsey Clark wasn't going to stay away from this one. He went in front of Ted's cameras, telling Ted's television audience that he saw no military targets that were hit by American bombs, but that he saw a great deal of damage and destruction to civilian targets and a great many deaths of civilians. Ted, of course, listened without any adversarial questions to ask his old friend.

Ted was being treated like a king. The Iraqi government brought him to a bombed-out bunker on the outskirts of Baghdad where Ted reported just what they told him. "This was a bomb shelter for civilians, the U.S. blew it up, and many clustered civilians were killed in its destruction."

Senator Alan Simpson of Wyoming called Ted Murphy a Saddam Hussein "sympathizer."

Military analyst Major General Perry Smith said that he had seen bunkers all over the world and this one was "a classic command bunker, heavily fortified with reinforced concrete, camouflaged on the roof and surrounded by a perimeter fence. A standard civilian bomb shelter does not have a perimeter fence because people have to be able to get into a bomb shelter quickly when the siren warning of an air raid goes off, and to get out fast if the shelter is bombed. Many members of the United States military are highly upset by the coverage of the bomb damage in Iraq that is appearing on various TV networks.... I would hope that all viewers will view the TV tape coming out of Iraq with considerable skepticism, especially when it focuses on bomb damage and civilian casualties. It may not tell the whole story. In fact, it may be telling precisely the story that Saddam Hussein wants to tell."

Desert Storm was the beginning of the end for Ted Murphy, as his credibility was falling through the cracks, the cracks deepening each night of Desert Storm until Kuwait was liberated in a four-day ground assault by the United States and its allies. Ted Murphy was sent home to a frosty welcome. Even his coalition of supporters turned the other way from him in view of the victory of Desert Storm and the false prophecies of thousands of filled U.S. body bags.

Ted had been appreciated more by Saddam Hussein and his Iraqi government hosts than he was by Linda and his American audience. The yellow ribbon Linda had wrapped around the tree in front of their house didn't help.

"It was for you," Linda explained as they sat in the living room facing a mute television screen that was displaying an ad for feminine deodorant. "It was meant to show I was thinking of you."

"Yeah! Yeah! Yeah! Yeah! Yeah! Look at that. They're advertisin' that stuff now?"

"You did a wonderful job in Iraq, honey. All those critics are jealous."

"Yeah."

"You're the only one who really spoke out."

"But that's dangerous stuff these days. They think I was Saddam's lackey."

"Well, someone had to be!"

It was that kind of thing that made life so miserable for Ted. She just didn't have a handle on her brain.

Linda wouldn't stop. "Do you think Bush should have gone on and captured King Hussein?"

"King Hussein? He's in Jordan. You mean Saddam Hussein, don'cha?"

"Yes, that Hussein. A lot of people are saying Bush should have gone to get that particular Hussein. The real one."

"Well, they're wrong. The only smart thing Bush did is finally stop the war."

"A lot of people say we shouldn't have left him—"

Ted interrupted, "A lot of people are wrong!"

"You're right. That's what I think."

The ad for feminine deodorant was done and to Linda it was a lot better than the image that followed. It was the image of Anne Whitney. And she looked good. Linda had come to despise Anne, knowing that Ted would have taken her over Linda if he had the chance.

"Look, honey," Linda said. "Anne Whitney or Daschle or whatever she calls herself. Look how she's getting so old looking. I don't think she's taking care of herself. Poof! She looks terrible. I mean I think we're about the same age, maybe I'm a little younger, but she looks terrible, doesn't she?"

"Turn the mute thing up!"

"What mute thing?" Linda asked.

"The remote! Punch the mute thing!"

"Here, honey. You do it."

In Linda's usual helplessness, she handed the remote switch to Ted, and he quickly pressed the mute button to the audio position. As much as Linda preferred the pictures of feminine deodorant to Anne, and Ted didn't, Ted should have left the mute button alone rather than hear what Anne was saying.

"—ought to be in jail!" Anne said. Now she was wearing a small metal yellow ribbon lapel pin on her blouse, replacing the larger one of fabric she had been wearing, and still there was the yellow strand of ribbon in her hair. "No!" She corrected herself. "A federal penitentiary! That's where

Theodore Murphy ought to be! Lawton Federal Penitentiary! He acted as a surrogate for Saddam Hussein while our troops were in harm's way. Further, he gave television time to Ramsey Clark who, just like Ted Murphy, has consistently taken the other side in every recent conflict with the United States, be it North Vietnam, Iran, Nicaragua, Libya, Panama, or Iraq. Clark–and Murphy gave aid and comfort to the enemy, which the Constitution defines as treason."

Linda interrupted. "Were you on Libya's side? I don't remember that one."

Ted was not happy. If only there was another war for which he could leave Linda. Surely someone should be willing to declare one.

"That was a very surprising and courageous commentary!" Jeffrey Stempka told Anne at the night time meeting she arranged. She was sitting very close to him at the most remote far corner-booth in the darkest bar in Washington. It was Wisconsin Avenue's The Cave Bar and Grill that had no grill.

Anne nodded, giving approval of the compliment he gave her. "I'll leave it up to someone in the Congress to follow through. Maybe it will do some good and they can get him for aiding and comforting the enemy."

"Sorry, Anne," Jeffrey Stempka said. "Constitutionally, Saddam Hussein wasn't our enemy. That's because we weren't in a declared war. We went through this when some congressmen wanted to prosecute Jane Fonda, Tom Hayden, and Ramsey Clark after they got back from North Vietnam years ago. No luck."

"Then, Mr. Stempka, the Constitution should be amended to define the word 'enemy' to apply for both declared and undeclared military engagements. How's that?"

"Well, go ahead and try to move that through the Congress if you want to, but even if it passes the Congress and even if it's ratified by the states, you can't make it retroactive, so Murphy can't go to jail for what he did."

"Then your agency should kill him."

"There's a law against that, too. Don't joke about it. We've been through that kind of thing, haven't we?"

"Too many laws," she said as she looked down at her daiquiri. Then coming closer to the point, her arm brushed his, and she said, "The reason I asked to see you is that I have three secrets for you, Mr. Stempka." Four. The fourth one was her age which was near invisible in the darkness.

"Three secrets?"

"Three."

"I'm all ears."

"You know who started all this, Mr. Stempka?" She asked, getting even closer to him in the booth so her forearm rested against his.

"All what?"

"The war. The Persian Gulf War."

"Yes, I know who started it. Saddam Hussein. His invasion of Kuwait."

"He was part of it. The other part was our State Department. Do you know what happened eight days before Saddam Hussein invaded Kuwait?"

"What?"

Anne's eyes opened twice as wide as normal. She was sure she had his attention, and she was sure she had a story that would astound him. "Our Ambassador to Iraq, April Glaspie, met with Saddam Hussein in one of his palaces eight days before the invasion. You know what she told him?"

"Yes, I know."

"Do you know this? She told him that 'we have no opinion on the Arab-Arab conflicts, like your border disagreement with Kuwait.' That's an exact quote. No opinion! That's what she told him! It was an engraved invitation for him to invade. Eight days later, 30,000 of his troops walked into Kuwait and took the country."

"She should never have said anything like that, but that isn't my agency's business. Are you saying State wanted Saddam to invade?"

"No. I'm no kook. I'm saying that those State Department types get so intent on being friendly to a foreign leader that they don't use common sense. I'm saying that State, through April Glaspie, gave Saddam an all-clear signal to do what he wanted across the border. Did you know that she had specific instructions from Secretary Baker to emphasize what she said? Then she got into all her language of diplomacy that Saddam couldn't possibly understand. She said we'd support our friends in the Gulf—but which ones? She had already claimed U.S. friendship with Iraq. Did she mean we'd support him? Defending herself, she says that she told him that we're opposed to the use of force. But did that mean to him that he shouldn't use force, or we wouldn't use force if he did? If Glaspie had talked to his Foreign Minister Aziz rather than Saddam, maybe Aziz would have asked the right questions, but Saddam is no sophisticate. In talking to Saddam she should have said, 'If you invade Kuwait, we'll blow you to Kingdom Come!'"

"Interesting. That's very interesting. But that isn't the business of my agency. That's States' problem."

"It's the nation's problem."

"What else do you have?"

"Don't shun it off." She backed away. "It's important. If we want to stop conflicts, our State Department can't continue to give signals that invite disaster. You and your agency can have all the spies you want in Iraq and all over the place, when the problem is being enhanced right here in Foggy Bottom at State."

"I understand. You're just talking to the wrong man. That's something you have to discuss with President Bush or Secretary Baker. Now, what else do you have? You said you had three secrets to tell me."

"The Russians still have a germ warfare program going—and it's been ordered to work at a faster pace than ever before. They're working on a contagious germ. It kills people in an instant. An instant!" She snapped her fingers. "It attacks every organ and tissue in the body. They're testing it on animals in Kazakhstan."

"How do you know?"

"Sources. When I was in Moscow. Just sources."

"Anne, I'm not asking you for a source in your role as a journalist. I'm asking you in your other role."

"As a spook?"

"As a very good spook."

"Sex. I found out through sex. Do you want to know with who?" Then she corrected herself. "Whom? Or is it who?"

"I want to know your source. I don't need to know the details. We don't authorize things like that, you know. What laboratory in Kazakhstan?"

She nodded and dipped into her purse. "Here's a map of Kazakhstan. I marked the place where the laboratory is located."

"You are something!"

"You want to know who I seduced?" Now she came closer to Jeffrey Stempka than she had been all evening, which meant that she was pressed against him.

Jeffrey Stempka hesitated, then nodded. "I want to know your source."

"A bellboy at the Belgrade One. These days, everyone in Moscow wants to sell or buy something. I saw him in the lobby around six at night, talking to some old KGB men. They were talking for about half an hour. After they left, I went to the bellboy and asked him to bring some vodka and cheeses up to my room at midnight. He said he gets off work at 10 o'clock. I gave him ten American dollars and I told him that what time he gets off is of no interest to me, I want the vodka and cheeses at midnight."

Jeffrey Stempka nodded. "So it was a bellboy."

"Yes."

He nodded again. "Okay. What was his name?"

"It never got to names."

"And what's your third piece of information?"

"Don't you want to know what happened in my room?"

"No. That's your business. What's your third piece of information?"

"I'm afraid, Mr. Stempka, that my third piece of information cannot be understood until you know more about my second piece of information. They connect."

"Go ahead."

"The bellboy knocked on the door. I answered and I was fully dressed. No nightie or anything that obvious. I thought that would be too planned, too easy, too common. He looked disappointed. He expected me to be seductive, but I wasn't. I told him to pour some vodka for me, and that was all. I knew he had just spent two hours doing nothing but thinking about what was going to happen at midnight, and the way I was dressed and acted, he was just sick. Good so far, huh?" She put her hand on his hand and got so close to him that from shoulders to foot, there was no space at all between them.

"Anne. Don't. Please don't."

That was it. Anne received the confirmation of what she hoped would not be confirmed. She wasn't being successful even at a rendezvous in the dark. She drew her hand back and stopped the pressure against him.

She was embarrassed as well as devastated.

The look on her face was enough to make Jeffrey Stempka sorry he had not shown some interest in her. He tried to repair the damage. "I have genuine feelings for you, but my job doesn't permit me to do anything about them." He meant it. He was controlling himself from her femininity. She didn't believe him.

It was the word "genuine" that gave her the most pain. He could have said he had "passionate feelings" for her or "longings for her" or something even more direct. But he chose to say "genuine." She nodded. "I understand," and she understood what he didn't mean. "Well, that's really all I have. That's all the information I have for you."

"But you said you had three things to tell me. What's the third?"

Anne shook her head, feeling tears swelling. "No. I was just kidding. I only had two things."

"Please, Anne."

"That's all!"

"Anne, I–I–"

"The third thing is that I'm not wearing any underwear! Does that answer your question?" And she gathered her purse and her coat and she slid out of the booth and walked hurriedly toward the door of The Cave Bar and Grill. He didn't follow after her. As a man, he wanted to follow after her. As an agent, he felt he couldn't.

"Just like Mark," she told herself. "Are they all through with sex? I just don't have the stuff anymore."

She walked down Wisconsin Avenue looking at all the young people of Georgetown walking in pairs and in groups. Some were laughing. Some were holding hands. Some were running from the cold into one place or another. Men were not staring at her. Maybe one or two were glancing with interest but it was probably because they recognized her from television. They just passed her by.

She almost felt like offering herself as a prostitute just to see if she still had appeal. But she didn't do it because it would be degrading, it would be dangerous, and worse than any of those two factors, she was afraid that no one would buy. "It always comes in threes," she said to herself. "There's always three things to consider."

Not always. There was a man, somewhere between youth and middle-age, wearing Levi's and a leather jacket walking toward her, and he smiled at her and winked at her as they passed, "Hey, good lookin'!" he said.

He didn't know it, but he was a blessing.

She wanted to look back at him. She wanted even more than that, but she kept on walking with her eyes straight ahead. If she turned to look back at him he might have thought she was desperate.

And no matter her desperation, she could never afford to give that impression.

She took the yellow strand of ribbon from her hair. She thought it must look silly. No more ribbons. Not at her age.

But that guy in the leather jacket did look at me with it on! She looked at the yellow strand of ribbon in her hand. The ribbon was all right. *It's my hand that needs a good pressing.*

Anne was making a terrible error. She decided she had to forget about being an appealing woman. When she decided that, she ended the appeal all by herself.

SEVENTY-SIX
THE YEAR OF THE WOMAN
1992

The '92 black Ford of the U.S. Consulate stopped on an unpaved road of Wo Hang in the upper part of Hong Kong's New Territories. The driver came out quickly and opened the doors for Moose Dunston, General Jonas Valadovich, Andrew Fung Kai-hung, and Irene Goodpastor.

"Are you sure she's your daughter, Moose?" Irene asked, as the group walked toward the inlet that led to the sea. This was the third time she asked the same question since the drive started at the U.S. Consulate building.

"She's my daughter, Irene." Moose was walking by her side while Jonas and Andrew were walking close behind them down the narrow lane.

"Don't fib me, Moose. If I were to repeat that she's your daughter, I would be doing it as a representative of the United States, and it's very serious. I wouldn't want to be wrong."

"You won't be wrong."

"I wish someone made a record of that twenty-one years ago."

"Wai-yee wanted Dr. Yeung recorded as Liberty's father on all the records. And she was right in doing that. It's the way it is, and if either one of them were alive, they'd be the first to say exactly what happened. There was no secret. Wai-yee and I created Liberty."

"Mrs. Goodpastor," Andrew said, "Liberty knows all that. As Mr. Dunston says, there was no secret. But anyway, what difference does it make? This man we are going to see is not an official. He is just a young worker who is a friend of Liberty and mine. Not even a friend. He is an acquaintance."

"I represent the United States no matter whom I talk to."

"I see." He had noticed the sternness in her voice, and Andrew had no desire to be a victim of her disapproval. "That is good. That is very good."

Mrs. Goodpastor gave a quick and abrupt glance back at him as they were walking toward the inlet. "Andrew, how long has Liberty been involved in smuggling refugees into Hong Kong?"

Andrew shook his head. "I don't know, ma'am."

"You know," Jonas said softly. "Don't you, Andrew?"

Andrew was surrounded by authority, and there was something about Jonas that made it impossible for Andrew, or anyone else, to do anything but tell the absolute truth to him. The quick answer to Mrs. Goodpastor didn't last long. "It's been going on and off, on and off, for about two years, sir."

"All right." Jonas turned to Moose. "Moose, let me do the talking here to whomever this guy is. You're too emotional. You let me ask the questions. All right?"

Moose nodded. "Okay."

The young man Andrew said would be there was there. He was waiting on the end of the walkway to the inlet. He was tall and thin, with a round face that hadn't been shaved for days. He was leaning against a rail with the inlet behind him. When Andrew, Moose, Jonas, and Irene reached him, he nodded slightly to each new face. His thumbs were left hooked in the pockets of his Levi's. He smelled like fish. But so did everything smell like fish in Wo Hang.

Andrew told him Moose was a writer, Jonas was a general, and Irene was a representative of the United States government. That caused the young man's relaxed, almost arrogant attitude, to make a quick shift into a soldier's posture. Andrew's entourage was not to be treated lightly.

"We are so glad to see you, Kin-shing," Andrew said. "It was a good trip here. This is the first time I've been up here to the inlet in the daytime. It's very nice."

"No small talk, Andrew," Jonas said, and quickly turned to give the young stranger a cold stare. "Where's Liberty?"

"Yes. Liberty. Miss Liberty." He was scared.

"What is it you know?" Jonas asked, and then added, "All of it."

"We have been dealing with snakeheads," he started to answer.

"I don't want a biography, I want to know what happened to Liberty."

"Yes, sir," he said, "But I must explain. Snakeheads are the ones who bring refugees from China into Hong Kong. We have been dealing with them. Late Monday night, it must have been after two o'clock in the morning, a boat was coming from up there," and he gave a gesture with his shoulder. "From China. Miss Liberty was helping the people off the boat, just lifting, you know, under the arms, when two soldiers came with guns. I thought at first they were Hong Kong police. Then there were seven of them. They took Miss Liberty and the others to their own boats, and they went away. It was very quick. They were not Hong Kong police. They were not snakeheads, but they were from the mainland. They were in uniforms of the P.L.A., the People's Liberation Army. They were in Hong Kong territory when they took her and the escapees. They can't do that. It is illegal. But they did it. They took her away with those she was helping. It was illegal."

"Everything done was illegal. What's your name?"

"Kin-shing."

"How do we get her back, Kin-shing?"

He gave a nervous laugh. "Oh, I don't know. I don't know."

"Do you know what a broken neck feels like?"

"Jonas!" Irene almost yelled.

Jonas was unruffled. "Kin-shing, do you know what a broken neck feels like?"

Kin-shing gave that nervous laugh again. "Oh, no, sir. I don't know about that. Not about broken necks and things."

Moose couldn't stay silent. He quickly intervened. "Liberty is my daughter. I want her back, and I'll pay you $10,000 American. Tonight. You be here tonight with Liberty. I'll be here at ten o'clock with $10,000 American. That's $78,000 Hong Kong."

"Oh, I–I–I don't know how to–"

"You can be a rich man tonight, Kin-shing."

Irene and Jonas exchanged a quick glance.

"I hope you know," Irene quickly said, "that Mr. Dunston is speaking for himself. The United States government does not stand behind that, nor do we endorse it."

"Seventy-eight thousand dollars Hong Kong," Moose repeated to Kin-shing. "Tonight, at ten o'clock."

Andrew was biting his lip. "Mr. Dunston, I do not think he has the ability to get Liberty free no matter the amount of money. He has no contact with the People's Liberation Army."

"He has contact with smugglers."

Kin-shing nodded. "Yes, I do. Snakeheads."

Moose didn't care about terminology. "Someone wants money. You want it. Smugglers, your snakeheads want it. The People's Liberation Army wants it. I have it. I want Liberty back."

"Mr. Dunston, I want Liberty back, too." Andrew's voice broke. "I want Liberty back! What can Kin-shing do? I think this has to be done at a higher level. I think it has to be done by someone in the upper echelon of the Hong Kong government who has the ear of the upper echelon of the Mainland government. Someone has to go to see the new governor."

That night, Moose went back to Wo Hang alone. Kin-shing was waiting for him. But Liberty wasn't with him.

"I cannot do it, Mr. Dunston. Do you have the $10,000 American with you?"

"I have the money and a gun. I have no hesitancy to use either."

"I have tried, Mr. Dunston. I have tried so hard. I know so many snakeheads and I asked everyone. Can I have $5,000 for trying?"

"You don't get ten cents for trying."

"You see? I am honest. I do not know anyone in the People's Liberation Army in China. But there are some snakeheads who know them. You must give me more time. I will keep on trying. You must pay me for trying."

"I must do nothing! The moment you have success, you contact me or Andrew. Here's my number," and he handed Kin-shing a folded piece of paper. "Day or night. Then, and only then, when I have her in my arms, all the money is yours. There will be nothing before then. I don't want to be milked. I want Liberty home."

Irene Goodpastor sat opposite the new governor, the Right Honorable Christopher Francis Patten, in his high-ceilinged office in Government House on the Hong Kong side. His desk was bordered by two flags, one of the Union Jack and the other one was blue with a small Union Jack on its upper left corner, the seal of Hong Kong on the right. The governor's hands were folded in front of him, resting on top of the desk. His graying hair seemed almost premature for his young, full, round face. "Mrs. Goodpastor, let me own up to you right away. Chinese officials are always very sensitive about incidents like these, as is my government. The fact that she was fathered by an American has deep and, I may add, justified meaning to your government, but in this case her heritage has no significance under the rule of law that must be upheld here."

"Governor, Mr. Dunston worked for presidents of my country and is a very prominent journalist here in Hong Kong, maintaining his American citizenship."

"In tuning up for this job, I read his articles with regularity. I still do. I read *Asia World Weekly* religiously. I'm an admirer of many of Mr. Dunston's editorials, and I have respect for his background and his talents and many of his views. But we cannot have different rules for the prominent and the admired than we have for the unknown or shunned. Isn't that the essence of American law, as well as our own?"

"Of course it is. I just want you to know that this isn't a story that he will allow to be out of the spotlight. He has a reputation and a vehicle to reach thousands, millions of people. He will use every device he can to get her out of there."

"So would I if I were him. Mrs. Goodpastor, I'm sure that Prime Minister Major will do what he can, but my influence may be somewhat limited both within my own party at home, surely with the opposition, and with Deng Xiaoping in Peking." It seemed strange to hear someone use the word "Peking" rather than "Beijing," but the Governor steadfastly held on to the old pronunciation of the city's name. "You must understand some things so you understand why I am limited in the Dunston matter. I'm sure your consulate knows that London and I have had our tiffs regarding my plan for increasing democracy here. London feels I am upping the pace too far and that I'm violating the Basic Law with my plans for democratization. To complicate matters further, Peking feels I am doing too much, that I am the worst governor Hong Kong has ever had. They call me irresponsible, imprudent, the whore of the East, a serpent. I have been called names here in Hong Kong, too, by business people and others. Hong Kong, with all its flash and dash really is one of a kind: chop sui generis, so I must deal with many elements. To put it charitably, there is dissatisfaction with me among many elements. If I had my way, there would be a totally democratically elected Legislative Council, so both Prime Minister Major and Deng Xiaoping are greatly bothered by my upping the pace of democratization. This, I'm afraid, may affect my influence in the Dunston matter."

"We at the U.S. Consulate have nothing but admiration for what you're trying to do here. We always refer to you as a different sort of governor than those sent here before. Governor Patten, can you 'up the pace' to get Mr. Dunston's daughter back home?"

He smiled and shook his head. "There have been remarkably good governors here. Sir Edward Youde was a strong-minded and immensely popular governor, fiercely loyal to Hong Kong, and perhaps as a result was regarded in London's private historic assessment of its custodianship of Hong Kong, as a tad awkward. The only reason I want you to know the present progress of my relationship with both London and Peking is so that you understand that I may not have the ability that some other Hong Kong governors might have had in getting the Dunston matter solved. I have been cashing in my chips very early here."

It was the voice of former president Nixon's assistant, Kathy O'Connor, coming over the intercom at his home in Saddle River, New Jersey. "It's Moose Dunston on the phone, Mr. President."

"Who?" President Nixon asked, talking into the intercom and putting down his yellow pad and pen on the small desk near his heavily cushioned chair, his legs resting on the ottoman.

"Moose Dunston."

"Oh, Moose! Moose!" He picked up the phone. "Moose! Hello. Where are you calling from? Hong Kong?"

"Yes, sir. First, sir, is everything all right with you?"

"Oh, fine. Fine. We have an election coming up, you know, and I think Bush isn't playing things well. He has to concentrate on foreign policy and he's talking about all kinds of things that he doesn't care about. You know?"

"I haven't followed it."

"Well, you don't need to. But here he was coming out of the Persian Gulf War with 91% approval ratings, and he campaigns on the Democrat's issues. Those approval ratings, you know, those polls, they're way down now. Can you imagine if Clinton wins? A draft dodger. A man who went overseas to protest our policy! But now tell me what's on your mind. How are things in Hong Kong?"

"Not well, sir. I have a real problem."

"What's going on over there?"

"You remember, Mr. President, that girl I knew in Hong Kong that you said I should marry—and I didn't—and I told you what happened in—"

"Tiananmen. Awful. Tiananmen Square."

"Yes, sir. That daughter of hers that I told you about—Mr. President, what I didn't tell you is that we—that daughter is ours." There was a long period of silence. Then Moose continued. "She's 21 years old now. We're very close, as you can imagine. She's my daughter. And Mr. President, she's a marvelous girl and she's been helping refugees into Hong Kong."

There was another long silence, then, "from the mainland? You mean from the mainland, or from Vietnam?"

"From the mainland."

"That's dangerous business, you know. Does she know how dangerous that is?"

"Yes, sir. The P.L.A. got her. She's gone. The mainland police, or military, took her. They're all the same there. The People's Liberation Army got her."

"She's in China?"

"Yes, sir."

"In China, itself?"

"It gets worse, Mr. President. She was the model for the Goddess of Democracy statue that was erected in Tiananmen Square in '89. I don't know if the authorities there know that."

The president was quiet.

Moose didn't like the pause. "I hate to ask you anything, Mr. President, but I need a favor. They have tremendous respect for you there and—"

"Back in '89 or whenever it was, I told you I would go to Beijing myself if I had to, if she got in trouble, didn't I? When you told me about her, isn't that right?"

"I'm not asking you that, Mr. President."

"We're going to get her out, Moose. Now, let's see how we do it. I think it's best if I start out by writing Deng.

"You will? Deng Xiaoping? It was what I was going to ask you. I want her back."

"I'll fax him. He has a machine now, you know. I don't think we'll make mention of that statue business. That way, if he knows, he can pretend he doesn't know. What's your daughter's name?"

"Liberty. Her family name is Yeung. Yeung Tso. But I don't know what she told them, so I think it's best to identify her as the girl they took into custody last Monday night at the border of Hong Kong. Near Wo Hang."

"Wait a minute. Give all the data to Kathy, will you? I'll get her on the line. Give her what needs to be said to identify her, and I'll do what I can. Now, you just be patient. All right?"

"Yes, sir."

"You just be patient."

"I will."

"You take care of yourself."

"You, too. Thank you, Mr. President. She means everything to me."

"I may have to make Deng some promises—like she'll never do anything like that again—and keep it all quiet, and all that. You know what I mean?"

"I think so."

"All right. All I can do is try with Deng. Believe me, he can do it. He's the Paramount Leader, they call him. He has no counterpart anywhere in the world. The Paramount Leader. He doesn't even hold a real position anymore. You know what position he holds? He's the Bridge Commissioner. And that doesn't have anything to do with bridges over rivers. It's the game of bridge. A card game. So there you are, the Bridge Commissioner. But he's the Paramount Leader. He doesn't have to run for office for that. Maybe Bush can be Bridge Commissioner if he loses to Clinton! Then he can be Paramount Leader!"

Moose faked a small laugh.

"You be patient. You take care of yourself. All right?"

"Yes, sir."

"Moose, if it comes to going there, I will."

Throughout their thirty-two years of marriage, Ted and Linda Murphy had argued about many things, but never about politics until it came to Bill Clinton. It wasn't that either of them were for the re-election of George Bush, it was that Linda had a Clinton-Gore-'92 bumper sticker on her car and wanted to work for him as a volunteer, and Ted did not want her advocacy to be advertised. "It hurts my credibility, honey. Clinton's goin' to win this thing with or without your bumper sticker and your volunteerin', and his folks know that I stand behind him, so where's the benefit? What's the percentage?"

Linda was, as usual, being relegated as a supplement to Ted rather than regarded as a separate human being. "But what if he loses–and I could have helped him win?"

"He won't lose. The only dumb stuff he's doin' is actin' like an interventionist when he dumps on Bush for havin' Most Favored Nation status with China, and callin' Bush a guy who coddles dictators. And then blastin' Bush for not doin' anything in Bosnia. Those are the only things Bush's done that's right. Clinton should stick to domestic stuff. Foreign policy is the only dumb stuff he's doin'. If China and Bosnia were the only issues, I'd vote for Bush. He's at least leavin' China and Bosnia alone. Maybe Clinton's just tryin' to get some votes from the right wing, I don' know."

"Honey, it's called the Year of the Woman, and I think as a woman I ought to be active, and I think that would be good for you, don't you think so?"

"You'll be active when he wins. We'll be dancin' in the East Room. I'm helpin' him every night on television–but we can't be right out in the open. Get it?"

She got it.

"It's the most sexist label I've ever heard! What if they called it the Year of the Man?! Would anyone stand for it?" Anne was the only one who could get away with saying something like that, because the television audience knew her as more of a woman than some of the most prominent women running for office around the country. It was Anne's last commentary on television. "Those organizations who coined that term as the Year of the Woman aren't for women, they're for women of one political party with one political philosophy. When I ran for office they didn't lift a finger for me. For that matter, they didn't lift a finger for Margaret Thatcher in Great Britain. She should be their idol–her picture should be hanging on every one of their office walls–that is, if they truly believe in women in government. But you won't hear a word about Margaret Thatcher in those organizations. She wasn't, after all, their kind of woman. Did you ever meet the leaders of those organizations? I think they're mad at God for making them women. Not me! I loved it!" She made a mistake by putting it in past tense. "And I still do," she said quickly. "They're men-haters, except for those jerky-men who publicly bend to them."

Every phone in the news room was ringing. It was the "jerky-men" comment that, above all others, brought so many viewers to register their complaints and compliments, some with demands she leave the station, some with requests that she be given a longer segment. But all they heard in response was "One moment please," followed by a beep and a recorded message: "We thank you for your comment. We are always interested in the reactions of our viewers. We regret that Anne Whitney will be leaving 'Crossed Swords' and we wish her the best in whatever endeavor she chooses to pursue in the future."

At three o'clock in the morning, four days after the phone call between Moose and President Nixon, a black, wooden boat passed through the inlet that led down to Wo Hang. There was no one there to greet the vessel. In an unprecedented display of courtesy for such a mission, five uniformed officers of the People's Liberation Army surrounded her as she disembarked. It seemed as though all five of them were trying to help her off the boat, each one eager to prove their devotion to her safety. Orders that came directly from the Bridge Commissioner, Deng Xiaoping, could not be taken lightly.

When she was safe ashore, the five officers went back on their boat and headed north to China.

As she stood on the bank above the sea on the inlet, she said in a very loud and strong voice, "Thank you, Ma! Thank you, Father! Thank you, God!"

Liberty was home.

SEVENTY-SEVEN
FAMILY
1993

The last time Moose was on Sunshine Island was in 1964 with Wai-yee. That was when the world was different. And now he was there with their daughter who was close to the same age her mother was when the two of them walked up the island's hill with three big dogs accompanying them to the home where Gus Borgeest and his family lived. Now the island was visibly desolate, not even the house was there, but the island was filled with the scent he hadn't inhaled since that day so long ago.

"I think she's here, don't you?" Moose had to say it to Liberty because it was impossible not to feel Wai-yee's presence.

Liberty answered as they walked up that hill. "She's everywhere I go and everywhere I look and everything I think. She's here, but she's everywhere." Moose felt no one, other than her mother, could ever compete with Liberty's soul.

"What do you want to do here now?" Moose asked her.

"Just walk and see it as it is today and make our plans. Today I want to do anything. Nothing." So much like Wai-yee. "Let's see what we'll do with Sunshine Island."

By the time they reached the top of the hill, Moose was out of breath. "Can we sit? That's some climb. I hate to tell you but I'm beginning to feel those things. My calves are a little tight."

"Let's sit right there," and she walked about ten yards from where they were. Did she, somehow, know that she picked the place where her mother and Moose had sat? Now there were no chairs on which to sit. There was no table, and no tea being served—no tea with bugs. They sat on overgrown weeds.

Sunshine Island was Liberty's reward from Governor Patten for promising never again to be an agent for smugglers of escapees from the mainland to Hong Kong. One thousand Hong Kong dollars a year was the fee Great Britain was charging her for the lease of Sunshine Island, and she would turn the island back into a training ground for refugees to learn a craft. But now the refugees would not be Chinese as they were years ago, they would be Vietnamese who she would select from the remaining camps of Hong Kong.

Moose had regained his breath. "You know that I'll take care of those things you need—for any facilities you put here, and whatever you need. Before Jonas went back to L.A. he said he'd come back here any time you need him for anything. He wants to help, too."

Liberty smiled. "I know. I don't need anything." Again came the consistency of Liberty to say the unexpected. "Ma and Father are taking care of all the funding."

Moose looked sharply at her.

"They left me more than I'll need here. Honest. I didn't spend everything on smugglers. I couldn't. I don't get it all at once. Honest! But do you know what I wish?"

"What, Liberty?"

"I wish they had known Governor Patten. He's quite a great man, isn't he?"

Moose nodded. "He's the best thing to happen to Hong Kong in a long time."

"Maybe Ma and Father sent him here. How do we know?"

"We don't. We don't know."

"Are you rested, old man?" Liberty smiled.

Moose nodded with a reciprocal smile. "Hey, what do you mean, old man? I'm more than ready! I was just being considerate of you because I knew you were out of breath and you didn't want to admit it to me. I made up a phony reason for wanting to rest."

Liberty got up quickly and extended her hand for Moose to use as a brace. "Now, don't move too quickly. I don't want your bones to creak!"

Moose grabbed her hand, and got up almost as quickly as she had gotten up. "Thanks, kid!"

"Kid! I'm no kid! Let's see what we want to do with this island. Just tell me when you want to rest, which, it seems to me, will be every few minutes."

Given the magnitude of Liberty's hopes, the island was small. "There should be a school there! A real classroom! Maybe two classrooms! Not just for children, but for every one who comes here. We'll need two teachers, won't we? Over there—that's where the living quarters will be. Now, I want a shed over there for the farm equipment. All of that land over there can be used for planting—planting whatever will grow. Let's go over there. Do you know what should be right here? A clinic! That's what I want! And not just to treat the refugees who come here, but to train every one of them in at least a little something about medicine so they can help each other when they leave here. And I want a place for artists—to paint or write music or what ever they want. That's important!"

"Liberty, you're talking pretty big."

"Every one in Hong Kong talks big and they make it. I'm just following what other Hong Kong people have done. If a shopping mall can be built every other week on Hong Kong Island, we can put the sunshine back on Sunshine Island. The refugees, themselves, will do most of the work. Refugees built Hong Kong."

"How long do you think all this will take?"

"It must be done in six months because the governor gave me a one year lease. By the end of that time I want him to see the merit in extending it for another year, and three more leases, all the way to 1997 when he leaves, and the takeover comes. Can Irene Goodpastor come out here when it's done? I'd love to have some representative of Ma's Consulate see what we do."

Moose gave a hesitant shrug. "Oh, the consulate knows all about your lease and I'm sure someone from the consulate will come out here when it's done, but I'm not sure it will be Mrs. Goodpastor. Irene is a political appointee and she had to write her resignation letter to President Clinton. That's the way it goes. That's the procedure. I don't know whether or not Clinton will accept her resignation."

Suddenly a loud far-away masculine voice yelled out, "Ahoy! Ahoy! Anybody home?!"

Liberty and Moose looked at each other quickly. "Who's that?" Moose asked. Liberty quickly went to the edge of the hill with Moose huffing and puffing to catch up to her.

"It's a man!" Liberty said.

Moose watched the man struggling to get up as he held a black leather case in his hand. A sampan was waiting by the other sampan that brought Moose and Liberty. Moose smiled. "It's Jack Edwards."

"Father's old friend? Mr. Edwards?"

"That's Jack!" Then Moose yelled down, "We're home, Jack! Come on up!"

When Jack Edwards got to the top of the hill he was breathless and sat down on the weeds, resting his leather case beside him. Moose and Liberty sat next to him.

"How do I rate?" Liberty asked. "How do I rate being on a beautiful desolate island with two old men who can't walk without gasping for air?"

"This, my dear, is how you rate!" Jack said as he opened the two clasps of the case. He reached inside the case and pulled out something very light, wrapped in white tissue paper.

"Two of your father's old friends—and one of them is me—wanted you to borrow this—for a day." He handed it to Liberty.

"A gift?" Moose asked.

"Not for you, you big piece of lard! And it isn't a gift for the girl, either."

"Oh, am I just the girl? I don't have a name?"

"That's right, girl! Open it up."

Moose said, "Would you rather be called a big piece of lard, like he refers to me?"

Liberty carefully unwrapped the unsealed tissue paper, and there was the folded flag of the Union Jack of Great Britain. Liberty looked mystified. "What is it, Mr. Edwards? A flag?"

"It's not just a flag. It's *the* flag!"

Moose's mouth was open. He recognized what was in that tissue paper. "Honey, do you know what this is?"

"A British flag," she answered. "The Union Jack. Thank you, Mr. Edwards."

Moose shook his head. "No. It's not just a flag. It's the flag Arthur May put up on the Peak to reclaim Hong Kong for Great Britain near the end of the war."

"Oh, my God!" Liberty said in sudden understanding. "The famous flag!"

"It got the Japs to surrender!" Jack Edwards just couldn't get used to saying "Japanese." Liberty gave a startled look and a stare until he explained his vocabulary the way he always did. "Not the good guys. They're Japanese. I'm talking about the bad guys. They were Japs."

Moose said, "Forget it. This is quite an honor, Jack."

"Arthur and I wanted it to wave over the rebirth of Sunshine Island. I have to bring it back, but you know who suggested it? Louise. My wife. Louise and I were over at your Consulate for a lunch yesterday and we were told you'd be out here today and Louise said, 'You should bring the flag out there so it's the first flag Dr. Yeung's daughter puts up over that place now that she's leased it.' I told Arthur what she said. He wanted it done just as much as Louise and I did."

"Oh, my!" Liberty was excited. "That is so wonderful. Thank you, thank you, Mr. Edwards!"

"Now how do we put it up?" Moose asked.

"Get a stick!" Jack Edwards said. "Get a big stick. Get two big sticks, or three. I brought rope and tape in this box in case we have to attach a few sticks together! I know how to do it! When you're a prisoner of the Ja—Japanese you learn how to do everything!"

It was Liberty who found a branch that must have been six to eight feet in length, that was on the ground.

"We're going to have a fit ceremony!" Jack Edwards said. Between Moose and Jack, the work was done and the branch was carried to the top of the hill and planted in the ground while on top of it flew the grand flag.

Only Jack Edwards would suggest it. And they did it: the three of them stood by its base with hands over their hearts as Jack Edwards sang, "Rule Britannia." Moose and Liberty didn't sing it. They didn't know the words.

"I have some more goodies in this box of mine," Jack said as they sat by the flag. He reached inside his black leather case and took out waxpapered sandwiches and three cans of Coke. They sat there eating the lunch that Jack's wife had prepared, and drinking from the cans of Coke. "You know, old lady Goodpastor is going," Jack Edwards said.

Both Moose and Liberty stopped eating.

Jack Edwards nodded. "Clinton said, 'Bye-bye.' She's a good old lady. I'll be sorry to see her go."

Moose put down his sandwich. "I was afraid of that. She is a good woman. When did you find that out?"

"Yesterday when I went to your Consulate."

"What was her mood?"

"Oh, fine. I don't think it was a surprise. It's your custom isn't it?"

Moose nodded. "For political appointees, yeah."

Liberty was downcast. "I wanted her to come here when Sunshine Island is in full use. I like her. She was very good to Ma. She put her picture up in the reception room of the Consulate."

Jack nodded. "I know. I agree. She can't be replaced. Liberty," and she was glad he actually remembered her name, "what do you need for this place?"

"Everything. But I can take care of it."

"No, you can't. I want to help. The Royal British Legion wants to help. I've been very successful you know, in getting what I want—as long as what I want is right—and it always is. I succeeded at getting British passports and pensions for those who fought in the war, you know."

Moose nodded. "You were on that campaign for years, weren't you?"

"More like decades, but it's done. Now I'm going to make sure their widows are taken care of, too. London has to do it before 1997—if there are any war widows still living here then." He turned his head to Liberty. "But if you need any help to do anything, you ask your old Uncle Jack."

Liberty smiled. "I will."

Moose took a swig of his Coke then asked, "When is Irene leaving back to the United States?" The swig was too quick. Moose gave an involuntary burp. "Sorry! Excuse me! I'm sorry!" It just wasn't something Moose normally did.

"Moose!" Liberty said. "How gross!"

"I told you he was a big piece of lard. Now, what did you say, Dunston, if you can talk without embarrassing yourself and embarrassing Liberty and me?"

"I said when does Irene go back home?"

Jack Edwards shrugged. "Soon. That's all I know. I think they leave pretty quick when the president accepts a letter of resignation. Right?"

Moose nodded. "I'll see her tomorrow."

Irene Goodpastor was standing among large brown cardboard boxes all over the floor. Two of the boxes were on her desk as she sorted out what would stay with the consulate from her desk drawers and what were her own things, to be sent home to Washington. Moose was in his usual position sitting on the chair facing her desk, but her chair was way off to the side, and Irene kept standing, sorting as she talked. "I'm just fine, Moose," she said. "I have plans. That's one thing I've learned by this age. Always have plans. If you don't have plans, God will know it and He might just shrug His giant shoulders and say, 'She's been down there on the Earth long enough.'"

"What's your plan?"

"Moose, the next time I come back here it will be 1997, just like I originally planned. And when that happens I'm going to come back as the head of a Think Tank in Washington. My own Think Tank. I want it to be better than the Heritage Foundation, Rand, Hoover, Hudson, and Brookings—all put together."

Moose nodded. He was getting used to the bold plans of women. "Not bad. Do you have a name?"

With some pride she announced, "The Goodpastor Center."

"I like it!"

"Can I buy you away from *Asia World Weekly*? I want to buy Jonas away from his freelance life, too."

Moose smiled. "I'm staying here, Irene. Thanks, I'm flattered, but I'm staying here. I want to be where Liberty can get to me in an instant. As for Jonas, I don't think there's enough money in the world to get Jonas to go to Washington. I don't blame you for wanting him, but he really dislikes that place."

"I know. I already knew that. But I thought I'd ask."

"Write Jonas in L.A. It will make him feel good. Just be prepared for a negative response. When do you leave Hong Kong, Irene?"

"Next Tuesday."

"Www! That soon?"

"Why delay it? I got the word last week. Even if Bill Clinton wanted me to stay, I don't think I would. Did you hear what he said last Tuesday?"

"I did. 'The United States should not become involved as a partisan in a war.' Irene, he doesn't understand foreign policy. As I recall, we were partisans in World War I, World War II, Korea, Vietnam, Grenada, Kuwait. What do we do in a war if we don't take a side? It seems to me that President Clinton wants the military to become a uniformed Peace Corps."

"We're going to pay a very dear price for that."

"Irene, you're beginning to sound like a Brit. Maybe you've been here too long, after all."

"What do you mean?"

"You said we're going to pay a very dear price. What American uses that expression? That's the influence of this British government that's in you now! Right?"

She gave a short laugh. "You're right."

"Isn't that funny? I mean funny–strange. We're all part of one family here, aren't we? We're all Hong Kong people. It's family."

She nodded. "Yes."

"Irene, you're going to be missed. Very much so. This place won't be the same without you."

"I won't be the same without it."

"You'll be better off. The consulate won't be."

"I'm going to get some good people to be part of my Goodpastor Center, and put the consulate in the past."

"Why don't you ask George Bush? He's out of a job."

"Oh, no. He's planning his library."

"Dan Quayle?"

"The Hudson Institute beat me to the punch. But I have someone in mind that I'm going to ask to work with me–and it's someone who will give the center immediate interest back home."

"Really? Who?"

Irene started nodding. "Guess."

"Well, I don't know."

"Just guess."

"Let's see. You have enough former senators and congressmen to choose from after the last election. That's what think tanks normally do, isn't it?"

She shook her head. "Not a former senator or congressman, but you're getting close."

"I have no idea."

"Sonny Bono."

"Sonny Bono?"

"Sonny Bono! 'I've Got You, Babe!' 'The Beat Goes On!'"

"Why do you want him?"

"You'd know if you knew him. Did you ever meet him?"

"No. How would I have met him?"

"He's very unique, and underneath that happy face is a very deep man."

"Okay. I don't question your judgment, but I just don't–I mean, he's a rock star, not a political thinker."

"Don't be so sure. He's a superb political thinker."

"How did you meet him?"

"I didn't. I watched him on television. I wrote him. He wrote me. We've talked on the telephone."

"That's all?"

"You know how everyone says they like people? He really likes people. You can tell. I followed what he did when he became Mayor of Palm Springs. He was very successful, an excellent mayor. Then, last year, I read everything I could about his run in that California primary for the U.S. Senate. I followed what he was saying. And he came out of that beyond anyone's expectations. He was good! He was very good!"

"I didn't know all that about him. That's fine, Irene. I didn't follow his career. Will he join you in D.C.?"

She hesitated. "I don't know." Then she shrugged. "Maybe, but I'm not counting on it. Like you and Jonas, he has his own plans. I already talked to him about it. He's very hesitant. He's thinking about it. He's debating with himself about his future plans. I'm going to make another offer–as attractive a proposal as possible."

"What's he debating about?"

"A friend of his is trying to talk him into running for the House of Representatives next year, and if he does, he has to start campaigning right away. Originally he was thinking of running for Lieutenant Governor of California, but now he doesn't know. So he's debating between lieutenant governor or congressman or coming to work for me."

"And if he decides to run–for something?"

"I'll support him. But I'd rather have him supporting me."

"Good luck. I feel odd. I don't have any new plans. Liberty is ready to rebuild Sunshine Island, you're going home to start a Think Tank. I feel like I'm stagnant. But I have to stay here. And I have to admit–it's not a bad place to have to stay."

"Hong Kong? It's Shangri-La. And your daughter, Moose. She's a real live angel, isn't she?"

Moose nodded with his lips tight. He could talk all day about the goodness of Liberty, but when someone else did it, he choked up.

Irene continued. "Is she going to marry Andrew?"

"I don't think so. I know he's crazy about her. But why wouldn't he be? Sure, he'd love to marry her. I don't think she's thinking of marriage. She's thinking about–I don't know–she's always thinking of grand things. She's thinking about Sunshine Island now."

"There's something about her that's beyond me."

John Travolta looked down at the living room in confusion. He had seen so much from his perch on the wall of the home on Crocodile Hill, but this was something he had not witnessed before.

There was this seated eighteen-year-old boy who called himself J.F.C. of all things, who couldn't keep his mouth closed as he stared at Liberty. He kept shifting in his chair. He had a yellow legal pad on his lap and a pen in his hand. And there was her boyfriend, Andrew Fung Kai-hung, sitting next to Liberty on the couch, and he didn't seem to enjoy the company of J.F.C. at all.

J.F.C. was not subtle about his feelings toward Liberty. It wasn't just his mouth that he couldn't close, it was that his eyes watched her even when he was writing on the yellow pad. He was, after all, eighteen years old, the age in which he seemed to be aroused every two minutes for no cause, and Liberty was not a minimal rationale for his excitement. Although he was four years Liberty's junior, this "older woman" could simply not be ignored as something beyond his interest. And, just like her mother when she was her age, she knew how to wear a cheong-sam.

"What does J.F.C. stand for?" Andrew asked him.

"John Fitzgerald Cooper." J.F.C. didn't like Andrew any more than Andrew liked J.F.C. What could Liberty possibly see in him? "I was named after President Kennedy."

"So no one calls you John?"

"Some, maybe. But almost everyone calls me J.F.C."

"How old are you, John?" Andrew asked. He had to do it. He had to reject the initialed name and at the same time he had to let Liberty know right off, if she didn't know by figuring it out herself, that this was no more than a boy compared to Andrew, who had long since passed adolescence. Well, passed it, anyway.

"Me?"

"Yes." Who else?

"You mean my age?"

"Yes. Your age. How old are you?"

Liberty knew that Andrew was trying to embarrass him. She knew that John was taken with her. She knew Andrew was upset. She knew what was going on inside both of them. Her rescue was instinctive. "Oh, I'll bet, deep inside, you're really twice or three times the age everyone thinks you are."

"Well, I've been—"

She nodded before he said anything of meaning. "Of course." Of course what?

Andrew wasn't going to let this get too friendly. "Aren't you in school, John?" That was a dirty trick.

"Oh, no. I graduated long ago." Six months ago.

"From secondary school?"

"I was studying at the English Schools Foundation. But now I work over at the Kai Tak Vietnamese Migrant Transit Center."

"You work with your mother over there?" Andrew wanted to say "mommy" but restrained himself.

John's father went through this kind of thing with an Eisenhower appointee, but John didn't know it. "My mother doesn't like administrative work. That's why she wanted me to come over here today so I could handle it for Liberty. My mother tends to the refugees and I tend to the business end. Over at the center I do all the coordination between her work and the Hong Kong government, the Civil Aid Services, the U.N. High Commissioner for Refugees, and all the agencies that deal with refugee services."

Liberty seemed impressed, which was his objective. "That's wonderful! That's just the kind of experience we need! Did Moose tell you about all our plans for Sunshine Island?"

"Yes, he did. And Governor Patten gave you the okay?"

"He did. And Jack Edwards over at the Royal British Legion said he'd do anything to help us."

"I hope you know, Miss Liberty, that all financial aid for Vietnamese refugees is a cooperative effort between the Hong Kong government, the U.K. government, and the U.N. High Commissioner for Refugees. Then independent humanitarian efforts like us at the World Refugee Mission help when we can. The kind of thing that you're talking about reinstating on Sunshine Island would be very difficult to fund. The appropriations are not—"

"It's funded. I don't need funding." Liberty interrupted.

"You don't?"

"No. Maybe later, but not now. I don't want to get into all the necessary paperwork and difficulties that go into getting funds. This isn't going to be a fund-raising effort that goes on for years while nothing happens. And besides, I assured Governor Patten all I want is the island and I would take care of the rest—just like Gus Borgeest did many years ago."

"How many refugees do you want there?"

"Fifty to begin with."

John wrote it down on his yellow pad, like any good administrator, but he didn't look down at the paper as he wrote. "That's no problem. We have around 30,000 Vietnamese refugees still at the camps here in Hong

Kong. We can devise a pretty good selection process. When will the island be ready for them?"

"That's where you can help. I need to know the architects, all that. I have blueprints that I made, but they aren't professional. I want it done quickly."

"I can steer you in the right direction." He jotted down something on his pad.

"And I need something else."

"What's that?"

"You touched on it. The selection process. I want particular refugees."

"What do you mean?"

"I want the ones who escaped from Vietnam to China—and then escaped from China into Hong Kong."

John shook his head. "Oh, no. That can't be done. They only have refugee status once. We call them ECVIIs, the Ex-China Vietnamese Illegal Immigrants. We reached an agreement with the PRC to repatriate all the ECVIIs in our camps here. They're sent back very quickly."

"Not anymore, John." Liberty looked stern—almost frightening to him.

"Liberty wants them on Sunshine Island," Andrew warned. He was anxious to show his authority in all this. Andrew had been a listener too long.

Liberty didn't need Andrew's authority. She was no amateur in getting her way. "J.F.C.?" Her tone changed from threatening to subservient, confusing her guest. She said his initials as though she was in need of him.

"Yes, Miss Liberty?" He answered as though he just fell out of bed.

"I'm sure that with your experience in refugee affairs and your expertise in administrative matters, that you can figure out a way to bring Vietnamese who escaped into China and then escaped into Hong Kong, to Sunshine Island."

There was no answer.

"Can't you?"

He couldn't help but nod. "I think I can do that."

"Oh, good!" She leaned over to Andrew and kissed him on the cheek.

Why kiss Andrew? What did he do?

Oh, well. She was a woman. She didn't need to be understood.

SEVENTY-EIGHT
THE DEMOCRACY OF DEATH
1994

During the day the clouds were gray and then black and the downpour was immense. That was rare for Yorba Linda, California, in April. Ron Walker held an umbrella over the Reverend Billy Graham as the two slowly walked from the entrance of the Richard Nixon Library to the pathway where the long black automobile was pulling up to discharge the remains of the former president. As the automobile stopped there was a slice of thunder so piercing, so reverberating, so powerful, that the electricity in the library was extinguished. The rain increased in intensity.

The representatives of the media, witnessing the outdoor ceremony of the automobile's arrival, were without umbrellas in this unexpected storm and they had no shelter from the deluge of rain. One of the totally drenched reporters, his wet clothes stuck to him, and getting more and more soaked, turned to Jonas and said, "All right! He wins!"

The library remained open that Tuesday night and the lines of people exceeded the horizon, some waiting seven hours to walk by his coffin that was protected by the flag of the United States of America. The street lights of Yorba Linda illuminated the figures in their very slow walk forward, and created sad reflections in the rain-soaked sidewalks.

Downstairs, beneath the reception room of the library building, the series of glass-enclosed offices were occupied by the staff of the library who were disassembling their first plans for a private funeral with family and friends, and preparing for an official state funeral to be attended, not only by the current president, Bill Clinton and his wife, but by all four living former presidents: Ford, Carter, Reagan, and Bush, and their wives.

At the far end of that series of glass enclosed offices was the room with a conference table and a Xerox machine. Seated around the table were John Taylor, the Director of the Library; Sandy Quinn who was putting together all the plans to accommodate the White House, the Secret Service, the State Department, and foreign dignitaries; Kevin Cartwright who had the unenviable job of accommodating the press; Don Bendetti, an old friend of President Nixon who had volunteered to take care of the burial itself; Susan Naulty, the library's archivist who was putting together a massive exhibition accompanied by bouquets of flowers received from around the world; and Loie Gaunt who had served President Nixon since he was a senator.

Loie Gaunt was still serving him, reexamining every name she had put on the invitation list. She knew, by memory, the friends of president Nixon through five decades, and remembered the oldest and most random acquaintances. She said it was "his wish that his friends were to have the preferred seating tomorrow." This was the second night in sequence that she remained sleepless, only leaving the library to get a change of clothes. "No," she said, "he shouldn't be invited. And her–she's all right, but not a purple button." The purple buttons were for friends of the president.

"How about General Valadovich? He isn't an old friend, but the president liked him."

"Purple," she answered. "He liked him a lot. He got to know him after he left the presidency. He knew him through Dunston."

"Is Moose Dunston coming?"

Loie nodded. "He phoned. He's flying in from Hong Kong. Now, purple buttons for Janet and Elyse Bresnahan. The president was very fond of them."

Upstairs, in the reception room that housed the flag-draped coffin and the military honor guard, General Jonas Valadovich was in uniform standing next to the president's coffin with Steve Bull, who had been the president's appointment secretary in the old days at the White House. Recordings of President Nixon's favorite songs were being played one after the other. Lines of people filed by. Steve Bull was choked up. Even in the toughest days of those White House years, he had retained his sense of humor but it seemed as though he lost it tonight. When he recognized that the general saw his eyes with tears, he wiped them quickly, he swallowed, then smiled, and gesturing toward the flag-draped coffin he said, "This tragedy isn't so tough for the Old Man compared to what he's been through. This is an easy one for him. He'll be back."

Somehow, a gray-haired woman reporter, notebook and pen in hand, seemed to appear out of nowhere and was suddenly standing next to Jonas and Steve Bull. "Mr. Bull, General Valadovich, I don't know if you've been outside in the last couple hours, but the line goes all the way down Yorba Linda Boulevard. You can't even see the end of it. A lot of them are Vietnamese who live in Orange County. There's a whole group of them among the others. Do you think all these people mean he's now been forgiven?"

"Forgiven for what?" Steve Bull asked.

"Well, I mean–Watergate–for all that."

Jonas looked at her sharply. "The question is, do they forgive you?"

The following day, after all the guests were seated outside before the burial, each president and his wife were announced separately and they walked to the center stage behind his coffin.

"Shy and withdrawn," Henry Kissinger said, "Richard Nixon made himself succeed in the most gregarious of professions and steeled himself to conspicuous acts of extraordinary courage. In the face of wrenching domestic controversy, he held fast to his basic theme that the greatest free nation in the world had a duty to lead and no right to abdicate."

"I believe the second half of the Twentieth Century will be known as the age of Nixon," Senator Robert Dole said. "To know the secret of Richard Nixon's relationship with the American people, you need only to listen to his words: 'You must never be satisfied with success,' he told us. 'And you should never be discouraged by failure. Failure can be sad, but the greatest sadness is not to try and fail, but to fail to try. In the end what matters is that you have always lived life to the hilt.'" Senator Dole's strong voice broke as he concluded, "May God bless Richard Nixon and may God bless the United States."

Governor of California, Pete Wilson said, "In 1960 many urged Richard Nixon to contest one of the closest and controversial elections in American history. But Richard Nixon said no, he would not go to court. He refused to fight, and he urged others not to on his behalf. He would relinquish the prize that was his life's ambition. Why? For a simple, but these days, remarkable reason. It was because he so loved his country that he refused to risk it being torn apart by the constitutional crisis that might ensue."

The Reverend Billy Graham said, "John Dunn said that there's a democracy about death. It comes equally to us all, and makes us all equal when it comes."

Jonas leaned over to a very tired Moose Dunston, and whispered, "Do you remember when President Nixon recited Ecclesiastics to us? He had every word perfectly memorized—that there is a time to —and he itemized them—all the things—all of them—and a time to be born and a time to die."

The democracy of death came that very day on U.S. Highway 193 and the 48th Avenue turnoff in College Park, Maryland, when Ted Murphy and a young woman, identified later as a secretary at the Department of Health and Human Services, were killed in an automobile accident, smashing at high speed, into a parked van.

SEVENTY-NINE
BENEFICIARIES
1994

There were fourteen people sitting in Linda Murphy's living room. The cushioned chairs, the davenport, the wooden chairs brought in from the kitchen, and the folding card-room chairs were arranged in a messy almost-circle. The fourteen people weren't there to mourn the loss of Ted. That had already been done. They weren't there to romance Linda. No one wanted to. They were there because she was an opportunity.

"With your name, with the devotion people have to Ted, with Vice President Gore having attended Ted's funeral, and with the Year of the Woman having been an American celebration two years ago—Linda, it's your time, if you do what you have to do. You have two years to do what's necessary to put yourself in the Congress of the United States of America! How does that sound?" It was the political consultant, Gordo Halleck.

He was the one who had approached Linda about this a month ago. There was no question that she was excited about the prospect. There was no question that she would follow his lead. She was used to following. Gordo had gathered his political allies who had made a career of political campaigns, and he quickly took charge at the Saturday morning meeting. He sat with a big black open notebook on his lap.

"It sounds good," Linda said, nodding.

"All right, then. Now we're going to go through what has to be done for you. This is your team, Linda. That is, if you want us. With your heavy loss of Ted, you have the inside track. It might sound like a long way ahead to you, but two years is a snap of the fingers in politics and if you want to do this, we have to start now. These people here are the best in the business. Emily Stouton, Ralph Cosgrove, Terry MacDonald, Sherry Rinders, Ross Novak, their assistants. They're pros. We're all professionals. I started putting this group together as soon as I knew you had the promise of a winning candidate. We all worked on big campaigns in the past, I don't need to itemize all of them. A lot of the folks here worked on the Clinton campaign. I worked on congressional and senate campaigns. We know what works and what doesn't work. Okay?"

"Okay."

"Okay?" He asked again, to be sure.

"Okay. Are you the campaign manager?"

"That's right."

"That's good."

"Now, the first thing you have to do is move."

"I do?"

"You can't run against Clayton Denman. You can't run against an incumbent in your own party. That's what you'd be up against, see? The party won't like that. You see? You follow? You see?"

"Oh."

"So you have to move."

"Where to?

"Another congressional district. That's all. Legally, you don't even have to—but it's better."

"Really?"

"You have the money?"

"Now I do."

"We'll find the district. There's a couple without an incumbent. They'll call you a carpetbagger, but that's nothing. Look what Bobby Kennedy did. He moved from out of state, here to New York to become Senator and he made it. You can move to another district for the House of Representatives easy with your appeal. They loved your Ted."

There were some quick glances, one to the other, among the members of the group. The glances were not questioning what Gordo said, but seemed to justifiably imply that Linda Murphy did not have the status of Bobby Kennedy.

Linda was a nodding machine. "I can do that if I can keep this place, too."

"Now, first, how are you physically? You don't want to have to duck out after a campaign begins, like Anne Whitney did in what was it, the 4th District there? If you have some physical problems, tell us now. Maybe we can deal with whatever it may be, or maybe you should decide not to run right now. You see? You see how that works?"

Linda looked scared. Would they all walk out of her living room and give up her candidacy if she wasn't well? "Oh, no! I'm healthy."

"More important, and you better think deeply into your past on this one. Did you do anything—anything that could be used against you?"

"Like what?"

"Anything. Sorry to ask, but it's better that I ask than let someone else ask—or charge you with something. Were you always faithful to Ted?"

"Always."

"Even before Ted. How did you behave? In the next few weeks what you should do is try to think of anything you did that could be an embarrassment to you. Anything, ever. I worked for a candidate, and our researcher found out that years back her opponent and his girlfriend were with some married couple, and after they went out to dinner, they all went to a nightclub that had strippers in the show there. So on the Friday before the election, when the polls showed him running within a point of our candidate, we used it. You have to put an opponent on the defensive when it's tight. Linda, it's hardball. See?"

"What did his wife say?"

"He wasn't married. Who cares? It worked. And he had the best team in the world; Khachigian, Peschong, Renfer, Rodota, Klein, Taylor, Leipzig,

Thimmesch, Steinberg, Riley, the best. But we won. We had the Hoover. They never even bought one."

"What do you mean?"

"To win nowadays you not only need a good staff, you need a good vacuum cleaner. And you need someone who can empty its bag and sift through it. So give thought to everything you ever did. Now, Ralph here, is the best opposition researcher in the business. He'll find out everything there is to know about your primary opponents in our party if anyone's dumb enough to run against you, and then he'll do the same on whoever runs against you in the general election. You see how that works?"

Ralph, who had been introduced as the best opposition researcher in the business added, "Now, what we have to be careful about is that you don't end up being on the defensive. And if they can't find anything, they'll make it up."

Gordo nodded. "But they'll take something that has a grain of truth to it, just a grain, that's all, and that's enough. Then you can't deny it in entirety without lying, see? An opposition researcher used to mean a person who looked up an opponent's record, how the opponent voted if the opponent was already in office, policies the opponent advocated. Now that's a minor part of it. Now it means detective work. But you have an advantage. They'll have to tread softly on you. It's touchy for them because you'll have the sympathy factor working for you. You're a recent widow, and the widow of Ted Murphy, no less."

The best opposition researcher in the business added, "But you can't be sure. Don't say that, Gordo. You can't be sure. When it gets to a close-call on the voters, widow or no widow, they won't play softball. Ever smoke pot?"

"With Ted, years ago," Linda answered. "You know, we were children of the 60s."

"Well, just say you didn't and Ted didn't until I think this thing out. Anyone around when you did it?"

"At parties sometimes."

"Well, if anyone comes forward, they're liars until I think this thing out. Write down a list of who you remember were there. Okay?"

"Okay."

"How about your son? He wasn't at Ted's funeral. Is he a problem?"

"No. He's not a problem." She was scared. "He sent beautiful flowers."

"Will he campaign for you?"

"I think so. But he's living with some people—"

"With some people?"

"We aren't as close as we used to be. I mean, he's a man now, not a child. The people are friends."

"Women? Men? What are you talking about when you say people?"

"He's living with a woman, but I think some other couples have moved in. He's in Arizona. He's a fine young man. His name is Tommy." She said it as though knowing his name was proof that she cared about him and he cared about her.

The best opposition researcher in the business was shaking his head. "I want to talk to him. Do you mind if I talk to him?"

"No," she said, "Why would I mind? I'll give you his phone number and address and everything!"

The best opposition researcher in the business looked over at Gordo. "I'll take care of that one."

Gordo took charge again. "All right. Let's go to issues. Mac is your man. He's your issues man. All the things you believe in, see?"

Linda nodded. "Good."

Mac took over. "You're pro-choice, aren't you?"

"Yes. You mean abortion, isn't that what you mean?"

"Of course. But never use that word. That's the last time I want that word to come out of your mouth. You don't want to put that picture in anyone's head. Always say 'pro-choice.'"

"Okay."

"How are you on Affirmative Action?"

"For it. Blacks, right?"

"Blacks. Women. Remember, it's women, too. That's what you accent these days. And don't ever say quotas or preferences. It's affirmative action."

"Okay."

"Gun control?"

"I'm for it."

"Good. Then do you know how to answer questions on the Second Amendment?"

She shook her head.

"We'll give you the material. You have to be careful on that one. There's a lot of shooters in some of the up-state districts, and we don't know what district you'll run in. Unions?"

"I'm good on that. I was in the Retail Clerk's Union once. I worked for the A&P when I was sixteen. I still have the buttons. We got a different color button every month. We all wore them on our smocks at work. The smocks were green, so sometimes the color of the button didn't match."

There were the quick mystified glances, one to the other, among the members of the group.

"All right. And I don't need to ask you, I assume you're against crime, for education, against pollution, for the disadvantaged and the disabled, you want to cut defense, and you want to strengthen Social Security. Right?"

"That's right."

"You'll win. You like Clinton?"

"Love him."

"Don't use that word about him. Say you respect him."

"Okay."

"How about foreign policy? Ted fill you in during all those years?"

"Not really, but I went around the world once. It was on our honeymoon. We went to fourteen countries in one trip."

"Your honeymoon was a long time ago, wasn't it?"

"Yes, but since then I've been to—" and she was about to say Nicaragua and Barbados but caught herself, "some other places."

"But I mean the current hot spots on policy. Haiti. Bosnia. Iraq. China. The Mideast. Russia. You know about what's going on in those places?"

"I respect them all."

"You respect them all?"

"Well, you know what I mean. Isn't that what you said?"

"You can't say that. You don't respect them all. Say you support Clinton on foreign policy. We'll give you some talking points we can get from the White House. You know what's going on in Rwanda?"

Linda shook her head, and then thought better of it. "Not everything."

"Genocide is going on there."

"Yes. I think so."

"We'll give you a paper on it. Are you good at memorizing?"

"I was in drama in high school. I was one of the leads in 'Life With Father' and 'Melody Jones' and 'If I Were King.' I memorized very well."

"You ever been to China?"

"No. But I've been to Hong Kong."

"Uh-huh. Maybe between now and the election in '96, you can take a trip to China. I know some big money people there."

"Are they Chinese?"

Mac closed his eyes in frustration, and nodded. "Almost everyone there is."

Gordo quickly interjected, "One thing you have to remember. You're going to win because people will see you as an extension of Ted, see? That's important to know. You mention him in every speech you make. You have to sound competent on your own, but remember why people want to see you, why they want to hear you, why they want to touch you. Now, you play that to the hilt. Sorry to put it that way, but that's the truth. Now, this is Sherry. Sherry is the woman you're going to learn to hate. Sherry is your scheduler. She's the one who has to supervise your calendar and judge all the requests from people who want to meet with you, groups who want you to speak, fundraisers, all those things. You'll think she's running you too hard, but that's the peril of any candidate and scheduler."

Sherry smiled. "We'll work together just fine, Linda. A campaign has a natural build, so right at the beginning it will be slow and you'll wonder why you don't have enough to do. But it will take on a life of its own until you don't think you can take one more event."

Gordo looked back at his open notebook. He turned the page. "One of the daily events at the beginning of the campaign, even before it begins, all the way through the end of the campaign, are the phone calls you'll have to make for money. It will start with what we call an exploratory committee. Let me introduce you to Emily. She's the fundraiser. She'll be treasurer temporarily, too. We'll get a full-timer later. The treasurer is the one who goes to jail if something goes wrong." There was some laughter, most of all from Emily. "Emily?"

"Not on this campaign! No jail sentence on this campaign! Every day I'll give you a list of fifteen people for you to phone and ask for money. The law allows a maximum of $1,000 a person. That's $2,000 a married couple. A child can be another thousand, so we look for families. When one of those people doesn't give the maximum, you want to call them back after we cash their first check, and you ask them to max-out. If they still give less than the maximum, we never stop until they do. Once someone gives a dime, it's like a subscription to our appeals—your appeals—until they max-out. You up to it?"

Linda nodded and then shrugged. "I'm not proud."

Gordo looked back at the open page in his notebook. "The events are Ross' business. You know what meet 'n' greets are?"

"I guess it's meeting people, and greeting them."

Ross answered. "That's correct, Mrs. Murphy. These are mainly fundraising events. Some of them aren't, but whatever they are, you walk around, no wallflowering, you shake hands with everyone and make small talk. I'll walk with you telling you who the most important people are, the high rollers. When it comes to luncheons or dinners, you come to the receptions on time and work the room with me by your side. Then we'll have photo-ops for the big donors. You just pose with them. That's all. A typical event like a luncheon in someone's home or hotel or something might be one that costs $50 with another $50 if they want to come to the reception and want the photo. Then you call them in a week or so after they get the picture, and ask them to max-out."

Gordo nodded. "Now, direct mail is even more important. Direct mail is how your campaign will get more money than any other device. Lou, here, will write the material, you approve it, we send it out to a top-notch list we have, see? It's right up-to-date. High rollers, medium rollers, low rollers. In the first direct mail we'll have a mix of 20% positive and 80% negative. Good stuff about you, bad stuff about your opponent. We enclose a contribution envelope with every mailing that comes out of headquarters. Make sense to you?"

"That sounds good."

"We don't have a press secretary yet, but I know a gem. A gem. He's on some fishing trip right now in Maine. He'll speak for you when you can't do it. You have to work closely together. We also have to get a campaign chairman—not the campaign manager—that's me, but a chairman. The person has to be someone of prestige.

"Do you think we could get Dulce Hoffman?"

Gordo gave a sigh. "She was for Reagan—three times. She was for Bush—twice. No, she wouldn't do it. Look, it has to be for our things, not against them. Whoever it is doesn't have to do anything except maybe sign some fundraising letters for you, and maybe appear at some dinners for you, things like that. Then a finance chairman. He has to do the same kind of things as the campaign chairman, but our finance guy has to be known as someone who's very rich—someone who's important enough to have CEOs pick up the phone when he's on the line. It's going to be someone who they feel obligated to answer positively when he asks for money. And we need a good pollster. A pollster can tell you more than if you're ahead or behind. He can tell you the issues you use, and when and where you use them."

"Really? There's a lot of things, aren't there?"

"It's like setting up a corporation. There's more. There's office managers, people contacting county chairmen, a lot of things we don't need to bother you with yet. There's media buys, too. I'll take care of that. That's buying radio and TV time."

"There's a lot of things, aren't there?" Linda asked again.

Gordo nodded. "You want to go ahead? You up to it? Are we your team?"

Linda now made quick, short nods, afraid to exhibit any sign of hesitancy. "Oh, yes. I'm up to it. You're my team."

Gordo closed his notebook and put it on the floor. "Ted would be proud of you, and I think he's going to be proud of all of us."

Ralph, the best opposition researcher in the business said, "You'll win. You're terrific!"

There was no question that he was right on his first point and wrong on his second point, but his second point wasn't all that important to Ted Murphy's beneficiaries.

"You see how this works, Madam Congresswoman?" Gordo asked.

Linda nodded excitedly. "Oh, yes!"

"Congratulations!"

EIGHTY
I GOT YOU, BABE!
1995

While Linda was planning her campaign for the 1996 election, the 1994 elections brought some surprising results. Democrats lost majority control of both houses of the Congress for the first time in forty years. Beyond that surprise was another one: it was one of the new congressmen. Sonny Bono was standing with the other freshmen taking the oath of office on the floor of the House of Representatives. Most Washingtonians didn't know how to handle him because he was so unlike them.

Sitting in the visitor's gallery at the inaugural, in the section reserved for guests of the new members of the House was Irene Goodpastor. In front of her seat was an aluminum walker, which she used ever since her return to Washington from Hong Kong. She simply kept falling. It was her good fortune that she never broke any bones, but her legs didn't work right anymore. That wasn't all that was wrong with her. She had difficulty in separating the important from the unimportant. She would lose patience with people and things for no logical reason. With all her problems she managed to put together the Goodpastor Center, or at least financed it, and she was its founder and president. It gathered quick prestige by the hiring of the right "thinkers."

She wasn't able to get Sonny Bono since he chose to run to represent the 44th Congressional District of California, but in attempting to make him part of her think tank, they became friends, and he invited her to be in the House chamber for that grand moment.

There, on the House floor were some of the leading legislators of the nation, and they were outshined by that humble man who was unimpressed with celebrities because he had already been one and knew what it meant, and more importantly, he knew what it didn't mean. What would they do with him in their midst? His wonder-filled eyes and his broad smile was foreign to them. His style put them in an unusual position. He had learned to talk and be understood, and so many of them had learned to talk and say nothing. He had the innocence of a child and the wisdom of the aged, and so many of them had neither. Beyond that, he had an innate humility, rejecting those who reeked of self-importance. They couldn't understand a man among them who was filled with talent, while so many in that chamber were filled with ego. Some were jealous, some ridiculed him, most had no idea of what he would mean to the institution.

He was sworn in again at a private ceremony in the office of Speaker Newt Gingrich, both of them wearing their new red lapel pins which identified them as members of the 104th Congress. They stood with Congressman Bono's wife, children, and a few friends including Irene Goodpastor.

"Northwest," she said to Congressman Bono as they walked out of the Speaker's office, the small group following them to the Capitol Subway to the congressman's office in the Cannon House Office Building.

"Huh?" He didn't know what she meant.

"You have to learn, Mr. Congressman, that the city is divided into compass points." She almost sounded mad. "Don't forget to tell the taxi driver it's K Street Northwest when you come to my Goodpastor Center. 18th and K Northwest."

"Oh, yeah. I know. The Capitol Building is the dividing line of the compass points, isn't it?"

"That's right. Northwest has everything you'll ever need. You don't need to go to Northeast or Southeast or Southwest for anything. Just remember that K Northwest is the street with the islands."

"Islands?"

"Those islands on either side of the road you sort of have to drive around to turn right if you're driving." Irene was talking goofy. Surely there were more important things to discuss on this golden day. But out of courtesy Congressman Bono acted intensely interested.

"Oh, now I know what you mean. Sure, Irene. I'll remember that. I think those islands are meant to ease the traffic."

"If they ease traffic, why did they just do it on K Street? Why not every street? You might work on that now that you're in the Congress."

Not his first passion. "That's good, Irene," he said kindly. "That's a good idea. I never thought about that."

"And how come there's no J Street?"

"There isn't?"

"It skips J."

"Is that right? Hey, that is funny!"

"You might find out. Something should be done about that. It's very mysterious. Maybe now you can find out what's going on."

Irene was full of Washington information and advice hardly needed by new members of the Congress.

That night Congressman Bono and his guests went to The Monocle to celebrate. They sat in a private room upstairs and although everyone was happy by the victory of the host, he looked grim.

"Bosnia," he said to Irene.

"What?"

"Has your Center released a paper on Bosnia?"

"Yes."

"What does it say?"

Irene looked confused. "I don't remember."

"It's a general backgrounder," Brian Nestande, Congressman Bono's Chief of Staff came to the rescue. "I read it, Mrs. Goodpastor. It tells the history of Yugoslavia and about Tito and what happened when he died, and about Milosevic, and what we've done so far to stop the genocide in Bosnia."

"We haven't done anything, have we?" Congressman Bono asked, and he didn't wait for an answer. "Milosevic is a genocidal dictator. Bush seemed to push that aside. Before he left office he said that the United States was prepared to use military force if the Yugoslav civil war was expanded to Serbia's Kosovo province. Why did he wait until that happens? Now we have Clinton, who was critical of Bush doing nothing in Bosnia, and since he's been president he's been worse than Bush. He's been saying that he has no interest in NATO becoming involved in that war, or trying to gain advantage for one side over the other. He said he doesn't want NATO to change the military balance there. I don't get it. I'm going to go there. I want to find out what ever I can learn over there. We're not doing what we should there."

"You're going there?" Irene Goodpastor asked.

"Yeah. I got to find out what's going on."

"To the war?" She thought the mysteries of K and J Streets were enough to think about for a while.

"Yeah. I don't want to sit around here listening to all the legalese. I asked a few of them about Bosnia and they talk in legalese. I don't think they know. If they don't know what's going on in Bosnia, then who does? I'm going."

Irene Goodpastor nodded slowly. She liked what he said. "Sonny–Congressman–will you do a paper on whatever you find out for my Center when you get back?" There were those periods of time when she would be just as she used to be. It came in waves.

Sonny gave a big smile. "I can't, Irene. I have to do everything now as a member of the Congress. You can reprint anything you want, but I'll give my paper to the House International Relations Committee–to Chairman Gilman, and maybe to President Clinton."

"Before me?"

Sonny looked apologetic. "You would be Number One, but I can't–Brian, what can I do?"

"She has to be Number Four. It's protocol. You had it right, Sonny. First, Chairman Gilman, then Newt, the president, then Irene Goodpastor. But that's pretty good. That makes anyone else Number Five."

"I Got You, Babe!" Irene Goodpastor said.

There was his big smile again, and then his laugh. The Monocle was bathed in his personality, and the District was not immune.

Sunshine Island was no longer desolate. It was filled with Vietnamese refugees who were working and being trained in farming and practicing crafts, and the children were attending school in the island's two schoolrooms by two Hong Kong teachers. All the Vietnamese refugees on Sunshine Island had fled from Vietnam to China, and then escaped to Hong Kong, therefore being illegal immigrants. Governor Patten was not told. If he knew he surely would have had no desire to argue with Liberty, but he would have had to disallow her to continue.

The two young men who directed the construction of the island's new facilities, under the leadership of Liberty, were John Cooper and Andrew Fung Kai-hung. John Cooper was falling in love with Liberty, but who wouldn't? Andrew Fung Kai-hung was already in love with Liberty. Liberty was in love with Sunshine Island.

EIGHTY-ONE
THE HOUSE OF ONE HUNDRED LANTERNS
1995

Moose was holding onto a corner of the Central Plaza Building to keep from being blown across the street by Sybil. October was supposed to be a month of ideal weather but Typhoon Sibyl had no interest in what was supposed to be.

It was a struggle for Moose to get inside the building. He edged to the entrance and made it into the lobby, leaving all the inverted umbrellas and papers and small objects to blow in the wet.

Moose had been trying to get to the Kowloon side which, he thought, was the simple task of walking to the Wanchai Ferry Pier outside the Convention Centre and taking the Star Ferry, as he often did. But nothing was simple in a typhoon. Walking the two long blocks was near impossible and even if he reached the pier he would have found that no ferries were in operation. Hong Kong Harbor was closed because Sibyl closed it.

There was an irony in Central Plaza rescuing Moose from Sibyl. Ever since the building was completed three years earlier in 1992, Moose despised it. He would often eat lunch in that building for the same reason Guy de Maupassant ate lunch in the Eiffel Tower. De Maupassant hated the Eiffel Tower and so he ate there because it was the only place in Paris from which the Eiffel Tower couldn't be seen. Central Plaza, with its 78 stories, was the place where Moose couldn't see Central Plaza. It was the tallest high-rise not only in Hong Kong, but in all of Asia, and Moose didn't like its domination of the Hong Kong skyline. Even though one "tallest building in Hong Kong" after another had been built so often, none had ever dominated the skyline as Central Plaza did. It had architectural similarity to the Empire State Building, adding what appeared to be gold-painted pipes of an organ engraved on its sides.

He was drenched, water pouring down his face, his clothes sticking to him, and water inside his shoes. It was obvious which people standing in the lobby of Central Plaza had been outside in recent minutes. There was an arrogance of those who were dry as though they were the smart ones, destined for heaven after death as a justified reward for having taken preventative action on this day.

"You are so wet! You shouldn't have gone outside! The warning signal for the typhoon is up to Eight!" a young Chinese woman said to him. She was one of the dry, arrogant ones who, under the conditions, felt it was her right, even her duty, to approach the drenched and impress them, as well as God, with the brilliance in which she had prepared herself for all things.

"An Eight? When I left my office just twenty minutes or so ago, it was a Three."

"The scale goes from One to Ten, but there is no Four, Five, Six or Seven."

"It goes from Three directly to Eight? It's been so long since there's been a typhoon warning, I don't remember the numbers."

"There is no Two, either," Miss Smarty-pants remembered.

"Well, that's sort of a strange scale, isn't it?"

She laughed. "No. It is the proper scale. It is important to remember." She made him feel as though he should apologize.

"Why don't they just make it One through Five? Why is it One through Ten with five numbers missing?"

She shrugged, and ignored his question, not willing to admit there was something she didn't know. "You are going to catch a cold." She wanted to add, "I, of course, won't," but it was unnecessary. She walked away looking for someone else to guide through life.

Scattered throughout the lobby were small groups of dry Chinese, American, and European men in business suits with white name badges on their lapels. Written under their names was "1997" in red, and a small replica of the flag of the People's Republic of China. Beneath all of that was printed "Minus 633 Days." They were talking and laughing and practically all of them were holding briefcases. No cheap ones. Good ones made by Bally and Gold Pfeil and Kenneth Cole. They didn't kid around when it came to an excess of rivalry in things of which Moose had no interest.

One group was talking about the handover of Hong Kong to the People's Republic of China in which one totally dry businessman said "will make absolutely no difference, or if it does, it will be a change for the better." Another group was talking about the recent Hong Kong election of the Legislative Council in which democracy advocates won an overwhelming victory, and pro-mainland candidates suffered devastating defeats. "That election last September 17 doesn't make any difference. Do you think Beijing will keep them in office after July the 1st of 1997? It will be good riddance to see Martin Lee and Szeto Wah thrown out of office."

"But they were elected for four-year terms. That should take them to 1999. That's trouble," another name-plated-badge analyst said.

"They'll be thrown out by the Chinese government the minute the Chinese government takes over in '97."

A young Chinese man with glasses, dressed in a vested black suit came from an elevator and made an announcement in Cantonese, followed by his translation in English, "Mr. Wu would like you to come up now."

Like the quick turn of a faucet, the groups stopped their conversations and quickly headed toward the bank of elevators and some of them went up the large stairway, not wanting to wait for an elevator. A few were going two steps at a time.

Moose watched the scene, open-mouthed. He had seen it before in the Old Executive Office Building in August of 1974 when some of President Nixon's trusted assistants, one after another, raced up the stairs to embrace Vice President Ford. It was exactly the same. As the handover to the mainland government was coming nearer, Hong Kong was becoming a massive August stairway.

Businessmen were eager to meet and impress their new masters, the representatives of the People's Republic of China. Their eagerness was part of their religion, because their religion was a wallet. They all had fat ones, and they wanted to increase their fatness. Good wallets made by Bally and Gold Pfeil and Kenneth Cole.

Moose walked out of the lobby, going back outside. At least with Sibyl he felt clean.

Very clean. Again, he stayed close to buildings, his arms outstretched behind him, rubbing against those buildings as though he was trying to be invisible from the rain and wind. It didn't work. The rain and wind wouldn't permit such a vain attempt. They were as arrogant as that woman in Central Plaza. He walked only a short distance before he surrendered. There was a shelter among a cluster of Wanchai bars and untypically, there were no barkers outside the bars with invitations to "Just look, sailor! No cover! No minimum! Just look!" Only an Eight could prevent such living advertisements. Moose's new shelter was a nightclub or dayclub called The House of One Hundred Lanterns.

Only ten of the one hundred lanterns on the tables and the bar and on shelves were lit, and that was probably a good thing because the few bar girls there during a day like this were so ugly that it was best not to be able to see them.

The bar girls laughed after he entered and they saw how wet he was. "It's an Eight, sailor! Come on in!" How could they possibly think he was a sailor? His appearance was a great distance from Popeye. "Good to be on your vessel," he said to make them feel good.

"Want some company, sailor?" Miss Ugly asked.

"No thanks. I have to get back to the ship. I just came in to chart our voyage after the storm." She didn't know what he was talking about, but neither did he.

"What's your name?" she asked as he walked passed the table where she sat with a drink.

He yelled back at her on his way to the bar. "Captain Bligh." There was a television set above the bar and it was beaming some special in Cantonese on the acquittal of O.J. Simpson. "He's guilty as sin," Moose said to himself. For the past three days there had been nothing but television shows on the acquittal and this one was showing a montage of Judge Ito, Johnnie Cochran, and Marcia Clark. "She was terrific!" Moose said.

One of the women who sat at a table with two other women, got up and walked behind the bar to become the bartender. "What will it be, sailor?"

"That jury let him get away with murder," Moose said to her. "Coffee. Can I have a cup of coffee?"

She shrugged her shoulders. "No drink?"

"Coffee's a drink. Can I have some hot coffee?"

She half-nodded and half-shrugged. "It costs the same as a drink."

"How much is that?"

"Fifty Hong Kong dollars. But it's a two-drink minimum. So one hundred."

Moose gave a disapproving shake of his head but said, "Okay." She just stood there doing nothing which meant she wanted it in advance. He reached in his pocket, then plopped down a Hong Kong one hundred dollar bill. She was probably the type who thought O.J. Simpson was innocent.

For two hours Moose stayed there waiting for the storm to end, walking back and forth to the door to judge the status of the typhoon. He was spending hundreds of Hong Kong dollars on coffee, while being entertained in the second hour by Kato Kaelin, Barry Scheck, and Mark Fuhrman.

Then, as suddenly as Three had become Eight, Eight became Three and turned into an unhostile One. Sybil was on her way to other places. Just as Moose was leaving, six men, whose name tags indicated they came from Central Plaza, came in. Five of them were Chinese and one was not Chinese. "Moose Dunston!" that one said, extending his hand. Moose looked confused but shook his hand. "I'm Peter Fielding," the man said, "with the American Chamber of Commerce here in Hong Kong. I work with Frank Martin. You're with *Asia World Weekly*, right?"

"That's right."

"Good. Good writer. I recognize you from your picture they put by your articles. We read every word of your magazine at the Chamber. I can't say I always agree with you, but you write good editorials. Hey, what are you doing in this place?"

"The same thing you're doing. Now we can blackmail each other!"

Peter Fielding laughed. "Can we buy you a drink, Dunston?"

"You see, Dunston, where we disagree with you is over this whole Most Favored Nation status business. You keep writing against it and your arguments would be convincing if it wasn't for things you haven't considered. If we were to take away that status from China we'd be hurting the people there, damaging their civil liberties."

"What civil liberties? How could we hurt civil liberties by punishing the government when they violate civil liberties? Clinton has de-linked civil liberties from Most Favored Nation status which means that now Deng Xiaoping can do what he wants to his own people and we'll continue trade as normal. What kind of moral code do we have with that cockeyed trade policy?"

"What you miss, Dunston, is the power of trade, of our people working with their people, of their people and our people buying each other's products. That's the way they're going to come around to greater freedom for their people, it's the way to bring about civil liberties, and eventually to bring about democracy."

"If the death of the Soviet Union's totalitarian system was due, in large part, to economic failure, why should economic health cause it to end in China?"

"It's different in China."

"Nothing is different. This is basic stuff. You don't free slaves by embracing their masters."

"You're one of the last journalists around here saying and writing things like that."

"That's because some of the journalists have been fired by cowardly editors and owners. Some of them—probably most of them—are censoring themselves. They're so scared that, in fact, they're bringing about everything they fear, all by themselves."

"You're not afraid?"

"No, I'm not. But I have to admit that I work for a boss who doesn't interfere with my work. You've heard of Hanson Alpert?"

"Who hasn't? We know you work for him over at *Asia World Weekly.* What kind of man is he?"

Moose shrugged. "I never met him. I don't think he's ever even seen his own offices at the magazine. But he lets me write what I want."

"Well, good for him. Good for you. I would think a man as successful as Alpert would be politically savvy enough to know he risks paying a heavy price for your articles. He has investments in China, you know."

"I do know."

"I don't think anyone else with investments up there would let you stick it to the PRC the way you do in every issue. He must respect you, Dunston."

"He respects freedom of the press."

Fielding laughed. "I'll buy that. But I'll bet you, Dunston, that his magazine closes down, or you get pushed out. Either way, you're going to lose out. No smart businessman can make a zillion dollars in Asia by sticking it to China. Not these days. If you think a guy like Alpert is going to continue to think some writer or publication of his is more important than all his Asian investments, you're pretty naive. You can ease his problems by just bending a bit."

"You don't know him."

"Neither do you. Didn't you say you never even saw him?"

"Seeing him isn't the test. I've lived under his policies for fifteen years. He leaves the editorial writers alone, no matter what. My column has a by-line so everyone who reads what I wrote knows that what's written are my thoughts, my beliefs. When he writes an editorial, he signs his name. You guys just don't understand freedom of the press. Or maybe you do and you don't care about it."

"We care. We care about you, believe it or not. I think you ought to see things from a wider view, and write from a–a broader outlook, and save yourself and your boss a lot of grief."

"A wider view? A broader outlook to include a salute to a bunch of dictators? All I want is for that government in Beijing to act civilized."

"Dunston, we want the same thing. We just disagree on what will bring it about."

"I don't think so. I think you guys care more about profit than human rights."

"Really?"

"Really."

Afternoon was ending. One of the ugly women started lighting the other ninety of the hundred lanterns, and when it was done, some pretty girls started to come in and the ugly ones left. They had to leave because nighttime catered to a different clientele. Like the Government of China and its advocates, the House of One Hundred Lanterns knew how to make a profit. The only difference was that you could walk out of the House of One Hundred Lanterns.

EIGHTY-TWO
1997 IN A HURRY
1996

The calendar indicated that it wouldn't be 1997 until next year, but the calendar was having a tough time keeping its pages in place. It was trying, unsuccessfully, to push 1997 to stay out of 1996.

More and more of the coins in the pockets of Hong Kong people had a picture of a Bauhinia flower rather than the familiar picture of Queen Elizabeth. A picture of that flower was beginning to appear all over Hong Kong in 1996 as it would be the predominant part of Hong Kong's new flag: a white five-petaled Bauhinia with a red star on each petal, against a revolutionary red background.

"Rice Paddy Babies," teddy bear style dolls that used to be sold throughout Hong Kong were now difficult to find. Each "Rice Paddy Baby" had worn a necklace with a miniature British passport attached, asking the potential buyer to take the particular doll out of Hong Kong before July 1, 1997.

It used to be that Hong Kong Television News used the term "the Tiananmen Square massacre." Now it was described as "the June 4th incident."

Larry Feign, the anti-PRC cartoonist who authored and drew the comic strip, "The World of Lily Wong" which had been published for eight years in *the South China Morning Post*, was out of a job. The publisher said he was let go because of "budgetary reasons." Feign responded, "Self censorship in the Hong Kong media seems to be an AIDS-like virus that is spreading rapidly and for which there is no cure."

When the motion picture documentary, "Mainland China 1989" was screened in a Hong Kong art theater, 17 minutes from the 78 minute film were missing. Deleted were interviews with mainland dissidents and pro-democracy leaders.

Hong Kong reporter, Xi Yang, was seized while visiting Beijing for his mother's funeral, then tried and sentenced to 12 years imprisonment for disclosing to his Hong Kong newspaper, Ming Pao, that the PRC planned to meet its debts by selling gold. The PRC charged that he stole state secrets.

Chan Ya was a columnist for Hong Kong's *Express Daily News* who wrote a column in support of the imprisoned Xi Yang. Chen Ya's column was discontinued.

All Hong Kong reporters were issued a warning by Zhang Jun-sheng, Deputy Director of the PRC's Xinhua News Agency. He said that Hong Kong reporters should familiarize themselves with Chinese laws and culture "to avoid trouble," and that Deng Xiaoping's three principles of patriotism are meant to "respect one's own race, support Hong Kong's return to the motherland, and maintain Hong Kong's prosperity."

Jimmy Lai, Chairman of the Board of Giordono retailers, and publisher of the Hong Kong magazine, *Next*, regularly printed articles critical of the PRC. The PRC closed down Jimmy Lai's Beijing branch of his Giordono store until he resigned as company chairman.

A Preparatory Committee was appointed in Beijing's Great Hall of the People to arrange the handover of Hong Kong. Jiang Zemin, president of the PRC under the "Paramount" leadership of Deng Xiaoping, said the committee faced a "heavy task as the return of Hong Kong to the motherland is the first station in our Long March. After that there is Macau and, finally, Taiwan." The Preparatory Committee voted 148 to 1 to disband Hong Kong's elected Legislative Council when the PRC takes over, and to install an appointed body to run Hong Kong. The lone dissenter was Frederick Fung, the Chairman of the Hong Kong Democracy and People's Livelihood organization. For doing that, he was immediately stripped of the right to vote for the chief executive of Hong Kong, and was told he would not be eligible to be part of the Provisional Legislature.

Governor Patten called the 148 to 1 vote "a black day for democracy in Hong Kong. . . . A Chinese appointed body of Chinese government officials and hand-picked Hong Kong advisers have voted to tear down a legislature which was freely, fairly, and openly elected by the people of Hong Kong in the most democratic election in our history." The governor praised Frederick Fung, saying Hong Kong would "salute him."

Martin Lee, Chairman of the Democratic Party said, "Hong Kong's elected leaders will not roll over and accept being ejected from office when China takes over on July 1, 1997. As legislators, we were elected to a full four-year term of office by Hong Kong people, and we intend to fulfill our duty to them—in the legislature or out of it."

Governor Patten said his government would "do nothing whatsoever, that's nothing, spelled N-O-T-H-I-N-G, nothing whatsoever" to undermine the elected Legislative Council.

In one day, to beat a deadline for obtaining British-issued travel documents, 54,178 Hong Kong people who were not born in Hong Kong lined up outside Immigration Tower for applications. A sports field was opened to accommodate the waiting people. The travel documents given out were British National Overseas Passports which did not even confer British citizenship, or right of abode, but simply allowed residents of British and former British territories to travel without a visa to Great Britain and travel, visa-free, to more than eighty countries.

It was announced that after the handover, Beijing would close down the consulates in Hong Kong of the 13 countries that maintained diplomatic relations with the Republic of China on Taiwan. They could stay only if they broke relations with the government on Taiwan.

The Preparatory Committee chose a committee of 400 members to select the new leaders of Hong Kong. The Selection Committee chose Tung Chee-hwa, a Hong Kong businessman friendly to the PRC, as the new Chief

Executive to take over on July 1, 1997, and named those who would serve on the Provisional Legislature to replace the elected legislators. Among the selected were ten Pro-Beijing people who had run for Hong Kong's Legislative Council and lost.

Governor Patten called the selection of those on the Provisional Legislature a "bizarre farce" and a "stomach churning" process.

In Beijing's Tiananmen Square near the area where the statue of the Goddess of Democracy had once stood, there was now a large electronic clock. It did not tell the time. Its purpose was to count down the days remaining between the current date to the Hong Kong handover of July 1, 1997. Soon there was another countdown clock, this one on the border bridge at Shenzhen. Then another one in front of the Tianjin train station.

Such clocks did not appear in Hong Kong. Hong Kong people needed no reminder. They knew the number. On the calendar, the date was Saturday, December 21, 1996. But that was unimportant. The coutdown number, which was important, was 192.

At four o'clock in the afternoon of 192, Liberty looked like Scarlett O'Hara sitting above a small stairway with two young men, one sitting on each side of her. They weren't the Tarleton brothers, they were Andrew Fung Kai-hung and John Cooper. And they weren't on the porch of Tara, they were sitting outside the main door to the Xinhua News Agency that represented the People's Republic of China. Liberty was holding a small microphone which was attached to a speaker resting near the door of Xinhua.

She turned off the microphone. "Late!" she said to Andrew, and then she turned her head to John. "Martin Lee is always late! How long does it take to walk here from Charter Garden!?" But just as she said it, there was the clatter and voices and chants of demonstrators coming from somewhere, and then there was the sight of them emerging around the corner.

Liberty stood up, her action immediately followed by her two young living bookends.

Even though Martin Lee was surrounded by others in front of the long uneven line of demonstrators, there was no question that he was in the lead. He was the standout, wearing bright yellow pants and a bright yellow polo shirt with a round collar. This was not a man who blended in. He walked up the small stairway to stand by Liberty and her companions while his followers stayed across the street. He turned to face the expanding crowd as more and more of his followers came from around the corner holding placards that in both Chinese and English read, "Democracy!" "Human Rights! The Rule of Law!" "Down with the Selection Committee!" "No More Tiananmen Squares!" "Against Provisional Legislature!" "Universal Suffrage for Chief Executive!" "Fake election!"

Liberty turned on the microphone and handed it to Martin Lee. His voice boomed over the public address system. "A Provisional Legislature is not in accord with the law," he said. "There is no such provision in the Joint Declaration between Great Britain and the People's Republic. And even if such a legislature would be deemed legal, how could that appointed body do any formal legislative work before July 1 of next year when the Special Administrative Region of Hong Kong is born? How can the baby start to work before the mother is born?" There was much applause and cheering.

"And we are not referring to Mr. Tung as the Chief Executive until next July the 1st. For these months, he is merely the Chief Executive-designate. Likewise, Provisional Legislature members are only designated members! My friends," and if Liberty resembled Scarlett O'Hara, Martin Lee sounded like Franklin Delano Roosevelt. "The only fear of Hong Kong people is that China will remain communist. China must become a democracy. That is the only solution for the future of Hong Kong people, and for the people on the mainland! My mission is to see to it that Big China becomes Great China!"

Again, there were loud cheers of approval. Martin handed Liberty a petition. She took it, and with Andrew and John serving as an accompanying delegation, she walked into the building to present the petition to the authorities of the People's Republic of China.

It was entirely appropriate for Liberty to enter the building holding the petition. They probably wouldn't have accepted a petition handed to them by Martin Lee, as they had labeled him a "subversive." But how could they reject anything from Liberty? As long as the representative of the PRC was a man, he would have accepted a poisonous snake from her.

When Liberty, Andrew, and John emerged from the building, Martin Lee handed Liberty the microphone. "Your message to Deng Xiaoping has been delivered," she said to the crowd. "I cannot guarantee he will receive it, but the message was accepted. You should also know that I not only presented his representative with your message about the illegality of their Provisional Legislature, but I gave them a personal letter of further demands that I believe are important. I have with me Mr. John Fitzgerald Cooper, the son of Gloria Cooper and, of course, the late Cody Cooper, who will tell you about the other letter I presented which was signed by Gloria Cooper of the World Refugee Mission."

Andrew was not a happy man. She was giving John more importance than him. She didn't even mention Andrew. On the bright side, he thought, John had to be introduced by explaining that it was his mother who was prominent, and not him.

John said, "As you know, my father died for the well-being of refugees, and my mother is living for them. One of the orders of Deng Xiaoping is that the British Government must get all Vietnamese refugees out of Hong Kong by the time of handover. There have been riots of thousands of refugees who would rather be incarcerated in camps than be sent back to Vietnam. They risked their lives to get out of Vietnam. Can Deng Xiaoping be so inhumane as to insist they go back? Our letter to Mr. Deng demands that they be able to stay in Hong Kong even after handover, unless or until a third country accepts the remainder of those 18,000 which remain in Hong Kong camps as of today. Do we have your approval?"

There were the loud cheers again, and applause.

John gave the microphone back to Liberty. She knew that Andrew was jealous of John and she felt guilty that she didn't give him equal importance in front of the crowd. With Liberty's inherent sensitivity, she made an addendum to the program before the crowd dispersed. "I would like you to meet Mr. Andrew Fung Kai-hung, who has been the architect of the re-born Sunshine Island, which is housing Vietnamese refugees, and will continue to house them until the midnight that will separate June the 30th from July the 1st, and will separate freedom from daily apprehension. He has a message for you."

Andrew was both startled and scared stiff. He had no idea what to say, even as Liberty handed him the microphone. There was applause for him, not that anyone ever heard of him.

"Good afternoon," he said. There was a long pause. "I want to say—" and he paused again, this time as he tried to think of something with which to conclude his sentence. So he just repeated, "I want to say." He thought of something. "I want to say that being here is very important. To have you here is having you here—to hear a delivered message. A message that has been delivered." Liberty was nodding as if to signal to the audience that his words better be respected. "And that message is going to go to Deng Xiaoping—I hope. So what you have done, and all that, what you are doing is very, very important." On second thought, he could add even more importance. "Very, very, very important." He nodded to show that he agreed with himself, and handed the microphone back to Liberty.

Liberty put the microphone under her arm and started the round of applause for him. John was glad that Andrew didn't do well. *What a contrast,* John thought, *between what I said and what he said.* But he applauded for Andrew. It was only right. In fact, it showed he was a mature fellow. No one said his applause had to be done energetically.

Liberty thought that Moose would be at the demonstration, but she didn't find him in the crowd. He had told her he wanted to be there because he wanted to write an article about the demonstration. That was before he found out that if he did, no one would read it.

For the first time since his job started, he received a letter from his ultimate boss, Hanson Alpert. It started with a compliment, but Moose knew that could be a bad sign:

"You have done exceptional work through the years for which we at *Asia World Weekly* are grateful. Regrettably, with our conversion to new computers and a long overdue heavy investment in the mechanical end of our business, along with the enlargement of our Singapore Bureau, the budget no longer permits us to retain all the editorial talent we have enjoyed over the years. Although your columns will be suspended immediately, please be assured that we will continue your salary for six months. If I can be of any additional help to you, please let me know.

"Sincerely, Hanson Alpert."

It was all over. And, of course, Moose knew it had nothing to do with new computers, or investments in the mechanical end of the business, or a larger Singapore Bureau. It was just as he was warned in The House of One Hundred Lanterns.

He was simply joining Larry Feign, Chan Ya, Jimmy Lai, and so many others, as 1997 arrived early.

EIGHTY-THREE
LIFTED VEILS
1997

Nostalgia is most frequently thought to be nothing more than sentiment over times past, but it can be a repeating cannon-fire that's triggered from somewhere inside a person, and that's why Anne went back to India. Her earlier visit was moving inside her for thirty-five years like an unborn, struggling for delivery. It isn't that she loved India back then, she despised it. But with the experiences that the years had given her, the hatred dissolved into a strange kind of passion for it.

And so she went, and there was the smell of night ashes again, inhaled as soon as she walked from Indira Gandhi International Airport, re-named in a commemoration of a woman who was their dictatorial, assassinated leader, unknown by almost anyone when Anne was first there. There were other changes. The road into the city was now well paved, and the Embassy of the USSR on Shanti Path was now the Embassy of Russia, and the Ashoka Hotel was no longer the esteemed place for visitors, relinquishing its previous crown to the newer Oberoi, Taj Palace Intercontinental, and Le Meridian. But there were still Tibetans selling their wares on carpets over hotel lawns, and there were still Harijan "Untouchables" sweeping the streets. and there were still child beggars with their hands extended, pathetically requesting "Bahksheesh!"

She wanted to embrace it all, and protect it all, and mother it all.

It was Anne who had changed more than India. There was no search for a Sadhu this time. There was, instead, a strong desire to see Benares again where Hindus went to die. Although she dreaded the sight of those long stairways by the Ganges River and dying, naked men with their arms in the air, and she dreaded the cremation ghats, and the chants, the fright of all those things created her longing to confirm the unconfirmable–that it was not really the way she remembered. Or if it was, maybe it had changed for the better.

Those were futile hopes. It was as though no time had passed at all. They appeared to be the same people in Benares, all the same age as they were thirty-five years ago. People unchanged. There. That angry man with the mustache with a knife strapped to his waist. There. That old woman in the wet sari. There. That grinning man panning in the Ganges for gold teeth of the cremated. There. That naked dying man.

What had not changed in Anne was the quest to rescue. And she did: unappreciated rescues as she fed one after the other after the other with food she bought at stands in the back streets. Again, the scowling crowds around her.

She argued with herself as to whether she should leave, having satisfied her nostalgic quest, or stay there forever and be some kind of good

Samaritan. Leaving won the quick argument. She was not Gloria Cooper. And she surely wasn't Mother Theresa. She was Anne. And that had to be good enough. It was quite good.

There was something else that provided incentive to leave. In her purse was the airline ticket that was taking her around the world, including to Hong Kong for the meeting that had been planned 37 years ago. She hadn't been back there since, and so every memory of it was seeped in 1960, and of those in Hong Kong who created her 1960. Of all those people, it was Mark who was the dominant figure. He was the boss, he was young, he was authoritative, he was angry at her while she was angry at him, and he always wore a silly bowtie.

How could the reunion take place without him? And he should officiate at the reunion. He was the leader back then. He was the host. He was the one who had invited them to the Kennedy-Nixon debate.

Mark Daschle didn't know who sent it, but he had a good idea, and a deeper hope. It was a first-class ticket to Hong Kong, for arrival on June 28 and an open return, with a week's reservation at the Holiday Inn. Irene Goodpastor received a letter from Anne, telling Irene that Mark would be there, and that Irene should give thought to letting Mark officiate as he did so long ago.

Irene Goodpastor would come to the Goodpastor Center on K Street every day in a taxi with her four-legged aluminum walker. She could have afforded to have a companion or even a full-time nurse, but she wouldn't hear of it. She insisted she needed no help.

As soon as the letter from Anne was received from India, it was read to her by her deputy, Thad Markey. "Didn't you want to officiate, Irene?" he asked her. "Or do you want Mark Daschle to officiate?"

Irene smiled. "I will sit at one end of the table and he can sit at the other end," she said, "just as I let him do when we were first there."

"It sounds right!"

"Did I ever tell you about that meeting?"

"Just a little," he said because he knew she would tell him no matter what he said. And she did, countless times. In fact, he knew she wouldn't start talking about the meeting in Hong Kong without going back to preface the story with something in her childhood.

It was common for Irene to sit at her desk and talk about her life. The recent American Consulate stories had little resemblance to the truth, even little resemblance to the same story, as told on a different day. But her friends and workers all laughed and nodded at the appropriate times, and questioned nothing. It wasn't that she had to do this to make her role at the consulate better than it was, she had become the star of the consulate. It was that she couldn't stop exaggerating just like people couldn't stop eating or sleeping.

"Linda? Hi. Bill Clinton." He said it in the same way Bill Beesley who ran the cleaners would announce who was on the phone to let her know her clothes were ready. No drum-roll, no "Hail to the Chief," not even a secretary on the line. "How you doin', Linda?" He abandoned most of his "g's" just like Ted did, but even with that habit, he didn't sound like Ted. President Clinton's abandoned "g's" were subtracted from a southern accent combined with an added sandpapered tone that made him sound as though he was close to tears.

Linda's new partnership with Washington was fast becoming a narcotic for her. It allowed her to fall in love with herself.

President Clinton knew he didn't need to phone Congresswoman Linda Murphy to ask her not to vote for revoking his Most Favored Nation status for the People's Republic of China, but he wanted to insure she wouldn't do it, and there was no question that a phone call from him would bring about that insurance.

"You know, we even have Newt Gingrich with us on this one?" And he laughed. "Dick Armey, too! Even they seem to realize that we have to engage China, not isolate it."

"Oh, I know! If I see some wavering around here, I'll take care of it!"

"I know you will. That would be helpful. You know, we're gettin' ripped apart by some of those right-wingers who say I shouldn't have de-linked human rights from MFN status, but what they don't understand is that the way to influence the Chinese is to be engaged with them."

"Of course, Mr. President!"

"Now, how are you doin' up there on the Hill? I hope you're havin' some fun up there along with all the good, hard work you've been doin'."

"Oh, I enjoy it. And I want to thank you, Mr. President, for all you did during the campaign. Having Hillary do that fundraiser for me put me over the top. I'll always be grateful."

"She's good at it, isn't she?"

"Oh, yes! We made 1.3 million dollars in that one night."

"We'll do it again for you in '98. But I don't think you're goin' to have a rough time. You're doin' such a good job up there."

"Thank you, Mr. President."

In her previous life she had never received a phone call from the president of the United States.

Linda wished Luis Angel Cajina was alive. He regarded her as a pretty woman. If he could only see her now, he would realize she was so much more than he thought. And if Ted could see her, he'd realize she was more talented than he ever thought. But she had no time for thinking about the past. Well, a little time.

After the president's phone call, another phone call was received, this one from Tung Chee-wah, the appointed Chief Executive-designate of Hong Kong.

It was just a "friendly chat." Tung Chee-wah didn't ask her to do anything, but the reason for his call was apparent. He didn't want her to be influenced by what would surely be on U.S. television before the day was done. "It's a difficult day," he told her. "I wish some of the few, but very loud Hong Kong people, would put down the baggage of the June 4th incident and start looking ahead. We cannot allow Hong Kong to become a base of subversion. There should be an emphasis on obligations to the community rather than the rights of the individual."

"Oh, I agree, Mister Chief Executive. You're right!"

A president and another chief executive in one hour.

It wasn't just a few Hong Kong people. It was 55,000 of them in Victoria Park to commemorate the eighth anniversary of the Tiananmen Square massacre, and before the day was done the Hong Kong demonstration was beamed on major television newscasts throughout the United States.

As it had been for the seven years previous, the demonstration was led by Szeto Wah and his Hong Kong Alliance in Support of the Patriotic Democratic Movements in China. The demonstrators were singing songs about freedom, and speeches were made demanding an end to China's one-party system, and demanding that all political prisoners be released.

Liberty was handing out buttons from a supply of 30,000 for the event. The buttons carried the face of a clock with the numbers 4, 6 , 8, and 9 deleted, meaning the massacre's date, the 4th of June, 1989 washed away the numbers.

Hong Kong's Trinity Engineering, with the help of Andrew, had the courage to install the sound and lighting, and Alex Productions took a chance on future repercussions by producing the three-hour show.

Miniature plaster copies of the Goddess of Democracy were being given out by Jack Edwards and a team of his followers, throughout the demonstration.

The only hesitancy was that of Metzger and Richner, a Swiss Company that refused to store or set up a 26 foot high sculpture of 50 bodies piled on top of one another called "The Pillar of Shame." "We are a neutral forwarder," was the company's excuse. "As guests in foreign countries, we should not get involved in political things like this."

"You're cowards!" Liberty told their representative who she found in the crowd. "And we'll remember this! I am not a fan of your company or your country. Neutrality! Neutrality is knowing what is right, but out of an overriding quest of safety, refusing to do what is right no matter the consequences to others. Do you know what Dante said?"

He did not know what Dante said. He shook his head. Liberty had inherited Dr. Yeung's Rolodex of Quotations that was transferred to her brain from his.

"I'll tell you what he said. He said, 'The worst place in hell is reserved for those who are neutral in times of crisis!'"

The man from Switzerland nodded.

"And do you know what Elie Wisel said? He said, 'We must always take sides. Neutrality helps the oppressor, never the victim. Silence encourages the tormenting, never the tormentor.'"

At night, when the demonstration was done, Liberty went back to Sunshine

Island which now had 350 illegal Vietnamese refugees who had gone through China to Hong Kong. She was informed by the Governor's office that by the end of June all of them had to be turned over to authorities. She had no intention of doing it.

It was still called Cocoa Beach but it wasn't Cocoa Beach to Jonas who didn't live through its transitions. Unlike Anne, who had gone back to India because she hated it on her first visit, Jonas went back to Cocoa Beach because he loved it on his first visit. But Cocoa Beach had changed. The aura, the humidity, the flatness, the sweep, the carpet of Florida roads were all still there, but they were serving as antiques in what appeared to be another place.

Cape Colony, once owned by the original astronauts, was now the Econo Lodge. Ron Jon Surf Shop had been constructed on the site once occupied by Cocoa Beach's general store, the U Tote 'Em. And there was no Jack Bishop's gas station, no Ramon's Restaurant, no Sea Missile Motel, and no Jake's Bowling Alley. Even the magnificent, giant, inoperative missiles that stood outside Patrick Air Force Base's main entrance had been taken down.

"We meet once a year at Ocean Landings," Bill Zeeba of the Pioneers Club said. "The Pioneers Club has a restricted membership of those who worked at the Cape during the 1950s and 1960s. We meet at Ocean Landings because it used to be the Starlite. Then it became the Carriage House, then the Atlantis, and now Ocean Landings. And we sit around and lie. The more of us die, the bigger the lies become since there are less and less pioneers to challenge us. I've told some whoppers myself, recently. My stories have gotten better every year. When I die, who's ever left will really tell some big ones. I wish I could hear them. Liars!"

Jonas drove to the Cape, but now anyone could drive there. No longer was the badge that had been designed by Adam a necessity to get onto the Cape. Tourists were now invited during daily visiting hours. And no longer was there a single road to the south gate from A1A, passing the orange juice factory and around the port to the entrance.

No longer the secret message on a large sign that told, in code, what pad was scheduled for a rocket's launch. Most of the old pads couldn't launch anything, anyway. Pad 14, the birthplace of Atlas launches, had overgrown fields of grass and weeds and other uncut things, and the gantry that was once so proud in its formal clothes of red and white was now covered with brown rust, but its monument to the Mercury 7 astronauts, designed by Eugene Keefer, was still there. Pad 26, where the first satellite of the United States had been launched, was now part of the U.S. Air Force Space and Missile Museum. At least care was given to it. Its huge computer room housed the technology that was now exceeded by a pocket computer.

Most of the operational launching pads, including the ones for the Space Shuttle, were across the Banana River on Merritt Island, which to Jonas' disappointment, also had a Visitor's Center.

"Just like a woman," Adam whispered to him. "When the Cape or the city or the woman allows the mystery to be gone, the imagined nudity becomes nothing more than overt nakedness. Don't ever lift the veil too far. When will the mysterious learn to retain their mystery? Jonas, it's time to go to the handover in Hong Kong. Get there before Hong Kong's mystery isn't there anymore."

EIGHTY-FOUR
THE VICTORY OF CLOCKS AND CALENDARS
1997

The British Crown Colony of Hong Kong was almost done. According to all historical records, the year of handover was becoming the year of the greatest rains to pour on Hong Kong since before the first treaties were signed between Great Britain and China, 156 years ago.

There were four consecutive days of holidays, the last two days of June claimed by the British, the first two days of July claimed by the People's Republic of China. On the first afternoon of those four summer holidays, which was Sunday, an old man was standing in the rain on Upper Albert Road at a side door of Government House. The old man was carrying a Marks and Spencer carrier bag to the mansion that housed Hong Kong's governors since Sir John Bowring in 1855. One of the Governor's assistants came to the door of the white mansion. "Ahh, Mr. Edwards. Come in. Come in. The governor is waiting."

Governor Patten had asked Jack Edwards to deliver to him, "without any fanfare," the British flag that Jack Edward's closest friend, Arthur May, had raised on the Peak, giving possession of Hong Kong back to Great Britain at the end of World War II.

Jack Edwards was ushered to the governor's office. Governor Patten stood up from behind his desk. "Good afternoon, Jack."

"It's good to see you, Governor."

"Sit down, sit down. Is Mr. May coming?"

Jack Edwards shook his head while sitting down. "Arthur is now 91 years old, Governor. He's pretty well glued to the bed these days. He's thrilled that you called about the old flag."

"Does he know I want it run up the flagpole before we get out of here tomorrow night?"

"Yes, sir! He asked me to thank you. I have it in here." Jack Edwards lifted the Marks and Spencer bag and placed it on the Governor's desk. "I thought this sack looked unobtrusive enough."

The governor took a quick look inside the bag. "I apologize for the secrecy in all this, Jack. There is so much protocol and diplomacy and riff-raff over the handover, I needed to receive it without flash."

"May I be there when it's raised tomorrow?" He hadn't been invited but he knew it would be all right for him to watch the flag go up.

"Your presence is required. I'm not sure of the precise hour. Sometime in the late afternoon here outside Government House. Probably around 4 o'clock or so. It just needs to be done before I go to all that pomp and circumstance and glitz down in Wanchai."

"You name the time, governor, and I'll be there."

Governor Patten nodded. "That flag was first up, and it should be last down. We'll leave it on the pole here at Government House until I get done with the public farewell ceremony at East Tamar. Then one minute afterwards, this one will come down. So it will be the last one down."

Jack Edwards tightened his lips. "Right!"

"Did you know that during the Japanese occupation that this flag ended, the Japanese added something to this old house that was quite nice?"

"No, sir."

"They remodeled the whole place and put on that pagoda style roof."

"Well, they did one thing that didn't do any harm, didn't they?"

"I'll miss the old place."

"What do you think things will be like a few years from now, Governor?"

"My anxiety is this—not that this community's autonomy would be usurped by Peking, but that it could be given away bit by bit by some people in Hong Kong, itself."

"The business folks?"

Governor gave a quick nod. "And self-censorship. If we in Hong Kong want our autonomy, then it needs to be defended and asserted by everyone here."

"Will it be pretty rough for you tomorrow night?"

"Anybody who actually thinks that I regard our departure as an opportunity for triumphism must think I have all the political intelligence of a wardrobe. I want the last hours handled decently, in a way which gives some credit to Britain and China, who have resolved an issue reasonably amicably—an old issue left over from the last century. Now. Now, what other than our little ceremony here is on your schedule, Jack?" Every one had something on their schedule for the handover.

"First, tonight I'm putting on my white dinner jacket and my tux pants and I'm going to do something that's never been done in Hong Kong before. 1997 will be the first and the last time. It's the Last Night of the Poms. We've moved it this time from the Royal Albert Hall in London to the Academy of Performing Arts here in Wanchai, and I'm going to belt out 'Rule Britannia' and 'I, Vow to Thee My Country.' There'll be five thousand there saluting the Union Jack."

"Good for you!"

"We're celebrating 156 years!"

"Right. And tomorrow?"

"Moose Dunston invited me to drop by at lunch time on the Peak. You know, old lady Goodpastor from the States is going to be back in Hong Kong, and she's holding a reunion of Yanks at the Peak Restaurant. It seems that—I don't know how many years ago—but a long time ago they pledged to be here at handover. Dunston is one of them. I'm just going to go to pay respects of the U.K. on our last day. That's what Dunston wants. I don't know exactly what the reunion of the Yanks is all about, really."

Governor Patten smiled. "I know the story. She told me all about it fifteen times. It was when Sir Robert Black was Governor. She said they were in love with each other. I never knew the chap, but I don't believe it. Irene's a great old lady but she's a storyteller. She said Prime Minister MacMillan put a stop to their secret rendezvous. Once I asked her if the Queen knew about it. I just asked her to see what she'd say. She said she holds any conversations she's had with the Queen as private and confidential. Besides, she said she deals more often with Prince Philip. You're going?"

"To pay respects of the U.K."

"I'll jot off a note for her and you can give it to her. Is that all right?"

"That would be very nice to do, governor."

"Is Irene in good health? I heard she was failing."

"I don't know. I heard the same thing. She's alive. For that alone, she should be grateful."

Poor Brian Nestande. The respected administrative assistant of Sonny Bono didn't know that accompanying Irene Goodpastor to Hong Kong was going to be what it became. Brian, who was deeply involved in the Congressman's foreign policy pursuits, was glad when Congressman Bono asked him to go to Hong Kong for the handover. The Congressman gave Brian a leave of absence to take the trip, and the Congressman paid for it out of his own pocket. "I think I should do it this way," Sonny told him, "or they'll call it a junket for you, or a payoff for Irene from me, or government money being used for Irene, or something. I don't want even the perception of doing something off-key. But I couldn't let her go there by herself. Irene is 92 years old! Imagine making a trip from Washington to Hong Kong at 92! She's in a wheelchair. I don't know what happened to her. She fell or something. I think she fell a lot of times. She's too proud to bring someone along to Hong Kong to help her. That's the way she is. She's sharp—at times. And then she gets pretty senile. So you go over there for me, and so she won't know you're looking out for her, I'll tell her I'd like you to take the same plane as she does so that you can get some insights on Hong Kong first-hand from her. Sound okay, Brian? When she gets to the hotel she'll at least have the hotel staff there to take care of her. I'll let them know to check in on her."

It sounded more than fine to Brian. He had never been to Hong Kong, and this was such an historical time to be there. But it wasn't fine at all. Irene Goodpastor didn't sleep one minute during the flight from Washington to Anchorage or the flight from Anchorage to Tokyo or the flight from Tokyo to Hong Kong. On those flights Brian found out that Sonny had evaluated her correctly. Sometimes she was thoughtful and lucid and sometimes she was nuts.

Congressman Bono had arranged for a limousine with a wide rear door to pick up Irene and Brian at Kai Tak. As they rode through the afternoon streets of Tsimshatsui, Irene did something that was a symptom of age. Every time she saw a sign with its words written in English, she would read the words out loud: "Rolex Zurich Watch Co. Yashica. Sony. Dr. Michael C. Y. Yuen. Chinese Arts and Crafts. Daily Steam Bath Court. Yue

Hwa Chinese Products. Emperor Watch & Jewelry. Tops Optical Company." She read them all aloud as though they had some meaning to her.

Brian escorted her to the hotel. Fifteen years ago she had reserved a block of rooms for the handover at the Hong Kong Hilton and she received a confirmation certificate. But, in typical Hong Kong fashion, in 1995 after a multi-million dollar renovation, the hotel was closed and then demolished.

Mrs. Goodpastor did not suffer in at least getting a substitute for herself. She booked a 28th floor suite in The Peninsula Hotel's 30-story tower. The tower had been added and completed in December 1994, because without it the view of the harbor for their guests had been obscured by the new construction of the Civic Centre and the Space Museum across the street. Brian's room was down the hall without a view of the harbor, but a view of the streets of Kowloon's Tsimshatsui district.

The later it got, the more difficult Mrs. Goodpastor became. Once safely sheltered, she became convinced that Margaret Thatcher was staying in the suite directly above hers. "Brian?"

"Yes, Mrs. Goodpastor?"

"Invite Margaret down here to my suite for tea."

"She's at the Mandarin Oriental across the harbor, Mrs. Goodpastor."

"She's here!"

"She's at the Mandarin Oriental on the Hong Kong side, Mrs. Goodpastor. I know she's there."

"She moved?"

Brian nodded.

"Then call her there!"

"To ask her to come across the harbor?"

"Who cares?"

"Well, I–"

"And then call Lai Ting-kar, the butler over there. I know him. Tell him to come over here with Margaret. She likes him, too."

It was getting wackier and wackier.

"If you don't phone her, Brian, I'll tell Congressman Bono that you wouldn't do it for me, and I'll call Margaret myself!"

"Calling her just isn't a good idea," Brian said softly. "Lady Thatcher is very tired."

With suddenness she became sympathetic. "Oh. Then she should go to bed."

"I agree."

"Is Johnny Carson on?"

"No. He retired, Mrs. Goodpastor."

"If Margaret can't come here for tea, I wonder if she would like to come to our reunion tomorrow."

"She can't. She has engagements and she has to rest some time. I checked."

"Oh." Then she added, "Poor dear!" Then she added, "the old battle-ax!"

Congresswoman Linda Murphy was at the Grand Hyatt Hotel on the Hong Kong side. Through a series of indoor walkways, the Grand Hyatt was attached to the Convention Center where the handover ceremonies would take place. The reason she was in Hong Kong and staying at the plush and convenient Grand Hyatt, had nothing to do with the reunion. She was one of the 130 Americans invited to be guests of the People's Republic of China for the handover ceremonies. There was a Washington rumor that the government of the People's Republic of China was helpful in her campaign and there was no question, not a rumor, that Linda Murphy was very helpful to the People's Republic of China. She was a leading advocate for continued Most Favored Nation status for that government and she was a key influence in allowing the Department of Commerce to decide what high-tech equipment should be allowed to be sent there, instead of the authority remaining in the Department of Defense and the Department of State, where it had been.

Congresswoman Murphy's office had sent a message to Irene Goodpastor that she was not positive she could come to the reunion, but would try to "make a drop-by."

Anne walked through Shamshuipo in the rain. The old apartment building in which she used to live, wasn't there. She wasn't even sure exactly where it was because the whole neighborhood had changed so radically. The blocks of buildings seemed to have been taken out in full and replaced with other blocks of buildings. Anne had an urge to go into every shop and every apartment to see if her Persian rug was on some floor. But what would she do about it if she saw it?

There was something about being in Hong Kong for the first time since she left so inelegantly, that made her long even more for her former boss and her latter husband. She had never known Hong Kong without him. He was, to her, as much a part of Hong Kong—even more a part of Hong Kong—than the Persian rug or Shamshuipo or the Star Ferry or the Peak.

The question of who would call for and accompany Liberty to the Peak became a crisis. She was going to represent her mother at the reunion and John Cooper was going to represent his father. "That," he said, "makes it natural for us to go together."

The reunion was not a natural for Andrew who did not represent anyone, but wanted to go because Liberty was going and because he didn't want anyone else to take her there, and certainly not John Cooper. Andrew was direct. "It's such a big day and such a big event at the Peak for you. I want to be there with you."

Liberty didn't answer.

"I'll take you and end the whole problem," Moose said when she told him about her prospective escorts.

"That doesn't make sense! You'd have to come across the harbor to pick me up to go back across the harbor! It's no problem unless I make it one." She paused for a moment and then came to a conclusion. "I'm going to ask Andrew to take me. If I didn't ask him to come to the reunion he wouldn't have any invitation, and that isn't true of John. He can come with his mother. Mrs. Cooper and John both have a right to be on the Peak tomorrow to represent Mr. Cooper."

Now if only Andrew could contain his glee that he not only would be able to take Liberty to the reunion, but that there was an added prize in John having to come with his mother.

There was a heavy rain on the night of the 29th when the flight of Korean Air landed at Kai Tak with Jonas aboard. Even though it was the night before the handover, rather than after the handover, already there was a different feel when the airliner's doors opened. It had never been that when Jonas landed at Kai Tak that he thought of Great Britain as its overseer; but its jurisdiction of libertarian freedom had always been in the air, and now it was fading. It had never been that when Jonas landed at Kai Tak that he thought of the Legislative Council or the Governor or the Royal Jockey Club, but now he thought of them because they were going. When landing at Kai Tak there was always the feeling that Hong Kong was mystical, because it was. It was a city that existed in its own style. Now it wouldn't be its own style, and the mysticism that had been thick in the air was drifting down the South China Sea with the rain, washing away what was left of it.

Even Kai Tak itself, was preparing for its closure. Another year and Kai Tak would be replaced with the massive Chek Lap Kok Airport on Lantau Island with a new tunnel, new expressways and new bridges, one of them already named Tsing Ma Bridge, the world's longest suspension bridge carrying both road and rail traffic. And there were helicopters scheduled to take airline passengers after they landed from Chep Lap Kok Airport to destinations in Kowloon and Hong Kong Island in minutes. Chep Lap Kok were words Kai Tak didn't want to hear, but it kept hearing them. Kai Tak knew it had little time left. It was old. It had been around since the 1920s with short hops, and since 1936 for flights between Hong Kong and Great Britain, and then it became a world-wide international airport, and by the time 1997 came, it was the third busiest airport in the world. 1997 saw a noticeable lack of maintenance at Kai Tak as the date got closer. Why repair it when there was only one more year of life left in it? It was like an old man deciding not to have a tooth filled because it wasn't worth the pain of the dentist's drill considering the length of his life that was left. Chewing sweets on the other side wouldn't be difficult, and dying with a cavity would not be important. So repairing Kai Tak was not important.

As usual, a uniformed driver from the Regent Hotel picked up each guest at Kai Tak. Generally the car was from the hotel's fleet of Daimler limousines but at handover time everything was different. It was a gold

Rolls Royce Phantom VI. Every moment was to be different for this unique period of Hong Kong's history. Jonas sat back in his seat as the driver headed to the hotel. Riding on Salisbury Road he saw more lights than at Christmas-time and Chinese New Year's. The buildings on the Kowloon side were decorated with coats of colored lightbulbs that covered the harbor side of the buildings, and the view across the harbor on the Hong Kong side was a spectacle. Almost every waterfront building was adorned with color in some electric words or symbols to commemorate the handover to China. Some of the buildings were simply outlined in lights, some had animated pictures of a jumping white dolphin which was the mascot of the handover, there were animated junks, a replica of a Roman candle exploding with many of the designs disregarding the law that prohibited moving lights. What government would lock them up? Great Britain? China? Who was in charge, anyway? Under the Sheraton sign there was a big '97, below an Olympus sign and a KAL sign there were dragon heads looking at each other, Jardine House had colored lights spelling a huge "Hong Kong 1997," Hutchinson House had more than 10,000 colored bulbs in their display of three symbols: the year "1997," the Bauhinia flower symbol-to-be of Hong Kong, and the jumping white dolphin. There were all kinds of electric pictures of the Bauhinia, even an electric Bauhinia on each side of Central Plaza, the towering, pompous building which had never agreed to be decorated for anything before.

And there on the harbor's edge of Hong Kong Island was the brilliantly lit white Convention Center Extension from which the handover ceremonies would take place. There were still workmen finishing it after three years from its design to completion this evening. It was a vast rounded building with a roof that appeared to resemble something between the wings of birds or the waves of the sea, with four massive overlapping convex panels on top.

In the harbor, just to the west of the Convention Center was the Royal Yacht Britannia that had brought Prince Charles to Hong Kong, and was scheduled to leave with Prince Charles and Governor Patten after the handover ceremonies. Just to the west of the Britannia was a gray British destroyer guarding the royal yacht.

Jonas' driver headed up the semi-circular oval drive to the Regent Hotel. The entrance was adorned with its usual lights and its unusual rust-red imitation junk-sails by the sides of the doors. Beneath the sprawling portico was a uniformed and beautiful young woman waiting for Jonas. She opened the door for him. "Good evening, General Valadovich," she said, "We're so happy to have you back at the Regent, and especially to have you with us for this historical event. Your usual room, 1614, is all ready for you. Your plane was a little late, wasn't it?"

She saw him to 1614, the room adorned with champagne, chocolate candies, and flowers. Soon the bellboys arrived with his luggage and, as was the custom, other bellboys arrived with tea and fruits. One of the bellboys pulled the drawstring on the drapes and not as custom, there was the display across the harbor of the lighted landscape for handover.

After the bellboys left, Jonas closed the drapes. Although the view was beautiful, its meaning was not beautiful, and he didn't want to sleep with it.

Jonas was up early on the last day of British rule, to officiate at a session of a Handover Conference down the street at the Shangrila Hotel. Szeto Wah, the great democracy advocate and member of the Legislative Council, was speaking to a group of one hundred Americans from government, industry, and finance, who had come to Hong Kong for the period of handover. Szeto Wah, who had once been a teacher, was a small, humble man in his seventies, hated by the government of the People's Republic of China who labeled him as a subversive. Since the Tiananmen Square Massacre, he had organized most of the Hong Kong demonstrations against China's human rights violations. In appearance, he would have looked more appropriate holding a bamboo stick on his shoulders with pots on either end, running through the streets of Hong Kong barefooted, than to be in a suit and tie, speaking to foreign visitors at a conference. But that was his style. He pretended nothing. He would be Szeto Wah no matter where he was, and he was correctly respected for that.

Szeto Wah could only speak Cantonese, although he understood some English. There was a young Chinese woman who acted as translator for his speech. Jonas sat between them, all three in front of the audience of Americans.

That was when a surprising incident took place.

As the woman gave a translation in English from Szeto Wah's Cantonese, Szeto Wah would often look disturbed at what she was saying. His understanding of some English told him she was being inaccurate. When that happened, Jonas found himself automatically correcting the translator. Szeto Wah would nod in approval at what Jonas said. This happened over and over again, with Szeto Wah looking at him for a correction of the woman, and Jonas then re-translating to Szeto Wah's satisfaction. The translator, who was often stumbling, then followed Szeto Wah's example. Before she made further errors, she would look at Jonas for his expertise, and he supplied it.

What was surprising about all this was that Jonas didn't understand a word of Cantonese. It just happened. Somehow, his appreciation for Szeto Wah gave him an ability he never had.

When the conference was over, Szeto Wah and Jonas couldn't even talk to each other because of the language barrier. But Szeto Wah looked deep into Jonas' eyes, while Jonas looked deep into his, and they gave a strong handshake between them, both recognizing that something wonderful and unexplained had happened.

At 11:30 that morning, Brian Nestande wheeled Irene Goodpastor into the Peak Restaurant for the reunion that was planned thirty-seven years ago.

The Peak Restaurant was being renovated like everything was. Now it was called the Marche on two levels, the yet to be completed new Peak Tower looking like a luxury liner standing on four pillars. Irene Goodpastor and Brian were one half-hour early, as she wanted to be. The table by the window, set for twelve, overlooked all of Hong Kong. But the window only exhibited occasional glimpses of the view, revealing and disappearing between the low clouds with rain coming from the high clouds. "Only six of the original twelve will be here, but there will be others," Mrs. Goodpastor said to Brian. "At the end, Brian. I should be at this end of the table. I'm officiating. Mr. Daschle will sit at the other end. I don't think there's enough places. Tell them there should be more places. A longer table. I didn't tell you but I'm expecting Margaret Thatcher, Governor Patten and Sonny Bono to join us. Tell the staff here to make the table longer!"

Brian closed his eyes in total frustration. "Sonny can't come, Mrs. Goodpastor. That's why I'm here. And the other ones you—"

"He'll be here. And so will the others."

Brian put aside the chair at the head of the table and wheeled Irene to that position. "I'll tell them to make the table longer, Mrs. Goodpastor."

He walked away from her without any plan to tell anyone to make the table longer. He knew she would forget her request by the time he got back to the table.

He came back with something better than a longer table. He came back with Anne Whitney. "Mrs. Goodpastor!" Anne extended her hand. "I'm Anne Whitney. Do you remember me?"

"Dear Anne! My dear Anne!"

Anne bent down and kissed Mrs. Goodpastor's cheek. "Am I on time? Didn't you say twelve o'clock noon?"

Mrs. Goodpastor nodded. "I did!"

"Www! I made it!"

"Dear!" Irene Goodpastor said. "Dear Anne! Sit down next to me. You should be next to me."

"May I go to the other end? Near the other end? I want to be near Mark. Will Mark be here?"

Mrs. Goodpastor looked confused. "I hope to smoke a pig!"

Brian Nestande extended his hand to Anne. "I didn't tell you but I work for Congressman Bono and I'm, sort of—I'm sort of with Mrs. Goodpastor." Sort of.

"I'm Anne Whitney."

"Oh, I know who you are. It's so good to meet you, Ms. Whitney. Sonny watched you, and my family used to watch you on television all the time. I wish you were in the Congress with Sonny. I hope you run again."

"Thank you. I don't think so. Did you see Mark yet?"

"Ms. Whitney, I don't know. I'm just here with Mrs. Goodpastor. I don't know all the people. I didn't handle invitations or anything like that. I just came here as a representative of Sonny."

Then came Jack Edwards who walked directly to Irene, lifted her hand from the table, and bent to it and kissed it. "Mrs. Goodpastor!" he said,

"The governor sends his best. I can't stay, but I bring the respects of the U.K."

For a moment Irene Goodpastor didn't recognize Jack Edwards, but he said the magic words. "The governor? Did he? Will he be here?"

"He felt he might be an intrusion at your rather private reunion—so I came to intrude! Moose Dunston told me to come by—and I mentioned it to the governor. And the governor gave me this," and he dug into his inside jacket pocket and gave her an envelope. "He gave me this to give to you on this important day."

She almost grabbed it from his hand. "He did?"

"He surely did, Mrs. Goodpastor."

"I know you! You're the man with the flag! Did you bring it?"

"It's at Government House. It's going to be raised up the flagpole before the PRC takes over. I'm going over there. I just came by for one drink and I have to be off."

"So it isn't here? I told Moose to invite you so you could bring the flag!" At least she was honest.

"You mean it wasn't so we could be together?"

"Of course it was! You don't have it here?"

"No. The governor wants to raise it. But he said to give you a big kiss from the Queen—no, he said that she sends her greetings, but I'm to give you a big kiss from Prince Philip, and from the entire United Kingdom, and especially from the governor, himself! That's what he told me!" Jack Edwards was no fool.

Entering the restaurant and being shown to the table were two men who were both imposing figures. Moose looked as distinguished as he was big in his dark blue suit, red tie, and gray hair. Jonas was in full-dress uniform. In a quick moment, Anne rushed to Jonas and embraced him. "It's so good to see you, General. If it wasn't for you, I wouldn't have had a good campaign or a television career! You gave me so much ammunition for any number of debates!"

Jonas smiled. "You're greatly exaggerating the little help I hope I gave you. Besides, ammunition means nothing if you don't know how to load it, how to hold the weapon, and where to aim when you pull the trigger. You made your own success."

Anne shook her head, and with a big smile she said, "Without bullets, what good does all that do?"

Jonas even gave a bigger smile. "I told you, you don't need me. Is Mark here?" He either didn't know they were divorced, or he was pretending he didn't know.

"He'll be here," Anne said.

In moments, Gloria Cooper and John were there, who Mrs. Goodpastor knew well, followed by Liberty in a beautiful white cheong-sam, looking so much like her mother. She was carrying a large white purse whose edge kept bumping Andrew, who was by her side. He allowed her purse to pound him with every step without a complaint.

Everyone was standing and talking, with the exception of Irene Goodpastor who was sitting and looking distant. For those who were there in 1960, they thought the others looked 37 years older, but not themselves.

"Okay," Moose said to Jonas. "I know you're dying to show me your new watch. I saw it on your wrist in the car. It is a new one, isn't it?"

Jonas nodded and raised his wrist. "I got it at a little shop in Kowloon. This one is out of this world, Moose. Look," and he pressed a button. "See? The hands are moving, going automatically to what ever place you want! They revolve to any city when you press this. And when it's daylight savings time you don't do a thing! It automatically adjusts for it."

"How could that be?" Moose was faking interest because Jonas didn't get excited about many things, but world-time watches was one of those things.

"They programmed it that way. And daylight savings time starts on different days in different cities, but they're all programmed! Can you believe it?"

Suddenly, in a voice louder than the collective voices of all them, Irene Goodpastor yelled, "It's time to eat!"

That got their attention, as well as the attention of most people in the restaurant.

They sat down and a waiter poured wine for them. It was Irene at the head of the table with Brian next to her, then Jonas, then Moose, then Liberty, then Andrew, then an empty chair for Mark at the far end of the table, then Anne, then Gloria, then John, then an empty chair for Linda Murphy, then Jack Edwards.

Anne smiled. "He'll be here." Then she looked around the table, asking no one in particular, "Mark was late at the lunch in 1960, too, wasn't he?"

Moose stood up with his filled wine glass in his hand and faced Irene. "A toast," he said. "Please join me in a toast to Irene Goodpastor who has kept her word to reunite those of us who are left, just as we all pledged to be together again. And we not only toast Irene for that, but for being such a strong force for all the best in Hong Kong."

"Here! Here!" Jack Edwards said.

There were scattered voices saying, "To Irene" and to "Mrs. Goodpastor." Irene said, "To me!" Then they drank the wine.

Anne took only a sip. "This is what got me in trouble last time!" she said to no one in particular.

Jack Edwards stood to excuse himself. "I didn't come for lunch. I have to hurry off. I just wanted to give my respects and the respects of the U.K.!" He went around the table and shook hands with every man, and kissed the hands of all the women. He fulfilled his mission. His mission was a last touch of Great Britain.

"Stay!" Irene Goodpastor yelled.

"Oh, I must–"

"Stay! Stay! Stay! Sit down, Mr. Edwards! Did you hear me!?"

Jack Edwards heard her. He sat down where he was seated before. His shaking of hands and his kissing of hands were all for nothing.

Anne kept looking toward the area near the entrance. She was not waiting in vain. Before lunch was done, Mark came in. He was dressed in what was obviously a new suit and a starched white shirt and a blue tie that was not fixed as a bow, but hung straight down his shirt.

Anne stood up. It was only because she was conscious of not doing the dramatic that she didn't run to him and embrace him. "Mark," she said so softly that it couldn't be heard by anyone, not even Mark who saw her lips move to say his name.

Mark came to Anne. They stood and stared at each other. Everyone else turned invisible to both of them. Anne's lower lip started trembling until she put her bended index finger against it, holding its tremble back.

Mark asked, "You're not going to make a speech telling us Mao Tse-tung's a great revolutionary, are you?"

That stopped the tremble without her bended finger against her lip. She released it and smiled, then laughed, then embraced him. "Maybe!"

"How about Ike?" he whispered. "Do you still think he should have apologized to Khrushchev?"

"You remember all those things I said?"

People at the table started talking so as not to eavesdrop, not that they could do it very easily because the two were talking barely above a whisper.

"Of course I remember," Mark answered. "I remember everything you said. Every crazy thing you did. Maybe I didn't know it, but–and," he fumbled with words that were incomprehensible.

"Sit down, honey," Anne said. He didn't.

"Do you think I stopped loving you?" He asked her.

Anne nodded.

"Not a chance, Anne. Not a chance."

"I have some new adventures planned! You won't believe them!"

He embraced her very tight.

Irene Goodpastor was bored by their private conversation that she couldn't hear. "Sit down, Mr. Daschle!"

That did it. He sat down. And so did Anne, next to him.

Anne introduced him to those he didn't know, as best as she could; to Liberty and Andrew, to Gloria and John, to Brian Nestande and to Jack Edwards.

Irene was impatient. "Now stand up, Mr. Daschle. You are the co-officiator here, and it's your turn to officiate."

Mark stood up. "Our thanks to you, Irene. You said you'd keep in touch with us and make sure we came back here. You did what you promised. Very few people do what they promise."

There was some scattered applause and a few "yes's".

"First," Irene said to him, quickly taking back the officiating position, "I have something here." She waved the envelope Jack Edwards had given her.

Brian intervened. "She has a message from the Governor. Jack Edwards here gave her a message from Governor Patten."

"Read it!" Jack said.

"I want you to read it aloud, Mr. Daschle!" Irene said. She hadn't even opened the envelope.

"Okay?" Brian asked Jack Edwards.

"Of course."

Irene handed the envelope to Brian who handed it to Jonas who handed it to Moose who handed it to Liberty who handed it to Andrew who handed it to Mark at the other end of the table.

Mark carefully opened the seal and read: "'Dear Irene. I regret that I am not able to attend your lunch and the reunion of your friends, most of whom are from your country. I want you to know my deep feelings for the United States. American power and friendship have been more responsible than most other factors in rescuing freedom in the second half of this century. America has been prepared to support its values with generosity, might, and determination. Sometimes this may have been done maladroitly; what is important is that is has been done. On behalf of me personally, I appreciate your friendship, and on behalf of all of us who have had the good fortune to serve in this vibrant community, we appreciate your dedication to Hong Kong over the years. Respectfully, Christopher Patten.'"

There was applause. Irene Goodpastor had listened to the reading with her eyes glistening. She couldn't wait to have it framed and put on her parlor wall back in Georgetown. "Is it handwritten?" she asked Mark.

"Yes, it is," he answered. Mark put the letter back into its envelope and handed it to Andrew who handed it to Liberty who handed it to Moose who handed it to Jonas who handed it to Brian who handed it back to Irene. Irene petted the envelope as though it was alive. To a great degree, it was.

"That's a marvelous letter, Irene," Mark said.

"Yes," she agreed. Her voice was never softer. Then she almost yelled at Mark. "Go on! You go on and officiate!"

Mark nodded. "Some of the group isn't here. They're with the angels, aren't they? Ambassador and Mary Fairbanks are with the angels." Then he looked at Liberty. "Your mother is with the angels. I knew her so well. She worked for me. She worked with Anne and me. She was an angel herself, even then. We all knew it." He looked over at Gloria and John. "Cody Cooper is with the angels. He was some man, Mrs. Cooper. He'd be so proud of you, John. You're named after President Kennedy, aren't you?" John nodded. "President Kennedy never had a greater loyalist than your dad. He knew the importance of loyalty. And you, Mrs. Cooper have been everything he could ever have wanted. You have done so much for so many—especially for this city of refugees. Who did I miss?"

Jonas said, "Adam. Adam Orr."

"Of course," Mark nodded.

"I'm not sure he's only with the angels," Moose said. "He's—he's..." and he looked over at Liberty with some hesitancy, and then he looked back at Jonas. "I think he's making love to them." Liberty laughed. She knew all about Adam. Then Moose whispered to Jonas, "Since he got up there, there's been a rash of pregnancies in heaven."

"The Murphy's aren't here," Irene said. "Ted is dead, of course! Dead as a doornail! Linda said she'd be here. I don't know where she is. I hear she's become very hoity-toity."

Mark shook his head. "We'll see if she'll be here. Now, if I remember correctly, we all predicted what would happen when—what would happen when this time would come. Frankly, I don't remember what I said, but if we can just think back, we are going to find out who was right and who was wrong."

"I was right!" Irene Goodpastor said.

"I'm sure you were," Mark agreed.

Anne said, "And we all gave our ages in 1997, didn't we? How old we would be."

"I remember that," Mark said.

"And now we are those ages. We shouldn't be unhappy at that. We survived." And then she felt bad that she said that because Liberty and Gloria and John were there because of those who didn't survive. "But I think even those who we don't think are here—are here."

Irene wasn't done with the previous topic. "I'm the only one who said what would happen."

"What did you say, Irene?" Jack Edwards asked. "I wasn't there but I'm interested to know what you said."

"I said everything would happen, that finally did happen."

"Did you say that the Soviet Union would be gone, and Red China would be run by Jiang Zemin?" Jack asked. He was kidding her. No one even heard of Jiang Zemin in 1960.

She nodded, the nods being very long movements of her head.

"And did you know back then that China would take more than the New Territories?"

Her nods were even longer. "See!?"

"I think you did say that, Irene," Mark was helping her. Truth was of no consequence.

"I know I did!"

"Do you remember what you said, Anne?"

"God, I don't know. I probably said the whole world would be communist!"

"General Valadovich?"

"I don't remember. Whatever it was I was probably wrong."

"Moose?"

"All I remember is I couldn't take my eyes off Liberty's mother. I'm afraid I wasn't thinking of politics."

"Well then, Irene gets the award. For those of you who don't know, Irene heads the best think tank in the United States."

Irene asked, "What did you say, Mr. Daschle?"

He had to repeat it.

Irene nodded. "The Goodpastor Center."

"The Goodpastor Center," Mark confirmed.

Anne said, "I don't know if you remember, but Ambassador Fairbanks told us all about his idea for a world organization of democracies that, in time, would mean the ultimate replacement of the U.N. At the time he had some unsolved problems with it, mainly because of the threat of the Soviet Union. But now that it's gone, Mark and I are going to see what we can do to bring that organization into reality. We call it NOLA, the Nations of Liberty Alliance. We think that NATO could eventually become NOLA if it expands, eventually beyond North America and Europe into Asia, Africa, and Latin America. If we have to wait for the next president, we'll wait, but we're going to prepare for it and write its charter."

Mark was surprised by what she said, but he nodded. The guests thought that Anne and Mark had privately decided to do this together, and had decided to announce it to them. Mark let them think it. "Anne and I want your help. Ambassador Fairbanks would want you all to be part of this. He felt comfortable enough with all of you to tell you his idea back then."

Then there was an interruption. Coming toward the table was Linda Murphy surrounded by an entourage of what appeared to be assistants of one type or another. Mark recognized her instantly and looked away. He stopped his officiating.

One of the women with Linda leaned down to Irene Goodpastor. "It's a drop-by," she said. "Congresswoman Murphy wanted to say hello, but she has a meeting with Prince Charles on the Royal Yacht Britannia and, you know, she can't be late for that."

Linda went around to one guest after another. She was an expert at working a table. Mark excused himself before she got to him. She would have worked the entire room if anyone gave the slightest encouragement. Everyone else at the table was little more than cordial to her except Jack Edwards who didn't know all the inside stories. "Well, Congresswoman, how good to meet you! Now, what did you predict would happen when you were one of the group up here years ago? What did you predict would happen come 1997?"

"Oh, my!" Linda said. "We did all predict, didn't we? " There was no answer. "Now, let me see! Well, I didn't know one thing back then! I didn't know it would all be for the good—that the handover would be good for Hong Kong, and that we would have China as a real strategic partner of the United States! Our two great countries are partners! I wish I had predicted that, but I don't think anyone knew that back then."

Moose whispered to Jonas. "They don't know it now, either."

"What?" Congresswoman Murphy asked Moose.

"No. No. I was just thinking back to those days."

Liberty stood up. "Will you pardon me for a moment? I want to get some air. It looks like there's a break in the rain, and I want to go outside for a moment. It's stuffy in here."

"I'll go with you, honey," Moose said.

Liberty looked hesitant, but nodded. She grabbed her large purse that had attacked Andrew. Liberty and Moose walked out together.

"What's up, honey?"

For a moment the clouds had parted below them and the magnificent skyline could be seen, if only for a moment. The dark clouds that were higher than the Peak formed a small clearing of blue directly above them.

"I just wanted to get out."

"You don't want to tell me? Was that toast okay? Did I say something wrong?"

Liberty gave a small smile. "Oh, no, Moose. You never say anything wrong."

"You wish your mother was here, don't you?"

"Ma's here, Moose."

"I know. I know."

"No, I mean—Moose?"

"Yes."

"I brought the ashes." And she gave a slight upward movement of the large white purse, and lowered it again. "I brought the urn."

Moose was unprepared for this. For a while he said nothing. Then just a simple, "Oh."

"Do you mind turning your back? I want to do this alone."

"Do what, honey?"

"I want to scatter them while the city is in sight, and I want to talk to her when I do it. I always planned on doing it today, on the day of the reunion that she wanted to go to—and I want to do it while Hong Kong has not yet been handed over."

With obedience to Liberty's request, Moose turned around.

It was perhaps only two minutes, but they were such long minutes to be turned away from what he knew she was doing.

"It's done," Liberty said.

Moose turned around. There was no evidence of what Liberty had done. The urn was obviously back in her purse.

Moose came to her and embraced her, and she embraced him. "Moose?"

"Yes?"

"Ma told me about you and her at the Miramar."

"Did she?"

"She said that ever since that day with you she couldn't walk on Nathan Road by that plaque of the Miramar Hotel without stopping to rub it."

He could hardly get the words out. "Me, too. I always rub it when I walk by. We did it together once."

"Moose?"

"Yes?"

"I took some of her ashes there today before coming over here, and I rubbed them into the plaque."

Moose did what it seemed he had only done around Wai-yee and now with Liberty. Tears. Among so many things she had inherited from her mother, was that ability to make him cry. Liberty embraced him even tighter than before. It started raining again and he was glad it was raining so Liberty might think the back of her neck and the shoulder of her cheong-sam was wet from the rain.

She knew it wasn't the rain. She cherished the wet of his tears. "Pa!" she said.

Moose quickly released his embrace and backed his face from her. That word she said was the greatest gift he had received since her mother had given him her love. "Liberty! You called me Pa!"

Liberty stared at his eyes that were wet and quickly getting red. Liberty gave a small and delicate smile and a slight cock of her head, the way her mother did. There were tears in her eyes, too, and she so rarely cried. "Pa! Thank you and Ma for giving me life!"

They were both sobbing in the rain that was quickly getting heavier.

She managed to say, "I love you, Pa! You are such a good Pa! You're my Pa, you know!"

She went into the ladies room and he went into the men's room, both of them needing to straighten themselves before going back to the table.

By the time they got back to their places, Congresswoman Murphy was gone and so was her entourage, and Mark was back to his position of officiating, just the way he used to. "Now we have China taking over, saying that it will be one country, two systems for fifty years. That means in 2047 it will be one country, one system, doesn't it?"

"That's right!" Irene yelled.

"Which will it be? Which system will it be in 2047? Anyone care to make some predictions?"

There was some laughter. "Again?" Anne asked.

"Well, I guess most of us won't be here then. Irene, I'm confident you will. And you will, Liberty. And you will, John, and you will—" and he forgot the name of Liberty's escort. John was glad he forgot.

"Andrew," Andrew said.

"Yes, of course. Andrew. You three young people are so likely to see it happen. Why don't you come to the Peak then—for a reunion?"

There was an embarrassing silence of rejection. Mark, of course, didn't know that John and Andrew were not the best of friends since both of them were rivals in love with Liberty, and that one of the last things John and Andrew wanted to do was to be doomed into a pledge of being with each other in fifty years.

With the cold reaction, Mark added, "But I suppose it wouldn't be the same thing."

Jonas leaned over to Moose and said very softly, "I hope you don't mind, but while you were out, I told Mrs. Goodpastor about your job—about the letter you received from Hanson Alpert."

"Sure. That's fine. It's no secret."

"She was delighted."

"Delighted!?" Moose quickly turned to Mrs. Goodpastor. She was looking at the ceiling. "Well, she's a little on the senile side."

"No. It isn't that. She was delighted because she wants you to work for her Goodpastor Center."

Moose shook his head. "She asked me before. Jonas, I'm staying in Hong Kong. I'll find something here. I want to be where Liberty can get hold of me when she needs something. I didn't marry her mother because I thought I couldn't live here. Then I ended up living here, anyway. I don't want to make another mistake by going home again—this time leaving my daughter when she might need me."

"You're getting possessive in your old age, buddy. She's a woman who can take care of herself, don't you agree?"

"Yeah. Sure. I don't know."

"Maybe it's you who can't take care of yourself without taking care of her."

Moose thought about that for a while. "Maybe." Then he looked over at Liberty to make sure she couldn't hear him. She was talking to Andrew, to Andrew's great delight. Moose looked sharply into Jonas' eyes. "Jonas, she just called me 'Pa'!" And he said it again. "'Pa'! Do you know what that means to me?"

Jonas could see the joy all over Moose's face. "Yes. I do know what that means to you."

"Do you, Jonas? I've had good things happen to me in my life—so many good things, but nothing like that. I don't even care what happens to me now."

Jonas nodded with his lips tight against each other. "That's wonderful."

"She always called me Moose. Since she was a little girl, she's been calling me Moose. Jonas, I'm 'Pa' now!"

"She loves you. She truly loves you. The kind of love that isn't dependent on anything except you being you."

"Wai-yee is 'Ma," Dr. Yeung is 'Father,' and I'm 'Pa.' My God."

"Just think over what Mrs. Goodpastor suggested. That's all."

Mark Daschle jiggled the spoon in his glass. "General, the last time we were all together, if I recall correctly, you were a lieutenant. You have been helpful to Anne, and to me. Your career has been a great inspiration to all of us. Do you have any words of wisdom for our rather unique group—that knew you 'when'?"

Jonas stood up, and when he stood up, people paid attention. He looked twice as tall as he was because of his manner, his uniform, and the suddenness of his rising. Mark sat down to give Jonas the floor by himself.

"No. No words of wisdom. Just some comments regarding today and tomorrow. On this day, June the 30th, there is an elected Legislative Council here—like our Congress. Tomorrow, on July the 1st, those elected legislators won't be in office. Today we can demonstrate without a license from the police. Tomorrow, we will need their permission. Today we can call for the independence of Hong Kong, Taiwan, and Tibet. Tomorrow it will be illegal. Today Hong Kong's Bill of Rights is in full force. Tomorrow it will be cut. All of these things will be ignored by the business interests and by the tourists. The great shopping malls will still be here. The luxury hotels will still be here. The spectacular skyline will still be here. The Peak will still be here. Many will say, 'Nothing has changed. Everything is the same.' That's because the changes will be silent and invisible.

"Hong Kong will still look like Hong Kong, but it won't be Hong Kong. This city will be under the threat of a storm. Go outside and you can feel it in the air, like a typhoon that's a One and can jump to a Ten. All Beijing has to do is say it's a Ten. It may never happen, but to know that it can happen transforms the atmosphere of libertarianism under which Hong Kong has lived so long, into a fear of losing it at any minute.

"My belief is that Jiang Zemin will keep the typhoon at a One. In that way the Government of China can claim the success of 'One Country, Two Systems' here, which they will use as an example to bait Taiwan. Once they take over Macau on December the 20th of 1999, they will probe Taiwan in some manner. At the same time they will probe the United States to find out how much the United States will tolerate.

"And they will wait to create the Ten, either in Taiwan or here in Hong Kong, or in both.

"Would the United States be willing to go to war to defend the people of Hong Kong? As of tomorrow, the People's Republic of China can claim it is part of China, and therefore any difficulty is an internal affair under their 'One Country, Two Systems' formula. Would we, in fact, go to war to defend the people of Taiwan? We act as though we're frightened of getting China's officials mad at us. So, like some little kid, we cater to them. Somehow, they have become the principal of the school, and we have become the child.

"Evidence seems to indicate that the United States will tolerate a great deal, and Jiang Zemin knows it.

"The last time all of us were together in 1960, we listened to presidential candidates Kennedy and Nixon debate whether or not we would go to war over Quemoy and Matsu. There was, however, no disagreement on Taiwan. Both candidates were in total accord that we should and would defend Taiwan. Would our current leaders have the same position? The fate of Taiwan and Hong Kong are tightly connected.

"To Liberty, to Andrew, to John, I apologize for my generation leaving this malignancy in Beijing to fester, and even deeper apologies for my generation providing the means for the government of the People's Republic of China to become a major threat to the liberties of people who want to be free.

"We leave you to have better sense than us, a higher standard than us, a deeper understanding than us, and the necessary will to insure the liberty of all people. You can do it. You can bring liberty to the world. It is not impossible. If there is anything my generation knows, it is that nothing is impossible.

"When this group met in 1960, and I was close to your age, I thought a lot of things were impossible. But those things turned into reality through the years that followed our meeting. Both triumphs and tragedies that I thought were impossibilities came to be.

"I thought it would be impossible for a U.S. president to be assassinated. That was the stuff of long-ago history with people in high hats and costume. But in 1963 a president was assassinated.

"I thought it would be impossible for segregation to end in the nine southern states. But in 1965, the signs of 'colored' and 'white', separating the races, came down.

"I certainly thought it would be impossible for man to land on the moon. That was the stuff of Jules Verne and Buck Rogers. But in 1969 it was the stuff of Neil Armstrong and Buzz Aldrin.

"I thought it would be impossible for a president of the United States to resign from office. But in 1974 a president resigned.

"I thought it would be impossible for an ally of ours for whom we fought, would ever be driven to surrender by our impatience. But in 1975 we saw the fall of Saigon and Phnom Penh.

"I thought it would be impossible that my country, the United States, would ever trade diplomatic relations with the Republic of China on Taiwan for the People's Republic of China on the mainland. But in 1978 that is what we did.

"I thought it would be impossible for the people of my country to reject a defense from missiles. But in 1983 we ridiculed, then rejected such a defense.

"I thought it would be impossible that I would see the Soviet Union die, and its empire dismember. But it happened in 1991.

"Nothing is impossible. Nothing. Our country can be paradise or imperiled. It is entirely possible that in the same length of time that passed from our first meeting to this day, that you will see everyone in the world living in liberty, and it is entirely possible that you will see liberty expire everywhere in the world.

"Witnesses and bystanders are unimportant. Those roles are beneath you. You, Liberty and Andrew and John, you be the leaders who bring about a world where everyone is free."

Just as Governor Patten promised, the flag that was raised on August 18, 1945, on the Peak was raised outside Government House on June 30, 1997. It was raised in the rain at 4:30 in the afternoon, and just as Governor Patten planned, it was done "without flash," with only family, staff, friends, including Jack Edwards, and tears present.

The headstone of the grave of Pickles the dog, the long-ago mascot of the British army, had been taken from the ground outside the barracks building, to give it a more secure shelter in London. It was one among many remembrances of the Crown Colony that had been packaged and taken to Kai Tak to go to London. One of the most difficult items to pack was the huge Korean War Memorial that honored the British soldiers who fought against North Korea and against troops from the People's Republic of China.

Outsidc the PRC's Xinhua News agency was a crumpled man, Zhou Xiupinga, who was camped out by its door. "This is where I'm going to be for the handover," he said. "Three years ago, that government took my travel documents away. I want them back. They took them because I was calling for democracy in China, and I wanted to talk to political prisoners in China. I make no claim that the British are Gods, but they're not devils, either."

A number of police inspectors said they would refuse to abandon their oath of allegiance to the Queen. They did it knowing they could face disciplinary action as deserters, and their pensions could be forfeited if they failed to report for duty on July 1.

Members of the April 5 Movement were on the streets in demonstration, burning pictures of Li Peng. Another demonstration of protestors were carrying a picture of Sun Yat-sen. Thirty thousand Buddhist monks announced they were going to pray for the city's future at Hong Kong Stadium on the first day of July.

The *South China Post* had a new consultant. It was 76-year-old Feng Xiliang. His background included being one of the PRC's top propagandists.

As of midnight Hong Kong would issue its own passports for the first time. The blue-colored cover said "Hong Kong" in both Chinese and English, with the words beneath it, "Special Administrative Region, People's Republic of China." Below that was a gold emblem featuring Tiananmen Square, and the five stars of China. It replaced the green cloth-covered Certificate of Identity.

The passport to have by residents of Hong Kong was the passport that had a burgundy colored cover and a coat of arms beneath the words, "United Kingdom of Great Britain and Northern Ireland." It was the British National Overseas Passport.

After Governor Patten bid goodbye to all at Government House, he and his family headed to the British Farewell Ceremonies on the waterfront home of the British Navy at East Tamar. Ten thousand British Nationals and Hong Kong people were waiting for him. They stood at attention for the Union Jack flag-lowering, the last time that flag would feel the companionship of that pole. Then it was the turn of the blue-fielded Hong Kong flag to come down. It was sunset, and an intense fog was replacing the rain.

One minute later the flag at Government House was lowered.

Jiang Zemin and Li Peng were supposed to be there at the British Farewell Ceremony but they didn't come. They would wait until the Handover Ceremonies. Missing the British event was their revenge for Prime Minister Blair's decision to boycott the inauguration of the Provisional Legislature that was to take place following the official Handover Ceremonies at the Convention Centre.

After bagpipes played, the governor, with tears in his eyes, gave his farewell to the crowd. It was his last public event this June the 30th other than the Handover Ceremonies themselves later in the evening. He said Britain had contributed to "the scaffolding that enabled the people of Hong Kong to ascend: the rule of law, clean and light-handed government, the values of a free society, the beginnings of representative government and democratic accountability. This is a Chinese city. A very Chinese city with British characteristics. No dependent territory has been left more prosperous. I have no doubt that when people here hold on to these values which they cherish, Hong Kong's star will continue to climb."

And then the orchestra played "Auld Lang Syne." Who had ever heard it before without a New Year's celebration? Without invitation, a few voices of the crowd started singing its words until by the end of the song, every one was singing that song that always signaled the end of something known and the beginning of something unknown.

Liberty had made a semi-career of disappearing without telling anyone her whereabouts. The most important midnight of Hong Kong's history in 156 years was part of that semi-career. There were so many who wanted to be with her, with invitations from Moose, from Andrew, from John, and from Martin Lee and Szeto Wah and other members of the Legislative Council to be in the Council Chamber. She declined them all without excuse. They all knew her well enough not to ask her where she would be. She wouldn't say, "It's none of your business," but worse: they knew that asking where she would be would mean she would look at the victim, and her eyes would deliver a silent but painful obscenity.

Since none of her friends wanted to celebrate the entrance of the new government, and none of them would be with Liberty, most decided to forgo watching the fireworks extravaganza planned for the handover. Besides, it seemed that being in the public crowd at the harbor, watching the show might be perceived as a form of approval, or at least of acceptance. It was almost as though being there could be a personal surrender.

Gloria sat with her son, John, in the almost barren office in the wooden barrack building of High Island Detention Center for refugees. It was the last refugee center left in Hong Kong. The Kai Tak Vietnamese Migrant Transit Centre had been closed in March, and Whitehead had been boarded up just before the June 30 deadline. High Island was becoming vacant. None of this was because there was a shortage of those who wanted to be there. 1,721 had tried to get into Hong Kong in 1997 but were sent back, as were thousands and thousands of others under what was called the Comprehensive Plan of Action, which was scheduled to have its work completed at midnight. In all, Hong Kong had returned over 60,000 refugees since the program started in 1989, and only hundreds were left for resolution.

"I received a new assignment, John," Gloria said to her son.

He knew it was coming, but he didn't know it would come on the last day of British rule. She handed him the letter from the Headquarters of the World Refugee Mission. She watched John read the letter, hoping she would see some sign of his acceptance. It wasn't there. He put the letter down on the otherwise vacant wooden table and looked at his mother, attempting not to show too much emotion on his face. "Are you going to Bosnia, Mom?"

"There's nothing to do here anymore. There's over two million refugees in the Balkans. We're needed there."

It was the word "we're" that he had to erase quickly. "You're the one they want, Mom. They don't need me."

"You don't want to come?"

"This is home. We've been here since I was six years old, Mom. I'm 22 now." He knew that by stating his age he was telling her he was considered to be an adult by law, and he was able to make his own decisions. "Can't you stay here?"

"Seven. You were seven. But it is home. I know that. John, I have to go where I'm needed." She had changed the "we" to "I" but then reminded John that he was a part of all this: "It's why we came here in the first place. Your Dad and I decided that's what the three of us would do with our lives."

He nodded.

"You weren't in on the decision, were you?"

John shook his head. "No."

"And you're in love with Liberty, aren't you?" She hit it.

He nodded while he was biting his lip.

"I can't criticize your taste. But I don't think she's ever going to marry anyone. She's the most independent young woman I've ever known."

"I'll bet if I leave, she'll marry Andrew."

"What if we asked Liberty to join us?"

"In Bosnia?"

"Why not?" Gloria tried a small forced smile. "I don't know if the Mission would go for it, but we could try."

"Mom, she loves Hong Kong more than anything else. She won't leave here. You know, she's the Goddess of Democracy!"

"What can she do here now? Hong Kong is China now. Or it will be in a few hours."

"I know what she'll do. She'll be keeping this place free."

Gloria stared at her son and then nodded. "You have to make your own decision. You're of age, aren't you? I want you to go with me, John. But if you stay here, don't do it just because of Liberty. She has her own plans. Where is she tonight? On this important night, she's not with you."

"I know."

"Do you know where she is?"

"No."

"Did you ask her where she'd be?"

"No."

Gloria gave a real smile this time. "Then you are an adult. Don't ever ask. Don't ever be a child again." She didn't say it, but she was thinking that his father had been a child too long.

Jonas had accepted the request of the World News Network to go to the Lok Ma Chau Checkpoint Border Crossing to give a military analysis when the World News Network received word from Shenzhen that the People's Liberation Army was on its way into Hong Kong. They wanted him to wear his uniform which he refused to do, since he did not want to be caught in a situation where exchanging salutes would have been proper.

The word came in the early evening and the network sent a car for him. Miraculously, through the rain and the crowds and the police barriers all over Kowloon, the driver made it. Jonas was driven through Kowloon, through the New Territories, and to Lok Ma Chau, outside the border.

At 8:25 P.M. it started. An advance element of 509 soldiers led by Major General Xiong Ziren entered Hong Kong in 21 armored personnel carriers, followed by some busses and some dark green wooden slab trucks with soldiers standing in seven rows of threes in each truck, each lead soldier holding the flag of the People's Republic of China.

"What for?" Jonas asked, talking into the microphone held by the American newscaster, Jim Moranne, who was totally unfamiliar to Jonas. "If nothing else, this is poor public relations. They could have waited until after midnight. In fact, they could have stayed across the border in Shenzhen forever. What country threatens Hong Kong from which they're protecting Hong Kong? The only threat is China, itself."

"Why, then, do you think they're doing it, General?"

"To show who's in charge. There can't be any other reason. Look at those armored personnel carriers. Those are WZ523's complete with turrets, 12.7mm machine guns and grenade launchers. Those personnel carriers can hold 10 troops in each one along with the soldier in the turret. All I can tell you about them is that they're newer and more effective than those they used in the Tiananmen Square massacre. And those assault rifles the soldiers are carrying are all state-of-the-art."

"General, do you suppose this is the whole contingent?"

"No. This is just the beginning. They said they would send in 4,000 troops tomorrow, including seven helicopters with anti-ship missiles, and they're sending attack ships loaded with Eagle Strike Missiles as well as anti-aircraft guns. Those 4,000 troops are going to come through here and through Man Kam To and Shataukok. I think these advance troops that are waving at us are on the way to Prince of Wales Barracks. If I may add, my guess is that soon those barracks are going to be re-named."

When the interview was done, Jim Moranne told Jonas that the producer wanted him to come back on-camera some time after the handover for an analysis of the day. Jonas declined until he was told that Irene Goodpastor agreed to appear on the show, and he wouldn't have to travel anywhere to appear. "We're doing it on that half-roof of the Regent Hotel through Room 1600, just down the hall from your room. We'll need you at around 2:30 in the morning. It's for our *Above the Fold* program. It's a big show. The host is Laurie Lespada. I'm sure you've seen it."

Jonas said, "No," but out of courtesy he added, "but I heard about it."

Anne and Mark were walking on Nathan Road in Kowloon, holding hands over the stem of Anne's open yellow umbrella, like two young lovers. The crowds were so immense and the thousands of umbrellas added so much to the congestion that in the interest of order, the Hong Kong police had erected barriers and signs, ordering pedestrians they could only walk one way. If pedestrians wanted to go north on Nathan Road they had to be on the west side of the wide road, and if they wanted to walk south they had to go to the east side of Nathan Road. To cross Nathan Road to walk in the opposite direction was a journey, as there were few corners without barriers.

There were flags on the antennas of taxis, most of the flags being the new red Hong Kong flag with the Bauhinia flower, some of the flags with just the numbers 1997, and some of them had a picture of the white dolphin, and some said, "Joy to the Reunification."

"The last time we were here, you were such a nuisance," Mark said.

"You fired me."

"I didn't fire you. I sent you home."

"I sometimes wonder what my life would have been without you."

"I know what it would have been."

"What?"

"You'd have been where Yeltsin is now."

"The president of Russia?"

"Not exactly. You'd have been the president of the Soviet Union. You would never have lost the Cold War. The world should be very thankful to me." She tightened her hand around his.

"Boy, did I goof up by allowing you to change my life, didn't I?"

"Or maybe you'd be over at the Convention Center tonight instead of Jiang Zemin. You could have taken over China after Deng Xiaoping died."

"Then I would be the master of five hundred million!"

"Anne, the population there is over a billion."

"I only count the men."

"Still?"

"Always!"

He shook his head. "I should have known I could never change you."

"Would you want to?"

He didn't answer.

She tightened her hand again.

"Never," he answered.

They were jostled by the crowd, forcing them to be even closer than they would have been. They had no problem with the jostlers, only the umbrellas. With the exception of politics, to Mark and Anne, Hong Kong was even better in 1997 than it was in 1960.

Irene phoned Brian and invited him to her room. He couldn't resist accepting the invitation, since he had a view of the streets and she had a view of the fireworks over the harbor. This was to be the greatest fireworks exhibition in the history of the world, with its record to be held for only one day, since the following night, when Hong Kong, under the People's Republic of China's government, planned their celebration to exceed the British.

At times the clouds were so low that the Peak wasn't visible and then, in an instant, the fog disappeared, with clear weather playing the referee in a fight between the fog and the rain. Irene could see the thousands of people standing on the Promenade Harbor Walk across Salisbury Road. Off to the west entrance to the harbor, hundreds of ships were motionless, the harbor closed to all traffic other than the vessels in the extravaganza. Not even the Star Ferry had a pass to enter.

Then the harbor sky was host to the fireworks of one color and shape after another. Their reflections in the water turned to red, then green, then red again and green again, and the entire harbor was used as a stage. The sounds were intense, and the crowds were cheering, even screaming. The windows of the Peninsula reverberated from the explosive noise of the fireworks. "Brian!" Mrs. Goodpastor yelled. "Quick! Come to the window!"

They sat there until they couldn't see it any more because fog was covering the window. "Stop the fog, Brian!"

He thought she was on the verge of her all-too-familiar drift into strange-land, but she was right. Brian could control it. He realized it when he wiped his hand over the window, discovering not all the fog was outside. It was the air conditioning that was fogging the window from the interior.

With the motionless mural that had been Hong Kong every night now off the government's leash, the lights were like a wild animal that had been caged and suddenly found the door open. The spectacle was sweeping east to west and west to east and high into the sky and deep into Victoria Harbor in a kaleidoscope of colored explosions.

Tall vertical spouts of light came from the sea and then disappeared and appeared again high above where they had left off, and the spouts changed to different colored balls that expanded and expanded and then other balls came from those balls and expanded, and then additional expanding balls from the newer balls, and they were all over the view.

The skyscrapers enjoyed it because they were part of it. There was even scaffolding of an incomplete building that had entered the display of lights before there were walls.

When it was done, Brian tried to talk Irene into having a quick sleep, since she had agreed to a television interview for "Above the Fold" at 2:30 in the morning on the roof of the Regent.

"I'm not tired. Will you tell the management here to bring me some oysters?"

That wasn't what he wanted to hear. He wanted her rested for such a public appearance, or she could make a fool of herself. "You're going to be very tired at 2:30, Mrs. Goodpastor. I'll tell them to send someone to help you get to bed. You should get some sleep. Sonny will be watching you on television tonight. I know that. And he'll want you to be alert!"

"I'm as alert as a twenty-year-old. Oysters!"

"I'll be by for you at 2 o'clock with a car waiting. The Regent's just across Salisbury Road, a minute away by car."

"I know where the Regent is! I lived here for four years you know, Mr. Hong Konger!"

"I'll be waiting for you."

Suddenly her voice was very soft. "I should never have hit that girl. I hope I didn't hurt her. I hope she's all right."

Brian didn't know what she was talking about.

Moose was with Andrew in a crowd, but not in any of the crowds watching troops enter, or watching the spectacular show of fireworks, or any of the crowds in the hotels and clubs that were celebrating. Moose was standing with Andrew under two umbrellas in the Charter Garden crowd of more than one thousand standing outside the Legislative Council Building. They were staring up at the balcony in which the members of the Democratic Party including Martin Lee and Szeto Wah, were standing. As a courtesy from the heavens, the rain diminished to just occasional drops and one umbrella after another was closed, and put down by the sides of the people.

"I know you'd rather be with Liberty," Moose said, "but you have to be satisfied with me."

"Yes, sir," Andrew said in agreement.

"In honesty, Andrew, as much as I like you and welcome your company, I'd rather Liberty was here than you–so we're even."

"Yes, sir."

Moose shook his head. There was no way to excite Andrew, and when Moose spoke lightly, he never knew if Andrew thought what he said was funny or was taken seriously.

Moose thought it was good that at least someone was with him who understood Cantonese. But Andrew was always short on words. Martin Lee, standing on the balcony with twenty other elected legislators, was talking and talking and talking and Andrew translated Martin Lee's speech into, "He said we should have an elected legislature."

"That's all?"

"That's what he said."

"In all that time?"

"He said he wants an early end to the Provisional Legislature. That it's illegal."

"What else?"

"Wait." Martin Lee was still talking. Again it was a long dissertation.

Andrew made his translation. "He said Hong Kong must survive."

"Andrew, what else?"

"Wait."

Then Martin Lee gave the longest dialogue of all.

Andrew turned to Moose. "He said that if there's an election in May of next year as Tung Chee-hwa says, the new electoral rules will insure there won't be a lot of democrats in Legco, and that's not good. Something like that."

"What else?"

"Wait."

This time Martin was saying something short. He kept repeating one phrase again and again, to the audience's applause and cheers each time he said it.

"It's okay," Andrew said.

"What do you mean, it's okay?"

"He's good."

"What's he saying?"

"Wait."

Happily some woman behind them translated for Moose. "He's saying, 'Long Live Democracy!'"

"That's right," Andrew said, confirming his role as translator.

"Let's go," Moose said, as there was a sudden new cloudburst, and a quick opening of thousands of umbrellas.

Liberty was not intimidated by the pouring rain. Neither were the 262 Vietnamese refugees standing in a circle around her on the highest hill of Sunshine Island in the black of night. Umbrellas were not among the more necessary conveniences of the island.

They could hear the rumble and sharp noises of fireworks from far-off. They knew that thousands of people were watching the handover festivities. It meant that neither the old authorities of Hong Kong or the new authorities of Hong Kong were watching anything on Sunshine Island.

"We have rented thirty sampans," Liberty said. She, and all the others, looked like they were showering in their clothes. "The sampans are waiting for you. They will take some of you to Lantau, some to Kowloon, some to Hong Kong Island. When you dock, you disperse. Families together, but the rest of you get away from each other. I want you to integrate with the people. You may have to stay on the streets for a while, but you know how to work, you know crafts, you know how to survive. Whatever you do, don't get in trouble. If you do, there is nothing I can do for you. Governor Patten will be far away, and the new government under Tung Chee-hwa will not help you. They will send you back to either Vietnam or China.

"All of you, when you get aboard the sampans you will be given 'lei see'. In each of the red envelopes there will be money to keep you going for a month or so—for even more time than that, if you're frugal. They are gifts from Gloria Cooper. She's the only one who knows what we're doing here tonight. Take anything you want from Sunshine Island, other than from my place, but be sure you aren't burdened by what you take. When the new government comes to inspect this island in the days ahead–and they will be here–I want this place to have nothing but vacant shelters. I wish you well. I wish you good fortune, my friends from Vietnam!

"Now off! Make quick preparations, and go down to the sampans."

The rumble and sharp noises of the fireworks from far-off continued. Liberty was where she wanted to be on the night of handover.

It was not long before the Vietnamese were all down the hill with roped together bags and possessions, getting on the waiting sampans. After they left to their scattered destinations, but before Liberty went down the hill to take the sampan that was waiting for her, she went to her tent which was a large khaki canvas. Under it were a number of things she had made on the island, and a number of things she had brought from home.

Those things she had made on the island included a paper stethoscope and a paper tea-kettle and a paper necklace and a paper on which she wrote some of the sayings of K'ung Fu-tze, Confucius.

Those things she had brought from home were two bags of already popped popcorn and a blank pad of prescriptions and a new patterned cheong- sam and ten small bags of M&M's, and a recording of "Tammy and the Bachelor" and the movie section of the *South China Morning Post*. And there was the painting of John Travolta.

She waited for a break in the rain to take the canvas tent down. Then, quickly, she did it: with a torch she burned all the objects she had laid out, for their deliverance to the spirits of Dr. Yeung and Wai-yee.

Linda was a star at the Convention Center, but not as big a star as she had expected to be. Before she had left the United States she knew she was one of a small number of Americans invited to be an official guest at the handover, but she was not aware that there were 3,899 other people who were invited from 44 countries around the world. It seemed as though inside the new extension of the Convention and Exhibition Center all of them were on the escalators at the same time that night. Her major concerns were her hair because it got wind-blown outside, and her shoes that got wet from the rain when an umbrella held by her driver was not targeted correctly for a moment, and a hope that she would be asked for an interview by one of the many U.S. television reporters who were covering the event. She was told time and time again from her advisers that some 6,500 media representatives were covering the event, but not to waste her time on interviews for any of the ones that wouldn't get back to American audiences.

She took out a small hand mirror from her purse while she was on the escalator. There was hair hanging out straight from the back of her head like an arrow. She brushed it back and looked down at her shoes. There was a big brown blob on the otherwise yellow of her right shoe. She leaned down to see if it was solid or loose, when she saw a camera crew aiming at her and undoubtedly caught her doing all the things she didn't want seen on U.S. television. There was no attempt to interview her.

Most of the crowd was dry since they were coming from the State Banquet in the Center, hosted by Britain's Secretary of State for Foreign and Commonwealth Affairs, Robin Cook. Linda didn't go because she had received a phone call that afternoon from a representative of President Jiang Zemin of the People's Republic of China. "It is your decision, Congresswoman Murphy," she was told. "But President Jiang and Premier Li Peng will not be at the banquet the British are giving this evening. As you know, Prime Minister Blair is not attending the inauguration of our new legislature after the handover ceremonies, nor is your Secretary of State, Madeline Albright. They are sending lower level officials. Under such circumstances we do not consider it correct for our president and premier to attend the British banquet. Only our lower level vice premier, Qian Qichen, will attend. Perhaps then, under those circumstances, you would want to reconsider the invitation from the British. Of course, the decision is yours."

"I won't go, either."

"We will see you then at the Handover Ceremonies with the rest of your country's delegation. And then we will see you again, without your top officials, at the inauguration of Mr. Tung and the Provisional Legislature."

The Grand Hall of the Convention and Exhibition Center Extension was as magnificent as the exterior of the building. The thousands of invited guests were not only witnesses to history in the handover from Great Britain to the People's Republic of China, but they became the audience of the first event in an architectural wonder of creativity. The Grand Hall was so massive that nothing was crowded. Just as the exterior of the building was a cross between a bird and the sea, the interior gave the audience the feeling of being beneath the wings of a bird, or beneath the breakers of the sea. Few theaters have windows, but to exclude them from this theater would have been criminal. The entire wall behind the stage was glass with intervening blue curtains, the glass exhibiting the magnificence of Victoria Harbor looking toward Kowloon.

On the west side of the stage was vice-chairman of the central military commission and chief of the People's Liberation Army General Zhang Wannian, chief executive Tung Chee-hwa, Vice-Premier Qian Qichen, Premier Li Ping, and President Jiang Zemin, representing the incoming government of Hong Kong. On the east side of the stage was Charles the Prince of Wales, Prime Minister Tony Blair, Foreign Secretary Robin Cook, Governor Christopher Patten, and the Territory's Commander of British Forces Major-General Bryan Dutton, representing the outgoing government of Hong Kong.

Also on the stage were two flagpoles on the west side and two flag poles on the east side. The ones to the west were vacant. The ones to the east had the Union Jack and the flag of Hong Kong. The ceiling of the Center was so high that the flagpoles were full length exterior flagpoles with a great quantity of room to spare above them. In addition, there were giant boards with the painted flags of both Great Britain and the People's Republic of China hanging from the ceiling between the stage and the glass wall.

Among the 3,900 invited guests, Congresswoman Linda Murphy was queasy. She felt indebted to the People's Republic of China and wanted to please their authorities, yet she did not want to be so close to them that her own constituents would suspect her of strange international loyalties. She was trying to be careful to give equal public respect to both countries.

The voice of Prince Charles was strong and firm and, above all, dignified, as he said, "Most of all I should like to pay tribute to the people of Hong Kong themselves–to all that they have achieved in the last century and a half. The triumphant success of Hong Kong demands and deserves to be maintained. Hong Kong has shown the world how dynamism and stability can be defining characteristics of a successful society. These have together created a great economy which is the envy of the world. Hong Kong has shown the world how east and west can live and work together....

"Ladies and Gentlemen, China will tonight take responsibility for a place and a people which matter greatly to us all. The solemn pledges made before the world in the 1984 Joint Declaration, guarantee the continuity of Hong Kong's way of life. To its part, the United Kingdom will maintain its unwavering support for the Joint Declaration. Our commitment and our strong links to Hong Kong will continue, and will, I'm confident, flourish as Hong Kong and its people themselves, continue to flourish.

"Distinguished guests, ladies and gentlemen, I should like on behalf of Her Majesty the Queen, and of the entire British people, to express our thanks, admiration, affection, and good wishes to all the people of Hong Kong who have been such staunch and special friends over so many generations. We shall not forget you, and we shall watch with the closest interest as you embark on this new era of your remarkable history."

The timing of the event was also remarkable, run with the precision of a stopwatch. When the Prince of Wales was done, three soldiers of the People's Liberation Army goose-stepped up the center steps to the red-carpeted stage, the middle soldier holding the folded flag of the People's Republic of China in his outstretched arms, forming a tray. Then three British soldiers joined them in goose-step. When the delegation of six reached center stage, five of them saluted the Chinese leaders while the sixth held the flag. Then they separated, with the three representing the People's Republic of China marching to a vacant flagpole, and the three representing the British Government marching to the flagpole that was flying the Union Jack of Great Britain.

The flag of the People's Republic of China was then clipped to the rope of a vacant flagpole. It was not raised.

Then three white-uniformed police of the Hong Kong Special Administrative Region marched up the center steps to the red-carpeted stage, the middle policeman holding the folded Bauhinia flag of the Hong Kong Special Administrative Region in his outstretched arms, forming a tray. Then three Royal Hong Kong police joined them. When the delegation of six reached center stage, five of them saluted the British leaders while the sixth held the flag. Then they separated, with the three representing the British Government marching to the flagpole flying the flag of Hong Kong, and the three representing the Hong Kong Special Administrative Region marching to the last vacant and unclipped flagpole.

The flag of the Hong Kong Special Administrative Region was then clipped to the rope of that vacant flagpole. It was not raised.

A voice announced, "The Union flag and the Hong Kong flag will now be lowered and the national flag of the People's Republic of China and the Hong Kong Special Administrative Region flag will be raised." Then the same announcement was made in Cantonese.

As the Union Jack and Hong Kong flags were lowered simultaneously, the orchestra played "God Save the Queen." Prince Charles and Governor Patten, two strong men, were trying unsuccessfully to hold back tears, as were the others in the British delegation on stage. There wasn't a citizen of Great Britain in the audience that wasn't crying. And so were most of the Hong Kong people who attended. And so were most of the Americans there.

When the orchestra was done, there were only fifteen seconds left until midnight. For fifteen seconds there was silence, only interrupted by sniffing.

Midnight.

The flags of the People's Republic of China and the Bauhinia flag of the Hong Kong Special Administrative Region were raised simultaneously as the orchestra played the National Anthem of the People's Republic of China.

It was done.

A cable written previously at Government House was sent two seconds past midnight to the United Kingdom's Secretary of State: "I have relinquished the administration of this government. God save the Queen. Patten."

The guests went to one of three major destinations. The chief destination of Americans was to go to their hotels and get out of the public spotlight, following the lead of Secretary of State Albright. As the highest representative of the U.S. government, she went to the Handover Ceremonies but was boycotting the inauguration of the Provisional Legislature up the escalator from the Grand Hall. That destination was a protocol duty of the United States Consul General Richard Boucher who knew he was being used as a representative so that the inauguration would not be a total snub of the U.S. government. Prime Minister Tony Blair boycotted the inaugural, and sent Great Britain's Senior Representative to the Sino-British Liaison Group, Hugh Davies, and Consul General Francis Cornish. Clearly, Richard Boucher, Hugh Davies, and Francis Cornish would rather not have attended, preferring to be at the third possible destination.

That third possible destination was the one favored by those guests who were proud to publicly exhibit their preference for Great Britain over the People's Republic of China, by going to East Tamar Naval Base where the Royal Yacht *Britannia*, an honor guard, and three British naval vessels bathed in white lights, were waiting for the Prince of Wales and for Governor Patten and his family.

It was a five minute ride of the motorcade from the Convention and Exhibition Center to arrive at East Tamar. Waiting was a crowd of thousands of Hong Kong people. Helicopters were circling overhead. Just above the helicopters and above the ships and above the crowds were many low and dark clouds, but those clouds disciplined themselves not to break and cause rain during the departure of the British delegation.

There was waving and tears from the *Britannia*, and waving and tears from the crowd.

At 12:40 A.M. the *Britannia*'s engines started, and then the Britannia left the pier for its last official voyage before being decommissioned.

"Rule Britannia!" Jack Edwards yelled at the departing ship. And then others yelled "Rule Britannia!" as well.

Slowly at first, the *Britannia* headed toward Kowloon, followed by the British destroyer and smaller escorting Royal Navy vessels and police boats. And then the *Britannia* and the procession of ships turned sharply eastward, passing the Convention and Exhibition Center, and headed to the harbor's exit and to the entrance of the South China Sea. Dozens of lights on ships in the harbor blinked at the departing yacht.

The crowds on Hong Kong Island and in Kowloon walked quickly, unsuccessfully trying to keep up with the movement of the ships. Then their quick walk became faster steps until they were running. Of course they couldn't keep up. To the crowds, the *Britannia* and its escorts were gone much too fast.

One hundred and fifty-six years were over.

The low clouds could no longer hold back. They broke, and there was a great rain again.

Inside Hall Three of the Convention and Exhibition Center, Linda applauded the president of the People's Republic of China, Jiang Zemin. And then she applauded Premier Li Peng as he inaugurated the new unelected legislature of Hong Kong, Special Administrative Region of the People's Republic of China.

At 2:45 in the morning, General Valadovich walked the short distance to Room 1600 which was the headquarters of World News Network. With the handover of Hong Kong from Great Britain to China done, it was the prescribed time for his television interview.

"General Valadovich! Come right in!" He did, and as soon as he crossed the threshold, the young woman put a can of unrequested Diet Coke in his hand. "Have one!" She had on red slacks and a Tee-shirt with a picture of the Union Jack over one breast, and a picture of the flag of the People's Republic of China over the other breast, with 1997 written above them. The room was full of cables, slates, camera batteries, cups, Coke cans and open white boxes with pizza slices in them. "We were getting worried about you. I was just going to call your room. Wasn't it exciting? Did you see the Royal Yacht *Britannia* leave?"

"No. I missed it. I don't want any Coke, thank you." He handed it back to her.

"Coffee?"

"No. I'm okay."

"We have a room full of stuff. Did you see the *Britannia* leave?" she repeated. "Prince Charles sailed away with Governor Patten."

"I know. I missed it. I didn't want to see them sail away."

She wasn't listening to him. "Wasn't it exciting?"

"I don't know. I didn't see it."

"It was so exciting. Now, you just need to get into makeup right away and then we'll get you on the roof. It's still raining out there so it's sort of a mess, but we have a tarp so you won't get wet while you're on-camera."

"Is Mrs. Goodpastor here yet?"

"Oh, yes. She's in place outside. She's on a wheelchair you know."

"I know."

"Poor thing. How old is she?"

"She's up there. I think she's passed her ninetieth birthday."

"She has a young man who's taking care of her out there."

"That's Brian Nestande. I met him earlier today."

Whatever he had to say was unimportant. "You'll be interviewed by Laurie Lespada," she said with raised eyebrows, a smile, and a nod, as though the general was to be awed by such a presence. He nodded in pretense that he had heard of Laurie Lespada. He hadn't, although most of the world knew who she was. "Now," she added, "let's get to makeup. Would you like a Diet Coke?"

Was this woman listening to anything except her own voice?

The camera was capturing the image of Laurie Lespada with the brilliantly lit skyline of Hong Kong Island behind her from across the harbor. Rain was beating on the tarp above her, and while the camera didn't show the tarp, the microphone couldn't deafen the noise of the rain beating on it. Laurie Lespada looked at the camera with a wide smile. "Welcome back to 'World Network News' and *Above the Fold*'s coverage of the Hong Kong handover! And where else could we be but Hong Kong on this historical night? W.N.N. continues its coverage from the roof of the Regent Hotel. Sitting with me now on this rainy night are two distinguished Americans who have become very familiar to all of us through the years, and who should have some valuable insights into what's happening here in Hong Kong. Irene Goodpastor is here, founder of the Goodpastor Center in Washington." The director cut to Mrs. Goodpastor who had her eyes closed and her mouth open. He held on her until he realized she was not about to open her eyes or close her mouth, and he cut to the camera that was on General Valadovich as the anchor-woman promptly continued, "And we have with us Retired Brigadier General Jonas Valadovich. General, let's start with you." Could she do otherwise? "What's your feeling about the handover? Optimistic? Pessimistic?"

"I'm saddened by it. How can we celebrate the reunification of Hong Kong people with China when it was the Hong Kong people who escaped so as to be disunited from the PRC?"

"The PRC—the People's Republic of China," she felt her responsibility to the audience to show how knowledgable she was. "The government there."

"Yes, ma'am." *Ma'am* for Laurie Lespada?

"But why should things change here in Hong Kong, General? The late Deng Xiaoping promised One Country, Two Systems. Doesn't that give you some assurance?"

"Tragically, the world is defining Hong Kong's system as capitalism, and that's the way Deng Xiaoping thought of the system here. But Hong Kong's system is liberty. Capitalism is no less or more than the economic dimension of liberty. It's part of liberty but not its roots." He knew television well enough to just keep talking about what he wanted to say or the anchor would turn to another subject. "And although you can't have liberty without capitalism, you can have capitalism without liberty. That's what Deng brought to his own people. It's true that China is turning more and more to capitalism, but without political as well as economic change, China is becoming more of a fascist state than a communist state."

Laurie Lespada dismissed that. "Jiang Zemin and Li Peng said that this night ends a century and one-half of China's shame and humiliation from the British Opium Wars. Isn't that true? Now the shame and humiliation is over."

"What they're really ashamed of is how well these Chinese people did without the government of the People's Republic. This is the pearl of Asia. The pearl is not Shanghai and not Guangzchou and not Beijing. That's the PRC's shame. And there's more reason for shame; shame for their support of Pol Pot's genocide in Cambodia. That happened in this generation, not 156 years ago during the Opium Wars by people who have long been dead. Why aren't they ashamed of what they did in 1978 to kids who were putting up posters on Democracy Wall? Why aren't they ashamed of their massacre in 1989 at Tiananmen Square? That was ordered by Deng Xiaoping and Li Peng. Li Peng is here tonight! He did tonight what you just did, ma'am. He talked about the shame of the Opium Wars and by saying that, he allowed himself to avoid the obvious. The British shamed his government all right—by the British letting Chinese people be free. And look what they built!"

Enough of that for Laurie Lespada. "Mrs. Goodpastor, tell us why you and the General and some of your other friends are here. We know about your Institute in Washington—the Goodpastor Center—but I understand you aren't here for the Center. There's a fascinating story behind this visit of yours, isn't there?"

Too bad, but Mrs. Goodpastor didn't answer. She wasn't rude, she simply didn't hear her. Her eyes were open now but she wasn't looking at anything special, certainly not at Laurie Lespada or at the camera. Her mouth was still wide open. The director knew enough now to cut back quickly to a two-shot of Laurie Lespada and General Valadovich.

General Valadovich put his hand on top of Irene Goodpastor's off-camera hand and she gave an off-camera start. Then, surprisingly, she started talking very clearly, although her thoughts were a little off subject. "Is General MacArthur dead yet?"

The director quickly cut back to her.

General Valadovich tightened his hand on hers. "Oh, yes. He's been gone for a long time," General Valadovich answered.

"Thank God!" It was a little difficult to figure out what she meant.

The director cut to a tight close-up of Laurie Lespada who performed her duties perfectly, as though Irene Goodpastor had said something of note. "Well," she said, "you never stop being controversial! Now, tell me, Mrs. Goodpastor or General Valadovich, either of you—tell me about that fascinating story behind this visit of yours."

General Valadovich nodded. The director cut back to the two-shot. "Yes, ma'am, it is fascinating. Irene Goodpastor was visiting here in 1960. That's 37 years ago now. So were some others here then, including me. Most of us didn't know each other, but nine of us were invited to the American Consulate to listen to one of the Kennedy-Nixon debates on Voice of America. I forgot by now which debate of theirs it was, but we all sat around a conference table and listened to it with three people from the consulate. So there were twelve of us all together. Afterwards we had a discussion about what would happen here in Hong Kong in 1997. Somehow, and again, I don't remember exactly how it happened, but we pledged to come back here—to be together during the transition of Hong Kong from Britain to China."

"It was my idea!" Mrs. Goodpastor yelled out. There wasn't any warning so the camera wasn't on her, but she was heard.

"That's right," General Valadovich said. "Now, the ones that are still left—who are still alive—were reminded of the occasion continually by

Mrs. Goodpastor, not that we needed a reminder. The living are here. Some of the kids of the originals are here, too."

"She didn't have the Goodpastor Center back in 1960, did she?"

"Oh, no. Not back then. I don't believe there were many real Think Tanks back then. Maybe just the Brookings Institution. Anyway, we all fell in love with Hong Kong. What American wouldn't? This city has come a long way since then and this night is a sad one. God made it rain."

"What did you do tonight during the handover, General?"

"Prayed."

"You're a very religious man, aren't you?"

He hesitated as though he didn't want to answer. Then he nodded.

"Were you in the service back then at that 1960 meeting, General?"

"Yes, ma'am. I was a lieutenant then."

"That was quite a prominent group here, wasn't it?"

"At the time, not really. Other than Mrs. Goodpastor, none of the others in the group were well known back then."

"Well, the years have changed all that! They practically all had brilliant futures, didn't they?"

"Yes. Two of them went on to be assistants to U.S. presidents; Moose Dunston, and he's here in Hong Kong tonight, he's a close friend, and Cody Cooper. His son is here."

"Cody Cooper was a presidential assistant? What president?"

"President Kennedy."

She lurched her head back in a start. "I didn't know that."

"You weren't born then, ma'am. Cody was quite a young fellow himself back at that meeting. He went on to go to the White House, then the State Department, then he left government to become the man that gained such great prominence."

"Congresswoman Murphy was with you too, wasn't she?"

"Yes, ma'am. She was here back in 1960 with her husband, Ted. They were on their honeymoon. He did very well on your medium, didn't he?"

"Absolutely! One of the best television journalists of all time!"

There was no reaction on General Valadovich's face. And he didn't say anything.

Laurie Lespada didn't like pauses, so she added, "Congresswoman Murphy is in town now to be with all of you?"

"She was over at the handover ceremony tonight as a guest. The government of the People's Republic of China invited her. She's a guest of Li Peng."

"Really? That's prestige!"

Again, General Valadovich ignored a remark of Laurie Lespada. "Did you ever hear of a man named Adam Orr? He was here then."

The camera cut back to a close-up of her. She was squinting and giving a slight shake of her head. "No. I don't think so." The camera zoomed back.

"He's become my mentor. Whatever I am, I learned from him. He became my teacher. Not just mine. He did the same for Moose Dunston."

"Go on, General. Who were the others, although I think I know who some of them were."

"You know who Anne Whitney is?"

"Oh, yes. She was the one in Iran during the hostage crisis–and then she–"

"Anne's here," he interrupted. "She's here. In those days she worked at the Consulate with a Chinese girl who, indeed, became very celebrated. Do you know who I'm talking about?"

"I certainly do, General. I'm afraid I forgot her name, some Chinese name–I just don't remember, but she was the one who was in Tiananmen Square, wasn't she?"

"Yes. Tso Wai-yee. Her daughter is here. She lives here. Back in 1960 her mother and Anne worked for our Public Affairs Officer at the Consulate, Mark Daschle. And back then, there was a visiting Ambassador and his wife at the Consulate too; the Fairbanks. He was never known among the general public but he was known among practically all the foreign service officers back then."

"And you all kept in contact with each other through the years?"

"Irene kept in contact with all of us but, for the most part, because of our careers–foreign service, military, television, some who became a part of one administration or another, our lives couldn't help but cross – in different places throughout the world."

Suddenly Mrs. Goodpastor yelled out, "How about Johnny Carson?" The camera zoomed back to include Mrs. Goodpastor in the shot.

"Ma'am?" General Valadovich asked Mrs. Goodpastor.

"Is he dead yet?" she yelled.

"No. No. He's alive. He's fine. He's retired but he's fine."

"That's good," Irene Goodpastor said with a sigh of relief. The Assistant Director gave Laurie Lespada a hand gesture of expanding his fingers on both hands, then closing them and expanding them four times, in a sign that she had forty seconds left.

Again Irene Goodpastor yelled out, this time looking off to the side to her off-screen escort. "Tell Sonny Bono the fireworks were beautiful!"

It was not exactly the way Laurie Lespada wanted the show to wind down. "General, Hong Kong was a great deal different back then, I'll bet." She was struggling to quickly get the show back on base. "I'll bet there were no skyscrapers here back then, were there?"

"No, ma'am. But not just that. Everything was a great deal different back then. Every city. Every life. It was another world."

"Better or worse? Can you tell me in fifteen seconds? We have to go to a break."

"No, I can't," General Valadovich smiled. "The different world took 37 years to get here. It would take less time to tell you those things that are the same. Time changes so much we used to know. And it will change again from what you know tonight. It has to be that way. We can only assume that's what God wants. So Hong Kong's face will change. And so will all of our faces change. Are my fifteen seconds up?"

She turned from him to the camera. "This is Laurie Lespada for *Above the Fold* at the Hong Kong handover for 'World Network News,' on the roof of the Regent Hotel in Hong Kong. And now, on this exciting night, we can say it differently than we ever said it before—we're broadcasting from Hong Kong, a Special Administrative Region of the People's Republic of China."

EIGHTY-FIVE
AFTER THE HANDOVER
1997

Black.

Through the window of the airliner there was nothing to see, but the woman who was in her late sixties or early seventies stared at the black with intensity, as though she would miss something if she looked away from that window to her left. She took a long inhalation of her cigarette. There was a queenly elegance to her from the way she sat with rigid posture on the purple airline chair that her presence had turned into a throne. And her blue dress with a white lace collar exhibited that flying was an experience she respected. Seated next to her in the first class cabin of Korean Air Flight 61 was Jonas. He had been sleeping, but he woke when the plane hit some turbulence.

"I think it's okay now," she said to him with the assurance of a nurse as the plane made a quick climb. "I think he went above the storm—or whatever it was. That was pretty bumpy." She took another long draw of her cigarette.

He nodded and smiled. "It woke me up."

"You're General Valadovich aren't you?"

He smiled. "Yes, I am."

"I admire all you've done, particularly in Vietnam."

"Thank you, ma'am."

"Were you in Hong Kong for the handover?"

Jonas hesitated, then nodded, a grim nod, with his lips tight together. "You, too?"

"Yes, for a week of rain, wasn't it? I'm glad to be out of there."

"You don't like Hong Kong?"

"It's because I love it that I don't want to see it again. Now it's different. It's just different," she said.

"Yes. I know. I feel exactly the same. You've been going there for a long time?"

"Back and forth since I was a young woman. Once, I thought I might even live there. Anyway, I'm glad to be going home. I flew from Hong Kong to Seoul and then this flight from Seoul."

"You took Korean Air for the same reason I did?"

She gave a broad smile and there was a youthful sparkle in her eyes that were not young. "To smoke! I think it's the only airline left! I used to take Cathay Pacific, then they wouldn't allow smoking. Then Delta and they stopped. Then United and they stopped. If Korean stops—I'll stay home."

"They've gone nutty over it," Jonas said. "You're made to feel like a criminal if you smoke. You can get away with murder, but not smoking."

"O.J. Simpson got away with two murders. Lucky for him he didn't smoke!"

Jonas nodded. "You have something there."

"You know while you were sleeping they showed the Hong Kong handover on CNN." She nodded toward the motion picture screen that was now showing Mike Tyson biting Evander Holyfield's ear.

Jonas didn't want to talk about the Hong Kong handover. "Did you hear they're even going to get rid of Joe Camel and the Marlboro Man?"

"Well, they won't get rid of the Marlboro Woman! That's me!" And she stomped out the small remainder of her cigarette in the ash tray. "While you were asleep they showed all the fireworks over the harbor, and Tung Chee-wah giving that speech."

"That's when I closed my eyes."

"You don't want to see it again?"

"I don't–no–I don't."

She accommodated his pained expression and changed the subject for him. "Did you hear that Jimmy Stewart died?" Not a very good way to change the subject.

"Yes, I know. He was a marvelous man. That's a shame. He was the real 20th Century American. Not just in his acting. You know, he was a pilot, a colonel in the U.S. Army Air Corps it was called back then. Then he stayed in the reserve and made brigadier general. He was great. Bob Mitchum died too, you know. He died. He was terrific, too."

"I loved all his movies."

"Did CNN have anything about the Mars probe?"

"The what?"

"Pathfinder. It was launched seven months ago exactly. Today's Independence Day, the Fourth of July, so it's supposed to land on Mars today."

"No. They didn't have anything on it, but it's a tape here. That's not a live newscast on the plane."

"I know. Where are we right now? Do you know? I slept so long."

"We're nowhere," she answered with total assurance.

"Nowhere? We have to be somewhere."

"We're nowhere. That's why I enjoy it. Flying over the sea at night is the nearest you can come to feeling what it was like before you were born, and after you die. Up here we aren't in time or place."

Here was a woman who was right up Jonas' alley. Or was she trying to please him? She knew he was General Valadovich and she might have heard of his obsession with time. "I think you have a point there!" he said.

"I know I do. I can prove it to you."

"Go ahead."

"What time is it?"

"Where? Here?" He looked at his new world-time watch he bought in Hong Kong. "I don't even know where we are. I still have my watch on Hong Kong time." He looked back up. "I don't know where we are, but they'll have it on the screen. They have that map –that computerized map showing where we are—and then they tell what time it is where we were and where we're going. There. It's in Korean. Wait. They'll change it to English. See? It's 6:14 A.M. right now at our destination—in L.A."

"But I mean here. What time is it here?"

"I'll have to wait for the map on the screen. It shows where we are. Then I can figure out the time."

"That blasted computerized map! That ruins the whole thing!"

"What does it ruin?"

"The whole thing, that's all." Then she lowered herself in the seat, sulking. "There is no time up here and they shouldn't try to create it."

Jonas was smiling. "You're a very wise woman. Since you know who I am—who are you?" And he extended his hand.

She took his hand but she didn't tell him her name. "When I'm on a plane, I'm not who I was or will be. No name, please, because there isn't any time up here."

"All right."

She sat up straight again and reached in her purse and took out her new dark blue passport. "See this?"

"Your passport."

"Yes. It's Suzy Drew the Fifth. Can you imagine? This passport is valid until 2007. It's like science-fiction come true. Then I'll get Suzy Drew the Sixth."

"You name your passports?" He was smiling.

"Of course."

"You name them after you?"

"I named her after Nancy Drew. I read Nancy Drew when I was a little girl."

"Okay!" Jonas reached in his pocket for his cigarettes and pulled out a Camel 100s pack. As he put a cigarette in his mouth, she reached in her purse again and this time she took out a very old and tarnished lighter. Some of the silver had worn away, exhibiting some areas of yellow shine. She lit his cigarette for him.

"Thanks! That's quite a lighter!. I haven't seen one of those old Ronsons in a long time. It's a real antique!"

"It's Wyatt." she said.

Then she felt a hand on her thigh. She looked at Jonas sharply. But his hand that was nearest her was holding his cigarette and his other hand was on the arm of his airline chair.

The woman smiled. She knew who it was. "Stop it!" she whispered.

Jonas could have sworn he heard a deep voice say, "Marry her!"

BRUCE HERSCHENSOHN has been a television and radio political commentator for the last two decades. After service in the U.S. Air Force he began his own motion picture company, and then was appointed Director of Motion Pictures and Television for the United States Information Agency. During his tenure the U.S.I.A. received more awards for film and television productions than all other departments and agencies of the U.S. government combined, including the Oscar from the Academy of Motion Picture Arts and Sciences. In 1969, he was selected as one of the Ten Outstanding Young Men in the Federal Government. He received the second-highest civilian award, the Distinguished Service Medal, and then became Deputy Special Assistant to President Nixon.

He has traveled to over ninety countries, Herschensohn taught "The U.S. Image Abroad" at the University of Maryland, occupied the Nixon Chair at Whittier College teaching "U.S. Foreign and Domestic Policies" and was chairman of the board of Pepperdine University. He was appointed a member of the Reagan Transition Team. Herschensohn was the 1992 Republican candidate for the U.S. Senate in California and was defeated while winning over one million votes more than the national ticket of the Party in California. He was a Fellow at the John F. Kennedy Institute of Politics at Harvard University for spring 1996, teaching U.S. Foreign Policy, and was a Distinguished Fellow of the Claremont Institute, 1993-2001.

He is currently teaching "The World Leadership Role of the United States" at Pepperdine University's School of Public Policy, and is an Associate Fellow of the Nixon Center for Peace and Freedom, and serves on the Board of Directors of the Center for Individual Freedom.